Lieutenant-Colonel de Maumort

Lieutenant-Colonel de Maumort

Roger Martin du Gard

Translated by Luc Brébion and Timothy Crouse

A<small>LFRED</small> A. K<small>NOPF</small>   *New York*   2000

THIS IS A BORZOI BOOK
PUBLISHED BY ALFRED A. KNOPF

Copyright © 1999 by Luc Brébion and Timothy Crouse

All rights reserved under International and Pan-American Copyright
Conventions. Published in the United States by Alfred A. Knopf, a
division of Random House, Inc., New York, and simultaneously in
Canada by Random House of Canada Limited, Toronto. Distributed
by Random House, Inc., New York.

www.randomhouse.com

Originally published in France as *Le Lieutenant-Colonel de Maumort*
by Éditions Gallimard, Paris, in 1983. Copyright © 1983 by Éditions
Gallimard. Édition d'André Daspre. Bibliothèque de la Pléiade.

Knopf, Borzoi Books, and the colophon are registered trademarks of
Random House, Inc.

Library of Congress Cataloging-in-Publication Data
Martin du Gard, Roger, 1881–1958.
[Lieutenant-Colonel de Maumort. English]
Lieutenant-Colonel de Maumort / Roger Martin du Gard; translated
by Luc Brébion and Timothy Crouse.
p.   cm.
ISBN 0-679-43397-X
I. Brébion, Luc.   II. Crouse, Timothy.   III. Title.
PQ2625.A823L513   1999
843'.912—dc21   98-50912
CIP

Manufactured in the United Sates of America
First American Edition

We dedicate this translation to André Daspre.

CONTENTS

Contents

II. LETTERS OF LIEUTENANT-COLONEL DE MAUMORT (31 DECEMBER 1944–JANUARY 1945)

III. THE FILES FROM THE BLACK BOX

Contents

TRANSLATORS' INTRODUCTION

Martin du Gard is the example, a rare one indeed, of one of our great writers whose telephone number nobody knows. He exists, very strongly, in our literary society. But he has dissolved himself in it as sugar does in water. Fame and the Nobel Prize have favored him, if I may so express it, with a kind of supplementary darkness. Simple and mysterious, he has something of the divine principle described by the Hindus: the more he is named, the more he disappears. Furthermore, there is no calculation in this quest for obscurity. Those who have the honor of knowing him as a man realize his modesty is real, so real that it appears abnormal. . . .*

—*Albert Camus, 1955*

THE BIOGRAPHY of Roger Martin du Gard is largely the story of a writer working at his desk. Aside from time devoted to his friendships (a source of deep satisfaction), his marriage (an ordeal for most of its forty-three years), the raising of a daughter (whose behavior as she grew up disappointed him), and occasional travels, his life was spent in methodical pursuit of his calling. During his adult years he lived in the country—chiefly in the Orne, west of Paris, in a house called le Tertre. He made only brief forays into the capital and, although he had socialist leanings, turned down all invitations to contribute to periodicals or pronounce on political issues. Everything he had to say went into his books or plays.

A man who has a vocation to write full-blown, intricate novels, and seriously dedicates himself to it, cannot afford many distractions. Yet in view of the fact that Martin du Gard's achievements are absurdly underrecognized, one could say that what Camus called his "quest for obscurity" was all too successful. While his books are considered part of the literary canon in France and are translated and studied in non-Francophone countries as diverse as Iran and China, his name remains comparatively unknown. The English-speaking world in particular has been slow to appreciate his genius.†

**Lyrical and Critical Essays*, translated by Ellen Conroy Kennedy.

†This despite the fact that many of Martin du Gard's works have been translated into English: *Jean Barois, The Thibaults* and *Summer 1914* by Stuart Gilbert; *Recollections of André Gide* and *Vieille France* (as *The Postman*) by John Russell. *Confidence Africaine*, with no translator credited, can be found in anthologies of Nobel Prize authors.

It may well be that his self-effacement has left him at a disadvantage in comparison with many authors of lesser accomplishment whose ceaseless self-advertisement while alive has stood their posthumous fame in good stead.

A further impediment to the spread of his reputation stemmed from the fact that his masterwork, *Lieutenant-Colonel de Maumort,* composed during his final seventeen years, was left in an unfinished state that caused its publication to be delayed until 1983, twenty-five years after his death, by which time his most ardent champions, writers like Camus and André Malraux, had themselves passed from the scene. In addition, the very audacity that makes the book so extraordinary may have dampened its initial reception. In his earlier novels, Martin du Gard had adopted the stance of a skeptic who nevertheless cherished generous aspirations for humanity. However, as he experienced the century's relentless violence and as he scrutinized his own ethical makeup and that of others with an ever-increasing acuity, his observations led him gradually to abandon hope until, in his culminating work, he arrived at a deep, bravely borne disillusionment with man. The critique he delivers in *Lieutenant-Colonel de Maumort* is universal, aimed at the human race as a whole, but since the book is set in France, it is French people who happen to be, so to speak, in the immediate line of fire. This may help to explain why French reviewers, although many of them praised the book for its modernity, its psychological realism, or the perfection of its prose, often tended to treat it simply as a kind of historical novel, a brilliant evocation of life under the Third Republic (1870–1940), and almost entirely failed to confront the profound, disturbing, timeless themes that constitute its very essence. True, the book's inclusion in the Pléiade series instantly ratified its status as a classic, and it had a *succès d'estime.* But if the author cannot precisely be called a prophet without honor in his own country, the fact remains that his ultimate achievement has yet to receive anything like full appreciation there.

What originally drew our attention to *Lieutenant-Colonel de Maumort* was a lecture by the poet David Rosenmann-Taub, and many of the insights we gained from him inform this introduction. The penetration and eloquence with which he analyzed Martin du Gard's novel and placed it in the context of world literature not only sent us to the book but gave us the impetus to make it available in English. In truth, we undertook our translation as much for the opportunity it provided to further explore the novel's riches as out of the wish to bring these to the attention of a wider audience. During the seven years we were engaged in the project, people often asked why we chose to invest so much time in such a formidable task. Our reply always remained the same: that *Lieutenant-Colonel de Maumort* stands as one of the greatest novels of the twentieth century.

. . .

Roger Martin du Gard was born on March 23, 1881. The scion of a long line of lawyers and financiers, he grew up in Paris and attended a private religious school while also taking courses at the Lycée Condorcet. When he was around nine, his vocation was awakened by the sight of a schoolmate declaiming a tragedy of his own composing. "This need to write, which has tormented me all my life, was born, I think, on a spring evening under the charm of the dramatic works of my friend Jean." Martin du Gard became an avid theater-goer but a laggard student. When he was seventeen, one of his teachers introduced him to *War and Peace.* He would thereafter return continually to Tolstoy's masterpiece, "always with the same fervor, always with the same delighted surprise," and it would have "the most decisive and durable of all influences" on him.

Between the ages of eighteen and twenty-four, with time off for compulsory military service, Martin du Gard studied at the École des Chartes, a school devoted to training paleographers. He obtained a diploma for his thesis on the Norman Abbey at Jumièges, and came away with a respect for the historical methodology he had learned, which he would employ in documenting his fiction.

He soon began writing novels, producing in quick succession *Une vie de saint* (1907), *Devenir!* (1908) and *L'une de nous* (1909)—all of which he later dismissed as juvenilia.

In 1913 (the same year that saw the publication of *Swann's Way* and Apollinaire's *Alcools*), Martin du Gard brought out his breakthrough work, *Jean Barois.* The hero, Jean, after a provincial Catholic upbringing, becomes a biology teacher and begins pondering scientific questions that eventually lead him to renounce his faith. In Paris, he rises in left-wing circles, edits an anticlerical socialist review, espouses the cause of the unjustly convicted Captain Dreyfus (whose trial and its repercussions are vividly evoked), and becomes internationally famous as a proponent of science over religion. Ultimately, however, the persistence of his early beliefs proves stronger than his lifelong determination to emancipate himself. Falling mortally ill, he is unable to face death without the promise of immortality, and ends by rushing, terrified, back to the solace of the creed he has scorned.

Martin du Gard originally intended to call the book *S'affranchir?* (*To Break Free?*), a title that could be applied to nearly all of his novels. Few of his characters are able to liberate themselves from their inner conflicts. Among the exceptional ones who do is Jean Barois's mentor, the freethinker Marc-Élie Luce, who declares: "I do not acknowledge two moral standards. One must attain happiness, without being the dupe of any mirage, through truth and truth alone." Commenting on this statement, Camus would write: "One could hardly give a better definition of the enlightened renunciation of happiness. But let us simply remember that the first portrait of men who reject all forms of hope, determined to confront death in its entirety, who later swarm into our literature, was traced in 1913 by Roger Martin du Gard."

That said, it must be added that certain elements in the book—the bright prospects of science, the high expectations of a nascent socialism, as well as the pardon of Dreyfus—imply a hopefulness despite the stark denouement. At this stage of his life, Martin du Gard still held a relatively sanguine view of man's possibilities.

Jean Barois opened new territory in French literature. It treated politics not just as a background element but as an active force, practically as a character, and in doing so made startling use of a documentary, almost cinematic form—scenes of dialogue interspersed with letters, diary entries, and brief descriptive passages. The book spoke powerfully to a generation that had wrestled with the competing claims of materialism and religion. It also earned Martin du Gard the esteem of many important intellectuals, including several luminaries of the newly founded *Nouvelle Revue Française:* Jacques Copeau, who would encourage him as a playwright; Gaston Gallimard, who would publish most of his books; and André Gide, who would become his literary confidant.

With the eruption of the First World War in August 1914, Martin du Gard was mobilized as a noncommissioned officer in a motor transport unit responsible for supplying the First Cavalry Corps (the same corps with which he would have Maumort fight in the trenches). While many of France's most illustrious authors actively promoted the resort to arms and succumbed to the patriotic fever sweeping the nation, it is clear from Martin du Gard's letters that he found the war a despicable folly and both sides barbarous.

During the war, he jotted in a little engagement book some notes on his activities, and afterwards found this fragmentary record so valuable as a reminder of important facts he was "on the point of forgetting forever" that he adopted the practice, between 1919 and 1949, of scribbling down events as they happened to him—"a personal incident, an emotion, a worry, a meeting, a talk with a friend, a confidence received, a difficulty that arose in the course of my work." This diary would be published by Gallimard in three volumes during the early 1990s.

His many readings of Tolstoy, Martin du Gard once wrote, had disposed him to "the long-drawn-out novel, with numerous characters and multiple episodes." In 1920, he embarked on just such a project—*Les Thibault (The Thibaults),* a saga that would run to eight volumes (each published as he finished it) and would take him nearly two decades to complete. In many ways, it was his own, distinctive, latter-day *War and Peace,* with World War I as the background conflict.

Martin du Gard's original inspiration for *The Thibaults* arose, he tells us in his *Souvenirs,* from seeing "the possibility of being able to give simultaneous expression to two conflicting tendencies in my own nature: my instinctive need to escape, to rebel, to reject every sort of conformity, and the instinctive need for order, for moderation, for the avoidance of extreme courses which I owe to my heritage." He accomplished this by portraying two brothers, Jacques and Antoine Thibault, radically different in temperament yet marked by the similarities of common ancestry. The maverick Jacques begins his career as a dissident with an abortive attempt to run away from a tyrannical home life, and ends it, at the onset of hostilities, on a disastrous airborne mission to shower the contending armies with pacifistic leaflets. The older, levelheaded brother, Antoine, allows his existence as a dedicated and ambitious physician to proceed largely unexamined until his last days, when, his health destroyed by the effects of gassing in battle, he realizes the vital importance of the self-knowledge he has never attained.

The novel encompasses the lives not only of the Catholic Thibaults and of another family, the Protestant Fontanins, but also of their friends, mistresses, dependents, servants, etc.—a network of relationships whose complexity is all but unmatched in the modern French novel. Although the spirit of Tolstoy hovers over *The Thibaults,* Martin du Gard in many ways manifests an independent sensibility. For instance, the account of the deathbed agonies suffered by the brothers' autocratic father can be read as a harrowing rejoinder to the relative idealism of "The Death of Ivan Ilyich." Martin du Gard was also generally far more open and at ease about sexual matters than Tolstoy had been.

In *L'Été 1914 (Summer 1914)*—the seventh volume of *The Thibaults* and the one for which Martin du Gard received the Nobel Prize in 1937—the causes of the war are elucidated from Jacques's point of view, as he sees his desperate efforts in behalf of peace crushed. By the last volume of the saga, *Epilogue,* two generations of Thibaults and Fontanins have been largely wiped out, and the prewar order has been swept away. In painting a dark period darkly, Martin du Gard allows only one spark of hope: Jacques's little son, Jean-Paul, the representative of the new order, may carry forward the defeated aspirations of his parents' generation. The last word Antoine commits to this diary, before injecting himself with a fatal overdose of drugs, is "Jean-Paul."

During the period in which he labored on *The Thibaults,* Martin du Gard also managed to write two plays: *La Gonfle* (1922–24), a peasant farce, and *Un Taciturne* (1931), a psychological drama concerning homosexuality; *Confidence Africaine* (1930), a brilliant novella about sibling incest; and *Vieille France* (1932), a scathing fictional study of small-town types.

Épilogue appeared in January 1940, and Martin du Gard began the process of feeling his way toward the subject of a new novel. He was still searching six months later when the Germans overran France. The day before they reached le Tertre, he fled to Nice. Although the debacle left him temporarily disoriented, eventually it provided him with his inspiration. On the night of May 1, 1941, plagued by insomnia, he constructed in his mind the outline of a book: a colonel in his seventies, confined in the wake of the invasion to the library of his occupied château, begins a diary which soon expands into a book of memoirs—of his childhood, his campaigns in Morocco with General Lyautey, the First World War, his marriage. The colonel's diary would record "the thoughts of an old liberal Erasmus who has seen everything." He would "resurrect the past, drawing pictures of people he has known." To an astonishing degree, the whole novel, with many of its characters and incidents, came to Martin du Gard in the course of that one sleepless night.

Originally, Martin du Gard intended the book to begin with the German onslaught. In conceiving Maumort, his first impulse may have been to give a more expert and effective voice to his indignation over the French defeat. His hero is a prescient officer whose calls for a stronger air force, had they been heeded by his superiors, might have saved France; furthermore, he embodies a high level of culture. As models for Maumort, the author chose men whose careers included both army experience and literary achievement: the Marquis de Vauvenargues (soldier turned Enlightenment aphorist), the Comte de Vigny (soldier turned Romantic poet), General Lyautey (conqueror of Morocco and man of letters), and Martin du Gard's friend Colonel Émile Mayer (a Cassandra who had clamored, with Charles de Gaulle, for France to modernize its armament, but also a grammarian and military essayist whose straightforward style the author admired).

A word must be said, however, about Martin du Gard's ambivalent attitude toward the weight to be given historical events in his novel. As he wrote:

> It is tempting to shape one's oeuvre out of the serious problems being debated in one's time. It seems legitimate to enrich one's work with the contribution of contemporary thought and experience. This is a stupidity which is always fatal. . . . The social question clutters the work of Balzac. Historical questions, that of Tolstoy. In *Middlemarch,* everything that is a general idea about medicine, political life, even the dissidence of religious sects, is so much dead weight. . . . The supreme problem for the artist is precisely to separate what is time-bound from what is permanent, what is the current, short-lived debate of contemporary humanity from what is the anguishing enigma of eternal humanity.

Martin du Gard realized that in both *Jean Barois* and *The Thibaults* he had become overly concerned with political and social issues, and he was determined not to repeat this mistake. Yet more than once during the composition of *Lieutenant-Colonel de Maumort,* he awoke, as if from a trance, to realize that he was focusing on the events of the war to the detriment of his novel as a work of art. Despite his warning to himself to "beware of the war," it was in the section of the book concerning the German invasion and occupation that, caught up in the turmoil of the present, he found it especially difficult to take a detached view of the history he was living through. The writing of these passages involved a recurrent struggle to free himself from the illusion that his particular time and place were more momentous than any in the history of mankind.

Martin du Gard's usual method of creation was to settle upon an outline, then tell himself the story of his characters. The point was to "objectify" his fictions. He noted in his diary: "The novelist in me does not move easily except in the past, in a world re-created by memory. Whence the impossibility of using in my work events, experiences, sights that are recent. Whence, as well, my way of working: a first rough sketch that I let lie for a while; when I return to it, the scenes that I have vaguely imagined, glimpsed, become for me like so many personal, authentic 'memories' that I try to bring back to life." He launched into his new project by collecting every news report that might have reached the sequestered Maumort during the summer of 1940 and by annotating each item with the colonel's alleged comments. However, it soon dawned on Martin du Gard that, having broken his own rule by neglecting to establish his character before all else, he was being seduced by the use of the first person into writing down his own thoughts in his own voice. Immediately upon realizing this, he instead set to work creating Maumort's biography in order to provide himself with the substance of a separate life. From then on, the work began to flow more easily, and for many months he happily created the raw material he planned to put into Maumort's diary. He drew not only on his imagination but also on his own diary and on the notes and clippings which, as an inveterate string-saver, he had amassed since the earliest days of his career.

For Martin du Gard, matter came first, style later: "I've chosen my hare, I skin it, I cut it up. When I have all the pieces of the animal before me, well prepared, I turn my attention to the sauce . . . Not before." It was the making of this "sauce" that would cause him problems throughout the writing of *Lieutenant-Colonel de Maumort.* Having adopted the diary form for the sake of its immediacy, he soon began to find it constraining. He excitedly considered, then rejected, the possibility of doing the book as a series of interrelated short stories told in the third person.

By 1946, he had decided that he could not limit Maumort's point of view to the period of the invasion: too much had already been written about that by other authors. Maumort must be given greater perspective; his diary should begin in 1945. From this point on, the book began to assume the more expansive shape of a memoir, with long set pieces (mainly extended portraits of people who played a crucial role in Maumort's life).

Bouts of exhilarating productivity were followed by episodes of discouragement. Once in 1948, and again the next year, he read long sections of the book to André Gide, who found them superior to anything else Martin du Gard had previously achieved, and who assured him that he had never written anything "more solid and more personal."

In 1952, Martin du Gard decided that almost the entire novel should be written in the form of letters from the colonel to his best friend, Dr. Gévresin—"which gives me a more relaxed tone than the diary and which allows me mostly to skirt current events." We cannot know if Martin du Gard would have persisted in this course or would once again have cast the book as a memoir, but the hundred or so pages of the "Letters to Gévresin" that he managed to complete show a remarkable vigor, range of feeling, and technical virtuosity.

In his final years, poor health, personal difficulties, and literary chores took him away from *Lieutenant-Colonel de Maumort* for long intervals. He prepared his *Oeuvres complètes* for the Pléiade Collection, began to arrange his papers for donation to the Bibliothèque Nationale, and reviewed his correspondence with Gide (who had died in 1951) with an eye to its publication. In the summer of 1958, he went back to his novel. Finding the manuscript in an "indescribable disorder," he asked a family friend, Marie Rougier, to help him sort it out. A teacher of French who had aided him in the past as a secretary, Mlle. Rougier managed to arrange the various drafts so that he would be able to proceed without getting lost in the complications of the many story lines he had invented. Toward the middle of August, Martin du Gard had recovered his full confidence and affirmed that he was ready to resume work. On August 22, at the age of seventy-seven, he suffered a fatal heart attack.

MARTIN DU GARD intended his final book to be a *livre somme*, reflecting the totality of his experience. In reaching what was to be the pinnacle of his work, he used many footholds: the knowledge he had acquired through the composition of his previous works; his close acquaintance with the novels of Tolstoy; his reading of Proust (with special attention to the representation of human contradiction); and his constant study of others—including, one may imagine, his observation of the hypocrisies inherent in the lives of authors whose writing he regarded highly, such as Goethe, Thomas Mann, and Gide. Above all, he drew on an extraordinary talent for introspection, and a canny awareness of the factors that can distort self-examination.

Martin du Gard's delineation of Maumort obviously cannot be taken as an exact self-portrait—for one thing, by making Maumort a career military officer, the author imparted to him a dimension absent from his own biography. Nevertheless he did, in certain fundamental ways, create a character similar to himself: a venerable intellectual, writing in anticipation of death, whose life has revolved around solitary reflection and who has for many years kept a diary as an ongoing assessment of his moral state. To what extent does Maumort's memoir constitute a disguised confession by Martin du Gard? We can only speculate. The more one delves into the book, the more one feels that this was his essential statement about himself. In the early novel *Devenir!*, the protagonist's best friend, Bernard Grosdidier (a character partly modeled on the author), says: "The difficult thing is to be true to oneself, resolutely enough and long enough to discover how to be really authentic." And he adds: "Nearly everyone fails." During the last seventeen years of his life, Martin du Gard himself appears to have taken up this challenge. While *Lieutenant-Colonel de Maumort* is not plot-driven, it nevertheless pulses with a suspense that springs not just from a superb storyteller's practiced technique but also from a peculiar tension—the tension, it seems to us, of the writer's mind closing in on a revelation that it is loath to confront. In *The Thibaults*, written in the third person from an omniscient point of view, Martin du Gard gave the impression that he stood above his characters. In the first-person narrative of *Lieutenant-Colonel de Maumort*, the judge seems to sit among the accused. Is this the record, transmuted into fiction, of the author's rigorous effort to divulge his truth while battling the temptation to suppress it?

Early on, Martin du Gard had determined that the book would not appear until after his death. We may suppose that he had decided to write it for himself alone, with total freedom, baring himself: before the world could react to this outrage, he would be beyond reach. *Lieutenant-Colonel de Maumort* addresses one of the most tormenting of human conundrums, which could be expressed as: *Why, knowing what is right, do I do wrong?* Many are the books that present characters who embody either good or evil, or protagonists who are torn apart by internal paradoxes. But the supreme contradiction of an ethical person corrupted by his own negative tendencies has never been broached with such thoroughgoing veracity and skill. Perhaps, given enough time, Martin du Gard might have lost his nerve and begun to soften his indictment. Chance forestalled this possibility. Death, like a good editor, snatched him away from his manuscript.

Lieutenant-Colonel de Maumort falls into three sections:

1. The memoirs of Bertrand de Maumort, a nobleman, intellectual, and soldier. By far the largest portion of the text, these memoirs are written by Maumort in his old age and mostly cover his life from his childhood in the 1870s through his young adulthood in the 1880s, but also afford glimpses into his experiences as a husband, as an officer under General Lyautey in North Africa, and finally as a septuagenarian suffering the occupation of his home at the beginning of World War II by German troops.

2. A block of letters written by Maumort to his best friend, Dr. Gévresin, toward the end of the war, reminiscing about shared experiences, reflecting on his own past, and describing the spiritual and material difficulties he faces upon returning to his wrecked château.

3. A lengthy final section, called "The Black Box," of entries on a variety of subjects ("Freedom," "Skepticism," "Revolutionaries," etc.); most of these are ascribed to Maumort as an old man, but some are left in the undisguised voice of Martin du Gard himself.

Born in 1870, the young Maumort grows up on an estate in the hills of the Perche region, west of Paris, neglected by his sullen, widowed father but warmly mothered by his older sister, Henriette. Possessing goodwill, curiosity, and an intelligence far above the average, he receives his early schooling privately from enlightened, imaginative teachers. At twelve, he is joined by a sickly, precocious cousin the same age, Guy Chambost-Lévadé, who, sent to regain his strength in the country air, arrives trailing clouds of Parisian sophistication. Guy's father, a powerful professor, dispatches one of his star graduate students, Xavier de Balcourt, to tutor the boys. Two years later Guy dies, and when Maumort subsequently goes to study in Paris, Guy's grieving parents, Maumort's Uncle Éric and Aunt Ma, take him into their home as a surrogate son. Thanks to this stroke of fate, he finds himself in the company of his uncle's friends, the finest intellects of his day (Renan, Pasteur, Turgenev, Daudet . . .), while courses at the Sorbonne introduce him to the deepest minds of the past. (He will also attend Saint-Cyr, the French military academy.) Keenly aware of the responsibilities implied by his many advantages, contemplative by nature yet bent on a life of action, Maumort stands as an exemplar—the flower of European civilization at its zenith.

What Maumort claims to value beyond everything else is self-knowledge. "At a certain level of cultivation," he writes in his memoir, "an individual consciousness can recognize what rounds it off, makes it grow, and what diminishes it: its 'good' and its 'evil.' It ceases to have faith in the commonly held set of values, and judges thoughts, actions, their consequences, according to a scale all its own." Aspiring to rid himself of all dogmas and prejudices, he has, since his student days, kept a diary as "a means to self-improvement, to intellectual and moral progress." Indeed, his entire memoir appears to be an exercise in impartial self-exploration. As we read it, carried along by Maumort's authoritative voice—so experienced, so disarmingly candid, so apparently wise—we are tempted to agree with the colonel's own essentially approving assessment of himself. But certain dissonances emerge, contradictions that undercut the narrator's testimony.

Some of the discrepancies seem relatively minor, but betoken an inner disharmony. For instance, Maumort congratulates himself on bringing a "lucid objectivity" to the matter of sex, which he understands to play a preponderant role in the formation of the personality. And indeed his claim is justified by his sharp, subtle scrutiny of such topics as his feverish discovery of gender differences; his cousin Guy's tantalizing of the homosexual Xavier de Balcourt; the hothouse atmosphere of his boarding school, where the inmates raid one another's beds; and his long, anguished, eventful quest to shed his virginity even while stubbornly clinging to it. Yet at the same time these passages are incongruously studded with censorious epithets—"depravity," "perversity"—that betray an unreconstructed puritanism.

A more egregious example is his attitude toward his first mistress, an attractive, older Creole woman named Doudou, who, partly to console him, takes the still uninitiated nineteen-year-old Maumort to bed. An idyllic affair ensues. Remembering his visits to Doudou in her aerie in a Martiniquais colony in the rue Mouffetard, and the calm happiness they brought him, Maumort the memoirist pays homage to her kindness, her openness, her sane judgment and maternal generosity, as well as her sensual charms. However, this does not prevent him from harboring idiotic, bigoted assumptions about her culture and her race that a moment's sober reflection should have led him to dismiss. Although he never says so to Doudou, he considers her countrymen a lesser species. The "colored Martiniquais," he asserts, are "fundamentally ineducable. . . . What makes them so little qualified to advance is their natural, instinctive, irreparable indifference to any improvement. Progress holds no interest for them."

The man who recognizes Doudou's qualities is obviously not a racist; the man who stereotypes her is. Yet it is the same person speaking. He is forthcoming: if it were not for his frank account of both parts of himself, we would not have the means to accuse him of bigotry. All the same, despite his horror of clichés and biases, he condones his own prejudice. He cannot be excused as merely succumbing to the commonplace beliefs of his era, since he prides himself on belonging to that aristocracy of freethinkers who over the centuries have transcended convention. Maumort embodies a major human paradox: equipped to see the injustice he is doing, he nevertheless remains indifferent to it. Even though prejudice goes contrary to his better nature, he makes no move to discard it. The irony of his remarks on the Martiniquais' putative resistance to progress is that they apply precisely to himself: his lazy indulgence of his inner dividedness thwarts the personal development by which he sets such store.

Maumort, let us be clear, is nothing so simple as a hypocrite. Rather than someone pretending to be better than he is, he remains a man who wants to act ethically, who sometimes does act ethically, and who is capable of acting ethically at every moment—but who, in crucial ways, permits himself to do the opposite. This contradiction has no solution because on some basic level he does not want to resolve it. Again and again, he even insists that he contains no contradictions when he patently does. In this respect, Maumort, for all the particularity with which the author portrays him, represents a universal phenomenon: irremediable moral ambivalence as the defining characteristic of mankind.

He also, to some extent, represents Roger Martin du Gard. For when Maumort expounds his ideals, he is closely echoing his creator, who in his Nobel Prize acceptance speech declared himself to be one of those "whose constant care is to develop their personal conscience, in order to keep their inquiring mind as objective, as emancipated, and as fair as is humanly possible." Likewise, when he disparages people of color, Maumort is in substance repeating observations that Martin du Gard confided to his diary on a 1939 trip to Martinique.* By means of his protagonist, the author is asking himself, in effect: *If someone who contains so much goodness, also contains such a strong tendency to sanction what is bad in him, is it possible for an entirely good human being to exist on earth?*

The book's implicit answer to this question is an almost totally unqualified *No.* In his later years, Martin du Gard conceived a dichotomy between the human being per se, whom he regarded as full of excellent potential, and human behavior, which he had come to see as essentially irredeemable. By the time the Second World War started to unfold, Martin du Gard's experience of human aggression and perversity had considerably darkened his vision.

---

*But not all the examples of prejudice in the book can be attributed to Martin du Gard himself. A passage in "The Black Box" has Maumort quoting with approval Dr. Gévresin's wish for a day when the "female species will disappear from the globe . . ." Another passage, propounding Maumort's largely favorable opinions of the Jews, nevertheless leaves the unsavory impression that he regards them as a race apart, and includes the comment that "the State should try to rein in the Jews' worldly appetites, which are insatiable." Since these appalling remarks occur in what amount to preparatory notes for the book, we cannot be sure how the author would have disposed of them in the final text, but it appears that he at least considered the possibility of having Maumort sink even deeper into his contradictions. However, it must be pointed out that, from what we know of his life and work, Martin du Gard himself did not subscribe to misogyny and was emphatically not an anti-Semite.

Through various figures besides the central character, the author approaches from different angles the phenomenon of good people giving in to destructive impulses (or of not-so-good people trying unsuccessfully to behave well). In one of the book's most dramatic chapters (presented as a segment of Xavier de Balcourt's diary which has fallen into Maumort's hands), Balcourt, billeted for a few days of army training in a small town, sets his cap for a local baker's apprentice, whom he hopes not only to seduce but also to rescue from an oppressive existence. After much difficulty a tryst is arranged, but just as the affair seems on the verge of consummation, a final obstacle arises, tempting Balcourt into an act of selfish recklessness that puts the youth in harm's way and turns what might have been a liberation for both men into a tragedy.

In another episode, Maumort's high-minded sister, Henriette, enthusiastically adopts an orphan girl; however, neither Henriette's intelligence nor her piety prevents her from letting her snobbishness undo her altruism, with damaging effects on both herself and her ward.

There is also the case of Maumort's uncle, Éric Chambost-Lévadé, a scholar of genius whose wife has created around him a salon that attracts the most celebrated writers, academics, and scientists of Europe. The professor's specialty is the evolution of moral consciousness through the ages; his exhaustive researches have led him to conclude that "the enlargement of knowledge must, in the last analysis, purify primitive moral ideas and contribute to moral progress." He belongs to that generation of 1880s thinkers who, as his nephew recalls, "imagined themselves as part of the vanguard of a new, privileged humanity which was suddenly awakening after centuries of trial and error and which had at last arrived at the threshold of the Truth." The members of the Chambost-Lévadé circle—the "light of the world," as Maumort admiringly calls them—have faith in the power of reason and knowledge to perfect mankind. But the struggle for mankind's development must be carried out within each soul. Here Chambost-Lévadé, the paragon of erudition, the herald of moral progress, falls short. Like Maumort he is divided, but in a more theatrical and tortured way. "He was, no matter what he did, stuck, entangled in that double personality—of the ugly monkey that Nature had created in the bosom of Madame Chambost-Lévadé, his mother, and of the great modern humanist, with a generous heart and a virtuous soul, who he desperately wanted to be, and whose outer behavior he mimicked, for lack of anything better."

Unconvincingly, Maumort concludes that his uncle is "the prey of successive sincerities" and has become incapable of noticing the contradictions between his theory and his base behavior. Maumort does not raise the obvious questions: What is all the savant's learning worth if he cannot recognize the truth about himself? How can mankind be said to have progressed if its most advanced types are like Chambost-Lévadé?

Maumort and his uncle are of different generations, but both belong to an epoch when, in Maumort's words, "pacifism was a noble ideal . . . endorsed by everyone." Yet this halcyon age became the spawning ground for two world wars. The reason for this, the book implies, can be traced to the same fundamental problem of human ambivalence. Society is only the individual writ large and contains all his baneful contradictions magnified many times over. For a single person to let his own prejudice thrive unchallenged may affect solely his own moral growth. But multiply his weakness a million-fold, remove certain inhibitions, and the result is Nazi Germany. To consider a people inherently inferior is to believe it deserves to be dominated. As long as there is racism, there will be war.

In a letter to his friend Gévresin, Maumort explains: "At Rabat, at Casa, beneath my victor's dolman I harbored—I would have qualms about writing: the heart of a *pacifist;* that would be paradoxical, in spite of all, and would demand too many qualifications and commentaries; but let's say: that of a pacifier, of a soldier-colonizer, of a messenger of civilization, who was reluctant to admit the supremacy of force, of a patriot who was not blinded by nationalistic idolatry." The sleight by which Maumort shifts from "pacifist" to "pacifier" in an effort to skate over the moral gulf that separates the two words only serves to proclaim the disingenuousness he is attempting to hide from the world and from himself. This would-be humanist never wishes to contemplate the murderous consequences of his military activity or the army's role as an instrument of aggression. Never, in decrying the Germans' invasion of his own country, does Maumort allow himself to draw a parallel with France's conquest of Morocco—or to consider that, in subjugating an "inferior" nation, France was not so different from Germany.

At the end of Maumort's life, this underlying disingenuousness quietly asserts its triumph. To Martin du Gard, death represented a final test of integrity, a last chance to cast aside self-deceptions. Thus, a crucial measure of each human being was the manner of his passing. A bad death provides the climax of *Jean Barois:* the protagonist dies clutching at religious consolations which he has hitherto rejected as specious. As for Maumort, the idea of a bad death is built into his very name, whose derivation can be found in the family motto: *"De male mort Dieu me garde!"* ("May God save me from a bad death!"). At first glance this prayer would seem, in his case, to have been answered. Maumort dies calmly, having pronounced himself "a happy man." But has he really made a better exit than Barois? Coming as it does after the many moral lapses the colonel has revealed, his statement of ultimate contentedness is the book's crowning irony. In order to recover an authentic picture of himself, the failing Maumort should have gone back and reread his own memoirs; he has conveniently overlooked the ongoing self-betrayal they describe. By leaving them behind, he is, as it were, saying to posterity: *Please, since I am dead, read my beautiful, horrible memoirs for me. Luckily, I will not be around to hear what you think. Oh, and by the way, dear Reader—what has your life been like?*

However forcefully Maumort may claim to be content, there is no immediate comfort to be found in the vision that his creator presents, through him, of man's destiny. Such light as may exist glimmers faintly at the end of a tunnel almost infinitely long.

> The sense I have of human stupidity and villainy is very close to despair and despondency. I try hard to fight against being dispossessed of the little faith that remains to me and is precious to me. I try hard to convince myself that the situation is not irreversible, that the perfectibility of the human animal remains true in itself, but that he is still only at the beginning of the beginning of the ascent, and that he will need thousands of years and thousands of steps backward in order to advance a single centimeter.

In this passage from "The Black Box," Martin du Gard's own lament can be clearly heard: mankind, though dressed up in the trappings of culture, remains still at the stage of barbarism. His prophecy of a *possible* improvement barely discernible on the farthest horizon of the human time line, though drastic, is by no means cynical. Only when the lies and illusions have been swept away can the hope arise that civilization may, at long last, commence.

WHEN ROGER MARTIN DU GARD DIED in 1958, the fate of *Lieutenant-Colonel de Maumort* was uncertain. Seven years before, he had drawn up a literary will, including instructions to a hypothetical editor of his final novel: "If I disappeared now, it would obviously not be easy to turn the fragments of 'Maumort' to good account. Not impossible, however. The devoted and industrious person who accepted this task would above all have to familiarize himself very carefully with the many preparatory files which make up my outline, and so manage to establish a complete and detailed biography of Maumort and of the various characters I have already placed about him."

The will called for a committee of his close friends—including Albert Camus, André Malraux, Gaston Gallimard, and Marie Rougier—to assume responsibility for the faithful carrying out of his instructions. Two attempts to assemble the disparate elements of the manuscript into a coherent whole failed to come to fruition. Finally, Mlle. Rougier led the committee to André Daspre, a professor of twentieth-century literature at the Faculté des Lettres de Nice, whom she knew because he had consulted her while doing his graduate thesis on *Jean Barois*. Daniel de Coppet, Martin du Gard's grandson and executor, gave his approval to the new candidate. Daspre turned out to be just the "devoted and industrious person" the author had envisioned.

The bulk of the manuscript had been packed, for protection, in a sturdy iron trunk. Thanks to Mlle. Rougier, the material was partitioned into folders, envelopes, and binders. For each episode or chapter, there were one or several versions of the narrative, plus supplementary material: story outlines, chronologies, sketches of floor plans, character studies, lists of possible names for people and places, rough drafts of secondary narratives, letters, newspaper articles, quotations. Sifting through this mass, André Daspre, over the course of five years, pieced together the text we now have. Whenever possible, he used the last version Martin du Gard had written and gave its text whole, without cuts. In instances where the text was not complete, or where different versions conflicted, the choices he made testify to his taste and scrupulousness. He also added a first-rate critical apparatus: two hundred pages of notes containing variants and subsidiary texts, background concerning Martin du Gard's intentions, and insights into his methods. These provide a unique view into the underpinnings of a masterpiece and the creative process of its author. We have included some of Daspre's notes in this volume, mainly as headings at the beginning of the less finished chapters. For the rest, we would urge readers with a knowledge of French to consult the Pléiade edition of *Lieutenant-Colonel de Maumort*.

The organization of the novel as Martin du Gard left it is linear; events are reported in chronological order. The author's "Summary" (p. 3) shows that he meant the book to be divided into seven sections, corresponding to the seven main periods of Maumort's life. André Daspre has respected this division of the text, although Part V ("The First World War") and Part VI ("Old Age at le Saillant") do not appear, since Martin du Gard did not have time to write them. The finished portion of the novel stops around the time of Maumort's marriage, but the author also produced two independent chapters about Maumort's sister, Henriette, and drafted accounts of two other periods of his character's life: his campaigns in Morocco under Lyautey, and the occupation of his château by German troops in 1940. There is also the beginning of the epistolary novel which might have replaced the memoirs.

In addition to the iron trunk, Martin du Gard left a smaller black cardboard box. This contained a collection of documents assembled for the writing of *Lieutenant-Colonel de Maumort: pensées,* fleeting observations, and brief essays, some drawn from notes that he had made over the course of his life, others composed from scratch for the new novel. "On many essential points," writes Daspre, these notes "express the heart of his thought." They have therefore been included as the final section of the book.

Like Proust's *Remembrance of Things Past* and Musil's *The Man Without Qualities, Lieutenant-Colonel de Maumort* remains an arrested work-in-progress, and for the same reason: it is not a mere novel but an entire universe, illimitable by its very nature. Martin du Gard understood this well and also saw the advantages of a jagged ending. A year after beginning *Lieutenant-Colonel de Maumort,* he wrote in his dairy: "It is a work that can grow and be perfected indefinitely: a work which will never be finished for me yet which may at any moment be interrupted by *my* death. An ellipsis and an editor's note will suffice: 'Here ends the manuscript of Colonel de Maumort, felled by a stroke on the night of . . .' " No life is rounded off; each, no matter how long or apparently complete, is cut short. Since reality hardly ever contrives tidy finales, there is something far more compelling in Martin du Gard's solution than in the more "perfect" denouements of so many conventional novels.

In fact, circumstances collaborated with Martin du Gard to bring about in *Lieutenant-Colonel de Maumort* the naturalness which he so wanted to achieve and which he felt had to some extent eluded him in his prior works. What might have detracted from the book ends up heightening its artistic value. The repetitions, the disunities, the mixture of different literary forms, combine to give the novel an invigorating rawness and make the reader feel as if he were an intruder peering into private papers he was never meant to see. Whether or not all of this was intentional on the author's part is finally beside the point. What matters is the miraculous vividness of the end result.

Lieutenant-Colonel de Maumort is Martin du Gard's definitive autopsy of human behavior. It takes a certain mettle to open oneself to the full brunt of his inquest, but the reader who does so will find his fortitude lavishly rewarded and will understand what Albert Camus meant when he called Roger Martin du Gard "our perpetual contemporary."

Luc Brébion / Timothy Crouse
March 1999

TRANSLATORS' ACKNOWLEDGMENTS

IT IS to a poet of the highest magnitude that we owe the adventure of having translated *Lieutenant-Colonel de Maumort.* David Rosenmann-Taub, the author of *El Cielo en la Fuente* and *Cortejo y Epinicio,* at once recognized the novel as a masterpiece in which Roger Martin du Gard had surpassed all his earlier creations. Hearing Rosenmann-Taub's analysis of the book—its multiple levels, its transcendence of its own time and place—inspired our effort to make it known to the English-speaking public.

André Daspre, the scholar responsible for bringing the unfinished manuscript of *Lieutenant-Colonel de Maumort* into its present state, and former head of the International Center for Research on Roger Martin du Gard, has been a mentor, sharing his erudition with us, and has become a friend. In the course of our work we were constantly guided by the critical apparatus he assembled, and we have drawn on his informative introduction to the Pléiade edition for our own introduction, particularly in relation to the circumstances surrounding Martin du Gard's composition of the novel.

We are indebted to our agent, Lynn Nesbit, for her trust in our vision, her perseverance, and her commitment to literature.

The book was skillfully shepherded through its various stages at Knopf by Jenny McPhee, George Andreou, and Melvin Rosenthal.

Gwyneth Cravens, with her novelist's eye and expertise as an editor, devoted herself unstintingly to reviewing our manuscript and made invaluable suggestions throughout. Kathleen Riordan Speeth lent her psychological knowledge, and Virginia Odessky her perceptiveness to the correction of our text. Chris Crawford gave the proofs a final going-over.

Barbara Epstein's comments helped us to refine our introduction.

Valerie Steele answered our questions concerning turn-of-the-century Parisian couture. Jean Paul Carlhian elucidated the vocabulary of design.

In Paris, Jean-Dominique and Françoise Lafay responded graciously to our many queries concerning arcana of the French language. Colonel Jean Vasche advised us on military terminology; Henriette Tarlier, on matters of decoration and period furniture.

The completion of this project was made possible by the generosity of the Peter Gruber Foundation.

FOREWORD

Soon after the publication of *Le Lieutenant-Colonel de Maumort* in 1983, fragments began to be translated into various languages, but it is in English that the first complete translation has been achieved. I am all the more delighted by this since Luc Brébion and Timothy Crouse have shown not only a care for precision down to the slightest details but also a remarkable sense of the author's intentions. They have found so many felicitous solutions to the difficulties of the text that I hope those who attempt the translation of the book into other languages will use this version as a model.

I cannot imagine a better presentation to the English-speaking public of this masterpiece by one of the world's greatest novelists.

André Daspre
*Director Emeritus, International Center
for Research on Roger Martin du Gard,
Toulon*

Nice. Saturday 30 April [19]49.

This afternoon at Gide's bedside, at the Belvédère Clinic where he has recently been seriously ill, I informed him of my intention to dedicate Les Souvenirs de Maumort *to him, and he was visibly—and joyously—moved.*

—————————

If the publication of this book is posthumous, I request that this be remembered, and that the following be inscribed on the first page:

"I dedicate this book to the memory of André Gide, whose exceptional friendship has sustained me, guided me, and wonderfully enriched me during the second half of my life."

R.M.G.

Lieutenant-Colonel
de Maumort

Summary of Maumort's Biography

I. Childhood and Adolescence (1870–1887)

July 1870:   Birth of Bertrand de Maumort at the château of le Saillant, in the Orne. (His father, a former artillery officer, had resigned four years earlier to attend to his estate; in 1870, he rejoined General Chanzy's army. His mother, née Suzanne Chambost-Lévadé, dies of complications from the delivery.)

1870–1882:   Lonely childhood at le Saillant, with his widower father and his sister, Henriette (his elder by nine years).

1882:   Guy Chambost-Lévadé, a first cousin Bertrand's own age, the son of a professor at the Sciences Politiques, comes to live at le Saillant. [The two cousins work with the Abbé Adry.]*

October 1882:   Arrival at le Saillant of a young tutor, Xavier de Balcourt, assigned to teach the two boys.

October–December 1883:   Guy's illness.

1884:   [Death of Guy in the spring. Bertrand continues to work with Xavier.] In October, Bertrand enters the Saint-Léonard School in the Orne, as a boarder.

1885–1886:   Year of *rhétorique.* Onset of puberty. Fails the *baccalauréat* at the July sitting.

Summer 1886:   Spends the vacation in the home of M. Nacquot, a teacher, and his wife [in Gevrésy]. Passes the examination in October.

1886–1887:   Year of *philosophie* at Saint-Léonard. Passes second part of the *baccalauréat.* Summer vacation at le Saillant.

II. Early Adulthood (1887–1891)

October 1887:   A decisive event: Maumort leaves his provincial home to live in Paris with his Uncle and Aunt Chambost-Lévadé, where he prepares for both his *license ès lettres* and his admission to Saint-Cyr.

1887–1889:   Life as a student in Paris. His schoolmates in the Latin Quarter;

---

*Material within brackets has been inserted in the Summary for clarity's sake by the editor, André Daspre.

3

[Blaise Saint-Gall and his family]. Xavier de Balcourt [and his mother's salon; the Hector Chambost household.] The academic world that revolves around his Uncle Chambost-Lévadé, a member of the Institut. Sunday gatherings of all the official, university, and intellectual celebrities.

[*1888:* Xavier in Aunay: the drowning; Xavier's suicide.]

1889: [Spring:] first love affair, with Doudou [born in 1861 or 1862], a Martiniquaise. [Her niece Zabette (born in 1872). Admitted to Saint-Cyr.]

III. BEGINNINGS IN THE ARMY, MARRIAGE (1891–1907)

1891–1892: Second lieutenant at Versailles. Second serious affair (with Raphaële Dancenis).

1893: Maumort falls in love with the sister of his friend Saint-Gall. Engagement. [Death of Pauline Chambost.]

1894: Death of his father at le Saillant. Marriage to Claire Saint-Gall.

1895: Lieutenant of spahis.* Stationed at Batna with Claire. Birth of his first son, Didier. Henriette's marriage to a neighbor in the Orne, Viscount [Adolphe] de Pontbrun [born in 1858].

1896: Stationed at Constantine† with his wife and son. [Death of Anna, Henriette's daughter, in the spring; then of Adolphe in November.]

1897: Maumort stays alone in Constantine. Claire's return to Paris for the child's health; she falls back under her family's influence. In spite of frequent leaves, the separation severely affects the couple's relationship.

1898: Birth in Paris of Alain, Maumort's second son. Dreyfus Affair, trial at Rennes. Maumort has serious disagreements with his superiors and his fellow officers in Constantine. He intends to leave the army, and begins by obtaining a two-year leave. His political attitude leads to a break with his in-laws. Claire continues to live with her parents. Marital dissension.

1898–1900: For two years, living at le Saillant with his widowed sister, Maumort devotes himself to the management of the estate.

1900: Shake-up in the high command in the wake of the Dreyfus Affair. Maumort returns to the army. Appointed captain of Hussars at Alençon,‡ under the command of Colonel Lyautey, who takes a liking to him. [Henriette adopts Emma.]

---

*Native Algerian horsemen serving under the French.
†Town in northeastern Algeria.
‡Town in northwestern France.

1901–1903: École de Guerre. Difficult readjustment to married life with his wife and children in Paris.

1903: Promoted to the general staff. Rejoins Lyautey's regiment in Alençon. Claire does not agree to leave Paris. [Summer vacation with his two sons at le Saillant.]

1904: Claire (born in 1874) dies of a sudden pulmonary condition. Maumort, a widower at thirty-four, with two boys of whom the elder is nine and the younger six, contemplates resigning. Lyautey, appointed general and sent to the frontier of Morocco, offers him a position on his general staff. Maumort leaves for Africa, leaving his sons in the care of his in-laws.

1905: At Aïn Sefra.* Introduction to Moroccan problems. [Death of Uncle Éric Chambost and his brother Hector.]

1906: After Algeciras, Lyautey is appointed major general at Oran. Maumort accompanies him there. Preparation for the first Moroccan campaign.

IV. MOROCCAN CAMPAIGNS

1907–1908: First Moroccan campaign. Maumort is sometimes at Lyautey's headquarters, sometimes assigned missions in the Moroccan bled.†

After the victory, Lyautey, appointed high commissioner, keeps Maumort with him, in Casablanca.

1909–1911: Lyautey, appointed corps commander, is called to Rennes.

Maumort, promoted cavalry major, stays in Morocco. Various garrisons on the border between Algeria and Morocco. Life in the bled; local skirmishes.

1912: Insurrections in the north of Morocco. Lyautey returns to Morocco as Resident, and summons Maumort back to his side. Second campaign. Conquest: Fez expedition, abdication of the Sultan, etc.

1913–1914: Maumort resides in Rabat or in Casablanca, attached to Lyautey's staff. Eighteen months of colonial politics, city planning, organization for the pacification of Morocco.

---

*French military hub in southwestern Algeria.

†Arabic term, adopted by the French, for the North African backcountry, or alternatively, a rolling plain or other open stretch of land.

V. THE FIRST WORLD WAR
(1914–1919)

August 1914:   Mobilization. Despite the efforts of Lyautey, who wants to defend his conquest and keep his officers with him, Maumort insists on leaving for France with the first colonial conscripts.

Disembarkation at Marseille on August 20. Called to the general staff of the First Cavalry Corps, which he joins immediately at Saint-Quentin. After Charleroi, the cavalry protects the retreat and participates in the Battle of the Marne.

In September, his elder son, Didier, having enlisted as a volunteer and been wounded on patrol, dies, at nineteen, in the hospital at Meaux.

Winter 1915:   In the Woëvre, Éparges sector.

Summer 1915:   Long summer with no battles. At his request, Maumort leaves the general staff but remains in the cavalry corps; he receives the command of a squadron of Dragoons.

1916:   The cavalry is partially dismantled. Maumort, appointed lieutenant-colonel, is placed in charge of an armored regiment. Life in the trenches.

1917:   Death of his sister, Henriette, who never ceased to live at le Saillant and to oversee its management.

Winter 1917:   Maumort has his knee smashed by a shard of shrapnel one evening when off duty, in the Soissons sector. Two months in the hospital in Compiègne.

Lame for life, he finishes the war in Paris, in a government office.

September 1918:   Ten weeks before the armistice, his son Alain gets killed in a tank, at twenty. [Death of Aunt Ma.]

Winter 1919:   Maumort leaves the army for good with the rank of colonel.

VI. OLD AGE AT LE SAILLANT (1919–1939)

Spring 1919:   Maumort retires to le Saillant. (After Henriette's death, its administration is left to the smallholders.) Maumort is going on fifty. He is alone in the world: he has lost his wife, his two sons, his sister; he has neither relatives nor friends (his colonial life has kept him away from France for twenty-five years).

1919–1935:   Lame but still very active and capable of staying in the saddle several hours a day, he divides his time between life outdoors (managing the land, riding, animal husbandry) and reading. (After the death of his Aunt Chambost-Lévadé, he inherited, at le Saillant, the eighteen thousand volumes of his uncle's library.)

1935:   Fall from a horse, on a morning of black ice. Breaks his pelvis. Long treatment at a clinic in Le Mans.

1936:   Disabled for good, unable to direct the farm work, he converts the four smallholdings into farms and resigns himself to a reclusive and studious existence.

1939:   Second World War.

VII. SECOND WORLD WAR
(1939–1945)

June 1940:   Invasion of Normandy by the German army. Le Saillant is occupied. Maumort refuses to have anything to do with the occupiers and lives confined to his study.

August 1940:   He leaves le Saillant and takes refuge in the "free zone" with Dr. Gévresin (whom he helps to organize the Resistance in the Piérac region).

December 1944:   Maumort's return to le Saillant.

Winter 1945:   Founding, at le Saillant, of a home for rest and work for the students of the university of Paris.

Remodeling and organizing.

October 1946:   Arrival at le Saillant of the first student boarders.

In December 1950, Maumort is struck down, in the night, by a heart attack. He is eighty.

I

Memoirs of Lieutenant-Colonel de Maumort

PART ONE

Childhood and Adolescence (1870–1887)

CHAPTER I

The Origins of the Maumort Family

MY SLEEP has always been light and intermittent. If I had kept an hourly log of my mental activity, it would in all likelihood turn out that I have spent many more nighttime than daytime hours engaged in thinking. These bouts of insomnia have taken on a chronic character over the years: when I have slept four or five hours in a night off and on, I consider it to have been an exceptionally good one. I always have a pad of paper and a pencil within reach, to catch on the wing this turn of phrase which strikes me as felicitous, that idea which I hope to be able to examine more closely in the light of day. Adversity has its uses . . .* I will even admit that, all things considered, these forced meditations bring me more pleasure than annoyance. It is only at the end of the night that I sometimes give in to impatience. All of my brethren in insomnia will, I think, know that anxiety which precedes the dawn, that interminably tiresome moment when one sits up every five minutes to see whether or not the day is going to decide to break, as at the end of a journey, at night, in a railway carriage, one constantly presses against the window to watch for the lights of the station where one is to arrive . . .

---

*These three dots are not ellipses and do not indicate any deletion of material. Rather, they are suspension points. Roger Martin du Gard uses them liberally throughout the book to suggest a wide range of nuances: a trailing off of thought or speech, a lapse into reverie, a pause for further reflection, an unfinished list, a statement left evocatively or discreetly incomplete, a tentative quality, a sense of breathlessness, etc. Although suspension points are not conventionally used in English, they are so much a part of the author's style of punctuation that we have elected to keep a large number of them.

All footnotes, if not attributed to Roger Martin du Gard or André Daspre, are the translators'.

This morning I am eager to set up a preliminary outline in accordance with the clear and almost panoramic vision which I had, last night, of my life—not that I intend to follow this chronological order, but this outline will help me all the same.

The only sensible arrangement to adopt for Memoirs would obviously be chronological order. Last night it seemed to me that my existence could be divided into a certain number of *parts*.

But I am straying from the purpose that made me take up my pen this morning. And when one decides at my age to set about such an undertaking, there is no time to lose.

Here begin the Memoirs of Colonel Bertrand de Maumort, born right here at the Château du Saillant on the first of July, 1870. I have always had a very accurate memory; I've been lucky enough to have kept it intact: I count on it for carrying out the task that I embark upon today.

Now I am very eager to gather the childhood memories that I have of my father. But before beginning, I shall first briefly note what I know of the ancient Maumorts.

A former dean of Menneville whom my grandfather encouraged to do research in the parish archives discovered the baptism, in 1505, of a male child with the Christian name of Loïs-Pierre, "son of Geoffroy de Maumort, former equerry, and of his wife, Marie Félicité de Littry," dwelling "in the place called le Saillant, abutting the forest of Mesneville." It seems likely that this Geoffroy de Maumort was the first of that name to settle in le Perche* in the last years of the fifteenth century. But where did he come from? A mystery. The ending "ort" is not from the area; it would indicate some other origin.

Since that date, the Maumorts, clinging firmly to their Saillant, have figured continually in the registers. It is in the middle of the sixteenth century that for the first time the family name Maumort was followed by the title of Comte de Saillant, which has been borne successively by all the Maumorts down to my grandfather, who styled himself simply: Général de Maumort. Nevertheless, in my childhood I still heard the old gardener say "our late Madame la Comtesse" to refer to my grandmother. Neither my father nor, of course, I myself ever made use of this nobiliary title, the authenticity of which I have not even verified. Among the old portraits set into the paneling of the white drawing room, thus pre-dating the eighteenth century, there are two that bear, in one corner, the arms of the house: a green shield on which three pretty little gray birds are arranged in a triangle. I believe this is rendered in

*Region of northern France on the border of Normandy, mainly in the east of the Orne département. Famous for its breed of draft horses (Percherons).

heraldic language as: *de sinople à trois merlettes d'argent.* And on a vermeil snuffbox which my sister made into her pin box (what has become of it? it must have been pinched by the Germans), the same blazon was painted in enamel, with a streamer on which could be read the motto of the Maumorts: *De male mort Dieu me garde!* *

The designation "château," applied to our manor house, does not appear until the end of the seventeenth century in the parish registers. From this my grandfather drew the conclusion that the present dwelling, although pure Louis XIII in style, had been built by one of our own in the late years of the reign of Louis XIV. This is possible: the master masons in the province were regularly fifty years behind the architects of the Île-de-France. The hypothesis seems confirmed by the date 1692, legible on the keystone of an arch which is embedded in the masonry of an outbuilding and which marks the site of an old carriage door, today walled up.

Among my archives that were reduced to a pulp by the damp, I used to possess a family tree drawn in a naïve style by my grandfather; I did not unfold it often and I have only a vague memory of it. A line of soldiers and landowners, with no merchants or lawyers—which, I confess, rather pleases me. The estate came together little by little, plot by plot, through successive acquests, sometimes by marriage, until it reached its present area: one hundred eighty-four hectares† of fields, pastures, and woods, in which the grazing meadows predominate, and which were divided up among our four tenant farms: les Houderettes, les Fouquerolles, la Clergie, and le Liardon.

Am I under the spell of their familiar sounds? They would, I think, have charmed the poets of the Pléiade.‡ Whichever way one puts these four names together, they have an exquisite ring to my ear. I always hear and utter them with rapture: les Fouquerolles, le Liardon, les Houderettes, and la Clergie.

I know little about my great-grandfather apart from the fact that he accepted the Revolution of 1789 and adhered to its principles—to the great scandal of the family and of the local gentry; and that after having spurned the Empire he ended up enlisting in Napoleon's armies. The breastplate he had worn as a colonel of cuirassiers remained in the attic. My sister gave it away, along with our grandfather's uniforms, to the Costume Museum. But we have kept that mediocre portrait of him which is in the hall; certain features—the salient arch of the eyebrows, the hooked nose, the mouth, the upward-jutting chin—call to mind my father's face (and my own).

Although I never knew him, I am better informed about my grandfather,

---

*May God save me from a bad death!

†About four hundred fifty acres.

‡Group of seven poets of the sixteenth century, led by Pierre Ronsard, whose aim was to elevate French to the level of the classical languages.

Général Bertrand de Maumort, whose Christian name I bear. He died during the Second Empire, senator for the Orne. He was only sixty. They die young in my family: my father died at fifty-six. To judge from the daguerreotype that I have of my grandfather, he was very different from us: stocky, squat, with a flat face whose mustache continued along his jowls in those close-cropped sideburns that used to be called "muttonchops." In his senatorial tailcoat it is impossible to guess what a great warrior he was. His life was one long feat of arms.

Second lieutenant in the artillery at the time of the Restoration, he was part of the French expeditionary force sent to the Peloponnesus to liberate Greece from the Turkish yoke. Scarcely had he returned when he went off to fight in Algeria in the army of General Voirol, who decorated him after the siege of Mostaganem. But he was repatriated in 1833 after the defeat at Constantine, in which he was wounded. A bad wound, inadequately tended, which festered during the crossing and caused him to be hospitalized in Marseilles, then in Arles. It was there, during his convalescence, that he met in Arlesian society the one who was to become his wife, Mademoiselle de Cambosc, a rather well-to-do orphan who introduced into the family a taste for very fruity olive oil and that ridiculous middle name of Angélina which she handed down to my sister Henriette, whose godmother she was. Settled in at le Saillant, my grandmother never returned to her Midi*; but she was homesick for it and never got used to our rainy climate. We owe to her the construction of our grape hothouse, which for a long time was the only one in the region. She consoled herself for not having been able to acclimatize the cypress to our forest fogs by planting nearly everywhere in the park those thujas which still flourish there.

I have always liked the idea that this little velvet-eyed Arlesian slipped a few drops of Southern blood into my Percheron veins. My natural laziness— I mean this meandering of thought (which I call my "purring")—would then have for an excuse its origin in that Provençal race—refined through centuries of Mediterranean civilization, passionate when so inclined but carefree and full of idle curiosity—which was able to push so far the subtle art of wasting one's time and of relishing those solitary amusements which daydreaming and the spectacle of the world lavish on inquiring minds.

Marriage did not keep my old trooper of a grandfather in his Perche for long. When he heard that a new expedition was preparing against Constantine, he buckled on his sword-belt and set off again for Africa, despite being on the wrong side of forty and without even waiting for the birth of his son, whom he was to get to know only ten years later. In November 1837, he savored his revenge and entered Constantine with the victorious army. He

*The south of France, including Provence.

was wounded at Sebdou, treated on the spot, healed, then attached to the staff of General Lamoricière, whom he did not leave until the end of the campaign, until the surrender of Abd el-Kader. Finally, he made up his mind to go back to France. But again this was only a short respite, since two years later, in '49, he was in Italy with General Oudinot, took part in the siege of Rome, and received the blessing of the Holy Father, whom my grandfather helped to repossess his States. (I still have, on the landing, two engravings that he placed on either side of his bed: one depicts the capture of la Smalah, the other the Pope's return to Rome.) This time, however, it was retirement, with two stars. His first concern, upon reappearing at le Saillant, was to pull his son, who was thirteen, out from under the maternal skirts and to pack him off to the Jesuit school at Sées. My father held this against him, and it is no doubt to this that I owe not having been sent to boarding school until after my fifteenth year.

My grandfather had, like all of us, a taste for things of the earth; but his turbulent life had not afforded him much experience with farming and raising cattle. He had the wisdom to let his farmers do these things. But he was bored; and I think it was to escape the vexations of his rustic idleness that he lapsed into politics—for which nothing had prepared him. In 1852, after the coup d'état and the promulgation of the new constitution, our département,* which had remained one of the most obstinately loyal to the monarchy, chose this general of Louis-Philippe's to represent it in the Senate. His career as a senator was rather short and unglamorous, except for the very last day: after four years, on that rostrum which he had so very rarely mounted, a seizure struck him down as he was finishing a speech demanding the abolition of the regulations that were hampering the grain trade. My father, then a student at the École Polytechnique,† summoned posthaste to the Senate infirmary, found him paralyzed, aphasic, dying. And it was in his coffin that my grandfather was brought back here. My grandmother was to outlive him by six years. Doubtless she scarcely missed her husband: he had got her used to doing without him. She lived long enough to be present at her son's wedding and at the birth of Henriette.

And here, after having put a little order into the family lore, I have quite naturally worked my way back to the biography of my father, Hippolyte de Maumort.

HE LIVED his entire childhood by his mother's side in the country and had a liking only for country life. But soldiering was a tradition in the family. I

---

*French territorial division, the largest unit of local government.
†The premier engineering school of France, established in 1794.

have various reasons to believe that, forced by my grandfather to prepare for a military school, my father opted for Polytechnique rather than Saint-Cyr* in the hope of afterwards getting a civilian job. This hope was disappointed: his rank in the class required him to be an artillery officer. Meanwhile, his father had died. No doubt my father would gladly have left the army; but he could do that only after having fulfilled the service commitments made at the time of his admission to the École. There were a few years to wait out. After a training period in the east—at Stenay,† I believe—he obtained, I do not know how, a post in the offices of the Department of the Artillery, in Paris, which brought him nearer to le Saillant. This young provincial, who might have had a rather heady sojourn in Paris, scarcely took advantage of it. He went out little and performed his bureaucratic duties punctiliously, while awaiting the moment when he would have leave to resign . . . Writing this, I suddenly realize that what I am stating here as though I had it on good authority is pure invention on my part . . . This is how I have always pictured my father's life in the capital, and, in good faith, I have turned this fiction into a truth. (History must be crammed with "truths" of the same sort.) The more I think about it, however, the more inclined I am to believe that I am mistaken, a victim of my own imagination, or rather my lack of imagination. For if this young lieutenant of twenty-four who waltzed at the Institut‡ Ball with the woman who was to be my mother had so resembled the man I knew, widowed and taciturn, retired to his land, living with his small-holders, it is hardly likely that he would have so greatly captivated the young Parisienne, or that she would have fought so hard against her relations to marry him.

Here is what I know of that marriage.

My maternal grandfather, the physicist Chambost-Lévadé, who was a member of the Institut, happened to be in charge of a course at the École Polytechnique. My father had thus been his student, and—this has been confirmed for me by my Uncle Éric—one of his favorites.

My father's taste for science, and particularly the very keen interest he took in modern discoveries in physics, was always quite pronounced: up until his final illness, the only reading he did on winter evenings and on Sundays was in the scientific journals to which he still subscribed; he put them away, stuffed with markers and references, in the big wardrobe in his bedroom, and each month he took the trouble to draw up an analytical table of the most instructive articles. These details have their importance. I shall

*The French national military academy, founded in 1803 by Napoleon and located until 1944 in the town of Saint-Cyr-l'École, near Versailles.

†Town on the Meuse River, near the border with Belgium.

‡A body composed of the scientists, artists, and writers belonging to the five French academies.

come back to them. There is certainly a connection between this curiosity for scientific questions and the liberal-mindedness that my father displayed, contrary to the traditionalism of his family and to the upbringing that he had received, in regard to religion as well as to the "reactionary" politics favored by his set.

As regards religion, my father showed himself to be respectful and indifferent. He was not seen in church except on the year's major holidays, and this was manifestly in order to conform to custom. All the men in the parish acted the same in those days, with the exception of a very small clan of notorious anticlericals—café politicians, uneducated and loud, unanimously disapproved of in the district. I never heard my father utter a remark against the faith or against the clergy. Five or six times a year, on the major holidays, he entertained the Dean of Menneville at his table and showed him a deferential friendliness. One point will always remain unclear for me. What were my father's religious opinions before his marriage? I have never known if the company of the Chambost-Lévadés—where the tone was rather resolutely "Voltairean"—had had an influence on my father's feelings and had contributed to distancing him from religion; or if, on the other hand, he had not been all the more attracted by that emancipated circle since, with his naturally free thought, he felt at ease there.

How, when he was posted to Paris, did my father resume relations with his former teacher? How did he come to attend the Chambost-Lévadés' salon assiduously and to fall in love with their daughter? It doesn't matter. What is certain is that my parents' union was a marriage of love and that they had much opposition to overcome in order to achieve their ends. The one who advised against this marriage the most vehemently—he told me so himself—was my uncle Éric Chambost-Lévadé, my mother's brother. At that time a young *agrégé* fresh out of the Normale,* he lived in close intimacy with his younger sister, whose education he was rounding off by including her in his reading, in his work, in his study trips to Germany and Italy. I can quite well understand that the love of this young "intellectual" for a big, strapping officer who was ruddy-faced and built like Hercules (my father, like me, was six foot one), who came from the provinces and did not hide his impatience to get back there to farm his lands and raise his livestock—seemed an inexplicable whim, an absurd piece of nonsense, to this Normale-trained brother who was highly cultivated, had grown up in the shadow of the Institut, and was scarcely acquainted with the country except through the *Georgics*.†

---

*That is, he had passed a special competitive examination (*agrégation*) at the end of his teacher's training at the École Normale Supérieure, qualifying him to become a professor in a lycée or a university.

†Virgil's treatise in verse on husbandry.

Therefore he did everything in his power to dissuade his sister from this pre-posterous plan and to foster the lack of enthusiasm that my grandparents showed for this marriage, which threatened to keep their daughter shut away far from Paris. But the obstinacy of the engaged couple finally triumphed over all obstacles, and the wedding ceremony was celebrated with great pomp at Saint-Sulpice in December of 1860 before a very Parisian crowd, present among whom, I imagine, were distinguished representatives of the five academies,* and among whom my paternal grandmother, who had come up specially from le Saillant, must have felt somewhat out of place.

My father's resignation and the installation of my parents at le Saillant, where Grandmother still held sway, followed close on their marriage. I know very little about the life of the young couple in the years that followed: a few events, a few dates. In November of '61, my sister was born. In the winter of '62, a bereavement: the death of my grandmother. Between '62 and '64, reform of the way the place was run, by transforming the farms into small-holdings. Then years pass. And, in the first days of July 1870, my mother died while bringing me into the world.

The birth of my sister, nine years earlier, had already come close to cost-ing my mother her life. Her health had remained frail as a result, which probably explains why my parents waited eight years before having another child. It is not even certain that my birth was desired, and I may be the inop-portune fruit of an inadvertence. Unless my father—who always encouraged and took the part of large families in the area—deliberately, and against the advice of the doctors, took the initiative in attempting this second experi-ment. A hypothesis, but not totally devoid of foundation. I know, on the one hand, that during her second pregnancy, which was particularly trying, my mother lived in terror of a day of reckoning that she sensed would be mortal; so much so that to ward off ill fortune she had planned a pilgrimage to Lourdes, which her weakened state made impossible; so it is reasonable to suppose that she did not risk this new pregnancy of her own free will. On the other hand, Aunt Ma—my Uncle Éric's wife, my mother's sister-in-law (about whom I shall speak at leisure, I hope, later on), for whom I felt the liveliest affection and at whose side I lived during my whole adolescence in a trusting intimacy—said to me, one day when I was complaining to her about my father's lack of warmth toward me: "What can I tell you, my child? He's never been able to forgive himself for your birth . . ." I can still see us, alone together, in that little blue sitting room in the Hôtel de Fleurus where I often

*The five academies that make up the Institut de France (founded in 1795) are: the Académie Française; the Académie des Inscriptions et Belles-Lettres; the Académie des Sciences; the Académie des Beaux-Arts; and the Académie des Sciences Morales et Politiques. Their sessions are held at the Palais de l'Institut in Paris.

went up to chat with her. "To forgive himself . . ." I did not immediately understand what she was implying by that; but the words had struck me, I turned them over in my mind, I never forgot them.

My sister always remembered the uncanny beauty of that translucent face, with its eyelids turned blue, which rested on the pillow, and which had, one last time, smiled. My mother remained lucid until the end: it was at her insistence that I was baptized at the foot of her bed by the Dean of Menneville, who had been fetched in the carriage for the last rites. I had our old gardener for a godfather; and my sister for a godmother. A few moments after having received Extreme Unction, my mother passed away, without suffering, following a new and critical loss of blood.

For my father, the shock was such that his entire life was marked by it. I can only say what I know about it from my sister. She often repeated: "It was the war that was his salvation; without the war, he would have lost his mind." In the family, it was said that this premature widowerhood, after ten years of unclouded happiness, had "turned that poor Hippolyte into *another* man." That is no doubt correct. Indeed, my father was like a cripple; beneath his robust and healthy appearance, there was something indefinably abnormal. Which makes sense, if one considers that he was no longer himself: his character had been deeply altered, transformed by a cause external to its nature; his hypochondria, that inner hardness which one surmised beneath the cold and detached exterior, that unconscious selfishness, and that fundamental indifference, and a score of other failings from which we, and my sister above all, had to suffer—were caused, and excused by, an incurable wound. And I repeat to myself that sentence of Aunt Ma's: "He could never forgive himself . . ." Considering the morbid form that his despair had taken, I am really inclined to believe that my father secretly bore the feeling of an irremediable responsibility, whose venom never ceased to gnaw at his heart.

"It was the war that saved him . . ." Indeed, two weeks after my mother's death, France declared war on Germany.

From the very first days, my father, seizing on that patriotic occasion to escape his sorrow and to flee this house where everything reminded him of his misfortune, did not hesitate to throw himself into the fray. My sister and I remained in the care of old Zélie, my grandmother's former chambermaid, who had come from Provence with her at the time of the marriage and had been part of the family for over thirty years.

My father spoke little in general, rarely about himself, and hardly ever about the war of '70. I have been told, however, that the battery he commanded belonged to the First Army of the Loire, under Aurelle de Paladines, then to the Second, under Chanzy; and that after the battle of Vendôme, in the December snows, he had to fall back on Le Mans, where he came down with a case of typhoid fever from which he nearly died (and from which he never completely recovered) and which kept him several months in the hospital at Laval. So that he did not come back to us until May '71, even though the armistice of Versailles had been signed in January, and Chanzy's army had been disbanded at the beginning of March.

Then, in the austere solitude of le Saillant, the three of us—this thirty-three-year-old widower, this ten-year-old girl, and the wailing baby that I still was—began that cloistered, monotonous, and joyless existence which continued until my departure for boarding school fifteen years later.

Cloistered, monotonous, and joyless . . . And yet the distant memories I have of my early childhood are not darkened by any sadness. Probably the vitality of youth, and the continuous presence of my sister, and the absence of comparison with other, less morose family lives prevented me from feeling the dismal atmosphere of the house. An atmosphere which perhaps had its effect on my character: it was probably in the course of those first years that I acquired, if not a tendency to melancholy, at least this ability to get along easily without gaiety, and this taste for reverie, which have been, which still are, among the oldest and most constant characteristics of my nature.

My father, in those days, was at the height of his powers. His blooming robustness, his extraordinary resistance to fatigue, had something excessive, insolent about them. In him there was a mixture of roughneck soldier and gentleman, of vulgarity and distinction. Very tall, very straight, rather stout, with a wide chest, an athlete's shoulders, powerful and hairy hands, a lush reddish-blond beard, a brick-colored complexion, small eyes, a worried gaze, eyelids that were usually screwed up; always in boots, always with a large wind-and-rain-faded felt hat on his head, he embodied for me not just physical strength and health but also order, courage, and authority; and though not producing actual terror in me, he inspired a respectful fear, shaded with admiration and perhaps with envy, which ruled out, on my part, all attraction, all openness, all affectionate familiarity.

Besides, he never paid much attention to me. He no longer seemed to have any role, any interest in this world, other than the running of his estate.

I was not the only one to be intimidated by him. And this, I believe, was largely due to a physical peculiarity of his. Prone to stiff necks, he always had a slight tautness in the neck muscles, and when he turned towards an interlocutor, he shifted his shoulders at the same time—which, in this simple and unaffected man, gave an indefinable insistency and manneredness to the most natural remarks: the most insignificant question, posed with that movement of the entire chest, immediately took on a solemn character; and the slightest assertion, a peremptory one. He appeared inflexible, and only for lack of muscular suppleness.

I remember a page from the chapter "On the Affection of Fathers," wherein Montaigne reports to us the confidences of a friend whose son has just died: the father grieves that he had made himself so little known to his child, that he had, through an excess of affection, brought him up with a rigid severity, and had deliberately hidden his tenderness in order to give more bite to his scoldings, with the aim of better tempering his son's character. Disconsolate, in short, at having loved him so poorly. I have never been able to read this passage without emotion, not so much because it reminds me of certain traits of my father's as because it brings out the lack of understanding between fathers and sons. Nothing more pathetic, certainly, than those warped family relationships in which, from one generation to the next, despite mutual efforts—and however genuine the atmosphere of affection—strained relations set in and irreparable misunderstandings develop between two persons of the same blood. I have looked up the text. I had forgotten the last lines, which so well bear out that kind of melancholy which takes hold of me each time I think about my father: "There is no sweet solace for the loss of our friends other than that which is given us by the knowledge that *there was nothing we forgot to tell them, and that we had with them a perfect and complete communication.*"

My attitude towards my father went through very few variations during the twenty-four years of his life that I witnessed: a habitual affection, without outward signs; and in his presence, a shifty deference. I seldom argued and I never rebelled; moreover he did not often give me the opportunity, although he basically had an authoritarian temperament, which he controlled. With me he was firm on certain points but otherwise accommodating: probably out of kindness, but also out of that mixture of indifference and aversion to quarrels which so resembles kindness and is the most common form of it.

What changed, from one age to another, was the judgment that I passed on him: I can almost say it is still changing.

As a child, I felt for my father a timorous reverence, of which, in reality, spontaneous tenderness formed no part. Was this his fault or mine? I don't know. I avoided him—without premeditation, by instinct: I preferred to stay out of his way. We said little to each other. He had a solitary, silent nature; and, completely absorbed in his active life, he showed himself to us only at meals. He was not particularly strict; but the kindness that he demonstrated toward me was distracted; he scarcely spoke a word to me except to correct my table manners, to question me about my work, to advise me to be well-behaved. As for me, I had nothing to say to him: it was with my sister, who was nine years my senior, that I chatted openheartedly, but away from the paternal presence.

Around the age of fifteen or sixteen, I began to judge him. At boarding school, for a start, I compared him to my teachers, to those whose influence affected me. Later, as a student in Paris, I compared him to those brilliant men with whom I rubbed elbows in the academic society of my Uncle Chambost: they seemed to me so superior to my father that I stopped venerating him. The verdicts of youth are absolute. I had consigned him once and for all to the mediocre category of ordinary people wholly absorbed in the practical life; he really seemed to me far too lacking in those intellectual capacities which, at that time, I prized with a single-minded fetishism. Certainly I respected his hard-working, free, uncompromising existence; but with a shade of disdain, the tone of which, I may add, my uncle very discreetly set for me. I thought of my father as a backward relative in the provinces, bogged down in his habits and his humble rustic virtues. I was happy to get back to him at vacation time, to see my sister and le Saillant again. I gladly took part in his existence, I went with him on his rounds, I questioned him about the farm work in progress, but I did not speak to him about the things that were on my mind. I did not even notice the pleasure that he took in having me near him and that he never expressed in words. When I felt at odds with him, it was of no importance to me. Given his attitude, I never was prompted to tell him. At le Saillant, I willingly complied with his wishes, which were not at all tyrannical. In Paris, when his authority made itself felt at a distance (softened, besides, by my uncle's interventions), I submitted to it, all in all, without great impatience. To tell the truth, I thought about him little and didn't much wonder about him: he did not interest me. Not even enough to make me want to free myself from his distant supervision.

It was then that he fell mortally ill and that my way of being toward him changed abruptly.

I clearly remember that brief May break of 1888 that I went to spend at le Saillant. My father had just been laid low by the first attack of that urinary ailment of which he was to die, but not until six years later. I believe that until then I had never had occasion to see him in bed (he was always up much earlier than the rest of us). I remember coming into that bedroom with its drawn curtains, its table cluttered with phials, and that huge fourposter bed where he was lying like a felled giant, humiliated. After the first few days, during which he had tolerated only the doctor from Menneville and old Agathe, the coachman's wife, at his bedside, he gradually consented to let Henriette take care of him; then he no longer wanted to be looked after by anyone but her. I remember my sister, attentive, skillful, silent, coming and going around the patient, and her white apron moving in the half-light. She was twenty-seven. She was beginning her apprenticeship in that occupation of nurse that she was to perform for him until the end, without complaint, without a touch of weariness or ill humor; and I learned only long afterwards just how hard that bondage had been on her.

Two months later, I returned to le Saillant with my tail between my legs. I had landed that title of *licencié ès lettres** which my father regarded as an

*A degree awarded by French universities, falling somewhere between an M.A. and a Ph.D.

inessential luxury, but had failed the examination for Saint-Cyr on which he set such store. Nothing cost me more than to make this confession to him. He laid no reproach on me; I was only the more ashamed. I had the excruciating impression that he was going to die soon and that I had deprived him of one final joy. I promised him to devote the following year to preparing seriously for my entrance examination, and I faithfully kept my word. (What determines our destinies? If Father had died during the summer vacation of '88, when several times we thought to lose him, there is no doubt about it: I would never again have sat for Saint-Cyr. And if he had not still been around when I graduated, I would, most probably, have resigned. It was largely to please him that I became an officer . . .)

From the day when my father ceased to be the sturdy, active, headstrong man that I had always known, new feelings awoke in me: a need for submission, a fear of disappointing his hopes. Now that his reduced authority could no longer weigh on my behavior, I would have reproached myself for taking advantage of that physical weakening; I had lost all desire to resist, to shirk. I held my own preferences cheap. I met him more than halfway. It seemed to me that I was acting like this out of affection, and I would have been indignant if anyone had accused me of loving my father very little. That would have been the truth, nevertheless. I see it clearly at a distance. These new feelings forced themselves upon me without any deepening of my filial attachment. Pity entered into it much more than tenderness. I foresaw that approaching death without feeling sorrow. It even happened a number of times, in the course of the six years of waiting, that I wished for the end. Of course, someone might say to me: for your father, you wanted a conclusion to this long agony; for your sister, liberation from a crushing servitude; nothing could be more natural . . . False excuses! My father was not suffering so badly that one could call his death a deliverance; and as for Henriette, she performed her task with a smiling abnegation that concealed from everybody, including me, the heavy yoke she bore. No. The truth is something else. I did not care if my father lived. I had no need of his presence in my life. No, it was first of all for me, in order to free *myself* from that constant worry, from that haunting sight, that I was so willing to see my father disappear. And it was a purely selfish relief that I felt, if not on the day itself, at least soon after his death. What is more, I was not conscious of it. I thought I sincerely missed my father, and it was in good faith that I imagined I shared Henriette's grief. I would have loathed myself, I would have thought myself a monster, if I had doubted my filial suffering. Such is the strength of learned, conventional feelings. But today I am no longer the dupe of these conformist illusions. I have lost my two sons; I have known that heartbreak, that open wound, and that relentless despair which the death of a tenderly cherished soul leaves behind. I felt nothing like that at my father's grave.

Probably I would have suffered more if I had understood him better when he was alive, for I would have loved him more. It was not until many years later, unconsciously, as I was getting on in years—perhaps under the influence of a heredity that had become more pronounced or perceptible—that I saw my errors of judgment, my injustices, and that gradually, through my memories, I saw his true face, unrecognized for so long, emerge more and more clearly from the façade that had hidden it from me.

In truth, things are not so simple as I have just said. During the ten years that followed my father's death, I did indeed pass through a crisis of filial piety, and I progressively revised the incomplete and overly harsh judgment that I had of him in his lifetime. We spoke of it often, my sister and I, and through a belated need for fairness, combined with remorse, I managed to paint an extremely flattering portrait of him, which resembled him just as little, really, as the previous one. But when Henriette was no longer around to maintain this excessive veneration; when, after 1918, I found myself back here, alone, in this setting where the impressions of the past were rekindled for me and were encountered daily, it was yet another image of my father that took shape in my mind. I had to correct my vision anew. With objectivity, I was forced to recognize that, out of an excess of repentance, I had indulgently overrated his moral qualities, his intellectual merit, his concern for duty. In the light of my memories, I noticed irrefutable signs of a certain dryness of mind, a certain narrow rigidity; of a certain mediocrity of character, also; even a certain hardness of heart . . . Not without a struggle, not without pain, I came to grow away from my father, to refuse him that posthumous glorification in which, for a while, I had indulged. It was as though I was losing him a second time. And the heartbreak that I felt, in my clearheaded solitary meditations, was certainly much crueler for me than his death had been.

I WONDER WHY I take the trouble to put down these details, and if, in doing so, I am not yielding to some unconscious and vain self-indulgence. I have often been called an *"aristo"*; in general, this annoyed me; sometimes, I admit, it did not displease me. Would I dare claim that I feel no pride in being a Maumort? Pride is perhaps putting it too strongly: a secret satisfaction. The idea that I could be named M. Durand—be the son of some tradesman grown rich thanks to wheeling and dealing—makes me wince involuntarily. Yet never, in the choice of my acquaintances, still less of my friends, have I taken name into account; and in fact, a few exceptions aside, I have had hardly any friends with the nobiliary particle. Nevertheless: I confess that I am not insensible to the sonority of an old patronymic; and the man who bears it, if by chance he is introduced to me—especially if he should also have a certain distinction of good breeding in his manners—is, I must admit, from the first moment, someone towards whom I am favorably biased . . . When my father used to say, with a disdainful expression: "He's not from *our set*," I sensed perfectly well what he meant by that, and though not as categorical as he, I was not without some prejudice against the fellow.

I hasten to add that, even in my youth, this foolish respect for a caste took on a different focus for me. If I kept the word *aristocracy* in my vocabulary, it was with a completely different content: in my eyes, quite early and exclusively, it indicated a set of values which do not necessarily pertain to birth: a collection of superior physical and moral qualities, among which I attribute a certain role to that bearing, that elegance in manners, those refinements, which are developed by a good upbringing and a comfortable financial situation but in which the dominant place is left to character and intelligence—steadfastness of spirit, courage, sense of honor, rigor of conscience, intellectual cultivation, independence of judgment, etc. No, really, I have never been infatuated with nobility. On the contrary, I am more demanding and severe with those whose mediocrity dishonors a great name; and our old families, one must admit, are for the most part breeding-grounds for degenerates, sensualists, and imbeciles. The only nobility of any worth is a high level of perfection, and it is in this sense that I like to use that expression of the old regime: "a person of quality." What is more, I am as far removed from utopian egalitarian prejudices as from stupid prejudices of the nobility. Nietzsche maintains that any improvement of humankind is the work of aristocratic societies. I like this thought, but that is not the only reason I have remembered it: historically, I consider it indisputable.

If there remains in me any atavistic residue of caste-consciousness, it is perhaps this tendency I have always had to feel and to want to be *distinct* while giving this word, I admit, a nuance of superiority. Yes, I have to confess to myself, at the risk of sounding smug—which, in all sincerity, I don't for a moment think I am—that this feeling of superiority which the Maumorts unfairly based on the sole fact of belonging to their family possesses me as well; and this since my earliest youth; and I might add that there is nothing of which I am more instinctively, unalterably certain . . . I can't do a thing about it: I consider myself a felicitous outcome as a human being, deserving of respect. This good fortune implies duties, by the way; and I have striven to fulfill them. But it also confers rights (I am actually tempted to write: "royal" rights); and as for those—ah, I confess that I have not refrained from using them!

This presumptuous attitude goes back a long way. I do not know if my case is exceptional. I do not think so. The fact remains that, very early on, while still a child, I had an unformed sense of my personality, of an "I" more real and more important in my eyes than all the rest of the universe: a kind of impregnable citadel, standing at the center of myself, where I could always find refuge against what was strange and hostile in the world of adults; a haven of happiness. (And I was not mistaken: I have carried that citadel around with me throughout my life without its ever having disappointed my hopes or gone back on its promises; many ruins, shades, and memories have gathered there over the years; but this walled hideout still stands fast. Death will find me there, amidst my treasures.)

I was still in school when I stopped short before a word I did not know that opened unsuspected and heartening perspectives, a word I immediately made my own: *esoteric*. If my memory is correct, Plato distinguishes two well-defined orders of knowledge, analogous to our elementary education and higher education: an everyday philosophy, accessible to any average intelligence; and a more subtle philosophy, the prerogative of a few exceptional minds, and to be divulged only with caution. An "esoteric" philosophy, in other words; reserved for the rare initiates. This discovery delighted me. It fit in with an amorphous but deeply rooted notion in my adolescent pride: the notion of an elite, of selection. I had this intuitive conviction in me that certain beings—of whom I felt myself indubitably to be one—had, from the quality of their nature, the right to live and to think according to their own directives, that is to say as outlaws, legitimately excused from submitting to the traditional rules.

At a certain level of cultivation, an individual consciousness can recognize what rounds it off, makes it grow, and what diminishes it: its "good" and its "evil." It ceases to have faith in the commonly held set of values, and judges thoughts, actions, their consequences, according to a scale all its own. It thus creates its own law. Not, to be sure, the cynical "everything is lawful" of old father Karamazov, but: "Being who I am, I have the right, so long as it does not result in any collective harm, to grant myself, under the supervision of my conscience, certain freedoms which I feel are useful to my development and which, nevertheless, I feel must be forbidden to most others." These are things that one can ponder, liberties that one can take, but that one is obviously well advised to keep to oneself. The best attitude in this regard seems to me to be that of conforming outwardly to the rules of the social game (insofar as one can do so without giving up essential freedoms); and of abstaining, with good grace, from any occasion for scandal which can be avoided without this causing serious inner damage. A question of moderation and of good sense. The collective morality is indispensable: it is for this reason worthy of respect, and it deserves certain personal sacrifices by those who are most disposed to compromise it. The main thing is not to lose sight of its relativity and of the fact that, in the end, it is nothing more than a set of conventions and police regulations, advantageous to the harmony of the city-state, codified by custom and long experience, and whose usefulness is confined to assuring a little order in the activities of the hive.

I have always deliberately hidden my "esotericism." I confessed it—and even then, in exceptional instances—only to co-initiates, to peers. I have, I may add, come across a great number of these. I will even say that, among the people of value it has been given me to meet, I have not found any who were not, more or less consciously, "esoterics." This is an observation that I was able to make while very young, as soon as I was introduced into the circle of my Uncle Chambost: an intellectual society, an aristocracy of the mind, where freedoms were broad, and where, right away, I felt very much at home.

And when I entered Saint-Cyr, the idea that I had of a military career further strengthened in me this sense of aristocratism, this principle of a human hierarchy. (Moreover, in the army, the duties that derived from this seemed to me much more important than the rights; and nothing upset me more, in my neophyte's fervor, than to meet a superior whose intelligence, character, or conduct did not do credit to the functions of a leader.)

My whole private existence was thus spent, with neither scruple nor remorse, in that "no-man's-land" which stretches beyond the written law into that free, airy, "esoteric" zone (but also steep and sown with pitfalls), where the members of the secret aristocracy live, the men who are not of ordinary stature, who know it, feel it, and cultivate themselves as such; and who, for this reason, consider themselves alone authorized to define the scope and bounds of their freedoms; in other words, to observe a moral code of which they themselves have set the terms.

What was this code? I shall have to explain it if I tell the story of my life. For the moment, I am speaking about the Maumorts, and so I end this digression.

One more parenthesis, however: I remember one of my first encounters with Lyautey,* at Alençon, when he was still only a dazzling original, rather pretentious in appearance, unbending in his likes as in his dislikes, very much in the public eye, wildly controversial and difficult to get along with. The conversation had come round to Tolstoy, whose complete works were then appearing for the first time in French translation and whom Lyautey, with his generous ardor, declared he admired without reservation. Long before, my Uncle Chambost had had me read *Anna Karenina* and *War and Peace* in the Hachette edition; and he had spoken to me copiously of Tolstoy, with whom he had maintained, through letters, a curious argument as to the manner in which the relationship of history to reality might properly be understood, and with whom he had later had the good fortune to spend some time during a season at an Austrian spa. I thus had the advantage over Lyautey of possessing facts about the man; and, I no longer know how, I was induced to say that Tolstoy had an unbridled temperament, consumed with passions, and that his inner life seemed a daily struggle against his demons.

*General Lyautey, conqueror of Morocco. See Chapter XXI.

These details appeared to make a deep impression on Lyautey, to touch particularly sensitive points in him. I remember his tensed face, the sharp glance he shot at me, his silence in which the threat of a storm seemed to hover, and, all of a sudden, his curt shrug. Then, without opening up further, he did an about-face, as was his wont, and launched into a brilliant improvisation on the character of Prince André. But his bearing, his gesture, had so struck me that I recorded them in my diary that same day and have not forgotten them. I regret having lost those notes. The interpretation that I straightaway gave and still give today to that surprising movement of the shoulders could pretty exactly be expressed as follows, and it is why this memory comes back to me: "How absurd it is, when you have the stature and the mission of a Tolstoy, to go and squander your energy in struggling against your petty human instincts!" After years of collaboration with Lyautey, I do not think I am misreading his secret reaction; and since then I have often wondered, while seeing him at work, if that economy of strength, that "esoteric" refusal to let moral constraints encroach upon his reserves of energy, did not in part explain the extraordinary creative power that he was able to devote exclusively to building a world.

But let us now return to le Saillant.

I SHALL SOMEDAY describe my Saillant, at the end of a fine spring afternoon, as it stands on the leafy spur that gave it its name, above the tiers of foliage in the park: as one sees it from afar, upon leaving Menneville; or when one comes back out of the forest, as one suddenly glimpses it from below through the last tree-trunks of the border. I shall also describe it from closer up, as it presents itself to the new arrival, as I found it still on that morning of my return after four years of exile, all pink between the stone pillars of its old gate, at the far end of its ivy-garlanded courtyard, with its high windows all in rows, and its mossy front steps, and the horns of plenty sculpted above the central doorway. And perhaps I shall even attempt to describe the façade on the park side, seen from the end of the terrace, as it appeared to me so many times at the close of a hot day, as I walked back along the pond and sat down, out of breath, on the curb of the pool, to look caressingly for a moment at the pure order of that architecture, the contemplation of which has always touched and soothed me.

It is the hour when the patina of the sunset warms the whiteness of the stones and sets the bricks ablaze; the hour when the heavy mass of the slate roof that gives this Louis XIII manor house, built low, long, and narrow, its volume and its nobility stands out most sharply against the sky; the hour when the sharpness of the shadows underlines the harmony of the proportions; when the serenity of the evening adds still more to the adorable distinction of that dear old thing and makes its silence, its isolation, more palpable.

I do not think it is immaterial, since I am writing my autobiography, to point out that the happy medium, the harmony of its proportions, is the main feature of the setting where I was raised. I believe in the influence of the forms that a child has always before his eyes. A boy whose youth had been spent in the weird, wild scenery of one of those medieval "burgs" that Hugo liked to draw at the summit of a rock would have strong odds of being quite different from his little brother whose early years had been spent playing at marbles beneath the colonnades of the Acropolis. Is it only due to chance if this architectural balance, this exact proportion, this harmony which strike one about le Saillant also happen to exist in my mind, in my sense of proportion, in my mental balance, in my tolerance, my intellectual probity, my *tastes,* and form the architecture of my mind, and if I may say so, the standard for my *judgment?* The true and *only* foundation, in short, of my *morality?*

CHAPTER II

Early Childhood

I AM TRYING to recall my early childhood, to find deep down in myself a few images, a few impressions around which I could reconstruct this past misted-up in the distance, without distorting it too much. A delicate operation, full of surprises, which reminds me of the fishing with a ledger line that my sister and I so liked to do. The line consisted of a long sturdy cord to which were attached, at intervals, little lead balls alternating with hooks of various sizes that we baited with worms and cooked wheat. In the morning, at the crack of dawn, we would go leaping in the dew down to the pond to pull up the line which the evening before at nightfall we had lowered with the cautiousness of conspirators. It required the greatest attention to pull the cord back up from the depths without getting it tangled, without breaking it, without snagging it on underwater plants or shrubs along the bank, weighted down as it was here and there with eels and perch that had taken the bait, a cluster quivering with life and struggling with incredible violence. There were cries of joy each time a new catch appeared on the surface of the pond; cries of triumph when we had managed, with our net, to get the fish out of the water without its slipping off the hook and to land it in a safe spot far from the bank. But I'm making fine phrases and losing sight of my comparison . . . What I meant is that similarly, at the bottom of my memory, it is as if there lies an unending rosary of memories which are buried and which I think lost, and which are so curiously linked to one another that I have only to recover one of them by a stroke of luck and gently haul up the rope in order to see another soon rising in tow, then a third, and finally to pull from oblivion a whole string of little facts which, magically, bring my entire past back to life in a flash.

But—and in this respect my comparison remains legitimate—the thread that ties all these memories together is so fragile that the slightest inattention may easily break it and plunge the spoils of this miraculous catch back into the inaccessible depths.

For example, this morning in the corridor, while going by, I opened the drawer of a dresser where we once stored old packets of candles. The Germans didn't leave a single one. Heading down the stairs, why did I suddenly recall the walks that I used to take in the park, as a very small child, *riding piggyback on my sister*? It took me a few minutes to follow the sequence of my associations back upstream. Whence sprang this distant recollection? From the drawer with the candles . . . An old magazine, spread out, still lined the bottom of it, and my eye had fallen for a second on the picture of a full-breasted black woman carrying a baby on the small of her back, held in place by the folds of her lappa. At the time, I had not made any connection. It was by an unconscious operation, similar to the capricious linkages of thought in dreams, that there came back to light this completely forgotten detail from the time when I was still wailing. Indeed, my sister—she, too, struck, perhaps, by some travel illustration culled from our collection of *Tour du monde*—had made a sort of harness that allowed her to carry me on her back and to go about her business without having to hold me in her arms.

I have gently hauled up the cord, and here I bring back to the surface a whole small fry of memories.

We lived, Henriette and I, with Ernestine, the chambermaid, in the other wing than the one I occupy today, the three top rooms, the one whose windows open onto the park.

I can see myself, between three and five years old, on autumn mornings, impatient to get out of bed, in the depths of the alcove with its blue percale curtains where I still felt a prisoner of the night. I can see the fog that whitened the window panes and the pink wool shawl that was wrapped around my shoulders while, sitting up in bed, I awaited my bowl of hot milk and my slice of brown bread. I can see Ernestine, a fat, stumpy girl, her hair tucked under the wide, flat-topped, embroidered bonnet that was the local headdress, squatting in front of the hearth, rekindling last night's embers with blasts from the bellows, and performing the miracle, each morning, of making a bouquet of joyous flames burst forth in the dark hole of the fireplace. I can see, behind the firescreen, the kettle where the water for my wash-up gurgled away and the wobbly tripod, painted yellow, where my sister used to place the basin for my ablutions. It was Henriette who washed and dressed me. I was very docile with her, but much less so with Ernestine, whose movements were rough and who couldn't comb my hair without pulling it and making me howl. For me she represented only an accidental, usurped authority, and I made her feel this without pity. I was not unaware that in my father's absence the supreme powers devolved exclusively upon Grandmother's former servant, old Zélie, an excellent creature, omnipotent and motherly, but constantly consumed by the worries of her responsibility, which made her loud, excessive, talkative, and quarrelsome. I saw my sister herself, despite her thirteen or fourteen years, submitting to the instructions of Zélie, whose vitality filled our gloomy dwelling with a slightly sacrilegious din, peppered with a Provençal accent, in which jokes and laughter alternated continually with scoldings, imprecations, and threats. Age had made her squint-eyed, breathless, and hunchbacked. I had a holy terror of her, and it was her traits—her brisk and heavy walk, her outbursts, her tortoise neck, her gray locks beneath her little black Arlesienne's bonnet—that my imagination lent to the wicked fairy Carabosse.* One morning she was found lifeless at the foot of her bed. She had let herself die more quietly than she had lived. I must have been six or seven. I remember clearly the strange, suffocating sensation of emptiness that abruptly swept through the house; for a long time the notion of death remained associated in my child's mind with that of silence.

From the cradle on, I had been for Henriette a living doll sent by nature; she had entirely assumed the burden of watching over me, the sole object of her activity and of her entertainment. From the day of my birth she had renounced all other games and left girlhood behind in order to enter straightaway into motherhood. The pleasure that she took in playing her role was contagious: everything became fun with her, everything, even the worst daily chores—face-washing and dressing included—right down to prayers, which she made me mumble on my knees beside her when my washing-up was done and which were often accompanied by laughter and kisses. She was not only sweet, conciliatory, and cheerful: she instinctively possessed the supreme art of command, that adroitness with authority, which—as I noted time and again in the course of my military life—is the rarest and perhaps the most useful secret talent of a leader. She never seemed to be aware of the rights that she had over me. She did not make me feel her yoke, and so I

*A fairy of French legend, old and hunchbacked.

submitted to it without even noticing it. And nothing shocked me more than sometimes hearing my father—if, for example, I did not rush to her fast enough when she called—say to me: "Come on, *obey* your sister!" Obey? My father seemed to me to commit a puzzling error there, and one which had in it something insulting to Henriette and to me. I knew very well what it was to obey and that obedience implies an opposing will which asserts itself and prevails. With my sister, how could I have to obey, since I never had to restrain myself, since in doing what she had suggested I do, I always felt I was acting spontaneously, carrying out an idea that we'd had together?

Around nine o'clock we would hear, in the little staircase of our wing, the skipping step of Mademoiselle Fromentot, a former schoolteacher retired in Menneville. A rawboned old woman with a pointed nose and not much chin is reminiscent of a fowl; but if, moreover, she walks with her head forward, craning her neck, and is decked out in a string bonnet that caps her with a crest of crumpled ribbons, the resemblance is so striking that it cannot escape a child. Most disrespectfully, we called her "the black hen." Every morning, no matter what the weather, she would come to the château on foot to give my sister lessons until it was time for the family meal, which she shared with us. In winter Henriette used to install me with my toys near the stove in the back room, which was called the schoolroom, and she watched over me out of the corner of her eye while conjugating her verbs. In summer, the lesson was given outdoors in the "circle," a terreplein cut into the thicket at the junction of the park and the terrace fifty meters from the house, and fitted out with garden chairs. There I had my shovel, my wheelbarrow, my sand pile and, between two beeches, a swing put up by my father onto which I could hoist myself alone, and where I would sometimes stay perched all morning long without a second of boredom, letting my mind wander while swinging in the sun-dappled shade. This "circle" has scarcely changed; nor I; I still daydream there. But the terreplein has widened and become bare, the thicket has turned into full-grown timber, many of the trees have died; and when, not long before the war, Bocca* had to cut one of them down, I was no less surprised than he at finding an iron hook encysted in it: the last vestige of my swing.

My father rose at daybreak to make the rounds of the four smallholdings on horseback. Even in winter, not a fence was put in without his having had the ground staked out himself; not a hedge was cut back, not a plot of pasture drained, not a wall re-stuccoed without his personally having deployed the workers and got the job started. It took a snow flurry or torrid heat to force him home before "dinner." (We used to "dine" at eleven, according to

---

*Pietro Bocca, Maumort's orderly in World War I and man Friday thereafter; for a description, see Chapter XXII.

the country custom, and we "had supper" at six in winter and at sunset in the summer months). At five to eleven, never late, he would come back up the hillside at a walk—sometimes on foot, with the reins over his arm—would go through the gate, and would stop in the middle of the courtyard (which was pompously called, according to age-old custom, the *cour d'honneur*,* to distinguish it from the other, the *cour des communs*,† separated from the first by an openwork portal, both sides of which were always swung back). He would cast about a circular glance from which nothing escaped—not a forgotten rake or a half-open window which should have been closed or a piece of paper littering the ground or a fresh imprint of wheels in the gravel—and then with his palm he would slap the rump of his horse and let it go back to its stable by itself, where the punctual Gaspard would be waiting to rub the animal down. Then, as my father was coming up to the front steps, old Zélie, on the lookout for the master's return, would materialize on the threshold and ring the bell. I really don't think that either my father or anyone else had laid down these rituals in such minute detail: they had established themselves little by little, without anyone's knowing how; and our style of living was so regular, the unexpected so exceptional, that they took place, immutably, to everybody's satisfaction.

(Correction: in reality, my father was rather fussy, and he probably had played more of a part than I think in the organization of the daily round— what the old French chroniclers so aptly called "the *coustume* of a house." I remember that Zélie, who spoke her mind in front of Henriette and myself, would say drolly: "Monsieur? What will be hardest for him when he passes on to the next world will be having to change his habits!")

The presence of Mlle. Fromentot brought some excitement to this eleven o'clock "dinner." She had a talkative, sprightly nature. Her little gray curls, her black dresses, a certain consideration that my father showed her, made her seem to us very old. She wasn't. I remember her round face with cheeks that were full and still fresh, although slightly blotchy; her youthful laugh; her quick and vivacious gestures; her swiftness of movement, her agility even, whenever my sister, after the meal, would be allowed to play a game of badminton or *grâces*‡ with her. And I have every reason to believe that this extreme old age did not exceed fifty. In the course of her career as a schoolmistress, she had taught in various corners of the canton, met many kinds of people, heard, gleaned, and remembered lots of stories.

Nosy and something of a gossip, but pleasant, ready to help, generous with her time and always full of good advice, she was respected, and her

---

*Literally "the courtyard of honor"; i.e., the main courtyard.
†The courtyard of the outbuildings.
‡A game in which hoops are tossed back and forth on slender rods.

services were called upon by one and all. In Menneville she knew everyone, was fascinated by each one's private life, gladly passed things on, and every day at the table treated us to a wealth of local news. "And what does the Gazette have to say today?" my father would ask, when he was less sullen than usual, as he unfolded his napkin. But in general he would not hear out the inexhaustible talebearing of Mademoiselle, whom, by the way, this lack of attention did not in the least deter from babbling merrily away, less to amuse us, I think, than to indulge her itch to tattle. Henriette (and I, as soon as I was old enough to understand) listened to her openmouthed. She often repeated herself, and we could have finished many of her anecdotes without her help; it pleased us all the more to hear them again and to laugh with her at the good parts. Mademoiselle and her stories occupied an important place in our young lives. She kept our curiosity piqued, she introduced the spice of news items into our becalmed and bland existence. Thanks to her, the austere isolation to which we were condemned by our father's unsociability was peopled with almost legendary characters, sometimes ridiculous, sometimes tragicomic, doubly deformed by the literary romanticism of the narrator and by our childish imaginations. From one season to the next we followed, as in a serialized novel, the development of their peculiarities, of their adventures, of their familial intrigues. Sometimes the story would end in a tragic fashion: pitchfork stabbings, tavern brawls, ferocious acts of vengeance, poisoning attempts, fires, sequestrations, suicides, prison . . .

At that time, the peasants of the Perche were rough, fierce, not to say cruel. The sunny narratives of the Comtesse de Ségur,* whose château was some ten leagues from our house, give no idea of the brutality of our country, which, however, diminished very rapidly in the wake of the First World War: one cannot say how much the intermixing of populations in the mud of the trenches modified regional characteristics and contributed to the unification of the people. We knew by sight some of the tragic heroes whose adventures the old maid recounted to us. We sometimes got a glimpse of them on Sunday at High Mass; but their appearance always disappointed us; they seemed to us drained of all their storybook prestige by their incarnation into real beings.

Dear Mlle. Fromentot! I enjoy going on about her at such length. It seems to me that I am belatedly discharging a debt in rendering to this forgotten phantom, whose name and virtues I am today probably the only one left to recall, the homage that is due her. I have said nothing of her knowledge of botany, zoology, even medicine. The thing deserves mentioning, however. Was it not this taste for the natural sciences which gave her the taste

*Sophie Rostopchine, Comtesse de Ségur (1799–1874), author of classic children's books.

for scrutinizing and wanting to understand the village fauna that she had before her eyes? I have made fun of her compulsive gossiping, the epic disposition that she had for magnifying the little events of Menneville, for darkening and dramatizing the motives of her neighbors in order to give a certain pathos to the news that she was retailing. In spite of all this, it seems to me, from a distance, that even in her deformations of reality Mademoiselle showed a rather rare understanding of humanity and a psychological insightfulness, quite subtle at times. I can well understand my father's irritation in the face of this prattling; but he was wrong, I think, to have seen nothing in it but the weakness of a prying, scandal-mongering old maid. And—at the risk of using words a bit too grand to fit the case—I'd be prepared to maintain that these indiscreet investigations actually betrayed the driving desire that Mademoiselle had of deepening her knowledge of people through the observation of their oddities and disorders. All in all, a worthy concern, which very likely had an influence on us, and one that deserves to be pointed out.

Indeed, today I wonder whether, without suspecting it, and however young we may have been, we didn't derive from this daily gossip-fest an indirect benefit whose consequences were by no means negligible. Wasn't it from listening to her, from conceiving a passion for the stories of those unknown characters, that there was born in Henriette, as in me, this marked tendency to take an interest in individuals, to search beyond appearances for their secret, to ferret out, even in their very unconscious, the inner motive of their behavior? In my own case, this disposition—I was about to write: this mania—later grew even more during the years that I spent in Paris at my uncle and aunt Chambost-Lévadé's, in the circle of scholars and literary men where "psychology"—a word that the novels of the young Paul Bourget had made fashionable—was the usual seasoning for the Sunday conversations. This insatiable *curiosity*—which, since adolescence, all specimens of human nature (and especially those which deviated most from the norm) have inspired in me, whether offered up to me by the world or by books—I have applied also, and above all, to myself. I will by no means speak ill of it: I owe too many happy moments to it, and even more: the best of my intellectual development. Age has managed neither to extinguish it nor scarcely to diminish it; it seems to have been a spontaneous and authentic manifestation of my taste for life. Well, the more I think about it, the more I am convinced that I caught the germ, in childhood, from my contact with Mlle. Fromentot. Henriette, too, was a victim of this contagion; and this shared inclination was not the least of the ties that, for half a century, so perfectly bound the two of us together. It fed our talks endlessly; it allowed us to chatter away about others for hours without tiring, and more readily still about ourselves;

it gave birth to a whole special vocabulary; it created between us an atmosphere of amused complicity and of almost total openness, the like of which I have not found in any other relationship.

UPON LEAVING the table, my father used to retire by himself to the little room which has become the linen-room and which he had set up at that time as a study. Ernestine would take him his coffee and the decanter of calvados. In the wintertime he would stretch out in his Voltaire armchair with his legs to the fire and doze off for a moment. We caught him many times. At the slightest noise, he would open his eyes and quickly bend forward to grab the tongs, ready to claim that he hadn't been sleeping. In the warm season, he would take off his boots, lie down on the tapestried chaise longue, and give himself up to a nap—which in this case he would admit to without shame. In winter at one o'clock, in summer at three, Gaspard would lead up to the front steps whichever of the two horses had not gone out in the morning, and my father would get back in the saddle to go survey his domain until sunset. He thus spent six or seven hours each day on horseback. It was only when he had business in town, or when he was going to meet his smallholders at the local fairs, that he had the "rattletrap" hitched up—a kind of low-slung buggy with two wheels and a broad hood. At those times he put on gloves of reddish leather and donned his top hat. Besides this light carriage, the carriage-house also contained a cart, specially reserved for Gaspard's outings, as well as an ancient coupé we hardly ever used that had beveled windows and was upholstered in dingy satin; lastly, a large break, and an old calash with yellow wheels. It was the break that Gaspard hitched up on Sunday mornings to drive the whole household to High Mass in Menneville. My father very rarely came with us; only on Christmas, Easter, and All-Saint's Day, out of respect for tradition. I adored Sundays, the spectacle of High Mass, this weekly outing with Gaspard driving in his opera-hat and blue carrick with silver buttons. On rainy days, our open umbrellas covered the carriage with a bumpy, streaming carapace, from under which squeals and laughter burst forth. On days when the road iced over, the drive was made at a walk, and Gaspard, grumbling, his nose red, his mustache bristling with icicles, led the horses on foot. Then it would take more than an hour to get to the church; and that huge, resounding vessel, freezing cold, where the steam of many breaths rose like incense smoke, seemed to me, chilled to the bone as I was, a warm refuge offered by the Holy Virgin, whose painted plaster statue awaited us at the entrance to the nave, arms gently extended in a gesture of welcome.

But I am letting these childish memories run away with me. I want to add this: the calash was not used except on rare occasions when my father felt he had to attend a funeral or when he went to visit our nearest neighbor, the old Comte de Pontbrun. This was, I think, the only acquaintance he had kept in the area; partly because, since his bereavement, he was in a solitary mood; partly too, it seems to me, because he shared neither the opinions of the local squires nor their way of life. At that time all the estates in the neighborhood still belonged to people of high birth. These petty nobles had remained, for the most part, arrant monarchists who seethed and plotted in a vacuum, in defense of a lost cause. My father did not much care to see them, but I suppose that they kept him at a distance as well. In the eyes of these dreary survivors, my father—who had always refused to affiliate himself with an opposition party; who on principle would not stand to hear the government and the institutions of his country run down; and whose votes, along with those of the "rabble," had contributed to the triumph of candidates of *"la Gueuse"**—must have been seen as a felon who had betrayed the honor of his caste. Quite rightly so, what is more. As far as this fossilized aristocracy was concerned, my father could only be a dangerous representative of what were then known as "advanced ideas"; he may even have been called a "socialist"!

What in fact was he? If I had to pin a label on him, I would say that he was of the "moderate republican" stripe, as much removed from the far right—which he damned for its haughtiness, the blindness of its routine, its selfishness, its contemptuous indifference toward the people—as from the far left, whose disorderly violence shocked him, whose anticlerical fanaticism he condemned, and whose revolutionary demands seemed to him a threat to the maintenance of order and to France's prestige abroad. A nationalist before the term came into use, ardently patriotic, Catholic by tradition and natural tolerance (but personally detached from religion), a supporter of universal suffrage and parliamentary representation (but hostile to all demagogy and convinced that the people could not effectively gain access to power except through the mediation of leaders who were educated, well-bred, and chosen from the liberal bourgeoisie) he was resolutely respectful of republican institutions and thought that a good government ought to be strong, honest, independent, and authoritative.

Actually, he was not much involved in politics. He always shied away from the solicitations of the Republican Party of the Orne, which would gladly have backed his candidacy for the Conseil Général.† He never even accepted the mayoralty of Menneville. I have never really understood his reasons. It seems that he, who in every area had a punctilious sense of duty, had

*Derisive name for the Republic.
†Deliberative body composed of members elected in each département.

no sense whatsoever that it might be incumbent upon a man of his position to devote a part of his time and energy to public affairs.

BUT I RETURN to our life at le Saillant.

Mlle. Fromentot, who could, with no breach of manners, have gone home as soon as the meal was done, usually tarried with us and took part in our games, either in the schoolroom or outside on the terrace, weather permitting. I wished to see her leave so as to have Henriette to myself. When the time came, we would generally walk her to the entrance gate and watch her as she went toddling down the slope with her big lawyer's briefcase under her arm.

Then there began for me the best part of the day, which lasted until teatime. The servants were attending to their chores: Michel in the vegetable garden, Gaspard in the stables, the women in the kitchen, in the pantry, in the linen-room, under the supervision of old Zélie. My sister and I alone were free, left to ourselves and our whims. I was supposed to be in her charge. And in fact I was: she would not have let me wander around in the rain, or keep my muddy high-topped shoes on in the house, or climb up on the curbstone of the pool, or venture off alone in the direction of the pond. But I didn't give her the chance to exercise her birthright. I hadn't the slightest desire to misbehave or act reckless. As I have already said, my sister's tutelage was so easy that I never felt its weight: quite simply, I lived in her company. From the day when I could get about on two legs, I followed her from morning to night around the house, into the courtyard and into the schoolroom when she was doing her homework. To be in her life was enough to make me constantly happy. Close to her, I could take no credit for always being in a good mood; none for always being well-behaved. Up till my tenth year, I never left my sister's skirts; I never for a single day escaped the rounds of family life; no roughhousing brat, insubordinate or sulky, taught me to act wild and unruly; and I had too little natural deviltry in me to invent naughty things to do all by myself. I don't remember having ever got a scolding, either from Henriette or from Mlle. Fromentot. I blush to have to make this confession, for I know of nothing more insipid, less winning, than a docile child: to give me any hope for its character and its future, youth has to rise up and kick over the traces.

Alas, I must confess it: I had nothing of the rebel in me. My nature was submissive and rather apathetic. While still quite small, I could already stay crouching under a table or behind a bush in the garden for half an hour at a time, daydreaming. I did not know what boredom was. (And never have, my whole life long: I have always found too much satisfaction in doing nothing and in giving myself up to my reveries.) However, I did not lack either health or liveliness or even deftness and agility when I had to bestir myself; but I would gladly stop, on the slightest pretext, in order to stay endlessly immobile in a kind of vague, carefree meditation that I savored with delight. This is what I later called my "purring" time. I shall have to come back to this peculiar disposition,* which, in the career I chose, certainly caused me some setbacks, but, all things considered—and especially at present—has brought me many joys.

From the disciplined, compliant, easily led boy that I was then, one could scarcely have predicted the uncompromising, ill-tempered person that I was to become and that I have remained. It is around the age of puberty that I place the first signs of this transformation, but only much later did it become really pronounced, and I began to see it only in the course of my military life, when I could no longer mend my ways. Lyautey often upbraided me for my "bullheaded" character, but he tempered his reproofs with a half-mocking, half-affectionate smile which always let me think that this roughness of temperament did not inordinately displease him . . . All the reverses in my career are partly explained by this mulish streak. I have always come by respect more easily than friendship. Understanding and tolerant, basically, through effort and reflection, I was brusque in my relationships and lacking in natural affability. My men—less sensitive, more intuitive, who saw me share their hardships and exert myself to make their existence less harsh—were generally very attached to me; on the other hand, I had few friends among my peers. I scared them away with the freedom of my personal opinions, the severity of my criticisms, a frankness that did not know how to spare sensitivities. I was thought to be haughty, cocksure, scornful.

BUT LET US go back to my childhood, and to Mlle. Fromentot; for I realize, reading over what I've written, that I have not finished with her, and that if I confined myself to the caricature I have sketched, I would feel quite unjust and quite ungrateful.

I too was her pupil, and from my earliest years. It was she who taught me to write and to count. I was only five, but already I could read. Henriette had taken this task upon herself without saying anything about it to anyone, and had accomplished it perfectly, as she did everything. She used a kind of ancient lotto dating from the First Empire, the counters of which bore engraved letters of the alphabet. My memory (which has been, I can say, prodigious, and, in all truth, is still excellent for my seventy-seven years) has always been rather visual. And so, playing to beat my sister, I very quickly came to recognize the letters, to arrange them on the cards, and to compose

*See File 51 in The Black Box, p. 744.

syllables, then words, which Henriette taught me to spell. My father, who suspected nothing, was very surprised the evening my sister had me decipher in front of him the title of a scientific journal he had just received. (Although I had no trouble performing that tour de force which is learning to read, I am always amazed to see that the most obtuse children succeed in passing this formidable test and in miraculously overcoming this first obstacle, which seems to me the most diabolical of all those that stand in the road to Knowledge.)

Writing has always been a pleasure for me, even at the time when I was only connecting dots. I progressed swiftly and effortlessly. Mlle. Fromentot's lessons were lively and varied, and I applied myself with pleasure. I owe her a lot. Eye-memory allowed me to remember without difficulty the spelling of the words I was reading, and as soon as I could write I began to do dictations. Mademoiselle did not lay much stress on grammar: the principal rules, backed up with clear, easily retained examples. Never any compositions. But she gave a lot of dictations. This was one of the bases of her teaching, and she knew how to make this exercise pleasant and fruitful. She taught me not just to spell correctly but also to understand a text, to discern, to the extent of my abilities, the unexpected in an unfamiliar thought; and each of these dictations was a pretext for instructive digressions, the occasion for a science lesson, a lesson on history or morality, a little work on the association of ideas and on reasoning. I can still hear her reedy voice when she dictated a fable by La Fontaine, for whom she had a decided predilection and a kind of emotional kinship. She had a somewhat simpering but quite piquant way of putting the best passages into relief, of bringing out the irony, the vividness of a turn of phrase, the verbal skill, the subtleties of the text. Then, unexpectedly widening the horizon, she would apply a storyteller's moral to this or that little fact of our everyday life, and, with vivid, concrete examples and imagery, would get me quite naturally to reflect on subjects which went far beyond my age and which I would certainly not have been able to translate into words but which I nevertheless perceived quite well.

After several months of this daily exercise, I found that I had effortlessly, and with growing interest, accumulated an incredible number of elementary concepts that were valuable in a variety of ways. My mind had opened up to all sorts of curiosity. The constant presence of my sister, who was nine years my senior, accelerated this development even more: the older I grew, the more she treated me as a peer, appealed to my serious side, confided her ideas to me, her judgments on many questions that I would never have thought about on my own. I matured quickly on this nourishing diet. The dictations became more and more educational without ceasing to be attractive: Mademoiselle lost no time in leaving La Fontaine behind for more difficult authors—Fénelon, La Bruyère, La Rochefoucauld, Vauvenargues.* (Is this not a surprising selection for a humble schoolteacher from that distant era?) At eight or nine, I was familiar not only with the names of these great writers but with the cast of their minds as well. It also seems to me that I was already vaguely aware of the rhythm, the music of the sentences, the choice and combination of the words—in sum, of style, of the genius of the language. I am convinced that something of this stayed with me. The commentaries that these moralists prompted in Mademoiselle were deft lessons in good sense, judgment, politeness and intellectual rectitude. I am hardly exaggerating. She gave me a taste for seriousness and quality. She taught me to think. And this without excess, without doing violence to my maturation, without having used methods that resembled in the slightest what horticulturalists call "hothouse forcing." She required only that I perform in a way that was comfortable, natural and in keeping with my abilities. But she certainly possessed a sort of genius for discovering and using to the maximum the resources of a child's brain.

I see yet another proof of this in the extraordinary use she made of teaching sums and of analyzing sentences. I remember her arithmetic lessons, and the little problems, more and more complicated, that she put to me each day. She was much less concerned with the correctness of the computations than with how the mind made its way towards the solution. With a perseverance and ingeniousness that I now admire, she excelled at leading my groping thought-process from deduction to deduction until the expected, hoped-for denouement, which I sensed with a joyous impatience, gradually appeared through the darkness, as one sees the daylight break at the end of a tunnel. And the accuracy of the result mattered little to her if I managed to work out the problem by a correct and well-organized course of reasoning.

It was exactly the same goal that she aimed at with the exercises in sentence analysis. In that department, Mademoiselle was truly incomparable. The gratitude I owe her has only grown with time. With a few months' training, I achieved a kind of mastery. I took apart, with unerring skill, any period in the *Oraisons* of Bossuet,† even those that were the most convoluted and fraught with parenthetical clauses.

I had already dimly understood that a rather long sentence, if it is well

*Jean de La Fontaine (1621–1695), French poet, known chiefly for his fables; François Salignac de la Mothe Fénelon (1651–1715), French prelate and man of letters; Jean de La Bruyère (1645–1696), French satiric moralist, author of the *Characters;* François VI, Duc de La Rochefoucauld (1613–1680), author of the *Maxims;* Luc de Clapiers, Marquis de Vauvenargues (1715–1747), French soldier and moralist, author of *Introduction to the Understanding of the Human Mind.*

†Jacques-Benigne Bossuet (1627–1704), French bishop, author of sermons.

constructed, owes its balance to the fact that it is built the way the various pieces of a framework are fitted together; that its pieces are not juxtaposed at random but assembled with an intelligent architectural precision. Today I would be quite hard put to find my way through the tangle of subordinates, to give the different types of clauses their specific names, to distinguish the *relative* from the *conjunctive*, to recognize the *adverbial*, the *causative*, the *temporal*, or the *comparative* . . . But at ten, I was so conditioned to this exercise in dissection that it was mere play for me to separate the various elements of the most involved thought, to detach the central kernel, to grasp the skeleton of the sentence beneath the profusion of words, and to arrange these multiple scattered materials according to their nature, their function, and their respective relationships. This work of anatomical dismemberment, arrangement, and rational classification, which puts off so many schoolchildren ill-prepared for the task, pleased me more than any other. Starting at that time, I found mental satisfactions in it that I could not describe. I can today. Mademoiselle's "analyses" put logic in my head, once and for all; which, upon reflection, is not so common as is supposed. Among the men of the first rank that it has been given me to meet in the course of my life (and it turns out that chance has served me rather well in this respect), how many times have I not been dismayed by the confusion of thought, the stumblings, the lack of straightforward reasoning in these eminent, cultivated, educated persons, whose intelligence could not be denied, but whose logic, one had to admit, was "unsound," and of whom I used to say to myself: "That fellow didn't do enough sentence analysis . . ."

CHAPTER III

The Pond with the Girls.
The Abbé Adry

IT WAS QUITE foolish of me, when I began, to want to get away from chronological order. I imagined that this constraint might spoil my pleasure. This showed a poor knowledge of myself. I have too much rigor in my brain to escape from logical order, and it is in their historical sequence that past events quite naturally come back into my mind. Which, besides, does not in any way imply that I henceforth deny myself unchronological digressions. No set positions, no preconceived discipline: I let my pen run on according to the wishes of my fancy. But the fancy of an old rationalist is less capricious than I had imagined . . .

So I return to the point where I left myself the other day.

That year (I was going on ten), in the spring of 1880, my father purchased a pony and put me in the saddle. I think he attached as much importance to this enthronement as I did. My pony had a thick coat of a beautiful glossy black, with a white lock on his forehead and big languid eyes the color of mirabelles. His name, Cettivayo,* was less strange than it would appear today: the English had just brought the king of the Zulus to his knees, and the death of the Prince Imperial in the course of this expedition had made the details very familiar to the French. Despite this name of a warlike Kaffir, Cettivayo, who was no longer all that young, had an easygoing nature. Gaspard gave me a few lessons at the end of a leading-rein, in the *cour des communs;* and soon I knew enough to accompany my father and my sister on their outings. Henriette had long since become quite the Amazon, and often, when the days grew long, my father and she would take a ride through the forest in the cool of the evening after our six o'clock supper. I was more than a little proud to be trotting along at their side. I have kept a glorious memory of those excursions; of the heavy silence of the woods, where the horses' legs would sink deep into the thickness of the dead leaves; of the coppery sunsets, whose last rays seemed to make the peeling trunks of the pine trees bleed.

Someday I shall have to sing of this Menneville forest, among the most beautiful in our Perche region, which boasts admirable ones. Our pines, exceptionally tall and straight, have for ages past been dedicated to the boat yards of the Royal Navy to mast its ships; and our beech groves, up until these last years, could proudly claim some of the oldest specimens known. One of them, "Blanche of Castile's† Beech," still exists, and is a neighbor of mine. Even yesterday, while shaving, I could, from my window, make out with my naked eye its sovereign head, raised among the rusts of the forest. I won't swear, as legend claims, that it was planted by Saint Louis as a child; but it must have taken it a good four centuries to grow so tall, to spread out and make so much room around itself. Though I have known this giant for over half a century, its majesty still astounds me. Its trunk, massive as a tower, turtledove gray, shoots up without a branch, without a lichen, without a scar, to a height of thirty-four meters before thrusting its first boughs into space and unfolding the splendor of its foliage, in whose shade a battalion on a war footing could easily bivouac.

---

*Cetewayo (1826–1884), last great king of the Zulus and leader of their doomed uprising against the British in 1879. During this war Napoleon III's son, the Prince Imperial, in search of adventure, joined a British expeditionary force and was killed in a surprise attack.

†Blanche de Castille (1188–1252), wife of Louis VIII of France, and mother of Louis IX (Saint Louis).

Yes, one day I shall speak with an open heart of our forest! It bounds our lands along two kilometers, and has always been the natural extension of the park: scarcely breached, seldom visited, as deserted and as much "our own" as the park itself. We could wander for hours in its undergrowth, on foot or horseback, without meeting a human being, without hearing any other noise than the rustling of the treetops in the wind, the cry of a jay, the splashing flight of a buzzard, the cooing of a pair of wood-doves, sometimes the frightened gallop of a bevy of does caught by surprise, or even, along the ground, the slithering of a grass snake through the ferns, and the melancholy, persistent, silvery trill of an invisible little spring in the thicket.

The following year, I sat a horse so well that during the vacation, on certain days when my father's rounds were to be shorter than usual, he took only me along with him to oversee the fieldwork. We exchanged but a very few words. I had never had any sort of intimacy with my father; those hours when we rode side by side in the shade of the hazel trees, down the short cuts that led to the smallholdings, are perhaps the only ones that have left me with a memory of closeness, of secret communion, of silent accord.

It is not enough to say that he was an excellent horseman: he was truly as one with his mount. The first time I found the word *centaurus* in a Latin assignment, and had to understand its meaning, the image that spontaneously forced itself upon my mind was not of a mythological monster but of this bearded colossus with broad pectorals, half-man, half-horse, whom I was accustomed to see looming up in the break of a hedgerow on his steaming mare, or galloping across the meadows, stretched out over her neck to clear the low branches of the apple trees.

For it was around the same time, between my tenth and eleventh year, that my father, having put me on a horse, also thought of putting me to Latin. This was not so easy to do. There were, in Menneville, only two people capable of giving me lessons: the old dean and his curate. It was the latter, the young Abbé Rumpert, who undertook to initiate me into declensions. But what was required of Mlle. Fromentot could not be asked of the curate: he did not have the time to bring his Latin to the house; it was up to me to go to him. In spite of Henriette's objections, my father declared that I was of an age to follow the example of every country schoolboy, to go on foot, with my satchel on my back, from le Saillant to the presbytery, three times a week. My sister wanted to come with me, at least for the first lesson. My father would not allow it.

So I ventured the empty Menneville road all by myself on a misty and nippy October morning. A red-letter day in my life . . . Those three kilometers, which I had always traveled by carriage, seemed interminable to me; but, performing this exploit with no witness, I felt more pride than fear. For the first time I was tasting sensations that I would later surrender to unreservedly: the elation of solitude, the intoxication of freedom.

I remember all the details of that marvelous adventure. As soon as I reached the first houses, I slowed down so as to pass through the town unobtrusively. I had not counted on the early-morning bustle of a weekday, very different from that of Sunday and altogether intimidating for me. Obstacles rose at every step, forcing me off the sidewalk. Women swept their doorsteps, shop-assistants spread out wares at the entrances of the stores; in front of the blacksmith's, horses stirred every which way among unhitched carts. Coming up to the school, I nearly lost all courage. The schoolday was about to start; all the boys and girls of the district, gathered in a swarm before the iron gate, were waiting for the bell and blocking the street. I had to push my way through those shouts, those laughs, that buzzing hubbub. I did not suspect that, so near le Saillant, the universe could offer up the scandal of such disorder, such ill breeding. Finally I arrived beneath the vault of the old ramparts and found myself in the square in front of the church. The high portal of the presbytery was closed. I gently pulled the chain, and did it several times over before setting the bell in motion. The dean came and opened the door for me. I was half an hour early. The curate was finishing his Mass. I had to go into the kitchen, answer the chitchat of the old maidservant, accept a bowl of hot milk from her, and roast my face at the fire so that I "wouldn't catch cold."

One must imagine what my existence had been until then, devoid of any surprises or departures from habit, devoid of contact with any stranger, in order to understand what that morning represented for me: a total dislocation, an incredible series of adventures, each of which took my breath away and drove the blood to my temples . . . I was both passionately interested and very unhappy. I do not think it was so much the unexpectedness of the events that produced this discomfort in me, as the worry, above all, that I would not have the requisite composure in the face of these peculiar situations. (A feeling of possible inferiority . . . I have often suffered from this in my life: facing a difficult mission or on the eve of an attack, it was not the risk I was about to run that sometimes made me sweat with anxiety, but the dread of a moral or physical failure, the fear of lacking decisiveness, presence of mind, or courage.) At ten, fortunately, my thoughts did not go so far. I was saved by my reflexes. (In war, too, by the way.) My attitudes, my reactions were instinctive. So, when the housemaid put that buttered bread and that bowl of milk in front of me, I, not daring to refuse, not knowing how to decline this kind of offer, politely thanked her and sat down at the table in the most natural way in the world. I was not really fearful, having never yet had a reason to become so.

The Abbé Rumpert came at last. I followed him into the dining room, where his breakfast awaited him, and I sat through his meal in silence. Petrified with surprise . . . The abbé did not eat at all like "us": he first crumbled all his bread into his coffee, mashed it down for quite a while, then, leaning over his bowl, he attacked this blackish, spongy pulp by large spoonfuls, which he wolfed down with a sucking noise. I could not turn my eyes away. I was horribly embarrassed. Finally my torture ended; the bowl was empty. The housemaid came to clear the table, and I had my first Latin lesson.

From that day on, everything in and around me took on new colors. Very little is required, really, to transform a child's life radically and bring forth his personality. I had stopped living as an adjunct of my sister, of the maids, of Mlle. Fromentot. I had left skirts behind. I was roaming the world, exploring the unknown. The fledgling had flown the nest and discovered the power of its wings . . . I am not exaggerating at all. I feel not so much that I passed a watershed in my development at that precise date, as that I truly became *someone else.* The little boy whose first memories I have recounted was not I: my cocoon, at the very most. It was on the Menneville road that I was born; and it is only with this little ten-year-old Bertrand, sauntering along between the hedges with his satchel on his back, that the elder Maumort recognizes bonds of nature and continuity.

I SPENT three mornings a week away from le Saillant. These solitary rambles delighted me. Wind, rain, frost, it didn't matter to me: in order to have the leisure to dawdle as I liked, I was never late. I knew every row of apple trees, every ditch, every pile of flint, every meadow gate, every trough. I always stopped at the top of the hill, less to catch my breath than to triumphally take in the horizon. From up there, I towered over the countryside. In front of me, on the hillsides, the winter forest stretched out in its rusty fleece like a recumbent beast. My gaze swooped down into the valley, where some mists always lingered; I made out the roofs of the farms, I glimpsed that of le Saillant, which barely stood out over the trees of the park, whose wall I saw as a chalk line zigzagging across the pasturelands, and which, seen from the outside, was no longer the center of the world for me but a private, bounded enclosure, lost among so many others. Passing through town no longer frightened me. Everything was fun. I was interested in the shops, in the people. I knew their habits. I put names to the faces.

Market morning was a festive day. Carts, driven along at a good clip by Percherons with powerful cruppers, passed me on the road. Sometimes, one of these would stop abreast of me; I would be invited to climb aboard. Thrilled, I would hoist myself up among the bushels of vegetables, the trays of cheese, the crates with chickens inside. On those days, I had more time to hang about in the square, watching the women put out their wares, listening to the laughter, the chatter, the arguments . . . When I returned, the market was in full swing, it was a fair. I liked to let myself be carried along on this wave of gay, boisterous street life. I went back to le Saillant regretfully, my eyes bright, my head stuffed with images, with things to tell. I did not mention them to my father; but with Henriette, I gave in to the pleasure of reliving my world tour by confiding my secrets to her. She listened to me smiling, with an indulgence tinged with misgivings. She was the only one to fathom the importance of the transformation I was undergoing, and not without (unconsciously perhaps) taking a certain amount of umbrage. I was dimly aware of this. Yes, I am sure I had this intuition, for I remember very well that I was a long way from telling her everything. Not, to be sure, by way of concealment; but because I sensed that she was vaguely saddened at seeing me attach so much value to these new and foreign joys that I was now finding far from her.

By way of concealment too, sometimes . . . I am thinking, as I write this, of a certain discovery which I made during one of my innocent truancies and which shook me so unexpectedly that the memory of it is still not erased: my first encounter, if I may so put it, with the eternal feminine! . . . It must have been during the following summer. To satisfy my explorer's whims, I sometimes changed my itinerary and struck out across fields. That morning, on my way home, tempted to avoid the sunbaked and dusty road, I had taken the sunken, grassy lane that runs between the barns of le Liardon and by a roundabout way at the far end of the valley joins up with the edge of the park. The hazel trees, planted on the banks, had not been pruned for a long time, and kept it cool and shady. The path is winding, and I was going along it, dallying, when, at a bend, I heard, in the pastures on the far side of the hedge, fresh young voices, childish laughter. I was about to turn back; but, hidden by the thickness of the border, I could proceed without attracting attention. Suddenly, through the curtain of bushes, I saw strange pale shapes moving. Roughly ten meters off, naked young figures were splashing about in a cattle pond: three girls, around my age. They had thrown their dresses and slips on the grass, and were playing at chasing and splashing each other. The water barely reached their knees. I stayed there, for one long minute, holding my breath, my heart topsy-turvy, my eyes taking in every detail of those naked torsos whose little breasts were scarcely more swollen than my own, and I did not immediately grasp the *difference* . . . Then, seized by a panic fear, I turned and fled, running, dumbstruck, back to the road.

The capacity for dissimulation and the science of lying must certainly be innate in children for me to have been able to return to le Saillant with my everyday face on, go upstairs and kiss my sister, answer with all naturalness her questions about how I had spent my morning, act like my usual self at the meal, and go about my normal business as if nothing had happened. I had nevertheless received a brutal shock, whose traumatic effect continued to be felt in the depths of my being. I am trying to remember, to rediscover impressions that I am sure of. It seems to me that in this undeniable disturbance of my deepest part, the discovery itself counted for rather little: the surprise that it had produced, very sharp at the time, vanished fairly quickly. And yet, until then my ignorance in these matters was total: I did not have the slightest idea of the dissimilarities between the sexes; I had never thought about the matter; the paintings, the statues, that I happened, very rarely, to have seen, did not show any form unclothed; and nothing, ever, could have caused me to suspect that girls lacked this natural attribute—which old Zélie, washing me, had once and for all christened "the li'l gentleman" and which I believed common to all human beings. But, on the whole, it was not this unexpected revelation that hit me so hard: the intimate peculiarity of which chance had just made me aware simply became for me one more of those familiar notions, I mean those external differences of face, hairstyle, size, clothing, occupations, which, ever since I could remember, had in my eyes divided humanity into two distinct categories: men and women. Then what was the source of that near-anguish which gripped me at the memory of the three naked girls? A precocious, physical stirring, advance sign of the first impulses of sexuality? Certainly not; rather an absurd feeling of *guilt*, of unwitting guilt, which awoke in me the pangs of a shame and a remorse that were equally unjustified. I was conscious, at one and the same time, of having committed some unconfessable offense and yet of having done nothing wrong. I had discovered, unbeknownst to anyone, a secret having to do with those parts of the body which must not be mentioned; an "indecent" secret that I was certainly not supposed to know, since care had been taken to hide it from me . . . I had therefore violated some unspoken prohibition; had crossed, without wanting to, a forbidden threshold. And for weeks I remained crushed under the weight of my scruples and my sin.

But at the same time the train of my solitary reflections had found a new direction: slowly, surely, from deduction to deduction, my thought followed its course. I began by casting inspectional glances at the anatomy of domestic animals: the furtive examination of the housedog, and of Gaspard's bitch, confirmed and solidly established my recent knowledge. From that to asking myself indiscreet questions about the people in my circle was but a step: inevitable . . . What was the physical conformation of the maids, of the gardener? I did not immediately dare associate those close to me with these guilty thoughts. It was only a little later that I said to myself: "My father is certainly built like me . . . And Henriette? She must be like the girls at the pond: she must not have one either . . ." I very well remember the day when I slipped down that fatal slope. It was one morning, in the hallway; I had just knocked on my sister's door: "No, don't come in!" she had cried out. It was early; she was still washing herself. At once, and for the first time, my imagination pictured, with a sacrilegious precision, Henriette naked, Henriette and the secret of her body . . . I felt an intense stirring, and of the same sort as the one that had sent me fleeing down the Liardon lane: a sort of fright, panic, denial, and shame, which for several days kept me insuperably apart from her. It's quite strange. For several days, Henriette's nakedness haunted me, scared me out of my wits. And then I got used to this idea, very fast, surprisingly fast, so much so that I no longer thought about it at all. In fact, this did not in any way change my behavior toward her: I continued, with the same guilelessness, to appear naked before her, as I always had when she came to make me change my linen or to check to make sure that I hadn't given myself just a lick and a promise. (I even had so little modesty in front of her that, the year after, when my down had started to grow, I ran to show her the thing . . . but this is, in many respects, a curious episode in my childhood. I still have the scene very present in my mind, and I shall relate it in detail someday.)

I think I can state that until then my curiosity had nothing ambiguous in it: no sensuality accompanied these first reactions. For example, I remember that, clambering onto a stool, I examined myself on several occasions quite meticulously in the mirror; and I conducted these inspections with the seriousness of a physiologist . . . But a few weeks later a temptation in which I think I see a sign of nascent sensuality took hold of me: to return to the pond, to go back down that sunken lane which I had avoided with a vengeance since the incident. I hesitated for a day or two—out of timidity, not out of virtue. Then the call became irresistible. One morning, resolutely, I set off on the adventure. And all for naught: the pond and its surroundings were deserted. I went back there afterwards almost every day, and each time in vain, but without getting tired of it; each time with greater excitement, even. My heart started to pound as soon as I had left the highway; the blood rose to my cheeks as I drew near the bend; but I had acquired such a taste for that febrile, delicious state that I found in it a marvelous compensation for my daily disappointment. Soon I had even lost all hope of witnessing a new bathing scene. It was a rainy summer, the warm weather was coming to an end. But for all that I did not give up taking the sunken lane. What was I looking for there? To resurrect the vision of the girls? No. Simply to reawaken the thrill of the first day, to revive in myself that short, acute, intimate arousal, delightfully painful. Sensuality? . . . I would stay for an instant on the edge of the bank, standing on tiptoes, mesmerized. Then, fearing I would be discovered in this strange posture, I would run away with my voluptuous secret . . . That stagnant water lined with willows, that corner of pasture which I glimpsed through the hazel trees, are forever etched in my memory.

A fence has replaced the hedge, the willows are dead, a cement drinking trough occupies the place of the pond, spreading apple trees shade the meadow; but it is rare that I pass by there without seeing again in my mind the setting of bygone days.

Sensuality, no doubt, but a diffuse and very chaste sensuality in which experienced psychologists might have descried the coming of the sexual age, but which, in my opinion, did not yet harbor any trace of sexuality. Really, at that time my innocence was complete. I sinned neither "in thought" nor "in deed," as the catechism bluntly puts it. I did not even suspect what it could be. And if my mornings ended more often than not with an excited pilgrimage to the neighborhood of the pond, my nights were still of an angelic purity. At night, in the warmth of my bed, waiting for sleep, I would think of all sorts of things but no obsession of a sexual nature haunted my reverie. Not only had I never had the idea of indulging in the slightest touching, but I never even lifted the long nightshirt in which I was wrapped, to caress my body. As unbelievable as this may seem to those who have had the experience of a precocious perversity, the disquieting apparition of those naked girls splashing about in the water remained linked for me with the setting where I had discovered them, and I never had the vaguest desire to recall their preadolescent figures anywhere else than in the countryside, at the fateful turning in the sunken lane.

I am rereading what I have written. And I must admit that I am a little surprised at having expatiated so self-indulgently on these childish things. It is because, rightly or wrongly, I attach a certain importance to them. All my life I have thought a great deal about the phenomena of sexuality—of mine in particular—and I have always done my best to approach these problems without self-deception, with a lucid objectivity. I have questioned a number of different people, collected a good many confidences; I have assembled quite a few curious documents on these questions. Let's just say that this is one of them. This insignificant adventure deserved, in my eyes, to be analyzed at some length for two reasons which lead me to believe that it has had not inconsiderable repercussions on my unconscious. Is it not indeed surprising that after seventy years of a very full life, my memory should still have retained such a precise, such a lasting, impression of this episode? And, furthermore, is it not telling that this children's skinny-dip—which, in itself, contained nothing obscene or even very exceptional—should have been seized upon by my morbid adolescent's imagination several years later, should have been revived, magnified, perverted, enriched with scabrous details, and given a place of choice in that lascivious imagery in which my depraved schoolboy's dreams wallowed? I shall have to return to this subject. What unsuspected conclusions would a psychoanalyst of today draw from my story? The least one can say is that on the morning of my tenth year when

I had that fleeting revelation of the female sex, I received a deep jolt which struck a secret, and hypersensitive, spot in me. Also, it is testimony that I should regret having withheld.

If I have attached so much importance to this incident it is because I think it was the first emotional shock that set off reactions in me of an absolutely personal nature; the first that compelled me to keep a secret, and, as a result, to free myself from the family universe; the first that gave rise to an expression of inner life; the first, finally, that awoke in me a consciousness of people's impenetrability, as well as the proud, expansive, intoxicating, and invigorating sense of our solitude.

THE BRIEF PASSAGE of the Abbé Rumpert in my life hardly counted. He was not even my confessor. It was to the old dean that I went twice a year, from the time I was seven, to ask absolution for my sins.

The lesson lasted two short hours: a little Latin, a lot of catechism. The dean, who marveled at my good memory and who doubtless trusted in my virtue, had guaranteed that his curate would be able, within six or seven months, to make me worthy to receive Communion. Comparing the dates, I notice that this ceremony, celebrated each year with great pomp on the first Sunday of May in the church at Menneville, must have preceded slightly (by a month or two perhaps) the adventure of the pond with the girls; and so I am surprised that these first sensual stirrings were not complicated by religious scruples and pious repentance.

In these visions, these "immodest" thoughts, how did I not sniff, fearfully, a trap by Satan? Though I had never shown an exalted devotion, my first Communion nevertheless had the importance of a solemn act, an initiation, in my life as a good boy. I should have had a troubled conscience, should have fought, struggled, sought out spiritual help against my obsessions. Yet I have no memory of any such thing. I don't even think I alluded to these matters when, on the 15th of August, I went to confession. Did my innocence perhaps immunize me against the very suspicion of evil? Perhaps, too, my natural reserve was repelled by embarrassing confidences which, in all good faith, I felt I could do without. The fact is that I never believed I should involve anyone in this business, neither the Good Lord nor His minister; and this instinctive refusal pretty well foreshadows the attitude that I was later to take towards religion.

As I said, I have scarcely any memories of my first teacher. At any rate, he left the area during the summer holidays. I have a good many more of his successor, the Abbé Adry, with whom I worked for three years. His influence on my education was much more active. I feel that I am going to have a great deal to say about him and that I will enjoy it . . .

Where did he come from? Not until later on did I know, did I become acquainted with his life. He was a southerner by origin, by temperament, by education, whom chance had set down in the Perche. One of those beings in whom an inner fire burns, whose flame can be felt by all who come near him. (It is not his faith that I mean.) He had an astonishing resemblance to the Bonaparte of the Brumaire. Much taller, but as thin; a long, nervous, febrile body; warm coloring, hair black as ink; a deeply sculpted face; a dark, caressing gaze, hemmed in under a bony brow with a black forelock across it; a hooked nose, sunken cheeks, a consumptive's cheekbones, a jutting and pointed chin. His lips were thin, turned up at the corners, and extremely mobile; he had an easy smile; but this smile, tempered and weighed down by the slightly feverish sadness of his eyes, endowed his physiognomy with more vivaciousness and ardor than cheer.

The first time I saw him it was in the pulpit, at High Mass. The dean had stepped aside to give him the opportunity to make his debut in the parish. A sensational debut. This tall devil, who did not stand still, made a disconcerting contrast—with his waving arms, warm, sonorous voice, and that fiery eloquence which gushed forth—to the easygoing ways and the dull Sunday sermon to which the good dean had accustomed us. Impossible to remain indifferent: from that first day on, the impetuous curate had his partisans and his detractors. "A real clown!" muttered old Zélie as she climbed back into the break. Henriette and I, whom this flight of oratory had surprised and captivated, felt instantly won over.

I was all the more so after my first lesson. The radiance of the Abbé Adry was such, the atmosphere that he created by his very contact was so effervescent, that his slightest words had a stunning resonance. He taught, as he lived, in a kind of perpetual spontaneity, improvisation. I listened transfixed. Habit gradually diminished these first reactions; but for a long time his presence alone was enough to put me into a state of receptivity bordering on the hypnotic. I very well understood, later on when he became a popular speaker, the reason for his hold over crowds.

With him I took to the classics for good, and happily sailed through the thankless period of the first notions of grammar. Prepared early on by Mlle. Fromentot's analyses to taste the satisfactions of logic, I at once found myself strangely receptive to the rational jointing of the Latin sentence, its rectitude, its ingenious concision. Yes, I got off to a good start with my studies. At an age when few schoolchildren can do so, I learned to grasp, to love, the dialectical virtues of the Latin mind. I am not afraid to say that on certain days the precision of Latin syntax threw me into a kind of rapture. And I bless the circumstances that saved me the time lost in repeating the rudiments by rote in an overcrowded classroom where the most gifted are made to keep step with the backward. Only later did I experience that lazy academic mastication which removes all flavor from the food—and often all the nutritional value.

It was not that the new curate had fixed methods, or even great experience in teaching. But he was intense, capricious, and grammar bored him: he preferred to strike out into the texts; and like Mlle. Fromentot with her dictations, he excelled at choosing them. I was just in my first year of Latin, yet he threw me into the *Eclogues** and the *Georgics*. We translated without preparation, diving directly into the text. He didn't much care if I was panting to keep up. He forged ahead without lingering too long over explanations of syntax. His melodious southerner's voice, in love with meter and with rhythm, scanned the cadence of the lines for me. The poet's finest strokes of inspiration enchanted him, and his enthusiasm was contagious. Emotion in him was spontaneous, generous, infectious, and on his lips the dead language regained a colloquial and living accent. He swept me along in his wake, got me drunk on idyllic images, and everything became present to me: the existence of the young shepherds, their country romances, their games, their reed-pipes, their meadows, their murmuring springs, their siestas in the shade of groves, their graceful frolicking in pursuit of a kid. I discovered not only the Latin tongue but Antiquity, pagan youth, the joy of living, the splendor of nature; and also the spell of poetry, the transformation of the universe through the magic of art. Some passage by Virgil on plowing or sowing, on harvests or grape pickings, would remind the abbé of a quatrain by Horace, a poem by Ronsard, some verses by Leconte de Lisle, a stanza by Lamartine or by Hugo. His memory was prodigious: he knew by heart all the poets that he loved. Thus, in a single incantation, the hymns of the past merged with the songs of all the centuries.

As I left those lessons, which I now had daily, the world appeared to me transformed. That countryside which I thought I knew, those pastures, those flocks—I looked at them with a new, Virgilian eye. A music arose in me which stayed with me all the way to le Saillant. I had always paid attention to the aspect of the seasons, to the colors of autumn, the shivering of the trees in the wind, the cavalcade of clouds above the forest; but I was sensitive to it in an entirely different way since I had become aware of being so, since I had learned that one can translate one's impressions into words. And this I did not shy away from doing: the exercises in French which the abbé gave me once a week and which had replaced Mademoiselle's dictations were a source of enjoyment for me—I will even say: of delight . . . "What do you know about the life of the animals in the woods?" "Tell about the return of the homing pigeon to its nest," "Describe a morning in spring," etc. I threw myself with a sort of lyrical intoxication into this new domain of writing, of

*Virgil's ten pastoral poems.

expression. I did it to my heart's content; I indulged in descriptive debauches; I was indefatigable; and my unbridled imagination brought me unsuspected pleasures that dimmed the austere satisfactions which logical reasoning had been able to give me at the time of arithmetic and analyses. I could not resist the temptation of reading my "compositions," piping hot, straight from the oven, to my sister. She smiled ambiguously, but I could see the surprise that she did not admit, and I was flattered by it. I had never confided in her or in anyone else that a vocation had been born in me, and that I would devote my life to writing poems. She had guessed it. One evening in the forest when my father, concerning some error in riding, had begun his reprimand with: "If you want to become an officer . . . ," Henriette had exclaimed: "Bertrand an officer? . . . but he's going to be a poet! . . ." My father, amused, started to laugh. He seemed to me quite narrow-minded that evening.

But the abbé's teaching held other revelations in store for me. We soon abandoned Virgil and his bucolic pastimes to tackle Sallust and Caesar. Then Livy, Cicero, Tacitus. A complete change of horizon. I suddenly entered Roman history; and, through history, the politics of all eras. A precocious initiation, at age eleven . . . But I have no regrets. I think that even in the field of pedagogy, chance often manages things quite well. I have noticed, in any case, that failed educations are generally those that have been the most rigidly planned.

It was in connection with Flaminius, Marius, or Spartacus that I perceived for the first time what a spate of muddled and legitimate demands was embodied in the abstract terms "democratic revolution" or "proletarian insurrection." I became fired up over the "resistance" of the Gauls, roused against the iniquitous invasion of the Romans. For me, the victories at Pharsalus and Philippi tolled the death knell of liberty. On the subjects of Jugurtha or the Punic Wars, of Brutus, of the "agrarian law," the abbé, without being too concerned as to whether I could follow him, enlarged upon the themes that were close to his heart. For he was one of those generous souls who are haunted by "social injustices," "the poverty and exploitation of the workers . . ." His digressions took on another tone. Poetry played a lesser role in them. He read to me from Rousseau, Lamennais, Montalembert.* He did still speak to me of Hugo or Lamartine, but it was to recite *Les Châtiments*†

---

*Félicité de Lamennais and Charles, Comte de Montalembert, were liberal Catholic writers who in 1830, with Henri Lacordaire, founded *L'Avenir* ("The Future"), a journal advocating the separation of church and state. Lamennais was later excommunicated for a poem attacking the papacy and the monarchs of Europe.

†Collection of poetry by Victor Hugo published in 1853, in which he condemns the mediocrity of the Second Empire while exalting the poor and the oppressed.

for me or to initiate me into the Ateliers Nationaux* and the revolution of '48. I tried hard to interest my sister in these exhilarating discoveries; but in front of my father I let nothing show. And when he asked me evasively, as he unfolded his napkin: "Did you work well this morning?," he was far from suspecting that the abbé and I had spent the morning in the company of Sylla or Sertorius, of Danton and Saint-Just, and that the proclamation of the *Rights of Man* held an infinitely greater place in our discussions than the rules for the relative pronoun or the ablative absolute.

It was not without consequences that these explosive notions burst into the malleable brain of a provincial boy. It is rather titillating to think that this premature emancipation and, if I may say so, my revolutionary novitiate, were the work—the unconscious work, it seems to me—of the godly priest who had been entrusted with the task of instructing me . . . I learned indirectly to judge without leniency the caste into which I had been born. I particularly recall a fiery diatribe by the abbé against the "propertied classes," who, he maintained, "will not enter into the kingdom of God!" (Occasioned, I believe, by a page of Plutarch on the proscriptions, the ruthless massacre of the "rich" by the triumvirs.) But a day that stands out above all the others I remember is the one when, dumbfounded, I heard the Abbé Adry curse almsgiving and pronounce a scathing indictment against charity. On that day I truly felt a whole side of my childhood certainties topple, one of the most stable foundations of my family tradition collapse.

I had been brought up to respect charity as the virtue par excellence; and for me charity was expressly the practice of almsgiving. From time immemorial at le Saillant, we had had our "poor day." A sacred ritual. The evening before, at market, fresh bread and pennies were laid in. Then the next day, Saturday, winter and summer alike, starting at dawn every beggar in the canton—the destitute, the needy, the miserable wretches, the old alcoholics from the welfare services, the cripples from the hospice, the ragged wards of the State, the dregs of the slums—was permitted to come through the iron gate of the château and to receive as his due a two-sou piece and his half pound of coarse bread, which was, more often than not, stuffed with a chunk of bacon fat, a bit of cheese, or some left-over meat. A whole disorderly and ragtag procession of toothless old women, beggars on crutches, pregnant girls, snot-nosed and rachitic children, who were often joined by a few passing vagrants, some of those wandering tramps who are the roving aristocracy of the underworld (and who at that time were jokingly called "senators") filed into the *cour d'honneur,* transformed that morning into the *cour des*

---

*The "National Workshops," a sort of emergency relief agency set up in 1848 at the insistence of the provisional government, and partly led by the poet-deputy Alphonse de Lamartine.

*Miracles.** The doling out was done in the kitchen doorway. My sister presided over it, as a rule. She had for each a word of welcome, of cheer; to those whose penury was particularly deserving she sometimes slipped a little something extra, a used petticoat, a pair of clogs, some socks, or a muffler she had knitted. And she accepted as the most natural thing in the world the "God-will-repay-you-for-it-my-good-lady's" which went with the salutations, the little bows, the protestations of respect and appreciation. And I too, up until then, had found this exchange of generosity and gratitude to be quite straightforward and even edifying. But the abbé's condemnation was so categorical, his indignation so vehement, his arguments so convincing, that I had to concede he was right. From that day on, that tattered procession on Saturdays seemed to me like a scandal, an inexpiable offense against the dignity of those human creatures. I undertook to persuade my sister that the renunciation of surplus wealth was the first duty of the rich; and that almsgiving was a degrading act, which demeans the donor as much as the debtor. She listened to me with attention and surprise. She did not say no. Then she ended up smiling: "Well, good Saint Francis," she said, "find something else. What do you suggest? Do you want to give away your linen, your clothes? Give them our carriages, your pony? What?—put them all up in the house, invite them to have lunch with us?" And as I remained stubborn and ill at ease: "In the meantime," she added, "the best thing, believe me, for them as well as for us, is not to change anything in the routine."

I choose this example among many others. It shows well what sort of intellectual attainments, moral broadening, and elevation I owe to the Abbé Adry's sometimes injudicious improvisations.

This was in 1881. His social dream seems to me to have been ahead of its time. Priests of his type were not numerous. Our venerable dean certainly did not approve of the "advanced" ideas that the "socialist vicar," as they called him in the town, professed in the name of the Gospel. But he put up no systematic opposition. I imagine, however, that he had not authorized without debate, and that he must have followed with distrust, the innovations which the fiery abbé, in order to combat the parish's humdrum somnolence, had hastened to introduce into the religious life of Menneville. Immediately upon his arrival, he had reorganized the girls' youth fellowship according to his own lights, and instituted weekly meetings for the housewives and monthly lectures for the men. He gave of himself without stinting. But he had mainly concentrated his apostolic fervor on the creation of an association, christened the "Cercle Lacordaire," which every evening and on Sundays, in a room loaned him and fixed up at his own expense, brought

*In the Middle Ages, an area of Paris known for its disreputable population; see especially Hugo's *Notre Dame de Paris.*

together the young men from sixteen to twenty—between apprenticeship and military service. There one found a few newspapers, a small library, a billiard table, decks of cards. (I was very surprised to learn that smoking was not forbidden there.) Every Sunday, at the end of the afternoon, the abbé would give a reading or a talk on some topical subject, followed by an open discussion that would sometimes go on all evening. These sessions caused quite a stir. The abbé put all of his gifts as a social director into them, and he quickly managed to gather round him all the young people of the area.

My father was not exactly unaware of this activity, since he had consented to appear on the list of founders of the Cercle, and was discreetly helping the abbé by means of gifts which, from time to time, I was assigned to take to the presbytery in envelopes with a red seal. Was he perhaps only seizing this opportunity to thank the teacher for his devotion? It surprises me that he was not somewhat worried by the influence that the "socialist vicar" might have on his pupil. In fact, he never seems to have taken offense at this. And without really knowing whether I should attribute this attitude to goodwill, to gratitude, or to indifference, I put it down in any case to his credit.

The remainder of the story is tragic. I shall summarize it briefly.

Recalling the fervor of that proselytizing, I was not surprised, a few years later, in Paris, to see the name Pierre Adry in the table of contents of the *Sillon,* a "Christian Socialist" review founded by Marc Sangnier. I wrote immediately. I got his address, I ran to see him. I found him in a garret, on the top floor of a run-down hotel in the rue de Vaugirard. Thinner, more sallow, more gangling than ever, with his black forelock plastered to his forehead, his lilting voice and his feverish gaze, that heavy and caressing gaze whose insistency contained so much charisma and authority. He had left Menneville for Sées, summoned by the bishop to take charge of the Catholic societies of the diocese, but with the secret plan of founding a militant socialist newspaper there that would also be a religious newspaper. He had done it, in spite of all opposition. He had sunk into it all the funds he had been able to raise, and it bankrupted him. Consumed with debts, in trouble with his bishop, he had ended up in Paris, where he was living as an unaffiliated priest, without means, haunting public gatherings, meetings, open universities; writing articles, pamphlets, tracts; battling from morning till night. I remember that, at one moment, as if something in my look had let him know, he abruptly interrupted his monologue to look me in the eye: "How you've changed! You haven't lost your faith, have you?" "Why yes, Monsieur l'abbé. A long time ago. Supposing that I ever had it . . ." "My God . . . You? No? Is it possible?" He was stammering with emotion. He no longer had all his self-confidence. He was staring at me now: "Oh, my boy, my boy . . . This is not good."

A few months later, one morning, very early, he arrived in the rue de

Fleurus, at the home of my uncle Chambost-Lévadé, where I was living. I had just got up. I went down to greet him. He had been shown into the library. The housework had begun, furniture was cluttering the way, and he was waiting for me at the back, at the far end, sheathed in his thin cassock. Seeing me, he attempted a strained smile and threaded his way to me through the armchairs and tables, with the litheness of a loose-jointed marionette. "Forgive me, Bertrand . . . I've come . . . It's the first time . . . I swear to you that never, never again . . . I need . . ." (here, a pathetic sum: something like "a hundred and thirty or a hundred and forty francs"). He was terribly embarrassed; and I even more so. I went upstairs to get the little money that I had in my possession, and I brought it to him. Five or six hundred francs, maybe. He looked at the bills that I handed him and said to me, humbly: "But I have no change . . ." I stuffed it all into his hand. His eyes filled with tears. He did not say thank you to me. "It's the fifteenth . . . The rent for April . . . Ah, you don't know those dates, do you? . . ." He did not want to sit down. He left, still holding the money in the palm of his hand. I followed him. On the doorstep, he turned around and smiled at me tenderly. Then his features became grave: "Bertrand . . . Every morning, you know, every morning I pray for you!"

I never saw him again. I wrote, shortly after, to the rue Vaugirard, and the letter came back to me. I had news only much, much later, in '98 or '99, during my vacation at le Saillant. The priest who had just been named to the deanship of Menneville came to pay his respects to Henriette upon arriving. During the conversation, which was flagging, I happened to mention the abbé's name. "Pierre Adry?" The dean had known him quite well, they had been fellow students at the seminary in Sées. I sensed immediately that he did not like him. Is what he told us completely accurate? Was it only the echo of the malicious gossip in the diocese? I will never know.

Here, in any case, is what I remember: The abbé had published, under different pseudonyms and without ecclesiastical authorization, various books and pamphlets of which two, in particular, had unfortunate repercussions: *Commentary on the Gospels* and *The Socialism of Christ*. The uproar surrounding these works having attracted the attention of the elder clergy, the identity of the author was discovered. Scandal. Placed on the index, etc. And the dean had heard that things had gone quite far, to the point where the abbé had found himself stripped of the right to celebrate Mass. He had then given up all his activities and had gone to seek refuge in the corner of the Vaucluse where he had spent his childhood. He had vegetated there for a few years, in great poverty, and had died at the hospital in Avignon before turning fifty. I can imagine poor Adry's distress, holed up like a pariah in his native village, half-priest, half-layman, suspect to the curé, suspect to the mayor, treated as a "creeping Jesus" by some and as a "defrocked priest" by the others. I have never been able to think about that miserable end without a pang in my heart. I hold it against the Church, against Society, that they could not make a place for this born apostle, on fire with evangelical faith, altruism, self-sacrifice, and true goodness.

I would wager that until his last day he prayed each morning that I would be touched by grace. The sainted man, fortunately, never suspected that he himself, in an indirect but distinct fashion, had helped with his pious hands to clear the way in my child's mind for that fearsome path of unbelief upon which I would soon so deliberately set out . . .

THE FACT is worth noting. One day as we went into the big room at the presbytery, our attention was attracted by a large framed engraving standing against the sideboard. The dean, who prided himself on loving "antiques," had probably been given it by one of his flock. It must have dated from the seventeenth century, and represented *The Hebrews Gathering Up the Manna from Heaven*. A crowd of men, women, and children, dressed in the Roman style, were hurling themselves pell-mell at the ground while a long slanted ray slid down between two clouds and fell from the sky upon this pompous disarray, arranged like a ballet at Versailles. The abbé said to me: "Guess where this word 'manna' comes from . . . Well, in Hebrew, to ask 'What?' 'What is it?' you say *Man hou?* When, one morning, the Hebrews saw their campground covered with manna, they looked at each other in amazement and they called to one another, shouting *Man hou? . . . Man hou? . . .* as the Romans would have said: *Quid?*"

I found this very amusing. "You laugh . . . but do you even know what manna is?" Of course, I knew. The abbé had taught me my Bible history. And nothing, except perhaps the pathetic scene of the sacrifice of Isaac by his father, had moved me so much as the distress of the poor Hebrews in flight, who were lost without provisions in the desert and would have all died of hunger if God had not answered their prayers and made that mysterious food to rain down upon them every day. Yes, I knew, but I made no answer, so as to delay the beginning of the lesson and to hear the abbé repeat such a beautiful story.

The abbé smiled, happy to surprise me once again.

"Well, I'm going to tell you what it is. You think it's a kind of edible snow that fell out of the sky? Not at all. Manna is a kind of tiny white, sugary, floury mushroom which grows in certain areas of Arabia, and whose scientific name I have forgotten. You can eat it just like that. But it often happens that no one is around to pick it. Then this moss dries out in the sun, the wind carries it far away like dust. And, during the night, when there is dew, these little beads swollen with moisture get bigger and after a few hours become like little pellets of bread."

"Good to eat?"

"Especially when you've got nothing else. The desert animals are fond of them, and understandably so. The caravans themselves make do with them, on occasion. The pellets are ground, are turned into flour, which is then kneaded to make cakes . . . A sort of hardtack . . . In Persia, they had known this for a long time, too: the warriors in Alexander's army who found themselves, like the Hebrews, lost in the desert, were also saved from hunger because they had the luck to find manna."

How simple it was! I was dazzled. It had been quite a while since I believed in Père Noël, but it would never have occurred to me to question a miracle that the Good Lord was involved in. I found myself suddenly as if *freed* of something. Of what? Of a constraint, of a weight, from which I hadn't suffered much, to tell the truth, but whose oppressiveness became noticeable in retrospect. Ah, how much lighter the abbé's explanation seemed for me to carry than the other, and how much more satisfying for the mind! A washed, luminous, transparent horizon spread out before me. I tasted the combined joys of discovery and of the obvious.

I wanted to say: "Then everything is clear, and the Good Lord has nothing to do with it?" But I had an intuition that this would have been to put my foot in it and I kept this logical and sacrilegious conclusion to myself. And just as well. For the good Abbé Adry, assessing in a flash the consequences of his imprudence, would have been quick to run me through the twists and turns of his dialectic and convince me that botanical explanations took nothing of the supernatural away from the miracle of the manna, since it was clearly through the express will of God that this lichen grew on barren soils; and since, besides, it was thanks to His almighty goodness that an ample harvest of the precious foodstuff had been "providentially" within reach of the Hebrews on the very day when they were all about to perish.

No one suspected what had happened in me that morning. Not even Henriette, to whom I did not breathe a word. I would not actually dare to claim that from one day to the next I revised my notion of the supernatural or looked with an informed and skeptical eye at all the marvels with which Biblical history and the Gospels are crammed. That must not have come to pass so quickly; those developments are timid and slow in an eleven-year-old's brain. It is very likely, nevertheless, that from that day on, while in Sunday sermons I was hearing our old dean allude to the resurrection of Lazarus, for example, or to the multiplication of the loaves, I said to myself, irreverently: "Another of these cock-and-bull stories that ignoramuses attribute to mysterious and unverifiable causes. Tall tales for the gullible . . . There's got to be some very simple explanation for it, like the trick of the manna."

Thus, the amused smile of a priest and a few words of good sense were enough to immunize me against spiritual mystifications and to implant in my mind forever the germ of *doubt*. I ought to call this chapter: "First application of scientific observation to a seemingly miraculous phenomenon . . ." My case must not be exceptional. I think that in religious teaching there is nothing more delicate, nothing riskier, than to put on guard against superstitions a young and fervent soul whose convictions we are trying, at the same time, to avoid upsetting. Credulity, nowadays, is fragile. A physician who administered a stimulant and its antidote by turns would be playing a dangerous game . . . There is a fine line between superstition and belief. As soon as a mistrust in the correctness of the interpretations of legends is born, it becomes an exercise in acrobatics to maintain a distinction between the truth of the mystery of the Incarnation and that of the miracle of the manna. The argument of the "Revelation" is too convenient not to be terribly vulnerable. The authority of "dogma" has suffered a setback. And I have a hard time understanding how so many minds, once their critical sense has been awakened, can reject superstitions as so many crude fables and yet stop dead on that slippery slope.

ALL THE MYSTERY that surrounded religion had always puzzled me. For example, death, eternal life, heaven, hell. All this seemed to me so strange, so difficult, that I wasn't far from smelling a rat. There was a time when I pestered Henriette with questions: Mama had died, she was in heaven . . . Well, which heaven? This big, cloud-filled uninhabitable sky that hung above the terrace and the forest? No? Behind this visible sky was another space, invisible and sacred, bathed in sunshine, radiant, where the Good Lord gathered his elect? In what form, those elect? Had they become angels? I had never been able to believe in that guardian angel, invisible, untouchable, and present, who fluttered about me and protected me from evil. I had quite early placed him, with his wings, among devotional props for children, of the Père Noël variety . . . And the Resurrection? The miracles . . . Too many grownups claimed that Jesus was risen for there not to have been some truth in it. But it seemed to me rather hard to swallow. And if resurrection was something possible, why hadn't the curé of Menneville, of whom everyone said "He was a saint," brought Mama back to life?

My sister Henriette, after a pious if not fervent youth, had, it seems to me, gradually freed herself from religious observances. She avoided talking about these things, perhaps even thinking too much about them. She had those of the servants who wished to go driven to High Mass on Sunday, but she went with them only rarely, on the major holidays: out of habit, rather than to satisfy a need of her inner life. As for my wife, she was a believer and practiced when she felt like it, as a matter of upbringing, of tradition, as her relatives did, as is expected when one belongs to a certain social milieu. We never discussed these questions together. I attached no importance to these outward displays and made no attempt to dissuade her from them, not even to make her clarify her real position in her own eyes. In the same way, my disbelief, which I never hid from her, seemed to leave her indifferent, probably because it remained discreet and because I never flaunted it in such a way as to cause a scandal around us. It is likely, for example, that if I had tried to shield my sons from all religious education, Claire, supported by her family, would have stood up to me and been violently opposed to it. Fortunately, I did not wish any such thing. I had pondered this at some length as far back as the birth and baptism of our eldest boy. And I had decided to let my wife do as she pleased.

I thought—and I still think—that in the present state of our moral evolution it doesn't really damage children to subject them, at least in their first years, to a Christian discipline. On the contrary. Christian education, properly understood—as it is, fortunately, by a large number of priests who have the responsibility for imparting it—is above all edifying. It opens the child's eyes to his conscience and develops it in him. Freethinking contains something negative and arid, which it is advisable to attain gradually and which is not assimilated without some danger by young sensibilities, young intelligences. Just as it is helpful to guide a child's first steps so that he acquires a sense of balance and gets used to walking upright, so it can be wise and beneficial to provide him with one of those moral beliefs tested by generations. I was counting on my sons' reason to discard, sooner or later, all the dogmatic and supernatural nonsense that was taught them along with everything else. At least religion had the incomparable advantage of implanting in them solid and just principles, which were, on the whole, my own, and which I doubtless would have been clumsy at inculcating in them without the intermediation of faith.

Of course I do not deny the possibility of a purely secular moral code taking hold in a young mind, although the attempts of this kind that were given me to follow seemed to me to produce mediocre results more often than good ones. But it is an arduous and hazardous task which neither my natural abilities nor my career as an officer in particular allowed me to undertake with any chance of success. Certain friends, more uncompromising than I, reproached me for this passive attitude. All the more so since I sometimes maintained to them that the broad mass of men are neither good enough material nor naturally provided with enough moral judgment to set out in life with only the compass of their common sense. Now, what matters for the good order of a society is not so much that the individuals who compose it should all be free spirits, emancipated from superstition, but that they be capable of recognizing the right path without hesitation and be determined to take it without delay—for which Christian morality, whether separated or not from dogmatic faith, can be quite useful. I would almost go so far as to assert, from my own experience, that people animated by a sincere belief and an authentic fervor generally have a morality rather superior to that of the majority of unbelievers. The cheats, the hypocrites, the hard-hearted are certainly no less numerous among the freethinkers than among the faithful. However, I am wary of going any farther down that road, and I am quick to protest against those who claim that religion is forever indispensable to the order of the state, and that it will always be the only solid foundation for a practical morality. Nothing is less certain. Nevertheless, one has to acknowledge—and I know this from having observed it at close range, not only in France among the Catholics or the Protestants, but in Africa among the Islamic populations—that religious feeling is a human feeling, unquestionably natural and enduring, and that faith, in our time, is still necessary for the spiritual equilibrium of certain natures. This is a fact, the observation of which is enough to make me respect faith when I come across it.

For myself, however, this is a moot point. Few people, I think, are as lacking in religious sense as I am. I cannot help looking upon every believer as a poor *duped* fellow (duped by myths, on which his childhood was fed and of which his reason has not rid him in good time; duped by vain hopes, with which he soothes his fear in the face of life and in the face of death; duped by that desperate need for divine protection which leads him to imagine a personal God, loving His creatures; duped, finally, by himself—Heautonmystificomenos*—I mean duped by that famous "will to believe" which is at bottom the most solid but also the most illusory basis for Christian faith).

Whenever I encounter someone who prays and convinces himself that God listens to him, or even that *He* answers and that *He* will grant one's wish, I cannot help thinking of the old Zélie of my childhood, whom I caught so many times, at the close of her life, jabbering away all by herself in the kitchen and imagining that she was talking to someone. *Atheist* I am—as completely, I believe, as a man of our times, who has, after all, twenty centuries of Christianity in his veins, can be; but *anti-theist*, no.

This is all I wish to say on that subject.

---

*A play on the title of Terence's comedy *Heauton timoroumenos (The Self-Tormentor):* here, "The Self-Mystifier."

CHAPTER IV

Guy at le Saillant

I NOW WISH to recount in its entirety my cousin Guy's stay at le Saillant. This is a new period of my early youth.

In March of 1882—I was going on twelve—my Aunt Chambost-Lévadé and her son came to spend Easter vacation with us.

I did not know either of them. My father, even before his widowerhood, had never been on really intimate terms with his brother-in-law. His retirement to the country, his bereavement, his unsociability, had not helped to expand their relations, which were limited after my mother's death to exchanges of cordial but infrequent letters.

I have already noted that my mother and her brother Éric were the children of the chemist Chambost-Lévadé; and that, in this Parisian and scholarly family (my grandfather was a member of the Institut), the marriage of my mother to this officer, with his provincial origins and rustic tastes, who had quit the army, had not been unreservedly welcomed. Éric in particular had done his utmost to dissuade his sister. In vain. He was vindictive by nature and had never forgotten this defeat. My uncle, since then, had pursued in Paris what is usually called a brilliant career. Upon leaving the École Normale, spurning a career in teaching, attracted by both philosophy and historical studies, he specialized in the history of human societies. His work, which was beginning to be accepted as authoritative in Europe, made him, along with Leroy-Beaulieu, one of the principal founders of the École des Sciences Politiques.* Since then, he had given a well-attended course there each winter in comparative sociology. He naturally had the Institut on his mind, and coveted a chair at the Collège de France. Between the two brothers-in-law, nothing in common. My father got along better with my Aunt Chambost, who was of an affable character and whom my mother had loved tenderly. It was with her that he corresponded two or three times a year. Our secluded life at le Saillant and the hardworking and highly social existence that my uncle and aunt led in the capital did not make for get-togethers. Since my mother's funeral, the Chambosts had not returned to le Saillant.

A fortuitous combination of circumstances at the end of that winter of

---

*A *grande école* founded in 1871 for the purpose of training future businessmen, managers, statesmen, and academics in political science.

'82 suddenly brought the two branches of the family together. The Chambosts had only one child, a boy a year older than I, whose health, long fragile, was at that time giving new cause for worry. The doctors insisted that he be taken out of the Parisian lycée where he was a student, and live for a year or two in the fresh air. The Chambosts had heard good things about a religious school located in our region, in Gevrésy, in the hills of the Perche near Menneville. And my Aunt Madeleine had contacted my father to ask his opinion and to request that he make further inquiries around the area; she did not conceal how hard this separation was for her; but, she said, the ordeal would be less painful if she knew her son was in our vicinity.

I remember what an event the arrival of this letter was for us. At my sister's instigation, and probably affected by the urgent tone of this appeal, my father, after many hesitations, consented to suggest to the Chambost-Lévadés that all three come to le Saillant over Easter vacation, in order to decide for themselves, on the spot, whether the Saint-Léonard School corresponded to their wishes. My aunt wrote back at once: Uncle Éric was detained in Paris by the preparation of his course—which produced visible relief in my father and Henriette; but Aunt Madeleine eagerly agreed to come spend Easter week at le Saillant.

Pandemonium in the house! We never entertained anyone. Most of the bedrooms had been closed off since my mother's death; and I actually believe I had never crossed the threshold of the little suite, made up of two rooms and a bath, that Henriette reserved for our guests. Time, humidity, and mice had combined to do their damage there. We had to hurry to set everything to rights. I can still see my sister conferring with the chimneysweep, the carpenter, the upholsterer from Menneville. She was already quite good at that sort of work. In three weeks everything was ready.

Henriette, back then, was in the full radiance of her youth. We had celebrated her twentieth birthday in November. For many years, she had spiritedly taken on the running of the household. I always admired her practical sense, her organizational gifts; and still more that art which she had of making light an authority that was in fact rather inflexible. Never nitpicking, yet precise in her instructions, she kept an eye on everything, and, without seeming to give orders, got what she wanted from our two maids, who adored her. One of her secrets, I think, was knowing how to lend a hand and set an example, unostentatiously, while giving generously of herself.

AUNT MADELEINE HAD set Easter Monday as the date of her arrival.

I remember my agitation that day, while my sister and I were awaiting the return of the victoria in which my father had gone to get our guests at the station. For the first time I was going to live in close quarters with a companion of my own age. I should have been overjoyed. But our stay-at-home existence had made me so little sociable, so stupidly in a rut, that I felt neither pleasure nor impatience nor curiosity. On the contrary: a feeling of animosity mixed with anxiety, almost dread.

Henriette had dispatched me to stand sentry in front of the gate. That April afternoon was as springlike as one could wish. I was sweltering in my Sunday best. The moment I saw the carriage burst onto the sunlit road and turn off, in the distance, under the trees of the drive, I ran to give the alert, and we took up our positions on the front steps. The ride up the slope seemed endless to us. Henriette was hardly less feverish than I. At last, the carriage came out onto the terreplein. Seized with panic, I ran out on my sister and retreated into the hallway, from where I could see everything without being seen. Gaspard, sitting up straight—he had his holiday air about him, in his triple-collared carrick with its silver buttons gleaming in the sun—showed off by putting the horses at the trot to go through the gate, and by executing a stylish turn in the courtyard. But I had eyes only for Guy. Perched on the jump seat, his thin face barely visible between his round hat and the otter collar of his Inverness cape, he seemed to me smaller in stature than I had dared hope; and, as such, less intimidating than I had anticipated. I decided to rejoin my sister. Guy jumped down first from the carriage and, having removed his hat and presented his forehead for Henriette to kiss, he came up to me, un-self-conscious, with his hand out. Then and there, I felt won over. More, even: the prejudices I held against him vanished instantly; and I felt drawn to him by an inordinate liking which nothing yet justified. I was already a victim of his power to bewitch.

I shall have many occasions to speak of my aunt, and at length. She was, with Henriette, the most tender attachment of my youth; I can even say: one of the beings who has held a dominant place in my life. However, when I conjure up that first encounter, I remember only my amazement. The innovations of Parisian elegance reached our Perche countryside several years late, and my Aunt Madeleine, who always loved clothes although she was short and prematurely stout, had a weakness not just for following fashion but for brazenly outstripping it. I recall, as she got down from the carriage, the astonishment that the strangeness of her figure aroused in me. I had never before seen a bustle; I had no idea of the device that was involved; I saw in it evidence of some secret and shameful deformity; I felt as much embarrassment as repulsion. She wore—and not ungracefully, I must admit—a long "visiting costume" with a large purplish leafy design of cut velvet on a background of black satin; it was trimmed with otter at the hem, cuffs, and collar: a sort of redingote, which reached down to her ankles, cinched in at the waist, tight around the bosom but quite full in the skirt, and shamelessly hitched up in the rear by means of a voluminous, mobile and elastic cushion, which emphasized, as it swung, the slightest movements of her hips. As the height of ridiculousness in my eyes, her face was entirely hidden under a veil of thick white foliated lace, whose ends fluttered about the nape of her neck and which half-covered a tiny and springlike bonnet of mauve straw adorned with a bunch of pansies and held on by violet moiré ribbons loosely knotted under her chin.

Among the old children's books—jetsam of preceding generations—with which my sister had taught me to read, I remember a certain blue-and-gold illustrated volume whose title was *A Mother's Counsel.* It must have dated back to the time of Charles X. A manual of "comportment" for the use of young society ladies, in which the virtues of the perfect young woman were celebrated in alexandrines. From it I have retained only this one verse, because Henriette and I used to enjoy quoting it:

Modest in her bearing, proper in her dress . . .

Well, it has to be admitted: Aunt Madeleine did not at all fit this model of good form.

Fortunately, no sooner had she stepped into the entrance-hall than she hastened to remove her coat and her veil. In spite of the strangeness of a dress of plum-colored silk with a very close-fitted bust and a skirt, composed of lappets with layers of flounces, that puffed out around her rump like a hot-air balloon, I was soon enough won over by the expressive vivacity of her face, by her laughing eyes, by the simplicity and sunniness of her manners; but it took me some time to get used to the false rotundity of her hind-quarters . . . I scarcely suspected then that this grotesquely got-up Parisian lady, whose spontaneous ways, easy laugh and bursts of loudness offended my notions of good behavior, would one day be the confidante of my adolescence and the most maternal of friends.

Henriette, as a child, called her *Aunt Ma.* That was what I had always heard her called around the house. My aunt remembered it, and from the outset asked us please to keep this friendly diminutive for her. Which I did until her death.

But I return to Guy.

Henriette, as soon as our guests arrived, had ordered tea served and had placed my cousin and me next to each other. In an undertone, he asked me friendly questions about my tastes, my games, my schedule, and he spoke to me about himself from time to time, without being insistent, in a semi-confidential tone that filled me with a tender pride. I marveled at his ease, his kindness, his refinement. ("Our little Parisian," said old Zélie, thrilled, in

Perche dialect, "oh, but he has pretty manners.")* Never before had I met up with a boy my age, a "fellow creature." And I was going on twelve. The experience was enthralling. No wonder that my first impulse towards Guy was not one of camaraderie but of love. How to call by any other name that obsessive attraction, that fascination, to which in those first days I surrendered myself with delight? I was under a spell. He was there; I reported everything to him, I couldn't move a step away from him; nothing counted but his presence, his contact. I remember that after tea he wanted to take a tour of the house. I went with him from room to room, like a dog. I did not take my eyes off him, I hung on his every gesture to anticipate his wishes. Henriette had entrusted me with the task of taking him to his room. I helped him unpack his things; I did not tire of touching his clothes, his toiletries; everything that belonged to him was endowed with magical virtues. I watched him come, go, get up, sit down, with inexhaustible rapture. I had lost all shyness, as if under the effect of a mild intoxication. I did my best to answer his questions; never had I felt so talkative, so cheerful; and when I did not know what to say, I smiled at him. I smiled at him with my lips, my eyes, my entire being. But he? He did not seem in the least surprised by so much attentiveness: in a sweet way, he let himself be adored. I asked nothing more than to have a place in his universe.

If, although my elder by a year, he was markedly smaller than I, it was because I was exceptionally tall for my age. My torso, to tell the truth, was still not on the scale of my limbs, and only my arms, my hands, my long ungainly foal's legs heralded the six-foot Saint-Cyrian that I was to become. (Always the first in my class or my year: by order of size . . . "*Grand dépendeur d'andouilles*,"† as Lyautey called me when he was in a good mood.) Menneville did not have a photographer, and my father cared little about keeping the family album current (in which could be seen the imposing figure of my grandfather in his general's uniform, wearing the senatorial sash of the Second Empire). Thus I have no picture of the boy that I was in that year of '82. If I examine in the mirror, as I just did a moment ago, my old Punchinello's visage—my balding brow, my hooked nose with its curving nostrils, my big weary mouth, with its thin and sinuous lips, its drooping corners and the two commalike furrows which frame it and today give it a closed, bitter, and stubborn expression—I have some difficulty imagining the face, probably unattractive but definitely youthful, of the fair-haired boy that I was at twelve. However, under the bushy bulge of my Tolstoyan eyebrows, I catch a bluish gaze, still sharp and clear, which life has perhaps hardened but which must be fairly similar to the one which in those far-off days

* "Not' ch'tiot Parigin, ah, qu'il a donc de *jolies magnières*!"
†I.e., a man tall enough to take sausages down from the rafters.

I fixed with curiosity on the brown curls, the little starched collar, the necktie, and the black velvet jacket of my cousin. I suddenly felt very awkward with my bare neck, my big blue canvas sailor's collar, my short trousers, and my farm boy's hair, mowed with clippers by Henriette.

Guy had all the natural grace that I lacked. We must have made an amusing contrast: I, a tall sunburnt country oaf, plainspoken, with sudden timidities and sudden audacities, overly brusque movements, the awkwardness of a young animal in full growth which has not yet really taken the measure of its own limbs; he, a slightly built city boy, nimble and artful, reflective, wily, talkative, all subtlety, already wise to the world. Next to me, he seemed even more frail, with his weakling's bones beneath his transparent girlish skin: a tender skin, with velvety shadows, a smooth skin, milky white, although, like his mother, he had hair of a brown that was almost black. I have at this moment a vision of him so precise that I want to take advantage of it to put down certain details which tomorrow I will perhaps have less present in my mind. His physical peculiarities seem to me to correspond so closely with his character, with his good qualities and his defects, that I consider them significant. Perhaps more than they are? Nothing harder to analyze than these mysterious relations between the outer and the inner. For myself, I cannot dissociate his external appearance from his psychological idiosyncrasies. I will draw his portrait, then, with the greatest possible accuracy.

What struck one first: the *triangular* shape of his face. It was not oval. It was inscribed within an equilateral triangle set on its point: the line that the arch of the eyebrows traced from one temple to the other was equal to the two oblique lines which ran symmetrically down the cheeks to form the acute angle of the chin. This singularity remained etched in my memory because there was, at the time, in the church at Menneville, a painted plaster statue of the Virgin, in a blue robe, hands together, eyes to heaven, crushing with her bare foot the triangular head of a slant-eyed snake, which was shooting out a forked tongue. When I wanted to get Guy riled, I would tell him: "You look like the Holy Virgin's snake!" And it was true. He had that flared, rather flat forehead, and those eyelids slightly turned up at the corners, and, below his cheekbones, that hollowness of the flesh down to his pointed chin. But the resemblance became outright comical when he was hunched over his homework and the effort of attention made a little tip of wet tongue stick out between his lips.

No less characteristic was the way he held his head. It sat on a thin, elongated, flexible neck—from which came a graceful mobility, giving him an air of being always on the lookout, with a certain indefinable spontaneity, ingenuousness, offhandedness that had great charm. Walking along next to him, I liked to put my arm around his shoulder and to hold that fragile little nape in the palm of my hand.

I have said that he had inherited his mother's dark curly hair. From her he also got beautiful golden-brown eyes, long-lashed, with a dense and velvety glow. However, the expressions in their gazes were altogether different. Aunt Ma's was witty and cheerful; Guy's could have impish glimmers, but it was generally serious, and it settled on people with more weight, insistence. My aunt's shone with goodness; Guy's was tender rather than good, and even cuddlesome rather than tender; he knew the power of it; he used it, instinctively, with a devilish cunning. Finally, my aunt's gaze had an unfailing limpidity and openness; my cousin's was often evasive and as if veiled, in its blackness, by a bluish halo. All in all—and never mind if I anticipate—he had that slightly clouded gaze, at once insistent, superficial, and vacant, of people whose attention falls prey to a secret preoccupation (by which sexual obsessives in particular give themselves away). Of course, I was too young to be aware of this; but I am surprised that around Guy no one—neither his parents, nor the Abbé Adry, nor my father—seemed to notice it. Yet there was no lack of signs which should have put them on their guard. I would not want, at this remove, to exaggerate and paint too dark a portrait. However, I cannot help thinking, in connection with Guy, of those urchins one sees wandering in the streets of capitals in search of some adventure, who seem to be wavering still between good and evil. He, too, had that slightly dubious audacity, that disquieting slenderness and prettiness, that hint of something too svelte in his figure, too lithe in his walk, too warm in his gaze . . .

And I have said nothing of his mouth. Yet it deserves to be described. In that thin face, it looked quite big. It was fleshy, highly colored, easily moist. Its line was soft, sinuous, shifting; bulging a little in the middle, which must have been due to the structure of the upper jaw; it turned up at the corners with a very pronounced movement, parallel to the slanting of the eyelids towards the temples, then disappeared into the hollows of two dimples. This shape of the mouth constantly gave Guy the look of being about to smile, which contrasted with the habitual gravity of his gaze and often lent an enigmatic expression to his physiognomy. This ambiguity had a way of exasperating my father. Probably he saw in it, and quite wrongly, the sign of a sneaky character. At table, frequently, he could not restrain himself from addressing my cousin with a certain brusqueness: "And you, Guy, what are you thinking?" Then, before the surprised and embarrassed face of the boy—whom he greatly intimidated, and who, I believe, did not much like him—he would turn toward my sister as if to apologize, and would mutter with a deliberate good-naturedness that sounded false: "You never know what he's brooding about, that little fellow . . ."

I would not dare claim that this difficult-to-decipher mask did not annoy me too, somewhat. In the beginning, at least. I was accustomed to less secret faces. But this difficulty of interpretation rather stirred my curiosity, and did nothing—quite the reverse—to diminish the irresistible attraction which my new companion exerted over me.

The day after Guy's arrival, I remember that I got up early and ran to my sister's bedroom, eager to compare my impressions with hers. The room was empty: Henriette was already going about her domestic chores. A great silence reigned in the house. My father, faithful to his habits, had left at dawn on horseback. I found Henriette in the pantry: she herself was preparing the tea tray intended for Aunt Ma. Guy had been invited to come have his café au lait with us; on his account our breakfast had been delayed half an hour. My sister had various orders to give, and for once paid no attention to my chatter. I was trembling with impatience and emotion. At eight o'clock, finally, the bell rang; and Guy still was not there. I offered to go get him, or to call him from the terrace. Henriette persuaded me not to. She had sat down at the table, filled the bowls and buttered the toast with a truly disconcerting lack of concern. The appearance of Guy suddenly dispelled my feverishness. The moment he came in, he gave me a caressing look. He apologized to my sister and offered her his forehead with a childlike sweetness which delighted me. I had noticed immediately that he was wearing neither his traveling outfit nor the dark suit in which he had dined the night before but instead a blue pea jacket and short pants: short pants, like me! But fastened at the knees with a metal buckle, over plaid socks; and the collar of the pea jacket was adorned with two gold anchors.

(I will note in passing that one of the first effects of Guy's presence was to awaken in me a notion which was totally foreign to me: that of clothes-consciousness; up until then, I had only that of cleanliness. Guy naturally concerned himself with his outward appearance; without affectation, moreover, and even without showing off excessively; as much to please himself as to please others. When he came near a mirror, he never failed to glance at it in order to fix his hair, straighten the knot of his tie. Before dinner, he did not content himself, like me, with going and washing his hands in the kitchen: he went up to his room, changed his collar, often his shoes, sometimes his outfit; each evening he also got out a fresh handkerchief on which he splashed a drop of eau de Cologne. These refinements prompted my surprise: the surprise of the savage before the customs of the white man. But I soon realized that the attentions he took with his little person played a certain part in the charm that emanated from him, and as a result I sorely felt the meagerness of my wardrobe. I complained about it to Henriette, who had the good grace not to make fun of me and who suggested that I put on my best things for the evening. Cold comfort: I now loathed that sailor's blouse, whose sleeves no longer covered my wrists, and I was ashamed of my short pants, of my long bare legs and my thick wool socks!)

For that first morning, I had dreamed of doing my cousin the honors and showing him thoroughly around my kingdom, and I eagerly anticipated introducing him to all my favorite nooks in the park, one after the other. What this first walk was, I remember quite well: the dawn of my first friendship; but above all I remember how it ended for me with a very unexpected scene.

Scarcely had he munched his last piece of toast than I whisked him out of the house. In the distance it was misty: trails of fog were lying on the low ground at the edge of the forest; the dew, in patches, still whitened, here and there, the long rectangular lawns which separated the central walk from the terrace. But the sky was pure, the sun radiant, the air already balmy, and the day promised to be glorious.

Guy was sensitive to the seductions of nature. From the doorway, he gazed round the horizon, momentarily contemplated the rectilinear plan of the terrace, which was laid out between two paths covered with bare lindens. "It's a little like Versailles," he commented. However, he admitted to me that he preferred "English parks" to "French-style gardens." I listened to him open-mouthed; I didn't know a thing about the art of gardens . . . In two leaps, he rushed down the front steps and ran off to the left, drawn by the big trees. I immediately gave up the idea of taking him to the great pool, of showing him the fountain of Flora, of having him admire, from the top of the "pierhead," the green expanse of the pastures and the view of the forest; in short, of following the itinerary that I had lovingly worked out. I understood instantly that one had to submit to his whims. I did so gladly: my first abdication.

I was immediately rewarded for it. When I caught up to him, he turned towards me and, while continuing to walk, took hold of my hand and kept it in his. We started off like that, side by side, down the path to the circle of Diana, whose statue, less mossy than it is today, glistened in the sun at the end of the airy vault that the interlacing of the leafless branches formed above us. That little child's hand, warm, slightly moist, which clasped mine, gave me an impression of sweetness, of tenderness, of trust, which I have never forgotten. Drawn to him by a passionate affinity, I was already interpreting that grasp as a marvelous promise of reciprocity. He, I have to say, did not seem moved in the slightest. He merrily swung our hands to the rhythm of our steps, turned his alert bird's head right and left, looked at everything, assessed everything, and chattered like a magpie.

What did he talk about? About himself, his parents, his classes, his "pals," his "profs," alluding to a whole school universe whose existence I did not suspect, to a thousand circumstances of his Parisian life which awoke in me nothing that I knew, no echo. But although I was thrown off by everything in this impromptu monologue—broken up with digressions, with jokes—when he laughed I obligingly let myself be won over by his laughter, without really understanding, for the sole pleasure of being in unison. I was dumb-founded by everything that this improvisation revealed of diverse knowledge, by all that experience he had effortlessly acquired without even realizing it, solely due to his having lived his thirteen years in Paris, attended a lycée, listened to what was being said in the drawing room as well as in the servants' hall, met the famous people whom his parents entertained, strolled in the streets, ridden the omnibus, been to the theater, taken a trip to Switzerland, another to Brussels, spent vacations at Trouville, at Royat, in the Dauphiné, seen the sea, hiked in the mountains, sailed on Lake Geneva, fished in Lake Annecy . . . So much maturity dazzled me. I suddenly gauged my ignorance of the world.

Was he trying to impress me? I don't think so; that was a failing he did not have. No, he carried on purely for amusement's sake, without pre-meditation, with the joyful abandon of a schoolboy on vacation. He was very far from imagining how different were our educations, our habits, our ways of life. I myself was sorely aware of it. I felt wrapped in my crust of provincialism—to such an extent that I did not believe anything would ever succeed in stripping me of it. Guy noticed nothing: I appeared very interested, and I was. But I said little in reply, for good reason . . . The attraction he exerted over me would perhaps have inclined me to confidences, if I'd had something to tell. Even so, I'm not sure. By nature, I have never been one of those people who open up easily; and then, up until that time it was for Henriette that I had saved my effusions: I wasn't at all prepared to speak freely in front of anyone else.

I remember that concerning a schoolmate with whom he had fallen out, he concluded sharply: "For starters, he gets on my nerves. You see, he's too *girlish* . . ." And after a pause which gave weight to his judgment: "I liked you right away, because you aren't at all." It was certainly the first time I had heard the word *girlish* used in an obviously pejorative sense, and I did not very well understand in what my superiority consisted. I nonetheless felt a flush of pride rising in me. (And this reminds me of another of his traits. Much later, the following year perhaps. One afternoon when we had bickered in our schoolroom, and when, fed up with his needling—for he was more of a tease than a fighter—I had beaten him up, he had run out of the room, furious, eyes ablaze, with a threat on his lips. At teatime I went down-stairs alone. Was he sulking? Was he preparing some revenge? I was expecting the worst. I found him in the dining room, chatting with Henriette. He greeted me as if nothing had happened, and, in front of my sister, I made no allusion to our quarrel. Before going back up to work, we were allowed a recess in the park. So we went out together, as usual. Hardly were we out of sight when Guy drew near to me; I remember how he took my arm and held it tight against him in a real burst of affection, telling me something to this effect: "I really like you, *because you're strong*!" I have forgotten the exact words but not their meaning, nor their tone, nor the ecstatic expression on his face; nor, for that matter, my surprise, in which the flattering feeling of an unsuspected prerogative was involved—one which, by the way, I have never known how to take advantage of.)

But I return to our walk on the first day.

While conversing, we had gone all over the park. I had resumed my role as guide, and did not spare him anything. I suddenly noticed that he was limping slightly. One of his ankle boots had hurt him. We were rather far from the house, at the lower end of the park, close to the Round Tower, which at that time was concealed in the middle of a thicket. I took him there so he could sit down. He was enchanted by this old ruined building in the depths of the woods, a true witch's house, with its heavy bolted door, its two loopholes hung with cobwebs, its dome with the flaking ceiling, its blackened stone fireplace. It was furnished with a few folding stools and a rattan chaise longue on which, sometimes, on summer Sundays, Henriette used to come and be by herself with a book. I made him lie down and helped take his shoes off. It was nothing: a crease in his sock had left a red groove across his instep but the skin was not cut into, and there was not even the threat of a blister. The incident amused us both. He did not mind being fussed over, and I was thrilled to have a chance to lavish care on him.

Next to my big suntanned legs, his looked strangely spindly and pale. He pointed this out to me.

"But," he immediately added, as he showed me, not without pride, the light brown down which shaded the outline of his calf, "*you* have hardly any hairs."

"I do too!" I replied sharply. "It's because they're blond that they don't show up well."

"And there? Blond, too?" he said, bringing his hand back towards his belly.

The gesture was so unexpected, so precise, and the question so shocking, that my cheeks turned crimson. But Guy's look was serious, insistent, questioning.

I answered, without lowering my eyes: "Of course."

"And you have . . . a lot?"

Increasingly embarrassed, I tried to get off with an evasive nod of the head. Before I had time to overcome my surprise, he nimbly dropped his pants.

"As much as me?"

No matter what, I was determined not to lose my composure. I forced my glance to fall on this unforeseen exhibition, and surprise immediately supplanted my discomfort. My modest "li'l gentleman" suddenly seemed so unworthy of being compared with this imposing fellow creature that I would certainly have thought my cousin afflicted with a monstrous disability if I had permitted myself to question his omniperfection. In all honesty, I stammered: "Oh, no . . . not as much."

"Show me."

This time, I could not repress a start. He smiled, with a surprised and mocking air.

"Don't you dare?"

Impossible to back out.

In a sudden burst of courage, I hastily undid my belt and in a second half-opened my pants. He showed magnanimity: "Well, you know, almost as much. Only, you . . ."

And with a freedom of language that brought my dismay to a peak, he launched into a detailed comparison that was quite mortifying for me.

Then, while he, in his turn, unhurriedly pulled his pants back up, he asked me in the same casual tone:

"Have you smoked yet?"

"Me? . . . No."

He explained to me how, at the lycée, they made cigarettes by stripping dead leaves. I liked this subject infinitely better than the other. I promised to find him some tissue paper and matches.

And since the bruise on his foot was no longer hurting him, I suggested that we go back to the house. My heart was still pounding a little. The feeling that I had was neither shame nor pique; I did not worry about my inferiority. My sense of modesty had been violently ruffled, but I was not displeased with myself: all in all, I had behaved in this situation with quite a lot of pluck.

He seemed to think no more about it. We set off again for the house, talking about this and that, without any allusion to the scene at the Round Tower, either on that day or ever again, I believe.

FOR ME, the memory of it remained very vivid. (It is a platitude to observe how much certain moments of the most distant past, probably those which have produced the most violent reaction in our sensibility, become deeply embedded in the memory—especially the visual memory—while so many less distant and more significant facts leave no clear image in us. Each man as he grows old experiences this himself and remains baffled by it.) A hundred times over, during our shared existence, I had the chance to see my cousin come and go before me in the altogether. He loved to be naked. No more modesty than a young dog. However, when I recall his nakedness, it is as it appeared to me so briefly, that morning, for the first time. The sight of that young body in the semi-darkness of the tower, fully lit by the ray of sunlight coming through the loophole, and the shock that I felt from it, are as fresh in my mind as if it had happened yesterday. The pants had slid down to his knees; with his left hand, he kept his shirt pulled up to his chest; with the other, distractedly, with his fingertips, he lightly touched the object of our contention. I again see the purple mark of a nipple, and the flat little belly, and the vertical groove at the center of which the navel, instead of going in like mine, formed a little bulge of flesh under a fold of skin. This slightly convex navel, because of its oblong shape and that sort of eyelid, brought to my mind the idea of an eye without a pupil, of a "blank eye," I thought—in the sense in which Mlle. Fromentot used to say "a blank map." I again see the graceful curve of the trunk, the right hip slightly raised—a vestige of the cox-algia which had kept him in a plaster cast for two years when he was very young; he had retained from it a barely visible deviation which sometimes became pronounced following an overlong walk, and then gave him the hopping gait of an injured bird. I see everything again. First vision of a sex organ that was not my own . . . Ponderous living cluster, swollen with youth . . . tender fruits of flesh, silky and diaphanous as the petals of a trilo-bate flower.

I have already expressed the conviction that the analysis of Guy's physical particularities shed light on those of his character and his behavior; thus I will not leave in the dark certain intimate details which I believe can provide significant clues to his nature. Beneath the black patch of the pubis, the sex showed, light-colored, and seemed to me of a surprising bulk. It was. In the middle of that frail body, of that narrow pelvis, it was all one saw. The con-trast between the development of those organs and the frailty of the consti-tution was striking; and I cannot help establishing a connection between this disproportion and a certain moral imbalance, of which I shall soon have examples to cite. The one seems to me to be the illustration and, so to speak, the concrete representation, of the other: the genitals occupied on this child's body that excessive and cumbersome place which erotic obsession held in Guy's imagination.

Guy had arrived at that "sexual age" which all human beings go through, and which, depending on the individual, the circumstances, the climate, generally takes place between the eleventh and the eighteenth year: an inevitable transformation, both physical and psychological, which should be only natural, which is frequently more or less morbid, and the influence of which can have incalculable consequences for moral development. At thir-teen, Guy was already fully involved in the upheavals of puberty. (I was not.

My "sexual age" was rather late: between my fifteenth and my seventeenth year. I shall speak later of this growth burst, which was of an extreme virulence. It is closely linked to my memories of boarding school. Must I hold the school, the boarder's life, specially responsible for it? I think not, even though the crowding together of shameless schoolmates, who underwent the same evolution, the same revolution, as I, greatly fostered these disorders; I think it fairer to say that my stay at boarding school accidentally coincided with that tumultuous period in the life of boys when their sexuality suddenly turns virile.)

But I shall come back to all this, for I feel no embarrassment at elaborating on all these psycho-physiological details; I even mean to linger over them at leisure, with a total candor and an assiduous accuracy. When one approaches the domain of sexuality, one must not be stingy with personal confidences nor be afraid of dotting one's *i*'s: it is by stepping unhesitantly into the labyrinth of self-investigation, then by making the most unveiled confessions, that one has some chance of avoiding common errors and getting away from clichés. The interest that I have taken in these problems for many years was quite often, in the past, called indulgence by certain of my friends. Now, probably it would no longer be so. The importance of these questions is hardly disputed anymore; and doctors are no longer the only ones to be aware, for example, of the crucial action which the condition and functions of the genital glands, whether masculine or feminine, exercises on the life of the body and the mind, on the general health, on the temperament, the behavior, the psychological orientation, of the human being.

In this area, lying and concealment have too long been the rule. If so many mysteries of sexuality still remain obscure, the blame must be laid on traditional hypocrisy, that of individuals, that of society. I have questioned many friends from every walk of life regarding this, have obtained many confessions; and I have become convinced that few indeed are the boys of fifteen who escape the "depravities" of what has been very well termed "the sexual age"; the special and ever-so-varied forms which they assume, their violence, their more or less obsessive nature, their duration, are among the most revealing elements of this essential and unique transformation in a person's life, which marks adolescence, the attainment of manhood. I have, furthermore, made this observation: whereas many of our memories of youth are half-erased and hazy, all those which, at some point, are linked to our sexual discoveries have, in a surprising fashion, kept their distinctness, their freshness, their intensity intact. This finding everyone, or just about everyone, can confirm for himself. Is there a more obvious proof of the impact of these initiations and of the primordial role that these first curiosities, these first experiences, play in the maturing of the personality? They have a decisive effect on the character, the tendencies, the entire existence of the adult. Here is the key to the man.

Tell me what your puberty was like, and I will tell you who you are.

THE VERY EVENING of her arrival, Aunt Ma had questioned my father about the reputation of the school where she was thinking of placing her son. Maps had been unfolded, and my father had offered to go visit it with her, two days hence. The weather was exceptionally fine for the season: one had better take advantage of it.

The old priory of Saint-Léonard, at that time converted into a boys' school—since bought back by the département and today transformed into a tuberculosis preventorium—is situated twenty-two kilometers from here, on the road to Laigle, on the northern outskirts of Gevrésy. A real expedition in those days: you had to set out quite early to leave time for the horses to rest several hours between going there and returning. I had hoped for a moment that my cousin and I would be included. But apart from my aunt's fearing the strain of such a long ride on her son, there would have been no room for us, since my father wanted to take the victoria, the body of which was lighter than that of the break; and Henriette, having never gone beyond the boundaries of the canton, had discreetly expressed a desire to get to know Gevrésy, where they were to have lunch. Doubtless, I easily got over my disappointment, at the prospect of spending a whole day, alone and free, with my new companion. I no longer recall anything about it: with very few exceptions, the subsequent memories of our life in common are superimposed on those of the beginning, and I cannot properly tell them apart.

What I remember is that my aunt came back very disappointed by this outing. All her plans were dashed. The monastic austerity of the dormitories and the study halls, the odor and the sadness of the dining halls, filled her with dread for Guy, who was accustomed to the freedoms of a day boy at a Parisian lycée. And the sight, in the deserted schoolyard, of a half-dozen boarders, slovenly, vagrant, idle, stranded there because their parents lived too far away to have them come home for Easter vacation, was all she needed to wring her heart. My father twitted her about her oversensitivity. He did not at all share her way of seeing things. He had spoken at length with the superior, and came away with a favorable impression of the school. (It is, in all likelihood, to this visit that I owe my becoming a student at Saint-Léonard three years later.) He sought in vain to dispel his sister-in-law's anxieties. Nothing worked. All week long, there were letters exchanged with my Uncle Éric, and interminable discussions every evening in the drawing room, after we had gone to bed. Henriette, always trusting in me, kept me informed. Did she suspect that I was telling everything to my friend? Thus we learned that my father, who had always shown special consideration for Aunt Ma, had finally said to her: "Well then, since this boy needs to live for a while in the country, why don't you leave him here with us? He'll share Bertrand's life. They'll work together. Come summer, you'll decide. There will always be time to put Guy in school for the start of the new term in October." My aunt had accepted with gratitude. But Uncle Éric dragged his feet. Finally he gave his consent, provided that Guy's studies did not suffer too much from this arrangement.

My aunt and my father went immediately to the presbytery. The Abbé Adry agreed to direct our studies; and, after some hesitation, the old dean granted his vicar permission to devote his mornings to us on a regular basis. But as my cousin had to be spared any excessive physical exercise, and the journey from le Saillant to Menneville might well have tired him, it was agreed that every morning my father would send the carriage to fetch the abbé after his Mass, and that, when he had taken his noon meal with us, he would return to town on foot for the parish service. In the afternoon, we were to do our homework and learn our lessons for the next day, following a rigorously established schedule that was subject to the approval of Uncle Éric. It was decided that several days later Aunt Ma would go back to Paris, leaving her son in the care of my father and Henriette.

At that point, a new existence began for me. I have the impression that the month of April '82 marked the end of my childhood. Overnight, I ceased to be "the little one"—an anonymous and asexual specimen of the family fauna—to become one of those noisy, disorderly, voracious young males, known collectively as "the boys," whose life in the house was organized apart, whose initiatives and whims seemed unpredictable and fearsome to all, and to whom the maids, laughing, pretended to give a wide berth, as if to a public menace.

All things considered, Guy's stay at le Saillant had the most salutary influence on my nature and on my formation. Until then, under the matriarchal authority of my sister and the old maidservants, I had enjoyed special treatment, the overpampered life of an only child. Suddenly I had a brother; and even an older brother; and what was more, a brother in delicate health who required coddling, who became the focus of everyone's attention and concern. I dropped at once into second place; I became of minimal importance. If I had been more egocentric, my self-esteem might well have suffered. But in fact, I rather experienced relief; I gained from it in independence; even Henriette looked after me less. And then, the daily presence, so close, of the one to whom I had immediately consecrated an idolatrous worship, truly brought me too much joy and exaltation for there to have been any place in me for feelings of petty jealousy.

(I note it in passing: jealousy is a disease—and an incurable disease—from which, by luck or by nature, I have never suffered.)

MY AUNT'S DEPARTURE took place on a gray showery morning, which left me with a few distinct images. We were all gathered at the top of the wet front steps. My father alone was taking my aunt to the station. It was no longer raining, but the sky remained so overcast that the old coupé had been hitched up. I awaited this departure in a fever: I longed for Guy to be all ours; and, inanely, the idea had not occurred to me that he might not share this joyful impatience. I saw him throw himself silently into the arms of his mother, who lifted her white lace veil to kiss him, and whose face appeared drenched with tears. He was not crying, but his lips trembled, his gaze was fixed, and grief contorted all his features. And when, once the carriage had passed through the gate and before it disappeared down the drive, Aunt Ma leaned one last time out the window, he suddenly burst into sobs. I believe I did as well. I vowed to myself to console him, to make him happy, to protect him always. Henriette drew us to her, kissed us, took us back into the hall-way. Then, to create a diversion, she told us to go get the gardener; she needed his help in tidying up the house.

We took off running, and since it was beginning to rain again, and Guy's coat was of a light material, I offered to shelter him under my cape. He did not need coaxing. (He was like a cat: he had a nervous horror of water. In our quarrels, when he had pestered me with his teasing, to make him stop I had only to dunk my brush in the water can and threaten him with a sprinkling.) So he came right away and snuggled up under my armpit. The cape covered his head: I was the one who led the way. Enjoying ourselves, with our arms around each other, we raced to the kitchen garden looking for Thomas. Well before having found the gardener, I must say I noticed that Guy had regained his good spirits and seemed to have completely forgotten the heart-rending departure scene. I played along; but such a quick turnabout struck me. I was less fickle; and this inconstancy in feelings seemed to me an unexpected sign of puerility in Guy. I suspected that I had perhaps exaggerated my cousin's maturity. I was a little disappointed by this observation, but pleased, deep down, to see a diminishment of that superiority which I had too quickly attributed to him, and a melting away of that distance between us which, a few days earlier, I had imagined insuperable. In fact, I loved him all the more for it; but already he impressed me less.

To shelter ourselves from the shower, we took refuge in the grape green-house, asking the gardener to let Henriette know so that she would not worry about our absence. We must have lingered there, talking, quite a long while, for my father was already home again when we got back to the house;

lunch was about to be served, and Henriette was just finishing off the fitting-out of what would henceforth be called "the boys' apartment." She had, as always, taken her task to heart, and all morning long there was a general commotion, for which she had mobilized every available hand. The prospect of this moving in, about which there had been long talks with Aunt Ma, delighted both Guy and me in advance; and when, after the meal, Henriette took us to visit our new domain, it was sheer delirium.

The room where my sister had once done her homework, and which for years had gone unused—the one where, as a baby, I had crawled about on all fours during the lessons with Mlle. Fromentot—was transformed into a study room, and minimally furnished with two similar tables, a few chairs, and two quite different bookcases. (It is the large room paneled in gray with blue fillets which occupies the west corner of the second floor in the wing across from the one where I live.)

The bedroom in which I had slept since my early childhood became Guy's. It was then all hung with that shiny percale patterned with bouquets, of which the last remnant presently hovers, as a canopy, above the alcove where the Boccas* sleep. The small adjacent room, paneled in white, where I'd worked until then, had been fitted out for me with mahogany furniture, consisting of a bed, a wardrobe, and a commode with a washbowl. These two rooms formerly communicated by means of a large door that my father had ordered taken down long before so that, during the winter, the stove in the small room could also heat my bedroom. Thomas had found the two flaps of the door in the attic, all right, but so warped by the damp that he could not manage to get them back on their hinges; and Henriette was about to seek the help of the carpenter in Menneville. Guy entreated her not to do any such thing, maintaining, with much talk and cajoling, that it would be far more "practical" for us to have free access between the rooms. I don't know if this argument convinced my sister or if she found it simpler not to have to get old Pilate to come out; anyway, the dusty flaps went back to the attic, and the door was never put up again. At the time of Henriette's marriage the partition between the rooms was pulled down, and this setting of my youth no longer exists except in my memory.

A part of the day was spent in putting our things away, in happily taking possession of our home. And that same evening, we used our communicating bedrooms for the first time.

I have so many varied memories of the life we shared in those two rooms that I no longer recall very well the beginnings of that lack of privacy. It is likely that I felt somewhat embarrassed getting undressed for the first time in

---

*Maumort's servants, Pietro Bocca and his wife, Rose.

front of my cousin. (I would probably have felt even more so if things had not been simplified in advance by the scene in the Tower.)

I have never known anyone who took as much pleasure as Guy did in being naked. He spurned the simplest precautions for hiding his anatomy from me. For instance, in the evening, I was in the habit of taking off my pants only after having changed my day shirt for my nightshirt, whereas he would proceed in exactly the opposite manner, beginning by removing his shoes, his pants, his underpants, and then tossing off his shirt. Stark naked, hopping about and jabbering away, he would wander endlessly from one room to the other before making up his mind to put on his nightshirt and slip between the sheets. Upon awakening, from the moment he jumped out of bed, and despite the morning chill, his first move was to get rid of his shirt; he would then resume his chattering and his traipsing, would drag out washing up, and would delay as long as possible the moment of getting dressed. His great fun was to perform, on his bed, in his birthday suit, a series of somersaults and acrobatic feats which generally concluded with what he called "doing the Y"—an exercise that consisted of his standing on his head, his open legs serving as a balancing-pole.

Admittedly, there was a bit of exhibitionism in his case; but much less than one might think. No doubt, what he sought above all was a physical satisfaction; the pleasure of experiencing the suppleness of his bare limbs, the enjoyment of feeling his skin freely exposed to the air. These are the voluptuous sensations that today the enthusiasts of nudism know well, and that most of them savor, as Guy did, with a genuine guilelessness. But nudism is a recent invention. I am speaking of a distant time and one so prudish that in the summer, on the beach at Trouville, the most brazen Parisienne would never have dared to walk out of her cabin without having concealed her form in an ample bathing costume with a collarette, basque, and skirt which covered her decorously from her chin to her ankles! Not only was nudism socially unacceptable, the word itself did not exist; and as for the thing, it would have aroused a scandal hardly to be imagined. Guy was a young pioneer!

His lack of modesty was so complete, and above all so natural, that it was inevitably contagious. I quickly got used to changing my linen without paying any attention to his presence. Later, during the summer, I too acquired a taste for living naked: in the evening I hastened to take off my clothes, every last item, and in the morning I was in no hurry to get dressed, wanting to savor for a longer time that feeling of emancipation which nakedness gave me. The monitor at a seminary would have judged our behavior very "indecent." It was, nonetheless, perfectly chaste.

Perfectly chaste. I insist on this point. Guy, whose thinking wallowed in sexual obsessions, and whose usual talk was so constantly licentious, never in my presence yielded to the temptation of an obscene gesture. Obviously, in the course of his inexhaustible chatter, he did not hesitate to use one of those crude words that came naturally to his lips. But, this said, it was enough that we be back in our sleeping quarters for him to desist, on his own, from broaching any scabrous subject. Yet these moments of tête-à-tête would have been more favorable than any other for the conversations he was fond of. We were safe from any eavesdropping. My father never ventured into our wing, and when Henriette had some message to give us, she would always knock on the door, would delay pushing it ajar, and would only rarely cross the threshold. Well, Guy took no advantage of these favorable circumstances. It seemed as if in the intimacy of our bedrooms, it satisfied his lustfulness to romp around without restraint. (This detail deserves to be underlined. It would have delighted the nudists, I believe. Do they not claim that the surest way to purge minds of all unhealthy curiosity is to freely bare bodies?)

Be that as it may, I hasten to say that my cousin did not lack other opportunities, and that he knew how to take advantage of them. If he respected our "home," he made up for it when we were outside, in the depths of the park, or, better still, on Sunday when we both went for a walk in the forest. There (was it because he felt far from the family hearth?) he would feverishly give himself up to his demons and seemed to do everything possible to have me share his obsession. If he never entirely succeeded, he at least managed to get me deeply stirred.

I think I have already pointed this out: when Guy made his appearance in my existence, I was still, if not completely ignorant, at least quite authentically innocent. All my knowledge in these matters was limited to what the sight of the three girls at the pond had accidentally taught me: that women did not differ from men solely by their occupations, their clothes, and the fullness of their blouses, but also by the absence of a certain attribute, to which until then I had devoted but little attention, and which suddenly seemed to me to merit special consideration, if only because it represented one of the most tangible male properties. This was as far as I had got. The surprise and the agitation that this discovery had momentarily aroused in me subsided soon enough. After that, I hardly asked myself any additional questions. Not that I lived like a simpleton: but there was in me an exceptional mixture of great naïveté and precocious seriousness. Having never had anyone but adults for company, my concerns were not childish; it was to rather austere problems that I felt myself drawn. That of death, for example. I remember that it periodically took over my thoughts: each death in our circle brought back muddled reflections on the hereafter and plunged me into painful perplexities. Then, fired up by the Abbé Adry's passionate improvisations, I became quite familiar with the general ideas that the study of history awakens. Of course, at eleven or twelve I could only touch lightly upon these abstractions. The fact remains that, without wanting to pose as the little prodigy, I can say that I was more concerned with the future of the world, the destiny of man, his social role, than with his physiological functions. I thus escaped the curiosity that children of that age ordinarily share and that gets them so worked up.

The mysteries of procreation, for example, did not in any way intrigue me. I had never thought about them. I did not even see anything mysterious about them. What I knew about maternity was enough to satisfy my biological preoccupations, and I had never wondered what the secret of fertilization was. Having lived since birth in cattle-breeding country, I used to hear it announced at certain times that this cow or that mare was pregnant, and I attached no more interest to it than to their other animal functions; I would see their belly grow heavy; then, one morning, I would learn that during the night they had "had" their foal or their calf. Did I realize that women "bore young" in a similar fashion? Probably. I don't remember. I had certainly noticed, if only among our farmers' wives, the change in shape of the pregnant women, and I was not unaware that after a number of months they became mothers and breast-fed their babies. All the same, I made no connection between the fecundity of the fillies and the anatomy of the stallions, any more than between the swelling-out of a woman big with child and the presence of her husband in the conjugal bed. Had I ever even thought about the "conjugal bed"? I do not believe so. My father was a widower; I had not known my mother; unlike most children, I had never seen my parents living in the intimacy of a single bedroom. Gaspard, the coachman, was an old bachelor. As for Thomas and his wife, they lived in one of the outbuildings, where each had a featherbed with individual pillow and comforter, in separate alcoves on either side of the fireplace. Where would I have picked up the notion of conjugal relations?

However, the day that Guy, with a blunt offhandedness, tackled this subject head-on, I suddenly felt an avalanche of incoherent thoughts and images release itself in me, which must, without my knowing it, have been accumulating over a long period in my unconscious, and were only awaiting a stroke of chance to link up and take shape. I perfectly remember this shock, and its effects. In a few seconds my brain roughed out a series of deductions and arguments which, in the minds of other children, must require months of groping investigations, of approximations, of errors progressively corrected. Above all—and instantly—I intuited that this phenomenon, to which I had never paid attention—the making of a living being—was the thing of all things to know, a key whose possession was going to give me the explanation of the world, a point of departure, the origin of a multitude of problems of the highest interest; and, long before having understood, I felt that this fundamental acquisition was going to stir up serious disturbances in me and throw my whole universe out of balance. I was not mistaken.

But I should reconstruct the scene as accurately as possible.

It happened not long after Guy's moving in at le Saillant, on a clear Sunday in April, in the middle of the forest, in a spot that I can see again distinctly, underneath the Saut-du-Roy beech grove, not far from the little bridge where we often sat for our afternoon snack.

We were walking along, conversing. All of a sudden, in his most natural manner, Guy said, without looking at me:

"So, do you know how kids are made?"

The blood rushed to my cheeks. It was at that precise moment that I became aware both of the extent of my ignorance and of the importance of what I did not know. I did not hesitate to make an affirmative sign. He looked surprised:

"You know, really?"

"Of course."

"Who told you?"

"No one."

He stopped dead and stared at me mockingly:

"You expect me to believe that you figured it out all by yourself?"

"That's right!"

"It isn't possible. If no one has explained it to you, you don't know!"

"Leave me alone. I'm telling you I know!"

I had started walking again as much to disguise my embarrassment as in the hope of creating some diversion and discouraging his insistence. I had lied spontaneously, not so much to hide my inexperience as to dodge, instinctively, an explanation that I sensed would be upsetting and that I trembled to hear.

He took several steps without saying a word. He was thinking things through. In spite of all, my repeated assertion had him puzzled. A strange supposition crossed his mind.

"You've seen a guy and a girl . . . together?"

I certainly did not understand what he was picturing, but I jumped at the lifeline he was throwing me:

"Yes."

"No kidding?"

"I'm telling you!"

He came up to me and grabbed my arm:

"So, let's hear it!"

"No."

I was well aware that I was getting in deep, but how to retreat?

"Why not?"

I stammered:

"These are things you don't talk about."

He adopted his coaxing tone:

"Come on, with me, you can perfectly well . . ."

"No!"

Obviously, he smelled the lie; nevertheless, before doubting such vigorous assertions, his imagination, which was never in short supply, searched for plausible hypotheses about them:

"What? Did you promise not to tell?"

This time, it was not a lifeline but a buoy! By grabbing onto it, I was saved.

To raise my bid, I put on a solemn air:

"I even took an oath!"

Of course, at a distance of sixty years, I don't guarantee the literal exactitude of this dialogue. But almost . . . (My memory, which, I have already said, is mainly visual, is peculiar in that auditory recollections have often stayed etched in it owing to visual recollections. Just as, in reciting a lesson, I saw the words printed on the page of the book, so, after having listened attentively to a class, my memory, which had instantly registered the physical appearance and movements of the professor, at the same time retained, associated with the recollection of his gestures, that of his voice, his intonations, his words, and consequently their meaning. Thus a great many sentences heard long ago which I ought to have forgotten have remained present to me solely because they are tied to a visual recollection of the person who uttered them, as if imprisoned in the surroundings, the moment, in which I heard them.)

However that may be, this dialogue, exact or not, well conveys the strange and bumpy turns that these sorts of conversations between us used to take. Guy did all the work. To break my silence, he resorted to trickery; he proceeded by insinuating interrogations, which greatly embarrassed me, but which, more often than not, and without his noticing, also suggested to me plausible fabrications that I would have been quite incapable of coming up with on my own. All unsuspecting, he educated me, and generally without my having to ask for explanations.

This is what happened that day. I see us again, sitting on the parapet of the little bridge. I, my features tense, eyes on the ground, taciturn, evasive, barely controlling my inner turmoil. He, on the contrary, calling the tune, titillated, talkative, speaking to no one in particular, brow lifted, eye darting, with, in his gaze, those murky glints which I knew well and which increased my uneasiness while whetting my curiosity. He was unrelenting. Not being able to obtain from me—and for good reason—the account of the suggestive scene I claimed to have stumbled onto, he badgered me with questions so specific, and of such an evocative indecency, that the most realistic descriptions would not better have taught me the facts of life. In less than a quarter of an hour, the secrets of generation had ceased to be hidden from me, and I was as informed about the mechanism of the sexual act as one could be without having experienced it personally.

But this was not without harm.

I am being careful to avoid all exaggeration, to weigh my words. The shock I suffered that day truly had the brutality of a trauma: in those few minutes, without any transition, I went from the temperate climate of innocence to the scorching climate of impurity. The myth of Genesis: Adam tastes of the forbidden fruit he is offered, and the irreparable is done; at once, the paradise of his luminous and drowsy childhood closes before him. He has entered the cursed circle; he has lost his peace; he has sunk into the complexities of his animal nature. But, by the same token, if he loves life, he takes stock of his possibilities, counts his assets, and discovers how to use them.

That an event so banal could have produced such a revolution in the mind and sensibility of a boy who was no longer a child probably seems incomprehensible. It was because, as far as certain things went, I was still in my childhood. I have said that my physical development was late. Here, I must be more specific. At twelve, I was not yet pubescent. If a certain state of organic arousal was not unknown to me—and I suppose that even at that age it must already have been fairly familiar—at least my dormant instinct had not yet been led to take, and to look for, pleasure in it: I had not yet experienced that heady wonder of the adolescent who suddenly learns to avail himself of his body. In short, I knew nothing of orgasm and its effects—of which Guy already had an inordinately cultivated knowledge. I was actually so far from any personal experimentation that I did not manage to grasp, through my cousin's allusions, what the fertilizing role of the male consisted of; what his essential participation was, in the couple. So much so that to clear up this annoying enigma I had to shyly request certain details, sacrificing all self-respect. Of course, Guy supplied them immediately; and not just obligingly, but with a disquieting eagerness—which makes me think that at that instant I would not have had to insist too much for him to have offered a personal demonstration. Probably our relationship would have been abruptly altered by it, and our friendship—which, except in words, had never ceased to be chaste—would have taken an altogether different direction. Perhaps it only hung by a thread. I never even thought of eliciting that additional information. And Guy, despite the propitious isolation of the forest, did not dare to push the initiation that far. Besides, the meticulous explanations that he lavished on me were so explicit that I had not the slightest need of seeing in order to imagine. I add that never, subsequently, did he try to make me share his propensities. Would it perhaps have been less difficult than he supposed? . . . No, I am wrong in writing that. I am letting myself be influenced in doing so by the memory of my depravities as a school boarder. At the time of which I speak, my senses were still asleep, or, more precisely, inanimate. Guy was only able to awaken mental curiosity in me; and certainly he did not fail to do so. But, if I willingly lent myself to these conversations, if I sometimes even sought them out, I would, I believe, have very stubbornly refused to accept a less platonic complicity.

(And, to illustrate this assertion, here, between parentheses, is a little occurrence that comes back to me at this very moment. In the course of the summer, we were both roughly shaken one night while sound asleep by the din, quite close by, of a storm; at the same time, a gusting wind, suddenly unleashed, violently flung open the not-quite-closed window of my bedroom. While I, sitting up, was trying to strike a match, Guy, quicker than I, had jumped out of bed and rushed to my aid. The rain, lashed by the wind, was coming into the room, and he had to struggle for a moment against the blast to pull the shutters in and shut the window. I had, without getting up, lit the candle on my bed table, and we were already beginning to laugh over this incident when a fresh clap of thunder shook the house. Did Guy get scared? Did he pretend to be afraid? He suddenly came over to my bed: "Let me get in beside you . . ." And before I could protest, he had lifted my blanket and already put his knee on the mattress. Seeing that I would not succeed in pushing him away, but quite determined not to share my bed with him, I jumped out the other side, into the space by the wall. And as he had curled up in my sheets and seemed to be taunting me, I wanted to reply in kind, and ran over and slipped into his bed. He could have come after me. No: he shouted at me, "Good night, idiot!," blowing out the candle; and a few minutes later we had fallen back into a deep sleep, both of us, where we were. Had he had some daring intention, that night? I don't think so: if I had given in to his whim, I honestly believe we would have gone to sleep beside each other, very innocently. But why had I shied away from him with such frightened suddenness? What had I been afraid of, what liberties? . . . This proves, in any case, that I was on the defensive, and that if my cousin had ever had the wish to make me a part of some depraved game, I would not have let myself be drawn into it without strong resistance. Out of virtue? No. Out of a sort of instinct, rather, and one I find very hard to understand.

I realize, moreover, before closing this parenthesis, that this is not the only time in my life when I have, by fleeing, eluded the possibility of an affair. I am thinking of the incomprehensible behavior with which I refused Mme. Nacquot's advances, several years later. I shall return to this at the proper time and place.)

AT ANY RATE, between Guy and me this is the only memory of this sort that I can recall. And I want to stress that he always respected my presence.

If, in the lack of privacy of our rooms at night, I gradually had occasion to suspect my cousin's personal habits, at least he took care to keep them secret. He hid from me to indulge in them and never spoke of them to me, even in innuendoes. I was grateful to him for it, and I always pretended not to notice anything. (Between brothers, I suppose that these half-concealments, these tacit complicities, must be fairly common.) Was he fooled by my apparent blindness? I would not be surprised if he naïvely believed that I noticed nothing.

What puzzles me, when I think about it, is that his example did not prompt me to imitate him. Here again, the backwardness of my development is the only possible explanation. I probably tried, without result or appreciable enjoyment. I was not yet mature. Pleasure, voluptuousness, still had no meaning for me . . . It was definitely not because of moral considerations. I am trying to recall my state of mind at the time. I had never been warned against these solitary practices, I did not associate any notion of sin with them. I was well aware that it was improper to allude to them, as it was unseemly to speak of so many other intimate functions; but I did not attribute any particularly reprehensible character to them. (Reason and experience later confirmed, besides, these intuitions of my natural good sense. I shall have occasion to say what I think about them when I come to my life as a boarding-school student.)

Thus we were able to live side by side for three years, Guy and I, without taking the decisive step that leads from "bad words" to "bad deeds"; and the catechism is very wise to set up this essential distinction. But just as we were restrained in our acts, so were we unbridled in our talk. I say "we" too loosely: it is more accurate to say "Guy." He had turned me into an informed and willing listener; he could think out loud and initiate me into the visions that fed his reveries night and day; he enjoyed himself to the full. As soon as we were alone, away from indiscreet ears, it was to those subjects that his chatter inevitably turned. His cynicism got the best of what remained of my shyness, which, at heart, asked only to be bullied. At first, he enjoyed the advantages of the offensive. In these scabrous discussions, he was the inexhaustible instigator; I was always lagging behind. If I encouraged him to go on, it was mainly by the attention I paid him. On my part, no confidences. And not only because I had few to share: I could have told him about my encounter with the girls bathing in the pond; yet I am sure I never breathed a word of this to him. Hobbled by my lack of experience, above all fearing to incur a condescending or mocking smile, I took pains to hide my ignorance, my surprise, my curiosity. When he guessed I was a little ashamed, a little reluctant, he had a winning way—very skillful, incidentally (but was it skill? these soothing ways, in him, were spontaneous and completely natural)—of slipping his arm through mine, and, to dispel my embarrassment, of telling me, in a low voice: "Between two friends like us, you see, there mustn't be anything secret, not even this." No more was needed: immediately, as if by magic, I felt my reservations melt away, and let the awakening of a diffuse sensuality steal deliciously over me, the magnetic attraction that I savored more with each passing day.

I AM REREADING these last pages. I would be angry with myself if, very much without meaning to, I had presented Guy as a fiendish boy, whose influence on me was pernicious. It is undeniable that his revelations deflowered me. But doesn't each of us have to meet his initiator one day? Guy was for me the instrument of chance. And I think about all this without the slightest blame, without the slightest regret.

I will go further: all in all, I consider that Guy's intervention was a healthy event for me. I do not in any way make a fetish of purity. The impure fermentation of the yeast gives the dough its character. I believe in the virtue of the stirrings of the flesh. All my experience of myself and others confirms this conviction: it is from his full sensual bloom that a person draws the main part of his strength and his inner richness. "If the salt have lost his savor, wherewith shall it be salted?" says Scripture. If the flame of our sexuality is lit but burns low, how will our temperature rise? From what source do we draw our vital impulse? All the excesses, all the disorders of the senses, are preferable to a sterile and sterilizing purity. So praised be he whose impure and wholesome breath set blazing in me that fire which took so long to catch. For him I have only affection and gratitude.

I NOTICE THAT I have omitted to put down a detail to which I attach a certain importance: it is to Guy that I owe having learned to lie.

What is lying, for a child? A means of defense against an authority that irks him, against prohibitions that he considers abusive and that he has decided to evade; it is a protection against the adult, the secret weapon of the weakest, whose effectiveness the child, with use, quickly recognizes. As for me, before Guy's arrival at le Saillant I had scarcely had the chance, or the temptation, to rebel against those who took care of me: neither against my father, who meddled very little in my upbringing, nor against the soft and persuasive Henriette, nor against the kind and not very authoritarian Abbé Adry. My cousin, for his part, had been brought up differently: quite early, he had got into the habit of deceiving grown-ups, because he had to be on his guard around them and had many secrets to hide from them. I do not think I am mistaken in pointing out here that it was the example of my cousin that showed me the usefulness of lying; and, particularly, from the time when his confidences and our naughty conversations made dissembling indispensable for me, as for him.

EVERY MORNING at eight o'clock, the carriage would bring the Abbé Adry to le Saillant. He would shut himself up with us in the study room and make us work, with frequent but short breaks, until lunchtime.

In spite of our difference in age, my cousin was not ahead of me. In French composition, he was superior to me. Endowed with a sense of subtlety that I still lacked, and having read, heard, and seen more, he had, if not more judgment, more imagination and ingenuity, a richer vocabulary, a less awkward style. For the rest, his knowledge showed incredible gaps. Mine was more rounded and better established. He was handicapped by a defective and poorly exercised memory, while I had been lucky enough, from my earliest years, to possess an excellent—I can say exceptional—one, which had always been trained with care. Certainly he was intelligent, but perhaps less so than he seemed at first. His quick-wittedness created a false impression; and, what was worse, he seemed afflicted with a hopeless inability to reason: he had missed out on Mlle. Fromentot's "logical analyses."

After having compared our strengths with a view to deciding on a joint curriculum, the abbé made up his mind to forgo teaching us new material and instead to dedicate those three months that stood between us and vacation to a general review of what, at our age, we needed to know. It was, for Guy, a way of catching up; as for me, I would get all the benefits to be gained from interrupting my march forward in order to consolidate thoroughly the knowledge I had already acquired.

If my cousin drew but little profit from this curriculum, it was not the same for me, and few trimesters have been so fruitful. In his teaching of Greek and Latin, the abbé did not content himself with drumming the particulars of grammar and syntax into our heads: he tried hard, and managed, to make us feel the subtlety, the wisdom of the Greek mind, the stature and harmony of the Latin order; to introduce us to the ancient world, to steep us in Mediterranean civilization. If, at eighteen, I profited so greatly from the influence of that gathering of humanists with whom I rubbed elbows on Sundays in Paris in my Uncle Chambost's library, I owed it to the Abbé Adry; it was his direction that had prepared me. I also remember his history lessons, and how, in about fifteen sessions, he took us through the entire history of France and of Europe. I had studied those centuries one by one during the preceding years, but the knowledge I had of them remained fragmentary. Thanks to him, I became familiar with the great trends of history; I got a comprehensive view of this millennium during which Europe became compartmentalized and France became larger, stronger, united. I remain grateful to him for it. Those synopses that he presented with broad strokes, in fiery flights of improvisation, are etched in my memory; there they formed frames, honeycombs where there gradually settled the additional notions that I have been able to gather over the years, everything that I learned from day to day about the political, military, civil, economic, administrative, and moral development of my country and of our neighbors. An irreplaceable grounding, which has helped me, which still helps me, in the efforts I have always made to follow—from a certain distance, and with an overall historical sense—the political upheavals of the present.

Moreover, the invigorating presence of the abbé made itself felt beyond school hours: it altered the atmosphere of the house, opened its windows, drove out the musty smell. At the noon meal, which he usually took with us, his substantial, stimulating talk visibly interested my father, cheered him, and forced him out of his silence. The abbé, I think, easily sniffed out the traces of that Voltairean spirit in my father, which, as a matter of courtesy, he evasively called "the spirit of the century"; but they hit it off marvelously on the subject of social reforms. These lively conversations also captivated the quiet Henriette, awakened her curiosity, caused her to reflect. The abbé often urged her to express her opinion. He spoke to her of poetry, of ethics; he advised her on what to read; he lent her books: *Paul et Virginie, Les Orientales, Graziella,* as well as Vigny, Michelet, Paul-Louis Courier. Yes, really, if my memories do not deceive me, that spring of '82 was an enrichment for all of us.

Except for Guy. At table as in class, his attention was only sporadic. A strange nature . . . He did not lack vitality, but he shied away from the influences surrounding him. He had willpower, but not much energy or application. Any effort put him off. He seemed to live in a world of his own, a vague world, and to take only an intermittent interest in the world of others. As animated as he showed himself with me in our private conversations, on our walks, when he was steering the discussion, so, elsewhere, did he appear apathetic and detached. Not intractable: he scarcely ever tried to avoid the work that was given him, but he scamped it as if it were a punishment assignment. He made no progress, and he did not care: no pride, no competitive feeling. The abbé, discouraged, told Henriette when my father could not hear him: "An incorrigible slacker . . ." Easy to say; it explained nothing. I am sure that this apparent laziness had causes beyond his control: his physical condition and his obsessions. He had gained weight since he had been with us, and we did not fail to express enthusiasm over his appearance, in which we were pleased to see the good effects of the country. It would have been wise, rather, to worry. That puffy look betokened nothing good. Nowadays, nobody would make this mistake: everyone knows that a boy who appears lymphatic, who is tired out by any exercise, who works poorly, and whose untoned flesh tends to bloatedness needs to be watched closely so as not to become a candidate for tuberculosis. As for his obsessions, of which I have already spoken at length, I will say only a word. Without going along with the conventional moralists, I think that "bad habits"—as natural and almost inevitable as they may be at the age of puberty—can damage a child's organism, when isolation, leisure, excessive development of the imagination, facilitate their abuse; all the more so if the physiological condition is not good.

Now this was the case with Guy. Imagination was his ruling faculty, and it was almost exclusively directed toward eroticism. Obviously, to such dispositions our existence at le Saillant offered only too favorable conditions: a maximum of solitude, independence, and idleness. What was he dreaming about during those afternoons of schoolwork while I was sweating over some translation into Latin and while he mooned for hours, chewing on his penholder, over the page he had begun, or amused himself, like a compulsive doodler, scribbling drawings that he showed me from a distance, laughing, and hurried to tear up right away, or while he became lost in dubious explorations in the ancient *Dictionnaire de la langue française* that Henriette, in her naïveté, had thought it good to bring up to the boys' quarters? (It would have been even worse, probably, if I had let myself become infected and had followed suit. That could have happened. His proximity and example often did affect me. But I made it a point of honor to do my homework conscientiously, and would not consent to conversation before having completed my task. Outdoors, on our walks, things were different: I let myself go, and showed myself, in words, to be as outrageous as he. But in the house, and especially during study hours, my apparent indifference, my protests when he disturbed me in my work, forced him to keep the ramblings that obsessed him to himself. The habit had been formed.)

One must really have no experience, in one's memories of youth, of what obsessions of this type are like, to be surprised that they could have totally paralyzed Guy's capacity for study. It was because he was thinking only of *that* that he could not get interested in anything else. At an age when the mind needs to be free to lend itself to the extraordinary gymnastics that school curriculums require of adolescents, those whose temperaments deliver them over helplessly to their haunting obsessions have a brain that is blocked, unavailable. I met, at boarding school, many "paralytics" of this sort. The laziness of dunces often has no other cause. The majority of today's educators are aware of this. The Abbé Adry probably was not. (I would be quite hard put, anyway, to say exactly what he would have had to do to release Guy from his spell . . .)

I had been taught to take studies very seriously, and Guy's nonchalance, his indifference to bad marks, scandalized me; the blind admiration that I had accorded him was badly shaken. Other character traits, which I discovered gradually, disappointed me. He often got on my nerves. For instance, I remember my stupefaction on the evening of the first of May, when I saw him place on the night table, between two lighted bits of candle, a statuette of the Virgin that he had gone for in the next room: "What's got into you?" I was about to lose my temper: I thought that he had some prank up his sleeve and I found it inappropriate for these devotional articles to be part of it. "It's for my month of Mary," he explained, seriously. "A vow that I made when I was sick." I said nothing in reply. He knelt in silence and drew from his pocket a mother-of-pearl rosary that I had never seen in his hands before. During the month we had been living together, I had not noticed any religious ardor in him. Never did he say his prayers. He went to Sunday Mass with us and the maids, but without the least devotion; and he even behaved rather badly there: to such an extent that I had asked Henriette to sit between him and me because he gave me the giggles during the sermon by whispering into my ear funny remarks inspired by the sudden risings in the voice of the dean, whom he called "old Punch." (I had no more fervor than he did, but in my eyes religious ceremonies formed part of the order of respectable things; and above all I felt strongly that on all occasions le Saillant ought to set an example of good breeding.) For several evenings he continued his devotions between the two little flickering flames. Then, when the candle ends were burned out, he did not bother to find others, and took the Virgin back to where he had got her.

This memory leads me to ponder Guy's piety. I did not notice other outbreaks of it. But, putting little details together, I think I can say that he would have been rather inclined to mystical exaltations if he had been pushed in that direction by his family circle, if he had been under less levelheaded influences than that of the Abbé Adry. He would have been capable of frenzied confessions, excessive penances, "novenas"—for all I know, of mortifications, fasts, the hair shirt . . . There was in him the credulousness of a primitive being, a taste for the miraculous. I remember his attraction to supernatural terrors. He loved darkness because it made him tremble with fear. Sometimes, in the evening, when we were alone on the stairs, he would suddenly blow out our candles; and, with beating heart, would feel his way along in the resounding gloom of the corridors, walking with muffled steps, enjoining me to be silent, shivering with curiosity, deliberate fright, and pleasure; and he savored these minutes of dread with a delectation that always made me feel uneasy. If, by chance, night overtook us in the depths of the park, under the trees, he would huddle up against me and implore me to run with him to get out of "the dark" more quickly. I felt him to be so little master of himself, so anxious, that I hesitated to make fun of him. I asked him one day: "But come on, you know the park, what are you afraid of?" He answered me strangely: "You never know. The devil . . ." Saying this, he smiled; but he had suddenly lowered his voice; to what extent was he joking?

What an easy prey he would have been for all superstitions! He liked to deform reality, to dismiss simple and sensible explanations, which seemed to him disappointing, tedious; he preferred to imagine, scattered out in the beyond, all sorts of evil forces by which he felt threatened. He was ready to believe in premonitions, omens, exorcisms, ghosts. Of course he had never heard, any more than I had, about occultism or magic. Nevertheless, by himself he invented strange rites, incantations. Thus, to seal our friendship forever, he had fashioned two rings of twisted copper wire: each of us had to scratch his calf, smear one of the rings with blood and slip it onto the other's finger while swearing an oath of eternal fidelity. We wore them for several months. Then one day as I was playing, mine broke and I lost it. I was laughing when I told him about it; however, confronted with his dismayed expression, his eyes brimming with tears, I saw clearly that he was very upset; he was convinced that I was going to die; and he would not rest until he had put his ring on my finger, to ward off fate . . .

What did I think of all this? Sometimes with annoyance, sometimes with amusement, always with surprise, I went along with his whims; but I considered them childish, unworthy of us, and I looked down on him, really, for attaching such importance to absurdities. I was much harder still on certain tendencies in his nature, ones which I unreservedly disliked. I have not forgotten, among other discoveries of this kind, the first time that, playing checkers with him one Sunday when the rain kept us from going out, I noticed that he was cheating. I was more taken aback by it than offended: for he was cheating out of mischievousness, for pleasure, rather than out of dishonesty. He was like those little Arabs I have often watched squatting around a game of knucklebones: for him as for them, cheating was not a reprehensible act but rather a proof of skill, a difficult and profitable trick reserved for the most artful. With a pickpocket's nimbleness, he did not hesitate, if I took my eye off the board, to spirit away a piece or two in order to win faster. When I caught him red-handed and let out a howl of indignation, he would hasten to put the pieces back on their squares with a disarming smile, only to begin again the moment I was distracted. He found nothing immoral and dishonorable about this whatsoever. I was so thrown by such cheekiness, and so ashamed of him, that often I preferred to appear to have seen nothing and to lose the game in silence. But he put so much natural unconcern, so much prankishness, into robbing me that once the first flash of outrage was past, I harbored no grudge against him for it. I am inclined to believe that I already had some propensity to refrain from holding people entirely responsible for what they do, for what they are. However, his prestige suffered in my eyes, and I was imperceptibly led to revise the too-flattering judgment that I had passed on him.

Otherwise, he showered me with attentions, with kindnesses. Even when he played a mean trick on me or when his teasing made him insufferable—he could, on certain days, be as pesky as a gadfly—I never doubted the solidity of his affection. Our squabbles did not last, and our breaches were rare. Neither of us could resign himself to discord; and I have to say, to his credit, that he was generally the first to make peace. I see again his sweet little triangular face with its too-ruddy cheeks, and his repentant half-smile, and that caressing way he used to gaze at me: I never loved him more than during those reconciliations.

I was not the only one to fall under his spell: except for my father, all the members of the household were captivated, and tried to outdo one another in spoiling him. Moreover, he was not unaware of his power to bewitch, and did not fail to take advantage of it. With his mother—I had noticed it from the very first days—he made cynical use of it: he knew how to throw himself into her arms, and call her "Mama dear," at the exact moment when he wanted to bend her authority. But it would be unfair to claim that he was always conscious of the charm he exerted, and keen to exploit it. No: he used it instinctively; and if he got something out of it, it was often not because he had deliberately sought to do so; for his nature was so fundamentally loving, he always had such a superabundance of good feeling to spare, that his cuddling remained sincere even when it was motivated by self-interest.

The abbé's preference for me was nevertheless obvious. It certainly put my cousin out, not only because he was jealous by nature but also because he had a compulsive need to feel himself approved of and fussed over by everyone. But I do not recall that he ever complained about it or showed me any resentment. As for me, I found this preference more painful than gratifying: I would have wished for Guy to be perfect, for no one to find any fault in him; and, from the abbé, I would have more gladly accepted, even at my own expense, an unfair leniency toward Guy.

In the same way, I was distressed by the attitude that my father displayed. He could not hide the annoyance that was caused him at table by certain unconsidered remarks or certain distracted silences on Guy's part, by his way of judging things according to whether or not they were "amusing," his slowness in eating, his capricious lack of appetite. For instance, my father was exasperated by Guy's habit of "picking at his food," as we said at home; of always leaving scraps on his plate, of eating only the eye of the chops, the lean of the ham, the crust of his bread; and my father did not always refrain from making a disagreeable allusion to it, which I found hard to forgive him. He definitely felt less attraction than pity for this sickly, refined, pusillanimous little Parisian, who did not ride and had no wish to learn, who was afraid of going out in the rain, of staying out in full sunlight, and whose strength constantly had to be conserved.

By contrast, I was grateful to Henriette for the maternal care that she lavished on my cousin and for her indulgence toward his shortcomings, doing her all, without seeming to, to cover up everything in Guy's behavior that would have unfailingly irked my father. I have since come to know that she was not taken in by either his deft caresses or his little lies. Perhaps this clearsightedness was sharpened, without her realizing it, by a slight feeling of jealousy toward this newcomer with whom I had so quickly become infatuated and whose presence, after all, was detrimental to our intimacy. However that may be, she saw and guessed many things. I did not learn until later how much she feared Guy's influence over me. Today, reflecting on what that influence was, I refuse to think it deplorable. The new curiosity that Guy had awakened in me rather upset my inner balance; but this initiation was bound to happen someday, and I was certainly old enough to lose my innocence. As for all the rest, Guy's coming resulted in gains: he took me out of my childhood, introduced me to friendship, taught me to look at the world with new eyes. I have always remembered our walks, his infectious joy in the presence of natural beauty, his emotion when together we penetrated the mystery of the tall forest; those summer evenings when he would pull me away from the family circle to go contemplate the sight of the setting sun, so beautiful, viewed from the edge of our terrace, when the forest against the light resembles a recumbent beast and the red disc sinks slowly behind the black fleece. This enchantment of a twilight over the forest, to which I still often give my marveling attention—it was he who opened my senses to it. I had never, before his arrival, tasted moments like that; they are, along with so many others that I owe to Guy's friendship, among the most delicate memories of my youth.

But I take so much pleasure in evoking them that I am really lingering over them inordinately. I will cut this short and go straight to the summer vacation of that year of '82, marked by the first and not very promising contact that I had with my Uncle Chambost.

IN ORDER TO SPEND a part of the vacation with their son without his having to alter his regimen, Guy's parents had accepted my father's invitation to come at the beginning of August and stay at le Saillant for six weeks. Henriette had gone to great trouble to prepare comfortable accommodations for them. She seemed to reconcile herself quite patiently to this inconvenience. My father, much less so . . .

The way in which he announced to his guests, on the very evening of their arrival, that the administration of the estate and the labors of the season would not permit him to change any of his working habits, made me understand that this stay was far from being for him what it was for me: an amusing diversion from the normal round. He must have dreaded this forced intimacy with his brother-in-law. I have already mentioned that Uncle Éric had at one time openly disapproved of my mother's engagement. My father had never forgiven his brother-in-law the underhanded insistence with which for several months he had tried to talk his sister out of this marriage. Nor had my uncle forgotten those attempts, and all the less so since they had been in vain. There remained between them, in spite of the tone of polite cordiality that they affected toward each other, a latent and sporadic animosity that was aggravated, besides, by a total divergence in outlook, in tastes, in lifestyle, and even in vocabulary. Nothing in common, no possible ground for understanding. My uncle, more often than not, did not even pretend to take any interest in my father's country activities; he did not utter a word about them; or, all of a sudden, out of the blue, he would begin to hold forth to no one in particular, in a nasal, pompous voice full of such an obviously excessive deference that this unexpected and inordinate interest looked like impertinence, a thousand times more wounding than the disdainful silence of the other days. The spirit of conciliation was not his strong point, any more than was generosity of heart. As for my father, who had never taken an interest in anything but science and agriculture, and who felt himself a layman in all the branches where his brother-in-law's intellectual superiority flourished, he never ventured the slightest allusion to the eminent position that my uncle had gained in Paris in the world of the university, political science, and literature: one would have thought he knew nothing of it. This deliberate tactlessness put the nerves of both parties on edge. Fortunately, these seeds of discord were rendered close to harmless by the skillful vigilance and good humor of Aunt Ma, by that overflowing vitality which issued perpetually from her presence. I have already sketched her portrait at that time. It is of Uncle Éric, as he appeared to me that summer, that I would now like to say a word.

A strange fellow! I had never met him. I knew practically nothing about him. He was hardly ever mentioned around the house, and Guy spoke only very evasively about his father. Thus I was not at all biased against him. In the course of that first evening, I watched him from a distance, with increasing uneasiness. He inspired at first sight an invincible aversion in me, mixed with fear, which it took me years to get over. I could not better compare this mixture of surprise and dread than to a feeling of the same kind that I experienced later, in Morocco, one night when, at a forward post south of the Atlas, I found myself face-to-face, in a hut glaringly lit by an acetylene lamp, with a rebel chieftain, reputed to be fearsome, who had just been captured by our scouts: a little Arab with a foxy face, sly lips, piercing eyes, who did not even get up when I came in and did not deign to answer any of the interpreter's questions. Frozen in a haughty silence, indifferent, smirking, unreachable to the depths of his nomad's savagery, he fixed me with an indecipherable gaze, and I have rarely felt so ill at ease as during my brief interview with that feline of the high plateaus. Of course, my Uncle Éric had nothing of the wild beast about him. But for the sensitive child that I was, this taciturn, sardonic, disquieting character likewise awakened the idea of a strange and rather terrifying specimen of humanity: altogether different, in any case, not only from the people I had had occasion to meet until then, but also from the simple and approachable sort of man I had learned to respect. His exterior was supremely disagreeable to me; and even later, when I lived on intimate terms with him and took pleasure in his company, I could never get used to his physical appearance.

At that time he was near fifty. His body was small, muscular, nervous and brisk. His sparse hair was beginning to turn gray, while his goatee, whose tip did not point forward but curved back toward his neck like a billy goat's, remained black and thick. It was in his eyes that the enigma of the man was concentrated: they were deeply set in their sockets, and the highly mobile pupils, which had the cold luster of jet, flashed a cutting glance, always on the lookout; I won't say a glance that sparkled with intelligence, because it didn't really conjure up the idea of a thought or an inner meditation, but one that sparkled with intensity, rather, like a bright gleam. His nose was short, flat. A sort of aggressive energy resided in the jutting jaw, the volume of which was increased and the prognathism accentuated by the badly trimmed beard. The mouth, hidden by the mustache, was nondescript. On the other hand, because of their odd structure, his ears had a revealing character: they expressed an alert curiosity; stuck flat against the skull, they moved away from it at the tops, and ended in points like those of cats; at certain moments, one would have sworn that they were quivering . . .

This face—because of the eyes, perhaps; also because of that too small nose, wedged between the jaw and the brow—had something apelike about it, which I could never get used to. I was surprised that Guy could, without repulsion, offer his forehead to that goatee to be kissed. To shake my uncle's hand, morning and night, was hard for me for quite some time; almost impossible when our first encounter of the day happened to take place unwitnessed on the stairway, or at the turn in a corridor; then my heart would pound when I caught sight of him, and to get away from him I would quicken my step while stammering a hasty "Good morning, Uncle Éric" as I went past, so much did I fear that limp and prolonged handshake, and even more the expression on his face, which produced in me an unbearable feeling of insecurity—an expression of malevolent inquisitiveness, vaguely mocking, vaguely suspicious, a look as if to say: "Aha, you rascal . . . Are you scared of me? So you have a guilty conscience?"

His son did not like him much, and I soon noticed that he avoided him as often as possible. I refrained, of course, from pointing this out to Guy. (We spoke together about everything, very freely—except about our fathers. Perhaps because each of us still hesitated to define, even in his heart of hearts, the embryo of sacrilegious judgment that he was already bringing against one of the divinities of his childhood pantheon.) Sometimes Guy was summoned by my Uncle Éric to the room that Henriette had fixed up for him as a study. There, for twenty minutes, lolling back in his armchair, he would keep his son standing under his gaze, like a cat on a griddle, and put embarrassing questions to him about his work, his grades, his health. He always displayed sadism in these interrogations, which he conducted with the tenacity and wiliness of a master torturer. I, in my turn, was to experience this later on. Professional habit, perhaps? He always went at it with a disconcerting politeness, fraught with elusive ulterior motives. The accused would feel the discussion steered insidiously, without his quite knowing how but to his detriment, toward a premeditated point that he endeavored in vain to discover. My uncle visibly savored the protracted discomfiture of his whipping boy—until the moment when, having probably reached his enigmatic goals, he finally dismissed him with an ambiguous smile, as often as not letting fly some double-edged taunt whose victim never knew whether it was an unhoped-for compliment or a treacherous rebuke heavy with threat . . . Guy would come down from his father flushed, tense, irascible, short of breath. He did not allow himself to comment; he seemed eager to forget the ordeal; but from the way in which he would suddenly shake himself like a dog who has had a forced bath, or burst into jerky laughter on any pretext, or lose his temper over nothing, or, on the other hand, would come up to me and slip his arm through mine to walk me to the park, I guessed what a toll the session with his father had taken on his nerves.

The most incredible thing for me was to imagine that such a simple, direct woman as the adorable Aunt Ma could love that spiteful ape and share his existence so intimately. Uncle Éric went out very little; he worked all day long, and most of the time my aunt did not leave his side. She had a dual role of servant-secretary. My uncle was at a loss before all the demands of practical life. It was my aunt who unpacked and lined up on the shelf the books they had brought in their luggage. It was she who sharpened the pencils, filled the inkwell, and cut his lined schoolboy's paper to the desired size; she filed the index cards, fetched the volume her husband needed, looked up words for him in the dictionary, checked his references for him, recopied his preliminary course notes in her tall hand, which slanted up the page; or, sitting near the window, she brought their copious correspondence up to date.

"Connections" held a sizable place in their existence; and that was a preserve which my aunt kept exclusively for herself and ran with a cheerful mastery. I remember our astonishment in the first days, after lunch, when we saw Aunt Ma plunge into the newspapers from Paris to go over the society pages with a fine-tooth comb. "Chambost!" she would cry (for she never called her husband by his first name, and this too did not fail to disconcert me), "the old Comtesse de Chaslin just died; remind me to send condolences . . . And Florency announces his son's engagement to a Mademoiselle Pezon . . . Is that the surgeon's daughter, or the law professor's?" Uncle Éric listened attentively. My father drank his coffee with a look of indifference while watching out the window for the moment when Gaspard would bring his horse to the front steps and he would have an excuse to slip away; the intrusion of this Parisian town talk into his home no doubt annoyed him. As for me, I sat agape: to know so many people, and all famous enough for the newspaper to print their names!

The gatherings that followed the meals were the only moments of communal life. Always sharply cut short after lunch, when everyone was in a hurry to return to his pursuits, they lasted a little longer at the end of dinner, especially since after the hot August afternoons, the evenings on the terrace were a feast of coolness. We sat there in a semicircle, with faces that were amiable, self-assured, and closed. Family get-togethers, the ritual of which had been established for generations, where everyone cautiously kept his own thoughts and worries to himself, and where the discussion revolved interminably around what the weather had been like today, what it would be like tomorrow: too red a sunset was a threat of wind; a light haze over the fields meant another spell of even hotter weather . . . It happened, but rarely, that a careless remark sent the conversation sliding toward a topical subject—the protest by M. de Lesseps over the occupation of Suez by English troops, the latest inflammatory speech by Paul Déroulède . . . And there would then be, between my father and Uncle Éric, an unsettling back-and-forth of clashing assertions and reticent retorts, to which my aunt hastened to put an end through some ingenious diversion. In general, Guy and I, once we had gulped down our dessert, would clear out, to escape into the park; and sometimes Henriette would join us. I noticed that, with acquaintance, she did not much like the Chambost-Lévadés, although she denied it when I questioned her. The estrangement that she felt towards my uncle seemed to me amply justified; however, I had a hard time understanding why she was not more attracted to Aunt Ma, whom I really liked a lot, and every day a little bit more. But precisely that impetuous frankness, that perpetual and slightly noisy cheeriness—just a shade common, perhaps—which caused me to delight in my aunt, alarmed my sister; and that incisive wit, which spared nothing and no one, offended her natural reserve and her notions of good form.

At table, Uncle Éric spoke little. A silence which might have been explained, after his long sessions of hard toil, by his preoccupation with the work in progress; but he did not seem to remove himself at all from the conversation—which my aunt, Henriette, and my father kept going. On the contrary: attentive to everything that was being said around him, he would aim his gimlet eye at whoever was speaking; and he refrained from intervening. It took Aunt Ma to turn to him and urge him to give his opinion. Then, for several minutes, he would hold forth in a precise, clearly accentuated voice; and what he said was always surprising, not only for the ease he showed in handling long sentences, the impeccable correctness of which was a little out of place in our home, but also for the subtlety of his thought, the clarity of his reasoning, and even more so for the unexpectedness, the originality, or often even the whimsicality of his viewpoints. No one found anything to object to, anything to add; the question seemed to be exhausted, for good. However, these pertinent interventions had an incongruous nature, like a firecracker set off in the midst of a party: they never failed to produce a moment of silence and of general embarrassment. Did he perhaps notice it? Did it perhaps even cause him pain? And if, most of the time, he preferred to remain silent, wasn't it because he never felt in tune with us and because he feared casting a chill? For one who came to know him well and saw a lot of him, as I was later able to do, there is nothing implausible about this hypothesis. At the time of these memories, my thoughts did not run so far: his abstract turn of mind seemed sibylline to me and his affected elocution ridiculous. I found him more boring than the most soporific of my textbooks. And foolish, what is more, indubitably foolish, because of his inability to perform the most elementary acts of everyday life. Nothing seemed funnier to me than his clumsiness in untying a knot on a parcel without his wife's help, in opening up one of our folding chairs in the garden, in winding his watch, in cutting off a duck's drumstick. Add to this—just to scuttle him in my eyes once and for all—his incredible ignorance of country things: he couldn't tell a shovel from a spade, a wasp from a bee, a young artichoke plant from a clump of asters . . . I saw him avoid crossing the lawn one scorching day for fear of finding dew on it. He was just this side of believing that there were cream cows the way there were milk cows . . . One day when my father and the gardener were talking in front of him about that circle in the park dubbed the *"Boulingrin"** because it was covered with turf, I heard him, with my own two ears, say to my father, with a naïveté that was not in the least put on: "My dear friend, you must show me your *boulingrin*. I really don't believe I know this shrub . . ." For me, such examples of incompetence were flagrant proofs of stupidity. I was a long way from imagining the respect

---

*Derived from the English "bowling green": a well-manicured lawn.

and affection that I was to feel for him a few years later in spite of his short-comings; and I suspected even less the influence that contact with this exceptional intelligence was to have upon the formation of my own.

Such a basic incapacity for everyday life would suffice to explain, in a couple where the husband was constantly making such a show of authority, the ascendancy that my aunt had acquired and the actual power that she wielded. Her skill, altogether feminine, consisted in not attacking her tyrant's obstinacy directly and in never openly encroaching upon his prerogatives as head of the household. A policy of subtlety, of circumventions, of apparent concessions, thanks to which she always ended up having the last word, as much in the little matters as in the big ones, including my uncle's professional existence, of which she had secretly taken charge and which she steered in the way of honors with a very sure flair for diplomacy, without ever overlooking anything that could further his career or enhance his fame.

A fine illustration of Aunt Ma's know-how is the masterly way in which, during that month of August, she managed to prevent her son's being sent to boarding school in the fall. The decision, made a long time before, seemed irrevocable; my uncle did not want to budge; what was more, my father had let it be understood that he did not much care to keep my cousin a whole winter at le Saillant. My aunt, that time, had little chance of success. But the vision that she'd had at Easter of the dormitories and dining halls of Saint-Léonard haunted her nights. Her maneuvers were prudent and unrelenting. Her master stroke was to secure the collusion of our old doctor in Menne-ville, a gallant and obliging man who, whether in response to the polite attentions of this comely Parisienne or because the boy's health worried him, helped her, very firmly, to convince my uncle that precautions still appeared to be essential and that they were not compatible with the harsh regimen of a boarding school. The game seemed to be won. The whole scheme fell through, however, the day the Abbé Adry came to inform my father that he had been assigned by the Bishop of Sées to run the Catholic clubs in the diocese and that he would have to leave Menneville as early as September. Aunt Ma was shrewd enough to seem to yield before this unexpected blow; and, for a few days, Saint-Léonard again became the only possible solution, not only for Guy but also for me; for, given the point I'd reached in my studies, my father feared abandoning me to the abilities of the little country curate who was going to replace the Abbé Adry. That is how things stood when we learned that Uncle Éric was leaving for Paris. He stayed there three or four days. And as soon as he returned, Aunt Ma ran looking for us in the park to tell us joyously that my uncle had come to an understanding, in Paris, with one of his former students, a young university graduate who had agreed to spend the winter with us at le Saillant as our private tutor.

Needless to say, at the time I was incapable of discerning by myself the role that my aunt had played in the matter. It was Henriette who opened my eyes. She was so hostile to the decision that had been made, and disapproved so strongly of the hiring of a tutor sponsored by the Chambosts, that, in spite of her usual reserve, she confessed to me that she had done her utmost to get my father to refuse. It was evening, in her room, where I had come to say goodnight to her. I see the scene again. She was sitting on her bed, wrapped in her dressing gown, and was winding into a ball a skein that I was holding between my open arms. The glimmer of the little oil lamp, which never left her bed table, lit up her brow; her head was lowered, and the rest of her face was in shadow. I was looking at her from below, huddling, with my knees pulled up, on the footstool where, since my early childhood, I was accustomed to sitting. "A tutor!" she said to me with an acrimony of which I scarcely would have thought her capable. "As if there weren't already enough intruders around here! They've spoiled our Saillant!" I thought I was joining in with her by deploring the presence of Uncle Éric. "Bah! *She* fools people, but *she's* no better than he!" she went on severely. "Without seeming to, she's always getting other people to do what she wants!" I made no answer. I was loath to believe her. I thought that my sister was unfair to Aunt Ma, whom I continued to hold dear; and I suffered in my affection for these two women who, for obscure reasons, did not like each other. "And what experience can *he* have in teaching?" Henriette continued in an angry tone. "*He's* twenty-three! *He* has never taught! It's absurd! A tutor twenty-three years old!"

CHAPTER V

Xavier de Balcourt at le Saillant

A TUTOR . . .

He arrived two days before the October term. The Chambost-Lévadés had been back in Paris for several weeks.

My father and Henriette had spoken to us very little about him, and for good reason: they knew nothing. The only one who could have filled them in, Uncle Éric, had naturally taken a malicious pleasure in evading all questions. We knew only his name—a fine old name, what's more: Xavier de Balcourt. Aunt Ma had never seen him, but she used to run across his mother at the receptions of a certain Mme. de Portville, to whom the Balcourts were related and in whose house they lodged.

Xavier de Balcourt . . . Writing that name, which was to become so familiar to me, I am assailed by memories. Xavier was only about ten years older than I, and when, as a young man, I met up with him again in Paris, where my uncle had engaged him as a secretary, our difference in age no longer counted and a real friendship developed between us. Subsequently, circumstances led me to see him at very close range; I received very intimate confidences from him; I was the only one, I believe, to know the whole underside of that existence, its joys, its acts of folly, its dramas of passion, its struggles of conscience; the only one to understand him, to love him in spite of all; the only one, probably, to fathom the secrets of his miserable end.

But I anticipate. I shall come back to all that at length. Today, I would like to forget everything I know of this strange character—one of the most touching, most unusual, most pathetic I have met—to put myself back in the shoes of the schoolboy that I was, at the beginning of October '82, when, from the window where Guy and I were on the lookout, we saw the cabriolet, driven by Gaspard, enter the courtyard and our "tutor" leap out agilely onto the front steps.

"Quite the little greyhound!"* Guy whispered to me.

He indeed had the greyhound's close-set eyes, the pointed muzzle, the lean-flanked body, the springy manner. Next to Gaspard, a sturdy bulldog with a great broad snout, he looked like a little lapdog. His appearance was most reassuring: not at all "respectable."

Followed by Guy, I stepped forward to greet him. (My father was out on the farms, and Henriette had decided not to appear before teatime.) He won us over immediately with his simplicity, his cheerfulness. There was nothing he wanted less than to impress us. The ice was quickly broken. His first move was to look me up and down good-naturedly: "How tall you are, for a twelve-year-old! I'm going to be ashamed of my size, I am . . . A good thing giants don't usually much like to pick fights . . . Now Guy here is less intimidating!"

The voice, unexpected in that little body, was unusually low, resonant, warm, and stirring, like the sound of a cello.

All three of us helped the coachman remove the luggage from the carriage—a basket of books and a trunk, bulky but not very heavy—and to take them up to the bedroom that Henriette had prepared near ours. M. de Balcourt seemed delighted. He ran to the window, marveled at the design of the terrace, the view, the russet coloring of the forest. He turned toward us, his face lit up: "It must be grand to live here! I love the country, the big, real country . . . What walks you must be able to take! Are you good walkers? We'll go on wonderful hikes, the three of us!" He took stock of his room like a child, thrilled with the sculpted doves on the pediment of the old wardrobe, with the clock, in a glass bell, that was adorned with a bust of

*The word in French, *levrette,* denotes the small, delicate Italian greyhound.

Aesculapius, and very amused by the contrast between the two engravings that hung on either side of the fireplace: one showed a thin General Bonaparte bending over the plague victims of Jaffa; the other, a pudgy Napoleon who was advancing, potbelly sticking out, over the bridge at Tilsit to meet the Czar. (I have them still.) Though I discreetly suggested that we leave him alone to unpack, he unaffectedly had us stay and help him. The trunk was an ancient battered leather portmanteau whose handles were coming off, whose buckles were covered with rust and whose lock was unusable; it scarcely did him justice. He probably realized this, and expressed indignation at the railroad employees, as if he hoped to have us believe that their rough handling alone could be responsible for such a degree of dilapidation.

Guy asked him with a straight face: "Was it new, sir?"

"Not entirely," admitted Balcourt, embarrassed. "But those brutes smashed it to pieces!"

He took from it a few articles of linen and some worn clothes, which he had us put away, following his instructions, in the wardrobe and in the dresser drawers. He caught Guy's glance at a pair of ankle boots he had just handed him. He seemed to look for something, explored the bottom of the trunk, and exclaimed, in a tone of sharp annoyance:

"How stupid! I forgot my new ankle boots in Paris . . . Two pair in patent leather . . ."

We said nothing. He launched into a detailed explanation: he'd packed in a hurry, the day before, after dark, while talking to his mother . . . He'd made a mistake: he'd taken these old laced walking boots . . . which, as a matter of fact, he had just been meaning to give away . . . or throw out . . .

"Bah," he added, "it doesn't matter. In the country, stylishness is no big thing, is it?"

The bell for tea rang as we finished unpacking the books, whose number and forbidding titles had suddenly filled us with respect for our charming little tutor.

Henriette was waiting for us in the dining room; her ceremonious demeanor did not bode well. Guy shot me a quick look. Nevertheless, my sister had a few words of welcome; she apologized for my father's absence. A conversation started up about life in the country and the work of autumn. Balcourt slipped in a well-chosen compliment on the architecture of the house and the perspective of the gardens: nothing could have served him so well with my sister. Things could not have gone off better. I quickly sensed, with a feeling of elation, that the newcomer was making a favorable impression on her, and, already won over myself, I was convinced that it would not take her long to drop her prejudices. For his part, Balcourt seemed at ease. I should have guessed that he wasn't; but his experience in society helped him hide his shyness. Henriette recommended that we take M. de Balcourt to the end of the terrace, to give him a view of the countryside; and when I saw that she was coming with us, I caught Guy's eye.

"He passed!" he whispered in my ear. "With flying colors!"

The walk developed into a tour of the park, so that my father was back when we returned to the house. He showed Balcourt into his study and shut the door.

"Did you see the trunk dodge?" my cousin asked me, as soon as we were alone.

I immediately added: "And the boot dodge!"

"And the boot dodge," Guy repeated, nodding his head.

It did not occur to us at all to laugh about it. We understood, from the moment we met him, that M. de Balcourt was poor and that he must be vain, since he did not shrink from the most childish lie to cover up his poverty. We also guessed that he was touchy, unhappy with his lot, and perhaps prematurely embittered; that he must have suffered not only from his lack of means but from many other things as well—like having a greyhound's muzzle, like being small and having to wear excessively high heels to gain a few centimeters . . .

For he was small, so small that on the tall chairs in the dining room he seemed to be perching rather than sitting (which was also due to his habit of throwing out his chest in order not to lose any of his height). However, he was small without appearing slight, because his limbs were muscular, he was broad in the shoulders, and the whole was of balanced proportions. As for his ugliness . . . I eventually became so used to it that I no longer found it unpleasant. Besides, that unattractive face was, to the very end, saved from ridiculousness by the intelligence, the meditative softness, of the eyes. Admittedly, however, his features had no grace. The narrowness of his face, accentuated by the thrust of the thin and overlong nose, gave him, at moments, a foxy expression. His complexion was gray; his hair, lifeless and too thin, made one think of chick down; a sparse mustache, washed-out blond like the hair, emphasized the long slit of the mouth. I am tempted to write that on his countenance he wore his destiny as a failure, a man without luck. This is because I have great trouble separating the brisk and jaunty image of the young Balcourt, turning up at le Saillant in his twenty-fourth year, from another vision which haunts me: that of the thirty-year-old bohemian, the down-and-outer with the face of a madman: I can still see, on the tile floor of the hovel where he was hiding his loneliness and his despair, that grimacing corpse, and, behind a half-raised eyelid, the bluish eye of a piece of game on the butcher's block . . .

Everything that I was to learn later about his family and his early years clarifies and explains that touchy vanity which our children's common sense had detected through trifles. I am anticipating again, but briefly.

The Balcourts had not always been without means. Xavier had been born at the château de Balcourt, in the Ain, where his father lived off the income from his land. Like many other idle members of the lesser nobility afflicted with the business demon, the senior Balcourt had not resisted an offer to lend the respectability of his name to a firm of swindlers—who lost no time in going bankrupt. Accountable as chairman of the board of directors, the imprudent M. de Balcourt thus found himself compromised, and the first victim of this fraudulent collapse. To avoid the disgrace of prosecution, he threw himself one night into the moat of the château. His death spared his family a sensational scandal, but did not save them from ruin. Mme. de Balcourt did not hesitate to sell the property to pay off the local people of modest means whom her husband had dragged into the business, after which she found herself without a penny to call her own and with a child to raise. Thanks to the compassion of her Portville cousins, who offered her a home, she was able to come and settle in Paris. "That poor Émilie," as the old Comtesse de Portville used to say, lived there by her wits and on discreet charity. She obtained a scholarship for her son, and Xavier, a good student, a future prizewinner in the Concours Général,* became her sole reason for living.

I grew very well acquainted with Mme. de Balcourt, whose death preceded her son's suicide by only a few years: she sometimes had the look of a grande dame and sometimes of a secondhand-clothes-seller. She was an odd sort of woman, and I shall speak of her again. Tireless and shameless, she seemed to have no other care than to render people services they hadn't asked for—which gave her the right to everyone's gratitude and consideration. "That poor Émilie" had managed to get herself received everywhere. The needy and social couple that Xavier and his mother made is a picturesque specimen of the Parisian fauna of the day. When I moved in their circle, they gave, in their four-room apartment, literary and musical gatherings to which they often succeeded in drawing well-known names and to which starving "decadent" poets, young lecturers with no public, and virtuosos just out of the Conservatory came to get a hearing before the oddest, most motley audience imaginable.

Xavier, to whom his father had bequeathed nothing but the character of a thin-skinned aristocrat, had suffered cruelly since childhood from his position as a scholarship boy and from the financial difficulties with which he saw his mother wrestling. To cap his misfortunes, the gibes of his schoolmates did not let him forget either his diminutive size or his unprepossessing physiognomy, and these physical defects, at least as much as his feeling of social inferiority, contributed early on to the warping of his character. Fool-

*Prestigious competitive examination for pupils in top forms of French secondary schools.

ishly, he tried hard to conceal his poverty beneath a misleading façade, as he saw his mother doing, and gratified his vanity by flaunting his nobiliary particle and his connections. But he was too clear-sighted to be able to deceive himself: he knew that his family name was somewhat tainted, and was never able to forget that those brilliant connections treated him as a poor relation. As he grew up, his natural pride became even more ticklish. Although he had a tender reverence for his mother, he could not without annoyance endure her inordinate pliability of character, her obsequiousness as a beggarly grande dame toward those blessed by fortune, from whom she relentlessly wangled favors. He soon affected a recalcitrant attitude which drove Mme. de Balcourt to despair and did not make her maneuvers any easier: on Sundays, he would shut himself in with his schoolbooks and refuse to go along on her self-seeking rounds. This spitefulness of a humiliated child gradually lost its edge, after the *baccalauréat*, as his scholastic achievements gave him confidence in his superiority and justified his secret ambitions.

When he landed at le Saillant, it was the first time he had escaped from maternal tutelage; the first time, too, that he could show himself to be natural, pleasant, and considerate without feeling that his dignity had to suffer. He finally stopped being the son of "that poor Émilie," whom people took in and fed out of compassion. With us, he was coming to hold a job that he deemed honorable, that he knew was difficult to perform well, and for which he had been flatteringly chosen and sought out by Professor Chambost in person. He showed up with head held high. In exchange for our hospitality and the price of his lessons, he gave us his time, his abilities, his learning. He was not a teacher in need: he was a *licencié ès lettres,* * had a diploma from Sciences Politiques, and was considered an up-and-coming young man by eminent authorities. He was hoping to have the leisure to do his own work in the evenings, and fully expected to have his doctoral dissertation accepted the next year. He could then, armed with serious credentials, launch out on that career as a writer and polemicist which was, for so many years, the unavowed goal of his efforts.

Granted, he did not have much experience; he had never taught. About that Henriette had been right. But for this new task he felt he had abilities, personal ideas, an inclination. He did not exaggerate his gifts. I consider them to have been real, and I owe much to his teaching.

I have already had occasion to mention that it was only after Guy's arrival at le Saillant that I learned to make use of lying, an invaluable expedient and quite often the only one that the child has at his disposal to protect his secret universe against intrusion by adults.

The presence of Xavier de Balcourt made me take another step in this

---

*I.e., held an advanced degree in literature.

direction, and a very important one. I suddenly had a notion of the place that lying holds in social life; its obvious necessity was revealed to me—and, to a certain extent, its perfect legitimacy. I gradually made this discovery, fraught with consequences, while observing Xavier up close; and first by noticing how different he was in his relations with us, particularly with Guy, from the Xavier that my father and Henriette knew. I understood not only that the same person could present very different aspects of himself according to the people who were around him, but also that he could do so without hypocrisy, without any of those various aspects being a mask, a sham. Xavier's demeanor at the family table showed no signs of deceitfulness: the correct, serious, respectable young tutor who kept a watchful eye on our deportment at meals while exchanging polite remarks with my sister or conversing with my father about social reforms, the Tonkin affair, the question of the Far East; and the overgrown boy, unrestrained and joking, whom I had as a companion in the schoolroom; and that slightly overaffectionate older brother who was stirred by Guy's cuddliness—these were disparate but equally genuine facets of the same individual. In each of these personae, so divergent in appearance, Xavier remained himself, perfectly homogeneous, perfectly sincere: he did not have to counterfeit himself in any way or put on a disguise. He passed instantly from one to the other without having to think about it; and in each of them he was so naturally at ease that he did not even seem to remember the one he had been the minute before: wholly in each by turns, and with absolute good faith.

Obviously, I would have been hard put at thirteen to come up with the slightest comment concerning these alternations, and still more to draw any psychological deductions from them. Nevertheless, I think it was an unconscious but edifying revelation for me: an awakening, a first glance into our psychological complexity, a first contact with that extraordinary ability to divide ourselves which has not yet ceased to surprise me. In the course of my life I have met (and I hope, in what follows, to be able to give some curious examples) a prodigious collection of these people with several personalities, with several contiguous and insulated existences, with successive sincerities, with multiple authenticities. I have come to believe that this ability to divide ourselves is one of the most marvelous gifts of human nature, all the more developed when the nature is richer; so much so that that reasonable stability which causes certain individuals not to have any reverse side and to be, as they say, all of a piece, is generally the sign of an irremediable poverty of temperament. But let us go back to Xavier.

I would like to note an example of his ingenuity as an educator: what he called "the dictionary exercise." I actually think he invented it, for I have never seen it used or recommended anywhere else. And yet I know of nothing more entertaining and instructive. The exercise consisted quite simply of coming up with definitions of words. Each day, Balcourt had us devote an hour to this work. He began with common expressions: "If you had to write a dictionary, how would you explain the meaning of the following nouns: *book, pen-box, bedroom, corridor*?" The point was to find a phrase that was general, exact, complete, concise. Each time there was a different problem to solve. I was helped, at the beginning, by the excellence of my visual memory: the concrete things that I was in the habit of seeing I described with sufficient precision and felicity. The difficulty began with the abstract terms. From week to week, Xavier chose thornier words: *helix, fidelity, shadow, sacrifice* . . . The definition of certain verbs presented real puzzles, and the most ordinary were not the easiest to explain: *to be able, to wish, to persuade, to surprise* . . . A number of words had several meanings, which we had to track down and classify, beginning with the etymological sense. It was fascinating. Even the listless Guy came a little to life with this sport. We competed as to who could find the aptest solution. Xavier judged. He brought to this role a rare sagacity, a critical mind, an incomparable refinement of invention. Sometimes he rejected our suggestions out of hand; sometimes he accepted one of our formulations; but he would qualify it, condense it, improve it endlessly. There would ensue a stormy debate in which each vied with the others in subtlety. Then, when we had exhausted all our resources, Xavier would measure our result against that of the two or three good dictionaries that we had at le Saillant, and the comparison would set the dispute going again. Sometimes we had the surprise of finding our definition nearly word for word in one of our dictionaries, and it was a validation that had us shouting with joy. Guy tired of this exercise more quickly than we, but Xavier and I were literally indefatigable at it, and we often continued it, out of pleasure, well beyond the set time. My mind even became so warped by it that I ended up paying more attention to words than to ideas: at table, like a man obsessed, I would lie in wait for difficult words, catch them on the wing, and not refrain from interrupting my father or my sister to fling my spoils triumphantly at Balcourt. I could be heard to proclaim, all of a sudden: "Gear-wheels!" or "Vacillate!" or "Speculation!" . . . Xavier winked, as a connoisseur: "Excellent," he would say. "To be remembered for tomorrow!" My father shrugged, but he smiled: he had too much of a taste for precision not to have approved of this game and understood its import.

I have not forgotten a certain bout which, unusually, took place away from the schoolroom, one spring evening, on the terrace, and in which my father himself took part with unwonted liveliness. To be determined were the exact meanings of three words particularly difficult to define: *misappropriation, embezzlement,* and, if I remember correctly, *malfeasance.* Of course, I kept my peace. The sparring match was confined to my father and Xavier. And I must say that on that day, through the pertinence and clarity of his remarks, my father won in my eyes—and very likely in Xavier's—a prestige that, until then, we had not granted him.

Probably one would need to have practiced this exercise oneself, and every day, as I did in that winter of '82–'83, to see that, beneath its childish surface, it is a matchless means of education. Not only does it enrich the child's vocabulary very quickly and effortlessly, but it shapes and sharpens the mind; it teaches one to concentrate the attention; to clarify one's notions and put them in a rational order; to set each thing in its proper place. I have had a good many opportunities to recount this experience to experts, to specialists, even to the bigwigs of the Instruction Publique; and I have never struck a chord. They deigned to smile, admitted vaguely that the method was ingenious, but their approbation was only graciousness and polite indifference. In fact, with my propaganda for the "dictionary exercise" I have always and everywhere come across as a crank and a bore, without ever convincing anyone of its effectiveness . . .

To boost the attention of the boys that we were, Xavier displayed a surprising ingenuity. One example among a thousand comes to mind. He had asked us to read the translation of the last book of the *Iliad* in order to make a summary of it. And as we seemed to him to lack enthusiasm in the face of those fifty somewhat dense pages, wishing to awaken our curiosity and stimulate our zeal he began to improvise for us a picturesque, colloquial, and vivid account of Priam's visit to Achilles.

It went something like this:

"It's a wonderful episode in the Trojan War. One of the most beautiful things in Greek literature. One of the most beautiful things in any literature . . . But listen. Hector, the Trojan, the son of the old King Priam, had killed Patroclus, the friend whom Achilles cherished above all others. So, determined to avenge the death of his dearly loved friend, Achilles sets off in pursuit of Hector . . . He is about to catch up with him. And what does he see? Hector has got hold of the remains, and as if to taunt Achilles, has put on Patroclus' armor . . . Mad with rage, Achilles rushes at him, takes aim at a joint in his breastplate, and sinks his javelin into him right between the neck and the shoulder . . . Hector falls . . . mortally wounded. But, before expiring, he has time to address a final plea to his vanquisher:

" 'Return my body to the Trojans, Achilles, so that at least I am buried by my own!'

" 'Never!' roars Achilles. 'Your corpse will remain naked and unburied! Devoured by the jackals and the vultures!'

"And he ties up the feet of the dying man, he fastens him behind his chariot, he whips his horses, and he gallops several times around the ramparts until the corpse is torn to pieces by the stones. Finally, when the body is in tatters, he leaves it on the ground, and he goes and shuts himself up alone in his tent, to weep for the friend he has lost."

All of Balcourt's teaching had this improvised and vivid quality: because he was not a professional, because he did not think of applying any learned method, because he was merely intelligent, educated, conscientious, and inventive. He presented himself less as a tutor than as a fellow-student: he lived with us; during school hours, it was at his side, bent together over the same book, that we worked; and if, suddenly, an association of ideas, a personal thought, a memory, prompted him to make a worthwhile digression, he did not hesitate to push the book aside and open up a parenthesis, which took us out of our study program and put us in direct contact with life, with reality.

Of course, this method of teaching, friendly, impulsive, and without punishments, scarcely resembled the one which is inflicted elsewhere on schoolboys our age; but it had much in common, I think, with the one that the tutors of the seventeenth and eighteenth centuries applied to the children who were entrusted to them. It could have drawbacks. It did not for me. I cannot say as much for my cousin. Guy was far too keen on exploiting the situation not to have very quickly grasped the advantage he could take of a teacher so easygoing and so little concerned with his prestige. Since Balcourt willingly let himself lapse into chat, Guy soon excelled at multiplying the insidious questions that postponed the moment of learning the lesson or of writing the homework. And since Balcourt saw his role as an informal collaboration, Guy quickly gave up making the slightest effort and soon contented himself with writing what Balcourt whispered to him: a little more and he would have had his hand held, so as to reduce still further his share of personal effort.

In exchange for this, Guy did not miss a chance to be thoughtful and willing to help. He watched out for all of Xavier's wishes, in order to gratify them. He had noticed that Xavier liked to drink big glassfuls of ice water: he saw to it that the carafe was always full, and kept it in a cool place, on the windowsill. He knew that Xavier had a passion for flowers: at the risk of catching cold, he took advantage of the slightest sunny spell, ran to the garden without a coat, in slippers, picked the last chrysanthemums or the last asters that the autumn frosts had spared, and without saying a word put them in the opaline vase that Xavier had in his bedroom. These were attentions that I would not have thought of, or that, out of self-consciousness, I would never have dared perform . . . If Xavier reproached him for a slapdash homework assignment, far from putting on a sulky face or a contrite look, Guy would present him with his most angelic smile, with his most enveloping gaze; and Xavier, disarmed, would return his smile with an affectionate indulgence and even with something more, with a hint of amusement, of tender surprise, with a look as if thinking: "This little fellow is irresistible."

Between Guy and me, Xavier showed a very clear difference in attitude: that difference which families set up between the elder son, who is treated as a responsible grownup boy, and the younger, the Benjamin, who is brought up a little like a girl and who tends to get away with everything. I never resented Xavier's demands on me. His liking for me was obvious, and I could only feel proud of the serious tone he took with me. I had the better part; how could I have been jealous? I wasn't, but Guy's behavior, certain liberties he took, caused me frequent annoyance; I guessed that they were premeditated; they struck me as unseemly. For example, when Guy called on Xavier to help him translate into French a sentence over which he had dawdled for some time, he gave him his chair with too marked an eagerness for my taste; and he went and sat down at his left, so close, so sweetly, with such apparent spontaneity and abandon, that Xavier quite naturally put his arm around his shoulder, drew him near, sometimes even sitting him on his knee, and, while writing, caressed his nape the way one strokes a kitten. Xavier permitted himself these familiarities with a distracted but obvious indulgence; and Guy, to prolong these cuddles which he had shrewdly angled for, pretended to have trouble understanding and requested explanations with a look of interest that did not fool me. To what extent did it fool Xavier?

Little by little, these touches, these brushes, became a habit with Guy, a need. Thus the slightest scratch, the slightest bruise, served as a pretext for him to call on Xavier's solicitude. It was now always to him and not to Henriette that he went to show his booboos, as if he took pleasure in displaying his cut calf to him, in having him feel his naked arm. Xavier shrugged: "Aren't you soft! A real girl!" He laughed, but he was not insensible to that trust; and, while making fun of him, he did his best to pull the splinter out gently, to put an arnica poultice on the black-and-blue spot. And I found both of them ridiculous.

Since the arrival of the "tutor," Henriette had deliberately stopped taking care of us. The neatness of our bedroom, the supervision of our washing up, the choice of our clothes according to the temperature, all this thenceforth became the responsibility of M. de Balcourt. In the early days, Xavier's vigilance in this secondary sphere was relatively slight. At night, we would go upstairs together, the three of us, with our candleholders, and Xavier would leave us in front of our door, not to reappear until the following morning at seven, our wake-up time. Which he presided over, but from afar: contenting himself with sticking his pointed muzzle in the half-open doorway and wishing us a resounding and collective good morning; then, lamp in hand, because the day was just breaking, tiny in the long greatcoat of reseda wool that served him as a bathrobe, he would wait until one of us—and it was always I—sat up and lit the candle. He would then slip away and would only reappear three-quarters of an hour later to take us to the dining room. He soon realized that so much freedom was not without certain drawbacks: in the night-chilled bedroom, we balked at getting up; we waited until the last minute to leave our warm sheets; we reduced our washing to the minimum, indeed to a mere show; and we were never ready to go downstairs with him when the bell rang. He had to alter his methods: to wait, before returning to his room, not only until we had a light, but until we were both on our feet and well awake; and to come back once or twice afterwards, to check that we were not busy misbehaving instead of getting dressed. To this thankless role of nanny he brought a constant cheerfulness and much consideration: thus, he never entered our room without having knocked and received our assent. Of course, when I was caught between two shirts, I would hurry to get dressed before saying: "Come in." At first, Guy did the same; for, if we no longer felt any sense of modesty with each other, things were different in front of this stranger. Soon I had the surprise of noticing that Guy, in this respect, was growing progressively lax. Example: if Xavier knocked on our door when I was almost dressed but Guy was still traipsing about in his underpants with his chest bare, and if, so that he would have time to cover up, I called out: "Just a minute, please, *monsieur*," Guy would protest: "Why not?" and he would go himself, just as he was, and open the door to Xavier. Then, as if he took pleasure in showing himself off that way, he would be in no rush to get dressed; often he would even force Xavier to examine a red blotch that he had discovered on his torso, or a little pimple that was coming up under his armpit. I was surprised that Xavier did not rebuff him and lent himself so willingly to this waste of time. Although I uncovered secret intentions in Guy's behavior—which I attributed to this need that he always had of making himself the center of attention—until then the suspicion had never crossed my mind that there could have been, on Xavier's part, anything more than kindness. It was only at the return of spring, and after my Aunt Chambost's second visit, during Easter vacation, that the relations between Xavier and Guy began to alter noticeably enough to put me on the alert.

AND THIS LEADS me to take up another aspect of the life of our trio.

I had not been surprised, at first, to see Guy use his charm to get into the good graces of the newcomer: it was altogether in his nature. But soon he no longer contented himself with Xavier's paternal leniency: Guy visibly wanted to conquer him. His game changed in appearance, took on a character of more insistent and less hidden flirtatiousness in direct proportion to the growing evidence of my superiority as a good student and as Xavier, by the way in which he devoted himself to me during the lessons, let it show that he was more interested in my progress than in my cousin's listless performance. As if, in order to get his own back for his mortified pride, Guy had said to himself: "Well, I too know how to catch his attention." (I am oversimplifying: Guy was not cunning enough to make such a Machiavellian calculation; but really, it all happened as if he had devised and progressively carried out a systematic plan of seduction.) The most ingenuous girls are sometimes aware, very early on, of the appeal that their freshness offers and know instinctively how to use it, with a sureness of touch that the most artful of whores would envy. Without any doubt, there was a "whore" side to Guy's nature . . .

I distinctly remember the insidious way in which doubt crept into me, on the day when, for the first time, I thought I detected, in Xavier's foxy expression, a change, a sort of concealed stirring. Naturally, I had no word by which to call this strange agitation; I could not make out where it came from; however, its reprehensible, vaguely dubious character did not escape me. It was during a little scene, the details of which have remained very much with me precisely because of the embarrassment I felt; a distinctive embarrassment, an embarrassment which I had not yet experienced but which Xavier's demeanor was often to make me feel later on.

It happened one Sunday morning. For us, Sunday was not only the day of Mass but also that of the weekly bath. We got up an hour later than during the week; we went downstairs, before washing up, to have our breakfast, at which the café au lait was replaced by Sunday chocolate; then we went back up to our rooms, each with a big cauldron of boiling water. In her luggage Aunt Ma had brought a strange basin of painted zinc, very wide, round, and shallow, which she used every day for her bath. She must have found our habits of hygiene inadequate, for she had left us this object, making us promise to use it once a week. At le Saillant it had been dubbed "the boys' *barbotière*;"* only Guy insisted on saying "the tub."†

That morning, I was, as usual, ahead of Guy. Washed from head to toe, dressed in clean clothes, I was putting on my shoes when the warm voice of Xavier called out to us through the door:

"Are you ready in there? May I come in?"

I turned towards Guy. He had just finished washing up. Standing in the *barbotière*, his back arched, dripping wet, he was drying his hair. Swiftly, he jumped out of the water, wrapped himself in a bathrobe that was lying on the floor, and shouted joyfully:

"Yes, *m'sieu!*"

It was the middle of April: a white sun lit up the bedroom, and one could guess that, outside, the mild air already had a hint of spring in it. At break-

---

*Noun coined from *barboter,* to splash about.
†English in the original.

fast, we had planned a long hike for the afternoon, and Xavier was bringing us the big map of the forest, which he had taken down from the wall of the landing so that we could choose a beautiful route together. He sat down on one of our unmade beds, where Guy came and curled up beside him, and they both bent over the map. I continued to button up my boots, and a lively debate started up over the possible goals of the walk.

Suddenly, Xavier noticed that Guy was shivering with cold:

"But your bathrobe is soaking, *mon petit*! You're going to catch cold! Your teeth are chattering!"

It was true.

"I got the wrong bathrobe," Guy explained.

In his hurry, he had grabbed mine, which covered him like an icy shroud. Xavier became agitated:

"Quick, Bertrand, bring him a dry bathrobe!"

In vain I rummaged through the room's disorder in search of Guy's bathrobe. And, as I turned around to ask where on earth he could have put it, I stopped dead: without waiting, he had let the wet garment slide off him, and he was standing in the middle of the room, completely naked. The blood rose to my cheeks. There was certainly no great cause for this, but—as I have said—I was still, despite everything, a prudish boy. I will add, by way of an excuse, that Guy's nudity was the most indecent possible: that male organ, capped with its black triangle and grafted like something artificial onto that body as pale and slim as a little girl's, had about it something unexpected, provocative, a sort of ostentatious immodesty . . .

Xavier, intimidated, was pulling at his mustache and, to keep his composure, grumbled:

"Hurry up! You're going to catch cold! . . . Where's your bathrobe?" Guy, struck by the curious gaze that had been fixed on him, was stealing a glance at Xavier, a smile on his lips. Suddenly he burst out laughing and moved towards the bed with a hopping step, swaying his hips a little, which he did when he was naked:

"You're sitting on it, *m'sieu . . .*"

Xavier got up hastily to hand the bathrobe to Guy. But, as if he were giving in to a secret impulse, he changed his mind, and, concealing his embarrassment beneath a resolute tone, he brusquely ordered:

"No . . . Lie down there! I'm going to give you a rubdown first . . ."

More and more amused by this whole unforeseen event, Guy stretched out obediently on his bed, from which Xavier had just thrown back the covers . . . And, rolling up his sleeves, he began to rub Guy's chest, arms, and thighs vigorously, which Guy let him do, laughing. He lay across the mattress, legs and arms spread, and, his head back, his mouth open, let out little yelps, as if he'd been tickled.

"Flip over, now," said Xavier, sliding his arm under Guy's body and turning him like a crêpe.

He was probably starting to get tired. He was no longer expending the same energy as at the beginning. With his palm, he softly massaged the back, the small of the back, the jutting little buttocks. Guy was silent and remained motionless, his nose in the bolster. I was standing at the foot of the bed. It was at that moment. I remember very well. I was looking at Xavier. He had his eyelids lowered, his breath came a bit short, and his gray complexion colored. He lifted his eyes, and I met his gaze . . . What could the stirred gaze of an adult reveal to me at that age? Nothing specific, nothing but that stirring itself. Yet that stirring struck me deeply. And I had the impression, at that second, that something was happening in Xavier, something new, something unavowed, something unavowable, something that certainly was not "good" . . .

Xavier had suddenly stopped, as if my attention bothered him. Guy still did not budge. Without explanation, without covering him, Xavier picked him up in his arms and carried him briskly to the other bed, where he thrust him under the covers.

"You, stoke that fire some," he snapped, without looking at me. "Make sure he doesn't get up before he's good and warm."

And, as if some urgent task were calling him, he left the room.

Scarcely was the door closed when Guy sprang out of bed and performed a series of somersaults ending with a masterly "Y," head down and legs in the air, which reassured me completely as to the recovery of his circulation.

"Well," I said, when he was back on his feet, "you really don't mind exposing yourself like that in front of him!"

"Bah," he replied, laughing, "that'll show him!"

He had planted himself in front of the mirror and was smugly running his fingers over himself.

"Do you think he's built differently than us?" he went on, without taking his eyes off the mirror.

And while striking ballerina's poses—a pantomime he liked to do on tub day—he ventured various incongruous suppositions concerning Xavier's anatomy with such a fanciful ribaldry that it was not long before I was sharing his hilarity.

We only saw Xavier an hour later, when he came to tell us that the break was waiting in the courtyard to take us to church. The three of us raced down the staircase jostling each other like youngsters. I noticed nevertheless that Xavier had not asked Guy about his chill; and that, in the afternoon, during our walk, neither Xavier nor Guy seemed to hear a humorous allusion that I made to the scene of the morning.

The incident, however, was not over. The next day, Guy woke up with a stuffy nose, an achy head, a feverish eye. It was fortunately only a mild cold, which ran its course in three or four days during which Henriette, alarmed, made him stay in his room and drink an herb tea that she prepared herself according to a family recipe, with marsh mallow roots, hyssop leaves and poppy flowers. It was supposed he had caught cold in the forest. With a tacit complicity, none of us breathed a word about the wet bathrobe.

But the following Sunday, although he was completely recovered, Xavier did not allow him to take his bath. And the Sunday after, he demanded, in an authoritarian tone that was not usual with him, that Guy let himself be rubbed down upon getting out of his tub.

This was henceforth the new Sunday ritual. As soon as I had finished my washing up, I would go to get Xavier. He would come immediately. Guy would be waiting for him, sitting cross-legged in the *barbotière,* and he would greet him with a roguish smile. Xavier witnessed the soaping, serious, his brows knitted, issuing advice in a gruff tone that did not ring very true; and when he himself had poured two pitchers of hot water over Guy's shoulders, he dried him off, rubbed him down, stretched him out on the bed, and solemnly massaged him; then he returned to his room, without forsaking his sullen air, without responding to the jokes from my cousin, who was never more facetious than during that quarter hour of self-exhibition. As for me, I saw no harm in it. Xavier's assiduity and his prolonged rubdowns were perfectly plausible; it was essential to avoid another chill. It was no different from the thousands of precautions that I had seen taken by Aunt Ma, by Henriette, by my father himself when Guy's health was at stake.

I noticed though, with a certain annoyance, that Xavier was no longer applying the same discretion when it came to entering our quarters and taking part in our private life. He still knocked, but he no longer waited for our reply, so that I often had just enough time to turn around and hastily cover myself in order to be decent. I even remember a day when Xavier almost walked in on me as I was finishing drying myself after getting out of the *barbotière.* I had the presence of mind to wrap around me, like a waist-cloth, the towel that I was holding. But I was put out by the lack of consideration with which Xavier, without a word of apology, came over to talk to me; and was made uncomfortable by the look that he ran, while chatting, over what, quite against my will, I let show of my nakedness.

Other details come to mind. I note them in no particular order.

One day, Xavier realized that Guy never thought of cutting his toenails. "With horns like those, you could hurt yourself walking," he said. "I'm going to trim your claws, since you're too lazy to do it." During the time that he took to go get the scissors in his room, my cousin, who was still in his nightshirt, could easily have put on his pants. He did nothing of the kind. And I can still see him, sprawled on his bed, with no concern for propriety, stretching out first one leg then the other toward Xavier, who, to get a better grip, had knelt on the rug.

How many times, during the increasingly frequent visits that Xavier paid us, while I usually waited for him to leave again so that I could finish washing up—how many times did I see that imp Guy prancing shamelessly across the room with his undershirt floating about his thighs and pushing his indifference to the point of getting down on all fours if his socks or his slippers had got lost under the bed! Or, in this skimpy attire, indulging in his acrobatic capers to amuse Xavier, and, under the guise of balancing and gymnastics, having him admire the famous exercise of the "Y"!

This shocked me, but not much, really; and I laughed with them quite wholeheartedly. At twelve, one easily accepts whatever happens; and all the more so if something recurs with regularity. I was already very accustomed to Guy's exhibitionism; I quickly got used to not being the sole witness of it. As for the sensations which the display of that young nakedness, and his brushing up against it, could arouse in a man of Xavier's age, vested still in my eyes with the prestige of a grownup—how, despite the look that I had intercepted, could I have imagined them? I had not as yet experienced anything comparable. I thought no more about the look, having failed truly to understand its significance. And Xavier concealed his secret stirrings perfectly. The serious, concerned, and slightly displeased expression that he affected at those moments put me off the scent. I did not have Guy's nose.

Since the arrival of Xavier, Guy's "obsessions" did not seem so virulent; at least, I found myself much less involved in them. Xavier was constantly with us, at work and at play. But when our bedtime came round we were alone, and we often took advantage of it to pick up our habitual conversations again. On certain nights, our whisperings went on rather late, from one bed to the other. Guy would imprudently raise his voice, and I would always tremble at the idea that Xavier could hear us.

"Not so loud," I would say. "If he knew what we were talking about . . . !"

"You think he doesn't suspect?" Guy would placidly reply.

"You're too stupid," he told me one day. "Haven't you figured out that as soon as he's by himself, that's what he thinks about, too?" He let out a little knowing laugh, which left me all befuddled. "And," he added with assurance, "he'd even be quite willing to talk about it with us if we gave him the chance."

One night, getting undressed, he complained of a little break in the skin in a very awkward spot, which he had already mentioned to me the day before and which he now had me look at.

"How about if I show him?"

I thought he was joking.

"Why not?" he said, with a wink.

And—out of bravado, I thought—he picked up his candleholder and started for the door.

"Guy! You're crazy!"

He had already lifted the latch. He turned around to enjoy my astonishment, smiled an enigmatic smile, and disappeared into the hallway.

I was sure he wouldn't go. I remained sitting for a moment, expecting to see him come back. Then I felt the cold creep over my legs, and I got into bed. Finally—maybe a half an hour later (which seemed interminable to me)—I saw him reappear. His eyes were shining and he had the same smile, full of innuendoes.

"I can't believe it—you didn't really go in there!"

"No?" he said, coming closer. "He even put some ointment on me!" He took the candleholder on my table and held it low. "Look, moron!"

It was true. I was so stunned that I didn't know what to say. He went off in silence, finished undressing, got into bed, and blew out the light.

I was a long time falling asleep. My first thought, upon waking, was about the break in the skin. "He's going to tell me," I thought. I was wrong. He whistled as he washed; he seemed less cheerful, less of a chatterbox than usual; a little distant, a little pensive.

And I never knew any more about it.

THIS INCIDENT STANDS out in my memory. It was from that day on, it seems to me, that I noticed new and disconcerting changes in their relations. To analyze these is difficult, especially since my recollections more or less overlap one another. What struck me above all was that between Xavier and Guy the temperature became extremely unstable. Until then it had been the opposite: perpetual fair weather. And suddenly, as if their relationship now found itself subject to imperceptible atmospheric fluctuations, it became so changeable that it was impossible to forecast in the morning whether the day would be one of harmony or of discord. That alone, if I had had more experience, ought to have alerted me to the romantic nature of their friendship. To be sure, harmony remained the habitual note, and quarrels, in spite of everything, were rare. Xavier continued to appear uncontrollably receptive to Guy's kindnesses and defenseless against his allurements and liberties, which were each day more indiscreet and more daring. Xavier beheld Guy with a melting eye, gave back smile for smile, and I constantly had the impression that there was a secret between them from which I was excluded. (I also had the feeling that I was the only one in the house to notice it. Indeed, their way of being together, looking at each other and talking to each other when we were among ourselves, and their demeanor as soon as they found themselves in the presence of other people, offered a revealing contrast and rendered the mysterious complicity that united them more blatant.)

But sometimes I saw in Xavier's attitude a sort of inner resistance, a refusal. Without ceasing to be nice, he seemed on the defensive. As if he had sought belatedly to reestablish distances, he adroitly deflected Guy's overtures, put on an indifferent, distracted air; when necessary he went so far as to pretend not to have noticed a considerate gesture or not to have heard the kind word that Guy had just said to him. At times, unceremoniously, he would even stop paying attention to him; he would hardly speak to him, or only with a deliberate chilliness. He took pleasure, one would have said, in finding him at fault; he suddenly noticed his sloppiness, reproached him for his laziness, or made fun of him with a kind of spiteful irritation. Guy, the good sport, answered this short-lived detachment with an impertinent smile, a mocking silence. I would sometimes say to him at night: "So, you had a falling-out?" He would shrug slightly, and his evasive look was indecipherable. But he didn't give me any explanation. On the subject of Xavier he was always reserved with me. For a long time, even, he avoided uttering his name. A taboo subject . . . And I have to say that I did nothing to elicit confidences. At heart, I think I dreaded receiving any.

At other times, the roles were reversed: I was very surprised, one fine morning, to see my cousin entirely change his usual behavior. He stopped all cuddling, gave up his spoiled child's faces, and even, for a whole walk, ignored Xavier and did not address him directly; or else he would cut him short, argue, arrogantly stand up to him. He seemed at that time to have the advantage over him and to be able to get away with anything. To my astonishment, on those days, instead of reacting, calling Guy to order, Xavier generally showed a conspicuous weakness: he beat a retreat and made no retort to Guy's impertinences; one would have said that they hurt too much for him to have thought of taking offense at them, that they only awakened bewilderment and pain in him. He would then have an unhappy, repentant look which I did not understand, and which gave me a keen sense of discomfort. What did he have to be forgiven for? . . . This would always end with a long tête-à-tête in Xavier's room, whence Guy would return red-eyed and less communicative than ever. After which, to my great relief, everything would seem to be forgotten.

I have retained the memory of one of these falling-outs because of its repercussions. It had lasted a whole week, without letup or reconciliation. Sunday came. Since the famous morning of the wet bathrobe, Xavier had never failed to attend my cousin's Sunday wash-up and to give him his rub-down. That day, Guy got hold of the *barbotière* before me, and when he was rinsed and dry, he knotted the belt of his bathrobe with a decisive gesture and phlegmatically left the room. When he returned, a long time after, bright-eyed and whistling, I realized that peace had been made. And, from then on, it was behind closed doors, in Xavier's room, that the Sunday rubdown was performed.

About this subject I asked myself many questions. Why in Xavier's room? What was going on there between them?

It is very hard for me, today, to describe clearly the suppositions that were forming in my head. Of course I could not help vaguely sensing something dubious in the air. But from that to being able to imagine with exactitude just what a respectable man of Balcourt's age and a boy like Guy could do together, there was a big step to take; I was too inexperienced; my conjectures remained very muddled. They did not become clear until later, when the lack of privacy at boarding school had stripped me of my innocence for good. When I then thought back on le Saillant, on Xavier's and Guy's attitudes, I at once naturally suspected the worst, I did not hesitate to think that their liaison had taken them both as far as possible in the practices of which at the boarding school I discovered so many examples around me.

Well, it was a mistake. I know now that I was wrong. I know that in Xavier's and Guy's tête-à-têtes there was *nothing* going on: nothing more than in my presence. As improbable as that may seem, it is so.

I have it from Xavier himself, who gave me his assurances several years later. And his veracity cannot be questioned. At that time, he was speaking to me very openly, and I had already received from him a good many of the most cynical confessions. If his love for Guy at the time had not remained platonic, he would have told me in so many words. On the contrary, he repeated to me any number of times: "But it was in front of you, Bertrand, that I allowed myself the most things! In front of you, I could risk going to the limits of the possible; I was sure I wouldn't go as far as the irreparable. In your presence, I felt sheltered from myself, reassured . . . On the other hand, as soon as the boy and I were alone, I felt at his mercy; and above all, at my own! . . . Then, I was so afraid of myself, afraid of him, that I didn't dare even touch him, I shunned even his gaze, I no longer thought about anything but throwing him out of my room, on any pretext whatsoever, to put a stop to that infernal struggle with my desires!"

But he did not readily talk about this: he had never got over Guy's death, and dreaded reviving his memories. I did not actually know the real story behind all this until after Balcourt's suicide, when I had to go through the private notebooks, the notes, the manuscripts found in his drawers, of which he made me the heir. Yes: it was only at that moment that the relations between Xavier and Guy finally seemed to come clear to me, in their true colors; when I discovered, among those papers, the rough draft of a short story which he had quite explicitly entitled *"Détournement de majeur."** (Many other experiences of his love life were thus disclosed to me by going through his notes. I am thinking, for example, of the drowning of a baker's apprentice, the subject of another story,† which is itself extremely revealing. I intend to recount, at its proper time, that appalling adventure, which was not without relevance to his death, since it was one of the causes of the nervous breakdown that preceded his suicide.)

The short story, *"Détournement de majeur,"* had as its setting an orphanage in the country, where, during the vacation, a few boarders who had no relative to take them in had stayed on, watched over by a student supervisor. Laxer discipline, long walks, outdoor games, etc. The drama slowly developed between one of the little outcasts of fortune—a disquieting boy, for whom it was not the first experience—and the young tutor, who progressively let himself be stirred by the bold and quite intentional provocations of the child. Although the young man had never been affected before by any temptation of this nature, he yielded little by little, out of curiosity, out of weakness, to the perverse tricks, to the increasingly explicit liberties that the boy allowed himself. For the latter, it was only a premeditated pursuit, a baiting, a depraved and cynical game. For the teacher, it had almost immediately become a consuming, irresistible blaze—to which he had surrendered himself without restraint, in defiance of all prudence . . . The rest, as far as I remember, was melodramatic and much more banal (probably because it was entirely imagined, divorced from any autobiographical element). The relationship, betrayed to the neighbors by the tattling of the other students, became a subject of scandal in the village. The police were alerted: investigation, damning testimony, interrogations, imminent arrest . . . The final pages contain only cursory, rather contradictory, notations; I remember that Balcourt, for his denouement, was still hesitating between the suicide of the tutor and his trial in criminal court.

Obviously, the adventure with Guy is only a pale image and, as it were, the timid foreshadowing of the intrigue that Balcourt was to imagine, amplify, "romanticize" later, in order to compose his tragic story of the orphanage. But the very fact that he had the idea of this subject so long afterwards and the pathetic tone in which he was able to present the passion of his young tutor were a revelation for me. Especially since the portrait of the boy, whose triangular face, wide sensual mouth, bright and caressing gaze—in a word, everything, down to the slender body and the little bird's neck—glaringly conjured up Guy's physical characteristics.

Corruption of an Adult, with a play on words: a *majeur* being the opposite of a *mineur*.
†Martin du Gard instead relates this incident as recorded in Xavier's diary. See Chapter XIII.

Despite appearances, there were thus, at le Saillant, only preludes: on Guy's part, an attempt at *Détournement de majeur*, but nothing more than a hesitant, inexpert, half-conscious one; on Xavier's part, nothing that resembled the corruption of a minor . . . Admittedly, my cousin carried on quite a diabolical game: less premeditated but similar, all the same, at least in its effects, to that of the little delinquent at the orphanage. As the female senses the male's urge, he had, with his sensual young animal's antennae, detected the arousal in the adult; but he did not know to call it by its true name: desire. Heedlessly attracted by the temptation of the new, of the unknown, pushed by his greedy curiosity rather than by a physical goad, and, I think, without quite knowing where he was heading or what he might be in for, he did everything to bring about the irremediable. And the irremediable did not come to pass. Why? Xavier told me himself that if he had been more forward, Guy would not have defended himself; and I can easily believe it. Moreover, he did not conceal that if such an opportunity had been offered him several years later, when his sexual tastes had been definitively set, no scruple would have been strong enough to hold him back. But at that time it was his *first* temptation. Whatever the intensity of his lust might have been, he was still too much of a novice, too timorous, to give in to it. The shock that he had received while contemplating that androgyne's body in its tantalizing nakedness had shaken him to the depths of his instincts; but his instincts still lay dormant. So long as he lived at le Saillant, he succeeded in keeping them repressed. He knew all the torments of the imagination; he allowed himself everything, in thought; but in thought only. He confined himself to playing with fire; to feasting his eyes, as often as possible, on the spectacle of that blooming flesh; he granted himself all the contact that any pretext could camouflage, make licit. Nothing more. A hundred times, he told me, he was, in a fit of giddiness, on the verge of explicit fondling. Each time, his timidity was stronger: a sort of panic seized him in his gut, made him break off the rash movement which he had already begun; which, in his dreams, he had so many times completed . . . Abruptly, with a frightened start, he would stop short or take flight. And I remembered, listening to him, the brusque way that he sometimes had of leaving us suddenly, his features tense, without a word. He himself marveled at having had the courage so many times, at the last second, to stay his hand and turn the boy out of his room, and to run off somewhere by himself, until walking and solitude had calmed his longings and dampened the fever that was consuming him. The passion he had had for Guy was, if you believed him, the first, and by far the most ardent he had ever endured. "Le Saillant?" he said: "my *Season in Hell!*"

When I had the draft of his short story before my eyes, the profound impression that he had kept of this unconsummated adventure appeared to me with blinding obviousness. I happened in fact to be the only reader informed enough to recognize, between the lines, all the elements of the past. I remain convinced that this dubious yet chaste passion had a decisive influence on his existence: that it was at the source of that sexual orientation which he himself confessed to me, and which we discussed often and freely in the course of our friendship. Was that orientation inscribed from the beginning in his psychic and physical nature? I believe it was, and I often had occasion to tell him so. In conversation, he would not refute this; on the contrary: he seemed to find in it some sort of justification that he needed. But in his heart of hearts he must have doubted it: otherwise, he would have blithely pursued his inclination with complete freedom, as have so many of his kind. Yet he did no such thing. In reality, and until his death, I caught him struggling ceaselessly against his instincts which, however, neither his reason nor his ethics succeeded in condemning. Periodically, some obscure regret, some haunting feeling of guilt, of malediction, would slip into his conscience and taint the pagan wellspring of his joys. It was quite strange. Never did he truly consent to accept himself as he was; never did he manage to free himself altogether from that insidious inner disapproval. He sought in vain to combat it, deny it: it weighed on his entire life. His very suicide gave me the ultimate proof of this, and would remain inexplicable for me if I did not know that a few weeks before the fatal act he had once again toyed with the chimerical hope of reforming his nature, that he had rashly considered the antidote of marriage, and that he had only made up his mind to disappear after having suffered a mortifying failure.

But let us return to le Saillant.

I IMAGINE THAT it was, above all, to flee a situation which had become untenable and to escape a temptation the opportunities for which the holidays would have inevitably multiplied if he had spent them with Guy, that Xavier, on the pretext of visiting his mother, left le Saillant at the end of July and went off for two months to be with Mme. de Balcourt in Paris.

Besides, the notion that I have kept of that summer of '83 is very vague. Did Aunt Ma come back to see her son? Probably; but her stay must have been brief. I am sure, in any case, that I did not see Uncle Éric again. That was the year, I believe, when the trip of which he spoke so often must have taken place, the one he took with my aunt to Sweden and Norway in order to study the interplay of institutions there; a trip that was the origin of one of his best books: *The Social Question in the Scandinavian Countries.*

Balcourt made his reappearance for the start of the new school year, and our academic existence resumed its course. A few weeks later, Guy took to his bed; and the fact that looms over this period for me, blotting out all the rest, is Guy's illness.

After an exceptionally mild month of October, one night, without any transition, a sudden drop in temperature plunged us treacherously into the midst of winter. We woke up freezing, with frost on the windowpanes. Hurriedly, the stoves were stoked. The schoolroom was soon warm; but our bedroom, with its two rooms communicating by a wide opening, did not heat up so easily; and the corridors were icy. Guy, less robust than Xavier or I, and always careless about covering up, caught a chill. The old doctor from Menneville, whom my father summoned immediately, thought at first that it would only be a bad cold. The patient was made to stay in bed. But three days later he began coughing and the fever slowly rose. It was already no longer being spoken of as a cold but as bronchitis when one morning, after the daily auscultation, the doctor, worried, murmured the word "pneumonia," advised that the Chambost-Lévadés be informed, and asked for a consultation. Alerted by wire, Aunt Ma arrived at le Saillant accompanied by a specialist from Paris, the same who, eighteen months earlier, had prescribed the stay in the country for Guy.

It is not easy for me to sort out my memories. It seems to me that this illness kept us in suspense for an interminable time, and that these oscillations between fear and hope disrupted the routine of our life for months. In reality, there must have been three or four weeks of serious anxiety during which Aunt Ma stayed with us, then two or three more weeks of convalescence. I have two reference points; Guy fell sick in the very first days of November, and for Christmas he was on his feet—I can still see him, pale, thinner, having supper with us in the dining room, which was decorated with candles and festoons of ivy.

I especially remember the very distinctive atmosphere which permeated the house during those weeks of uncertainty. A collective state of mind was spontaneously established which seemed to abolish individual peculiarities, differences in character, habits, functions, and even social distances: a warm unanimity, without precedent and without sequel. The coachman, the gardener, the maids, were just as affected by the irruption of this shared preoccupation in their everyday existences as Xavier, Henriette, and even my father, who had partly given up his rides on the estate and seldom left the corner by his fire anymore except to wander the corridors in search of news. The barriers which as a rule separated the material and moral life of the inhabitants of le Saillant had miraculously disappeared. An altogether special understanding was created among Xavier, Henriette, Aunt Ma, and me, who were the only ones to take turns at Guy's bedside. And what struck me most was my sister's new attitude regarding Xavier. They had already lived an entire year beneath the same roof without her having dropped her reserve. Obviously, the feeling of preconceived hostility that she experienced at the beginning toward the tutor chosen and imposed by Uncle Éric had rather quickly subsided; she had appreciated his perfect manners, the deference he showed her, the respect with which he surrounded my father, his discretion, the genuine liveliness he brought to meals; and, insofar as she could judge it, she recognized the intelligent zeal that he put into fulfilling his role with us. Nevertheless, she continued to treat him with a polite indifference; she never joined in any of our walks, she avoided all private conversation with Xavier and addressed him only in a tone of distant amiability, which seemed always to remind him that he would never be for her anything but a passing stranger.

Within a few hours, this entire line of defense vanished as if by magic. The metamorphosis, if I may so put it, took place under my eyes right at the start of the illness, on the evening when the state of the patient seemed to worsen and when, my father being absent, Xavier and Henriette had to confer together to cope with the unforeseen.

Late that Sunday, after some hours of abatement, Guy's temperature had suddenly risen to a hundred and four. It was the first serious warning sign. I saw clearly that it worried Xavier. He left me alone at the patient's side and ran to tell Henriette. My father had left at dawn for the fair at Térouges and would not return until quite late in the evening. Henriette went over to Guy, who was lying in the hollow of the bed, short of breath, curled up like a sick little marmoset. She smiled at him, pushed back the forelock that the sweat was making stick to his forehead, plumped the pillow, and slipped her fingers under his wrist to take the pulse; then she turned back towards Xavier, who was watching her, and they exchanged a glance. It was this glance that surprised me. Under the circumstances, it was, in itself, nothing extraordinary. But it showed, suddenly, a tacit complicity; and for me, accustomed to the discreet chilliness of their relations, that complicity was something unusual. I was as shaken by it as if Henriette had told me: "Guy is in danger." I did not have time to be further surprised. As if he had only been waiting for this glance to put into execution a plan worked out in advance between them, Xavier motioned to me to give him a hand. Henriette was already moving the bed table away and rolling up the rug. Guy's bed was alongside the partition: it had to be gently moved and placed with its head to the wall in such a way that one could move around it to take care of the patient more easily. Guy followed us with his eyes, in silence: no matter how weakened he was by the fever, he always took pleasure in being fussed over.

Henriette sent me to look for the folding table which was used in the summer on the terrace. When I came back, Xavier and she were busying themselves around my bed: they were making it up with Xavier's sheets, which he had got from his room. They had both decided that a cot would be set up for me in the schoolroom, and that from now on Xavier would spend his nights in my place. It was only natural; but that Henriette should help

Xavier make his bed, without asking Ernestine to do it, was one more proof of that unexpected familiarity, of that pact of companionship, which had just been established between them.

The bed made, there was a brief exchange in undertones, and my sister quickly left the room. I helped Xavier unfold the garden table, cover it with a towel, and move it over to the patient. When Henriette returned, everything was ready to receive the strange appurtenances she brought on a tray: an alcohol lamp, a wad of cotton wool, and a dozen little balloon-shaped glasses whose purpose I did not know. My arm trembled slightly as I kept the candlestick raised above Guy's puny back while Xavier took one after another of the prepared glasses that Henriette handed him; he would deftly set the cotton ball alight, and, with the confident movement of a torturer, apply the cupping glasses to either side of the spine. I watched with fright as the skin reddened and swelled up, surprised that the victim let it be done so meekly; motionless, his face in the pillow, he merely gave out each time, as if to keep score, a lambkin's bleat that went to my heart.

I have another very clear memory from that same evening. It must have been rather late. My father had long since come back from Térouges; he had immediately paid a visit to the patient and had a long conference at the head of the stairs with my sister and Xavier. Then Henriette came to kiss Guy and to check that Xavier did not need anything: she had made him promise to knock on her door if anything happened and had given him, as she left, a frank and affectionate handshake, quite different from those they normally exchanged. At that point, I remained alone for an instant at Guy's bedside while Xavier got undressed in his room. The cupping glasses had momentarily stopped the cough. The patient, relieved, was beginning to fall asleep when Xavier reappeared in his greenish bathrobe, a book under his arm and his lamp in his hand. At the noise of the latch, which it was impossible to avoid making, Guy reopened his eyes and smiled at him.

"Now you need to get some rest, Bertrand," said Xavier in a low voice.

He went over to the bed as I was walking to the door. Turning around, I saw him lean down, slide a hand under Guy's head, and, tenderly, press his lips to his forehead.

I must have been stirred by this gesture of Xavier's for the image to have been etched with such precision in my memory. It was, in fact, the first kiss that I saw him give Guy. This surprises me today, when I think of the familiarity of their relations. Xavier did not mind stroking Guy's nape in front of me, encircling his waist, or pulling him up against him when they were bending together over a page of the dictionary. And, on the first fine spring evenings, when Guy would take us, at twilight, to the far end of the terrace to watch the sun disappear behind the forest, and, on the stone bench where all three of us squeezed together, Guy, like an easily chilled little monkey, would snuggle up to Xavier and in a tender voice ask him the names of the first stars, Xavier did not hesitate to put his hand on Guy's head, the better to press it to the hollow of his shoulder. How did he resist the temptation to kiss the little face that was held out to him? My presence almost sanctioned it. However, he never did it. Never. And I have every reason to believe that what he did not dare in front of me he forbade to himself even more severely when they were alone. Yes: the kiss which, from the doorway, I saw him place on Guy's feverish forehead I am certain was the first; and I am also certain that this kiss was almost as chaste as the one given a few moments before by my sister. For there is no doubt in my mind that Xavier's feeling changed character under the pressure of worry. From the day when the tempting little demon who beset him with his provocations became, nestled in his damp bed, only the listless body of a sick child, racked by coughing, which Xavier had to soothe, succor and bring back to life, his passion was suddenly purified. He no longer had to repress that love which was poisoning his blood. He no longer even had to keep it secret: Guy had become the permissible object of everybody's attentions, the center of all solicitude. No token of tenderness was any longer excessive or suspect. On the contrary, everyone was grateful to Balcourt for the attachment, the measureless devotion that he showed for our patient.

Who can say what sensual flame still smoldered, perhaps unconsciously, beneath his zeal as a nurse? The fact remains that, in his new role, Xavier proved to be truly outstanding. His vigilance was tireless, his intuitions always right, his care of a proficiency, a skill, that was incomparable. He had a feminine gentleness for handling those aching little limbs. No intimate duty repelled him. He would get up five or six times a night to keep the fire going, give Guy his spoonful of syrup, prepare an inhalation for him, make him drink his herb teas. At the slightest increase in perspiration, he would change the linen and replace the little hot water bottle at Guy's feet. My aunt Chambost herself, who, as soon as the pneumonia set in, had hastened to her son's side and was preparing to send for a nun, was forced to admit that Xavier was irreplaceable; and it was she who insisted that he continue to sleep in Guy's bedroom. Night and day, he remained on watch: it seemed as though he sensed peril. And if no complication arose during the night when Guy first spat blood, it was surely thanks to Xavier's vigilance and his presence of mind. He knew that in such a case, absolute immobility, calm, and silence are the primary indispensable precautions. He did not alert anyone, for fear of provoking panic, noise, disorder; he took, by himself, the initiatives that were needed. I have forgotten what they were. Mustard plasters, I think, and dry cupping glasses. What I remember is that his performance that night earned him the congratulations of the doctor, summoned at daybreak.

And I also remember how much that first hemoptysis upset us all. Inexperienced as we were, we all thought that Guy had just escaped death. I know now that these complications, if they are always a serious indication, are quite common in the course of a pulmonary ailment and that they rarely put the life of a patient at risk. There was in fact a second, then a third, at intervals of a few days. My aunt, frightened, then had the specialist from Paris return. He declared that the present crisis was in remission and that Guy's condition gave him no immediate concern. But he did not hide the seriousness of the case or the necessity for protracted treatment. He insisted that my aunt take Guy for an eight- or ten-month stay in the mountains as soon as he recovered enough to withstand the strain of a trip.

I place these hemorrhages at the end of November. A month later, for Christmas, Guy was back on his feet. Meanwhile, his mother had returned to Paris to prepare their departure for Switzerland. She came back to fetch Guy shortly after New Year's. Uncle Éric, detained by his courses, could not get away: it was Xavier who was given the responsibility of going with my aunt so that she would not have to make the trip alone with the convalescent.

I remember their departure, in the old coupé, one clear morning in January. A timid sun lit up the courtyard without managing to melt the heaps of snow gathered in the corners. All the servants were around us, at the top of the front steps. Aunt Ma bustled about to benumb herself, counted and recounted her numerous pieces of luggage, said goodbye to us with tears and laughter in her voice. My father and Henriette had thoughtful faces, and remained silent. I was very moved. I wept. I somewhat held it against Guy that he could not conceal the amusement he felt at this whole commotion, of which he knew himself to be the cause. Xavier wrapped him in a great green checked blanket, made a snug hood for him, then picked him up in his arms to carry him to the carriage. My father drew his watch from his fob, helped Aunt Ma into the coupé, and gave the signal. The equipage turned in the courtyard, went out the gate at a jog trot, and disappeared around the bend.

I can see again, at that moment, half hidden in the folds of a wool plaid, a small face with sunken cheeks, an impish smile, and, beneath tired eyelids, an amused and cuddlesome look fixed on me: the last vision that I retain of my little cousin Guy.

Xavier's absence was brief: about a week. Nevertheless, when he came back to us, the life of le Saillant, so deeply disrupted during the autumn, had had time to resume a quiet course; which went on, it seems to me, all winter long. Curious, how few memories I have kept of that year 1884 . . . Caught, and as it were smothered between two of the most significant episodes of my childhood (the eighteen months of life shared with my cousin Guy, and my entry into the Saint-Léonard boarding school), that final and sedate year of familial existence has almost entirely faded from my memory. Thus there are, in the motion pictures of our past, inexplicable gaps, reels of almost unexposed film from which it is impossible to extract a meaningful series of clear and coherent images. Yet that was the year of Guy's death; and this event had such an impact, although momentary and circumscribed, on my nervous stability that it must have left an indelible mark on me.

Guy passed away at the beginning of the spring of '84, after six months of a progressive weakening which no treatment had been able to check. Nothing had prepared me for this outcome. Why had so much care been taken to hide from me the more and more alarming letters which Aunt Ma wrote from Switzerland? I do not remember how I learned the truth, but the shock must have been terrible, since the doctor had to be sent for in the night. I have been told that I was put to bed for several days in a dark room, my head wrapped in cold compresses; and I took, it seems, a good week to recover, to regain enough calm to be able to resume my studies with Xavier.

What I recall quite well, on the contrary, are the two memories, particularly insistent, which haunted me. Sometimes I would see Guy again in his sickroom, just as when I had sat up with him, alone, on a certain evening in the autumn, while his mother, with Henriette and Xavier, were showing the doctor to the door and lingering with him downstairs. A bedside lamp lit the emaciated little face. I again saw the waxen transparency of his forehead, the unhealthy rosiness of his cheeks, the shadow which hollowed out his eyesockets, and, in the pupils enlarged by fever, a fixed gaze which did not seem to see anything. Never have I been able to forget the scare which that absent gaze gave me—surprised, motionless, of an abnormal, unbearable brilliance. And now that Guy was no more, it was thus that I imagined him on his deathbed, certain that he had had that same gaze at the fatal moment.

At other times, when, obsessed by this notion of his death, a strange one for me, I tried hard to visualize Guy as an inanimate cadaver, it was an older memory, an image at once cruel and tender, which came to mind.

One torrid evening the previous summer, we had gone up to bed. The windows were wide open, the room without light. While Guy began to get undressed, I had leaned on my elbows at the window in search of a bit of coolness, and I remained there to daydream, unable to tear myself away from the fairylike scene of the terrace and the countryside beneath the moon. Surprised by the prolonged silence which was scarcely like my cousin, I turned around. Guy, entirely undressed, arms and legs stretched out, had thrown himself across his bed and dropped off into a deep sleep. Head thrown back, lips parted, eyelids closed, limbs spread, he lay there in a state of abandon, at once supple and inert, like a freshly mown sheaf. I went over to him and, for one long moment, holding my breath, I contemplated that young flesh which lay before me in the semidarkness, and from which there seemed to well up a kind of light. Then I cautiously moved away and went to bed without waking him up.

These two visions, so different, moving in such different ways, imposed themselves on me in turn. They were linked to my little cousin's death; they were like a plastic representation of it. And, many years later, whenever I happened unexpectedly to think back on Guy's tragic fate, it was inevitably one or the other of these two images that would be projected before my eyes.

GUY'S DEMISE WAS my first encounter with death. A few months earlier, he had been among us, vivacious, sprightly, happy-go-lucky; and suddenly, for no reason, he had ceased to be that living Guy, real and tangible, to become no more than a shade, an imaginary character, referred to by a name, as in books . . . He had been forever deprived of that material existence without which I could no longer imagine him, without which he was no longer anything but a flimsy, distant, almost foreign memory . . . For no reason! In spite of all the care! Neither his mother's tenderness, nor my affection, nor that need which all of us had of his bodily presence, had been able to save him from that incomprehensible destruction! That, above all, I could not accept. Everything in me rose up against that inconceivable hoax, that monstrous injustice of which he was the victim and all of us with him. My grief was nothing beside that burst of impotent rebellion which set me wholly against death. Of course, with Henriette, with Xavier, only at the mention of Guy's name I felt my heart melt and I could not hold back my sobs. But that feeling of distress, of sorrow, of despair, was far more intermittent in me and much less violent than my indignation, my revolt. I came up against that inexplicable fact as against a wall. Until then, all of my experiences had been discoveries of life. I became aware, suddenly, of nonbeing; and faced with nothingness I was, above all, *disconcerted.*

I am rereading what I have written. I believe that all of it is strictly true, that this really was the essential character of my reactions at the time.

And yet, if I want to remain truthful, I also have to confess this, which seems in contradiction with what has been said so far: I quickly, incredibly quickly, resigned myself to the death of my cousin Guy.

Is this to say that I am less sensitive in my affections, less vulnerable, more self-centered, than another? It may be. At any rate I have had, since birth, an obvious disposition not to rebel for long against what comes to pass, and, however painful it may be, to accept the fait accompli when it is beyond my power to alter anything. In other words: an instinctive incapacity for prolonged and futile regrets . . . I admit that I have done nothing to suppress this tendency in my nature. I have even sometimes cultivated it, encouraged it. I have none of what I call the fetishism of suffering which is so widespread in so many various and insidious forms. After the loss of a loved one—at the death of my sons, for example—I have never had the temptation to which so many others yield, to settle into a funereal self-indulgence, in my mourning: I have never held against myself, as a selfish weakness or a posthumous infidelity, the effort I have made, knowingly, to dismiss memories and sentimental obsessions as much as possible and to welcome, to instigate if need be, all the diversions likely to relieve my thoughts of a sadness which could only be unproductive.

Not so my father, who was unable to resign himself to his widowerhood and whose latent grief, unexpressed, incurable, weighed down my entire childhood and my sister's adolescence with the stifling atmosphere of a silent and frozen existence. The austerity, the monastic monotony, of that family life were not deliberate; not even conscious; they had become established gradually, as expedients to make the course of the days and the passive wait for death less noticeable.

Henriette, on the other hand, was like me: submissive to the event, little given to regret, she lived effortlessly in the present. Which did not prevent her, any more than it did me, from attaching the greatest value to the past and from thinking of it often, but with a cold, detached lucidity, and without ever seeking in it a reason to become emotional.

When she and I found ourselves together again at le Saillant, we did not tire of returning interminably to our shared life of the past. How many evenings—in the winter by the fire, in the summer on the terrace, lying side by side beneath the great black twinkling sky—did we thus devote to comparing our memories, conjuring up the departed, precisely limning, thanks to the perspective of many years, their faces and their characters, rummaging together through every nook of that half-forgotten universe where there always remained things to clear up, to understand better, to judge more fairly, sometimes even to discover—truly. And this was where the kindred similarity of our temperaments plainly came to light; those forays, which fascinated us equally, were a diversion for us, to which was added on rare occasions a fleeting hint of melancholy.

I see again, turned towards me, Henriette's beautiful, spirited face, her open smile, her eyes sparkling with joyous complicity; I hear her voice melt suddenly, vanishing in a throaty laugh, which was so young, so infectious, and which she still had at the age of fifty . . . Facing what was past, though it was one of the happiest periods of our youth, we had a sort of historian's impassiveness, a lively curiosity to find our trail again and pursue it, but no feeling of regret; we accepted, both of us, without any difficulty, that the past was past.

I REALIZE, reading over what I have written, that my feelings regarding Guy's death evolved in a manner less simple than I at first let on. It remains true that I resigned myself to this loss with a strange rapidity; but, in fact, my mind was occupied much longer by this death than I have said, owing to a sort of transference: it was through Aunt Ma that I continued to suffer. I accustomed myself easily enough to the idea that I would never see my cousin again, but I did not stop thinking about my aunt, about her solitude, about her immense pain, and as soon as I tried to imagine what this mutilation was for her, I felt a refusal from my entire being, a physical contraction, a laceration far more agonizing than my personal grief had been.

In that, I detect a deep, secret, unconscious, and already very keen emotion. I was smitten with Aunt Ma. Without suspecting it, I must have loved her ever since I had met her, since the day I had seen her get out of the carriage at the front steps of le Saillant, in her coat with its bustle and beneath her white lace veil.

This child's love—born in the very young heart of a boy of twelve who had not known his own mother—nourished itself, during that winter of 1884, on such an intense compassion that it took deep root in my unconscious. And if this attachment did not always have a solely filial character, as I have long believed, it was probably because at that time, under the guise of pity, a new element of a more passionate nature slipped into it.

But I will have to explain better the unique role that Aunt Ma played in my life and that sort of adoptive guardianship which she exercised over me a little later, during the most receptive years of my adolescence. I simply note here the effect which, indirectly, the death of my cousin had on the development of my emotions. And on those of Aunt Ma, besides. A double effect; for there is no doubt that my aunt's attitude toward me would not have been entirely the same if Guy had lived. When, as a young man, I came to live with her in Paris, I am not saying that I occupied a place which Guy's death had left vacant but rather that I benefited spontaneously from a maternal tenderness of which her misfortune had prematurely deprived her.

I ought to be able to say a word about Xavier's grief, about his attitude towards me during that winter, about our work in common, etc. It is surprising that this period of my life left so few impressions. I think I see the reason for it. That was the year of my puberty. (On this point, I have reference marks: during my cousin Guy's whole stay at le Saillant, I had remained a child, in spite of my long legs and my young peasant's shoulders; whereas, a year later, when I arrived at boarding school, I was sexually formed and already so completely so that my self-esteem hardly had to fear comparison with those of my schoolmates who claimed to be the best endowed.) That year had therefore been of the utmost importance in my physiological development. And this evolution, which was belated, which, in short, had been rapid and probably rather drastic, doubtless suffices to explain this gap that I find in my memory. Several times in the course of my existence I have had the chance to observe boys who were going through this critical age. I have often been struck by their uneasy, absent expressions; it was obvious that they were seriously shaken by the secret operations which were taking place in their bodies, were affected deep down by the development of their organs, and seemingly overburdened by the momentary disorder that this unstoppable rising of sap produced in their physical equilibrium. Well, I must have been like that, continuing to lead my daily life, my life as a good student, but entirely beset by obscure forces, withdrawn, prostrate, passive, and so little attentive to external circumstances that not a single memory of them has stayed with me.

CHAPTER VI

Year of Rhétorique* at Saint-Léonard

THE SAINT-LÉONARD SCHOOL was located at the very top of the old town of Gevrésy, next to the church of Saint-Léonard, in what must have been the outbuildings of the former priory. After going through the forest to the high road and then four leagues in a straight line across the Perche countryside with villages on either hand, you reached the railroad crossing of the train station at the foot of Gevrésy, and the town rose in tiers before your eyes, dominated at the top by the steeple and the tall buildings of the school. You climbed the long slope at a walk; you entered what was called the old town, whose cobbled, narrow streets ran between hovels and residences with imposing portals; as a shortcut, you took a cobbled alley with a gutter down the middle where two carriages could not get by each other; you went along the apse, and, in the square that opened out behind the church, you finally arrived at the old gate of the school.

It was run by Jesuits.

The gate opened only to a ring of the bell and through the good offices of an old porter who was both the sacristan of the chapel and the keeper of the

*In the lycée system of the time, the grades went in the following order as one advanced: quatrième, troisième, seconde, rhétorique, philosophie.

poor garden, behind which rose the main building and to which the students never had access. Having entered, one had to walk round a lawn, at the center of which stood a statue of Saint Léonard in the middle of a bed of sun-broiled geraniums, and to climb some front steps before reaching the flagstone-paved vestibule, onto which the double door of the parlor opened.

It was the eve of the fall term. A young priest, seated at a little table in the vestibule, smiled at the arrivals, wrote down their names, and directed the new boys into the parlor.

A few new boys, having come early like my father and myself, and accompanied by a parent, were waiting silently in small groups in the large room, whose three curtainless windows overlooked the senior boys' yard. The parlor was furnished with chairs covered in blue rep. At the center, in a jardinière of house plants, was a statue of the Holy Virgin. Black-framed blowups of old priests, the school's former superiors, hung in a line on the walls, and the largest panel was reserved for the honor roll, where the names of the previous year's prize-winning students and those who had passed the *baccalauréat* were inscribed on little gilt-edged cards.

I was quite overcome. My father, dressed in black as when he went to a funeral, wore an unusual expression, at once formal and offhand. Seated on a chair too low for his long legs, he looked like a squatting giant. From the carriage the porter had taken the little black wooden box and the old straw carry-all into which Henriette and I had piled my books and my clothes, so that my arms were left dangling and I did not know what to do with my hands. This wait was like those at the dentist's. A door opened, a priest with a beautiful old man's face, bald and fine-featured, leaned out and with a broad welcoming gesture motioned a mother and her son into his office. Then silence fell again.

Finally it was our turn. My father let me go in front of him. The superior had us sit down and went back to his seat, behind his big table loaded with record books, files, letters. The interview was short and very cordial. It touched on the studies I had completed, about which the superior did not hide his disapproval: it was rare, he said, that a student who had not followed the general academic program of the school system could keep up with the class he was put in. However, he admitted with good grace that my entrance examinations, the marks of which he found immediately in a file, were very good. He made some laudatory remarks about the fathers who were going to have me in their classes. Then the conversation, up to that point rather conventional, took, to the priest's visible satisfaction, a social turn, veering off towards some of the region's notable families, whose offspring were going to be my schoolmates, and suddenly became animated when my father and the superior realized that they had many acquaintances in common among the local squires. Names followed names. The superior smiled as if he had been at a procession of friends. He knew all the nobility of the Perche: "See," he said, "we have something in common." Finally, he got up, patted me on the shoulder, and said a few affectionate words to me. My father kissed me and went out through a door; the superior told me: "You'll see, my boy, you're going to be very happy with us." Then he showed me out through another door, and I had the sudden feeling of being caught in a mousetrap.

There was first a long and wide corridor; at the end of it two fathers were waiting for me, serious and indifferent, sitting in front of a table on which file cards were stacked. I had to answer some questions relating to living languages—I had mastered none—gymnastics, and my musical knowledge. They also asked me if I had chosen a spiritual adviser. Upon my negative response, I was enjoined to make this decision as soon as possible, at any rate before the eighth of October—the feast of the Virgin, and a day when the whole school took Communion. Then a door was pointed out to me; behind it I would find a corridor where I would have to look for door number 4. I did so. It was my class's study hall, and stuck with four thumbtacks onto the door, in capital letters, was the prestigious word: *Rhétorique.* Six or seven students were happily chatting with a young monitor who had left his platform to mingle with them. By the silence that fell upon my arrival, I understood that I was a "new boy" and that they were all "old boys." I was even "*the* new boy," as I was told, with a friendly handshake, by the young monitor, who broke away from the group to greet me and who led me back with him. There was only one new boy that year in *rhétorique,* and it was I. The old boys, whose names and nicknames the monitor mentioned for me in succession, along with jokes which set off bursts of laughter and which alluded to facts which were legendary and known by all, an entire school folklore of which I understood nothing, stared at me with curiosity and a certain coldness. The monitor put me on the spot by asking me various questions about my age, my studies, my preferences and abilities. Luckily I was simple enough to be scarcely ever intimidated, at least not in too obvious a way. Young people are ferocious but cowardly. Any timidity, any weakness, would have done me in. The coldness of my future schoolmates, the arrogance with which they were perhaps preparing to make me feel their superiority as old boys, disappeared pretty quickly, thanks to my natural and unpretentious demeanor and the monitor's good humor. This first contact probably seemed satisfactory to them. I did not strike them as unlikable. Fairly soon their welcome even became congenial and set the tone for those who, from one hour to the next, during that afternoon, came to join our group. Naturally that first day I was somewhat left out of things among that merry band of twenty or so boys who had known one another for a long time and noisily displayed their joy at meeting again after the long break of the vacation. But neither on that day nor on those that followed was I the object of any especially unpleasant hazing. And, from the first classes on, the consideration the teachers showed in examining me made me accepted once and for all as a good student and a good schoolmate.

IT WAS A strange and rather exceptional experience, at fifteen, to discover boarding school life and comradeship. I had large gaps in my knowledge, large areas of naïveté. I remember in particular that one of my discoveries in the first days was to learn that a certain secluded place which at le Saillant was humbly called *"les cabinets"* was indelicately named *"chiottes"* * in the students' slang and, solemnly, "latrines" in the teachers' vocabulary, as witness a sign posted in the dormitory: "It is forbidden to leave the dormitory without permission to go to the latrines. Any student who finds himself indisposed in the night must see the Proctor and ask him for the key."

I understood only later how well advised was this measure, which at the time seemed to me incredibly aggravating.

All in all, I have only excellent memories of my first days of incarceration. I was old enough to take pleasure, without suffering, in that change of existence and that totally new scenery. I also benefited from Guy's school memories, which had prepared me for this communal academic life.

So many new things entertained me more than they disconcerted me. The somewhat aggressive curiosity about the "new boy" quickly disappeared among those sixteen-year-olds. I was soon integrated into the herd and soon took up its ways and its language.

This acclimatization was also facilitated by the gratifications of self-esteem which were given me from the outset. I was appreciably stronger than my schoolmates. In the first translation from Latin, I was at the head of the class. I was among the first in Greek, in history, in geography, in mathematics. The studies I had accomplished, apart from any academic program, had already taught me most of the notions that were new to my schoolfellows. On the other hand, they were ahead of me in French composition, in Latin prosody, in religious instruction, and generally in all subjects where there was an essay to do. I had less training than they did in that exercise. My knowledge about it surpassed theirs, but I was poorly prepared to make use of that advantage. I did not possess the clichés, the tricks, the dexterity which allowed them to hide what they did not know and to hand in four pages of copy containing vague generalities drawn out with set formulas. In my first French composition, I was at a terrible loss to create a conversation, in the Underworld, among the shades of Virgil, Ronsard, and Jean-Jacques

Cabinets, literally "closets," for "water closets." *Chiottes,* from the verb *chier*—roughly, "shitter" or "shitcan."

Rousseau, whose works and place in literature I knew well enough and of whom I had read and retained many more pages than my competitors. I produced an essay so inept that I would have been placed in the bottom of the class if I had not at the last moment been clever enough to quote almost verbatim, from each of them, a text that I knew by heart.

This awkwardness in my compositions (for lack of having learned the technique, over the years) is rather surprising, if I think about it, for a man who has spent all the leisure hours of his life covering paper with an easy flow and who has certainly never seemed to lack either facility in writing, or skill. I believe, without vanity, that I have been passably talented at this exercise. However, for as long as my classes went on, I was handicapped in this regard. Rare were the graders who accepted a special, free manner of writing, outside the traditional rules, and who gave me credit for the ideas which I expressed in my own way, which was concise, direct, and independent, and could never be bothered with ready-made formulas which, at the time of my studies, were indispensable for being placed among those who "wrote well." Across my French compositions in history or philosophy the teacher would comment, usually, in red ink: "Interesting but poorly written" or "Knows the subject but expresses himself without elegance." This weakness, or at least what passed in the eyes of the grader for a weakness, hampered me till the end of my studies. I improved a little later on. But this complaint still followed me when I sat for the *licence ès lettres* and for Saint-Cyr. I would doubtless have received a higher ranking in those two examinations if I had known naturally how to turn that somewhat ornate, balanced, and oratorical phrase which the professors liked (I learned the trick fast enough, and unfortunately it stuck with me) and if these conventional embellishments of form had been added to the solid qualities of content. It was a price that I had to pay, I think, for the fact of having worked two years under the guidance of Xavier de Balcourt at the important moment when I was learning to express myself: Xavier, who had remained immune to academic deformation, or had freed himself of it, was a born writer who had a horror of "frills," as he said, and who, far from criticizing a certain dryness, a certain precision, a certain maladroitness even, preferred these defects to redundancy and the conventional elegance. And if I happened to try my hand at it clumsily, he would make fun of me and would read me a page of Voltaire, Montesquieu, or Stendhal.

I stayed a whole month without going back to le Saillant. Our first break was on the first Sunday in November. My father came to get me in the carriage on Saturday afternoon. I brought with me a monthly report card of which I had every reason to be proud, and I looked forward to the pleasure of reading it to him on the way. This pleasure was snatched away from me by the superior himself, whom we met up with in the vestibule, and who, in a few words that made me blush, declared that I was an excellent student, that I would do honor to the Saint-Léonard School, that I was, if I applied myself, destined for the most brilliant career. And he concluded, laughing, that he apologized for having at the first meeting expressed doubts as to the results of private instruction outside of the school system and that my example was just the thing to make him revise this common opinion.

My father did not conceal his pride. The main topic at le Saillant was my good grades. Henriette alone displayed only a moderate satisfaction. "You don't seem surprised that I'm getting on so well," I decided to tell her, slightly put out. "Why, no," she answered me imperturbably. "It's the opposite that would have seemed surprising!" I did not forget this observation, so touched was I by that calm confidence in me which she expressed with so much natural sincerity. It was with such reserves of feeling for me that she secretly and solidly supported me throughout my life; and, after having lost her, I keenly felt that I would find it more difficult than before to be an honorable man.

IN SPITE OF my attempts at retrospective gratitude, I cannot convince myself that I owe a lot to the Jesuits of Saint-Léonard. My stay in their school had a great importance in my moral—or rather immoral—formation, but that is another story, and their personalities, their influence, went for nothing in that department.

Father Desnuits, the superior, was, I think, a good administrator, or had been. When I met him, age had already seriously dulled his faculties as head of the community. He excelled in his relations with the outside world, the parents of students, and the diocese. I remember an old man with a worldly affability, who, without much discrimination, spread a generalized affection about him. The mothers ate it up. He knew how to give each one the conviction that her son was the object of a special fondness on his part, and remembered little details designed to soften maternal hearts, calling each student by his first name, even by the diminutive used in the family. He would smile kindly, saying: "Your little Pierrot is coming along well, he's got a heart of gold; a little unruly, but that goes with his age, doesn't it? We'll make a good Christian of him." Or: "Your little Bob has grown too much, these last months . . . He should be sent to the infirmary for tonics . . . Don't worry about his poor grades. It's growing pains. After a good vacation with his family, he'll have a fine fall semester . . ."

Pressed by the deadline that had been set for me to choose a spiritual adviser, and swayed by the charm of the welcome he had given my father and me, I had appointed him my confessor. I was not his only penitent: half the school confessed to him, and on the days before a feast day, we would jostle each other in the parlor awaiting our turns, since he nearly always heard our confessions in his office. It was not unusual for him to dispose of sixty or so absolutions between four and seven o'clock, which comes to an average of twenty an hour. With him, confessions were quick and easy! Whatever the admission may have been—and I tremble to think of those he must have received—you would get off with a few words of exhortation, a little pat on the cheek, and a *Pater* "for your penance." You would rise again reassured, with the conviction that you had been quite wrong to consider yourself a great sinner, that the father must have heard much worse, and that your chums were wickeder than you were.

I owe to this indulgent and distant "supervision" my never having found in religion a curb, an obstacle, to the crisis of sensuality that erupted in me during my stay at Saint-Léonard. I do not regret it. I remember certain schoolmates, tormented in vain by pious scruples which were not enough to keep their passions in check and added agonizing terrors, fears of eternal damnation, to the disturbances that their puberty, their temperament, and nature unleashed in them. Quite a useless addition to the torture they were already enduring. I rather regard as a lesser evil my having been able to surrender myself without a struggle to that impure flow which sweeps our adolescences along. I do not see what I would have gained by those pangs of conscience, those nocturnal fears, those raptures of piety following on excesses of lubricity. Balance was restored all by itself, at the proper time, by the force of circumstances. There are fevers which it is better not to bring down abruptly with doses of quinine . . .

THE CLASS in *rhétorique* had been entrusted, for over a decade, to Father Huxler, who worked wonders and obtained exceptional results in the examinations.

He was helped in his task by other fathers, of whom one taught history and geography, another German, another mathematics. Lastly, the chaplain, Father Bazelin, gave the course in religious instruction. But it was with Father Huxler that we had daily contact for French, Latin and Greek, which were the major subjects of the curriculum.

Father Huxler's life was an unceasing fight. From the start of the year, he took possession of his team of candidates and did not let up on them an inch. There was a distant and difficult goal to attain. Out of twenty students, the success in the examination of seven or eight, on average, was almost assured in advance. That left a dozen doubtful ones whom he needed, at all costs, with a minimum of failures, to turn into graduates at the end of the year. The honor of the school and the personal honor of Father Huxler were at stake. He went at it with a fierce and infectious determination. He worked us up into a frenzy. He was inured to this exhausting job, knew all the tricks for turning a mediocre or weak student, through an intensive and methodical cramming, into a solidly prepared candidate with two chances in three of being able to win the race, if not by giving proof of mental sharpness or of critical sense, at least by answering, by rote, the questions which would be put to him, and of which the father knew the whole series inside out.

Under his rule we spent a fiendish year. Everyone knew it. People began to get ready for it in the *quatrième*. The worst dunces, in the anxious hours when they saw before them the fateful ordeal of the *bac*, told themselves to put their minds at ease: "Yes, but Croupion's here . . ." (That was his nickname.*) And they were right. They were the ones that Croupion especially hounded. To coach a good student, or a fair one, was not interesting. To lay hold of a dunce, force all the subjects in the curriculum down his throat, give him every semblance of knowledge in ten months, and have him snatch, from under the noses of examiners who were taken in by that semblance, a prize he did not deserve—this was a fine piece of work.

When the tests were over, Father Huxler was exhausted. Each year, he packed his bag, took refuge at a Swiss inn, spent two months there drinking milk, breathing in the mountain air, sleeping fifteen hours a day. In those two months, he would bounce back. Three days before the new term, he would reappear, plump, paunchy, bright-eyed, his muscles in shape, ready for the ring. And from the moment he was put back with his two dozen future candidates, he would set to work on a new year of stubborn striving for victory.

Is this just an idea? It seems to me, from a distance, that he looked precisely like what he was. He was small, squat, stocky. He wore soutanes that were too short, raised in the front by his silk-strapped belly. From there emerged two burly legs, solidly rooted to the ground by thick-soled mountaineering boots. His head, round as a ball and always close-cropped, was too big for his body, and too near the shoulders. Of his face, I see three parallel horizontal lines: three strokes: the eyebrows, the big mouth with dry lips, and the flat underside of a determined chin. The nose, wide and upturned, rather resembled the tail end of a roast turkey. This nose, his small size, the short soutane, contributed to giving him a slightly comic figure. But his eyes did not invite laughter. A gray, piercing, keen look, with the intelligence and the will always on the alert. His criticisms were biting. He never expressed his satisfaction. Even to the best, he prophesied only failure, inability to pass. You didn't much like him, but you were attached to him for that Newfoundland-like devotion. You were grateful to him for that unflagging enthusiasm in behalf of our cause. We felt our fate, our future, that diploma which we had been taught since earliest youth to regard as the indispensable

---

*A *croupion* is the "parson's nose" on the rump of a fowl.

key to adult life, to be in his hands. We felt that he was our salvation, that we would owe victory to him.

He was, one heard, a son of Norman peasants. He had inherited their robust and tireless energy, their patience at work, their tenacity, their greed for gain: his gain was our success.

From the time school started, he grabbed hold of us, convinced us that we knew nothing, that we still had our whole education ahead of us, that there was not a minute to lose; he multiplied the exercises, the charts, the word lists; he embedded in our memories everything we had to be able to answer in order to pass the *baccalauréat*. He did not much care about developing our intelligence; that was time wasted when it came to the precise goal that had been assigned him. And I admit that as coach for the *bac* he was a marvelous trainer. He would have shaken up the inertia and indolence of a Mussulman. He battled from morning till night against human stupidity and laziness. He put into the spading of the ground of our intelligences and the coaxing of its seeds to send up shoots the ruthlessness that his forebears had put into turning over and sowing the most barren soils.

This tough man did not have many penitents. But the ones he had under his thumb he kept well in check. I heard, through schoolmates' confidences, what an extraordinary confessor he was. He invested the same energy in clearing out a soul as in sprucing up a dunce. At confession, he changed the usual procedure. He did not wait for admissions. He provoked them, with a prying and holy ardor; he rummaged through hearts with his subtle and penetrating questions. He needed to possess the consciences that had been surrendered to him down to their most intimate recesses. His penitents left his confessional red, ashamed, panting, put through the mill. He set to work on their consciences, outlined for them a plan of progressive reformation, a veritable regimen of moral therapy. He took on faults by order of importance, the cardinal ones first, as a devoted doctor settles in at a patient's bedside until he has tracked down the illness and got it to subside. And this, apparently, without violence, without excessive severity which would have dampened spirits and soured goodwill. I suppose that his toughness could, in the privacy of the confessional, appear affectionate and that his aim was to convince the penitent that he was a victim of evil, not entirely responsible, and that each sin was a point won by the Devil, who was determined to do harm, and that the salvation of the soul depended on this struggle in which he, Father Huxler, was personally participating. They were two, the confessor and the confessant, defending the threatened terrain against the diabolical marauder who takes advantage of all weaknesses to come and sow his bad seeds. I was always surprised by the somber fondness that his penitents had for him.

But to finish up with the fathers, I shall also sketch Father Billadon, known as "la Bille,"* the bursar. Short, too, but rather rotund and always on the move, he indeed called to mind a marble, or rather a rubber ball. His portliness was carried in such a sprightly fashion that, even physically, he at once revealed that indefatigable activity which was central to his nature. His soutane was generally hiked up in back by one of those nickel-plated clips that country women wore at the time to keep their heavy skirts raised, and it uncovered big feet shod with square-toed shoes with buckles. The face was framed by a graying mop of hair and by an almost white, closely trimmed beard. The very expressive forehead furrowed and wrinkled in accordance with the agitation of the bushy arch of the eyebrows, and this elastic mobility of the upper part of his face contrasted with the quiescent calm of his bluish gaze: a calm which did not preclude the liveliness of his glance or the merry twinkle in his eye. This gaze had an almost indefinable glint, which was healthy, direct and young, almost childlike, sometimes ironic, without meanness, and compassionate if need be, without weakness. The treasure of balance, of mental health, which he kept under that heavy bodily casing, showed in his joyful and determined gait. He was seen running, bounding I could say, all day long, from the kitchens in the basement to the dormitories, taking nimble strides with his stocky legs. One came across him everywhere, and he accosted everybody—teachers, students, monitors, dining-hall waiters—with the same cheerful question, tossed off to no one in particular, without waiting for an answer: "How's it going? Working away?"

Because he himself worked from dawn till dark. I would wager he never had an hour of idle melancholy. Or rather, was that exuberant activity a hedge, a preventive against wistfulness? He was highly regarded at the school. I believe he was the dean, if not by age, at least by seniority. The whole town of Gevrésy knew Father Billadon. He'd had his appointed tradesmen for thirty years. On market days he was even seen with two servants in tow loaded down with baskets. He impressed everyone with his vigorous good-heartedness, that well-disciplined strength which shone forth from him. The students had little personal contact with him, and I scarcely knew him. But I always thought that this big bouncing man, constantly busy with material things, must have an exquisite sensibility, a lenient, understanding, fatherly soul, and I often regretted not having chosen him as my confessor.

I WOULD NOT want to paint too dark a picture. Nor do I wish to blame the outburst of sensuality which marked my stay at Saint-Léonard on the moral dissipation of those young men among whom I suddenly found myself. But I want to tell everything frankly, bluntly. And I must observe, at the outset,

*"The Marble."

that in this little closed circle of adolescent boarders there fermented a riot of imagination and, for some, a moral freedom which were incredible.

From the very first day, I was in a position to judge all this from the surprisingly raw remarks that my schoolmates swapped as they recounted to each other the adventures and escapades of their vacations. I suppose there was scarcely a word of truth in those debaucheries, cynically confessed and proudly, smugly described. For in that era especially, the lives of young men and girls were in general anything but free, even at the beach, and the circle of the bourgeoisie and minor nobility to which all those boys belonged was quite straitlaced. It was rather unlikely that in the family existence of the summer vacation they had found so many chances for depravity. There was not only a shameless boasting in those lies: what was more serious, they revealed that these boys had probably not in fact practiced any of the lewd acts which they vied with each other in describing, but had lived them in imagination during their morbidly obsessed nights. And this applied particularly to the boys whose daily lives (on those estates and beaches where they had chastely played croquet with their sisters and their girl cousins, or gone shrimping, or danced a polka on Sunday afternoon at the casino under their mother's watchful eye) were the most innocent and domestic. Each of those fellows with a bawdy look and scandalous cynicism quite certainly reverted, at home, to being a good little boy who avoided hurting his mother, blushed at table when his father allowed himself a slightly risqué innuendo in front of a guest, refrained, out of timidity, from raising his eyes to the chambermaid or letting her come into his room while he was dressing, and played checkers with his sister or spent his rainy days in a corner of the drawing room with his herbarium or his stamp album.

But this, which I understand today, I did not suspect back then. And I listened gaping with a stunned credulity to those lecherous boasts. Perhaps what surprised and shocked me most was not the subject of those titillating stories, but the freedom, the absence of reserve and secrecy with which those boys flaunted before one another their exploits as well as scabrous details about their anatomy and the use they claimed to have made of it. I did not know then that this absence of all modesty was the fruit of five or six years of boarding school and living together at close quarters. I did not know either that these boys who were so lacking in verbal restraint would, most of them at least, have hesitated a little to undress in front of one another to go swimming in a river, and would have wrapped themselves carefully in a towel to take off their bathing trunks.

Thus, from the first day on, I was thrown without warning into that unhealthy fermentation of the imaginations of those sixteen-year-old boys, and the shock that I got from it, made worse by the state of relative innocence in which, despite Guy's stay at le Saillant, I still remained, owing to a slightly backward and dormant nature, this time shook me to the depths and brought on that crisis of puberty which for me overshadows all my memories of boarding school.

I have already said that I attach the greatest importance to these questions. What goes on in the head and in the senses—but especially in the head—of a boy of fifteen determines to a certain extent an entire part of his future character and his behavior. One cannot devote too much attention to that hellish age of solitary and nocturnal passions. My arrival at Saint-Léonard in part coincided with—in part triggered—my entry into that sexual age which others come to know much earlier: the age of nighttime imaginings, erotic hallucinations, insistent, irresistible obsessions, unbridled desires, solitary never-satiated pleasures. In that entire class of twenty students I was probably one of the worst affected, one of the most depraved, because for me this crisis sprang up all at once, with its full force. By coincidence I found myself both in possession of a fully developed body, suddenly insistent and perpetually erupting, and plunged into an ambiance, a lack of privacy, which, when it came to perversity, encouraged all the instincts by a sort of competitiveness.

I say that I was the worst affected because that headlong slide into hell had the most corrosive influence on my work, to a degree that none of my schoolmates experienced. And there is an explanation for this. They had all long since become acclimated to their vices, as addicts are to their drug. The harmful effect was dulled in them. They had passed that stage of puberty where the frenzies of the libidinous imagination occupy all of a person's faculties. They were already at the age when, on the contrary, some gradually begin to settle down again. This allowed them both to live an almost serious life during the day, a life of work, wholly taken up with relentless worry about the examination which awaited them at the end of their school year, and, at night, in their beds, to give themselves up to their propensities and their unwholesome dreams. In short, those *rhétoriciens* split their lives in two. Their eroticism did not significantly prevent them from working and from making the enormous intellectual effort which was demanded of them that year.

During one of the previous years, they had already known and grown out of that cursed phase when lust becomes mistress of the whole being. But *I* entered it fully, and I was unable to make any room for serious work. Against the flames which were suddenly devouring me, my schoolmates were half fireproofed. Not I: I exposed my youth, all healthy and combustible, to the blaze. And I was its prey. They were too, still. But they could burn out a firebreak for themselves. I could not.

And all the less so since I had not entered that *rhétorique* class like them, with their anxiety about the examination and their resolve, even among the laziest, to make a great effort that year in order to land the diploma. Xavier had led me to believe that I would easily pass that examination; and this calm had been further bolstered in me by the place I had taken, at the start, among the first in the class.

But I was not to keep that place for very long.

I am trying to recall in approximately what order I arrived at the secret of my schoolmates' sexual preoccupations. The conversations, from the first day on, had starkly revealed their obsession to me. At first, I listened without saying anything, confining myself to cravenly knowing smiles. More was not asked of me. I showed in this way that I was as informed as they, and that I would not betray them.

But a few days later, my neighbors in the classroom, the study hall, or the refectory began to pay attention to me and ask me indiscreet questions about my personal experiences, to which I responded quite evasively, and for good reason, with a false bravery and timid particulars.

From that instant on, it was my turn to feel haunted. The little girls at the pond, the only memory of my youth that I used, in my confusion, to clumsily make up a kind of affair, started to obsess me; and what I had invented by a stroke of improvisation took on substance for me and developed like a daily and nightly film until it prompted, on certain nights, the first uprise of my natural sap. As strange as it may seem, this was a great jolt. Until then I was unacquainted with the spasm. I suddenly discovered how naïve I had been in likening certain harmless secretions, which I had long experienced, to those emissions about which my cousin Guy had formerly spoken to me. I understood better the purpose of the handkerchief that he took to bed with him at night. I understood, most of all, the importance that my schoolmates attached to that little intimate occurrence, and the appeal they found in it, and the impatience they felt to repeat it. I was then exactly fourteen years and ten months old. All my classmates in *rhétorique* were over fifteen and some were already sixteen.

Most of them had chosen, at school, among the younger boys, one with a sweet face and pleasant appearance, towards whom they directed their romantic and poetic need for love. These deviations from a natural urge at that age were among the more familiar phenomena in the existence of those young men. With very rare exceptions these feelings remained absolutely platonic. Concrete face and form had to be given to those awakenings of the heart, parallel to, but very distinct from, the awakening of the senses. To that end, each of them had what was known at Saint-Léonard as a *"chouchou"** — something like a *"gamin de leur pensée,"*†as the troubadour rhymesters had a *"dame de leur pensée."* It was quite often a student in the *cinquième*, or in the

---

*Pet or favorite.

†Literally, "kid of their thought," as *"dame de leur pensée"* is "lady of their thought."

quatrième, that is to say an eleven- or twelve-year-old, somewhat girlish-looking, from whom we were completely separated, since the life of the older boys and that of the middle boys had nothing in common, neither the building nor even the play yard. Thus one would not see one's *"chouchou"* except on very rare occasions, and always from afar, in the chapel for example, or, sometimes on Sundays, on our walk, when chance had it that the lines of the older boys crossed paths, in the countryside, with the lines of the middle boys. More often than not, the *"chouchou"* would be unaware that he had been chosen. Sometimes also, with the collusion of a brother or younger friend, one would manage to make the fact known to him through some impassioned note. This lack of meetings, this hopeless love, made things all the more obsessive. It was among the first secrets one confided at the beginning of a friendship, and one could not wait to point out to one's new friend the silhouette of the distant object of one's infatuation. All the literary clichés of love fed that secret ardor. Certain of my schoolmates secretly filled notebooks with childish poems celebrating the beloved object in the most conventional forms, in doggerel, dripping with tenderness. I am thinking especially of my friend Raoul de Luzac, who was quite unplatonically sensual but who cultivated in another sealed-off part of himself a romantic of the most sentimental stripe. Madly in love with a little blond cherub in the *sixième,* he succeeded in showing him to me one day at a window of the infirmary. He had managed to find out his name: René or Robert Ledoux. He affectionately called him "Doucette"* in the verses which I helped him get up more or less onto their eight feet and whose refrain I have remembered:

> *Doucette, gentil damoiseau,*
> *Pour toi, je perdrais un royaume!*
> *Ah, si j'étais petit oiseau*
> *J'irais becqueter en ta paume!*†

Each had his *"chouchou"* and we knew their pet names: *"la Bichette," "Beau coco," "Pomme d'amour."*‡

It did not take me long to become infected with that same need. My attention was attracted by a schoolboy who, I realize only today, in trying to describe him, looked somewhat like Guy: a boy with a frail body, a sickly complexion, dark velvety eyes, a rather shy gaze, the same black forelock as

---

*"Little Sweet One," feminizing the name Ledoux.

†Doucette, sweet sire,
  For thee, I would forfeit a kingdom!
  Ah, if I were a little bird,
  I would go and peck in thy palm!

‡"The Little Doe," "Beautiful Darling," "Love Apple."

my cousin. I have forgotten his surname. His first name, which seemed to me as melodious as a chord on a harp, was Emmanuel. I vowed a sublime affection to him. He was in the *troisième* and he played in the same yard as we, but on another part of the field. My eyes searched him out from a distance among the others at every recess. I had the joy of discovering that he confessed as I did to the superior, which gave me the very secular emotion of sometimes finding myself fairly close to him in the parlor on the day before religious holidays. But I then would avoid his gaze. He never knew that I was dying of love for him, that I wept out of tenderness while repeating his name and calling up his features. I never attempted to talk to him: what would I have said? It was in the silence of my heart that I spoke to him. It was when I thought about him poetically, in relation to a text by Racine or the lyrical stanzas of *Le Cid,* that he was most present for me in my heart. A vague longing, the awakening of an affection different from the one I had for Henriette, the first summons of sentimental love, first projection onto someone of all the poetry of a child's soul.

I unfortunately did not content myself with these furtive and platonic emotions. Emmanuel occupied my lovestruck dreams, but my nascent sexuality urged me towards less ethereal, more animal satisfactions. Starting on the day after my arrival, I had noticed, in Latin class, some distance away, a student with a chubby face, freckled like mine. He was seated at the end of a row in such a way that I saw his entire body, bent over his desk, his left hand always buried in his trouser pocket; the other hand twiddled a tuft of hair while he followed the text being analyzed, and my attention was drawn by that distinctive posture, until a surmise came to me which sent a flush to my face. That hand in those pants, despite the casual naturalness of the pose, had something particularly strange about it which caught my eye. I watched him in spite of myself, and although I at first dismissed the suspicion that was crossing my mind, I caught a shifty look that he cast about him as if he was afraid of being observed. At that moment, the teacher called out: "Luzac, continue!" He hastily pulled his hand out of his pocket, nudged his neighbor for help, and was unable to carry on. His diligent air notwithstanding, he was not following and did not know where we were, which earned him a zero.

He was charming. He had all the marks of the country boy: the pale eyes, the hair the color of bread right out of the oven, and above all the face of a comic-opera peasant, round and naïve, with round eyes, round nose, fleshy mouth. I would say that he looked like a girl if he had not been the opposite of effeminate: a big overgrown baby boy. A girlish side all the same, but of a beautiful farm girl, round and fresh. And this lovely child of nature, who bore one of the old names of France and a purebred distinction in his rough, infantile features, was quite close to being a monster of perversity. Badly put: he had nothing of a monster in him and, on the whole, nothing much perverse. He was a free, naked instinct, lustful as a young animal in the mating season.

The next day, a Wednesday, the day when we students had the afternoon free, we set off in double file to take a walk outside the town, and on the way back it so happened that I was paired with this Luzac. We chatted cordially. I found him delightful. I quickly forgot what I thought I had found out. Surely I had been wrong. I learned that his name was Raoul de Luzac and that he was the only son of the Comtesse de Luzac, widow of a landowner of the region, whose name was well known to me. His conversation was cheerful, simple, good-natured, very chaste, and it enchanted me; I took pleasure in maintaining the same tone. We had a thousand things in common. He knew le Saillant by sight from having often had picnics in the Menneville forest. He rode horseback and on vacations led the same sort of life I did. We parted friends. We had spoken at length about the year's teachers, not all of whom I yet knew, particularly about old Father Müller, an Alsatian, in charge of teaching German. Luzac, who had had him for two years as teacher of modern languages, told me about the uproars that were traditional in the class, and when we took leave of each other to go to study hall, where we were placed rather far from each other, he said furtively: "Tomorrow, if you want, for the first German class, you'll come with me, I'll show you which are the good seats." I accepted, quite happy with this attention, which proved to me that my doltishness had not put him off too much.

The German class was held in a small room, long and narrow, where the tiers rose in height, and which, unusually, was still furnished with old desks, which had been replaced everywhere else by tables. These desks were joined up in twos, and they had the feature of being fitted out underneath with a shelf closed off on three sides by solid panels that allowed things—food, etc.—to be hidden.

This room has remained very present to my mind, for it is associated with the most dissolute memories.

In that setting, Luzac took pleasure in enjoying himself conspicuously and in artlessly stretching the material of his pants so that I could make out the uneven contours of his manhood. It was not long before I timidly imitated him and also put a hand in my pocket. Then he allowed himself a first discreet and very superficial touch, brushing my fly with his hand to make sure that I was in the same state as he, and this initial and brief contact affected me so strongly that I pushed him away with a sharp knock of the elbow. But soon I waited for, hoped for, that brushing like an incomparable thrill, and not only did I no longer push him away, but offered myself willingly to his examinations, always found his touch too brief, and was grateful to him for prolonging it when he unabashedly put his hand on me. And when he started to feel me more insistently, I so enjoyed it that this rough pressure through the cloth was the same for me as the most sensual caress, and almost instantly set off my pleasure. I learned then to make that moment of preliminary exhilaration last for as long as possible, slipping away from his hand when I was afraid of seeing that delicious instant end too quickly, then offering myself once again as soon as that dangerous minute had passed and I felt able to receive his caress without immediately succumbing to climax.

Having arrived at that point, the initiation went on for several weeks without progressing further. We had our habits. It became a ritual, the resumption of which I awaited for a week, with a feverish impatience of imagination. No sooner had the class begun, and Father Müller, oblivious to the general indifference and to the noises, whispers, drummings of his pupils, had started to write out on the blackboard, in the flowing letters of his Gothic hand, his examples of *"grand-mère,"** as he said, we would settle in, Luzac and I, for our shared game. He would stretch out his legs a little, thrust out his chest, dig his left hand deep into his pants pocket, and put his other hand on my fly. I pretended to apply myself to the book open in front of me, over which I was bending, elbows on the desk, hands on my temples. And I gave myself up to his caresses, by turns shying away and yielding myself until I could no longer delay the end of my pleasure.

Probably Luzac grew tired of doing the same thing every Thursday. (The initiative always came from him.) One day I felt his hand hunting for the opening of my pocket and sliding between my thigh and the cloth of my trousers. As always at each new stage, I tried at first to pull away. But he kept at it, gradually crept in, and, through the lining of my pocket, as he pushed aside the change-purse, the piece of string, the eraser, and everything that a student buries in a pants pocket, I felt his fingers come near and take hold of me. From then on, this more direct fondling became a new habit, and I let it happen without attempting to defend myself. I even made his approaches easier for him by emptying the contents of the left pocket into the right before going into class, and the moment that I devoted to these preparations was already one of intense excitement.

But this strange boy did not content himself even with that. A few sessions later, I felt his hand enter my pocket, then come out again. I did not understand right away what he was rummaging for against my leg. I only figured out his Machiavellianism when he put his hand back into my pocket and I suddenly felt his warm fingers on my skin. He had slit the lining of the empty pocket with a deft flick of his penknife. I no longer had on me the usual touch of his hand gloved with cloth and stopped by the bottom

*Father Müller, with his Alsatian accent, pronounces *"grammaire"* (grammar) so that it sounds like *"grand-mère"* (grandmother).

of the pocket. I had his bare and moist hand on my belly, and, as he extended his arm, nothing kept him any longer from indulging in the most complete investigations. I shuddered with a new arousal, I leaned forward, bent double, pressed my thighs against each other to prevent that daring break-in. But I could not long resist the temptation that had seized me, and soon, on the contrary, I surrendered with delight to that incredible increase in pleasure. His was no less acute. Our cheeks must have been burning, our mouths dry. He ran his caressing hand over me softly, tenderly, taking a slow, passionate and meticulous inventory of my most intimate treasures, and the expert gentleness with which he handled me produced a sudden spasm which I could neither delay nor hold back. I was terribly ashamed and thought that he would involuntarily let out a cry of disgust. Not at all. He had not even tried to remove his hand and went on stroking me softly. Had he not noticed anything? I looked at him out of the corner of my eye. He had his eyelids half-lowered, a vague smile on his lips; I did not meet his gaze; but at the very moment when I gave him an uneasy glance, I saw him put his head imperceptibly back, I saw his smile congeal, an intense and unknown expression pass over his features. At the same time I felt a slight contraction of his hand and I realized that a few seconds more and we could have merged our double pleasure into the same instant.

From then on, I got used to turning my eyes stealthily towards him at the moment I was watching for his spasm, and I would revel in the sight of his ravished, somber, almost pained face. *I have always liked to give pleasure.*

Henceforth, this conjunction of climaxes was our principal aim, and we soon became as skillful as two experienced lovers in perfect unison.

I dwell on all this with an indulgence that I cannot help. The echo of those enchantments is not far from being awakened in my old carcass. Not only have I no regret for that deplorable way of learning German, but I do not hold the slightest grudge against Luzac for having led me into those weekly debaucheries. He introduced me to shared sensual pleasure and I feel nothing but gratitude to him for it.

I almost hold it against myself today that I never consented to return his practiced caresses. For he soon asked me to do so. By signs, at least, for we never exchanged a single word in the course of these amorous exercises: quite often he took my hand and wanted to put it in his pocket, but I would hold out against his prompting and he would not insist, he did not even seem to resent it and did not at all decrease his attentions towards me. Two or three times, however, driven by an insidious curiosity and taking advantage of a moment of greater boldness, I slipped my fingers into his pocket: the lower half was cut out; my fingers almost immediately encountered the warm flesh of the thigh, and I hastily withdrew my hand. I still do not know today just what feeling of absurd modesty (absurd because modesty had long since been left behind), timidity, shame, or repulsion I was obeying. I could not bring myself to place my hand on his naked flesh. I too was sometimes gripped by a passionate urge to go through the inventory, to know every secret detail of his body, yet I could never resolve to satisfy that curiosity, though it was sometimes very strong. Never, in my faltering investigations, did I venture beyond the fold of his groin, whose warmth, whose silky smoothness, made me shiver with a sort of mixture of attraction and disgust that was impossible to curb, and I would snatch my hand away from his pocket as if I had burned myself on a red-hot iron. My willingness to oblige did not go beyond what he himself had done to me at the beginning of our adventure. I gladly consented to place my hand on his clothes, on his belly, and by means of an elastic and well-gauged pressure through the material, to produce his spasm at the very same instant when his hand, deeply buried in the throbbing warmth of my body would, with no sign of disgust, touch off my pleasure; and when, with an irrepressible glance, I would surreptitiously watch for a few seconds, on his face, the sharp and fleeting ravages of his climax.

The strangest thing is that our intimacy had no other chance to express itself than there, once a week, for a whole year, during that hour and a half of proximity in Father Müller's class. We never exchanged a single confidence. We never spoke of what we did together. We acted exactly as if each of us served as the other's partner without knowing it, without noticing it.

The rest of the week, we had the most ordinary of schoolboy relationships. Neither a word nor a knowing look passed between us. If we were in line or at recess, we would not avoid each other altogether, but we would not seek each other out. It was as if nothing had ever happened between us. By chance, on certain Wednesdays or Sundays, I found myself next to him on walks for two hours in a row; we would seem to take the most innocent enjoyment in being together then. We would talk about our families, our life at Luzac or le Saillant, our horses, our vacation plans, country things, school things, schoolmates, teachers. The Comtesse de Luzac might have listened to us during those two hours without finding fault with anything, without even hearing a coarse word that could have shocked her.

Perhaps there was no other schoolmate with whom I had, outside of Father Müller's class, relations so pure, so simply and openly friendly. He was the only one, I believe, to whom I spoke readily of my sister, of our rides in the woods. And he spoke to me of his mother with adoration. "My mother does such and such . . ." To which I would respond: "My sister also thinks such and such . . ." Together, once away from the double desk which was our joint hell, we were two good, well-behaved little boys. He was the only one with whom I did not think myself compelled to be worldly-wise and churlish, and I found it pleasant. And everything led me to suppose that he felt as I did.

It happened that we were not at the same table in the refectory, or on the same side of the study hall, or next to each other in any class except German, and that our beds, in the dormitory, were quite far apart. Thus we did not live very much together. We needed the chance of being on the same side in a game of prisoner's base or soccer, the chance of a walk, where there was a certain latitude in the choice of one's partner in line, and where we would sometimes say to each other: "Want to pair up?" I never knew if he took advantage of the freedoms of the dormitory with others. Moreover, I believe that the restraint of our private relations outside of the "German" promiscuity was not solely due to our lack of contact. I think that even if we had been neighbors in the dormitory—where a lot went on!—nothing would have happened between us. So, at least, it seems to me. Our companionship had taken a certain "correct" turn that could no longer be reversed, I think, and that we would not readily have let be reversed. Basically it was a relationship between two shy natures which only forgot themselves at a certain moment, under certain circumstances.

I had the opportunity to see the nakedness of many of my schoolmates, either fortuitously or because they deliberately let it be seen in the dormitory or in the washroom. I knew nothing at all of Luzac's nakedness.

What sort of life did he lead with the others? I would be rather hard put to say. It is too easy to think that he did with others what he did with me. However, I am inclined to doubt it and even not to believe it. First, in the other classrooms there were no double desks but instead long benches with a board containing holes for inkwells. You could not get away with indulging in those licentious excesses. You "worked the pocket," if I may so put it, by yourself, but cautiously and not without risks.

I tend to believe that he engaged in solitary games at night, behind the curtains of his bed, and that this was the only gratification of his instincts. And that with no one else did he seek to take the liberties that he had gradually come to take with me. I even think that he would have been on his guard against others. That what made him so open with me was the sort of trust I inspired in him by the name that I bore and by my relatively correct and polished manners—more correct than those of most. I defy ridicule by adding that he felt me to be of "his set" and was reassured by it, freer with me than with the others.

But these are suppositions. In reality I know nothing about it.

I WRITE all this for myself, out of pleasure, for the pleasure of going back and watching, with my eyes of today, that past which I lived with the inattention and spontaneity of youth.

But in writing for myself, I am not sure that I am writing only for myself.

By dint of writing entirely for yourself, it happens that, without having planned to do so, you find that you have also written for everyone.

I HAVE SO FAR said nothing of the extreme liberties that the dormitory made possible for most of my schoolmates. I have to go back to the first weeks of the fall semester. It took me at least a fortnight to realize what was going on in the dormitories. There was a dormitory on the top floor of each of the three buildings. (The dining halls were on the ground floor, the study halls on the second, the classrooms on the third, and the dormitories on the fourth, in the attic.) The "junior boys'" dormitory, the "middle boys'" dormitory, and the "senior boys'" dormitory. This "senior boys'" dormitory, which was ours, brought together for the night students in the *troisième*, in the *seconde*, in *rhétorique* and in *philo*: it was vast, containing seventy or eighty beds, each of which was chastely surrounded by white canvas curtains. No furniture: a little shelf to empty one's pockets onto, and a chamber pot below. One sat on one's bed to get undressed, and one put one's clothes at the foot of the bed, or generally on a little woven mat. After the evening prayer, I would hasten to get to this tent which I would close hermetically by drawing the curtains, and where I would feel deliciously alone in my own home.

I soon noticed that, despite the regulations, most of the curtains remained half open, but in such a way that the opening was not visible from the central aisle, where the monitors would pace up and down, chatting in undertones, until it was time to put out the lamps. These monitors were two young lay brothers and a father.

The father slept in the middle of the dormitory, in a sort of cell formed by half-partitions of paneling. The two monitors had, at either end of the dormitory, beds slightly larger than ours, also surrounded with white curtains. But each had a night table, a little wardrobe, and a bedside kerosene lamp that remained dimly lit through the night.

Silence was the rule, and strictly observed as soon as everyone was in his place. You heard a shoe fall onto the floor, or a bedspring creak, that was all. But, through the slit in the curtains, from one row to the next, extremely risqué and animated conversations took place in sign language. Obscene signs, naturally. A whole exhibitionistic ritual, at once brazen and shy. This conversation of deaf-mutes could have been translated thus: "Pull your nightshirt up a little, and I'll pull mine up.—No, you go first . . . No, after you . . ." Finally, the bolder of the two would decide to act, and the other, keeping his tacit promise, would comply in turn. Then silent and solitary acrobatics on the bed, to "display the goods." And stifled laughter and insatiably curious looks. However well they knew each other, having adjacent beds, every night they would begin this game again with a glee that was always fresh. Until, the lamps being put out, and the darkness being almost complete (for the lamps of the monitors, who were sleeping or reading behind their curtains, gave off only a faint and distant glimmer), the game would cease to be fun. Then each would slip quietly into his bed and begin his solitary ramble amidst his dubious images and his private dreams.

Most of them, I have to say, confined themselves to this little show of exhibitionism, which in fact revealed more playfulness than true depravity, and to their onanism, the nightly prelude to their sleep.

But in the course of my first year of boarding school, I was witness to a few less childish debaucheries, which I want to record as well.

Among the occupants of the twenty-five or thirty beds in my vicinity, there were only two or three more wildly dissolute boys who were past masters in the art of slipping into a schoolmate's bed without making either the floor or the bedspring creak. One of them, whom I particularly recall, was literally crazed with daring, and on certain nights managed to reach beds quite far from his own. How is it that the monitors never noticed anything? Obviously, these incidents happened mainly in the rows that were farthest removed both from the father's cell and from the monitors' beds, which is to say as far from the center of the dormitory as from its ends. Moreover, these singular "explorers" went hunting only in the dead of night, or at least very late, at the time when most of the sleepers, including our guardians, had sunk into their first slumber. I was nevertheless surprised that none was ever caught, not at any rate during my time. Indeed, I sometimes wondered whether the father supervising our dormitory, who, if only from the whisperings of the confessional, must have suspected something, and the monitors, who were used to the habits of the boarding school and its clandestine customs, didn't willingly close their eyes and ears for fear of unleashing a scandal that would have embarrassed them as much as the victims. I also imagine that these teachers, familiar with all the secrets of the boarding school, had arrived at a kind of fatalistic indifference in these matters. Something like: "You're never going to stop it, and besides, it isn't so important . . ." In short, whether from naïveté, indifference, laziness, or fear of any scandal, and perhaps for all of these reasons put together, I saw that those dormitory debaucheries, provided they were carried out with the stealth of Indians, in fact enjoyed a total impunity.

I am thinking especially of one of those "explorers," because I was, on certain nights, the object of his attentions. It is with this episode that I want to close the chapter of the dormitory.

His name was Couraud, René Couraud . . . (You don't forget any of the details of that age.) He was the son of an employee of the forestry service of Alençon. He was skinny, swarthy, with a rather unattractive face, but with a big sensuous mouth and little gimlet eyes whose murky gaze was veiled by long black lashes. His particular sadism was to strip his schoolmates of their innocence and force the timid ones to serve him as partners. For a long time I believed that those whom he boasted of having "bedded," as he oddly said, were in cahoots with him, and that, if I may so put it, his nocturnal visits only took place by appointment. I learned to my cost that on the contrary he liked improvisation, and knew how to impose himself without warning. I received a visit from him one night towards the middle of winter, before Easter. I had for quite a while already ceased to be the innocent "new boy" whom my father had entrusted to the Saint-Léonard School. It was at the time when I had begun to have delectable experiences with Luzac. However, if Couraud had ever made me propositions, I would without a doubt have rebuffed them through a mixture of natural modesty and terror of a possible scandal. I did not have to make this decision. I woke with a start from my first sleep, feeling a supple body slide up against mine, while he hurriedly whispered in my ear: "Sshh! It's me, Couraud." My initial reflex was to shove him out of the bed. At any rate, I honestly think so. But he was clasping me strongly, and the least resistance, the least struggle, would have set off, in the thick silence of the dormitory, a racket that could easily have got us both caught. This was enough to paralyze me. I scarcely had time to be tempted to push him away when already other feelings arose in me: curiosity, a heady mix of *fear* and *desire*. It was a cold night. He murmured: "Warm me up," and slid his body up against mine; his icy legs wound around mine, his brazen hands slipped under my shirt and stroked my flesh, as Luzac did. I struggled feebly to turn my mouth away from him. Of course I was no longer at all ignorant of sensual pleasure, but I was not acquainted with kissing, and those hot moist lips produced in me, for a brief instant, the most intense loathing. Then, as his hands became emboldened, I shivered with desire, I surrendered myself and gave him my lips. I have to say that he "kissed well," and I owe to him the discovery of what a deep kiss adds in savor to pleasure. All in all, I see that I owe much more than I thought to that little devil Couraud . . . I did not return any of his caresses but let him fondle me and held him tight in my arms. I wanted him to snuggle up against me, for us to end the night softly dozing in the same warmth. But he hated "sentimentality." As soon as he had finished with me he took care of himself, and the moment the thing was done he withdrew without saying a word, crept out of bed, and vanished into the darkness, leaving me alone, quite bewildered, and very disgusted in the midst of my soiled sheets. I do not know if I managed to fall back to sleep.

He returned. Not the next night, nor the night after, despite the silent invitations I made him in the secrecy of my instincts. He came back, however, a few days later, unexpectedly. And this was much less pleasant. I wished only for a repeat of our first encounter. But he liked change. He took liberties with me that seemed unbelievable and which deprived me of the pleasure of his mouth. I gave in to him for a short instant with a voluptuous surprise, then I roughly tore myself away, seized with acute shame. And when he asked me to do the same to him, I gasped and thrust him away with horror. Then, furious, he let go of my head which he had grabbed by the hair, after having shaken it in a rage, and, without taking his pleasure, he abandoned me. I never had another visit from him; nor from anyone else. And these were, really, the only two experiences of mutual pleasure (or even displeasure) that I was to have until my twentieth year, until my encounter with Doudou, the beautiful Creole woman of my first amorous adventure, my first affair—I can say: my first love.

I HAD A FRIGHT that I still remember on that Saturday in May when my father came, at the usual time, to pick me up to spend the first Sunday of the month at le Saillant, and when, as we were crossing the town in a buggy, he told me in his gruff tone: "Guess who came to visit me this week? The Comtesse de Luzac . . ." I thought myself betrayed, found out, dishonored, lost.

I must have started shaking in every limb, while a burning sweat stood out on my forehead. My father, caught up in curbing the pace of the mare as she made her way through the carts of the laggards who were going back to their farms after the ritual libations of an afternoon at the market, did not notice my terror. He went on: "Why did you never tell me that you had a Luzac in your class? It's an old family around here. After your grandfather's death, it was the Comte de Luzac who succeeded him in the Senate. I knew him well, and your mother and I often met his son, your schoolmate's father. But I didn't know his widow. What kind of terms are you on with the boy?" Where was he heading? I mumbled some unintelligible words. He added: "You can make friends with him. They're a very good family." I breathed a bit more easily. I had imagined the worst: Madame de Luzac, informed of our behavior, coming to tell my father . . . The truth, fortunately, was altogether different. And my father, who hardly suspected the scare he had given me, told me the story in detail all the way home. A young farmhand from the Luzac estate, a godson of the Comtesse's whom she had last year made a coachman, had met the daughter of a cattle-breeder of ours at a wedding; these young folk had hit it off, the marriage was set, and the Comtesse wanted information about the girl; looking after her own interests, my father added, since the boy had asked that his future wife be taken on with him at the Luzac château as a housemaid.

That Sunday at le Saillant, the Luzacs were mentioned several times, and each time my father and especially my sister pronounced that name I felt a violent and fleeting queasiness at hearing it from their mouths, and I resented Henriette for making me in some way associate her, it seemed to me, with the memory of the German classes. I responded with so little enthusiasm that she was convinced I had no great liking for my schoolmate.

This matter of a country wedding formed the subject of an exchange of gracious letters between my father and Madame de Luzac which ended up with an invitation to me. The Comtesse urged my father to allow me to come spend Pentecost Sunday* and Monday at Luzac, and my father, certain that this invitation had been contrived by Raoul and me, and pleased us both, accepted. I was very annoyed, but after my father's acceptance I could not decline. I thought that Raoul would be as annoyed as I, but I was mistaken. He came up to me during recess a few days before the vacation and said, in the most natural way in the world: "So you're coming with me to Luzac on Saturday?" He seemed very happy at this prospect, and rattled off the various diversions he meant to provide me, the horse that he would have me ride, the fishing trips we would take to the pond at la Trappe, etc. He seemed to have completely forgotten the sort of "diversions" we usually had. And during the forty-eight hours I spent with him, not once did he seem to remember them, not once did he make the slightest allusion to the German class.

AT TEN O'CLOCK, Madame de Luzac sweetly bade us go up to bed. There was a table in the hallway where candleholders were lined up. The servant lit them and handed them out. We said good night and each went to his room.

I followed Raoul, who led me to mine and went in with me.

"You see," he said, opening the doors which communicated with his room, "we can talk. It's only us on this side of the house."

I was about to get undressed, vaguely uneasy, fearing and wishing at the same time that something would happen—when he returned with two big stamp albums to show me his collection. It had been begun by his father and the albums were full of good specimens. I knew nothing about philately, but I admired the stamps on faith. We were leaning over the table side by side. I was wondering whether these albums had not been a pretext to come back to my room. But after having leafed through them and commented on some of the rare items, he shut the albums and said to me: "Well! We need to get to bed."

I remained alone, and hastened to undress. I heard him going back and forth in his room. The doors were open but positioned in such a way that we

*The seventh Sunday after Easter.

could not see each other. He called to me: "Tomorrow, if you want, we can take a stroll in the park before High Mass."

"Sure."

I hurried to get into bed, my throat a little tight.

"Everything all right?" he called. "You have everything you need? Do you want me to lend you a book to read before you go to sleep? I've got some here that I like a lot. Have you read *La Vénus d'Ille* by Mérimée?"

"N . . . no," I went, slipping between my sheets.

"It's great. You want it?"

"No, I'm putting out the light."

I did not do anything of the sort. It seemed to me that the light was a protection, and that he would only try something in the dark.

"All right, good night!" he called.

"Good night!"

I hesitated to blow out my candle. Finally I did. There was still light in the next room.

I was sitting up in my bed, staring at that lighted doorway, ready for anything. To do what? To defend myself? To yield? I didn't know.

The light did not go out. He must have been reading in his bed. This lasted for what seemed to me a long time. Finally the room went dark and I heard the bedsprings creak. Was he lying down to sleep? Or getting up to come in? I stared wide-eyed into the blackness, pricking my ears for the slightest noise, holding my breath, at once anxious as to what might happen and let down that nothing did.

And indeed, nothing happened. I do not know how sleep overtook me. I woke up in broad daylight.

Shortly after, I heard him stir. I coughed awkwardly.

"Are you awake?" he called.

"Yes."

"Sleep well?"

"Very well."

"Shall we get up?"

"If you want to."

I heard him getting up. I stayed in bed, thinking that he was going to come in and preferring not to be seen in my nightshirt, with my legs bare.

But he did not come in, and I finally decided to get out of bed and put my pants on. I heard him moving his water jug and washing up.

"How are you coming?" he called. "Have you washed?"

"No. I'm starting."

"I'm almost done. Hurry up!"

A little later, I heard him utter this surprising sentence: "When *one* can come in, tell me!"

"Yes," I said.

As I was finishing knotting my tie, he repeated: "*One* can't come in yet?"

"Sure you can," I said, slipping on my cardigan.

He came right in. He had on his best-behaved look, his good-little-member-of-the-youth-club look.

"You're taking so long!" he said. "It's beautiful out. I'm going to ring for the tray to be brought. And afterwards I'll show you around the park."

So it happened. And all of his plans for entertainment came to pass one after the other. He was so natural, and this simplicity was so contagious, that I gradually stopped thinking about the German classes. And it was truly as if my Pentecost companion was not the same as my imperious desk-mate in Father Müller's class.

High Mass.

Lunch.

Horseback-riding in the Laigle forest.

I had really forgotten the Luzac from school. Scarcely did the haunting thought flit through my mind, in the middle of the day, when we dismounted to rest and to eat the snack that had been sent along with us. He had chosen a mossy nook, completely isolated, under the trees. When I saw him lie down beside me, on his back, with his arms spread out, I was certain that he was going to extend his hand towards me. But he stayed lying down, his eyes half closed.

"This is the life . . ."

Then he propped himself up on his elbow to unpack the food. And the siesta ended without anything happening.

And evening came round, the two rooms, the open doors, the darkness. And my enervating anxiety. And sleep, without anything happening.

ON MONDAY, we were to take the governess-cart and the Comtesse's little mare to go fishing in the pond at la Trappe and to have lunch together there on the grass. Which we did.

Here again, I was surprised by Raoul's behavior. The weather was lowering, stifling. The fishing had been fun, and quite satisfactory. Other groups, on the banks of the pond, were swimming. Raoul had brought his bathing-suit. We had spoken about it that morning, in front of his mother. I had confessed that I did not know how to swim, that my sister had never wanted me to go swimming in the pond at le Saillant because of the water-weeds, that there was no point in Raoul's lending me a pair of trunks. A wicked curiosity had seized me at the idea of his taking a swim before my eyes. I well knew that he would do it with modesty, and that he would go to get undressed in the bushes that bordered the pond, a few yards from the edge.

But I was curious to see him in swimmer's garb, to guess at his forms under the clinging suit. I urged him to go for a dip. But despite his being worn out by the heat, he claimed that the water was dirty, that he didn't want to. And I remain convinced that he was dying to, that he would certainly have done it if he had been alone, or with strangers, or with anybody but me. He did not want to show himself to me half-naked.

I realize that this supposition, of which I am certain, may seem difficult to accept. How could the boy who gave himself so freely in German class and who sought from me liberties which I always refused, how could this same boy be embarrassed to show himself to me in a bathing suit? Nevertheless, I have no doubt about it. And I see nothing in it at odds with what happened that same evening.

It was Pentecost Monday, our last day of vacation.

That night, we had to be back at the school by nine o'clock. There were a good two hours to be spent in the carriage. The Comtesse gave us dinner at six, and as a rather violent storm had broken at the end of the afternoon and a torrential rain was still coming down when we left the table, she had the broad-hooded victoria hitched up to drive us.

Raoul and I settled down alone in the back of the carriage, with the top up and our legs protected by a great leather apron. We went on talking while the rain whipped all around, both of us entertained by this unforeseen circumstance. The sky was dark, night fell quite fast. The road was long, we let ourselves be jostled about over the potholes made by the rain. We were silent. I had no bad thoughts. And all of a sudden, I felt my companion's hand alight on my leg, exactly as in German class, without a word. I did not move, the leather apron protected us better even than the desk in Father Müller's classroom. Stretched out beside me in the darkness of the old rattletrap, Raoul in no time lapsed into our habits and our favorite games. The rest of the trip drew to a close in total, but extremely active, silence. Nothing more, though, than in the German classes. As usual, I let him take the initiative in these indiscreet explorations. I confined myself to putting my arm on his leg and bringing about his pleasure through his clothes. Leaning backwards, he seemed to be thinking of something else, and if the coachman had suddenly turned around in his seat, he could never have suspected that we were not dozing.

Why had he waited for that moment? Had he been thinking about it, then, as I had? Why had he not taken advantage of the proximity of our rooms, of the open door between our beds, or of the bushes in the woods when we were lying beside each other, or of the thousand opportunities that had offered themselves to us during that stay at Luzac? I still wonder. I am inclined to believe that, in order to satisfy his desires, this enigmatic boy needed certain exceptional circumstances, and above all to re-create the routine that was associated with our excesses. He also needed, somehow, to dispense with my consent, to not have to seek it. Perhaps he also needed me to be placed in such a way so as not to see his face, not to meet his eyes. I don't think that he would easily have brought himself to approach my bed at night to say "Do you want to?" or in broad daylight, in the woods, to make those forward gestures that he was used to making in the rear of the classroom. But there, in the back of that carriage, side by side in the twilight, in silence, he again found all the conditions that he required.

In short, he had more true modesty than I.

The next day and the day after, we had frequent discussions in the courtyard. This sojourn had finally united us. We laughed together over our common memories. And in a tone of fully innocent and trusting camaraderie. We were a little like childhood friends.

And the next Thursday, our silent debauch began again, exactly as before, under the myopic gaze of good Father Müller.

THIS STAY AT LUZAC was an oasis in the middle of that last trimester which preceded the examinations. Father Huxler was on a rampage. From morning till night, even during the recesses, he spoke only of the menacing tests, hounded us with questions, took us aside to make us recite his "general review tables," which he had had hectographed so that each of us would have a copy and which contained in the smallest possible space all the subjects of the examination. A fever had taken possession of us all. We too spoke only of the examination, sharing our terrors with one another, gathering in the courtyard under the trees, instead of playing, to review difficult questions, to go over our "tables" again. The father badgered the weakest ones, rounding them up in the evening for extra studies which lasted until the hour of lights-out. And often, in the already darkened dormitory, we would hear the returning of this little band of "desperate cases," whom the father had just finally let go and who, exhausted, obsessed, got undressed in the dark. Our bodies felt the effects of all this. We had all lost weight, and looked unwell. Many had toothaches, whitlows, all manner of physical woes.

I think I suffered a little less than the others from that contagious terror, that fear of the millennium, that panic. I was still living with that certainty of passing which Xavier de Balcourt had instilled in me and which had prevented me during the year from doing my utmost. At certain moments, though, I shook with anxiety like the others. At night, I, like them, had nightmares in which frightening examiners harassed me with incomprehensible questions, in which I found myself suddenly mute, incapable of uttering a sound, and which caused me to wake up in a sweat. Not only did these academic worries fail to diminish my sexual obsessions; I believe that they exacerbated them, and that I never abused myself more than during those hot nights, agitated as I was with sudden dreads.

In fact, I had made no progress during the year. I had more or less kept up a decent average in French, Latin, Greek, but I was in the lower half of the class in mathematics, algebra, geometry, and at the very bottom in German composition.

The time of the examinations finally arrived. The last days were exhausting. The heat was scorching in those final weeks of July, and the intensive intellectual effort was a torture. Father Huxler himself took us by train to Alençon, where the examination was given, and I can still see those second-class cars in the light of dawn, filled with scared, noisy candidates to whom Father Huxler was, one last time, handing out advice. Then we were shut up in a large room for the written tests. There was no written test, luckily, for math or German. As soon as I had skimmed through the text from Tacitus, I felt half reassured, and I did my best to give an elegant turn to my translation. The Greek text was a fragment from Thucydides, which I got through without too much trouble. I arrived at the test in French composition pretty sure of myself. I do not remember all three topics that were offered us. But I have not forgotten the one I chose: "Letter from Virgil to Maecenas thanking him for his generosity and praising the charms of the villa that he had given him." I did not try to make it too long, but took care over my style and handed in a paper four pages long, neatly recopied, in good French, from which it was obvious that I knew my Virgil and that I could put a sentence together.

Father Huxler was waiting for us on the way out. He took us to have lunch at a *pension* where a large room was reserved for us. The meal was spent going over the rough drafts. When my turn came, the father smiled and said to me: "I think it'll do."

I had indeed passed the written test.

There were still the orals.

Seized at last by a healthy panic, I used the few days that separated the oral from the written to cram geometry and irregular German verbs. It was for nought. In spite of the satisfactory grades that I had received in the Greek analysis, the compliments I received for an analysis of a letter by Pliny the Younger, and my good answers in the commentary that was requested of me on a soliloquy from the last act of *Phèdre,* these high marks did not suffice to make up for the 7 out of 20 that I got in mathematics, and above all for the dismal 2 which the examiner in German inflicted on me with the most insultingly ironic scorn.

My father, with Henriette, had traveled to Alençon to witness my success. When the list of those who had passed was posted and I did not see my name on it, I was shattered. I reread it twice without being able to believe my misfortune. I did not dare go back to my father and my sister. The sky could have fallen on my head and I would not have been more stunned. Father Huxler was checking off the lists in his notebook. He so little expected this failure that he had not noticed the absence of my name. I rushed over to him as though he could help me and grabbed him violently by the arm. He saw my distraught face, my tear-filled eyes, looked over at the list, and finally understood. It was he who had the charity to tell my father. He must have done it in terms such that my father, rather than letting his disappointment and humiliation show, came up to me with a forced smile. "Well, what of it? These things happen . . . You qualified for the oral, that's what counts. You'll pass in October, nothing's lost." He was even considerate enough to say: "It's my fault more than yours. I should have made you take German at home."

Henriette said nothing. She too had tears between her beautiful lashes. They took me, with the wind knocked out of me, to the station café, where my father had me drink a cold toddy "to buck me up." And we went back to the platform, where the little train for Menneville was already made up. Henriette was kind enough to get us seats in the first car, in order to avoid people we knew.

The return to le Saillant was gloomy. We remained silent, all three incapable of dissembling. I went to bed without being able to eat my supper. My father, trying to joke: "Don't look like a man on death row . . . There are other ordeals in life besides failing the oral . . ."

The next morning, early, he came to my room, which he never did. I was still sleeping, after a night of leaden slumber. He sat down at the foot of my bed.

"You're going to rest, without opening a book, for a couple of weeks. After Assumption, we'll see where we stand. I'll be quite surprised if, in two months, you won't be ready for the exam in October."

CHAPTER VII

At the Nacquots'

TWO WEEKS AFTER my failure in the *baccalauréat* and my return to le Saillant, my father and I were coming home on horseback one evening from la Clergie, where the threshing of the wheat had begun. We were silent, and this was so normal for us that we did not even notice it. However, as we rode at a walk up the slope of the drive, my father turned to me and pointed out that if I wanted to avoid having to repeat the year, I would soon have to consider getting back to work. I knew that he was corresponding with the father superior of Saint-Léonard but not that he had already made a decision about me.

"Here, alone, left to your own devices," he went on, "you won't get anywhere. The superior advised me to contact a mathematics teacher at the lycée in Caen who is from this area, has a house in Gevrésy, and comes every year with his wife to spend his holidays there. They sometimes board a student. I wrote to him. He's willing to take you in until the beginning of the school year, and he'll prepare you for your math oral."

My father must have read on my face the distress I felt at the idea of going to live with these strangers:

"They're the right sort of people, I've been told. I've had reports from the notary in Gevrésy. The man is an *agrégé*.* An old local family. What do you think?"

What did I think? I preferred not to say. I only asked what their name was.

"M. and Mme. Nacquot."

We finished the climb in silence. I was so grateful to my father for the stoical way in which he had, contrary to my expectations, accepted my setback that I did not dare let him see my vexation.

Before dismounting, he added laconically:

"Next week, I'll drive you to Gevrésy."

IN FACT, the following week, because of the threshing, which had been late that year, he was forced to abandon this plan, and it was my sister Henriette who went with me to the Nacquots'.

We seized on the opportunity to inaugurate the phaeton that my father had just bought. This strange four-wheeled vehicle was not as light as the buggy, but it could hold three; the seat-back did double duty: the occupant of the rear seat turned his back to those in the front seat. For the occasion, my sister had dressed up. A loose dust-coat of light-colored silk protected her flower-patterned lawn dress, which we never saw except on holidays and which I disliked on principle. "It makes you look too much like a *lady*," I had been telling her since childhood, each time she abandoned her everyday outfit. I took the reins. Henriette sat down next to me; and Gaspard, done up in his blue livery, wearing his cockaded beaver whose ruffled nap gave off bronze lights in the August sun, took his perch behind us, gripping between his knees an old tin trunk of my father's into which Henriette and I had

---

*I.e., has passed a high-level competitive examination for teachers and commands a certain position in the profession.

stuffed my books and my clothes. We had to allow a good two hours for getting to Gevrésy. The trip was dreary. This separation at the beginning of the holidays saddened both of us. Without my wanting to admit it, the new existence that awaited me at the Nacquots' was causing me acute apprehension. To crown everything, for a few days a deplorable eruption of pimples, which I kept inflaming by touching them, had spotted my forehead, and this physical disgrace, at the moment of making my debut in the world, added still more to my dark mood.

The Nacquots lived at the foot of the town in the place called le Pré-Jeannet, on the banks of the Clayette. The woman guard at the railroad crossing showed us the shortest route. Instead of climbing the slope that led to the center of Gevrésy, to the marketplace and the church, we needed to stay in the plain, drive along the edge of the fairground, and go through the suburb of le Jars to get to le Pré-Jeannet, which was amid the truck farms at the edge of the open country. I did not know this district, located at the other end of town from the suburb of Saint-Léonard and not among the usual destinations of our schoolboy walks.

The Nacquots' little property was separated from the road by a small, well-tended garden surrounded by a fence. The gate was shut. On one of the brick pillars was fastened a plaque that I can still see precisely: enameled, adorned with flowerets, and announcing in Gothic letters, *Manoir du Pré-Jeannet.* We were pleasantly surprised by the fine appearance of the house. To tell the truth, it had nothing of a manor about it but was only an honest country dwelling, doubtless built with love at the start of the century by some retired legal worthy or local notable: what was so prettily called at the time a *"demeure de plaisance."** I cannot recall without emotion that attractive house where, during that summer of 1886, I spent a few fruitful weeks which made a real difference in my life as an adolescent. It no longer exists except in my memory. It was torn down during the construction of the gas plant; subdivisions have turned the laughing meadows that were watered by the Clayette into a suburb.

It was a long building; two stories high, roofed in slate, and with two rows of windows placed symmetrically on top of each other, their green shutters standing out against the freshly whitewashed wall. The façade's only ornament was a narrow peristyle in the manner of the First Empire; it sheltered the steps leading up to the central door; stems of jasmine twined around the two columns that supported it. In the center of the garden, a bed of little pink begonias filled the middle of an oval lawn.

*Country house; literally, "pleasure residence."

AFTER HALF A CENTURY AND MORE, my memory of our arrival still makes me smile. No sooner had we got down from the carriage than a white-and-tan spaniel, with which I would soon make friends, bounded up to the gate, barking. Right away, an old housemaid in a headdress who must have been watching for the arrival of the "boarder" came out to meet us, tying, over her hindquarters, the strings of a formal white apron. She opened the gate without raising her eyes and without answering our greeting. Then, as we followed her around the lawn, the peristyle suddenly came to life, like the set of a marionette theater: a couple of little figures, who from a distance resembled the tiny man and woman in our Swiss barometer, emerged from the shadow between the two columns and stood motionless side by side with the light full on them at the top of the steps. They were the same size. He, somewhat portly, in an alpaca frock coat, white vest, and trousers of fawn-colored nankeen; she, noticeably younger, plump and spruce in a gossamer heliotrope-colored dress. Without moving, but smiling, they let us come up to them. M. Nacquot bowed to my sister.

"And here's our young man," he said good-naturedly, looking me over before holding out his hand.

Mme. Nacquot had charmingly slipped her arm under Henriette's, and showed her into the front hall. She spoke loud and clear with an Alsatian accent, which, without being too prominent, added weight to what she said and a sort of importance to her whole person. She turned to me and smiled, apologizing for not receiving us in the drawing rooms, which were still under their dust covers. She explained that they had been detained at Caen by the prize presentation ceremony and had arrived only two days before. We were ushered into the dining room, where a light "lunch," she said in English, had been prepared for us. Henriette made excuses for my father's not having been able to leave the estate. Her even voice, her rather slow gaze, her calm features struck me as if I were noticing her simplicity and natural distinction for the first time. A conversation started up about the quality of the harvest, the heat of the day, the dust of the road, the length of the trip. The entrance of the old servant created a diversion. She brought in a brass-bound wooden pitcher and two misted carafes on a tray. M. Nacquot extolled the coolness of his well. He introduced her simply as Césarine, who, he said, had been a part of the family for more than forty years—the caretaker, and, he added, "the true owner of the manor since my mother's death." Césarine did not appear to have heard herself mentioned, and she left the room without the slightest sign of affability having lit up her weathered and mustached face.

"She always makes me think of Félicité in *A Simple Heart*," *Mme. Nacquot confided to us, laughing.

A silence ensued. I wanted to question Henriette with my eyes; but she had lowered her head with a polite, extremely vague smile.

Meanwhile, Mme. Nacquot, moving her hips, fussed about the table, cut the tart, prepared glasses of syrup water. She was wearing a rustling silk dress in several shades of purple. It was her Sunday finery, and I had so many chances to see her in that outfit later on that I have not forgotten either the bodice with its deep V-neckline or the slightly ballooning sleeves that stopped at the elbows, or the long pleated skirt over which a loosely draped piece of material formed a rounded pinafore that went down to the knees and was gathered up over the hips in two cleverly ruffled lappets. Next to her, my sister seemed subdued and very simple, with her white straw bonnet, her floss-silk mitts and her lawn dress dotted with little bouquets.

Until then—it is true—I had been in contact with very few women—none, at any rate, of Mme. Nacquot's type. Even more than by the elegance of her dress I was disconcerted by the somewhat affected offhandedness of her movements; and also by the oddness of her hairdo: little-girl's bangs that hid her forehead and gave her eyes, her smile, her whole face an indescribably girlish expression. I caught a glance that surreptitiously examined me, and my thoughts turned at once to my pimply brow . . . I was rather intimidated, I admit, and participated in the conversation as little as possible. But I only observed the better, with a mix of surprise and uneasiness, this pair of strangers, who seemed to me so different from what I had imagined.

I took to M. Nacquot from the first. While conversing with Henriette, he threw me a quick glance from time to time which made me immediately look away but in which I did not sense any disparaging curiosity—rather, interest, a serious interest, and one disposed to leniency. There was indeed a mischievous gleam in the bright, keen look which came and went beneath the creased eyelids, but a mischief that did not rule out kindness. One was drawn to him by the courtliness of his manners, his congenial physiognomy. His air of tidiness as well: he seemed to have just got out of his bath; an English baby's† complexion, with closely shaven chin and lips; the skull—an ivory ball, perfectly round and polished—had an appetizing nakedness about it; two short side whiskers, nicely combed, foamed at the level of the ears. His age? I would have put him—overestimating, I may add—at sixty.

He nibbled his slice of tart with greedy lips. But when his wife offered him a glass of syrup water, he shook his head negatively, smiling. Mme. Nacquot turned towards us as if calling us to witness her husband's peculiarity:

*Flaubert's story about an elderly housemaid.
†English in the original.

"The professor, being a true Norman, never gives up his '*bolée*'. . . Even in the middle of winter, if we have a few friends in for the 'five-o'clock,'* you can't get him to drink a cup of tea!" She was poking fun at him, but her eyes were filled with tenderness, and it was obvious that she took pride in the "professor's" slightest quirks. (For that was how she always referred to him, when she spoke of him. Just as, at the Élysée, Mme. Grévy† would say, "the President.")

She took the wooden pitcher and poured the clear cider into one of those rustic cups, cylindrical and squat, made of thick, decorated earthenware, which are no longer found today except in the windows of antique stores, but of which our housewives at the time possessed whole multicolored collections that they hung by their handles on rows of hooks under the shelf of the hutch.

M. Nacquot gallantly raised his *bolée,* smiling at my sister, and gulped down its contents, with a wink at me.

Henriette proffered some remarks about the coming apple harvest, which was shaping up as disastrous; it was not a "fruit year." Then, as the snack was over, we exchanged a look, and she got up to take her leave. Which instantly set off a duet of protest: "Leave without having visited the house?" "You haven't even seen your brother's room!" "Or the vegetable garden!" "Or the river!" "Besides," said M. Nacquot, "the coachman has certainly unharnessed. After twenty-two kilometers, even the best horse, at this time of year, needs a rest!"

Henriette, who was dreading the moment of separation, easily let herself be swayed. I don't think she was sorry, either, to carry out her mission to the end in order to be able to give my father a full report about my new abode.

"Well, let those who love me follow me!"‡ exclaimed Mme. Nacquot with a throaty little laugh. The graceful but determined movement with which she lifted her skirts to lead off the sightseeing party, and the authority with which she opened the hallway door, gave fair warning that she was not going to spare us anything.

I ought to take this opportunity to describe the plan of the house, the function of the various rooms, the look of the furnishings, the topography of the garden. But, really, I balk at the task. Those surroundings in which I lived are too present in my mind for me to be able to give a careful description of them without getting bored. I shall speak of the places as I go along, when they come up in the narrative. For the moment I shall simply note that the entrance hall occupied the center of the "manor." To the right, as one entered

---

*English in the original.

†The wife of Jules Grévy (1807–1891), then President of the Republic.

‡*"Qui m'aime me suive"*—a popular saying, attributed to Philippe VI (1293–1350), who was urging his reluctant barons to join him in a winter campaign.

through the peristyle, there was the small drawing room and then the large one; to the left, the dining room, leading into a pantry and a kitchen. These rooms on the ground floor were lit both by the windows of the façade looking out onto the garden and the road, and, on the other side, by French doors, which opened straight onto a vegetable garden that sloped down to the river. A charming staircase with Directoire balusters led from the hallway to the floor that contained the Nacquots' quarters, located above the drawing rooms, and two guest rooms, above the dining room and the kitchen.

MY FIRST DINNER at le Pré-Jeannet must have been a fairly sensational event for me. I recall nothing much in particular about it. On the other hand, I have retained the memory—the burning memory—of an incident that occurred before the first meal.

I had felt a slight twinge in my heart as I watched Henriette climb onto the seat of the phaeton next to Gaspard, take the reins in one hand, and, before putting the horse to the trot, lean down towards us and give a last wave goodbye. By a tacit accord, we had not kissed in front of the strangers. I helped M. Nacquot close the gate.

"Now you're a prisoner, young man," he said archly as he gave the key a sharp twist in the lock. I forced a smile. Did he understand that I was somewhat distraught? He tried to put his hand on my shoulder; but I was quite a bit taller than he; he settled for taking my elbow in a familiar way and walked me with short steps back towards the house, to which his wife had already returned.

"Do you want to go for a stroll in the meadows? We have more than an hour before dinner. Or would you rather unpack?"

"Yes, I think . . . That would perhaps be best . . . ," I stammered, anxious to be alone. And I went to my room, as a refuge.

It was the second bedroom at the end of the corridor: "A tiny bit less cool than the other, because it's above the kitchen, but more spacious," Mme. Nacquot had pointed out to my sister. "Your brother will be more comfortable there." (Which had kindled a brief glimmer of irony in Henriette's eyes.)

The room was hung with a rather cheerless, grayish wallpaper imitating upholstery but was brightened by the red of the floor tiles and by the ancient pink chintz curtains on which white birds fluttered. I liked my room at first glance. It was isolated from the rest of the floor by a minuscule private foyer created by expropriating the far end of the corridor. As a continuation of this antechamber, a cubbyhole of like size, but reached from the bedroom, formed a sort of alcove curtained off by a chintz portiere where the washstand and a little closet had been installed. (I can still hear the shrill grating which, in spite of my best efforts, accompanied the sliding of the portiere on the rusty curtain rod.) The mahogany furniture consisted of a sleigh bed, a wardrobe with a looking-glass, and a chest of drawers. A locally made table of light cherry placed in front of the window was meant to be used as my desk, as was attested by the crystal inkwell which stood out all by itself on the varnished surface that shone like a mirror.

Closing the door behind me, I felt I was taking possession. I stopped in the middle of the room and took a good look around. The window was wide open. I hesitated to go over to it for fear of being seen. From where I was, I saw the foot of the vegetable garden, the hedge with its white gate, the shimmering of the river among the meadows, a whole countryside beaming under the warm light of a beautiful afternoon that was drawing to a close. I felt a slight intoxication on the threshold of this new life; and I approached it with trust and joy, full of wise resolutions. The mirror in the wardrobe, reflecting the image of my pimply forehead inflamed by the sun and dust, plunged me back into mortifying reality. I went and bathed my face in cold water, and began putting my things away.

I quickly unpacked, hung up my clothes, filled the drawers of the chest. At the bottom of the trunk were books, notebooks, dictionaries. I wanted to put them out on the table. A volume slipped from my hands and knocked over the crystal inkwell. The splattered ink spread over the table. Certain memories are like sleeping bells that one stroke is enough to set clanging. As much as I would like to smile today over that childish experience, the echo that it wakens in me is one of poignant anguish, and the rush of blood which, at this moment, makes my old temples throb, is what sharply rose to my face when I saw the viscous black flow oozing over the varnished wood. The Nacquots' beautiful table! On the day of my arrival! I scanned the room with a distressed look. Stanch it, instantly! But with what? Neither blotting paper, nor a rag, nor even an old newspaper . . . Call out? No, not for anything in the world. Heroically, I pulled my handkerchief from my pocket and pressed it into the pool. The material quickly became saturated. I took a second one from the chest of drawers. Then another. Ready to sacrifice the dozen . . . I was sweating with fear. What was I going to tell them? A gust of wind? Absurd . . . A cat! A cat that had come in through the window? No: "It was hiding under the bed, Monsieur; then, when it saw me, it jumped up onto the table . . ." I ran to fasten the latch; someone could come in, catch me . . . The third handkerchief was barely spotted. The coat of varnish had protected the wood, the ink hadn't had time to soak in. An immense surge of hope—the memory is as present to me as that of my panic . . . With a fourth handkerchief, dunked in the pitcher, I washed, mopped, rubbed, so much so that there soon remained only one slightly dull area and a barely visible slate-gray sheen. Delirious with joy, I backed off a few steps to judge the effect: really, you needed to be in on the secret to notice that slight bluish halo . . .

Saved! I still had to get rid of the handkerchiefs, scattered on the tile floor. I crumpled them into a ball, which I jauntily tossed onto the top of the wardrobe. Tomorrow I would tie a stone to them and drown them in the Clayette . . . I could not get over my luck; I was short of breath, my heart was pounding, and my legs were shaking. I can still see myself sitting on the bed, dazed, trying to regain my composure, ears pricked like a criminal, and holding my stained hands in front of me . . . I had a half an hour to recover, before dinner . . . There was plenty of time to remove the last incriminating traces from my fingers, scrubbing with a brush and a pumice stone. (I shall confess all, shall follow my memory to the end. A triumphant exaltation had succeeded my fright. To celebrate my deliverance and soothe my nerves, I could not resist the temptation of resorting to pleasure . . .)

Such was my first hour of solitude in my room at le Pré-Jeannet.

DESPITE WHAT I SHALL HAVE to tell later on, I do not think that I have ever met a couple who, after twenty years of married life, had stayed so amorously close. This was revealed to me on the first morning by a detail which may seem so ridiculously insignificant that I hesitate to mention it, but which in reality was quite telling, since it struck me so strongly that it has stayed with me to this day.

Before us on the table were coffee, milk, a round loaf of whole-wheat bread and a plateful of *fromage frais*. In front of Mme. Nacquot's chair, a kettle sat on an alcohol stove, which M. Nacquot had lit when he came in and which he was keeping an eye on. As soon as the water began to boil, he left off eating, took a little silver teapot, warmed it, threw in two pinches of tea, and poured in the water. He then turned his attention to a tray on the sideboard, on which were set out a dish of butter and two little milk rolls, those smooth, pale, slender *pains de gruau* with the very white crumb, which bakers have stopped making since the war and which used to be called *pains mollets*. M. Nacquot sliced the rolls in two, buttered them, sprinkled them very lightly with salt, put them on the tray along with the teapot, next to a cup, a sugar bowl and an English porcelain creamer; then, lifting the whole thing, he winked at me:

"Take your time over breakfast, I'll be back."

There wasn't a day when I saw him fail to perform this ritual. Each morning he would himself prepare his wife's breakfast with the gestures of an officiant and would take it up to her in her room.

Probably I remember this so well because those kinds of attentions were surprising to me. Since my birth, I had lived with a widowed father. I had no experience of what the existence of a couple could be like, especially of a childless couple whose rapport is perfect and who enjoy maintaining the tender zeal of newlyweds. The Nacquots' daily life was animated by a never-ending exchange of little services, kindnesses, teasing words, coy expressions and familiarities that I found quite childish and rather shocking in people who could have been my parents. I have never been particularly sentimental. This open cuddling often caused me a certain embarrassment, and it took me some time to get used to it. However well informed, however little prudish I may have been, I was still at an age when it was hard to imagine that the games of love are not the exclusive prerogative of youth and that between a teacher in his sixties with graying whiskers and his wife in her forties—though she be as vivacious as Mme. Nacquot—there could exist anything other than the affectionate and quiet routine of cohabitation. It was only after some time that certain suppositions crossed my mind. To tell the truth, I am not very sure of this. But it seems probable that my suspicions did not really take shape until later on.

Monsieur Nacquot was not long in returning and we finished our breakfast talking about this and that. He was no longer wearing his respectable frock coat of the day before. In his brown canvas jacket with bronze metal buttons, and the leather leggings that fastened tight around the lower part of his pants, he brought to mind a gamekeeper more than a teacher of mathematics.

"And now, let's talk work," he said, pushing his empty bowl aside. He struck his touchwood lighter and lit one of those thin, short cigars that he called "ninas," whose acrid bluish smoke I had already noticed; then he folded his plump hands on the table and, looking at me attentively, addressed me something like this: "You've come here because you want to make up for lost time and pass in October. Success depends on you more than on me. I don't intend to treat you as a dunce whose memory must be force-fed so that he can fool the examiners into thinking that he knows something. It is to your intelligence and your conscience that I shall appeal. For this morning, here's what I propose. You're going to settle down in your room with the syllabus for the examination and your textbooks; you're going to think about your deficiencies and draw up for me, as you see fit, a draft of a timetable to achieve the best results, distributing the work among the six weeks that stand between us and the first of October. This afternoon we'll go over your draft together, and we'll set up a final work plan."

I was very surprised, a little taken aback, but flattered to be treated as a serious young man. I sat down at my big table, with all my books around me, and as best I could drew up a schedule to suit me. I did this spadework with a kind of exaltation, appetite for learning, and desire to make the most of my time. I was expecting to see M. Nacquot appear, and to feel that he was supervising me. But he did not come. The lunch-bell brought us back together in the dining room. "Well," said M. Nacquot, "are you happy with this first morning? Is your study program coming somewhat clear?" I timidly pulled from my pocket the chart I had made and copied over. He glanced through it and put it in his pocket: "We'll go over it together later. It doesn't look bad to me."

Naturally, this outline was very sketchy and imperfect. M. Nacquot, during the hour he spent in my room, discussed it point by point, but in a tone of collaboration, of complicity, putting his objections to me, giving me a say in the matter, asking me repeatedly if I agreed. "You're the one most concerned. You know better than I what you lack. Don't you think that two hours a week would be enough for the history of literature, which you have pretty well down, and that you should devote a few more hours to algebra?" Even while revising my program from top to bottom, he saw to it that I was left with the impression that it was my handiwork, that it was not imposed by him, that in working according to the agreed-upon schedule I would be submitting to my own orders.

"Now," he said, "we're going to go out together and on our walk drop in on Father Müller and finish off your plan with him as to German."

Father Müller received us in the empty school, where he had stayed alone, as he did every summer, with a reduced staff. I realized that this was how he paid for his inadequacies as a teacher in comparison to the other fathers, and that if they let him hold on to the duties that he discharged so poorly during the school year, it was partly because he was willing to forgo a vacation and watch over the school during the holidays.

We agreed that I would come four afternoons a week to have a two-hour lesson and that I would devote a good hour and a half every morning to making translations from French into German and vice versa. I was quite pleased to learn that these lessons would take place in the fathers' library and not in the German classroom, of which I had such impure recollections. These recollections, I have to say, were nearly obliterated from my memory, so different did these large deserted and silent buildings seem from the ones where I had lived and so different was Father Müller, seen this way in private, from that myopic and baited teacher that the students knew. I remembered an incompetent and ridiculous figure. I discovered a dedicated man, who was full of heart, shy as a child, very capable in his field, and who, in those few weeks, introduced me so intelligently to the German language, choosing texts by Goethe, Schiller, Lessing, and even Heine, well selected to please and interest me, that I made very rapid progress. I owe to him the taste I have always kept, cultivated, and developed for Germanic culture and literature. Goethe always had a place next to Montaigne in my officer's trunk.

M. Nacquot worked in an attached cottage that looked out on the vegetable garden, and that I never knew what to call. As an old *normalien*,* he had christened it the *turne*.† Césarine, faithful to tradition, always said *le caviot*.‡ As for Mme. Nacquot, more fanciful, she varied her names. Now she said the *Workshop*, now *the Arbor;* sometimes *Diogenes' Lair* or *the Cyclops' Cave;* but more generally, *the studio.* It was in fact an old storeroom, built as an extension of the kitchen but separated from it by a woodshed where Césarine piled her firewood for winter. The structure, shallow and rather low, was attached to the wall of the vegetable garden. It was entered from the garden by going down two stone steps. The door was one of those old stable doors that allowed the horse to put its head out: the upper panel could be opened like a shutter while the lower remained closed.

The walls, whitewashed and mottled with saltpeter, supported venerable, dust-colored rafters. The floor was packed earth. A homey disorder reigned. The blackboard, covered with equations or with geometrical figures, was set on an easel next to a tall, cluttered architect's table. M. Nacquot liked to write standing. To read, however, he would sink deep into an armchair near the window; it was a roomy wicker basket, all askew, whose crushed cushion retained in its hollow the posterior imprint of its master.

The back wall consisted entirely of a set of shelves loaded down with books and pamphlets, where the seventeen volumes of the big Larousse stood side by side with the collection of *La Revue des Deux Mondes,* to which the Nacquots had remained faithful since the year of their marriage: they called it *La Revue* and seemed not to be aware that other magazines existed (literature was relegated in the house to a shelf on the landing: Madame's library). A grandfather clock, the living, beating heart of the place, stood in its blond cherrywood case in one of the corners. And I can still see, leaning in the opposite corner, the July 14th flag in its moleskin sheath, the bundle of fishing rods next to a small shelf on which M. Nacquot stored his boxes of fishhooks, and the jar in which he kept his earthworms. This old polychrome jar from Rouen, on which, intrigued, I spelled out some Latin pharmacological formula made even more mysterious by its abbreviations, would today occupy a place of honor in the drawing room! To complete this overly indulgent description—which has nevertheless been entertaining to compile and provides an idea of M. Nacquot's various activities—I still must mention a little arched door on the right through which one reached the shed for garden tools: a foul and dusty jumble, where watering cans, spades, pickaxes, pitchforks, and rakes, many worn out, had been accumulating for years; and where there was even to be found, under a carpenter's workbench, in a small

---

*Graduate of the École Normale in Paris.
†École Normale slang for a student room.
‡"Little cellar" in local dialect.

domed box like a child's coffin, an old set of lawn bowls that was called "the Kugel" because it had been left there, in '70, by the "Pruscots"* billeted in the manor. Mme. Nacquot was fond of showing it off, with a mix of repulsion and patriotic pride, as a trophy of war; but if you reached your hand out, she would quickly shut the lid. She would have been scandalized if you had wanted to get up a game.

As soon as he had crossed the threshold of his *turne,* M. Nacquot, professor of mathematics, proved to be a wholly different man from the one I have sketched up to now. M. Nacquot—it is time I said it—remains for me one of the most distinctive and richly gifted minds I have known. He was in addition a wonderful educator, free of all professional tics, having long put his mind to the problems of pedagogy and having acquired exceptional experience, assurance, and subtlety in that domain. I emphasize this; not everybody recognized his merits.

He never shared the results of his experiments with me, still less revealed his methods. As little doctrinaire as possible, he distrusted theories, but he distrusted intuitions just as much. The opposite of an improviser. With him everything was thought through, reasoned out, and he never took a random tack. His principles of education definitely rested on proven foundations. What were they? He valued nothing but personality, and by inclination strove to discover its secret clues wherever possible. I imagine that he divided students into two categories: the ordinary ones; and those in whom he thought he detected gifts, distinctive worth. For the first, implementation of syllabuses, a standardized education, broad and airy but with no chancy initiatives. For the second, on the other hand (the only ones to whom he could, I think, give his total, conscientious attention), a custom-made program, judicious but departing from the norm: every attention, every innovation, even daring, risky ones if necessary. He began, it seems, from this conviction: nothing is more important than self-realization. Therefore the educator must, without hesitation, set apart the individuals with a special quality, deliberately exclude them from certain general, restrictive rules, from certain overly active influences that threaten to jeopardize their integrity; he must apply himself to singling out among their buried abilities those that are most personal, those that contain the most promise and thus deserve to be cultivated first; he must make these exceptional natures aware of those secret seeds, teach them how to distinguish their most characteristic traits; and, while protecting them from fatuous presumption, he must encourage them, in short, to want resolutely, continuously, obstinately, to be themselves.

In thus endeavoring to set out some of M. Nacquot's principles, I may be bending them a bit in my direction and lending him views dear to the old

*Slang for Prussians.

individualist that I am. But wasn't he fundamentally an individualist himself? In fact, no, I do not feel I am misrepresenting him. I can, at any rate, vouch that in my case he behaved as if these precepts were indeed his own.

I am trying to remember clearly what our master–student relationship was like.

Without losing any of the simplicity or smiling good-naturedness that ordinarily made up his charm, with no concern for defending prestige or making authority felt, M. Nacquot immediately seized my attention with the pure brilliance and genuineness of his intelligence, the passionate interest he showed in the life of the mind. With what suppleness did he go from the particular to the general! With what ease did he instantly raise the level of the slightest question he approached! How naturally he moved in the field of his knowledge! I remember connections that he improvised on the spot between the most disparate subjects or categories of thought; luminous connections that poured out of him, full of novelty, daring and usefulness, even for the mediocre listener that I was. He used no technical jargon, no term that was not instantly accessible. He was at pains to have me feel always on an equal footing with him. He explained every difficult point with concrete images and examples that were all the more striking and easy to retain for being borrowed from daily life; and he never went forward in his argument without checking to make sure that I was keeping up.

I have the name Socrates on the tip of my pen . . . Of course, it would be absurd to overdo the comparison. All the same, M. Nacquot was not unlike the Greek philosopher, or at least the legendary figure whom I still find in my memories from school. That southerner Socrates was certainly more talkative and fanciful, although my Norman teacher was not lacking in impishness, even if he tended to save it for family conversation. If I persist in making connections between them, it is because certain details come back to me. The deliberately informal tone with which M. Nacquot handled abstract questions, the range and sometimes the whimsicality of his viewpoints, the visible pleasure that he himself took in his conjurer's exercises; and above all the pains he took to get the listener to participate in the discussion through the very Socratic device of questioning, then the effect he obtained from the surprise when, after having directed one's thinking through subtle twists and turns, like switchbacks on a mountain road, he would lead it progressively up to the summit and suddenly unveil some unexpected truth in all the radiance of its self-evidence. And, as in the teaching of the Socrates of old, this revelation usually had some practical extension, some consequences for moral behavior.

I would like briefly to describe all that I owe to M. Nacquot. I note first the most tangible fact: it was obviously thanks to him that I passed the October exam; and with quite a good grade: the marks I got—especially in mathematics—earned me not just the diploma but honors. This success had very happy results: in healing the wound that the stinging mortification of July had left me, it gave me back that precious self-confidence which Xavier's instruction had once been able to awaken and sustain, but which my year in boarding school, crowned by that failure, had sorely shaken; come the fall semester, I was in a whole new state of receptivity; and that last year of my secondary studies was the most profitable of all, even though the teaching of *philosophie* at Saint-Léonard was quite mediocre.

Another benefit, of a general nature, that I took away from my stay at Gevrésy was that there I learned how to work. A science less widespread than one would think. And extremely useful. To become someone exceptional it is not enough to know how to work (and I am the best example of this); but among the people of worth with whom I've been acquainted, I do not see one who doesn't have this trump card in his hand: knowing how to work. Some people remain convinced that it is a grace, that one must be born with this gift. I don't believe it. It is an ability that can perfectly well be acquired, but only by a concentrated and personal effort. It is here that the providential role of a teacher becomes apparent: without a nudge from outside, this personal effort would never be set in motion. An intelligent educator knows how to induce it, to steer it, and above all to render it conscious—which ensures that the beneficiary will be able to summon it up whenever he wants.

Like the master craftsman standing over the novice who feels his way and wastes materials so long as he does not know how to "handle the work," M. Nacquot taught me to bend my whim to the demands of the task, to begin at the beginning, to make a good start, to attack a problem the right way, always to prepare a summary of my lessons before memorizing them and before rushing into the writing of an assignment, to draw up a plan that was complete, well-balanced, and satisfying for the mind. It was he who taught me rigor. It was he who instructed me in composition. I had an aptitude for writing. He quickly noticed it. Instead of giving me a topic from literature or history to develop in ten pages, which would have taken up the morning, he gave me, for the same amount of time, ten different topics to prepare, for which I had to show him only the outlines, a few lines in diagram form, clearly legible, with divisions and subdivisions numbered and arranged in a logical order. Nothing was more instructive than to see these literary outlines corrected by a teacher of mathematics.

And when it comes to this overall training of the mind, I am not forgetting the contribution of reconciling me to mathematics, about which I had always been foolishly obdurate. Yet another discovery that I owe to M. Nacquot. I have said that he taught me how to work. I add, remembering his math lessons, that he also taught me how to *think*. He eased me so intelligently into this initiation that with him I not only "took to math," as my father used to say, but fell under its spell.

Until then I had a taste only for the humanities. With mathematics, I suddenly entered another world. I escaped from the more-or-less, from appearances, from doubt, from a realm where all solutions have a concrete, provisional, forgiving, fluctuating character, where truths are numerous and unstable, easy to grasp and yet ungraspable, because they are always approximate, experimental, subject to interpretation and ingenuity. In the field of mathematics, everything is strict and solid. There I have known the satisfaction the mind derives from perfect logic. There the air one breathes is rarefied and exhilarating. There one lives in the abstract and the self-evident. Uncertainty recedes and vanishes as one advances, truth exists, certainty becomes possible.

I do not pretend to have become a mathematician. I lost none of my literary tastes; always, with me, they have remained the strongest. But the contact with mathematics opened my eyes to a sense of the perfect, the excitement of the absolute. The real, most naked, purest joys of intelligence: it was by arriving at mathematical truth—if I dare say so—that I tasted these. The Q.E.D. brings an explosion of mental elation that I think is known only to mathematicians—when, having made their way through the labyrinth of a rigorous argument, they suddenly arrive at the indisputable.

I am probably exaggerating my impressions of that time, mixing them up with those that I would receive later on from mathematics classes in Paris. I want only to emphasize that M. Nacquot's teaching of mathematics opened new perspectives for me and offered me the possibility of a new direction. Without him, I would never have been able to prepare for the entrance examination to Saint-Cyr, and my life would have been completely different.

LET'S NOT EVADE the sexual question. I had not turned into a little saint because I was boarding in a professor's proper household, and because I had made and kept good work resolutions. All the less so since the abundance of fine fare, overly rich and spicy dishes, a meat diet, a sluggish digestion after meals, enriched my young blood excessively and had an effect on my temperament. The demon hadn't left me. At the very most I could say that it had somewhat changed its aspect and modified the images by which it tormented me. A curious thing, which I note to begin with: during the day, in that room where I spent so many hours alone and where the demon had leisure to visit me and offer me distractions, I was good, most of the time, and very rarely turned away from my chaste application to work. Not only because I feared that M. Nacquot might enter unannounced, or because I always worked with the two windows open, and these windows, which went quite low, exposed me to the view of people in the vegetable garden. Perhaps it was for no other reason than that I was truly determined to work, and that this work, which I took seriously, interested me enough that each day I was impatiently intent on completing the program set by my schedule.

I believe that in these matters, habits—the "bad" as well as the good— play a great role. I had got used to reserving the moment just before sleep for my dissipation: it was in the darkness of night and in bed, beneath the mosquito netting, where I often lay naked on the sheet because of the heat, that my erotic fantasies were given free play. The habit was formed. I had my special time for lustful excitement, and if my demon did not manifest itself exclusively at that late hour, at least I hardly ever, except at that moment, gave in to my practices and obtained the satisfaction that my temperament demanded.

Something else even more curious. Since I had left boarding school and no longer had either boys or their example around me, or Luzac's indiscreet companionship, my imagination had, as it were, changed register, and the images with which it beset me were distinctly transformed. As far I can remember, during my life at boarding school, in the silence of the dormitory, the naked bodies that haunted me were usually male. From the time of my stay with the Nacquots onwards, they were quite exclusively female. And I am seeking the reasons for this very important transformation. I see several. I attribute this change partly to the absence of my schoolmates and partly to the feminine presence of Mme. Nacquot. The thought that the Nacquot couple, whose large conjugal bed I knew by sight, were sleeping not far from my room prompted me to envision their mating and to feed my imagination on wildly lascivious scenes in which they were the players. There was a lot of naïveté in this. But it must be said that their behavior, Mme. Nacquot's flirtatiousness toward her old graybeard of a spouse, certain familiarities that he permitted himself in my presence, such as lightly touching the curly hairs on his wife's nape with a caressing hand when she was sitting at the table and he passed behind her to get to his seat; certain ways, in the evening at the river's edge, of helping her lie down in the hammock or get up from it; even certain very tender kisses that I happened upon, either to end an argument or seal a promise she had obtained from him; a certain twinkle in the husband's eye on days when Mme. Nacquot was particularly perky and had amused us with her remarks—all this somewhat justified the ideas that my perverse innocence concocted of their intimacy at night.

There were also daily walks, in the town and its immediate environs, which constantly put the bodies of young women before my eyes. All this was rather novel for a child whose youth had been spent in the deserted park at le Saillant and who had never been away except to find himself thrown in with a community of males.

The fact remains that it was at the time of my stay in Gevrésy that woman and her sexual attractions truly burst in upon my life.

AROUND MID-SEPTEMBER, a letter from the Nacquots' nephew set off a great commotion in the calm and industrious regularity of our existence. Gustave Nacquot announced his appointment as teacher at the lycée in Alençon and suggested to his uncle and aunt that he stop off for two or three days in Gevrésy before going on to take up his post at the beginning of the school year, so as to let them get better acquainted with his young wife, whom M. and Mme. Nacquot had met only briefly on the day of the wedding, in July. This proposal was greeted with joy, and they immediately began to prepare the house for the young couple's arrival.

Over and over they read out loud the "missive" from *Tatave,** which seemed a model of the epistolary art. "How prettily he writes!" marveled Mme. Nacquot. And I blindly agreed.

The first thing they did was to talk to Césarine in order to lay in ample provisions. To reserve a whole calf's head, with tongue, at the butcher's. To arrange with the poulterer to procure, in due time, a good fat goose or a young turkey, not to mention a couple of grain-fed chickens. M. Nacquot set up an appointment with a neighbor who owned nets to string across the river, so that he could try to catch a big pike to keep in a fish tank.

The drawing room was stripped of its slipcovers, the furniture beaten in the garden, and one day I watched Césarine and a cleaning lady spread out on the lawn a rug I had never seen except rolled up under the piano, and get down on their hands and knees to brush it with damp willow leaves.

Then all the furniture from the big guest room next to mine was taken out onto the landing, and an entire day was spent in cleaning the room from top to bottom, hanging the freshly ironed tulle curtains, and putting on the tables little round white crocheted doilies that had been washed in bluing.

Finally came the memorable Monday when the young couple was due at the Gevrésy train station. A hired barouche arrived to pick up M. Nacquot an hour before. Mme. Nacquot timidly hazarded the idea that I go along with him "to help." But M. Nacquot was against it and made a point of saying: "I'm terribly afraid that the visit of my niece and nephew may cause you distractions from your work. But they will stay for only three days. I ask you

*I.e., Gustave.

to change nothing in your schedule, and I am counting on you not to let your work suffer. Of course we will have our lesson every morning, as usual."

But no sooner had he left for the station than Mme. Nacquot called me to help her to rehang, above the young guests' conjugal bed, the mosquito net, whose string had just been broken by a draft. Then, together, we took stock of the room one last time, and she sweetly asked me if I would be so kind as to go and look in her bedroom for the big Japanese screen, which she wanted, as a final touch, to put in front of the visitors' washstand.

"I know quite well what it's like to be a very young woman," she told me. "Even if they've been married two months, there are details of one's personal hygiene that one doesn't like having to perform in front of the other . . ."

She laughed her throaty laugh. We were together in this room that was going to be the scene of the young couple's amorous romps. We were moving back and forth around the bed, with its two pillows. Everything was suggestive. I imagined all sorts of things . . . I had the feeling that Mme. Nacquot was thinking about them too. There was an indescribable new sense of companionship, a certain slightly ambiguous complicity between us. While bustling about, she told me little memories of the first months of her marriage, laughing over various instances of childish modesty, speaking with an unprecedented freedom, as if we were the same age and had the same experience of life.

Then we stood at the window to watch for the arrival of the carriage, which could be spotted about four hundred meters off as it came out of the street from the station into the road. We were leaning side by side, chatting.

She was not wearing a dressing gown but rather a foulard dress with a low-cut décolletage bordered by a narrow piece of pleated lace against the skin, and with rather wide flared sleeves from which her forearms, adorned with charm bracelets, emerged. There was a black ribbon circling her bare neck.

"There they are," she said suddenly. "Quick, get going, so my husband doesn't scold me for keeping you from your work!"

I went back to my room, and even though I did not dare look out the window, I overheard the arrival, the hugging and kissing, the joyful shouts. The whole house sounded like an aviary. I heard the four Nacquots come up the stairs and enter the room next to mine. I noticed that the wall was thin enough so that voices could be made out rather easily, when they were raised even a little. And ideas of spying began to arise in my head.

I heard the hosts leave.

"We'll let you settle in," said Mme Nacquot. "You'll see if you have everything you need. But really, my dear, no dressing up for dinner . . . We're in the country. And besides, the bell's going to ring in twenty-five minutes . . . Just enough time to unpack. We'll let you be . . ."

M. Nacquot came into my room before going back downstairs. But he had the tact not to check my work too carefully and to make only a quick and absent-minded appearance.

As soon as he was gone, I ran to stick my ear against the common wall. I heard a muffled murmur of voices, a moving-around of trunks, then giggles, and a silence that I imagined full of passionate kisses. Then the murmur started up again, the bureau drawers, the sliding closet door. They were unpacking, putting things away.

I went downstairs sooner than they did, before the bell rang, and as I was crossing the landing, the door suddenly opened. The nephew, in shirtsleeves, was coming out to put a pair of dusty boots on the threshold. He pretended not to see me, and hastened to shut the door. But not fast enough so that I didn't have time to see, at the back of the room, in front of the washstand, a young woman in corset and petticoat, her upper chest exposed, her beautiful arms lifted to twist the blond plait of her hair into a bun. I also had the time to say to myself: "Ah, they've got rid of the screen . . ."

Ten minutes later, they hurtled merrily down the stairs and joined us in the drawing room, where we were ceremoniously awaiting them.

They were a very handsome couple, pink and fresh, both blond, with smiling mouths and laughing eyes. Their joyous entrance, in light-colored outfits, into that sad drawing room with its curtains and armchairs of garnet red velvet, where dusk had already made it necessary to light the two lamps on the mantelpiece with their frosted globes, was like the coming of happy youth. Juliette was wearing a full dress with flounces of lawn embroidered with a sprinkling of little roses; she seemed to dance as she walked. Her husband had on trousers of a pale shade, and a white vest. A pretty blond mustache curled above his lip. He seemed, to the schoolboy that I was, the incomparable paragon of ease and good taste. They would appear quite stuffy to the young people of today. But back then, and in that provincial context, they brought a note of independence and almost of cheek that left me transfixed with admiration.

The dinner was interminable and sumptuous. A real wedding banquet. Under the hanging lamp M. Nacquot himself, his napkin tucked into the top of his vest, carved the braised leg of lamb, then the fat, crisp chicken. A set of glasses that I had not seen before was lined up in front of the place settings, and Césarine brought M. Nacquot one dusty bottle after another, which came from his grandfather's cellar and the tasting of which gave rise to admiring comments and endless comparisons.

During the two and a half days of the niece and nephew's stay, the abundance and quality of the fare were maintained morning and night. The star attraction of these feasts was the famous pike, which weighed close to five pounds and which the neighbor with the nets had managed to capture and to kill, in shallow water, with a rifle shot. All five of us vied to do justice to the dishes. The young couple displayed an insatiable ravenousness, and Mme. Nacquot, smiling, filled their plates while uttering ribald little innuendoes: "We know what it's like to be newlyweds . . . You need to restore your strength . . ." I was almost shocked by these startling insinuations and would have experienced great discomfort if I had felt that they ever so slightly embarrassed the pair they were directed at. But it was quite the opposite. They seemed delighted to be reminded at every turn, and even gratuitously, of what obviously was occupying all their thoughts. The atmosphere of the old house, and the hosts themselves, seemed to be transformed, and to succumb to some lascivious contagion. Even Césarine, a confirmed old maid, wreathed the young couple with looks that testified to a kindly tolerance for the weaknesses of the flesh. "Come on, off to bed, lovebirds!" M. Nacquot would say at night when the steeple clock chimed ten-thirty. And they didn't have to be told twice. "The lovebirds' tray," Césarine would say, preparing their bread and butter in the morning.

I don't know how to describe the kind of blithely sensual fever that reigned in the house. Mme. Nacquot had suddenly grown younger. She did not look much over thirty. She had something blooming in her flesh, lustful and languorous in her walk, equivocal in her cooing laughter, rapturous in her smile, and misty in her eyes.

I submitted delightedly to this contagion that exacerbated my senses. I was in a better position than anybody to be obsessed by what was going on in the lovers' bedroom. At night, in my nightshirt, I would remain for hours with my cheek glued to the wall. In my mind I was living in the neighboring room, from which all the noises, all the murmurs, stifled laughs, sounds of the basin, were suspect to me and were translated by my imagination into orgiastic scenes. In truth, I could not make out a single word, and I had great difficulty interpreting the confused rumblings that I succeeded in picking up. In the nocturnal silence of the house, I managed to make out certain noises more clearly and to identify them. I heard the couple getting ready for bed, bantering in lowered voices, and I pictured them, undressed, performing their ablutions.

One evening, I clearly heard them running after each other across the room barefoot, then throwing themselves onto the bed, laughing. The bedsprings gave off a few muted cymbal clashes. And silence fell. I kept on listening awhile, holding my breath, tensely rooted to the spot and trembling all over with morbid curiosity. But as I heard nothing more, I was certain, in my lack of experience, that they had gone to sleep. I felt my way back to my bed, but I was still straining my ears in the direction of the love chamber, and suddenly it seemed to me I perceived a creaking of the bedsprings. I leapt over to the wall, just in time to catch something vague, a sort of smothered moan, scarcely audible, incomprehensible to me, which sounded like the sigh of someone turning over in his sleep. Then, after a few minutes' silence, I distinctly caught the murmur of the two voices. Were they awake, then? So much so that, to my great surprise, I heard them moving around in the room. And immediately came the clink of the jug against the marble and a sound of water, very clear—and what was quite odd, hardly an hour after they had washed up. "Don't catch cold," I thought I heard. It was the husband's voice, just on the other side of the wall, where their bed was. So it was Juliette who had gone to the washstand. I was straining to figure out these strange clues. And in a flash I understood. I had heard them making love.

When silence returned, I finally decided to go back to bed. I slept hardly a wink. Several times in the night I woke up, obsessed, and rushed over to the wall. Sometimes I heard the two of them breathing, and sometimes nothing.

During the day, I scarcely saw them. I went on strictly leading my normal life. But during the meals, I could watch them at leisure. Or I would see them from my window, in the late morning, finally ready, heading down toward the river with their arms lovingly around each other's waists. I saw Gustave chase his wife through the grass along the bank, pick her up in his arms, and carry her to the hammock. Then suddenly lower his face to Juliette's. I saw Juliette's arms close around him, pressing her husband's head against her cheek. They kissed. Furthermore, they felt no constraint in front of us, and kissed greedily at the drop of a hat. "Now, now, lovebirds, behave yourselves," Mme. Nacquot would coo, gazing at them laughingly with sparkling eyes.

On the third day, in the morning, they left in the barouche. M. Nacquot had called me to say goodbye to them in the entrance hall. I immediately went back up to my room. As I passed my neighbors' door, I noticed that it had remained ajar. From my window I saw the barouche in front of the gate. I saw the group crossing the garden. M. and Mme. Nacquot flanked the young couple, who were in traveling garb. Césarine and the housemaid followed with the luggage. I suddenly realized that I was alone in the house. Then I swiftly returned to the landing, opened the door of the adjacent room, and stopped on the threshold. It was in a suggestive disarray. The unmade bed, the washstand bucket full of soapy water, damp towels bunched up on the marble of the mantelpiece. A bidet, without a lid, was pulled out in front of the washstand, with a damp towel wadded up inside. It had something solemn and aggressive about it; it stood out there, on the parquet floor, like a symbol. I furtively went to the bed, pulled the covers further back, sniffing, searching for something, some traces, some proofs . . . A distinctive smell of perfumes, toothpaste, unmade bed, filled the room. I looked all over the place, inhaling, devouring every detail with my eyes, like a policeman on the prowl. Then I grew afraid of getting caught, and I went hastily back to my worktable.

THE MAGIC VIRUS that the couple had brought did not stop working after their departure: it was precisely then that it spread through our veins with its maximum efficacy.

As soon as they left, I felt that Mme. Nacquot had become another woman and that our relations suddenly entered a new phase. The animation she had exhibited during those three days persisted in her smile, her chatter, the cheerfulness of her expression, the brightness of her eyes. M. Nacquot, who had immediately resumed his work life, not sorry, I believe, that everything had returned to normal, scarcely responded in kind.

It was to me that Mme. Nacquot addressed herself, it was towards me that she directed that light and laughing fever. Through jokes, sweet little gibes, increased attentions. I had assumed more importance in her life. She would take advantage of an absence on her husband's part to call me, from downstairs, to help her put a piece of furniture back in place in the drawing room, to carry something heavy, or even to eat some fruit that she had just brought in from the garden.

It was the very end of September, night fell early, but the evenings were mild, and she would not give up spending them by the water's edge. M. Nacquot stayed in the dining room, where he had placed an armchair under the hanging lamp. We would see him, from down below, immersed in his *Revue des Deux Mondes*. He could not have heard us even if we had raised our voices, but she took pleasure in speaking low, stretched out in her hammock, with a shawl over her shoulders and me sitting close by. The moment we were alone, the conversation would immediately turn towards the couple. That young and sensual love haunted her, as it did me. And she very quickly fell into a whole new freedom in her remarks, making insinuations about that love, the proximity of which still intoxicated her in retrospect. I enjoyed this game, flattered to be treated by her as an adult with whom anything could be discussed. I probably only half-understood her allusions, but I bluffed it out and answered in the same tone. She asked me for my impressions of Juliette, pointing out her physical charms, the quality of her skin, the fullness of her figure. And disparaging details. "I saw her getting dressed the other day. She has no modesty, it's amazing. She'd let me in, she was in her nightie. She has something extraordinary for a woman, blond hairs on her legs, can you imagine, like a boy . . . She hardly tightens her corset, which is a mistake, I took the liberty of telling her. She has a very large bust for a woman so young, and low-slung. If she doesn't watch herself, she'll have big flabby breasts before long. Don't you think? Especially if she has a child. And

that could certainly happen, though they appear to be taking precautions . . .
They're so smitten with each other that they're not sensible. Did you notice,
Wednesday morning, the dark shadows they both had under their eyes? I
don't think they can have slept much. At their age, I can understand it . . .
And you? Do you like her, I mean as a woman, is she your type?"

I laughed with an air of collusion. "Yes," I said, "that night they moved
around a lot in their room . . ." I let her suppose that I had overheard much
more than I actually had. "That's right, the wall's so thin. Well, well, you
must have had a good time! . . ." I pretended to be reticent in order to provoke her questions, which I enjoyed. She pressed me to confide in her.
"Come on. You can tell me . . . You see how freely I speak to you . . . If my
husband could hear me . . . I'm sure you were listening at the wall, you
naughty boy! And so? what? Kisses? Yes? Did you hear what they were saying?
The poor bed, the springs must have been working overtime those three
nights!"

I was more embarrassed than I let on. Those "precautions" opened up
horizons for me. I was finding out many things. I understood those sounds
of water . . .

Laughing, she told me some facts about Gevrésy.

"Just imagine, weddings are always held on Saturdays, because the hair-
dresser's bathtub is available only on Fridays and Saturdays, and the bride
and groom, you see, do like to have had a wash that day. As well they might!
People are so dirty in the country! I always wonder what gets into men that
they run, as they do, after these farm girls or girls from the suburbs, who
hardly wash . . . It can't be appetizing . . . But when they really want it—
right? Ah! men are disgusting . . .

"Do you know about the black bidet? No? It's a local legend. Dublé, the
upholsterer, rents it out at five francs, for marriages. Yes, for the wedding
nights! And do you think that they hide the fact, that they have it brought
round at night or wrapped up in a cloth? Not at all! Dublé's assistant brings
it, and he crosses the whole countryside with the black bidet on his shoulders. Nobody is surprised by this. They say, 'Ah, he's going to So-and-so's.' It's
one of the assistant's perks, he's sure to get a good tip. And he goes to get it
the next day, or sometimes the day after that when it's the fastidious ones
who've rented it for two days, the ones who don't niggle.

"Juliette told me about her wedding night. I shouldn't be telling you
this . . . If she knew! But you're discreet, aren't you? I haven't even talked to
my husband about it. Oh, young women aren't as ignorant as they were in
my day. She told me that she knew almost everything through the confidences of a married girlfriend. And just imagine . . . Oh, I don't know if I can
tell you this . . . They didn't even wait for night. It's incredible, don't you
think? Gustave must have been in a real hurry . . . At five in the afternoon,

while people were dancing, after the banquet, the newlyweds slipped away. Juliette went to her room to take off her wedding dress and get into her traveling clothes. They were to spend their honeymoon at Le Tréport . . . Gustave came in while she was getting undressed. That's what she told me, but you know very well that if she'd wanted, she could have locked the door . . . or told him to go away. And it was there, right in the middle of the afternoon, in the room she'd lived in as a young girl, while people were dancing and her parents were downstairs receiving the guests at the buffet, that it happened . . . Bing, bang! Eh? You don't find that incredible?

"Especially since, the first time, one can't assume that it's so pleasant, for a girl . . . At least, it's not something I'll soon forget! . . . I laugh about it now, but at the time! Especially since I wasn't expecting that at all . . . Oh, I knew, roughly what was supposed to happen. And then my mother had made me a long, embarrassed speech, poor Mama, to warn me that I might perhaps be surprised, but that a husband had the right to all sorts of liberties, and that I had to submit nicely . . . But I was pretty naïve . . . Would you believe . . . Well, it's very difficult to say . . . What a story you've got me started on! . . . I knew that little boys were made differently from little girls. But I had never seen anything but babies or young boys . . . I didn't suspect what a man was like . . . And a man in love . . . Because my husband was handsome, you know, and very smitten, and young, in those days . . . Well, he was thirty-four, and I nineteen . . . But I liked him so much that I accepted everything. Only it can't be said that for a young woman it was a pleasant beginning . . . No . . . Fortunately, you get a taste for it pretty quickly . . . So much of a taste that you can't do without it!"

All this, written out, seems quite harmlessly banal. I myself have to make some effort to fathom the stirring created in me by those poor idle remarks of a provincial woman, a petty bourgeoise on the brink of middle age, whom the visit of an amorous couple had left all aquiver, succumbing to her inner turbulence, like a stagnant pond that seems quite limpid but that a dog's slightest splashing turns all muddy.

That "you can't do without it" was accompanied by a look which I guessed in the darkness to be fraught with a secret and persistent questioning that I heard in the voice.

Her appetite for amorous things having been whetted by the stay of the young marrieds, it appeared that, quite naturally, the curiosity with which she had spied on them had carried over to the young virgin she had under her wing. Virgin? I quite obviously was one, but I'm not at all sure that she realized it. Or, at least, I'm sure that it would have taken little to raise doubts in her. And this little I provided her, with a skill that consorted oddly with my shyness and my inexperience. For, while answering in a falsely evasive manner, I put on airs and assumed a knowing tone that led her to believe that I already had a certain acquaintance with these titillating matters. And though it may seem odd to say so, I think she was scarcely aware of all that can go on in the mind and senses of a young man, and the particular experiences that he may have had at boarding school. What's more, I would rather have been burned alive than to have started confessing those things. But she did not even give me the chance. It was obvious that while circling inquisitively around the extent of my sexual initiation, she was miles from suspecting how perverse and peculiar it truly was. "Has he already had an affair with a woman?" was definitely the only question that occurred to her. Tall and strapping as I was, it must have seemed probable to her that temptations and opportunities had come my way and that I had given in to them. I entered into the game at once, both to render more impenetrable the darkness in which I was anxious to shroud my real schoolboy depravities—which, at this time, already seemed to me like the shameful acts of a child, boyish pranks that a man does not admit to—and also to invest myself with prestige: for I sensed quite strongly that by assuming the air of a young man who has had affairs with women, I would be giving myself more importance in her eyes. An importance that I understood all the better since, at school, we had a jealous respect for those among us who had, or pretended to have, slept with a woman.

From hesitancy to hesitancy, from half-admission to half-admission, by less and less veiled references, I did everything necessary to convince her that I had already proved myself as a male. Quite naturally it was around the "girls in the pond" that my imagination, caught unawares, invented a vaguely plausible story. I let her gradually suppose that in the country, one summer, at a swimming hole, I had happened onto a local girl, very beautiful and not overly bashful, whom I had chased into the bushes, and that a "liaison" had ensued. And I did it in a way so that everything seemed to suggest that this rustic nymph did not represent my first such experience.

From then on, the theme of her conversation changed. It was hardly ever about the newlyweds anymore, but about me and my aquatic affair. I had to give a name to the lady of the pond and gradually expand on the circumstances of our meetings. There were tumbles in haystacks, at night; trysts in the straw of a lonely barn; I was even so shameless as to mention a farmhouse bedroom whose window was kept ajar for me and where I went to spend nights of pleasure.

All this happened very fast. In a few evenings by the water's edge. (Cooler and cooler evenings, what is more; such that we deserved credit for staying so late outdoors. "You're both of you crazy," M. Nacquot came to tell us at ten o'clock. "You're going to catch cold! Léone, you're just as foolish as Bertrand!")

She obviously enjoyed being alone with me and speaking about my affair.

She did it with an affectionate complicity, freer and freer. She spoke to me as if to a student whose casual love affairs are known and who has to be cautioned. She went so far as to advise me to be careful, which I did not immediately understand. Careful, first of all, on account of my health. "With these country girls, you can catch a nasty disease . . ." Careful, also, because of the consequences. And this was what I did not grasp right off, so little did it occur to me—I still wondered, every night, how women were made—that I could get a farm girl pregnant . . . But those allusions to the precautions taken by Gustave and Juliette had vaguely prepared me to understand. The "sounds of water . . ." I pretended to be sure of myself, claiming that I knew perfectly well what had to be done, and that my bathing beauty and I were not running any risk . . .

Her attitude towards me had also changed a great deal. At the table, she looked at me in a different way. I would catch something collusive and ambiguous in her eyes. Thus, quite naturally, with that Machiavellianism that comes instinctively, I did everything necessary to make her fall for me. I paid her unexpected attentions. From my walks I brought back little wild orchids of many different kinds which grew by the roadside and under the bushes and whose delicate filigree always enchanted her. She would pin the bouquet to her blouse, and keep it there till evening. I gradually grew bolder in winning her over. I did not know it was so easy and already so far along. If she said of a bunch of jasmine, "It has a lovely scent" and pressed it for an instant to her face, I would say, "Show me," and bury my own in it for a long moment. Then I would look at her, smiling, and would delight in seeing that she was stirred. In the evening, I helped her get into her hammock and I spread the shawl over her with a solicitude that was altogether new.

The strangest thing is that I was working all the same, and a lot. Work occupied another part—the most important—of my life. I very keenly wanted to pass, I saw the enormous progress I had made, I was working with relish and without distraction. The flirtation with Mme. Nacquot was my recreation, an incidental habit, a game for the evening. And nothing had changed in my solitary nights, either, except that the image that obsessed me most persistently was that of Mme. Nacquot and of her nakedness. It was even easier than before to imagine her saying: "Look how I'm made . . . Am I different from your girlfriend?" And she would half-open her dressing gown and I would see her statuesque body, white as alabaster, with its bloodless pallor, its smooth belly, its round thighs. Or I would imagine myself confessing to her: "I lied to you a little . . . I'd like to know how women are made." And just like that, smiling, she would give me a slap as she sometimes did: "Naughty boy . . . Here, look at me." And I would feast my eyes on her nakedness.

Sometimes, during the day, I would look at her and mentally undress her.

With an impassive air, at table, as I cheerfully replied to her teasing, I would contemplate her bosom and suddenly see her two bare breasts.

And I occasionally daydreamed about a scene that was set in the hammock. I was admitting to her how much I wanted to know how women were made. And she, in the darkness, yielded herself to the investigations of my hands that I slipped beneath her dress to discover the warm secret of her flesh.

One night when a storm was brewing, we had stayed down by the river until the first drops of rain. "Quick, let's go in," she said. "Help me get down." I went over. I was against the hammock, in exactly the position where I had imagined myself in my fantasy sliding my hand along her legs. I held the netting steady so that she could get down. And, as she sat up, I felt the flesh of her thigh, the weight of her body, on my hand as she glided to the ground, brushing against me. I experienced in this contact, so close to what I had wished for in my fantasy, a desire that went all the way to spasm, a sudden, horribly painful stirring, such that I brusquely pulled my hand away, letting go of the hammock, and she almost went sprawling. She steadied herself on me and unquestionably took advantage of that moment to prolong the contact. I instantly freed myself, with the same involuntary brusqueness. "Clumsy," she said. "A little more and I'd have fallen."

There was in this cry very little of reproach, no impatience, and a strange and languorous tenderness. It was the same tone in which she might have said: "You're mean, I don't love you anymore!"

What did I feel, during this whole business? And she? Yes, what did we feel?

It had started, for both of us, as a sort of game. For my part, the game consisted mainly of an instinctive flirtatiousness, an ambiguous pleasure that I took in getting close to what I vaguely sensed to be a smoldering fire; but I did not perceive this fire clearly, and, of course, was never aware enough, or vain enough, or experienced enough to say to myself: "She feels something for me." Even less: "Maybe she desires me." Shy, naïve, very young, completely unaccustomed to relations with people and especially with women, of whom I knew none in a family consisting only of my sister and my father, I found it *unthinkable* that there could ever be an affair between Mme. Nacquot, the wife of my elderly professor, and myself.

And she? I believe that she was a very decent and faithful wife, and I would bet that she had never had any lapse for which to blame herself. But there happened to be, at that moment of her life, a combination of very diverse circumstances: the idleness of the holiday, that summer's stormy heat, the languor of a frivolous, novel-reading woman with nothing to do who was approaching her difficult forties; the presence in her life, an unprecedented presence, of an adolescent with whom she had to live every day at very close quarters; the chance and heady visit by that young couple in full sensual effervescence whose contact struck incendiary sparks; finally, the game I had begun to play with her, which might have led her to surmise a juvenile passion, or—who knows?—one of those *chérubinades* that no woman of mature years can experience without an emotion that is half physical, half maternal. To this was perhaps added an indefinable attraction for my seventeen-year-old's freshness, for my apparently healthy innocence, a certain temptation to tease my ingenuousness, to see how far the thing would go . . .

And then, I think that she had got caught up in her own game, that she had begun to lose control, and that, as conversations progressed to confidences, light touches to more insistent ones, her crisis became more acute, which alone can explain what followed.

When I discovered, naïvely, that my game was becoming less harmless and that she was leading me beyond what I had dared wish for (the evening of the hammock, for example), I abruptly pulled back. I was gripped by a kind of fear, and all the fun of the game vanished. From the moment I began to suspect that she was capable of going further, I had only one reflex: to evade, to flee, no matter what. And this is something very strange, which I have often since pondered. But let us not anticipate.

The scene of the hammock was followed, the very next day, by another, which I wish to recount: the scene of the cat.

A little tabby, very young, with white fur and a pink muzzle, taken in by Césarine at the beginning of the vacation, that Mme. Nacquot had christened "Herminette" and that she often kept in her lap or on her shoulder. I too had grown attached to that warm and silky, soft, yielding, purring little ball, and it sometimes spent the whole afternoon perched on my shoulder, motionless, refusing to budge while I worked in my room.

That night, we had not been able to stay outside. The storm of the day before had thrown the weather off kilter and triggered the autumn equinox; it had rained all day long, the air had turned downright cool, summer seemed truly over. We had spent the evening in the dining room, while M. Nacquot, in his armchair, read with his back to the light. Although the unpleasant impression of the day before had stayed with me, I had recently become so used to our free after-dinner chats that I felt a keen disappointment at spending my evening there, in a chair, leafing through the newspaper and keeping up a trite conversation with Mme. Nacquot, a continuation of our table talk, which the presence of M. Nacquot prevented from veering into confidences and which seemed to me bland, so much had I developed a taste for that suggestive fencing in the evening with just the two of us. Mme. Nacquot had the cat curled up in her lap and was diverting herself by brushing a finger along the head of the dozing little animal, which, at each stroke, shook its ears in an amusing way with a sudden nervous movement. She was looking at me and sometimes smiled at me strangely, as if she were trying to continue our low-voiced riverside conversations by means of these looks and knowing smiles. This dumb show behind M. Nacquot's back, despite the fact that he could not detect it—there was no mirrored mantelpiece in the dining room, only an old white porcelain stove in a recess—gave me a painful feeling of disquiet. The game was beginning to overstep the limits I deemed acceptable; everything in me resisted going further. Was this because of my affection for M. Nacquot and a kind of remorse at taking advantage of his trust in this way? Wasn't it mainly an anxiety that had come over me, since the day before, at being carried away by the game? A kind of fear? I did not respond to these signs of connivance, or did so with an annoyed, sullen, disapproving air. I visibly refused to participate in this silent and hidden exchange. I read an intended reproach in her eyes, as if to say, "You're not being nice tonight . . . ," full of sadness and tenderness. And this too was unbearable for me. Luckily, M. Nacquot turned around to us, his magazine in his hand, and explained what he had just read, a very well-researched article about I no longer remember what, which, he said, brought very original views to the matter. And, as he sometimes did, he offered to read us the author's most salient conclusions. I had moved and sat down facing M. Nacquot in such a way as to be under his gaze and separated by him from his wife, at whom I purposely stopped looking.

When he was done reading, Mme. Nacquot got up. She was the one who usually lit the candles that Césarine, after having cleared the table, set out in their holders. The candles happened to be so burned down that M. Nacquot, who needed one to read in bed, commented on it and went to get fresh ones from the box on the top shelf of the wardrobe on the second floor landing. Mme. Nacquot and I found ourselves alone, standing next to each other in the dim light of the dining room. The door was open. We heard M. Nacquot go up the stairs and pull out a chair in front of the wardrobe to reach the box. "Sad weather . . . sad night," murmured Mme. Nacquot, shooting me an extraordinarily new, warm, compelling look. Flustered by this glance, I answered evasively and turned my eyes toward the kitten that was sitting on her shoulder. And to avoid looking at her, I pretended to be interested in the little creature and put out my hand to caress it. M. Nacquot was already coming back, and while he took his penknife out of his pocket to pry the old candle butts out of the candlesticks and put in the new ones, after having wrapped each end with a scrap torn from the newspaper I had left on the table, and while both of us, standing in the same place, watched him do this, I felt Mme. Nacquot's chin and then her cheek nestling against my hand, which, mechanically, continued to caress the cat. I came close to pulling my hand away with a brusque movement, and restrained myself only so as not to attract M. Nacquot's attention with this sudden gesture. Then, almost immediately, I doubted what I had felt, so implausible did it seem that she had permitted herself that brazen caress, that sort of invitation, right there in front of her husband, and I went on teasing the cat's silky fur with the tips of my fingers, convincing myself that the touch could not have been intentional. Then I felt Mme. Nacquot's lips pressing heavily, passionately on the back of my hand with a kind of abandon, of distress, so affecting to me that I shivered, furious, and, this time, in spite of myself, vindictive. I pulled back my hand as if I'd been burnt with a red-hot poker, and brusquely stepped around the table to hand M. Nacquot the box of matches without raising my eyes to her.

Candles lit, we went upstairs. The custom was to bid each other a cheerful good night on the landing, in front of the couple's room. She had gone first. I followed. M. Nacquot brought up the rear. As soon as I was on the landing, I turned towards him and wished him good night in the most natural tone I could muster. Then I went past Mme. Nacquot, who had arrived at their door and had turned around, waiting for me. I flung at her a look literally crazed with anger, said a dry "Good night, Madame," without extending my hand to her, reached my room in three steps, and quickly closed my door.

I sat down on my bed. I was outraged. Quite odd what was going on in me at that moment. So odd that I remember it very clearly, and yet I cannot explain why I felt that rage, that sort of hate. Yes, I detested this woman who, far from insulting me, was offering me her affectionate friendship, perhaps her love. I detested her because the game she was playing seemed to me dishonest toward the good M. Nacquot and also dangerous, for I trembled with shame as well as with fear at the idea that he might have caught her making signs at me or kissing my hand on the sly. But if those had been my only reasons, I would not have been so utterly vexed with her. I detested her, I think, because, never having had the slightest feeling for her except a boy's foolish curiosity, I saw her taking advantage of the situation, which I had treated as a game, in order to change the nature of that very game and lead me onto a terrain where I was terrified of slipping. As for that terror, there lies the heart of the mystery and the thing I cannot explain. And that terror was so strong that it motivated my whole behavior in the final and decisive scene on the following day.

THE NEXT DAY at breakfast M. Nacquot said: "I'm going to give you your lesson right away, because I've been summoned to City Hall and I might as well do various errands in town. I'll probably get back late for lunch, which will be delayed by a quarter of an hour."

Now, this was a Saturday, "wash day," which I had completely forgotten in the upset that the business of the previous evening had caused me. Had so completely forgotten it that at nine-thirty, when I went back to my room after my lesson, I devised a little scenario that would give me a chance to show Mme. Nacquot how much I resented her attitude and to put a stop to her carrying-on. Since M. Nacquot would not return until lunchtime, I would wait for the moment when Mme. Nacquot began her singing exercises* to go down to the drawing room. I would walk right in, and without saying hello, I would impudently tell her: "Listen, if you start that stuff again, I'll tell M. Nacquot." It was an absurdly boorish plan, quite unworthy of someone my age and most unlike me, for I had an instinctive horror of tale-bearing, and would have been quite incapable of ever executing my threat. But alone in my room, forced into a situation which seemed to me inextricable and dramatic, I had not hit upon anything better.

Except I had forgotten that Saturday was the one day when I did not have to wait for lunchtime to see her, or make special arrangements to speak to her privately. If I had thought about it, I would have prepared myself to receive her in my room as she deserved. Instead of which, I was so caught off guard that it was only when I heard her coming toward my room, her mules clacking, that I abruptly realized what day it was, the futility of my plan, and the danger I was in of seeing her enter at any moment. A defensive idea occurred to me, of answering: "Don't come in," as if I were changing. I was sitting at my table, with my back to the door, which opened. A wave of anger swept over me, reviving all my rancor. She was trifling with me; she was, for the first time, entering without knocking, as if to foil my strategy in advance; she was hunting me down in my refuge; she was invading my territory . . .

Taken unawares, I was in a ridiculous pose. I remained bent over my book as if I had not heard her come in or did not want to see her, my elbows on the table, my fists against my temples. Heart beating, holding my breath, I froze in that position for a time that seemed to me interminable. She had put the clean laundry on my bed. She was heading over to the washstand to change the towels. Suddenly I felt her bare arm slide between my wrist and my cheek. I had the flesh of her arm on my mouth. With a tender and maternal gesture, she tried to make me lift my head toward her. I felt her face come to rest on my hair, her lips glide onto my forehead, while she murmured in my ear: "Bertrand, my darling, why do you want to hurt me? . . . Why are you so mean to me?" She had forcibly raised my head, and I saw, leaning over me, very close, her face. Her eyes were closed, and in the features seen from below there was intense voluptuousness, supplication, suffering, desire, something overwrought . . . Then I did this insane thing: I got up roughly and struck her jaw so hard with my head that she could not suppress an "oh!" of pain. I was standing, and while I shook with a kind of panic fear, my eyes

*In an earlier version of this chapter, Mme. Nacquot was a singer.

glittered with a cold rage. Although I had not done it on purpose, I shouted at her, like a schoolboy fighting with a classmate: *"Serves you right! That'll teach you!"* She had taken a few steps back. She stared at me, stunned, suddenly furious too, and all at once she burst into sobs and ran out.

I was left alone, disheveled, out of breath, as if after a fight. I experienced no regret, no pity for the pain I had read on that face, for that spurned tenderness. On the contrary. I had a feeling of insolent, prideful satisfaction. I deemed myself the stronger—impervious, unbending before that distraught woman who was sobbing—and I had a wicked sense of triumph.

Today I puzzle over that incomprehensible cruelty. All this may seem unbelievable. Nevertheless, it was what happened.

Who can understand it?

I dreamed about nothing but physical love, for months I had been eaten up with curiosity. The chance to satisfy it appeared. I did not have to lift a finger, utter a word. I had only to surrender myself. In coming to me that morning in my room, half-naked beneath her dressing gown, with her husband gone, it is hardly to be doubted that she was prepared for the complete initiation. I dreamed every night of seeing her naked. I had only to let her take off her dressing gown and offer herself to me.

Not only did I not feel tempted for a second, but I felt a kind of horror of her as well.

Why that chaste reflex of a virgin hurling himself into the void to keep from being raped? How strange it is! And how strange to think that I was plagued by this sexual anxiety until close to the age of twenty without daring to take the decisive step. An instinctive fear of what irreparable act? Does losing one's virginity carry a concrete, direful sense of *defeat*? There is something of that, no doubt. Is it a matter of absurd pride? In surrendering, I would have somehow been ceding her the upper hand. By repulsing her, I remained victorious. As a matter of fact, in my room I had the feeling of having remained master of the battlefield, of having routed the enemy. The enemy?* There must also be in this a vestige of the struggle, the hatred, between the sexes. I triumphed by not yielding. I was ready to give everything I possessed to get any slut to undo her filthy blouse, and I had just turned this beautiful body of an appetizing woman out of my room. Who can understand it?

What I know for sure is that I was thus obeying an urgent, irresistible *reflex*. The instinct of the virgin? It was not after having weighed the advantages or the risks of an affair that I had made up my mind. I acted, as it were, in spite of myself, and in spite of my morbid desire for a sexual experience. Yet I was neither abnormally shy nor excessively modest. In any case, these

---

* *"L'ennemie"*: feminine.

obstacles natural to youth should easily have disappeared in the face of desire.

I cannot even claim that, though I desired a woman, I did not desire that particular woman, since she was a part—indeed, the jewel—of my nocturnal harem, and in my fantasies I had thrown myself at her body many times over. Besides, the contrary would have been quite preposterous, for Mme. Nacquot was still a very fetching morsel, and I had only to undress her in my imagination to experience all the fires of lust.

These phenomena of that age when virility establishes itself and wants to fulfill its function, and when the adolescent cannot decide whether to take the leap that nonetheless obsesses him, are very little studied, I believe, and very poorly understood. I provide my personal testimony. I draw no conclusion.

There is nothing stranger than this dramatic inner tug-of-war between the unbounded sensuality of that age and the instinctive modesty which seems both to desire and to fear the act of initiation, as if there were a terrible peril in losing one's innocence and tasting the forbidden fruit. A survival in us of moral prohibitions, of preachings against the sins of the flesh? I circle in vain around these frights of the inexperienced without advancing a step further in my analysis.

Why did I feel an aversion to her so strong, so spontaneous, so irresistible, that not only was I not afraid of hurting her by repulsing those unhoped-for advances, but I also deliberately wanted to do so, to shout my disgust and my refusal at her with a brutality that today seems to me revolting and unforgivable? Virginity was like a natural element in me, like a force, aggressive and fierce, from which I could not escape. And it existed in me along with the most urgent sexual desire, thanks to a disconcerting contradiction which prevented me from going frankly towards the goal to which all my natural energies were pulling me. Adolescence is not the time of frank impulses, and even the biggest cynic, at that age, is bound by unimaginable restraints; he does not want to look straightforwardly into himself; he does not know how to distinguish the feelings that are moving him; his overexcited desire is so keen that he ought to be able to observe it with precision and grant it its due; but he only experiences the vertiginousness of it, forbids it to speak out, does not know either what to call it or how to satisfy it. No one is less cynical, at heart, than the most cynical boy of seventeen!

As mysterious as the instinctive shrinking of certain flowers at the approach of a foreign body.

This state has been described in female virgins. That fear of the male which sometimes instinctively makes little girls wary well before they know what they have to fear is generally explained by their dread of the brutal wound of rape; and that instinct, by women's dread of the consequences of the act. But nothing similar exists for the boy. He knows full well that intercourse will afford him only pleasure and that he has no need to worry about the outcome.

AFTER MY CHILDISH and furious "That'll teach you"—(I wonder if, having blurted it out, I wasn't aware of the foolishness of my remark, aware that I really could have come up with something better)—I ended the morning alone, without daring to leave my room. If I try to retrieve my feelings, it seems to me that they were two-sided, or, to put it more precisely, alternating. By turns, I enjoyed a kind of victory, the pride of having had the last word, of having shown character, of having imposed my will, of having not let myself be pushed around, of having offended and punished this woman whom I still detested, for the fright that she had given me. And I enjoyed the sort of vengeful hatred that one has, that nearly all children have, for the victim they have beaten. At other moments, I must admit, I was quite nervous and did not much feel like swaggering . . . I had no idea how things would turn out. I did not doubt, despite the sobs, that I had made a terrible enemy. I knew intuitively that a woman never forgives having been placed in such a foolish position. And I did not hide from myself the fact that she was much stronger, more powerful, and better armed than I, that she could, with a word, set her husband against me, cause me lots of serious problems—who knows?—get me sent home to my father. But on what pretext? I also knew, with an intuitive certainty, that she would never admit the truth. That what had happened would forever remain a secret between the two of us. And in all fairness to myself, I must say that I felt honor-bound to keep this secret and that not for an instant, even when I imagined M. Nacquot unjustly turned against me, did the thought ever cross my mind of defending myself by making accusations.

Lunchtime had arrived. Césarine did not ring the bell. M. Nacquot probably was not back yet . . . Finally I heard his footfall on the front steps, and the door of the entrance hall close. Then a consultation with Césarine, the words of which I could not make out. All this unusual activity, which might still have been explainable for simple domestic reasons, added to my agitation, my anxiety. This turned to dread when I heard him coming up the stairs with heavy and rapid steps. I had been standing in my room for ten minutes, listening hard, not knowing what to do. I thought he was going to burst in on me like a thunderbolt, and, panic-stricken, I quickly sat down at my table and opened the first notebook at hand. No. He was going into their room. Unexpected things must indeed have happened to have prevented lunch, at the hour it now was, from being served. A good five minutes passed, during which I remained cowering in my chair, unsure what to think, feeling an awful danger hovering over me, one whose nature I could not guess. His bedroom door finally opened again, but not with the violence I had already imagined. Then mine. I turned around, ready for anything. I saw M. Nacquot, standing in his frock coat, halted on the threshold, a finger to his lips (I was expecting anything but that . . .). "Come to lunch, my boy," he said in a hushed voice with a nice friendly smile, "but don't make any noise, Mme. Nacquot is sleeping. She has a frightful migraine . . ." My heart leapt with joy in my breast. I got up without answering and followed him on tiptoe.

That lunch which I had so feared was charming. M. Nacquot seemed quite entertained to have me at table alone opposite him. Contrary to his habit, he was very talkative and particularly hearty, even confiding. "Don't be concerned," he told me, "Mme. Nacquot's indisposition"—she always said "my husband" in speaking of him; but he never said "my wife"—"isn't at all serious. A very severe headache, and a bit of a temperature. After a day's rest, it will go away . . ." And as I concealed my discomfort beneath a very questioning look, he hesitated for a minute and went on, smiling: "You are old enough to be told certain things. You perhaps know that women, around the age of forty, all go through a period of transformation . . . which is accompanied, to a greater or lesser degree, by little disorders . . . by certain problems of an intimate nature . . . In short, what is called: change of life . . ." I nodded acquiescence, as if these pathological matters held no secrets for me. I listened to him with a show of gravity. "Mme. Nacquot," he continued, "has already had certain symptoms, certain ailments like this one . . . So there is no cause to be concerned." He was smiling with a certain bashfulness, somewhat embarrassed at having permitted himself this confidence. "We're talking here man to man," he added, with a serious and trusting look. "Of course, Mme. Nacquot would be very put out if she suspected that I had spoken to you about these private matters . . ." I again nodded, which seemed to seal a pact between us. Then he started to tell me about his morning, good-humoredly and even with an unaccustomed zest. And I made an effort to reply to him in the same tone. The two of us seemed a little like schoolboys on vacation.

Mme. Nacquot prolonged her absence for two full days. She was served her meals in bed. "What will happen when she comes out of her room?" I wondered.

Nothing happened. Two days later, going down to lunch, I found her arranging flowers in a vase. M. Nacquot was not there yet.

"Good morning, Bertrand," she said, holding out her hand to me across the table, with her most natural smile. "It was high time I came back down," she announced, in a laughing voice. "Look at these flowers! I don't think it would have occurred to either of you two to throw out this wilted bouquet . . . men really don't see anything! . . ."

M. Nacquot appeared. We sat down and the meal took place as though nothing had ever disturbed the harmony of our trio.

But the harmony of the duo had been ruined forever. As lively and convivial as Mme. Nacquot acted in her husband's presence, so did she become silent and closed off if by chance we found ourselves alone for an instant. Which happened very rarely, for both of us were devilishly careful to avoid a tête-à-tête.

Those moments were excruciatingly painful. Her expression would change instantly, becoming hard, hostile, disdainful, with a haughty and ironic crease in the mouth, a sideways glance as sharp as a steel point. Ah, I had not been wrong to imagine that she held a deadly grudge against me. If she spoke to me at those moments, it was in a curt, sarcastic, wounding tone, and usually to give me an order. "Shut the window!" "Light the lamp!" "Give me the matches," as if to a servant. It was quite childish. And I had the good taste, or the shrewdness, not to seem to notice it. But the moment M. Nacquot reappeared, it was her cooing laugh, "Bertrand's always the same . . . ," lighthearted teasing, familiarities, near-kindnesses. I had a first and effective lesson in how nasty and duplicitous a decent woman can be . . .

What helped make this situation bearable was that we had arrived at the month of October. The evenings around the lamp and the first fires in the fireplace were short, and did not go on like the evenings at the water's edge. Then too, the examination was approaching. I was totally involved in my work. M. Nacquot and Father Müller were monopolizing most of my time for a general review of everything they had crammed into me during those two months.

M. Nacquot went with me to Alençon for the oral session. I was to go directly back to boarding school, without returning to their house. Mme. Nacquot's farewells were made in the professor's presence, on the front steps, while Césarine and the coachman took my bags to the carriage. At that point she wished me a successful exam with her most affable smile, and I stammered out a somewhat muddled sentence thanking her for her hospitality. She listened to me with a sort of involuntary little grimace. She was doubtless searching for something hurtful that would be understood only by me.

"Don't thank me," she said. "One deserves no credit for taking you in, you're so little in the way, so discreet . . . You count for so little . . ."

"That's not very nice, what you just said," remarked M. Nacquot, laughing. "Come on, enough of this kowtowing—let's get going!"

He went first. I was about to follow him, turning one last time to Mme. Nacquot, who was standing in the front door. Then she did this little vengeful thing. She made as if to put out her hand. I took two steps up to her, with my hand inanely extended. But she had placed her hands on the frame at either side of the door, and I found myself nose to nose with her, looking foolish.

"Goodbye, *Joseph*," she whispered very low, with a grin truly hideous in its spitefulness and scorn.

Why Joseph? Joseph just happened to be the name of the coachman who would be driving M. Nacquot and me. Why tell me, "Goodbye, Joseph"?

CHAPTER VIII

*The Year of Philosophie**

THERE WERE FIVE of us who had failed the oral in July. Most had not worked much during their vacation, and I was far and away the leader of the pack. The session was on October 13, at Alençon. I was the only one who passed with honors. My father had come. He took me back to le Saillant in triumph to spend the two final days of the week there, and on Sunday evening I returned to the school to be part of the *philosophie* class.

It had been agreed, the previous year, that I would major in *philosophie* and not in mathematics. But from the first month on, I regretted it. M. Nacquot had given me a taste for math, and I envied my schoolmates who were preparing for the *bachot*† in math, among them my friend Luzac, whom I scarcely ever saw anymore except at joint recess periods. I never learned how he was doing with his erotic diversions or whether he had found a neighbor in German class as obliging as I.

I see that I do not remember much about that second and final year of boarding school. Possibly my memories of Saint-Léonard for those two years have overlapped, and in my narrative I may have mixed up my memories of *rhéto* with later ones.

I have the impression that the atmosphere of that second year was considerably different from that of the first. Perhaps it was mainly I who had evolved: there were only a dozen of us *philosophes,* and we formed a more "serious" set than our former group of *rhétoriciens.* It seems to me that there was much less corruption, and I do not recall a single affair, that year,

---

*At that time, *philosophie* was one of the two branches of study possible in the last year of the lycée, i.e. humanities, the alternative being *mathématiques élémentaires,* or *"math élem."*
† *Baccalauréat.*

between boys, involving either me or my classmates. The fact is that all my scabrous memories of the school are set in the *rhétorique* class. It also seems to me that the lascivious talk (for I don't want to make those *philosophes* out to be a collection of little saints—far from it!) had taken on another tone, less childish, I would say, more removed from locker-room conversations. I think that a number of my classmates, not so complicated or reticent as I, had taken advantage of opportunities on their vacations to have their first experiences with women, and this alone was enough to alter the tone of their jokes and their stories. Their success in the *bachot* probably had something to do with this emancipation: it made them feel that their schooldays were over, that they had become men; it may also have given them more confidence in themselves and freed them from the shackles of their shyness. When the chance came, they had seized it. Doubtless these experiences, far from diminishing their obsessions, had in a certain sense increased them; but they felt less of a need to flaunt their experiences, and in their memories kept certain domains private, only to be hinted at. It is indeed a matter of common observation that, in communities of young men—boarding schools, universities, barracks—the least licentious talkers are always the ones who have had actual affairs; and the ones who sound off the most obscenely are usually the virgins, who are subjected to a constant hallucination by their unsatisfied desire and who compensate for it with crude boasting about the feats they dream about and have not been able to bring off.

As FAR AS I am concerned, I think I can state that my erotic obsessions were, at that time, directed exclusively towards women, and that if I had found myself back in German class that year next to Luzac, I would not have let myself be drawn into the same games. I am not certain of this, but I sincerely believe it. And I even find it rather hard to envision a Luzac in *philo* taking the same liberties and having the same curiosity. The Luzac phase was over. There cannot have been many "slit pockets" in our class of *philosophes,* and I do not remember a single classmate who "played with himself" in class or exhibited himself in the dormitory.

That year, I spent most of my solitary nights elaborating on the theme of Mme. Nacquot. It is rather ironic, incidentally, to think that this woman, whose only memory of me must have been the mortifying and ridiculous one of my rebuff, can never have suspected the blaze she had ignited in my erotic imagination, can never have known that the almost chaste and maternal initiation that she had offered me had degenerated, in my dreams, into extravagant orgies where I ascribed the most shameless positions to her, excesses worthy of Messalina, and where, for a year or more, we abandoned ourselves to the most unbridled pleasures.

I also note, as contradictory as it may appear, that from that time on, and together with this almost nightly concupiscence, my thoughts took a totally different turn, very pure and chaste: a *sentimental* turn. I do not know if my case is special or fairly normal. At any rate, it was during this period that my attraction to young women was born, and to the most ethereal, most poetical, least prurient aspects of love. The carnal debauches to which I abandoned myself with Mme. Nacquot's lewd body did not prevent me from cultivating in myself, at certain times of day, the most naïve hearts-and-flowers that ever bloomed in the breast of a shy and mawkish adolescent. I had both a dissipated mistress and an innocent fiancée. My senses no longer absorbed me to the exclusion of all else; my heart began to have its demands and to claim its share of my juvenile imagination. A phenomenon that I am tempted to believe is rather widespread, for I very well remember certain confidences received that year from my classmates: they had an entirely new ring to them. Most of these young men had a chaste love in mind and allowed love's fledgling attraction to materialize around some girl met during the vacation, some cousin in long skirts and with a demure bearing. These confidences were no longer about nakedness or fondling, as they had been the year before, but about timid admissions, blushes, regrets, and hints of betrothal.

I was quite embarrassed, in this new mode, by the strange, restricted existence that I had led. When you came right down to it, I didn't know any young women. My sister hadn't a single woman friend worth speaking of, and our very rare dealings with a few neighboring squires featured very little in the way of girls. None, in any case, that I had been able to see at sufficiently close range to pledge her that loving devotion which I was burning to render unto some chosen being. So, for want of anything better, I fastened my tribute of ardent and unchanneled affection onto the first comer, onto the merest silhouette I happened upon in which I found some charm. Thus, in the course of that strange year, I was successively smitten with the daughter of the druggist on the main square, a little thing with brown braids on a frail catlike neck; with a classmate's sister glimpsed in the visiting-room on Christmas Eve; and then with a girl in an otterskin toque whom we had passed near the church while out walking double file on a shivery afternoon in March. For weeks, in class, in study hall, I devoted my moments of idleness to one after another of them in interminable daydreams that were fed by all the poetical clichés of love, to which my boundless fervor imparted an invigorated, rejuvenated freshness. I reread the poets in our school anthologies, I recited to the object of my love sonnets by Ronsard, monologues of Titus to Bérénice, stanzas of the *Orientales*, of Musset's *Nuits*. I am not sure I did not plagiarize the doggerel of a popular ballad, in order to dedicate a poem by me to one of my distant heroines. And when I succeeded in learning that my classmate's sister, a tall flaxen-haired girl, was named Giselle, I spent several days carving an interlaced B and G into the wood of my desk. It did not bother me that I knew nothing about these girls, and I made do with the most fleeting image. For a while I was in love with a white arm I had seen closing a shutter, on the outskirts of Lormoy-sur-Mareuse, while I was going past in a carriage with my father one Sunday evening when he was taking me back to Saint-Léonard. The love of a young man of twenty addresses itself to a person, it is an individual passion. The love of a boy of eighteen is frequently impersonal. What I loved was not anyone in particular, it was "the girl," "the chosen mate." It was to the species "girl," to the ideal of a "girl," that I gave my heart.

And, of course, nothing sensual could be allowed to tarnish such pure sentiments. Never would I have committed the sacrilege of luring any of those graceful and inviolable forms into my solitary nightly hell. Between those two types of fantasy, the barrier was impenetrable. The beings that I loved in this way had only a feminine shape, barely a corporeal outline, and I would no more have entertained the criminal idea of undressing them in my daydreams than I would have thought about my sister's body when I watched her coming and going around me in the house.

IN DESCRIBING THESE four or five years of my life between the ages of fourteen and nineteen, I may seem to be recounting a case of turpitude and juvenile depravity. This is neither my wish nor the impression I have had in going back over my youth. I am telling the story of a normal and healthy lad with an ordinary temperament under usual circumstances. This sexual obsessive was a gifted, serious boy with a scrupulous conscience; an upright sort, very adequately equipped for life, someone *good*. Let any of my contemporaries, or better, any man of good faith, who reads me, look carefully and unblinkingly into his own "awkward age" without placing a screen of hindsight in front of his past, and I am sure he would have quite a similar confession to make. The details would be different. The essence of the sexual obsession will be more or less the same. I consider myself neither better nor worse, in those years of my adolescence, than the average man of my time, or of any time. My only peculiarity may be the repugnance I have for drawing a veil over my youth. Out of simple concern for human truth. Without cynicism and without prudishness, without vain impudence and without conventional shame.

.   .   .

DURING THAT YEAR, I had a painful encounter with my own character and a painful experience with friendship. Why does a friendship suddenly come about between two people who until then have only been classmates?

A certain René Chénereilles had been in my class the whole previous year, yet we had not felt particularly drawn to each other. We had very cordial relations and often chose to pair up with each other on the walks. So we had a natural affinity and enjoyed conversing. And yet our easy rapport had never gone beyond the bounds of ordinary camaraderie. He, like me, had flunked the oral; he had been the only other one to pass at the October session. We had arrived together in the *classe de philosophie,* and we both had to catch up for having started two weeks late. We were the pair of newcomers. In all the classes, we found ourselves sitting next to each other in the remaining seats. This special position we shared helped us get to know each other better. But that hardly bound us closer. The spark was struck between Chénereilles and me much later, towards the middle of the year, and I no longer have any idea for what reason. I am inclined to think there was no reason. Our friendship was born of itself when its time had come, and with an urgent, powerful impulse which, within a few days, made the two of us inseparable.

I must note here that my "difficult" character—as my masters said—had become quite pronounced since my arrival at the boarding school, especially since I had felt myself freed from the constraints of my home life, and perhaps even more after my stay with the Nacquots. I suppose that many of my schoolfellows must have found me proud, violent, curt in discussions, contemptuous perhaps, self-satisfied, fierce—unsociable, in short. I may have appeared to be all these things, but I cannot in complete sincerity subscribe to this verdict. I was too unsparing of myself, too lucid about my inadequacies and shortcomings—even to the point of exaggerating them and imagining myself always inferior to others, incapable of doing what they did, of never being sure I had done my homework well or knew my lesson; I was also too scrupulous, and too given to admiring everything that I was not, to be guilty of pride, smugness, conceit, disdain. My violence in the discussions seemed to me to have two causes: first, my *mental maturity,* which came from my very advanced education at le Saillant and which naturally led me to take things of the mind seriously and even passionately. (The habit I had acquired from conversations with adults—the Abbé Adry, Xavier de Balcourt, M. Nacquot—made me judge my schoolmates' muddled chatter severely.) I was obviously aware of this maturity; I tended to see childishness in boys my age; and I relied all the more on this sense of maturity since in general I felt my schoolmates far more experienced than I in a large number of areas: they had big families, brothers, sisters, cousins; they had moved in different circles, they had traveled some, their horizons had been far less limited than mine. (I remember in particular the sort of furious shame I felt when I had to confess that I didn't know the sea.) They had the advantage over me of a whole other experience of life, of social diversity.

The second cause of some of my heated replies in the discussions came from a certain *logical* makeup of my mind, the original source of which lay in the analyses of Mlle. Fromentot and which my initiation into mathematical thought and rigor by M. Nacquot had further reinforced. Nothing exasperated me so much as the difficulty that my potential opponents experienced in following my line of reasoning and answering it with logical, methodical arguments; the feminine foible that they had, for instance, of suddenly veering off the topic, of interrupting an ideological discussion with attacks of a personal order, of passing indiscriminately from one plane to another, and, cornered by a precise literary or philosophical question, of escaping with an aggressive "Oh sure, *you* always have to be right . . ."

The fact remains that my demeanor with my classmates did not spontaneously elicit warmth. I was on good terms with most of them, but not much sought after. I do not believe I deceive myself in thinking that I was generally accorded a certain respect, owing to my academic successes, and credited with a certain steadfastness of character, a certain moral cleanness that made me incapable of the slightest cheating, of any serious lying, of the least impropriety in my dealings with my schoolmates. But I was hardly popular. And I remember that when we set out on our Wednesday and Sunday walks, for which many of the students, at the sound of the bell, formed pairs according to plans made in advance ("I dibs you for the line on Wednesday"—for we were given this right to choose one another, on the condition that these friendly partnerings were not exclusive or too frequent), I most often found myself in the middle of the schoolyard, after a part of the procession was already formed, in the group of the unchosen, those who had not been "dibsed" and had not "dibsed" anyone; and usually I ended up taking the walk with a random partner, someone unchosen like me.

Chénereilles was one of these. I seem to remember that he was not particularly well liked. His unattractive looks went against him, and also the social class to which he belonged. His grandfather was a cattle dealer whom everyone in the area had seen making a quick fortune, who had been known *"en blouse,"** as they said; and although his father had stopped making the rounds of the cattle fairs and had bought a château near Mamers, where he led the life of a landowner entirely similar to that led by many students' fathers (aside from the fact that he was "greeted" by the closed and jealous society of the region's petty nobility, but not "received"), those mercantile origins still had not been forgotten, and the students did not much bother to

---

*The blue smock typically worn by peasants and workmen.

socialize with him, even though they did not try to make him feel different, either. At Saint-Léonard, those things counted.

The amusing thing is that, in the midst of those descendants of aristocrats or of bourgeois reactionaries solidly established and accepted in the region for several generations, many of whom had the build of hardy peasants, a ruddy complexion, a thickset body, and the wrists and ankles of a farmhand, Chénereilles had all the delicate signs of high birth. He was the "last of his line," and could have been named Luynes or La Rochefoucauld. I can still see a beanpole with a sickly look, a bony head somewhat thrown back and rather too heavy for the thinness of the neck, a big, very seventeenth-century nose, spindly wrists, pretty hands, and, in the whole of his demeanor, the indolence of a degenerate offspring. But that overly fine skin and that pseudo-blue blood were prey to acne and boils. The downy circumference of his mouth was spotted with half-picked pimples, and on his nape the boils proliferated with such pitiless regularity that nearly every morning he spent the first half hour of study hall in the infirmary and came back with his neck bulging with plasters, wrapped in a welter of bandages bristling with safety pins, after having gulped down, under the incorruptible supervision of Sister Eulalie, a big bowl of bitter and blood-cleansing herb tea that she had brewed herself for those of us whose awkward age proved to be too persistently pustular. The proverbial foulness of his breath had earned him, among the lower grades, a rather revolting nickname the validity of which I, for my part, never ascertained.

Such was my friend. Something of pity was no doubt involved in that choice. His outer unsightliness lent an unexpected luster to his virtues, which were real. Although his absent-mindedness kept him from being a good student, he was very intelligent, and in a way I liked: I found his judgment sound, with an aptitude for reflection and observation that matched mine. The accident of several walks side by side allowed us to see that we had many ideas in common, the same way of taking an interest in people's characters, and convinced us both that everything marked us out to become friends. Unlike love, friendship is always born of a certain reciprocity of fellow-feeling and attraction. I was perhaps not sorry, either, to flaunt a choice that would surprise my circle, and thus to present myself as unconventionally independent: there was a bit of defiance in my kindness to Chénereilles, but also a lot of genuine warmth. For his part, he was probably not loath to become the friend of Maumort, who was known to be difficult, who was thought to be disdainful, and whose attentions brought him a little more esteem than he was used to receiving in the class.

Contrary to what one might suppose, what also appealed to me in Chénereilles was a great core of purity. He was neither more reserved nor more prudish than the others, and I do not think he was spared the sexual obsessiveness of that age any more than the rest of us. But he was "pure" in spite of this, in the sense that I myself was; in the sense that I consider my boarding-school depravities to have been of a passing, accidental nature—I will say: normal—and without any truly harmful effect on my basic character. This—which, of course, I did not analyze back then—I sensed vaguely. I felt that I was profoundly, essentially different from some whose names I could still remember if I wanted to and whose depravity had reached the deepest fibers of their being and was creating a kind of inner rot, attacking their hearts and minds. In me, this depravity could, at certain times, bring out the worst in me, as we have seen, but there remained something superficial about it, despite those falls into the abyss. It left me intact. The rest of my life has proved it. I do not say that the existence of the particular classmates I have in mind has been continually depraved, but I am certain that they were deeply, indelibly stamped, and that there has always remained in them some tendency to baseness. With them, perversity had touched the soul's very quiddity, and I am sure, however their lives may later have appeared, that they bore in the most secret part of themselves a speck of decay, of gangrene, localized perhaps, and, as it were, encysted in their flesh, but incurable.

Chénereilles, in this aspect, resembled me. I sensed in him, as in myself, a solid inner cleanliness. We shared many confidences with each other. I do not want to say that we kept our friendship completely apart from whatever sexual preoccupations we might have had; we very freely acknowledged certain things that aroused our curiosity, and we pooled our theoretical knowledge to enlighten each other on points that remained obscure. But in reality these conversations had nothing obscene or crude about them. They had a serious, almost abstract note to them. We spoke about intercourse in the same tone as about the reproduction of plants, and our curiosity about the sexes led us to explanations of the same order, of the same didactic nature, as botany lessons about the male and female organs of flowers. I am almost sure that we never permitted ourselves confessions about our nocturnal habits. On the other hand, our confidences were unbridled, frenzied, inexhaustible, when it came to the "objects" of our passions. Chénereilles was in love with a girlfriend of his sister, and he would speak to me about it for two straight hours during the walks, without my tiring of it, and without his tiring of it himself. In the same way, I disclosed my "feelings" for the daughter of the pharmacist on the square, or described to him the "bare arm" at Lormoy-sur-Mareuse, without his wanting to smile, so brotherly and natural did these preoccupations seem to him.

It surprises me, when I think about it, to realize how many boys of sixteen or seventeen remained children, in a provincial backwater sixty years ago . . .

There were a few weeks of infatuation between us, rather like a honeymoon. Then a less effervescent period, which lasted a few months, when the friendship put down roots. Then we had a stupid falling-out, which ought to have been insignificant, but which deeply, absurdly, shook our relationship. Things would have straightened themselves out in spite of everything, I think, when an incident occurred which caused a certain stir at the school, which upset and shocked me profoundly, and which made me break off the friendship outright.

The falling-out is so silly that I smile as I note it. It must be said that, since our horizon had ceased to be obstructed by the terrifying obstacle of the first *bachot,* our eyes had opened wide to the prospects that the future offered us, and the choice of a permanent calling, of a career, had suddenly assumed for everyone an immediate, urgent importance, upon which all our thoughts were focused. It was the principal, the endless, subject of all our conversations. "And what do *you* want to do later on?" The two avenues that had been laid out for us since the start of the school year, *philo* or *math élem,* had already brought about a first selection among us. On the one hand, the mathematicians, those who were headed for the *grandes écoles,** Polytechnique, Grignon, Saint-Cyr, Borda; on the other, the more hesitant group of the *philosophes,* relatively impervious to mathematics, who were considering liberal careers, law, medicine, letters. To tell the truth, among that circle of a local and agricultural bourgeoisie, many among us, if they had been free to follow their natural, atavistic inclinations, would have quietly gone back home after having passed the second part of the *bachot* and led the same life as their fathers, as landowners, riding and hunting, looking after their live-stock and their farm. But there were the three years of military service, which terrified the sons of well-to-do families and forced them all to go after one of the higher degrees that would exempt them from two of those years in the barracks. It was well worth pursuing one's studies and stretching one's school life into university life in order to obtain one of the exemptions connected with diplomas of *licenciés en droit* or *ès lettres.* So the university classes had recently been cluttered with young candidates who were studying for a *licence,* with no other purpose than having to spend only one year in the army.

I found myself in a somewhat special situation. For a long time I had discussed these questions of my future with Xavier de Balcourt, and even with Uncle Éric. Without having any very specific resolve, I was, at any rate, quite determined not to live the same life as my father at le Saillant; at least not

*Small non-university establishments, entered by competitive examination, which award highly respected diplomas. Most have close links with industry. A diploma from a *grande école* is comparable in prestige to an Oxbridge degree in Britain. *(Larousse)*

before having done something else. My father approved of these views, and his wish was that I enter the army. I had never clashed with him head-on, but until my stay at the Nacquots', my lack of appetite for mathematics made me reject any possibility of going to Saint-Cyr, and, with even more reason, to Polytechnique.* I toyed with the dream of continuing the study of literature, for which I had a very pronounced taste, and of preparing for my *licence*. My Uncle Éric had said in passing, one day: "You'll come to our home in Paris, to study at the Sorbonne." These words, which were casually tossed off well before Guy's death, and which he probably no longer remembered, had sprouted in my young head and become the focus of my future hopes. I did not quite know where my studies would lead me. I dared not envision a career like Uncle Éric's, who seemed to be endowed with exceptional genius and to be living on a summit of intelligence inaccessible to ordinary mortals, but I vaguely imagined it all the same. And I told myself that in Paris, if I reached the intellectual peak that the *licence ès lettres* represented for me— who knew?—the Chambosts, who seemed to me all-powerful in those spheres, would perhaps find me an intelligent occupation where I could show what I was capable of. In any event, the study of literature engrossed me sufficiently, and sufficiently to the exclusion of all else, that it made me think of the attraction that letters exerted over me as a kind of vocation.

At certain moments, however, this whole shaky structure would collapse under diametrically opposed forces. The interest in mathematics that M. Nacquot had been able to inspire in me often made me regret not having entered the *math élem* program. Sometimes it seemed to me possible to repair this error and to make up for lost time. I even occasionally dreamed of Saint-Cyr, of an officer's life. I had been brought up to worship the army and military honor, and, in my heart of hearts, I was close to conceding, on certain days, that this was the career of the elect, and that any other ranked lower than that of arms. On those days, even the fame of Uncle Éric, member of the Institut de France, seemed to me mediocre, fusty, lacking both heroism and glorious renown: a merely civilian existence.

But those days were, on the whole, fairly rare, and, at the time of which I am speaking, during the height of my friendship with René Chénereilles, the only goal of my eager rush toward the future was a life dedicated to books and things of the mind. Chénereilles, who shared the same tastes, did particularly well in French, and was even a poet when the spirit moved him, the class poet—almost officially so: a poem of his, an occasional poem glorifying the martyrdom of some missionary who had just been butchered in China, had been read the previous July, at the formal assembly where the prizes were given out. He dreamed of becoming a great poet and like me had adopted

*The *grande école* for engineering.

the *licence ès lettres* as his way to an exemption. This shared aspiration had been no small factor in binding us together when we confessed it to each other. We would both become transported in the course of interminable conversations, during the biweekly walks, about our dual destinies, united in the future as they were in the present under the sign of letters.

But, all of a sudden, Chénereilles' vocation faltered. He devoted himself, with a more and more exclusive passion, to the study of natural history, for which he had discovered in himself an unsuspected aptitude. A top mark and the teacher's praises, following an essay test on the circulation of the blood in the human organism, completed the transformation. And he categorically declared that he was giving up all of his vague and childish literary projects and that one course alone was henceforth open to him: medicine. I protested, in despair. I felt betrayed. I tried everything to make him reverse his decision. It was irrevocable. Our endless arguments about this subject grew so very acrimonious, owing to the intransigent passion each of us put into wanting to be right, and wanting to convince his opponent, that our friendship was profoundly affected by it. There was a week of coolness. I had been so wounding, so peremptory, I had so mercilessly denigrated that career as a great physician of which he was dreaming and which I reduced to the level of the two or three country doctors I had known, that he refused, several times in a row, to pair up with me and hitched himself to another walking companion, less authoritarian and more understanding. I was mortified.

This was how things stood, and perhaps they would have sorted themselves out in the long run, since his affection for me was real and I had a lively attachment to him, when a rather dramatic incident occurred that established the break for good. I have said that we sat next to each other in class. We were accused of having copied from each other during a geography test. It was an extremely serious charge that nearly got both of us expelled, for the fathers did not take that sort of cheating lightly. I was absolutely incapable of doing such a thing. I considered it ignoble, and I was incensed at being accused of it. I defended myself with the most violent indignation. I believe that this very violence in the office of the prefect of studies, where we had to explain and defend ourselves before a tribunal composed of two fathers and the prefect of studies under the chairmanship of the rector, and where my indignation led me to overstep all bounds and utter very disrespectful words, since I could not let this suspicion stand—I believe that this outburst, for which, what is more, I was severely punished, saved me. That indignation had the tone of innocence about it.

Chénereilles defended himself less fiercely. But he refused to confess. The facts were obvious. The subject of the test was "Spain." We had both handed in a map of Spain on which the same gross errors were to be found. These errors I knew I had committed on my own. How did they wind up on Chénereilles' paper? Of course, I had not asked him anything during the test, and he knew me well enough not to seek any help from me. I was a real stickler for the academic code of honor. Only one explanation made sense to me: Chénereilles had taken advantage of a moment's inattention, or of the fact that his proximity prompted so little distrust in me, to glance at the map I had made and to draw regrettable inspiration therefrom. The errors were so singular and so exactly repeated that one could not for a minute suppose an unfortunate coincidence. I did not want to accuse my classmate. But I stood up for myself with ferocity and anger. The rector, very put out at not being able to extract a confession from either of us, and convinced, I think, of my innocence—he was my spiritual adviser and knew me to be strictly honest in that sort of thing—handed down a verdict of both guilty. We were not thrown out of the school but very stiffly punished, and we were made to change seats in class in order to prevent our being neighbors.

In the corridor on the way back to study hall, I had a short, vehement, terminal confrontation with Chénereilles. I forced him into a corner, looked him in the eye, and shouted at him: "You're a cheat, a liar, and a bastard!" My fist fell on his big nose. I was clenching my teeth: "I forbid you ever to speak to me again." And I left him there, crushed and seething.

I was deeply shaken, sickened by this business. I must say that neither my teachers nor my classmates harbored any doubt about me. It seemed to them manifestly impossible that I was guilty. The unanimity that I felt around me helped me get over the experience. But I nearly became ill from it.

My break with Chénereilles was without appeal. I held tight to my resolve. Not once in the two months before the examinations, during which we continued to share the same existence, did I speak a word to him. Nor he to me.

I never saw him again after leaving Saint-Léonard. But I sometimes came across his byline in *La Depêche du Perche,* where he used to write critical articles on literature and drama—and I always recalled the map of Spain. I was told that he had lost his father soon after the end of his studies, married early, and settled down with his wife in his mother's house to manage the paternal estate. The last time I saw his name mentioned, many years ago now, it was in the bulletin of the Société de Folklore Percheron, of which he was a member, and where a long obituary, highly laudatory, was devoted to him. Poor Chénereilles! May he rest in peace . . .

TWO MONTHS after this painful episode, which for a long time left a splinter in my flesh owing to my perception that I had not been able to have my innocence publicly acknowledged and that a suspicion of cheating might hang over me—I see that I still have not forgiven Chénereilles after half a century—I was to leave Saint-Léonard with a flourish: I passed my *bachot* with high honors, which were very seldom awarded.

I returned to le Saillant with my schoolboy's trunk. The period of secondary studies was over. I was seventeen and a half, and fully aware that I had become a man. My father and Henriette reinforced this illusion, without meaning to, by treating me in a new and flattering fashion. Until then I had been the Benjamin, the child of the house. Heretofore my sister, nine years my senior, and my father formed a party of adults by which serious questions were settled and from which I was excluded. From now on, I was no longer made to feel that exclusion. They involved me in their conversations and even, to a certain extent, consulted me, which I very much appreciated. I was instantly part of the family.

My father took me to Le Mans, where the most highly respected gunsmith of the area lived, and bought me a hunting rifle. He got a license for me, and at the end of August I went on my first "opening day," all newly fitted out and provided with a pointer named Strogoff, a particularly affectionate animal with a short, white, ginger-spotted coat, "M. Bertrand's dog," whom I was privileged to have sleep in my room, most often at the foot of my bed, and who was always at my heels. I had a great love for Strogoff, whose eyes as they looked up at me were always swimming with tenderness and the skin of whose skull was satin; and I remember being very sad fifteen years later when I learned, in Constantine, through a letter from Henriette, that he had ended up dying of old age at le Saillant.

With Henriette, I very quickly recaptured the intimacy of our childhood, which these last years had inevitably somewhat weakened. All difference in age seemed—to me perhaps more than to her—done away with. That first fortnight in August after my return home remains a radiant period in my memory, as if a prelude to all the quiet joy that our exceptional sibling harmony had in store for us.

WITH MY FATHER, I cannot say that I took up old habits. We had hardly been close. But the best memories that I have of him date from that time. He had stopped treating me as a child, or rather, he had begun taking an interest in me because I was no longer a child. Although he had a morose and not very communicative disposition, and was very careful to maintain that unsociable solitude in which he wallowed, he tried to make a place for me in his life, and never again turned me away. On the contrary, he drew me into his office after meals, opened his cigarette box, and, sitting across from me on the far side of my mother's little sewing table, upon which, as had always been his custom, he had the coffee tray and the decanter of old marc set down, he made obvious attempts to start up conversations. I went along with this willingly enough, but I now tell myself that I could have rewarded his efforts better, and, instead of leaving it to him to make all the overtures, spoken to him more freely about myself, asked him more about that past which he wanted to share with me—I almost said, bequeath to me. For those discussions had only a few subjects, always the same. He generally began by speaking to me about domestic matters, little difficulties he had encountered that day in the farm work, repairs he was planning to make, improvements he dreamed of being able to carry out and was putting off from one season to the next. When he was in an expansive mood, he would make some allusion to the past that I ought to have guessed was shyly deliberate, and if I seemed ever so slightly interested, or responded with a question, he would take an obvious pleasure in telling me about the family's history and its characters, all the anecdotes about my grandfather. At the time I was slow to guess his secret wish to make me the depository of those things that only he still knew. I ought to have been struck by certain phrases, which were like confessions: "You'll remember that, when I'm not around anymore," he would say in conclusion, holding my gaze for an instant. He would have been happy to know that I was listening to those details with an ear infinitely more attentive than I let on, that I have remembered them, thought back on them quite frequently, and recorded bits and pieces of them in my diary.

With Henriette he was more at ease, and without dropping his attitude of authority, actually consulted her about everything and generally let himself be guided by her.

Very rarely—I can even say almost never—did he speak to me of my mother. But he talked about her to Henriette, in that same reticent, tentative manner which I described just now. And Henriette took in those retrospective monologues almost the same way I did, with a slightly distracted air, an uneasiness that kept her from revealing that those confidences were precious to her and moved her. We have often reproached ourselves since for that attitude, which we were both led into by a sort of inner stiffening that we could have done more to resist.

But my father's most immediate worry, that year, was the direction I was going to take and the sort of future I was going to prepare for. He adopted a serious and concerned tone which immediately froze every impulse towards spontaneity in me. For it was not trust that I lacked, but spontaneity. I was on the defensive, as if I had to overcome his resistance. I was evasive, reticent, silent. With a nod of the head, with an mm-hmm, and in a way that did not fool him, I agreed to his advice which, I have to say, he slipped me with as much hesitation, as many reservations and convolutions, as I employed in answering him. But what good does it do to analyze all that awkwardness which, on both sides, warped our relations? I shall have said everything, alas, when I write: those were the conversations of a father and a son.

For my father, an old *"pipo,"** there was only one *grande école*: Polytechnique. If I had wished to go there, he would gladly have accepted my seeking a civilian career and shying away from the military profession: one could remain a civilian as long as one was an engineer trained at Polytechnique. He barely acknowledged that one could be an engineer trained at Centrale; those who went there were, for him, second-raters. But he realized that I did not have enough mathematical aptitude to stand a chance of getting into Polytechnique, and above all of going from there into a civilian career. Which was true, but less true, perhaps, than he thought. He did not know about the initiation into math that I owed to M. Nacquot, and that might, perhaps, have allowed me to do higher mathematics and wear the cocked hat of the *polytechniciens*. And it is one of my regrets, by the way, to have failed to give my father that joy. Not the joy of seeing me aspire to Polytechnique but of being able to talk with me about mathematics, which he always loved. And, at the level to which M. Nacquot had brought me, we could have had general conversations which would have drawn us together. But I was careful not to dispel my father's conviction that I was unsuited for mathematics, since I was counting on this to induce him to let me study for my *licence ès lettres*.

As soon as I had revealed my intentions to him, however, he strongly opposed them and pushed me hard toward a career as an officer. The *licence ès lettres* would not lead to anything except to exempt me from two years of service. And after that, what would I do? I would come back to le Saillant for lack of anything better, and, at twenty-three, would lead that life of a young gentleman farmer of which there were so many specimens in the neighborhood; and he disliked that prospect intensely. To tell the truth, his arguments seemed reasonable to me. I was not at all averse to the idea of being an officer. I would know how to avoid the boredom of the garrisons: I would go into the colonial army, which was beginning to be much talked about, and would have a career as an officer, traveling, exploring, pioneering, and colonizing. This possibility did not displease me. In reality, I had no pressing vocation, and I was attracted as much by my taste for things of the mind as by a certain enthusiasm, a certain inclination, for endeavors involving activity, energy, and heroism.

The visit of the Chambost-Lévadés decided my immediate future.

Aunt Ma had not had the courage to return to le Saillant since Guy's death. For eighteen months she lived in her grief, and was just beginning to

---

*An alumnus of Polytechnique.

regain a certain balance. My Uncle Éric had been named, during the winter, to the Collège de France.* It had been a big event for them, a major advancement, and Aunt Ma was so much a part of "the Institut set" that this flattering appointment, much celebrated in Paris, had been for her, as strange as it may seem, a diversion from her grief, her first joy after her great sadness, and a chance to start entertaining once again. She had seized the opportunity, forcing herself, she said—and believed. In truth, she had so much vitality, such a need to use her energies and have people around her, to receive and be received, that this resumption of a social life, which she accepted as a necessity of her situation, allowed her to shake off the mourning and the semi-confinement that weighed horribly on her and prolonged her suffering. The wound was never healed in her heart. But she was not made to live in sorrow. Her whole nature drove her to be happy in spite of all, to let herself be carried away by the social whirl and Parisian life.

Within a few weeks, she saw that this routine was transforming her, bringing her back to life. It was she who asked to come see us during the summer.

That stay was of great importance to me. I had immediate and frank discussions with the Chambosts. My uncle was too much in agreement with my taste for letters not to encourage my plans very strongly. I think at that moment he began to have an inkling that I could perhaps become his disciple, his spiritual son, his successor. Aunt Ma, who was shaken by this return to le Saillant, which she had left two years earlier with Guy ill, showed me, from the moment she arrived, a special affection. I reminded her of Guy. This might have been a reason for her to distance herself from me. But she was too effusive, too loving, to suffer from any such grudge. The memory of Guy only brought her closer to me.

They convinced my father that it was wise not to rush the choice of a career. Uncle Éric was able to persuade him that the *licence ès lettres* could be an incomparable educational bonus for me. It was agreed that I would simultaneously carry on the preparation for Saint-Cyr and for my *licence*. This combination spared everyone's sensibilities. It was likewise agreed that at the beginning of the fall semester I would come and settle in Paris, at the Chambosts', and would work at their house, under their supervision, preparing for Saint-Cyr at the Lycée Saint-Louis, and studying at the Sorbonne for the *licence ès lettres*.

This solution thrilled me. The attraction that Aunt Ma exerted over me had only grown in the course of the two weeks they spent with us. I went for

---

*This place of learning near the Sorbonne holds public lectures given by prominent academics and specialists. It is not a university and does not confer degrees, although it is controlled by the Ministry of Education. (*Larousse*)

long walks with her. She spoke to me of Guy, and I sensed that she was entirely prepared to transfer her wounded affections to me. I felt tremendously at ease with her. I talked to her with a fluency, a trust, a freedom that I had not yet shown anyone, not even Henriette. I foresaw my life in Paris with Aunt Ma as an entry into adult existence, the doorway to happiness. And I also had an entirely new relationship with Uncle Éric. He intimidated me much less. He displayed a sort of consideration for me that flattered me deeply and that I owed, I think, to the honors in the *bachot*. He was surprised by certain areas of ignorance that I shamelessly admitted, said he would send me books, prepared me a whole little reading program for the end of the vacation; and, once back in Paris, dispatched the promised volumes to me.

The end of that vacation came quickly. I divided my time among many activities. My debut as a hunter enthralled me, although the countryside, broken up by hedges and not very well stocked with game, did not much lend itself to hunting with a pointer. I rode, sometimes with my father, sometimes with my sister, sometimes with both. During the hot part of those September days, I would stretch out on my bed, in a breeze, and for two or three hours devour the books that Uncle Éric had sent me. I no longer recall what they were. I only remember that among those that opened up new horizons there was the *The Origins of Contemporary France* by Taine, which I read, pencil in hand, filling a notebook with quotations and notes. I scarcely suspected then that I would inherit my uncle's library and that those volumes would one day come back to le Saillant. I can see, as I write these lines, the brown backs of the ten volumes of Taine, and I suddenly realize that I have hardly opened them again since that month of September '87, when they were a sort of revelation for me . . .

That vacation marks the end of my childhood and the threshold of my youth. Life in Paris had such a great influence on me, I was so deeply transformed by my studies there and the milieu in which I lived, that I was no longer to be the same, and the grown child who left le Saillant at the beginning of October never returned.

PART TWO

Early Adulthood
(1887–1891)

CHAPTER IX

The Chambost-Lévadés: Uncle Éric

MY ARRIVAL IN PARIS, on a fine morning in October 1887, my settling in with my uncle and aunt Chambost-Lévadé, was, I think, one of the two great and important events of my life (the other being my encounter with Lyautey).

At the end of the nineteenth century, the coming to Paris of a young provincial barely eighteen years old was inevitably a major jolt, nothing like what a person in the same situation would experience today. The differences between life in the provinces, its routines and ways of thinking, and those of Paris, have gradually diminished with the automobile, the ease and frequency of travel, the intermingling of countryfolk and Parisians during World War I, etc. But for me this jolt was even greater than for many others.

Not only did the schoolboy of Gevrésy suddenly become a student at the Sorbonne; not only did the country boy, brought up in a château in the Perche where scarcely anything, neither physical habits nor mental ones, had changed since Louis-Philippe, suddenly find himself involved in the private life of a very 1880s Parisian household, where his complete disorientation both bewildered and exhilarated him; but there was also this, which infinitely magnified the importance of that precipitate transplantation: I went straight from my backwater into the most cultivated, the most intellectual circle of the capital; my first time out, I reached what was then one of the peaks of European thought and civilization: the crowd that revolved around the dome of the Institut.

The extent of the shock and its repercussions will be better understood when I illustrate my disorientation with a precise, tangible fact. I arrived in Paris on a Friday. I had spent my final days at le Saillant packing and sorting out my books, with Henriette's help; the day before leaving, I bade farewell to the farms, riding with my father one last time on his daily round. I oiled my hunting rifle and put it away, commended Strogoff to my sister's care; my father drove me to the station himself in his old buggy, and Henriette followed on horseback. A few hours later I got off at the Gare Montparnasse, where Aunt Ma was waiting for me; and a cab with a roof rack carried us, through the din of the congested streets, to the Chambosts' in the rue de Fleurus. There I found Uncle Éric in his library, at the foot of a rolling ladder on which Xavier de Balcourt was perched, putting books away on one of the top shelves. And on Sunday, *the next day,* I found myself, intimidated and lost, in that same library, among a dozen old gentlemen, and I was introduced successively to M. Renan, to M. Albert Sorel, to M. Boutmy, to M. Leconte de Lisle, to M. Berthelot, M. Brunetière . . .* Reason enough, I think, to be a bit disoriented!

I cannot emphasize all of this too much.

To have some notion of what it meant for me to be adopted by the Chambosts-Lévadés, one would need to assess, as I alone can do, the degree of intellectual poverty that was mine when I landed in Paris—although, back home, I had been a little prodigy of sorts, an exception. Thanks to the Chambosts, I was all at once admitted to a world whose level of civilization and brilliance I naïvely believed I had guessed from afar, but of which, in reality, I had not the faintest idea. It hit me like a lightning bolt. The first Sunday at-home which I attended at the rue de Fleurus, in that autumn of '87, sufficed to reveal to me the entire scope of the new world in which I had been set down; to make me understand and feel things which could be shown me only there; to render me, for life, discriminating and hard to please; to impart to me a sense of quality, a permanent respect for things of the mind; to sharpen forever the cutting edge of my critical sense; to acquaint me with a supreme hierarchy of values which, for the whole of my existence, served as a solid basis for my judgment.

Luckily I was clearly and immediately conscious of it. I had the giddy sensation that at a single bound I had cleared a series of steps that would have taken me an entire lifetime to pass through if left to my own devices (even

*Ernest Renan (1823–1892), philosopher, historian, author of the *Life of Jesus* and *The History of the Origins of Christianity;* Albert Sorel (1842–1906), historian and writer, author of *Europe and the French Revolution;* Émile Boutmy (1835–1906), political writer and professor of constitutional law; Charles-Marie-René Leconte de Lisle (1818–1894), poet; Marcelin Berthelot (1827–1907), chemist and statesman; Ferdinand Brunetière (1849–1906), literary critic. These and the other intellectuals mentioned in this chapter enjoyed an immense prestige in their day.

supposing I had been especially gifted). Life at the hôtel Fleurus presented me, on a platter, the best of European civilization in my time, without my having to make any effort except to absorb it. My awareness of this, even as it happened, helped me avoid wasting any of the exceptional advantages that were offered me. I did not shy away from this magical windfall. The intoxication that I felt made me throw myself all the more avidly at that substantial nourishment which each day placed within my reach.

I changed more during the first trimester of that stay in Paris than I have over the entire course of my life since. From then on, I have only evolved, ripened. In that autumn of '87, what happened in me was a *metamorphosis.* Within a few weeks, I was changed in the same way that Cinderella's fairy godmother changed a pumpkin into a fancy coach . . .

The Chambost-Lévadés occupied, in the part of the rue de Fleurus that has since been destroyed to let through the Boulevard Raspail, a small three-story townhouse that had been built by the senior Chambost, the chemist, at the beginning of the Second Empire.

It requires no effort for me to picture that place where I lived for so many years; which was my home for five years, from '87 to '92, until my graduation from Saint-Cyr; to which I returned so many times afterwards; in which I always had "my" room. And I want to give myself the ultimate treat of describing and inventorying it in detail.

The front door, dusty green bronze in color, opened onto a paved entryway. Immediately to the left, a glass door led down to the kitchen, which was in the basement, lit from the street by two half-windows with bars. You climbed five steps, carpeted in blue, and found yourself in the actual front hall, separated from the entryway by a French door that had leaded panes of stained glass, white framed with blue. This front hall was fairly spacious and the whole far end of it was occupied by a wide staircase with oak balusters, over which, on certain days, Aunt Ma would drape lamé stoles and chasubles with golden fringes. The walls were covered with rough, sized canvas painted in oil the color of a stormy sky, blue gray, on which heraldic lions, stenciled and symmetrically arranged, stood out in dark blue. The stairwell, lit from above by a glass roof, was hung with this wall-covering up to the third story. The ground floor, higher than street level, contained only two vast adjoining rooms, whose tall doors, never closed, both opened into the left wall of the entrance hall: first the drawing room, whose three wide windows looked out on the street; then the dining room, extended and lit, along its entire breadth, by a sort of conservatory filled with house plants, which opened onto the garden. There was a butler's pantry behind the big staircase; from it one could go straight down to the basement. The garden, enclosed by walls, was small but surrounded by other gardens that were planted with trees, which turned that side of the house into a leafy landscape. The drawing room, large and abundantly furnished with mahogany Empire chairs upholstered in embossed golden-yellow velvet, was not often occupied. We lived on the second floor and seldom went down to the first except for meals. The dining room, paneled in mahogany, with its many chairs, contained two large glass-fronted sideboards adorned with Empire brass; in one were displayed pieces of old silverware and in the other a porcelain service that was not used and whose many pieces, exhibited there as if in a museum, decorated with flowers, butterflies, and golden garlands, were the work of Aunt Ma, who, in her youth, had been very fond of painting on porcelain. That ground floor, normally deserted, nevertheless had one faithful and decorative occupant, chained in perpetuity to its perch in the middle of the conservatory amid the potted palms and aspidistras: Iroquois, Aunt Ma's parrot, a noisy white macaw with a superb yellow crest, whose mysterious tantrums sometimes provided a deafening accompaniment to the mealtime conversations. Its quirk, during lulls, was to shriek surprised and furious "What?"s, which created the impression of having a deaf and inquisitive guest at the table. These "What?"s sometimes fell so comically into our talk that they set off fits of hilarity.

On the second floor, the stairway led to a fairly spacious landing, furnished with various and comfortable chairs, which was a favorite living area. The whole front of this second floor was taken up by a very large room, which occupied the entire space above the drawing room and the entrance hall, had five windows on the street, and was truly the heart of that house: the library. All the walls—apart from the windows, the doors, and the tall mantel of sculpted oak, whose central pier featured a large portrait of Aunt Ma as a young woman done by a student of Winterhalter's around 1860—were lined with books, nearly all of them leather-bound. Uncle Éric, who had inherited the books from his father and his father-in-law, possessed a remarkable library. It was in that vast hall, with its many rather ill-assorted chairs, that we usually gathered; it was there that the Sunday at-homes took place. The room lent itself to those gatherings. The armchairs, the sofas, the tables, the lamps were distributed in such a way that people could either divide up into little groups for private discussions or form a big circle when the conversation was general. Without a doubt I spent the best hours of my life in that place. I can still see all its details. I can see the little Directoire "*sabot*,"* in crimson silk, where Aunt Ma usually sat, to the left of the fireplace, next to a screen decorated with real flowers. I can see those wide, red-velvet armchairs striped with bands of Louis-Philippe tapestry, the Karamani curtains, the Chinese vases converted into oil lamps with their great lampshades of light-colored silk and their ruched flounces. I can see the five or six

*A type of easy chair fashionable at the end of the eighteenth century.

Spanish Renaissance armchairs of Cordovan leather with brass nails. I can see the tall, dark, wooden ladder, fitted with a Gothic handrail like a miniature staircase, on the steps of which my Uncle Éric liked to sit, perched on one buttock, in an affectation of simplicity, asceticism, and ostentatious humility. (How vexed he secretly was when we failed to notice it and when none of the young men came to beg him to assume a pulpit less uncomfortable and more worthy of him for his holding forth! . . .)

I can see the strange catafalque which, at the back of the room, formed a counterpart to the mantelpiece—a sort of circular couch done in padded cherry-red damask whose center harbored a jardinière with a thicket of house plants soaring out of it. I can see the two folding tables, ebony inlaid with mother-of-pearl, each holding a big round brass tray engraved with Arabic inscriptions, on which refreshments, invariably consisting of Marsala and English biscuits, were served. I can see the three Dutch polished-brass chandeliers, in which the gas burners whistled as they were lit by the butler who came to draw the curtains and who was equipped with a bamboo pole to which a wax taper was affixed. And I can still feel under my soles the cushiony wool of the huge red, blue, and green Smyrna rug, which put a finishing touch to the room's contemplative atmosphere.

Uncle Éric's study was at the rear of the room, off to the right. It was above the dining room, lit on the garden side by a wide picture window that looked out onto the glass roof of the conservatory, whence there sometimes rose the furious questions of the parrot. The double door that communicated with the library was almost always open, even in winter, although my uncle was sensitive to cold, even while affecting a philosophical indifference to the contingencies of the weather. It must be added that the house was heated from top to bottom by one of those old hot-air furnaces, whose vents spat out as much soot as heat, and that the temperature was always sixty-eight degrees.

When there were a lot of cigar-smokers present and the gas of the chandeliers was lit, the air became completely unbreathable. Aunt Ma would then light a little smoke-absorbing lamp that someone had brought her back from London. And everyone, to please her, would carry on about the genius for invention and practicality on the far side of the Channel.

The study was a private extension of the library. The walls were also lined with shelves loaded with books, but books for his work, mostly paper-bound and filled with markers and note-slips. The master's place was indicated by a leather desk chair, with sculpted lion's heads, behind an immense medieval table piled with folders, publications, writing materials. A big modern bronze inkstand, representing Clésinger's *Sappho,* I believe, sat enthroned amidst the clutter. It was a gift presented to him by his students on the occasion of his appointment to the Institut. Behind this chair were the shelves for textbooks and dictionaries. He scarcely ever sat there except to receive a visitor. He mostly worked at a little lightweight and portable chess table that he moved several times an hour, settling himself now over the vent of the heater, now by the window if the weather was a little overcast, now, once evening had come, under a big church lamp—a wrought-iron lantern that had been modernized and adapted for gas.

Next to the study, above the butler's pantry and behind the stairwell, was another room, narrow and long, also looking out onto the garden, that was pompously called the archives room. It was simply furnished, like a notary's office, with numbered green cardboard files. It was there, at a black pearwood desk placed between the windows, that my uncle's secretary—Xavier de Balcourt—worked.

The floor above, the bedroom floor, was the private kingdom of Aunt Ma. The couple's bedroom was hung with wallpaper featuring a scene of greenery and contained a wide bed with spiral posts. The room looked out onto the street and had the three windows in the middle of the façade. There were smaller rooms to the right and left. One was the couple's bathroom. The other was the sitting room. This was where Aunt Ma lived, and where I went to chat with her. Here she had gathered the furniture from the house they had moved into after her marriage in 1863, and today it would provide, for a retrospective exhibition, a curious example of the Empress Eugénie's style. A few low chairs in quilted sky-blue damask trimmed with piping, fringe and tassels. On the floor, a moquette carpet with a beige background and blue flowers. Two little marquetry tables ornamented with brass; one, with a top, was a sewing table and the other a jardinière always filled with flowers in pots.

The walls were hung with shiny satin of a soft moonlike blue, considerably lighter than that of the chairs and curtains. A small white marble fireplace, where gas flames whistled among the hollow cast-iron logs. On the mantelpiece, a gilded bronze clock surmounted by a Clodion nymph, wriggling in the arms of a satyr, and flanked by two Chinese vases converted into gas lamps and topped with frosted glass globes. On the wall, a big etched crystal mirror from Venice, which Aunt Ma had bought on her honeymoon. And, all around the room, personal souvenirs, little family portraits, daguerreotypes, and two framed porcelain plaques showing butterflies, dragonflies in reeds, works of her youth which must have brought her great compliments, and for which she had retained a touching fondness. I am forgetting a little Louis XVI marquetry *"bonheur du jour,"** which today is at le Saillant, and where she kept her accounts and wrote her letters, usually at night, till an ungodly hour.

---

*A tall escritoire.

In my room, the bed was Guy's, an English brass bed. A white marble mantelpiece with an heirloom, a copper-faced Boulle clock that was crowned by a chariot with four gilded horses and was a little too monumental for the room. The window was wide, with three panels, and looked out onto the garden. To the left of the window, between it and the fireplace, a big table set up as a desk, and above it some shelves for my books. An armchair, upholstered in red velvet, and, in front of the table, a mahogany Louis-Philippe armchair with bands of tapestry bordered in red rep, completed the furnishings.

To the right of the window was a bathroom, narrow but as long as the bedroom, with an ample white-painted wooden closet running much of its length, where I had plenty of space for my linen and my clothes, so that my bedroom served as my study.

IT WAS, in truth, a very odd marriage, that of my uncle and aunt Chambost.

They were ten years apart and more, if not in appearance at least in spirit. Aunt Ma, despite the mourning that had broken and aged her, despite the portliness that weighed her down, was still so fresh in mind and heart, had such a need to use her energies and to live despite all, that she seemed young for her forty years. Uncle Éric, on the other hand, although still very spry (he clambered up the library ladder twenty times a day) and with keen hearing, excellent eyesight (he died without having worn spectacles), a full head of hair (it was only at the end of his life that his hairline receded), an exceptionally active brain, and no disabilities, seemed to be several years past the age of fifty, which he had just reached, because he was slow in his movements and awkward in his everyday actions, and his beard and hair were gray; above all, because he led the sedentary existence of an old man and made no effort to combat his physical laziness.

This son of a great chemist had, through a natural process of opposition, turned to letters. Upon his graduation from Normale, rich enough to dispense with a career as a university professor, he had abandoned pure literature and criticism to apply himself mainly to sociology, in its connections with philosophy, ethnology, political economy, the mores of man across the centuries and the continents. His first works, appearing in the journals, had brought him notice. His doctoral thesis, *Origin and Development Through the Ages of Respect for Truth and Good Faith,* soon followed by another volume, *Origin and Development of Altruistic Feeling Through the Ages,* made his name. It was the era when, with a neophyte's zeal, everyone was trying to trace problems back to their roots, to the time of their genesis. "Origins" were in fashion. M. Renan was looking for the "Origins of Christianity";

M. Taine, for those of contemporary France. Uncle Éric took on the Origins of moral ideas. Thanks to his father, he consorted with all the distinguished minds of the world of the Institut.

The multiplicity of moral ideas, their differences, their contradictions, the incredible variety of traditional notions as to what is good or bad, compulsory or irrelevant, and, moreover, the large number of cases in which the moral imperative outlived the reasons that had given it birth seemed to him, early on, one of the principal enigmas that arise in the human mind and one whose solution had to be pregnant with consequences. It was to this research that he devoted his life, exploring all that could be discovered about moral consciousness throughout past civilizations and the present state of humanity.

This expert on folklore, who, for his work, ought to have spent his life covering the globe, had scarcely traveled at all. "Everything can be found in books," he would say. In fact, this sedentary man possessed an unparalleled collection of documents on the institutions, laws, customs and, in general, the mores of every race, country, and century. It was from this treasure trove of psychological, historical, ethnological, legal, and theological notes that he drew innumerable references. But his goal went beyond the curiosity of the historian. What fascinated him was to compare these historical data in order to seek out the origin and pursue the evolution of moral ideas throughout all times and places and, finally, to determine the nature of humanity's moral consciousness.

Unlike the philosophers who had specialized in the study of moral laws and who nearly always contented themselves with limiting their investigations to the present state of moral consciousness in the civilized countries, he had arrived at the conviction that there was no moral Truth, that the source of all moral concepts was purely *emotional,* that moral judgment had no other foundation than moral emotion, and that, in consequence, morality was identical with ethics and that its only purpose was to control the behavior of people in society.

He liked to claim that duties towards others have an obvious tendency to increase, to multiply, with the evolution of moral consciousness, and he believed, it seems to me, in the *progress* of moral ideas with time.

Although he based moral ideas on moral emotions, he admitted the growing influence of intellectual considerations on the moral judgments of the civilized individual. Moral ideas seemed to him generally more enlightened today than a thousand years ago, because discernment, exercise of reason, reflection, and methodical research into motivations now had an increasing effect on moral concepts. The enlargement of knowledge must, in the last analysis, purify primitive moral ideas and contribute to moral progress.

He predicted a constantly expanding importance for altruistic feelings in the future, a decrease in the sentimental influence of likes or dislikes over judgments of morality, and an increase in the influence of reflection.

The evolution of moral consciousness goes from lack of reflection to reflection, from ignorance to knowledge.

He published little.

His first book, which had brought him attention, was a short treatise bearing the title *On Approbation and Disapprobation* and subtitled *Essay on the Nature and Origin of Certain Moral Ideas.* It takes as its epigraph these sentences from Montaigne:

> I reckon that there is no notion, however mad, which can occur to the imagination of men of which we do not meet an example in some public practice or other and which, as a consequence, is not propped up on its foundations by our discursive reason. . . .
>
> *The laws of conscience which we say are born of Nature are born of custom;* since man inwardly venerates the opinions and the manners approved and received about him, he cannot without remorse free himself from them nor apply himself to them without self-approbation.*
>
> (MONTAIGNE, *On Custom.*)

And these from Pascal:

> Custom is the whole of equity, for the simple reason that it is accepted. This is the mystical basis of its authority. Whoever tries to bring it back to its first principle destroys it.
>
> (PASCAL, *The Need for Justice.*)

From that time on, my uncle was considered by his peers the most qualified investigator of the human conscience.

In 1872, at the time of the founding of the École des Science Politiques, Boutmy had the idea of entrusting Chambost-Lévadé with the mission of setting up the school's first library, and he accepted. Soon afterwards, he obtained permission to start, on the fringe of the normal curriculum, a course in "practical philosophy and sociology," which could have been called "General History of Mores."

The school had as its unofficial objective the formation of a republican elite and as its official objective the preparation of its students for certain competitive state examinations to enter Affaires Étrangères, Conseil d'État,

---

*The M. A. Screech translation. Italics added by Martin du Gard.

and Inspection des Finances.* It then occupied a modest apartment in the rue Taranne. Shortly before my arrival in Paris, the influx of students, who were approaching three hundred in number, necessitated a change of location; thanks to a generous bequest, it was able to find a home in the rue Saint-Guillaume, where it still is.

But by the time I came to Paris, my uncle was no longer teaching there. A chair had been offered him in 1879 at the Collège de France, and it was to his course there on the Evolution of Moral Concepts that he devoted all his efforts. But he remained on the staff at Sciences Politiques, administered examinations, and stayed in close contact with the school's whole faculty. Among the regular Sunday guests at the rue de Fleurus were Boutmy, the director; Alex Ribot, the specialist in parliamentary history; Léon Say, specialist in financial history; Anatole Leroy-Beaulieu, professor of contemporary politics; Albert Sorel, specialist in diplomatic history; Funck Brentano, who gave the course on human rights.

During the winter of '84, my uncle reached what he considered the summit of his career: his appointment to the Institut, as a member of the department of moral and political sciences. Aunt Ma hoped to see her husband one day enter the Académie Française. But I do not think that my uncle ever really hoped for that.

Each Thursday, he went for two and a half hours to the Collège de France. And each Saturday, early in the afternoon, he walked down the rue de Rennes to the Institut, where the *"sciences morales"* were meeting. On other days he seldom went out, and if he did, it was almost always to consult some rare book at the Bibliothèque Nationale. Aunt Ma, who went out herself every afternoon, often suggested that he take advantage of the hired carriage, which came each day at two o'clock and parked at the door of the house. But my uncle Éric preferred to walk. "It's my only exercise," he would say.

I have always wondered if he had some trace of Saracen blood in his veins. There was something vaguely Negroid in his features. And yet, if I had to describe his face, I would not know where to place signs of an African ancestry, for he looked very French, very Latin. All I see that could be cited as "Saracen" characteristics are his slightly swarthy complexion, the somewhat frizzy density of his mop of gray hair, perhaps also the fleshy thickness of his lower lip. The blackness of his irises, too. He had the keen, round, piercing,

---

Affaires Étrangères: the Ministry of Foreign Affairs; *Conseil d'État:* the Council of State (a body of 200 that acts both as the highest court to which the legal affairs of the state can be referred, and as a consultative body to which bills and rulings are submitted by the government prior to examination by the *Conseil des Ministres*); *Inspection des Finances:* the government department responsible for monitoring the financial affairs of state bodies. *(Larousse)*

mobile, and ungentle eye of a bird, of certain raptors. My memory also calls up a faunlike quality that I attributed to that animal alertness of the gaze, to the short beard, to the prominent cheekbones, but still more to the little, jutting, pointed ears which he concealed by letting a tuft of hair, slightly simian, grow over each of them.

THE LEAST I CAN say of my uncle is that he was a strange character. I believe I have already mentioned this. I lived for many years in close proximity with him, I experienced, successively and sometimes simultaneously, the most diverse feelings towards him, ranging from the most overpowering antipathy to the sincerest attachment, passing through every shade of irritation, admiration, affection, even pity. I think I can state that, next to Aunt Ma, I was the one who was closest to him and knew him best. And yet, even today I sometimes ask myself whether the true, secret depths of that complicated and enigmatic figure were ever clearly revealed to me and whether I am entitled to sketch his portrait. All the same, I shall in a little while try. And in doing so, I shall attempt to overcome that sort of curse which makes it so difficult to be able to speak anything but ill of him, so obvious and annoying were his faults, his shortcomings—and so hidden his good qualities. These latter nevertheless did exist, and they were considerable. If one were inclined to underestimate or deny them, it would be enough to recall the place he held, the many and exceptional friendships he formed.

Ah, but he was difficult to know! I shared his daily life for several years, and I still ask myself questions about him that remain unanswered . . . I could not even say if he was good. I know of gestures of great kindness that he made. But when his self-esteem was wounded he was capable of the stubbornest grudges or even of the most treacherous and savage vindictiveness.

And this reminds me of an anecdote.

That summer, Xavier de Balcourt had taught Aunt Ma a certain parlor game that was then all the rage in the Latin Quarter: the game of Analogies. Here is how it was played. The group was divided into two different sides, separated by an empty space. The members of one side huddled and agreed among themselves, in an undertone, on the name of such and such a personage, well known by all, living or dead, chosen from among the great men of history, the heroes of literature, the celebrities of the present day, or from people familiar to the company. This done, the two sides sat down facing each other, and on each side a leader was in charge, one of asking questions, the other of answering them, after whispered consultations with his teammates. The side which did not know the name had to find it out through "analogies," according to the answers made by the other side.

Aunt Ma was absolutely crazy for Analogies, and for one season every Sunday, around teatime at the Chambosts' summer house in Neuilly, she would not rest until a game had been got up. I have to say that, played by cultivated and subtle minds and when expert swordsmen like Alphonse Daudet, Berthelot, Taine, Jules Lemaître, Renan, and Sully Prudhomme* tried to outdo each other in shrewd inspirations, it could be entertaining, and laughter rang out.

Now one day, some mischievous friends chose the host, Uncle Éric, as the subject! The gathering was particularly large, and witty. The game lasted a long time, either because the riddle was especially difficult, or perhaps because those who had a clue hesitated to say that they recognized Uncle Éric through the analogies, most of which were satiric and some downright cruel.

I was on the side of the questioners, and it took me a long time to dare to guess . . . That session had an effect on my life. I was so struck by some analogies which suddenly illuminated certain aspects of Uncle Éric that I took the trouble to write them down that night. I have forgotten almost all of them today. Here are the ones that I find in the depths of my memory.

"If it were a flower?"

"The thistle," whispered someone.

"No," corrected the team leader, "the thistle is a homely flower with no scent. It would be a rose, but with all its thorns."

"If it were a monument?"

"A pointy tower."

"If it were a garden?"

"A parterre in the French style, with a maze."

"If it were a play?"

There were long consultations among the group. They whispered: *"The Liar, Tartuffe."*

Finally, someone tossed out the title of the comedy by Diderot: *"Is He Good, Is He Bad?"* and there was, from the side giving the answers, an explosion of laughter and bravos.

"Living or dead?"

"Very much alive."

"If it were a surgical instrument?"

"A scalpel."

"If it were a book?"

"A dictionary."

---

*Alphonse Daudet (1840–1897), novelist and short-story writer; Hippolyte Taine (1828–1893), philosopher, critic, and historian, author of *The Origins of Contemporary France;* Jules Lemaître (1853–1914), critic, short-story writer, and playwright; Sully Prudhomme (1839–1907), poet, essayist, winner of the Nobel Prize for Literature (1901).

"If it were a fabric?"

"A waterproof material."

"If it were a statue?"

"Janus."

"If it were a mythological character?"

"A faun."

"If it were a great politician?"

"Machiavelli."

"If it were a piece of furniture?"

"A drawer with a false back."

"If it were a fruit?"

"A nut, but in its green shell."

"If it were an animal?"

"A bookworm."

"If it were a painter?"

"Greuze."*

UNCLE ÉRIC WAS phenomenally cultivated in the classics, in literature and philosophy, in history and sociology. Writing this, I am not a victim of the illusions that a young provincial might have entertained, showing up one fine day at the Chambost-Lévadés and comparing Uncle Éric's intelligence and knowledge with the general learning possessed by the teachers at Saint-Léonard. No. The exceptional scope of my uncle's erudition was something recognized in his circle, which was one of the most cultured in Europe, and earned him the esteem of the Taines, the Renans, the Sorels, the Lemaîtres, of all the great minds that had hobnobbed with him. People were surprised that he did not produce more. The books he left were all remarkable, but few.

His great work, the one on which I saw him toiling his whole life, *The Moral Evolution of the Human Mind,* which was to be the general history of moral ideas throughout the ages and all known civilizations, remained unfinished. Only the first two volumes appeared during his lifetime. The third, which was published after his death, contains a large number of finished chapters, but the whole was not in its final form, and the second half of the volume contains only outlines, rough drafts, short completed fragments, and a multitude of notes. The rest of his files were left by my aunt to the archives of the Bibliothèque Nationale and will probably be plundered by researchers who will not cite their source. But while he was alive, he dissipated the substance of this historical monument that he was planning, first in his courses

*Jean-Baptiste Greuze (1725–1805), French painter. Martin du Gard adds in a note to himself concerning Greuze: "[Grandiloquence and mawkishness.]"

at the École des Sciences Politiques and then, a little later, in his courses at the Collège de France.

For one who saw him live and work, the relative meagerness of his output cannot be a surprise. He was far more interested in tracking down ideas than in developing and implementing them. He spent his life accumulating documents and notes, which he meant to use later, adding his comments to them; and the work of classification, of writing, which was all done in his head as he proceeded with his research, seemed to him nothing more than a mere unchallenging game that he was sure of completing when he finally got around to it, and the deadline of which he was always postponing. It was nothing less than a miracle that twice in the course of his investigations he consented to halt in his quest so as to profit from what he had gathered and allot a period of close to a year to composing each of the first two volumes of his *Moral Evolution*.

There is another reason for this apparent sterility. I think that if he had led the life of a small-town librarian, without friends or connections, the need to broadcast his ideas and discoveries, and to face the public, would have made itself more strongly felt. Probably he would have published more regularly and more prolifically. But this necessary contact with minds capable of understanding him, of taking an interest in his views, of discussing them, was offered him every day in Paris, through his teaching and his conversation. It was there, in his courses and his meetings with friends, that he spent without stint the treasures patiently accumulated through his work. This gave him immense daily satisfaction. But when, in his chair at Sciences Politiques or at the Collège de France, and also at the Sunday get-togethers, he had generously poured out in small change the results of his inquiries, of his reading, of his meditations, he would feel very little inclined to pick up his pen to make a book of them. When he went back to his desk, it was to dart off on new trails. His work was squandered in speech. He talked his books instead of writing them. Those subjects that he had turned over and over while chatting and teaching became a bit shopworn for him. To go to the trouble of writing a book, he needed to be sustained by the impression that he had a secret to reveal and that there was no other way of disseminating it. But well before he contemplated putting down the first chapter, the secret was already an open one; all the substance had gone into talks, digressions, teaching, discussions, and had lost its juice. At least for him. My regret is that his lectures were not taken down in shorthand, then collected in book form after his death, when we could not hope ever to see his work brought to realization. Unfortunately none of his students recorded a complete text of his courses, and he himself left nothing of his lectures but brief and muddled notes. For he extemporized, like all true improvisers, and never read a prepared text.

I think of another great mind who, at the same period and with more or less the same methods, the same steadfastness in his labor, the same ambition to extract laws, had slowly built up a body of work: Taine, and his *Origins of Contemporary France;* Taine who too came, quite regularly, to the Sundays at the hôtel de Fleurus and who, like Chambost-Lévadé, might have yielded to the temptation to squander in his conversation all the fruits of his solitary toil. But Taine usually spoke very little. Above all, he made no effort to steer the conversation, as my uncle Éric so naturally, so irresistibly did. Taine accepted the conversation that was offered him. He listened attentively to everyone, spoke his piece, sometimes took the floor a bit longer if the gathering was not too large; what he said, however, concerned topics put forward by others, not by him. Where my uncle could not resist the pleasure of tossing into the discussion his preoccupations of the week, the discoveries that he had made, Taine, for his part, reserved his life as a writer for his solitude and did not spoil his work beforehand in desultory talk. For the circle of the hôtel de Fleurus, which spent several afternoons a month with Taine, each volume of the *Origins* was, I won't say a surprise, since he did not keep the goals he was pursuing secret to that extent, but an innovative book, chock-full of unexpected revelations.

Normally, Uncle Éric would appear before his guests with a vague plan of discussion, certain topics that he wanted to broach and put into play, either because these subjects had a connection with his interests and researches that week or because he had a personal, original opinion about them that he was pleased to exhibit and highlight in front of an audience well equipped to appreciate its subtlety. What makes me think this is that sometimes, at the arrival of a new guest who was a little late, he would rather suddenly change the subject, as if he had said to himself: "Ah, here's Berthelot . . . (or Taine . . . or Renan), now I can trot out what I have to say about the primitive pharmacopoeia of the Chibchas of Bogotá, or about the Revolution (if it was Taine), or about pre-Christian Antiquity (if it was Renan)."

Though he had the preconceived and despotic intention of directing the discussion to suit himself and of imposing his views, he played the part of the liberal host who first lets the others have their say and remains in the background. Each time he broke in, he prefaced his intervention with absurd circumlocutions which were a mannerism of his and which always produced smiles: "If I may be permitted, my dear friend, to add a word to your remarkable presentation . . ." And, when he at last relinquished the floor to let some interrupter get a word in, he would start mincing again: "I apologize for having monopolized your attention for so long. I return to the no-man's-land of the listeners . . . I'm stepping aside, dear friend, excuse my chatter—among you I'm nothing more than a hyphen . . ." Which did not prevent him, two minutes later, from cutting in on someone to say: "I will again permit myself a brief word, which I believe goes right to the heart of the matter . . . ," etc. All this uttered smilingly, with a humble shrinking motion—a ludicrous expression of reticence and modesty.

If the talk did not allow itself to be led in the direction he wished, he would maintain a glum and disapproving silence. But he was preparing his revenge. At the end of the discussion, he would finally intervene: "Before we break up, I think it would not be unprofitable to sum up what has been said and round it off." Then, under this pretext, he would quite shamelessly graft onto the conversation in which his premeditated intentions had been betrayed a conclusion diametrically opposed to the one arrived at but in keeping with his personal view, which he had reached long before the appearance of his guests.

And everyone, with good grace, let him do it. They were used to his quirks and forgave them all the more easily because more often than not his summing-up served him as a pretext for very instructive and meaningful digressions.

I can see why my uncle took pleasure in conversing. He was a dazzling talker, a phenomenal improviser, because he had a glib tongue, a vocabulary at once rich and simple which allowed him to express the most novel ideas without resorting to any pedantic terms (he was especially wonderful in philosophical discussions, on account of his ability to say everything in clear language with the most ordinary words, and I think that he did this deliberately, that he prided himself on speaking as a philosopher without borrowing anything from the technical jargon of the professors of philosophy), and he came up with felicitous and striking phrases that you never forgot; because he drew from an extensive, precise, and inexhaustible erudition, effortlessly making unexpected connections between the events of every era, between the doctrines and works of all the great minds that had stood out as landmarks over the centuries, between the thinkers of all countries, quoting, in the same sentence, Callimachus, Milarepa, Kierkegaard, and Gibbon, comparing the dismemberment of Cyrus' empire, the Peloponnesian Wars, the Italian struggles of the Renaissance, and the wars of the nineteenth century. "Forgive me for these banalities, but you all remember," he would say with a serene and impish show of ingenuousness, "that famous text from the *Olynthiacs* of Demosthenes . . ." or "the very beautiful passage by Apollinaris of Sidon . . ." or "the curious letter of Ballanche." And he would recite the fragment in question from memory. And this was not at all to give fresh evidence of his learning: it always turned out that the text to which he alluded and which he was the only one to know, or at least to recall, was not merely a "master-text," as he liked to say, one of those important texts, full of meaning and implications, which stand as a milestone, but a text which had the most direct connection with the topic under discussion, and gave it new impetus, and shed a new and decisive light on it. It was not unusual to see Taine, or Brunetière, or Jules Lemaître, pull a notebook out of his pocket and jot down, like a schoolboy, one of these precious tidbits that my uncle tossed off while chatting, sometimes in a short aside or a quick parenthesis, as if he found it indecent to linger any further over something that must be so well known by all.

This insolent and guileful way of expressing himself was his mannerism, one of the signs of pettiness in him, and one of the most enigmatic features of his nature.

I never clearly understood, either, what purpose was served by this bizarre game:

"A play from the seventeenth century, which created something of a stir in its day, and which I could not too strongly recommend that you read if you should run across it," he would say, for instance, turning amiably toward one of those present, Taine perhaps, or Faguet;* "I am referring to a play entitled *Le Cid*, by Pierre Corneille . . ."

But, on the other hand, he would say:

"I will not have the presumption to remind you of that fragment from the *Philosophoumena*, which everyone remembers, and in which Origen gives such precious information concerning the condemnation of the Monarchianists by Pope Zephyrinus."

Or again:

"Regarding that respect for the life of animals, so firmly rooted in the traditions of ancient Persia, you are all familiar with the beautiful lines from the Zend-Avesta where Zoroaster, in one of his most moving gathas . . ." etc.

Or:

"You know better than I the role of Lord John Somers in the accession of the Prince of Orange . . ."

Or:

"You are all aware of the formal lines of the *Institutiones*, wherein Gaius declares illegitimate the children born of a marriage between a *civis romanus* and a woman belonging to a community that did not have the privilege of the *connubium* . . ."

He would cite by turns Procopius and the Sar Dar, the *Établissements* of Saint-Louis, the *Opera* of Eusebius, Gregory of Nazianzus, or the *Lex duodecim tabularum* . . . as if it were impossible for these texts not to be present to every memory.

Although it might appear so, there was no hint of pedantry in this sort of

---

*Émile Faguet (1847–1916), French teacher and critic.

talk. These works came spontaneously to his mind, and in quoting them he was doing no more than thinking out loud.

But why did he give his remarks that affected, somewhat smarmy twist, and that form of crude hoaxing? I swear that when he turned to Taine or someone else to suggest to him, as he would have done to an illiterate, that he read *Le Cid,* he had no intention of ridiculing him, or of satire, or mockery of any kind. I don't even think he had the slightest wish to make a joke, except perhaps at his own expense. Yes, I would be tempted to believe that he was being ironical for his own personal amusement. He could, in certain cases, let fly with cutting shafts, and at those times he would wield irony with a sort of ferocity. I was sometimes its victim, in private. He occasionally liked to question me in order to catch me out in some flagrant piece of ignorance, and, under the guise of an exaggerated courtesy—which was also very much his style—he would mercilessly humiliate me.

The cruelty of these satirical tendencies grew with age. Towards the end of his life, already ailing (I remember a visit he made to le Saillant in 1904, the year before his death, while I was garrisoned in Alençon), he gave in almost continually to his bitterness. He seemed to harbor resentment against the whole world for the disappointments he had suffered. Not in his career, which fulfilled his ambitions (although he must have been sorry not to have been admitted to the Académie) but in life, in his contacts with mankind. And here I see a proof of his sensitivity, usually so little visible. To have been so disappointed in people, when he had had so many friends and such a deferential entourage of the great men of the day, he must have had high and generous hopes as to the quality and perfectibility of human nature, of institutions, and of the Republic.

He nursed his grudge against the world, and found his peace of mind, his balance, by indulging in critical denigration. He practiced this with wit, with an unflagging zest. He expected nothing of Man, still less of Society. He had found his form of happiness in this witty sniggering which never deserted him, which could be intuited, piquant and active within him, even when he was silent, his mouth fixed in a sardonic half-smile, and his eye sparkling with a sarcastic gleam beneath its half-lowered lid.

All this is more complicated than I am managing to say. I am right when I maintain that in suggesting to Jules Lemaître that he read a play called *Le Cid,* he was not in the slightest trying to be ironical at Lemaître's expense. But he was ironical with no purpose, for the fun of it, to amuse himself, because irony was one form of his thought, entirely natural. He was putting on a show for himself, it seems to me, without considering for an instant that anyone could feel hurt by his irony, which was aimed at no one in particular.

How to explain some of his behavior? Why, almost every time we found ourselves together in front of a door, did he make the ceremonious gesture of stepping back in deference to the young man that I was? I am quite certain that he would have been deeply mortified if I had taken advantage of this invitation and gone ahead of him. Then why did he make the offer, with all that fuss, that insistence? If it had been to test my good manners, he would have stopped this game early on, having established that I obstinately refused to go first. But he did this all his life, almost mechanically. Here again, I think he was putting on an act for himself.

I remember a strange scene of the same type. On a certain Thursday, when I was going to attend a classical matinee at the Théâtre-Français, I left the house at the same time as he. He was going to the Collège de France, for his lecture. He always walked there, and that day, as usual, he was early. "You'll never be at the Français by two," he told me. "Take a cab." We proceeded together as far as the Boulevard Saint-Germain, where there was a carriage stand. I said goodbye to him and headed towards the first cab in the rank. I thought that he was continuing on his way. But he was at my heels. And when, having climbed into the old hack and given the driver the address of the Théâtre-Français, I wanted to close the door, I saw him hurrying to close it. And as I watched him with surprise and embarrassment, he solemnly doffed his hat with a broad courtly gesture and stood stock-still on the sidewalk, hat in hand, until the cab had started off—with no hint of mockery, with the greatest and most genuine seriousness, as if he had escorted the President of the Republic to his landau . . . What did this attitude signify? I still wonder. Did he mean to underline that I, a callow youth, was riding in style, while he went on foot? Surely not, for it was he who had urged me to take that cab. And he could not blame me for being late, since the fault was his: he had gone to the funeral of a member of the Institut that morning and had not returned till one o'clock for lunch. Nor could he have meant that I might have suggested he get into the carriage, since we were going in completely opposite directions. No. Here too, I cannot explain this absurd piece of business except as a need to play a role for himself.

I shall come back to this curious, entirely gratuitous instinct for ham acting, which was blatant, for instance, when he gave a reading. He was considered an exceptional reader, but I never found this to be true. He read with a consummate knowledge of effects. He was not content merely to read with intelligence, pointing up the nuances contained in the text by means of his tone and his delivery. He exaggerated the author's intentions, altered his volume and pitch from one moment to the next, took pauses, suddenly accelerated his delivery, raised his voice, then lowered it to a murmur, and accompanied his reading with all sorts of faces, much too expressive, overdone, as if instead of being seated in his home amid a circle of friends he were before the footlights, performing to a packed house.

Xavier de Balcourt confessed to me one day that hearing my uncle read always caused him an unbearable discomfort that even prevented him from understanding the text. And he added drolly: "He reminded me of the one-man band, you know, that Diderot describes in *Rameau's Nephew*." I could not forget this quip, and every time I had occasion to hear my uncle read, I thought of Diderot. I have just reopened my Diderot to search for that quotation. As often happens, I ran across something different but apropos: a letter from Diderot to Mme. d'Épinay, explaining to her why he will not go to see the King of Prussia: "This king is certainly a great man, but flighty as a parakeet, wicked as a monkey, and capable at one and the same time of the grandest and smallest things. He's a miserable soul, and, I'll speak plainly, mean-spirited as they come . . ."

This appearance of overacting was never more painful than when he evoked Guy's death and his fatherly grief. I do not want to be unfair. He had felt his son's illness keenly, and not just because it had forced Aunt Ma to leave him alone for months on end, or just because his pride had been bruised, for this remarkably intelligent man was sufficiently petty to feel humiliated at having to say, "My son had to interrupt his studies and go to a sanatorium," but also because he loved that son as much as he was capable of loving. And Guy's death had, without any doubt, profoundly affected him: for two weeks he had not appeared at the Collège de France, and for two months he had lived, prostrate, in the midst of his books, unable to interest himself in anything, unable to resume his work. But at the end of two months he had begun to revive, to see people, and from that moment on he had gradually freed himself from his grief by turning it into literature. He staged for himself, and in public, the spectacle of his despair. He mimed his sorrow. Everything that can be said, in moving phrases, of such suffering, he had said, and repeated it to all and sundry. Dressed in black (to the point of using handkerchiefs bordered in black and having a boater dyed black), displaying an ostentatious mourning, he put on a face of silent, concentrated fortitude; a sad, fleeting smile played about his lips; he seemed to say to everyone: "Look, I have the inner strength of a sage; but my heart is broken; my life is over." From then on, he recovered his appetite and his sleep. He had externalized his pain. He compared himself to Priam coming to retrieve his son's corpse and quoted Homer, in Greek. I have these details from Xavier. When I came to live with my uncle, he had long ceased to play the part of the anguished father. But many a time I heard him allude to Guy's death, I saw him conspicuously "hold back" his rekindled pain, speak of his "father's heart," his "eternal mourning." And, very sincerely engrossed again in his role, he would create in himself the emotion he was conjuring up, his mouth would tremble with grief, his voice founder on the brink of a sob, his eyes mist over with real tears. These were not hypocritical affectations. He had the power to summon up this private drama in a literary way, so much so that he relived it fictively and was utterly shattered by it.

I remember one detail. I have already said that the Chambosts had given me Guy's old bedroom, which had not been reopened since his death and which had been repapered and refurnished for me. My aunt, as she took me to it, had told me with a staggering simplicity: "You see, it was his bedroom. I had never wanted to come back to it. But it's better this way. You too will be a son for me." The next day my uncle knocked on the door. And, on the threshold, he stopped, theatrical and "speechless." Then, making a conspicuous effort to overcome his emotion and regain the power of speech, he said: "Forgive me, Bertrand. A father's grief . . . You will understand, later on, when you have children . . . 'Aux larmes, Le Vayer, laisse tes yeux ouverts!'"*

At that moment, I was close to believing him incapable of real suffering, too self-centered for that. This was shortsighted and wrong. Today I think that what I broadly call his "overacting" appeared to deform his deep feelings but that these feelings had some reality to them. His manifestation of them was distorted by that strange compulsion to play a part, to assume the semblance of a character. I would no longer even dare to say that he magnified his feelings, that he betrayed the truth through exaggeration. A little, maybe, yes. But quite little, really.

I am thinking, as I write this, of Lemonnier, that actor at the Odéon who was a reserve officer and whom I had as a secretary for six months in 1915, when I took command of my regiment. I saw him at quite close range, and ended up becoming attached to him. He was a genuinely sensitive, genuinely patriotic, genuinely courageous fellow, although he had such a disagreeable way of twisting the expression of his thought and of his true substance through theatrical posing that everyone around us had long taken him for a swaggerer, a braggart, a rather contemptible phony. This was a serious error in judgment, and I was the first to realize it and to make the officers of the regiment reconsider the unfortunate impression produced at the beginning by this man, who was instantly nicknamed "The Showoff." He was in reality very simple, very loyal, with an intense and cheerful nature. But he was an actor, and he had the characteristic of always needing to "immerse himself in his role." In the war he was a soldier, a lieutenant, and he fancied himself "the typical officer," strapped tight in his uniform, puffing out his chest, his forage cap cocked over one ear, his voice curt, his walk full of vigor. In the trenches, he was "the officer at the front," dirty, muddy, bolting down a piece of cheese in the doorway of his dugout; at the look-out slit, binoculars

---

*"Let your eyes, Le Vayer, give way to tears." The writer François de La Mothe Le Vayer (1588–1672) received these sympathetic words from Molière upon the death of his son.

screwed to his eyes, attentive, hunched over, tensed up, he was "the sentry watching out for the enemy." In our billet, he was the "*colon's** secretary," a staff officer with a dilettantish air, close-shaven, impeccable, peeling his pear with a fork, raising his little finger to drink, and when one of us in the mess told a funny story, he had an insufferable way of laughing, a stage laugh, rippling, a sort of gargle with cooing modulations, putting on the face of the "man laughing" from the books on human physiognomy. Aside from that, he never spoke of the theater, or of his creations, as would have been natural. And this was not out of modesty: it was because an actor who is acting, who is immersed in a character, forgets all his former characters. Lemonnier was playing "the officer at war," he forgot all the rest, forgot that he had caught Tosca in his arms, at nineteen, as a supernumerary dressed as captain of the guards and that the Tosca was Sarah Bernhardt; and that he had created a role in *Chantecler,* and played *Cyrano* on tour . . . It was through questioning him that I learned of these exploits. (I even remember a rather amusing quip of his, the day when I asked him, seeing him writing a long letter, whether he was married. "No, *mon colonel.* I'm divorced. You know, *mon colonel,* in the theater, one is sometimes married, but one is always divorced, and often more than once . . ." The letter he was writing was intended for Jeannot, a five-year-old he was bringing up, the child he had had with some well-known actress and who had sent him one of his little dolls, which Lemonnier kept in his tin trunk as a mascot.)

Well, Uncle Éric had somewhat the same shortcomings as Lemonnier. The emotions he felt, the thoughts he expressed, had as their immediate effect the creation of a "character" in which he would promptly immerse himself, for an instant. And when he thought of his little Guy, the secret wound reopened, and he became the old Priam, and recited a speech from the *Iliad. He became the old Priam* does not mean that he sought to pass in the eyes of his interlocutor for a father stricken to his paternal core. It was in his own eyes that he appeared magnified, sublimated, clad in old Priam's grief.

There are people whose lives are entirely controlled, and thrown out of balance, and whose personalities are, as it were, dislocated, by the need to cut a figure. My uncle felt this need in the extreme, and constantly: but the need to cut a figure in his own eyes. And he was capable of acting out the tragedy or the comedy for himself, in front of others. Capable of any hypocrisy, admittedly, but in order to deceive himself, and to make himself believe that he was different, better, greater, more noble, more sensitive than he was.

When you lived with him, and you had leisure to see the extent to which this man could, in private, be basically hard, selfish, vehement, unjust, and

*Short for *colonel.*

intolerant, you felt a sort of indignation at also seeing that he always had in his mouth the words Charity, Justice, Fraternity, Tolerance, Kindness, Greatness of Soul. From there to considering him a monster of duplicity and falseness was but a step.

This would have been completely unjust. I ended up understanding that my uncle was the prey of successive sincerities. He was no more himself, nor less, when he behaved with a fierce grudge than when he professed magnanimity and forgiveness of wrongs. He was sincere in both of these attitudes.

I believe that the secret of this double game was quite simple to explain. I believe that my uncle was born wicked. I believe that bad fairies had bent over his cradle and that he had been born with a violent, vindictive, unfair, vain, selfish disposition. But a good fairy had also presided at his birth. And she had grafted onto his heart a very genuine ideal of moral perfection. He was born evil, and he made a cult of virtue. He was a nasty devil who would have liked to be endowed with the nature of Saint Vincent de Paul; a beast whose ideal was to resemble the sage Emerson. When, in words and in his public actions, he was affectionate, humane, devoted, modest, compassionate, generous, selfless, prompted solely by noble motives, he spoke and acted at those moments in accordance with that ideal of moral beauty which was an integral part of his soul. And when he committed some mean little misdeed, vented his spleen, was unfair, spiteful, mendacious, malevolent, indifferent to the misfortune of others, brusque, bilious, intransigent, authoritarian, curt, he was obeying, at those moments, his imperfect, vicious nature, against which, I believe, he struggled sincerely but in vain. Xavier used to say: "No one will know if his great intelligence has ever allowed him to see himself as he is." As for me, I do not doubt it. I think that his secret life was a constant conflict between two forces, that every day he was the battlefield of Good and Evil, of Ormazd and Ahriman, of Light and Darkness. He was, no matter what he did, stuck, entangled in that double personality—of the ugly monkey that Nature had created in the bosom of Madame Chambost-Lévadé, his mother, and of the great modern humanist, with a generous heart and a virtuous soul, that he desperately wanted to be, and whose outer behavior he mimicked, for lack of anything better. I believe that his life was a secret martyrdom. And here as well, he pridefully misled people. There was no virtue with which this man, torn by base passions, forever unhappy and dissatisfied with himself, yearned more to adorn himself than that of inner peace and intellectual serenity.

One day he gave me a very sensible piece of advice in which I think I see still another explanation for his overacting. "We must strive," he told me, "to like that which we instinctively dislike; it is the surest way of improving ourselves."

The insincerity that one often observed in him was probably connected to this precept. His assertions were sometimes a reflection of his natural instincts, of his tastes, and sometimes, on the contrary, the result of factitious acquirements that he tried to force on his nature. Hence, for those of us who saw him up close, an apparent contradiction, which made us accuse him of lying.

There is yet one thing more to say about my uncle's relative sincerity. His double game had been going on for so long that he had had the time to alter his true nature to the extent of having, in certain respects, replaced it with a borrowed one, which, fictive to begin with, had ended up being a "second" nature. Concerning certain things, he had adopted a way of speaking to which he was sedulously accustomed, and faithful. He probably no longer realized that his ways of acting almost invariably belied his professions of faith. These contradictions between his theories and his behavior, so disconcerting, so distasteful to others, he had, I believe, become incapable of noticing.

It goes without saying that the daily exposure to that perpetually skewed personality created, for those around him, a constant uneasiness. (For those in his immediate circle, that is—since the care that he took to give himself the appearance of virtue was generally convincing, and even among those who regularly attended his Sunday at-homes, there were few, I believe, who had seen through him. Moreover, most of these, not being much for psychology, were rather ill-equipped to detect that subtle split. They knew, and wished to know, and contented themselves with knowing, only the phenomenal scholar whose sparkling conversation was an endlessly replenished enrichment.)

As for myself, I could never shake off that feeling of insecurity and discomfort. I alternately felt a genuine attraction and affection for him, and an insuperable dislike, according to what day it was, or what hour of the same day. But scarcely ever, in my admiring fervor or in my animosity, did the feeling of unease, of malaise, irritation, awkwardness subside, and it sometimes caused me such annoyance that I was repelled, outraged, offended, and unfair in my turn. With him, all exchanges rang false, and to live in his wake one had to keep a constant check on oneself, dissemble, put on an endless act as he did. In general I avoided private conversations, hid myself from him, let him see only a superficial and well-rehearsed side of me. I did not stop looking up to him, consulting him, listening to him; he had me deeply under his influence; but I could never trust him; and to put it all in a nutshell, this man to whom I perhaps owe the best that is in me, I was never able to love.

I owe it to myself, I owe it to truth and justice, to elaborate a bit more upon the influence that Uncle Éric had on my intellectual formation and upon the incomparable good that this influence did me. I would be ungrateful indeed if I did not acknowledge an immense debt to him.

Granted, he was often hard with me. He spared me no disagreeable observation, and he did it in his own way, which was usually wounding. I never saw politeness, irony, and sternness dealt out so perfidiously. At the start, this horrendous mixture, so new to me, cut me to the quick. Then I got used to it. His reprimands were like certain electro-cautery treatments that bite deep into the flesh and make a painful lesion but leave the area decontaminated and swift to heal. It did not take me long to experience the benefits, and quite soon I began to endure the cruelty of the cure with pluck because of its efficacy. Moreover, in the final analysis, this was (let it be said in passing, and without pride) to my credit. I had faults, but I was not foolish enough to refuse to see them or to not wish to correct them. I soon recognized, underneath my uncle's severity, the interest he took in me. Because he did not, after all, get sufficient pleasure from inflicting hurt that he bothered to fire his shafts at those who left him indifferent. For him to scold me so, he had to love me. I had it in me to prefer severity to indifference.

I quickly noticed that once he had discharged his venom and satisfied his penchant to indulge in irony, the man he let show was not impervious to human feelings. And our talks then took the following turn. For several days running, at meals, in front of my aunt, or during our brief meetings in the library, he would toss at me enigmatic, allusive witticisms, whose meaning I did not immediately fathom. Then, taking advantage of some opportunity, he would draw me into his lair, ostensibly to speak about a text or a book that he wanted to lend me. He would sit behind his desk, leave me standing and very self-conscious in the middle of the room, and in a calm, soft voice in which the mockery was wrapped in an excessive politeness, he would begin his diatribe, and always with plenty of preparatory remarks: "You're old enough to take on responsibilities . . . What I want to tell you is only a suggestion . . . Feel free to think otherwise . . . God save me from encroaching on your independence in the slightest . . . I must, however, enlighten you . . . I believe it my duty to call your attention to things I think I have noticed . . . Perhaps I am mistaken, but it seems obvious to me that . . . etc." There followed the bitterest moment of the session. In a few scathing sentences, he would deliver some merciless truths about me, about my character, about my work, about a faulty mental habit, a bad tendency, a weakness . . . Experience had taught me that I needed to receive these assaults without flinching, to avoid the argument that would set him off again and in which he always blithely kept the upper hand; that I had to let him pour out his bile; that it would always exhaust itself rather quickly if it did not meet with any contradiction. I did this with a hypocritical humility.

Soon the tone would change. He would cease to put things on a personal plane, would leave off denouncing this or that deficiency of mine in order to broaden the subject, to enter into general ideas and abstractions. Which always brought about a change in him, soothed him, restored his peace of mind. Then, under cover of generalities, I could start up a conversation with him, and an unexpected cordiality would gradually seep into his remarks. Through my interventions, if I managed to show him that I had understood him well, that I sided with him as to principles, that there was acceptance and agreement on my part, he would surrender himself to the pleasure of improvising, would smile, but no longer satanically, would gesture for me to sit down, and the conversation would finally take another turn. I could then cautiously come back to my case, timidly present my defense when I judged his criticisms unfair, or, on the other hand, if I considered that he had aimed true and hit some defect of my nature dead on, I could plead guilty, acknowledge my fault, draw his attention to the extenuating circumstances, demonstrate a desire to improve and to cure myself of my failings, ask his counsel. It was not uncommon, at this stage of the session, for him to assume a paternal, conciliatory role and to lavish judicious advice on me. Never, at any rate, did he use a confession to condemn me. And we would sometimes spend the whole rest of the evening chatting frankly, freely; I questioning him, calling upon his knowledge and experience; and he exerting himself unstintingly to help and better me.

Poor Uncle Éric! Strange phenomenon . . . Reflecting after all these years on him and our odd relationship, I see nothing to reproach him with. I have only gratitude for the good he did me. I wish for every adolescent what I found in him: daily intercourse with a great and encyclopedic intelligence.

This scholar, who lived absorbed in history and folklore in order to collect and classify the evidence of the evolution of the human conscience, was an astute psychologist.

Quite the opposite of a theoretician. Always ready to bow before a fact, and never more confident than when he was relying on experiments. I was one for him. He was sufficiently interested in my development to appreciate the trust I showed him by speaking plainly about myself. My sister Henriette had, from my earliest childhood, prepared me for these psychological investigations into others and ourselves. I too had a taste for analyzing myself, understanding myself, elucidating myself. I did not try in the least to conceal the particular features of my character, however little edifying they might be. I was never loath to make a confession that could enable me to profit by an enlightening response, a helpful piece of advice.

Yes, I owe much to the understanding intelligence and psychological experience of my Uncle Éric.

That was a time in my life when I was both torn with doubts about myself and buoyed by limitless ambitions. Uncle Éric helped me to see more clearly into that shapeless tangle of real gifts, imagined gifts, hidden and significant flaws, and flaws conspicuous but superficial. The unsparing judgments he passed on me allowed me to perceive where my natural limitations lay, to operate neither below nor beyond my potential: an insight that has served me all my life. I believe that nothing in the world is more essential to the leading of a life than a lucid vision of what can be undertaken and of what exceeds our abilities. Uncle Éric made me aware of what was childish and fanciful in certain of my hopes for the future; and, at the same time, he made me see what was justified and legitimate in certain of my aspirations. In so doing, he effectively contributed, if not to dispelling my adolescent unrest, at least to lessening its danger, its harmfulness. And in teaching me to see better into myself, he gave me that balance which is achieved only when one has accepted oneself and does not suppose oneself to be anything but what one really is.

I arrived in Paris as the provinces had made me, filled with boldness but also with timidity, powerfully attracted to people but also very reticent, very secretive, fiercely reserved. I arrived all puffed up with covert pretensions, and if I had a foolishly vulnerable pride, I was also capable of underrating myself to the point of despair.

With his way of mixing me in with the eminent men who came to his house, now and then permitting me an exchange on the fly with this or that well-known professor, stinging me publicly with his irony if I allowed myself to slip in a word too many or if I made a blunder, Uncle Éric taught me to be sociable with discrimination, always to maintain good form, gradually to assume the place that was fitting for me, neither higher nor lower—that of a deferential student with an open mind. It is to him that I owe my lifelong ability to be at ease anywhere and to shed neither simplicity nor naturalness in the most diverse surroundings. He gave me that psychological tact, indispensable for social harmony, which is generally lacking not only in young men but in many adults as well.

He cleansed my mind and, without turning me into either a snob or a dupe, gave me a foundation of wisdom at an age when this cannot be acquired without help. He gave me faith in myself, in my strength, which is to say the courage to strive. He taught me to correct my faults and not to be satisfied with concealing them. To feel at ease with myself; to be frank without either presumption or insolence; to know men and myself in such a way as to take others into account while not fearing, in certain areas, to pit myself against others.

In everything, he taught me moderation.

With his chiding, about which I harbor no bitterness, he disciplined my character, tempered my natural ardor, relieved me of the smugness that good students have, and, through his straightforwardness with me, without humbling me for his own amusement, without belittling me, he reassured me about the life that was opening before me, and allowed me to take wing with everything working in my favor.

CHAPTER X

The Chambost-Lévadés: Aunt Ma

I HAVE ALREADY mentioned the strong attraction that Aunt Ma had exerted over me since my childhood. An attraction that truly assumed every possible shading, emotional, moral and, I am not afraid to say, physical, to the extent that so many sons are, without knowing it, tenderly in love with their mothers. For I liked her bodily presence near me, and the pleasure that I took in watching her—in following the reflection of her feelings, her reactions, in her beautiful eyes and in the expressions of her face—undoubtedly had something sensual, not to say voluptuous, about it, and added much to the charm that I found in conversing freely with her.

Yet she was not pretty. She had a squat body, which might once have had a certain plump freshness to it but which was weighed down with middle age by the time I knew her. There was nothing delicate about her features, but they expressed so much kindness that one forgot their irregularity. The lower part of the face had thickened; the mouth was big, its line slack and too fleshy; the nose, too fat, too wide at the base, too round at the end, was downright homely and gave a coarseness to the face. But the forehead was quite beautiful, the smile vivacious; and as for the eyes, they were magnificent. Such eyes alone can make a woman attractive. I am sensitive to the quality of eyes, and have loved many beautiful ones. But my Aunt Ma's had a somber brilliance which is rare to such a degree, and as much fire as softness, which is also rare; above all, what made them truly incomparable was the intensity of their blaze: that merry brightness which twinkled in the coal-black of the iris, that joyous sparkle which was like a talisman and which electrified me, even as a child. No: I have never encountered a more laughing gaze. And that shining sprightliness, although occasionally mischievous, was not fed by irony: there was a continual goodness and a warm reflection of the heart in that magical incandescence.

Her body, though not slim, was neither without grace nor without distinction. She had been born Madeleine Lizzy de La Place and contained enough blue blood in her veins that this stout and rather plebeian exterior did not make her seem inherently ordinary. Those who found Mme.

Chambost-Lévadé "a bit common" had not observed her carefully. I can easily see what gave rise to the misapprehension: an exaggerated Parisian elegance which well-born ladies generally dispense with and which is usually the mark of the parvenu.

Well, all right: I admit that at first sight there might have been a hint of the parvenu in what I call Aunt Ma's Parisianism. She had excuses. She had been left an orphan very early on, had been, between the ages of ten and eighteen, shut away in the provinces, near Saint-Just-en-Chaussée, in the Oise, with a very old and disabled grandmother. An austere beginning, with quite a narrow horizon, for an ardent nature eager to live. Her marriage, the circumstances of which I have forgotten, had suddenly taken this provincial young woman to Paris, curious about everything and already prepared to let Parisian life go to her head. She brought my Uncle Éric a tidy fortune for the time, and this detail is not without importance: it gave her the power to insist from the beginning on a fairly sumptuous and frivolous existence. Thus her first whim had been to convince my uncle to rent by the month one of those coupés that the Compagnie de l'Urbaine provided to people who did not want to go to the trouble of keeping horses and carriages of their own. At the time it was a rather unusual luxury. Likewise, she had wished to have her box for the "Tuesdays" at the Théâtre-Français. (When I went to Paris, she had it still, and I made liberal use of it. It was there that I gradually saw the entire classical repertoire and all the new plays of the time.)

And, quite naturally, she had begun to follow fashion with a somewhat childish frenzy that would doubtless have been more easily forgiven her in any other circle than that serious society in which her marriage required her to live. Probably she was at fault not to have been more aware of the effect that her young-woman's clothes might produce in the solemn Left Bank gatherings to which she was invited. I even suspect her of impishly wishing to shock the ladies of the Institut with the somewhat showy boldness of her dresses and of having rather too often forgotten that she lacked the figure required to launch the season's new styles. However, I am only speaking from hearsay: when I first met my aunt at le Saillant, I was not old enough to distinguish between genuine elegance and that over-daring Parisianism of which she was fond. And when I came to live with her in Paris, her son's death, the incurable wound that stayed in her heart and had already deeply transformed her, had also sobered her attire. She continued to attach a great importance to her wardrobe, had not stopped going to the best-known dressmakers, and could not resist the temptation of following the changes in fashion as closely as possible; the habit was formed, and she could not imagine things any other way. But as she had decided to remain in mourning for the rest of her life, I always saw her in black. And if the number, the variety, and the cut of her clothes still revealed a constant concern for elegance, if she retained an inordinate taste for beautiful embroidery, laces, and sequins, this indulgence, at least, remained discreet. The woman I knew was a very fastidiously dressed Parisienne, but no longer with anything of the fashion plate about her. And, to be frank, I will add that I was not indifferent to that sartorial refinement. It made me very happy to see her so attractive. When I went to chat in her little sitting room at night, I loved sitting next to a woman with well-cared-for skin, manicured nails, hair always waved, and admiring the silken folds of her housecoat; I was ready to claim that my aunt was the best-dressed woman in Paris. Especially, I repeat, since she was so used to this personal luxury that it was a part of her; one never sensed either affectation or intention in it. Settled in beneath the lamp to read, in her little blue-upholstered easy chair, clad in a loose black velvet robe with a jabot of old lace, perfumed, hair done, with beautiful rings on her fingers, wearing silver mules trimmed in white fur, she looked as much at ease in that outfit that seemed to have been arranged by a painter of society portraits as another woman would have in a merino bathrobe, with a black crocheted shawl over her shoulders and worn-down slippers on her feet.

Yet I was not seduced and blinded to the point of overlooking her shortcomings. For example, she was intelligent—very intelligent, even—but relatively uneducated. Or rather, her education lacked solid foundations. What she knew she had learned here and there, through the Sunday conversations, by listening to her husband hold forth, and through her reading. But as this had been going on for twenty years, her stock of knowledge was considerable, and she held her own among the scholars and artists she invited to her at-homes. All the more so since she did not claim to be an intellectual; on the contrary, she never passed up a chance to admit her ignorance and to correct it by asking questions. "Monsieur Renan," she would say, "you know I'm an ignoramus. Then tell me what the difference is between . . ."

Or to Berthelot: "I'm sure that if you would take the trouble to explain it to me, I'd eventually get an elementary idea of what this Carnot's principle is that you're always talking about . . ." This in all sincerity, without the slightest pretense, with that real and commendable simplicity that everyone found so attractive. People often said, in a tone of affectionate warmth: "That charming Mme. Chambost."

Her tour de force was to assemble the elite of the French intelligentsia several times a month in her home and play her role of hostess to perfection without being a bluestocking; to run one of the leading academic salons of the era without displaying any of the insufferable traits of women of that type, without changing her true nature in any way, but remaining cheerful, a bit frivolous, and effortlessly witty without even seeming to suspect that she was, always saying everything that came into her head, presenting herself exactly as she was, sympathetic and good, quick to laugh, happy to be alive, happy to be healthy, happy to be rich, happy to entertain, and making herself liked by means of this very spontaneity and steadfast good nature. People like Alphonse Daudet, Albert Sorel, Paul de Mun, and Anatole France took obvious pleasure in leaving the male groups to go over to her on the little Directoire sabot where she normally sat, and talk with her one-to-one. This happened frequently. But it was not unusual either to see some solemn academic like M. Taine, or some historian like M. Ribot or M. Leroy-Beaulieu (when it was not M. Renan or M. Berthelot who was lapsing into "social chitchat") lingering with her over a private conversation full of simple intimacy and laughing gaily at her unexpected sallies. For she had a spontaneous spirit that she liked to let run free if she was even slightly encouraged, and the soundness of her intuitions always gave quality and solidity to her judgments. The most austere among the guests could at times let themselves appreciate her *enfant terrible* charm, and laugh with her wholeheartedly. I do not think I am giving way to personal impressions in supposing that her presence, her joyous affability, her good humor added something irreplaceable to the appeal of the receptions in the rue de Fleurus and that if my Uncle Éric had become a widower the regular attendance of those gatherings would perhaps have rather quickly fallen off.

There was, in Aunt Ma, an artist's temperament lying fallow. What would she have become, would she have created works of her own, if her instinctive potential had been noticed in time and been developed, cultivated, given direction? I really don't know, but I have the idea that she would have made something of her innate originality. Her life seems to me not like a failed work, certainly, but rather like a plant rooted in an unsuitable soil, which, lacking competent care and proper fertilizer, grew any which way, without attaining normal growth, without managing to bloom. In that serious and academic circle she occupied a special and very enviable place; she used it to foster intelligence and played her allotted part to perfection. But I imagine that in a more exclusively artistic set—of painters in particular—the gifts that remained dormant would suddenly have flourished.

The paintings of her youth, her decorations on porcelain about which we twitted her and which were certainly not in any way works of art, nevertheless demonstrate, by the inventiveness of their designs, the combination of their colors, the variety of their compositions, a painter's eye which could have been trained. I have exquisite little pastels by her of flowers, of birds. It must not be forgotten that these efforts were the hobby of a seventeen- or eighteen-year-old, cooped up in the provinces, who had never met an artist, never taken a trip, never set foot in a museum, and whose entire artistic education consisted of the counsels of an old maiden lady, an art teacher to whom the bourgeois society of Saint-Just entrusted its daughters, when they left the convent school, to give a certain polish to their "accomplishments."

(A young lady of that era was supposed to know how to play a polka on the piano, do embroidery, and paint a few flowers in watercolor.) After studies on that level, Aunt Ma would have needed a driving personal genius to have become a great artist. She made do with becoming more skillful than her peers, more demanding as well, more enterprising, and with displaying in her schoolgirl attempts more taste than the others. After her marriage, she gave up these activities that were, in the eyes of the world, merely the pastime of a young woman waiting for a husband. But she still had a gift for that kind of thing, and I see indications of a frustrated talent in a thousand details of her life as a society lady, including her propensity for dressing up, for pretty materials, for fashion; in her interest in interior decoration and her liking for beautiful old furniture at a time when French upholsterers and cabinetmakers were outdoing one another in the unimaginativeness and bad taste of their conceptions; in her passion for the knickknacks with which she covered the tables, mantelpieces, and shelves; in her curiosity about the painting exhibitions to which she went by herself and for her own pleasure. I see another indication too—a more subtle indication—in her very nature, that gay and overflowing vitality, that freedom of spirit, that spontaneity in her repartee, that whimsy in her remarks, which against all expectation charmed that circle of pure intellectuals she was a part of but which surprised and sometimes shocked them; and I now feel that all this would have been much more apropos, much more appreciated, in some painter's or sculptor's studio, and that living amid paintbrushes, chisels, and models, Aunt Ma would perhaps have found an opportunity to develop, channel, and give expression to her gifts.

When I think of Aunt Ma, it is her gaze that haunts me. That gaze revealed at once her innermost being, her prodigious vitality, an insatiable appetite for life. That zest for life stood out in her whole demeanor. Despite her portliness, her movements were brisk, jaunty, never sluggish or tired. This vivacity in her gestures even extended to a certain graceful brusqueness in her way of swiveling to answer a remark heard from behind, for she had a keen ear, and in her drawing room or at the table, she always seemed to take in all the comments, all the asides, simultaneously.

Her need to live to the fullest, to participate in every expression of life around her, seemed constantly in play. She did not refrain from interrupting people, tossing a word in here or there all around the drawing room, enlivening every group with her pervasive presence, going from one to another to add her sparkle to it.

Her natural wit continually erupted in funny quips, in unexpected associations. It is quite difficult to define what this witty turn of her thought consisted of. She did not seek to be clever. Never did she "plant" an anecdote as so many "brilliant talkers" in her drawing room did, skilled as they were at leading the conversation onto ground where they had a story all set to bring out, one that they had already used somewhere else and whose effects they had, like good actors, consciously prepared. She rarely repeated herself, and never in the same terms. Everything with her was improvised; it sprang forth fresh. She was not trying to entertain an audience. She was amusing herself with ideas that came to her unexpectedly, and was doing so out loud. Happy and thrilled, of course, when she found herself understood and appreciated, when she felt that her public was participating in her private enjoyment. But she immediately passed on to some other subject and never exploited her success, often not even seeming to notice it. More concerned with the *accuracy* of her remark, with the sense of what she had said, than with the way she had said it. She seemed to be saying, "Isn't that how it is?" and never, "Isn't that funny?"

Sometimes, with an apt word, struck like a medal, precise, clear, suggestive and graphic, she would sum up an entire discussion. This trait occasionally led to quite daring remarks, which would have been shocking in any other woman's mouth. I imagine that our eighteenth-century female forebears allowed themselves to make similar ones, those great ladies with their libertine talk of whom it was laughingly said, "She's no prude."

That inborn, impulsive wit was the single thing in the world to which my provincial life had least accustomed me. From the beginning at le Saillant I had listened to Aunt Ma with rapture, without always understanding the opportuneness or unexpectedness of her retorts at the table but vaguely seduced by that amusing manner in which she said the most common things, and also often getting the humor of her sallies and taking pleasure in it. But I quickly realized, upon seeing her again in her home, among her friends, that she restrained herself somewhat when she was at le Saillant, and that, in front of Henriette and my father, she knew to keep a certain reserve. Altogether different was the freedom of her talk in Paris, and I imagine that she must quite often have scandalized certain professors' wives, who came from the provinces, were a bit stuffy, and must have found her Parisian manners very daring. I myself more than once felt a certain surprise, and to be frank, a certain embarrassment, when her liberty went all the way to license.

I will quote an example, which comes to mind because of a story Aunt Ma told in front of me within the first few days of my arrival at the rue the Fleurus and because I remember quite particularly how squeamish it made me, so obscene did it seem to me. And in fact it was. This was during one of our first evenings together; there were no guests, just the four of us at dinner: my aunt, my uncle, Xavier de Balcourt, and I. The press that day was full of the arrest in the Bois de Boulogne of a "satyr" whose misdeeds, though harmless, had been in the news for a few weeks, and whom the police of the Bois had finally nabbed. A pervert who was frightening unaccompanied women by exposing himself without warning at the bend of a deserted walk, or by popping up out of a bush.

Upon leaving the dining room, my aunt, while straightening up the newspapers that were lying about on the library table, cheerfully exclaimed:

"What a fuss about this poor satyr in the Bois! It's becoming perfectly ridiculous . . ."

"Perhaps you wouldn't be so lenient, Madame," Xavier said with a smile, "if you found yourself nose to nose with him in a deserted pathway . . ."

"Nose to nose," said my aunt, laughing. "Your euphemisms are well-chosen . . . Do you think I'd have called up the whole Parisian police force on that account? Listen, when I was a young woman, here's what happened to me not in the Bois but right on the terrace of the Luxembourg . . ."

"Madeleine," scolded Uncle Éric.

But my aunt was off and running:

"At the end of a beautiful October afternoon, we had lingered on, a woman friend and I, with our children . . . so mild was the temperature. Night was falling, the terrace was deserted. A man in his fifties, an old glazier in a white smock, with his frame on his back, who appeared to be peaceably heading home from his work, came up to us, smiling slightly, as if he was hesitating to ask something . . . And suddenly, three steps off, point-blank so to speak, he lifted his smock . . . My friend, who was newly married, let out an awful shriek, as if she'd seen the devil. As for me, I looked at him, the devil, quite calmly, and said: 'Thanks, my good man, but we've got better at home.' "

"Madeleine!" repeated Uncle Éric, casting a glance at her in which there sparkled more glee and admiration than reproach.

Xavier laughed. I was the only one who felt horribly embarrassed.

"I must have hurt his feelings, poor man," my aunt wound up. "He closed up his smock and slipped off without a word, with his treasures . . ."

She was delighted that she had been able to tell her story and seemed, in those instances, to congratulate herself both for the drollness of her anecdote and for the boldness she had shown in flouting convention. This irreverent side of her was combined with so much good-heartedness and such a wholesome, solid background of distinction that her most indecent remarks were never vulgar or out of place. But the straitlaced milieu in which I had been brought up had left a strong stamp on me, and it took me quite a while to get used to Aunt Ma's liberties in expressing herself.

Strangely enough, for a long time this kind of unabashedness in speech made me more uncomfortable in tête-à-têtes than in large gatherings. I remember certain conversations, between just the two of us, at the beginning of my stay, which literally made me blush. (The day when, describing a ball gown seen the night before whose shamelessly low-cut bodice amounted to hardly more than two thin shoulder straps, she concluded, laughing: "I mean, one of those décolletages to make all the fly-buttons pop . . .")

But these liberties were thankfully rather infrequent, and our conversations, in general, were of a more serious turn, although the tone always remained light, smiling, punctuated with youthful laughter evincing a happiness that came less from the talk than from the pleasure we felt in being together.

My uncle, immediately after the evening meal, went back up to his office, and we went with him. The dinner conversation would continue there for a brief quarter of an hour. Then my uncle would settle in at his desk until midnight. My aunt would take up a book, or her sewing. Sometimes I stayed with them to read, but more often I went back to my room to work. Around ten o'clock my aunt would come up to her room to get ready to retire. Then, in her bathrobe, she would settle down in the little sitting room next to her bedroom and, working, would wait for my uncle to come to bed. This was where I went, nearly every night, to spend an hour with her, for the pleasure of chatting freely.

At those times she was quite different from the way she was in my uncle's presence. We were a little like two children who feel freer in the absence of their parents. I very quickly fell into the habit of confiding in her, telling her about my encounters and impressions, speaking to her about my friends, thinking out loud in front of her, as I might have done with a friend my own age. I had complete trust in her discretion, and never had to regret that trust. I knew that she would not repeat my words to my uncle, that our intimacy was secure and secret. This discretion had nothing furtive or disagreeable about it. We did not hide from my uncle to talk together. Quite simply, what we said there remained between us.

This intimacy played an important part in my development. I gained from her experience. Her friendship offered me what one finds in the company of a close older friend. The gusto she brought to living, the violent love she had for existence, the interest she took in everything, the concrete way she had of approaching every question, that sort of insatiable appetite that life inspired in her, had a large, contagious influence on my development. Not only did I learn, from knowing her, to appreciate people like her, those who live intensely, joyously, generously—an appreciation which, later on, to some extent guided me in the choice of my friends—but with her I came into my own zest for living. A zest I still have, deep within me, now that I am past seventy. A zest which was of course always in me—the taste for living is not acquired: one has it or one doesn't—but which became more compelling thanks to the example I found in Aunt Ma at a time when the personality takes shape and becomes more pronounced, when the attitude that one is going to have towards life for all the rest of one's days is permanently set.

This inner, irresistible vitality had saved her from despair over Guy's death. And I have always thought that my presence in Paris, physically taking the place of the departed child in her home, had also helped her forget her grief a little.

For, having noted the comradeship that existed between us, I have to say that comradeship does not suffice to describe the true nature of our relationship. There must be added, on Aunt Ma's part, something maternal in her tenderness, and on mine, something filial. Yes, really, my aunt had transferred to me a maternal instinct that had fallen into disuse. I had not only usurped Guy's bedroom, his chair at the dinner table, and his napkin ring: I had also taken his place in Aunt Ma's heart: or rather, I was occupying that place, and she was pleased to have it occupied.

Our rapport even had certain characteristics of mother with son. We understood each other without spelling things out. At the table, or during the Sunday at-homes, a mere exchange of glances created a collusion between us, a subtle comprehension, which exists only between intimates. Even our attitude towards Uncle Éric was that of a mother and son before the head of the family.

Since I had not known my mother, it was through my relationship with Aunt Ma, even more than through my closeness with my sister, that I experienced what filial attachment could be: because in my affection for Aunt Ma there was a suggestion of deference that I never felt for Henriette. The nine years that separated me from my sister had indeed created, during my childhood, something filial between me and her; but that difference had quickly waned with time. When I left le Saillant for Paris there hardly remained any appreciable discrepancy in age between her as a young woman of twenty-six and me as a student of seventeen. I had somehow caught up with my sister. With Aunt Ma, who was my senior by more than twenty years, I had found a maternal friend, a woman of forty.

I REMEMBER—it was a few weeks after my arrival in Paris, at the moment when I had begun to get to know Uncle Éric—having wondered, with dismay, if Aunt Ma was really happy, and how she could love her husband. It was the time when the admiration (distant but unreserved) which Uncle Éric had inspired in me during his visits to le Saillant gave way to a great disappointment, soon followed by an insuperable dislike, now that, seeing him from closer up, in his private life, at home—seeing this strange animal, if I may so put it, "in his natural habitat"—I was discovering his monstrous selfishness and his ugly disposition (a passing phase, however; the admiration regained the upper hand, eventually, and the dislike quickly lost its intensity as I came to understand the remarkable qualities that made up for his dreadful faults).

In family life, my uncle was demanding and gently, inflexibly tyrannical. He found it quite natural that the rhythm of the household should revolve entirely around him, his habits, his requirements. I recognized that this was understandable enough, actually, given his position, his work, his merit. Thus, I was more annoyed by the hypocritical form of his despotism than by that despotism itself. For this peaceful tyrant, who, without appearing to, had his eye on the smallest details and intended for everything to be carried out according to his particular views, exhibited the most complete indifference towards the running of the house, and in general towards the whole concrete side of existence. Here, too, he had created a character for himself. He played—and to a T—the role of the scholar entirely absorbed in his spiritual life, the "absent-minded professor," the savant in his study, lost in his books, who lets himself be led by the people attending to his material needs, like a blind man by his seeing-eye dog. He assumed the distracted and bemused look of a pure spirit who descends from his clouds to commune with ordinary mortals and who feels utterly awkward and hobbled when it comes to everyday chores. If the carafe on his desk had, by accident, not been filled with well-chilled water as he required, instead of ringing for the valet to have it done, he would be seen wandering on the stairs, climbing up to the third floor or going down to the kitchen, a glass in one hand, his pen in the other, his face worried and intimidated, looking bewildered, seeming to not quite know the way to the butler's pantry, to be opening the wrong door, like a humble person who hesitates to ask for something, until he ran into my aunt and thus prompted a rebuke to the servant who had failed in his domestic duty. I could go on and on with examples. He cut the servants no slack, seemed to look for any chance to let them incur a reprimand, and this with an air of apologizing for his tiny needs, with the air of someone who is trying to take up the least possible space in the house. All of the servants without exception hated him and feared him like the devil, although he never scolded them and avoided giving them orders. I never saw him cede to my aunt's objections or take problems into account. When he wanted something, nothing could make him relent. He never took the obstacles head-on. He appeared not to see them, diverted the conversation in order to buy time, returned gently to the charge, dismissed the difficulties one by one, and always achieved his ends. This manipulative hypocrisy irritated me more than anything else. All the more so since the motive for my uncle's obstinacy was always the same: as casual as his insinuating proposal might at first appear, as general and often altruistic as the reasons might be that he invoked to get it accepted, I always ended up discovering the innermost, private, secret, self-interested cause. He would have sacrificed human lives to obtain the slight personal gain that he coveted—the trifling advantage to his well-being, to his selfish gratification, that his treacherous and roundabout scheme was supposed to win him.

I simply could not understand the endless concessions, capitulations, and bendings by my aunt, who always yielded in the end, without realizing it, by falling into the trap. I sometimes resented her for not knowing how to give a firm and reasoned refusal to the authoritarian whims of the Master.

I now believe that a peculiar blindness completely prevented her from detecting what was shifty, duplicitous, wily, and underhand in my uncle's behavior. She endured the pressure of that relentless maneuvering with an unbelievable credulity. I think she never perceived anything of her husband's diabolical powers of simulation.

She loved him. She saw him as she had loved him at the moment of their engagement. And she was the only one in the house not to see him as he was. (The lowest chambermaid, the lowest kitchen maid, after a month of service knew more than she about the character of Monsieur.) Love creates a zone where the sharpest critical sense and the most clear-sighted intuition have no purchase.

She had totally dedicated herself to her husband and put all her strength, all her abilities, at his service. Such devotion, so complete, so exclusive, seemed to both of them altogether natural. She took no more pride in this than he felt gratitude for it. But they both derived great satisfaction from it.

I have to say that it would be wrong to imagine that my aunt was entirely enslaved. My uncle adored his wife and admired her beyond measure. He relied on her for many things, and not of a minor order, nor only in the realm of the practical. He scarcely ever contradicted her, and showed her a tender respect through which he expressed an unremitting consideration and trust. He attached the greatest importance to her judgment, and, on a number of points, notably the conduct of his life in the world at large, let himself be guided by her (and with good reason). He well knew, in so doing, that he was acting in his own best interests. Thus, it might be said that in letting himself be led by his wife, he gave a fresh proof of his selfishness.

Aunt Ma's love was a fine example of conjugal love. I would almost say: the love of the Chambost-Lévadé couple was a model of what love is in marriage: a strong and lasting sentiment, rooted in the past, cultivated in the present, exclusive and peaceful, the product of a deep passion and indelible habits. My aunt hardly ever called her husband by his first name. She said: "Chambost," and this corresponded, for her, to a particular reality. Perhaps she had wed Éric; but it was to Chambost that she was married; and it was to Chambost, more than to Éric, that she had dedicated the entire activity of her ardent, enterprising, energetic nature.

She certainly no longer distinguished the man, the spouse, from the philosopher, the professor, the member of the Institut. She was the opposite of certain enamored wives who can only with a jealous impatience bear the professional existence, the vocation, the career of the man they love, and who, all week long, wait for Sunday to finally enjoy a husband freed from his job and have him entirely to themselves. Aunt Ma had married her husband's career; she had devoted her Sundays, for years, to the cult of that career.

I was not present at their start in life; I cannot give my word that, from their first years as a couple, my aunt had taken an active part in the creation of that eminent circle of which my uncle was now the center. But I would swear it was so. In any case, it did not take her long to make that circle her own, and to do everything possible to keep it developing further. At the time I knew her, her whole life was entirely taken up by that role, and it was she who was fully in charge of my uncle's connections. It was she who master-minded his social advancement, kept up relationships through personal con-tacts, distributed invitations, and above all remained on the lookout for anyone who had a name in the intellectual world, not only in Paris but in Europe as well; she was always the first to hear about those whose fame was beginning to spread, about the foreign celebrities who were visiting France, about the books that one had to have read, the old or newborn journals that one had to follow closely, the name of this or that young professor whose the-sis presentation had drawn attention and who ought to be enticed to the rue de Fleurus. Whatever the *précieuses ridicules** and other learned ladies do to maintain a "literary salon" where reputations are manufactured, where mem-berships in the Académie are handed out (which is so disagreeable), my aunt did to keep a select crowd around my uncle. And it seemed to her she was doing the very least she could, which was to help a man of "Chambost's" merit to have a circle of friends and an audience of followers and peers who were truly worthy of him and of the exceptional rank which she assigned to him among the great contemporary minds. The whole elite of the time, everyone that counted intellectually in France and in Europe, had to more or less gravitate toward "Chambost." And indeed, she succeeded. One has to believe that there was something natural about those connections, that they were not due only to an artificial assemblage or the machinations of an ambi-tious woman, since the hôtel de Fleurus was without any doubt the meeting place, the locus, where, in Paris, the best of the intellectual world came to gather—the fidelity of friends such as Renan, Berthelot, and Taine, to men-tion only three, making it quite clear that my aunt's social efforts had noth-ing purely contrived about them, and corresponded to a real phenomenon,

*From the comedy of the same name by Molière: ridiculously affected women.

independent of her, which more than justified the trouble she took with her "salon."

It was strange that this intelligent woman—whom love had caused to sacrifice her entire personal existence in order to concentrate all her efforts, all her thoughts, on making a successful life for the great man she had married, and who, so little greedy on her own behalf, was resolutely and insatiably ambitious for her husband—should bring her ambitions to bear only on the most brittle, most fragile, most ephemeral, most uncertain, most illusory, most inconsistent, most superficial part of this fame: she attached more importance to connections, to outward influence, to the oral expression of my uncle's thought, than to actual, consistent, productive labor with a lasting result in the form of a written body of work. I cannot avoid thinking that if she had devoted a quarter of the trouble she put into securing my uncle an audience of great minds and maintaining it around him, into protecting his solitude and his work as a writer, he would have left behind one of the great oeuvres of the nineteenth century . . . If she had not so willingly provided him with opportunities to fritter away in conversations his many original and profound views for the pleasure and profit of those who came to hear him, and if she had pushed him harder to complete his projects, to finish the books he began, to make use of his enormous research, to write down the conclusions he had reached and that he scattered about in brilliant pyrotechnics, she would have better served his fame and better fulfilled the mission she had set herself.

Obviously, in this error, in this wrong interpretation of the values that count, in this overly feminine conception of true fame which caused her to mistake the incidental for the essential, she found an accomplice in my uncle. He was too inclined to be satisfied with this glory in the present, and he neglected to guarantee himself a future fame through enduring works. He gave very little thought to posterity. His almost too eclectic intelligence led him to bestow his attention upon all problems at once, so incorrigibly curious was he about every expression of the intellectual, philosophical, literary, moral, and social life of the Europe of his time. The number of disparate books, of French and foreign journals that he indiscriminately devoured each week, unable to resist the curiosity that drove him to inform himself about the questions most remote from the subject of his own work, casting his thought in every direction, gave him a proficiency that was limitless but that would have gained in depth and effectiveness if he had known how to concentrate it. His mind was a pane through which passed all the rays of every light; he would have done better to make it into a *lens* capable of focusing the rays into a single, intense beam.

This man who spoke so well about boundaries and who lectured me with such wisdom about the usefulness of knowing one's limitations and of staying within them in order to lead a fruitful life, refused to accept his own, and was the most typical example of the fault he was pointing out to me. His range was too broad. After a Sunday when he had shot off his fireworks and illuminated ten obscure, complex, disparate questions with his personal wisdom, or after a day spent in the library immersed in some impromptu incidental research, he thought he had done more than if he had written two more pages of his *Evolution of Moral Ideas*.

DID MY AUNT see him as we did? Did she see him as he was? I have already asked this question. I do not think so. She loved him too much to really see him. And it was probably because she did not see him clearly that she was able to love him so exclusively.

But how to accept the fact that such a bright woman—gifted with a lucid mind as well as her innate common sense, and above all with an active intuition which made her feel intensely even what she did not understand fully with her intelligence alone—could be so mistaken? How to believe that this love could blind her so completely, after twenty years of such close married life?

Thus I am led to suppose that there was, in my Uncle Éric, another man than the one he showed us, a secret, private person that she was the only one to see; a person who must have been the vestige in him of the child and the adolescent he once had been, of the young man she had married for love. Probably the moment he was alone with her he was very different from what he was with us. They were a very tight-knit couple. They shared the same bedroom, the same bed. I would not dare to venture into that intimate, impenetrable zone. I lack the simplest clues. That secret was theirs, and nothing could penetrate it. But here may lie the explanation for Aunt Ma's amorous blindness, or what seemed like a blindness to me, and which may have been, to a certain extent, quite the opposite: a more complete vision, a vision in which elements invisible to outsiders got superimposed onto the ones that we could see. I find the hypothesis appealing. All in all, I am inclined to believe that Aunt Ma knew him much better than we did. And I like to think that he probably deserved to be loved more than we could love him with the incomplete information that daily life provided us.

Another thing, and one that I do not know where to place, because it introduces into my analysis of the couple a factor that could alter everything: my uncle, as much in love as he was with his wife, was not insensible to the charms of other women. He had "crushes." I would put my hand in the fire that he never had an affair, never fell into an actual, outright infidelity. But unfaithful he was, after a fashion. I would even say childishly so. Because there was something puerile in the sudden and immoderate way in which he would become enamored of this or that young woman whom he scarcely knew, a former student, an auditor at his lectures, one of those intellectual ladies from abroad who did not want to pass through Paris without being received at the hôtel de Fleurus. He was demonstrably stirred by their presence, spoke about nothing but them for a month, wrote to them, lent them books, read their manuscripts, wasted precious time giving them advice, helping them in their bibliographic research, etc. At those times he had the naïveté of a schoolboy, a sentimental emotion that he could not conceal; the name of the object of his affection was constantly on his lips and prompted teasing from Aunt Ma. He was taken in by appearances, attributed a wholly exaggerated worth to these women, put much stock in their judgments about his course, their opinions of books or of the masters. Aunt Ma took no umbrage at these successive and purely intellectual flights of enthusiasm, at these platonic and poetic passions. She openly and indulgently laughed at them, and lent herself with good grace to all that he required of her on behalf of the chosen one, taking charge of her, if my uncle asked her to, welcoming her with every consideration, showing her around Paris if she was a foreigner, taking her to the Louvre, to the Carnavalet . . . I remember a Swedish student, a gorgeous creature with a dazzling Nordic complexion, whom my uncle was taken with for several weeks and whom my aunt had the kindness to accompany on a freezing winter morning up to the highest platform of the Eiffel Tower, from which the winsome Viking wished to write a postcard to the fiancé who was dreaming of her at the University of Uppsala.

I make a point of mentioning these "crushes," as Aunt Ma called them. They may provide a clue, more revealing than I think, to that unknown "other" person who probably inhabited Uncle Éric, and whom my aunt was the only one to know and love. In any case, they demonstrate that a quivering, pure, slightly ridiculous adolescent, a child-poet, can remain alive in the soul of a serious professor at the Collège de France, and that a remarkable intellectual can fall prey to a very genuine puppy love. I do not want to make too much of the conclusions that can be drawn from this. At least it goes to show how complex my uncle's character could be, and how difficult to reduce to a simple equation.

I can also add, on this subject, that this austere man indulged in a childish and idealized worship of Woman in general, which one so often finds in the hearts of old bachelors. He was capable of interrupting an important discussion when a woman came into the room and of leaving the circle of the Renans and the Taines to flutter about her with gallant, old-fashioned manners, to take her to see his archives, to show her his rare editions. All the ladies were mad for him and were grateful for the attentions he unsparingly lavished on them. I saw him, in Neuilly, walk away from his friends to go to the far end of the garden and pick some roses to offer Mme. Alphonse

Daudet; and he was seen returning, with bloody fingers, awkwardly holding a poorly arranged little bouquet of flowers, which shed their petals before they could be presented to their intended recipient.

I don't believe I have yet spoken of that property in Neuilly which holds as much of a place in my memory as the hôtel de Fleurus.

It was in '72, just after the war (my Uncle Éric's widowed mother died in Paris during the Commune) that they left the little apartment in the rue Bonaparte, where they had lived for the nine years since their wedding, and settled in the rue de Fleurus, in the senior Chambosts' old townhouse. Guy, born in '69, was three.

At the same time, they inherited the little country house that the Chambosts had in Neuilly, on the boulevard Bineau.

This was a glorious time for Aunt Ma. In Paris as well as in Neuilly she carried out remodelings, expansions, and improvements, so as to settle in for good. Her goal was to entertain, to create a center where select friends might gather. The trial runs in the rue Bonaparte had been encouraging.

There was a housewarming party in rue de Fleurus that was a minor event in Parisian life.

From that day on, every Sunday, the Chambosts were at home, without fail, starting at three o'clock. People came unasked, at least once they were among the regulars. And almost always at seven o'clock there was a little dinner for eight or twelve, invited beforehand. Sometimes more friends came to spend the evening, but usually those little dinners and the Sunday nights remained intimate.

On the first of June, my uncle and aunt emigrated to Neuilly, where they stayed until the first of October. The country house had been enlarged with a vast, high-ceilinged room that was called the "hall"* and that was bright and cheerful, first because it was hung and upholstered in a pink percale with multicolored flowers, and then because it opened through three wide French doors onto a half-covered terrace, looking out on the "English" garden— a round, fine-bladed lawn surrounded by sanded paths and adorned with two flower beds, one of petunias, the other of geraniums. A walled courtyard, covered with gravel, separated the façade from the boulevard so that on the garden side there was only greenery, silence, and the chirping of birds. At the far end of the garden, my aunt had had a vaguely Chinese "kiosk" built, where we went to have tea. And behind the kiosk, screened off from the rest by flower beds that rendered it discreetly invisible, lay a little vegetable patch, with fruit trees. The plums there were particularly tasty, and I remember M. Renan, in alpaca frock coat and white ducks, after being led to a mirabelle plum tree by Aunt Ma, busily shaking it to make the fruit fall.

*English in the original.

For the "Sundays" continued at Neuilly during the summer. But these gatherings had a different character, more intimate and rustic. The visitors were never so numerous there, and most had been invited to lunch. They came on the horse-drawn trolley from the Pont-de-la-Jatte, and departed, as a group, around six. We walked them as far as the stop, which was fairly near the front gate, and it was quite a spectacle to see those members of the Institut clamber aboard a usually packed vehicle as they sometimes continued with Uncle Éric, until the horses started off, the discussion interrupted when they had left the house. These guests were nearly all close friends of the family, and many came with their wives and children. In June and September, when the heat was not oppressive, a game of croquet on the lawn sometimes reduced the length of the afternoon. There was also, at the center of a grove forming the rough outline of a maze, a *jeu de tonneau**: I saw my uncle Éric, in a nankeen suit, accompanied by a few serious colleagues such as Albert Sorel and Leroy-Beaulieu, tossing disks down the frog's mouth, all the while planning some bold reforms which might alter the destinies of the Sciences Politiques or the Collège de France. I also saw Alphonse Daudet, limping, grab the garden hose and threaten Guy de Maupassant with an improvised shower. Daudet was by then already very sick, though, and his beautiful emaciated face winced with suffering from time to time. I remember that one day he took my arm to walk back and forth on the terrace, so bad were his nerves, and occasionally I felt his leg give way under him. "Nobody can imagine what it's like," he told me under his breath. "It's as if my leg became a telescope whose tubes suddenly collapse when I put weight on them." But this martyrdom prevented him neither from coming every so often nor from cheerfully taking part in the conversation: he only needed, it seemed, to have a memory, an anecdote to tell, to immediately forget all his pain. Mme. Daudet was always with him. She hardly ever took her eyes off him, and his delicate face, in which tenderness and agony mingled in an indefinable expression, is as present to me, as I write these lines, as if I had it still before me.

These regular get-togethers were a source of continual concern and work for Aunt Ma. She had to plan, invite, organize, write. She thought constantly about all this. It was her life.

I pause. Aunt Ma, in the garden at Neuilly . . . I can see her, at this moment, with a clarity that moves me, leading her guests towards the kiosk for tea . . . She is wearing a long, full foulard dress, black with white polka dots, and a big garden hat. This hat had a crown made from an antique bonnet of embroidered tulle and a wide brim, which swayed about her face,

---

*A game in which metal disks are pitched at the open mouth of a large metal frog.

bordered with a flounce of white muslin that set the laughing gleam of her eyes back into a pale shadow . . .

This must have been in 1889 or '90 . . .

Does this type of intelligent woman still exist? Probably. Yet I'm not sure. I knew other intelligent women in my own generation, which followed Aunt Ma's; they still had features in common with Aunt Ma. But in the generation that succeeded mine I have for the most part met only "female intellectuals." And that is very different. The young woman who was twenty after World War I, liberated, and leading the free existence of a student at the Sorbonne, today abounds. She has something to say in the most serious conversations and does not hesitate to cut in. She usually says precise, bright things, she is well-informed, she handles philosophical jargon or the vocabulary of modern criticism with ease. But what she says does not seem to come from her. She appears to be stating theorems, reciting a lesson, taking an examination, and there is more erudition than intelligence in her talk.

The memory I have of Aunt Ma is altogether different. She was always tentative about joining in the general conversation. Yet she did not lack for assurance or for things to say. But she could not let go of her conviction that the role of women is mainly to listen. If she ventured to take the floor, it was in a lively, concrete, easy tone, full of naturalness and modesty. No matter how much she might know about the subject, she never tried to show it. With her amused smile, she seemed to be slightly making fun of herself and to be apologizing for stepping in, as if on a childish whim. It was rare, however, that what she said was not rich in meaning. Above all, her talk had a personal character, seemed to arise spontaneously from her, spring from her temperament, have its roots in her own observations, in her life. Her intelligence did not seem to be the laborious result of her reading. Hearing her, one felt that books were not instruction manuals for her, that she came to them fully equipped with personal experiences, with a mind fed on reality, and that she wanted nothing more from them than a verification of what she had established through living.

Such must have been the "philosophical" *grandes dames* of the eighteenth century, who were the confidantes and entertaining friends of the Encyclopedists—Mme. d'Houdetot,* Mme. d'Holbach,† etc.

I do not want to insinuate anything disparaging about the learned ladies of our day. Yet I think that one would be hard put to find in them the simple

---

*Elisabeth Françoise Sophie de la Live de Bellegarde, Comtesse d'Houdetot, was made famous by the chapter in Rousseau's *Confessions* in which he describes his unrequited passion for her.

†Charlotte-Suzanne d'Aine, who in 1756 became the second wife of Paul-Henri Dietrich, Baron d'Holbach, one of the leading contributors to Diderot's *Encyclopédie*. The couple presided over a salon which became the main social center for the Encyclopedist movement.

charm, the sprightly, spontaneous spirit, the maturity of heart and intelligence, that Uncle Éric's friends loved in Aunt Ma.

ONE OF MY SURPRISES, or rather one of my gradual discoveries, during the first weeks of my arrival in Paris, was to find myself in an environment where the Catholic faith, and religious practice, had no place.

As I have said, I had no piety of my own. I had never genuinely had any, so I cannot really write that I lost it. But I had been brought up very religiously and had never been away from a circle of believers. My sister Henriette was intensely pious. My father, while not a devout man, attended High Mass in Menneville every Sunday with his whole household, in the side chapel that had, from time immemorial, been reserved for the "château." He took Communion at Christmas and Easter, maintained steady relations, both deferential and friendly, with the presbytery; and I had always heard those who did not go to church judged very severely in my family. Piot, the veterinarian, considered the ringleader of the little radical republican group in the region, was spurned, and my father refused to let him be called when an animal was sick, although he was renowned for his skill; my father preferred to turn to an imbecile, the veterinarian in Mamers, who had to travel five leagues to le Saillant and usually arrived too late. In the family vocabulary, "anti-patriot," "socialist," "anticleric," "anarchist," "communard" were synonyms for "outlaw," and a person who was indiscriminately stigmatized with one or another of these ignominious labels was execrated and feared like the Antichrist.*

I had never much reflected on these questions and had by and large adopted this way of seeing things. There was no real rationale behind my fellow feeling for the blue-bloods of the region and the bourgeois in our towns, who exhibited their Catholic beliefs and conservative opinions in their words and deeds, but I acknowledged as a general principle that they made up the "right-minded society," which set a good example for the masses; the little minority of rebels who thought differently were the "rabble," the dregs of the populace, a local disgrace, lawless people, a hotbed of rioters and agitators, capable of any crime, who put order and homeland in peril by fomenting revolutions.

My summer stay with the Nacquots had already imperceptibly changed my habits of mind. At least concerning the religious question. Mme. Nacquot

*According to André Daspre, this portrayal of the father as a religious and political conservative was probably an earlier conception of the author's. At some later point, Martin du Gard decided to present the father as an independent spirit, breaking away from the ideas honored in his circle—the picture that is given of him in Chapters I and II.

and I went to Mass every Sunday, but M. Nacquot came with us only once, on the feast of the Assumption. I was quite struck by this abstention. Although I never once heard him make a statement that could be interpreted as a denigration of the faith or a criticism of the Church, the very fact that religion did not at all figure in his conversation proved that it scarcely did so in his life. And since, in everything else, he appeared to have a great intellectual and moral honesty, with which I was much impressed because of his learning and his character, and since he seemed more open-minded and sharper-witted by far than all the men I had met up until then, particularly my teachers at school, and than my father, I began, quite naturally and without even thinking about it, to esteem this man in whom I sensed a lack of religious observance, in whom I even vaguely suspected a rejection of the teachings of the Church, indeed an intelligent and reasoned opposition to them. My personal coldness in regard to faith made me sympathetic to M. Nacquot's freedom of thought, and I was inclined to give my respect, my trust, my private support, to a man who had escaped the constraints of religion.

That is more or less where I stood upon arriving Paris in October '87: much closer than I myself might have suspected to taking the last step between half-hearted, superficial observance of the creed and complete indifference; between a de facto, unconscious lack of belief, stagnating behind a screen of habit and convention, and freely acknowledged emancipation. It did not take much to sever such slack and fragile bonds.

The thing happened of itself, without the slightest jolt, and without my even clearly sensing a break. So much so that my attention was not even drawn to the phenomenon taking place in me. It is not through clear memory but by means of reflection that I am today able to analyze the subtleties of my inner life.

I did not realize, right away, that there was no religious dimension at the rue de Fleurus. I cared so little for it that I did not feel its absence.

In our shared daily existence, I gradually noticed many differences between, on the one hand, what my uncle and aunt were like, what they thought, what were their actual tastes and their attitudes towards life, and, on the other, what I knew or had understood of them until we lived together. And it was not their mental attitude towards religion that struck me first, or most strongly. It was a whole attitude, made up of very diverse elements: I found that all of a sudden I had completely changed atmospheres.

I must, by the way, immediately make an important distinction between my uncle and aunt. Uncle Éric was a freethinker, pure and simple, as this term was then employed. (A term he never used, let it be said in passing. He did not say "a freethinker" but "a free mind." And, for him, this meant much more than a mind emancipated from faith in religious dogmas: a mind freed from every sort of dogmatism, a mind wide open to all branches of knowledge.)

He was the son of a mother who believed and a father who did not. The old chemist Chambost-Lévadé, risen from the working class, brought up by the priests of the Restoration—who were, I am quite sure, of the worst sort—always nursed a bitter grudge against the clergy for the constraint and deceit that had been imposed upon him during the first fourteen years of his life. Later on, his resentment was blunted by success, renown, the Institut. He strove for the tolerance that he preached, the absence of which had so tyrannized his youth. He never prevented his wife from practicing or from raising her two children in the Catholic faith. She remained devout. My uncle followed in his father's footsteps and quickly freed himself from all religious belief. But he had not the reasons his father had to be aggressive. The Parisian circle of the Institut, which my uncle had known since his childhood, included many men respectful of the state religion. He did not profess anticlericalism at all. He had married and had his son baptized in Notre-Dame-des-Champs. And when he came to le Saillant, he went with the household to Sunday Mass, out of politeness.

For my aunt, it was very different. She had been something of a believer in her youth, but without exaltation or great fervor. A "respectable" religion, as befitted Madeleine de la Place, daughter of a magistrate under Louis-Philippe and granddaughter of an émigré.* Her faith was so undemanding, however, that the lack of any religious feeling in her fiancé had not for a moment delayed her acceptance of his proposal. For this marriage was a marriage of love, and the feeling that Éric Chambost-Lévadé inspired in her was of a force altogether different from that which she brought to matters of religion. All the same, she had never renounced her family beliefs. At that time, such things were hardly ever done. A freethinking woman would have been a kind of monster that Parisian society would have regarded with horror. A woman went to Mass. Aunt Ma had the good taste to go on practicing her religion, after a fashion: a worldly religion, respectful of the clergy and of the principal dictates of the Church. She had her son baptized first privately, as a precaution, then publicly, and gave a dinner for thirty on the day of the baptism. (A dinner, moreover, attended by her priest-eating father-in-law, as well as by the parish priest of Notre-Dame-des-Champs.) And I know that she went to Easter Mass until Guy's death. At which point, things changed rather abruptly. Grief might have driven her back to piety. The opposite happened. She refused to accept that trial like a good Christian. She felt herself hatefully

---

*I.e., her grandfather was one of the royalists who became refugees at the time of the Revolution.

victimized by an unjust, inhuman mutilation. She still believed enough in God to hold Him responsible for her misfortune but no longer enough to bow obediently beneath His holy will. She rejected the *"Fiat!"** She would not forgive God the dreadful blow He had dealt her. And she snubbed Him almost until her death.

After becoming a widow in 1905, thirteen years before her own demise, she had to live the most wretched period of her life. There was no reason for her "Sundays," interrupted for two years before Uncle Éric's death because of his condition, to be resumed after he died. Aunt Ma let it be known that she would be at home every Sunday. The first year, people paid her occasional visits of condolence, especially women. They sat around her, in a corner of the vast library, stayed twenty minutes, and left. General conversation no longer took fire, even if chance brought together five or six of the guests from days gone by. Then these visits became less frequent. My aunt, faithful to the tradition, did not go out on Sunday. But she sat in her little blue sitting room on the third floor, and her Sunday was spent waiting for a few close friends, alone with her memories.

I was hardly ever in France at that time; it was my Moroccan period, then came the war. I was never quite sure what happened, but religion later became a solace to my aunt. Aunt Ma took refuge at le Saillant during the summer months. Henriette's piety may have encouraged her to go back to God. During the war, from 1914 to 1918, the year of Aunt Ma's death, she led a lady parishioner's existence of good works, entirely centered on her faith, never missing her daily seven o'clock Mass at Notre-Dame-des-Champs.

This digression has perhaps been of some use in clarifying the exact extent of Aunt Ma's religious coldness in the years '87, '88, '89, when I lived in close contact with her. She no longer set foot in church, except for social chores, marriages, or funerals. But she made no hostile remarks. She seemed to have written God off once and for all.

It is understandable, when one knows how unsympathetically disposed towards religion I was when I arrived from my province, that the ambiance of the hôtel de Fleurus should have precipitated the evolution of my break with the Catholicism of my fathers without my even being aware of it. I repeat, I did not realize it myself. It was a few months later that, suddenly plunged back into the atmosphere of a Catholic family and the close proximity of a very devout sister, I abruptly noticed that for six months I had not thought once about matters of religion.

---

*According to the *New Catholic Encyclopedia*, "The single word 'fiat' . . . exemplifies the attitude that every Christian must have toward God as expressed in the Our Father: '*fiat voluntas tua*—thy will be done.' "

Since this question of religion has led me to speak of Aunt Ma's old age, I want to use the occasion to write down some particular features of her later years.

During the final period of her life, this woman, so cheerful by nature, so outgoing, so sociable, had become gloomy, misanthropic, shut away in a pessimistic and disillusioned sadness which seemed beyond remedy. This woman whom I had known to be so lively, so exuberant even, so easy to amuse, who liked and was interested in everything, had become a mournful old lady, impossible to entertain, apathetic and almost cross. Such a metamorphosis is practically unbelievable. Having spent little time with her in that last part of her life, I would refuse to believe it had I not gathered so many precise details from my sister that I cannot doubt it in the least.

As a young woman, Aunt Ma had made social life her entire center of gravity. That gusto which made her a radiant focal point, that contagious, irresistible gusto which beautified life around her, found its basis, its springboard, in the Sunday at-homes, in that crowd which regularly revolved around the hôtel de Fleurus. And all the attentions, letters, errands, visits that the organizing of those at-homes required filled the gap from one event to the next, kept her constantly busy towards the same end. In reality, more even than caring for my Uncle Éric, my Aunt Ma's *raison d'être* was to create and maintain that select and artificial universe around him. All her thought, all her vitality, was aimed at that goal.

I understood this only later. Aunt Ma had little inner life. She was not centered on herself, but on the outer world, on a collection of frivolous, social things. When, during my uncle's illness, then after his death, this support failed her, she found herself plunged into a barren atmosphere, dark and stifling. She was not capable of solitude.

She bore a grudge against that capricious society which had abandoned her. She had become, not backbiting, but mercilessly severe. On every side she saw nothing but the ugly aspects of human nature, selfishness, self-interestedness, indifference towards others. She fell from a long dream, a long easy happiness. She was no longer young enough to find another equilibrium within herself. Religion helped her by bringing her a little of that elusive equilibrium.

And now, I remember certain things that did not strike me in the past. I see something of a first sign of that state of prostration and misanthropy, something of a prefiguration of that slide into a kind of disillusioned nihilism, in certain details that at the time were so fleeting and so infrequent that they did not attract anybody's attention. On Mondays, it often happened that my aunt was not entirely her usual self. Always less lively, less gay. Sometimes even a little irritable, as if crestfallen. More silent, more apathetic. In the state, one might say, of a schoolboy who has dreamt all week of his day off, and who, on the evening of that holiday, is overcome with sadness, regret, a vague disenchantment.

On Monday, Aunt Ma sometimes spoke somewhat harshly about people, about her guests of the day before. On that day there sometimes seemed to be in her a well of weariness, from which rose bubbles of ill humor that burst at the surface. It was nothing. It did not prevent her from being cheerful, active. I only think of it because of that dismal old age that awaited her, of which those lapses in mood strike me as a foreshadowing. A practiced eye would have detected, in those slightly drab Mondays, how much her life was composed of effervescence and froth, and how different it might have been without them. On those days she seemed to be paying for the elation and excitement of the day before, as she seemed, at the end of her life, to be paying with an incurable despondency, a desperate nostalgia, for the glamour of her youth and of her thriving maturity, for the perpetual fireworks she had provided.

Existence without Uncle Éric and Sundays without academic intrigues, without the tidbits of intellectual news, seemed to her suddenly empty of all interest. I attribute to that aimless appetite, to that social disappointment, the awakening in her of religious concerns. Faith alone was an answer to that call, a cure for that thirst, a use for her objectless hope, an occupation for her thought, an explanation for that great void which had opened before her and which only an intense inner life could fill. She was then seen reading pious books, undertaking good works, visiting the poor and the hospitals, compelling herself to attend Mass daily. She thus restored meaning to her life. She filled the gap.

But she found neither calm nor rest in these activities. She was like those theatrical celebrities who, aging and forced to abdicate, die of starvation, so much do they miss the need to be a star, to be worshipped, applauded, to play a role, to shine.

A sad end. One of the regrets I have is that I was never able to soften those hardships with my presence, my affection, my steadfast loyalty. I was at the front, in June '18, when she died. I only received the news two weeks after her death.

CHAPTER XI

The Intellectual World of
Paris around 1890*

UNTIL ENTERING SAINT-CYR, I lived in Paris with the Chambost-Lévadés, from the autumn of '87 to the autumn of '89. But during the years that followed, while I was at Saint-Cyr, then during the years when I was stationed at Versailles, until I left for Africa, that is until 1895, I never stopped coming back to the rue de Fleurus, as to my home base, my family.

During those eight years, I was thus able to see at very close range Parisian intellectual society and the academic world in particular. At the "Sundays" in the rue de Fleurus, I saw all those who were considered "stars" in the realms of philosophy, literature, history, and the University. I also met many artists, scientists, and foreign notables there. I witnessed all these luminaries in a setting they enjoyed and liked to visit, where they were free, relaxed, and informal.

It was an experience whose full value I sensed even at the time. But I did not understand until later how lucky I was, at an age of great eagerness and spiritual receptivity, to live in such close contact with the leading men of French thought.

IN THE YEARS 1880–90, that enlightened, liberal, reasonable, hardworking French intellectual society played a predominant role in Europe. I do not think I am exaggerating when I say that it was something like the light of the world. And it had an unquestionable influence on public opinion in France, and even in Europe. With hindsight, am I perhaps inclined to overestimate its importance and to see it as greater and more beautiful than it was? Possibly so. It seems to me, though, when I think of Uncle Éric's circle, that all the rest of my life has been spent in a world that failed to measure up, a world

---

*André Daspre assembled this chapter from two main fragments, one a survey of intellectual life in Paris between 1880 and 1890, the other a portrait of Ernest Renan at the rue de Fleurus. Martin du Gard's intention, at one point, was to include sketches of a score of great intellectual, artistic, and political personalities—all of them supposed frequenters of the Chambost-Lévadé salon. He was unable to realize this plan. However, to give the reader a sense of what the author envisioned, M. Daspre has included, following the portrait of Renan, a number of short sketches Martin du Gard had drafted of other members of that circle.

disrupted, incoherent, credulous, sectarian, passion-driven, and lacking in grandeur.

By that decade, it seems to me, all beliefs had collapsed. Every problem posed by philosophy, science, religion, art, and sociology was again up for discussion. All those thinkers liked to point this out. Rightly or wrongly, they imagined themselves as part of the vanguard of a new, privileged humanity which was suddenly awakening, after centuries of trial and error, and which had at last arrived at the threshold of Truth.

They believed in the progress of civilization through knowledge and reason. Because, though they doubted everything, they still had their dogmas. They respected moral consciousness. They debated everything but in fact accepted as imperative those elementary rules of right and wrong that dictate our natural conscience, provided we are born with one. They were not systematic, anarchistic destroyers. They accepted a certain order, a certain sense of the good, as a necessary postulate, as a preliminary, indispensable rule that must be adopted experimentally, without fanaticism, that must be taken for what it is: a relative, practical truth, which is of benefit to the moral perfectibility of man, useful to the broad mass of people for the conduct of their lives, and which, in that way, offers a guarantee of progress and is of great value to society.

Whatever trust and hopes all those skeptics and freethinkers may have placed in the evolution of civilization through science, they were only partly deluded as to the slowness of that evolution. They were too intelligent to completely escape the reasoned pessimism characteristic of observers. And certain among them, if pushed a little, might not have been far from admitting that those religious beliefs whose bases they had undermined would be, for some time to come, the only cure for the bad instincts of the average man, and that religion was not without use as a temporary check against universal Evil.

What is more, had not all of them been formed in their hereditary nature and their primary education by Catholicism or Protestantism? More or less unconsciously, they retained its deep imprint. In their most subversive, most emancipated remarks, when they spoke of morality, of conscience, most of them employed—with an amusing inconsistency—a Christian vocabulary. In Renan, this was glaring. But in the others too. It was not unusual to hear two famous freethinkers, two learned members of the Sciences Morales, solemnly discussing sin, salvation, temptation by the Devil, and of course God, because these locutions seemed convenient and were natural to them, although they meant something quite different by these religious terms than the designations they had learned in their years of catechism.

These men had all achieved a remarkable intellectual eclecticism and liberalism. Which they conveyed to each other through this slightly childish distinction: the unbelievers would say "freethinkers"; the believers, "free-minded thinkers." And they felt themselves to be first cousins and lived together on the best of terms.

I was often struck, in particular, by the religious tone that endured, especially among the Protestants who had become freethinkers. However fundamental and well established their lack of belief may have been, however total their emancipation from dogmas, in their puritanical austerity they retained something of the preacher about them.

I instinctively viewed the freethinkers with a Protestant education as more distant from me, and less likable, than those with a Catholic background; they always gave me a certain feeling of falseness that made me uneasy. I have long believed, and I still to some extent believe, that there is, among Protestants, a sort of innate and instinctive falseness, a lack of forthrightness with regard to their frailties, a need to *appear* upright, a constant need to "save face." The most honest among them almost always demonstrate some trace of hypocrisy. I attribute this tendency to that dread of scandal so ingrained in them. The terror of being a bad example makes lying preferable, in their eyes, to admission of guilt. "There is some cynicism in every confession," a friend of Protestant origin told me one day, reprovingly.

This survival of blind belief was so strong that Xavier de Balcourt and I used to put our heads together quite irreverently to divide the Sunday guests into two categories: the *idolaters* and the *scholiasts,* depending on the direction in which they tipped—some towards the spiritualism of believers without dogmas, devout souls without a church, like Renan and like Berthelot, that high priest of science as a universal panacea; others towards bookish hairsplitting, according to the best critical methods of contemporary German erudition, which had a prevailing influence over the French university establishment. And I have to say that the clan of our *idolaters* was by far the more numerous: from the idealistic freethinkers like J. Simon, Boutroux, Boutmy, Fouillée, Guyau, Sully Prudhomme, etc., to the liberal Catholics like the two Vogüés, Albert Sorel, Pasteur, de Mun,* all the shadings of what we called *idolatry* were represented. And, observing them, I mockingly thought of a sentence from Ballanche,† often quoted by my uncle, in which

---

*Jules Simon (1814–1896), French political leader and philosopher; Émile Boutroux (1845–1912), French philosopher; Alfred Fouillée (1838–1912), French philosopher; Jean-Marie Guyau (1854–1888), French philosopher; Charles-Melchior, Marquis de Vogüé (1829–1916), French diplomat and archeologist; Eugène-Melchior, Vicomte de Vogüé (1848–1910), cousin of Charles-Melchior, French diplomat and writer on Russian literature; Louis Pasteur (1822–1895), French chemist and microbiologist, inventor of vaccines against rabies and anthrax; Albert, Comte de Mun (1841–1914), French Christian Socialist leader and orator who advocated Roman Catholicism as an instrument of social reform. For Boutmy, Sully Prudhomme, and Sorel, see note, Chapter IX.

†Pierre-Simon Ballanche (1776–1847), author of the *Essay on Social Institutions.*

I found an excellent definition of idolatry: "To create objectives as an aid to an intelligence that lacks them."

Over these more or less skeptical *idolaters,* there hovered, in spite of all, a Montaigne-like air of doubt, which rescued their *idolatry* from narrowness and vapidity, added spice to their remarks, gave a seemly modesty to their more chimerical hopes, and protected them from overly emphatic assertions.

This elite gathering was entirely recruited from the bourgeoisie—but from that upper layer of the nineteenth-century bourgeoisie that had more respect for conscience and things of the mind than for money.

(Those first thirty years of the Third Republic were probably the final apotheosis of the old French bourgeoisie that had sprung up in the wake of 1789, consolidated its social position during the Empire, grown rich under Louis-Philippe and Napoleon III, and, firmly seated on its worldly goods, believing itself invulnerable, found in those last years of the century the freedom to exercise its peaceable rule to the full, and showed itself to be a happy, satisfied, well-balanced class that had arrived at a summit of civilization.*)

Most of them were neither poor nor rich; they generally scorned wealth but were much attached to their modest incomes, which freed them from material worries, provided they contented themselves with a restricted and

---

*The Third Republic (1870–1940) would, after a shaky start, manage to sustain a (relative) social and political calm such as had eluded France earlier in the nineteenth century. The century had begun, politically speaking, with Napoleon's coup d'état of Eighteenth Brumaire (November 9, 1799) and the establishment of the Consulate (1799–1804). There followed the Napoleonic Empire (1804–1815) and the Bourbon Restoration (1815–1830). The revolution of July 1830 established the constitutional monarchy of the "Citizen King," Louis-Philippe, a member of the Orléans branch of the royal family. This July Monarchy in turn ended—after a slump in the economy and a wave of discontent among both the working class and the bourgeoisie—with the populist February Revolution of 1848, giving way to the brief and troubled Second Republic (1848–1852). Louis Napoleon, a nephew of Bonaparte, was elected president; after a coup d'état, he contrived to become Emperor Napoleon III. His Second Empire was divided into an authoritarian period (1852–59) of political repression, economic expansion, and successes abroad, and a liberal period (1859–70) of increased civil liberties, fierce political opposition, and blunders in foreign policy. A series of diplomatic miscalculations by Napoleon III provided the Prussian premier, Otto von Bismarck, with the opportunity he had been seeking to goad France into declaring war. The humiliating defeat of the French forces by the Germans at Sedan (in northeast France) on September 2, 1870, brought down the Empire and ushered in the Third Republic. Paris, however, held out until January 1871, when a Prussian siege finally forced its surrender. The Republican government, based at Versailles, agreed to pay Prussia an enormous indemnity and to give up most of Alsace and Lorraine. In Paris, a leftist, largely proletarian Commune took control, rose up in protest against these concessions, and demanded economic reforms. The communards set fire to public buildings and killed hostages; in reprisal, they were crushed with extreme violence by government forces, which slaughtered over seventeen thousand people. With its suppression of "the reds," the Republican government won over moderates and conservatives, solidifying its base. The patchwork Constitution of 1875 proved sufficiently forgiving of instability to allow the whole gamut of parties, from the Socialists to the Monarchists, to coexist.

orderly existence in which their only luxuries were those of the mind. They were never heard to allude to money, to the slenderness of their means, to the pecuniary difficulties that certain of them may have had. I do not believe they thought about it. Their wives usually thought about it for them.

Such a community is an adornment for a country. An *aristocracy.*

Most of them had come of age under the Second Empire. Some had lived in a state of restrained opposition, faithful to an ideal vaguely reminiscent of 1848. Others, without accepting the Bonapartist regime in their heart, had more or less rallied to the "liberal Empire"; without renouncing an ideal of greater freedom, they had given their de facto support to the Empire of 1860 and to the economic reforms as to a lesser evil.

And all had been deeply marked not only by the defeat of 1871 but also by the tragedy of the Commune.

All had enthusiastically approved the new Republican Constitution, which promised them the realization of their secret dream: *liberty within the law,* and the solution to that *social question** that the Empire had failed to understand or had actually ignored.

Even those who had feared the coming of the Republic and were afraid that the triumph of democracy would "pull France down," as they said, had ended up accepting it as a fact. This virtually unanimous acceptance was accomplished in '83. There was a widespread attitude of fairness towards the new regime, which prevented people from snubbing it out of resentment or backward ideology. It had already given proof of order, and that was all people cared about after the terrible experience of the Commune. They yielded, ungrudgingly, to the new state of affairs. Their duty was to serve the country, no matter what regime the majority had freely chosen. Political passions had to give way to concern for the future of France.

From the social point of view, this intellectual crowd passed for "progressive" in the eyes of the reactionaries, but how timorous, how reticent, they seem to us now! The most daring thinkers among them remained very "conservative," too opposed to revolutionary disorder to encourage militant socialistic action, sincerely hoping for important reforms but fearing the sudden shocks that might jeopardize the stability of institutions.

I remember having heard these problems broached in the Sunday discussions. The guests showed themselves to be strongly taken with the idea of an intellectual aristocracy sitting at the controls, limiting the excesses of popular demands. They were apt to talk about "the mob"; they disapproved of strikes almost as much as of riots and barricades. They dreamt of an aristocracy of skills, to which the people, the good minds among the workers, would have plenty of access through education and diplomas. They wished

---

*I.e., the plight of the proletariat, as presented by statesmen and polemicists of the Left.

for a government of the just, anxious to alleviate poverty, curb the privileges of the wealthy, increase the number of hospitals, and expand social services, making the courts free of charge, for instance, etc. They believed this possible; they even thought it realizable in the near future.

This moderate attitude might have been enough to alter human relations deeply and to institute fair and comprehensive social legislation, if it had been widely held, if it had been that of the industrial bourgeoisie and not just of an intellectual elite. The important reforms that were carried out in certain European countries, notably Sweden, during that same period and that reduced polarization and took the poison out of the class struggle, show what could have been achieved in France and elsewhere. But such untroubled progress was able to take place in Sweden because this political ideal, rather than remaining the exclusive conviction of a few men in the cabinet, was also the ideal of the employers.

I mean that the reason for French delay in the matter of social evolution must be attributed far more to the insurmountable selfishness and lack of understanding of the industrial bourgeoisie than to the moderation and timidity demonstrated by the Republican intellectual circles. The trouble came not so much from that pluckless caution of the thinking elite where social policy was concerned as from the fact that this goodwill was criticized, attacked, and even condemned as anarchistic and wildly dangerous by the heads of industry and the financiers.

This state of mind only grew between 1870 and 1880. The old political parties were dying. The death of the Prince Imperial at the hands of the Zulus, and of the Comte de Chambord, had tragically dethroned Bonapartism and Legitimism. The princes of the house of Orléans, in exile, idle, and not very popular on the whole, rallied only fossils from the Faubourg Saint-Germain to the cause of Orléanism.*

The national conscience had become unified and consolidated around the Assembly of 1875.

---

*Louis Bonaparte (1856–1879), the only son of Napoleon III by Empress Eugénie, put forward by the Bonapartist party after his father's death in 1873 as the official pretender, was killed by the Zulus while trying to gain military glory that he hoped would win him the crown. Henri Dieudonné d'Artois, Comte de Chambord (1820–1883), was the last heir of the elder branch of the Bourbons and, as Henry V, pretender to the French throne from 1830. The passing of these two figures left the Bonapartists and the Bourbon Legitimists bereft of any candidate for the throne. The July Revolution of 1830 had overthrown the "legitimate" Bourbon monarchy and transferred the throne to Louis-Philippe, head of the collateral line of Orléans. The House of Orléans became, by the usurpation of 1830, so odious to the Legitimists that some of the latter, when the "legitimate" line died out with the Comte de Chambord in 1883, declined to recognize the head of the House of Orléans as the rightful pretender to the throne. Most Legitimists, however, followed the final advice of the Comte de Chambord by recognizing the rights of the House of Orléans to France. (*Encyclopaedia Britannica*).

When I arrived in Paris, in 1887, the Republic had a good press. France's new government was giving obvious proofs of stability. The political crew, as a whole, enjoyed the respect of the majority. Of course, as always, the same as yesterday, the day before yesterday, or today, disgruntled folk complained about the political mess, favoritism in high places, the waste of public funds, general slackness. It was good form to jeer at parliamentary demagogy, to treat the men in power as thieves and social climbers. This happens with all regimes and in every age. (During the fifty and more years that I have watched the show of political life in France, there has not been a single year when I have not heard it said that the State was undergoing "a serious crisis," and that the regime was "rotten.") In reality, the Third Republic inspired trust and a sense of security. It worked away at its job and let the trouble-makers carp. It felt strong enough (and this alone was a sign of flourishing health) to grant the country broad liberties. Between 1875 and 1905, France lived under the freest regime, by far, that it has ever known—that any country, I believe, has ever known.

Yes, if I were not afraid of being called *laudator temporis acti,** I would come right out and say that it was good to be alive in France back then!

In any case, the atmosphere was sensible. Among the young men in the Écoles, at the incitement of Déroulède,† there was still a lot of patriotic clamoring for "revenge." But the bulk of the nation as a whole wanted peace, became quite upset when some incident with Germany occurred, and sadly but seriously tried to get used to the amputation of Alsace and Lorraine. From '83 on, the revanchist movement that still bothered the young heads of Saint-Cyrians, Polytechniciens, and military men had found a glorious outlet in the unchimerical dream of colonial expansion.

I shall have to return to this.

The intellectual world of Paris stuck to a balanced liberalism. Equally opposed to all sectarian systems, to all assertions that were too rigid, they drew reasons for mutual tolerance from the daily practice of a moderate skepticism. I believe that this liberalism is an attitude profoundly natural to the French mind, which distrusts extremes and sees in liberalism the most practical solution for reconciling individual differences. The Frenchman willingly accepts the notion that the convictions of others have to be respected, since he very much needs to see his own respected. Among the thinkers at the end of the nineteenth century, the notion of the relativity of ideas, the complexity of the universe, was too widely accepted to allow for

---

*A praiser of past times. (Horace, *Ars Poetica*).

†Paul Déroulède (1846–1914), French author and revanchist politician. After having been wounded and taken prisoner by the Germans at Sedan, he published in 1872 a patriotic verse drama *(Chants du soldat)* that made him famous.

extreme dogmatism, and they were too bent on keeping their minds free to be partisan—at any rate, to be so consciously or with premeditation. It is no lie to say that all those men I knew made a sincere effort to be as little partisan as possible.

The memory of the 1870 defeat nevertheless remained sharp enough so that, without being excessive or blindly fanatical, France and, curiously, the intellectual set of the Institut and the University, were infused with an enlightened and ardent patriotic sentiment.

This sentiment was further inflamed, kept at fever pitch, by the presence on our borders of a triumphant, arrogant Germany, whose threats, during that decade, had so many times seemed about to materialize that many believed in Bismarck's wish to knock us back down, just as we were recovering, with a fresh attack and a fresh defeat. It was said that, in German ruling circles, a new war, to finish off the extraordinary French national vitality once and for all, was considered a necessity. The pessimists always believed themselves to be on the eve of a conflict. As a matter of fact, the difficult Franco-German relations did keep things in a constant, indefinite, unnerving state of alert. Or at the very least, among the less fearful, in a state of insecurity.

We simplify—to the point of inaccuracy—the position of France, its intellectual circles, and the French university vis-à-vis Germany, when today we condemn the French craze, around 1880, for Germanic science, historical method, and philosophy. Two distinctly different viewpoints have to be recognized in the attitude of cultivated Frenchmen. On the one hand, it is true that the Sorbonne and the Institut were profoundly influenced by that German erudition, by the host of scholars and historians who had revived criticism with a new scientific apparatus, by the methodical realism of the German professors and the spirit of documentary precision they brought to their researches, often making it possible for them to reconsider most of the great questions posed by the past on a new basis. An historian of the Michelet school looked like a poet and an amateur. The name of Mommsen* was revered, and his works found a following in France. Of this there is no doubt. (And it was for the greater good, the regeneration of French criticism.)

But this legitimate admiration, which can be faulted only for its blind exaggeration, did not prevent the great majority of French intellectuals from condemning the realpolitik of a Bismarck and from repudiating, as a barbaric code, such Prussian expressions as "Might makes right," etc. These axioms seemed to the French mind, heir to the Latin jurisconsults, a pure

---

*Theodor Mommsen (1817–1903), German historian, author of the *History of Rome,* winner of the Nobel Prize for literature in 1902.

denial of justice, a brute regression, a spiritual bankruptcy, which imperiled the most precious essence of civilization, the integrity of the human conscience. I can only compare this upsurge of unanimous reprobation to the hue and cry in France that followed the first manifestations of the Hitlerian ideology. There was, at that earlier time, the same rejection, the same instinctive revolt against what seemed to everyone a blasphemy and a return to a prehistoric savagery that threatened to annihilate that moral civilization of which we were all so proud.

At a distance, that era seems quite "literary" to us, especially in the light of current events. It is somewhat surprising that this company of thinkers should have attached so much importance to literary endeavor, and that these critical minds should have had so much indulgence for contemporaries who, today, with hindsight, do not always seem to us those whose work and impact the history of letters and of philosophy will consecrate. I cannot help smiling when I remember, for instance, that none of those learned professors doubted the importance of a Leconte de Lisle, a Coppée, a Sully Prudhomme, a Catulle Mendès, or even an Eugène Manuel,* at a time when Verlaine, or Mallarmé, or the young Rimbaud had already begun, in the shadows, to revolutionize contemporary poetry. When I recall what serious and impassioned discussions the latest play by Dumas fils, by Émile Augier, or by the young Sardou gave rise to, when Becque had already written *Les Corbeaux* and *La Parisienne* . . . And how much importance these writers gave to the *vie des boulevards* and to the theaters, in spite of pretending to scorn them!

At that time, this academic world had the *Journal des débats* as its daily organ. A moderate organ, full of gravity and high standards, one of the only dailies to which one could contribute without demeaning oneself, written entirely by respected, cultured authors, competent in the subjects with which they dealt. Often, during the week, one or several articles in the *Débats* would create a sensation and would become food for the Sunday conversation, like intellectual events. It was the newspaper of respectable people. The defender of liberal politics. Many academics who were concerned with social problems wrote for it regularly. A shared faith in the law, in justice, was proclaimed quietly, unpolemically, but firmly in its pages; and freedom, in the best sense of the word, was defended in them. The initiates, writers, and subscribers did not have to spell things out to one another, and one could say anything in it, provided one said it with seriousness, finesse, and courtesy. Civility was valued, in those distant times . . . The *Débats* had a wide audience among the literati of Europe. This Parisian newspaper enjoyed the authority

---

*François Coppée (1842–1908), French poet; Catulle Mendès (1841–1909), French poet, playwright and novelist; Eugène Manuel (1823–1901), French poet and man of letters.

that was then granted, almost universally, to the quality of the French critical mind: no celebrity could shine without first having been anointed by it.

Twice a month, my Uncle Éric contributed a column to the *Débats.* I especially remember the series of articles that he did one winter on the Albigensian heresy, in which he distinguished two separate heresies—the Cathar and the Waldensian—and whose importance was so unanimously recognized that several publishers requested permission to collect them in a book. He agreed. It is the little volume that he called *Note on the Crusade against the Albigensians, Considered as a Reaction against Feudal Disciplines.* (He had a genius for these cumbersome, confusing, absurd titles; he stuck to them obstinately, because of the exactitude that he got into them. It made no difference to him that they were not . . . enticing! On the contrary, he liked to discourage the overly frivolous curiosity of the majority, as if he feared having a best-seller, which would have prevented him from regarding himself, and from being regarded by his set, as unappreciated. This was the despair of his publishers; and perhaps the fun of playing a dirty trick on them by refusing to yield to their very sensible advice, which he called "commercial," had something to do with his stubbornness.)

MANY OF my Uncle Éric's friends were alumni of the University or the École Normale Supérieure, and many held chairs at the Sorbonne, the Collège de France, or the Sciences Politiques; some of the younger ones (Faguet, for example) were professors in lycées.

To one degree or another, these men all had the habits and quirks of the teaching profession of that time. Since the advent of the Republic—and in ten years its state of mind had taken root—the University, defiant under the Empire, freethinking, Voltairean, had lapsed openly into anticlericalism. This attitude was tacitly encouraged by the Republic (there were a lot of University men in the regime). The government was counting on the secularization of the rising generation to solidify the republican spirit in France. The clergy was in the opposition. The fall of the Empire had been a defeat for the Church, and a threat to it.

We had seen, since the beginning of the Republic, a Minister of Public Instruction like J. Simon propose reforms that tended to reinforce secularism and to spread among the young its principles, which differed from those that the Jesuits and the parochial schools were teaching. Under the Empire, a Victor Duruy* had already worked on the expansion of education among the people—but with respect for religious and moral traditions. The republican University cared more about leading the young towards a nonreligious phi-

*Victor Duruy (1811–1894), French historian and politician.

losophy, and, in spite of its theoretical protestations of tolerance, virtually entered into a battle with the Catholic influence. Let us say, in the University's defense, that the Church was openly hostile to the Republic.

I shall not venture further into this debate. I only want to note a certain cult of the secular within that professorial milieu. An anticlericalism which was not that of the demagogic parliamentarians but which instead came straight out of Kant and which derived its legitimacy from German philosophy far more than from the French tradition of the Encyclopedists or Voltaire.

On those occasions at the "Sundays" when the professors were in the majority, a special atmosphere was created. The tone was stuffier than on the days when the gathering was full of artists and writers. One professor after another took the floor, as if at the lectern. The others listened without interrupting too often, waiting their turn. The conversation did not have that light, lively, spontaneous quality, peppered with interruptions, that the artists or the critics without university training brought to it. Each spoke as one used to an audience that does not argue back or contradict, and with that verbal complacency peculiar to those who are accustomed to speaking in public and know how to repeat the same idea several times in slightly different forms, so as to give themselves time to prepare the rest of their lesson. That slightly pedantic eloquence of the professors, studded with rather heavy humor, which seeks less to please than to instruct, is quite different from political or judicial eloquence. The politician, the lawyer, does not speak, he pleads, he has a trial to win. He defends a thesis, he has to convince, and any means will serve his purpose. He speaks as if he had a voter in front of him to indoctrinate, or a judge to take in, or a "distinguished opponent" whose mouth he has to shut by clobbering him with unanswerable arguments rather than by means of subtle reasoning.

I must add that these university men had almost all gone through the Procrustean bed of the École Normale. They were the cream of the crop. They had kept hardly any of that childish vanity, that upstart distinction, that florid and offhand glibness which forever marks the mediocre *normaliens* and makes them stand out from the crowd at a gathering of provincial notables, at the prefecture ball (and that light sort of playfulness that always makes one think of a successful speech at a prize presentation).

All the same, the professors were sometimes quite irritating. A mixture of inexperience, naïveté, and erudition; the awareness of having learned much and the delusion of mistaking knowledge for intelligence, the conviction that a familiarity with texts opens the mind to all the world's domains; a particular way of being irreverent, in the manner of the Voltaire of *Candide,* and of laughing to themselves as if they were the only ones worthy of savoring the choiceness of their wit. These sprightly little tics contracted at the École nearly always came out at some point or other, for an instant, even in the best of them.

*

Renan was then a big fat man who seemed to me very elderly, and who must have been scarcely more than sixty in 1887. Xavier impiously called him *Our Holy Father Macrobius*.* His lameness had aged him before his time. I can still see him, as he appeared to me many times, from the landing of the library, struggling up that staircase which I took in a few bounds, his head down, his neck in his shoulders, and blowing like a sperm whale. His black frock coat, unbuttoned over his prominent belly, hung amply about him. Before going into the library, he stopped for a moment to catch his breath, and plunged his hand into the skirts of his coat, grimacing at the effort, to extract a big handkerchief like a country priest's, with which he mopped his brow and his blubbery mouth. Then he made his entrance, headed with unexpected briskness over to my aunt, who was usually sitting not far from the door, in the corner by the fireplace, bowed with a great show of courtesy, and held for a moment in his two big paws the hand that she extended to him. "Chambost," she would call out, "here's Monsieur Renan."

Uncle Éric, who generally held court at the other end of the room, at once broke off to rush over to his illustrious friend. Renan's fidelity to the "Sundays" was one of the secret prides of the Chambost couple.

My uncle would show him to "his seat," a capacious upholstered armchair, not easily movable, placed with its back to the window (for he was afraid to face the daylight, and when he had it in his eyes, his heavy lids would blink in his flat face, calling to mind a barn owl), and he would gently collapse into the wide chair, filling it with his mass of flesh, which seemed boneless. He did not stir from it until he left. A circle formed around him. My aunt brought him a "finger of Marsala" and two cookies which he nibbled with a discreet greediness. The newcomers were introduced to him, but this did not happen often; he knew all the regulars, remembered their names, their distinctive characteristics, everyone's intellectual "specialties," had for each a gracious word, and, smiling, asked them for news about their work, never getting anything mixed up.

His urbanity was one of his charms. For an indisputable charm emanated from this good, stout giant. His smile had kept a certain freshness, a certain childish purity, and a great kindness; a natural kindness, no doubt, but also *an intentional kindness*. Indeed, the sly look which filtered through and at

*Ambrosius Theodosius Macrobius, Latin grammarian and philosopher active around 400 A.D.

times shot forth between the thick, creased eyelids gave sufficient indication that his good-naturedness did not betoken any unawareness, that the benevolence of his usual talk and the politeness of his judgments could not be taken for a lack of observation or a naïve conception of men or institutions. He could be very biting, but always with more playful roguishness than malice, and never with any acrimony, resentment, or bias. Even when he alluded to the clergy, to the Church, of whose virulent attacks he was still the object,* he really never showed any personal bitterness. Perhaps it had not always been so. But when I knew him, he had had his revenge; his European fame and the respect he enjoyed probably smoothed the way for that generous attitude of skeptical tolerance. The nastiness that he was still forced to endure was so well offset by the flattering friendliness shown him by the intellectual elite, and by the honors he received, that it was easy to accept with a smile.

Such was Renan, in that broad armchair at the rue de Fleurus. Languid, huge, static, giving the impression of a mass in repose, extraordinarily stable, indeed immovable. Thighs apart, belly heavy beneath the cascade of folds in the immense black vest with its gold chain; gesturing little and only with his hands, he was expressive through his physiognomy alone, although the face, too, was almost immobile. But the smile that hovered about his mouth, and the keenness of his eye, twinkling and quizzical, were enough to give a great deal of life to that face thickened with whitish fat, which was rather unhealthy-looking. A man who, as any doctor could have seen at first glance, did not take good care of himself.

In general, he kept his counsel and listened. On certain Sundays, even his silences had about them something weighty, which occasionally paralyzed the conversation. "Today, Buddha is digesting," Xavier would say.

His speech resembled his style. Undulating, fluent, musical, with a fine rhythm to it. He finished all his sentences, and gave them a harmonious turn. Very simple words, neither common nor crude, nothing trite in his choice of vocabulary, and yet a total absence of pedantic terms and affectations; a smooth style, an exceptional ability to use ordinary words in their proper sense. This fluent ease of the words in the sentence, of the parts of the sentence, even when it was long, this felicitous equipoise, recalled a dance, a

---

*Renan had counted on the writing of his life of Jesus to secure election to the chair of Hebrew at the Collège de France. He was elected, before the book was ready, on January 11, 1862. But in his opening lecture, on February 21, he referred to Jesus in the words of Jacques Bossuet, a French bishop and historian of the seventeenth and eighteenth centuries, as "an incomparable man." Though this was, in his eyes, the highest praise one could bestow on a man, it was not sufficient for the clericals, who took advantage of its implied atheism and the uproar caused by the lecture to have Renan suspended[. . . .] When the *Vie de Jésus* did appear in 1863, it was virulently denounced by the church. (*Encyclopaedia Britannica*).

well-choreographed ballet, or, better still, the sure and supple grace of a good skater.

The scholar in him came out only in his passion for quotations. Not only did he like to slip into his sentences a phrase from Herder or from Hegel, or often a verse from Scripture, but he also constantly stopped after a word used in its precise etymological sense, to give the Latin word, briefly, as a reference, as if between parentheses. He often said after a gibe: "*Cum grano salis,** gentlemen . . ." (And he even added sentences such as: "Irony is a gift from the Lord, and we would be very ungrateful not to use it . . .")

To Aunt Ma, who scolded him one day for complaining about his health and congratulated him on his youthful spirit, he made this response, which Xavier and I remembered and repeated to each other, laughing: "Yes, yes, dear Madame, *Spiritus* is still quite *promptus,* but how *iam infirma* is *caro!*"†

I believe he was aware that Aunt Ma knew no Latin, and that he took a particular pleasure in embarrassing her. To no avail, though, since Aunt Ma, with her usual straightforwardness, never failed to cry: "Translate, Monsieur Renan, translate, please!"

He was otherwise charming with my aunt, and I think that he very genuinely savored her spontaneous turn of mind, her tone of conviction and assertiveness. He listened to her with a smile and never bothered to rebut what she put forward with the confidence of a pretty woman but turned, laughing, to Uncle Éric, a gleam of mischief slipping through his eyelids: "*Quod gratis, asseretur, gratis negatur. . . .*"

"Translate, Monsieur Renan!"

He did so immediately, with good grace: "We mean by this, *chère Madame,* that what we gratuitously declare one day, we just as gratuitously deny the next."

He always seemed to be amused "within" by what he himself was saying as much as by what had just been said by others.

His voice was clear, with soft inflections and a kind of ecclesiastical unction.

Nothing common in all this: an undeniable nobility in his good-naturedness.

He rarely spoke at any length. At least, in the general conversation. If someone pulled up a chair and had a personal, private word with him, he became suddenly animated and, in an undertone, might make a long speech. But for the most part, from the depths of his episcopal throne, motionless, he contented himself with brief remarks, smiling or serious, which showed that he was following the talk with attention, that he had views of his own

*"With a grain of salt."
†"The spirit is still quite willing, but how weak is the flesh!"

on all the subjects but did not care to impose them and preferred to learn and reflect as he listened rather than defend his opinion. He had a visible horror of holding forth. There was nothing pontifical about him. He was treated somewhat as a pundit, of course; my uncle, when Renan was there, always turned in his direction and addressed his long speeches to him— and the others as well. But this pontifical character came from them, not from him.

However, as I write this, I suddenly recall a little personal anecdote. He had just quoted some article from a German review, and my Uncle Éric, so as not to interrupt the conversation, had told me: "Bertrand, do take that reference down for me in writing." I went over to M. Renan, who dictated the text of the quotation to me in a low voice, and the complicated title of a German archeological review. All of a sudden, I felt his fat paw on my shoulder. "Your lines slant up so!" he said, taking the sheet from my hands. "You need to correct that defect, young man. You need to use ruled paper, as I do. One must write straight. One must love straightness in everything." Then he handed me back the sheet and resumed his dictation. But this pontificating behavior was a real exception.

Perhaps, after all, not as much of an exception as I make out . . . Other memories come back to me.

That way he had of saying, when a sally of my Aunt Ma's made that learned assemblage laugh till it cried: "Let's laugh . . . We need to be merry . . . Merriment is the sign of a good conscience." Or again: "Laugh, laugh, *chère Madame*. I like to see you laugh. Our moments of merriment are certainly pleasing to the Lord . . ."

He also said: "If the clergy had known how to laugh, there wouldn't have been an Inquisition." He often returned to this matter of merriment. According to him, it was the universal panacea. "Those people never laugh," he said of his enemies.

What also might be seen as pontification was that habit, when concluding a discussion or at the moment when he hoisted himself out of his chair to leave, of declaring, as he lolled his head and smiled at no one in particular: "Ah, gentlemen, seen from Sirius, none of our little controversies is so very important, is it?"

Or, if there was reason to lament some occurrence, the cold, the snow, a flood: "Ah, gentlemen, let us not forget that the laws that govern the universe have other ends than that of accommodating our puny selves."

He himself was aware of what was called his "benedictory tone." "I was born to preach," he sometimes said. "What a good old country priest I'd have made, if that had been the Lord's intent."

This "benedictory tone," for which his listeners at the Collège de France sometimes criticized him, was, in my opinion, fairly rare in his conversation.

I never heard Renan teach a class. But, at the end of the '88 academic year, Xavier and I attended the prize day at the lycée Louis-le-Grand, which he was presiding over, in order to hear him. I well understand that "benedictory tone." I did not much like his speech. Something mushy in the diction, and, what is more serious, in the thought. A sort of overly facile "wisdom." I have forgotten the precise subject of that address. But it was only a pretext for preaching sweetness, tolerance, love of life to those young students. To the best of my recollection, it could be summarized in this way:

"My dear children, enter life with trust; it is sweet, it is good to those who accept it as it is, who do not ask the impossible, and who approach it with love. Cultivate reason, do not be too optimistic, nor foolishly pessimistic; the good makes up for the bad. Be tolerant in order to remain fair, always think for yourselves, be sincere, love freedom but respect that of others," etc.

Such words were perhaps less insignificant at that time than today, but I recall the disappointment Xavier and I felt, and the impression of banality that this philosophic humanism left us with. It certainly was not Renan at his best.

One sentence, I remember, struck us in particular. Something like this: "Your generation is undoubtedly marked out to do great things, for you will undoubtedly witness an unprecedented upheaval of the world." People always rouse the young by promising them an exceptional destiny and a great task to accomplish.

I have a personal reason for believing that on that day, M. Renan stooped to a bit of demagogy and was looking to please his audience. (He always made some effort to please, and you felt he was anxious to make himself liked.) For I remember that, one Sunday, seeing Xavier de Balcourt, Léon Daudet, and myself heatedly discussing something or other, and saying "we" with a certain amount of impudence, he leaned forward, smiling, to listen, then waved us over to him and favored us, from his armchair, with an unctuous little speech that went something like this (and which completely contradicted his attitude in the auditorium at Louis-le-Grand): "My dear friends, believe me, do not run too ardently after the truth . . . Nothing is ever gained by running, anyway . . . Do not forget that up until now humanity has only gone from one error to the next . . . That will make you more humble . . . Do you really think it is reserved for your generation to finally show the world the truth?"

I can see him smiling like a porcelain Buddha, shaking his big skeptic's head which, seen from up close, appeared so enormous, so shapeless, so heavy with flesh: "We know so few things, young men! And above all, so little of what we would most wish to know . . . Let us not deny anything. Let us not assert anything. The only reasonable attitude is to *hope*."

In '83, he had just brought out his *Souvenirs*. He presented a copy to Aunt Ma with a somewhat coy dedication; I have the volume in hand: "To

Madame Chambost-Lévadé, who in her kindness will perhaps not be too hard on these ramblings of an old man on the decline," etc.

He was often wont to mention his age.

"I who am now an old man on the decline" was an expression he had got us all used to. He liked to start his friend Berthelot's imagination going on the subject of scientific progress. It was an excuse for him to say, with a smile: "I'll die before having seen that . . ." He had settled comfortably into this superannuated attitude. He used it unrestrainedly. Or else, having told, with that muted wit and those rectorial circumlocutions that were peculiar to him, some slightly frivolous, slightly risqué anecdote (or one that seemed so in the mouth of M. Renan), he would apologize: "At my age, one should only be concerned with eternal truths . . . But one remains a big child to the end . . ." "Young men," he would sometimes say, with a comical seriousness, addressing a group of friends in their fifties.

At that time, he was completing his *Origins of Christianity* with his *History of the People of Israel. Saint Paul, The Gospels,* and *Marcus Aurelius* had appeared. Naturally, among the Chambost crowd, this work was regarded as a monument of imperishable scholarship. I had read only the *Life of Jesus,* and with delight. Xavier de Balcourt, who, I never quite understood why, wasn't very fond of M. Renan, did not encourage me to open his other books. Xavier congratulated Rome for having forbidden the reading of them and for having placed these works on the Index, saying drolly:

> *Le Très Saint-Père eût fait bien pire*
> *En nous ordonnant de les lire!**

I wrote down certain remarks of Renan's that I have not forgotten:

"Some of us here belong to the tribe of those who want justice," he once said, in a rather severe tone, to the young Drumont,† who had been brought that day to my uncle's by Alphonse Daudet, I believe, for the first time and who had just launched into a diatribe against the Jews. (Drumont was then preparing his book, *Jewish France,* which was to cause such a stir, and create so many divisions, and do so much harm two or three years later.)

"Everything is possible, dear friend," Renan said one day to Berthelot, who had just put forth some brilliant hypothesis. *"Even God . . ."*

He liked joking about religious questions. One day, an initiative by the Vatican that seemed quite unfortunate to everyone was being discussed: "Eh,

---

*"The Most Holy Father would have done worse
  If he'd ordered us to read them!"
†Edouard Drumont (1844–1917), French politician, one of the leaders of the anti-Semitic party.

gentlemen, how could the Pope have clear views about matters of religion? He still believes . . . To understand something about faith, you need to have had it but to have lost it."

He had several bêtes noires. Bossuet was one of them. "That big windbag Bossuet," he used to say.

He was quick to make fun of himself. "An old defrocked priest like me," he would say. With a charitable indulgence, very much "forgiveness of trespasses," in which there was perhaps more self-control than actual indifference, he took a wicked pleasure in reporting the vicious remarks that were heaped on him in anonymous letters. As proof I cite the following: a ridiculous slander, which was still circulating in certain rigidly conventional circles, accused him of having been paid by the Rothschilds to write his *Life of Jesus*. Well, in fact he must have thought about this a good deal, since he jocularly alluded to it often. He obviously went on being hurt by it. I heard him say one day, with a laugh, but with a subdued note of irritation:

"The year the book came out, I received only thirty pieces of silver, like Iscariot. A year later, it was a thousand francs. Today, it's a million. But there's worse to come. They'll end up publishing a copy of my receipt . . ."

"Ah, Monsieur Renan," my aunt carelessly said to him one day, "you never take anything seriously!" "It's because I hold my peace of conscience very dear, *chère Madame et amie*," he answered. And he added, after a pause, "I have always possessed *the art of being happy*."

It was true, I think. His perpetual good mood was more than a pose. That childlike gaiety, that guileless serenity, came from a satisfied conscience. He had served the truth as best he could and was growing old pleased with himself, pleased with the world and with his life. To pessimists, he often said: "How unfair you are to the age, how hard you are on Man." Or: "How impatient you are! Wait a little! *Justice will come in the end*." His forbearance, like his stability, stemmed from his awareness of his profound honesty.

"I have always been a very lazy sort," he used to say. "I am incapable of any hard effort. I have always *had a good time working*."

He was annoyed by overbearing people (and quite a few came to the rue de Fleurus), by harsh, arrogant critics, by fanatics. On those days, he paralyzed everyone with his ruminant's silence. Or else, he would hazard a timid comment, which he prefaced with an "I, who am *a moderate* . . ." or even, if the fierceness of the argument had irritated him too much, "I, who am not in *possession of the absolute truth* . . ." I remember having heard him say (to the young Brunetière, I think), "Look, young man, at my age, one prefers to be only half right . . ."

". . . Your God!" some anticleric flung at him one day. Renan smiled: "Would it occur to you to say 'your' Infinite? 'your' Absolute? Of course not. Then why do you say to me 'your' God?"

When he said of someone, "He is a *seeker,* a *lover of truth,*" one felt it was the finest praise he could bestow, the praise he most wished to deserve. The pursuit of truth was, in his eyes, his reason for being, his mission. His "religious" attachment to the Collège de France came from that: it was, for him, the temple of our day; the temple of free thought and independent research.

This worship of the truth never led him to believe that he had attained it. No one pronounced the word *truth* more often than he, but no one thought less than he that he possessed it. To such an extent that he never said of an opinion different from his own that it was wrong but that it was questionable, simplistic, specious, ill-informed. Thus, when my Uncle Éric, less timid in his judgments, would exclaim, as he often did, "So-and-so is wrongheaded," which meant that the person did not think as he did, M. Renan would always correct him, nodding gently: "*Limited,* my dear friend, *limited . . .*" And this distinction, to which he seemed very attached, was indeed revealing. In principle, he accepted all opinions. He did not judge them as "true" or "false" but as emanating from a vast and expansive intelligence or from a short and limited outlook.

"AH, MONSIEUR RENAN," Aunt Ma would sometimes say to him, "how disappointing of you to doubt everything . . ." He would laugh softly: "Not at all, *chère Madame,* what is disappointing is to be a man; that is, an animal endowed with intelligence and reason, who is part of an infinite world, who knows it, and who also knows that in this infinity he doesn't amount to much more than a zero . . ."

I always thought that too much importance had been given to that sentence in his *Souvenirs* in which he calls history a "conjectural little science." This was just one of his quips. There was also a certain amount of affectation and coyness in his habit of repeating that he was only a philologist, a bookworm, a rifler of old texts. He apologized for this as he would have apologized for an inadvertence, for something childish. As if he had been caught playing jacks or making paper birds. In fact, he believed in history as he believed in science, of which it is a branch. He was expecting the progress of humanity as much from the scientist who approaches the truth through his experiments as from the historian and the philologist who approach it through documents and textual analysis.

He liked history for other, more personal reasons, I think. That panoramic vision he achieved, through history, of man's past brought him a higher peace. I often heard him say that the study of centuries gone by leads to serenity, to wisdom. He excelled at showing that the fiercest, most sectarian adversaries, in mercilessly battling each other, collaborated without knowing it in that common endeavor which was the progress of human civilization.

If my interaction with Uncle Éric did me the great service of teaching me to doubt—that is, in short, to think—I certainly owe something of this as well to those encounters with Renan. I will admit that the youth in me sometimes became slightly annoyed. I was at the age when one likes to take sides and to judge. When, at the conclusion of a lively argument, one of the protagonists turned to the silent Renan to ask him: "What do you think, Monsieur Renan?" and Renan, smiling, replied, with the gravity of an oracle, "To deny it would be quite foolhardy, I agree. But would it not be just as much so to affirm it?" I caught Xavier's eye, and I was relieved to see that his exasperation was as keen as mine.

But I did not escape the profound influence of that environment. I was, by nature, reflective, and on the whole, for a young man, moderately self-assured in my changing opinions. The respect that the Chambosts' circle inspired in me, the habit that I formed—by living at close quarters with my uncle and attending, each Sunday, those conclaves of all the prelates of contemporary thought—of seeing every question debated and of witnessing doubt, if not negation, always honored as the highest, most dispassionate, most transcendent position of the mind before the enigma of the universe, held the greatest sway over my education. I might snort, back then, and kick over my traces. I was nonetheless marked by it. A few years later, with experience, I myself noticed the errors that can be produced by dogmatism, presumptuousness, making a cult of the absolute. And it was then that the lesson of the hôtel de Fleurus, the memory of Uncle Éric and of M. Renan, bore their fruit. To them I owe the form of my intelligence as well as my horror of fanaticism, which has only grown and asserted itself in the course of my life, although that life, by a strange contradiction—more apparent than real—has been that of a man of action, after all. But a man of action who never passed up a chance to philosophize while acting and to defend himself against the distorting effect that action can have on thought.

This horror of fanatics M. Renan had to the highest degree, thanks to reflection and personal experience. He had encountered them along his way; it was at their hands that he had most suffered.

But even on this point he avoided unqualified assertion, and found a way to doubt. I remember having heard him debate with M. Taine about the men of the Revolution. He knew a great deal about the history of that chaotic time, and M. Taine himself rarely caught him in a mistake. One day, M. Renan, having voiced his agreement with the friends who were gathered that afternoon, and having condemned even more indignantly than the others, with proofs, anecdotes, unpublished documents to support him, the stupidity, the naïveté, and above all the abominable cruelty of the leading revolutionaries, did a very surprising about-face, and pointed out that these monsters with human heads had nevertheless been the architects of an imposing and highly civilizing piece of work. Then, generalizing, he presented the idea that, in the current state of humanity, certain essential reforms perhaps cannot be accomplished by reason, moderation, justice. In short, he made the case for the usefulness of the fanatical and the violent: "One must accept them," he said. "Let them do their ugly job, and then, as soon as possible, get rid of them . . ." He smiled, delighted with his idea. "Who knows if this hideous collaboration of evil is not indispensable for the coming of a great good? Criminal and abhorrent, insane and detestable, they certainly are. But the endeavor that humanity is dimly trying to perfect, and that goes beyond them, and that is glorious, needs their madness and their crimes to blossom and to establish itself in a lasting way." I have not forgotten this position of his, which was disconcerting at the time but which undoubtedly contained a profound and pessimistic view of evolution, of the stage of evolution which is that of our era. I am sure he would have followed the history of Bolshevism in Russia since 1917 with a mixture of horror and trust, disapproval and hope.

Thus there are, in the depths of my memory, certain words, certain viewpoints, that I heard from M. Renan and that certainly left their stamp on me, since half a century of active life has not managed to erase their memory.

For example, I remember a conversation on *original sin*. I can still see M. Renan, who was in a talkative vein that day, explaining with a great many analytic proofs that this story of the first man's transgression (which seemed to me the basis of Christianity) does not appear in the various texts of Genesis, except for one. I have naturally forgotten all the details. I only recall that his luminous account made it as clear as day that this mythical episode—fundamental since the time when Saint Paul built on it one of the essential dogmas of Christian doctrine—has only a minor importance, and that this legend could very well have been forgotten, have gone unmentioned, never to reach either Saint Paul or us, since it played no part in the religion of the Hebrews.

This was my first contact with exegesis. I listened open-mouthed. I was suddenly discovering the fragility of those beliefs on which I had been brought up and the part that chance and invention played in them. That day I understood how right my intuition had been to make me doubt and on what a fragile foundation of fictions, symbols, and poetical imaginings dogmas were based! A decisive step for me! I knew, from that day on, that my instinctive dissent, my detachment, my lack of belief, could be backed up by irrefutable historical arguments. To tell the truth, I was not a worrier, and my religious doubts did not torture me. All the same, this assurance that in my ignorance, in the darkness of my lack of cultivation, I had on my own found the correct and reasonable way, the way that knowledge shows to seekers, brought me in those matters a conclusive peace that I have never lost.

*

M. Berthelot* had been brought to the rue de Fleurus by M. Renan; he rarely appeared alone but came fairly often with M. Renan. Their friendship was celebrated. It went way back, perhaps forty years, to the time when the young seminarian of Issy† had, as they used to say back then, "gone over the wall."

These two men were a curious sight together. M. Renan deferred to his friend with a humility in which some thought they saw a bit of playacting, but which, I believe, was real and sincere, and of very long standing: it was M. Berthelot who had opened M. Renan's eyes to science, at a time when he had just wrapped his gods in the famous "shroud of purple"‡ and felt himself at a loss. M. Renan had unconsciously transferred to science all the religious feeling and need to believe that remained in him. A fairly widespread attitude at the time in scholarly circles. It was the era of science-worship. Everything was expected of it. M. Renan showed a naïve, touching, absolute admiration for his friend. "You who are lucky enough to have taken the only path that has a chance of leading anywhere," he would tell him, visibly pleased at rendering him this public homage. Never did he display so much hope in science as in his friend's presence. He hailed M. Berthelot's scientific explanations with pious little sentences such as "The resources of science are truly limitless!" or "The future of science is the least chancy of our certainties . . ." or even "If we had no other reason for loving and pardoning humanity than that it had produced science, this would be enough to justify our love." (He had a way of saying "Science" that implied a capital "S.") And I would not be surprised if his respect for morality was founded, in part, on the conviction he sometimes expressed that "honesty is the defining virtue of a true scientist."

M. Berthelot accepted these tributes like a priest hearing God praised. "Our temporary errors don't matter much," he would sometimes say, "what matters is the result: from error to error, the pyramid rises. We will never see it finished, but it is already standing on its foundations, and someday it

---

*See footnote, p. 222.

†I.e., Renan, who left his seminary and the Roman Catholic Church in 1845.

‡"Le linceul de pourpre où dorment les dieux morts" ("the shroud of purple in which the dead gods sleep"), a much-quoted line from Renan's "Prière sur l'Acropole," which appears in his *Souvenirs d'enfance et de jeunesse.*

will tower above the desert in all its loftiness." For M. Berthelot, doubt was only a means of approaching truth and of partially attaining it. A fact, scientifically proven, was for him *absolutely true.*

M. Berthelot's presence always gave the Sunday gatherings a special tone. When he was there, it was around him that people clustered, and on those days my Uncle Éric would "let him spout," as Xavier said.

He was a stunning talker. I think that he regarded the rue de Fleurus somewhat as a vacation and that this assemblage of philologists, of literati, seemed to him an audience of ignoramuses who forced him to confine himself to a popularizing approach. He clearly tried to amuse this congregation of uninitiates, and to give it only what it could understand. His favorite game was to indulge in dazzling predictions as to the applications of science in the future life of humanity. Then his French workman's face, honest, energetic, reflective, would become animated, shining with enthusiasm and naïve faith: he reminded me of certain donors shown with an ecstatic gaze in the corner of a religious painting.

It seems to me, today, that none of his fantastic prophecies has come to pass.

One idea of his that has stayed with me is this: He foresaw the moment—and he claimed it would be soon—when a man's brain would no longer be able to encompass by itself the scope of the science of his time. He even said that his generation might be the borderline generation, the last in which the powers of a single brain could still store the gist of established scientific findings in its memory. He cited his own case and made us feel how difficult it was for him to keep up with the work of the scientific community in Europe, to read and absorb the reports of the hundreds of researchers who already were publishing their findings in seven or eight languages, to collate everything, to compare all their different contributions.

It is an idea that I have heard seconded since, and in an especially moving way, by a young aeronautical inventor, Robert Esnault-Pelterie.[*]

BRUNETIÈRE[†] CAME fairly often, perhaps more often than he was wanted. His very friends, who defended him when necessary, seemed to detest him in spite of themselves. He was treated with care nevertheless. I naïvely believed

---

[*]Robert Esnault-Pelterie (1881–1957) invented ailerons, produced early studies of high-altitude rocket flight, and coined the term "astronautics."

[†]André Daspre: Brunetière is particularly vituperated by Martin du Gard for at least two basic reasons: he was among those who launched the noisiest attacks on the scientific spirit by proclaiming the failure of science; and he placed himself, not long after, among the first ranks of the anti-Dreyfusards, at the side of those who organized the campaign against Zola and the "intellectuals."

it was out of fear of his verbal thrusts, but in fact he ruled the roost at the *Revue des Deux Mondes,* and people had sniffed him out as the future editor.

Uncle Éric, who tore him to pieces in private, was among those who also had the courage to stand up to him, and let fly some of his most finely honed poisoned arrows. I was not present at that "Sunday," thereafter renowned in the annals of the rue de Fleurus, when, after a vicious and trivial diatribe by Brunetière, Uncle Éric began with these words: "Our young friend, *who knows how to wield a platitude . . .*" He was at least fifteen years older than Brunetière, and never failed to call him "our young friend." The catty trick which he usually employed was, when Brunetière had aired his views—in that overly refined and heavy language of his, not flowery but pompous, all festoons and astragals, massive sentences overloaded with parentheses, like furniture with multiple drawers, which seemed a pedantic and less-than-splendid pastiche of the noble style dear to the *grand siècle*—to take the floor and sum up, in a few brief and very simple phrases, the young orator's long tirades, as if the primary and essential thing was, for a start, to explain to the gathering what Brunetière might have been getting at: "Our young friend, if I've understood correctly," he would say, not looking at anyone, "simply wants to state that . . ."

Supreme insolence . . . But he brought it off so naturally, with such perfect courtesy, that Brunetière was always forced to accept the lesson. The most mortifying thing was that my uncle would of course manage to reduce Brunetière's argument to some insignificant truism but without, however, misrepresenting his victim's thought, thus depriving him of any pretext to remonstrate. Brunetière took a beating.

Brunetière struck me as a man with a twisted mind of the worst sort: the kind that never notices that it is off target. This systematical mind otherwise reasoned with a logician's great skillfulness and always presented its thinking in the form of syllogisms that made it appear irrefutable. He was methodically wrong and persisted in his error with complacency. But the keen blades that were the wits of Taine, Renan, or Uncle Éric lost no time in finding his vulnerable point and bursting his hot-air balloons.

He was very young still, in comparison with the average age of the regulars at the hôtel de Fleurus. He cannot have been over thirty-five. But, although his way of speaking was always very academic, he obviously lacked all deference toward his elders and had not the slightest respect for anyone. He contradicted on principle, and quite speciously. And I never heard him admit that he was wrong. He was invariably and unshakably of an opinion opposed to that which had just been uttered by one of those gentlemen. He did know a lot, and took advantage of this to talk about everything with the same pedantic aplomb. His intelligence was undeniable. But it operated in a vacuum, never engaged with reality, and gave me the impression of a very complicated clockwork operating under a glass bell-jar, or better, under an airless bell-jar.

My aunt did a killing imitation of him. I remember a story she liked to tell about her meeting Brunetière in front of the Institut on a very windy day. Brunetière's opera hat had rolled onto the sidewalk. "I am reminded," she said with a comical solemnity, "of that memorable day when the Académie was preparing to receive Monsieur de Renan into its bosom and when Monsieur de Brunetière, who was conversing with me on the stairs, suddenly had his headdress spirited away by Aeolus . . ."

He usually arrived late, his hair disheveled, pince-nez askew, and plunged into the discussion with the rage of a quarrelsome cur and the arsenal of a professor of dialectic. He was not easy to refute head-on, and my uncle acted prudently in getting around him with irony. I suppose that he was reasonably aware of the general hostility and that he enjoyed confronting it. If not, why would he have come so often? Who knows? Perhaps for him those sessions were an exercise in argument, in which he was sharpening his future weapons. When, later on, I read his essays on literature and his famous book *The Failure of Science,* it seemed to me that he had not relented and that he was belatedly taking his revenge both against Taine's critical methods and against the Renans' and the Berthelots' belief in scientific progress. I would wager that the "Sundays" at the rue de Fleurus were not without their influence on the direction taken by this doctrinarian.

THE WRITERS and artists were mainly my aunt's guests. I think that they rubbed Uncle Éric somewhat the wrong way, since, if there were a lot of them, the conversation soon lost its serious, or at least its professorial, tone. Accustomed to the witty talk of the salons, they did not play the game, and broke in with quick, preposterous comments, not observing the "rule," a tacit convention among professors of patiently accepting the monologues of the others so as to be able to take one's own turn when the time came.

I saw the principal literary figures of the day there. Flaubert was dead, but once I was lucky enough to catch a glimpse of Turgenev, at one of the first "Sundays" after my arrival. He died during the course of the year. I do not remember if he was already ill. I would be tempted to think not, so robust is the image that remains in my memory. I can still see a figure out of a fairy tale, an old ogre with a ruffled white mop of hair, but a kind and merry ogre who was not at all frightening, even when he did an exaggerated mime of surprise by arching his bushy eyebrows; extremely talkative, outgoing, colorful, with a head voice that had stayed young, a brisk and cheerful voice, warbling and modulated like birdsong. Although expansive and noisy, he was not the least bit slovenly, but almost overly courteous in his attentions, very lordly. He really ought to have been seen on his estates, in boots up to his thighs. He danced attendance on Aunt Ma, sat by her side, and spoke to no one in particular, laughing out loud. In his honor, tea was served that day; he gulped down three cups, scalding himself and munching sugar. In ten minutes of monologue, he managed to conjure up so many memories, to tell so many anecdotes, that all of Russia burst in on the library at the rue de Fleurus, with its snow and its steppes, its sunbaked muds of spring, its birch forests, its troikas, its drunken mujiks, its peasant girls in motley kerchiefs, its vodka, its samovars, its kopeks, its bast shoes . . . All this picturesqueness, later made familiar to us by the Russian novels, then had a strange and heady flavor that truly intoxicated me.

AMONG THE SCIENTISTS, I have forgotten many personalities, many names. I remember hardly anyone except Pasteur and Charcot.*

The latter was frankly insufferable. Leconte de Lisle and he are probably the reason for that mistrustful dislike that I have had all my life for the handsome countenances of Roman emperors . . . And perhaps they were the primary victims of their imposing faces. I could easily believe that the self-satisfied and egotistical authority which one generally observes in those who bear that imperial visage are due mainly to the smug pride awakened in them by the noble and commanding regularity of their features.

Charcot flattered himself, as doctors rather often do, that he was, as well, not just a man of great culture, and well-read, but also an artist. It is to this superior and calculated dilettantism that I ascribe the rather surprising constancy of his visits to the rue de Fleurus, especially during the winter of '89. His piercing and inquisitive alienist's gaze always made me extremely uneasy when he happened to let it rest on me. He had a tyrannical way of fixing his eyes on yours which made my flesh creep, as if it were only a matter of his clinician's whim to dispatch me, for the rest of my life, to some padded cell in the Salpêtrière. This impression was almost confirmed by the way in which he spoke of the poor mental patients he was taking care of. Did he take care of them? One might well wonder. He seemed more concerned with observing them, in order to gather material for his works, than with curing them. Not a gleam of human pity in that keen and self-satisfied eye, as he laid out with complacency—and in my opinion, with a reprehensible indiscretion, a total lack of any sense of professional secrecy—the mental woes of

*Jean-Martin Charcot (1825–1893), one of the founders of modern neurology and a teacher of Freud. In 1862, he began a lifelong association with the Salpêtrière Hospital, eventually opening there a neurological clinic which became famous all over Europe.

his clients, not omitting their names, ages, and professions (from the habit of scientific precision, no doubt). I was sometimes horrified to hear him smilingly describe an attack of violent and clear-cut insanity which he would ingenuously admit to having knowingly brought on the day before in order to prove the validity of a diagnosis in front of his students and to be able to teach *in anima vili.**

He had founded a society for psychophysiology, to which, if I remember correctly, M. Taine, M. Renan, and M. Daudet belonged. He was quite fond of promoting periodic interchanges of views, under his chairmanship and at his prompting, among the doctors (more particularly the psychiatrists) and the intellectuals (especially the philosophers and writers preoccupied with psychology), to establish a closer relationship, and one he deemed useful to scientific progress, between the clinician's observations about patients and the novelist's about the common man. One felt, in all of this frightening man's remarks, that he perceived only slight shades of difference between the insane in the asylum and each of us, between society ladies and the "hysterics" he was treating in his practice. And that, if it had been only up to him, he would have put the whole of society under treatment behind the bars of his hospital.

This also explains his presence at the rue de Fleurus.

It is fair to add, though, that he did not confine himself to recounting his most recent clinical experiences in the Chambosts' library, and that he knew how to join in the general conversation, not without wit, and in questions far removed from his specialty. It seemed he prided himself on being cultivated enough to talk about philosophy, literature, even painting and music. He was particularly interested in politics, and when that subject arose he would patronizingly toss into the discussion peremptory aphorisms, inspired by the principles of 1789, for he was extravagantly republican and anticlerical. In that area more than any other he was loathsome, with his regal airs, his weighty judgments, in which he did not even take the trouble to conceal the general contempt that men inspired in him, his interlocutors included. Nothing aristocratic about this "emperor"—very Napoleonic in this respect: a false grandeur, a false nobility: those of a usurper. I remember him as a tyrant whose onerous importance had to be endured, a hard tyrant, fixed in his ego, perched on the pedestal of his pride, and to whom all homage was due.

Completely different, of course, was Pasteur. He came to the rue de Fleurus only on very rare occasions, at least in my day. For that matter, I do not think that this prodigious worker ever went anywhere. If a precise and personal memory of him has stayed with me, it is due to particular circumstances. As fate would have it, I ran into him in the corridors of the

---

*"On a lower being": i.e., he would use a human guinea pig for his demonstration.

Sorbonne, in the month of July, one or two days after he had appeared at our house. There was a crowd, since just then the results of various examinations were being posted, and he looked utterly lost. I took the liberty of going up to him and introducing myself again. He was searching for some lecture hall where they were giving the oral part of the second *bachot* to a student whose uncle he was, I think, or perhaps only the guardian in Paris, and in whom he took an interest. It was on the other side of the courtyard, one flight up, and I offered to take him there. On the way, he chatted simply with me and spoke to me about his young man and the tests he had had to take. I recall this detail: he was amazed by the question which had been asked that morning in the chemistry exam, and he stopped walking to tell it to me. With his country accent that came down heavily on the *a*'s, the *o*'s, and the diphthongs, and made the nasals resonate, with his eyebrows raised in surprise and reprobation, his naïve gaze peering over his pince-nez, his feet planted on the ground, completely absorbed in his subject, he repeated: "What a question! I'd have a hard time answering it myself! And to seventeen-year-olds! Can you imagine that?"*

CHAPTER XII

Xavier de Balcourt in Paris

I HAD NOT SEEN Xavier de Balcourt since his leaving le Saillant after the death of my cousin Guy, and my memory of him was rather hazy. We had exchanged a few letters. I had informed him of my success in the *bachot*. I knew that he was continuing to see my uncle Chambost and to work for him, but I had not realized that in his capacity as secretary he had become part of the hôtel de Fleurus, and I was surprised to find he was a fixture there and that he lunched with us several times a week.

My uncle had relegated him to the room next to his office, behind the staircase, which was called "the archive." It was a room longer than wide, lined entirely with numbered green cardboard boxes, and its two windows looked out onto the garden. Xavier had a desk there, between the two windows. His duties were many. He was in charge of answering business letters; he corresponded with publishers and with journals, according to the instructions that my uncle gave him in the morning at nine o'clock, when the mail

---

*"Une pâreîlle questi*on*! Mais je serais embârrâssé d'y répondre môâ! Et à des gâmins de dix-sept ans! *C*oncevez-v*ous* celâ?"

came. This took place in my uncle's study. My uncle opened his mail in Xavier's presence and handed him the letters he would have to answer, with a few words of explanation. After which, Xavier went back to the archive room while my uncle got down to work. A little before noon my uncle would call for him to bring in the outgoing letters to be signed. The scene was rather comical. Xavier read out loud the answers that he had drafted. My uncle interrupted him constantly to make sarcastic remarks to him about his style, about the incorrectness of certain words. Never did anything Xavier had written meet with his approval. From the library my uncle's ironic voice would be heard: "Are you positively not on speaking terms with the agreement of tenses, Monsieur de Balcourt?" (My aunt called him "Xavier," and my uncle too, at meals; but in his study, never anything but "Monsieur de Balcourt.") "I would have preferred, I confess, the imperfect of the subjunctive. These are antiquated habits that die hard with me, I'm afraid . . . Allow me also to point out to you that the verb 'dériver,' derivare, has a precise meaning, which is to follow the current, to go drifting off, and that it would have been better to use the verb s'ensuivre . . . ," etc. After this he would nevertheless usually sign the answers prepared by his secretary without making him do them over, happy merely to have imposed a few minutes of daily humiliation on him.

One of Xavier's main duties was to file my uncle's notes in the folders contained in the green boxes, a process he had mastered thoroughly. Several times in the course of the morning, my uncle would summon him: "Monsieur de Balcourt, would you be so kind as to give me everything having to do with the disputes between Louis XIV and Innocent XI about *the matter of regalian rights* . . . Monsieur de Balcourt, we have, if I am not mistaken, notes somewhere concerning the influence of the French *philosophes* on the discussions of the deputies assembled by Catherine II during the *Grande Commission pour le Code,* correct? I would be obliged if you would find them for me." In general, Xavier gave prompt enough satisfaction to my uncle, who usually ran his eye so cursorily over the items his secretary brought him that I often wondered whether those complicated researches answered a real need on my uncle's part, or whether he didn't take a sadistic pleasure in checking up on Xavier's skill and the efficiency of his cataloguing. Frequently, too, my uncle would dispatch his secretary to Sainte-Geneviève or to the Bibliothèque Nationale to check some references or to take notes on a work he did not have at the rue de Fleurus. Xavier was sometimes gone for several days in a row, and during this interval my uncle got along so well without his services that I really had to ask myself whether this "secretary" was so very useful for my uncle's work, and whether he didn't simply find in him the opportunity to have a whipping boy continually within reach.

My aunt, on the other hand, was very sweet with Xavier. He had been her son's tutor, and everything that related to Guy's life (I experienced this myself) remained dear to her. Xavier had a photo of Guy in his office, and I never knew if it had been put there by him, as it seemed, since it stood, in a plush frame, on his table, or if it had been placed there by my aunt. There was a similar photo in the library, and another on the wall of my uncle's study. Xavier and I never spoke about Guy, at least during the first year of my stay. Was he embarrassed to talk about him in front of me? We spontaneously avoided this subject, along with everything connected to the memories of his time at le Saillant.

I was so close—relatively—with Xavier later on that I have trouble precisely recalling what the tone of our relations was at the beginning of my stay at the rue de Fleurus. It seems to me that our dealings, apparently cordial, were rather reserved and somewhat cool. I could no longer show him the deference of before, when I was a child and his pupil. I was seventeen, and he twenty-seven. In my uncle's house, we were the two "young men." There was also something uncomfortable about our respective positions. I was there as the son of the house, and he was Professor Chambost's secretary, the one to whom my aunt gave her letters to be mailed, the one my uncle sent to get a book from the library, the one of whom small, vaguely menial services were requested. He was nevertheless treated with a good deal of courtesy.

In the beginning, Xavier's attitude had surprised me somewhat, and displeased me. I perceived in his behavior a hint of servility. I had known him more independent and prouder at le Saillant. Less docile, less eager to please. As if he had undergone a certain decline when he moved from the rank of tutor to that of secretary. With my father, he affected a sort of polite restraint, which was not without style, and which I found attractive. With my uncle Chambost, he seemed to me to have relinquished some of his dignity.

He had excuses, to be sure. My uncle, under an exaggeratedly courteous exterior, never stopped humiliating him. Xavier suffered greatly from it. He needed respect, and all the more so since his duties were minor ones. His pride was continually wounded. My uncle had a way of showing him uncalled-for considerations, which offended him. I saw my uncle rush to pick up a page that Xavier had dropped on the carpet, and Xavier redden with confusion and mute resentment. I saw my uncle get up to retrieve a marker that had fallen out of a book which Xavier was leafing through, which was a way both of reproaching him for his clumsiness and of producing in Xavier a moment of confusion, and of thanks, and of excuses, which my terrible uncle seemed to relish inwardly.

At the very start of my time at the rue de Fleurus, I hazarded questioning Xavier about my uncle Chambost, as to precisely what I no longer recall: "You know my uncle well," I said, "how do you explain . . ."

He interrupted me: "I know M. Chambost very little; I know only what he lets everyone see: the least genuine part of himself."

And as I seemed surprised—since I actually was—Xavier smiled and said something like this, which made so great an impression on me that I have never forgotten it: "You know, every man has two very distinct and often contradictory lives: his social life, that is to say his life in front of others, with his family, in the world; and then his secret life, or to put it bluntly, his sexual life, about which no one around him generally has the slightest inkling; a life completely hidden and disguised, in which each of us lives his true character; a life totally apart from the public existence, and in which each of us has tastes, passions, habits, quirks, a way of behaving, even a face, even a vocabulary, absolutely different from the tastes and demeanor by which he is known. Well, then, remember this: You don't know a person until you've been able to penetrate this secret labyrinth. And that is very rare. So we truly know none of the people we are around, even those we're close to . . ."

If I have not forgotten this remark, it is because it had a profound impact on me. At the time, it left me stunned. But it made me think. It crystallized vague impressions, vague experiences in me. I quickly grew accustomed to what at first had seemed to me only a cynical paradox. The more I considered this point of view, the more I sensed its importance. I took stock of myself and had to admit, deep down inside, that as far as I was concerned, Xavier's observation proved to be cruelly accurate. Between the person I was to those around me—even to my best friends—and my real, secret self, whose past was freighted with the experiences of boarding school, who gave himself up, at night, to his lustful obsessions, there seemed to be no resemblance. In fact, I was forced to acknowledge that nobody knew me, since I was concealing from everyone the part of me that was most vigorous, most passionate. I understood, by the same token, that this duality was not peculiar to me, that all people have deep-seated areas which they carefully screen off from everyone, and that, behind the façade known to others, they harbor jealously guarded oubliettes where clandestine things go on, Bluebeard's chambers entered only by the occasional accomplice. And I already guessed that these secrets were not the same for each individual, that these faunae and florae of the depths were boundlessly varied, that everything was to be found among them, from pure feelings warily hidden out of a sense of modesty to the worst aberrations, which one would never dare reveal to anyone. No, I was not an exception. Everyone I knew, or almost, had his own hell, belonging to him alone.

From that day on, I possessed one truth more, and, as it were, one of the keys to the world.

But this remark struck me for another reason as well. I could not separate it from the person who had made it. Xavier suddenly appeared to me with his true face. I remembered all sorts of details of his stay at le Saillant, of his affection for Guy. In saying that to me, he had unwittingly unmasked himself. I scented mysteries in him. I was on the track of a discovery.

MY AUNT WAS outright friendly with Xavier. She would even often adopt a tone of special companionship with him, asking his advice about people, laughing with him over certain failings they had both observed in some guest of the day before, putting questions to him about a certain side of Parisian life with which she was not familiar, the *cafés-concerts,* the Opera balls, the theater gossip, the little scandals of the boulevards and of the artists' circles.

And Xavier was charming with her. Sweet in a way that was both affectionate and respectful but not overly solicitous; cheerful, amusing, helpful, trying always to make her happy, bringing her the first number of a new magazine that had just been published, pointing out the reviews that he knew might interest her, mentioning the exhibits to go and see, reporting the quips that were going the rounds of Montmartre or the boulevards. She twitted him about his quirks, about his unique sartorial style, with a gracious gaiety that he could not find wounding.

For he was rather oddly dressed, with a mixture of simplicity and pretension that was in very bad taste. Xavier was very concerned about his clothes. He wanted to deck himself out like a dandy. But his very restricted means forced him to outfit himself at mediocre tailors and prevented him from refurbishing his wardrobe. And as he could not bring himself to go unnoticed, to be dressed like just any employee or tutor, he put all of his effort into the accessories. He had an old badly cut jacket, trousers that were baggy at the knees, shirts of thick percale; but he compensated by wearing starched collars of a romantic style, with black satin cravats that wrapped around his neck three times and on which he pinned old family jewels, a costume brooch, or a paste brilliant. He spruced up his jacket by having light-colored piping sewn on it; he loved gaudy waistcoats of velvet, tapestry, or silk brocade cut from an old dress of his mother's; he drew attention to his tired old boots by wearing light-colored gaiters, and smartened up his lapel with a flower; he always had at least one ring on each hand. And as he could not afford to have his top hat attended to every morning, he would brush the silk, which had turned a little reddish, with a lightly-oiled rag which, at a distance, enhanced its luster and produced a great impression, but which, up close, made it look like a coachman's or an undertaker's beaver.

A strange lapse of taste in this otherwise refined and cultured man, whose literary judgment was that of a true artist. Yet even here, he had shortcomings. He liked Ronsard, and for the best reasons. But he also had a rather unpardonable weakness for certain "decadent" poets (as they were then beginning to be called). And even his penchant for the poets of the Pléiade revealed, if examined more closely, a certain patience with the mawkish, the precious, the showy appurtenance. I am not sure that the poems by Baudelaire that he preferred were really the best. But he liked Baudelaire and stood up for him with fervor and discernment; this, at the time, was proof enough of a genuine sense of poetry and beauty.

From the pains he took with his clothes, one could guess how much he suffered from being poor, slight, small (he always wore very high heels, which gave him a slightly jerky, theatrical gait). He also suffered on the intellectual side: he knew enough about genius to realize that he had none, and also to be inconsolable about it.

He was haunted by the fear of being a failure. He performed his duties as secretary conscientiously, which was commendable, since he was well aware that he was superior to them. Superior: enough to suffer from it, not enough to produce an oeuvre and gloriously escape from his menial tasks.

All of this remained mysterious to me for a long time, and it was only after his death that I understood his character. Very much of a piece and easy to decipher, really.

At the period when I met up with him again at the rue de Fleurus, he got on my nerves. I mainly noticed his pretensions, and they seemed to me uncalled for. At that time I had a taste for the serious, and a strictness in my thinking that made me harsh, unfair. I was somewhat surprised by Aunt Ma's indulgent friendship for Xavier. I understand it better today: my aunt had a sound intuition, and there was certainly much insight and a discreet hint of pity in her attitude with him. She did not judge him solely on appearances. I am certain that she guessed Balcourt's secret sufferings. She would not have clearly defined their nature, as I now can, but she sensed some painful and nobly borne enigma.

He was only twenty-seven, but one would not have known what number of years to assign to his face, which had noticeably aged, or, more precisely, had withered a good deal since his departure from le Saillant two years earlier. He had those Nordic looks, pale and blond, whose eternal youth gradually fades without getting old. This had happened: he had lost all freshness. His fine and colorless skin had gray shadows, especially around the eyes. His features were delicate, but as he had got a bit thinner his nose had become more prominent, making him look, in profile, something like a greyhound. He had always been a little hard of hearing in his right ear, which caused him to hold his head somewhat askew, tilted towards the right shoulder. All in all, he was not without charm, thanks to his clear and light blue eyes and the sensual expression of his wide-cut, thin-lipped mouth, whose slightly disdainful smile remained very boyish. Thanks also to his voice, strangely warm and rich, vibrant like the sound of a stringed instrument.

He came from a very good family. But since the unfortunate matter in which his father had been involved—I never really knew the details; the scandal had not, however, had any legal consequences, because his father committed suicide—his mother had withdrawn from all family relations and no longer appeared among the Faubourg Saint-Germain set to which she had once belonged. I think that they must have had a few very lonely years until Xavier formed other connections. When I knew them, they went out a lot, saw many people, but in a circle absolutely different from that into which they had been born: a circle of young artists, intellectuals, painters from Montmartre, theater folk, cabaret singers—the public of the little avant-garde exhibitions. Parties were given often and very simply, in the evening after dinner, in modest little apartments, bachelor flats, artists' studios. All these people were poor, or even needy, and were obsessed with a concern to push themselves forward, to become recognized, in order to sell some canvases, to do some portraits, to place a poem or an article in some newspaper or magazine, to find some lessons to give, etc. Those evenings had a practical intent. People took turns performing. The musicians, the virtuosos, the cabaret singers, the poets, were given a hearing. The hostesses strove to attract some potentially useful celebrities—the head of a theater or a newspaper, a publisher, a patron of the arts—who were seated in the front row and to whom everyone paid court. Everyone's goal was the same: to get ahead in the world, turn his little talent to account, make ends meet . . . They helped one another, with the understanding that the favor would be repaid, and all the while running each other down on the sly.

I was introduced by the Balcourts to these circles during my first year in Paris. I could not be of much service to them, but I was the nephew of Professor Chambost, whose academic receptions were famous. And besides, I was harmless, I wasn't competition.

That is why I was invited by Xavier to his mother's "fortnightlies."

Mme. de Balcourt and her son lived on the noisy rue des Martyrs, in an exceptionally quiet little entresol at the rear of a courtyard, at the top of the street, not far from what were then called "the outer boulevards." Two bedrooms and a "drawing room," with a tiny anteroom where the hats and overcoats were piled up, and a little kitchen three meters square, from which, toward midnight, a few carafes of cold tea lightly laced with rum were extracted, along with a few plates of dry little cookies that left a taste of sand and dust in the mouth. I scarcely exaggerate when I say that I could have touched the ceiling with my hand if I had stood slightly on tiptoe. The three rooms were adjoining. The last one, which was Xavier's, was locked. I suppose that on the nights when they entertained, they crammed into it everything that was not supposed to be seen. The guests, of whom there were often about forty, used Mme. de Balcourt's bedroom and the drawing room. This made for precious little space in which to stand, since the rooms were small and abundantly furnished, the Balcourts having stuffed them with everything that remained of their former prosperity: upholstered armchairs, mahogany commodes, mirrored wardrobes, gilded consoles, showcases in which antique fans stood side by side with lengths of lace, scent-bottles, Venetian glassware, Sèvres porcelains, white and gold Empire cups, and ancestral decorations on squares of crimson velvet. In the drawing room, the parlor grand piano took up an unseemly amount of space. On the walls, daguerreotypes and a few beautiful old portraits. The lighting was provided, after a fashion, by the two bronze standard lamps with globes and small chains, which stood on the mantelpiece and were lit by gas. Two or three oil lamps were placed about on the consoles. The odor of burning gas and cigars was quite formidable after the first hour of the gathering.

Mme. de Balcourt entertained with a remarkable skill, which would have been worthy of a more sumptuous setting. She was like a spider whose web had suddenly been invaded by a swarm of gnats. She slipped from one corner to the other, through the groups, introducing the newcomers, and not haphazardly but always in the way most advantageous to them. She had her eye on everything, a word of overblown praise for everyone; nothing escaped her, one felt that her brain never stopped working. The evening had to give each guest the maximum in value, or at least in hope. She hatched her schemes, helped the timid to shine, heaped encomiums upon the vain, spoke to each of his talent, to the painters of their latest canvases, to the journalists of their latest articles, to the poets of their latest poems. Then, when she had her crowd well kneaded and the hubbub was going strong, she would ask, with a mysterious smile, for a bit of quiet, and the presentations would begin: the musicians sat down at the piano to give their latest melody an airing, the singers premiered some unpublished song, the poets, in front of the little Chonbarsky stove that scorched the skirts of their frock coats, recited their verses. She introduced everyone as an exceptional phenomenon, and always found, in the embarrassed silence which followed each piece, some ponderous compliments to lay on the performer, prompting the crowd's indulgent applause. For everything was applauded indiscriminately, with good grace; in this way, each bought the bravos that he was counting on for himself when his own turn came.

These receptions took place twice a month, on the first and the fifteenth; I did not immediately grasp the useful purpose they served for the Balcourts. For a long time I lived with the idea that Mme. de Balcourt was an excellent person, compulsively obliging, whose whole pleasure, after a trying life, was to assemble the largest possible crowd around her so as to give her son's friends a chance to win recognition and earn a little money. I also told myself that this society lady, who had had a fairly brilliant past and been forced to live for several years in solitude and humiliation, found in this something of a compensation for her destiny, and enjoyed playing, in that world of semi-failures, the social role that she could no longer assume in the circle from which she came. This opinion seemed all the more justified since the kindness, the good-naturedness, the affability towards everyone, and even that admiration which she lavished on the most mediocre, were, quite obviously, natural and sincere.

I gradually discovered that the principal goal of this tireless activity, and its principal achievement, was to serve Xavier, to create a network of useful connections for him, to give him importance, to provide him with chances to become known; and that Mme. de Balcourt's true motive was a blind and boundless maternal love. Without those receptions, without that constant touting, Xavier would have been deprived of those little satisfactions of self-esteem which kept alive his hope of becoming someone and of making a place for himself among what Mme. de Balcourt ingenuously called "the elites." This art dealer or that gallery director, whom Mme. de Balcourt had managed to lure to her house to meet a woman painter or an American lady who did watercolors, and to organize an exhibit, agreed at the same time to entrust Xavier with the task of writing a few pages as a preface to a catalogue or to assign him several articles of criticism in the magazine he ran. An editor of some journal or rag, who had come to drink a glass of punch at the rue des Martyrs and had let himself be treated as an important man in front of that audience of losers, would not refuse to let Xavier write his "Monthly Column" or to commission from him a study of some literary question of the moment. It was thanks to his mother that Xavier sold his little efforts; it was she, through her subtle acts of thoughtfulness, her unflagging helpfulness, who opened for him the back doors to the minor publications, the literary coteries, the new publishing houses. I scratch your back and you scratch mine . . .

And thus, with the best of intentions, she rendered him a terrible and dangerous disservice. He frittered himself away in modest, poorly paid endeavors which gave him the illusion of getting ahead and which, in reality, prevented him from tackling anything that was worthy of him. For he was infinitely superior to those middling projects. I remain convinced that Xavier de Balcourt had exceptional gifts and that he could have risen to the highest level, not just as a critic but perhaps also as a novelist. His conversation, on certain days, was scintillating, full of fresh perceptions, unexpected parallels, invention, boldness, perspicacity, proficiency. His cultivation was real and vast. He had personal views on contemporary literature, fed by his thorough knowledge of the classical authors, the ancients, the Greek tragedians, foreign literatures. His taste was very sure, and he admired only the best. In contemporary writing, he immediately recognized the true talents, without letting himself be influenced by what was currently in fashion. He could have had a major influence on the taste of his time. I found in his papers, after his death, notes on Diderot and an unfinished essay on the Encyclopedists; a long piece on Locke; another, dashed off at one go, on Hobbes. Each of those slim folders could have been the starting point for an excellent work of criticism. He had been among the first to understand the genius of Stendhal; and everything that he said about him, well before Bourget's studies, would have formed the material for a book absolutely original in that era, and which might have had a considerable impact.

I may be the only one to know that he had the makings of a novelist in him. Perhaps he only lacked enough confidence in himself, and the nerve to get down to it. The two unfinished short stories, left in the state of notes, which I found in his drawers—and which helped me to lift a corner of the veil under which he proudly and painfully hid the dubious secret of his private life—testify not only to an acute and very personal psychological judgment but also to a gift for storytelling, for portraying characters, for measuring out suspense, for creating life through fiction, that was altogether remarkable. The disappearance of those notes, along with most of his papers, causes me a keen regret. I plan some day to write down the rather precise memories that I still have of them.

LITTLE BY LITTLE, we became close during those years. At the beginning of my stay in Paris, our relations were hesitant, and, in fact, rather false. It took some time for us both to forget that I had been his pupil and he my tutor, and for the distance that the ten-year age difference created between us gradually to be erased. To truly become friends, there was still a threshold to be crossed, and that did not happen right away. I remained the former pupil, the junior, a new arrival to Parisian life and the student life of the Latin Quarter, who needed information, warnings, advice. He enjoyed this role of mentor, which flattered his self-esteem. And I, foolishly enough, did my best to appear less at sea than I was, avoided asking him for guidance, or decided to do so only when I had no alternative. I wanted to fly with my own wings and was annoyed by the knowing, slightly superior tone he took with me. But at the end of a few months these little causes of friction disappeared by themselves as I settled into my new existence and felt more self-assured in it. I must also say that our friendship found a common ground in the collaboration of sorts that grew up between us in regard to my uncle Chambost. I helped him to sidestep the traps that my uncle constantly set to catch him out. The nitpicking and overly polite tyranny that my uncle exerted over his secretary exasperated me. Xavier soon realized that in the tacit daily conflict, I was on his side, without, however, getting involved. We spoke freely about my uncle and his insufferable faults. In his presence, a look exchanged between us sufficed to make us accomplices, and these glances did much for the birth of our friendship.

I really had a great and loyal affection for Xavier de Balcourt, and his death, in 1888, by depriving me of a closeness which was very dear to me, caused me deep pain, quite apart from the dramatic and rather mysterious circumstances which surrounded that suicide. I reproached myself strongly at the time. When someone we love reaches such a degree of lonely despair that it leaves him no way out but death, we inevitably imagine that a more forthcoming, more vigilant affection might have averted the fatal act. With hindsight, I see nothing to blame myself for. Balcourt had arrived at a point at which no amount of friendship could have reconciled him with life or with himself. I shall tell that story, with all its details, in due time.

I WANT to try to delineate Xavier's character a bit more precisely, to describe him as he was before his mother's death. What had attracted me to him from the very beginning was the special quality of his intelligence, that natural way he had, in conversation, of invariably going to the heart of the question, of delicately cutting through extraneous matter and appearances to get to the root of a problem, and of having, almost always, a personal, profoundly original way of thinking. This originality was all the more remarkable in that he was very well educated, had an excellent memory, and might have dispensed with thinking for himself and remained content with making the opinions of others his own. Which is what is done by so many intellectuals whose knowledge is vast and constitutes practically their entire worth. In Xavier, substance and style were always unexpected and piquant. No pedantry. He made no display of his learning, even with me, whom he might easily have dazzled.

So little did he do so that I did not immediately realize the importance of his intellectual attainments, and, fooled by the glibly witty turn he gave to this thinking, I imagined for some time that he was mainly a quick and somewhat superficial improviser.

I did not always like his personality. I was harsh, as people are who have never come up against any serious difficulty. He was capable of flattery, even of a certain momentary obsequiousness with those who could do something for him. I wish I had had no reason for suspecting the deferential gestures he lavished on famous men, on people in high places, but I could not avoid seeing self-interested behavior.

Poor Xavier! I understand him better today, and I pardon him. He was aware of his worth, and he was ambitious in the best sense of the word. Lacking wealth, carrying inside him the shame of bearing a name his father had disgraced, needing to support himself and his mother, wanting to achieve the position that his merits and the quality of his mind deserved, how could he have appeared as detached, as independent, as I would have liked? He could easily be forgiven for humoring the powerful, seeking out profitable connections, or pushing himself up in the world through self-seeking moves. I loathed what I called *in petto* his social-climbing, opportunistic side. I would have preferred to see him more uncompromising and prouder. Proud he was: insofar as he nursed a secret grudge against the maneuvers that necessity forced him to employ. He got his own back with an insolence that was scathing but prudently disguised and with a judicious contempt for men in general. But he concealed this contempt and his bitterness as he did his inner arrogance.

If he had been a man of means, he would have pursued his literary projects, would probably have become an esteemed critic, an "essayist" as we say today, or—who knows?—a famous novelist. Poor, he had to keep afloat no matter what. In such a case, courage and good sense dictate that people find a profession with which to make a living, but a profession completely divorced from their intellectual life, so that they make a clean division in their existence: keeping for their intellectual exercise and production the leisure time stolen from their remunerative labor, in such a way as to be independent writers and to maintain the integrity of their thought and talent. But, like many others, Xavier had neither the courage nor the good sense to do this. He was willing to cash in on his talent. Since he needed to work to survive, he began to chase after intellectual jobs, to practice journalism, to support himself with his pen. He had been a tutor at le Saillant. He had done research in archives and libraries for pundits, had written pieces that others paid him for and signed in his place. He had become a secretary for the Chambost-Lévadés. He hung about newspaper offices, obtained an assignment here or there for which he received several francs a line and in which he had to express someone else's opinions, flogging their political program or furthering their schemes. He agreed to doctor comic-opera librettos and compose songs for well-known cabaret singers who gave him three hundred francs for verses he did not sign and from which they made a small fortune. He wrote prefaces for art dealers' catalogues. I found in his papers rough copies of pharmaceutical prospectuses, financial articles . . . He got into the habit of dashing things off helter-skelter, without correcting them, without even reading them over. His facility saw him through. But by playing this game he debased his talent, strayed farther and farther from the ideal of his youth. He had told himself for many years: "If I could make a little name for myself as a journalist and find a steady, well-paid and not too demanding job

with a good salary, I could finally devote myself to endeavors worthy of me."
But all of his undistinguished and accommodating projects led him increasingly away from those endeavors, which he never could make up his mind to tackle.

All the same, he had in him a very noble ideal, and deep reserves of truly selfless generosity. He probably never abandoned this, and I saw him desperate over the trap in which he had got caught. He needed to make a living, pay the rent for the rue des Martyrs, and hide his poverty.

What drew me to him was this wretchedness from which he suffered. Too weak to be a hero.

I am rereading what I have written. Xavier was far superior to the portrait I have just sketched. And yet I have made no inaccurate statements; I have not exaggerated his failings and flaws or glossed over his good qualities. How hard it is to be fair and to catch the likeness . . . All the features are very much Xavier's, and yet the likeness is not there.

In depicting him as I have (and indeed as he was)—badly dressed and pretentious in his cheap-looking getup; intelligent; industrious; educated but without that secret strength which makes creators; scorning the powerful but carefully shining up to them; capable of rendering services with his own interests in mind, as grasping as if he were destitute; envious of others' talent and above all of their fame and success; severe in his judgments but covering up the opinions that might have worked against him; a party to the social ploys of the conniving Mme. de Balcourt; lending himself to all the chores of a hack, to all the dishonest compromises of low journalism, but faithful, at heart, to the noble conception of a man of letters that lay behind his sternness, his indignation, his rebellions, and maintaining, despite his weaknesses, a scale of genuine values—I have here drawn the portrait of a mediocrity, a commonplace failure. And he was the complete opposite of that! I swear it, and I am not blinded by friendship, or by the pity I feel for that botched destiny. If he had really been as I described him, would he have been looked up to and sought after by all those in his generation who had real worth? Would he have been liked and consulted by that little intellectual elite composed of the best artists who at that time were beginning to establish themselves and who, to a man, have left behind a name and justly renowned works? Would he have been among the close friends of young writers like Paul Bourget, René Boylesve; of young painters like Signac, Toulouse-Lautrec, Degas; of young musicians like Debussy; of young doctors like Babinsky, Georges Dumas, Pierre Janet?

I mention here only the names of men I met several times in the little entresol of the rue des Martyrs, at Mama Balcourt's fortnightlies. Their presence was enough to raise the level of those gatherings. Of course, they were not regular visitors for the most part, and one felt from various signs that they had come out of friendship for Xavier rather than for their own enjoyment. But they had come, and they demonstrated a cordiality that was full of goodwill. Yet it was not to them that Mme. de Balcourt was the most attentive. They were all young and still unknown. They stood in the window recesses and good-naturedly endured the performance by the Hungarian virtuosa or the recitation by the "decadent" poet who was billed as the evening's main attraction. But they did not treat Xavier as if he were a failure. They would scarcely have been surprised if they had been told that Xavier had a fine career as a writer before him, and they attached more importance to his good qualities and the subtlety of his intelligence than to his faults.

There must have been more to Xavier than I have been able to convey for all those gifted men to have respected him, enjoyed seeing him, trusted his judgment; and, on the other side, for Xavier to have chosen so discerningly among the young men his age and sought out the friendship of those whose importance the future would ratify. He did not let himself be taken in by false values, by false promises of talent. His very sure taste is already the mark of a personal gift. In those young coteries, he felt himself among peers and was received as such. I cannot find a better corrective for the deficiencies of my portrait.

GIVEN HIS PERSONALITY (and sometimes, with his bright-colored spats, his motley waistcoats, his loud cravats, he was as absurdly, as comically ridiculous as if he had stepped out of a novel by Dickens), Xavier was at once insufferable and endearing. Insufferable like all unbalanced people; and endearing due to his undeniable basic virtues, a loving and unhappy heart, and a certain charm that I cannot put into words because I cannot define it.

Full of contradictions.

This person who was social to the point of snobbism was also a misanthrope. A natural and genuine misanthropy that the trials of his youth, the misfortunes of his family, had made still worse. This misanthropy came out again and again in private. He criticized everything and everyone. And indeed, in such a subtle, intelligent, always apt way, without ever lapsing into inaccuracy or unfairness, that you really were forced to go along with him even if you disapproved of his excessive severity. Still, the very unpleasant aspect of this severity was that you sensed an uncontrollable desire in him to disparage everyone in order to exalt himself; to exalt himself not so much in the eyes of the listener as in his own eyes. Which revealed a suffering, a secret anxiety, for which I had tolerance and compassion.

Certainly he felt that he was a man apart. In fact, when he was among those he trusted, without other witnesses, he let this show openly. So openly that it was sometimes quite annoying, and you wanted to tell him that he was exaggerating, that he was less special than he thought. The awareness of his peculiarity was obviously a source of pride to him. It never crossed his mind that this deviation from the norm might be the cause of his difficulties and disappointments. He preferred to make the world, society, responsible for his problems. (For example, he admitted that his homosexual tendencies created an abnormal life situation for him; but it never occurred to him to regret being that way; he was not the one who was wrong in opposing common moral standards; he did not hesitate to accuse society, which was obviously out of joint since it placed obstacles in the way of his freedom and forced him to conceal his inclinations.) Never did I hear him consider that he ought to be other than he was or act differently: if society hampered him, he concluded unquestioningly that society needed to be reformed.

He was thus constantly in revolt against everything: men, institutions. And it was a strange contradiction to see this perpetual rebellion in a man who never sought solitude, who never ceased to mingle with that society which he deplored, who led an existence the opposite of that of misanthropes and malcontents, an entirely outward, determinedly social existence. In this, he was his mother's very willing accomplice and could imagine no other way to succeed than by securing the most extensive contacts. This rebel constantly pursued the world; he sought it out and could not accept it as it was; he was taken with society yet could not adapt to it. This impossibility of acclimation was not the least cause of his pessimism, and also kept his rebelliousness alive.

I would not hesitate today to place Balcourt in the category of *waverers*. It is a judgment that I did not pass on him at the time I knew him. I was under his influence, and I let myself be convinced that his repeated setbacks were not due to any personal reason, and that, actually, it was circumstances, lack of money, the difficult conditions of his life that always hindered his intentions and regularly prevented all his fine plans from coming off. But I was wrong. He was really a waverer by temperament and he was primarily to blame for his constant failures. I recall several cases in which I saw him reverse himself for no good reason by suddenly abandoning a project that was being carried out and that might have succeeded; I also saw him, at the time of an important decision, make an abrupt about-face that nothing justified, and do exactly the opposite of what he had wished and prepared for.

What explains my error, even more than my friendly credulity, is the kind of genius that he had in these cases for making arguments—in good faith, I think—and presenting the event in such a way that you were not able to disagree with him.

Not only did he refuse to acknowledge the setback to his project—which he might have, without admitting his guilt, by putting the blame on others or on bad luck—but, on the contrary, he proved beyond a doubt that what he had done, which was precisely the opposite of what he had previously claimed to want to do, was very carefully thought out and preferable to any other solution. In acting this way, I think he was mainly giving in to his pride. He deceived himself in order to have a better opinion of himself.

When he had gone off on a tangent and acted contrary to the plan he had devised, when the setback was blatant and irreparable, he had a diabolical ingenuity for explaining away what had happened, for showing himself to be the victim, and, finally, for extracting from those unfortunate circumstances the maximum of self-justification and self-esteem. Pride, always pride. I have never seen anyone put such skill into coming up with excellent excuses for his worst blunders, for his most glaring weaknesses, and even for his little acts of moral cowardice. And here again, I was not the one he wanted to mislead. He was sincere, and his specious reasoning was entirely aimed at deluding himself.

I AM EAGER to get to the question which, for me, is the central one, the one that provides the key to that unhappy existence, and that, to my mind, sheds light on everything which in Xavier's life, death, and character would otherwise remain forever obscure: the question of morals, the sexual question.

Today I have some difficulty understanding why it should have taken me so long to discover Xavier's secret. It required chance circumstances to open my eyes; it even required reluctant confidences on Xavier's part to make me certain that my suspicions were well-founded. This surprises me. I had every reason in the world to be on the right track: I had only to remember Xavier's attitude at le Saillant and to recall the markedly dubious nature of his affection for my cousin Guy Chambost. But these memories remained dormant in me, in a strange fogginess which I made no effort to dispel. With hindsight, all this seems quite simple to me, its clarity obvious. It was not so when I met up again with Xavier in Paris and struck up a friendship with him. All the same, the stirrings of my own sexuality, and the sensual licentiousness of my life as a schoolboy, ought to have made me more perceptive. I had specific experiences in my own past that should have enlightened me. As odd, as unlikely even, as it may seem, nothing of the sort took place. In fact, I think I had forgotten those personal experiences. I must never have thought about them. Or, if I ever did happen to think about them, they seemed to me like the childish acts of a boarding-school boy, without consequence or sequel, with no deep connection to me, to the young university student I had become; they were simple lapses of behavior that were part of my completely bygone, outgrown schooldays, in the same category as certain rumpuses, certain periods of sloth, certain skipped classes, certain cigarettes smoked on the sly, etc. A boy's pranks.

Yet I had not given up my bad habits, and periodically my nights were haunted by erotic fantasies and solitary debauches. But for at least two years these lubricious imaginings had quite naturally taken on a wholly heterosexual character, and the naked bodies that filled my visions were solely female.

It is difficult, from this distance, to grasp all this with exactitude. I am trying to remember. It seems to me that at that time—the time when I was beginning my studies at the Sorbonne—I had no notion of the role that homosexuality plays in society. The games of two boys seemed to me a stopgap due to the absence of the female sex, and understandable as a result of puberty's awakening in the close quarters of a boarding school. I really don't think I am exaggerating when I say that I did not imagine that those games could continue among adults, or that a grown man, living in the world and able to have affairs with women, would, out of personal taste, go looking for other men. This may not have been so clear in my mind as I am writing it here. But that is roughly how it was. And in any case—of this I am certain—I had no idea what homosexual *love* was. I mean I was not aware that relations between men could be anything but a joint exercise in onanism as I had experienced it at Saint-Léonard; nor had I ever thought that such relations could partake of amorous passion, exactly like the love of a heterosexual couple. Such was my naïveté as a "precocious" and "vice-ridden" boy . . .

The fact remains that for many months I developed an increasingly friendly and close relationship with Xavier without becoming aware of his private life and without attributing a sexual cause to the oddities of his nature. Especially since I saw him being very solicitous with the young ladies who came to the rue des Martyrs. I even envied his ease, that cheerful rapport shaded with a hint of tenderness in his smile and his gaze, which was obviously attractive to women. I even suspected him of several affairs with the woman artists to whom he appeared particularly considerate; with whom he had animated private conversations in an undertone near the piano, revealing a suddenly serious air, a flash of the eyes, an insistency in the smile, a look of covert accord and intimacy. His shortness, his manners that were at once brusque and gentle, the warmth of his voice, gave him the appearance of a cherub grown old in the company of women. I knew that he had a few friendships with women; I had several times met him at the theater or at a concert with young ladies, actresses, musicians, whom I had seen at the rue des Martyrs and whom he called familiarly by the diminutives of their names. In the small volume of free verse that he had managed to have published by Lemerre, a collection some thirty pages long, in Elzevir type, on glossy paper, bearing the discreetly melancholy title of *Nostalgies,* most of the poems were dedicated to women: a first name followed by a mysterious initial. How could I have suspected any trickery in that? Who could guess, apart from those involved, that those first names of women were, most often, the deliberately feminized first names of men, and that this *Jeanne S.,* this *Paule R.,* this *Georgette B.,* were young male friends. I discovered this only after Xavier's death, by finding in his papers an early draft of that booklet in which he had not taken the trouble to camouflage the first names; a draft that contained a few erotic poems as well, which I permitted myself to destroy without a scruple, since they were more revealing than successful.

BUT XAVIER had left behind much more serious confessions: in a diary, which he had kept during a period of service in the army, he told how his passion for a boy in the village where he was staying had ended in the most tragic way. Now that all the witnesses to that drama have disappeared, I see no reason not to reproduce this pathetic story which shook me and disclosed to me the secret of Xavier's suicide.

CHAPTER XIII

The Drowning

PART ONE

Saturday 7 July 1888.

Arrived this morning around 11 o'clock—the whole company, without one straggler—at Aunay-sur-Marne, after a final stretch of eighteen kilometers. (Blister on my right heel. Done in.)

It was the Tonkinese* who had taken command of this strange company of eighty noncoms in field dress, and our entrance into the village caused a sensation. The lieutenant had left on horseback before daybreak to arrange the billet. He was waiting for us in front of the town hall. He'd kept his word: we were all quartered with the citizenry. He had emphasized to the town council that we were no rank privates but rather a special platoon of future reserve officers, come for ten days of instruction and training; and he got eighty individual billeting orders out of them. Before giving the command to fall out, he announced a schedule: every morning, assembly at 5:25 in front

*I.e., a veteran of service in Indochina.

of the church; field exercises till 10 or 11; time off till 3 in the afternoon for lunch and a nap; from 3 to 5, classes in the meeting-room at the town hall. As for meals, four messes—one per section—in each of the four main local cafés.

In short, everything bodes well: a lot more spare time than in the barracks at Châlons!

I'm jotting this down while waiting for lunch at my section's mess, which is set up at the Trois Écus; as luck would have it, the Trois Écus café is three minutes from my house. An odd house, to which the accident of a curious encounter led me . . . But I'll put all that down later.

8 July.

This morning, first field exercise—cut short because it's Sunday. And no class this afternoon. "Off duty," as the Tonkinese says.

I've fled my comrades, who are smoking and playing cards at the local inns, and have come out here to the bank of the river with *L'Immortel,* the Daudet that was just published and that I had the pleasant surprise of spotting yesterday in the window of the foremost stationers-cum-milliners of Aunay. But first I want to use this day of rest and freedom to bring my diary up to date: a pleasant way of reliving the emotions of these last twenty-four hours . . .

The spot is deserted, and as fine as one could wish. The Marne is navigable, I believe, only after Épernay. So no canal-boat ventures along here. Nor any hikers, it seems. The river, it's true, is a good kilometer from the town, and the road that brings you here is fully exposed to the sun, treeless, wind-blown, and dusty; it skirts hideous building plots, a few swampy fields where one sees neither man nor beast; and it finally ends at the Marne, crossing it by way of a brand-new brick bridge, which is stuck there like an intruder—and which, I'm afraid, will never quite manage to blend in with the countryside. Aside from three small children with their pants rolled up who were splashing about in the water at the foot of the bridge under the supervision of an old grandfather dozing stretched out by his fishing rod, I didn't see a living soul. I took the footpath that runs along the bank, and here I am ensconced on a bed of moss, my back propped against the trunk of a poplar. The water is flowing two meters below me, cool, green, and deep, and the current that sets it gently throbbing makes it alive. Overhead my poplar throbs as well and murmurs in the breeze; I am quite content. I'm going to be able to spend the day here with no risk of being disturbed and to write down everything that's on my mind.

Is Aunay going to be the site of a wonderful adventure for me?

I'd noticed him yesterday, as soon as we arrived in the square. The assembly in front of the town hall of our four sections of NCO's, when the lieutenant and the Tonkinese handed us our billeting orders, had attracted a small gathering of busybodies, worn-out old winegrowers, and the whole gang of village brats. He was practically the only youngster his age. I'd taken him at first for a plasterer's apprentice because of the white dust that covered his clothes, his bare arms, his mop of hair, and even his face.

Dressed in large canvas pants and a short-sleeved knitted jersey with blue-and-white stripes, he was somewhat off to one side, sitting on the edge of the fountain with his legs crossed, his bare feet in espadrilles, his torso tilted backwards, leaning on one hand, which made his thin shoulder stick out through a rip in the jersey. Immobilized as I was in the ranks, ten meters away from him, I observed him at leisure. He wasn't smiling, but his ferreting eye, which missed nothing of the show, sparkled with pleasure, while a sort of natural mirth, of mischief held in check, played at the corners of his lips.

As soon as we fell out, I took advantage of the platoon's scattering to go over to the fountain with my eyes lowered on my billeting order and a worried, hesitant look. Two steps away from him—he hadn't moved—I looked up. Our eyes met. Mine were questioning:

"The widow Dumesnil, rue des Reservoirs. Whereabouts is that?"

His face immediately brightened as he uncrossed his legs and sat up straight.

"Old mother Dumesnil?"

"Yes, I'm billeted with her."

"No." He laughed rather strangely. I moved closer.

"You don't believe me? Look, if you can read."

Amused, he briskly took the paper that I held out to him and deciphered in an undertone:

"Ser-geant-de-Bal-court . . ." He lifted his flour-dusted face toward me. The rims of his eyes, which had remained a dark pink, set off the laughing twinkle in his irises. "That's you, Sergeant Balcourt?"

"Yes."

"How come they put you with that old lady?"

"I have no idea. Is it far from here?"

"Pretty far . . . It's behind the Reservoirs . . . And besides . . ." (He shrugged cheerfully.) "She may not let you in. She's always in bed . . ."

He had nonchalantly let himself slide off the curbstone and was standing before me.

"You want to go there?"

"Really, I'd rather not, if it's as far away as you say . . . Can you point me to a decent bunk somewhere closer?"

"A what?"

"A room . . . A vacant room."

As he thought this over, his Pierrot's face suddenly took on a seriousness and even a sort of melancholy that were surprising. He answered, slowly:

"We've got one at our house, a room, except . . ."

"Except, what?"

"The owners won't want to."

I was now absolutely determined to try my luck.

"What do you know about it? And if I offered to *rent* this room for a few days?"

"Ah, if you're going to rent it . . . Listen, you can always try and see . . ."

He seemed so happy to have found a role to play, so happy to be of service:

"Come on, it's not far: up there, past the bend."

I settled the pack on my back again, the gun on its strap, and off we went side by side; I, loaded down like a private on maneuvers, dragging my clod-hoppers over the old cobblestones of the square; he, arms hanging loosely, back supple, light on his rope soles, which gave him the silent tread of a cat, adding even more to the gangling grace of his walk.

"And what does your boss do?"

"My boss is M'sieu Deuillot."

How could anyone be unaware of M. Deuillot's profession? Not pressing the point, I changed the subject:

"Do you have your family in Aunay?"

"Me? No . . ."

This "no" pleased me. And what followed as well.

"Where do you live, then? With your boss?"

"Yes."

"Yes," "no": he wasn't talkative. From timidity, maybe; not from suspicion, at any rate. He smiled so sweetly, turning his face towards me . . .

"Where are you from?"

He contented himself with an evasive answer:

"Before, I was apprenticed near Épernay."

"And what's your name?"

"Yves."

"Yves what?"

"Yves Janvier."

"How old? Nineteen? Eighteen?"

"Seventeen and a half."

"And how come you're not at your job at this time of day?"

"Mornings we're always done early."

We'd entered a little side alley that came out into a wide street, or rather roadway, lined with houses and shops. When we arrived a short distance from an old white building, slightly set back, newly stuccoed, whose carriage door was half open, he stopped:

"It's over there. Work it out with them . . ."

Obviously, he didn't care to introduce me to his boss. I said "Thanks" and put my hand in my pocket, as a Parisian used to tipping. Seeing the movement, he guessed my intent and took a step back. In the embarrassed look that he gave me, then immediately averted, I thought I read a little wounded pride, a little reproach, a little temptation also, perhaps . . . He now seemed in a hurry to go. I took my hand out of my pocket.

"We'll be seeing each other, I hope, *mon petit*?"

He smiled with a quick nod of agreement so spontaneous, so friendly, that I was staggered by a mad hope . . . Then he turned on his heels. I was heading for the white house when he caught up to me in a couple of bounds to whisper in my ear:

"Go in through the front door, but don't turn left into the shop: the mistress will say no . . . Talk with the old man first, in the storeroom, to the right."

Was he so set on my lodging there? Or rather was it simply that he wished to see a move he'd sponsored succeed?

Under the arch, to the left, I did indeed see the window of a shop: a bakery, though there wasn't any sign. My plasterer's apprentice was a baker's boy . . . On the right, in a sort of shed whose door was open, an old man with a goatee was weighing flour. Churlish and deaf, this geezer. He began by flatly refusing. But I gave him to believe that there was a risk of the room's being requisitioned by an officer, and he'd be better off renting it to me. I offered forty sous a day and to pay ten days up front. I took a louis out of my pocket. The gold coin decided him.

My "room" is no more than a garret under the roof, barely furnished. It smells of flour dust; you suffocate there. What's more, it's a passageway: it's at the head of the stairs and commands the entrance to the attic. Never mind: I've gained a foothold! From my window I can see everything that goes on in the courtyard and in the bakehouse, situated on the ground floor of the building across the way. I've achieved my ends. I was afraid the old man might change his mind, and to take possession of my new home I left my equipment there before going off to have lunch at the mess in the Trois Écus.

As soon as I'd gulped down my meal, I went back to the bakery. It must have been one o'clock. The Deuillots' kitchen was just under my room. I had to go past it to get to the stairway. The window was open. They were still at table. Silent. I recognized the blond mop. He had his back turned to me.

A quarter of an hour later (I had swapped my boots for slippers and was stretched out on the bed), there was a knock on my door. It was he, with his sly, pretty smile and his light tightrope-walker's step.

"Am I disturbing you?"

"Not at all, *mon petit*. Come in!"

What was he up to? Heart pounding, I sat on the edge of the mattress and looked at him, smiling like him, shy like him.

"You see, I'm having a little rest . . . It was a long haul."

He had wiped his face; he looked less like a Pierrot. I saw in better detail the particularities of his features, the thin and straight line of his eyebrows, the long slits of his eyelids, between which sparkled a remarkably blue gaze, the little urchin's nose, the line of the mouth, thin and long and straight, paralleling the line of the eyebrows . . . How to describe in words the mysterious charm of that face, its oddity, its childish bloom beneath the maturity of adolescence?

"So, soldiers get Saturdays off?"

"Yes, and every afternoon until three. And you?"

"Oh, we work nights and mornings. We sleep in the afternoon."

He had gone past the window and was near the door to the loft.

"So where are you going, in there?"

"Goin' to get some sleep . . . till five."

"In the loft?"

"No, in our room, over there."

He pointed toward the window, and indicated, on the other side of the courtyard, the wing across the way, the bakehouse building, where two windows set into the roof stood opposite mine.

" 'S'only one staircase, I always got to come through here, it's a pain for you . . . 'specially at night, when we'll be goin' down to make the bread . . ."

He had opened the door, he pushed it wider; he turned his head to add, sweetly:

"Don't worry, we'll be quiet, so's not to wake you up too much . . ."

I'd leapt up from the bed to follow him:

"Show me what it's like in there."

He looked at me, laughing:

"Why, it's like any other loft, of course!"

"Show me."

We entered a huge loft all white with dust, filled with heaped-up sacks, and well lighted by a wide opening that gaped onto the street. To stretch out the visit, I pretended to be surprised, I asked questions. He, too, seemed to take pleasure in this chitchat. He explained to me how the sacks were hoisted by means of a pulley hung from a cross-bar fastened to the façade above the opening. Since this window was flush with the floor, without a guardrail, I put my hand on his shoulder to lean outside, and I took my time in this position while inspecting the view, the roofs, the slopes planted with vineyards on the horizon. I can still feel, when I think about it, the warmth of his skin through the rip in his jersey . . . I didn't dare move my hand too much. While chatting, I nevertheless made bold to graze, with the tips of my fingers, his little bird's neck, which was mainly bare. And as he remained impassive, I gently placed my palm on the nape of the neck. He looked up and smiled at me. Nothing equivocal in that smile, nothing ambiguous in that look: a child's eyes, with a disarming candor. He was obviously far from imagining my agitation. His passivity, his trust, were those of an animal that one pets in passing, of a little tot whose cheek one caresses. Nothing more, nothing more . . . And his affectionate smile seemed to say only, "You are kind to me; that makes me happy . . ."

As the silence was beginning to weigh, I think he felt the polite thing was to break it. He said, with gravity, looking out at the sunburnt countryside, that faraway blaze of greens, yellows, and ochres that seemed to quiver with heat beneath a cloudless sky of intense blue, "This time of day, it really beats down . . ." Then after a pause, "In the summer, it's hard to sleep, during the day . . ."

"So where do you sleep?"

"Over there."

He used this to free himself quite naturally; and I drew my hand away. With my eyes fixed on his pale little nape, with its light golden down, I followed him along the narrow passage left between the sacks to the other end of the loft and into a long garret where there floated the same very fine flour dust that was everywhere, a lumber room rather than a bedroom, with old tubs and cast-away tools lined up along the walls; and, in the middle, in the remaining open space, two beds—one of iron, the other only a pallet—two dilapidated chairs, a crate turned upside down and covered with disparate objects: a candlestick, tumblers, a comb, an empty bottle, old newspapers. Some clothes hung from nails driven into the posts of the framework and, across the window, socks, a faded bathing suit, and some linen were drying on a line.

"Watch out, don't step in the rat poison!"

My foot had stumbled over a dirty plate placed on the floor in which some gluey old breadcrusts were going moldy.

"You'd be better off setting a trap if there are rats . . ."

"You get rid of more with this . . . But there's not much you can do about these vermin! I was bitten again the other night . . . Look!"

He rolled up his pantsleg and showed me toothmarks near the knee. The leg was slender, very clean, white, and smooth, with delicate joints and soft skin, like a woman's; but a real boy's leg, all the same: solid, wiry, muscular. I drew closer.

"Show me . . ."

He had already let his pantsleg fall back. Was this to avoid the touch of my hand? I think, rather, that he didn't want to seem a sissy.

"It's nothing . . . But it really smarted for two days . . . *You* don't have to worry, with your bedstead. You'll hear 'em running around underneath you, but they won't dare climb up to get a taste of your hide. But I . . ." He pointed to the pallet lying directly on the floor.

"That's where you sleep?"

"Yup."

"And the other bed, who's it for?"

"For Honoré . . . Honoré, the owner's nephew. He's the one who gives me my orders."

"You get along well with him?"

My question made him laugh.

"Why not? He's always yelling, that's how he is. But he's not a bad guy . . ." Encouraged by my attentive look, he suddenly became more talkative. " 'Cause he's got a whole lot of work, right? He does all the mixing, the kneading, the baking . . . He's the guy does it all . . . So naturally he's not always in the greatest mood . . . The boss's old, and since his stroke he can't take the night shift. He only helps in the shop on days when his sister has too much business . . . See, the mistress isn't his wife, she's his sister. He brought her in with him to do the selling when he became a widower . . . You don't know her yet? You'll see: she's a real Deuillot! She's even peskier than her brother! She noses around down there, she's always finding fault with something . . . And deaf! As bad as the old man, if not worse! You ought to hear them talking at the table . . . It's a riot, I'm telling you . . . They get all balled up when they talk to each other, one thing for another, pass me the bread and I give you the mustard . . . And then they get mad, they want to have it out and it's even worse, they can't drop it!" He'd put his hand over his mouth like a child to chortle freely, and, somewhat intoxicated by his chatter, his eyes laughing, his other hand thrust into his pocket—a pocket into which the arm disappeared up to the elbow—standing, with his espadrilles riveted to the ground, he rocked his lithe, pretty body from side to side. His winks, his sly smiles seemed to add to his improvisation innuendos of which only he appreciated the aptness but which must have been full of mischief and piquancy. I'd sat down on the little iron bed and did not take my eyes off his lively face, his moist and mobile mouth. I was thinking: "Still a child, in spite of his size, in spite of his age . . . He has no inkling of the attraction he exerts . . . How can he not be embarrassed by the insistency of my look, even if he doesn't understand it? Nothing more daunting than that kind of guilelessness, that kind of trust . . ."

He had stopped smiling; he seemed for an instant to ponder very serious matters. And over his features for several seconds again fell that veil of solemnity, of sadness, so unexpected, which I had noticed before. Then, suddenly, in a resolute tone:

"Let me tell you . . . Baking, that's something I'd like, for later . . . Because it's clean . . . And you've got time, during the day . . . And then, of course, you're in town . . . And then, it's not as hard as winegrowing at any rate, don't you think? Now, I'll tell you, I wouldn't want to go back to farmwork . . . The only thing I miss is the horses . . . That, yes! I used to love the horses . . ."

At that moment, a grating voice behind me made me jump: "Hey! Make yourself at home!" I turned around. In the doorway had appeared a strange individual, squat, his face covered with flour, at once thickset and puny: a broad torso mounted on small legs, with a big head, black hair, a low hairline, bulging eyes full of menace. He was somewhere between twenty-five and thirty. His massive, naked neck emerged from a flannel vest that was sleeveless and white with dust. Arms crossed, he stared at me fixedly with the obvious intention of scaring me. He succeeded, the animal! I knew better than anyone that what had led me to this room was anything but blameless, and, although my attitude was not in itself at all reprehensible, I had too much of a bad conscience not to fear some kind of troublesome fuss (I'm trying hard to recall the details of that ridiculous scene). I got up, and stammered while straightening the bed I'd used as a seat:

"Excuse me . . . I was taking a tour of the house with . . ." He brusquely cut me short: "There's nothing to visit here!" He went over to the window to spit out the fag-end he had between his lips, and over his shoulder threw at me: "Especially since it's time for my nap!"

Rather sheepishly, I took a step toward the door:

"I understand . . . I'll let you sleep . . . And, if you'll excuse me, I'm going to do the same . . . A cigarette, before I go?" I had taken out my case and offered it to him, attempting to smile. He hesitated a couple of seconds. He would have liked to decline—and didn't dare, I think. But he didn't say thank you.

Then I turned towards Yves, and as naturally as I could:

"And you, *petit,* do you smoke?"

He shook his head "no," without looking at me. His physiognomy had totally changed expression. No longer any trace of a smile. A discontented look, slightly cunning, slightly servile, and clearly disapproving; as if he had adopted the other's animosity and was endeavoring to show it. I put the case back in my pocket, mumbled: "Sleep well!" and went back to the loft, whose door had remained open. I heard Honoré slam it behind me.

But I wasn't done with the evil spirits of the place. Upon re-entering my room, I found the old lady there, putting sheets on the bed. I immediately tried to get in her good graces. "I'm causing you a lot of trouble, Madame."

"What did you say?"

I'd forgotten her deafness. I turned up my smile and repeated my sentence. She corrected me sharply:

"Mademoiselle!" And as I stammered an apology, she went on without dropping her crabby tone:

"You've got no business in there! Can't have the help bothered!"

The untamable shrew . . . A few gray bristles on her chin, like her brother; and like him, little ferret eyes rimmed with red, a blotchy complexion: sanguine types.*

I was quite determined to make myself pleasant.

"Would you permit me to help you?"

Her only answer: a shrug. Moreover, she performed the task very well by herself, showering blows on the bolster before rolling it deftly in the sheet. Without looking at me, she grumbled:

"And when you have your nap, you'll have to take off your boots!"

I lifted my slipper-shod foot.

"Already done, Mademoiselle."

I hadn't given up hope of getting a little chat started:

"You must often have troops around here."

"Too often! But we don't put them up! The room isn't on the books! There's no shortage of others in the village." She'd grabbed the red comforter and the blankets she considered superfluous at this time of year, and was heading for the door. In profile, beady eyes, a sharp-pointed beak, the trembling of her head adorned with a crest of black lace gave her the stupid solemnity of a hen. Before crossing the threshold, she turned back:

"In my day, soldiers used to sleep in barns! They didn't dirty people's sheets."

I laughed good-naturedly, as if I were savoring all the wit of her jest. Nonplussed, she stared at me with her piercing eyes, then disappeared down the stairs with her load as I called out, feigning good humor:

"Bye-bye, Mademoiselle . . . Many thanks!"

No use pretending that I haven't fallen into an openly hostile environment. All the same, damned if I'll let them throw me out. Were I to have no other pleasure over the next ten days than feeling Yves so close, seeing him in the courtyard, trading smiles with him from time to time—I'd be sufficiently compensated for all their rebuffs. He is exquisite. In this village populated by

*I.e., having blood as the predominating bodily humor.

leering, red-faced, alcoholic louts and more or less degenerate, rachitic children, he seems to belong to another race, this tall Pierrot with his slender silhouette, that nonchalant distinction, that look of a young prince disguised as a baker's apprentice. No trace of flirtatiousness: he is irresistible, and all the more so, perhaps, because he doesn't even suspect it. I feel him to be so willingly trustful, so sensitive to the slightest attention . . . No face has ever attracted me so . . . Only to think of it undoes me . . . That smile, at once humorous and caressing . . . Those eyes that don't turn away, those big frank eyes, so blue, of the first water! And his mouth? How to describe his mouth? It doesn't have a pretty form: too broad, with indistinct, colorless lips . . . A child's mouth . . . A sensual mouth nonetheless, but with a sensuality that is still unaware of itself, that is no doubt already searching for itself? He has never, I would swear, kissed other lips; and yet, this mobile, slightly swollen mouth looks as if it were distended, softened with kisses . . . I don't know what time it is, I've stupidly forgotten to rewind my watch. But to guess from the light, it can't be later than four o'clock. I'm not in any rush. And I get so much pleasure from thinking about him, I'm so perfectly peaceful on this deserted bank with no other company than this living river at my feet and all my memories of yesterday in my head which allow me to go on unhurriedly re-experiencing every detail of that first day.

Where was I?

After the old witch left, I, unable to bring myself to leave the house, stretched out on my bed. Much too restless to sleep, I thought. Yet I was dozing when around five o'clock the door to the loft suddenly flew open without anyone having knocked and in came Honoré followed by the boy. They crossed the room wordlessly. Honoré didn't even look in my direction. But Yves, closing the door to the stairs, shot me a friendly glance and flashed a smile.

I leapt to my window. It has no glass curtains, but is fitted instead with an old wooden rolling blind that I'd taken the precaution of lowering. Between the foot of the blind and the windowsill, there remains just the space one needs for observing the courtyard; and as the sill is rather high above the floor, I have only to sit in front of the window to have this space at eye level. So, while comfortably seated, I can keep a lookout without being seen from the courtyard. I only risk being surprised by someone entering my room, my doors having neither locks nor bolts; but the staircase is sufficiently noisy so that I'd hear someone coming.

I saw the two apprentices heading for the pump to perform their ablutions. Honoré, his chest exposed, was already soaping his face and neck while Yves was still taking his time in laying out some toiletries on the bench in orderly fashion: his comb, his soap, his towel, a clean shirt. Is it my imagination? Twice I thought I caught a furtive glance thrown toward my window, as if he vaguely suspected my presence; and he was half turned away when, with a quick motion, he made up his mind to pull his striped jersey over his head. I confess that I awaited that moment like a boon . . . His young, naked shoulders gleamed in the sun. The wide canvas pants accentuated, by contrast, the slimness of his torso. From then on, I didn't take my eyes off him again. He walked over to the pump. Honoré, sniggering, gathered water in the hollow of his hands and threw it in Yves' face. As the boy stepped back laughing, Honoré grabbed hold of his body to shove his head under the spout. But Yves put up a struggle, and, with a supple roll of his back, succeeded in breaking away. Next to the big hairy chest of the adult, how milky-white it looked, how tender and sleek, that adolescent breast, with its two mauve marks like two flower petals. The satiny young shoulders, the fleshy roundness where the arms attached, the shifting muscles in the back . . . in the sun. Crouching behind my blind, I didn't miss one of his movements! Just thinking about it, my hand shakes . . . I left the window only when I'd seen them slip on clean shirts, comb their hair one after the other before a broken piece of mirror nailed to the wall and disappear under the arch, chatting away.

Basically, what am I hoping for? Nothing. Really: *nothing.* I'm not crazy. I'm too afraid of unleashing the catastrophe, the fatal "scandal" that breaks your back and from which you don't recover . . . However much I may be tempted, no, the danger is too great! Here, more than anywhere else, I must forbid myself any imprudence . . . Even if I was sure that I could, within these few days, make him overcome his resistances and love me, the risk is such that it would be absurd, insane, to give in to this infatuation, no matter how violent it may be! In these country towns, nothing stays hidden: behind every shutter, eyes are watching, malign imaginations are busy suspecting; the slightest clue is spitefully interpreted, blown up, and quickly broadcast from mouth to mouth . . . A man like Honoré, if he suspected the slightest thing, would be a terror! And a scandal, at this moment, in this uniform! . . . The military courts are implacable! Careful, careful! I must constantly remind myself that the slightest lapse on my part could have appalling consequences . . . It's my future, my whole life that are at stake . . . No! However thrilling such an initiation might be, and however bitter it may be to give it up deliberately in advance, the sacrifice must be made, I have no choice! No, no: I must be content with this waking dream; to ask nothing more from the luck of this delightful encounter than these hours of intoxication, this feast for the eyes . . . Isn't it already wonderful to be living under the enchantment of this spell and to give myself up, without risk, several times a day, to this secret, ineffable rapture, which his presence alone is enough to plunge me into without his even suspecting it—the magician!

But time is passing, and I'm still a long way from having exhausted all my memories of yesterday and this morning!

First, the evening. Before dinner, I wandered around the village for an hour. I was vaguely hoping to run into Yves . . . The heat was less oppressive, the day was gently waning. Our red trousers added a touch of brightness to the streets. Girls hung about the fountain jabbering. The shopkeepers were taking a breath of cool air in the doorways of their shops. Every so often, a winegrower's cart crossed the square at a walk, bringing the workers and their tools back from the slopes. At the Trois Écus, the meal was slow and noisy: several fellow trainees boasted that they'd started affairs . . . When I returned to the bakery, night had almost completely fallen. Everything was silent. But Mlle. Deuillot was waiting for me in the dark, leaning on her elbows, perched rather like an old owl in the window of her kitchen. She'd lost none of her charm.

"Here we go to bed early because of the work. You'll have to come in earlier!" She handed me a brass candlestick. Before taking it, while stammering excuses, I mechanically pulled out my box of matches. The candlestick immediately withdrew into the shadow:

"Here we don't burn up candles to light the courtyards!"

"You're right, mademoiselle, I'll light it upstairs . . ."

I put out my hand. She decided to give me the candlestick.

"Thank you, mademoiselle, and good night!"

She closed her window without a word.

I groped my way up the staircase. The "help" must have been asleep. One of their windows had been left wide open, but their garret wasn't lit. I struck a match to set my alarm for five o'clock and went to bed in the dark.

They wrenched me from my sleep in the middle of the night, coming through my room to go down to the bakehouse. The moon had risen, and its diffused glow rendered more ghostly the appearance of those two pale specters with naked torsos, their legs disappearing under their heavily pleated "baker's skirts" which flapped about their ankles. Honoré walked in front, swinging a lantern. Waking with a start, I muttered:

"What time is it?"

Yves' voice answered me:

"Two." (It's odd: from the sound of his voice, I would swear he was smiling at me . . .) He had stopped, letting the other go ahead. His graceful silhouette stood out against the blind; a halo of bluish light caressed his neck and shoulders. He was there, so close! Already, he was at the door to the stairway. How to keep him for one instant more? Prompted by a sudden inspiration, I nimbly hid my alarm clock under the bolster.

"Listen, *mon petit* . . . I'm afraid I won't be ready for assembly. Since you're up, you wouldn't want to come shake me at five?"

"No problem."

"You'll remember?"

"Sleep easy!"

But I thought no more of sleeping. I went and sat in front of the window. Two lamps hanging from the ceiling lit the bakehouse very brightly. Through the big glass roof, I could follow their work. Honoré, directly in the light, bending over the kneading-trough, was already making the dough while humming a ballad. Yves was busy in the left-hand part of the spacious room, which was darker. Off and on, I would see him appear, his arms loaded with firewood, and move off towards the rear with long springy steps that made his full-length waist-cloth flutter. Then, once again, I would lose sight of him. But I heard him singing, and I did my best to make out his young and hesitant voice, which was mingled with Honoré's vulgar warblings. Suddenly, the rear of the room flared up, and I saw Yves' shadow running about against the incandescent reddish glow. He kept disappearing off to the left, only to reappear suddenly with an armful of wood that he would hurl full force into the mouth of the blaze. With each of his movements, the reflection of the flames danced on his bare skin, bringing out the shadows, throwing his flesh into relief, and he looked like a young demon who had sprung from the fire . . . Then everything went dark again; he had shut the doors of the oven.

I spent a long while yet watching their comings and goings behind the dusty glass. I heard the church bell toll three. Finally, overcome by sleepiness, I decided to go back to bed.

I think—I'm almost certain—that I was dreaming about him when, opening my eyes, I saw a pale torso standing close by my bed in the dawn's rosy light . . . Yves was actually there, powdered with flour up to his eyelashes, disheveled, smiling, with a mocking look in his eye:

"Hey, you know, you could sleep through a cannon going off! It's almost five."

Feverish from my night, still hardly lucid, and not quite able to control myself, I instinctively thrust out my arm, and, before he had time to step back, encircled his waist—but without trying to pull him close to me.

" 'Morning!"

" 'Morning!"

He had answered me, like an echo, in the same playful, chummy tone, smiling all the while, without averting his caressing gaze, without trying to pull away from me—without even thinking of it, apparently. My hand was resting on the small of his back, at the top of the waist-cloth that girded his loins. He smelled of sweat and baked bread. His skin was soft and moist.

"You're going to catch cold, you know, you're drenched in sweat . . ."

I avoided looking at him, afraid to betray my emotion, and I struggled against the temptation to pull him closer. Did he guess what was going on in me? He laughed suddenly as if I'd tickled him (had I perhaps done so, with an inadvertent brush of my fingertips?) and he disengaged himself with a deft half-turn which put him a meter from the bed. From there, he sauntered off towards the staircase.

"You're leaving?"

"Better get back downstairs . . . Who'll keep my fire going?"

Twenty minutes later, I was kitted out, buckling on my sword-belt, when a very faint creak made me turn my head. It was he. He had silently opened the door again, and was looking at me, smiling, with a finger to his lips. On cat's feet, he came over to the table and put down two croissants fresh from the oven. Then he vanished on tiptoe. The croissants were still piping hot. I breathed in their scent for a long time before biting into them: their steaming dough gave off the same aroma as his body.

I'm reproaching myself with the liberties I took this morning. No; to be honest, I reproach myself with nothing, I'd be lying if I wrote that I regret what I did: the pleasure that I stole has left me with too heady a memory . . . As long as I remain within the limits of these friendly familiarities that cannot scare him away (and that clearly amuse him, flatter him, please him), as long as I am master enough of myself to abstain from any gesture that might put him on his guard, there's no cause for alarm; nothing serious can happen. (But, careful! It's a slippery slope . . .)

All morning, I could think only of him . . . During the exercise, the Tonkinese assigned by the lieutenant to go inspect the sentries surprised me standing guard at the edge of a small wood; he stumbled onto me without my even having heard him coming:

"Hey, there, Sergeant! You dreaming about your love life?" It was all I could do not to smile . . .

I won't go beyond that for today. It's high time I got back to the mess. I'm happy.

Monday afternoon.

They're having their nap in the room across the way. Blinds lowered on account of the sun: I can't see anything . . .

Disappointments, all down the line.

First, this morning, waking up well ahead of time, I waited, waited for him, all atremble with hope . . . Does he mistrust me? Instead of coming to my bedside, as he did yesterday, he stayed near the door and merely called out:

"It's five!"

To force him to come close, I pretended to be sleeping. But, without budging, he repeated: "It's five!" clapping his hands. I still didn't move. Then he decided to come in further, but only as far as the head of the bed, and he began to drum on the wooden panel near my head, louder and louder. I had no choice but to pretend to wake up. I heard him laugh:

"Up and at 'em!"

I raised myself on an elbow: just in time, before he disappeared, to glimpse, in the morning twilight, in the narrow opening of the door, his blond mop spotted with flour, his friendly, slightly mocking smile . . .

The other disappointment is more serious.

When, at eleven o'clock, upon returning from the field exercise, the platoon fell out in the square, he was there in his striped jersey, sitting on the steps of the town hall. He was looking around for me. I met his gaze and immediately guessed that he'd come there for me, that he had to talk to me. I didn't dare go over to him openly. Unhurriedly, I started down the road to the bakery. I hadn't reached the bend before he'd caught up to me. How sad his face can be, the moment he stops smiling! He looked so worried that I took fright. I questioned him with my eyes. I was relieved to hear him say:

"He won't let me go up and wake you in the morning . . ."

It was only that! I laughed:

"Honoré? What's it to him?"

"You know, that's how he is . . ." This, scarcely audible, with a sulky pout, a raising of the eyebrows, an evasive, resigned movement of the head, a whole gamut of expressions that were marvelously suited to his Pierrot: a Pierrot who has been around and is no longer surprised by the whims of adults.

I went on laughing.

"Well, what can I say, *mon petit,* I'll try to wake up on my own . . ."

But he didn't see it that way. He'd thought it over, he had his solution all ready:

"No way! It's too chancy. What if you miss roll-call? No, no . . . Leave it to me . . . To wake us up, we have an alarm clock. So while I'm getting dressed, without letting on, I'll turn the hand to five, and, when we go down to the job, on my way through your room I'll put it on your table on the sly. And then, as soon as you're gone, I'll run up and put it back in our room. Who's going to know? . . . That way, you'll sleep easy . . ."

He too was smiling now, excited at having explained his trick, proud to have thought it up, thrilled to be of service. I put my hand on his shoulder:

"Listen, *mon petit,* I wouldn't want you to get into trouble on my account . . ."

"Tsk! Leave it to me, I tell you!"

He obviously had his mind quite made up. And it was easy to guess, from his confidence, that this wasn't his first time out in the art of disobedience and of putting one over on people without getting caught.

We came to the opening of the alley. He took advantage of this to slip away rather abruptly. No doubt he didn't care to be seen in my company. But as I watched him go off with big supple steps in his espadrilles, he turned halfway round to shoot me a joyous and complicitous wink.

He's a charmer, that boy . . .

But why did the other one forbid him to come up to my room in the morning?

Tuesday.

I'm leading an absurd life. All my free time I spend here, keeping a lookout. He makes no effort to get close to me, the little monster . . . You'd almost think he's avoiding me . . . Yet he makes touching gestures. Last night, true to his promise, he surreptitiously slipped the alarm clock onto my table. This morning, he even added a brioche and a bar of chocolate that he must have snitched for me from the shop.

It unnerves me to stay here day and night skulking behind my blind, my throat dry, my eyelids burning, prey to this sort of a fever—which I know all too well, alas, and which is exhausting. I hardly sleep, and badly at that, because it's mainly at night that I can observe him best, for the longest time, through the glass roof of the bakehouse; because it's then that he appears before me in all his gracefulness, his torso naked, his waist-cloth, tied around his hips, fluttering. I'm all eyes when he comes out into the courtyard, when he goes to empty the ash pan or to draw water from the pump: on these moonlit nights, a silvery halo plays about his shoulders, his arms, his shoulder blades glistening with sweat . . . And that deep, vertical shadow that plunges under the waist-cloth, down the small of the back . . .

On top of that, the training is hard. For five hours at a stretch, the Tonkinese has us racing around the vineyards with all our whole gear on. By eight in the morning, the heat is already scorching. We come back bathed in sweat, dead beat after hiking our eighteen, twenty, twenty-two kilometers . . . As soon as I've had lunch, I come and fall into my bed and am out cold until the moment when, after their nap, the two apprentices come through my room to go down to the courtyard. Then I can't stay in bed anymore, and I sit down at the window to observe their washing-up. I hardly have time, then, to wash my face before dashing to the town hall, where the lieutenant gives us an hour and a half of instruction. After which I often wander around the village in hopes of running into Yves. What can he be doing at that time of day? A game of belote, maybe, in some café, with Honoré?

At eight o'clock, I've rushed through dinner and quickly make tracks for the bakery. That's when the apprentices go to bed—without light, but with the windows open, so that I hear them laughing, or bickering, or singing mawkish songs in two-part harmony. I strain my eyes to see them coming and going as the day wanes. When Honoré is in bed, he sometimes lights his lantern to skim the newspaper before turning in. The light is too weak for me to be able to make out Yves on his pallet. Is he reading, too? Is he dreaming? Of what? . . .

Yesterday evening I got back a little earlier—lucky for me that I did! There was more light than usual. They were not in bed: leaning side by side in one of the windows, they were leafing through a booklet together, a sort of popular pictorial, a collection of songs perhaps? . . . Oh, but the boy looked beautiful to me, in that attentive pose! And with a newfound beauty, for it's the vivaciousness, the mobility of his features, that usually make for his peculiar charm. Last evening, he stood there motionless, his brow bent forward, his eyelids lowered, his mouth serious, with a face I didn't know on him, a rapt face and one that is, as it were, imbued with *silence* . . . This unexpected gravity recalled—I am not exaggerating—certain oriental masks, the contemplative gentleness, the somewhat sorrowful, somewhat dramatic nobility of certain Egyptian statues . . . (I am thinking especially of the oblong face, sad and serene, still childish yet sensual, of some adolescent pharaoh whose polychrome bust is in the Berlin Museum.) Anyone catching him unawares at that moment, knowing nothing about him, would have thought, I'm sure, that that pensive, vaguely melancholy expression was the reflection of a secret and tormented inner life . . . Suddenly, I don't know why—had Yves turned the page too quickly?—Honoré, stupidly testy and brutal, dug an elbow into his ribs. Yves bridled; and all of a sudden over the mask of the oriental prince I saw the mischievousness of the Pierrot reappear. Fleetingly, without dropping the booklet, he vanished into the semidarkness of the room. The other chased after him. But Yves threw a chair at his legs, and, while Honoré was stumbling, jumped up onto a crate, then with a great leap, onto the bed, where the other caught him. I realized then that they were both in their nightshirts, with bare legs. In spite of his agility, it was the youngster who got the worst of it. Honoré, grabbing him around the knees, had thrown him off balance; and although Yves struggled bravely, Honoré succeeded in pinning him down, pressing his shoulders into the mattress with both hands. I had a view of Honoré from the back, bearing down with all his weight on the boy, and I heard him repeating breathlessly:

"Say you're sorry, you son of a bitch! Say you're sorry!"

But Yves wiggled like a devil, not wanting to give up. Then Honoré seized him around the waist, hoisted him on his shoulder like a sack of flour, went and threw him onto the pallet. Then he came back triumphantly to settle in again at the window, with the booklet; and, a few seconds later, Yves, all disheveled, his collar unbuttoned, laughing, took his place again beside him. As if nothing had happened, they went back to their reading, while there was a little daylight left.

And I am writing this down, in complete detail . . . That's how far gone I am.

Wednesday the 11th.

At the Trois Écus, waiting for lunch.

A good morning. Shooting practice. I spent two hours dozing, stretched out in the shade of a small pine wood.

I've never felt so wretched. Besotted, and without hope . . . The hostile atmosphere of this Deuillot house, to which I return again and again, where I spend all my free time, like an addict whom nothing can prevent from reverting to his drug, is, in the end, almost asphyxiating. My cowardly attempts to play up to that bear Honoré fail, one after the other. Yesterday, as they were still at supper when I came back to the bakery, I thought it would be politic to make myself pleasant, and, crossing the courtyard, I went over to the window of their kitchen to say good evening. They were there, all four of them, sitting in silence around a dish of cabbage. Honoré, seeing me, buried his face in his plate. Yves, looking uneasy, chewed steadily without raising his eyes, without seeming to suspect that my gaze was seeking desperately to meet his. Only old Deuillot seemed aware of my civility. He asked me if the training was hard, and if I was having a good time in the area! I even think he was going to propose that I try a little of his wine when his sister pulled the bottle out of his hands, shouting at him to finish eating; she was clearly enjoining him to be done with this inopportune conversation forthwith. I can take a hint, and I'm not about to renew my overtures!

It's Honoré, mainly, that I'd do well to cultivate. But he's a tough one. When the two of them come through my room to go down and wash up in the yard, I do my best to exchange a few words with them. Honoré doesn't answer me, and, looking cross, continues on his way as if he hadn't heard . . . If I offer him a cigarette, he takes it and sticks it behind his ear, without looking at me, with a surly motion of his head by way of a thank-you. I hate him! He has a low and mulish brow, a flattened nose, and bulging eyes; and, however puny he may be, this ill-made brute gives an impression of strength because of his short legs, his broad pelvis, his heavy tread, his gorilla's jaw. Yves himself would gladly chat, I'm sure; but he daren't hang behind because of the other; he's content to smile at me as he goes by.

Ah, the spell cast by that smile! I'm obsessed by it . . . It's by his smile that he caught me, by his smile that he holds me . . . A spontaneous and frank, bold and mischievous smile, which goes so well with the winsome look that flows from his eyes . . . A defenseless and unsecretive smile . . . All the freshness of childhood, and yet nothing puerile, not the slightest affectation of innocence. So alluring, and yet, in spite of all, so unprovocative, that smile, so artless, so trusting, that it compels you to constraint, it paralyzes desire . . . I'd be less intimidated by a sulky mien, by a hostile and shifty look, than by the perpetual offering of that irresistible smile—which offers nothing! . . .

I SCORE A point!

I hasten to write it down even while keeping an eye on the courtyard, where they're washing up.

They've just come through my room, after their nap; I succeeded in talking to him. He had thrown over his shoulder that washed-out blue bathing suit which I'd seen drying in the window on the day of my arrival.

I had pulled my table and chair closer to the window in such a way as to obstruct the passage between the head of the bed and the wall. It was therefore necessary for me to move. This took several seconds, which I made use of, while pushing the table away, to ask, without addressing either of them in particular:

"It's so hot today! It's stifling . . . Isn't there some place along the Marne where you can touch bottom and where I could take a dip?"

Naturally it was Yves who answered:

"At the landing."

"At the landing?"

"Yes, at the landing, that's the best . . . to the right of the bridge, they call it the 'landing'. . . Where they have the contest . . . It's wider, and there's not much current . . . But as for touching bottom, you can't, it drops right off." Honoré, without waiting, was already on the staircase. Yves was getting ready to follow him.

I pretended to be surprised:

"A contest? What kind of contest?"

"Swimming, of course! On the Fourteenth of July . . . with a prize of a hundred francs!"

"Have you ever entered, yourself?"

"No. To begin with, I wasn't in Aunay."

"But this year, you're going to enter?"

"Why not?"

He smiled, but kept turning towards the staircase, as if he expected to be called.

"You know how to swim?"

"Of course!"

"And you go swimming often?"

"I like it a lot . . ."

He had reached the door, but, seized by a belated scruple:

"Well, swimming, I'm no champion, you know . . . I've never learned diving . . . But when it comes to the breast stroke, I can keep up with the best of 'em . . . And you?"

"No. I don't know how to swim. That's why I was asking you for a place where one can touch bottom."

"Really, you don't know how to swim?"

"No, not at all. And I really regret it. Because we could have gone swimming together . . ."

"Yes, it's a shame . . ."

With what spontaneity he said that! I was so moved by it that I said, in a low voice and with a gaze that must have been much too tender:

"I'd like to learn, with you . . . If you wanted to give me lessons . . ."

Without hesitating, he shook his head negatively, and his face became serious:

"Oh, no! With the current, that would be asking for trouble! . . . No, here there's way too much current to be able to learn with!"

Then he smiled at me one last time and disappeared.

I spied on them as usual while they were washing up at the pump. I saw Yves going off with Honoré, his towel rolled up under his arm. I'm going to try to follow the boy.

Thursday the 12th.

I didn't manage to catch him yesterday. First, because he and Honoré left the house together. Then because, just when I was about to go downstairs, I heard voices in the courtyard. Old Deuillot and his sister, both done up in their Sunday best, were chatting with two ladies dressed in black, whom they were giving a grand tour of the bakery. I had to wait until they'd gone into the bakehouse and come out again and returned to the shop before I could slip away. It was too late to pick up the trail of the two of them. At least, I could go survey the vicinity of what Yves called the landing.

I took the alley, to be in the country more quickly, without having to go through town, and, via bits and pieces of little-used roads, I reached the Marne, at a certain distance downstream from the bridge.

This north bank on which I had arrived was planted with thick bushes packed one against the other and just tall enough so that a man could move about there without being seen from any direction. Between these bushes winds an irregular path. Passersby must be few there, for the track is scarcely visible. To reach the area of the bridge without attracting attention, it would be impossible to dream up an approach better shielded from view. Soon I heard from far off the echoes of laughter and shouts that the river carried to me. But on the side where I was, the vegetation was so dense that it was difficult to get to the bank. I had to thread my way through the brush, getting scratched by the branches, to make out, finally, several swimmers' heads on the dark surface of the water. In no time, I spotted a blond mop bobbing among the eddies. At that moment, a damned stray dog that was coming in the opposite direction took fright at finding me in its path and started to bark furiously. I didn't dare move any closer to the swimming place. I didn't dare stay there watching, either. Enraged, I turned around and went back to the village. At least I'm sure that Honoré wasn't with Yves. There were only half a dozen of them, and all rather younger than Yves.

I was terribly disappointed. I'd have been much less so if I could have foreseen what the evening held in store for me. But I want to put everything down in detail, so as not to let a single bit of this memory be lost.

Well, at eight o'clock last night, coming back in, I was struck as I passed under the arch by an unusual sound of voices. The kitchen was lit up for once, and I slowed my pace upon seeing, around the table, an unwonted number of guests. Old Deuillot was presiding, flanked by the two ladies I'd noticed that afternoon in the courtyard. Honoré, in a jacket, standing bent over, was uncorking a bottle. Yves, well combed, was sitting quietly at the end of the table. As I passed by, Mlle. Deuillot, with her crest of black lace, was carefully placing a splendid cake, crowned with white icing, under the hanging lamp.

Nobody paid any attention to me.

I was seized by the temptation to use the opportunity to go take a look around the apprentices' garret. If I did it quickly, I ran no risk of getting nabbed. Stealthily, I made my way through the loft. The door to their room was half-open. The two beds were unmade. I went over to Yves'. His striped jersey, his canvas pants were lying there in a heap. I couldn't resist picking them up, sniffing them. I recognized his special smell. By the head of the bed, on an upside-down crate, lay a wadded handkerchief, a bit of soap, a box of matches, and on the floor, among old newspapers, a greasy book with its binding falling apart: *Babylon, or the Vices of the Capital.*

On the illustrated cover stood a half-naked girl, candyish pink, with a black domino on her face, a black corset, black stockings. The titles of the chapters were suggestive: "Sweet Little Sins," "Prostitution in the Suburbs," "Harlots in High Society," "Lust and Crime". . . I was too afraid of being caught to hang around longer. I returned the booklet to its place and rushed back to my room.

This boy . . . Is it possible? I'm trying to define what I'm feeling. This discovery, did it disappoint me? A little. I'm surprised, mainly. And, at the same time—I must say . . . —encouraged!

How ill-matched that book is with the limpidity of his gaze, the ingenuousness of his smile! The striking fact remains: Yves doesn't mind this sort of reading; and, what's more, he doesn't hide it from Honoré. For that matter, who knows if it wasn't from Honoré that he got the book? And who knows if this wasn't the very booklet which he was browsing through the other night, next to Honoré, at the window—with his eyelids lowered, with the beautiful face of a thoughtful angel?

Downstairs, the meal was merrily drawing to a close. Finally, the kitchen lamp was doused, and the guests came out into the courtyard. They were talking loudly, all at once. I thought I heard that a carriage was waiting for the ladies at the Cheval Blanc, to take them to the station at Ay. There was still a little daylight. Old Deuillot and his nephew were finishing a cigar. Yves was keeping slightly off to the side. At one moment, he raised a quick glance towards my window. Did he guess that I was on the lookout, behind my blind? . . .

The old man said:

"No, don't be silly, my sister and I will see you off."

All six of them disappeared under the arch. The gate swung shut, and immediately I heard the sound of running feet: Honoré and Yves had only been as far as the threshold, and, left alone in the house, returned to the courtyard chasing each other. I saw Honoré grab a half-full pail in front of the pump and toss the contents full force at the legs of the boy, who avoided a soaking by leaping like a billygoat. Then, one behind the other, they bounded up the stairs. I barely had time to get away from the window before seeing them burst through my room and hurtle, laughing, into the loft.

It wasn't light enough so that I could see them, even though their windows were open. But I heard their revels clearly. In the scuffle, a chair fell with a crash. Then the shouts, the laughter, the roughhousing came closer, and I suddenly realized they'd come back into the loft that separates my room from theirs. The chase got even wilder. As a precaution, I again left the window and lay down on my bed. A good thing, too. The door sprang open again, and in came Yves. He had a head start on the other. He had time to slam the door behind him, before making a dash for the door to the stairs. He had already opened it when, suddenly changing his mind, he came straight at me, cleared my bed with a single bound, and slid like an eel into the narrow space between the bed and the wall. The ploy was a good one. Scarcely had he vanished when Honoré appeared in his turn. Seeing the door to the stairs wide open, he had no doubt that Yves had gone down, and blowing like a walrus, he plunged down the stairs four at a time and rushed headlong into the courtyard.

I had not recovered from my surprise when Yves got up from his knees, panting, disheveled, bursting with laughter like a child. I had him there, close by, on my right, in the semidarkness, trapped by the bed, a prisoner of his own stratagem. Determinedly, this time, I encircled his shoulders with my arm. His shirt was damp with sweat. Caught up in his game, cocking an ear toward the courtyard, he let me do it. I tightened my embrace. Was it in seriousness, was it out of embarrassment, to keep his composure, that he said:

"Sshh . . . Listen."

But there was nothing to be heard. Honoré, down below, was rummaging in vain through every dark corner, the bakehouse, the stable, the old coach-house, the henhouse, the shed.

I held the boy with a steady arm. I was pulling him toward me timidly. Beneath my palm I felt the living mobility of the muscles in his back, a feline suppleness that quivered under the caress of my fingers. I breathed in his smell, a smell of youth, of clean linen, warm and wholesome. My cheek touched his temple, my mouth grazed his hair. He said nothing, did not move, made no attempt to flee. I couldn't see his face, but I knew he was no longer smiling . . . My lips were about to reach his. Only then, with a swift and seemingly involuntary movement, he averted his mouth. Oh, without trying to pull away from me, on the contrary: simply by lowering his head, and pressing his cheek tenderly onto my chest. We remained several seconds without moving, holding our breaths. I heard our two hearts beating. Then, with my free hand, I took hold of the lower part of his face, and, gently, brought it toward mine. He no longer resisted. My kiss slid from his hair to his forehead, from his forehead to his eyelid—ah, the fluttering of his eyelashes beneath my lips . . . —from his eyelid to his cheek, from his cheek to his closed mouth, which tightened at first, then very slowly opened halfway and surrendered itself . . . Ah, how cool, wet, deliciously unskilled, his lips seemed to me . . . but how docile they became, suddenly, and how willing! And when I disengaged myself from him for a second to take a breath, with what a hunger for tenderness he came back to meet my kiss! The arm that I'd first slipped around his shoulders had moved progressively down the length of his slender body, and my hand stretched out to feel the hard curve of his hip, the joint of his thigh . . . the other hand, resting on his chest, had succeeded in slipping between two buttons of his shirt, in sliding under the cloth, and my fingers advanced gradually along his soft, moist, sinewy flesh. I had him all vibrant against me, motionless, rigid, probably overwhelmed by what he was feeling—already open, perhaps, to more.

Down below, the door to the bakehouse slammed, and I heard the footfall of Honoré, who was crossing the courtyard and entering the stairway. As for Yves, he was no longer listening and heard nothing. It was I who had to shove him brusquely away, who pushed him back into the space between the wall and bed.

Honoré burst into the dark:

"Where is he? I know he's here!"

"Who?"

"Don't play dumb! I tell you he came back up! Where did he go?"

He struck a match, and lit the candle that was on my table.

Oh, how I hated him at that moment! I could have wished him dead! However, I had enough of a grip on myself to reflect; Yves was inevitably going to be found out. There was a chance that the game would take on a dangerously equivocal, premeditated character in Honoré's eyes. He mustn't be allowed to think that there could be any collusion between Yves and me; better to give the boy away than to seem to be hiding him behind my bed.

Honoré had picked up the candlestick and was coming over to the bed.

"Where's he holed up, the bastard?"

Then, like a coward, with a smile of obliging connivance, I winked toward the little space. He brought the light forward over the bed, in the direction that I'd pointed out, and he saw the boy flat on his stomach on the floor.

"Oh, you son of a bitch, you're going to pay for this!"

But Yves, seeing himself caught, shot up like a spring, and, with a backhanded blow, put out the candle. Then, taking advantage of the darkness, he jumped over the bed and dashed for his room, followed by Honoré.

I got up to close the doors and take my place at my window. But I saw nothing. From time to time I heard the boy's purling laugh rise up out of the midst of Honoré's profanities and curses. Then the noise of the carriage door abruptly shut them up. The owners were coming home. The old man, whistling to himself, went to urinate in a corner of the courtyard before returning to his room. And everything ebbed into the silence of all the other evenings.

I went back to bed, feverish, my mouth burning, unable to get to sleep, reliving the slightest details of that minute when I'd held the boy in my arms. At two in the morning, as usual, they came through my room to go down to the bakehouse, and Yves put the alarm clock on my table. Naturally I pretended to be asleep. But for the whole rest of the night, I remained awake, with the absurd and stubborn hope that Yves would find a way to come back . . .

Since this morning, I've been living in a dream. We did five hours of maneuvers . . . I walked like an automaton. I came back dog-tired. I can no longer think of anything except that brief moment when I had his satiny skin beneath my fingers, his wet mouth beneath my lips . . . A few seconds more, a few seconds more, and he'd have surrendered! . . .

Saturday the 14th.

Mad with joy! We're to meet this evening at eight o'clock. A whole evening, alone with him! It's too wonderful, I still can't quite believe it . . . a whole evening! I'm having wild dreams . . . more than five hours to wait!

I can hardly write, I'm so excited. This evening! All the same, I'd like to put down everything. A way of killing time, of knocking off these few hours, and my impatience . . .

This morning, several circus wagons were parked in the square in front of the town hall, where the platoon breaks up around noon upon returning from maneuvers. The gypsies were unloading cross-bars, small beams, motley tent-poles. Yves was there, naturally, and every brat in town, and a few old idlers. Recognizable from a distance by his flour-covered jersey, with its blue and white stripes. A beanpole in a red body shirt, who had climbed up on one of the wagons, was hanging a calico poster on a frame. Le Grand Cirque Stella-mare, whose troupe includes the most celebrated star, the most hilarious clown, the most extraordinary acrobats of modern times, was offering the inhabitants of Aunay three sensational shows: the first, this evening, Saturday, at eight o'clock; the other two, tomorrow, Sunday. As soon as we'd fallen out, the platoon, dusty and sweaty, forgetting its fatigue, went to swell the crowd of rubberneckers, and I took advantage of this to go over to the boy. More of a Pierrot than ever: his hands in his pockets, raising his little powdered nose, his eyes on the poster, his thin neck wholly exposed by the opening of the jersey, his blond mop hiding his forehead down to his eyebrows . . .

At first he pretended not to have seen me coming; then his blue gaze furtively met mine, and I saw his long eyelashes flutter. A bit later, with his nonchalant dancer's step, he detached himself from the group and started ambling off in the direction of the bakery. I had no trouble catching up with him before the bend.

He turned around, making a poor pretense of mild surprise.

"Oh, it's you . . . you saw the circus?"

"Listen, you wouldn't want to come see it with me tonight?"

"You bet!"

"Well then, if you like, I'll get two seats, and I'm inviting you."

"Tonight?"

He smiled, obviously tempted.

"Why not? The performance is after dinner. It'll be over well before you start your night shift. So, are we on?"

He looked in front of him, without answering. I felt that he was per-plexed. As for me, I was desperately attached to my scheme.

"What? The boss can't find anything to object to in that, since it's your free time . . . What's more, if necessary, I can speak to him about it . . ."

"Oh, no, don't do that!"

"Why not?"

"Better not get the boss mixed up in this . . . To begin with, on Christ-mas Eve, I was out with Honoré until after midnight, and the boss didn't complain."

"You want me to talk to Honoré about it?"

"No, not that! . . . I'll tell him myself."

"So, are we set for this evening?"

"If you want."

"And after the show we'll go back to the house together."

As he said nothing, I awkwardly added:

"The two of us . . ."

He lowered his head, for an instant: then, suddenly, he turned around, and he smiled at me with a surprising tenderness. I asked for no other answer. We took a few steps, without speaking. But we were thinking, for certain, about the same things. I finally said, in a low voice: "You know, *mon petit,* I had a hard time getting to sleep last night . . ."

I wavered, and, even lower, I muttered:

"How about you?"

He kept his head down. From the side, I couldn't see his face clearly. I was afraid I'd put him off; I quickly changed the subject and my tone:

"You don't go very often, to the circus?"

"Oh, no . . . in fact, I've never been."

"Never? They must come here, though, from time to time."

"Of course . . . but I wasn't here, I told you."

"And where you were, the circus never came through?"

"I was on a farm . . . Placed there . . ."

"Ah? On a farm? Did you like it?"

An evasive shake of the head.

"The work must have been harder than at the bakery?"

Still the same silence. But a vague movement of the shoulders that seemed to say: "That's not it." I tried to explain his muteness to myself. It didn't seem to me that he was refusing to talk, nor that he found me importunate or too inquisitive; but rather that his thought was following another direction than mine, that he was thinking about something somewhat difficult to explain, perhaps, yet which he'd have tried to say if only I'd known how to help him.

We continued on our way in silence. I was going to ask him, "What are you thinking about?" when he stopped short. Then he started walking again, and, without turning towards me, with a tautening of his neck and a bit of defiance in his voice, he suddenly declared:

"If you want to know, I'm an orphan . . . A ward of the state."

It was I this time who couldn't find anything to reply. But I laid my hand on his shoulder, and I put so much gentleness into this gesture, such affectionate feeling, that he immediately raised his head and smiled at me. His eyelashes fluttered, his eyes were dimmed with tears: I discreetly took my hand away and made an effort to go on in a playful tone:

"Well, Yves, I'm going to introduce you to the circus! See you at ten to eight, by the fountain . . . And then, you know, if you're not having a good time there, at the circus, well, we don't have to stay till the end . . . We can always leave, eh? Go back to the house early . . . or take a little walk together, if you like . . . a little walk, before going home . . ."

I watched him. He hadn't shied away. What was he thinking? I couldn't refrain from persisting:

"Wouldn't you like that, a little stroll together, in the night . . . the two of us?"

By way of an answer, he stopped and turned towards me as if he were offering me his face. A face in turmoil. The lips closed. The pupils dilated and staring, staring . . . I was trembling with emotion. I looked deeply into his eyes. I repeated, very low:

"Would you like that, *mon petit?*"

Then, abruptly, his features relaxed, his eyelids half-closed; finally, slowly, with an adorable abandon, he decided to smile. Then he left me, running.

Tonight, at ten to eight, by the fountain. I'm counting the minutes . . .

I've taken two seats, but in the last row, near the exit.

Sunday afternoon, the 15th.

I'm alone in the house. The old folks just left for vespers. And the two apprentices, at this moment, are at the circus!

I'm doing my best to keep calm. Perhaps all is not lost.

Yesterday, I was busy writing the preceding pages when they came through the room as they do every day, after their nap, to go down to the pump. Yves docilely walked behind Honoré, his towel in his hand, without raising his eyes. But as soon as the other had gone out the door to the landing, he turned back to me with an extraordinary expression, at once dramatic and childlike, and, before disappearing down the stairs in his turn, he made a bizarre gesture to me with his hand as if to ask me to follow him. What did he mean? Follow him? Where? When? Apparently not right away, or into the courtyard . . . If he wanted to talk to me, it couldn't be in Honoré's presence . . . Just in case, I shut my notebook, quickly put my shoes back on, and, hidden behind my blind, watched them perform their daily ablutions. Several times, Yves looked up toward my window.

As they were finishing up their washing, a boy came up and joined them. I knew him by sight, I'd noticed him because of his red hair and his flat face, with no eyebrows, covered with freckles. Much younger than Yves: eleven years old, maybe. There was a brief confab. Then, all three headed off toward the street.

Yves' gesture had been so precise, so urgent, that I went downstairs without waiting any longer. As I came out of the carriage door, they were turning the corner by the pharmacy. I followed them. Coming to the bend, I was pleased to see Honoré enter the café, leaving the two boys to go on by themselves. Yves turned around, saw me, slowed down. Without a doubt, he wanted to talk to me. I took a shortcut down the little rue des Halles and arrived before them in the market square. There was a crowd around the beanpole in the red shirt who was leading about town a white horse on which sat enthroned a little marmoset adorned with plumes. I stopped. Yves came up to me, with his redhead in tow.

"Honoré's against it."

I was so little expecting this that I was left speechless. He looked at me, his eyebrows raised, his mouth twisted into a forced smile. He finally added:

"Because there's a lot of work for tomorrow . . . He says I'd be tired."

This wretched pretext made me furious:

"I'm going to talk to him: you'll see!"

"Oh, no! Not that! . . . No, no . . . He's against it, there's nothing to be done . . . and the circus, he said he'd take me, himself, tomorrow, in the daytime . . ."

I was determined to do the impossible.

"But you are free in the evenings. That is nobody's business. There's no work, at that hour . . . You have the right to do what you please!"

"He's against it . . . You can see, he's like that . . ."

He shook his head, obstinately, with the same grimacing smile, the same winsome and resigned look. I saw that I was wasting my time preaching revolt. My anger was dissolving into powerlessness and despair. This must have been visible on my face. I saw his lashes flutter, and tears sprang to his eyes. Was this because he, too, felt frustrated, disappointed? He threw a quick look around us. The crowd had moved along slightly, the redhead had gone off to follow the beanpole, we were more or less left to ourselves. Then, he lowered his eyes and stammered:

"Another time, maybe . . ."

"But the platoon leaves Aunay Tuesday morning!"

He didn't know this. He seemed to have received a shock:

"Oh! You're not going to leave?"

I caught a glimmer of hope.

"Yes, *mon petit*, we leave Tuesday morning. But between now and then . . . two more days . . . in two days we should easily find some way to be together, if you want to!"

The redhead was coming back in our direction. I saw him getting closer. There wasn't a second to lose:

"Do you want to, tell me? . . . You want to? Then come up with something, *mon petit* . . . I don't know . . . in my room? No? Then, where? Outdoors? But when? Think, *mon petit*! Find a time, a place! . . . Tell me, you promise to try?" The boy was only a few meters away. I questioned Yves with my eyes. He was no longer smiling; his nostrils were pinched, his mouth was open, his breathing quick.

I lowered my voice again:

"You promise?"

He answered *"oui,"* so feebly that I didn't hear it but guessed it from the movement of his lips. And this movement resembled a kiss.

The redhead had rejoined us. He looked us over with a curious, shifty glance. He nudged Yves:

"You coming or not?"

"So where are the two of you off to?"

With a movement of the chin, Yves pointed at his little friend:

"It's Ratel's grandfather who's expecting us, with his punt. We're going to help him with his trawl lines."

In a foul temper, I watched them head off toward the road that leads to the Marne. I didn't know what to do with myself and my heartbreak. Mechanically, I went in the same direction as they had. It seemed to me that perhaps, by staying in Yves's wake . . .

I followed them at a distance, by the track lined with hedges that runs parallel to the road; I saw them cross the bridge and on the other side join an old man in a flat boat. Yves and the boy took the oars, and they cast off sluggishly, against the current. I didn't cross the bridge; but I continued to follow them, keeping to the river: the punt went faster than I. And as the bank where I was was all choked with bushes, it didn't take long for me to lose sight of them. I couldn't even see the Marne, hidden by shrubs; but I heard, far ahead of me, the splash of the oars echoing on the water. Then the splashing stopped and I heard voices. When it seemed to me I'd come abreast of them, I left the path and went through the brush down to the shore.

At the place they'd drawn up to, the opposite bank was flat, grassy, planted with a few sparse poplars. Yves hadn't left the boat: alone, standing in the stern, he was keeping it in place with the help of a long boat-hook stuck in the mud. The old man and his grandson had spread out their lines on the ground, and, kneeling in the grass, seemed busy checking the hooks or baiting them. They both had their backs turned to me and were working in silence. I had all the time in the world to gaze at Yves in his new capacity as gondolier. I saw him in profile. With his arms half bared and lifted very high, he was leaning down on the pole with all his weight, his calves taut, his back arched, his chest swollen by the effort, his neck erect, his head thrown slightly back. How willowy and graceful was his silhouette against this landscape of water, greenery, and freshness! Those muscles in action, I had felt with my hands; that wiry body, I had, for a few seconds, felt quiver beneath my caress . . . I couldn't resist the wish to reveal my presence to him; to create this further complicity between us. The other two, bent over their task, couldn't see me. But the Marne is wide. How, from that distance, to catch his eye? I had no other cover than the row of particularly lush and leafy bushes that jutted out over the water. Perhaps, by standing up, by parting the high branches to free my head, I'd have a chance to be seen. But he wasn't turned in my direction all the time: the current continuously drifted the punt, which kept turning slowly around the pole as if around an axis. I had to wait for the right moment. I was trembling with impatience, never taking my eyes off him. As soon as he came opposite me, I stood up, raised my arm. In vain. Rapidly, with a piece of dead wood and my handkerchief, I made a flag that I waved over my head. And suddenly, without his having shown any sign of surprise, I saw his face, leaning against the pole, light up with a smile. Just in time! On the bank, old Ratel had got up and was scolding the boy. Quickly, I dove back into the shrubbery.

The old man and the redhead got back into the boat with the baited lines. Yves, without taking his eyes off the place where I was squatting, took hold of the oars. Ratel directed the operation. The punt, this time gliding with the current, went back in the direction of the bridge, keeping very close to the shore, while the grandfather and the grandson, leaning over the side, paid out the lines. And for as long as they were in my field of vision, I could see Yves, whose features I distinguished less and less, turned toward the spot where I had appeared.

I stayed there, in my thicket, lying down like a wounded beast. To face the noisy dining room of the Trois Écus this evening was beyond my courage. I gave up on dinner. The circus, too, of course. I had the two tickets in my pocket: I tore them into little pieces and scattered them among the dead leaves. Yet the quick smile of the boy standing in the boat and the memory of his promise—that *"oui"* on which now hung all my hope—somewhat tempered the bitterness of the missed opportunity. I didn't know all that was still awaiting me . . .

AT DUSK, I went back to the bakery without stopping at the mess. The circus band had struck up its racket to pull in the audience, and the roar of the trombones hit me in blasts at the street corners.

In the kitchen, the meal was finishing up.

I lay down without getting completely undressed. It was still daylight. I don't know what I was expecting. Maybe that Yves had been able to work something out? Maybe that he would manage to come up after Honoré and have a word with me as he passed? He had promised. I wouldn't yet give in to despair. But I heard them talking in the courtyard and climbing the stairs together, as they did every night. I was on the bed: I picked up a newspaper and pretended to read. Yves went first. He crossed the room with his silent and springy step, without looking at me, without even daring to grant me that "g'night" which he often tosses off to no one in particular, in a silvery choirboy's voice, and which for me is like a draft of fresh air at the threshold of my stifling nights. Honoré was at his heels. He always goes by without speaking a word to me, without seeming to see me. But yesterday, instead of going through the attic door after Yves, he closed it with a sharp movement and turned towards me.

"So you're here, are you? I thought you had such an itch to go to the circus tonight?"

The tone wasn't just cross as usual, but rather ponderously mocking, and tremulous, angry. I bore him a mortal grudge; nevertheless, I mastered my anger. I slowly lowered my newspaper, propped myself up on an elbow, contemplated him for several seconds—I think I even smiled—and calmly replied:

"Not really . . . what would have made me happy was to treat Yves to this show, because he's never been to one . . . But, since he wasn't free . . ."

Thrown by this good-natured tone, he at first kept quiet, for a moment. Then he raised his snout, took a step towards my bed:

"All this has got to stop! Understand?"

I put on a look of amazement:

"Stop what? Explain yourself!"

"Don't take me for an idiot! Why are you always trying to talk to the apprentice?"

He was less than two meters away, his fists clenched, a nasty look in his eye. I was afraid. And especially of a possible scandal. My first reflex was to leap from the bed, so as to be in a position to strike back. But I sensed that at the slightest movement, he would charge. Only my calm could keep him at a distance, force him into dialogue, prevent him from making a scene.

I succeeded in simulating the greatest naturalness:

"Why do I like talking to Yves? My God, if you want to know, it's because he's the only one among all of you here who's a bit polite, the only one who responds when you say hello."

He stared at me intently, his lips parted, his breath quick. But he didn't take a step forward.

"Keep your smooth talk! Nobody needs it! We don't gab around here. We work. Yves loafs enough already—he doesn't need any chewing the fat to take him away from his work."

He had hardly lowered his voice. Nevertheless, I was keenly aware that he was weakening, that the impulse had worn itself out, and that the worst was over.

One last time, he raised his fist:

"You've been warned, you son of a . . . and stop whispering with him, or I'll settle your hash, understand?"

Then he did an abrupt about-face. And he disappeared, slamming the attic door behind him.

All night long I could hardly sleep. Semi-nightmare. Terrifying visions: scandals, corruption of a minor, court-martial, etc. This brute would be perfectly capable of spreading an awful story around this little village if we were to let ourselves get caught unawares . . . A boy of seventeen, a noncommissioned officer . . . the army doesn't make light of such matters.

The wisest thing would be to clear out, to look for a room somewhere else. And above all to give up the boy . . . but we leave Aunay the day after tomorrow; is it worth changing lodgings? As for giving up the boy . . . after his near-acquiescence . . . how could I?

I ended up by resolving on a half-measure. The room, I'll keep. The boy, that will depend on him. I've sworn to myself not to make any approach during these final days: this morning, I did not attempt to talk to him; presently, I shall not go hang about the exit to the circus. But if the offer should come from him . . .

Monday the 16th.

He came! He spoke to me! In a little while, I'm to meet him on the bank of the Marne. Joy! Joy!

It was this morning while I was getting dressed that he came. The door from the landing opened noiselessly:

"Sshh . . ."

I sprang towards him. Silently, he leapt into my arms, snuggled up against my chest, and suddenly offered me his mouth. His naked breast was burning. We were both trembling. He whom I had in my arms was already no longer entirely the child of the other night; *he* was the one who leaned his whole body against mine, who pressed his legs trammeled in their canvas skirt against mine, and who crushed his young desire, awakened and impatient, against me . . . But that lasted only half a minute. He slipped from my fingers with the suppleness of an eel, and, as I tried to take him back, he caught hold of my two hands and held me away.

He had arranged everything, foreseen everything:

"This evening, on the river, at half past five . . . Like the other day, when we put out the lines . . . There's never anyone around there . . . You know where it is? You go there first, and don't let on. I'll be there at half past five . . . Sshh!"

"Kiss me!"

"This afternoon!"

He was still holding me by the wrists. He stepped back to the door and smiled at me. With so much promise of tenderness, such abandon, already!

"Sshh!"

He let go of my hand, and like a shadow vanished into the dim rectangle of the staircase.

Tomorrow, I'll have to go off and leave him here. But in five days, my tour of duty will be up, I return to civilian life. Who will prevent me from coming back? From coming back, this time, to take him away?

The day seemed endless to me. It was only three o'clock. I went back to the bakery as usual, instead of running right down to the river, as I wanted to do. My absence might have seemed suspicious to the other . . . On the contrary, I must show myself. I'll wait here until they go down to the pump, as I do every day. And when they come through my room, I'll take that moment to briefly say my goodbyes, since we leave Aunay tomorrow at dawn, and I am not supposed to see either of them again before our departure.

Three o'clock. They're across the way in their garret. He's taking his nap there, so close by. Is *he* sleeping? Can he sleep? I'm tossing and turning. Still two hours to kill, in this room where I'm suffocating, with this fever throbbing in my temples.

PART TWO

Sunday, 11 September 88.

What prompted me to get up, to go look for this notebook? It's been there at the bottom of that drawer for two months now. I've never had the courage to open it again. And tonight it's tugging at me. Oh, I have no intention of rereading it! What's the use of suffering more? But I want to add a few pages to it. Perhaps I'll find some peace in finishing off this confidence. Shall I perhaps rid myself of this haunting memory of mine? To examine the facts one by one, once again and more closely, to exorcise this feeling of guilt—absurd—which for two months I have not, I absolutely have not been able to shake. That will require no effort of memory. Everything is only too present in my poor head, worn out with sleeplessness. What a deep impression, what immutable precision of detail is left by the places, the circumstances, whose memory has been planted in us during the fever of desire!

That last evening in Aunay . . . Here is exactly, honestly, how the horrible thing happened . . .

Well then, the better to avert any suspicion, I had decided, as if I weren't to see the boy again, to say goodbye to him in front of Honoré, at the moment when the two of them would be coming through my room. I was rolling up my blanket and fastening my pack when they came in. I took a risk and spoke to Honoré as if no altercation had ever broken out between us.

"I don't know if I'll have a chance this evening . . . We leave tomorrow morning . . . I'm saying goodbye to both of you."

He'd stopped, with his head down, looking furtively up at me. I held out my hand. He finally took it, grumbling:

"G'bye!"

Yves, hanging back, witnessed this scene with curiosity. I went over to him:

"And you too, kid, goodbye!"

He smiled, a little embarrassed, without saying anything. But when we shook hands, he answered the pressure of my fingers. And when Honoré went out the door to the stairs, he turned to me briskly before following him. I questioned him anxiously with a look. He assented with a nod that clearly meant: "See you soon!"

I went downstairs almost immediately. They were under the pump, at the rear of the courtyard. I spotted the master and mistress in the kitchen and went over to the window to take leave of them as well.

"Don't walk off with our towel!" This was all that the old lady found to say to me . . .

The deaf old man was friendlier. He even asked me in to lift a glass with him. I declined and thanked him, and seized my chance to shout very loud, so as to be heard by Honoré, that I couldn't linger because that evening we had a final assembly of the platoon.

Determined to proceed with the maximum of caution, I'd studied the survey map that had been issued to each of us for our training period and had even slipped it into my pocket. To avoid the road to the bridge, where I might meet up with fellow soldiers, and in order not to pass within view of the little beach, where, at that hour, a few children sometimes came to splash about, I had decided to leave the village by the east, as if I were heading off in the direction of the vineyards, and then, after crossing the drained marshes that had been turned into poplar nurseries where nobody ever went, to come out at the place on the bank where I'd hidden the other day to spy on old Ratel's fishing. This spot was wonderfully suitable. Lost in the denseness of the brush, we were certain, unless we'd been shadowed, to elude any prying eyes, even if someone decided to come down the path—which was hardly likely, for in the course of my outings, I'd never run into a living soul on this uninviting bank, overgrown with brambles and bushes that kept you from getting to the edge. Besides, in this season nobody had time to come for a stroll along the river: the entire population was working in the vineyards, a very long way from there.

I had no trouble finding the exact spot where I'd crouched the other afternoon and where I'd made myself seen by Yves. But I needed to be patient. I stretched out on the dry leaves, tensing to control the throbbing of my blood that had me trembling in every limb.

Against all hope, here I was almost at my goal. The boy was about to arrive. He was going to lie down, close to me. The main thing was not to frighten him off by being in too much of a hurry . . . It was by sheer force of sweetness, of tenderness, that I wanted to complete my conquest of him, until he surrendered, until he delivered himself over to his pleasure . . . With what fire he'd thrown himself into my arms that morning! How he'd pressed his whole body against mine, and how beautiful was his upturned face, with his eyelids fluttering, in the half-light of dawn! With what eagerness he had offered me his mouth! What a fresh taste, full of promise, that too-rapid kiss had left me with! My imagination was preparing, down to the slightest details, the moment we were going to live. I had to turn this initiation into a marvelous, an unforgettable success!

A few more minutes and he'd be there . . .

They seemed interminable to me, those minutes. Every second, I glanced anxiously at my watch, astounded by the slowness of the hands. He was on his way . . . He was getting closer. Half past five. Any moment now, he would appear . . . Twenty to six . . . Quarter to . . . He couldn't take any longer. I was holding my breath, giving ear to every rustle, to the slightest flight of a bird, to the shivering of the branches, the clamor of the water . . . To soothe my fever, I took out my map and forced myself to examine it carefully, to trace the various paths that might bring him to me . . .

Six o'clock . . . What was he doing? Why this delay? So much precious time stupidly wasted! Was he hesitant about coming? But no, his nod of agreement on the doorstep, his complicitous wink . . . Had he thought it wise, as I had, to take the long way round? Or else, in this thicket, was he having trouble finding the spot again? I had to restrain myself from leaving my hiding place, against all caution, to go look for him.

Five after six . . . Ten after six . . . A terrible anxiety came over me minute by minute . . . I imagined things: Honoré might have stayed with him when they left the bakery, and Yves was maneuvering in vain to shake him . . . And if he didn't manage to get away? If Honoré, suspicious, stuck stubbornly to him?

Suddenly I thought I made out a peculiar whistle, some distance off. A

bird chirping? Or was it Yves? I got up, straining my ears. Nothing . . .
Then—a long time after, maybe a whole minute—a second time, the same
two notes. No doubt now: a signal, a call . . . But the whistle seemed to come
from far away, from the other side of the river; it couldn't be him . . . Someone from the village? A fisherman? Old Ratel in his punt? But who was he
calling?

I couldn't stand this uncertainty any longer. Slowly, with the caution of a
wildcat, I crawled toward the edge, so I could survey, through the branches,
what was happening on the other side of the water. No boat in sight, no one
on the other bank. I immediately recognized the grassy spot where, the other
night, the grandfather and grandson had been fixing their lines. And then,
another "Pee-weet" told me where to look . . . Goddammit! there he was in
his striped jersey on the opposite bank, lying on his belly in a little gully, his
head up, keeping a lookout. The whole river between us! . . . An agonizing
disappointment pinned me to the spot. How had he ended up over there, the
little idiot? Tears of rage and nervous tension blurred my eyes. What to do?
How were we to get together now?

I made a supreme effort to control myself. Before any rash moves I had to
make sure that neither Ratel nor Honoré nor anyone else was nearby. I
waited several minutes, watching him constantly. No, he did seem to be
alone. Leaning on an elbow, his hand shading his eyes, he scanned the horizon, now to the right, now to the left; observing the various approaches to
the bank where he was, without ever looking in my direction. And this
behavior suddenly explained his presence there to me: a stupid misunderstanding! He had told me: "On the river, like the other night, when they put
out their lines . . ." I'd thought immediately of the north bank, of the place
from which I'd followed the comings and goings of the punt, of that north
bank which was overgrown with vegetation and so perfect for a secret meeting; I'd congratulated myself on such a judicious choice, without for a
moment the idea dawning on me that Yves could be thinking of the other
side, the south bank, which presented nothing but problems: you could get
there only by crossing the bridge, which meant the risk of being noticed; and
mainly, you were entirely in the open there, since it consisted of a long
stretch of grass along the water sparsely planted here and there with a willow
or a poplar.

Absurd! Absurd! So near the goal! And he'd come! And he was there,
willing! Oh, to find a way to outwit fate, no matter what! And first of all, to
get him to see me.

I stood up and resolutely raised my head, my shoulder, my arm from the
brush. But he persisted in looking upstream, downstream, never across from
him.

I tried to whistle "Pee-weet!" I made three attempts at this, each one louder. Finally he turned his head, got up on his knees, and all of a sudden caught sight of me. I saw him jump with surprise. The river was too wide for us to hear each other without shouting; we had to make do with signs. We stared at each other for a few seconds, and together, with the same gesture of anger and despair, we spread our arms, then let them fall.

What to do, indeed? By gesticulating as best I could, I got him to understand that he should retrace his steps and come join me. I made this point several times without eliciting anything but negative movements of the head. Clearly, he had some objection to crossing the bridge again. And to repeat his gesture of refusal with such obstinacy, he must have had a serious reason. Perhaps he'd run into someone, perhaps he'd been seen by some fisherman whom he knew to be stationed there and whose attention he didn't want to attract.

He'd sat back on his heels, facing me, and he remained there like that, with his arms dangling, in a disheartened attitude. More desirable than ever! Ah, if only I'd been able to swim, wouldn't I have thrown myself into the water to reach him! . . . But what about him! Why not? *He* was a good swimmer! . . . Was it so hard for him to get across this accursed river? What kind of chance would he be taking? To be swept along by the current, to land on the bank some distance from me? What would the problem be? Once he'd crossed the water, when he'd landed on my side, I'd certainly manage to get to him through the brush!

Of course! This was our last, our only chance! With a lot of gesturing, making several breaststrokes in the air, I motioned him to swim to me. He understood right away, but again he shook his head negatively, and the movement of his hand indicating the breadth of the river clearly said: "No, it's too far!" Time was pressing. Impatience exacerbated my desire. I couldn't give up this supreme hope. I had to persuade him at any cost. I repeated my gesture, and so insistently that this time he seemed to waver. Slowly, as if with regret, he got up and went down to the water, leaning over to the right and to the left, examining the area, no doubt estimating the strength of the current, measuring the distance between the banks. Then he looked at me for a moment, thoughtful, perplexed. Was he going to refuse again? I kept on encouraging him with signs. He remained standing, his eyebrows knitted, his face expressionless, looking now down at the water, now over to me, without moving.

Obviously, he too was dreadfully disappointed, was suffering, and longed to join me . . . I thought I noticed a vague movement of his shoulders which seemed to say, "No, impossible . . . ," but which could just as well have meant, "Not easy, but worth a try . . ." Slowly, he went to the edge and stopped once again, with his fists on his hips, leaning slightly over the water; his tawny lock, lit by the setting sun, nearly hid his face from me. He no longer seemed concerned about me. He was gazing intently at the river. What was he going to do? Suddenly he straightened up, and with a decisive movement pulled his jersey and undershirt over his head. I shivered with joy.

He unbuckled his belt; then, modestly, he turned around. The pants, falling down around his feet, uncovered his loins, the curve of his thighs, his calves. With his back still to me, he gathered up his clothes and rolled them together into a turban that he secured to his head with his leather belt. Only then did he bring himself to face me. It was the first time that I'd seen him in his nakedness, that I'd glimpsed the manly secret of that body: a pale shadow barely crowned by a gingery tint . . . I was trembling . . . How beautiful he was! How pure and fresh that slender body seemed, how lustrous that young golden flesh showed against that background of greenery in the evening light! He avoided meeting my eyes. He bent forward, and all of a sudden his reflection appeared to me in the dark mirror of the water. Was he still balking? It lasted no more than a second. He sat down on the grass and silently let himself slide into the river.

He swam with a will, heading right for me. I watched him coming, my whole being taut with anticipation. He was already a good distance from his starting point, and the space that separated him from me did not seem to decrease. He was going at it, however, with all of his young strength. The splashes of water threw silvery spangles around his turbaned head. Intermittently I made out his features, a face that wasn't smiling, a somewhat grimacing face, with its eyelids almost closed, its lips shut tight, a forehead I didn't recognize under that heavy headdress that had caused the blond tuft to disappear . . . One stroke followed another . . . The space between us did not diminish. A dull anxiety crept over me. This crossing would never end! . . . Seconds, minutes passed. I couldn't stand that immobility, that concentration, that worry. How far he still was from the middle of the river! . . . And suddenly, for no precise reason, I was seized with the certainty that he was in danger. The attempt was insane, it couldn't succeed, it had to be stopped at once! Nothing mattered anymore: hope, impatience, desire, everything was swept away. I began to gesticulate to get him to give up, to turn around immediately. Finally he saw me, raised himself up from the water for an instant, smiled at me, and made a sign that no, he didn't want to. He'd taken on a challenge, he wouldn't accept defeat. And, yet again, he charged forward. But the movement of his head had upset the balance of the bundle: the turban, poorly fastened, slipped backwards. With his hand, he tried to put it back in place. Feeling that he wasn't succeeding, he decided to keep it on his nape, holding it there with the belt strapped around his neck like a dog-collar.

This brief pause had cut down his momentum. He started swimming again, but not so fast . . . Suddenly, something happened. His head seemed to swivel abruptly, and instead of seeing his face, I no longer had anything before me but the blond mass of hair and the bundle of clothes strapped to his nape: he was turning his back to me. I hoped for a moment that he was going to put back, that he was saved, that I was going to be relieved of this unbearable anguish. No: he'd only spun round under an unexpected assault by the current, and already he'd managed to resume his course. But the exertion must have been hard. With terror I noticed signs of fatigue: the face more drawn; the irregular strokes, now coming at long intervals, now rushed and choppy. My fear changed to panic when I saw him swivel again and yaw off sharply to the right. No more doubt: a calamity was about to happen! . . . I lost all control, I wanted to shout: "Yves! Go back!" As soon as the first syllable was out of my mouth, its harsh plangency over the surface of the water, in the terrifying silence of the valley, made me get a grip on myself and clap my hand to my mouth . . . Keep quiet, at all costs keep quiet. Besides, what was the use? He was now in the middle of the river, he'd have had as hard a time getting back to his bank as reaching mine. If there had been a boat there, any way at all to go to him . . . nothing! I kept repeating to myself, fearfully: "No, no . . . Keep still! Don't call out!" Anyway, it was too late . . . and then, there wasn't a single human being within earshot.

My fist in my mouth, petrified, powerless, desperate, shaking with every nerve, I was leaning forward . . . Terrified by what I saw, terrified by what I was going to see, wild-eyed, I watched my little one struggle against the flow that was carrying him off course . . . My life, his, hanging in that gaze . . . His strength was giving out. He tried, I think, but in vain, to turn over on his back. Apparently the violence of the current was too great. Was he perhaps also hampered by that bundle of wet clothes that was hanging from his neck and strangling him? He was far away, I couldn't see him well. A small blond spot half sunk in the water . . . It disappeared, then reappeared, then disappeared again, to reappear once more. An arm rose up, a stiff, motionless arm, held out in desperation. I couldn't bear the sight of that arm . . . My eyelids closed in spite of me. Two seconds . . . Ah, I confess it with a sense of shame, of horror: during those two seconds, with a precise and lucid terror, I thought of everything, but of myself first! . . . Death, suspicions, Honoré, inquest, examination, court . . . My life shattered . . .

The thought which at that moment took hold of me with a lightning clarity, I shall never forget. It was twofold. I first said to myself, in a flash:

"He's drowning. Impossible to hide. I'm done for!" And immediately, with an inexpressible relief: "Mama's dead. I'm the only one involved."

I grasped my jaw in my hand. Keep quiet! So that no one, no one would be able someday to denounce me!

Two seconds. But when I opened my eyes again, the Marne was bare . . . Without so much as an eddy. Horribly bare, silent, and forsaken, as far as the eye could see, all the way to the bridge.

For one long minute, still hoping for the miracle, clutching a bush, prey to a nameless terror, I stared at that smooth and shining surface, with frightened eyes blinded by tears. Then my fingers, gone lifeless, let go of the stem I'd been clinging to, and I slumped down into the midst of the brush. Sobs choked me: *"Mon petit . . . mon petit . . ."*

I AM TRYING to remember everything. The first thought that broke through the darkness was "Above all they mustn't find me here! Run!" Such a stinging thought that it gave me the energy to move. I grabbed my fatigue cap, which had remained caught in the branches, and, doubled over, I rushed forward in the direction opposite the current. Lashed by my panic, I went as fast as the thickness of the bushes allowed, muffling my steps, like a hunted criminal. I ran like that for five or six hundred meters, maybe more. I was exhausted. The brush, it seemed, was getting less and less thick. It would be reckless to go farther. Stay hidden until nightfall. Stop, think things over, decide on a plan of action . . .

It is excruciating to confess: *I was no longer thinking of the boy*! Fear wiped out all feeling. The instinct of self-preservation had created the void. To be lucid, I didn't even have to push aside my grief. Nothing counted but my own safety. The mentality of a killer . . . My whole being was dominated by the fear of being discovered and by the desperate wish to escape suspicion . . . Be calm, think things over. Now I could. The physical effort had restored the body's balance. The brain was working with an incredible clarity.

The thought that the platoon's departure just happened to be scheduled for the next day at dawn suddenly brightened me with a cynical comfort. A providential coincidence! Once far from Aunay, I was feeling almost saved already . . . Twelve hours to wait. Hold on until then. Appear calm, so as not to arouse suspicions.

I constantly repeated to myself: "Stay calm . . . stay calm." And I reasoned things out. He sank like a stone. No one saw anything. I'm the only one to know. The only one, absolutely the only one. Therefore everything depends on me, on my steadiness, on my self-control . . . Drowned men stay under water for a long time before reappearing. The body won't be recovered for a day, maybe not for two or three (I was thinking of "the drowned man," of the "body": I wasn't thinking of the boy). Besides, the current is continuing to carry it off. They'll find it a long way from here . . . unless it's stopped by one of the bridge piers? Not very likely . . . And even if they find it at the bridge, how could they locate the spot where the accident happened? No clothes on the bank. Not a trace. Even if they should interrogate me . . . But why would they interrogate *me*? First, I'll be gone. Because I'm leaving, I leave tomorrow at dawn. And who could think of me? It wouldn't even occur to Honoré . . . And then, what could they suspect me of? No one knows that we were supposed to meet up . . . No one in the world can guess what happened. No one! An accident. An ordinary accident. A drowning. I've never gone swimming with him, who could think of mixing me up in the incident? . . . And, supposing the worst, even if someone should run into me here, more than a kilometer from the bridge, haven't I gone off in the direction of the river many times, for the simple pleasure of taking a walk? . . . There would be no lack of witnesses . . . Nevertheless, I must take every possible precaution. Don't leave the brush before it gets dark. And get back to the village by a roundabout way. Suddenly, the idea came to me: "Suppose they stop me, suppose they search me! I've got to destroy my notebook!" I put my hand in my pocket, I felt it. It was all that remained to me of the wonderful, terrible adventure. Get rid of it? I couldn't bring myself to do it. I committed this mad imprudence. I kept it. There would be time to deal with it if I sensed suspicions coming round to me . . .

I looked at my watch. Seven-fifteen. The light was fading fast. Within an hour, it would be completely dark. Wait. Stay calm . . .

As I reassured myself, my memory awoke, the events of the drama came back to me again, stood out with a hallucinatory precision. I thought I would faint. My brow was covered with sweat. My teeth chattered. I had a sudden attack of hiccups; I vomited.

Stay calm, at all costs stay calm . . . As if I'd been standing before a judge, I stubbornly sought to exonerate myself. Had I forced him to come? It was he who'd suggested the meeting place. Could I have imagined? . . . He had assured me that he was a good swimmer. How could he not have been aware of the fierceness of the current? And hadn't I done everything to make him turn around and go back before it was too late? It was he, who, through his own rashness, his stupid obstinacy . . . And then my whole rationalization toppled . . . Who'd had the idea of this insane crossing? Who had forced the boy to attempt it, in spite of his resistance, in spite of his refusals? . . . I saw him again, standing on the bank, hesitating . . . I saw that adolescent body, standing in its splendor, in the light of the setting sun . . .

It was at this moment that remorse hit me. Flat on my stomach in the dead leaves, repeating through my sobs those two words that I murmur every night in my sleeplessness: *"Mon petit . . . mon petit . . . ,"* I howled with grief, my face buried in my arms.

The torture had only just begun.

After a long detour through pastures, in a darkness thick enough so that I could neither be seen from far off nor recognized from up close, I re-entered the town through the district of the water tower. It was the hour when the vineyard workers, who are numerous in that part of town and come home late, are still at supper. I ran no risk of being encountered except in the center by people who couldn't know where I was coming from. Indeed, in the village I did meet several comrades from my platoon who were chatting on their way home to bed and who paid no attention to me. Besides, I had an answer ready in case I was asked why I hadn't come to the mess. My aversion to long meals and drinking sessions was known; no one would be surprised that, precisely that evening, I'd avoided putting in an appearance at the Trois Écus, where our group had organized a "farewell banquet" with champagne.

The walk had somewhat allayed my fever, but not my fear: it kept growing, the closer I came to the bakery. What was awaiting me there? Would I be strong enough to face the unexpected? Would I be able to avoid getting flustered if they spoke to me of Yves' absence?

But this fear—this fear that had taken hold of me from the moment I'd had the foreboding of misfortune; which had kept me from crying out, from calling for help; which had given me the monstrous courage to run away without doing anything to get someone to search the river to try and find the body, and attempt, against all hope, to bring it back to life; this fear of perhaps being compromised in a dubious drama, of being treated forever as a pariah, stripped of an income, ruined, "sunk," I too, with no way out; this fear that had gripped the whole of my being for more than two hours was nevertheless what kept me standing, stiffening myself, and lent me the strength to return to the house at an easy, dawdling pace, with a cigarette trembling in my lips, like a man who knows nothing and has nothing to feel guilty about.

The street was dark and silent. The big door had been left ajar. For me, perhaps? I pushed it open, passed under the archway, crossed the courtyard in the dark. I avoided making noise, but I didn't try to muffle my steps. The bay window of the kitchen was shut, Mlle. Deuillot's shutters were closed, the bakehouse was dark, and dark as well were the windows in Honoré's garret on the second floor. I groped my way up the staircase. My room . . . Closing the door, I had the absurd impression that I'd arrived at a refuge . . . Without a light, I went over to the window; and it was really there, when I found myself again at that lookout from which, so many times, I had followed the boy's comings and goings, that the horror of the irreparable appeared to me in all its tragic nakedness. The straining of will that had allowed me to get that far deserted me. Bent double, my forehead on the blind, my shoulder leaning on the stile, my head empty and ringing, my arms lifeless, my hands like lead, I was shaking like a victim of ataxia. If someone had come in, I'd have been incapable of standing up straight, of uttering a word. This stark notion suddenly brought back some of my strength. I managed to pull myself together, to think. I tried to lend an ear, to catch a noise, a footfall, a snore, any sign of life in that dead house, but I heard nothing except the battering blows of my heart. Nevertheless, something had certainly happened here. The boy was so regular in his habits, so little independent, that since the beginning of supper his lateness must have been surprising, and, as time went on, must have become a cause for serious alarm . . . What had they done? Had they all gone off to look for him? Even the old ones? It wasn't very likely. They must have waited on the doorstep until nightfall, alerting passersby and neighbors; then they'd ended up going back in, no doubt, and going to bed, putting the matter off until the next morning in broad daylight, with that caution, that resigned patience, that reluctance to act so characteristic of the peasant race, which waits for the first sweats of the death agony before going to fetch the doctor. My gaze remained fixed on the enigmatic black rectangle of Honoré's window. Had he dropped off to sleep like a brute? Or rather, stretched out on his bed, was he still awake, all alone, keeping his ears open, turning all the possible suppositions over and over in his skull? . . . Had he heard me, did he know I was there? Wasn't he about to suddenly appear? To interrogate me? . . . I had to anticipate everything, be on my guard.

I made a superhuman effort to get back into my character: I was the one *who knows nothing.* I should, as usual, go through all my habitual moves, light my candle, go to bed. But there was a risk that my light would wake Honoré, conjure him up . . . It was a relief not to find the candlestick. It was no longer on the table. It wasn't on the dresser. It had been removed. Why? Everything that was out of the ordinary, that night, awakened my fears . . . It came to me, as I realized my towel had disappeared, that this was a stroke of the old lady's, her parting shot: she'd put away everything that the boarder might have been able to carry off when he went; she'd even had the nerve to strip the sheets!

I took off my shoes and stretched out, fully dressed, on the mattress. At moments, I went over my role again: "I'm coming back from a walk, I know nothing, I've seen no one . . ." At other moments, with a gasp, I saw it all again, the shimmering surface of the water, the little head floating . . . the naked arm that had risen, just like that, in a final appeal . . . Then, once again, I thought of Honoré. At midnight, he was going to open the door, come through the room to go down to his work. He'd talk, he'd ask questions. "I don't know anything. I didn't see Yves again . . . Me? I went for a walk out by the vineyards . . ."

But midnight rang, and Honoré didn't get up. Suddenly, a little before one, I leapt to the window: it seemed to me I'd heard the dull bump of the gate and made out a footfall under the archway. Indeed a shadow was crossing the courtyard slantwise, heading for the bakehouse. Honoré? The slow gait wasn't like him. The window lit up. It *was* he. Where was he coming from so late? From the police station at Ay? No, in the country people aren't in such a hurry to rouse the constabulary. All evening long he must have been prowling the village, questioning people, scouring the countryside. I didn't let him out of my sight. I saw him take off his shirt and his pants, put on his waist-cloth. Then he went out again. Was he going to come up? I hastily threw myself back onto my bed. No: he was working the pump. I went back to the window. In the light from the bakehouse I could see his naked torso and his movements in the corner of the courtyard. He filled a bucket. Before lifting it, he got down on his knees to stick his face in it, and I heard him drinking, like a horse. Then he went back into the bakehouse with the bucket.

I spent two hours standing behind my blind, following his silent silhouette with my eyes as it moved about behind the panes. I saw him plunge the upper part of his body into the trough and knead the dough interminably. Then he lit the oven. I was concentrating all my attention on his work, so as to think less.

The church bell tolled three. The quarter hour. The half hour. It was time for me to get ready for the assembly of the platoon. A growing anguish gripped me. Should I avoid Honoré? Or, rather, make the bold move, go in and shake his hand? But I'd said goodbye to him the night before, in the presence of the boy. Since I knew nothing, I could very well leave without starting my goodbyes all over again. By picking the moment when he was tossing wood into the fire, I could disappear without his hearing me.

But I hadn't allowed for the noise of my boots in the silence of the night, or for the clinking of the chain on my mess kit, balanced on top of my pack. I was scarcely in the middle of the courtyard when I saw, against the light of the fire, the shadow suddenly straighten up, turn around, lunge for the door. In two bounds he was on me, blocking my way.

"What the hell are *you* doing here?"

I was so far from expecting this kind of attack that I didn't have to put on a show of amazement. I had stopped and was staring at him. Strangely calm, suddenly: truly, at that moment, I was indeed the man I needed to be, the man who knows nothing, who doesn't understand.

"Me? I'm going to assembly, of course! Have you gone mad?"

He didn't seem to have heard.

"Where were you all night?"

"Me? Up there, in my room."

"Liar!"

"Wait a minute, Honoré . . ."

He'd come closer still. I could smell his sour breath:

"Bastard! You're lying! You didn't come home last night! You were with the apprentice! . . . Where is he?"

"What apprentice? Yves? . . . You're out of your mind . . . I came back last night the same as usual, and I went to bed. I haven't seen Yves since yesterday, with you."

The tone was even, so natural, and my good faith so well acted, that he was taken aback.

I immediately pressed my advantage:

"I have no idea what you're going on about. But what I do know is that you're a barbarian. Goodbye!"

And, walking steadily, I passed in front of him and went out under the archway.

He'd let me leave. I thought I was free. Suddenly, he sprang and caught me just as I was tugging at the latch of the carriage door. I felt myself knocked off balance in the dark, driven back against one half of the door—which, fortunately, I had opened. For an instant he had me nailed to the panel with his two fists crushing my shoulders, and he breathed into my face, in a low, panting voice, through clenched teeth:

"Listen, you bastard! If you've corrupted the kid, if he's taken off with you, I'm telling you: tomorrow you'll have every cop in the county on your heels. And you can be sure of one thing, I'll know how to find the both of you, and I'll shoot *you* down like a dog!"

"Moron!"

I shoved him away with such violence that he fell back a step. I was able to dart out and push the heavy door shut behind me.

Staggering under the weight of the pack, loaded down with my field gear, I plunged into the night, running. Everything was silent. He hadn't dared come after me.

I breathed again. It was over. In a few minutes, I'd have rejoined the platoon. In a few hours, we'd be far away . . . Today, tomorrow maybe, the body would be found. Honoré's suspicions would fall away of their own accord. A reckless act, a drowning. Who could accuse me? Three lines in the local newspapers . . . "Tragic swim" . . .

I was saved!

Sunday, 12 September.

No, it was only a prelude, the beginning of a new torture, more circumscribed, more secret . . . My thoughts going round and round . . . The beginning of this nervous collapse that's been gnawing at me for months, which has turned me into this wreck, incapable of any work. This will be the end of me, if Dr. Paillasse's treatment doesn't succeed in ridding me of my hallucinations, if I can't regain enough balance to resume a normal life.

A good thing I fainted on the march home! A lucky blackout, that made everyone, even the doctors, think that this fever, this mental agitation, are the aftereffects of sunstroke!

I'd still managed to keep up with the others, to stay in the ranks to march and march like an automaton for close to four hours . . . Leaving the village, I'd been able to look without flinching at that thin milky trail which, as the night drew to an end, floated over the valley and outlined the course of the fatal river. A single thought in my head: I'd left, I was moving away from the danger, I was putting behind me all the horror I'd been living through since the day before. Four straight hours, to the sloppy rhythm of marching songs . . . I was still keeping up. We were already nearing Châlons. It was nine or ten o'clock, the sun was starting to beat down hard. The platoon was going to stop for the final break before entering the outskirts of the town. Sweating, shivering, on my last legs, my eyes riveted to the pack swaying in front of me, I was putting one foot in front of the other like a sleepwalker . . . Hang on. Make it to the barracks, my room, my bed . . . And then, pow! Passed out . . .

MY TOUR OF duty was over; the platoon dispersed. After a few days, I'd been able to return to Paris. I convinced myself that with my escaping that accursed terrain, coming back to my old haunts, taking up my activities again, the inner torment would have less of a grip on me. What an illusion!

I hadn't been back two weeks when one evening, coming home, I found in my mail an envelope bearing the stamp of the prefecture of police. I was requested to appear, within three days' time, at the office of M. Mouraillon, police inspector, about a matter concerning myself.

My first thought was: "A good thing Mother's dead."

I envisioned all possible escapes: flight, going abroad, suicide . . . Yes, I said to myself, several times: "If I were to kill myself tonight, everything would be over, I'd be forever at peace . . ." To die, I didn't have enough courage. To leave the country, not enough money . . . In the morning, calmer, I thought things through. Once again I went over everything in my mind, down to the slightest details. No one could know. No one could even suspect the truth. I had lived in the same house as Yves, surely they wanted to call me in as a witness? . . . To run away—that was exactly what would focus suspicion on me!

At ten o'clock, I was shown into the office of the inspector, who stood up politely to greet me, almost apologizing for having put me out. I found myself in the presence of a man of my age, well dressed, with an open face and a cordial smile: quite different in every way from the wily and suspicious old policeman before whom I'd imagined myself having to appear. He was not alone: a young clerk, who was tidying up papers near the window, came in as I entered the room and sat down, with a notepad in his hand, at the same desk as the inspector.

This unhoped-for welcome had, right away, given me a great deal of confidence; and it was with the greatest naturalness that I settled into the armchair that was pointed out to me, and took the initiative, in a jaunty tone:

"So, what the devil is this about, Inspector?"

Before answering me, and as if he needed to refresh his memory, M. Mouraillon rapidly leafed through a notebook that he had in front of him. Then, after having checked my identity—and having said amiably: "A man of letters? We don't have much free time to devote to our reading, in our line of work, but I do seem to have come across your byline . . ."—he asked me if it was true that I had, last July, in the course of military exercises in the region of Châlons, been stationed in the town of Aunay-sur-Marne and lodged in the home of a certain Deuillot, a baker. I answered in the affirmative, without ceasing to look surprised.

The dreaded moment was approaching.

"What can you tell me concerning the accidental death of young Janvier?"

"Janvier?"

"A ward of the State, Yves Janvier, baker's apprentice."

"Dead? The apprentice?"

"Drowned."

"It can't be . . ."

By luck, the anxiety that choked me and altered my voice, instead of betraying me, served my purpose, I believe, by giving a plausible authenticity to the sympathetic astonishment that I affected. Yes, I remembered this boy called Yves, who was employed at the bakery . . . He hadn't seemed like a daredevil, though . . . Drowned? Owing to some stupid act, some wild stunt? . . . Poor kid . . . It had happened after my departure, obviously, since I remembered having seen him on the last day, and even having said goodbye to him, along with the assistant baker with whom he worked . . .

At that moment, the secretary broke in:

"No, *before* your departure . . ."

I had, several times, felt him staring at me. What did he know? . . . In an amicable way, we, the inspector and I, cleared up this question of the date. The platoon had left Aunay on Tuesday morning; the body had been dredged up on Wednesday evening; but the youngster's absence had been established as early as Monday evening. How, lodging in the house, had I known nothing of it? Because I'd left before daybreak, when everyone was still asleep at the bakery; and since then I hadn't had the slightest contact with the inhabitants of Aunay.

The inspector concluded:

"This being so, you can't give us any personal information regarding this matter?"

"None."

The secretary went back to writing. M. Mouraillon seemed neither disappointed nor even surprised by my answers. Once again, he apologized for having made me come in. He had been compelled to do so by a request from the police at Ay, whose report he had on his table; a report in which I was vaguely implicated, on account of statements of a certain Honoré Lebat, assistant at the aforementioned Deuillot bakery, who claimed rather confusedly that I might have been a witness to the accident. Moreover, added M. Mouraillon, although the sergeant who had signed this long report had asked that I be called in for my testimony before the case was closed for good, he did not seem to lend much credence to the vague and contradictory statements of the assistant.

While talking, he glanced at his watch. I sensed that the game was won. He was in a hurry to get it over with . . . He took the paper on which his clerk had continued to scribble throughout the interview.

"It only remains to write up the report of your deposition. Do you want to dictate it to my secretary, or would you rather that we do it for you, summarizing his notes?"

"Please, go right ahead, you're used to doing it."

"It will take about ten minutes."

And to make my wait easier, he genially handed me the dossier, with this terrible word:

"Have a look, if it *amuses* you . . ."

I took it, without flinching. It was a folder containing about twenty pages. I'd have had time to read it twice. I can't claim that I read it, for my heart was beating so hard, all the lines of that tiny laborious hand were dancing under my gaze. But what I did decipher and take in was enough to convince me of just how narrow an escape I'd had . . . That brute Honoré, incapable of logical reasoning, seemed to have been endowed in this instance with a sort of animal instinct that had taken the place of perspicaciousness and allowed him dimly but surely to sniff out the truth. With a diabolical patience and tenacity he had managed to build up against me, if not a formal case, then at least a series of plausible suppositions buttressed by a multitude of verifiable little facts, which, in the hands of a prosecuting attorney, could form a devastating whole.

Did the secretary know what was in the dossier? I still wonder. He stared at me several times with a strange insistence. In any case, Inspector Mouraillon himself had assuredly not taken the trouble to study that report, or else his interrogation would have had an entirely different tone and I would doubtless have been received not as a witness but rather as a suspect. I was the beneficiary of an incredible stroke of luck. I suppose that, having given me three days to come in, he was caught unawares by the swiftness with which I had answered his summons: he must have just had time to look up the dossier and hurriedly glance through its conclusions while I was waiting in the anteroom. Was the promptitude of my arrival perhaps also for him more or less vaguely a presumption in my favor? A man who has something to be guilty about doesn't generally show so much eagerness in placing himself at the disposal of the police . . .

But I was trembling with a retrospective fear as he showed me to the door of his office. And I tremble still whenever I think that that report hasn't been destroyed, that it still exists, that it's lying somewhere in the file of closed cases, and that the minutes have surely been kept at the police station in Ay . . .

Honoré's accusation was terrible: it led, pure and simple, to a conclusion of *murder*!

According to him, from the moment of my arrival at Aunay, I'd tried to get close to the boy; little by little, I'd beguiled and corrupted him; finally, on the eve of my departure, I'd lured him to the banks of the Marne, and there, taking advantage of the darkness and the loneliness of the spot, I'd undressed him and had my way with him. Then, seized by panic, afraid of being discovered and denounced by Honoré (who had several times stumbled onto my machinations and of whose suspicions I was aware), perhaps also afraid that the boy might confess, I hadn't hesitated to cover up all traces of the offense by doing away with my victim: I'd strangled the boy, as the bruises on the neck showed, and I'd thrown his body in the water, counting on his being carried away by the current and on his death being regarded as an ordinary swimming accident.

In support of this abominable thesis, he had assembled an impressive number of little "proofs." He had forgotten nothing that could be used against me.

Wasn't it obvious, to begin with, that since I, Xavier de Balcourt, a *noble-*

man certainly accustomed to the finer things, had immediately turned down my gratis billeting order which ensured me an excellent bedroom in the presbytery, in order to rent, at my own expense, at the bakery, an uncomfortable garret for which I'd paid in advance and a good price, it was with the aim of living close to the apprentice?

On the very first day, what was more, Honoré had caught me in Yves' room, in conversation with him; and he'd had to chase me away . . . To get the boy into my room, I'd asked him to come every morning to wake me up; and Honoré had had to put an end to this . . . Did I not already have the idea of taking the apprentice down to the banks of the river? I had, a day or two after moving in, insisted on knowing if there was a beach for swimming . . . One evening, after nightfall, Honoré had entered my room unannounced and had found Yves, half undressed, hiding in the space beside my bed, while I lay on the bed with no light . . . In order to spend an entire evening alone with the boy, I'd invited him to come with me to the circus; this shady scheme had fallen through only thanks to Honoré's intervention . . . He'd brought a boy from the village, Ratel's grandson, to the police station to give evidence that one afternoon in the Place des Halles there had been between Yves and myself an interminable conversation in undertones, that we had appeared to be plotting and to not want to be heard . . . Furthermore, wasn't my constant presence at the bakery during all my spare time revealing? Why, the moment I was free, did I come and shut myself up in that stifling garret instead of going to smoke and play cards with my fellow soldiers in the village's cafés? Why, if not because I was always on the lookout for a chance to meet up with the apprentice?

The day of the boy's disappearance, his attitude and mine had been particularly suspicious. Yves, to escape from Honoré's surveillance, had pretended that he'd sprained his wrist and had rushed off into town to get tended to by Pivert, the pharmacist . . . But after supper, when Honoré, worried, had gone to look for him, neither Pivert nor either of the two other pharmacists had received a visit from the apprentice. On the other hand, two little girls said they'd seen him taking off at a rapid pace down the road that leads to the bridge . . . As for me, just at the time when Yves was faking his sprain, I had told a barefaced lie to M. Deuillot, declining to take some wine with him on the pretext of having to be present at the platoon's final assembly, which had turned out to be untrue. And—a still more conclusive fact— I, who used to come home early to go to bed and who crossed the courtyard every evening before the end of the meal at the bakery, hadn't come by that evening. Yet, owing to Yves' absence, the meal had been served a half-hour late. Where was I?

That wasn't all. Day after day, Honoré had so painstakingly examined the riverbanks that he'd sure enough ended up discovering the spot that I'd stomped around on for such a long time while waiting for the boy: a place in the midst of brush, where, said the report, the leaf-strewn soil, deeply trampled, seemed to have been the scene of a struggle. And, quite nearby, he had picked up a survey map, which could only have belonged to a member of the platoon. (It was without a doubt the map I'd taken with me and that I must have forgotten on the ground.)

To identify the body, which had been found near Épernay, Honoré had gone to the county seat with old Deuillot; and he had drawn the attention of the lieutenant of the Épernay police to the bruises on the neck. He had been so insistent that the doctor previously in charge of the certification of death had to be called in. By good fortune, the doctor had discarded outright the hypothesis of strangulation: he affirmed that the death had no other cause than immersion and that it was accidental; he explained the marks, which anyhow were much more pronounced at the back of the neck than under the chin, by the prolonged chafing against the hair of the leather belt that was holding the bundle of clothes on the nape. Without this categorical declaration, which cut short any supposition of crime, what would have happened?

I only note, among the numerous details with which the report was crammed, those that struck me and that come to mind. The oddest was the writing in that report. One sensed in it the application of a police sergeant, hampered by the poverty of his vocabulary, concerned, nevertheless, with his responsibilities in case a prosecutorial investigation should ensue, but constantly torn between the desire to carry out his duty scrupulously and the distrust inspired in him by Honoré's tendentious and rambling statements. It was clear that the latter, with a stubborn and vindictive tenaciousness that nothing could deter, must have returned to the charge twenty times over, each time bringing supplementary details and new accusations against me in order to obtain an extension of the inquest and prevent the matter from being shelved.

However, one could easily see that the worthy policeman, while faithfully relating the accusations, the communications, and even the slightest suppositions of his informant, remained personally incredulous. The following skeptical formulations clearly implied the very limited credence that he attached to the successive denunciations of this narrow-minded, impassioned and biased witness: "We have today received a new deposition from one Honoré Lebat, who believes he can assert that . . ." "One Honoré Lebat claims that . . ." "According to the allegations of one Honoré Lebat, it would seem that . . ." "On this point, we have had no confirmation of the statements of one Honoré Lebat . . . ," etc.

The dossier reproduced, in conclusion, the doctor's report and the personal opinion of the Épernay police lieutenant, who both confidently came to the formal conclusion of an ordinary accident such as occurred every summer in the region.

Inspector Mouraillon had said as he took leave of me: "Will you be in Paris *for the next few days*? In case there might be some detail to check with you. But I really don't think we'll have to bother you again . . ."

That was six weeks ago. Officially, everything is therefore finished. But I have yet to regain my balance. My imagination, upset by the shock, leaves me only brief respites. My nights are simply a series of nightmares, where, as in a kaleidoscope, the same elements are always recombining . . . Ten times a day, without reason, at the moments when I'm the busiest or the calmest, or the most distracted—at my worktable, in the middle of a meal, during a conversation or a walk—suddenly an attack of fever sets my blood on fire, dizziness overwhelms me, my vision blurs, my breath comes haltingly, my forehead breaks out in a sweat, and any effort to stave off the attack is impossible for me: my will escapes me, my paralyzed attention cannot focus on anything else, I feel literally laid low, given over like an inert being to this absurd feeling of guilt which nothing justifies and from which no attempt at reasoning can set me free. Sometimes this lasts only a few instants and sometimes hours without my being able to stop my fall. The images of the tragic film unfold before my hallucinating vision with a merciless precision. Ideas, always the same, follow one another in my obsessed brain. Words, always the same, rise to my lips. And it's to the boy that I address this barren and unavailing monologue . . . "It's you who set the meeting place . . . It's you who got the bank wrong . . . Did I force you to cross the river? It was up to you to know if you could . . . I even did everything to make you give up while there was still time . . . You stupidly kept at it out of pride . . . How am I at fault? How am I accountable? In no way. Could I have guessed that you weren't a good enough swimmer? Could I have suspected the strength of the current? What reproach can you lay against me? None! . . . That I didn't call for help? But there was no one within earshot . . . And even if someone had been able to hear me, find a boat, get out there . . . You had disappeared so fast, the current carried you off with such force . . . To call out would have served no purpose except to unleash a scandal . . . A good thing I had the strength to keep quiet! A good thing I had the courage to witness the ghastly thing in silence! . . . No, you have nothing to reproach me with . . . Absolutely nothing! . . . So, *mon petit,* why, why . . ."

*

Xavier's notebook ended there, with that unfinished sentence. And it was less than two months after having written this second part of his diary that Xavier de Balcourt committed suicide.

CHAPTER XIV

Life as a Student in Paris

ONCE I ARRIVED in Paris, my life as a student was set up with my Uncle Éric's help.

It was agreed with my father that I was coming to Paris to study for my admission to Saint-Cyr, but I had obtained his consent to study at the same time, and secondarily as it were, for my *licence ès lettres.* In Uncle Éric's eyes, and in mine as well, it was the reverse.

I had thus enrolled at the Sorbonne, among the candidates for the *licence ès lettres.* But I was also a day pupil at the Lycée Saint-Louis in the class of the future Saint-Cyrians.

Thanks to the complicity and backing of my Uncle Éric, who had been at Normale with the principal of Saint-Louis, I had arranged to take only the main courses there, which gave me an even freer existence than that of the day pupils, something of a special status. To such an extent that I could even occasionally skip a class that I was supposed to attend without it occurring to the teacher to mark me absent. In a pinch, if my absence was motivated by a desire to attend a special session at the Sorbonne, Uncle Éric would not refuse to jot a word on his card to get me excused by the administration at Saint-Louis.

My father knew nothing of this.

I spent most of my days at the Sorbonne, where I not only put in a very regular appearance at the "seminars"—advanced, private classes reserved exclusively for the students preparing for the *licence,* where *explications de texte* were done in a small group, as well as the correcting of dissertations and of Latin and Greek translations (Tacitus, *The Bacchae* of Euripides)—but where I also attended certain large public lectures on Montaigne, Pascal, Thucydides. And I so enjoyed that atmosphere that I would often, out of curiosity, slip into this or that classroom where a course in philosophy, or philology, or history, or art history was being given. I would ensconce myself in a corner near the door, get a sense of the teachers, feverishly take notes and more notes on everything, and would become intoxicated as I discovered and explored the official humanism of the University of that time. More than once, rather than returning to work in my room at the rue de Fleurus, I went up and sat in the library of the Sorbonne, where I liked the free and studious ambiance, the big tables with their lamps, the collective silence, and where I had the most diverse books brought to me, and lost myself in endless reading, which I talked about later at dinner with my uncle in order to prolong my pleasure still further.

My taste for books, for being surrounded by books, was born at that period. There were none at le Saillant. My father, in his office, had a little rosewood display cabinet with wire netting where a few practical books were lined up—dictionaries, treatises on cattle breeding and beekeeping, as well as numbered clothbound folders in which he filed away gardening and supply catalogues. That was it. In a corner of the attic were stacked, right on the floor, a few piles of old volumes bound in calf, mainly incomplete sets, for the most part religious books (my handsome edition of *The Spirit of Christianity** comes from that scrap heap) and countless copies of *The Propagation of the Faith*. It was in Paris that I discovered the kind of spiritual atmosphere provided by the sight and constant proximity of books. At the rue de Fleurus, everything took place amidst books: the walls were nothing but rows of books, each of whose spines ended up having for every one of us a familiar, friendly meaning (those books, transported here upon the death of my Aunt Ma, are at this moment the comforting walls of my prison†).

I had so quickly acquired this taste for books that, quite often, on the pretext of having to consult dictionaries or to compare texts, instead of staying in my room to work of an evening, I would sit in the huge, overheated, shadow-filled library, at a corner of the big table, under the lamp. Nearby, my uncle was working too, in his study, its door usually open. He sometimes came in to get a book, and would take a minute to see what I was doing; each time he passed through, I would receive some cogent insight, some apt pointer, which he drew from his prodigious erudition and which spared me much wasted time and many a mistake.

Often too, in another lighted corner of the room, Aunt Ma, bent over some piece of embroidery or fixing a dress, would linger there, like us, in silence, with her brown poodle at her feet.

I delighted in being there, part of that life of work, happy to feel understood and helped, happy as well to be finally treated as a companion and no longer as the boy who, even the year before, was told: "It's late, you need to go to bed."

I took a childish pleasure in staying up. And sometimes I lingered there, past midnight, alone, in an indescribable state of well-being. And my aunt, before going upstairs, would come and put a glass of Marsala and some cookies by my side, "so that you don't go to bed on an empty stomach . . ."

---

*By Chateaubriand, 1802.

†André Daspre: In the first version of the novel, Maumort, after the occupation of his château by the Germans in July, 1940, voluntarily shut himself up in his library, where he wrote his memoirs.

Happy time! I would close my books, my notebooks, and stay there dreaming of the future.

An amusing memory: when I had math homework or technical drawings to do, then I would go work in my bedroom. That appealed to me somewhat less. But I liked my bedroom all the same, with its red leaf-patterned rug, its crimson velvet curtains with tapestry stripes, its big oak wardrobe, its old Venetian mirror whose glaucous surface, when I glanced at myself in it, gave me something of a romantic air that I didn't half mind. My aunt had placed on my mantelpiece a beautiful plaster rendition of the Victory of Samothrace, whose folds seemed to quiver as the evening shadows fell and which uplifted me, like a symbol of my passion for life.

This duality in my studies corresponded to a deep duality in my nature, which it took me years to recognize, and which has probably been the reason for my lifelong inability to give myself entirely and exclusively to whatever I was doing, to the projects that I ought to have pursued without hesitation. This duality is responsible for my having never, in anything, reached the very top.

There was in me, from the time I entered the University, a budding man of action who was attracted by the great colonial endeavors and by soldiering; and a meditative type who was not willing to give up intellectual ambitions and preferred the passive attitude of those who would rather understand than judge, dream than act, doubt than believe.

The fluctuations which, during my student life, swayed me, with a steady rhythm, now towards dreaming of a military future in which I could give expression to my active energies, now towards dreaming of a future as a man of letters and a thinker, have not ceased, my whole life long, to toss me from one extreme to the other, from action to contemplation, from movement to passivity. As an officer, I dragged two tin trunks full of books and papers along with me; I longed for the leisure time that allowed me to read and to work; and I spent my evenings sitting on my cot, scribbling notes in my notebooks, keeping my diary—in short, making literature out of the events of my professional life. I lived aloof from my fellow soldiers who, after action, rested, enjoyed themselves, gathered their strength for renewed physical exertions. I led the life of a man of letters swept by circumstances into a life of adventure.

And during the periods when I was not performing my military duties, during my leaves, during the two years I took off at the time of the Dreyfus Affair, and later after the First World War when I retired and came here to live among my books, I suffered from my sedentary ways, I did not know how to expend my need for physical activity, and I led the life of a man on half-pay who impatiently tolerates the idleness imposed upon him.

For this reason, I was neither an officer with a great future nor a talented man of letters. Pulled in opposite directions, I spread myself thin. In the army as in literature I was only an amphibious amateur. I retired as a lieutenant-colonel, which, from the military point of view, was a terrible rebuff to my ambitions as a young Saint-Cyrian. And, as a writer, I have produced nothing: there is not even a proper volume to be assembled from the articles scattered here and there in little technical journals; and the pile of notebooks in which I have recorded the facts and the reflections of fifty years are of no use to anybody.

That overloaded student existence made me live in an intense fever. What a marvelous age, when one first takes flight!

Everything contributed to my being intoxicated, to feeding a sort of great uninterrupted blaze in me: the exploration of the capital, the freedom given me by my uncle and my aunt, their Sunday at-homes where I immediately found myself with everyone who had a name in art and literature, the contact with the professors at the Sorbonne and with the other students, with whom I spent some time at the end of classes or in the Sorbonne's library—everything, even the physical blossoming of my eighteenth year, and the endless discoveries that I made around me, and my nascent ambitions taking wing. I lived in a state of perpetual inner joy. My curiosity, open to all subjects, was inexhaustible. The influence of my Uncle Éric, his table talk, his friends, the dazzling exchanges and clashes of ideas that I witnessed nearly every day—all this gave birth to a new and passionate being in the little provincial that I had been the year before. My aunt's presence added to this the charm of a feminine intimacy that put grace, gaiety, playfulness, and also the warmth of an understanding affinity into that intensely intellectual existence.

At the Sunday gatherings, my shyness and the respect I had for those celebrities rendered me silent, deferential; and, thank God, I knew to keep my place.

But this modesty was only apparent. It was a form of good manners, of politeness. A rather common form. The young people of that time were naturally and easily respectful. They had an awareness of their inexperience, of their ignorance, a high regard for learning, for achievement. This did not prevent them from judging their elders, and even with the severity of youth enamored of the absolute. But in that very severity there was a foundation of respect, and our iconoclasm was never irreverent. We did not have the presumptuousness to reject out of hand the worth of a well-known professor or writer of repute, to make light of his contribution, to regard him impudently as an established mediocrity. No. If we criticized him among ourselves or in our own minds, it was not with the peremptory offhandedness of today's youth. We did not summarily condemn him. We usually criticized him in the very name of the values that he represented or defended, and this in itself showed the esteem in which we held him. We blamed him for not being truer to his own ideal, for not being great enough, or pure enough. We blamed him for his weaknesses. In our juvenile intransigence, we demanded more of our great contemporaries than they demanded of themselves.

But beneath that modesty of bearing, I harbored, like every boy of eighteen, boundless ambitions. A whole life lay ahead of me. I had only reached the threshold. Nothing seemed inaccessible, no domain was closed to me. I had an entire life, that is to say an eternity, in which to attain the highest, farthest, hardest goals. I intended to relinquish nothing, no possibility. I did not accept any idea that would limit me. In every area where my intellectual curiosity ventured forth, I wanted to obtain the maximum, and I believed, sincerely, that I would obtain it. Enthralled by things of the mind, I firmly intended to become a great thinker, a philosopher, a writer of genius. Interested in mathematics and the sciences, I quite expected to become equal or superior to the greatest. And in the practical sphere as well. If I thought about a military career, I imagined myself conquering territories, colonizing a continent, and I saw myself not only as head of the expedition but as arriving at the highest rank, a field marshal, a great commander.

The life force that I felt welling up in me was so violent, and a human life span seemed so long, presenting so many twists and turns, opportunities, and different stages, that if you had asked me: "Will you be a member of the Académie? Président du Conseil? Generalissimo?" it was only decorum and the fear of being laughed at that would have prevented me from answering: "Why not?"

Luckily, this naïve overconfidence never came out. Not even in my cozy chats with Aunt Ma. With my friends, I dissembled less. The fact is, they were almost all like me. We did not need to confess to one another that we had the highest destinies cut out for ourselves. This went without saying. And none of us found the others ridiculous or presumptuous. This unbridled hope for glory we bestowed on all those among us whom our friendship had singled out from the crowd. We thought, ingenuously, without having to say it out loud: "*You* will be the great poet of the century . . . *You,* the great diplomat . . . *You,* a builder of cities . . ."

With my Uncle Éric, I avoided any mention of my future. It was with him that I was the most hypocritically humble . . . As one hides one's appetite upon sitting down at a friend's table where one is a guest. Partly because I dreaded the sarcastic irony of his gaze. Partly because, aware of my ignorance and my youth before that deep well of erudition, I really felt like a very little boy in his presence. Partly, also, for other, vaguer reasons.

Sainte-Beuve says somewhere—I think in regard to Rollin—that modesty is quite often merely the awareness that one has some secret, fundamental, perfectly undeniable deficiency. A judicious remark that I have many times had the opportunity to confirm; and especially for myself. But it is a remark that applies only to adults.

At eighteen, if you have a certain vitality, the appetite for living is so strong that it masks your inadequacies from you; or, if it does not mask them completely, you think you have so much time ahead of you that you always hope to correct your shortcomings; and no weakness seems beyond remedy. The awareness you may have of your faults, of your weak points, far from being grounds for discouragement or self-deprecation, whips up your enthusiasm and increases tenfold your desire to become perfect; and you hardly doubt that you will succeed. Self-confidence is instinctive in a youngster.

Thus I was not modest. At most, I tried to appear so, out of good manners. I do not even know if it was really out of good manners. I would be tempted to think that it was rather out of an excess of pride: the pride of disguising beneath a neutral and unassuming attitude the extent to which what I imagined myself to be, what I wanted to be, what I wanted to become, differed from the ignorant, timid, provincial boy that I felt I still was.

But I was privately so confident in myself and in the grandiose possibilities of the inexhaustibly rich life which offered itself to me that in my moments of solitude, my strolls through exhilarating Paris, I could barely contain in myself the youthful and exuberant explosion of that nascent personality, whose plenitude flooded me with pride and secret joy. I felt on the eve of a glorious flowering, I was all aspirations, euphoria, hope. The mere thought of the future left me saturated with intoxicating promises. I felt I had all the rights. To embrace life in all its forms. To assert myself in every field. Such a concentration of vital forces was seething in me that no goal seemed big enough. Reason could not make me accept any curb on this impulse.

If I concealed this inner drive, this urgent rising of the sap (and I must have concealed it very poorly; the sparkle of my eyes, my voracious impatience in wanting to know everything, in wanting to understand everything, to taste everything, the tense passion that quivered even in my silences, all this would have given me away to anyone who had observed me closely), it was because it would have been unbearable for me, in the state of confident certainty I was in, to encounter in others any doubt as to my potential. I preferred the torture of shutting up these consuming appetites in my breast, like the young Spartan's fox,* to the shame of seeming too cocksure even for an instant, or the slight that a skeptical glance from Uncle Éric would have caused me to endure.

---

*The reference is to a story from Plutarch in which a young Spartan, concealing a little fox under his cloak, let it devour his entrails without flinching rather than allow himself to be found out.

And, to be frank, I have to confess that I maintained this boundless confidence in my potential for quite a long time. Only very late in the day did I consent to acknowledge that reality could impose limits on my dream. And I turned sixty before admitting that my active life was over, that there were domains that I had to give up, possibilities that were henceforth closed to me. It is not so long ago that, as an old man, I was still capable of dreaming of some different and wholly new future, indulging in the most chimerical plans, and deluding myself for an instant with the "Why not?" of my eighteenth year.

My father, whose fortune far exceeded his needs and the style of the life he led, and who was naturally generous in matters of money, gave me a more than adequate monthly allowance. I no longer recall the figure. Every quarter, he sent my Uncle Éric an amount that they had determined together for my upkeep in Paris, my board and student fees. It was agreed that a small portion would be given me for my incidental expenses. I did not attach any great importance to these matters, not from lack of greed, perhaps, but because I had never known want. My uncle did not concern himself with these practical things. It was my aunt who had always held the purse strings. When I first arrived, she wanted to hand over to me the amount that I had been allotted each month. But I did not worry about having money in advance, and we agreed that she would keep this money and dole out what I wanted as I needed it, up to the limit of my monthly allowance. Things were organized in this fashion, and remained so until I entered Saint-Cyr. I would ask her for fifty francs when my wallet was empty. When I went to buy myself some article of clothing or a pair of shoes, I had them delivered to the rue de Fleurus, and the cook would pay. My aunt had a "Bertrand" book in which she wrote down the outlays. I never knew whether I sometimes went beyond the agreed-upon allowance. My requests were so reasonable, my expenditures so out in the open, that my aunt never made the slightest comment to me or preached economy.

I thus reached adulthood without ever knowing anything of financial difficulties. And this was, in a way, quite unfortunate. I think it is good to have had a less easy youth. Such were my circumstances that I led, albeit with limited means, the life of a lord, since my needs were so moderate that I could always spend without concern and never had to deny myself anything.

I do not think that this was very detrimental to me, in the long run. But it was not good training.

.   .   .

I HAD, in a few months, passed the stage which, around the seventeenth year, according to Léon Daudet,* separates *the sexual age* from *the age of speculation and abstraction.* There is some truth, I believe, in this observation. During my stay with the Nacquots, over the vacation in '86, I was still a boy given to obscene visions and erotic dreams; even so, I had acquired a taste for work, and I finally made it a large part of my inner life. With my arrival in Paris in the month of October—and the change of existence, of company— a veritable craving for things of the mind had taken hold of me, and this new passion had transformed me to the point of having become my reason for living. The rest was only secondary.

By "the rest" I mean my sexual obsessions; they continued to inhabit me, and if they were no longer exclusively the burning center of all my preoccupations, they still consumed me at certain times, and subjected me to their whims with a violence that had diminished in frequency but not in intensity. What was new was that they no longer jeopardized my physical and moral equilibrium. I had ceased to be in their thrall. Eroticism had found its place in my life, and remained deeply rooted there. But I was now only sporadically possessed by it. It no longer spilled over into my life as a whole. A sort of habituation occurred. I gave in to its demands; in exchange, it let me live and work in peace.

If I'd had a mistress, an easy and convenient liaison, I would have devoted two evenings a week to her and had a healthy, balanced, satisfied, perfectly normal existence. But I was a virgin, and my sexual needs, deprived of a natural outlet, required periodic satisfactions which the solitary vice alone could provide. Afterward, I would again be calm for a few days.

I admit that this situation was absurd, and today I have difficulty understanding how it went on for so long. At the Chambosts' I enjoyed an almost total freedom. I led my student life as I pleased. I went out in the evening, to go to the theater or to see friends, as often as I liked. At the Sorbonne I spent time with students, many of whom had mistresses or at any rate were having affairs; and the Latin Quarter, where I spent my days, abounded in opportunities. Why did I live in Paris for more than two years before getting rid of my dubious virginity? At this remove, I find myself at a loss to explain it. But it is a fact.

This is all the more mysterious in that I was not held back by any scruple or moral constraint imposed by an uncompromising conception of virtue. On the contrary, not only did I attach no price to that technical innocence, but, on the one hand, I was rather ashamed of it, and on the other, it weighed so heavily on me that I desperately wanted to take the plunge. I was so

*Léon Daudet (1868–1942), French journalist and writer, son of Alphonse Daudet.

ashamed of it that I hid it from everyone without exception, as a ridiculous and disgraceful secret. I was mortified by it as by an affliction. In my conversations with my friends and even through certain very free remarks that I made to Aunt Ma, I took great care to appear experienced and nonchalant; through veiled hints, knowing smiles, I did everything necessary to make people think that I had mistresses, and that it was due to my discretion that nobody could name any of them or had ever met me with a woman on my arm.

Furthermore, I lived in anticipation of that decisive step. Many of my erotic fantasies were about this initiation which I so desired and constantly deferred. Nearly every time I went out at night to go to the theater with an acquaintance or to spend the evening at a friend's home, I would prepare for the event, would take the money necessary for a chance bedding, would dress with care. I would say to myself: "Maybe today?" And I remember, without smiling, my absurd and anxious rambles through the dark streets, before I returned to the rue de Fleurus, seeking out an opportunity like a famished dog, walking quickly, hugging the walls, tramping along for twenty minutes in the rain or snow to pass a certain corner, in front of a certain doorway, where I knew that a streetwalker would be lying in wait for passersby, where I had already come and gone ten times before, my heart pounding wildly, pursued by calls and enticing offers that made me quicken my step and flee the place I had sought out expressly to hear them, flee as if pursued by the devil.

The scenario was almost always the same. I arrived at the spot that I had ardently thought about going to all evening long, where I would finally have the encounter that was to make a man of me. The way the woman looked, her voice, the circumstances, another pedestrian walking by or a car pulling up—all this would produce an insuperable disappointment in me, everything seemed different from what I had so much hoped for; a panic would seize me and send me darting off as if I'd escaped a danger. Then, usually, this is what would happen: on a street corner, at the moment when I was least expecting it, a silhouette would detach itself from the shadows, would whisper its invitation, would lightly brush my arm. Or some woman going by, whose path I crossed, would flash me a tempting smile. Caught unawares, I was incapable of a quick decision, and I would bolt. But scarcely had I lost sight of her than a terrible regret would overcome me. In my memory, the silhouette was graceful, the girl young, the voice fresh and innocent. I felt I had let an irreplaceable chance go by. I was beside myself. I retraced my steps, shivered with desire in the cold winter's night, tried to find the door again, or the woman who had passed by me. Too late. I went around the neighboring blocks, almost running, thinking only of finding the one I had so foolishly scorned. Too late, too late . . . I wandered about in vain, haunted by the image I had glimpsed, rejecting any other chance that might present itself, until the streets were empty, the hour late. Then I went home, feverish, exhausted, and as soon as I was in bed I fantasized about the missed opportunity, I imagined everything that would have happened if, instead of running away like a ninny, I had accepted that gift of the gods, had taken her to a hotel room, undressed her, possessed her . . . For a week, two weeks in a row, I indulged in that fiction, embroidered it, added wild details to it, used it for a time in my solitary debauches. Then a new chance of spending an evening away from the rue de Fleurus would arise. I would leave, with my mind made up to return, after the theater or the party, to the site of the divine apparition, and this time to carry out my plan. But either I did not find the woman again or she appeared to me so different from the one that my daydreams had embellished and transformed that I would take to flight once again in a paroxysm of disappointment and despair.

And this sort of thing kept happening, always in the same stupid way. And it went on for two years!

Why did I aim so low? Why were my principal, constant preoccupations at the time focused on that cheap prostitution of the street and of the brothels? Out of timidity, probably. Perhaps because I was thus continuing the unwholesome dreams of my last year at Saint-Léonard, in which the tits and brazen rump of the slut at the Beau Voiturier had played such an important part.

But mainly out of timidity. A timidity of two kinds. First, the girls of the Latin Quarter intimidated me because there was some sense of modesty, an appearance of decency left in them. As far as I remember, those girls kept up the tradition of the *grisettes* of the *vie de bohème*. They did not offer themselves like prostitutes. You had to conquer them. An easy conquest, obviously, but one which required certain attentions, maneuvers, sentimental declarations. They had lovers, they usually didn't sleep with just anyone. In order to win their favors, you had to single them out, follow them, invite them to the sidewalk cafés, pay them a kind of court, appear to be in love. Besides, the ones I chanced to meet were never available. I saw them with the students whose mistresses they temporarily were. With them, relationships took on the character of an affair, not a fling. To go to bed with one of them, I would have had to tell her that I loved her, and to prove it to her with a modicum of preliminary involvement. To take her dancing, invite her to restaurants, make friends with her before she became a mistress. But I had nothing but disgust for that romantic shamming. What I wanted was the initiatory possession, with no frills. I was not in the least attracted by the company of those girls. Their conversation bored me silly. Their vulgarity—which would not have hampered my lovemaking, quite the opposite—made sustained contact with them intolerable. I had nothing to say to them. They were completely foreign to me. And they certainly felt that I was foreign to them. They kept me rather at a distance. I imagine that they must have said to the classmate of mine who was their lover and who brought me to their table at the brasserie: "Your friend Maumort bores me, he's a poseur." They sensed that my thoughts, my life interests, were somewhere else. I was not incapable of loving—as I shall soon tell—but I was incapable of loving that kind of little tart; incapable even of pretending in order to satisfy my desires.

And then, my timidity would have prevented me from taking up with one of those girls, who had no secrets from anyone, who lived a public life in the quarter, and whose successive affairs were known by all. It would have been intolerable to my self-esteem for the other girls, and my friends, to have been aware of my choice and privy to my sexual life.

In that domain, I had consistently pretended to have a secret life which I did not let my friends in on. People assumed—I later learned—that I was having a long affair with a woman of the world, probably married and forced to be cautious. It was, for them, the only plausible assumption; it explained everything: the freedom of my remarks, the air of superior experience I put on, and also my detachment from the girls of the quarter and the infrequency of my forays into the brasseries and *bals musettes* where most of my fellow students spent several nights a week. I was not known to have any relationship, and it was quite obvious to all that I had long since lost my innocence: hence I had to have a mistress from the circle of the family I was living with, and about whom I spoke only evasively. The hypothesis of a steady liaison fitted well with my gravity, the seriousness I brought to everything.

Besides, with my friends the topic of love did not often come up. An allusion, a meaningful smile here and there about sexual matters, but never a confidence. Our conversations were only about the curriculum, and the work, the professors, their methods, their respective merits—as far as concrete matters went. But they were mainly about abstract questions and lofty problems of the intelligence. Religion, philosophy, history, literature. We read about all of that. The first question we would put to each other was invariably: "What are you reading these days?" It is not without surprise that I recall that intellectual fervor. We lived easily in that rarefied air. We could devote fifteen hours a day to that cerebral stimulation. I remember certain evenings at one or another of my friends' houses, when, after a whole day of work, attending classes, intellectual force-feeding, we could still spend hours together arguing tirelessly about the poets of the Pléiade, the loves of Bérénice,* the Revolution of 1789, the philosophy of John Stuart Mill or the theories of Proudhon, about the origins of Christianity, Kant's imperative or free will . . . Midnight struck, you could not breathe for the smoke in the

*Heroine of a tragedy by Racine.

room where we were wrestling with the great problems, yet we could not bring ourselves to part. And if one of us opened a book and began to read a page of Michelet, a translation of Emerson, or a poem by Sully Prudhomme, the conversation would start up again livelier than ever, our enthusiasms would clash unrestrainedly, and it was not unusual for the meeting to go on until two in the morning, before each of us resolved to break the spell and call it a night. Often we would continue the conversation, two or three of us, in the cold of the night and the black solitude of the streets, making enormous detours to "see each other home."

The few friends I am thinking of nearly all ended up having very ordinary lives and are all, at this point, dead. They formed a close circle entirely apart from the students of the *quartier* whom we met at school. The student population was roughly divided into two very distinct categories: there were what we called *"les types du quartier,"* students hailing from the provinces who had a room in some Left Bank boardinghouse, who gathered in the cheap restaurants for their meals and, at night, in the brasseries of the Boul' Mich'; they kept to themselves, saw the girls from the quarter, had mistresses, played billiards or *manille,** often argued politics, went to socialist meetings, were swept up by the election campaigns, and sometimes wrote for the newspapers. And then there were those whose families lived in Paris, young *bourgeois*, better dressed, more affluent, more refined in their tastes, who seldom showed up in the cafés, entertained each other at home, formed a clan apart, led a less free, less bohemian existence, hid their romantic adventures, and only rarely showed off their mistresses in public, when they had one; this latter group, to which I belonged, had only casual dealings with the former, at the start or end of classes, and looked down a little on the *types du quartier*, whom they found ill-bred, slovenly, somewhat common. Two "social classes," in short, which did not mix.

I NO LONGER recall the reason for my being invited to a late supper one night with a few of those *types du quartier*. The meal had been copious, generously washed down, and I had let the general vulgarity get the better of me. "Let's go to Mère Léontine's!" someone suggested. Mère Léontine was the madam of the Fric-Frac, a house of assignation on the Avenue du Maine behind the Gare Montparnasse, much renowned, quite expensive, and known for the number, the variety, and the attractiveness of its denizens. I have been to so many brothels in the course of my life, in all the towns of France and elsewhere, that I am not very sure whether my present memory of the Fric-Frac is scrupulously exact. I can still see a large room

*A French card game.

with gilded panels and mirrors, where you drank champagne at little tables that were placed on the periphery; and where some thirty girls in short dresses, their legs sculpted in black silk stockings, went to and fro with an amazing nonchalance.

From time to time, six of them would jump up onto a little platform and execute a cancan, providing the affecting spectacle of their pink silk panties, trimmed with several flounces of black lace. There were a lot of men of all ages, not just students. The women went from table to table, sat on the men's knees, and got the clients to offer them a flute of "bubbly." I looked around, all eyes, quite proud of my casualness, which might have led people to believe that I was one of the regulars. When a young swarm of these "ladies" descended upon our table, and a tall brunette sat down on my lap, I greeted her with a smile, myself surprised at not being more stirred. She took my hand and slid it into her blouse. I shivered and must have blushed at the touch of that firm and warm flesh which lay so naturally in my palm, but I betrayed none of my excitement, and went on laughing and joking. But when she drank from my glass, and wanted me to drink from it after her, I turned away my lips in spite of myself. She did not insist, and drank all that was left in "our glass."

Every so often, a client would rise, cross the room, and disappear, in the wake of the "lady" who had "picked him up," behind a large red velvet portière that concealed the bottom of a staircase. "Coming up, *chéri*?" my companion breathed into my neck. "No, not tonight," I said with the nicest smile and the most natural air in the world. "Really?" she said, sliding an indiscreet hand down. Gently, I pushed her hand away. Even if I had wanted to, not in a million years would I have dared to get up in front of my friends and cross the room after her (although three of our group had already vanished behind the red portière). But in truth I did not want to, in spite of my having been terribly aroused by the floor show and that physical contact. Strange yet true! I who dreamed of nothing but nude women and copulations, I who had been tortured almost every night for years by a longing for initiation, I who, so many times, in daydreams, had followed a woman of this type to greedily possess her, felt totally paralyzed by the reality, had lost all boldness and even all desire; and if that appetizing girl had dragged me to her bedroom, I think I would have fought like a madman rather than carry out with her what I had so passionately fantasized in my solitary nights . . .

If a precise, violent memory of that evening has stayed with me, this is why:

The three or four "proper" friends who had stayed with me in the room suddenly decided to leave. But we had to wait for the ones who were "partaking" upstairs to come back. Twenty minutes, thirty minutes went by, my friends grew impatient. Two had returned, the third was taking forever.

Stimulated by the champagne, they finally got up. But as they were going past the red portière on their way out, some diabolical idea occurred to them: "Let's go get Brideau!" and they pushed me over to the staircase, which I climbed with them. But the rooms were well guarded. On the second floor landing an assistant-madam was on watch, barring our way. She mistook our intentions, and leaning toward the one who was leading the party, said something in his ear. I did not grasp what she was proposing to him. "Ten francs if you like," my friend answered. "And we each get our turn." "Give her ten francs," my neighbor told me. I did so without understanding. "Go ahead, Maumort, you'll tell us if it's worth it." Not knowing where I was going, I followed the old woman. "No noise," she whispered; she opened a door, let me into a sort of closet with her, and closed the door behind us. I wanted to protest. "Shush!" she said. And slowly, at the level of my eyes, she slid back a tiny shutter that revealed in the wall a luminous hole the size of a ten-sou piece: "Look quick."

I clapped my eye to the opening. It took me a few seconds to identify a mass moving in the light. A naked woman was spread out on a harshly lit bed, and a man, whom I saw from the back, naked also, was kneeling with his head on her. "Enough, come on!" muttered the old woman. I stood there, glued to the wall. She wanted to pull me away from it, her hand felt me, probed further; no skillful caresses were needed to establish proof of my arousal. "Chéri . . . petit chéri . . ." said the woman. Then, almost immediately, she pulled the shutter to. "Give me another five francs, if you're happy." I slipped a hundred sous into her hand. She opened the door. I found myself back in the hallway, stunned by what had happened to me. "So, was it great?" the others asked me. "Well . . . yes . . . not bad," I answered in a blasé tone. "I'll wait for you outside." I had only one thing in mind: to regain my solitude. I let them go along with the old woman. I went down the stairs, out onto the sidewalk, and took off, without waiting.

It was the first woman I had seen naked. The vision—brutal, shattering—has never faded. The woman was beautiful, in full bloom. The man, with the posture of a supplicant, the active fervor of an officiant, had something religious about him. A sordid and beautiful spectacle, which I fed on night after night . . . A thrilling spectacle, and one which left me, in spite of all, with a feeling of grandeur.

How many times afterwards did I not come at night and prowl about in front of the Fric-Frac, without daring to cross its magic threshold? . . .

A strange phenomenon, those sharp attacks when all your desires suddenly well up, like an abrupt and virulent onset of fever; when all your demons, unleashed without warning, literally give you the feeling of being "possessed," in the medieval sense . . . You get up in a "state of purity," you start off the new day with gusto, full of noble appetites, with a readiness for challenges. The whole day goes by working joyfully, in good conscience. If you happen to think for a moment about some debauch of last night or the night before, you can scarcely believe it, can scarcely recognize yourself in the lustful person that you were. It seems that it's over for good, that you are cured forever, freed. You spend the evening talking with a friend, confiding to him in a climate of exalted intellectuality, of heroism in the air of mountaintops. How far you are from that animal in rut that you were the other night . . . And then the evening comes to an end, you go your separate ways, you walk home in the night soothed, all enriched by your vibrant conversation, bearing like a talisman the blessing of that intellectual friendship and those confrontations with youth's finest ambitions.

And, then, for no reason, a darker street, a couple that you pass, a woman waiting under a streetlight, and the sudden fit is on you, all the demons precipitously rush out from the depths of your being . . . It's like an inner volcano that erupts, and its acrid smoke suffocates you, makes you lose all control . . . Within a few seconds, you once again become the victim of your instincts. And nothing can hold you back. You have to yield to that torrent of your wicked desires . . . You change direction like iron filings pulled by a magnet, you turn off towards those places where you know temptation lurks, you quicken your steps, you run, with your head on fire, your heart pounding, to that rendezvous with the devil, like a sleepwalker or a hypnotic who cannot help carrying out the action he is ordered to perform by the hypnotist's induction . . .

And once again it turns into a night of raging, deranged chasing about, with the madness of the senses, the frantic desire for initiation, ruthlessly sweeping away all of that fine day's resolutions of work and inner peace . . .

*

WHOEVER DOES NOT WISH upon reading this to remember that wild summons which overwhelmed certain hours of his youth, laying waste to all sensible resolutions, making him capable of almost anything in order to attain his ends without delay; whoever refuses to cast this lucid gaze upon himself, refuses to see the appalling frenzy that the raw delirium of his senses can produce at certain impassioned moments, that person will not understand the fanatical violence of the feelings I am describing, or the patient indulgence I am bringing to this analysis, or even the interest, the profound human significance I attach to these fits of sensual madness, whose irresistible energy it is healthy to comprehend in order to have an exact and complete picture of what man is.

I know how quickly and with what *blindness*—in which all the vestiges in us of the centuries of Christianity and of traditional morality unconsciously collaborate—we forget those deep onslaughts of instinct once they have been satisfied and left behind.

*

I AM TRYING to remember the place that Love, with a capital L, occupied in my life as a young man during that early period of my time in Paris.

In my mind there was already a profound separation between this Love and the erotic obsessions that preyed on me. Was this separation as clear-cut for my friends? I believe it was. But I want to speak only for myself.

In the foreground of my daily preoccupations, there was that organic, sexual fire, that desire for copulation whose throbbing fever I staved off with onanism. I will not go over that again.

But in the background and on a higher level, there was also a certain fascination with romantic love, that of the great heroes of the literature of passion, that of the tragedies of Racine, of Musset's *Nights,* of Michelet's *Love* and *Woman,* that of *The Charterhouse of Parma,* that of Musset and George Sand. I did not doubt that there awaited me such a love, in which my entire being would find itself committed, physically and spiritually. And that total love was already in its early stages. In fact, as far as I go back in my memories, there has always been in a corner of my heart a chosen being to whom I pledged ardent and pure thoughts. In Paris, this niche acquired its statue right away, actually several, since I simultaneously installed there the images of a number of young ladies I had met in Aunt Ma's drawing room.

All this is so childish that it takes some courage to confess it . . .

But childish or not, admitted or not, that is how it was. And the only interest in writing it down is that it is a general phenomenon. This childishness is not the sole preserve of virginal boys. It also often goes with an adolescence that is full of flings. Quiz a random selection of twenty young men between fifteen and twenty-five—lycée students, apprentices, college students, employees, conscripts, students at the *grandes écoles,* second-lieutenants, engineers, notary clerks, sailors, workmen, school supervisors, salesclerks at department stores. Whatever social class they belong to, whatever they intend to become, nineteen or twenty of them, if they are sincere, will be able without hesitation to tell you the name of that more or less precise vision which haunts their romantic daydreams, the name of the girl, loved on the sly, or simply glimpsed, with whom they secretly unite for life. Some are having affairs, others are still only at the stage of lustful and unconsummated obsessions—it doesn't matter. In a blue patch of their sky there is a tangible and idealized image around which some instinct of the species, some natural passion, some human, all too human, need of loving and being loved revolves: each, at the bottom of his heart, inevitably and childishly worships some "fiancée" whom he perfectly well knows by name.

What they do not know is that this private worship which they bestow upon a real individual is not in fact addressed to that individual. It is only a personification. It is Love that they worship. They believe in good faith that they love a girl, a young woman. They believe it so thoroughly that sometimes they marry her . . . But it is Love that they love, and it is Love that they call out to, without suspecting it. And the glimpsed figure, which aroused that deep and lasting agitation in them, is in reality only a mirage, a trick of the instinct. What they love, at that age, is really only an abstraction that has clothed itself in human form.

I continue to examine myself. Was I thinking "marriage"? Yes and no. Yes, I was thinking of it, somehow. As a worldly complement to, a realization of, my dreams. As a practical, social way to pin my dream to a human future. But I only thought very superficially about it. If you had asked me, mentioning the name of the girl who at one moment or another "poetically," "literarily" personified my need for love, "Will you marry Arlette?" I would, sincerely, have answered yes. But if you had asked me, in the abstract, "Do you wish to get married?" I would certainly have answered no.

"Marriage," the idea of marriage, presented itself to me later on, along with other seductions and other spells. I remember certain times in my life when I felt terribly alone—around thirty, in the province of Constantine, and later, stationed at Alençon, and later still, even past fifty, after my retirement—times when the need to become attached to a weaker being, the need for the sweetness of a companion, for the sharing of two solitudes, overwhelmed me with yearning . . . But it was nothing like that stage of my youth when, having just set foot in Paris and overflowing with vitality, enticed by all the riches that adult life was offering me, I felt on the contrary an intoxication with solitude and freedom.

Beginning at that time, I had a natural aversion to marriage, to the eventuality of my marriage. I told myself, quite often and genuinely, "I won't marry." I was not in the least attracted by the desire for a home, for a family, for children. I was already very concerned with keeping myself unattached. I was inclined, by nature, to protect my future, my possibilities, from any commitment, any set plan: my first duty in terms of the future was to remain free for great achievements. I would have agreed wholeheartedly with that remark whose author I no longer remember: "To marry is to bring a *demanding stranger* into one's life."

This was even a fairly frequent subject of my conversations with Aunt Ma. She smiled at my intransigence. She told me, amused: "Someday I shall remind you of what you're saying here . . ."

I never gave her the opportunity.

CHAPTER XV

The Hectors

MY UNCLE CHAMBOST-LÉVADÉ had a brother two years his junior.

Hector Chambost (he had crossed the *Lévadé* out of his name) was quite different from my uncle. At forty-eight (in 1887) he was still a very handsome man, tall, very well groomed, very elegant, without a hint of white in his black hair. A broad, rather flat and slightly bulldoggish face, round eyes, a big black mustache. Not studied in his attire but richly dressed, with very fine linen; a patron of English shops, he favored impeccable jackets and starched shirtfronts, shiny as porcelain, on which a wide black satin cravat always stood out, held fast in the middle by a chased gold loop representing a chimera with unfolded wings. A heavy signet ring on his finger. Everything he wore was of the best, both luxurious and in good taste. The cigarette case that he drew from his pocket was solid gold, with his monogram on it. He chain-smoked English cigarettes that he fitted into white cardboard cigarette holders—he had them made by the hundreds and always had ten or so sticking out of his breast pocket—which he threw away along with the fag end. I cannot picture him except with his cigarette holder jutting out under his thick walrus mustache.

Having inherited his father's scientific aptitude, he studied advanced mathematics, entered Polytechnique, graduated among the first in his class, and underwent several years of training in the shipbuilding industry.

At thirty, he had fallen madly in love with a young orphan, said to be colossally rich, whose mother had been English and who lived in Paris with an aunt, her guardian.

Pauline was very young when Hector fell in love with her. She was eighteen, twelve years younger than he. He had married her in spite of her delicate health, and they had had a daughter, Éva.

Hector was still clearly in love with his wife when I met him, and he showered her with attentions.

Pauline was a child-woman, one of the most exquisite creatures I have ever met, of an infinite refinement. Tall and slender as certain English women can be, she looked like a long frail reed, bending in every wind. Perpetually unwell, spending several days each week in bed, catching cold at the slightest chill, she required the greatest care with her health. Their large fortune allowed her to lead the life of a permanent convalescent. They lived in a magnificent apartment on the Avenue Hoche right by the Parc Monceau.

The household was run by an old English lady who had reared Pauline, and who was treated with great respect. Mrs. Witcherly presided over a sizable staff, and Pauline had no need to attend to anything. Mrs. Witcherly was very distinguished, took her meals with the family as a matter of course, and wholly shared the Hectors' life. It would never have occurred to Aunt Ma to invite the Hectors to dinner without inviting old Mrs. Witcherly as well. She had a grand air about her, moreover, with her white lace pouf in her white, lightly powdered hair, her equine profile, her capacious evening gowns, her breastplate of jet necklaces, and the white silk ribbon, with its paste-jewelry clasp, that she always wore on her neck. Very much the dowager, she imposed respect; and her discreet graciousness, her humor, made her irresistibly endearing.

Éva, when I became acquainted with her, had just turned sixteen, but she had her father's build and appeared eighteen, although upon closer inspection her slight stoutness, her still fleshy form, brought to mind baby fat rather than the figure of a nubile young woman. The first time I met her, at a family dinner at the rue de Fleurus a few days after my arrival, an odd thing happened. I had eyes only for the adorable Madame Hector, but I convinced myself that I had fallen in love with Éva, next to whom I was seated at table and from whom I could not extract ten words. This mistake lasted several months (and would no doubt have lasted longer if, having been taken by my friend Blaise Saint-Gall to the familial phalanstery in the rue Saint-Guillaume, I had not become seriously infatuated with Laure Saint-Gall; out of sight out of mind, and the plump Éva, overnight, ceased to matter to me).

At any rate, that evening I had eyes only for Pauline, and I was not alone. The strange charm she exerted, without ever trying to, without seeming to notice it, was universal, and the moment she appeared, she was the center of attention. My Uncle Chambost became another man in the presence of his sister-in-law, and never stopped fussing over her with a tender concern.

She had an exceptional grace, and yet you could not say that she was a beauty. The too small head, the childish face, the rather undersized nose, the slightly oversized mouth, the pale complexion: nothing regular in her features: the face of a Parisian gamine.

The body was, it could be said, the opposite of a beautiful female body. Incredibly long, and so lean that there did not seem to be any flesh under the clothes, only a skeleton (besides which, in her face there was something of a death's head). How to describe it? Burne-Jones has painted those long women with spindly, disproportioned limbs and narrow hips. And I am thinking too of certain drawings by Rops, of his women with worn little faces, somewhat prominent cheekbones, sunken eyes, ultra-sensual lips.

But what exquisite grace in that fragility, what supreme distinction in that delicacy! A flower-woman, one of those beings whose pathetic slightness stirs all of a man's deepest fibers. How easy to understand that Hector, from the day he set eyes on her, had no other ambition than to dedicate his strong man's robustness to her, protect her, be her cavalier!

It was eight o'clock when she arrived. All three of us, my uncle, my aunt and I, had been sitting in the library for three-quarters of an hour. We were waiting. I had been warned that Pauline had no sense of time, that the Hectors were always late. When the hour hand neared eight, my aunt remarked: "If Pauline had come down with her migraine, Hector would already have let us know. They'll be here."

My uncle smiled over his *Débats: "Tarde venientibus ossa,"** he declared, turning to me. When it came to Pauline, he had unexpected reserves of patience.

At last a landau and pair stopped in front of the house; we heard the front door slam, the carriage start off again. Then the library door opened before Mrs. Witcherly and her jet breastplate, and behind her, towering a whole head above her, Madame Hector appeared. She came forward unhurriedly, sovereignlike, followed by the inseparable couple formed by her daughter and the young English governess, Miss Jordan, then by her husband; the folds of a mauve gown trailing over the carpet slightly impeded her gait; wrapped snugly in a large, embroidered white silk shawl with long fringes, she seemed, in her veils of mauve chiffon, a dream figure, a fairy-tale princess gliding over the waters. Her eyes, squinting a little, sought us out. Smiling, she graciously apologized for being late, like a spoiled child who can get away with any whim and knows it. My aunt introduced me. Pauline blithely settled her glance on me; I did not dare devour her with my eyes, and lowered my head, blushing, as intimidated as if I had found myself in the presence of the Empress of All the Russias at a court ball.

After dinner, Hector took me off into a window-recess and questioned me for a long time about my studies and my scientific abilities. This was very much his style. Precise, somewhat finicky, he always seemed to be pursuing an investigation, or rather to be attentively, meticulously conducting a laboratory experiment. Without the slightest pedantry, though, and in a comradely tone that flattered me. He inquired about the curriculum at Saint-Cyr. I confessed to him that my taste for mathematics, which M. Nacquot had developed in me, had been eclipsed, since my year of *philo,* by my interest in physics and above all in chemistry. His face lit up. Discreetly, he put a few posers to me, and seemed favorably impressed by my answers. At that moment, Aunt Ma came and joined us. She wanted to rescue me. Hector had a reputation for buttonholing people and not letting them go. "I'm sure," she said, "that you're quizzing him . . ." "Not at all," he said seriously, turning to

*"Latecomers are left with the bones."

me to back him up. "What your nephew is telling me interests me, and I hope I'm not pestering him . . . Well," he added, "since the problems of organic chemistry amuse you, I invite you to come chat about them with me. I have a small lab where I carry on a little research. I'll show it to you. Are you free Sunday morning? Come early, we'll work a little together. And you'll stay for lunch with us."

"You know," Aunt Ma told me the next day, "don't think you're in any way obliged to go to Hector's if it bores you. He spends all his time alone among his retorts, and he's always looking in vain for someone who's interested in his harmless hobbyhorses. Don't let him grab you . . ."

I protested. I truly wanted to accept the invitation. I was quite curious to learn about Hector's projects, and my interest in chemistry was genuine. Admittedly, the invitation to lunch might have added something to this temptation.

It was thus that I became for a time a regular visitor to the Avenue Hoche. Roughly every two weeks, I would show up on Sunday morning around ten o'clock, and I was ushered in to Hector, whom I always found in his smock, at work in his laboratory. He took an obvious pleasure in having a willing listener, and kept me abreast of his experiments (which, in his family circle, interested no one) and let me take part in them for two hours. He always seemed happy to see me come. He loved to teach and never got a chance to do so. I took advantage of this to ask him about the questions I was studying, and to perform with him elementary experiments which fixed in my mind the theoretical teaching I had gathered from my chemistry and physics texts. It was a pleasant way of prepping for my future examination for Saint-Cyr, to which I paid little attention, being mainly interested in my *licence* courses at the Sorbonne; I felt I was not wasting my time.

But clearly what counted for me on those mornings, what made me so constant, was the pleasure of being asked to stay for lunch and of finding myself involved in the Hectors' family life.

For I sincerely believed myself to be in love with the young Éva. It was, when I consider it, a rather comical story, completely absurd, a lamentable and stupid mistake, which really has only one very slight claim on the attention: that of having happened to a boy of eighteen who was not the worst of imbeciles, and who, moreover, had always trained himself to analyze his feelings and to be sincere with himself. Unbelievable!

As long as I'm at it, I don't want to hide anything; I will tell all about that folly. I, who had not written verses since my first year in boarding school, wasted precious hours composing little poems in verse and rhythmic prose in the tone of the most sickening sentimental romances, to "sing" my love. I leapt at any opportunity to burden my poor friend Vayron with my childish confidences . . . I stole from a drawer of Aunt Ma's a photograph, taken two years before, in which the object of my affection, in short skirts, seated on a pouf, her hair pulled back in a net, stared into Nadar's lens. In a studio on the Avenue de l'Opéra whose advertisement I had found in a newspaper, I had made, at great expense, a miniature print of that touching image, the size of a postage stamp, and I pasted it into my watch case, so as always to carry it with me, to be able to look at it at any time; and every night, in the solitude of my bedroom, hunched under the lampshade, I would contemplate it for a long while, with beating heart . . . What did I not do besides? I skipped classes to go and station myself, like a thief, in a bar on the rue d'Astorg, from which I could glimpse her for five seconds, leaving, escorted by her governess, a school where I had learned that at such-and-such a time, on such-and-such a day, she was taking a course in art history . . .

Yes, I loved her madly—*except at the times when I was in her presence.* On this point, my memories are scrupulously exact. I awaited, with an intoxicated impatience, that semimonthly Sunday lunch at which I was going to see her, spend two hours in the same room with her. And as soon as that moment arrived, I no longer felt anything, not the slightest emotion, not the least temptation to speak to her up close, to attract her attention—nothing, absolutely nothing but a surprising coldness, a total indifference just barely tinged with a sort of gloomy sadness, a vague disappointment.

But I want to remember how things unfolded. To begin with, the apartment building on the Avenue Hoche was magnificent. A double porte-cochère allowed carriages to come in under the double arch and to depart without having to back up or to turn around in the courtyard. A concierge in livery was, at all hours of the day, on guard beneath the arch, in front of a wide French door; it opened onto a sort of colonnaded gallery whose red carpet led to the foot of the staircase. The stairwell was spacious, decorated with slabs of reddish marble and bronze standard lamps. The Hectors lived on the second and third floors, which were joined by an inner staircase. But Hector's laboratory was located on the ground floor: a row of three big rooms, with imitation-hardwood linoleum flooring and a whole array of stoves, ventilation hoods, tiled tables, basins, sinks, glass cases, bookcases, shelves loaded with retorts, jars, flasks and carboys. In the rather handsome first room he had placed a large Renaissance table, which served as a desk, and the walls were covered with dark oaken shelves on which were aligned an extremely rare collection of old Flemish druggist's jars, with blue decorations, bearing on their bulging bellies the old Latin inscriptions of the ancient pharmacopoeia: *Asafoetida, Pulvis,* etc. A blackboard on an easel was set up near the curtainless, frosted-glass window.

I would ring at the ground floor. Hector would come and open the door to me himself, since the young assistant who helped him in his experiments had Sundays off. I can see his greeting, his brief smile, his worried brow and eyes. The sleeves of his smock were always rolled up to the elbows, and he generally held out his left hand to me because the other was stained with acids or powdered with chalk. I often interrupted him in the midst of a calculation on the blackboard, and he would finish noting down some cryptic formulas before attending to me; he also would often come from the back of his laboratory, a test tube between his fingers, which he would lift to the light of the window to point out some curious feature, some chemical decomposition that he had just obtained and whose interest he immediately explained to me. In general, my presence did not deter him from pursuing the work he had begun; he loaned me a smock and I served him clumsily as a stand-in assistant.

But when he had the leisure for it, he would sit me down in the front room, settle in at his desk, ask about what I had learned since my previous visit, give me advice, jot on the blackboard a few figures or formulas that he wanted to imprint on my memory, and we would chat freely. He kept up with the most recent discoveries, received technical journals from all over the world, corresponded with foreign scientists, and, being an avid specialist, dotted his conversation with fresh insights and unexpected connections, the essence of which I did my best to remember. The chief benefits I received from this desultory instruction were initiation into the tremendous leap forward that chemistry was taking at that time, and instant contact with a modern scientist, intelligently imbued with the scientific spirit, scrupulous in his claims, devoted only to the truth, strictly disinterested when it came to his research, and whose ambition confined itself to being a useful cog in the progress of knowledge. (I did not understand until later all that he owed to Marcellin Berthelot's friendship.)

Hector was known, not only in the world, among his old classmates at the "X,"* but in his immediate circle, as a sweet lunatic hobbyist and a weak character, who, at thirty, having become through his marriage the usufructary of a magnificent fortune, had become, by the same token, if not an idler, at least a scientist de luxe, who had turned away from all professional work, all social constraints, in order to devote himself to his favorite pastime. "Hector," they would say, when he came late to dinner, "is *amusing himself* in his lab." Of course, no one denied his intelligence, and that sort of "amusement" which people tacitly seemed to hold against him was certainly not the amusement of an idiot. They even wondered, once or twice, if he might not end up with some discovery, if he might not produce something useful with this "amusement." But he had disappointed even the most indulgent. Although he never spoke of his research—not even to Berthelot—it was somehow known that he had completely changed direction several times: for six months, he was busy with one thing, then the next year it transpired that he

*Familiar name for Polytechnique.

was busy with something altogether different. People came to believe that he had no consistency in his ideas, and that wealth, total freedom, the habit of luxury, had irreparably spoiled his gifts, made him slack and fickle. There was much truth in this judgment. Probably he would have borne other fruit if he had submitted to some constraints, worked in a team with other chemists, and accepted precise tasks. He needed more discipline. But he was not entirely without it, he knew how to impose it on himself and sustain it. Above all, he was the opposite of lazy, and led an industrious, silently engrossed life which deserved respect. Perhaps he was too intelligent, curious about too many things, to be able to plumb any one of them deeply.

What he lacked was less discipline than ambition. He never tried to draw attention to himself, never considered reaping the benefits of his discoveries, never took the trouble to publish an article or speak at a scientific congress. His self-effacement was complete. Out of modesty, and also out of indifference to success, and perhaps out of a certain contempt. He contented himself with writing down the results obtained in the various branches of the research he conducted, and in making files of them, which he bequeathed to the Bibliothèque Nationale. A bequest which went completely unnoticed until the day when a collaborator of Pasteur's chanced to stick his nose into it, and to sum up the gist of it in two substantial articles in the *Revue de chimie,* which appeared during the First World War and created a considerable stir in the circles concerned. At least that is what I learned then, without having the time to inform myself further, through a letter from the elderly Aunt Ma, a year or two before her death. Hector had died ten years earlier, at almost the same time as my Uncle Éric.

But let us return to the Avenue Hoche, and to the Hector I knew. As best I can judge, it was not out of sheer capriciousness that he moved from one line of research to another. He gave the impression of being a researcher who has his secret idea and who follows it through projects very different in appearance. This man of science, who had all the rigor of the great scientists, also had that intuitive, inventive side which often leads to important discoveries. No doubt he set up very precise relationships, perceptible to him alone, among his projects, and had a vital thread which linked together what my uncle and his friends treated as successive "fancies."

It is thanks to him that I had a close acquaintance with a free man who had given his life an overall direction, who pursued—without anyone's help, without even confiding his scientific preoccupations to anyone—a patient, obscure undertaking, and who remained faithful to it. He had a general goal: to be useful, in the place he had assigned himself, to the acquisition of knowledge, to the uninterrupted investigation that humanity carries on century after century into the phenomena of the universe. He did not worry about being rewarded or widely known; he only thought about learning, and everything with him was subordinated to this end, whatever the outer, luxurious, even frivolous appearance of his life may have been. He had chosen to be a chemist. He knew that civilization needs this sort of man, and he even sensed that he belonged to an era when, thanks to the chemists, science was going to make great new advances. And he aspired to be the best chemist possible.

Hats off to the memory of Hector.

And let us finally return, this time for good, to the Avenue Hoche, and to the young student, a bit bewildered, in whom a fifty-year-old man in a white smock was inculcating hieroglyphic formulas, while initiating him, without seeming to look down on that ignorant listener, into obscure endeavors.

The student listened and sought sincerely to understand. But one part of him was elsewhere; an important part, the most vital part of him, lent an ear to the outside noises and waited with a pounding heart for the doorbell to ring twice at ten before noon: the hour when Éva, returning from eleven o'clock Mass with Miss Jordan—and sometimes also with her mother—rang at the ground floor to say hello to her father, who got up early and was usually not seen before lunch.

I open a brief parenthesis concerning the religious question at the Avenue Hoche. Éva never missed eleven o'clock Mass on Sunday, which was, at that time, the fashionable Mass in the wealthy parishes. And, in principle, her mother always meant to go with her; but for that delicate, somewhat lethargic creature, it was a painful effort to be ready to go out so early, and three times out of four she stayed home for reasons of health, either because she'd had a bad night, or was afraid she might come down with a migraine, or simply felt tired and preferred not to overtax herself. As for Hector, he never spoke to me about religion, and since I always found him on Sunday mornings in his laboratory, working as usual, I had never doubted his religious indifference. Afterwards, I was bewildered by what I thought was his turnabout and used the term "conversion" to Aunt Ma. "But Hector has always been a very regular churchgoer," she told me: "the only believer in the family . . ." And I learned with surprise that at the time I knew him, if I had never seen him go to church with his wife or his daughter, it was because he used to attend a very early Mass alone, and not only on Sundays but also fairly often on weekdays. And that every year, during the holidays, he always spent about ten days at the abbey of Solesmes, on retreat.

So at ten to noon our serious discussion was abruptly broken off by the arrival of Éva, followed by her governess. She would kiss her father, who never showed any impatience at being interrupted in this way, and would shake my hand in a friendly manner. I had awaited this appearance with emotion, but I felt none in Éva's presence. She evinced neither surprise nor pleasure at seeing me. "Oh, hello Bertrand . . ." She was very far from suspecting that I was there because of her. To her I was a young student, a distant relation, her Uncle Éric's nephew, curious about her father's scientific obsessions, a future scientist devoid of interest who lived in her father's mysterious and slightly ridiculous world and who did not count for her at all. Nothing in my attitude, what is more, could undeceive her. If I spoke to her it was to join in the trite remarks that she exchanged with her father about the weather or the smell that she sniffed, making little faces, as she entered the laboratory.

She was always very well dressed—very expensively, at any rate—but with great ordinariness. She was tall, rather heavy, with a young blonde's nondescript pretty face and a fresh complexion, glowing with air and exercise. For she always walked to Mass when she went without her mother. In the winter she had on beautiful furs, in the summer light-colored dresses that made her sturdy hips look even broader. Often she would pull from her muff a little bunch of Parma violets that she had bought in the street, coming out of church, for her father, and that she sweetly arranged in a graduated beaker filled with water, and Hector would thank her as if this attention and those flowers pleased him enormously. But it was obvious that this was pure politeness. Their relations were odd: affectionate but without the slightest hint of intimacy. Éva considered her father an original who belonged to her familiar world but had no standing there; a crank whose life was on another plane than her own and whose harmless brainstorms one respected, with utter indifference. This was also to some extent Mme. Hector's attitude. No allusion was made to his chemist's pursuits, except to tease him. As for Hector, he treated his daughter with great kindness, like a spoiled child whom one pardons everything because it simply doesn't matter, and it was obvious that she was scarcely more important in his life than a somewhat precious pet; scarcely more important than Dick, the tiny Pomeranian who lived in his wife's lap; and Hector had the same indulgent smile when he planted a kiss on his daughter's brow as when he leaned down to pat the silken forehead of the favorite little dog.

Thinking it over, I cannot blame him for that lukewarmness. Éva was not at all endearing; she was nothing more than an unexceptional specimen of a young Parisienne, silly and utterly devoid of any special gifts; a young "Society" woman, the most ordinary imaginable. For a man of Hector's merit, who was already naturally inclined to treat all women as charming and slightly burdensome luxury animals, whose whims, little ready-made ideas, idle chatter, absurdities, naïve ignorance, triviality, frivolous stupidity had to be patiently borne, and who had their shortcomings forgiven on account of their grace, it was clearly not Éva who was going to induce him to revise this overall judgment of the weaker sex. She proved the rule. She was young, charming, innocuous, a stranger. He felt he was quits with her, since he never hindered her carefree life and asked nothing of her but that she be happy after her fashion. She was part of the household to which he was accustomed, along with Mrs. Witcherly or Miss Jordan.

This Miss Jordan had been in the family for more than ten years, although she was still very young: maybe twenty-six or twenty-seven. I recall a fresh little soubrette's face, a pert little nose, a bright and merry gaze, an exquisitely comical way of twittering French, a great natural simplicity, a constant eagerness to be helpful—deftly, attentively, competently, cheerfully, and without the slightest hint of servility. Next to her, Éva seemed a big fat hen coupled with a tamed lark: Miss Jordan's bursts of laughter were the only gaiety in the house. She was full of tact, to boot, and knew how to do little services without anyone even having to call upon her vigilant goodwill.

I admit it may seem in bad taste to compare someone with whom one confesses one was in love to a "big fat hen." I fault myself, in speaking about Éva, for only being able to find terms that present her as an overweight and doltish girl. I appear to be taking my revenge retrospectively for a disappointment in love. I also appear to be a simpleton.

A simpleton, yes—that's what I was during that absurd episode of my youth. But beyond any acceptable limit.

However, I am not telling myself my story in order to shine in my own eyes. I am trying to be honest and to understand myself.

If I keep on about this first love without sparing myself, it is because something tells me that my case must be comparable to others, and that this incredible misapprehension by an adolescent who wasn't an idiot must be an unexceptional phenomenon.

It must not be unusual for a boy of seventeen or eighteen, rather bookish, shaped by his reading, and having no experience of women other than that which derives from the works of poets and classical authors, to create for himself an altogether conventional conception of love and to become the victim of an error as gross as the one I fell into.

I had not yet spent much time with young women, and it seemed to me (from books, and from a certain emptiness, a certain unused capacity for tenderness that I felt within me) essential to bring romantic love into my life. Tolstoy has made much of this idea that love, the preoccupation with women, would hold a far smaller place in the thought and the lives of young men if they were not hypnotized and intoxicated from their earliest years by the world's attitude on this subject, the example of heroes in tragedies and novels.

Seduced, from the moment of my arrival in Paris, by the Hectors' world, attracted to the exquisite creature that was Pauline, flattered by the attention that Hector showed me, and meeting just then, in that family, a young woman whom I was to see again and again, with whom I was to be in close contact, and who benefited from the prestige that her parents had in my eyes, I focused on her all the emotional elements that I had in reserve. I needed a "love object." Éva appeared at exactly the right moment. I did not examine the matter, I did not ask myself if we were suited to each other. I did not even wait to get to know her better. The very evening of that dinner in the rue de Fleurus when I had been bewitched by the charm, the wealth, the kindness of the Hectors, I secretly declared myself in love with their daughter, having hardly spoken to her.

From that day on, there was a "love object" in my life who had Éva's physical appearance—an ideal creature, entirely the product of my imagination, who I persuaded myself was indispensable to my happiness. For nothing in the world would I have been willing to renounce the step I had finally taken towards adulthood by securing a "love object" for myself.

There were two entirely separate planes: the real plane of my relations with Éva, which was nonexistent (so nonexistent that I did not even feel any disappointment in spending two hours in her family circle, welcomed into its bosom, without speaking to her privately a single time, without broaching the slightest personal subject with her, without even paying much attention to her); and then the fictional plane where, while I was away from her, I euphorically developed the "love" theme.

How was this possible? I seem to remember the following, which is important and makes the error less incomprehensible. I believe that despite everything I was aware of the nonexistence of our relationship and able to see how uninteresting and ordinary Éva was. But what I loved or thought I loved in her was not so much the child of sixteen that she was as the young woman, the fiancée, the bride that she was to become. At the time I had this idea of the pristine fiancée, of the malleable, teachable woman in her first bloom, whom the man marries for her charming freshness and of whom he makes, through the miracle of love, the ideal companion, the other half of himself. It is only this that can to some extent explain what went on in me. I was not disappointed by how uninteresting Éva was, because, in truth, I was attached only to her future possibilities; and in that domain, my imagination had free rein.

She was not without charm, I might add. She was healthy and fresh, simple and sweet, and instead of discerning a meager character, an inborn stupidity in that lusterlessness and absence of personality, I simply saw one more opportunity to shape her in my own image and bring forth a choice butterfly from that commonplace chrysalis.

And then wasn't the fact that she had her mother's eyes enough to attract me? Irises of a strange shade, the shade of a pond at sunset, a gray with a lot of russet in it, a warm, golden gray (all my life I have remained susceptible to that particular color of the iris). And she also had that slight shortsightedness of Pauline's, not enough to correct with a lorgnette or with glasses but enough to make her screw up her eyelids very slightly and give to her gaze something hesitant, blurred, and attentive, which cast a deep spell over me.

THE HECTORS occupied the second and third floors; an inner staircase, with dark oak balusters, connected the antechambers of the two apartments. The third floor was reserved for the bedrooms, and I did not often have occasion to go up there. But the layout of the second has remained very much in my mind.

They spent most of their time in a spacious room located to the left of the antechamber and adjacent to the dining room. On the right there opened a row of three rooms, of which the first, the billiard room, and the last, the big drawing room, were very large; between the two was the little drawing room, smaller in size, but which anywhere else would have been a grand reception room.

The first time I was received at the Avenue Hoche, I had the impression of entering the Musée de Cluny. Contrary to the fashion of the day, Mme. Hector had not accumulated in her home those stuffed armchairs, poufs, and little tables covered with plush, trimming, and tassels, or that bamboo furniture which people took to be Chinese and which was all the rage everywhere.

During her childhood holidays in a feudal English castle, Pauline had developed a passion for the style of the Renaissance, and she had created for herself in Paris a sumptuous yet somewhat austere setting of very beautiful antique furniture—sideboards, chests, carved tables, all polished like mirrors. The French fifteenth and sixteenth centuries stood there side by side with English furniture from the Tudor and Elizabethan periods. However, comfort was not sacrificed to the plastic dimension. The chairs were of two types. First, there were carved gothic thrones; church stalls; straight-backed Louis XIII armchairs, hard as you could wish and upholstered with damask and figured velvet in purple and olive green, with cushions of antique silk; Spanish chairs of embossed Cordova leather, gilded like old bindings. And this would have been quite uncomfortable, despite the abundance of cushions and antique materials, if Pauline had not skillfully complemented this less than inviting furniture with excellent, softly-padded armchairs brought from London, where fashion had just created a Renaissance-inspired style that was much more welcoming than the medieval. Pauline's art consisted in knowing how to put these examples of various periods together without doing any violence to taste. This produced an ensemble that was splendid, staid and rich, somewhat formal, somewhat stiff, somewhat somber, but warm to the eye: a harmonious whole was formed by the old gilt and the wood grown shiny with age, by the tapestries, the draperies of Genoa velvet, the old reds, the old greens, the ancient Persian rugs, the silk brocades, and the seventeenth-century damasks that covered the walls. There were wrought-iron lanterns, ceilings with painted beams like those in the château of Blois, monumental fireplaces of stone and wood, with hoods, sculpted string courses, caryatids; there were lecterns, shiny brass sconces from Holland, multicolored and translucent glass chandeliers, ewers, clocks with silver dials in tall Venetian casings, old earthenware, old pewter, copper water-urns, ivory Virgins, enamels, every kind of luxurious bric-a-brac to dazzle the eye.

Pauline was twenty years ahead of that fashion for bric-a-brac which swept the bourgeoisie around 1890 and which is still illustrated, for social historians, by photographs taken in the homes of the artists of the time—the studios of the bourgeois painters of the *plaine Monceau,** Sarah Bernhardt's townhouse in the rue Fortuny, etc. Such a setting was wholly new to me and made a deep impression. It was very different from the furnishings of the hôtel de Fleurus, where mainly the padding of the Second Empire lived on. We also had some very lovely furniture at le Saillant, old wardrobes and sideboards mixed in with Louis XVI bergères, Empire mahogany bookcases . . . I had not been brought up to care for these ill-assorted old things, which were not, in our house, prized objects, chosen with love and put on display, but family heirlooms, vestiges of former times, worn with use, which we did not even look at. It seemed to me, when I walked into the Avenue Hoche, that I was entering a museum of rare pieces that created an imposing and exceptional decor around Pauline.

It is true that her tall, lithe figure, always wrapped against the cold in floating veils, scarves, and long-fringed shawls, was particularly well adapted to that somber and stately interior. She was the chatelaine of that old manor, and her languid poses, her way of reclining like a permanent convalescent among those draperies and embroidered cushions, took on, against that background, something legendary, hieratic, which made of her a precious object, beyond fashion, beyond the present.

She always greeted me with a special kindness, which flattered and captivated me. It was for her that I went there so gladly, but I was not aware of it. Convinced as I was that I loved Éva, I did not realize that it was with Pauline I was smitten, that it was Pauline's presence which warmed my heart, that it was with Pauline I felt myself in secret harmony.

She had an inner life that was rather private. She was a poet, and crafted strange, delicate, personal little poems, from which she derived no vanity and which she gathered from time to time in a slim deluxe volume that she had published at her own expense by Lemerre, anonymously, and not for sale. One of these little volumes, *Stele to Shelley,* had caused a certain sensation in the literary

*Area around the Parc Monceau in the sixteenth arrondissement.

circles of the day, and a few poems from this collection had appeared in translation, in a London literary review. But always ailing or imagining that she was, she worked little and yielded to her inspiration only intermittently.

She was as removed as possible from her husband's scientific concerns. They seemed very much in love with each other all the same, but their existences were quite separate. She lived on the third floor, in a bedroom which I never entered, but which I imagine to have been large, with the curtains constantly drawn, a bed with its back to the light, and a divan piled high with cushions. She did not tolerate daylight well, and always had the muslin blinds lowered in the windows of the rooms she was in, for fear of migraine. She fared better with the glare of lamps than that of sunshine, and lived more comfortably in the evening.

Her visitors generally did not call until the end of the day. She shied away from all the obligations of the Parisian round. But there was still a good deal of entertaining at the Avenue Hoche. Without ostentation, I would even say without invitations, and almost always on the spur of the moment. Those who were there and happened to have the evening free were invited by Pauline to stay for dinner. These were most often artists, bachelors, poets, young musicians. There was also a whole cluster of picturesque and parasitical characters that gravitated around the Hectors, attracted both by Pauline's charm and by the pleasure of having a good dinner in a select setting with people like themselves. Pauline liked to surround herself with friends who were beholden to her and with whom she did not have to make any extra effort, with whom she could be herself. Sometimes she sat down at the table with everyone, and then in the middle of the meal went upstairs to lie down. Sometimes she had her dinner in bed but reappeared suddenly at nine and kept her friends until all hours. Sometimes she was tempted to go to a concert or a play, and would dispatch the page-boy at the last moment to book a box with ten seats, where she would arrive, late, like a queen, followed by her little court. Hector accepted this behavior with a good grace that was quite surprising. But he adored his wife, down to her most bizarre vagaries, and perhaps because of them. He treated her like a delicate, pampered child whose fancies only added to her charm. And then, he never worked at night, he was free; the evening did not belong to him, his wife disposed of it as she saw fit. He rose very early, but as he needed little sleep, he did not mind staying up late. He even seemed happy to see his wife sought after, fêted, smiling, as if he had had a premonition that she did not have many years to live and wanted to let her take from life all the good it could still give her.

The table, large and rectangular, almost square, was lit, in the evening, by a wrought-iron chandelier, an antique which was originally designed for tapers and had been cleverly converted to hold a big oil lamp at either end, and a whole crown of candles.

It was around this table that we took our places as soon as Pauline, swathed in her trailing fabrics, and holding the Pomeranian that never left her lap in her thin, bracelet-laden arms, had finally descended from her bedroom. I was on the hostess's right, and Éva was on her left. Hector sat at the other end of the table, flanked by the two English ladies, the old Mrs. Witcherly and the sweet Miss Jordan, whom I thus had on my right. The meal was served by a liveried manservant under the supervision of Frédéric, the butler, who stood, in tails, near the door of the pantry, and who bestirred himself only for such special duties as serving the wines or carving the meat on the trolley set up under one of the windows.

The dining room was wainscotted to the height of about six feet with Gothic paneling, in black oak, which must have come from some old chapter room. The fireplace, in the same style, was of stone, quite beautifully designed and very simple; no other ornament than a string course decorated with sculpted foliage on which old traces of red and blue paint were visible; this string course was supported by two wreathed columns, and two tall wrought-iron andirons stood in the red brick hearth, where, in the winter, out of sheer luxury, since the building was heated, a wood fire was lit, gladdening the eye. Opposite the fireplace stood a tall piece of sacristy furniture in three sections, with the middle part jutting out into the room. In one of its corners was a low door to the pantry. The carved panels represented religious scenes, with several characters. The two other walls were bare; in one there were three windows with panes of old stained glass; in the other, two wide doors, paneled, one leading into the antechamber, and the other into the room where they spent all their time and which was called, I don't know why, the "hall."*

This Frédéric was my bête noire. I loathed his clean-shaven and ageless face, with its gray complexion, his hair plastered down *"à l'anglaise"* (as they said at the time), his heavy batrachian eyelids, and the keen, curious, cunning gaze, at once hostile and obsequious, which constantly slid between his lowered eyelashes. He was the impenetrable and informed witness. One of the most intimidating creatures I have ever come up against. If, when I began to speak, I met his stealthy gaze for an instant, I found myself paralyzed. When, by chance, it was he who opened the front door, I felt myself examined from head to toe, judged, seen through. "I know why you're coming": such was the thought I believed I read beneath his quick, unctuous smile. "You can deceive everyone else as to your secret intentions, but no one deceives *me* . . ." He zealously helped me off with my overcoat and took it into the cloakroom as carefully as if it had been a vestment sacred to some devout cult. He was, along with Mrs. Witcherly, whom he served as

*English in the original.

confidential adviser, aide-de-camp, and invaluable collaborator, one of the pillars of the house, and his presence contributed, I do not know how, to creating the sense of an excessive luxury. Never did he have to be taken to task, as he was the model butler; but he called to mind a white mushroom growing on a dung heap; and I am sure that if one could have read his secret thoughts, known the most private side of his life, one would have vomited with disgust.

At table, it usually happened that after a few moments of general talk there developed a private conversation between Mme. Hector and myself, another between Éva and her governess, while Hector and Mrs. Witcherly ate silently, hardly saying a word to each other. Hector was very courteous with her, even addressed her ceremoniously, always called her "dear Mrs. Witcherly," but he spoke to her little. And the old lady was busy keeping an eye on the courses, the diners' plates, and exchanging with the impassive and shifty Frédéric quick glances filled with mysterious meanings and conducive to the service. Invariably, at the beginning of the meal, Hector would ask about the menu like a sick man who has to watch his diet: "What are we having today, dear Mrs. Witcherly?"—and he would always seem very satisfied with the answer. But he rather seldom tasted the dishes that were presented him. He first refused all the dishes with sauce, rarely ate meat, did not touch the hors d'oeuvres or the salad. Then, around the middle of the meal, he would lean over to his neighbor and murmur a few words to her that seemed to be a friendly request. Immediately, Mrs. Witcherly raised her beautiful powdered face towards Frédéric, who would disappear into the pantry. He would soon reappear, himself bringing Hector a tray on which there were three fried eggs sizzling on a silver dish, and a Sèvres porcelain bowl filled with cold café au lait. Hector never varied this menu. And never did he allow this special fare to be ordered in advance. He persisted in sitting down at the table as if he had decided to eat some of everything. "What are we having today, dear Mrs. Witcherly?"—and it was during the meal that he would ask, excusing himself, as if it were a favor, an unexpected whim necessitated by the singular state of his stomach, that three eggs and a cup of café au lait be fixed for him. And nobody seemed surprised by it. This was plainly regarded by everyone as one of the endearing Hector's countless quirks and eccentricities. When he came to dine at the rue de Fleurus, he ate nothing, merely took a bit of ice cream at dessert, nibbled a few grapes or a few segments of mandarin orange. Aunt Ma no longer worried about it. She had it from Mrs. Witcherly that Hector before setting out had gulped down his eggs and his café au lait in his dressing-room.

. . .

I HAVE WONDERFUL MEMORIES of my talks with Pauline. She had read a lot, especially the poets. She had a thorough knowledge of English poetry, old and modern, and read Italian fluently. As a young woman she had made long visits to Rome and spoke of it nostalgically. She knew by heart long passages of Milton and Dante, which she translated for me in her soft and vibrant voice with a profound sense of poetry. We endlessly discussed the respective merits of the contemporary French poets, of whom I was less ignorant than of the foreign ones. She had a very sound, very personal taste, the taste of a dilettante, an enlightened amateur, without any pedantry or any conventions left over from school. She always surprised and delighted me with her naturalness, with the refinement of her preferences and the deep echo that poetry found in her. She never alluded to the poems she was writing. For her it was an intimate pleasure that she kept for herself alone, and she was as little a "woman writer" as could be. A spontaneously artistic nature. She had brought back from Italy a folder of watercolors, done in the Roman *campagna,* which would have delighted Goethe. Here too she had a personal talent, a precision, a delicacy, an ease of notation, which in no way resembled the somewhat conventional landscapes drawn by the young ladies of her time who cultivated the "decorative arts." Many of these studies remained unfinished, yet they rendered with freshness and appealing spontaneity a fleeting impression on which she had declined to dwell. A musician also when the spirit moved her, and enthralled by Chopin, almost exclusively. I never heard her play. When I met her she claimed not to be able to sit at her piano anymore because her back immediately would begin to hurt. But Aunt Ma told me that Pauline, at the time of her marriage, spent many hours each day at the keyboard.

I will not say anything about her poems. I thought I had two collections in my library but have not been able to find them. I would need to reread them to be able to do them justice. At that time their mysticism did not bother me, and I was sufficiently under the spell of the poetess to accept her Christian inspiration without reservations. I remember in particular a long poem about Teresa of Ávila, which had seemed very beautiful to me; it had appeared in an art edition by Lemerre, with an engraved frontispiece, the work of a Spanish artist. It came into my hands by chance; she had showed it to me, for the frontispiece, one evening when she was quite distressed: she had just learned of the sudden death of its young illustrator. As I was trying to convey a little of the emotion with which the reading of her poem had left me, she had gently silenced me by putting her hand over my mouth, the way one hushes an indiscreet child. I remember it perhaps less for the quality of the verse than for the feverish warmth of that palm brushing my lips. She had long narrow hands that prolonged her thin arms, with their sickly pallor: I discovered those hands again on the canvas where Velázquez painted his portrait of X.*

After lunch, coffee was served in the billiards room, and as soon as he had left the table, Hector, his cigarette holder stuck in his mouth, began circling the baize, making carom shots. He had a passion for billiards, had taken lessons with renowned champions, and was first-class at it. He happened to like to play alone, and became absorbed in his solitary game as if, with each carom, he had the satisfaction of confirming mathematical laws. His billiard table was naturally a marvelous instrument, made in America, of an unusual size. He devoted nearly an hour to the game after each meal and it was, he said, his only exercise, excellent for the health, and particularly favorable, no doubt, to the digestion of the fried eggs and café au lait.

Mrs. Witcherly generally slipped away after having inspected the coffee tray and made sure that Miss Jordan or Éva was in charge of serving. The two young ladies waited until the coffee was drunk to vanish in their turn. And Pauline, who dreaded prolonged exposure to tobacco smoke, usually invited me to follow her into the big room where she was most comfortable, to the left of the antechamber.

There she settled into a big English wing chair, well padded and furnished with throw pillows. It is there that I can envision her best, her shoulders enveloped in a scarf, her dog on her lap. Dick was a marvel of a dog, it goes without saying—a prizewinner several times over: I don't think I've seen his equal. He was a tiny Pomeranian, no bigger than a toy, with a silky coat of Havana brown, who never slept except with one eye open, in his mistress's lap, and his nervous body stood up quivering every time someone opened the door, to greet the new arrival with a sharp little yelp that pierced one's eardrum. I, of course, made every allowance for this companion of Pauline, but I felt especially warm towards him when I noticed the fierce dislike he had for the shady Frédéric, which he valiantly demonstrated with shrill barking, up on his little paws, his eyes blazing and all his little teeth visible under his curled lip, until the butler left the room.

Pauline and I chatted alone together and it seemed to me—it still seems to me—that the pleasure was mutual, and that her affectionate interest was not feigned. I did not in any way play the know-it-all, the grownup. I let her see my ignorance, my naïveté. I asked her advice, her suggestions as to reading. I was natural, unconstrained. And I think this was what she liked. No affectation in any of that. I conversed with her in the same tone as with my sister Henriette or with Aunt Ma. I believe that she appreciated this natural-

*The addition of the subject's name awaited Martin du Gard's final revision of the chapter.

ness, and that my youth, ardently taken as I was with literature, open to all sorts of enthusiasms, amused and rejuvenated her.

When Hector had walked his kilometer around his large billiard table, he came and looked in on us for a moment, sometimes even sat with us a short while, then went back down "to his alchemy"—as his wife said—after having leaned over and tenderly kissed her hair. I would then get up to take my leave. Sometimes she would keep me with her a little longer. But most often she seemed weary, and she would let me go, making me promise to return soon.

I usually had to put up once again with the sidelong glance and impassive obsequiousness, which I persisted in interpreting as ironical, of the silent Frédéric, before getting out the door. And I would return home to the rue de Fleurus, nearly always walking, for the Sunday gathering.

I would leave without having seen Éva again. Sometimes, while I was sitting beside her mother she would come in with her governess, both elegantly decked out for a walk in the Bois or a visit to a friend, and we would amicably shake hands. But as a rule I did not see her again. And I seem to remember that I was not much saddened by this. I went off with a happy impression of my intimacy with the mother, and scarcely gave a thought to the daughter at that moment. But the very next day, recounting the little occurrences of my visit to the Avenue Hoche to a friend, I would let myself go and embellish my banal encounter with Éva, and she again gradually became the haunting image of Love. And I would spend a couple of weeks daydreaming about her, adorning her with graces and imaginary intentions, senselessly getting myself all worked up.

My excuse, if I need one, is that this stupid mawkishness, this foolish romantic delusion, lasted only a few months.

I WILL BRIEFLY CLOSE by noting the end of the story of the Hector family. It is quite pathetic.

Towards the end of the winter of '87, at the time when, with a fresh enthusiasm, I was seeing a lot of the family of my friend Blaise Saint-Gall and was received as a regular guest at their home in the rue Saint-Guillaume, my Sunday visits to the Avenue Hoche became less and less frequent. The following year, the preparation for Saint-Cyr further reduced our contacts. I paid visits to Pauline, and always with a tender pleasure, and I always received from her the same friendly welcome. But I hardly went to the laboratory anymore. However, I saw the whole family fairly often at the dinners that Aunt Ma gave for them several times during the winter. Those meetings were rather unpleasant for me. I found Éva quite vacant, and I was mortified when I remembered the absurd place that she had, at one moment, held in my life. (Since then I had fallen in love, less foolishly, with Laure Saint-Gall. And it was at the end of the winter of '89 that I met Doudou, and knew the realities of love.)

My relations with the Hectors were the same during my time at Saint-Cyr. Even more sporadic. Pauline's health declined, she no longer went out at all in the evening, and several times I found her door closed to me.

When I finished my years at Saint-Cyr, she was in Switzerland, in a sanatorium outside Lausanne, where Hector and Éva had settled to be near the patient. Aunt Ma kept me informed.

While stationed at Versailles in the winter of '92, I learned of Pauline's death. Hector went back to Paris. I paid him a visit of condolence. He had not set up his laboratory again. He was barely recognizable. He had left Mrs. Witcherly, Éva, and Miss Jordan in Lausanne, where Éva had wished to stay on. There she met a Polish count, luxury-loving and bankrupt. Hector consented to their engagement and to his daughter's departure for Poland, where the count had vast mortgaged estates which he was eager to put back into cultivation with his young wife's enormous fortune. Miss Jordan went home to England. Mrs. Witcherly returned to Paris and moved into a convent that took lodgers, in the rue de Bac, to finish her days there. She sometimes came to the rue de Fleurus for a meal.

Hector stayed on for a few months in Paris. He had given up the magnificent dwelling on the Avenue Hoche and lived, with only Frédéric, in a furnished pension in Passy. Then he came and broke it to my uncle and aunt that he was renouncing the world to enter the Benedictine Abbey of Solesmes. He was fifty-five.

He was to live there for about fifteen years. He died in 1905, shortly after my Uncle Éric, while I was in Morocco.

I am forgetting to put down one piquant detail. In 1899 or 1900, my Uncle Éric was summoned, to his great surprise, by an examining magistrate at the Palais de Justice to testify on behalf of a rather disreputable character, the former manager of a house of assignation involved in a sordid case of swindling, who had named my uncle as a defense witness. It was Frédéric! Probably he had purchased a brothel with the fortune he had made out of what was squandered at the Avenue Hoche. I do not recollect the details very well. I only know that my uncle's testimony was quite reluctant, and that Frédéric was well and truly condemned to two years in prison, and that his fines were considerable.

Aunt Ma received very little news of her niece. She seemed to be more or less confined by her Polish count to a feudal castle, where she raised her numerous children. At least that was what Mrs. Witcherly claimed, before her death; she had had some Polish friends, whom she met at a spa, conduct a little investigation.

CHAPTER XVI

Blaise Saint-Gall and His Family

I VERY WELL RECALL my first contact with Blaise Saint-Gall, whose friendship was to last a long time and whose family was to become my own.

It happened in the little classroom at the Sorbonne where, once a week, Old Mellay had us translate *The Bacchae* of Euripides. The lesson had not begun. It was the very start of the school year, the third or fourth class in Greek textual analysis, and I still did not know my fellow students. I had arrived a little early and was rereading the text I had prepared the day before when I saw a tall, heavy boy, who stopped, hesitating, in the doorway. He met my gaze, came over to me, and asked if this was where the course in Greek was being held. Then, probably encouraged by my reception, he explained that he was enrolled in *licence ès lettres,* that he had just got over a minor illness which had prevented him from attending the first classes, that he did not yet have the required books, and that, if the seat next to mine was free, he would like to be able to follow the analysis from my text. All this was said with simplicity and geniality, with a sort of natural ease which seemed to me all the more likable since, up until then, I had kept apart from my classmates out of shyness and was suffering from this isolation. I hastened to make a place for him beside me and filled him in a little as to what had been covered in the previous lessons. I even offered to lend him my notes after class. The professor's arrival interrupted this friendly talk. We followed the lesson side by side, hunched over the same book, then we left together. I was so happy to have made a friend, and so eager to be helpful, that I suggested he come with me to the rue de Fleurus so that I could give him the reading list and the schedule of lectures and lend him my notebooks. He accepted without ado. So I took him to the Chambosts', brought him up to my room, and we spent the end of the afternoon together in warm conversation.

Such was the beginning of this friendship.

It was, without any doubt, due to external impressions that I was at once attracted to Blaise Saint-Gall: his ease, his distinguished style, his innate affability, the intelligence of his eyes (mischievous but with no disturbing irony), his obvious kindness, his naturalness, the fine cut of his clothes, his beautiful round and straightforward handwriting, something upright and solid about his entire person.

From our very first meetings, he became a model for me, the classic example of a certain order of things that I wanted to attain as quickly as possible. Not to put too fine a point on it: I still felt like an uncouth schoolboy, a schoolboy and a provincial; Saint-Gall, on the other hand, was a young Parisian student. I wore ready-made clothes bought in le Mans, solid boots with laces and round toes, neckties on the loud side. Having picked all of this out myself with Henriette, I was very proud of these expenditures for which my father had virtually given me carte blanche, and I was convinced that these clothes would be appreciated in Paris, representing as they did so much progress, in terms of quality and daring, over what I had formerly worn as a country boy and boarding-school student. I realized that, next to Saint-Gall, I was dressed like a rube in his Sunday best. Never would he have worn those dove-gray trousers with a black stripe, of which I had been rather vain up till then, or those light-colored neckties that called attention to themselves. He wore only dark suits, black or navy blue, and neutral neckties, but the fabrics were woolen and soft, his linen was the very best, his feet were shod in high-button shoes with thin soles and pointed toes. He had that sterling elegance which does not show, which comes from the quality of the material, of the good cut, a supremely discreet elegance of which he did not even seem to be aware, and which was due, in part, to the naturalness of his manners, to that air he had of being perfectly, intrinsically comfortable with himself.

I observed him attentively. No detail of his dress or behavior eluded me. I drank him in with my eyes. His hands were small and well cared for. He always seemed just to have come out of his bath, and had about him something appetizing, clean, refined, that enchanted me. He sported a very fine and freshly ironed handkerchief in his breast pocket, and he had an unaffected and offhand way of taking it out, unfolding it and putting it back without rumpling it, which seemed to me incomparable. He did not appear to attach the least importance to any of this. And indeed I believe that his socialite's manners had been a part of him for so long that he never thought about them. I never felt that he was conscious of this superiority. Actually, I have since learned that he regretted his irregular features, his heftiness, and, in short, his being rather unattractive, and that he envied my thinness, good build, litheness, and well-drawn features.

Perhaps, in hindsight, I am exaggerating how provincial I looked. Among my Sorbonne classmates, I was not at any rate the only one; and I think that in spite of everything—and in spite of the dove-gray trousers—I had a certain natural distinction which many lacked and which came to me directly from the Maumorts without any effort on my part.

But it was very useful for me to meet this pure-blooded Parisian soon after my arrival in Paris and to model myself rather childishly on him in order to cast off my provincialism. At that age, such a transformation takes place very fast. I put aside part of my monthly allowance in order to be able to modify my wardrobe as rapidly as possible; I did not hesitate, I recall, to have the dove-colored trousers dyed—with the complicity of Aunt Ma, to whom I often confided these sartorial worries, and in whom I found a sage and indulgent partner. She too did much to help me become, within a few months, the young Parisian I aspired to be. She never made fun of my efforts at metamorphosis. I am even certain that they pleased her and that she wished to make of me what her son would have been: a well-bred young man, accustomed to and fond of society, cutting a fine figure, and always at ease in whatever circle he found himself.

I was at the maximum age at which that natural ease can still be acquired. In the army I had friends of excellent country stock, who had left their province only to let themselves be shut away at Saint-Cyr, and who remained self-conscious all their lives, shy and awkward every time they had to appear in a drawing room or go out into the world. This is not in itself a very serious flaw. Its consequences, nonetheless, are often very unfortunate, and many a career has been hindered by it. One has to have gone through it, to have felt oneself clumsy and blushing, to have known the temptation of turning down every invitation in order to avoid undergoing that humiliating ordeal; one has to have been "provincial" in one's youth to appreciate the truly considerable advantages that social skills provide. The man of the world, who is comfortable everywhere, thereby gains an independence of mind, a freedom of movement, a liveliness, a mastery of his resources, an additional strength, and, besides, a charm, a hold over others, which are of great value in leading one's life. There exists, between him and a shy provincial of equal merit, the same difference as between an athlete and a cripple . . .

Our friendship quickly took solid root. This, clearly, was more my doing. I made repeated overtures and created favorable opportunities. I do not know if Blaise, on his own, would have become attached to me. He had always lived in Paris, had gone to school at Louis-le-Grand, possessed a few good friends and a large family with many connections, and it could easily have been that after having needed me, through force of circumstance, to get caught up on the first classes and make up for lost time, he would merely have maintained with me that sort of superficial friendship that he had with many others. But that was not how I wanted things to go. I was still very much at sea in the Latin Quarter, very isolated and unhappy about it. I liked Blaise enormously, all the more so since there was no other classmate whom I had been able to get to know; my meeting with him seemed providential. I was able to do him a thousand services in letting him benefit by my experience, and I did not fail to be helpful. I think that he took to me at first out of convenience, then out of gratitude. It was not in his nature to brush someone off after having used him. He graciously consented to my attentions. I did my best to direct our conversations, which at first had been purely about school, toward more general subjects, then toward personal questions. I noticed that I interested him, that he liked the way my mind worked. I happily tried to raise the level of our chats. He had enough intellectual curiosity to develop a taste for them. We fell into the habit of waiting for each other after classes, of walking each other home by turns—even, on certain days, of taking long walks on the paths of the Luxembourg. I spoke to him about my Uncle Chambost-Lévadé, described the Sunday gatherings, told him the remarks that had struck me, and mentioned the famous people I had met. This gave me a halo in his eyes that I did not hesitate to use discreetly to fix his attention on me.

At that age one makes friends quickly, once the ice is broken. We soon enough arrived at our first confidences. Our friendship took shape and developed on its own.

We naturally had a strong sense that we were profoundly alike, because, without even realizing it, we mainly focused on the many points we had in common.

In reality, though, we were quite different, even at that time.

He was already a very outgoing young man who always smiled when he spoke and did everything he could to be liked. To breathe easily, he needed to feel a welcoming atmosphere around him, one of well-disposed, open people. And he had that gift of always knowing what to say to make contact, whether with the ticket-taker on the omnibus, the girl at the post office, a grumpy classmate, or a cantankerous examiner. He effortlessly spread a human magnetism about him which made those he addressed sociable, susceptible to his good mood. He was witty. Above all, he had that mischievous look, with no malice in it, and an amusing way of putting everything he said that made it sound wittier than it perhaps was. I do not mean to imply that there was anything vulgar about this affability. His native distinction saved him from that. His ease even gave him a rather grand air, and he was able to allow himself many things without the slightest hint of slumming.

The shy and secretly proud provincial that I then was, frequently taciturn or even distant out of awkwardness, had much to learn from Blaise. The mimicry usual at that age, the need to imitate immediately what one admires in others, helped me change my rather surly manners. And as this welcoming attitude in fact corresponded to a certain sociability in my nature and did much to satisfy the curiosity I had about people, I did not adopt those manners only on the surface; I rather quickly made them my own, I felt good about them, and this only served to spur me on and make me persist in that direction. In truth, I had only to overcome my adolescent's shyness and surrender to a natural tendency to become friendly. I acquired a taste for it. And this taste I kept. If I have made myself generally liked in all the circles I have been part of over the years, I of course owe it to my rather accommodating character; but I also owe it to the example of Blaise Saint-Gall and to my luck in being exposed to this example at that moment of youth when the character is easily molded.

Yet our values were different.

Blaise—as the rest of his life would prove—was a fairly superficial person. He had no inclination to ponder deeply. He had never had any strong passion. He was facile, and contented himself with that. He did not demand much of himself. Nothing in him was very substantial. He had neither great defects nor great virtues. His ambitions were modest. He planned to take up law, wished to make an honorable place for himself in that arena, and hoped to succeed without much personal effort thanks to the connections that his family had maintained in the world of the courts: his maternal grandfather, whom he apparently resembled, Justice Forestier, a venerable magistrate of the old school, honest and right-thinking, had left a respected name in the profession, and his grandson was sure to be welcomed by the legal fraternity as one of their own. Blaise did go on to make a very creditable career in the courts, but not a brilliant one. He was a good corporate lawyer, conscientious and principled. In Parisian society, he was a perfect man of the world, widely known and congenial; he passed for a very cultivated and well-read fellow in a milieu where, to be deemed an artist and a thinker, it is enough to be a pleasant talker, keep up with the new books by reading several magazines, and touch lightly, in one's conversation, on all the literary, historical, and political topics of the season. He spoke about everything in an intelligent way, played light-handedly with general ideas, sprinkled his remarks with witty quips, subtle observations, amusing anecdotes, and allusions to celebrities; he was much sought after in the salons. He got on my nerves a little, because he had that lawyer's glibness—too easy, too fluent, a watered-down amalgam of ready-made ideas and clichés, of false intellectual audacities, of cheap and purely verbal skepticism. Also, he obviously loved the sound of his own voice. He would have made a perfect lecturer. I was surprised that with this type of oratory he could ever have won a lawsuit. I think that he pleaded a case better than he chatted, I mean with more strictness in the progression of ideas and with a less florid style. Yet this is not certain, and it is possible that the judges who, as we know, like to translate Horace on Sundays, and who have to hear a boundary dispute or the claim to an inheritance, are grateful to the well-spoken attorney who gives them the illusion that these prosaic debates are a feast of wit and literature . . .

But the subject, for the moment, is Blaise in 1887 and our friendship in its prime. Today I can discern what was superficial in him at the time. However it would have taken quite a practiced eye to notice it back then, and I was far too fervent in my friendship to possess that critical lucidity.

In those days, he was keenly curious and really fond of intellectual things. He had received an excellent education and his memory was reliable and well stocked. He had the advantage over me of having been taught by the cream of the crop at Louis-le-Grand, highly cultured *agrégés* who took pride in raising the academic tone to the level of general ideas and in shaping the taste and intelligence of their pupils—rather than cramming their memories—by peppering their lessons with indulgent digressions on contemporary literature, history, philosophy, and Parisian current events. Blaise had read many modern authors whose names I was only beginning to learn. He loved arguing and did not cheat at it; we both had a reverence for knowledge and the honest search for the truth in all fields. Anyone who had caught us sauntering in the streets or in the alleys of the Luxembourg after class, instead of rushing home to work, would have been quite mistaken to think that we were wasting our time. Our interminable talks on all subjects had a serious turn, passionately serious, and this intellectual contact between two young minds eagerly taken with ideas was extremely beneficial. With a generous competitiveness, we lent each other books and compared impressions as to what we had read. We were capable of going on a whole week about the relative genius of Aeschylus and Euripides, about *The Social Contract* and *The Spirit of the Laws,* about Virgil and Theocritus, about Joseph de Maistre and Proudhon, about Hugo and Lamartine. I recall that we discovered *Dangerous Liaisons,* and that it gave rise to effervescent debates concerning morality and love.

I GOT TO KNOW the Saint-Gall family without any preparation, without anything in Blaise's attitude resembling what I might feel at the idea of introducing him to the rue de Fleurus, which was for me a delicate event, necessitating a whole little plan, precautions, preliminary conversations, an entire diplomatic operation. For it mattered a great deal to me that Blaise should see my uncle and aunt in the best light, in favorable circumstances, and that this meeting should be such that the Chambosts should have the best possible impression of Blaise and that Blaise should at once take a liking to the Chambosts and respect them. As for him, it was obvious that my first visit to his parents was not an event of much importance. Not that he would have been very affected by a negative judgment of his family on my part. But I don't think that he even began to imagine such an eventuality. He had that mentality of members of large families—to which I shall return—who so worship their clan that they do not even suppose you could find anything in them to criticize or scoff at.

The Saint-Galls lived in the rue Saint-Guillaume, in that part of the street which runs from the boulevard Saint-Germain to the rue de l'Université.

Several times already I had walked Blaise to his door, a great eighteenth-century portal with a knocker, which was always closed. That morning, around eleven I think, we were talking as we went along about a French essay we had to hand in a few days later which we each had already written and about which we had differing views. When we arrived at his door, Blaise said to me: "Come on up a minute, I'll read you my composition." I had the time, since I knew that my aunt was attending a funeral at the Madeleine that day and that lunch was to be half an hour late; I accepted. I thought that he was going to take me to his room, as I had taken him to mine on the day of our first meeting to give him my course notes, and that I would not see any of his family. I did not yet know that you could not step over the threshold at the rue Saint-Guillaume without finding yourself swept up in the bustling life of the clan, whose comings and goings from one floor to another never stopped from morning to night, and whose members lived in casual and noisy togetherness. He rang, and we found ourselves in a paved courtyard where a girl of about ten and another of seven or eight were zigzagging along on roller skates. They dashed over to us with joyous cries and little faces reddened by cold and exercise. "Let me introduce my nieces, Jeanne and Lili," Blaise said to me, kissing them. They tottered along on their skates, which slipped on the little tile-smooth paving stones, and, jostling us, they hemmed us in and hung on to us to keep from falling, while breathlessly twittering all sorts of things: "*Tonton 'Laise,* Mama went to get Grampa. And Grandma said for you to come see her, *Tonton 'Laise.*"

"Right away?"

"Yes, when you came in, she said."

Blaise extricated himself, laughing, and led me toward a corner stoop at the rear of the courtyard. At that moment, a glass curtain was lifted in a ground-floor window, and an elderly lady made a sign to which Blaise responded affirmatively, with a nod. And as we arrived at the stoop, two muffled-up young ladies pushed open the French door. The older one, who seemed to be my age, said to Blaise in a lowered voice: "We're going to get the basket at the florist's." The other looked at Blaise, smiling: "Mama allowed us to go out, but I think she guessed where we were going." He kissed them both, and said to me: "May I introduce two of my sisters?" "You know," said the younger one, a pretty blonde still in short skirts, "we didn't have enough, it's twenty-eight francs, because of the cyclamens, so we each have to put up another franc twenty-five."

"No, a franc thirty-five," said the older.

They went down the steps and got thoroughly jostled by the skaters, who clung to their coats. Blaise opened the French door, which led directly to the stairs.

"How old are your sisters?" I asked.

"Laure is eighteen, like me, since she's my twin. And Clairette, the younger, is fourteen."

We had been friends for barely ten or fifteen days and I knew hardly anything of his family except that his father, an old navy man, had just been named Vice-Admiral and held an appointment at the Ministère de la Marine.

IT WAS a very old house on the Left Bank, probably a former *hôtel* that had been cut up into apartments.

Blaise's maternal grandfather—the one he was said to take after, Justice Forestier—had bought the house in 1865, when he retired, for the sake of the garden, where Mme. Forestier, blind since the birth of her daughter, Mme. Saint-Gall, could stroll in the winter and sit all day in the spring without having to leave the grounds.

The Forestiers had moved into the first floor. Soon after, the lease being up on the second floor, they placed the Saint-Gall couple and their children there. The Justice died. Mme. Saint-Gall, the only daughter, inherited the house. Upon the marriage of the Saint-Galls' son Jean, the Forestiers let the young couple have the third floor. So the entire house, or just about, was occupied by the family. A true *"maison de famille."*

The building did not have a façade on the rue Saint-Guillaume. A tall carriage door opened under an archway, between two old hovels fronting on the street. The Saint-Gall house consisted of an edifice from the eighteenth century, of which one façade formed the rear of the courtyard and the other looked out onto a garden slightly larger than the courtyard, about four hundred square meters. To this building were added two wings, the same height as the house and one room deep. One of these wings occupied the right side of the entrance courtyard. The bottom floor of this wing was set apart for the concierge's quarters and for various storage areas; above, three small stories, formerly rented by strangers of modest means but eventually taken over by members of the family: an old widower cousin, and a woman, also widowed, Mme. Saint-Gall's foster sister, who paid no rent and did small services. The other wing occupied the right side of the garden, and each of its three floors communicated with the floors of the main building and essentially formed part of the apartments, except for the top floor, the fourth, which was on the level of the floor reserved for the servants, and was used as an attic, a drying area, etc.

The stairwell that Blaise and I came to that morning was of vast proportions, and the big staircase, with its steps of worn stone and its eighteenth-century wrought-iron banister, would have appeared grand if the walls had not been daubed an unvarying, rather grimy chocolate shade. The foot of the staircase was cluttered with potted plants and in the winter served as a hot-house crammed with planters of little orange trees, pomegranates, and fuchsias which were thus being protected from the frosts and which, in the spring, adorned the garden.

A door on the ground floor opened halfway, and the old lady who had been keeping watch at the window called to Blaise, said a few words in his ear while smiling with a mysterious air, gave me a friendly little nod, and closed the door again.

"That's Aunt Adèle," Blaise explained to me, "an old cousin who lives with Grandma. I must tell you that it's Mama's name day, and we're all having dinner tonight at Grandma's . . . So the house is a bit topsy-turvy . . . We're very traditional in the family . . . Come on up . . ."

We arrived at the second-floor landing, where there were several doors. This landing did not look like the landing of a Parisian apartment house but rather like that of an old provincial hotel, for it was furnished with a large Norman wardrobe, a medieval chest above which was hung an Empire wall clock, and three or four gilded X-shaped stools upholstered in quilted black satin with yellow buttons. And the main door was half-hidden by a portière of very faded tapestry.

Blaise stopped in front of this door, hesitated a second, and tugged on the bellpull made of a passementerie ribbon. "Do you mind? It seems that Grandma has something to tell me. Wait for me a second."

But contrary to what he was probably expecting, it was his mother herself who opened the door. She did not seem in the least surprised to see me, answered my greeting, and spoke to Blaise: "Cousin Loisel died yesterday. A stroke. I got a wire from Josephine just this minute. Thank goodness she was in Orléans and he wasn't alone . . . with that creature. Isabelle has gone to the ministry to let your father know. But come in, dear. Come in, Monsieur," she said to me, as if I were a childhood friend. "I think that Isabelle is going to bring your father home and that he'll take the one-thirty express . . . I won't go. I don't even know if I'll go to the funeral. Josephine didn't come to Isabelle's wedding, or to Jean's, she didn't even put herself out for my father's funeral, I don't see why *I* . . . Anyway, we'll see. What I want to tell you, dear, is that I've ordered lunch for eleven-thirty. And then, can you go with your father to the station? I'm busy getting his things ready . . . But where's the leather satchel with straps, the small black one? I'll bet you've kept it upstairs . . ."

"You think so?"

"Look for it, will you, and send Élise down with it . . . Speaking of Élise, you still haven't given her your laundry this week, and it's Thursday already; this cannot be . . . Don't forget."

"Yes, Mama."

I looked at Blaise. A new Blaise, an unknown Blaise. A Blaise come down from the pedestal onto which I had raised him. No longer that adolescent with free ways, accustomed to independence, whom I considered, comparing him to myself, almost a grown man. A child Blaise, a filial Blaise, a Blaise who let himself be told everything he had to do, who showed no rebelliousness, no wounded pride, not even impatience at being treated thus in front of me. For that is what surprised me most. Here too, he appeared perfectly natural and at ease. Neither conceited nor foolish enough to be vexed because he was his mother's son, one of the children of the house, the next-to-last-born of a sizable family. That was just how it was. He found it quite simple and would never have tried to hide his submissiveness as a good son, any more than he would have tried to conceal his name or his father's career. And not only was he incapable of any dissimulation (I discovered this later), not only was he incapable of regretting that I had immediately witnessed his affectionate acquiescence to maternal orders, but he did not dislike it at all: I thus entered his world at once, and he loved that world, judged it better and more pleasing than any other, was proud of it. Blaise was the last person to say to himself, "Maumort is going to find that the house is untidy, inelegant . . . that Mama is a bore, with all her stories," etc.

In fact, he was right. I thought nothing of the sort. I even felt a great, indefinable satisfaction at entering into the specifics of Blaise's existence, at seeing him treated like a obedient little boy, at seeing him scolded for his dirty laundry . . . It brought him down from his sham pedestal, but, in my mind, it brought him closer to me. And then, from the first instant, everything I saw there—perhaps because it was Blaise's world—was to my liking. I found charming that old provincial house in the heart of Paris, where everybody knew everybody else. Charming, those little nieces, affectionate and teasing, who hung on to my overcoat with the greatest familiarity simply because, having entered the house, and being with Tonton 'laise, I could only be a friend. I had seen a great deal of kindness in the face of Aunt Adèle, glimpsed on the ground floor, and in her confidential air. And at that moment I found Mme. Saint-Gall very appealing, what with the informality of her greeting, her lack of affectation, the simplicity of her attire and her words, that trust she showed me from the first contact by speaking to her son exactly as if I had been a friend of his she had always known. This was partly true. But what I did not perceive was that it was neither out of particular trust nor out of spontaneous warmth that she acted that way. It was because she regarded me as negligible. It was because she never worried about what outsiders might think, those beyond the periphery of the clan. She was too preoccupied with that family universe of which she was the center, the cornerstone, to ascribe very much importance to the rest of the world. She led her life as queen of the hive, active and well-heeded. It did not matter to her if someone watched what she did or heard what she said. She was the mater-familias who, in days gone by, at the start of vacation, surrounded by two maids and her six children, would invade the car of a train, place everybody among the vacant seats in two or three compartments, go from one to the other, give her instructions in a carrying voice, tell the children to behave, get out the snacks, distribute the slices of bread, wipe the little faces smeared with currant jelly, send the small ones to the W.C. under the supervision of the older ones, call out to Julie and Ernestine at the far end of the car to make sure that the gas meter had been turned off before leaving and that they had not forgotten to put M. Jean's knitted underpants or Mlle. Paule's new corset in the trunk—all without maternal ostentation, without unnecessary shriek-ing, in a voice of command, firm, precise and friendly, as a powerful woman who has six children to raise and a commander husband whose last letter was postmarked Hong Kong or Bermuda, who has a weighty job, a thousand serious responsibilities, and much more on her mind than to wonder whether the old, childless retired couple sitting quietly in the compartment, or the single lady reading an English magazine, are going to find the children insufferable, or the mother too loud. Mme. Saint-Gall lived her life, equally welcoming and indifferent to everything that did not have to do with the life of the Saint-Gall clan. She had a way of saying "we," simple and peremptory, which revealed an entire special concept of existence. The concept of big families.

I became dimly aware of all this as I watched her speak to her son. We had all three of us come into the hallway. It was of medium size, cluttered with furniture and belongings—there was even, half hidden by a portière, a padded dummy, a busty and big-bottomed torso, headless, cut off below the pelvis, and standing on a tripod of black wood. This area, though lit by a window on the courtyard, was dark, owing to the panes of stained glass and a Turkey red wall-covering; it contained earthenware dishes, a wide, round barometer in a gilded wood frame, a display of antique swords, and a coat-rack overloaded with clothes.

Mme. Saint-Gall looked about fifty to me. She had in her hand a pair of black lisle socks which she had probably just taken from the admiral's wardrobe while packing his bag and which she mechanically folded and unfolded, slipping her fist down into the toe to make sure they did not have to be mended before putting them into the suitcase. She was dark-haired like her son and had somewhat the same features, thick, as if rough-hewn and unfinished. And that whole big woman's body, with its massive torso, had something heavy about it, carved from a block, something stable, too, and solidly balanced. I immediately understood that the dummy had been built from nature, and the glance I gave to the naked and mutilated trunk with its skin of pale drill suddenly seemed to me indiscreet.

Her body was built like a man's, and she must have taken after her father, Justice Forestier. Her voice itself was of a good-natured and simple coarseness, without many shadings, strong and straightforward, not very feminine. Neither the mind nor the tongue faltered over what they wanted to say. An air of going straight to her goal. Masculine, too, that indefinable authority which emanated from Mme. Saint-Gall. Her face, not beautiful, not delicate, had a certain charm all the same. She would have been a perfect model for a medieval statue, a Saint Anne or a Saint Barbara, for the chisel of a Burgundian sculptor, and it was very easy to imagine her large bust, her round shoulders, her fleshy features, her domed forehead carved out of the stone of Autun or Vézelay, and the lower part of the body lost in the thickly creased folds of an overflowing dress, covering the feet and spilling out over the plinth. These were the thoughts that came to me later, when I had become familiar with that sturdy appearance. It is thus that one pictures certain grand abbesses of Christianity, or certain authoritarian sovereigns, Elizabeth of England or Catherine of Russia.

She was kind, and this I had sensed right off, in the look and the welcoming smile she gave me when Blaise, showing me into the entrance hall, had introduced me, without even saying my name: "One of my classmates from the Sorbonne . . ."

We left her to go upstairs to the apartment on the third floor, whose door was wide open. Blaise ushered me into a bright anteroom, quite tidy, whose walls were covered with blue material. The kitchen door was also open and I noticed a young woman who was giving orders to a cook in a blue apron. I felt quite intrusive, and I hesitated on the threshold. But Blaise gave me a push, smiling: "Go in . . . I live here, at my sister-in-law's." The young woman turned to us. She did not seem in the least embarrassed at being surprised in her dressing gown by a stranger. She came over to us: "Don't make too much noise; Baby's asleep in the dining room."

She might have been twenty-two or twenty-three. Tall and lithe, an elongated face with pure features and big doe's eyes, a graceful gait and something fragile, almost sickly, romantic. Blaise introduced me: "My classmate, Bertrand de Maumort." She held out to me a wide billowing sleeve trimmed with lace, from which a long pale hand with a thin wrist emerged, and she smiled at me in a friendly way.

"Have you seen your mother?" she asked Blaise.

"Yes, I know, poor cousin Loisel."

"Jean is his godson; I think he'll go to Orléans for the funeral. And you?"

"Mama didn't speak to me about it. But I'd be surprised if she wants me to . . ."

They smiled at each other, as if they understood each other without finishing their sentences. Then she gave me a little nod goodbye, and went back to the kitchen.

We crossed a sunlit dining room. "Shhh," Blaise said to me, opening the door. A cradle was in front of the window, under a tulle veil on which hung a big ivory cross. Blaise walked on tiptoe. I did likewise.

We entered a hallway, off which was his bedroom. It was in the wing on the garden side. Big, silent, sunny. Two windows, small, but opening onto the garden. I went over to one of the windows. I saw a round lawn, encircled by a gravel path. The wall of a rather tall, windowless building closed off the far end, which was planted with a row of trees. On the left side, opposite the wing, a low wall separated the garden from a neighboring courtyard, quite large, surrounded by one-story buildings, and through this sizable breach the sun shone freely upon the wintry landscape of this little garden.

"You've sure got peace and quiet here," I told him.

The room did not have a very high ceiling, and was hung with a flowered percale showing blue morning glories on a cream-colored background; the same material had been used to make the curtains and the spread of the mahogany bed. A mahogany washstand, a little blond Norman wardrobe, and a wide table covered with a fringed rug of blue plush completed the furnishings. A rather large shelf with spindle-shaped colonnettes, placed above the table between the two windows, held books of all sorts.

"Sit down," he told me, rummaging among his papers in search of the essay that was the reason for my visit. But instead of reading it to me, as I was expecting, he folded it in two, without having glanced at it, and handed it to me. "Take it with you, you can read it at home. You'll bring it back to me tomorrow in Merleau's class, and we'll talk about it afterwards."

I slipped it into my briefcase and stood up.

"Oh, you can stay awhile yet," he said, turning towards the clock on the mantelpiece, beneath which burned a coke fire. The face showed eleven-twenty. "I still have ten minutes before going down to lunch.

"I've been living for a year with my brother and my sister-in-law," he explained, "because their apartment is too big for them, and because this way each of my sisters has her own room on the second floor; but I usually don't have my meals here. You know, with us it's open house. Everyone gets along well and we're always visiting each other.

"My brother Jean is a Centrale* grad, an engineer at the Compagnie du Nord; he never comes to lunch until twelve-thirty. They've only been married two years. My sister Isabelle lives across the street. Those were her daughters, down there in the courtyard."

* *Grande école* training highly qualified engineers.

"It's pretty hard to keep things straight," I said, smiling, "when you come for the first time."

"No. It's very simple, really. On the first floor, there's my grandmother, my mother's mother, who lives, since she's become a widow, with Aunt Adèle, the white-haired lady you saw downstairs. She's not a real aunt, she's a first cousin of my grandmother, an old maid who's pretty much always lived with us and who raised Mama and all of us too, more or less, because my grandmother is blind and can't do much else but knit for the poor, from morning till night.

"On the second floor are my parents, with my three sisters. Paule, a terrific girl, whom you don't yet know, and who's going to get married this spring to an intern whose whole family lives in Bourges. He has all his meals with us, he's already part of the household, a marvelous fellow, a scientist. Then Laure, whom you met on the front steps, my 'real sister,' as I used to say when I was little, my twin . . . Finally, the youngest, Clairette, who was leaving with Laure, you know . . . Are you with me?"

"Yes, I'm starting to be . . . There are four of you, then. No, five, with your brother, who's the husband of the young woman with the baby . . ."

"No, seven. Because there's also Louis, the oldest, and Isabelle, the mother of my little nieces. Louis was the youngest lieutenant commander in the French navy; he's thirty and we never see him, particularly this year when he's going around the world, and he must be, at this moment, in Peking, on his way to Japan and Alaska—and he's the great man of the family, you know, an amazing fellow, unique . . . If you know any sailors, you only have to mention him, you'll see!

"As for Isabelle, the oldest girl in the family, who's eleven years older than I, she's almost a second mother . . . She's married to Captain Bousseron. I love him like an older brother—a really nice fellow, everyone agrees on that. He's at the École de Guerre. They've taken a furnished apartment across the way, at Number 7. They have three children who are always at our house, naturally, three girls and a fourth on the way, a boy this time, they claim . . . Isabelle is a terrific woman, same type as Mama, competent, resourceful, who runs her whole little tribe just like clockwork, without ever seeming to turn a hair, always cheerful and happy with everything, in short terrific . . . Why are you laughing?"

"Because all your brothers are marvelous and all your sisters are terrific . . ."

"But it's the truth. If you knew them . . ." He seemed quite taken aback by my comment. He thought for a moment, and went on:

"Really. It's not because it's my family, but I don't think there's another like it, that's turned out so well. My grandmother, you'll meet her, a poor infirm woman who bangs into doors, is always smiling, never a word of complaint, patient, sweet, a saint . . . My mother, you've seen her, you can't judge, but she's an admirable woman, indefatigable, who thinks of everything, who runs everything, who gets whatever she wants from us without ever losing her temper, simply because she understands everything and is always right. You can tell her anything, she always understands . . . And like Grandma, always in a good mood, always happy when you bring friends home to her . . . Because all our friends come as often as they like, there's always room for one more at the table . . . And then there's my father. He's something altogether different, he's the way navy men are, somewhat reserved, somewhat quiet, but so kind, so understanding—him too—that you can't not love him. He's always been adored everywhere, by his crews, by his shipmates . . . You only have to ask about him in naval circles, Admiral Saint-Gall, everyone's face lights up, he's never had an enemy. He's made his whole career like that, through work, through being conscientious in his job, never asking a favor, always off at sea. He's only been in Paris for six years now, since he agreed to be at the ministry. For us, when we were little, he was a kind of legend, a hero, we followed him in the atlases, we imagined him standing on the bridge, in the midst of storms. And then he would appear and the house would celebrate, and it would last three, four, six months at the most, and he'd go away again . . . But while he was here he knew how to make up for lost time, he looked after each of us, and for each he wasn't like other fathers—he was a great friend . . . You know, I have a kind of reverence for Papa . . . I don't think I could do anything he disapproved of, even if it were something I cared about very much. And my brothers are like me, I'm sure. And my sisters too . . . But it's almost half past, old pal, we have to go down. It's the only thing that Mama's ferocious about: being punctual at meals. And really, since there are so many of us, it pretty much has to be that way . . ."

As we arrived at the second-floor landing, we met the admiral and his daughter, who were coming up. Blaise introduced me.

Mme. Bousseron seemed to me, from the moment of that first contact, a bit more ordinary than the rest of the family, and this impression was confirmed later on. Yet she somewhat resembled her mother, who had nothing common about her, quite the contrary. She was a beautiful woman of thirty, blonde and plump, with pleasing but fleshy features, surprisingly nimble in spite of her weight, dressed without the slightest flair. Light-colored eyes, an engaging smile, visibly indifferent to whatever opinion one might have of her, a loud, curt, even slightly cutting tone of voice, that of someone who knows what she wants and does not waste time arguing or convincing. A matronly body, tired at thirty. Her pregnancy hardly showed, and only in her gait, not in her figure. She left us almost immediately to ring at her mother's, and disappeared into the apartment leaving the door ajar.

I don't know why—because of his rank, maybe, or rather because of the way in which Blaise spoke of his father—I was expecting a man older and with a more imposing appearance. He was in fact approaching sixty, but looked fifty. He was of average size, rather small and made to seem smaller still by his flat-topped officer's cap and the coat that came down to his knees. He must have attached little importance to honors, from the way he wore that old uniform, with its faded braid; under his arm he held a weathered briefcase with a metal clasp. But his physiognomy was of the utmost distinction. A clean-shaven face between two closely-cropped salt-and-pepper sideburns, the lips thin, the nose straight and with a slender bridge, the chin quite jutting and well-defined, the eyes very limpid, observant, and thoughtful. From the way he stopped, had my name repeated, held out his hand to me with a quick nod, bade me put my hat back on, and told me that he was happy to make my acquaintance, I sensed a great natural politeness, and a concern to be courteous which was fairly unusual in that house where everyone, until then, had seemed to me to behave with a simple and rather offhanded casualness.

I immediately took my leave.

"I hope to see you again, Monsieur de Maumort," he told me, shaking my hand. "Blaise's friends are always welcome here." I stammered vague thanks and slipped away, leaving Blaise to go with his father.

But I was not entirely done with the family Saint-Gall. As I was crossing the courtyard and starting under the archway, the door to the street opened, and I recognized the two girls I had passed on the front steps. The younger was carrying the famous basket of cyclamens, wrapped in a large sheet of white paper from which peeked the bows of a big knot of cerise satin.

I doffed my hat as I went by them, but they stopped unceremoniously, smiling.

"Look how beautiful it is," said the younger, pushing the paper back to let me admire the flowers.

The brisk air and the walk had heightened her coloring, whose freshness had a very special glow. She was still only a child in short skirts, with the face of an English baby, a clear and winning gaze—but with a charm that stirred me.

"Clairette!" the older said with a smile, "you're bothering the gentleman."

I naturally demurred, and admired the basket.

"We're going to hide it with the concierge until dinnertime," Clairette confided to me. "What a shame that Papa won't be here this evening! . . ."

"And you, Mademoiselle," I said to say something, "when is your birthday?"

"June fifth. It's very nice, isn't it, since at that time of year you've got all the flowers you want . . . And this year, there'll be fourteen pink candles on the cake . . . Laure isn't lucky, she was born on November second, the day when you go to the cemetery and everyone is sad. So she gets her birthday on All Saints' Day instead . . .* And Blaise too, of course . . ."

I looked up at Laure, who was smiling, and we exchanged an amused glance. I noticed that if, in her features, she resembled her twin brother, she differed from him completely in her expression. She did not have his open and joyful face. Her smile was fleeting, a bit sad, and her eyes were mirthless, as if turned within, reflective, indifferent to the outer world.

"Come on," she said to her sister. "We're going to be late." She nodded to me, somewhat formally, and started walking again towards the courtyard.

Clairette finished pinning the white paper around the basket. She called to me in a familiar tone, "Au revoir!" and caught up to her sister in three joyous leaps.

I RETURNED to the rue de Fleurus without being able to think about anything but that visit (and I was far from suspecting its consequences, the place that the Saint-Gall family would assume in my life).

I was spellbound. I had just discovered one of the sources of the charm that Blaise had exerted over me for some weeks: he belonged to a big family, where everything is done in common, easily, gaily, simply. That affable easy-goingness that I liked so much in him came in large part from his life in such a big family, where the daily ups and downs softened natures, where there was no spare time for withdrawing into oneself, for nursing one's selfishness, for becoming the center of the world. The center of the world was the family. The individual was only an insignificant rung, one element of a whole.

I discovered a kind of universe, previously unsuspected. I had not known that certain children, because they belong to a big family, bask, from their childhood on, in that collective, many-sided, happy life which simplifies relations, lends interest to every moment, turns away sadness, seriousness, boredom, loneliness.

I had no experience of this sort. Probably, at boarding school, I had had classmates from families like the Saint-Galls, but I had not known it, and had never become acquainted with such a family.

In passing through the portal at the rue Saint-Guillaume, I found myself in an entirely new atmosphere. I entered a closed world that had its rituals, its customs, an ambiance of its own; where everything was full of life, relaxed, friendly; where one felt bathed in, sustained by, everyone's affectionate good mood; where one left the weight of solitude outside; where one entered into a kind of brotherhood whose rules were simple and gladly

---

*All Saints' Day, on November first, was, for Catholics, an occasion of celebration; November second, *La Fête des Morts,* was dedicated to commemorating the departed.

accepted; where there was neither touchiness nor friction nor stifling secrets; where everyone lived out in the open, in camaraderie; where the feelings that add so much sweetness to life—friendship, affection, trust, respect, admiration, devotedness—bloomed in the fresh air, did not hide beneath veils of modesty, pride, or shyness, but were exposed in a natural way, and were expressed at every instant in acts of mutual aid, generosity; where everything helped you, compelled you, to be simple, obliging, and cheerful. I had entered an earthly paradise.

I was not in the least a rebel, and was deeply attached to my relatives. It had seemed to me until then that there was nothing to criticize in my family, that what they thought and did was what people were supposed to think and do. I adored my sister, loved and respected my father, and was very fond of my Aunt Chambost. It would never have occurred to me to bemoan my fate, and I congratulated myself, on the contrary, for having been born into what seemed a prizewinning family.

The discovery of the rue Saint-Guillaume did not in fact result in estranging me from my own relations or in diminishing the admiration I bore for my kin. But I could not help comparing my childhood, my life at le Saillant, the mood of my father's house, with what I had glimpsed of the Saint-Galls' existence. And all of a sudden I realized the austerity of my youth.

To belong, like Blaise, to a large family seemed to me an incomparable bliss, the greatest luck that one could have in being born, the true form of happiness, a matchless ideal of life. To have such a refuge, to come home to that animation, that laughter, so many sibling hearts with which to share one's joy in living, became a secret dream in me, half-conscious yet compelling, which had an unequaled power of bewitchment over the rest of my adolescence.

I became convinced that everything I judged bad or reprehensible in myself, all the faults I knew to be there, all the shameful tendencies of my constitution, would not have taken root or developed in the Saint-Gall environment. This was rather naïve. It was perhaps not completely erroneous. I imagined that the disorders of my life as a schoolboy, the obsessions that still possessed me, all those demons of lust that hounded me, had more hold on an only son, on the isolated child who is not surrounded by the protective influence of his clan. And this is possible, after all. The salubrious air that a child breathes in the bosom of a big family is less favorable to the fermentations of puberty than that isolation in which I lived; and if there are exceptions, if there are a number of depraved, withdrawn, complicated boys among the offspring of large families, one has to admit that in general the usual mark of those whose youth has been spent in a house full of brothers and sisters, where the communal life prevents concentration on

oneself, is a certain simplicity of the instincts, an absence of the psychological complexities and the repressions induced by solitude, a healthy and open
appearance, the look of a hardy plant, a certain banality as well, the banality
of a single mold. Families with only children seem to produce a greater number of atypical, original, and abnormal persons, because they are seedbeds of
individualism.

I was surely right, in any case, when I thought that my shyness would not
have arisen in the Saint-Gall milieu, and that my nature would have been
easier and more sociable.

FROM THAT MOMENT ON, I looked for every chance to get closer to the
rue Saint-Guillaume, and I was very soon a close friend of the family. It was
easy. "Open house," as they all said, not without a touch of pride. And this
was true. They all welcomed you with a delighted smile. You never seemed to
bother them, so simply and naturally did they go on about their life without
letting themselves be interrupted by your arrival, and so quickly did they
bring you into their ambit. I noticed this on my second visit, which took
place, as circumstances would have it, on the day after the first. Blaise had
gone with his father to the station and had not been able to come in time to
the Saturday class, where I was to give him back his paper. On Sunday morning, around ten-thirty, I went by the rue Saint-Guillaume. In the courtyard I
met Mme. Saint-Gall and her two daughters, who were going to Mass. "Go
on up, you know the way. You'll find Blaise in his room." He was indeed
there but was about to go get a haircut. "Impossible to reschedule," he said,
"I've got an appointment, but I'll be back in twenty-five minutes. Make
yourself comfortable and wait for me." I wanted to leave, but he became
cross. "We've got to talk about the paper, and you have no good reason for
leaving." I gave in, and picked up a book to pass the time while waiting. But
he had hardly gone out of his room when he came back. "Come let me introduce you to my brother Jean." He was perched on a ladder in the entrance
hall, in slippers, with an old jacket over his nightshirt. He was repairing the
doorbell. "Don't let him get away," Blaise told him, disappearing.

Jean was a handsome man of twenty-six, blond, crewcut, with his father's
light-colored eyes but with a gay and open face.

"You've come at the right moment. You're going to help me. This will
spare me having to come down off my ladder all the time. Please pass me the
roll of wire . . ." He went on working at the top of his ladder, chatting away,
while I unwound the electric wire which he fastened to the bottom of the
molding. He moved deftly, taking special little nails out of his mouth one by
one and sinking them into the wall with a neat tap of the hammer. I was
fairly clumsy at that sort of thing, and I complimented him on his skill. "I

love to tinker. All my Sunday mornings are spent this way. There's always something to do in these old dumps." In five minutes, the wire was in place.

"Come with me, if you don't mind. Now I've got to clean the batteries." In the kitchen, Jean's wife, in a pink flannel dressing gown, was warming a baby's bottle. "Don't make a mess everywhere," she said to us, laughing. "On Sunday morning, Jean always turns the apartment upside down . . ." We set up at the sink. It was not just a matter of rinsing out the battery jars, but also of scraping with a knife the cells that had been fouled by the chemical reaction. Lotte came back with the baby in her arms. "You're lucky that Anna's out running errands, she'd throw you out of her kitchen for sure . . ." She took the knife her husband had given me out of my hands. "Jean, the knife for peeling the vegetables—are you out of your mind! Anna's going to throw a fit." She rummaged in a drawer, and handed me an old nicked knife. "This one you have my permission to do anything you want with . . ."

A tall young woman, slender and blond, with a sweet and serious face, burst into the kitchen.

"You're just in time, Paule," Lotte told her. "Can you take care of the baby for ten minutes? Nanny's at Mass, Anna's gone out, Jean is fixing things, I just have time to get dressed if I want to catch eleven o'clock Mass . . . Don't you know my sister-in-law Paule?" she said to me, seeing that I greeted the new arrival a bit formally. She introduced me. "A friend of Blaise's." Jean asked: "What have you done with your fiancé this morning?"

"Pierre is busy at the hospital until noon at least, he's not even sure he can come for lunch . . ."

"My sister Paule is engaged to a medic," Jean explained to me. "Strange idea, isn't it? A chap who dedicates his life to butchering his fellow men." "A splendid fellow," said Lotte, smiling. "When you see him, you'll understand . . ." Paule smiled silently, and her eyes were full of tenderness. She took the baby from her sister-in-law's arms, sat down on a stool, and bounced the child on her knees. "She's in training," Jean told me. "But she's an intellectual, my sister, she still doesn't have much of a knack, you see." The baby had started wailing.

At that moment, Blaise reappeared, out of breath from having dashed up the stairs. He did not seem in the least surprised to find me in the kitchen scraping the metal rods. Without removing his hat or his overcoat, he snatched up the baby, raised him at arm's length, twirled him around, laughing, and brought him down in a sudden dive. The child immediately became quiet and smiled at his uncle. Blaise, delighted with the outcome, returned the baby to his sister.

"Now come to my room," he said to me.

"But we haven't finished," said Jean.

"Well, you'll finish by yourself," replied Blaise, dragging me off.

. . .

IT WAS on this same day that I had my first meal with the family.

We had conferred a good half hour about the paper when I looked at the time and wanted to leave.

"You're going to lunch with us," declared Blaise.

"Are you crazy?"

"Why not?"

"Come on, I'm expected at home."

"Well, that's very easy. Lunch won't be served here until twelve-thirty today, on account of Paule's fiancé who's held up at the hospital. We'll go along, chatting, to the rue de Fleurus, you'll let them know that you won't be having lunch, and we'll get back here on time. It's sunny and cold out, perfect weather for a brisk walk."

I made various objections, but he held firm. Running out of arguments, I gave in.

"You're so formal! Here, no one ever needs to be invited. Mama's always thrilled when we bring her our friends. Come on, now!"

On Sunday mornings, Mme. Saint-Gall always had two or three extra places laid, just in case. The dining room was spacious, the table large, and there were a lot of us. Mme. Saint-Gall and the three girls who lived on the second floor, Paule, Laure and Clairette. The Bousseron couple, Isabelle and the captain (in mufti), with their three little girls, two of whom I had seen skating in the courtyard and who had come over to offer their fresh cheeks, as if to an old acquaintance. Jean and his wife, who had lunch and dinner at his mother's every Sunday. Blaise and I. A young lady who was a friend of Clairette's, and whom Mme. Saint-Gall and her daughters had run into at Saint-Thomas-d'Aquin and brought home. Finally Pierre Dormoy, the young intern, whom we did not wait for to sit down at table, and who arrived after the potage (for it was one of the family traditions to start the noon meal with a vegetable soup).

This made an impressive and merry table of fifteen or so people.

Jean had taken the admiral's seat, opposite his mother, and it was he who, in front of the steaming tureen, mumbled a short grace; everyone listened to this standing, and made a quick, sketchy sign of the cross at the start and finish. Another family tradition.

I was almost at the foot of the oval table, between Blaise and Laure, and for a few minutes I had the sense that I had been quite tactless to accept that impromptu invitation and that they were deliberately making me feel it by paying no more attention to me than if I had been, at that moment, sitting between Aunt Ma and Uncle Éric at the rue de Fleurus. Blaise, turned away from me, was explaining something to the girls seated on his left, his sister

Clairette and her friend. The person on my right, Laure, had got involved in a noisy family conversation among Mme. Saint-Gall, the captain, Lotte and Jean. So I found myself completely left out. Across from me, on the other side of the table, Isabelle, who was on the right of her brother Jean, was very busy serving her two little girls, grouped around her, and spoonfeeding her youngest, who sat next to her and was only three. And, opposite me, Paule and her fiancé, leaning towards each other, were chatting by themselves. No one paid me any mind, and I looked like an intruder. I could not join in the general conversation, which was a genealogical discussion about the degrees of kinship that connected the admiral, who was absent, to cousin Loisel, the deceased of the day before, whom the Bousseron son-in-law and Lotte, the daughter-in-law, did not seem to have known well, and about whom Jean and his mother supplied more and more information as they alluded to a thousand facts and very hoary anecdotes from the vacation of 1871, during the Commune, a troubled time when the whole clan had found itself gathered—I don't know why—on a family property called la Drette, located I don't know where. One felt that these private details had a special meaning for them all, that these stories were probably being told for the hundredth time, and that everyone was as interested in them as if they were historical events touching the fate and future of France.

The final point was made by Mme. Saint-Gall. Sedately, without raising her voice, but with the authority that emanated from her entire person, addressing herself more particularly to the two "add-ons," her son-in-law Bousseron and her daughter-in-law Lotte, who was across from her on Jean's left, she declared:

"In the family, there are things that have always been disapproved of . . . His wife doubtless had great faults, but her husband ought not to have acted as he did . . . When one belongs to a family like ours, my dears, one has to accept certain sacrifices in preference to the slightest scandal . . ."

This little speech, delivered calmly, with an imposing simplicity of expression and tone, but with an inner conviction that gave it a good deal of force, ended in the most complete silence. Blaise had interrupted his conversation with Clairette and her friend, and Paule had left off her tête-à-tête with her neighbor. But in this silence I felt there was no constraint, nothing but a general approbation, deferential admittedly, but of a spontaneous and natural deference, and the last words had resonated in the way a classical symphony finishes with a perfect chord that leaves in its wake only peace and satisfaction. And this silence was not followed by any embarrassment. Isabelle began tending to her children again; Paule resumed her talking with her fiancé in a hushed voice; Clairette and her friend went back to chattering together; Jean spoke to his wife; Laure, the captain, and Mme. Saint-Gall exchanged their impressions of friends met in church; and Blaise conversed with me about our studies in common and our preference for this or that course.

I quickly realized that I had been foolishly mistaken in imagining I was being left out. On the contrary: I was being treated so little like an outsider, was being so naturally incorporated into this family gathering, that it did not occur to anyone to deal with me as a guest and to give me preferential treatment. That is how they were. They lived their clannish life, and the presence of a witness changed nothing in their habits. Everything that came from the outside was of little interest to them, and merged into the fringes of their family life. As in the life of a country, the presence of foreign elements that filter through borders—the settling of a few Swiss or a few Italians in the populations of Savoie or Provence—in no way alters the integrity of the nation, and such newcomers are quickly assimilated. It also stemmed from a total indifference to the opinions of others, the absence of any concern as to "what-people-will-say," which was the natural consequence of that invincible awareness they all had of making up an autonomous group, a legitimate force, a special universe, sufficient unto itself, having its traditions and its laws. A deep, unassailable, quietly conceited awareness, bolstered by that secret pride each of them felt at being a member of the Saint-Gall family.

The oddest part was that this pride seemed shared as a matter of course by the recently inducted members. In this respect I was able to observe, later on, that Captain Bousseron and even young Pierre Dormoy, though he had not yet received the final investiture, seemed to have completely renounced their own origins, to have lost whatever, in their personalities, came from their respective families. In marrying a member of the Saint-Gall family, it was, above all, it seemed, the Saint-Gall family they were marrying. They were no longer either Bousseron or Dormoy except in name: in reality, they had become Saint-Galls. I leave out Jean's wife, née Lotte Gérard, because she was something of an exception to the rule. All her affection for her husband's family notwithstanding, she was the only one among the "add-ons" who had retained, in spite of her efforts, an individuality alien to the family and who had not succeeded in casting off her origins in any fundamental way. Probably because she too had been born into a large family, molded from childhood on by her clan, and could not break away from her personal universe as easily as a Bousseron, an only son and already an orphan, or a Pierre Dormoy, whose family was vegetating far away in a little town in Britanny, where his father was a doctor and a widower.

It was at this lunch that, placed between Blaise and his twin sister, for the first time I felt an attraction for Laure. But that is for another chapter.

Blaise's mother, née Caroline Forestier, had so thoroughly adopted the family of her husband, the admiral, that she ran it, was its soul. The wife of the eldest son, having never known her mother-in-law, who had died in '48, which is to say five years before her marriage, she had been the first lady of the family. She had, from the time of her marriage, at barely nineteen, presided over the family table opposite her father-in-law the admiral, she had been fêted and pampered by her husband's three younger brothers, and she had, from the outset, taken her new role so seriously, had so well occupied the throne left vacant by the death of her mother-in-law, that she was considered by the entire family to be the female head of the tribe.

But she had not for that reason given up her own family, and along with her position as head of the Saint-Galls, she held concurrently that of eldest daughter of the Forestiers. Her mother's blindness furthered her acting as leader.

Gathered about her, trusting in her authority, the two families had, in short, become one by the time I met them.

The merger had been further facilitated by this: Caroline Saint-Gall and her tribe had overrun Justice Forestier's Paris home in the rue Saint-Guillaume. But, in the summer, the holidays were spent near Melun, on the Saint-Galls' estate, la Popelière, which had remained undivided among the four Saint-Gall sons, but which, in reality, Caroline Saint-Gall managed alone, sure of everyone's consent. And as Maurice's family spent the summer in Alsace, Mme. Saint-Gall's brothers, Edgard and Joseph Forestier, had got into the habit of coming with their wives, their children, and their servants for long visits at la Popelière, where they considered themselves more or less at home, being at their sister's. So much so that Justice Forestier's country house, which was at Fontainebleau on the edge of the forest, and which had become too small to accommodate Edgard's and Joseph's families, was, by common accord, sold after the war, when Justice Forestier died.

CHAPTER XVII

Doudou

AS OFTEN HAPPENS, it was a series of trivial little coincidences that were to give birth to an event that had a great impact on my life.

The date? The end of May or beginning of June, '89. Over the two days' holiday we had been given for Pentecost.

I had spent Easter vacation at le Saillant, and I had only caught a glimpse of my friend Vayron* at the train station, before going back to school. I had found him in a peculiar, agitated state, and he had spoken to me with a furtive enthusiasm about an English girl with whom he was visiting the museums and art shows. Then, a few weeks later, I received a long, confiding letter from him. A great love had sprung from this encounter. Phylée had come to Paris to paint. She belonged to a well-to-do English country family and lived in Montparnasse in a studio she occupied alone, fiercely cloistered with her work, engrossed by painting, with no teacher, no friends. Vayron naïvely believed he had found his soul mate in her, and fell madly in love with this "pure" artist. They had run off to Bruges together for Easter, and she had given herself to him, solemnly, in a little hotel room resounding with Flemish church bells and carillons.

When we met, his eyes were shining, his gestures feverish. He barely asked me about my work, my chances for passing the exam, which was only a few weeks way. He admitted to me, not without embarrassment, that he had to give up the plan of having lunch with me. But in compensation he offered me the opportunity to meet Phylée: he wanted me to go with him to her studio at the end of the morning, when she always took a break from her work. I understood that he had spoken to her about me with his customary exaggeration as a character exceptionally worth meeting, and that a refusal on my part would have hurt him deeply. Therefore, somewhat put off, I accepted. He awaited the time he had set for this visit. He continually consulted his watch. Nervous, distracted, he sidestepped all conversation despite himself, and I had to get used to the idea that this meeting with him, at any rate, would be a waste.

Phylée lived in the rue Campagne-Première, on the second floor of a queer ruined cottage at the rear of an empty lot, a former garden, now abandoned, where there were still traces of paths, remains of flower beds, and where she was raising a white goat that she milked herself and whose milk she drank with a sort of religious feeling. He explained to me that she ate only dairy products and fruit. Arriving at the foot of the cottage, he called out to her. A strange creature appeared on the rickety wooden balcony, whose worm-eaten balustrade no longer had its balusters. A tall girl, pale and blond, her hair parted down the middle and pulled back in two flat curves over her forehead; she wore a long black velvet dress and held an enormous palette in

---

*This character, mentioned fleetingly in Chapter XIV, is one of those that Martin du Gard was unable to develop for lack of time. He was to have been modeled in certain ways on Gustave Valmont, a close friend of the author's. In the present chapter, a first draft, he is referred to as "V[almont]," and then simply as "V." However, Martin de Gard, in his notes, makes clear that he ultimately intended to call the character "Gustave Vayron." For the sake of consistency, we have taken the liberty of using this name in the few places where he appears.

her hand. She stared at us for a long time without smiling and finally gave me a little nod, which probably meant that she was granting me permission to come up. We entered that weird lair through a dusty cubbyhole that must have been a woodshed, for only a narrow passage between cords of logs allowed access to a tiny wooden staircase in the semi-darkness. We came out onto the balcony, where she was waiting for us. Two large pink shirts were drying on a line. She put out her hand to me, looking into my eyes with her watery, colorless, permanently ecstatic gaze, and I wondered stupidly whether Vayron's girlfriend drank . . . Then she preceded us, through the French doors, into the studio. The first thing I caught sight of was the body of a young black woman, naked, fleeing behind a screen.

"Oh, *darling*,"* cried Phylée in a deep and lilting voice, "but why? These are friends . . . artists . . ."

Vayron went over to the easel, and I did likewise to keep my composure. The sight of that golden-brown rump had given me a violent jolt. I hid my embarrassment beneath a knowing air, examining with the utmost seriousness the canvas she had begun. Fortunately, there was only the slightest connection between the adorable figure I had glimpsed and Phylée's artwork.

The painting evoked a chaotic and blackish landscape under a sky of storm clouds. A long darkish body, neither man nor woman, was lying on its back on the ground, stiff and somewhat emaciated like a Christ in the tomb. The pudgy clouds formed a kind of gigantic hand above her, a shapeless, pallid, puffy hand, like a wash-glove filled with wind. What I still had in my eyes was altogether different: a young and chubby little body the wonderful shade of a light cigar, with silky shoulders, as if gilded, and the small of the back arched, full of enticing shadow . . . I yearningly ogled the green plush screen.

Phylée, like us, silently contemplated her canvas with its thick crusts of paint. This impassivity made it even more difficult to say anything. Vayron came to my rescue:

"It's a *Creation of the World*," he explained hesitantly, looking constantly at Phylée for fear of displeasing her by revealing her intentions. "God's hand, which hovers in the Ether and which brings forth the first human body from the formless clay . . . Humankind will be born from this creative gesture . . ."

I stammered a few words about the infinite, space . . . the grandeur of the symbol.

Phylée left me to flounder for a moment, without taking her eyes off her work. Then she smiled:

"I have no talent whatsoever," she declared. "But that isn't what matters. I have to work, to work, simply to learn."

*English in the original.

I did not know what to reply to these enigmatic words.

"Darling," she said to Vayron, "come and sit down."

She led us to a corner of the studio, where four padded black satin poufs surrounded a little bamboo table on which there was nothing. We planted ourselves uncomfortably on those backless seats. And conversation would probably have been difficult if the young model had not emerged at that moment from behind her screen, wearing a dress of iridescent gray faille with lappets, and a little black silk mantelet with white ruchings around the neck and wrists that brought out the brown skin. On her black and frizzy mop of hair was stuck a little black straw hat, also trimmed with white ruchings, and a white muslin scarf, loosely tied under the chin, framed her delicious native-child face.

"Zabette is a bird who has come from the islands," said Phylée. "Sit down, *darling,* you mustn't go before your mother comes."

Vayron asked what country she was from.

"From the country of the rue Mouffetard," she said, bursting gaily into laughter, "where I was born seventeen years ago!"

She needed no coaxing to furnish other details. She had never left Paris. Her mother had been born in Martinique: having come to France in 1867, at twenty-two, she was a bookkeeper at a wholesaler's in the area of les Halles. Just then, "Zabette!" was heard from the garden. The girl leapt lightly onto the rickety balcony and motioned someone to come up.

"S'kiouse," said Phylée.

Chattering was heard on the staircase.

Two Martiniquaises made their entrance in rustling dresses. One, getting on in years and already going gray, was the mother of Zabette. The other, still young and quite pretty, was her aunt Célie. The mother could have been forty-two. The aunt, between twenty-five and thirty. They were coming to pick up the child but seemed in no hurry to depart. "Has she been a good girl?" said the mother. "I don't know how she can stay still to pose, she's so restless at home . . ."

Zabette did not like office work. She could have taken the Post Office exam like her aunt, who was employed at the central bureau of the Postes et Télégraphes. But it was not to her liking. She wanted to be a dancer. She studied music, gymnastics, dance. Her mother allowed her to pose, but very rarely, and never with gentleman painters.

I devoured her with my eyes, shamelessly. I had never met such a desirable creature. A dancer . . . I was no longer surprised by her grace, her litheness. Through the silky lappets of her dress, I still saw the brief appearance of her arched back, her fleshy rump in motion, her sinewy thighs.

All three of them had admirable eyes, of an extraordinary softness, filled with a dark glow.

But I could look only at Zabette. I caught the aunt's gaze resting on me. A gaze that smiled, that seemed to say: "You want the girl, I can understand."

The mother had a much darker complexion than the daughter. But the aunt had that same shade of a light cigar, that same smooth glossy skin, and that inborn grace in all her movements.

They suddenly decided to leave, after Zabette had promised to come back the following Sunday. And the studio, which had resounded with that noise of island birds, suddenly lapsed back into silence.

Vayron wanted to do me the honors of the house. He was eager for me to admire his girlfriend's works. But Phylée's indifferent silence, which I assumed was due to my presence, scarcely encouraged me to prolong my visit. Besides, I wished to be alone. The vision of Zabette's body had stirred me deeply, and I was obsessed by it.

I departed, disappointed by Vayron, annoyed by Phylée, and without anyone's much insisting that I stay.

I OPEN a parenthesis. I will probably never again have a chance to speak of this Phylée. And she was, in spite of all, a poor, curious character who deserves a few lines.

(I have never known how to spell her name. Phonetically, my friend Vayron pronounced "Phylée" in an enamored voice which seemed to stretch out the final vowel on a dying *e*.)

Vayron obviously found her beautiful, and one might, at a pinch, consider her so. She was mainly singular. A long face, regular and oval, crowned with a narrow, vertical forehead made narrower by the two flat *bandeaux;* her smooth and glossy hair was plastered on the ovoid skull; it was gathered at the nape in a sort of queue plaited like the tail of an omnibus horse. Commonplace eyebrows above colorless but rather luminous eyes; a little nose, unequivocally turned-up, which seemed to pull the upper lip slightly towards itself, to the point of forever revealing the long white ivories of her front teeth. This pug nose would have lent something mischievous to any other face. But Englishwomen can have a rather aristocratic way of carrying their nose in the air: Phylée's brought to mind that of the then Prince of Wales, the future Edward VII, and all the noses of the royal family.

She dressed in the "aesthetic" manner, with a childlike zeal. I never saw her except in long black velvet dresses cinched at the waist by a cord with golden tassels. The wide, drooping sleeves were like those worn by the lady of the manor in a fairy tale. She lacked only a lily in her hand. She was fond of barbaric jewelry: I remember certain earrings with crystal pendants that seemed stolen from a chandelier, large broaches, belt buckles made of silver plates encrusted with cloudy emeralds or sickly turquoises.

In spite of the nose, her expression was not without nobility. Her features had an extraordinary impassivity. She gorged on books about Hindu philosophy and in all circumstances affected a fatalistic calm that rounded off her character rather well.

She was the daughter of a rich London merchant, a remarried widower, who left her free and sent her checks. Keen on art, she had settled in Paris to work on her *painting.** She had no gift, no budding talent, and knew it perfectly well. But she believed in metempsychosis: she was certain that her soul would one day be reborn to inhabit the personality of a great artist. And sustained by this fixed idea of rebirth, she worked ten hours a day, without teachers, with the perseverance of a drudge, persuaded that all this effort would be rewarded, would serve the painter of genius in whom she was finally to be reincarnated after a certain number of necessary transformations. No setback could discourage her or dent her faith. All the pains she took had one precise goal: to reduce the number of transformations, to shorten the steps that would lead her to perfection.

I was furious at seeing Vayron so delude himself about this creature, in whom I really saw no merit. The most complimentary thing you could say about her was that she was kind, in the sense of "couldn't hurt a fly." I found her incurably stupid. If I appreciated anything about her, it was that she wore her stupidity rather modestly, and humbly concealed it beneath a muteness which Vayron found cryptic but which was simply dictated by a dearth of ideas.

I took a rather perverse pleasure in flushing her out of her silence. She spoke French with difficulty, with an accent that exaggerated the absurdity of her words. I sometimes tried to push her to the limit with merciless logical objections. But I only succeeded in making her return to her silence, with the self-satisfied smile of a person who *knows,* whom rational discussion cannot reach, who *alone* possesses the truth. And sometimes she even apologized for having let herself go and talked a bit: "*S'kiousez moi,* I lost my *self-control*† a little just now . . ." And her calm, mulish, satisfied face was that of a lunatic in an asylum.

I LEARNED through Vayron of a rather touching episode in her life. She had been engaged in England to a theology student, and was to marry him as soon as he became a minister. But a few months before the marriage she believed she saw that her fiancé loved another young lady and was only honoring his commitment out of duty. She came up with the following line

*English in the original.
†English in the original.

of reasoning, simplistic but worthy of a great tragic heroine: "If I truly love him, I have to wish for his happiness. Therefore I must step aside." And it was then that she had come to Paris. This had happened eight years before. "The most amazing thing," Vayron told me, "is that the minister never understood her bowing out; he's still unmarried, still in love with her, and has never given up hope of winning her back. But she assumes he's sacrificing himself on account of his former promise, and she's demanded that her father not even give him her address. He doesn't know what's become of her."

"BUT WHAT GOD do you believe in, then?" she asked me one day.

I got out of this with an evasive reply.

"So you don't believe in reincarnation?"

"No," I said finally.

She looked at me strangely for quite a while. Then she had a sort of explosion, in which certainty was mixed with a kind of joy: "Well," she cried, "you're sure going to get *oune siourprise!*"

Then she refused to go on with the conversation.

Her art was cheaply symbolic and absurd, like her. The painting she wanted to do was born obscurely in her brain, and she brought it into being as she had conceived it, without taking the slightest account of the models she had hired to pose so she could execute it. When I had examined some of her works, I understood better why, that morning when I met her, the delicious physique of Zabette's before her eyes had inspired nothing more in her than that large black and wasted body with which she dreamed of symbolizing the creation of humanity: a lump of clay assuming human form.

TODAY IT SEEMS odd to me that I did not understand, when I ran into Zabette's aunt several moments later on the corner of the Boulevard Montparnasse, that she had been waiting there for me. Seeing her gave rise to only one feeling in me: the hope of being able to meet Zabette again. That is how naïve I was; above all, that is how impatient I was to get back to that little brown body the sight of which had sunk a hook deep into my flesh. I wonder if I had ever been bitten by a desire so intense, so particular.

"Hey, there," she said, surprised. "I thought you were having lunch with Mademoiselle Phylée."

"No."

Possessed by my idée fixe, I added almost instantly:

"I'm having lunch by myself. And you? Aren't you having lunch with your sister and your niece?"

I realized right away that this was practically inviting her to have lunch with me, and I was terribly embarrassed at the idea of being seen in a restaurant tête-à-tête with this pretty mulatto. But thrilled by this unhoped-for encounter, which would put me back on Zabette's trail, I was afraid to see this last chance to meet her again (and who knew what else?) slip away from me . . .

"Oh," she said, "we live in the same house, but each of us has our own little place. On Sunday, I don't feel like cooking. You know what I do? I go get pastries, lots of pastries, and that's what I eat. Don't you like sweet things? Me, I can't never get enough pastries . . ."

I let her talk, not sure what I was going to do. Invite her out? She was quite attractive, quite conspicuous, and her exoticism would not go unnoticed anywhere. But she did not look at all like a tart. There was even something composed, serious, and decent in her manners which reassured me. I was about to risk an invitation when she made the first move:

"If you liked pastries, I would invite you to come have a snack with me."

I immediately saw a chance to worm my way into the house, into Zabette's family. I had fully intended to go spend the afternoon in Neuilly with my aunt, for whom this was the first Sunday of the summer at-homes, but I had the time, and nothing mattered more than getting close to Zabette.

Three-quarters of an hour later, loaded down with a selection of pastries, we arrived in the colorful hurly-burly of the rue Mouffetard, whose pavement, congested with stalls and little carts, was as animated as a fair. We were now chatting away like old friends. I found her very likable. She was open and gay, free, affectionate, familiar in a nice way, without any embarrassing coquettishness. She amused herself with her own inexhaustible chatter, laughing at everything like a child.

"There's our house," she said, showing me, at the top of the rue Mouffetard, an old seventeenth-century brick-and-stone residence with big windows, whose broad portal was wide open.

I scarcely suspected, crossing that threshold for the first time, that I would return there so often afterwards, and that it would be the scene of so many memories. Not long ago, around 1920, a big new pile replaced the ramshackle old building, and on my last visits to Paris I stopped making the occasional long detour to pass beneath the windows where I had known such sweet moments. But until the house was demolished I never spent a week in Paris without finding some excuse to make a pilgrimage to it.

It must once have been an opulent *hôtel* of the Ancien Régime. The ironwork of the windows was beautiful, and the great stone staircase, spacious and well lit, with its wrought-iron banister, would still have had a grand air about it if the surface of the walls had not been so smudged with the grime of generations; if the different landings, more or less stripped of their tiles, had not always been littered with straw, papers, peelings; and especially if it had not been, from top to bottom, a sort of communal annex to all the apartments of the house, a place where laundry was hung out to dry, where swarms of children were sent to play, where the women held court, called each other from one floor to another, laughed, jabbered, sometimes quarreled, and, in the summer, came to sew or peel vegetables in the coolness of the draft.

The house had been colonized by Martinique and Guadeloupe. I believe that not one of the many residents lacked some connection with "the islands," and the majority were colored. They hardly spoke anything but Creole patois. They lived on top of one another day and night. There was a constant coming and going to ask for services—to exchange utensils, to share supplies, to offer one another chocolate, barley sugar, pastilles, caramels— with endless palaver, the twittering of an exotic aviary, bursts of laughter, sometimes tears and sobs, all the excessive and childish expressions of joy and suffering; and from top to bottom the great resounding shack echoed with people warmly calling out to one another: *"Bonjou, ché? Comment va, ché? Comment ou allez, là-dedans? Toute douce, ché . . . Et où?" "Hélas, m'z'amis, voyez ce macaque!"* And the most unexpected names: Nounoune, Edoualize, Coroliane, Néphélie. I remember one old man, the color of ebony, who was named Hilarion and whose frizzy hair was almost white, and another, Tertullien, who had an eye covered with an opaque film. But the men were scarce. It was a hive of women and children, a matriarchy where married couples were not plentiful, where adult males came only to visit. The few men who lived there were generally old grandfathers whose daughters put them up, pampered them, and handled them roughly, sent them on errands, had them grind the coffee and wipe the children.

Aunt Célie lived alone at the very top of that strange phalanstery, in two large, bright rooms which continued into an attic; theoretically, she slept in one and cooked in the other, but there was a rocking chair and a sewing basket near the little stove, and the table in the bedroom was always cluttered with dishes when it was not the nightstand, since she often brought in her meal on a large wooden platter, which she called the *"tray,"** and ate leaning on one elbow, stretched out on the bed. Without the slightest embarrassment she ushered me into this incredible disorder, which seemed to me more magical than sordid, for everything was meticulously clean, and the sun was flooding in through the big open windows.

She sat me down in the bedroom on the sofa done in old golden satin with black tassels, which faced the fireplace, sat down herself on the rosewood bed, which was made and was covered with a sky-blue damask quilt, and, as naturally as could be, removed her bronze-colored kid ankle boots

*English in the original.

and her white stockings, for she always went about her household chores in bare feet. She cleared a table, which she pulled over to the sofa, laid a clean cloth on it, brought china plates with a flower pattern, goblets, a bottle of rum, set out the pastries that she had selected and I had paid for on a wicker tray, and began to prepare that Martiniquais "petit punch" to which I would take such a liking: half a glass of white rum, a piece of ice and a twist of lemon.

I thought about Zabette, listened to the noises of the house, desperately wished she would suddenly walk into her aunt's. And then? I did not know, had no precise plan, did not even suppose I could ever have her, but I remained stuck in my fixed idea, the little brown body, so lithe, Zabette, Zabette . . . And I did not even look at the beautiful woman sitting next to me; at least I did not look at her with the eyes of a man, I did not see her, lovely and desirable, and available, maybe. It did not even occur to me that this encounter, this impromptu snack, were quite unusual, quite encouraging. The look we had exchanged at Phylée's, when I had felt myself found out, made me believe in a sort of tacit collusion on the aunt's part, a possible obligingness which endeared her to me and led me to place something of a mad hope in that complicity. I was not completely wrong, since it was she who first mentioned Zabette, while I was still racking my brain for some subterfuge to bring the conversation around to the girl.

Célie's chatter, as she devoured the pastries, savoring them slowly, told me many things about her family. It was a respectable family from Fort-de-France, where her father, M. Cyprien, ran a store. What kind? She couldn't say. There, trade wasn't specialized. You were a *"ma'chand."* You sold everything, poorly: a little stationery, a little hardware, a little linen, seeds, fishing nets, even spectacles and small pieces of jewelry. Azaline, her older sister, had been the first to come to France, brought by the assistant manager of a rum distillery, who shortly left her, with Zabette, who had just been born. Abandoned, but with a job in a firm at les Halles where she was now a bookkeeper and where for eighteen years she had courageously earned her living. It was she who had drawn Célie, her younger sister, to Paris, in spite of their father's wishes, and had sent her money for the trip. Célie had landed alone in France at sixteen, twelve years ago. An excellent student at the school run by nuns in Fort-de-France, armed with a *certificat d'études,* having a taste for schoolwork, she had lived several years at her sister's, prepared for the post office exam, and got a job. She gradually rose in rank and at this point held a good position in the central office of Postes et Télégraphes. She had moved out of her sister's place a long time before. As soon as she could, she rented this little apartment on the top floor of the house. Azaline and Zabette had occupied various apartments in the building one after another, and they now lived in one of the best, on the second floor.

I had thus passed by their door without suspecting it, and I was very sorry I hadn't known.

I awkwardly questioned Célie about her niece, about Zabette's vocation as a dancer. She looked at me with an odd smile; then she got up and came back with a big garnet-colored leather album with an elaborate clasp, to show me the family photos. I first had to endure Mother Cyprien, a fat mulatto woman in Martiniquais garb, and Father Cyprien in white canvas frock coat, a true Negro, black, thick-lipped, frizzy-haired, whose belly was adorned with an imposing gold chain with charms on it. She turned the pages with emotion, flooded with memories.

"There she is," I said suddenly, spotting the photo of Zabette, at thirteen or fourteen, dressed for her first Communion, her little brown face surrounded by stiff white muslin.

"Who? Zabette? No, that's me, *ché.*"

I looked at her, disappointed. It was true that Zabette resembled her closely, and I had not noticed it before.

"Here's Zabette," she said, showing me a blackish baby, half naked, in the arms of Azaline. "And here she is again in school. And here she is when she made her first Communion. And here she is at her teacher's . . ."

The photo, which must have been recent, showed her in an exercise outfit, neck and arms bare, in bloomers, her long ballet student's legs sheathed in tights, dancing en pointe along a barre.

I stayed silent.

Sweetly, she put her hand on mine.

"You find her pretty, *ché?*"

I raised my eyes. She smiled mischievously and considered me with a kind of tender affection. She lowered her voice and asked me, in my ear:

"I did see that you found her pretty . . . You'd like . . . to be friends with her? No?"

I did not need to answer, my face must have been eloquent enough.

"But her mama always keep an eye on her, *ché* . . . She's already quite a flirt, the little devil . . . This winter, there was trouble, she had one boyfriend, and then another, and then another . . . Her mama found out . . . Woo, what a row! . . . Still, at sixteen, it's natural. But my sister want her to work, and if a little accident happen to her, you know, that would be it for the dancing and everything . . . An *'iche du bon Dieu'** can happen just like that, you know, *ché!*"

She gave me to understand that she was not as vigilant as Zabette's mama concerning the girl's conduct, and that she would be willing to facilitate matters and shut her eyes. But would Zabette agree? I thanked her fervently.

---

*A "little angel" in patois.

She offered to go and see if Zabette was in, and, on some pretext, bring her to me. I was left alone for a moment, with the canaries and the old cat. I was deeply agitated at the idea of seeing Zabette again in such favorable conditions. Célie's intervention opened possibilities to me for which I would not have dared hope. How would I have achieved my ends alone?

But bad luck had it that Zabette had gone out right after lunch with a neighbor family who had daughters her age. An outing to the Bois de Boulogne, on the island in the lake, a picnic on the grass, and Azaline didn't know when her daughter would be back.

I had the strength to somewhat conceal my disappointment.

"Come back tonight, after dinner," Célie told me. "She'll be back, I'll have seen her, and maybe . . ."

I left, affecting calm, but I was done in. It was too late to get to Neuilly; and it would have been awkward for me, since I had the next day off, to return to Paris that same night. Besides, I was in a feverish state that required solitude, and I had no wish to attend that day's gathering. I had to go to the post office at the Bourse to send a *pneumatique* to Aunt Ma. I used my work as an excuse: I was staying in Paris to prepare for certain parts of my exam with a classmate, and I wasn't sure I would be able to come the next day. I told her I would sleep at the rue de Fleurus. But in my mind, it was quite another night I was imagining . . . A first night of love!

This is just what befell me. But in a very different way than I could have foreseen.

I wandered all that Sunday through springtime Paris, from café to café, from one park bench to another, trying in vain to put my attention on the textbook I had in my pocket, and on some course notes. An interminable and anxious day.

At eight-forty-five, I was in the rue Mouffetard. I had impatiently waited for dusk to be more certain of climbing the stairs without being seen. The whole building rustled like an island full of birds. I met few tenants on the staircase, which was dark, but from each apartment, whose doors were open and lights lit, there rose laughter, cries, calls, sounds of cooking and of dishes, the sizzle of frying, the whole happy hubbub of Sunday dinners.

Célie opened the door to me. There were no lights on, and I was positive that this dimness was intentional and that Zabette was there.

I was wrong. Crestfallen, Célie greeted me with sighs and exclamations of *"hélas, m'zamis!"* as if a catastrophe had taken place. The family of neighbors had not come home, Azaline thought they had taken enough provisions to have dinner in the Bois and would not be back until late. At any rate, the thing had fallen through. Célie had no way of seeing Zabette alone tonight and testing the ground. There was nothing to hope for today.

I had lived the entire afternoon in such expectation, such reckless certainty, such nervous tension, I was arriving there so sure of finally having the adventure I had been seeking for years, that I was unable to brave it out. I could not respond at all. I took a few steps, like a man knocked senseless, and collapsed on the sofa, sobbing like a child. You can be almost twenty, even much older, and suddenly realize that you're still a very little boy . . .

Célie rushed over in distress: "Poor baby! . . . Poor baby! . . ."

She sat down next to me, slantwise, on the edge of the sofa, and not knowing how to console me, touched my arm, my hands, my knees. I felt as much at ease with her as if we had always known each other. That in her which was so affectionate, so maternal, made me forget the woman. I had placed my trust in her, I was counting on her to get to Zabette, I felt no shyness about letting her see my tears and know the extent of my disappointment.

And I found it altogether natural that she put her arm around my shoulder and softly pressed me to her, to comfort me. I even found this was the only thing that eased my sorrow, my vexation. I would not have had the courage to remain alone.

"Poor baby!" she repeated. "How sad he is, poor man! . . . How he love her already, his Zabette . . ."

She had moved closer, softly drawn my head to her in a very motherly, very sweet, very spontaneous gesture, and, letting myself go, I rested my temple on her bosom. She kept it there with a hand that stroked my hair, and her other hand was on my knee.

We stayed like that for a while without moving. She was not wearing her afternoon dress anymore, but a housecoat, full and loose-fitting, a light dressing gown of flowery percale, and against my cheek, through the material, I felt the soft warmth of her flesh. I was a little embarrassed when I noticed this and the shock of my first pique began to fade. All this was quite sweet, though, and there was so much simplicity, friendliness, in her attitude.

I did not move. But already I had ceased to think much about Zabette. I was thinking about the strange situation that I found myself in, cuddled by this woman whom I had only known for a few hours.

She was silent now. Night was falling fast, and you could barely see the objects in the room. I had the feeling that some change was taking place in her, in me. Our breathing became shorter, somewhat heavy.

Then she leaned down, brought her mouth close to my ear and whispered, very low: "You know, you wanted so much make love tonight, poor baby . . . *I* wouldn't mind with you . . ."

I was an idiot not to have thought of it. It was obvious that things had to end up this way. But it hadn't occurred to me for a single moment. At least, if the idea had crossed my mind, it had only done so a few minutes before.

But these words were enough to throw a spark and instantly electrify me. I completely forgot the unattainable Zabette in the face of this possibility I had suddenly glimpsed. I cannot say that I desired Célie. I desired love, initiation. And I felt so safe with her that I had no shyness, no apprehension of appearing awkward or inexperienced.

I did not answer, but let myself go heavier against her, and leaned my head more on her bosom. I felt her putting her hand there, undoing her dress. And my cheek felt her bare breast.

I said nothing. I had closed my eyes to keep my composure. I just let things take their course, like a simpleton, and I do not think she minded this artlessness, but even found it charming. It allowed her to treat me like a child, and given her motherly nature, this was what would have attracted her most.

Everything happened wordlessly. From time to time, breathing heavily, she murmured: *"Ché'i . . . Ché'i . . ."*

Night had come. She had not drawn the curtains. The darkness would have been complete if the glow from the street or the light of the nocturnal sky had not dimly lit the open window. Did she desire me? Probably. But she mainly wanted to make up for my earlier disappointment, and her primitive candor, her maternal instincts, had imagined only this "natural" way.

Had she, from the start, sensed my lack of experience? Or rather did she attribute my willing passivity to the fact that it was not for her that I was here? She must have noticed quickly enough that I was not at all used to lovemaking. For my desire had become obvious, and yet I made not the slightest move to participate. Her mouth, from the beginning, had sought mine, and at first I had shyly avoided her insistent kissing. But she had overcome this resistance, had taken hold of my mouth, and I gave myself up with the utmost passion to her deep kiss. Imperceptibly she had slipped out of her housecoat, like a butterfly from its chrysalis, and it was a half-naked woman who held me in her arms. She was probably surprised that I did not help her more. She took my hand and pressed it against her bare flank. She made all these moves with an incomparable softness, tact, naturalness, absence of obscenity. Touching that warm body, over which I now ran my feverish and hesitant hand, brought me so much sensual gratification that suddenly, gasping, I arched back in her arms.

She realized at once that I had let our pleasure get away. She would have been within her rights to hold this against me, to be miffed. She seemed on the contrary to sacrifice her pleasure without a second thought, and to become more tender as if wanting to spare me the shame of my clumsiness. A shame I did not even feel . . .

We remained silent for quite a while, sitting on the sofa, intertwined and motionless. It was I who gradually shook off the sweet torpor into which I had sunk. I propped myself up halfway, turned towards her, and sought out her mouth. As if she had only been waiting for this reawakening of my senses, she got up decisively: "Come over on the bed."

She was standing in front of me. She let her slip drop, and in the half-light I made out her naked figure. I stood up to grasp her and hold her tight. She stepped aside, and wanted to unbutton my vest. I too was eager to be naked, to press my body to hers. I quickly stripped, while, leaning towards me, she felt and caressed my shoulders and my chest as my last clothes fell away. Then she pulled me toward the bed, and threw herself on it first. I can still see that beautiful dark body spread out on the white sheets, as an offering. This time, I hurled myself at her, impetuously; and slowly, for a long time, intoxicated with virile strength, overcome with gratitude, I took her. I quite well recall the thrilled surprise I felt at causing that admirable instrument of pleasure to vibrate under me for the first time. Although one may know everything about love in theory, how, without having experienced it, can one form an idea of what that burning penetration is, and that unknown sensation of two people becoming a single merged being, and that echo of the other's pleasure in oneself, and the acceleration of those coupled movements, and that paired, headlong, dizzying race, down to the moment of the plunge, together, into the abyss?

Such was my discovery of physical love, at the age of nineteen.

I had long awaited that initiation. But I can say that I quickly made up for lost time. And that very night, I might add.

For I spent the night at the rue Mouffetard—or, more precisely, in Doudou's* bed, in her arms—and nearly all the next day, which was a holiday for her as well. It was my first night with a woman. We slept little, talked a lot, and partook copiously of pleasure. She seemed delighted to be my first experience, lent herself obligingly to my most indiscreet investigations, and even amused herself by anticipating the many facets of my curiosity. I thought no more about Zabette. By the hour I became more attached to Doudou. She had an admirable body, buxom and young, elastic and warm, a blithe body, a marvelous instrument of sensuality. But what charmed me even more, I think, was her sweetness, so difficult to describe yet so distinctive, that tender simplicity, that instinctive, delicate kindness, which made our relations so easy. She had a certain childish naïveté, and was so natural about everything that one would not have dreamt of mistrusting her, and could not have any more ulterior motives concerning her than she had herself.

"I'm almost nine years older than you," she told me with a melancholy sigh, "you'll leave me soon to run after Zabette . . ."

---

*Célie's nickname. Doudou is a common term of endearment for a woman in the Antilles— "darling."

I protested, sincerely. At that moment, I had ceased to lust after Zabette. The joy with which Doudou had filled me probably had something to do with it. But mainly, when I thought about Zabette, what came to mind was her mocking, coquettish youthfulness, and all my virgin's timidity returned. I compared her to Doudou, whose love was so comfortable, from whom I needed to fear neither rejection nor irony; to Doudou, whom I had neither had to court nor to conquer, who was not doing me a favor in offering herself up to me, and who so generously dispensed pleasure. In Zabette, as in every other woman, I suspected an adversary whom I would have to vanquish, subdue, entice . . . I was weary of this fencing match in advance. It would be paying too dear for the charming graces of that little body I had glimpsed.

In Doudou, I sensed, above all, a friend. I could abandon myself to the enthusiasm she inspired in me without remaining on the defensive. I was grateful to her for being so understanding, so accommodating, so selfless, even when it came to lovemaking. Of course, she was after her own satisfaction, and with the keen ardor of a not easily sated adult. But she had already, during that night, given me proof of her ability to yield precedence in order to gratify me; of the greater happiness she took in giving than in receiving; of the knowing, expert compliance that she lavished on me with such delicacy (I could almost say modesty), with an animal enjoyment that was sterling, without a vulgar word or gesture, because everything in her was healthy and fine.

We spent that Monday behind closed doors and windows, living off the provisions and a few leftovers that Doudou still had in her larder. When we were not interlaced as lovers, we chatted as friends. Several times, there was a knock at the door to the landing.

"Don't open it," I told her.

"And if it's Zabette? . . ."

"Even if it's Zabette!"

I left her, at nightfall. I was fulfilled, a little sad, not in the least tired of her, thinking only of seeing her again on my next day off, the first Sunday of the following month. I had spent twenty-four hours at her place. I had arrived a virgin and was departing as experienced, I thought, as if I'd had several affairs. And there was actually something true in that conviction. A profound transformation had, during those few hours, taken place in me. My sexual life had assumed a new direction. The reality of natural, physical love abruptly pushed into the past of my childhood the murky fictions in which I had wallowed, for lack of anything better, during the last four or five years. I had crossed a watershed. The nightmarish climate in which, up until then, my sensual activity had taken place, suddenly vanished. The female body, about which I had fantasized in a morbid way, was revealed to me in its most secret intimacy. I instantly recovered a sort of manly health. I will not deny that I persisted for some time yet in my solitary habits; but more and more infrequently, with diminishing satisfaction, and as a last resort, a distraction, the inadequacy of which quickly made me lose interest. I would have been cured of it at once, I think, if I could have lived with Doudou, and had her regularly within desire's reach.

Thanks to Doudou, I was not forced, at the outset, to separate lovemaking and affection, which always has fairly serious consequences. Thanks to Doudou, I knew deep, prolonged, intense kissing before intercourse, and I yearned for her mouth before her sex. This apparently insignificant detail left such a permanent mark on me that I have very rarely, in the course of my life and when the occasion arose, been willing to make love without kissing. This sometimes did happen to me. But each time that a vague disgust in the presence of a prostitute kept me from seeking her lips and I had to content myself with "dry" lovemaking, I felt a great dissatisfaction and regretted being driven by my lust.

However, it is only fair to add that those who do not "separate" the two things—those for whom physical attraction and the act of love are not possible without feeling, those for whom sex necessarily involves the heart and the mind, the entire self conquered and enthralled—are perhaps even more to be pitied. All such people I have known have been wretched, victims of romantic passions that hellishly complicated their lives and that often wrecked their careers, ruined their happiness, and caused everyone who loved them to suffer.

I very soon "loved" Doudou.

I do not want to embellish the memory of that first liaison. For me it was obviously not the first great love, that groundswell that surges up, irresistible, at the dawn of certain male lives, and which forever transforms them, gives them their flavor, their coloring, explains all that follows. No. But it was still love, and it was still my first love. It was not a romantic feeling that propelled me into her arms. As we have seen. But this feeling followed so closely upon desire that I can almost say that the two things coincided, and that, as I parted from her the morning after, I was leaving a woman with whom I was in love.

Doudou's love placed sweetness at the threshold of my existence as a man. Who knows? If I have remained, up to these last years, a man happy with his lot, happy to be alive, trusting in his fate, I may partly owe this to Doudou. Or, to frame this supposition in a less positive way, I will say that if I had, for my first sensual and romantic attachment, met a femme fatale, if I had needed to struggle against a wild, exclusive passion founded on jealousy, lies, torment, such a beginning would probably have left me bitter, haunted, hostile, diminished, disenchanted, and I might have spent my life cursing love and falling prey to it.

This affair lasted about two years. Two of the happiest years of my life.

From the start, contrary to what one might think—to what I thought myself, for I kept saying to myself, as I went back, that Pentecost Monday: "I have a mistress, my exam is done for"—I rarely worked so much or so well as during those two months which followed our meeting. Never did I apply myself to work more lightheartedly, or with all my faculties in better balance. The thought of Doudou obsessed me, and I impatiently awaited each opportunity to see her again. But this constant thought had no connection with the obsessions that had consumed my youth for five years. It was light and wholesome. I had chaste and refreshing nights. I was overjoyed, confident in myself and in my success to come.

And indeed, I passed the exam for Saint-Cyr with a very good grade.*

This introduction to love influenced me in a thousand ways. Among which I note right away the taste I developed for women of color: a taste which was not confined to only one, which I was lucky enough to be able to satisfy often during my life in the colonies, but which had got into me and which I still feel in myself.

Exoticism entered my life with the rue Mouffetard. During my Saint-Cyr years, I went there every week, and felt practically at home. Everyone knew about my affair with Doudou, accepted it, acknowledged it. I was "Mlle. Célie's Saint-Cyrian." I was soon acquainted with everybody there, since people lived at such close quarters that it was impossible to visit often without in some way becoming part of the house.

I have never been to the Antilles. But it is a little as if I had. I think that trip would hold few surprises for me, so much did I hear about the country, its inhabitants, the customs and beliefs there. I especially doubt that contact with the Martiniquais of Martinique would teach me much about the general characteristics of that race, since I had all the specimens I could want before my eyes.

That lack of privacy might have been unbearable. It was delightful. The friendliness, the receptiveness, the helpfulness of "colored people" is proverbial. This is no exaggeration. All of them, young and old, were incredibly kind to me. They adopted me. I was part of their big family.

The thought of the native island never left them. They withstood their life in France, I think, only because they had that common home, that oasis of the fatherland, which was the building in the rue Mouffetard.

It can be imagined how interesting this utter change of scene right in the middle of Paris was for one who had never traveled. Quite often, I stopped Doudou from sending away a woman visitor who had come to ask or offer

*This is presumably his second attempt, in 1889. In Chapter I, he has described his chagrin at having had to confess to his father, in 1888, that he had failed his first exam for Saint-Cyr.

some service, for the pleasure of looking at them, hearing them chatter in their Creole patois, of catching their natural instincts, their reactions, their habits of mind, their particular phobias, the childish things they did, the very special freedom of their ways. As soon as they were back home in the rue Mouffetard, they were no longer the post-office clerk, the cleaning woman, the waitress in a brasserie, the dishwasher in a restaurant, the clown in a fairground booth that they were when they crossed the threshold to the street to go to work at their various jobs. They seemed instantly to forget everything about their city life and to revert, in the strange surroundings of that great phalanstery, to what they had been in their corrugated tin shacks or in their straw huts, in the dusty alleys of Fort-de-France, on the fishermen's beaches, on the paths lined with hibiscus and jasmine, or in the tangled vegetation of the big hills. They promptly went back to their quarrels, their traditions, their superstitious fears, their incorrigible childishness.* I think this fundamental loyalty to their origins is very specific to them. Neither the Armenian colonies in the Jeanne-d'Arc quarter nor the houses full of Arabs in the Museum quarter offer, as far as I know, anything similar. Although those people instinctively banded together in the same area, they did not, like the Martiniquais of the rue Mouffetard, create a piece of their native land in the midst of Paris.

It was sometimes hard for me to get to Doudou's, on the top floor, what with so many friends whom I met on the staircase insisting that I pay them a visit, which was their roundabout way of saying "drink a *petit punch*." The less well-to-do always had some reserves of tafia in their cupboards.

That Creole amiability can become downright annoying. They cultivate it and display it ostentatiously, like a national characteristic. They all pride themselves on being friendly, generous. They make repeated advances, they want to be liked at any price and to be owed some gratitude. They won't let you get away without having given you something, a bit of cane sugar in a cornet, a handful of green coffee from the Antilles, two beignets in a scrap of newspaper, or a few candies in the bottom of a box. And they insist, excessively. On this point, they know no discretion. They abhor solitude and it never occurs to them that they must respect the reserve, the seclusion, the privacy of others.

They sometimes reminded me of those too affectionate, overly sweet young dogs that enter wherever they see an open door, walk around the room wagging their tail, sniff everything, offer themselves to be petted. You don't hold it against them, but you push them out. The Creole has his pride; he

---

*For a discussion of Maumort's racism—so blatant in the next few pages—and of its significance in the book, see Translators' Introduction, pp. xxiff.

knows very well when his feelings are hurt. But if you spare him, you let yourself be imposed upon. Such unflagging kindness is disarming.

Yet it cannot be said that they lack discretion, or even tact. They have very subtle responses, at times. Intuitions, which lead them to do things of great delicacy. As children sometimes do. But these responses are rare. Their lack of consideration is much more usual.

I did not suffer from it much, because they amused me and I went there only at relatively well-spaced intervals. And then, all in all, the contacts I had with that colony did not last more than eighteen months. I would probably have tired of their ways in the long run. At any rate, my liking for them did not keep me from seeing their faults, which are many, considerable, and, I believe, incorrigible.

Their vanity knows no limits. They have a naïve need to show off, which is winning. It is, as much as their natural sweetness (a sweetness which even involves a certain cowardice), one of the causes of their friendliness. Their boastfulness, their swaggering, breaks out in all their behavior. You could get anything from them by flattering them, by persuading them that you consider them important persons whose friendship you are courting. Most of them are not intelligent enough to be suspicious: the whole lot are ready to drop the cheese, like the crow in the fable.*

This question of the intelligence of mixed races is very delicate. At the outset, I was struck, quite often, by certain proofs of intelligence which I would not have expected from them, with my prejudices as a European and a white. But I very soon had to reconsider these. When one says of a Negro that he is very intelligent, it is in exactly the same way as one would say it of a child of twelve or thirteen, where one implies: "for his age"; with the black, one implies: "for a black." And this qualifier is very important.

The intelligence that one finds in many of them has, I don't know how to say it: a character of cleverness. One rather wants to say of such-or-such an intelligent Creole: "This one is clever as a monkey," and not to debase the word *intelligence*. Yes, many of them have a quick mind, an eager aptitude for imitating, for "aping" the European. Clever as monkeys, yes; and not much more . . .

This kind of intelligence is superficial, and basically nonperfectible. On balance, the impression I got from the colored Martiniquais was that he is fundamentally ineducable. He has gone as far as he can go. What makes them so little qualified to advance is their natural, instinctive, irreparable indifference to any improvement. Progress holds no interest for them. This can be perceived in the smallest things. When I entered Azaline's apartment

---

*By La Fontaine: a fox flatters a crow into dropping the piece of cheese it was holding in its beak.

or just about anyone else's (Doudou, actually, had a certain taste for European luxury), I was always struck by seeing that these people who were not without means, who bought dresses and jewelry, who treated themselves to the theater, who could therefore have spent a little money on their comfort, did not even think of doing so. They hammered nails, at random, into their walls, to hang their rags on; it did not occur to them to lay out forty sous at the dime store to buy themselves a coatrack, or to organize a closet where their clothes would be put away out of sight and protected from dust. They had no furniture. They piled up their linen in old potato sacks, or in grocery boxes. If one day they bought a mirrored wardrobe, it was because of the mirror, which draws the eye, and out of vanity: they were very careful to place it in the best spot that was visible from the landing, the door to which they generally left open. And those who had a mirrored wardrobe put nothing in it, as often as not, and continued to put their folded madrases and petticoats in their dusty old sacks. I saw Doudou wash her dishes, always the same way, squatting on her heels in front of a tub of hot water placed on the floor, with her ample skirt hiked up between her knees, forming knickers that made the roundness of her rump jut out. She did her laundry in the same posture, and sometimes stayed on her haunches for two hours. Why? Who prevented her from putting her tub on the kitchen table, or on her sink, or on a stool, so as not to have to hunker? The thought never crossed her mind. She had no concern for improving her habits. She had always done it that way. Her grandmother, a poor woman in a fishing village, had done it that way, for lack of equipment, crouching in front of the door of her straw hut. Her mother had done the same. Doudou was continuing the tradition. And to make sure her laundry was good and white, instead of buying some washing powder, or bluing it lightly, she did like her grandmother: she spread it out damp in the sun and wet it down ten times on Sunday, to achieve an immaculate whiteness through these successive dryings.

What attached me most to them was their childlike character. A cliché, obviously. But a strikingly truthful one. That race is a race of children. Their faults and virtues are those of children. Even the sense of justice which, with them, is so instinctive, so urgent, so unshakable, even among the thieves and criminals, is a sentiment innate in children. They have the child's easy kindness, and also the unexpected insensitivity, that sometimes goes all the way to cruelty. The child's incapacity for steady application, prolonged effort, the fickleness of mood, the involuntary lack of concentration. For them, as for children, no lasting sorrow: shrieks, soul-rending sobs, then, before their tears are dried, the slightest thing makes them smile; the storm has blown over. As with children, the taste for bright colors, metals that shine, mirrors, and the pleasure in making noise, not to say a racket, the need for talking loud, for roaring with laughter, for singing, telling stories till they're out of breath. And, as with children, the surprising mixture of modesty and immodesty; or to put it better still: they have the modesty of a child, and the immodesty of an animal.

It was enough to be with a young girl for a few moments, or even with a young woman in her own home, and certain of not being disturbed, for her to get the idea that you wished to take advantage of the circumstances: her smile became more mischievous, vaguely quizzical. You ventured, in response, a slightly pointed word or gesture, and immediately, with frightened looks, laughter, protestations, scoldings, threats, she would timorously flee in such a way as to be pursued, would make a stumble that landed her on the bed, on the sofa or on the rug, and would let herself be taken with the tenderest gratitude. On the other hand, even after she had generously given herself, you needed ten minutes of cajolery, maneuvering, and persuasion to undo her blouse, and even if you managed to get her in her slip, it was very rare that she would consent to remove it unless you had obtained her favors several times already, and the darkness was complete. She did not hesitate, if the urge took her, to go and squat on the pot in front of you, but you had to employ a great deal of patience and diplomacy to get a glimpse of her nipples.

The girls, as soon as they were nubile, were nearly all willing to lose their virginity, and appeared to attach only a very relative price to it. And as soon as they had some experience of lovemaking, they manifestly took the greatest pleasure in it, and scarcely turned down a decent opportunity. But they had a special conception of what was good and bad, and in this regard observed a rather rigorous code. Nothing more licit in their eyes than the sexual act; making love seemed to them almost as natural as eating, and the appetite of their sexual nature was as exigent as that of their stomach. But they retained, very strongly, the notion of sin, and surrendered to lovemaking without allowing themselves the slightest licentiousness. Apart from kissing and normal intercourse, to which they lent themselves obligingly and frenetically, every other liberty came under the category of vice, and was rejected with an indignant disapproval. In this domain, their dignity was very touchy, any suggestion at all racy seemed offensive to them, and the delectable variations with which our European imagination likes to enhance sexual play struck them as the utmost in perversity. I will not claim that they all were forever incapable of improvement in this respect. But even the ones whom many and diverse affairs had gradually led down the path of complications, and who had ended up developing a taste for them, never altogether abandoned the idea that they had entered the way of sin, and did not surrender themselves without a remnant of scruple and remorse to the most common practices of "civilized" love. I often discussed this with Doudou, who, in this area, had, well before my reign, advanced beyond the stages to which I am referring, and spoke freely of these matters. "You see," she explained to me, "making love is something you don't need to confess; but the rest is vice, and you need to confess it."

I think that the Jesuits who colonized and converted the Antilles are in part responsible for these rather arbitrary but not completely absurd distinctions between *lovemaking* and vice. I want to note the connection, in the people of the islands, between religion and the sexual act. From Doudou's stories about her childhood in Fort-de-France, it was clear that the clergy there, composed solely of Jesuits, confronted with the magnitude of the sexual instinct among the blacks, had had to come to terms with it and relax the strictness of their precepts. They had quickly grasped that it was absolutely impossible for them to prevent the pubescent girls from making love with the boys, and equally impossible to fight against the customs of the country, according to which a girl of sixteen who is pregnant is blessed by heaven; an illegitimate child is a "creature of the Good Lord," welcomed with joy by the family, and no stigma is attached to the situation of an unwed mother. The more children one has, the more one is respected.

"My cousin isn't married, alas," Doudou told me, speaking of a young woman back home. "But," she added proudly, and as if it had been an obvious compensation, "she already has five beautiful little ones." The clergy of the Antilles have had the good sense not to undertake a crusade which could only be a failure for religion. But they have contained the evil which they could not prevent. To make love is not a sin, as long as it is for the satisfaction of a pressing natural need. But any embellishment that erotic invention can add to it is a mortal sin, and jeopardizes one's eternal salvation. Ten generations of blacks have followed one another in the Antilles since Catholicism was established there. The terror of hell quickly got the better of the mediocre imaginative faculties of the blacks. They have contented themselves with the *lovemaking* that was permitted them, and have denied themselves, without undue pain, those extras and variations without which they got along quite well, considering. The habit is formed. "Honestly," Doudou sometimes said to me, laughing with pleasure, "how wicked you are, all of you, in France!"

IT HAPPENED in winter, during my second year at Saint-Cyr. I had met Zabette a hundred times at her aunt's, I had even been invited on many occasions to have a *petit punch* at Azaline's, and I never looked at the dancer's supple little body without feeling a fleeting desire. I saw Doudou almost every Saturday night, if possible. On one of these occasions she invited her niece, and the prospect of dinner with Zabette appealed to me. So I went. Outside it was cold. Doudou had fired up the stove white-hot, the room and the kitchen were warm, a candelabra with five candles was lit on a little shelf, the crêpes were fragrant with the aroma of melted butter and punch, they were crisp as could be; I had brought two bottles of good wine, and beautiful oranges, which were still rare in Paris at that time. Everything was a great success. The stove gave off so much heat that before the end of the meal Doudou, without ceremony, had stripped to her petticoat, Zabette had undone the top of her blouse, and I had hung my tunic on a nail. This general informality matched the picturesque disorder of the two rooms, and all this was done so simply that there was nothing offensive about it. After the meal, Doudou went to make the coffee. It was a sacred rite. Not for the world would she have roasted and ground her coffee a couple of hours before using it. To make coffee, for a Martiniquaise, is not to pour boiling water over the ground coffee. Lord, no! To make coffee is to take a handful of green beans, set them roasting on the little red-hot pan which is used only for this, then grind them very fine, and brew the result slowly. This triple operation is fairly long, and Doudou shut herself up in the kitchen so that the smoke from the roasting would not fill the room and force us to open the window onto the freezing night air.

So I was left by myself on the yellow sofa to chat with Zabette, in front of the table still covered with the desserts. She was savoring a blood orange and offered me a section. I refused at first, I don't know why, then changed my mind.

"Too late," she said, playfully, putting the tip of the last segment between her teeth, and giving me a defiant look.

I leaned forward and made as if to snatch the piece out of her mouth. We struggled for an instant. I had her thin little chest between my hands, she thrashed about, laughing, rolling her eyes, and the juice from the orange wet her lips. I pulled her to me and bit into the segment that she had in her mouth. It was a kiss à l'orange, utterly scrumptious, and it lasted much longer than the juicy pulp which had been its pretext.

When Doudou came back, with the tray loaded with three little covered cups and the steaming coffee pot, Zabette was on my knees and was letting me tickle her neck with my mustache. "If your mama could see the two of you," said Doudou, half laughing and half scolding. Zabette, teasing, refused to get up to take her coffee. "Well, you won't have your cup if you don't come get it," said Doudou, handing me mine. "It's enough for both of us," declared Zabette, without leaving my knees, and we shared the little cup, taking turns drinking gulps of the scalding mocha, which was delicious. Doudou eyed us, amused, feigning disapproval, and shaking her finger at her niece. "You better behave yourself, Zabette! You better mind your manners, you little fool!" She laughed, despite herself, and looked at us with her tender permissive gaze. "Well," she said, "a little girl who behaves so bad, it's too ugly a sight to look at! I'm going to blow out the light so I don't have to see this, and I'm gone!" She put out the candelabra with one puff and disappeared into the kitchen, leaving us alone in the dark.

Once in the dark, Zabette, who had mounted a stubborn resistance to my attempts so long as there had been light, helped me to undress her, and when she got down to her slip, whispered in my ear: "Carry me over to Aunt Doudou's bed."

So it was that I tasted of Zabette's exciting little body, while poor Doudou put her dishes away, quite happy in spite of all, I am sure, to have us enjoy ourselves—if a little concerned.

She had no reason to worry. That fling with Zabette was no more for me than a passing bit of fun which I did not wish to repeat often, and which rendered even more precious the satisfactions I found in my affair with Doudou. Zabette, fresh, impish, vivacious, and wriggly as a fish, was revoltingly selfish; she was after nothing but her own little pleasure, without the least concern for mine—her little pleasure, always early, always over quickly, which caused her to utter a little cry of surprise each time, as if she had never expected it, the short "ah" of someone who has inadvertently let something slip from her hands.

I slept over at the rue Mouffetard, and that very night I returned to Doudou with a rekindled appetite, which seemed to bring her both pleasure and regret.

I did not conceal from her that Zabette had disappointed me. She appeared saddened, as if worried.

I understood all of these nuances later.

That year, 1891, special reasons (a temporary worsening in the state of my father's health? the discouraged letters from Henriette?) forbade me from cheating either of them of my Easter vacation. I had already, because of Doudou, skipped the New Year's holiday. They had hoped to see me for the midterm break, and I had not come.

I thought that Doudou would be terribly let down by this, and I broke it to her gently. Contrary to my expectation, she greeted this news more with surprise than with regret. A strangely calm, almost happy, surprise. One would have said that this absence suited her. At the time, this did not make much of an impression on me. I was ready for a friendly little discussion about the need for this trip, and I had begun by laying out all the arguments. She did not insist, but rather accepted them at once and urged me to go. She only dwelled on one point, and with an odd tenacity: she made me promise that no matter what, I would not depart until the first day of the vacation from Saint-Cyr and that I would spend the night with her before leaving her for le Saillant.

I wanted the same thing myself. I had already lied to Henriette in writing to her of my arrival: I had announced that our break began the day after it actually did.

As far as Aunt Ma was concerned, I was going straight to le Saillant, without returning to Paris. So everything was arranged to give me an evening and a night at the rue Mouffetard.

I was so far from suspecting that Doudou could hide anything from me that I noticed none of the clues which ought to have opened my eyes, and which struck me in hindsight. I did not notice the elusive demeanor of Zabette, whom I met on the stairs and who barely stopped to toss me a quick hello, as if she did not much want to have a conversation with me that day. I did not notice certain changes in Doudou's apartment, the absence of certain furniture, certain objects; I had a vague idea that she had decided to tidy up a bit, that the rooms were less cluttered than before. I did not even notice Doudou's extraordinary nervousness, her vacant air, the tender, maternal, desperate look she sometimes shot me while I talked away. Or rather, since this could not have escaped me completely, I found it quite natural to ascribe this emotion to the disappointment that my trip was causing her. I was so tied down to Saint-Cyr that the vacations were the only times when my affair with Doudou had a sort of continuity. These were the milestones of our love, the chapters of our story. We said: "It was at Christmas . . . it was over New Year's . . . Easter . . ." It seemed to me quite normal that Doudou was affected by seeing me leave for le Saillant, since this visit robbed her of two weeks of intimacy—our best chance of the winter. Yet I ought to have understood, from the intensity of her transports, from the fit of weeping she had in the morning before getting out of bed, that such dejection hid something more serious.

That morning, something happened which I remember very clearly, about which I have often thought since. I had to go off without saying good-bye to Doudou. I was crushed, and a long way from supposing that this was the result of a diabolical little plan invented by her.

She knew that I had to take the eleven-fifteen train at Montparnasse, which was the only convenient one of the three daily trains, of which one left Paris at five-thirty in the morning, which is to say at an ungodly hour, and the other at five in the afternoon, which, at that time of year, would have forced me to arrive after dark, and to do the leg from Nogent-le-Routrou to le Saillant at night. While I lingered in bed, she heated the water for me to wash up. I heard her rummaging in the kitchen. Suddenly she came in with the breakfast tray . . . She was dressed to go out. "I have time to go do my shopping while you get dressed. Get up soon, darling, it's almost nine-thirty. Here's your breakfast. I had mine while I was getting dressed." She spoke quickly, without looking at me. "You see, if I miss my Sunday market, after that I'm in trouble all week long . . . I'm in a hurry . . . I'll be back in half an hour." Very rapidly she leaned down, pressed her lips to mine with a kind of ardor and desperation, then ran off.

I was disappointed. The routine was that she got back into bed with our big breakfast tray, and this little meal, together, side by side, the scalding Martiniquan coffee, the toasted bread with butter, the guava jelly, was one of the minor joys of my holidays.

I breakfasted alone, got dressed. She did not come back. Time was passing. I had a suitcase, not very heavy, but heavy enough that I had to take a fiacre. The time I would need to find a cab . . . I was seething with impatience. Ten-fifteen . . . Ten-twenty . . . I opened the window. The rue Mouffetard was a swarming market from top to bottom, the whole quarter let loose, calls, shouts, street-peddlers' yappings, an indescribable melee. At ten-thirty I decided to get started and slowly go downstairs. She knew the time of my train, she couldn't not show up . . .

I arrived downstairs without having run into her. I went out onto the doorstep. The noisy throng. No Doudou. What to do? Impossible to delay any longer. It was going on twenty to eleven. To find a cab, get to Montparnasse . . . Not a moment to spare . . . Henriette had told me she would come pick me up herself in the cart; I really couldn't miss the train.

I dashed, furious, through the crowd, still hoping to catch sight of Doudou, towards the Place de l'Estrapade, where there was a hackney rank. And I arrived at the station just in time to jump into the train, which was starting up. Jostled, running, with my casoar,* my suitcase, my sword, incensed with her.

Poor Doudou, poor dear Doudou! She had come up with this ruse to avoid farewells in which her despair might have betrayed her. That final, discreet gesture was so like her!

In the train, I wrote her a note.

I arrived at le Saillant with Henriette, who had met me at the station.

My father was having one attack after another. He was thin, his features drawn—hardly recognizable. The family atmosphere took hold of me once more. Still, I waited every day for a letter from Doudou. A week went by, I began to worry. I wrote to Zabette. No answer.

Three days before the end of the vacation, I finally received an envelope with Doudou's handwriting. As soon as I opened it, my eye fell on the date. This letter had been written two weeks earlier, before my last night at the rue Mouffetard, and had been mailed by Zabette according to her aunt's instructions, on the day when Doudou, from Le Havre, had sent her last message from France, a wire, at the moment when her boat was sailing.

A heartbreaking letter, in its brevity and simplicity.

*The plume on shakos worn by Saint-Cyr cadets.

"I will love you always," she wrote, "you have been the only love of my life. But I love my homeland, I could not live in France. Forgive me. I have tried, until the last moment, not to cause you too much pain. I let you leave without saying anything to you, without kissing you one last time. I did not have enough courage to tell you goodbye. We will meet again in heaven. Do not forget your Doudou."

The next day, a note from Zabette explained the rest to me. Doudou had filed for a transfer two years before. She did not speak of it, but she was always hoping, and privately intensified her efforts. In January she had finally received the promise of a post in Fort-de-France. She had prepared her departure in great secrecy. Only Zabette was in on it. Azaline had learned of her sister's leaving only a few days before the fact. She had burst out with threats, reproaches. But there was nothing to be done. The call of Martinique was stronger than anything. The two sisters had parted on bad terms. "Come see me," Zabette added. "We have the same sorrow, we'll console each other by talking about her."

All the details of those last months came back to me. I understood Doudou's hidden intention in letting me sleep with her niece. Naïvely, she was preparing a consolation for me . . . It was not a lover's gesture, it was a maternal thought.

I did not succeed in concealing my grief. I had made discreet allusions to Henriette about my affair. I confided my sadness to her. I alleviated my pain by speaking to her about Doudou, telling her about the rue Mouffetard, without dwelling on what would have shocked her too much.

I did not move up my departure from le Saillant. I did not try to see Zabette. I went straight back to Saint-Cyr, leaving my father convalescing and Henriette soothed by my stay with her.

It was only five or six weeks afterwards that I went back one Sunday night to see Azaline. She was much changed, she had been in torment since her sister's departure. She looked seriously ill to me. My presence seemed to irritate her. Everything that reminded her of Doudou reactivated her affliction, which was strange, animal, mixed with rancor, and was poisoning her like a venom in her blood. I have always wondered if she did not suffer from the same homesickness as Doudou and if there was not a lot of envy connected to her anger and her grief. For she could never leave France because she did not want to meet up with Zabette's father, who ran a rum distillery in Martinique.

Zabette walked me out to the landing after a visit which I cut short, disappointed. In the shadow, I was once again seized with desire for that little black body. We made a date for the following Sunday.

I took her to a cheap hotel, and there, in a seedy setting, I had my second experience with Zabette. I thought only of Doudou, I compared the niece to the aunt, and as soon as I satisfied my desire, I swore that I would never see her again.

Zabette was a flirtatious, cold, pretentious, insufferable little sort.

She who, every week, went and got undressed at some woman painter's or sculptor's, and remained naked for two hours in any pose, always made an unbearable fuss about letting herself be undressed. I very rarely held her completely nude in my arms, and always demurely hidden under the covers, in a totally dark room. She pushed modesty to the point of not getting out of bed until she had put her slip back on. I slept at least a dozen times with her. The only visual memory I have of her body is the one left me by our first meeting, at Phylée's, when I glimpsed, through the gap in the screen, her arched lower back and her little brown rump. She was very careful, and her fear of consequences made her always pull away at the moment when I would most have wished her to let herself go. I cannot really blame her for it. But Doudou had got me used to cozier ways, and Zabette's precautions left me with a lack of satisfaction which, every time, led me to vow never to repeat the experience.

Doudou had spoiled me . . .

Her attentive, maternal, entirely altruistic love, prompted by her desire to make me fully happy and to match her pleasure to mine, and not mine to hers, to anticipate all my whims, to consent to all my fancies (to sleep naked, for instance, naked all night long), her habit of placing the joy of giving far ahead of that of receiving (although she knew how to take her share of satisfaction with a greediness that wonderfully mirrored my own), had made me demanding and inclined me to judge Zabette's reluctant complaisance severely, along with her coquetry, her caprices of a little queen who wants to dominate, to keep men waiting, and to be desired—who, at bottom, despises males, etc.

We parted, each probably annoyed with the other, and without making a date.

I stopped going back to the rue Mouffetard.

Anyway, those last months of the second year required intensive work. I had to make up for lost time if I wanted to graduate high in my class. I buried myself in my work, and found my only solace in it.

TWO OR THREE YEARS afterwards, I ran into Zabette by chance on the Odéon-Batignolles omnibus. It was she who recognized me, and who gave up her seat to come and chat with me on the footboard.

This was how I learned that Doudou was married and that Azaline had died.

This death Zabette attributed to the deep and irreparable discontent which her sister's departure had caused her: "It's as if Doudou had *hexed* me . . . ," Azaline would say. In the spring and summer that followed Doudou's leaving, she had been more and more unwell, staying home for weeks at a time. She quit her accounting job and was consumed with worry at the thought of eating up her savings. She died in the fall, without having wanted to see a doctor, without any symptom of disease, as if devoured by her grief and her spite, and she had not reconciled with her sister, who wrote her from the island and whom she did not answer.

As for Doudou's marriage, it had just taken place when I ran into Zabette, and she had few details. With great pomp, in the cathedral, before a large audience, Doudou had wed a "politician," a Fort-de-France business-man, well-considered, appreciably older than she, a widower who was a city councillor. He hoped to become a deputy. He was a man of color. Doudou had left her job at the Post Office for this marriage. Her husband was rich and possessed an estate near Fort-de-France, a domestic staff, horses and car-riages, a whole retinue. There were two sons, thirteen and fifteen, and two daughters married to Martiniquan merchants. This was all Zabette knew about this marriage, to which she seemed rather indifferent. As for me, I remember feeling an immense pleasure. The idea that Doudou was happy, loved, surrounded by friends, allowed me to think of her without concern. It was a perfect ending to the Doudou episode.

I questioned Zabette about her own life. She spoke of it harshly, with a sort of grudge against society, against the world of dance, against men. She told me that she had a "friend." I promised to go at some point to the night club where she did a dance number (the beguine) with her "friend," and where she played a part in a little revue at the end of the show. But I forgot to go.

FROM A DISTANCE, the memory of my affair with Doudou appears to me like a moment of happy fulfillment: calm of the senses, calm of the heart. One Saturday night at the rue Mouffetard was enough to satisfy the demon of the flesh: a weekly bath of sensuality that left me contented, sated, with-out tiredness or obsessive curiosity. I really think that in the course of those years, I was unfaithful to Doudou only two or three times, and that each of those escapades rendered my affair more precious. Calm of the heart. I loved her passionately enough not to have anything more to ask of love. She was a perfect mistress and delightful friend. I liked to be with her, and found as much appeal in her cheerful and even nature, her sane judgment, her amus-ing exoticism as in her body always ready for pleasure. I invariably left her with regret and returned to her with impatience.

This smooth and untroubled affair put me in a mood for work. If I learned a lot at Saint-Cyr, I owe it to Doudou. I have nothing but gratitude and tenderness for her.

Another thing. It was during that year that there arose in me the desire for a colonial career. It would be foolish to attribute this inclination to Doudou. The France of that era was all abuzz with colonizing ambitions, and the influence of Jules Ferry* (the systematic glorification of our budding colonial empire, the intervention in Tonkin, the African explorations) is enough to explain how a young officer could dream of shirking the dull duties of garrison life to devote himself to faraway conquests. All the same, the encounter with Doudou at that time in my development, and all the exoticism that I breathed in her company, and the lasting attraction that a colored woman's skin exerted over my senses, contributed to the hatching of my colonial vocation. And I owe her this recognition.

*Jules Ferry (1832–1893), French statesman of the early Third Republic, notable both for his anticlerical education policy and for his success in extending the French colonial empire. *(Encyclopaedia Britannica).*

PART THREE

Beginnings in the Army. Marriage (1891–1907)

CHAPTER XVIII

Claire Saint-Gall. The Marriage.

[Translators' note: In June 1943, Martin du Gard recorded his intention to develop the character of Maumort's wife, Claire, and to describe their engagement, their marriage, and the Saint-Gall family seen from the inside. Time did not permit him to carry out this project as completely as he had hoped. The present chapter was assembled by André Daspre from four extant fragments.]

THE FIRST YEAR of my friendship with Blaise, I was invited to la Popelière. "Invited" is a quite unsuitable term: I was "brought" to la Popelière by Blaise to spend Pentecost Sunday and Monday of 1888 with him there.

La Popelière had been the Saint-Gall family's estate since the First Empire. Admiral Saint-Gall, the father of the present admiral, inherited it, I believe, from his mother. He had retired there, and had enlarged the house and the garden.

The property was located four kilometers from Melun, on the heights that overlook the Seine between Melun and Corbeil.*

I had already heard a great deal about la Popelière when I went there for the first time. The whole family loved this estate where every year for fifty

---

*Both Melun and Corbeil-Essonnes lie just southeast of Paris.

years they had gathered for the holidays, and where the whole younger generation of cousins had gaily spent the summer since their birth.

For all, old and young, this Popelière was a sort of real-life myth, an exceptional, half-legendary place, full of embellished memories. They did not speak of it as a particular corner of the universe but as a place out of time and space, which each of them imagined as children studying the catechism might picture limbo or the Garden of Eden. A spot that had nothing in common with outer geographical areas. And they were quite aware that they were stretching things. They sometimes said to those who did not know la Popelière: "Oh, it's not so much that the country is beautiful, that the estate is nice, it's something else . . . You have to know it, to have lived here, in order to understand . . ." And they smiled, laughing a little at themselves, as a concession to others. But with eyes shining with affection, as one conjures up a beloved object, knowing that one sees it through a distorting enthusiasm but pleased to see it that way.

You got off at the Melun railway station, whence an old family break, driven by the venerable Barthélémy, took you in half an hour to the estate, with the two horses at the trot.

You could see the walls from a distance, and the gate, always open. The carriage entered the shady garden, so refreshing, the horses slowed to a walk to climb the slope, and you came out in front of the house.

It was a mismatched assemblage, and in rather bad taste. You could easily make out what must have been the original house, a big square mansion with tall windows at regular intervals, a roof in the Italian style (that is, crowned with a balustered terrace), and an entrance that was a stoop of two steps under a little peristyle supported by two columns with Doric capitals. The top of the peristyle formed a balcony. At the center of the façade: a large clock, framed with stone.

To this first building, two very disparate structures had been added. On one side, a rather long wing, higher than the main building, presenting two rows of five or six windows and ending in a sort of low veranda or hexagonal rotunda, entirely glassed in, that was called—I have never known why—the "café chantant." This veranda looked out onto a long and narrow terrace from which there was a very beautiful view of the Seine valley.

On the opposite side of the main building rose another wing, absolutely different, a Swiss chalet with a pointed roof and flower-boxed balconies, entirely clad in wood painted brown. This part of the house, which was known as "the chalet," brought to mind the body of a gigantic cuckoo clock, and it would not have been surprising when the hour struck in the dial on the old house to see the middle window open automatically and a sculpted wooden bird appear.

The ugliness of the whole was certainly quite offensive. One has to imagine the look of that façade, where, all in a row, stuck on to one another, there were: a Swiss chalet; a little yellow stucco Italian palace from the First Empire; a building without style, taller than the others, with a blue slate roof, green trellises where roses climbed, and green shutters; and, to top things off, like a promontory, the glazed wart of the "café chantant," with its zinc roof glaring in the sun.

I got the impression on the first day—and had it during my whole life with that family—that I was the only one to see this ugliness, so blinded were they by their joy at returning to their dear Popelière and so unable to apply to it the most elementary critical sense.

And they were quite right. The deep, bracing, soothing satisfactions they came to seek there, and that they found without fail in the family atmosphere, had an importance of a different order from aesthetic satisfactions. Even Uncle Jean, the abbé, a man of taste who lived surrounded by beautiful proportions, did not seem affected by this shapeless architectural grouping, and on the day when I made so bold as to bring this to his attention, he had to admit that I was right, smiling and caring not a whit for this outsider's opinion: the evaluating gaze he cast, on my account, at the house where he was born, seemed to me to be the first critical gaze he had ever cast at it, and probably the last.

But I am far from having finished this overview.

When you had crossed the peristyle, you found yourself in a long, narrow entrance hall with a staircase at the rear. This entrance hall had been entirely restored by Mme. Saint-Gall in the Renaissance style: sculpted wainscoting, modern of course, covered the walls halfway up; the top was a painted fabric on which stenciled brown fleurs de lys were arrayed on a crimson background, in the style of Viollet-le-Duc. Two large doors, also with modern sculpted panels, opened to the right onto the first drawing room, to the left onto the dining room. In the back, to the left of the foot of the staircase, a low door took you into a corridor that passed behind the dining room, leading to servants' quarters and storerooms, and ended in the spacious kitchen and then the courtyard. This entrance hall was furnished with two big antique oak chests, on which shone copper pans, an old water-urn and two tall vases with handles. And the wainscoting always disappeared beneath a mass of hanging garments, garden hats, shawls for the cool evenings, and children's toys.

The dining room was huge, and the big square oak table could easily seat twenty. The walls were hung with old *verdure* tapestries, from the floor to the cornice. Three wide windows gave onto the garden. A pass-through near the old stone fireplace, with its tall andirons, communicated with the kitchen.

The first drawing room was of the same size, and also furnished with Louis XIII chairs and tables, with twisted legs; tapestry portières hung in front of the doors. On the walls, family portraits. On the tables, framed photos of all the members of the tribe.

The dining room and drawing room were the two main rooms of the original house. From the drawing room one passed into a brightly lit room on the courtyard, formerly the admiral grandfather's study, which had become Mme. Saint-Gall's office, the place where she did her accounts, received the gardener and the suppliers; from her worktable, she kept an eye on the courtyard.

The new building, which ended with the "café chantant," formed, on the ground floor, an enormous drawing room, quite cheerful, painted white, full of ill-assorted furniture coming from several different suites. There was plenty of space for everything there: an entire Empire suite, mahogany with Sphinx heads, upholstered in yellow patterned velvet; a whole Second Empire suite, padded, covered in a cretonne with yellow flowers and green foliage. This vast hall, where everyone always sat, was made even larger by the "café chantant," the middle of which was occupied by a round table, surrounded with four dark green moleskin sofas. The room was very bright because of the four large windows that looked out onto the garden and because of that veranda, entirely glassed in, which resembled a lantern and from which you could see the meadows going all the way down to the Seine, whose twists and turns you could follow as far as Melun.

Everyone had his own special setup in this room. The women left their sewing baskets there, the men their books, their cigar boxes, their stationery. This general clutter was very homey.

Behind this drawing room, there was in addition a former barn, converted into a library and billiards room, which received light from both the garden and the courtyard. You reached it either through the drawing room or Mme. Saint-Gall's study. It was there that the youngsters, mainly, took refuge. Often the uncles played billiards there as well. The glazed bookcases occupied the whole back wall. The collection was quite a hodgepodge. It was always locked, and you needed Mme. Saint-Gall's permission to borrow a book; she rarely entrusted the key to you; she came and opened the glass door, and entered in a notebook the name of the volume you were taking out. Not much reading was done at la Popelière. Life there lacked the necessary contemplative atmosphere.

The immense, stone-paved kitchen, with its big stove and its hooded fireplace, must have dated back to the time of the old house, but as a one-story annex grafted onto the central building. It was on top of this that the Swiss chalet and its high pointed gable had been erected. Around the kitchen there was an assortment of old storerooms, laundry rooms, a utility room, a larder, and a bathroom whose sheet-metal bathtub, painted like green marble, had a copper lining. To take a bath at la Popelière was a complicated adventure;

you had to fill the bathtub with the water that had been heated on the stove in big copper kettles. Three baths could be had of a Saturday morning. As there were never fewer than fifteen or twenty persons in residence, each one's turn did not come very often. For it never would have occurred to anyone to ask for a bath on a day other than Saturday.

You reached the second floor only by the big staircase. A long central corridor served the whole house, as in a hotel, and there were as many rooms on the garden as on the courtyard, about twenty in all, of different sizes and simply but adequately furnished. Some had communicating doors between them, and the various branches of the family thus formed apartments of sorts, always the same. There was the white bedroom that Uncle Laurent and Aunt Esther always occupied, and the adjacent rooms, reserved for their daughters. There was the blue bedroom, for the abbé. There was the Louis XIII bedroom of Admiral and Mme. Saint-Gall; the pink bedroom of Uncle Edgard and Aunt Marie, whose two daughters stayed in a communicating room with two beds. And in the Swiss chalet there was a big bedroom with an alcove, for Uncle Joseph and Aunt Armande. And then there were the Louis XVI bedroom; the bedroom of the fire (long famous in the family annals for the chimney fire there); the Louis-Philippe bedroom; the morning-glory bedroom; the shark bedroom (on account of a certain engraving in which poor castaways on a raft were threatened by the gaping maw of a shark). Grandmother Forestier and the faithful aunt Adèle had a little apartment on the courtyard with a wooden balcony, which they were fond of because it was cool and all covered with climbing roses.

The third floor was called "the boys' floor." It was reached by a spiral staircase at the end of the corridor on the new building side. It was also the floor of the servants, who had the garrets on the top floor of the old house. The rooms for the boys were small, with somewhat sloping ceilings; but they enjoyed a great deal of freedom there and escaped all supervision. They fought, hit each other with bolsters, played ritual pranks, got together for interminable whispered conversations till past midnight.

The garden was enclosed by walls, with paths that described circles among the tall trees, the planes and chestnuts. Certain areas had names: the "quincunx," the "boules area," the "parterre," the "little meadow," the "arbor." The admiral grandfather had bought a three-hectare lot to make a vegetable garden and an orchard there. He had had the dividing wall torn down, so that the old garden connected with the vegetable garden. Beyond stretched the orchard with its fruit trees, overgrown with grass. The vegetable garden and the orchard were surrounded by a hedge, always nicely trimmed. And, at the bottom of the orchard, at the two farthest corners of the new lot, the grandfather had had two little shelters built, latticework covered with climbers, where you could take refuge in case of a shower. There was a pretty view of the countryside from there, in the direction away from the Seine.

Behind the house was the courtyard, with a gate onto a back road. It was entirely bounded by buildings: stables, sheds, a kennel, henhouses, barns, etc. In the center stood a tall, ancient linden tree whose circle of shade covered a large part of the courtyard and around which there had been built a wide chicken-wire aviary with compartments where certain highbred hens, a pair of Barbary ducks, a pair of white pheasants, and a pair of golden pheasants were raised. After lunch, everyone observed the ritual of following Mme. Saint-Gall into the courtyard to watch her toss the birds crumbs and scraps of bread from the meal; then you returned to the drawing room via the office and the library, and on the table in the "café-chantant" you found the enormous tray of coffee.

In the courtyard also stood the old well with its pump, whose familiar sound we heard from dawn till dusk, since the providing of water for such a household was quite a task, requiring stoneware jugs and pitchers to be filled by the dozens. And in front of the pump there was the stone trough where the horses were watered and which was well-known to all the dogs and cats of the house. The courtyard was a rustic and noisy place where Barthélémy, the coachman, reigned; where the women servants laughed openly and spoke loud. Flocks of ducks and chickens wandered about freely, and the ground was always a bit miry. "Scrape your shoes," Mme. Saint-Gall always cautioned when we came back from the aviary and, in single file behind her, climbed the two steps that led to the study. And this order was not unwarranted, since we always brought in droppings on our soles. I can still hear the sound of the shoes on the scrapers that flanked the little stoop.

MY FIRST VISIT to la Popelière, in the spring of '88, has left me a memory of gaiety and easy living. There were the parents: the admiral and his wife, who, although the property belonged to all the Saint-Galls, had, by tacit agreement, the role of hosts; Aunt Esther, who came from Tours with her children, but without Colonel Laurent Saint-Gall; Uncle Edgard Forestier, the lawyer, the cutup, with Aunt Marie and the two girls; Uncle Joseph Forestier with Aunt Armande and their two children; and the abbé, Uncle Jean, who brought along a young seminarian, a distant cousin of the Saint-Galls.

There were a lot of youngsters, and they formed separate groups according to their ages. There was the twenty-to-thirty crowd: Isabelle Bousseron, Jean Saint-Gall and his wife, Lotte, and Paule Saint-Gall; Uncle Laurent and Aunt Esther's children, Frédéric, Emma, and Yvonne Dille, with her husband; and René Saint-Gall, Uncle Maurice's son, who came from Alsace.

These were the "elders," who played interminable games of croquet on the lawn in front of the house, and hardly ever left the estate.

Next came the fifteen-to-twenty crowd, of which I was a member, along with Blaise. These were the "big kids." There were Blaise's two sisters, Laure and Clairette; Uncle Edgard Forestier's two daughters, Françoise and Charlotte, a girl of thirteen, the youngest of the group, who followed Clairette around like her shadow; Guy Saint-Gall, Uncle Laurent's lastborn, a little younger than I, who was studying for his *bachot* in *philosophie.*

Then there were the "small fry," the ones under ten, a rowdy gang who were sent to play at the far end of the garden and who were kept firmly in line by Ernest and Louise, the children of Uncle Joseph and Aunt Armande; the three little Bousserons, Jeanne, Alice and Suzy; and the Dilles' children, Uncle Laurent's grandchildren, Simone and Pierre, toddlers of two or three.

Finally, in a cradle, the youngest of all, little Raoul, the son of Jean and Lotte.

I remember our bunch best. There were about eight of us. We went swimming in the Seine at the end of the afternoons. We played billiards in the evening after dinner. Blaise, Laure, and I were the eldest of the group, and the three of us often went off by ourselves, leaving Clairette, Françoise, and Charlotte to go their own way. Guy usually kept to himself in a corner of the garden, cramming for his exam.

I bloomed. I found that life heavenly. I had never known anything like it. Everything was entertainment, fun, jokes, all day long. I was, at the time, quite smitten with Laure. That happy camaraderie enchanted me. I felt "rejuvenated," I had never lived in such an atmosphere of purity and good cheer. I did not have a single unchaste thought in my head. Everything here was simple, easy, genuine.

Those informal meals with twenty-six or twenty-seven at the table, where all showed their joy at being together, were dominated by Uncle Edgard's resonant voice.

There was an atmosphere of noisy cheerfulness, like a perpetual party. They told hundreds of family stories, which everyone knew and heard afresh with tireless pleasure. From time to time, Uncle Joseph, the admiral, and the abbé exchanged more general ideas, and the conversation went up a notch. But it soon lapsed back into frivolousness and cordiality. It was soft and restful. Everyone here seemed to be effortlessly kind, and one felt oneself a better person.

I recalled the gloomy lunches at le Saillant, with my sister and my silent father; or the meals at the rue de Fleurus, the serious questions raised by Uncle Éric, the uneasiness that his strange, complicated character produced. At la Popelière, I discovered people who were happy simply to be reunited in a setting that they loved, and who had no mistrust of one another.

. . .

THE END OF MY TORTURED relationship with Raphaële Dancenis* had left me, at the end of 1892, in a state of nervous fatigue and deep sadness. I was still stationed at Versailles, with no hope of obtaining the transfer I was requesting, empty in mind and heart, worried over a start in life and career that was giving me no satisfaction, making short-lived plans which I abandoned one after the other without managing to stick to anything.

For two years, since Laure's entering the convent†, I had let my relations with the rue Saint-Guillaume lapse; in large part because the disappointment that Laure's vocation had caused me, and that no one in the Saint-Gall family except Blaise had known about, made my visits hard to bear; then, my affair with Doudou, my moving to Versailles, my affair with Raphaële had kept me busy and distanced me from my friends.

A case of typhoid, quite serious, which put Blaise's life in jeopardy during the fall of 1892, brought me quite naturally back to the rue Saint-Guillaume. Blaise had been moved down to the second floor to his parents' apartment, where Laure's room was free; and the family's whole existence during those anguishing weeks revolved around that sickroom, where a nurse who was a nun had been installed. I did not immediately learn that Blaise was sick. When I found out and rushed to the rue Saint-Guillaume, the illness was in its ascendant period, the fever was very high, the doctor was coming three times a day, and in spite of the inveterate optimism of the Saint-Galls, the family was in a terrible state of anxiety. Of course, one could not go near the patient. Brief conferences were held in the drawing room, where, in hushed tones, the latest news was passed on. There were not many people at these meetings; Grandmother Forestier and her faithful aunt Adèle were confined to the ground floor, away from any contagion; Jean had forbidden his wife and children to set foot on the second floor, where he came alone for news when he went out or returned from his job at the Compagnie du Nord. The admiral, busy at the ministry, was there only in the evening. Usually I found Clairette by herself, or sometimes with her older sister Paule (married for three years to Dr. Pierre Dormoy), who came every afternoon although she had her hands quite full with her two children, the youngest of whom, just

*André Daspre: Maumort's affair with Raphaële Dancenis, when, upon leaving Saint-Cyr, he finds himself stationed in Versailles, would have been a very important episode in the novel. Unfortunately, there are only two file cards on Raphaële, and some allusions here and there.

†M. Daspre has judged it inappropriate to include a section dedicated to Bertrand's infatuation with Laure Saint-Gall, since in it Martin du Gard reiterates the theme of a misplaced passion, already fully developed in the episode concerning Éva Chambost (Chapter XIV). At any rate, the situation is short-lived; six months after Bertrand's first visit to la Popelière, Laure announces her intention to take the veil.

born, she was nursing. I also ran into Dr. Dormoy there, and sometimes Jean. But most often I found Clairette alone.

Mme. Saint-Gall, from the beginning of the illness, had donned a white coat, turned herself into a nurse, and never left the patient she was caring for, except to be spelled by the nun. They had appropriated the bedroom of Clairette, who had emigrated to the drawing room, set herself up there as best she could, and was sleeping on a cot that she unfolded at night. She had interrupted her normal life, which consisted of taking advanced classes for young women in art history, French literature, English, and piano. She always went accompanied by her chambermaid, as befitted bourgeois young ladies of the day. She was rather idle, reading little, since her mother was strict about what she read; and she could not even entertain her friends, who were barred from entering the plague-stricken house. My visits gave her some distraction, made her visibly happy; and she detained me, in a sweet way, for as long as possible.

I found myself quite free at that time, since the instruction of the new recruits, to which I was assigned at Versailles, occupied me mainly in the morning from six till ten, and then at the start of the afternoon. The days were short in that month of November, the exercises ended at three, I left the barracks early, able to remain at large until dawn of the next day, and so nothing kept me from taking the train for Paris around three-thirty and from being at the rue Saint-Guillaume by four-thirty, where I often stayed until dinnertime in order to hear the outcome of the evening consultation. I went to dine at the rue de Fleurus almost every day and returned to Versailles to sleep.

There were two quite anxious weeks. The patient was very weakened and somewhat delirious. The doctor requested a consultation by leading medical experts, but as they could not deliver an opinion before a certain waiting period, it was necessary to follow the progress of the illness with great attention.

On certain days during that trying time, I found poor Clairette racked with worry, and I did my best to cheer her up, chatting with her to rally her spirits.

She was then eighteen. I had known her when she was quite young, at a time when I was eighteen myself and had treated that little girl of fourteen as a child. This created something like a childhood friendship between us. I had lost sight of her during these last few years. I now discovered a young woman, affectionate and simple, who treated me like a slightly older cousin. But that difference of four years between us, formerly so pronounced, had become imperceptible. I was surprised to find her so serious, so mature, although she still looked like a child, and I took great pleasure in this friendly intimacy.

Soon the news was more reassuring. The fateful waiting period was over. The fever went down a little. The illness followed its course. The patient remained very weak, but the doctors affirmed that the danger had passed, and that by avoiding complications through great vigilance we could hope that nothing unforeseen would occur.

Those anxious days Clairette and I had shared strengthened our closeness. Our minds grew freer as the fears diminished, and gradually the subjects of our conversations became more intimate, more personal. I fell under her charm without trying to defend myself from it, without really being aware of it. The frequency of my almost daily visits was quite natural for everyone, and for us, since the reason for them was Blaise's health. Circumstances played along.

I DISCOVERED CLAIRETTE little by little.

Her name suited her beautifully. Everything was *clair** in her—her coloring, her eyes, her natural gaiety, her good-as-gold heart, her easy and uncomplicated character, that extraordinary youthfulness which she was to lose only with life itself.

She still looked fifteen. And all the more so since around the house she seldom wore her hair in a chignon, but rather, as in the past, sported braids that she did up with a bow at the back of the neck. That impression of youth came from her Nordic fairness, her baby's complexion, her smooth skin, her pale, gray-blue, astonishingly limpid gaze, her frail and graceful body, her little hands, her brisk and mischievous movements, her smile like a beaming child's, her dazzling teeth—from that whole freshness of a flower about to bloom.

Aside from her coloring and the aqueous clarity of her eyes, there was nothing really exceptional about her. An ordinary face, if you analyzed it. Ordinary in its very regularity, because no feature was prominent. A rather long, rather flat face, with the eyes set a bit too far apart perhaps, and a cute little nose: no marked character. A plain mouth, but delicate and fresh lips with a ready smile, and small, very white teeth, quite straight, evenly placed in the pale gums. A gracile neck. Where did the charm of that face come from? From the gaze, obviously; the eyes were not particularly large, but were very light, with long golden lashes, and crystalline like those of certain blond children. I think the eyelashes were more golden than the hair, which was blond, but a pale and slightly ash blond, without much sheen to it.

She was quite shapely: slender but well-proportioned limbs, fragile shoulders, the bust of a very young woman, which was never spoiled by child-

*I.e., light.

bearing. Above all supple, graceful, the body of a young girl, quick and easy in all its movements.

Blaise always called her "Miss" to tease her, and she did indeed have the look of an English girl. Until her last illness, at close to thirty, she was addressed as "Mademoiselle" in all the stores, even when she was with her sons of eleven and nine, who both resembled her as if they were her younger brothers. And she looked so much like their older sister that if I was with them people constantly said "your daughter" when speaking to me of her. And I did not always correct them, since I took pleasure, a strange and secret pleasure, in this mistake. It was so much through her youthfulness that her charm worked on me! It was this freshness, this childlike fragility, the ingenuousness of the gaze and the smile that had made me love her and attached me to her so powerfully that we stayed together, indissolubly, even after so many deep differences had driven our lives apart.

The odd thing is that this physical appearance, so frail, so childish, so carefree, so gay, did not at all tally with her underlying nature. And this took me years to realize. She was always easy to live with, even-tempered, smiling, accepting me as I was without appearing to suffer from it. But beneath this easygoing, docile air was hidden a temperament that was headstrong, intractable, unswerving, and of rocklike solidity. No influence, no argument, no amount of shared living, of common interest or thought, had the slightest effect on that gemstone.

An unbending character. She was like a cut diamond, clear, transparent, full of sparkle and lights, which nothing, absolutely nothing, neither age nor life experience, nor feelings, nor love, could chip away at. Everything bounced off that smooth surface without penetrating it. We never had a violent disagreement. In fourteen years of marriage, I cannot remember a stormy argument. In the early years, at the height of our harmony, when our love was at its peak, when I lived with her in complete trust and without any dissembling, my tastes and personal opinions were reflected on that gleaming surface, with its mineral hardness, and I naïvely took that reflection for an expression of inclinations and points of view that were similar to mine. It was nothing of the sort. I came to understand this later. No influence, no outside power could make a dent in the solidity of that block. You could not cut her to the quick, charm her, advise her, persuade her, trick her, exert the slightest pressure on her. It was not recalcitrance on her part, or concerted resistance; still less female cunning, or the guile of a weakness that defends itself by avoiding every hold on it. Nor was it indifference. Nor stubbornness, nor self-satisfaction. No. It was how she was. With no rebelliousness in her, no insubordination, but passive, inert, closed off, mysteriously unreachable, yet with the most welcoming, least aggressive exterior one could imagine. To all appearances, she went along with everything, agreed to everything without seeming to force herself, rejected no advice, seemed to assent whole-heartedly, to understand and approve. But she behaved according to her nature, and had her own unpredictable, unfathomable responses, without ceasing to appear accommodating, without even seeming to notice that these reactions were contrary to mine. She had the flexibility of a fragile reed which is bent by the slightest breeze, and which, once the breeze has passed, per-petually straightens back up, according to its own law, its roots, its fibers, the upsurge of its sap—unbelievably strong, strong in the way that forces of nature, or the elements, are.

My male personality had no impact; it was always beaten by that almost imperceptible power of inertia. I realized my defeat only over the long term, and often when this defeat had ceased to have any importance to me. For instance, when our sons became ready for moral training and education, I would sometimes object to certain methods of upbringing, certain habits they were falling into, certain tendencies I saw arising, certain defects that would have been easy to put right, and at night, before going to sleep, we had long whispered discussions, filled with affection, in which I explained my discoveries to her, and she listened to me with an understanding air, a child-like support, which made me feel that I was opening her eyes to things she had not noticed, that we were perfectly in accord as to the pitfalls, the dan-ger of these things, and that she had the same ideal of perfection as I did as to what our children's character ought to be. And we would drop off to sleep in each other's arms with a sense of complete harmony (and I remain quite convinced that this sense of harmony was mutual); I am sure there was no hypocrisy on her part, that she was much too simple and honest by nature to hide an inner refusal from me behind a pose of seeming acquiescence; absolutely incapable of that "Keep on talking, little man, I'll just do as I please," which is the defense and secret evasion of so many women, who avoid head-on collisions the better to triumph under the guise of a feigned acceptance.

But three weeks or three months later, I would realize that my explana-tions had been totally ineffective, that nothing, absolutely nothing, had been changed in the direction I had advocated, that my advice had flowed over her like water over stones, and it was useless ever to hope it could be otherwise. She was impregnable. Time itself seemed to have renounced its malevolent powers over her: ten years went by without leaving the slightest discernible mark on her. Death alone . . .

It is not easy for me now to reenter that state of mind and to understand the kind of spell I was under when in the presence of the Saint-Gall family. A spell which is now only too clear, and which had irreparable consequences for my entire life.

It was, to a large extent, due to the fascination that this big family—

where everything seemed different and better than elsewhere—held for me, that I became smitten first with Laure, Blaise's twin sister, and then, a few years later, with the woman who was to become my wife and the mother of my two sons.

I shall have occasion to return later to an about-face in me so complete that it made the suffocating atmosphere of the Saint-Galls totally unbearable for me. An about-face which had consequences as serious in my private life, in my married life, and in my life as a father as the original attraction that had made me become so infatuated with the clan. I shall try to recover from my memory the date of the first symptoms of that detachment, which very quickly turned into a violent disaffection from all the members, including Blaise. The sole exception was Clairette, whom I continued to love deeply until her death, although my insuperable antipathy for her family (to which she remained closely connected, and with which, in the final analysis, she was never willing to break in order to follow me, except temporarily) had irrevocably strained the ties, strong though they were, which bound the two of us. It was, it seems to me, around the third year of our marriage, after the birth of Didier (1895) and before that of Alain (1898), therefore in the year '97, that my innate individualism suddenly regained the upper hand and made the hold that the Saint-Gall family continued to have over Clairette intolerable to me. Yes, I believe that what brought on this turnabout was the trip that I made to France in '97, after having lived alone for several months at my post in Batna, in Algeria. Clairette had not wanted to undergo the strains of a second pregnancy there, and still less to risk a second delivery far from home. She had not hesitated to leave me in order to go seek refuge with her mother, at the very heart of the clan.

When I came home on leave a few months before Alain's birth, everything that divided our two temperaments suddenly became terribly obvious to me. Probably because those few months of separation had allowed us to reassume our own personalities, I as a bachelor officer in an African garrison, she by returning to the fold and plunging back into her origins, putting herself once again under the collective tutelage of the clan—ecstatically, unrestrainedly, to satisfy a passionate, long-frustrated need.

I remember that soon after the arrival of little Alain, I found some excuse to cut short my leave, the sooner to escape that Saint-Gall ambiance which I had once so appreciated and which had overnight become absolutely foreign and insufferable to me. I went off to Batna by myself, in haste, with the feeling of a man who regains solid ground after having almost been sucked down into quicksand; like a bird which, without realizing it, has been caught in the birdlime of the trap, manages to break free, shakes its sticky feathers, and flies off into the open sky.

From that day on, it was over. The scales fell from my eyes once and for all. Not only did the charm of the clan, the sentimental well-being that the clan's warmth brought to its members, lose its seductive grip on me, but I came to detest it, and from then on I could see only the defects, the general blindness and vanity, the cheap and mediocre complacencies, the insufferable self-importance, the rigid enslavement under the family yoke. I saw the falseness of their peremptory assertions, beyond dispute for them but unacceptable to a broad-minded and thoughtful intellect. And, what was more serious, much more distressing, at the same time my eyes were opened to my wife's real character.

My recovered lucidity, which made me judge the clan without being deceived by appearances, suddenly revealed Clairette to me in her true light. I discovered her limitations, the narrow-minded stubbornness that hid itself beneath her sweetness and her childlike charm. I went on loving her, but while judging her. And my judgment was sufficiently severe that it was not very hard for me to drift away from her, to get along without her, to abandon her to the evil influence of her family ties, which nothing in the world—I now understood—could ever loosen, still less break. Although my love did not seem grievously stricken, I nevertheless ceased to have faith in her, to believe that our union could only bring us closer with time. I had already accepted, without suffering too much over it, that she was what she was: a Saint-Gall first and foremost, a Saint-Gall and nothing but, unable to find her balance at my side, separated from her loved ones, unable to live in any atmosphere other than that polluted, fusty, never-renewed air that they breathed in the clan, shut off from any other outlook on the world. I realized, when I saw her with her mother and brothers and sisters and their spouses and their children, that only among them could she bloom and be happy. And that I, her husband, the father of her children, could offer her only the trials of a kind of exile. I was an outsider.

At that point, our married life took on a new, looser form. We did not stop loving or respecting each other, but we no longer had much need to be together. We became like those marriages of so many seamen, the same as my father-in-law the admiral's marriage had been: the wife lives in Paris with her mother, and raises the children; the father is in Brest or Toulon, and most of the time is away on distant seas. The wife runs the household; she takes the initiatives. The father, from afar, seconds the decisions that have been taken. And when he comes home, he is a guest passing through, he is fêted when he arrives, a place is made for him while he is there, but he is soon allowed to leave again, without tears; the vacation is over, and with it a certain inconvenience; life resumes its course, lands on its feet, and there is an unconfessed relief.

Should I have given in so quickly, could I not have struggled a bit on the off chance, before abdicating? But the Saint-Gall air that I breathed in my own home, among my wife and my sons, was unpleasant for me and kept me from staying. I escaped from it with a sense of deliverance. I did not put up much of a fight because I too found advantages in that separation. Alone, far away, I led a life that was a bit too lonely and devoid of close affections, but free, and with plenty of time for my soldierly activities. And besides, what good would fighting have done? It would have poisoned our relations without any actual result. Thanks to my uncombative consent, we never had any real clashes. An affectionate and accommodating modus vivendi developed between us. We wrote each other long letters, and very frequently. We never loved each other so well as with the Mediterranean between us. The moment we were back together, any exchange became impossible or artificial. Our mutual tenderness fared well only in our correspondence.

I will have to try to be more precise, to see more clearly into this complex past. I still do not very well understand how it suddenly happened not only that this spell of the big family, which had bewitched me for ten years, ceased to act on me after three years of perfect married life, but also that, just then, the deep-seated individualism hidden in me rallied with such a vengeance, became irritated like a wound, and brought about such a strong repudiation. The reversal was, after all, quite abrupt. Just like that, unfairly, indiscriminately, I turned on my in-laws. Virtually from one day to the next, it became impossible for me to bear that togetherness in which until then I had found only charm, warmth, security, complicity. I had to flee from it at any cost, for fear of stifling. That general sharing of all that everybody thought and did had become hateful to me. Even if I thought as they did about a given subject, I refused to admit it and deliberately took the opposite side. Up until then I had gladly consented to follow their lead, to be "one of them." All of a sudden, I only saw intolerable sacrifices that were demanded of my nature, my character, my dignity, my independence. Until then, sentences like, "In our family, some things just aren't done," found me willing, effortlessly convinced in advance, and even happy to feel bolstered in my judgment by a collective verdict; calmer and more assured because I had voluntarily given my backing to the watchwords of the clan. And then I upped and rebelled, with all the vehemence of which I was capable. I actually broke off almost all relations with certain members of the clan who were simply too "Saint-Gall," like the Bousserons, like Blaise.

Did Clairette grasp this immediately? I mean, did she grasp the genuineness and irreversible nature of that opposition? No, certainly not right away. And I even wonder if, in her heart of hearts, she ever courageously faced reality. When it came to people's relations with her, she had a very sound psychological intuition and a great sensitivity. But she never gave this much serious thought. She had a tremendous talent for adapting to contradictions and for ignoring anything that could cause her to suffer. Very frank, she was at the same time quite elusive. I may be wrong in writing "very frank." She appeared frank because she was very simple and always very natural. But at bottom she tacked between reefs without seeming to see them, and without anyone knowing whether she saw them.

A strange temperament, exquisitely captivating, and yet disappointing. Never a reproach, never an outburst of anger, but, sometimes, in the case of hurt feelings, a sort of inner stiffening, and, beneath that sweetness, that affability, that natural cheeriness, that physical fragility, a sort of hardness which made her intractable. She always achieved her ends, without having asked for anything, without having admitted that she had a specific and ineradicable goal, and perhaps without knowing it herself. She forged ahead with an invisible strength, impossible to turn aside or block, like viburnum, like morning glories, those hardy plants that foil all obstacles.

Well before the decisive test of the Dreyfus Affair—which, in 1897, got me ostracized by the family for good and conclusively sealed the break—the disagreement, the imbalance between Clairette and me was an established fact. A de facto disagreement, almost imperceptible, and which we did not discuss. Simply this: she was a Saint-Gall far more than she was my wife. And from the day when I ceased to be a Saint-Gall, we were made of different stuff, like strangers (never was the well-known definition of marriage, "To bring a stranger into your home," more justified!).

You don't fight with a wall, you stop in front of it, your momentum runs out. We clashed little, and never violently. But all our natural reactions were conflicting. We noted the discrepancy, we silently stuck to our positions, and life went on with its demanding little details. Any merging had become impossible. I had dreamed of making her mine; I gave up. That's all there was to it. A Spaniard who has married a Norwegian woman must have some idea of what I experienced. It doesn't alter love, but it makes any real communion impossible.

We still had some luck, in that adversity. We might have turned married life into a hell. In the end, however, things sorted themselves out after a fashion. There was equilibrium, on another plane than the one I had hoped for. Helped along by circumstances: by my military life abroad, in which I found great satisfaction; by a certain aptitude for indifference, as well. I suffered from that estrangement but did not dramatically carry it like a cross. Nor did she. In our adversity we both had the good fortune to have characters capable of putting up with what would have been a misery for others.

I CAME TO LOATHE "big families" because I lived for thirty years in the shadow of one—ten years of bewitchment, twenty of hostility.

But today, when I have gradually broken almost all contact for what will soon be another twenty years, since the death of my sons in the war, I am reconsidering the question with a calm heart, with a more equitable eye.

Big families are annoying to their neighbors and repellent to individual-ists of my stripe who find themselves caught in their spider's web. But, as Le Dantec* says, "Let us not be blinded by the personal . . ."

For those who belong to such a family and are used to that slavery, one has to grant that it is an institution which offers them many advantages, and which is, after all, a justifiable form of happiness for the run of humanity . . .

In that huge and prolific Saint-Gall tribe, I really knew only relatively contented people—myself excepted—whose daily happiness was very largely drawn from the joys of family life.

Within such a clan, the children grow up in a warm crowdedness, which is healthy, probably healthier and undeniably jollier than in a smaller family. Their characters develop in a little circle of young folk, of peers, where the usual rough patches get smoothed over, where one undergoes a helpful apprenticeship for life in the world through reciprocal aid, good cheer, con-ciliation, tolerance, sharing. They do not acquire a proprietary sense; they do not become selfish or even self-absorbed. Their innate sensitivities blossom freely amid the general affection and friendship. They have the pleasure of being spared clashes, of living among people who have the same upbringing, the same ideas, the same tastes as they do. They are not tempted to rebel. They are proud of their group, they have that patriotic satisfaction of belong-ing to a tribe, preferring it to all others and deeming it better, indeed the only perfect one. Obviously, they all turn out alike, and humanity does not gain much from this mass production in which the difference of characters gets worn down very quickly with friction. In those ranks, it is rare for an origi-nal, creative, exceptional nature to emerge. The mark of the single mold is almost always stronger than attempts at particularity and independence. I realize that a born genius breaks all molds. But born geniuses are few and far between. Less so are original natures, whose role in society is quite important all the same and whose infinite variety makes for the worth and richness of a people and of mankind. Those natures do not thrive in beehives or termite mounds, or seldom in the disciplined regimen, the easy happiness of big families. The price paid for this happiness is the stunting of anyone with even a slightly distinctive character.

That cheerful atmosphere is also a plus for the adults. In the Saint-Gall tribe I did not come across those tormented and dramatic existences, those hatreds between close relations, those sharp disagreements between spouses which are not infrequent in the world. And I attribute that ease in human interactions largely to the healthy ambiance of the big family, to the peaceful

*Félix Le Dantec (1869–1917), French biologist.

setting that it creates, to the many distractions it affords, to the activities it produces and imposes, which deny the various members the leisure to turn inward and become poisoned with the toxins often secreted by solitude in smaller families. Not all couples belonging to large families necessarily have excellent marriages, but on the average they are rather good. In any case, differences of opinion develop less dangerously and are counteracted by those shared feelings consisting of family affections, pride in belonging to a privileged breed, limits to independence laid down by family rules, and the supervision created by the communal life of clans. In such a situation, a man is less likely to yield to the temptations of an affair. To everything that would restrain him to begin with is added the fear of being deprecated by his kinfolk. He also feels more bound by the moral laws that are honored by the group and that he has adopted as his own; he will not risk, as much as an isolated individual would, rushing into a cheap adventure. He has got used to not acting on his own initiative; he does not make decisions without consulting the family, and is vulnerable to their advice. Temptations of every sort have less of a hold on him; he is protected by the communal life of the group; he cannot do without the support of his relations; he needs their consent, their encouragement, in order to do anything; and he quite naturally finds in them a secret power that controls him and prevents him from making a false step.

The women, for their part, housewives, very involved with their children as well as with the collective life of the women of the tribe, have far fewer opportunities than other women to go astray. Even more than the men, they have developed a vital need for the approbation and respect of their family. Even more easily than their male counterparts, they submit to the accepted rules and are careful not to stumble. They have no truck with that evil counselor which idleness and frivolity can be. They feel a great pleasure in remaining within the established order. They do not listen to their every desire. Their existence as mothers is a life of duties, joyously accepted, the accomplishment of which forms part of their happiness, their equilibrium, their inner peace. They also benefit from the good dispositions that children of big families generally possess. Harmony reigns. The children are not recalcitrant, and the relations between children and parents hardly ever present those serious difficulties which cause so many knotty problems in smaller families. And then, parents who have four or five children do not make those tyrannical demands so frequent in families with an only child. They do not stake everything on one alone; they do not try to make each one into an exceptional being; it happens less often than elsewhere that a child is different from them, or bewildering, or disappointing, but if any of these things do occur, the parents do not get worked up or take the matter personally.

Rather, they accept more easily that the child is not what they had dreamed he would be. They do not turn this into a tragedy, but instead make up for it with the others, and as a result the relations of the parents with the children are not spoiled.

In big families, I observe above all that the parents grow old in a happier atmosphere. They have enough children to be surrounded by them without its being a burden for the offspring. In their turn, they benefit from the familial respect they bore their own parents, the departed heads of the family, whose place they quite naturally assume. In this they find great rewards of self-esteem and affection at an age when other kinds of satisfaction are becoming scarce. They can congratulate themselves on their progeny and see the proliferation of grandchildren who will carry on the spirit and traditions to which they have devoted their lives. These parents enjoy the sense of having accomplished a human mission, of having left something behind them; they are aware of continuing on in their children: old age and the approach of death are thus less bitter to them. Until the end of their days, they are spared that final trial of so many old people, loneliness. Solitude and idleness. For in big families, the old do not know the inactivity that gnaws at so many of the elderly. There is always something to do to help the children, a thousand chances to be useful, to receive, to give, to please this new tribe that has been born of their blood and perpetuates them.

I compare the solitary end of my own life to that of Blaise before his death five years ago. The very year he died, he saw the fourth or fifth of his grandchildren married, and he presided over a family dinner—a true banquet, for which a private room at a restaurant had to be hired—and where there were seventy guests, of which forty-six were Saint-Galls! . . . And not a single cousin could be invited: those forty-six Saint-Galls were all children, grandchildren, nephews or nieces, nothing but close relations!

A big family!

As for me, I am dying without perpetuation. My two sons are dead. My sister died childless. I carry the last drops of the Maumort blood in my old veins. Soon I shall take to my grave the last trace of the Maumorts on this earth where for four centuries or more their progress could be followed, I shall take with me everything I know of my kin, everything I know of myself, all my memories, all my experiences. Nothing will remain of the Maumorts.

These recollections? . . .

CHAPTER XIX

The Marriage of Henriette

[Translators' note: According to André Daspre, "Henriette is a character that Martin du Gard studied closely; this feminine figure would certainly have occupied one of the most important places next to Maumort. It may be supposed that the novelist would have examined the relationship between the brother and sister as he did that of the two Thibault brothers . . ."
M. Daspre goes on to describe the varied contents of the thick folder on Henriette, which included a number of notes, drafts, and sketches. From these he extracted two episodes, the description of Henriette's marriage and that of her adoption of the orphan girl Emma, making a chapter out of each. He inserted at the beginning of the present chapter a brief passage that Martin du Gard had considered placing after a chapter on early childhood.]

TODAY I WAS intending to go on with the account of my early childhood, recalling at leisure our late afternoons in the study room around an opaline oil lamp which was shaded with a globe and which you adjusted with the aid of a key—an operation that Henriette and I may have repeated more often than necessary, since it was always accompanied by a hilarious succession of gurgles, finishing with a loud belch, the impatiently awaited incongruousness of which never failed to send us into a state of jubilation; then the glum evening meal, where my father's silence weighed on us like an unmerited disaffection and seemed to render the dim light of the large dining room even more opaque; then the escape, after a distracted kiss on the hair, and the climbing of the stairs on all fours, and the scramble down the interminable corridor filled with a familiar darkness; and the undressing in front of the fire, and my sister's laughter and cuddles; and that mysterious moment that preceded sleep, when, buried under the Turkey red eiderdown, I watched the moving shadows projected on the ceiling by the last fluttering of the flames. I called them "the bats," and, while knowing perfectly well that they were only shadows, I was afraid of those nocturnal flocks, and played with my fear as I nestled under the covers . . .

*

I would like to go into some detail about the very strong, very special feelings that bound Henriette and me. They derived from a deep-seated communion that the relation of brother and sister alone cannot explain. Neither affection nor the interlocking of our lives would have sufficed to give rise to and so enduringly maintain that perfect harmony between two persons whose natures, characters, affinities, and tastes were in many ways disparate. Two saplings sprouting from the same stock can thus vary in details; they nonetheless have the same roots, which take their sustenance from a single soil, and it is one sap which rises in their stems and makes their foliage spread in distinct ways. The bonds that our secret and essential alikeness created between us were infinitely more powerful than all our differences in temperament. We understood each other intuitively, profoundly, before words, before explanations; we were open books to each other; a word, a facial expression, a pause, a look, revealed to us the other's intentions, the slightest fluctuations of the other's feelings or thoughts. No misunderstanding could find its way into our relations. We understood each other better than one often understands oneself. Naturally, we did not always agree. But in each of us, nothing surprised the other for more than a few seconds: the time it took to perceive, to grasp and, usually, to concur.

I think of my wife, of the few intimate friends I have had. No comparison. Neither love nor friendship ever manages to eliminate the basic and impermeable uniqueness that sets two people apart. As close as one imagines two parallels to be, there remains a space between them, mathematically and by definition irreducible. Between my sister and me this duality, this parallelism of nature, practically did not exist. A miracle of consanguinity! Which inevitably renewed itself with each contact, and filled us both with a feeling of complete security, in a serene, wholesome climate that no outer circumstance, no element of passion, no turbulence of our secret beings, ever succeeded in changing.

Still, in the course of our lives, events caused us to subject this wonderful harmony to perilous experiences. I will cite only one example. In 1898, at the moment when the Dreyfus Affair upset my career, when I left the army to take a two years' leave (which I was then planning to make final with my resignation), I did not hesitate—as I found it impossible to resume living with my wife and sons—to move back into le Saillant, with Henriette. It was risky. On that estate, from which she was never gone for more than two weeks, even at the time of her marriage, and which she had managed by herself after Father's death, in that house which she had remodeled to her taste and which she had every right to regard as her own (for I had never claimed my title as co-owner), the unforeseen cohabitation of that authoritarian, active, capable widow of thirty-seven and that heretical officer, who was no less independent-minded than she, could have brought into play a thousand points of friction and chances for conflict. (All the more so since I had resolved to take on the running of the estate with her and to experiment with certain reforms.) Whereas not only was there never the slightest disagreement between us, but those two years of daily closeness, of collaboration, of shared responsibility, so strengthened our bonds and made us so necessary to each other that separation was equally agonizing for both of us. As for me, it so grieved me to part from my sister that at the last moment I nearly backed out of putting the uniform on again. Higher and more pressing reasons than our personal inclinations were needed to decide me, and I can truly say that it was a sacrifice, performed out of duty. Up until Henriette's death, our dearest dream was one day to resume our sibling partnership. We mentioned it frequently in our letters; and if, during the terrible winter of 1917, that fatal pneumonia had not carried her off before her time, at fifty-six, in the prime of life, there is no doubt that after the war I would have returned to le Saillant and that we would have ended our days side by side, in a serene old age that would have been the crowning glory of our exceptional intimacy.

For me, Henriette's marriage remains surrounded by question marks.

It is a matter which I was never able to clear up to my satisfaction for any number of reasons, and in spite of the great frankness that prevailed between us. First of all, circumstances did not allow of an explanation:

1. Because I had been sent to southern Algeria shortly after my father's death and had spent nearly three years there with no leaves, and it was during this period that my sister got married.

2. Because I did not come to France until my promotion to captain in '97, for a short leave, and when I was reunited with my sister she had been a widow for several months. And her mourning made it hard to have a heart-to-heart discussion with her, to reexamine the strange choice she had made. Not only her mourning, but also the bitter grief that she suffered from her baby's death and from remaining a childless widow.

That is not all.

This question of Henriette's marriage was always a delicate subject between us. I learned of it through a letter of hers. A brisk, firm letter which did not seek my opinion. And for good reason. She knew perfectly well what I would think of her choice. For years we had made fun of the Pontbrun family and of poor Adolphe. She could not have forgotten this. Besides, I had a sort of instinctive hostility, of which she could not have been unaware, against marriage in general and against marriage for a woman like Henriette in particular. Which I don't even understand very clearly myself. Jealousy before the fact? Repugnance at seeing another man enter my sister's private world and take a place which, until then, I alone had occupied?

Her letters at the time of her engagement were short and colorless; I knew her well enough to read between the lines: "I am acting as I believe I must. I have my reasons. I realize that you do not approve. But my mind is made up. It is useless for us to cross swords about this." I responded in kind, evasively "delighting" in the knowledge that she was happy.

A little later, in '98, when I temporarily left the army and came to live with her at le Saillant for two years, a number of references to her marriage were made during our endless evenings of talk, and I saw a bit more clearly into the matter. But not much. The child's death, which remained an open wound, was mixed up for her with her husband's death, and threw over that whole period of her life a sorrowful veil which made any mention of it painful and brief. With the result that we both steered clear of that difficult subject. But I sensed a lot of things all the same, and here is how I think I can explain that marriage to myself.

The Pontbrun family, who lived in the little Pontbrun manor house, two kilometers from Menneville, on a path through the fields that led to the main road to Le Mans, was a very old family of the region, and remained one of the most highly regarded, even though for half a century a succession of misfortunes and follies had completely ruined the old estate, which was reduced to an ancient turreted hovel, cracked all over, and mortgaged. The Pontbrun I knew, who was my father's contemporary, lived there, a widower with an old pair of servants and a sickly son who was twelve years older than I. The four of them could be seen on Sundays at High Mass, at which they had the privilege of occupying the chapel in the north transept, while we occupied the one in the south transept. We would greet each other. They no longer kept up with anyone. Mlle. Fromentot spoke of them with a respect tinged with pity, but her mockery did not spare them.

Their adversity, their well-known penury, did not prevent them from being the laughingstock of the countryside. Not out of malice. People felt sorry for them but made fun of their poverty because the Pontbruns took pains to hide it beneath lofty airs. They had kept a carriage; they came to Mass in this broken-down old landau, the sort of coach that belongs to a poor bishopric, dragged by a caricature of a nag, and driven by the gardener, who wore a coachman's reddish beaver, and, in all seasons, a great-coat with several collars. Their entrance into the church—single file, with the Count in front, tall, stooping, bearded, in his threadbare frock coat, followed by his beanpole of a son, as tall, as stooping, and already as bearded as his father, then his "staff," the gardener and his wife, who carried the coats and the missals—was, though people were accustomed to it, a weekly source of mirth; smiling, sidelong glances followed them until they had taken their seats and crossed themselves.

Sometimes we rode along the path that bordered the wall of their garden, and we saw the cracked turrets, the ruined roof, the attic windows missing their panes, the faded and timeworn shutters, many of which were held on by nothing but a rusty hinge and hung miserably down the crumbling wall. Never did we glimpse a sign of life in the mansion. The Pontbruns lived there devoid of means, subsisting on the eggs laid by ten or so hens and the vegetables from the garden.

However, I do remember that once, with my father, I stepped through the always half-open gate which clumps of nettles would not allow to close, and entered the grassy courtyard.

The old Count, probably to alleviate his shortage of funds a bit, had gradually built up an apiary, and in the fall had his maid sell the honey at market. My father, who wished to put in a few hives at le Saillant, went to ask if he could see M. de Pontbrun's setup, and, if possible, buy a hive and a swarm from him. I was only ten or eleven, but I have forgotten nothing of that bizarre visit, neither the thin, vicious dog that greeted us at the end of his chain with ferocious barks and leaps, nor the vast sepulchral room which the maid ended up ushering us into and which must have been the drawing room. There we waited for what seemed to me an interminable time. From the ancient paneling issued a musty odor of mildew that caught in our throats, even when the old woman had opened the six windows and pushed out all the shutters, at the risk of seeing them tumble into the courtyard.

My father, who rarely smiled, pointed out to me, with amused but somewhat indignant surprise (for he loved order), a barrel, a chicken crate, some lintels and a punctured clothes boiler that sat in the middle of the room on the old inlaid parquet. Along the walls was lined up a good deal of antique furniture, which must have once been beautiful and which was damaged and dusty for want of care; also portraits and engravings, their glass covered with fly specks. At the windows hung splendid but completely faded curtains.

Finally, the Count appeared. Had he been tidying himself up all this time? He seemed to me old, dirty, almost in rags, with the look of a tramp. But, as Sainte-Beuve says somewhere about someone, in regard to the first sentence that came out of his mouth, "you sensed a man with a venerable name." He apologized very courteously for having kept us waiting, and with ceremonious and easy manners bade us sit down. Then his son entered in his turn. He looked like a marionette, in his clothes that were too large. Hand-me-downs from his father, perhaps? He was assigned the task of entertaining me while our fathers conferred, and he took me to visit his "livestock." I can still see myself, led by this tall ghost who may have been twenty-two or twenty-three, walking down a flagstone corridor where onions were drying on racks, crossing a saddle room with cherry panelling of a beautiful red orange, where the stands and pegs were entirely stripped of their harnesses, to come out in a sort of pen surrounded by a wire fence and divided into separate birdcages where Adolphe was engaged in the rearing of a few pairs of purebred animals—Barbary ducks, fantail pigeons, and angora rabbits— whose names and zoological particularities he ticked off for me in the most affable way.

Other than at Mass, it was the only time I saw him up close. All in all, I remembered that poor lad rather fondly. Probably I was grateful to him for not treating me like a child and for speaking to me seriously about things that seemed to interest him a lot, and which, hearing him, I wanted to be interested in too. I recall distinctly that he had a signet ring on his finger, which made me notice that his hands were emaciated and that his nails were worn down by labor like the peasants'. He was dressed like his father, and I now suppose that those clothes must have been cut from the handsome Elbeuf-cloth frock coats left by the previous generation. A black cloth that time may give a green or a red tinge to, or wear thin, but whose weave is indestructible.

And he wore one of those neckties that attach with an elastic and whose visible part consists of material backed with cardboard.

He had a strange thinness about him. I remember protruding ears that I could not help looking at, and hollows in the neck below the ears, and that neck itself, in which bobbed an acrobatic Adam's apple, a neck so long it formed a kind of handle on which the skull was fixed, like one of those long brooms for cobwebs that are called *"têtes-de-loup."** His ugliness was certainly remarkable, but not without a certain distinction. He did not at all intimidate me, despite the difference in age. He had a kind look in his eyes, simple and direct, a guileless smile. "I found him very nice," I told my father as we left. "But what a house! It's like Sleeping Beauty's Castle." At table, my father repeated the remark to my sister and Mlle. Fromentot, and from that day on, Mademoiselle never spoke of Adolphe de Pontbrun without calling him the Viscount of Sleeping Beauty's Castle.

These are the childhood memories awakened in me by the famous letter in which Henriette announced as seriously as could be, and even with a certain tone of solemnity, a sort of insistence, in a paragraph whose words seemed carefully chosen, between two blank spaces, that the priest of Menneville had, several weeks earlier, brought Adolphe de Pontbrun on a visit, that she had found him very likable, simple, with perfect breeding, and that she had been so happy talking to him about animal husbandry and farmyard matters that they had become the best of friends, and that the

*Literally, wolf's-heads.

young man had several times had occasion to come back to see her. These visits, she said, very pleasantly broke up the monotony of the winter's solitude. There followed a long digression about the unusual rigors of the winter that year, and the damage that had resulted on the farms.

Five months later, she informed me of her engagement.

I am willing to believe that the fiancé no longer completely resembled that Viscount of Sleeping Beauty's Castle whom I remembered from my childhood and whom I have indulgently allowed myself to caricature a little. The fact remains that this choice was incomprehensible for a hardy, refined, demanding person such as Henriette.

Adolphe had virtually never set foot outside Pontbrun. An attempt to put him in the little seminary of Mortagne, when he was around fourteen, had been deleterious to his fragile health. He had not been able to withstand the boarding-school regimen for more than three or four months. He might as well have never received any formal education. A former elementary-school teacher from the département, in retirement a few hundred meters from Pontbrun, on the road to Le Mans, had taught him as a child to read, write, and count. And he knew how to serve Mass. That was all. The background of a little country shepherd who has never finished his basic schooling. I do not say that he was stupid. He loved the things of the earth, had always lived in the fields, knew much about cattle, and would have ridden decently enough if he had had the means to keep a saddle horse and if his health had allowed him to risk the least fatigue, the slightest chill. But he was not at all cultivated, and, I am almost certain, had no world view, no view about anything. Colorless.

After his father's death, he had remained at Pontbrun without changing anything in his life apart from having resolutely expanded his breeding of animals and his apiary, and openly making a business of it, going so far as to shamelessly place advertisements for the "Pontbrun Breeding Center" in the rural newspapers, which his poor bashful aristocrat of a father would never have lowered himself to doing and by which he proved himself more intelligent than his elder.

At the time when the priest from Menneville introduced him to my sister, Adolphe was thirty-seven, three years older than Henriette. Of course, I always thought the Abbé Marion had some hand in that match. But to accuse him of being the instigator and the author of that marriage would be absurd. My sister was not someone to be married off; and however great her faith may have been, whatever heed she may have paid the priest's advice, she was incapable of being influenced on a subject so personal and serious.

No, it was independently and of her own free will that she dreamed up that unlikely union, and, being who she was, it was she alone who was responsible for it.

The mystery remains all the more impenetrable, and for me all the more puzzling.

MY FATHER, who had suffered for years from a bladder disease and had become almost an invalid, was forced to undergo a very serious operation in Le Mans during the winter of '94, from the consequences of which he died, without having returned to le Saillant. It was a bit later, in the spring, that Henriette got married.

What had happened with her during those few months?

I was, as I have said, extremely busy at that time in southern Algeria. But we exchanged long and frequent letters.

From my *bled*,* I had the impression that after those last, very painful years at the side of my ailing father, Henriette had felt a certain relief at settling into a solitary life at le Saillant. An impression that I formed from a distance, and that perhaps did not jibe as closely with reality as I believed. Yet my sister's letters exuded tranquillity, harmony, and activity. Although sick, my father had remained authoritarian until the end. Neither being able to issue all his orders himself nor to oversee the farm work in person, and annoyed at being kept from doing so, he appointed Henriette to replace him without leaving her the slightest freedom of action, and all in all, during the four years of his illness, the running of the estate increasingly suffered. My sister complained about it more and more in her letters. And so her first concern, as soon as she was on her own, was to energetically take back control over everything. In particular, certain changes in personnel had to be made. In this respect, she was a powerful woman, capable, shrewd, with a talent for command. We had naturally decided to continue our joint ownership of the estate, and for the first few months she made no decisions without wanting to consult me, which, given the distance and the time it took for letters to travel, often presented major drawbacks. I kept on replying that I trusted her completely, that I considered her the absolute head of the estate, that I would put my signature sight unseen to the important alterations that she was planning—purchase of properties jutting into our own, transformation of fields into pasture, acquisition of forty boggy hectares called the *bas-fonds*, which she was convinced she could drain by a method that was fairly new at that time. In short, all those big plans, and the heart she put into them, seemed to indicate that she had organized her life, as I had always thought she would, around taking charge of that land that was hers, that she adored, that she had never wished to leave.

*Term borrowed by the French from the Arabs of North Africa to denote the back country there, or alternatively, a rolling plain or other open stretch of land.

How to imagine that she could be considering marriage? Maybe I was naïve; but I not only thought her capable of leading a happy life without creating a family but also incapable of finding fulfillment as a wife. I did not see her as a born "old maid" but rather as an Amazon . . . She was in large part responsible for my way of thinking. I had never heard her speak of marriage except to rule out the possibility for herself with an unequivocal smile, a genuine firmness, a sincerity that was not open to doubt. And this for as long as I could remember, I mean at least ever since she had been able to speak freely with me about it. One day, in front of me, she told Aunt Ma something which Aunt Ma often quoted to me later, for it struck her as quite strange and she was never quite able to accept it. Henriette had said, with great conviction: "*To give one's hand, to share one's life* with someone? But, Aunt, all those words fill me with horror! My life belongs to me, I wouldn't give it up for anything . . . *To share* one's life, the very idea of such a *sharing* makes me shudder . . ."

Another time, on a summer's evening, when we were both up late on one of those breathtakingly pure starry nights which truly could not be enjoyed anywhere better than on that large bare terrace where so much of the sky could be seen overhead, we were talking about some English novel that she had just read (I think it was Wells's *The Passionate Friends*), and she said something like this to me: "You see, love in this world can only be a sham. For people of a certain quality, I mean. First, because it's not possible ever to be loved as much as we would like to be. And then because we are not able to love anyone as much as we would like."

Love "in this world." An important distinction. For what led me to so easily accept a life for my sister without earthly passion as something almost natural was her faith. I was convinced that she had placed her love elsewhere than "in this world" and that this mystical fervor, which filled her completely, protected her from all human experience and fully satisfied her.

On the other hand, I myself had such an instinctive aversion to marriage that there was nothing in my sister's attitude regarding this issue that could take me aback. In this, I was not like Aunt Ma.

And yet, Henriette got married. And she consented of her own free will—with no apparent necessity, without yielding, it seems, to any outside pressure—to the most unexpected, the most mediocre of unions.

I HAVE OFTEN sincerely sought to understand what could have militated in Adolphe's favor. I try to imagine, on the day when my sister considered the possibility of that marriage, what seemed to her to be its "good points." What arguments could she have made to convince herself?

First, probably, that it was not a misalliance. That a Maumort could become a Pontbrun. Those things counted for my sister and me. *Aristo.*

Then that Adolphe was a good believer. I think that this point may have worked in his favor. And yet, I also think that my sister was sufficiently intelligent that, in other circumstances, she might have married an intelligent heathen like me. For she always accepted my lack of faith. We had only one discussion on that subject, during the vacation that preceded my entering Saint-Cyr. I did not in any way hide from her my new views. She seemed more saddened than surprised by them, but I did not feel I had caused her real sorrow. She deeply respected the independence of others. She only said to me: "Will you tell Father?"

"No," I replied. "What for? I'll make every concession necessary so that he never suspects a thing." She seemed reassured. Never again did we tackle the religious question head-on. Until my father's death, each time I was on vacation at le Saillant, I went with Henriette to High Mass in Menneville, as in the past. After his death, I stopped doing so, and she seemed to find all that natural.

Poor Adolphe was puny, weak. I am sure that this also redounded to his credit and contributed to Henriette's determination. Her affection for him found its strongest support, I think, in that pitying, and perhaps maternal, emotion. In fact, from what I gathered of their existence, she spent two years of married life nursing him, and, at the very least, preserving him from any fatigue.

She also appreciated his being a gentleman farmer and a native of the Perche, as she herself was a farmer and a *Percheronne.* Moreover, in the letters where she spoke to me of her coming marriage, the agricultural skills of her future husband were often mentioned, and the aid he would give her in managing le Saillant. Actually, he understood nothing about running an estate. His competence stopped at bird-breeding, beekeeping, and the rearing of certain types of rabbits. He brought his "livestock" with him when he moved into le Saillant, and in the farmyard we still have a few degenerate descendants of his fantails and his Barbary ducks.

To all these logical reasons must be added another, less plausible one, the influence of the Menneville priest, the Abbé Marion—who would not have been attempting this for the first time, since his nickname around town, and with no pejorative connotation, really, was the Abbé *marieur.** He was indeed a matchmaker. Yet another reason might have been a certain weariness on my sister's part with her solitary life. But I don't really think so. First because Henriette liked solitude and because that solitude, put to very active

---

*"The Matchmaking Abbé." (*Abbé marieur* is a play on Abbé Marion.)

use—and doubly so, through the running of the property on the temporal plane and through her very absorbing religious fervor on the spiritual—left no chink through which boredom might enter. I was more willing to consider her possible desire to have children, even if it seemed a rather far-fetched explanation for a marriage which, in precisely this respect, offered such little hope. I would not hesitate to place this reason high among the most decisive factors if my sister, who was versed in animal breeding and knew the virtues of good stock, had, in order to start a family, chosen a strapping stud.

But I'll be damned if that was the case. Later events proved this. It was not only because their little girl was born two or three weeks prematurely that she died, since she lived for nearly two months. It was because she was weakened by rickets, like her father, and it is very fortunate for all of us that she was not able to survive: the doctors did not conceal the fact that her lower limbs would never have developed normally and that she would always have been a cripple.

To me, none of this explains that absurd marriage in a satisfactory way.

I have always had an idea in the back of my mind about the subject. But I have repressed it because it is not without a certain self-conceit . . . I have wondered if there was not, at the source of that mad decision, a gesture of pique stemming from a disappointment for which I might have been personally responsible.

My sister and I were attached as brother and sister seldom are. So much so that I sometimes said to myself that if it had not been for the affection, the companionship, the friendship, the tenderness, the close connection with Henriette, I might have been led, like anyone else, to someday consider marriage from a less severe and unfavorable angle. Well, what may have been true for me might have been all the more true for Henriette. I had my freedom as a man, my career, my adventures, countless diversions. She had only her life at le Saillant, and me. Is it conceit to think that, as things stood, I held in her Nordic virgin's life a place that was greater, even more special—more *romantic*—than she held in my life of an explorer and adventurer?

I have several reasons—vague, to be quite honest, and more intuitive than based on precise facts—for believing that after my father's death Henriette hoped that I was going to leave the army and return home to live with her. It was a dream that we had cherished long before, when I was still an adolescent. Then I went to Paris and joined the army, and if my childhood dream still survived, it was for much later, as a plan for my retirement, for the end of my life.

But Henriette? In all likelihood, this dream had stayed much brighter in her mind, had sunk much hardier roots. When my father died and she saw le Saillant without a master, it is not impossible that she thought: "The moment has come. He's going to return. And our beautiful life together will become a reality."

I must say that she never wrote me this. I cannot even say that she wrote me anything of the sort, in a formal way. But I base my assertion on two things.

First, the way in which she described her dismay to me as she faced the enormous task that fell to her lot of restoring the estate disrupted by my father's long illness, the problem this posed for a single woman, how much she missed my advice, how unfortunate it was that I could not visit for at least a few days and work out with her what needed to be done. At the time, I attributed all this to her recent loss and to her modesty. But upon reflection, it is very unlike the woman she was, determined, competent, active, never frightened by the most unpleasant chores, but on the contrary, finding in them a sort of intoxication, exaltation, and a source of energy. It was only afterwards, long afterwards, that a doubt occurred to me. Likewise her insistence, when it was quite obvious that I could not take a leave, on consulting me as to all the details of her initiatives, as if to prevent me from relying on her, as if to force me to consider them along with her, to have an opinion, to get involved, to do my part in the management. An attitude that only lasted a while, given the reluctance of my answers, and that had long since ceased when the matter of her engagement arose.

The second thing that aroused this suspicion in me is what happened several years after her widowhood, when I handed in my pseudo-resignation and announced my intention of moving in with her. There was an explosion of joy from her out of all proportion to the circumstances. I recall that I was, not wounded certainly—for that sisterly joy touched me too deeply, and flattered me as well—but somewhat shocked all the same, since for me it was the continuation of a distressing drama of conscience, the sequel to long and painful hesitations that had led me to upset my life, abandon my career, renounce all my great dreams for the future. I renounced, and she exulted. And in that rejoicing there was—it seems to me, upon reflection—something like a feeling of redress . . . "Finally, I'm going to have him to myself." It was, admittedly, quite natural.

But all this gradually fed my suspicion that Henriette's marriage had perhaps been, at heart, an act, I don't say of despair—but I repeat, for want of anything better, the words I have already written—of disappointment, and perhaps of pique.

Pique is a feeling with which I was somewhat acquainted at that time. The thought that that imbecile Pontbrun was moving in as master of le Saillant was, I admit, thoroughly displeasing to me. Of course, I never allowed her to see this. On the contrary, I declined every offer my sister made to let me withdraw from the partnership and sell her my share of our father's bequest. "What for?" I wrote her. "What has changed? What you did by yourself was fine. What you and your husband do together will also be. I agree to all your wishes in advance." And, hypocrite that I was, I in turn obligingly insisted on my brother-in-law's abilities and the godsend that his directives would be for the estate.

I very well remember the tremendous joy that came over me when I learned of his death. I took it as a gesture of courteousness, of tact. His presence in the family had poisoned my thoughts, but when you came right down to it, he really hadn't overstayed his welcome, and he withdrew like a perfect gentleman!

WHAT THOSE TWO YEARS of married life were like for my sister, I never really knew.

When I saw her again, Adolphe had been dead for two years, I was moving in in his place, perhaps forever, my sister was overjoyed at welcoming me, and our life together resumed immediately as if nothing had ever happened. My sister seemed to me more of a Nordic virgin than ever, in spite of her widowhood and her ill-fated pregnancy. Neither physically nor morally did she appear changed to me. At least she seemed no more changed than could be expected after those six years of separation, during which we had both matured. And I erased from my mind the unpleasant thought of that marriage, which, fortunately, had left no trace. I liked to think that Henriette had agreed to it out of an inexplicable lapse from who and what she was, that the marriage had not been a love affair.

Well, I was curiously, absurdly wrong. Henriette was deeply changed. She had loved with all her soul, with all her body, and the miracle had come to pass: she seemed the same, she was another woman.

How queer life is! I proved to be quite blind and quite naïve. I lived with her for weeks before suspecting those profound changes and for months before being sure and admitting them.

I only wanted to see the continuity in her attitudes and behavior, which remained roughly the same as before; but under that chaste reserve which deceived me there now burned a hidden flame I did not at first perceive. Not a consuming flame: a flame that gave light. Love, the quicksilver of passion, had coursed in her veins, and her whole being had been altered by it, forever enriched.

She had finally had her share, her full share of life.

She had known the great secret, attained the dazzling mystery which alone reveals us to ourselves; and without that fundamental shock, we remain always incomplete, unfinished, the odd one out.

It did not matter that fate used a dull descendant of the Pontbruns to strike the spark, bring about the marvel. It did not matter that he was so frail, so ungainly. For Henriette he was *the other*, the seducer, the sacred initiator. He had loved her. He had offered his whole self and she had surrendered herself completely. Together they had plunged into the eternal fountainhead. Together they had discovered not only love's embrace, but love's communion.

How could she not have been transformed by this? How could I have believed for so long that nothing in her was changed? Everything in her had experienced the magical touch. Body and soul were expanded, softened, opened up by it. And she was unconsciously aware of this. She felt no pride in it. But a sort of self-esteem, perhaps; in any case, a sense of newfound dignity. It was as if a calm strength, established for good, now inhabited her.

Henriette did not speak much about her "love," but, in spite of her extreme constraint and reticence, enough so that I can state that she did not escape the common rule and that it gave her great satisfaction to think that her love had been something absolutely *unique*, an unprecedented experience, of which no one could guess the intensity, the high-mindedness, the nobility, the blinding brightness, the fiery heat, etc. She did not see Adolphe as he had been. Thinking of him, it was of love that she thought; she remembered only his good and tender heart, his touching fragility, the way he had given himself completely, his unbounded love.

She virtually never spoke of him. One day, though, this surprising expression slipped out of her: "He understood me so well!" I was struck by it. "She sincerely believes it," I thought at first. Then I understood that she was probably right in believing it, and that it must have been true.

Ah, of all the enigmas that are presented to us each day, that of the human being is truly the most fascinating, if the most insoluble . . . I had taken leave of a young girl, I came back to find a woman. I had left the freshness of spring, its hesitant budding, its hazy promises. I had come back to find the steady warmth and refulgence of a summer laden with fruits. Our harmony, which had seemed to me, at the time of our youth, a rare and accomplished thing, only became truly perfect, I have since realized, after my return to le Saillant, after Henriette's encounter with love.

She seemed to be coming home from faraway adventures, and it was I, the traveler, the man of the desert, the man who had lived at the border of two worlds, on the threshold of another civilization, who sometimes listened to her with surprise and gazed at her in silence as if she had acquired the last word in wisdom and I could learn it from her.

I HAVE ALREADY mentioned that there was no real closeness between my sister and Aunt Ma. Henriette had announced her wedding to the

Chambost-Lévadés in a way that precluded any invitation to attend it. Probably, if Adolphe had lived, the Chambosts, during some holiday that coincided with my being home on leave, would have had an opportunity to return to le Saillant. But this opportunity did not arise during the two years the marriage lasted, and neither one side nor the other did anything to bring it about. I understand Henriette quite well. She did not wish to expose her husband to the facile irony of an intellectual like Uncle Éric; although he was not completely incapable, much less his wife, of appreciating certain luster-less virtues in the new spouse. Furthermore, the state of Adolphe's health prompted my sister to shut herself away and ward off visits. I do not exactly know what his condition was when he got married, or if that condition quickly worsened. But during the first winter, a case of pneumonia threat-ened his life, and my sister, who had almost lost him, lavished every care on him. She told me several times that he was very negligent about taking pre-cautions, saying that all his life he had had "bad colds" every winter and that this was trifling.

As far as I was able to ascertain, although he actually died of a pulmonary disease which would have carried him off sooner or later, and which got much worse during the two years of his life with Henriette, what in fact did him in was an accident that might have been avoided.

It happened at the start of November, on the day of one of the last autumn fairs. Adolphe, unwell, had not been able join my sister, as he usu-ally did, and Henriette had gone off alone in the English cart. During the day, Adolphe had an odd spell that ended with a slight spitting up of blood. He got frightened and went to bed. But towards the middle of the afternoon, feeling completely well again and not wanting my sister to find him in bed, he decided to get up. This first act of imprudence might not have been fatal. But he committed a second. No sooner was he up and dressed than, still feeling weak, he convinced himself that this was due to the fact that he had not eaten lunch; and he had himself brought a bowl of soup, which he gulped down very hot. The bleeding started up again a few minutes later. When Henriette came home an hour later, he was at the point of death. He died the same evening, I think. They had sent in vain to all the tavern-keepers of Menneville in search of ice. The doctor thought he could manage to suppress the bleeding. But it was too late.

My sister had wed in the spring of 1895. In '96, in the spring as well, she had given birth, prematurely, to a feeble child who had lived for two months. In November of '96 she was a widow.

I learned of this through a terse wire that was relayed to me via Constan-tine to an outpost in the south: ADOLPHE DECEASED.

And I could not help feeling a great relief . . .

CHAPTER XX

The Story of Emma

ANOTHER STORY, quite strange—I have never really understood its deeper implications in Henriette's life—was the adoption of Emma, or rather my sister's attitude towards this child whom she seemed to have made her daughter.

The origin of this affair goes back to the time when, having halfway resigned from the army, I moved into le Saillant, with the idea that I would probably end my days there without returning to the service.

Although my sister, as I have said, spoke little about her marriage and still less about the death of her child, I was quite aware that the wound of that short-lived motherhood remained raw and that it would have been a great solace for her if that matrimonial experience had left her a daughter to bring up.

During one of the rare references that she made to that added grief, I was so struck by her tone and the intensity I sensed in her sorrow that I recklessly said to her: "I am always surprised that in France adopting children is such an unusual occurrence. We all know childless couples who are in despair over their sterility, women whose mental life is even utterly unhinged by it. Why don't these disconsolate women satisfy their urgent maternal instinct by adopting a child? The Assistance Publique* is full of beautiful, bouncing babies, without physical or mental defects. By taking a few precautions one can really reduce future risks to a minimum."

"It's not the same thing," she answered me sadly.

"Of course, I don't claim it's the same thing. I'm only saying that it's better than nothing, a good deal better, and that a lot of infertile mothers would find a great compensation for their misfortune in this very simple solution."

This ill-considered conversation was not without bearing on the events that followed.

There in the Perche, we were in a particularly good position to know about the subject. It is one of the regions where the Assistance has always placed a good many nurslings. All around us, on the little farms and in Menneville itself, wives of farmers and graziers took in babies to raise. These children remained under the supervision of regional inspectors, most of

---

*The state agency that managed orphanages, supervised foster homes, and distributed welfare assistance.

whom performed this delicate job with intelligence and devotion, made frequent tours of inspection, showing up unexpectedly almost every week at the wet nurse's, and made sure that the infants were well cared for. We obviously knew of cases where the choice of the women was wrong, where the children were poorly tended to, not well fed, but this was the exception, and the bad wet nurses were usually soon spotted by the inspectors, stripped of their wards, and crossed off the lists of the Assistance.

I have already said that our farms, run without tenant farmers, were maintained by us—by my father; then, after him, by my sister—but on each we had nonetheless installed a sort of team leader who lived there and who we insisted be married; the husband managed the day laborers and the farmhands, carrying out the orders given by my sister; the wife handled the dairy products and the poultry, and prepared the meals, since the day laborers, even though they did not live on the farm, had their meals there.

It happened that for several years on one of our farms, la Prêtrie, we had had an excellent grazier couple, the Puchots; the wife had taken in a baby some time before and become so attached to her, although she had a boy of sixteen, that she had obtained permission to keep the little girl and continue to bring her up—a rather unusual favor, since the normal procedure was to rotate the children and never leave them in the same hands for more than a year. As Puchot's wife was a good-hearted and very capable woman, and the couple was living comfortably, my sister agreed to receive a visit from the inspector and plead the woman's cause. The little girl, who was named Emma, had thus grown up for four or five years on the farm, and she was so pleasant, so neatly turned-out, always so smiling and affectionate with my sister, that Henriette herself became attached to her, made clothes for her, gave her presents. And the child, whenever my sister arrived, clung to her. So much so that, at the start of the winter of 1900—I had then been at le Saillant for about eighteen months—when we were told that Puchot's wife had fallen very seriously ill with what the doctor feared was a bad case of appendicitis, and had been moved in great haste to the hospital in Menneville, my sister, seeing poor Puchot in despair and much burdened by staying alone with the girl on the farm, did not hesitate to bring the child to the château. I no longer remember the complication that arose in the case. At any rate, Puchot's wife was kept under watch for two weeks at the hospital; then, with the onset of a new attack, a surgeon had to be rushed in from Le Mans to operate on her.

She died several days later.

In Puchot's anguish, the idea of being forced to give up the little girl and turn her over to the Assistance so clearly increased his grief that my sister decided not to hasten things and to keep Emma at the château with her for a few weeks. She had a crib put in her room, and took care of the child all day long with so much affection and pleasure that I found myself pondering all this. I was afraid that the Assistance would insist on taking the child away from my sister, and without saying anything I resolved to go and see about it and if possible arrange things so that Henriette could keep the girl as long as she wished.

The head of the office at Alençon, the county seat, was, fortunately, an intelligent man, a sort of altruist, with whom one could talk. It was agreed that my sister would be considered as a volunteer worker by the civil service and that the child would be entrusted to her for the time being.

But Henriette had another idea in mind. What I had said to her about adoption had come back to her. Uncharacteristically, she used a childish stratagem in telling me: "Here's a perfect candidate for adoption. It's a pity we don't know a childless woman, with the means and the wish to adopt a child." I vigorously made the usual objections. The truth was, I now realized, that I had accepted the idea as long as it wasn't my family that was involved.

Henriette answered with such fire that I looked at her questioningly. She fell silent, without pressing further. My suspicions were aroused.

Emma was a five-year-old with blond curls, a flowerlike complexion, and firm muscles. Very lively, high-spirited, and unfailingly cheerful, she showed quite a touching affection for my sister, which at times left Henriette deeply moved. Without saying anything, I went back to Alençon, under the pretext of attending a fair, to see the head of the Assistance, and was pleased to find him understanding and discreet. He could not tell me the secrets of Emma's birth, but he promised to look into the matter and inform me as best he could. Thus I learned that she was not of peasant stock. The mother had since married a man who owned forests in the Ardennes; the father, who had never known the consequence of his affair, was a very young man, a medical student, who had come to vacation at the same beach in Normandy as the young woman's family. The clandestine delivery had taken place in May '95 in Alençon, at a private clinic. Never in four years had anyone bothered to inquire for news of the child. I got in touch with the doctor at the clinic. He remembered the matter quite well. Without violating any professional confidence (which he kept all the better since he had never known the young mother's name), he was able to state that she had a strong constitution and to give me every reassurance concerning the child's heredity.

We were at the start of the winter of 1900 and the changes taking place in politics already had me thinking about rejoining the army. I knew that my leaving would be an ordeal for Henriette.

This consideration was not enough to make me hesitate in my decision, but it strongly prompted me to speak up for the adoption of Emma, since that little one's presence at le Saillant gave my sister an even stronger reason for living than the management of our properties, and I would have gone off with a lighter heart if I had left Henriette with a daughter to raise.

I broached the question forthwith. Henriette at first shied away from discussing the issue or even mentioning it. I saw that here I was touching a subject that stirred her profoundly and that she wanted to pursue in complete independence, without yielding to the slightest pressure. It was she who, two weeks later, asked me to go over the matter with her. She enumerated all the "reasonable" objections, but I realized that she was giving in to an emotional impulse more potent than any rationale and that, in her heart of hearts, the decision had been made.

I knew that the formalities were very complicated, and I was half-hoping that some insuperable obstacle would arise. I went to see old Odier, the former *notaire*, who was still alive at the time and had always enjoyed my father's trust. I could count on his discretion. I was disappointed to learn that, if the formalities were long and costly (to begin proceedings, to wait for a judgment, etc.), at least in the present case there was no insurmountable legal problem, since the law required the adoptive mother to be forty-three years old and fifteen years older than the adoptee. Moreover, things were facilitated by the fact that the child had not been acknowledged by either her mother or her father. In a few months, the question could be settled.

Deep down, I was opposed to this project. I really don't know why. Bringing an outsider into the family, giving her rights over us, altering the balance of my sister's life. In case of Henriette's death, dividing up le Saillant with Emma, who might be married, etc. I was quite determined to stop my sister from going ahead with this adoption, at any rate for the present. Why rush into it? Didn't she have what she wanted? A little girl to raise. What would the legal adoption add? The wisest thing would be to wait a few years, try it out. To bring up the child as if she were her daughter. And if everything went well, if the child really deserved all that affection, there would always be time to make the situation legal.

These sensible reasons might not have been enough to change the mind of Henriette, who, in the first flush of her infatuation wanted to commit herself immediately and completely, with a decisive act. I was helped by an objection that had not occurred to me and that was the only one which gave her pause. Did she have the right to give to this little stranger the name of her husband, the surname of the daughter they had lost? She would have adopted her if she could have called her Emma de Maumort. She hesitated to call her Emma de Pontbrun (almost the same name as that of the little Anna de Pontbrun).

I obtained a formal promise that Henriette would not think about it anymore, or at least would do nothing for ten years. In 1910, the girl would be fifteen. We would know by then whether or not she should be adopted. For my part, I agreed to replace my sister in the event of her death, to look after the child and to adopt her if I had no serious reason not to. Calm finally returned to le Saillant after two days of heated discussion. And Henriette could freely surrender herself to that blaze of maternal tenderness.

Everything fell into place, even as to the details. One question that remained was the child's attachment to Puchot, her adoptive father. My sister did not dream of severing those ties. But in keeping Emma, she wanted to be the *only* one to take care of her, to remove the child from the environment in which she had been raised for five years, to make the girl utterly her own. Events simplified this little problem. Puchot, since his widowerhood, had remained in charge of the farmhands at la Prêtrie, but a woman was needed in the house, and his replacement by a grazier couple was necessary before spring. He himself came to talk to me about it.

"We were happy here," he told me, "and we would never have thought of leaving if this terrible thing hadn't happened. But everything is changed for me. All I have left is my son. He's never had the health or the hankering to work the soil. My late missus and I had thought about sending him to Chartres this winter, to my parents', where he could study and become a surveyor. He's had that on the brain for a long time. But now that I'm alone, I have no more cause to stay behind. I'll go back to the country around Chartres, which is where I come from, and I won't have any trouble finding work there." Henriette had already assured him that she would take care of Emma and would never give her back to the Assistance. When he heard that she was considering keeping her always, and that little Emma was going to become "the young lady of the château," emotion made him burst into tears. I believe that there was some bitterness in those tears as well: the sorrow of losing the child, a little jealousy, probably. His subsequent behavior was odd. We never again had word from him directly. Henriette, in the early days, sent him news of Emma. He never answered her letters. He seemed no longer to want to hear anything about this child who had been like his daughter.

Anyway, in 1900, when I got my uniform out of mothballs and packed my trunks to leave le Saillant, everything was back to normal. I left my sister with her maternal honeymoon in full swing. Over the last six months, I had seen how important the child had become in her life, and I could better assess what she must have suffered from being childless after her widowhood. Watching her become attached to the little girl after Mme. Puchot's death, I thought: "This is going to change her life." But what I had observed, in those six months, exceeded all expectations. I began to wonder how my sister had been able to exist until then at le Saillant; I could no longer imagine what her life was like before Emma.

My sister, at the time of her marriage, had altered the layout of the wing that we had occupied as children to make a sort of new apartment consisting of a bedroom, a bathroom, and a little sitting room and office that she still sometimes called, through an unconscious slip, "Adolphe's office." As a widow, she had kept this apartment, merely replacing the couple's bed with the old bed she'd always slept in, and I imagine that she had somewhat rearranged "Adolphe's office," which became a small, rather feminine room where my sister gathered various furniture from the bedroom she had occupied as a young woman, her worktable, her sewing machine, etc. It was this room, which was large and airy—my old childhood bedroom—that she could have given Emma. It communicated directly with her bedroom. But she wanted to have the child closer to her, and had a cot placed right next to her own bed.

She got her up, washed her, had breakfast with her. She visited the farms less frequently and almost completely stopped going there on horseback, as she had before. She had the cart hitched up so she could take along the girl, who adored these rides. Henriette's first concern was to have an entire wardrobe made for Emma, and the dressmaker from Menneville spent close to a month at le Saillant, being paid by the day, cutting slips and bloomers as well as dresses for the summer and early fall. The few pieces of clothing that the child had owned at the Puchots' disappeared. I even felt somewhat annoyed at observing certain excesses, certain white satin bows in the hair, certain little yellow leather ankle boots that had replaced the clogs and the faded woolen stockings a bit too quickly. I restrained myself from saying, "You're playing with a doll; it's charming, but you're not necessarily doing the child a service."

I went back to le Saillant a few months later for Easter vacation. In that interval, my sister's passion for the little girl had taken a rather disturbing turn. Emma was unrecognizable. The fresh little peasant girl had come to resemble the fancy doll she held in her arms all day long. From morning on, she was dressed as if for a party, in embroidery and lace, with bows in her frizzled curls, and delicate white ankle boots which forced her to lift her feet when she crossed the courtyard to avoid getting them scratched by the gravel, thus giving her the gait of a circus horse. I couldn't get over it.

My sister had always been very sober in her attire, not unkempt, but dressed "in the English style" as Aunt Ma used to say, which at the time meant in clothes with a casual cut, in a neutral shade, practical, not showing dirt, suited to the active life she had always led. It was so uncharacteristic of her to dress up her daughter like a little princess . . . I could not keep from making a remark about the white ankle boots. "It's because I've dedicated Emma to the Blessed Virgin until her first communion," my sister told me, "and so she can't wear shoes of yellow or black leather." Indeed, I realized that the little girl was always in white and blue, usually in a white dress with a sky-blue ribbon in her hair. Rigged out in this way, she had quickly lost her simple and natural manners. She had become very clothes-conscious, took great care not to get her outfits dirty or wrinkled, no longer ran here and there but walked with a sort of ludicrous self-consciousness. Her character had already changed, like her manners. She was always cheerful and smiling, but very concerned with what was due her, saying "my lunch, my tray, my toast," and, if not already demanding, then very well aware how to get the maid to wait on her. Although there was already lots of silverware at le Saillant, my sister had bought her little silver knives and forks with her initials on them, and a gilded silver cup, and an ivory napkin ring on which her name was engraved.

I remember my surprise, at the first lunch I had at le Saillant, where soft-boiled eggs were served, at hearing her ask the maid for "her" eggcup, which was not flowered faience like ours, but silver, like the drinking cup, with a matching teaspoon. My sister laughed to see her so meticulous, so pretty, so careful to eat properly. She gazed at her ward with such a look of perpetual admiration, of rapture, that I didn't dare make the slightest comment.

I loved Henriette too much to upset her during those few days I had come to spend with her. Above all I sensed, in that enthralled admiration, a maternal need, an instinct whose strength I had never suspected. I kept thinking: "How she must have suffered from not having a child, to be like this." I suddenly discovered a chasm in my sister's life that I had never guessed. I was more struck by this than annoyed by that inordinate indulgence and affection. I also supposed that it was only a phase, that things would settle down.

Our former study room was converted into a costly toy store, always neatly arranged. Dolls in a whole variety of shapes and sizes, put away in miniature cabinets; each had its bed with embroidered curtains, a little dressing table, etc. Though I went into this room a number of times, I never caught Emma playing with dolls, as she had, the winter before, with the rag puppet she had brought from the farm. Either she walked around the house carrying one of her "daughters" bedecked and coiffed as if for a toy exhibit; or she "tidied up," put the beds in a row, making sure that no disorder disturbed that dreary show of luxury. What Emma did with her dolls, Henriette did with Emma. The child, I saw, was only copying her new mother. Henriette did not take her eyes off her daughter, drew the child to her, touched her constantly to straighten the bow of a ribbon, repin a broach, check the clasp on a bracelet (for she already had a whole assortment of jewelry), as mothers of brides or first communicants do while waiting for the ceremony to begin.

Henriette looked younger, seemed deliriously happy. She spoke about Emma all the time, steering the most diverse subjects back to this single topic. She went on and on enumerating the virtues and the (very real) charms of this child, but to the point of ascribing the most extravagant perfections to her.

"You see what a sharp customer she is," she told me, elated, if the girl did not respond or seemed not to have heard. "When the question embarrasses her, she doesn't hear it."

"But I assure you, she didn't see that you were speaking to her," I tried to slip in. Henriette smiled, unbelieving. "She's more wily than you think!"

During that stay, I learned, from Henriette herself, that this adoption had caused a great deal of gossip and had been unanimously censured in Menneville and the surrounding area. People readily conceded that it was a great misfortune to be left a widow so young and to not have a child, but to take into one's home a little person whose background one did not know, the fruit of some illicit affair, one of those "lost" children of the Assistance, doomed by its origins to every defect and degradation, this was worse than foolhardiness: it was a reprehensible act, an act of revolt against the sacred laws of the family, against the laws of nature, against custom. Old Mlle. Fromentot, stricken with rheumatism and hardly getting around at all anymore, had made the trip from Menneville to le Saillant to observe the thing with her own eyes. She obviously did not accept my sister's genial explanations; I was told she shook her head, more indignant than surprised, and Henriette had not been able to draw from her any more cogent objection than: "No, I've never heard of such a thing . . . If the Count were still alive, he would never have allowed it."

Henriette had even received a scandalized letter from an elderly cousin of her husband's, a spinster who lived in the Périgord—one wonders how she could have heard the news there—and who, ostensibly because she was the only person in France, except for Henriette, to bear the name Pontbrun, protested in advance a prospective adoption which would expose the Pontbrun name to a shameful degeneration . . .

This general hostility, far from affecting Henriette, strengthened her in the decision she had made. She only surrendered herself more to the impetus of her new passion. To all the reasons that had decided her was now added a satisfaction in being contrary, in asserting herself, an element of obstinacy. And there was a slight chilliness in the clergy of Menneville, who, without actually remonstrating, found the example uncommendable and socially dangerous.

This attitude of the "châteaux" in the area and of the provincial petty bourgeoisie did not surprise me. I was more surprised to learn that this minor scandal was the main topic of conversation not only for the squirelings and civil servants but also for the common folk. The lower classes were not at all grateful to Henriette for having raised one of their own to the rank of lady. Quite the opposite. What did they find wrong in this? Perhaps they saw it as something like a success bought with wealth. "Those things are whims that the rich can afford."

A vague feeling of betrayal, too. They had been robbed of a child; she had been made to desert her class. Jealousy perhaps, as well. "That little tramp, picked up who knows where, has all the luck . . . more than our kids do . . ." I had already noticed how hard the working class was on foster children. They were always considered pariahs. One did not give one's daughter even to a good worker if he was a former ward of the Assistance. The Assistance usually arranged for them to marry among themselves. One accepted them then, and lived with them on neighborly terms if they proved industrious and helpful, but with a shade of condescension. They were not part of "folks from around here." Try as they might, they would never be locals. And at the slightest misdeed, the slightest lapse, which any native would easily have been forgiven, a fence went up around those unfortunates: "They're no-account people, children of the Assistance . . ."

I also believe that the widespread hostility, for example that which Henriette thought she sensed on the farms, was made much worse by the attitude that she had her daughter strike. When people saw that overdressed child who was afraid of getting dirty and who stayed obediently tied to her mother's apron strings, and whom they had known as a little girl, playing with the other peasants' children, half in tatters, doing somersaults in the hay and splashing about at the edge of ponds—when they saw her come to the fields, sitting next to her mother on the cushions in the cart, they called her "stuck up." They were not wrong, but it was not entirely Emma's fault.

I have not forgotten these details because that visit to le Saillant was important for me. I left, after a few days, in a state of mind very different from that in which I had arrived. For the first time, I was distinctly disappointed in Henriette. Her marriage had surprised, stunned, perhaps vexed me, but it had seemed more like something that was inexplicable for lack of information than like a weakness or a sign of mediocrity in Henriette. Her way of raising Emma, the transformation brought about so quickly by an undertaking that I had at first encouraged and whose effects on Henriette's character I had imagined very differently, showed my sister in a poor light, and I fell from such a height that I was dreadfully wounded. For the first time, I saw her rendered commonplace, debased by something. And that something was a deep feeling in her, a long-established feeling that had been suddenly set free and had bloomed. Not the maternal feeling, but a low and childish maternal vanity which made her so ugly that I was happy to leave, and experienced no regrets at going off for a long time—for as long as possible. Henriette's game with Emma was really too awful to watch, too difficult for me to bear. "What has become of her!" I repeated to myself, astounded. And the thing that perplexed me most was to observe: 1) the typically feminine *excessiveness* of this sort of small-minded passion (until then what I had liked in Henriette was her moderation, that quite unfeminine quality of not being excessive in anything), and 2) the *obliviousness* towards herself and towards me that allowed her to be this way (until then, I had so prized in Henriette that beautiful clear-sightedness which never spared anything or anyone, which had not spared her father, had not spared me, had never spared herself). She was no longer my Henriette. She was an ordinary female, in whom the base instincts of the petty bourgeoise had suddenly sprouted. She who put *quality* into everything she thought, felt, and did had fallen prey to a common, stupid feeling. And I was forced to admit that this feeling, born of circumstance, was in her nature, or it would not have burst forth so spontaneously, so brazenly. I had always been hard on women, but until then I had excepted Henriette. "Like the rest," I thought, despairing. "Worse than the rest!"

I MANAGED, though living in Paris, not to go back to le Saillant for the summer holidays of 1901, nor during my second winter in Paris at the École de Guerre* in 1902. I decided to go at the end of the summer holidays in 1902, in September, when I was made a trainee in the military government of Paris,† and just before taking up the post. During that whole interval, I could not tell from the letters I received where things stood. Emma figured prominently in this correspondence, but everything Henriette wrote me was generally very sensible, not overly indulgent, and she even sometimes said she had noticed in Emma certain little character flaws, which she was trying to correct, and about which she asked my advice.

I had gone for fifteen months (since the Pentecost of 1901) without putting in an appearance at le Saillant. Now I spent only a week there.

Once again I found things much changed, and not what I had expected. My sister came to get me at the station in the cart, and I noted that she had not brought Emma. I inquired after her and my sister spoke to me of her not at length but with great affection, telling me that the child was developing from day to day and was already "a little companion" to her, but right away the tone seemed different from the childish exaltation of my last trip. Everything was to confirm these first impressions. I indeed found Emma much grown, or more accurately "broadened," for she had thickened. She no

---

*A special school, established in 1878, to train lieutenants and captains for staff positions.

†For administrative purposes, the army was divided into two "governments," one in Paris, the other in Lyon.

longer wore blue bows in her hair. She went around in simple, washable white dresses, with little white canvas tennis shoes, and seemed slightly older than her seven years. All the ridiculous little habits of her earlier life had disappeared. Her place at table was set the same way as ours, and she no longer seemed to enjoy undue privileges. She did not sleep in Henriette's bedroom anymore. She had her bed in our old study room, where there were still a few dolls and toys, but ill-assorted and not neatly put away, and where there was also a washstand, which showed that she no longer shared my sister's bathroom, and a little table with a desk-blotter and some books, where my sister required her to study. Henriette showed me Emma's penmanship and arithmetic notebooks, ink-stained and not very attractive. In short, she seemed to have turned back into a normal little girl, pampered like every only child but not too spoiled, and I very soon noticed that Henriette did not hold back from scolding her. It even seemed to me that she did not display much patience.

The child was charming like this, with her sweet little country girl's face, fed on fresh milk and vegetables, her pretty, naïve smile, her clear gaze, her invariable good mood. She bore my sister's chidings with a docile sweetness.

"She's a little on the lethargic side," my sister told me. "Easygoing, almost too much so. There's a lot of indifference in that good mood. Nothing matters to her. She leads her steady little life like a house pet. I don't know if she'll be capable of a deep attachment. She's friendly by nature, and as much with just anybody as with us. Fairly selfish, I suppose, like all children. Have you noticed how she behaves at meals? She never seems to be listening to what's said. She doesn't pay attention unless she's spoken to. She has no curiosity, she takes no interest in anything going on around her, never observes, never thinks about anything. Her body develops, but her mind lags a bit behind. Oh well, she has an excellent constitution, that's the main thing."

When I pointed out to her that a little girl of seven was still a big baby and that it was too soon to tell what the future held, she said: "No, really, I mean it. For example, I make her study. It's clear to me that her brain is lazy. She doesn't do it out of ill will, but she never takes any initiative. She'll copy out a model of penmanship until I interrupt her. She never wants to change, to make an effort. Yesterday, she wrote me ten lines 'dada-dada' instead of one, because I'd gone to the kitchen. She'd have written three pages of it if I'd stayed away an hour, and with the same blinkered application . . ."

At another moment, she confessed to me, very quickly, in an undertone: "You know, I'm afraid that Emma may not be intelligent." I remembered the period when she had absurdly credited her with every perfection, and I thought that she was on her way to another exaggeration. Save for these somewhat harsh remarks, I would not have observed any shadow on Henriette's happiness. She often drew the child close to kiss her, and Emma snuggled up to her "mama" with a winsome cuddliness. But, alerted by these comments, I thought I could sometimes discern in my sister a bit of muted irritation towards the girl.

"Answer me, Emma!" she would say, with a kind of vehemence, when the child, embarrassed by some question, smiled ingenuously, in silence. Emma would then give her a surprised, innocent look, and it was clear from her frown that she was trying in vain to find some reply.

"I don't know," she would end up murmuring, continuing to smile disarmingly.

Everything I saw at le Saillant relieved my past fears. Henriette had completely stopped playing mommy. She spent much time taking assiduous care of her daughter, but she had completely resumed her own independent existence. She rode out nearly every morning, quite early, to go round to all the farms and give her orders, and came back at ten o'clock to tutor Emma before lunch. Often, she went out again in the afternoon, in the cart. She never took the child, and I even had the feeling that she did not take her on those occasions when she might have done so, for instance one day when we rode out in the cool of the evening to see the work done by the threshing machine at la Prêtrie. Emma watched us climb into the cart, and sweetly waved goodbye.

"Why aren't we taking her?" I asked in a low voice. Henriette did not answer, and I thought she hadn't heard. But when we had passed through the gate and the mare had begun to trot, she said: "You see, Emma has her little life at home, very set. It's what suits her. Don't suppose that she would have wanted to come with us. She doesn't like the unexpected, anything that upsets her routine."

"But what does she do at home?"

"She'll sit in the linen room, next to Louise, and chat, while sewing. And that's the spot where she's happiest. Everything that's housework, sewing, ironing, interests her. In fact those are the only things in the world, up to now, that seem to interest her at all."

This time I keenly regretted leaving le Saillant. Henriette had never been closer to me. Never had we had better talks. Never had her intelligence seemed sharper to me and her mind more mature. We had agreed on important repairs to be done on the right wing, whose roof had been in very bad condition for a long time. I went off with an excellent impression. My sister had recovered her balance. The girl occupied an important place in her life, but an appropriate one. As she grew up, this child was going to become a charming little companion, a younger sister as much as a daughter. I congratulated myself on the adoption.

. . .

I WAS KEPT very busy in Paris by my duties in the military government, and it was quite a while before I returned to le Saillant. But in March 1903, I managed to leave that post and get stationed again in Alençon, where Lyautey was still in command of the 14th Hussars and where he took me on as a captain attached to the staff of the colonel. The proximity allowed me to visit le Saillant fairly often. I had few if any long stays there during that spring of 1903, but several times a month I slept over on Saturday night and spent all of Sunday.

I did not realize that something had changed yet again in the relationship between Henriette and the child, so imperceptible still were the differences. It was only later, when I thought about it, that I understood I might have seen things more clearly.

I found it very natural that, during those Saturday evenings and those brief Sundays, my sister should have devoted all her time to me and neglected the girl a bit. We always had many things to tell each other and were always enormously happy to find ourselves alone together, and I was not struck by the readiness with which Henriette sent the child to bed immediately after dinner or put her in the maids' care for the whole of Sunday without even having her come take tea with us. It was only later that I wondered if this distancing of the child, which I had taken as a special concession in honor of my visit, had not become a daily habit and if Henriette had not gradually returned to her solitary tastes of before. Several times, during those Sundays, Emma did not even have lunch with us. I do not recall what excuse Henriette gave for her absence. Maybe: "Lunch is late because High Mass was so long, and I didn't want her waiting around, so I had her served in the kitchen" or something of the kind, in which I saw nothing unusual or deliberate.

Yet something did strike me during that time, and in an entirely different domain. I hesitate to mention it, since it is a delicate matter about which I am not very knowledgeable. It seemed to me, or more precisely I received, on several occasions in the course of my conversations with my sister, the very vague impression that her religious sensibility was going through a minor crisis, and it is from this period that I think I can date the beginning, not of a religious chill in my sister's soul, but at the very least of a gradual transformation which would lead to that freer religious attitude which she had during the final fifteen years of her life. It is very difficult for me to put my finger on just what formed the basis for this impression. I have already said that we never spoke about religious questions. But I noticed from small details that Henriette seemed to attach less importance to certain observances. For example, I learned that she had become accustomed, that spring, to going off on horseback earlier than before, and, as I knew that what had formerly prevented those morning rides was her habit of attending seven o'clock Mass nearly every day and taking Communion, which meant that she had to come back to le Saillant for breakfast around eight, I deduced that obviously she was no longer going as frequently to Mass. I also learned, by the bye, that she had changed spiritual directors, and that after having put herself in the hands of the new dean for a while, following the death of the old priest who had presided at her wedding, she had become friends with a former teacher in the seminary at Alençon whose fragile health confined him to a very cautious way of life and whom the bishop had installed as a country priest in the smallest village of our diocese, Breuil-sous-Menneville, where there was an old Romanesque church and a population of scarcely four or five hundred. During a horseback ride, she pretended to have something to tell him in order to go through Breuil and pay a little visit to the presbytery. In reality, I think she wanted the Abbé Deluze and me to meet. The encounter, as a matter of fact, was quite cordial, and the Abbé Deluze seemed to me a very fine mind. I was pleased to think that my sister had in him a confidant and a friend. Unfortunately for her, he lived only a few years, and his death left in my sister's existence a large void, which I perfectly understand.

The influence of this distinguished man, the affection which he very quickly seemed to bestow upon Henriette, the frequency of their meetings, certainly had something to do with her changes in religious feeling. I have referred to a "chill" but I am aware how inappropriate the word is. Who knows if precisely the opposite should not be said. I never felt that Henriette's deep fervor was altered, but from about that time on, it seemed to take a slightly different form. As if broadened, as if purified, and I am tempted to add: made more manly. Until about her forty-fifth year, Henriette's religion owed much to that somewhat elementary religious education she had received at Sunday school in Menneville and had kept up with little observances, occasional reading. As intelligent as she was, her religiosity nevertheless retained some flavor of the provincial youth club. The child-of-Mary ribbons, the processions and banners, the novenas, the indulgences, all were quite important to her. During the final period of her life, she neglected no religious ceremony, and her visits to church were not less frequent, but the spirit "that gives life" had won points over the letter "that kills." An example will help me make clear what I mean: in 1900, when she adopted Emma, her first concern was to pledge the child to the white and blue. Admittedly, there was nothing ridiculous in this . . . Nonetheless I am sure that, three or four years later, Henriette, having become Father Deluze's penitent and friend, would never even have thought of it.

I do not know why I have mentioned all this in relation to my account of Henriette's shift in attitude regarding Emma. Probably there is only a coincidence of date. However much I think it over, I cannot see how I could come up with the slightest connection of cause and effect between those two changes—the transformation of religious sentiment and what I can now call, without fear of error, the cooling of maternal feeling. Unless to infer that at the time, Henriette's thinking, her intellectual scope, made a leap and reached a new stage of growth. And that this development might have made her sterner about what was gradually pushing her away from her adopted daughter: the child's deep, irremediable lack of intelligence.

WAS SHE UNINTELLIGENT? My sister claimed she was, and never budged from that position. This was certainly no reason to withdraw from the girl, and to act as my sister, by successive steps, ended up acting. And Henriette knew it. What she forgave Emma least was not the disappointment, the wounded pride that Emma had caused her in not being the child that she had wanted to adopt, the one to whom she had given her name, the one that she wanted her to be at all costs: someone of quality, someone exceptional. No, what she undoubtedly forgave her the least was the remorse she felt over her own altered behavior towards the child, remorse that came rather belatedly, when it was too late to change things. But could she ever have voluntarily changed anything about those cold, misdirected feelings? I strongly doubt it! What she could not forgive the girl was her being the cause of a shabby mode of behavior, a mean-spiritedness of which my sister must certainly at times have been aware; was Emma's having blighted the end of her life with that feeling of dissatisfaction with herself, of injustice perpetrated, of secret shame, of inexpiable sin.

All this I am supposing. Never did anything my sister said allow me to be sure. I never reproached her, but I remain convinced that she would not have persisted in that determination to lower Emma in my opinion and to justify her grievances against the child if she had not, in the depths of her conscience, felt the weight of her sin and of an inner disapproval, whose voice she stifled. Henriette had staked too much on the child. In fact, she was not satisfied with loving the girl, she wanted to be proud of her as well, wanted her affection to be, as it were, justified by the child's exceptional qualities. I later remembered little facts which ought to have struck me more. For example, in the months following the adoption, during that period of absurd infatuation when Henriette could not utter two sentences without bringing in the idea of Emma, I recall that she was mainly preoccupied with the future. She seemed to adore the girl less for what she was at present, and for herself, than for what she would become later on, under the influence of Henriette's tutelage. It might have appeared touching—considering that this was a five-year-old girl, brought up on a farm, uncouth, speaking the country patois, not even able to tell one letter of the alphabet from another—to hear Henriette construct a whole distant future in her imagination and say: "I'll hire a live-in tutor, I want her to have the best education possible. Naturally I want her to get her *baccalauréat,* and if, as I fully intend, she wishes to get her degree, I won't hesitate to make the necessary sacrifices, I'll spend a few winters with her in Paris."

"But," I said to her, "this girl will love the country. You'd do better, once she comes of age, to introduce her to the life here, teach her how to manage an estate . . ."

"Certainly not," she retorted, pursuing the idea I had suggested to her, but in order to distort it, exaggerate it. "If she has a taste for the land, I'll encourage it, in a scientific way; I want her to go to an agriculture school, get her diploma, do her training in the big cattle-raising countries like England, or Denmark maybe . . . If she is to lead a life like mine I want her first to have acquired all the technical skills that I don't have . . ."

"Anyway," I said to cut things short, "what's the use of making so many plans? At twenty, a young woman usually gets married, and her whole life is changed; she follows the direction that the marriage takes her in."

At this thought, my sister grew suddenly gloomy. She fell silent, but I clearly felt her hostility in advance towards a son-in-law whom she would not have chosen and who might destroy or nullify all her efforts in educating, training, and guiding her daughter. Her concerns about Emma seemed to me childish and endearing. I did not see their secret importance. At that point I did not discern the unbridled ambition that she already harbored for her adoptive daughter.

Very soon, that maternal ambition was reduced to nothing. Ambition and affection were indissolubly linked in Henriette's heart. When she had to give up her dreams, the affection disappeared along with the thwarted ambition.

WHEN, EXACTLY, did this renunciation and loss of interest take place?

Circumstances prevented me from witnessing it. I caught a glimpse of the prelude during that spring of 1904 when I was in Alençon, but without suspecting the repercussions. During that summer of 1904, at the end of August, Lyautey, dispatched to the Moroccan border, took me with him, and this was the beginning of that long campaign in Morocco which kept me away from France from 1904 to 1914, ten years during which I took only two months of leave, in 1909 and in 1913 after the abdication of the sultan. Everything therefore happened in my absence. And what I can say of it is only a plausible attempt to reestablish the facts.

I did not even see Emma during my stay in France in the spring of 1909. Henriette had put her in Sainte-Anne, a Catholic school at Le Mans, where she had been a boarder for three years already, only coming home to le Saillant for vacations. My sister and I had just one conversation about her, upon my arrival, when I inquired after Emma. So it was that I learned—what I already knew from Henriette's letters, although she spoke very rarely of Emma—that the girl was way behind in her studies, and that she was, despite her fourteen years, in a class where all her schoolmates were two years younger, and in which she was bringing up the rear. The nuns had no complaints about either her character or even her willingness to apply herself. She was sweet, obedient, loved by everyone, very pious, but incapable of any mental effort. My sister did not even seem to feel bad about having to admit these things to me. She appeared to have completely given up her ambitions for Emma and spoke of her to me with a total detachment, as she would have done of a stranger. Emma had become a fat blondish girl, extremely healthy, but without any vigor or curiosity, lethargic, apathetic, living an animal life based on habit.

She enjoyed Saint-Anne, not suffering in the least from being regarded as a backward child, liking her teachers and her schoolmates without ever showing a preference for this one or that. She did quite well in sewing.

"You can't blame her for anything," said Henriette, smiling (and that smile surprised me at least as much as the details she was giving me, since it seemed to show so much indifference on my sister's part). "She hasn't any defects. She hasn't any strong points. She's neutral across the board. She's neither withdrawn nor hypocritical, but honest, open, unsecretive. She's even-tempered, always ready to do what she's told, silent with those who don't talk, gay and chatty with those who chat with her. Affectionate with everyone. She writes me once a month, on a set date, short, conventional letters checked by the sisters. I'm sure that she only thinks about me on that day. When she comes home for vacation, she seems happy to be here but just as happy to leave when school starts again."

"But," I asked, "when she's here with you, what sort of life does she lead, how does she spend her time?"

"In living, that's all. She gets up when I wake her, gets dressed, makes her bed as in the dormitory, tidies up her room, and comes down to have breakfast in the kitchen. I sometimes take her with me to the farms, when I walk or go in the cart, and she never declines to go with me, she follows me like a faithful dog, enjoying everything and at the same time indifferent to everything, answering the questions I ask her, never asking any herself, taking absolutely no interest in the work she sees being done right in front of her. When I'm a little weary of dragging her around with me, I tell her: 'Wait for me here, I'll pick you up on my way back.' I find her an hour later, sitting under the same apple tree, playing with a blade of grass or an insect, and we go home together."

"But what does she dream about, what does she think about, when she's alone like that for an hour at the foot of a tree?"

"I don't believe she thinks. She lives, like a plant, and that's enough to occupy her . . . Besides, these walks don't happen every day. I don't think she gets much pleasure out of them. She never asks to come along with me if she sees me going out, and I don't suggest it. What she likes best, I think, to the extent that a 'preference' for anything has meaning for her, is to live among the help, watch them working, and do whatever they're doing along with them. So I often find her in the kitchen, peeling vegetables or shelling peas with the cook; or in the garden, watching Thomas replant lettuces, or staking beans and helping him, as an apprentice might do, by handing him the lettuces or the raffia strings. But mainly she spends entire days in the linen room, with Mariette. Sitting on two low chairs near the open window with the basket of mending between them, they work together, day after day, chatting away."

"Maybe she confides in Mariette more readily than in you."

"Oh, it's not a matter of confiding. You know how Mariette is. She's a simple soul, too. When I say that they chat, it consists of: 'Where's the darning thread? . . . This dish towel won't last much longer, two or three more washings and it'll go to the dust cloths . . .' Their mind is on what they're doing, and their conversation is restricted to thinking out loud; there are neither questions nor answers. But they're happy together, there in the linen room, where nobody bothers them and it's cool in the summer. They have their little routine. At four, they have a snack, on their lap, of a piece of bread with a handful of currants or half a bowl of curds, and Emma enjoys her snack much better there than when I call her to have tea with me. I'm wrong to say 'better.' I should say 'as well,' since if you asked her to choose she'd be incapable of making up her mind."

These servantlike tastes explain to some extent what happened afterwards and has always remained mysterious to me.

I was, and, I confess, still am, less convinced than Henriette about Emma's preferences. That detachment, that lack of interest—though not coldness—which Henriette felt concerning Emma, and which had slowly taken over from a mad enthusiasm, the child, as limited as she was, as narrow as her sensibility was, could not but vaguely sense. She must have felt more at ease with Mariette. During the rest of my stay, Henriette, I believe, did not breathe another word about her foster daughter. Was she avoiding speaking of her, thinking about her? I rather suppose that she did not think about her, and did not care to think about her. In any case, the subject of her future was not brought up. Not only did I make no allusion to that date of 1910 which had been set between us for deciding about the adoption, and which was only a few months away, but I did not pose the question which sometimes came to my mind: "What will you do with Emma when she finishes school?"

I had brought from Africa a bundle of native fabrics and little objects which I gave as presents to Henriette and Aunt Ma. Among these souvenirs, I wanted for Emma to have a pair of embroidered babouches and an embossed silver necklace I had picked out for her there. I handed them over to Henriette for her ward, and I heard nothing more about them. I found that little package, with my notation "For Emma, Souvenirs of Morocco," much later, in 1919, two years after Henriette's death, when, having returned for good to le Saillant, I decided to order her belongings. I never knew if Henriette had forgotten to give them to Emma or had not wanted to do so. And to me there is nothing implausible about this last supposition.

I was soon back in Morocco and thought no more about the situation except when a letter from Henriette brought me news of Emma, which was not often. I nevertheless heard, two years later, that the nuns at Sainte-Anne, refusing to advance Emma to the higher grades, had discreetly broken it to Henriette that Emma could not stay on much longer as a boarder in Le Mans. My sister announced the fact rather evasively in a letter during the fall of 1911 in which she told me as an aside: *Emma just had a very severe sore throat, which momentarily raised fears of the first signs of scarlet fever. Have I told you that she has left boarding school for good? She is now in her seventeenth year.*

I WENT BACK to France in the spring of 1912. I did indeed find Emma living at le Saillant, and was very surprised at the position that she had been assigned. It was quite off-putting. I daren't write that she was a servant there. And yet . . . Henriette did continue to treat her as before, and there were nuances in the way she spoke to Emma as compared to that in which she spoke to Mariette or Clementine. But for a bedroom Henriette had given Emma a little room at the other end of the château, adjacent to the one where Mariette slept. And Emma spent almost all her time in the kitchen or the linen room. I say almost, because Henriette had gone on having lunch with her at noontime. In the evening, my sister, who had noticeably aged, did not sit down at the table but instead in an armchair in Emma's old bedroom, which she had turned into a little salon where she sat at night and where she had her dinner: a cup of warm milk and some cooked fruit on a tray. This tray was brought her by Emma, who took it away as soon as Henriette had finished, and who then dined in the kitchen with the servants.

I am well aware that those old servants were like friends, and that it was not as if Henriette had sentenced Emma to live with an ordinary household staff. However Emma, by the very way she dressed and behaved, belonged to the help, and was no longer one of the "masters." She was forever wearing an apron, which was not a cook's apron—except when she helped in the kitchen—but rather one of black serge such as housekeepers wear; all the same, she wore an apron, and it was like a sign of her function. At the mid-day meal, she admittedly had her place set at the end of the table, but she also did the serving, instead of Mariette, who no longer appeared in the dining room. It was Emma who took the dishes from the pass-through and cleared the plates; she did not sit down to her own plate until we were served.

In short, Henriette had gradually given her the role of a chambermaid specially assigned to her service. It was Emma who, in the morning, opened her shutters for her, brought her breakfast and the hot water for washing. It was Emma who did the room, as soon as my sister had left her apartments. It was she too who helped Mariette make my bed during my visit, and I came upon her more than once, in my room or in the hallway, with a broom or a dust cloth in her hand, doing the housework with Mariette.

Henriette seemed to find this arrangement so natural that she did not even take the trouble to explain it to me. I made no comment. I adopted the same tone with Emma as did Henriette, that which one would use with a nurse or a governess who was also a local child you had always known and addressed in the familiar: "Would you *(tu)* be kind enough to see if the cof-fee's ready . . ." I was more self-conscious when it came to speaking to her about Henriette, and I scrupulously avoided doing so, not being able to bring myself to ask her if "Madame" had already come downstairs, and no longer daring to say to her, as when she was little: "Is Mama in the garden?" I tried to determine if, when speaking to my sister, she continued to some-times call her "Mama." Of course, she did not speak to her in the third per-son. But, no matter how hard I listened, I was never able to make out how she managed it. I think that she quite simply avoided addressing her by name. I remember that, to announce the meals, she had this clever formula: "Luncheon is served," instead of Mariette's "Madame is served."

As soon as the meal was done, we left the dining room; Emma brought me my coffee tray in Henriette's little salon, and withdrew. She never sat down with us. And for supper, when I alone had a normal meal, Emma did not join us at the table but served me, going back and forth between the pantry and the dining room.

I note all these domestic details; as absurd and insignificant as they are, they are the only clues I could gather as to what the relationship between my sister and her ward had become. No familiarity, no intimacy, but nothing stilted either. It was the relationship that an elderly lady who lives alone and needs special care sometimes has with a hired companion or a sicknurse. On both sides a cordial attitude softened the demands of service.

I HAVE a still better reason to linger over these details: it was to be my last visit with Henriette at le Saillant. When I returned to France in August '14, I had to join, at the front, the general staff of the cavalry brigade to which I was posted, without going back through the Orne. Both of the two short leaves I took, a year apart—in the fall of 1915 after the failure of the offensive in the north and at the end of the summer of 1916 after the battles of the Somme—I spent in Paris, and it was my sister who made the trip to see me. I was not to go back to le Saillant until after the armistice of '18, and I would find the house empty. Henriette had died, in a clinic in Le Mans, at the end of the terrible winter of 1917.

Starting in September '14, she had taken over the running of the auxiliary hospital that had been set up, on her initiative and with the aid of well-off families of the region, in the hospice of Menneville. She had even taken an apartment in Menneville, to avoid going back and forth to le Saillant every day. For two and a half years she had assumed the heaviest burden in the management of this hospital for convalescents, without taking a single day off, except the one she came to spend with me in Paris on each of my two leaves (it was actually because I knew she had moved to Menneville that I had not taken my leaves at le Saillant).

During all this time, Emma assisted her at the hospital. I have little precise information concerning this collaboration. I think that Henriette had begun by keeping Emma at her side to do the accounts. Then a secretary capable of more initiative became necessary, and Emma had gone on to take care of the patients. I suppose it was by carrying out those simple duties that she discovered a penchant for taking care of the sick and that this fortuitous work experience had a great influence on the direction of her life.

The fact remains that in April 1917, my sister, who had been overtaxed by those thirty months at the hospital and whose physical resistance must have been seriously undermined, had a heart attack so severe that she was rushed to a clinic in Le Mans. Emma went with her, and stayed there. The military events at that time did not allow me to make the journey to Le Mans to see her. What is more, she had forbidden Emma to write me, and sent me her news herself in a cheerful tone which succeeded in reassuring me. I was even pleased about the forced rest that had been imposed on her. Only later did I learn of the gravity of her condition. There was one attack after another, despite all the medical attention. The doctors struggled for two full months but without managing to bring the illness under control. During the night between the twentieth and the twenty-first of June 1917, a new, more violent attack struck her down in a matter of minutes.

My regiment had been on the front line since the night before. The brigadier general, when he had the wire forwarded to me, offered to let me quit my post for three days. I refused. The men were worn out from six weeks of combat without any real replacements. The onslaughts kept coming constantly. Our positions were shelled every night. This was not the moment to relinquish my command, even for three days. And then, for what? Perhaps I would have hesitated if it had been a matter of seeing my sister alive one last time. I don't even think so then.

Aunt Ma was still living. She had been a widow since 1905, and was herself to die the following year, the winter of '18, without my having seen her again. It was she whom Emma notified. She hurried to Le Mans and brought Henriette's body back to le Saillant. There, she took charge of everything, and, after the funeral, stayed on for a week with Emma and the servants to set the house somewhat in order and to close it up pending the end of the war and my eventual return. I wanted the servants to be left there, since I had complete trust in them to look after the estate in my absence; and I put the most experienced of our graziers in charge of managing the estate as best he could. I also wrote Emma to tell her that she need not worry about her future, that I would do for her all that my sister would have done about providing for her; I added that the house naturally remained open to her, and that she could live there. She wrote me back a rather embarrassed and vague letter, a great deal of which I did not understand and which concerned her vocation and taking care of the sick. I thought that she was going to go back to her job at the hospice in Menneville.

It was a letter from Aunt Ma that filled me in and informed me that Emma had decided to become a novice in an order of nursing nuns in Le Mans. This order was actually the one which supplied nuns to the clinic where Henriette had died, and where Emma had spent two months at her bedside. Could it be that during that time she had felt her vocation awakening? I have always thought that if my sister had gone on living, Emma would have stayed with her. I do not believe she was capable of exceptional resolutions. But she let herself be easily influenced, and during those two months in the clinic, sharing the life of the sisters, perhaps receiving advice from some nun who had grown fond of her, she had fallen into the routine of that hospital life, for which her training in Menneville had already prepared her, and, suddenly deprived of support by Henriette's premature death, had found no better refuge than that community whose example had been right before her eyes. I do not question in the least the genuineness of her religious vocation. I only mean that she found there, at the same time as the satisfaction of her religious sensibility, a ready-made existence which was neither foreign nor unknown to her and which spared her taking any other initiative. The nuns knew her and welcomed her as one of their own.

I never saw Emma again. I know that after her novitiate years in Le Mans she took her vows, became Sister Véronique, and left Le Mans to become a nurse in a hospital in Lyon, where she probably still is. I had news of her from Mariette, to whom she wrote faithfully each year at Christmastime. Since Mariette's death, that is, for fifteen years, I have heard nothing more of her. She must be forty-five now, and is very likely still alive.

My sister, who had not foreseen her sudden end, had made no will. I am therefore not surprised that she had made no particular arrangement to provide for Emma's future. If she thought about it during her illness, it was certainly not with anxiety, since she was well aware that I would do everything necessary. At the time she died, I had even considered putting aside a little nest egg for Emma which would allow her to get married in a proper way. Her religious vocation spared me this expenditure.

When I say that Henriette had made no particular arrangement, I am forgetting that in one of the drawers of her desk I found a curious document whose purpose I have never quite understood. It was an imitation-leather notebook, kept current with the greatest care, in which were written down in the most minute detail all of the expenses occasioned by Emma since her arrival at le Saillant; and the precision of those figures was such that even the food and the laundry were roughly recorded for each month. At the end of each year, on a blank page, were noted not only the total spent each month and the annual total, but the addition of that yearly total to the totals of the previous years, after which my sister wrote, in red ink: *Which comes to . . .*

This notebook had been kept even during the first two years of the war. I think I recall that the final written page was dated the 31st of December, 1916, and that the sum total of all the expenses over sixteen years incurred by Emma's presence at home and the costs of her education amounted to something like a hundred twenty thousand francs. (The slightest outlays were mentioned: birthday presents, doctors' visits, medicines, even bars of soap and the resoling of a pair of shoes.)

The strangest part remains to be told. On the first page of this notebook Henriette had written, in a willful hand: *To be given to Emma after my death.*

As I did not find this notebook until 1920, when I set Henriette's apartments in order, and since by that time poor Emma had long since taken the veil, I did not think it my duty to carry out this posthumous wish, but I am still rather uncomfortable when I think about that notebook. The instruction written on the first page clearly shows that it was not merely out of a concern to keep careful accounts that Henriette compelled herself to perform that complicated chore of working out each month, for instance, how much, after the overall kitchen expenses, it cost "to feed" that extra mouth. It does appear that in Henriette's mind there was an obscure desire for some sort of revenge, a wish to humiliate her ward by making her understand in financial terms the price of the "good deed." This indelicate act is so unlike Henriette . . . To have yielded to that base temptation, to have had that devilish postmortem plan, she must have nursed hidden feelings against Emma which I would rather not attempt to bring further to light.

It makes one wonder in what spirit she received Emma's daily services. Did she not experience an ugly satisfaction in seeing her reduced to that servile role? How much she must have begrudged her being there, present at every instant of her life . . . What strength of character she showed in speaking to her amicably, smiling at her, when she must, in her heart of hearts, have wished her to vanish from sight forever. She must have imposed that presence on herself like a duty. "I have taken her in, I have not gone back on my word, I will keep her, I will put up with her for as long as necessary, and no one will suspect what I feel."

Who knows, perhaps Henriette's greatest merit, the greatest victory that she won over herself, was to resist, for ten years running, the temptation to make Emma her whipping-girl?

PART FOUR

The Campaigns in Morocco (1907–1914)

CHAPTER XXI

Lyautey* and Morocco

[André Daspre: Maumort's military life would have occupied a central place in the novel, mainly in this section, if one is to judge from the importance of the research that Martin du Gard assembled on this subject, but the outlines and chronologies alone give an idea of the scope the narrative might have assumed [. . .]†

On Maumort's life at Saint-Cyr, his postings at Versailles and Alençon, and his time in Batna and Constantine we have only partial information. The Dreyfus Affair is not dealt with, but we at least know that Maumort's pro-Dreyfus stand would have been explained by the influence of Uncle Éric. Maumort's double education, his intellectual and military duality, would have been at the root of a conflict whose dramatic power can easily be imagined.

---

*Louis-Hubert-Gonsalve Lyautey (1854–1934), soldier, writer, friend of writers and intellectuals, icon of French colonialism. Having passed through Saint-Cyr and the Staff College, Lyautey served in Indochina, fighting pirates, then in Madagascar, where he suppressed an insurrection and began to develop his personal style of colonial government. In 1902, Lyautey returned to France to take command of a regiment of hussars at Alençon (which is where the novelist has Maumort meet him). In 1904, he was sent as commandant to Aïn Sefra, the military hub of southwestern Algeria. With the protection and encouragement of the French governor general, he subdued various Moroccan tribes which were threatening France's position in the region. From 1906 on, as commandant at Oran, he succeeded, despite considerable political opposition at home, in pushing the Algerian frontier steadily westward.

†Dots enclosed by brackets indicate a deletion of material.

Thus a sustained narrative will not be found here, but instead a montage of rather diverse texts chosen from among the most significant, not simply to show the adventures of Maumort as an officer but chiefly to better understand the intentions of the novelist and to see the preparatory phases of his work of creation.

On the colonization of Morocco, on Lyautey, Martin du Gard assembled considerable research. One index card of his reading tells us that he had gone through eight books on Morocco and had ordered thirteen others from the library of the Sorbonne. On April 15, 1942, he noted in his diary: "Flaubert, writing his Sentimental Education, *ransacked the archives of the ministries to find out which battalion of the National Guard, and in that battalion which company, was on duty on such-and-such a night, in front of such-and-such a monument in Paris [. . .] In conducting this sort of research like him, I am obeying (like him) an urgent concern with reality. I am put together in such a way that, to create a character who is alive, I have to feel informed as to all the facts of his public and private life. It matters little, I admit, that, for example, Maumort's memories of the campaigns in Morocco, of Lyautey's general staff, be, from the historical point of view, scrupulously exact down to their slightest details. But, by fixing him in a strict historical truth, I confer upon Maumort a more precise reality, a sort of concrete consistency, and, at the same time, a greater human truth. The historical accuracy of the biography, which I am building up for him at this moment, helps me to focus his psychological truth."*

*

It is significant that the basic book on Lyautey, to which the novelist constantly refers, is that of André Maurois. This monograph appeared in 1931, that is to say the very year when Lyautey, named General Commissioner of the Colonial Exposition, organized a triumphal return to the political scene after having dramatically resigned his post as Resident General of Morocco in October 1925 (after the war of the Rif), and withdrawn to his native Lorraine. Maurois' work met with the expected success, and contributed considerably to spreading the legendary image of the great lord who wins the trust and respect of the adversary as much by his chivalrous way of waging war as by his administrative abilities. It was this representation of the colonial officer that Lyautey himself put forward in his books, and which the support of the government helped to impose upon the public. Martin du Gard is far from reproducing this image unaltered.

Besides, the novelist was not limited to information drawn from books concerning the influence and personality of Lyautey. He could turn to particularly reliable eyewitness accounts, and first and foremost that of Paul Desjardins, one of Lyautey's oldest friends, and also of Pierre Viénot, who was one of those close to Lyautey before becoming Undersecretary of State for the Colonies [. . .] Martin du Gard himself seems to have met Lyautey only once, on December 14, 1928, with Gide, to support the candidacy of Marcel de Coppet for the post of Governor in black Africa; only one letter from the writer to Lyautey is extant.

In this section of the novel, one has the impression that Martin du Gard would have been more interested in Lyautey than in Maumort. After having chosen to create the character of a great intellectual by inventing Uncle Éric, did the novelist not need, for the balance of the whole, a great military leader? Lyautey is an exceptionally effective, realistic man of action: what better guide for Maumort, who, after the intense intellectual activity of his Parisian period, is going to engage in military action, in combat, to follow the other fundamental tendency of his personality?

But what probably interested the novelist in Lyautey is that he had—like Maumort, one might say—the double education of a military man and an intellectual . . . Lyautey even had undeniable talents as a writer. He began his career in the Parisian salons, with the tastes of a "Swann in epaulettes," it was said; but, beyond aesthetic and social pleasures, he sincerely searched for a moral direction, a line of action that allowed the "gathering of the elite." Thus he became, along with Paul Desjardins, one of the founders of the Union for Moral Action, in 1892. And one sees clearly that it is always the same milieu that Martin du Gard intends to study: Lyautey, though the novelist may not say it, could also have frequented Uncle Éric's salon!

In his diary, on July 16, 1941, Martin du Gard writes: "Maumort has to be very different from me, if only through the training of his mind, his aristocratic background, his military career, etc. I already can see very clearly what sort of 'great figure' this can be. In the tradition of Luce in Jean Barois*—but crossbred with Lyautey (for the 'grand seigneur' side); very French and even rather eighteenth century, through a certain freedom of thought and manners." This statement allows us to understand the double function that the novelist attributes to the character of Lyautey: he is studied for himself and he serves at the same time for the imagining of Maumort, the construction of Maumort's personality. The historical character would have thus coexisted with the fictional character for which he would have served as a model. How both would have come through this confrontation we unfortunately cannot know, but the novelist's plan was fascinating.*

*

Why did the novelist make Maumort a colonial officer? At the time in which the novel is set, the desire to participate in colonial conquests was so strong, so widespread among the career officers, that the only ones who remained stationed in France were those with serious reasons for doing so. Maumort, upon leaving Saint-Cyr, stays in France because his father is beginning to be

seriously ill and he wants to help Henriette manage the estate; this is why he
requests posts close to Menneville—first Versailles, then Alençon.

Martin du Gard later sends Maumort to Algeria, then to Morocco. The
novelist knew Algeria well: after getting married, he had spent four months
in 1906 with his wife near Algiers. He had set a whole section of his first
major novel, Une vie de saint *(unpublished), in Algeria.]*

I. MAUMORT'S LIFE IN THE MILITARY*

In August 1904, during the maneuvers in Sarthe, Lyautey is appointed by
André, the Minister of War, to command the Algerian-Moroccan Division at
Aïn Sefra as brigadier general. Maumort is at the lunch where Lyautey
receives his orders. Lyautey requests Maumort for his general staff and takes
him to Aïn Sefra.

From 1904 to 1910, belongs to Lyautey's general staff, sometimes attached
to his office, sometimes given missions in Morocco. Takes part in the victories of 1908. Remains with Lyautey when latter made High Commissioner.
Works with him on organization, laying out of towns, etc. Witnesses birth of
Lyautey's concept of "native politics."

From 1910 to 1912, when Lyautey is recalled to France,[†] Maumort does
not remain with Regnault[‡] but is sent to the Algerian-Moroccan border as
major of a regiment of spahis,[**] in a forward position. It is from there that
he witnesses international difficulties from a distance. The Agadir crisis in
1911. Caillaux.[††]

In 1912, rioting in Fez. Lyautey, sent back to Morocco as resident general,
goes through Algeria and the region of Oran. He brings Maumort back onto
his staff.

---

*In the following notes, Martin du Gard sometimes speaks of Maumort in the third person
and sometimes has Maumort speak in the first person.

[†]In 1910 Lyautey was recalled to France to command the army corps at Rennes. October of
that same year saw a general rising of the tribes around Fez against the unpopular sultan Moulay
Hafid. Fez was besieged in March, 1911. In April and May, French troops were sent to occupy Fez
and pacify the district. This action angered Germany, which in July dispatched the gunboat *Pan-
ther* to Agadir, on the Atlantic coast of Morocco. An international crisis ensued—which was
finally resolved in November with a treaty by which Germany, in return for territorial concessions
in the Congo, recognized France's political protectorate over Morocco. In April 1912, with Fez still
in disarray, Lyautey was sent to Morocco as high commissioner and resident general to quell disturbances and to consolidate the recently declared protectorate. Immediately upon his arrival he
succeeded in relieving Fez, and initiated his work of pacification and colonization.

[‡]Eugène Regnault, French minister in Tangiers.

[**]Native Algerian horsemen serving under the French.

[††]Joseph Caillaux (1863–1944). In 1911, as premier of France, he negotiated the treaty which
gave his country the protectorate over Morocco in exchange for concessions to Germany in the
Congo—a compromise so unpopular among his countrymen that it led to his resignation.

From 1912 to 1914, with Lyautey on the Fez expedition. Lyautey made a member of the Académie in October 1912. In Rabat, 1913, pacification of Morocco.

World War I. Maumort lands in France on August 20, 1914, with his spahis. Is requested by the chief of staff of the First Cavalry Corps and joins up with Connaud's staff at the end of August, near Saint-Quentin.

He will leave Connaud's staff in the spring of 1915, at Auxi. Promoted to lieutenant-colonel, assigned to an armored regiment, in the First Corps. Presently the cavalry are unhorsed and become infantry. Maumort will fight in the trenches as a lieutenant-colonel.

2. MAUMORT THE COLONIAL OFFICER

2.1. *His colonial vocation (life of Gouraud*)*

In 1898, when I was stationed in Constantine and much occupied with the Dreyfus Affair; then at le Saillant in 1899 and 1900; then in 1901 and 1902, while I was in the École de Guerre, I received letters fairly regularly from my old friend and schoolmate X, who kept on fighting in Africa under Gouraud; fiery and enthusiastic letters, which moved me deeply every time and made me feel more bitterly the contrast between that active and heroic life and my home-troop existence, so dull, so thankless.

I envied him without, however, giving in to his appeals and without being able to make up my mind to join him.

2.2 *The colonial officer*

When one has seen colonial officers in action, one understands what a school of energy and endurance this could be for a man of our time and how toughened the character emerges from those superhuman trials.

2.3. *Important*

Maumort and colonialism
        Morocco
        the Moslem World

Correct the common opinion of colonial officers by closely rereading Daniel Guérin's article, *Temps modernes,* No. 87, January '53, on the true situation in Morocco, Algeria, and Tunisia. The article is titled: "Pity for the Maghreb."

---

*Henri Gouraud, French officer famed for his capture in 1898 of the Muslim leader Samory Touré, who had led the resistance to French colonial expansion in West Africa. Later one of Lyautey's most trusted subordinates in Morocco.

3. Maumort's Memories of Fez

- The green and pink sky of dusk, above the city walls, with the swifts and owls and harriers gliding, during the prayer of the *aâcha*. The white flags hoisted in the evening on the towers of the minarets.
- The gardens, cool in the evening, of the old neighboring town, Dar Debibagh, and its old casbah, and its chattering storks.
- Gouraud and his blue gaze, and his boyish, contagious laugh.
- Moroccan landscape: great, undulating pink and reddish expanses; hills with dark patches; douars* set up on the slopes; little enclosures with dry rock walls, where prickly pears grow. Not a bush, not a blade of grass. Charred. Baked earth.
- Those plateaus become covered with vegetation in the rainy season: crops, asphodels, grasses.
- Landscape. Islands of greenery, oases on the brick-red plain. Ancient olive trees. Cypresses. Geraniums, jasmine. Pomegranate trees. Red partridges rising slowly from the ground.
- *Famine.* I saw Shleuh children, south of Marrakech, in November, after months of torrid drought and famine, searching through the horse manure left by the bivouac for undigested grains, to take them home.
- Parties in the houses of rich Moroccans. The table laid in the inner garden, among the orange and lemon trees, the roses, the jasmines. The blue night. The guests lit by great candelabra set on the ground. The spicy dishes. Outside, singing, yelping, flute music coming from the red-light district.
- *Debarrasek!* "Get out of your own damn mess!" *Inshallah.*
- I saw groups of looters (harkas) who were surrounded let themselves be cut down by the charges of squadrons of infantry, without making a move to defend themselves. Only a few tried, before falling, to disembowel the horses as they went past. Most of them, motionless, standing, watched, as if insentient, the deadly whirlwind come, feeling all resistance impossible, facing the attackers with only their calm scorn of death, their fatalism before the inevitable.
- The native negotiators come forward, waving a white rag at the end of a pole and shouting: *Marahba bikoum!* (Welcome!)
- The souks of Marrakesh, very alive. Rugs said to be "the Glaoui's,"† with black and white stripes. Leather goods of every color. Perfumes.

---

*Douar: a small encampment of Arab tents grouped in a circle round a central enclosure for the cattle. *(Oxford English Dictionary)*

†A powerful feudal lord of the Glaoua tribe.

- Swarms of mosquitoes. The days of malarial fever when you toss and turn in your damp bed, with an unbearable anxiety in which you think that all is lost, in which you take your temperature every hour. A long, terrifying nightmare.
- Berber ethnography: to the north, the Djebel, the Rif; in the center, the Beni Ouaraïa, the Idrassen; to the south, the Shleuh (High Atlas).
- A *diffa:* a popular fair, a row of "mechouis"* spitted for roasting, calabashes, thick stews with spices, white couscous, cakes, sugar loaves, pots of honey, mint tea.
- In the distance, a clump of shrubs heralds a water hole.
- Arbors of roses in abandoned gardens. A riot of jasmines, so fragrant in the night. A wood of fig trees, clusters of oleanders on the bank of the wadi.†
- Spring. Fertile plains, fields of poppies, larks springing out of the grass, bees—all bathed in an admirable light.
- Gazelles, hares, partridges.
- A convoy of the wounded, returning from a local operation. Nostrils pinched, wrapped in bandages, limping, supporting one another. Finally, on camels, come the dead, funereal bundles in bloody tent canvases from which labels dangle.

  The men who watch this sinister parade pass by stand spontaneously at attention and salute.
- The *d'chours,* an enclosure with ruined walls, a single entrance, and square towers at the corners of those ramparts four or five meters high.
- The sandstorm, a yellow fog, hot as the breath of an oven; it stung the face with its blinding dust, parching the lips.
- Nights on bivouac, impossible to catch a wink. The mules, the horses always break their tethers, stray, snort. We go after them to tie them up again. The stallions are restless when they smell the mares. A shot is fired by a prowler. The dogs, always numerous and famished, fight with one another, baying, barking interminably at the night.
- The native looters attack, throwing themselves upon the camps at the gallop, two on a horse, a rider and a man riding pillion who jumps off and fights crawling on the ground.
- The "silos" of the tribes, crammed with grain, underground; narrow opening plugged with stones and branches.
- The soldiers' baths in the raging wadi; immediately shouts, laughter, chatter in the splashing of the yellowish water.
- I hear a shot. A young Shleuh has just put a bullet in his mouth, out of

---

*Sheep barbecued whole.
†A gully or streambed that remains dry except in the rainy season.

homesickness. He had said to a buddy: "Say hello to the captain, tell him I'm sorry, take him my rifle, my cartridges, all my gear."

- The first time I met Major X, he loomed up out of the desert, alone, on a chestnut thoroughbred, at the gallop. He was laughing. He had bet that he could, by himself, do a round trip of three hundred kilometers in a hundred hours, four days.
- A scorched country, yellow as a doormat.
- In January, lightning storms, low sky, torrential rains, hail. Invasion of rats and field mice, seeking shelter in our tents. Bursts of sunshine that set the soaked tents smoking and stretch them like drum skins. Muddy, foul-smelling trails. Fevers. Swarms of mosquitoes.
- Village: a few straw huts, a few palms and jujubes, two wells.
- *Kheima:* large camel-skin tent.
- What you find in the homes of the caids: a piano, a music box, a few wild beasts in captivity, a few birdcages, a camera, crates of flares, Bengal lights, tricycles, bicycles, clocks, a billiard table, umbrellas, mirrored wardrobes, English saddles, a bathtub with no plumbing, a chandelier, painted chests full of new but moth-eaten European clothes.
- A Meknasi: an inhabitant of Meknes.
- A big "marabout tent," set up on low dry stone walls. All the comforts!

4. LYAUTEY

4.1 April 1919. Jean Fernet.*

Until the age of thirty-nine Lyautey was an officer of hussars, a gambler, riding in horse races, spending his patrimony. Lived in Meaux, came constantly to Paris in the Vogüé† set (*Revue des Deux Mondes.* Discovery of the Russian novel. Taine).

Then, cleaned out, taking the bull by the horns, he leaves for the colonies, and there finally becomes a great man, the conqueror of an empire, and a legislator, organizer, proconsul.

4.2 Lyautey

G. Hardy, *Portrait de Lyautey,* Bloud et Gay, 1949.

Entered the army in obedience to family tradition rather than through irresistible vocation.

---

*Friend of Martin du Gard's from his student days; a naval officer who eventually rose to the rank of admiral. He first served in Morocco in 1911 and probably knew Lyautey. This note is based on a comment made by Fernet in 1919.

†Eugène Melchior, Vicomte de Vogüé (1848–1910), French writer, posted as diplomat to St. Petersburg, who, through his books, introduced the major Russian writers of the nineteenth century to France.

Employs force when necessary, but reluctantly, and as briefly as possible. Policy of friendship, persuasion, mutual interest.

Would have done better as a statesman, *as a diplomat;* but this man who was a man of action due to his career and circumstances was more fundamentally an intellectual.

4.3 Maumort and Saint-Cyr

If I became an officer, it was *like Lyautey,* out of family tradition, through force of circumstances and not at all through an irresistible vocation.

4.4 Suarès*

Grande revue, 25 April 1911, p. 839. On Petronius: "He has the steady brilliance of a great intelligence, for whom *life is a map to be read with care:* the calm self-control, the well-ordered memories, the swiftness in the decision that action suggests; the always ready will which cannot be surprised by any unsolved problem, which will not be stopped by any question that is posed."

[Below, written at a later date] = Lyautey.

4.5 Valmont.† January, 1911

Bismarck once quipped, concerning a foreign-policy position, that pike keep carp from sleeping at the bottom of ponds so that they don't taste of mud.

We all need pike around us to wake us up from time to time.

[Below:] Idea for Lyautey.

4.6 Suarès

Chronique de Caërdal, Nouvelle Revue Française, May, 1914, p. 661.

"Vanity is a universal weakness. Modesty is the sincerity of little people. The great souls do not need to be modest: they are sincere; and this virtue suffices."

[Below:] Lyautey.

4.7 On Lyautey: making use of circumstances

Maumort: What I admired in Lyautey was that he never let himself be mastered by circumstances. They were for him what cards are for the gambler: external factors, unmodifiable, which life flung at him and which he seized upon immediately, without vain recriminations, in order to get the most out of them, to work them into that personal oeuvre which his creative power never stopped improvising. This way of grasping the event to make it contribute to the creation he was pursuing often reminded me of a poet who

---

*André Suarès (1868–1948), French writer.

†Gustave Valmont, close friend of Martin du Gard's, killed on the front at Esternay in 1914.

catches the rhymes that are tossed at him and weaves them into a quatrain. If he always knew completely what he wanted, he had no idea in advance of the means by which he would attain his ends. It was always the chance occurrence, the inspiring fortuity, which suggested them to him.

4.8 On Lyautey: the leader

He was never more impressive, more surprising to watch, than at cataclysmic moments. With what violent and serene strength did he face the storm! "The boss can take it," said his staff, admiringly. Yes, he could "take it," as a big ship "takes" the sea.

4.9 On Lyautey

By a curious mechanism of his temperament, this man, who lived, it could be said, in the illusions that he himself created, drew from the very intensity of those illusions an excitement that brought the power of *wanting* to fever pitch. Between the idea and its realization, there is a murky and shifting zone where most people get bogged down. For Lyautey, this space did not exist. He crossed it with a single bound. The three steps of action—imagining, wanting, doing—happened in him almost instantaneously, carried along as he was by his uncontrollable momentum.

4.10 Lyautey: implementer only of the "possible"

I had the luck—one of the secrets of a happy life—not to be inclined to fanciful desires. This is how I am: I wish only for what is feasible, and very quickly give up any goal I am not sure I can reach.

On a different scale, it was also Lyautey's basic talent, and, to my way of thinking, an invaluable asset for a leader of men and a founder of empires.

For Lyautey, the passage from thought to action always happened with a dazzling rapidity. The only things he took an interest in and applied himself to were those that could be done. He enjoyed the difficult, but rejected the impossible out of hand, and his attention turned away from it automatically. Faced with a problem of strategy or organization, he accepted only hypotheses that were humanly attainable, that could be translated into workable action. In his councils, he always silenced those dreamers who told him, "*Mon général,* we should . . ." "Yes," he would say, "you're right: we should. But that's wanting to grab the moon. Let's not discuss it further." But once with his unwavering judgment he had felt and declared something to be doable, then he stuck to it doggedly, did not let go, followed it to its outcome no matter what.

4.11 Lyautey's conversations about the Moroccan war

Lyautey kept on repeating that the aim was not to destroy the enemy but to pacify him. Which meant turning the enemy into a collaborator in colonization who understood the material advantages he could gain from his submission. Military action was only a way to commence political action.

When it comes to political action, you have to make yourself feared without making yourself hated, to appear strong yet loyal and generous whenever possible. Force was only a means of giving the white man a lasting prestige.

He was opposed to quick and short-lived expeditions. The enemy's tactic in the face of the attack was to scatter, so as to regroup and return to the charge. No temporary or localized offensives. First subjugate, then immediately *govern.*

Lyautey knew how hard the war in Morocco was on the soldier, and kept an eye on the provisioning, hygiene, and care of the men.

*Victoria uti,** the Roman colonizers used to say. You have to know how to exploit any victory, even a partial one, very fast, reorganizing the conquered territory and bringing it greater affluence in order to disarm the hostility of the vanquished.

The Moroccan is susceptible to order, to good administration, to justice.

Avoid night combat, where the native has the advantage of knowing the ground, being mobile. Approach by night, but do not launch the attack until dawn.

The skirmish, the melée: the *baroud.*

To avoid night action, the great importance of the *camp,* which must be well positioned, with all precautions meticulously taken, well and easily defended. Assaults are seldom carried through all the way. What counts is not to get taken by surprise.

The Moroccan, be he Arab, berberized Arab, arabized Berber, or pure Berber, is brave and scorns death; he is observant, patient, cunning, and can perceive the slightest weakness in our armies.

They do not maneuver much but fight individually, with freedom of action, lying in ambush so as to spring up unexpectedly. More warlike in eastern Morocco than in the western part. Cannot in the long run stand up to modern tactics, which consist of encircling them. Ready to surrender once they clearly see the futility of resistance.

Fertile country if one knows how to farm it and irrigate it, but very poor and arid at the time of conquest. Impossible to live off the land. Hence the importance of well-organized supply lines.

*Make the most of victory.

4.12 *Maumort in Casablanca, 1914*

14 July '14. Lyautey comes to Rabat to review the troops, in the presence of the Sultan Moulay Yusef in a luxurious tent. The sultan's Moroccan band, dressed in red. The Sultan on a throne of red-and-gold velvet. Lyautey at the gallop, followed by his general staff, stops a minute in front of the sultan and salutes him chivalrously, like a musketeer, with a great sweep of his plumed cocked hat (very mindful, by these marks of respect, to give importance to the Sultan, the spiritual and temporal leader of the natives).

Maumort caracoles among Lyautey's general staff.

4.13 *Maumort detached from Lyautey*

Arriving in Morocco, I changed. Until then I was under the spell of Lyautey's prestige. During the war, Lyautey, at a distance, seemed to me deserving of criticism in many respects, because I mistrusted him.

Lyautey, despite his dynamism, is a man stuck in the past. A representative of something outdated, a bygone civilization. He is half a century behind the times. An exile in the present-day world. Anachronistic and off-putting. He is a feudal lord of the Early Middle Ages. Which accounts, incidentally, for one part of his appeal: he is outside of our history—even while making history; he has the charm that the past, the memories of former times, the *traditions* of old that appear to us clarified by distance, sometimes have— there lies his apparent *originality.*

All of us more or less go along with modern ideas. Not he. He refuses, and stiffens in that refusal. He thinks that modern civilization is a mistake, an absurdity, and that the world has gone the way of weakness, of decadence. He considers himself to be from another world, an outmoded world, which was more sensible and better. He has held on to its prejudices and sticks to them as the only possible way to live. He refuses any indulgence towards what others regard as a new order and what he judges to be an aberration fatal to Europe and Western civilization.

He declines to have even the slightest bit to do with the views of his contemporaries in any area. Holding firmly to his old convictions, he pronounces an anathema.

He was able to succeed in his project only because it took place, as it were, in a virgin field, and because he could act and decide utterly by himself, away from France, outside of his time. He is a monolith, a monument of the past.

Others are victims of an inferiority complex. Lyautey is prey to a *superiority complex,* far more serious. Has no doubts as to the high worth of his opinion.

Everywhere but in Morocco he has been a fish out of water.

5. MAUMORT, MILITARY LIFE, WAR

5.1

Maumort will say very frankly, right from the beginning: I took part in the Moroccan campaigns with the youthful ardor of a crusader, convincing myself that our conquering armies were bringing peace, justice, and order and that we were the missionaries of civilization. Much might be said about this, but that will be for another time. It was in the same warlike and civilizing spirit that I threw myself into the First World War, against a Germany which was greedy for conquests and whose triumph would have been, for Europe, a step backward on the path of progress. About this also much might be said. But the only thing I want to note today is that this fine impulse broke down in the course of the war. In the mud of the trenches, there was too much time to ponder.

5.2 *Maumort as officer. Important*

He will explain that:

1. Until the Dreyfus Affair, his aim was to be the great model soldier, disciplined, full of abnegation, virtue, humility, dedicated to the point of totally renouncing his own will, mystically accepting the hardest sacrifice for the sake of his ideal.

2. The Dreyfus Affair, *the great moral drama, the break.* Suddenly the soldier had doubts about his leaders, their honesty, their intelligence. And he had doubts about the army. He understood that his homeland was represented by justice rather than by the army.

Total change. The obedient, disciplined man, at one with the community, again became an emancipated *individual,* obeying only his own reason.

He had *two lives as a soldier,* entirely different in spirit: from '89 to '97; from 1900 to 1920.

5.3 *Choice of a military career*

Maumort: I confess that I did not go into the army with a frenzied desire to fight, nor even to give France back her lost provinces. By 1887, people had begun to be less wrought up about getting even with Germany.

As a matter of fact, in the discipline of military life I was to some extent looking for an employment of my energies which would not require the total sacrifice of my attention and intelligence. I saw in it a way to live usefully, within an established order, and to *pursue my personal development,* which was more important to me than anything. I was somewhat in the state of mind of those who, in the Middle Ages, embraced the monastic life: I was searching for a retreat where I could give myself over to reflection.

And, in fact, I found in the army what I was looking for. A steady and interesting activity; the sense of serving; a great freedom for the mind, which was not hindered by the somewhat mechanical daily routine of the garrison; and a healthy life, in the open air, for the body. I did not suffer from the mediocrity of that life; on the contrary, I derived many benefits from it.

5.4 Military career

In choosing a military career, I did not take the wrong path. Even today, I congratulate myself on having chosen it. I see no other sort of existence which would so well have allowed me to combine the demands of, I dare not call it my spiritual life—let's rather call it my "purring"—and an active, intense life, led by a man of this century who wanted to avoid being idle, wanted to "serve."

5.5 Maumort and the soldier's profession

My soldier's profession remains part of me. More: a central part of my human substance.

Perhaps I was made to be an "intellectual," as Uncle Éric wished. But the vocation of arms progressively got into my body and shaped me. I feel myself to be the brother of all the soldiers of the world, of warriors of every era, broken, put through the mill, made supple by the yoke of discipline. That fierce discipline which does violence to the man until it has subjugated him. That inhuman *exactingness* which you end up loving with a restive, rebellious passion for the *secret strength* that it gives to the soldier, that armature which allows him to perform, to surpass himself.

5.6 Military life

It was unforeseen that this fanatical tendency to meditative speculation would not kill the man of action in me.

However, it didn't. At certain phases of my career, whenever necessary, I was truly the man of action that I was expected to be, that my position of command and my responsibilities demanded. And effortlessly. And I demonstrated noticeable stamina. My subordinates as well as my superiors would simply have shrugged if you had told them, "Maumort is a dreamer, Maumort isn't cut out to be a man of action."

I explain this anomaly by the alternation of two natures within me. In the life of activity I found a diversion from my inner life. Like a schoolboy who leaps from his seat in the classroom to throw himself spiritedly into the rough-and-tumble of recess.

And those two worlds, those two expressions of myself were so distinct, with no interaction, that I scarcely tried to apply to my active life whatever ideas I might have had in my meditative life. Obviously, I was the same man, and my behavior in everyday life could not help being influenced by the results of my reflections. But in some sense *involuntarily,* and by force of circumstances.

At any rate, I never had the desire to try and put my speculations into practice. I thought much about youth, pedagogy, methods for educating young people. But I never used my men or my sons as subjects for experiments. On the contrary, in my relations with my sons in particular, I took care not to influence them.

I would not for anything in the world have wanted to stick my finger into the workings of politics, although I gave no small amount of thought to governments, institutions, and laws.

5.7 Military life, garrison life

I carried out what I had to do as well as I possibly could. And always, everywhere, I have had an excellent record. But in this I used only a minute and insubstantial fraction of my intelligence. My brain did not truly work except outside of my profession.

This duality was perceptible even in my outward behavior. *I was not the same man in uniform that I was in mufti.*

In uniform I walked briskly, stood straight, had a gleam in my eye, observed what was going on around me, really looked like a man of action.

In civilian clothes my whole being changed, and I was another character: my gait was slack, my gaze vacant and distracted. I went around in an endless state of reverie which filled my mind completely and screened off the outer world.

In uniform, I seemed a gay and lively man, capable of a quick response. In civilian clothes, a somewhat weary and preoccupied man who could not shake off his seriousness.

Isn't there a film in this? A *double* life. The stiff, professional life with its flair and its great deeds. The secret, private, ordinary life with its failures.

And finish with this: that the fellow is a hero nevertheless, because it is in his professional life that he is called to show his stuff, to run a risk.

5.8 Military life

That garrison life, despite its reputation for exuding an asphyxiating boredom, has left me with only good memories—of a well-balanced existence that catered to all my tastes. I saw people, I entered new circles with each move, I explored a microcosm, I amused myself with human beings. There were sports, exercise, action. I took enough of an interest in the profession, and was sufficiently attached to my men, to enjoy performing my role among them.

And I had a huge amount of leisure time for reading, writing, and daydreaming. I had whole afternoons and evenings for my woolgathering. I mixed all these things together—my experiences with the natives, my recent reading—and they kept my brain constantly alert and working, which has always been the greatest pleasure for someone of my nature: *to use everything as food for thought.*

I surprised my colleagues by my lack of ambition and my indifference to honors and promotions. What I liked in the gossip at mess were true anecdotes or anything that revealed character.

5.9 Maumort. Freedom

I have never felt *freer* in my whole life than during those years as a young officer in the outposts of Morocco, subject to the strictest order, in the most absolute solitude, narrowly limited, hemmed in, tied down to a discipline that was all the more relentless since the men I commanded and had to make obey me, by example more than by instructions, were watching me day and night, looking out for the slightest infraction on my part. It was the need for, and the intoxication of, this *true* and total freedom which must have led so many fierce and independent men to enter the monasteries of the Middle Ages.

The observance of military or monastic rituals, of *the rule,* by simplifying material life and limiting social exchanges, is, in many regards, a liberation. In my *bled,* there was a fraternity, simple and friendly relationships, but no intellectual exchanges, hence a total freedom of mind that I have not found anywhere since; even the soberness of the life, the absence of comfort, the elimination of politeness, the concessions to communal living, the return to elementary ways of washing and eating, foster this liberation of the mind. A lifting of social obstacles because the relations among men are governed by discipline.

The mental life, set free, exults in continuous meditation, which is no longer an accident, an exception, but a habitual state: and it expresses itself in the private diary and also in correspondence. This expression is a need. This is where I picked up the habit of the diary.

For my entire life since that period of intoxication in freedom and solitude, I have had the feeling that Moses must have had after Sinai of having come back down to earth, of having fallen.

5.10 Maumort the soldier

How could an individualist like Maumort have loved the army?

Because of its perfect (theoretical) organization, its rational hierarchy.

5.11 Maumort as officer. Authority

My fellow officers, my superiors, Lyautey, all concurred: "Maumort has *authority.*" I have to acknowledge that this was true. It was a natural gift, concerning which there is no cause for vanity. I cultivated in myself that secret strength of assurance, that energy, will, decisiveness, unbending perseverance in execution, which has a hold on others and compels their immediate trust. Never hesitate once the decision is made. If you do hesitate, never show it once you have taken a public stand. And I cultivated the trust of others by endeavoring to be "exemplary," in order to have "charisma."

It becomes a habit, and this habit increases the self-confidence and mastery of the leader. You end up believing yourself to be invulnerable, invincible, and this certitude (absurd, yet so precious) greatly magnifies those natural gifts of will-power and clear-sightedness.

I don't know if I had courage, but I *displayed* it, and that is all that is required. Your carcass stops shaking the moment you feel yourself to be the leader whom the men are counting on and *whom they watch* to help them be less cowardly. You forget the risk, whatever the cost, when you have to set an example and show yourself a superior being.

When not under fire, I let the men see me just as I was, very simple, natural. I did not hide from them to eat, to smoke, to sleep. I wasn't one of those who are constantly afraid of losing *prestige.* I think you have prestige by virtue of the man you are, and that the best way to have it is never to think about it and not to do anything with that purpose in mind. My familiarity with everyone never did away with distance: a hint of natural distinction took care of that. With the French, at least. And even with the Arabs. I never needed to withdraw onto a pedestal. The prestige I had was based on *the goodwill I inspired.*

I insisted on being obeyed as soon as I had given a command. But whenever I could I explained the reason for my orders, and it always seemed to me that with the French, to be *well* obeyed you need as much as possible to be *understood.* I noticed, with experience, that this method has an invaluable advantage: sometimes a given order is impossible to execute. If the men have understood the logic of the order and are prevented from carrying it out to the letter, they take initiatives in the right direction, and, as it were, stand in for their leader.

5.12 Maumort as soldier

I write: "the fraternity of arms." This appears to be an insipid cliché. Yet the hackneyed phrase expresses a solid, unquestionable reality. The fraternity of arms exists. And it is something other than love, friendship, camaraderie, something entirely different from family feeling or the bond among schoolmates.

It exists only after danger has been faced together. Until the hour of shared danger, the fraternity of arms is scarcely more than any association of clans or groups, the feeling of connection forged by mutual interests, cohabitation at close quarters, traditions, folklore, shared memories, hopes. This does not prevent the clashes, the irritations, the hatreds, the dirty tricks, the reprisals, the incompatibilities that occur in every group.

Comes the hour of danger and all that disappears in a flash. Everything that is not "fraternity" goes up in flames. The only thing that remains is what binds soldier to soldier, soldier to officer, officer to superior—as *brothers.* Each sheds the personality that was at odds with the personalities around him. Gone the disgust for one another. Individual communicates to individual through a kind of general osmosis, and the impermeable walls separating the various sacks of skin dissolve. This is the hour of the "fraternity of arms." In the trench, on the attack, at the lookout post . . .

After that, life resumes. You go back behind the lines. And all the causes of discord spring up again, and all the sacks of skin grow back their impermeable hides. But the miracle has happened, and it endures, *underneath.* This group of personalities, more or less at odds, hostile, in competition, in friction, remains united, in the depths of their bodies and souls, by this new feeling which has been born of danger.

This is the *"fraternity of arms."*

5.13 The senior officers

You seldom find a senior officer who is a despicable man. He might sometimes be a mediocrity, lacking substance, and a man who, moreover, would have stayed that way. But as a leader he feels eyes fixed upon him, and eyes that will not be taken in by appearances for long. The virtues he demonstrates he may not have had since birth; he may only have them because he is forced to demonstrate them. But it is as if he had them in reality; and in fact he does have them, he has acquired them: you cannot act fair, conscientious, and courageous for thirty years straight without becoming so.

5.14 Abuse of power

Maumort thinks: No officer capable of reflection will contradict me: you have only to be entrusted with a tiny bit of power to realize that you need to watch yourself constantly and keep yourself well reined in if you want never to yield to the temptation to abuse it (that poison which all too naturally oozes out of power and domination).

The most independent, the most rebellious of servants, the one who suffers most from having to obey, becomes a tyrant the moment he gets an assistant to order about (Bocca* and his day laborer).

---

*Pietro Bocca, Maumort's man Friday.

5.15 Maumort. Military life

I never worshipped rank. On the contrary, the more stripes a man had, the more I demanded of him. I judged officers very harshly, I knew many who were vain, nonentities, dullards. I obeyed them to the extent that discipline dictated, but I had little to do with them outside of work. I was thought to be pretentious. I was also criticized for being a demagogue because I willingly took an interest in the enlisted men and the noncommissioned officers. I passed for a dissident, though I never showed any hostile resistance to my superiors. But they felt that I could do without them, that I was not "part of the family," and they did not forgive me for it.

I never asked for a favor or requested a promotion. The moment a friend came into a position where he could be useful to me I avoided him, so strongly did I fear that he would take my friendliness and my overtures for a self-interested solicitation.

What is more, I deserved no credit for this. I had no career ambition. I only tried to provide satisfaction and conscientiously fulfill the job that was given me. I was never promoted except through seniority.

5.16 Military life

Perhaps I could have attached myself to Lyautey, got into his closest circle, become one of his right-hand men, his trusty liege man, like so many others who found happiness in that personal devotion.

As for myself, I was incapable of finding happiness in a *subordination* of that kind. Something in me always balked at the idea of such personal dependence on a man, though he might be the greatest I had met. Perhaps my *dignity* was too ticklish? Such a dependence implies that you are unreservedly subjugated: it inevitably implies a moral submission.

5.17 Why Maumort is a lieutenant-colonel

"Discipline is hard on the men, but at least it asks nothing of their minds; then too, I have often observed that blunders by those in command were well known around the kitchens, which serve as information centers for the privates. Discipline in the world of the officers is far more cunning, but it aims at the head even if indirectly; for it is understood that opinions are free and that critical remarks are listened to. But the underlying message is that *whoever dissents* will be slowed in his progress up the ladder as far as the rank of lieutenant-colonel, where he will stay stuck like a drowned man on a weir . . ." (Alain,* *Échec à la force,* p. 128.)

Nom de plume of Émile-Auguste Chartier (1868–1951), French essayist and philosopher.

PART SEVEN

World War II (1939–1945)

CHAPTER XXII

Maumort During the Defeat and Occupation (1940)

[André Daspre: We have no more sustained narrative, or even isolated fragments, which would tell us anything about Maumort's life from 1914 to 1940.* The texts we are going to read in this seventh part—reduced to the dimensions of a single chapter—are, chronologically, in their place, but Martin du Gard had originally intended to begin his novel with an account of the events of 1940 [. . .]

It must be recalled that this plan had two variants. In the beginning, Martin du Gard imagines that Maumort, cloistered in his library after the occupation of le Saillant by the Germans in July 1940, decides to write the diary of the invasion, then proceeds backwards and tells the story of his entire life. The novelist began this work in the summer of 1941 and he wrote in his own diary, on October 3, 1941: "I have worked well for a whole month now. And yet the toil is thankless. It is limited to preparing the historical ground for the opening of my book. When Maumort, in June '40, starts keeping a diary again, it is to record the events of the day (the campaign of France, the invasion, Pétain, the armistice, etc.); but gradually this diary becomes something else, a man's reflection, then the reflection of a past, the reflection of a long life; and it is only then that my book can begin to be worth something. All the same, this work of historical notations must be done: it is the framework of the whole beginning. Thus I am living through June and July '40

---

*According to the author's Summary (see pp. 6–7), Part Five would have covered Maumort in the First World War, Part Six his retirement to le Saillant between 1919 and 1939.

again. First, I had to do a meticulous examination of the press and of all the documents I have been able to obtain. Then to select the facts that strike Maumort, i.e., not only what is important but also what Maumort might have heard, true or false, in the depths of his occupied château. In addition to which I am adding his commentaries, his reflections. And this is very hard for me, because my character is far from being created: I still don't know him well, haven't sized him up."

Of all that work, there remains about twenty typed pages that contain the narrative, in the form of notes, of events of June, 1940; an attached card, dated Antibes, 17 May 1942, gives the date of the writing of the fragment: "This is the rough draft, done in the summer of 1941, at Évian, of the diary of Colonel de Maumort during July, '40. I am filing it away under 'Sainte-Hélène,' " and in pencil Martin du Gard has later added, in explanation of this term: "Code name of Dr. Roger Froment in Lyon"—in whose home he hid his manuscripts.

Then Martin du Gard changed his mind and decided that Maumort would begin in 1945 and relate the events of 1940 while gradually combining with this story other, much older memories. It is fragments of this second version that have been used to make up the single chapter of this seventh part.

Whatever the date of the writing of Maumort's diary, the situation at the root of the tale remains the same: it is the occupation of le Saillant, where Maumort lives half-secluded. The novelist had some hesitation when he then had to imagine the relations between Maumort and the Germans. He first thought that the colonel would refuse all contact with his "guests" and would leave le Saillant as soon as possible to join his friend Dr. Gévresin in the Lot. This scenario closely resembles that of Le silence de la mer *; it is not without grandeur but it establishes a radical break between the occupied and the occupiers, so that we can learn nothing important about them. The novelist found a much more dramatic scheme, since he devised a (forced) dialogue between Maumort and some of the Nazi occupiers: the old officer, sick or injured, is cared for by German doctors and orderlies to whom he has no choice but to speak!

This new plan is mentioned in a note in Martin du Gard's diary dated July 20, 1943: "I have seriously resumed my preparatory work. I am going to try to finalize the episode of Maumort's relations with the German general staff that is occupying his property: the political discussions that he has with them about Nazism, etc." It was thus right in the middle of the war, let us not forget, that Martin du Gard wrote the discussions about Nazism that we will read in the second part of this Chapter XXII.

The second plan is much better because it permits a fundamental debate

---

* *The Silence of the Sea* (1942), a novel about the Resistance by Vercors.

about the Nazi ideology. And we know that Martin du Gard excels in the dialogue of ideas, which here takes place between characters (the defeated officer, who has fallen under obligation to his occupiers) at a historical moment (the unprecedented defeat of France), which would give this confrontation a tension, a pathos, of undeniable power [. . .]

The Table of Chapters that the novelist made well after having sketched out these outlines anticipates a division of this episode into four chapters: "January 1st, 1945. The death of R. Rolland. Damage from the occupation of le Saillant. / Hatred of Germany. Atrocities of the Nazi camps. / Memories. Invasion of le Saillant in June '40. / Aftermath. Succinct: occupation of le Saillant, after having received care from the Germans."

But of this plan there remain only fragments. It seemed to me possible to indicate the broad lines of the episode by grouping these texts in five parts, of very uneven lengths:

 I. Invasion of le Saillant
 II. Maumort and the Nazis
  1. Rupert Gralt
  2. Maumort and his guests
  3. Kert
  4. Weissmüller
 III. Hatred of Germany
 IV. Responsibility of the French General Staff for the defeat
 V. The true nature of the Résistance: indignation.]

1. THE INVASION OF LE SAILLANT

Thirty degrees outside when I got up. Not a thaw, but it didn't snow again last night. Sunny morning. I wanted Bocca to take advantage of the weather to dig out the scrap of iron where they stuck their flag. They sank it above the front door the very day they arrived. Holed up here, in one of the armchairs in the library, I clearly heard the thuds that were breaking through my bricks. I can hear them still. During all those years of humiliation, each new wave of occupants, as soon as it moved in, hastened to unfurl the swastika in my courtyard. (To tell the truth, I saw it only in my imagination. From the moment the first wave took possession of le Saillant until the day I left to seek refuge in the Lot, I didn't stir out of my house, but kept to the three rooms of my wing, with the windows shut and the curtains drawn. But I remember recoiling, furious, one morning: Rose, after having cleaned the library, had forgotten to close the shutters; coming in, I glimpsed a great moving shadow that swept over the gravel in front of the window.) No use thinking back on all that. Besides, I had my little revenge just now as I watched Bocca, up on his ladder, chisel out the unholy iron!

It was so mild in the sunshine, as I was sheltered from the wind, that I lingered out of doors. A golden light, a spring light, flooded the pink bricks. For some reason the entrance gate we hardly ever close was closed today. As on that tragic morning in the spring of '40. I thought I saw, between the two stone pillars, their gray-uniformed horde massed behind the bars . . . The illusion was so strong that I went back in without waiting for Bocca to plaster up the hole.

I tried to read. Impossible to concentrate. I relived those hours of June '40. Everything has stayed so clear in my memory! I want to write it down.

First, the cannonade on the thirteenth. It was on the thirteenth, Thursday the thirteenth of June, at dawn, that Bocca came and knocked on my shutter: "*Mon colonel!* listen to the cannon!" I jumped out of bed and opened my window; but my deafness would not allow me to verify the observation. "It's pounding hard out there, *mon colonel!* . . . Began twenty minutes ago. . . . It's a long way off, but that's it. No mistake!" Bocca is no novice. We fought together for three years, from '15 to '18. He did not speak without being sure. That continuous muffled hammering, which seemed to reverberate to the center of the earth, does not fool the ear of a soldier who has been through the Woëvre, the Argonne, the Chemin-des-Dames, the Mort-Homme, Doublens.

I was less surprised than he. A week earlier, the Berlin radio, whose broadcasts I tried to pick up in spite of the jamming, triumphantly announced that a significant part of the Panzer Divisionen, massed somewhere between Abbeville and Amiens, had succeeded in breaking through the front. Our covering army, the Tenth (under Altmayer, my old friend from the general staff of the First Cavalry Corps in 1914), was cut in two. The German communiqué reported the shortcomings of the French air force, which had facilitated this lightning advance. With their first strike, the armored columns had reached Aumale and were heading towards Forges-les-Eaux and Rouen! I had immediately thought that the success of that audacious operation would have the gravest consequences for the western region. I had clearly sensed the threat of the invasion coming our way. And even more so on the following days, when Berlin announced that the bulk of the Tenth Army, forced to retreat, was moving towards the east to brace itself against the Oise instead of doing its utmost to defend Le Havre, Rouen, and the Basse-Seine.

For a long while, in any case, I had feared a disaster for France. Since the declaration of war . . . I had not foreseen either the suddenness or the incredible extent of it; but, alas, I was too well informed on military matters to delude myself as to our chances for victory. In my articles for *La France en armes,* in the pieces that I published from time to time in the *Bulletin des questions stratégiques* (the periodicals subsidized by the ministry rejected my studies), I had, between the two wars, often enough drawn attention to the inferiority of our air force, the insufficiency of our armored units, and often enough criticized the conventional notions of our high command so as to leave no illusions about the deadly risks that this new war would bring us. During the winter of '40, I kept silent, appalled by the optimism of the government officials: I knew that, for most of them, that insane confidence was sincere. Since the Germans' breaking through our lines on the Ardennes front—and even before, since May, since the attack on Holland—I had understood that we would meet our fate within several weeks, and I shuddered. It was obvious when the Panzer Divisionen came through Sedan that they were making for Paris. They were aiming for the heart. To be saved, we needed nothing less than a new victory of the Marne. Perhaps not even that would have turned things around. But miracles don't repeat themselves.

I lived for the German radio broadcasts, but the jamming had got more skillful. I ruined my eyes studying my maps. The enemy strategy could clearly be read in them from the first days of June: in the west, to forge recklessly ahead between the Channel and the Seine in order to sever all contact as quickly as possible between the French army and the British expeditionary force; in the east, to make a wedge between the troops that were fighting to the north of the capital and those that occupied the Maginot Line, in order to encircle Paris unhindered. Thus I was expecting the worst. Yet on that thirteenth of June none of those goals had been attained; our defenses, even according to foreign reports, remained partially effective.

The newspapers were trying hard to keep our hopes up: Weygand,* "the great old campaigner," was thwarting all the enemy's plans, one by one. He was "plugging the gaps." A pronounced sagging of the enemy offensive was noted across the entire front. American matériel was constantly rolling in. Interrogation of the prisoners left no doubt as to the poor morale of the attackers. Our fighter squadrons were slaughtering German airplanes, etc., etc. I was not yet willing to despair. The situation was far gone, but still not lost.

Bocca and I stayed outside on the terrace until the hour of the first broadcast. He standing silent, somber-faced, rolling cigarettes that he chewed on and continually relit. I, lost in thought, sitting on the low wall. Both facing the forest. When I arched my eyebrows questioningly and he answered me with a brusque nod, "Yes, they're still hard at it, *mon colonel*," it was always to the northeast, above the forest, that he stretched his arm, pointing his mutilated forefinger without hesitation in the direction of Laigle, Évreux, Les Andelys.

---

*Maxime Weygand (1867–1965). In World War I, served as chief of staff under General Foch. Recalled to assume command of the French forces in May 1940, as the country was already being overrun by German troops, he ended up advising capitulation.

The tip of his finger, sliced off by a splinter of shrapnel, was left, in March, 1915, in the mud of the Woëvre. Thanks to which Bocca is here . . . Without a fingertip to pull the trigger, he was officially unfit for service—which, incidentally, did not keep him from being one of the best shots in the squadron until the end of the war; or, even today, from bringing down a harrier with his first shell.

Bocca did not on any account want to go into the auxiliaries. One day, in the town square at Étain, where the general staff was billeting, he came up to me in a driving rain and told me his story. From the outset, this bushy-haired *poilu*—with his Corsican name, mulish brow, gruff tone, and faithful dog's gaze—who refused to shirk his duty, appealed to me. That evening in the mess, I pleaded his cause with the five-stripe sawbones. He told me: "One way would be to take him on as an orderly . . ." The next day, everything was arranged. We finished the war together. I brought Bocca here, and I took Rose into my service since he would, I think, have otherwise left his wife to follow me. And it will soon be thirty years that Pietro Bocca has been with me, still bushy-haired, gruff, stubborn, touchy, and demanding, as idolaters will be, but blindly faithful; and I am at the center of his life, as one is in that of one's dog.

At seven o'clock, I began listening again. The broadcast from Berlin was more cacophonous than ever. At the beginning, right when the jamming started up, I thought I understood them to be talking about a "broad bridge-head south of the Seine." Had the Seine been crossed?

I did not learn much from the radio in the morning. Less than from the postman's gossip. He said that the exodus of cars and refugees had increased considerably since the day before. People from Gaillon, questioned along the way, confirmed that during the night the German vanguard had crossed the river and reached Les Andelys. Others announced that Louviers was occupied and that motorized troops were speeding towards Bernay and Évreux. This would have explained the bridgehead and the cannonade. But were all those frightened tales to be believed?

My decision, at any rate, had been made a long time back: should le Saillant find itself in the combat zone, I would not abandon the estate unless forcibly evacuated from it by the French military authorities. But there were no troops in the area; no preparation had been made for its defense; how could there be fighting there? Besides, why assume that the Germans would push all the way to the hills of the Perche? After having secured bridgeheads on the Seine, they were concentrating all their forces in the direction of Paris.

But the noon radio report was alarming. It confirmed the crossing of the Seine and the march on Évreux. In the region of Senlis, the tanks were coming down the valley of the Oise, and our troops had been forced to fall back on the capital, which was being threatened to the east by the army that had crossed the Aisne at Château-Thierry. Crossing the rivers was hardly slowing down the enemy advance. Everywhere the penetration was accelerating.

It was on the same day, the thirteenth, at the end of the evening, that Reynaud spoke over the radio. I can still see myself listening, alone, in the very place where I am now writing. "This is the President of the Council." Distressing disclosures. The government was abandoning the capital to escape the imminent invasion . . . A desperate—and absurd—appeal had been sent by Reynaud to President Roosevelt . . . I scarcely recognized in that muffled, halting utterance the intonations we knew so well, the haughty assurance, the biting terseness, the clarion bursts of his normal voice. Only towards the end did the tone firm up, almost finding an echo of former days, to declare angrily that the government in flight would retreat from département to département and all the way to Africa if need be rather than surrender to defeat.

I did not go to bed. I spent the night filing papers.

On Friday the fourteenth, in the morning, unable to keep still, I went hobbling out* with Bocca to go fetch news in Menneville. No one in the fields, no one in the pastures; no one on our back road. On the main road, a swarm of vehicles, of people: a disorderly throng flowing in one direction only, towards Le Mans. The wealthiest in cars, the others in carts, and then the dusty, exhausted pedestrians, limping along, pushing wheelbarrows or baby carriages loaded down with clothes. We entered the stream. The automobiles had a hard time forcing their way through. As they passed, they brought the latest news: the enemy was surging towards us through the valleys of the Risle, the Iton, the Eure; he had put Lisieux, Bernay, and Évreux behind him . . . In front of us, mixed in with the civilians, soldiers of various divisions, gathered in a silent little group, were wandering aimlessly, leaderless and orderless, and several had neither rifle nor gear. I could not catch up with them, question them. But it was upon seeing them that I truly understood how vain was all hope. We ran into Fortin, the deputy mayor. Menneville was now emptying out. Many inhabitants, seized by panic, had, after having hastily prepared their departure, decamped on the sly at daybreak without saying a word to their neighbors.

It was close to noon when Brunet's cart kindly picked us up and took us back to le Saillant. In the courtyard, in front of the Boccas' cottage, the smallholders were waiting for me, gathered around Rose. The women had come along, and the children. I spoke to them. I had guessed, with one glance, what they wanted to know. I told them that neither I nor my servants would abandon le Saillant. Faced with my resolute attitude and Bocca's

---

*André Daspre: Maumort is lame either because of a war wound in the knee (1917) or because of a riding accident (1935).

somber look, no one dared admit that he had considered fleeing (as it turned out, none of them left his farm).

It was that Friday, at the end of the afternoon, that the airplanes with swastikas started to fly over us, so many of them that my deafness was not enough to protect me from their din. But that was only the beginning. The whole night long, and then all of Saturday and Saturday night, that is, for thirty-six hours in a row—for reasons that still escape me, since not a single bomb was dropped on either the forest or Menneville—more than one hundred and fifty aircraft, rulers of the sky, circled above us, ceaselessly retracing the same route, flying over the forest and the park, pressing on as far as the steeple of Menneville, then coming back above us, lower and lower, almost grazing the treetops and the roof, filling the court with an incredible racket that shook the windowpanes and set our brains vibrating in our skulls like the glassware in the sideboard. We had shut all the windows and closed the shutters tight. The electric power went out, we were left in the dark for thirty hours with no other lighting than the hurricane lamp from the shed.

By the same token, no more radio. Without news, in that funereal night, cut off like castaways, with that uninterrupted throbbing of the motors over our heads, Saturday the fifteenth was interminable. Were they fighting in Paris? Had Roosevelt responded to France's appeal? Bocca suddenly remembered the old battery-operated radio set, relegated to the cellar for ten years now. We worked five hours repairing it; that evening I could, after a fashion, pull in a few uninteresting scraps of the broadcast. I can still see the three of us, in those evil hours, skulking in the library. Rose, terrified, on the verge of a breakdown, had not dared cross the courtyard to go back to her home for thirty-six hours; her husband had not been able to leave her side; they had spent this whole time in the château, cowering, sitting in the kitchen or with me. Of course none of us had been able to get a moment's rest. Our nerves were raw.

Then all of a sudden, on Sunday the sixteenth, at dawn, the infernal merry-go-round stopped. But that abrupt silence, instead of relieving us, seemed so stifling that Bocca and I rushed out onto the terrace. The sun was not up; day was breaking. The sky, where a few stars still twinkled, was pale, immensely empty. Not an airplane in sight. No more cannons were heard. I went back in, and the early hour notwithstanding, I tried to pick up some bulletins on the radio; in vain.

To gather some news, I suggested to Bocca that we go down to the road and question the passersby. We were walking down the slope of the drive in silence when he suddenly said to me:

"If I were you, *mon colonel,* I certainly know what I would do."

"And what would you do, Bocca?"

"Well, I'd put on my uniform."

The idea seemed so preposterous to me that I couldn't help laughing.

The road, contrary to what I had expected, was completely empty. No more autos, no more refugees. I sat down sheltered from the wind while Bocca climbed the embankment to inspect the surrounding area. No one anywhere. The silence hovered, like a threat. Finally a bicyclist appeared at the top of the hill. Petitjean, the former road mender, who was hurrying back from Menneville, stopped when he saw us approaching him: *"They're com-ing, mon colonel . . ."* So distraught was his face that I thought he had seen *them* with his own eyes. No, it was a gendarme standing guard at the entrance to the town who had told him: "We're expecting them any minute now . . ." Laigle, Verneuil, Dreux, Chartres were overrun. La Loupe and Rémalard had been bombed and were in flames. Petitjean was shaking his head, his little red-rimmed eyes were open wide, and he kept repeating like a refrain: "So we ain't got any army left? It boggles the mind, *mon colonel!*" The mayor had posted lookouts all over the place, in the steeple, in the belvedere of the hospice, at the top of the electric transformer from which you could see all the main routes of access. During the night at Connéré, a last convoy of civilians had been ruthlessly machine-gunned. Petitjean had heard a sur-vivor describe the attack: the three-engined planes going into a sudden dive over the line of automobiles and carts, the whistling of the bombs, the blind-ing smoke of the explosions, the screams of the crowd as they tried to hide in the hedges and in the ditches, the pitiless rat-tat-tat of the machine guns, the blazing cars where the wounded, women, children, were roasting . . . "And how 'bout our planes, *mon colonel,* where're they now? And our machine guns, and our cannons, and our soldiers, what the hell are they doing?" He had remounted his bicycle; but before pedaling off, he turned to me once again with this grim parting shot, "It looks like we've been *sold out, mon colonel!*" This, too, he must have heard in Menneville.

When we came back, we both, without consulting each other, wanted to lock the gate to the courtyard. It took the two of us to do it, and we had to dig a furrow in the sand with our heels. Bocca went to get the heavy key in the shed. The lock had not been used for years. He had a hard time turning the key twice. I put the key in my pocket and we went back into the house. There was nothing more to do but wait.

That Sunday! Without news, without seeing a soul . . . We settled into the library. Rose sat in a low chair, her hands under her apron, fingering her rosary; Bocca crouched near the window, like a wildcat on the lookout, to watch the entrance to the courtyard. To appear composed, I picked up a book. After a moment, I went over to Bocca:

"Would you even be able to find it . . . my uniform?"

He didn't bat an eyelash, the rat. He answered me without unclenching his teeth, keeping his eyes fixed on the gate:

"Everything is ready in your room, *mon colonel.*"

And so it was. Breeches, dolman,* kepi were laid out on the bed, as if for an inspection. The buttons were polished, the decorations pinned on the dolman; the shoehorn was placed next to the patent-leather boots. He must have run up to the attic during the night and rummaged through the big camphor trunk where Rose stacks my old clothes. But why, instead of taking out the horizon-blue combat uniform, had he chosen that old dress uniform? Probably those red breeches, that frogged dolman, that kepi circled with braid, had seemed more decorative to him? (Besides, I would doubtless have done the same thing . . .)

I got dressed. I had lost weight over twenty years; the dolman fit loosely about my torso. As for the kepi, I had to forgo it. I had lost a lot of hair, and it came down to my ears. I left the room without having raised my eyes to the mirror.

That evening, on the radio, I was able to catch a few scraps of news. "The enemy advance is progressing . . ." Names of towns, incredible: "Auxerre . . . Dijon . . ." Then, around midnight, resignation of the Reynaud cabinet; formation of a Pétain government.

WE STAYED UP all night, around the single hurricane lamp on the table in the library. (I have to pay this tribute to the Boccas: they are not talkative. That Corsican and that Breton woman hail from two taciturn breeds. That night, I could not have stood servants' cackling.)

Day finally dawned. Still nothing: Bocca hastened to resume his lookout post; and Rose, at my request, ventured to the kitchen to make us coffee.

Suddenly Bocca's voice startled me: "*Mon colonel,* listen!" Instantly on my feet, I strained to hear, cursing my deafness. "Listen, listen . . ." repeated Bocca. But I detected no noise other than the pounding of my heart. At that moment, Rose rushed in. "They're here!" I still heard nothing. At last, I thought I made out the drone of motors. And abruptly, at the bend in our drive, fifty meters from the gate, two, four, six, eight armored vehicles climbed the embankment.

They loomed up together, tangled, almost abreast; and, at the same time, a horde of green uniforms, a cloud of locusts, sprang from the moving vehicles and swarmed over the roundabout. Concealed by the glass curtains, we looked on, breathless, paralyzed by the suddenness, the strangeness, of that wild parade. Motorcycles, armored cars, kept surging onto the terreplein, and from each one rushed greenish men in helmets, weapons in hand, who hurled themselves at the gate, shaking it to open it. There were about a hun-

---

*The uniform jacket of a hussar, worn like a cape with the sleeves hanging loose. *(O.E.D.)*

dred of them now. My gate is of wrought iron, sturdy seventeenth-century craftsmanship dating from the time of the château, and its massive lock would probably not have given; but the stone pillars to which it is fixed are in bad condition, and I saw the moment when, under the pressure of those lunatics, my two pillars were going to come crashing down into the courtyard. Right then, the soldiers suddenly stepped back to let through five or six officers who had just jumped out of a car with pennants on it. At that point, I motioned to Bocca and his wife: "Stay here!" All my calm had come back to me; I even felt the sort of relief that follows an interminable wait. I quickly went to the entrance hall. As I passed through it—I don't know why, perhaps to put on a brave face?—I grabbed my riding crop, which was hanging from a stag's horn. I slid back the two latches of the front door, and with one thrust I opened both the panels. I am thinking of that moment now: in the empty courtyard, the appearance on the front steps of that tall old man, six foot one, thin and lanky, alone, bareheaded, with his Punchinello's features, his baldness fringed with white hair, his red breeches, his old black dolman with the Légion d'honneur and the Croix de Guerre hanging on it, must not have lacked a certain picturesqueness . . .

With no haste, hobbling along, my riding crop under my arm, I descended the steps and crossed the courtyard. I might have been greeted with hoots and jeers. No. The motors went on throbbing where they were, but all the men, massed behind the bars and turned towards me, were hushed; and in spite of the din of the engines, I had the impression of an imposing silence. When I was six feet from the gate, I stopped. The eldest of the officers, a major whose role must have been that of chief of staff, asked me in a strong accent: "Château du Saillant?" I nodded. He glanced down at a paper he was holding. "Colonel de Maumort?" I nodded again. He brought his fingers to the visor of his helmet and stiffened, all correctness, to utter a short sentence in German, introducing himself. I noticed his iron cross, on the field-gray cloth of his tunic. I looked him up and down, without responding. He grabbed a bar of the gate in his gloved fist: "Open, please, order of the general." I took two steps, pulled the heavy wrought-iron key out of my pocket, and without moving forward, without saying a word, holding it at arm's length, I handed it to him through two bars: then I about-faced.

I was not even halfway up the drive when they had already opened the gate and burst into the courtyard. The major, still surrounded by other officers, had no trouble catching up to me. I heard, at my back: "*Bitte, Herr Colonel* . . . How many residents? You must lodging for the general-staff. Ten officers, one hundred fifty *Soldaten* . . . Have you supply of *Benzin?*" Without answering, without even turning around, I went into the entrance hall, leaving the door wide open, then I quickly returned to the library, afraid they were on my heels. But they had stayed on the top step. They had not dared follow me into the house right away.

Bocca and his wife were waiting for me with stricken faces; I turned the key twice in the lock and went over to the window. Standing in the center of the courtyard, a *Feldwebel*** was directing vehicles like a traffic cop at a crossroads: armored cars, motorbikes, came through the gate in order and turned, ploughing up the ground, to disappear into the *cour des communs* amidst guttural cries, whistle blasts, honkings. The two courtyards were teeming with men in green running in every direction, opening doors, breaking into everything. And my disability did not keep me from hearing, already, over our heads, a stampede of hobnailed boots down the corridors.

I told Bocca and Rose: "Go ahead . . . show them the bedrooms . . . Give them the whole tour . . . I don't want to see them . . . Tell them I'm keeping these three rooms for myself, that the rest is for them . . . They're the masters, we have to give in . . ."

Until then, I had held up. But those weeks of progressive anxiety, those last few days of anguish, of feverish waiting, the invasion finally materializing with that resounding of boots throughout the house . . . The moment I was alone, the resistance of my nerves gave way. A flood of impotent rage rose in my throat, as abrupt and violent as a hiccup. I remember I was standing over there, in front of the stove in the fireplace; I put my elbows on the marble, held my head between my fists, and squeezed my eyelids tight to keep from crying.

It was not at that moment, though, that I really touched bottom. Pétain's coming to supreme power had given me a bit of mad hope. Of course I was not one of his blind admirers. I knew his limitations too well. For fifteen years, in a series of articles, I had relentlessly opposed his conceptions concerning the future, the role, the organization, and the training of a modern French army; I had persistently taken him to task, had devoted a number of savage, well-documented attacks to theories that I considered outmoded and pernicious; and I attributed a heavy portion of the responsibility for the obvious weakness of our defenses to the baneful influence of his power as supreme commander. But I could not forget his glorious past. We had seen him at work in another poignant hour of our history: at Verdun he had displayed a sort of military genius, and through virtues very much his own had saved a situation which everyone thought to be hopelessly lost. And then, Weygand was at his side. For these two loyal soldiers, well aware of the present circumstances, to have been willing to assume control of the country's

*Sergeant.

destiny, there must still have been, beyond our defeats, some ultimate possibility, some reason not to give up altogether. Alas, these illusions did not last twenty-four hours. On the very night of the day when the Germans had taken possession of le Saillant, that same Monday, the 17th of June, Pétain officially recognized our rout and sued for an armistice. Could he have done otherwise? Would France's lot have been worse if he had tried to carry on the struggle? I have no idea. One can argue about it forever. There is no such thing as a control experiment in history. I only know that on that night, all the Frenchmen who were listening, those who felt shamefully betrayed as well as those for whom the "cease-fire" was a miraculous deliverance, understood, as I did, that at that precise moment an irreparable event had come to pass.

I AM READING over what I have written. I am thinking about those four months of the occupation that I lived at le Saillant, so close to *them* . . . Strange . . . My memory of it is not so dark, all in all. Four months of confinement. Four months of retreat, of reading, of work.

I had anticipated searches. They did not once try to force my door. I had refused any visits, any contact. They had no intercourse except with the Boccas. They were not unaware of me, though. They sometimes asked Rose for news of "Herr Colonel." They had got their hands on everything. Everything, save for my three rooms and the Boccas' little cottage. Le Saillant was turned into a barracks. The swastika hung on the façade. A sentry was on duty, day and night, in front of the gate. The general (who tried to pay me a visit and whom I never, of course, received) had appropriated for himself my sister's former apartment: the whole ground floor of the wing opposite mine. Ten or so officers and a few NCOs shared the rooms on the second floor. Their orderlies never stopped going up and down, dragging their hobnailed boots over the runners on the stairs and in the hallways; the rest of the time they hung about the kitchen and played cards in the servants' hall or in the linen room. The general and his head of staff had their meals alone, in the dining room. The white drawing room served as a mess for the other officers. In the billiards room, they had assembled a lot of tables, where secretaries worked. A telephone had been placed in the entrance hall. They had set up their duty room there. Day and night, motorcyclists brought orders; especially in the night, I would hear them come through the gate like racing cars, and turn into the courtyard with a noise like thunder, which stopped dead. The officers' cars were parked in a row that reached to just below the library window. In the outer courtyard they had pitched a tent and set up a repair shop for their machines. The courtyard was full of vans, small trucks. The garage had become a mess hall. The former stable, a *"Benzin"* depot. The mobile kitchens had taken possession of the two coach-houses. Naturally, from the first day on, the cellars, the woodsheds, the attics had been looted. The vehicles that had been put in the park under the trees ruined the thickets and dug up the walks, to Bocca's indignation. Under the lindens around the terrace, two sections of armored cars were lined up in battle order. All the hay and straw in the barn had been brought down to make litters—on the lawns, since almost all the men preferred to sleep outdoors. They also brought with them an incredible number of straw-filled and regular mattresses, stolen from who knows where, which they spread out at night on the grass. After the evening soup, they solemnly sat down together in little groups, forming circles, and sang. They had guitars, accordions, mandolins, harmonicas, and even phonographs. A loudspeaker fastened to the roof of the shed broadcast, several times a day, short programs in German, and, on Sunday afternoons, a concert that all of them, even the officers, came to listen to religiously.

I knew all this through Rose and her husband. I would have learned much more if I had been willing; but I had declared—without success—that I did not want to hear about them. Bocca and Rose could not refrain from keeping me posted about all their brushes with the "Fritzes." It was to "Madame Rosa" that the officers preferred to address themselves. She gave them sharp answers, knew how to make them respect her, bitterly disputed their slightest demands; as often as not they gave in to her and took her rebuffs with a smile.

Bocca, less bold, avoided encounters with the officers; but he kept an eye on the men. All day long, he wandered about with a scowl on his muzzle, fiercely scanning everything. To every question, he answered *"Nein!"* and turned his back. He stopped the soldiers from urinating in his courtyard, from cutting down his bushes, from stealing his plums, from raiding his vegetable garden.

The moment they resisted him, he ran and got a *Feldwebel,* and, by force, pulling him by the sleeve, led him to the scene.

I can easily believe that he was hated.

One day he came to me more bushy-haired, more infuriated, more wry-faced than usual.

"Mon colonel, you who can speak Kraut, what kind of an insult is *'der Starel chouanne'?"*

"Why?"

"That's what they call me amongst themselves. I've caught 'em at it a few times now!"

"Wait. I'll go check in the dictionary."

And after having leafed through the volume, to calm him down: "You're silly . . . It just means a *watchdog*. It's actually rather flattering!"

I was careful not to tell him that *der Stachel-schwein* means *the porcupine* . . .

I was living in seclusion, with the shutters closed, the curtains drawn, using electric lighting day and night. At mealtime, Rose brought me, as she does now since my return, a tray prepared in her own kitchen. Not once did I set foot outside; I did not even stick my nose out the window. I did not want to see them.

At the start, I had thought, "If this keeps up—and it will keep up—I'm going to croak with rage, idleness, and boredom." Well, no; it's odd, the unsuspected resources you have in reserve and that you suddenly discover in the event. Shall I even admit that my memories of that self-imposed confinement are not all that bad? In one blow, the whole temporal world was taken away from me. This estate whose safekeeping, management, and maintenance I had undertaken was—for the time being—left neglected, handed over to others. I no longer had anything to plan, organize, command. I no longer had anything on which to exercise my will. I had nothing to do but look out for myself. I have to conclude that I am selfish enough to be able to take care of myself day in day out, not only without weariness but with a sort of endless amusement. The radio kept me connected to the rest of the world. I had my library, my diary. I spent my time writing or poring over books, I reread Amyot's *Plutarque* in my beautiful edition, many plays of Shakespeare I did not know or had forgotten, the *Mémoires* of Saint-Simon. What else? Swift, Gibbon, Montesquieu, Tocqueville. I reread *Port-Royal* and I don't know how many volumes of the *Lundis*.* I reread almost all of Diderot. I took up German again; I went at it very steadily three or four hours a day. I filled almost a whole volume of my diary with notes suggested by my reading of Eckermann. I even began to study Greek again, with the ambition of tackling Thucydides and Polybius in the original. But I did not stick to it for more than two weeks, and made do with translations. I own a sizable portion of the Budé collection.† I have at my disposal a well-stocked shelf of line-by-line translations. Most invaluable. I have often consulted them, over the last twenty-five years, since I retired and can undertake long readings. It is the best way to go back to the classics: a lazy way, a dunce's way, but very much to my taste, and one that lets you follow right along with the text without constantly tripping over discouraging difficulties of syntax or vocabulary; a way of moving blithely forward without losing sight of the whole, without getting bogged down in the details like a schoolboy. Sequestered in a house

*Both *Port Royal* and the *Monday Chats* are by Charles Augustin Sainte-Beuve (1804–69).
†A well-known French collection of the classics.

full of Germans, I led that hermit's life for more than four months. And did not suffer from anything but my humiliation. Several times a day, often several times an hour, the roaring of an engine, an assembly in the courtyard, the noise of boots over my head, got the better of my deafness and produced a surge of unbearable, impotent rage in me. Then I would leave my armchair and my book, and hobble around my table for five minutes, like a wounded beast caught in a trap. After a while I'd end up going back to my seat, and my book . . . At my age, you get used to almost everything, I think, except humiliation.

At the end of the summer of '40, my friend Dr. Gévresin, who lived in the unoccupied zone, at Piérac, in the Lot area, managed to get a letter to me. He gave me to understand that he was organizing a pocket of resistance there and urged me to come. I decided to abandon le Saillant, where I saw myself condemned to inactivity, to go to the "unoccupied zone" and join my friend. Word had it in Menneville that the occupying units stationed in the area were daily expecting to be replaced. And I got ready to take advantage of this short respite, during which the house would probably for a short while be free of its locusts, to clear out.

II. MAUMORT AND THE NAZIS

[André Daspre: In this second part are gathered the preparatory texts that were to have been used for the writing of the other version of the events of 1940, according to which Maumort is forced to enter into dialogue with the occupiers who are taking care of him. Here is the first chronology of the episode: "Friday 18 Oct., fall, fainting spell. / 19 Oct., laid up in a cast—23 Oct., congestion of the lungs: 4 days, first reluctant discussions. / 22, 23, 24, 25: bad days. / 26, first day better; 28, convalescence. / 2 Nov., end of this congestion; 10 Nov., removal of cast: second free discussions (12 days). / 11 Nov. (Armistice Day, 1918). Schopfer's final visit."

As to the characters, we find these first indications:

"Major von Schopfer, born in 1894, Major of an armored-car group. Career officer, looks like Admiral Doenitz."

"Gralt will represent—as opposed to Kert, the defender of Mein Kampf, and the enemy of France—Hitler's conciliatory tendency after 1933."

Kert, the medical orderly, is partly inspired by Pierre Herbart*—a card makes it clear that Martin du Gard had met him for the first time in 1933 and had taken him then as one of the models for Paterson in Summer 1914.

"Dr. Frank Weissmüller, born in 1900. 40 years old, medical officer, member of the party, son of a ruined industrialist. Intelligent but not cultivated."

---

*Pierre Herbart (1904–1974), French writer, leftist Résistance fighter, friend to André Gide. In what way he served as a model for Kert remains a mystery.

The first of these characters will disappear; the three others are studied separately. About Kert and Weissmüller, Martin du Gard has written a sustained narrative, or at least a series of well-ordered notes; as for Gralt, who would perhaps have had the main role, there remain only isolated, unpaginated cards, but it seemed to me necessary to publish them as well, since it is quite obvious that each of these characters was created to give a particular point of view about Nazism. In the mind of Martin du Gard, these characters represent three typical kinds of Nazis; he tries hard to understand them rather than summarily condemn them. To understand does not mean to justify. As is his habit, the novelist means to conduct his study of the irrational and the monstrous as rationally as possible; he wants to analyze the Nazi phenomenon objectively, to explain the historical process—the economic, political, psychological conditions—that led his characters to become Nazis. To avoid a repetition of the evil, a precise knowledge of its causes, of its origins, is much more effective than the most violent of anathemas. Thus the novelist does not at all caricature the Nazis that he describes; on the contrary, he carefully shows the consistency in the behavior of each of them and he even makes Gralt into a good dialectician, able to hold his own with Maumort.

So it is quite evident how Martin du Gard would have organized this dramatic dialogue between Maumort and his Nazi guests. But wouldn't the tone of the novel consequently have changed? In 1940, Maumort does not mistake the Germans for the Nazis, even if he sometimes seeks in certain features of German culture that which might have fostered Nazism. Later on, when Maumort sees how Hitler's Germany wages war, when he learns of the systematic use of torture, the rounding up of the Jews, the existence of extermination camps, critical discussion is no longer possible, he is seized by indignation. The novelist titled a certain number of cards "Hatred of Germany" because, this time, it is the German people as a whole that is held responsible for the scourge [. . .]

Martin du Gard, who had a good background as a Germanist, was always attracted by German culture. He was among those who, before 1914, did not want to hear talk of revenge and keenly wished for a lasting reconciliation between the Germans and the French; he was among those who greeted Jean-Christophe* with enthusiasm. After the First World War, which he went through in a state of continuous outrage, Martin du Gard hoped anew that harmony would come to pass between the two old enemies. So strongly that he was hard put to see the danger of Hitlerism in its early stages, and brought back from a visit to Berlin in March, 1932, the impression

---

*In this novel cycle by Romain Rolland (1866–1944), the friendship of the young French hero with a young German represents the "harmony of opposites" Rolland hoped to see develop between nations.

that the German capital was a "city of freedom." He would change his mind later and, in 1938, would be frightened by what he saw in Germany. Under the occupation, he would, without hesitation, side with the Résistance, although he did not directly participate in the struggle as many of his friends did. His letters and his diary for those war years show that he was more and more scandalized by the behavior of the Nazis [. . .] Martin du Gard's indignation was all the stronger because he had always admired German culture, because he had trusted in the virtues of the German people; faced with the aberrations of Hitlerism, he was utterly dismayed. What an absurdity, to dream of a fraternal future with Jean-Christophe and suffer the law of the Nazis! It was very significant that at various points in the novel Martin du Gard mentioned the name of Romain Rolland, who, more than anyone, had taught him to love Germany but who had become "the most ferocious enemy of Hitlerian Germany."

I thought it wise to arrange the isolated cards that concern Gralt as logically as possible and to number them in order to facilitate references; and the same for those that the novelist called "Maumort and his guests." I have not done this for the texts on Kert and Weissmüller, which are written on pages as a sustained narrative.]

1. *Rupert Gralt*

[1] Born in 1910. Medical orderly. Resembles Schiffrin, Wanden.* Poor health, Protestant.

Son of a Rhenish minister. Began his theological studies reluctantly. Upon his father's death, parted with the Church, obtained his university degrees to teach history. Fervent Nazi, temperament of a mystic.

Volunteered at the start of the war, but drafted into the reserves. Medical corporal, assigned as secretary to a doctor.

Very cultivated, very courteous in debate. Very firm in his convictions. The intellectual Nazi.

Looks: beautiful, feminine hands, a bony face with prominent cheekbones, an already balding forehead. Sparse, unhealthy-looking blond hair. A greenish complexion. Yellow-green eyes, clear and attentive, very bright. Freckles. A hook nose. A sweet smile, a tender and compassionate gaze.

Not a member of the party.

[2] Maumort: *The Gralt delusion.* How hard it is to see clearly and pass judgment on what Gralt presents so well!

He expresses himself like a man who lives on summits (Goethe's reflection: "On all summits, one finds peace.") Everything he says comes from very high up, from an unquestionable nobility, from a supreme moral and spiritual elevation. And yet!

---

*Jacques Schiffrin: a friend of Martin du Gard's, Gide's, and Gaston Gallimard's, he conceived the idea of the Pléiade series. Wanden has not been identified.

And yet, take heed! In his doctrinaire presentation, I clearly sense (but how difficult it is to explain) that all that moral beauty, all that grandeur is there *like bait on the edge of a trap to make real moral beauty, real nobility, real grandeur fall into it.*

Renan says that it is hard to escape the web of snares that the theologians set for reason. In the same way, nothing is trickier, or requires so much mental vigilance, as to evade the supremely clever hold of that noble line of argument.

Nothing is more beautiful, greater, in appearance, than Nazism presented in such a way. Every noble mind, confronted with that dialectic, feels itself on the brink of conversion, of adherence. But it all rests on a seductive lie, all that fine verbiage about greatness is refuted by the facts, by concrete reality.

[3] Seen as Kert presents it, Nazism is odious. Seen as Gralt presents it, there is nothing more lofty in the political arena, nothing more attractive.

But Gralt has been drawn into a delusion, and all the Gralts of Germany along with him. It is Kert who is in reality. It is Kert's Nazism that has thrown itself upon Europe. It is Kert's Nazism that would spread its night over the world, if it succeeded in ruling it.

Do not be taken in by the Gralt delusion.

[4] GRALT: You say you are attached to the liberal ideologies. But one should not speak in such terms. In Germany I knew many people like you, who imagined that their opposition stemmed from their loyalty to old liberal convictions. Those people remained opposed to us solely because they did not understand. They were stuck in the past, with their eyes blinkered and their ears stopped, out of touch with their times. The least intelligent were shut off in decrepit out-of-date traditions. The most intelligent, the intellectuals, were shut off in the prison of their artificial system of thought, out of touch with the reality of life, lacking comprehension of the needs of the people, indifferent to the collective interest, incapable of adjusting to the present.

You, too—all this comes of your not understanding Nazism, or how Nazism responds to all the aspirations of modern man.

[5] You think that the coming of Nazism involves a lowering of the general intellectual level, a halt in the progress of the mind. What is threatened by Nazism is not the intelligence, it is the abstract dogmatism in vogue among intellectual Jewry, those pure ideas, detached from the concrete, from reality. The Nazis are fighting against this artificial intelligence but not against science and its development, or against the intellectual life of the elites. Nazism wants intelligence to apply to life, collective life. Thus Nazism restores to intelligence its true usefulness and raison d'être. This is not the end of science, but its reform and resurrection.

[6] GRALT: *Führerprinzip.* One of the essential rules of Nazism, one of the fundamental principles, is *Führerprinzip.* Joining forces under one leader.

The whole of Germany under Hitler. And each group, in every field of life, under a guide who is in charge and who is freely obeyed, because he knows, he feels, he confirms at every moment that his instructions express the common feeling, the collective will.

[7] GRALT: The foundations of the capitalist world of yesterday have now collapsed everywhere. In London, even, and New York. But to realize this, you have to know that he is never wrong because, with him, clairvoyance has the force of an instinct: he is a *prophesier,* a *seer.*

[8] THE COLONEL*: One must not think too much, it does no good. One must believe.

One must believe *in him.*

[9] The citizen who claims to participate in the governing of his country, about which it is obvious—and perfectly excusable—that he knows nothing, is like a traveling salesman in the grocery business who would presume to demand the job of the tram operator before getting on the tram.

An engineer is needed on a locomotive, and one who knows his trade. And all the passengers need to trust in his competence, and blindly let him drive.

[10] GRALT: There, in the new Germany, where you suppose there is *tyranny* and coercion, there is only a *mystical and spontaneous adherence* to an ideal of collective service and national greatness, an eager and brotherly submission to a common discipline, which generates benefits for the community. And not only benefits and material profits: culture, civilization are only the natural products of an *ordered society,* that is, one in which discipline imposes a strict order.

[11] Gralt always insists on the deeply Germanic character of Nazism. The very opposite of a political doctrine imported from somewhere else and imposed upon a people. No: Nazism was born in the very heart of the German race, whose instincts, aspirations, and dreams it totally expresses. Hitler both symbolizes and embodies every German man of today. It is this embodiment, of which there is no other example in history, which produces his greatness and his strength, which gives his voice the resonance of eighty million voices gathered into one.

[12] GRALT: The new German Nazi. As a base, the Germanic land and race. On which a true, solid community is established. No false abstract concepts, very few precise doctrines, no narrow philosophical systems, in order to allow all the transformations that reality will offer. Stay flexible in order to adapt to the shifting life of a country, of a race, in touch with the world, developing in a living, human context. No vain speculations, so dear to the Jewish quibblers.

The Nazi no longer makes a cult of reason, which has led the liberal,

*Not Maumort, but an otherwise unidentified German colonel.

socialist, and communist doctrinaires into ineffectual utopias. Everything boils down to life forces, to the reality of daily existence. Thus, no possible errors; one can no longer stray from a path that leads to concrete goals. Man's natural dynamism is freed from its fetters and expresses itself outwardly, freely.

[13] The Nazi then appears as a new man, simple, strong, direct in his drives, obeying natural and healthy reflexes, all of whose spontaneous movements converge in the collective good, in the national resurrection.* He no longer thinks of his individual goals, but of his task for the German and Nazi community. The new man is no longer an individual in the earlier sense but instead a member, a fraction of a whole people. His entire effort, his entire hope, is to do his part for the progress of this people's community. A vast national bond has welded together all the individuals of the former Germany.†

[14] GRALT: Hitler personified the German soul at a decisive and fateful moment of its history; and he rescued it from its death throes.

I say that the new German soul was born of *Mein Kampf;* I can say with equal truth that *Mein Kampf* was born of the eternal German soul. Nazism is not a personal doctrine preached to the people and accepted by them. Nazism is an expression of the Germanic race; it was born spontaneously from German suffering and ordeals; as a natural reaction, as a reflex to the shock of calamity. And it is profoundly German: it responds to the innermost nature and deep instincts of the race. It is not an opposition party turned victorious but a spontaneous product of the popular consciousness that reveals to it its true essence.

MAUMORT: So, how do you hope to impose it on foreign peoples, who have different, and perhaps contrary, aspirations?

Besides, what you're saying is not so true after all. Without Italian Fascism, would Hitler have written *Mein Kampf*? At any rate, would he have written the same book?

[15] MAUMORT: Characteristics of the German: perseverance and tenacity towards a goal, boundless application in pursuit of a single effort. Need for having a goal, a task to perform.

The opposite of a pleasure-seeker. Prefers work, effort, to ease in life. Only tastes the joy of living when he has a good conscience, when he has earned it through his devotion, his sacrifice, to a difficult objective. His recre-

---

*Roger Martin du Gard adds in a footnote: It is in this sense that Nazism is *totalitarian.* It has *united* everything into a single orientation, a single inspiration. It bears on the whole social, economic, political, familial, individual life of Germany, on *everything;* nothing escapes this transformation by inner force.

†Roger Martin du Gard: This is very striking in one small example: the Nazi brotherliness between the officer and the soldier, due to a common conviction, a similar goal.

ation, his relaxation, his Sunday's reward after the week of labor, is the simple, wholesome, sentimental satisfactions of family life. This attachment to his own is only the prefiguration of his communal attachment to his people. Need for harmony in a group, sociability, pleasure in filling his leisure time in the company of others: the opposite of individualism—a taste for communal living.

[16] So it is clear how little the German seeks out liberty, which is an individualistic taste. He does not care much about it, far less than about a well-ordered collective life.

[17] GRALT: For us, liberty is not, as here, the right of everyone to do whatever seems good to him; liberty is, for each of us, the sense of belonging, of feeling deeply that we are forming an integral part of a nation that is truly free because it is strong. Our liberty is that of Germany in the world. We came to understand this during the ten or twelve years when France and England starved, ruined, humiliated, and enslaved us: in the Germany of 1925 there were still quite a few individuals who on the whole enjoyed a "freedom" in their private daily life that was not so different from that of a Frenchman of the same era. But we suffocated under the servitude, and we learned at that time where true freedom was to be found.

[18] GRALT: And even if that false freedom which you value so highly in France had a certain sweetness, must we hesitate to sacrifice those individual advantages when it is a question of the salvation of Europe and the world?

[19] GRALT: You always claim your need for individual freedom. But the German Nazi has more true freedom than the Frenchman with his parliamentary system! In France, the free play of everyone's abilities was hampered by politics. In Nazi Germany, everyone feels free to exercise his abilities to the maximum, since those abilities are bundled in a single national aim, since each action corresponds to a clear, accepted duty which is the same for all, and in conforming to this guiding idea all act in the same direction, and all have the sense of acting freely, of acting as they wish. In each person, the individual consciousness has become the national consciousness.

[20] GRALT: You live according to an old ideal of liberty, which comes to you from the Rights of Man, in capitals—and without seeing that your false democratic liberties are only a caricature in practice when not just the opposite, for this preposterous and selfish concept of life seen solely from the viewpoint of individual interests reduces it to a stifling prison wherein each person's individuality suffers from constant dissatisfactions, from an isolationism which narrowly encloses it, impoverishes it, shrinks the world to a compass that is pitifully small.

On the contrary, it is when he becomes one with the community that man blossoms, finds an outlet for the complete deployment of his initiative, and enjoys a feeling of expansion, of plenitude, of calm, of real freedom, because his individuality grows, develops to the point where it identifies itself with the collective life. It is a broadening of individualism.

[21] Montaigne? An old fox who may have done France more ill than good . . . Oh, don't take me for a philistine: I myself was under his spell for a time . . . But that's over, I'm vaccinated now! Montaigne still amuses me, with his dialectic of a good well-read man of the Renaissance, keen on the Latin classics, and his Gallic gaiety, and his crafty frankness, and his quirk of turning little problems over and over, winking slyly, and his little audacities, and the pleasure he takes in thumbing his nose at the pedants, like a village rascal . . . Intelligent, of course . . . What is called, I believe, a "refined" intelligence . . . But so miserably, so hopelessly devoid of true greatness, true generosity! . . . *So devoid of any heroism!* The very model of the French bourgeois!

[22] MAUMORT: Gralt employs locutions that betray the Nazis' enormous indifference to the individual, to a person's right to think for himself: "shape the new face of Germany," "mold the German clay, in order to sculpt the man of tomorrow with it," "knead the dough of Europe."

(But, when he "expounds the doctrine," he denies that Nazism attacks individualism and he proves that Nazism not only respects but rests upon the human personality.) According to Gralt, in the new Germany, individualism has its part, which is huge: never has man been better ensured of the joys of a family, the love of his brothers, of his country, of his land; never has he been so eager to develop his personality as when he seeks, by perfecting himself, to enrich the community through his personal contribution, as when he is no longer a solitary egotist, everywhere an outsider; never has he so enjoyed his singularity as when he is no longer stifled, as when he breaks through his limitations and participates in the collective life. He has left the airtight walls of his individual being, has given up that paralyzing moral solitude which he took for freedom and which was a separation from humanity.

[23] GRALT: The great men of state, and especially those who belonged to the race of conquerors, have always bullied their subjects and demanded hard sacrifices of them. But these are the ones who have brought greatness to their country; and the people feel this so strongly that they soon forget their sufferings and proudly celebrate that glory which has cost them so dear.

[24] GRALT: A people of masters. . . . The age-old right that a man of noble blood has of using his strength to shape the world.

[25] THE COLONEL, *to Maumort:* Yes, yes, justice! . . . Of course, yes, justice! . . . But justice has never taken human societies a single step forward. Progress is spurred on by a genius who rebels—that is, by violence and injustice . . . Justice is a luxury of those peaceful and rather sluggish epochs when society rests up before setting off again on new conquests, when the warrior reposes before striking out once more for battle!

[26] GRALT: In a life devoted to great deeds, the little bourgeois virtues

don't matter. A few injustices, a few cruelties, a few crimes even, are only incidental, and in no way alter the greatness and legitimacy of a heroic life. The strong man can allow himself to also be, under certain circumstances, in the eyes of the common man, a criminal. Anything but the timid virtue of the mediocre and the moderate, which is the negation of action and enterprise.

[27] GRALT: The main question is how long France will take to accomplish its recovery—that is, to get rid of that "democratic" and "liberal" phraseology, which no longer corresponds to any reality in the world today, which has been the downfall of the republican parliamentary regime, and to which the French remain attached through pure routine and laziness about reappraising their values. You all sense the degradation of your political system, but you don't have the courage to look the evil in the face and denounce its true causes. You continue to delight in hollow formulas.

[28] The Frenchman, who does not like anarchy, who has a taste for order and well-organized things, deceives himself when he demands an absurd, unrealizable, pernicious form of total freedom. These are words that mask the true reality, the true necessities of a people's national life. Each Frenchman, in the commonsensical part of himself, knows perfectly well that social rules and just laws are needed for the family, the society, and the State to work. But he doesn't want to admit that he actually has a liking for rules. He swaggers about and clamors for an anarchic freedom which has never been granted him in any case and which he knows would be disastrous. At bottom, the Frenchman lives according to rules but does not want to be told that he does. He voluntarily gives in to necessary disciplines on the condition that they are not articulated and that he can tell himself that he is free from everything, obeying only his own fancy. How long will this childishness last?

You go on using an outdated vocabulary from the time of the Revolution of 1789, empty words from your Encyclopedists, from a purely intellectual lexicon; you stay faithful to an impossible and noxious *materialistic individualism,* or think you do, and you set yourselves apart from the new world, from the new Europe, born of *concrete* realities.

[29] GRALT: The Revolution of 1789 was noble, I grant you, but absolutely theoretical and utopian.

The Nazi Revolution is essentially different from it. It is based on strong ideas whose validity is confirmed by experience, but it has nothing chimerical or dogmatic about it, it aims only at practical and progressive realities. In Germany it has displayed both a contagious dynamism and a great caution, a great wisdom in its applications of theory to reality.

These achievements in the new Germany are the prefiguration of what will be the reorganized Europe. This role of precursor is quite obvious.

[30] GRALT: Before long, the theories of liberalism and capitalism will

have become as obsolete as Medieval scholasticism . . . People will study them as the social organization of Roman helotism or feudalism are studied.

[31] GRALT: The postwar pseudodemocracy could not last. It had against it the instinctive rejection by all the young. It had against it the vague and inner sense of the Germanic nature. An article for export, worn and outmoded, that the old Western nations might be able to get the Negroids in the Congo to accept, but from which a strong and eager, enterprising and realistic race could draw nothing useful. Abased and humiliated and bruised as it was, in its heart of hearts Germany had kept the obscure sense of its destiny, and a spark of its will to power still inflamed the blood of every German youth. When Hitler appeared and spoke, the general disillusionment had reached its height.

[32] GRALT: In France, the best minds can tell that the democratic government is running the country into the ground and that something has to be done to prevent a collapse. But they grope in the dark, like the Germany of Stresemann and Brüning.* They need to have the route pointed out for them, and the destination to be reached. Only the contact with and the example of National Socialism can reveal this to France.

[33] GRALT: Our occupation of France, which is justified by the complete military defeat, is not meant to weaken or despoil you. It should help in France's recovery and its regeneration, in its political and moral cleansing, which is necessary for the healthy life of Europe. Taking advantage of your strength and our disarmament, you occupied the Ruhr in peacetime, with Negroes, aiming to coerce us. You accelerated our commercial ruin by paralyzing our industry; you debased and humiliated us, abusing your power. We, however, extend our hand to you; Hitler has only one desire: to help your Marshal make a France that is purified and strong.

[34] GRALT: France, awake! Man has a vital need not to feel isolated, left to his own devices or to a shut-off, miserable existence, with no male ideal. A people has a *need* to be able to unite through the feeling of a lofty shared national mission, of a *"destiny" to fulfill.* This was the feeling that was utterly lacking in the people of the Third Republic. It is the stirring and dynamic feeling which National Socialism has given to the German people and which has made them invincibly strong. France, awake in your turn! Our mission is to bring to the civilized world, which is deteriorating, a rational and practical solution, satisfactory to all, for the problems that set the individual and the community against each other.

[35] GRALT: When will the French be sensible enough, realistic enough, to understand that the fascist evolution of European politics—an evolution

---

*Gustav Stresemann (1878–1929) and Heinrich Brüning (1885–1970), German statesmen who held high office immediately before the Nazis came to power.

guided and sustained by the example and the beneficent hegemony of the German National Socialist revolution—is a *historical necessity,* as inevitable as was the unification of the German empire begun by Bismarck and carried through by Hitler? Will the triumphant rise of German might always have to happen in spite of you, which is to say, against you? Isn't the experience of three disastrous and pointless wars enough to open your eyes?

[36] GRALT: It is a patriotic duty to collaborate. If you remain hostile, or simply neutral, passive, Europe will take shape without you, and you will be victims of your losers' pride. There isn't much time for France in its turn to enter into the rhythm of the political evolution that all of Europe is under-going, if it doesn't want to be left behind, written off, reduced to the rank of a fifth-rate power that submits to the new organization without taking part in it.

[37] GRALT: From whom to hope for the future understanding between France and Germany if not from men like you? This requires a fine mental clarity, honed by experience. It requires courage and tenacity. Also a strong patriotism; one must want one's country's salvation, almost against its will, in any case despite the instinctive reactions of public opinion. Nobility and greatness are needed, to keep from giving in to the petty grudges of wounded pride and to join forces intentionally with yesterday's victor.

But an example like yours would have a serious effect on the masses, since people would know that if you adopt this edifying attitude, it would not be out of personal interest.

Our first Nazi militants were familiar with this moral problem. They too had to fight against routine and suspicion and lack of understanding in order to reject the past and show the way of the future. They did it, and they secured the salvation of Germany.

[38] GRALT: You do not seem to have understood, or even seen, this great groundswell rising in Europe which has already swept it clean of that old lib-eralism whose degenerate effects still survived in the West, in Switzerland, in Belgium, in France, in England—in a few countries that were slow to evolve, asleep in their routines, suffering from slow death. Only in these nations—lethargic, backward, with no windows on the future—do democratic utopias still seem the monopoly of the parties of the left. Everywhere else the left (that is to say, the enterprising, revolutionary, independent minds) has rejected those worn-out, bloodless conventions in favor of a new, realistic policy, truly revolutionary and truly popular, born of the instincts of the peo-ple, based on strength and action. What characterizes these innovators is a complete renewal of values.

MAUMORT *interrupts:* What characterizes these innovators is the immorality of their politics, which consists of grabbing power, no matter what the cost, through violence, and of staying in power, no matter what the cost, through *violence* and *cunning*, which are outwardly proclaimed as lawful means, and the success of which proves their validity, regardless of law, agreements, or fidelity to justice. Pragmatists!

[39] GRALT: These innovators, whose names are Lenin, Mussolini, Pilsudski in Poland, Kemal Ataturk in Turkey, Salazar in Portugal.

—Hitler?

—Let's leave Hitler out of it for the moment. These innovators have slowly and surely made a European revolution, a revolution in the thought of Europe. They have known how to be more socialistic than the socialists, more nationalistic than the nationalists, more autocratic than the monarchists. They have combined all the old ideologies and systems into a new method, and they have fashioned a new, spirited, and effective morality in Europe, whose hegemony has triumphed almost everywhere and will end up triumphing everywhere. They have given Europe a new economic concept.

Hitler came along and synthesized all these new elements. He has provided the great example, from which there will finally emerge a European federation that can come about only through the dominance of a powerful central state. Germany is the only one that can play this catalytic role, owing to its position, its nature, and its intrinsic strength. The only one to give equal weight to the material and the spiritual. The only one to want both order and revolution. The only one to be able to gather all the National Socialisms of Europe around it.

[40] GRALT: What bothers you about Hitlerian socialism is that it has no connection with that demagogic nonsense advocated by the self-styled socialists of the nineteenth and twentieth centuries. As far as can be from the Marxes, the Jaurèses, the Vanderveldes, the Bebels.

This time we're talking about getting rid of appetites and personal gains once and for all, to set up in their place a communal ideal that will deserve the name of socialism.

[41] GRALT: Do not confuse the socialism of the Nazis with that Marxist socialism which, to do away with individual profit, *nationalizes* all human effort to an absurd extent; which ends up turning every individual into a slavelike bureaucrat, with no initiative, obeying a tyrannical entity, the State.

National Socialism preserves private initiatives and cultivates them to the maximum for greatness and the community: it curbs selfishness, almost reducing it to nil, but it develops the personality by opening up to it this unlimited field of service to the community, collaboration in the life of the people and the happiness of all. It has not emasculated man by castrating his individualism, but has directed that individualism towards the life of society, has transformed selfish and narrow-minded individualism into a *collective, communal individualism,* in the service of humanity for a common goal, for an always greater progress.

[42] GRALT: Do not call it a *"democratic revolution,"* that embryonic movement which in 1918 put the gravediggers of the Second Reich in power over the ruins of all of Germany's age-old values. That was not a political movement or any kind of contribution, but the passive acceptance of the collapse of all the vital Germanic forces. Germany then paid dearly for the absurd weakness Wilhelm II had always had for the socialists, those foreign and destructive elements that were gradually allowed to creep into the heart of the old virtuous, disciplined, hierarchical Germany. That was not a revolution but a general lapsing into material and moral decay.

The incredible thing was that this decay could have been tolerated by the majority of Germans who did not agree with the government but were temporarily stunned by the unexpectedness of the catastrophe as well as the usurpation of power by the Red anarchy and those Jews around Rathenau* who were monopolizing everything quite easily in the midst of that general breakdown.

[43] GRALT: Italian Fascism was, at the beginning, a *political theory,* a creation of the mind.

Nazism was born of a *popular feeling,* primordial in nature, and of the instinctive needs of the Germanic soul. The torments of the defeat, the poverty and the humiliation, gave to this popular, national resurgence its *intimate* strength. That popular, national movement suddenly, miraculously expanded because it was the act of a *preserving instinct.* The country had to be reborn or perish in ruination. Every German man felt it, and stood up all at once, with the energy of despair, to escape the deadly decay.

It was only after having secured their own salvation that the German people understood that they had found in themselves the cures for a sickness that was not specifically German but worldwide, and it was only then that they understood their mission towards Europe. They will bring to this general cause the same total, lighthearted, conscious devotion that they have given to their national community.

[44] GRALT: You're very close to calling us "the Prussians," as Déroulède† did in 1875. You live on baseless prejudices, on a false concept of the Germans. It is possible that in the past this concept may have been less unfair, less inaccurate, more in keeping than today with certain appearances, or even

---

*Walter Rathenau (1867–1922): statesman, industrialist, and philosopher who, after World War I, as minister of reconstruction and foreign minister, was instrumental in beginning reparations payments under the Treaty of Versailles obligations and in breaking Germany's diplomatic isolation.

†See note, p. 278.

certain realities, and I won't discuss that. But today I know and can affirm that it is fundamentally false. Open your eyes, learn to know us, see what we have become in the wake of an unjust defeat, years of humiliating privations which have given the Germanic soul new strength or perhaps tempered it anew, it hardly matters which; and relinquish your old erring ways.

You still believe in the romantic and fanciful Germany, the "feudal and military" Germany that people kept harping on to you after Sedan. We are bringing the world a new mysticism, a faith in the human community, a new morality, a new conception of duty and virtue, and an economic structure based on work and on authority freely accepted by the individual: enough to transform a continent and finally establish the unity of Europe and its prosperity.

[45] GRALT: A revolutionary era. In the space of hardly a generation, the prodigious experiment of the new Germany has totally altered the structures of social existence. Outmoded data have been replaced by new. The economic and social concepts credited for centuries have been rendered null and void. A new spirit is sweeping Europe. And new blood is instilled in it, which is regenerating the old body. The impulse is spreading throughout the whole civilized world. The so-called political wisdom of which we were all the heirs turns out to be false, pitiful, producing injustices and disorder. It is a social upheaval of such breadth that a moment of dismay and confusion is inevitable. But Europe and the world will just have to adapt to the new order. An era is drawing to a close and a new time is brewing. Woe to the blind and the fearful who try to cling to a dead past!

[46] We now have laws that are fair, easy to apply, easy to comprehend, and above all that are immediately and clearly understood to be made for all of us, for our national community, and whose application is in everyone's best interest. There you have the Nazi civil code. Compare this with your outdated code, which has never been able to stop injustice and privilege, and which has become complicated by a lot of secret deals improvised to satisfy this or that party in power, this or that set of voters.

[47] GRALT: Confidence in the lasting power of Nazism. The difference between Napoleon and Hitler is that Napoleon seems to have sensed that the revolution he made was fragile, with no certain future. It is this more or less conscious doubt that explains why he was in such a hurry to improvise new institutions in every field, solutions to every problem at once. The Nazis, on the other hand, perfectly sure that the movement they have launched has scope and a solid durability, perfectly convinced that they have given birth to a new order which will have all of time in which to develop and resolve human problems in their entirety, do not waste their strength, and, at the start, undertake to solve only certain precise and limited problems. Trusting

in the future for the total realization of the new order, the Nazis take on only urgent problems.

[48] GRALT: For those who can see beyond the immediate, Nazism is beginning an *era of peace* for humanity. Thanks to our restricting the ego-centricity of individuals and our steering human activity towards the great-ness of the community, man's selfish instincts will lose their virulence, the opportunities and temptations for conflicts will disappear, the national com-munities will merge into the great human community, and peace among men will develop by itself.

[49] GRALT: Don't you understand that it is *urgent* to end these fratrici-dal struggles, these wars and successive counterwars, to work together to organize Europe? You have seen that this is not easy. The League of Nations was a failure. Its methods were false and warped. Accept the German offer of a joint project with an organization which has proved itself in our country, so that the continent can get back on its feet, settle down to peace, and live through work. There is too much to do to protract our arguments about precedence, and go on quarreling like yappy little dogs.

[50] GRALT: Why should Europe dread the hegemony of German good sense, when it has put up with the British hegemony for more than half a century? And France in particular, which has lived in vassalage to England, and let itself be dragged by the British into the worst of material and moral disasters?

Germany, at least, is a continental power. The hegemony it offers, and that it will impose, if need be, on France, is the protection of a parent to which France is attached by a thousand family traits, and not a foreigner like insular Albion.

[51] GRALT: England! You have seen, at Dunkirk, how it understood its role as an ally . . . And at Mers el-Kebir* . . .

At the very moment of the armistice, Churchill, in a swaggering speech, counted out his millions of intact troops and airplanes, in reserve on his island. Insolent cynicism, since for three or four weeks England denied any help to the French generals. If those English soldiers and those planes had come *in time* to join up with the French armies, who knows if the Germans would ever have been able to cross the Oise and the Somme?—and if we would not be in the trenches today, as we were in 1915?

[52] GRALT: What do you expect from an English victory? A return to the parliamentary republic of comrades, a return to the Popular Front and its demagogic lies? A return to the ruination of France?

---

*French naval base in Algeria where, in 1940, British warships destroyed most of the French fleet at anchor to thwart a German capture of it.

[53] GRALT: The new Germany is the prefiguration of the new Europe. This will be its glory and its mission. It is also placed in the vanguard of the ongoing evolution of the civilized world.

It would be absurd to want to unify the elements of the new Europe to an extreme extent. The people of each country have their own skills and propensities. The future Europe will be made from this harmonious chorus.

[54] GRALT: But it is not Germany that has beaten you, it is not Germany that occupies France! Take a closer look! It is the *future of Europe* that is victorious, it is the *European revolution* that is already established in your country: we are only its representatives, its pioneers, and so to speak its symbols.

[56] GRALT: Hitler embodies the instinctive ideal of the whole of a vast and populous and powerful nation; he embodies the German *future.*

And, whether you like it or not, he also embodies the future of every European, the future of that European Community which only asks to be born, which the League of Nations did not know how to bring into being, and which Germany has had to forge on the spot, in blood, through the force of arms.

For a revolution so profound can be created only by a people endowed with an invincible material might.

[57] GRALT: Europe asks only to be realized. Europe is what Germany was at the start of the nineteenth century: a potential state made up of provinces in which the same blood circulates but which squabble out of stupidity, childishness, and vanity.

MAUMORT: Certainly not! That was also the idea of Wilson, who sinned through ignorance and dragged us all down in his tempting error. Back then we said: the United States of Europe. We thought of America before the Revolutionary War. A terrible mistake! The federation of American states was something natural and easy compared to ours. It was simple to fashion a coherent whole of those groups of expatriate colonists and stateless people who had scarcely a century of family quarrels to forget and so many common interests to bring them together. But in Europe, how to reconcile so many ethnic differences, rival ideologies, conflicting and mutually exclusive interests, so many fanatical nationalisms, twenty centuries of savage wars, invasions back and forth, inexpiable offenses, passionate claims, wounded vanities, hereditary grudges? At each other's throats *ad aeternum.*

[58] GRALT: Unification is inevitable nonetheless. It is a historical necessity. You yourself admit it, who have put such hope in your League of Nations. If unification does not come about through harmony, it will come about through force. You will not escape a yoke: a Tartar yoke or a Germanic yoke. If Europe wants to avoid suicide, she will agree to join in the German hegemony. Germany brings you everything you desire: a noble and workable socialism—which can be something other than an unleashing of material

appetites—peace lasting for centuries, an era of unbounded prosperity, and, what is more, a certain respect for your quirks and shortcomings, since we will not in any way touch your national personalities and only plan to arrange them like flowers in a bouquet.

2. *Maumort and his guests*

[59] Maumort and his guests. Talleyrand's quip: "The power to do anything doesn't give the right."

[60] Maumort with his guests: in the family of fanatics, the hero is not far from the villain, and the man with urgent, uncontrolled passions moves between heroism and villainy without there being any impermeable partition between the two.

It is the same "dynamism" and the same worship of strength that drive them both.

"I already observed this in the trenches," Maumort will think.

The opposite of wisdom is not folly but perhaps heroism—let us say: *passion.*

[61] MAUMORT: They are surprised to hear me one day bring out certain truths contained in some extreme doctrine and the next day do justice to whatever is justified and true in the opposite doctrine. Sometimes I have sensed the question rising to the lips of those fierce partisans: "But for God's sake, whose side are you on?" They have not yet dared express it aggressively, but their surprise, their insistent lack of understanding, and even certain discreetly indirect queries left me no doubt as to the nature of their curiosity. I have prepared my answer. It will be an apologue. I will not make any silly profession of eclecticism. I will only tell them that in the time of Erasmus, when some "believers" once questioned the old sage's friends to find out what party he belonged to, they merely shook their heads, smiling: *Erasmus est homo pro se.** (Epigraph from Zweig's *Erasmus.*)

[62] MAUMORT: The spiritual and moral foundations of four centuries of civilization are the stakes of this game. All the reforms you want, but in the direction of civilization! To destroy the essential groundwork in order to take a position opposite to all that the present world has gradually accomplished can only be a regression.

Will future humanity have to return to this concept of man as an animal who is superior owing to his strength and his cleverness? Is it by virtue of his "will to power" that he deserves to reign over the planet? Is it in conquest and domination alone that he must find his reason for living, and is there no other happiness for him than in the "heroic" life leading to success, to victory through daring and battle rather than through right?

---

*"Erasmus is his own man."

[63] MAUMORT will say: What I have before me is nothing less than the *dark forces of Germany.*

And what is happening in this room may be only an episode in the eternal clash between the German and the Latin . . .

[64] MAUMORT, *on Gralt:* When he describes to me the sickness from which we are suffering, I am sometimes tempted to agree with him. But when he suggests his remedy, the illness at once seems to me quite relative, quite tolerable. The cure that he offers is worse than the disease . . .

[65] MAUMORT will think: There are not many absurdities in what Gralt says. If I deplore the ways he thinks and sees, it is mainly because of the abyss that lies between his ideas about the world, the future, society, the facts—and the acts of the people he thinks are bringing this new order to the world: an abyss between what he advocates or wishes and the example given by the people who, in the name of this same doctrine, are turning Europe upside down.

I am ready to say: "All right. I admit that your ideas are valid. Now let's look at what those who put them into practice are doing. Well, the policy carried out for ten years now in the name of these fine principles is a denial of justice and human dignity."

He will answer me that the blameworthy life of one bad priest does not invalidate the religion.

But what to say of a believer who would defend and justify the vile deeds of a bad priest?

[66] MAUMORT thinks, while listening to the doctrinaire Gralt: Very well. Everything he says makes up a coherent body of doctrine. But the facts, the domestic and European policy of Nazi Germany, the acts of conquest, despoilment, deportation, terrorism, and persecution, are something else. And between the two, only people who are blinded like Gralt can establish a connection.

[67] MAUMORT: But they annoy me by stressing, as they do, French individualism and France's lack of "communal sense."

Is it the communal sense—which is also the "herd" sense—which matters in itself, like an abstraction? Or rather, isn't what matters simply that the individual, the member of society, contribute to the collective life, "serve" the community? Didn't people work in France? And all these individualistic individuals at whom the finger is being pointed today—weren't they all good, conscientious, courageous, skillful *workers?* Work? Well, isn't that precisely the main way of "serving" the community?

They may have served it without thinking too much about it, without being overly aware that they were doing so, but they served it as much as anyone in Germany or elsewhere.

[68] MAUMORT: To work for the community of the living, to devote one-

self to the good of all, can appear a very noble thought; but I believe, and will do so until I see proof to the contrary, that this is an idea which is, for the present, beyond the scale of man.

[69] MAUMORT will think: What often keeps me from rising up against Gralt's ideas is the thought that the real meaning of current events escapes us and will be perceptible only to posterity. It is in this way that a favorable doubt can creep into an uninformed mind.

We have a precise, overall idea as to what an epoch of profound and total recasting like the Renaissance represented for man and for European civilization. But what mind of that time could have had any notion, any awareness, of this?

And who can know whether a new era, following four centuries that will perhaps later be called the era of the Renaissance, is not being born before our eyes—whether humanism, individualism, materialism, capitalism are not flowerings of the era of the Renaissance which today are fading, breaking up, and are going to be replaced?

[70] An international elite. A big step would be taken towards the conciliation of nations if their intellectual elites alone were set against one another; if a people were not judged except by its elites. Their gathering could be the prefiguration of internationalism in the civilized world. The spiritual union of cultivated minds.

Maumort knew a time, from 1880 to 1890, when this higher internationalism, at first disrupted but then invigorated by the Dreyfus Affair, began to exist de facto and seemed on the point of becoming widespread. At that time it did not appear absurd to hope for the reconciliation of peoples through the intellectual and moral agreement of the better minds, in a common ideal of humanism and pacifism. We did not know that the old torch of national hatreds was still so flammable. The patriotic politicians took care quickly to relight it.

[71] MAUMORT, to Gralt: Don't people know how to think clearly anymore, or don't they want to? And why not?

The appearance of logical reasoning in words masks a great confusion in thought, a sort of delirious incoherence. A vague, resounding, and hollow vocabulary. An intoxication with certain key words, a metaphysician's way of leading brains astray and of muddying very clear, very simple things, the practical stuff of society. Everything gets wreathed in a halo, everything takes on the flimsiness and secret intensity of a myth. It is reminiscent of those smokescreens behind which convoys proceed, those roads covered by nets woven with branches beneath which armored columns advance. It is new strategy. Beneath this confusion, explosives are brought forward . . .

But who is commanding the operation? It is too deft not to come from some clear heads. Those who pour the wine keep from drinking it so their hand won't shake.

3. *Kert*

This Dr. Kert, the medic, whom Gralt calls the "Berliner," is young: twenty-five or twenty-six. He was an extern at a hospital in Berlin; he has not yet finished his studies; it seems that half his trunk is filled with books; he devotes every instant of leisure to work.

Nothing Germanic at first glance. Small, muscular, nervous; rather short-legged, with a broad pelvis, which does not prevent him from moving with an agility and a suddenness that makes you think of certain insects. His face is thin, narrowing at the level of the temples and the mouth, widening at the cheekbones, tapering at the chin; he has a ruddy complexion, large white teeth, a black and flashing eye, very black hair. One would think he had been born on the Côte Basque rather than on the shores of the Baltic.

Not much education. Gralt gave me to understand that he was of humble birth: the son of the owner of a village hardware store, from around Lübeck. Gralt also told me that Kert wanted to become a surgeon; this does not surprise me; he has decisiveness in his gaze and in his gestures, and strong, bony hands, dextrous but not at all gentle.

Since coming of age, a party member, and militant. One senses that he is not without knowledge but that he has no background or family traditions. A former scholarship boy, he made his own way, and wanted to succeed. It was at this moment that the party offered itself to him.

He says, very sensibly: "In your democracies, what you call *parties* are nothing: shades of opinion. Nowadays, there are only two parties in the world, ours and the Communists."

And here is his definition of what a party is: "A force which has gradually seeped in everywhere, has penetrated the entire nation, has made a solid bloc of it: what iron mesh is in reinforced concrete."

It was natural that he should tie his destiny to that of the great nascent Germany.

I imagine that his support was at first the support of an ambitious student, and one with no connections in the struggle against all the obstacles that a closed social regime still raises against the isolated individual. And what his realistic mind probably first admired in the new order was the swift expansion of a force able to impose itself without pointless scruples: such a force must have seemed exemplary to him.

His desire for power thus spontaneously merged with that of the regenerated Reich: he understood that the German triumph over a decadent, then enslaved, world would carry him, as if on the crest of a wave, towards the realization of his own ambitions. Of course, he does not say this. And he may not know it. It is possible that he believes, when he declares the individual is nothing, that only the *party* counts (he never says "the human community," as Gralt does). But I only have to see him, to hear him, to catch a certain glimmer in his eye when he expounds his future plans, to be skeptical about his abnegation as a militant: I did not tell him how much of his adhesion to the party I attributed to his *arrivisme,* but I made several allusions to the opportunists who know how to find in national upheavals a springboard for their ascent. Contrary to what I expected, he did not in the least deny that there were hordes of "profiteers" in the new Germany, but he seemed to think that this went without saying and that only a naïf would be surprised or shocked by it. For him, it appeared, any member of the National Socialist Party was, from this very fact and legitimately, someone who derives a personal advantage from his membership.

Without seeming offended by these realistic views, I pushed him further, and here, in short, is his position: every human undertaking, if it is to succeed and not be a pipe dream, must be founded on selfishness and self-interest. A revolution which wants to be deep and lasting has to provide concrete gratifications for its supporters: "The Third Estate," he told me, "compensated itself with state property." "A revolution starts with ideologues and mystics," he told me, smiling, on another occasion, "but a new regime is really founded only on voracious men of action, who have tremendous appetites to assuage. The first concern of those who seize power, if they want to keep it, is to hand out jobs and favors in order to secure loyal accomplices. A revolutionary government cannot endure unless the beneficiaries of the new order are well enough provided for, and numerous enough, and self-interested enough, to constitute a majority of satisfied and determined men who, for fear of losing the goods they've acquired, will stop at nothing to defend the people who got them those goods, and maintain them in power."

I DO NOT WANT to judge this Kert. I want to understand him. Until the age of ten, he hungered and froze in the shop of the village hardware seller, a disabled war veteran and a consumptive. His father dies. The boy winds up in an orphanage in Lübeck. When the eyes of this puny child begin to examine the world, in that Germany still wounded by military collapse and civil war, in that beaten, starved, humiliated, threatened, hated Germany, an excruciating sense of undeserved degradation turns the atmosphere unbearable. It is in the midst of all this that he grows up. When National Socialism comes to power, he is eighteen or nineteen. A delirious and contagious fever sweeps the country. Kert reads *Mein Kampf:* revelation . . . Now he has his holy book, the Tables of the Law, the answer to all the questions that he is asking himself. He suddenly realizes that Hitlerian victory brings him deliverance. Limitless prospects open up before him. He throws himself into studying, makes up for lost time. From nineteen to twenty-five, six years of frenetic work and hope; six years, during which his personal momentum keeps pace with the rise of Hitlerism, is sustained and magnified by it. And now, the heroic epic: the new Germany rushes triumphantly to the conquest of Europe, and leads its sons in its irresistible thrust, and includes them in its victories.

Kert's story is that of several million young people . . .

GRALT, VERY CLEVERLY I must admit, strives to justify the present war by the selfish and hostile policy of the victors of 1918, and more precisely by the threat of a fresh encirclement of Germany. His dialectic relies on reasons—some of which are unquestionably quite strong.

As for Kert, he does not go to so much trouble. Success needs no justification. His simplistic argument can be summarized as follows: German hegemony is legitimate because Germany is the only great nation that is virile and young, the beating heart of old Europe: that is the axiom he starts from. Given this, the grandiose task set out for the Führer's political genius was to implement, in three stages, a progressive plan for the rallying of forces and colonial expansion.

First stage: on the arbitrarily amputated ground left to the country by the *Diktat* of Versailles, to regenerate Germany through a new faith, reforge the race through the moral disciplines of National Socialism, give it back its confidence in itself and in its destiny, provide it with an invincible army.

Second stage: free from their servitude all the populations of Germanic blood unrightfully kept outside the borders of the Reich, and consolidate them with the central mass over an expanded territory.

Third stage: throw this mass, thus raised from its degradation and considerably increased, into the conquest of foreign territories. (In particular, Russia and the Ukraine, if my memories of *Mein Kampf* are correct. And, on this point, it seems that there has been an unforeseen reversal in the Hitlerian plans. But this is a parenthesis.)

For Kert, who has watched the first two phases come to pass, who has himself participated in the miracle of the national resurrection, who has witnessed the return to the motherland of all its enslaved Germanic brothers, and who is presently cooperating in the final phase, and sees one victory follow another, the crowning triumph cannot be doubted.

Today there must not be one German in a thousand who thinks otherwise.

I thought: "Yes, to keep the hounds whipped up, the quarry is indispensable." There have to be all sorts of Nazis. This Kert is of a completely different species than Gralt. Isn't it Bertrand Russell who distinguishes two classes of theoreticians: those who emphasize will and those who emphasize knowledge?

Faced with a dogmatic mind, I always think of a compass whose needle is stuck.

KERT IS A PERFECT PRODUCT of Nazism. Even his gaze . . . that gaze which is sharp and shallow, hard and icy. When you let him run on, you feel you are hearing the Hitlerian doctrine in its strict purity. Through him, the National Socialist doctrine appears just as it is: simplistic and coherent. Which, I think, suffices to explain its appeal to young intelligences and unsophisticated brains, that is, its success with the masses, always impatient to have things resolved, who are puzzled and wearied by the complexity of problems, who are satisfied by a cursory explanation as long as it is clear and easy to remember, and who are looking for certainties in order to be sooner rid of the pangs of hesitation, the strains of reflection, the difficulty of a choice, and the risk of having, like Sisyphus, to repeat this inconclusive toil over and over again.

They have clearly understood how fundamental a necessity it is for Nazism to achieve a total penetration of the masses, on the spiritual as well as the material level. And Kert, on this subject, let slip the adjective "brutal" in a way I want to note. It was the day when he was talking about the problem of education. He had begun by saying that the creation of a receptive social milieu was vitally important for the future of National Socialism and that such a milieu could be built up only gradually, by the molding of a homogeneous younger population. Thus the party had secured an absolute hold over the minds of the rising generation by removing the children from family authority and influences and by imposing on all of them, starting with the youngest and making no exceptions, an identical education, wholly imbued with Nazi doctrine. I pointed out to him that never since the monopolization of education by the Church in the Middle Ages had such a hoarding, such a confiscation of minds for the benefit of a "state religion" been attempted, in any country . . . "Do you hesitate to graft all the wild cherry trees in your garden to make good fruit trees of them?" he answered me. And he developed this theme, which I shall summarize. For anyone who holds the truth, there are two ways of making sure that it comes out on top: by proving it, in order to convince—this is the way of missionaries, this is the way of philosophers; we all know what it's worth! Fortunately there exists another means of imposing on an entire nation the faith which must regenerate it: to engrave the essentials on the blank mind of the child: "This method," he concluded, "is the one of men of action, and it is ours. It is *brutal* and infallible."

(Not the first time I observe this: the word *brutal* has no pejorative connotation in the Nazi vocabulary.)

GRALT'S NOSE ALWAYS lengthens and he looks shamefaced whenever I slip in a reference to what they did in Poland; with Kert, on the other hand, not the slightest embarrassment. This morning he so annoyed me with his attitude that—what is unusual for me—I got worked up. I told him that all the injustices of history and the horrors of the barbarian invasions themselves would seem like peccadilloes to those who will study the campaign of the Nazi armies in Poland; that it was impossible to imagine going further in disdain for human laws, in abuse of justice, in cruelty as torturers, in the massacre and plundering of innocent people, etc.

He was smiling.

These eternally brawling Germans have managed to attain the highest degree of civilization and at the same time preserve almost intact the instincts of primitive tribes (fleeting traces of which I have also found in certain country children): a natural ferocity, a bestial pleasure in misusing physical strength, a savage need to tyrannize the weakest by making them suffer.

A nation of born warriors, like certain native tribes.

How they all seem to love war! I made war, myself, for ten or fifteen years of my life, without loving it. With a sportsmanlike feeling, which is very different. Even in the army in Africa, there were few among us for whom making war was a natural vocation.

What an alarming light gleams in Kert's black eyes when he explains: "This war is a Caesarean operation, it is delivering Europe of a new civilization which was germinating in its unconscious." The surgeon who rolls up his sleeves and joyously pulls on his rubber gloves will say that he is going to save a human existence. But it is the operation to perform, the belly to open up, which arouses that delirious excitement in him, and not any eagerness to bring relief to his patient. The taste for violence is really in them like an animal instinct. Gralt himself . . . When he allows, with a shade of melancholy, "All that is creation, alas, can be achieved only through violence," it is a justification that he is seeking; and his "alas" is purely formal.

Frightening, this little Kert. A steel object, one of those new devices that didn't exist in my day. When he has stopped talking and he is here, in my bedroom, leaning with his back against the bookcase, his arms folded, silent, his presence causes me the same uneasiness as if I had at my side, on a corner of my table, a grenade with its pin pulled, ready to go off . . .

This type of overzealous neophyte is often more dangerous than useful to a cause. The leaders know it. I imagine that at party headquarters some intelligent section chief may have jotted in Kert's dossier: "Don't spare: use for a desperate terrorist attack . . ."

His doctrinaire dogmatism is the high all-purpose motive that he lends to an inner necessity, a personal instinct: his instinct to rebel. For that matter, this generation of young Nazis can be envisioned only at the impulse-rebellion stage. What would become of them in case of success?

And what would become of Hitlerism itself if it ever ceased to be a revolutionary force warring against an old world? If it imposed itself through an undisputed success across the continent? One wonders, and it makes one speculate. The day when, having established its mastery over Europe, National Socialism, suddenly stripped of its virulence, would no longer be a doctrine of combat and rebellion against a regime judged to be hateful; the day when no other task would be offered it than that of organizing a new order of civilization, its present supporters, disoriented, would, probably, lose their whole raison d'être and automatically break away from it.

They are nothing but momentum, movement; victory is not a goal for them; they prefer the fight and the hope of winning. In triumph, in the realization of conquest, they would no longer find anything to feed their desire for power and sustain their enthusiasm. Many would be seen throwing themselves into Communism and attacking their former myths. (And, in case of defeat, likewise.)

"THE IRRESISTIBLE STRENGTH of National Socialism," states Kert, "is to have considered life's problems once and for all as it should be done—in a concrete way, with an exact, illusionless vision of man and society." What does he understand by an exact vision? I know only too well. For Kert, law, justice, legality and illegality, etc. are truly absurd concepts, devoid of any positive content, any interest, any practical application. A race's instinct for self-preservation and fulfillment is expressed and imposed through violence. In every field, it is force that determines and success that decides. Such is his credo.

I wonder, as I listen to him, if the emergence and ascendency of totalitarian regimes in our old humanistic Europe—and particularly the triumph of Nazism, as it is symbolized for me, at this moment, in the "Kert type"—might be a spectacular demonstration that brutality, cruelty, absence of justice and kindness, the need to prevail by any means, constitute the only human constant, against which the dreams of the ideologues, the sermons and the hopes of the moralists, are always bound to shatter in vain . . .

This emergence, this rapid success of "totalitarianism" in a world which one might have believed, on the contrary, to be devoted to increasingly democratic and socialistic forms of government—does it mark the beginning of a new era in human civilization, or merely an abrupt and passing swerve in European society? *That is the question . . .** The hypothesis of a new era happens to be substantiated, for the moment, by this fact: that Fascism and National Socialism are unquestionable victories on the one hand over capitalism (autarchy and the state-run economy may indeed be decisive obstacles to the development of international capitalism) and, on the other hand, over Communism (since the stifling—apparent, or real?—of Communist expansion in the countries under totalitarian regimes, and especially in Hitlerian Germany, undermines all the revolutionary hopes of a Marxist hegemony in the world). Are these victories temporary, or definitive?

And what would man become, in this new world?

They justify their violence by citing the good that they are bringing to the world, because they are blinded by their own experience, since it is to the violence of their national revolution that they owe their salvation. "By the sword and the flame, since we must," Kert says somberly. It is the language of all fanaticisms; it is the cry of the torturers of the Inquisition, of the slaughterers of Saint Bartholomew's Day.

4. *Weissmüller*

I saw him close up, this morning, leaning over my cast. What a strange, shapeless, powerful face! Tormented? Yes, insofar as it resembles Mirabeau;[†] but serene as well, and thoughtful; it brings to mind the death mask of Beethoven. To describe that face, the exact words are hard to find. "Bloated" would be inaccurate; fleshy, rather; and lumpy; like a bunch of grapes, like a bag of walnuts. Every muscle juts out and forms a protuberance of hard flesh. A face all made up of little roundnesses: the bulges of the forehead above the eyebrows, the somewhat blunted tip of the nose, the nostrils convex like seashells, the cheekbones, the two parts of the chin divided by a notch down the middle. Archeologists have a word, *epannelé,* to describe the unfinished capitals that are found in dark corners of cathedrals, rough-hewn by the apprentice stonecutter and lacking the touch of the master's chisel. It also makes me think of a preliminary model, when the sculptor is still distributing its volumes and merely indicates where the reliefs will go by sticking onto the mass little pellets of clay, which he doesn't bother to smooth out with his thumb.

Gralt has given me some biographical information about Weissmüller, which clarifies things for me. He is a rebel, too. Family of big Hamburg

---

*English in the original.

†Honoré-Gabriel Riqueti, Comte de Mirabeau (1749–1791), one of the leading figures of the French Revolution.

industrialists. His father, ruined by the revolution of '18, committed suicide. His mother, his uncles, wanted him to go into business; but, from the time he was quite young, taking advantage of the confusion of the war and the slackening of family supervision, he had, by inclination, hung about with the working youth of the suburbs and the docks; he heard the demands of the workers and soon conceived a fierce hostility towards that bourgeoisie which always responded to the most legitimate claims of the proletariat with the same selfishness, the same inertia; which refused to improve working conditions or regulate the work; and which sabotaged the government's social reforms on the quiet. The bourgeois and capitalist milieu of his childhood inspired only horror in him. He began his medical studies in Munich; as a student, he joined political movements; he saw Hitlerism arise and became affiliated with the party early on. As soon as he had finished his studies, he went home to set up in Hamburg as a family doctor in a lower-class suburb and very quickly acquired a practice among the workers. He is not militantly political; but he has remained a member of the party and takes an active part in community service in Hamburg. I now better understand why he always boasts of the "social facilities" of the new Reich.

This Weissmüller must be a child of the century: I suppose he has just turned forty. Rose claims he looks brutal. This is from not observing him properly. He immediately inspired trust in me, as a doctor, I mean. The patient is a weakened being who needs to feel strength in the person to whom he surrenders himself. Weissmüller, with that athlete's physique, those shoulders, that chest, those hands, that heavy head, that massive brow, that broad lion's muzzle, right away gives an impression of energy, of power. Of judiciousness as well: he reflects before expressing an opinion, an order; and his face, at that moment, has something reassuring about it: the contraction immobilizes all its muscles; the lowered head presses the chin against the neck; the deep-set eyes, calm and thoughtful, wander here and there, seeing nothing: one senses that what he is going to say will carry weight.

When Weissmüller refers to his youth, however much in control of himself he may be, the blood rushes to his cheeks, his features tense up and stiffen; it is as if a flood of bile rises to his face, and I hear in his voice the same rancor that makes Gralt's lips quiver when he recalls his adolescent years. To understand them, never forget the inexhaustible spring of anguish from which they drank at eighteen . . . They came out of a childhood of deprivation and suffering with a mad desire to live. Round about them, the ruins of a bourgeois civilization in bankruptcy, the incoherent clashes of extremist doctrines, all the fundamental values undermined, disorder everywhere, a chaos. Germany, hated, rejected, humiliated, had stewed in its own cesspool for five or six years at least without receiving any aid, without obtaining the slightest understanding or fraternal gesture from the victors.

That is the darkness in which those young men who form the terrible Germany of today grew up, with no illusions. They reached manhood in that atmosphere of decay, finding no response to their anxious questions or any use for their fervor. In response to their frantic need for truth, for certitude, nothing: the void. "Our lives," says Weissmüller, "strove irresistibly towards a single goal: the discovery of an order, the creation of a stable universe in which man could finally bloom." To reach that vital goal, to achieve it socially and impose it on the world—why should it be surprising that those desperate young people have been capable of any heroic act and ready for any individual sacrifice? The potential for accumulated resentment, which for years has built up in the heart of that cursed generation, explains everything. The more I let them talk, the more obvious it becomes to me that it is out of this resentment that most of them stick so strongly to the ideology that has extricated them from their hell.

WEISSMÜLLER TOLD ME that he had come to Paris and to Brussels in the summer of '36, on the occasion of some congress devoted half to medicine, half to social welfare, and that he had been struck, in his relations with his French and Belgian colleagues, by the narrowness of their political views. "I met only the one-eyed," he cried, with a grimace of disgust: "Those men had a hopelessly distorted vision of the world, because they were looking at it with only one eye! . . ." Here is the gist of what he went on to say: "In your democracies, the *social* and the *national* are absurdly separated. The man of the Left sacrifices all the national problems to the social problems; and the man of the Right, stupidly nationalistic, stubbornly resists all social reforms. In Hitler's Germany, we have the synthesis: a national-socialist in our country is more patriotically nationalistic than your reactionaries and more generously socialistic than your socialists. The day when you throw off your blinkers, the day when all your one-eyed people start using their two eyes again and finally learn how to consider human problems from both the social and the national angle, you'll become normal men and you won't have any more trouble understanding us."

Unstoppable, once he starts extolling the social facilities of the Third Reich. If he is to be believed—and why doubt him?—National Socialism has accomplished veritable miracles, in record time, without despoliation, without conflicts, with the magical ease of a fairy wand . . .

He says: "Our factories are bigger, better constructed, better lit and ventilated than in any country in the world, and our workers are more comfortable than anywhere else. Our villages, our farms, are showplaces compared to yours, compared to the rural areas of Europe or America. And the press in the democracies still calls us 'barbarians!' The world denies the obvious.

Inform yourself! Ask me about the subjects I know well, the organization of our medical profession, for example, or the institutions that govern workers, or the operation of our housing projects, our insurance system, our pensions, our schools and universities, the progress we've made in pediatrics, the laws that protect women and children . . . You'll be astounded, *mon colonel*! No nation has yet reached the level of civilization and social organization that we have attained!"

I refrain from contradicting him. I take him at his word. But is all that truly the contribution of National Socialism? Isn't it more generally the result of the disciplined and organizing mind of the Germans? Before the First World War, wasn't Germany already, thanks to its social legislation, ahead of all the nations of the world?

On all these subjects, he is fantastically well-informed. He must have a flawless memory at his disposal, fed by the details that Nazi propaganda provides him.

Moreover, I find very typically German this wholly concrete way of reasoning by the numbers, of considering everything in the light of statistics, of measuring a nation's greatness solely by the square miles of its land, the sum of its inhabitants, the amount of its public debt, the number of its soldiers, cannons, tanks and warships, its factory equipment, its industrial output, etc. On that terrain, Weissmüller is unbeatable. And how to make him understand that the French have an entirely different scale of values? Another concept of a nation's greatness? A different assessment of strength? All Franco-German dialogue is contaminated at its starting point by an almost inevitable lack of mutual understanding.

LONG MONOLOGUE BY WEISSMÜLLER, which I want to put down. He began with something like this:

"The French, who are quick to pride themselves on being an ancient people—and indeed, in many respects for half a century France has appeared to be an aging, worn-out country—are also, in certain ways, a nation of children. What could be more childish than their mysticism about independence and their instinctive aversion to all authority?"

I thought to myself: "The German, for his part, is rather like a domesticated animal. He accepts the yoke; he has no need to live according to his fancy . . . And he has, in his blood, that disposition to obey an iron hand: Bismarck, Hitler . . . And wouldn't this be the line of demarcation between the Nordic temperament and the Mediterranean?"

But Weissmüller was rolling. And, what he said, I must admit, was quite beautiful and very moving. I summarize as best I can:

"Only children rebel against the rules. A grown man, a thoughtful man, knows that he needs to be reined in so as not to veer from the straight and narrow and to give his full measure. In France you think all is lost if your famous *republican liberties* are compromised, or only muzzled, by someone in power. As if authority and discipline were intolerable shackles! The mentality of stubborn mules . . . Probably you don't know what a chief is, and what it is to obey when the chief is a real leader of men . . . The German, on the other hand, not only is unafraid to submit to the orders of a just and enlightened chief, but wants to, because he is aware that he will find in him a prop against his weaknesses and a way of fulfilling his potential to the maximum. The real leader can be authoritarian without ruffling any legitimate sensitivity. Take the Führer. Even more than our leader, he is our guide: our blind trust, our absolute devotion, rest on the certainty, confirmed by experience, that the Führer does not represent an individual, isolated power outside of us to whose will we would have to arbitrarily submit, but rather that he constitutes an essential—and the best—part of ourselves; that he is, in some way, our conscience, our nobility, our energy, our feeling of national solidarity, our concept of duty, our sense of the good."

(I thought, "Isn't it Vauvenargues who says somewhere that servitude so debases man that it ends up making him love it?")

"The Führer," Weissmüller went on, "is our *common will,* centralized in a predestined brain. What he commands us is precisely what our secret conscience would order us to do and what, alone, left to our low instincts, to our individual anarchy, we would probably have neither the courage nor the perseverance to carry out; and what he forbids us is precisely what, abandoned to our human frailty, we might do but would be ashamed of having done. The Führer's presence at the head of the nation keeps each of us at his peak. That strength, that greatness, that will for good which are scattered, hidden deep within us, and which we only detect at certain moments of lucidity and moral elevation, the Führer has discerned, once and for all, with his infallible glance, and has voiced in vivid, concrete formulations, accessible to everyone, and he compels us to translate them into heroic acts. There you have the divine mission of a true chief. This magical power that the Führer has got over the German people comes solely from this: that he incarnates, in a way that for us is beyond questioning, the *continuity* of that *collective will* by which, down the centuries, the mysterious destiny of a race is expressed.

"Hitler is a Führer, a leader worthy of us, worthy of a people who do not merely consent but yearn to be led, because he always knows what is right for the vague desires of this people and because to bring about the triumph of that collective ideal, he alone determines the means and goes forward with an unbending brutality, free of any cowardly sensitivity."

Gralt was listening. When I found myself alone with him again, he could not help returning to the same subject: the Führer, the Führer . . . Of what he said, I select only this:

"This harmony between the chief and those who are under his orders is truly the German miracle. And this miracle has now spread to the entire army. I know what the relations between the officers and the soldiers were like in the other war. Today, those relations are profoundly changed. Our officers are not feared by the troops: they are respected and loved, like older, better-educated brothers. They don't *command* soldiers (in the *Prussian* sense): they *lead* men. They are their guides, their teachers. They have taken them under their care, they are responsible for them: and the obedience they obtain is freely given."

This could be. It tallies fairly well with what Rose and Bocca have often told me about the demeanor of the officers among their men.

LIKE THOSE FLEETING and occasional resemblances one glimpses in flashes between distant members of the same family, I often find in Dr. Weissmüller traces of that cold hardness that Kert has in his face, in his eyes, in his slightest remarks. Strange, that this Weissmüller, a doctor—that is, someone who has dedicated his life to the curing of illnesses, the relief of suffering—passionate about reforms and proud of the German social-welfare system, never seems to have considered the idea of the happiness, the well-being of individuals. On the contrary: several times now I have heard him say that it is healthy for a strong people to live in very harsh material conditions; deprivations, by eliminating the least hardy, automatically purify the race. Today he mounted a learned apologia for natural selection and a thorough-going attack on Christian squeamishness. The extinction of the weak is a natural law, of vital importance for humanity; by trying to thwart this law and limit its effects, society is committing a crime against life and against the species. The future will belong to the races that not only give free play to natural selection but also foster and hasten its effects by the deliberate, rational elimination of the mentally retarded and physically disabled. Insane asylums, homes for the incurable, are social nonsense, etc.

No pity for the lame ducks! Seen in this light, the ideal of society is the stud farm . . .

Maybe so. Everything in this concept of future humanity shocks me, but it is not illogical in itself.

The fact remains, however, that the whole effort of civilization has consisted of a struggle by man against the brutal laws of nature and that all the progress accomplished by intelligence and reason has been reached through fighting against natural instincts.

A SILENT SCENE, rather odd.

Today, for no apparent reason, he suddenly pulled a wallet out of his pocket and drew a snapshot from it, which he handed me without a word. Two beautiful children with light hair, a boy and a girl, between three and five years old, perched on either shoulder of a Weissmüller in mufti, whose leonine face, lit up by a broad and kind smile, occupies the center of the picture. His powerful hands hold the four little legs, delicate and naked, against his chest.

This man is married. He has a home, children.

I gave the photo back to him without saying anything, after having studied it for a long time. He solemnly returned it to his wallet, which he stuffed into the pocket of his tunic, and left the room in silence.

YESTERDAY, I NOTICED that Weissmüller, before withdrawing, lingered a moment in front of the bookcase and ran his eyes over several titles. Then, as he passed the orderly who opened the door for him, he muttered a few words in German. I was naïve enough to ask Gralt later whether the doctor would not like to borrow certain works. He could not keep from smiling: "You know the comment he made to me? He said: 'How can someone clutter up his house, and even his bedroom, with all that printed trash?' "

Such a reaction, in an intelligent, educated man who has certainly read a lot, left me very intrigued. Today I could not rest until I had got him going on this subject. The ideas that he professes about it, and with the greatest seriousness, are beyond belief. And the funniest thing is that I gather they are quite widespread in Germany; they are based on certain statements made by Hitler himself, in *Mein Kampf*, of which they are apparently only an exaggeration.

In a nutshell: Weissmüller considers reading to be one of the most harmful modern habits, one of the most regrettable legacies of the bourgeoisie, a social scourge that should be fought in the same way as alcoholism . . . Copious reading could only result in encumbering the mind with useless information, which congests it and leaves it paralyzed. It is to be wished that those who are responsible for watching over the nation's hygiene protect the minds of the younger generation from this parasitic invasion. Weissmüller strongly opposes the absurd worship of "general ideas," the source of all anarchy, a poison whose unrestricted use can only jeopardize the social order. "Access to public libraries should be severely regulated!" he says vehemently. "In the universities," he goes on, "there are far too many books lying around. The student wastes precious time reading at random; he should be able to get his hands only on technical works in which the teaching of his professors is set down and developed. The only valid aim of study is to allow the younger members of the community to acquire ideas necessary for the professions they want to enter, in order to become the best possible cog in the social machine." As for grown men and women, he admits that the exercise of reading might be beneficial, as long as it is used with moderation and good judgment, but it would not take much prodding to get him to say that government censorship should remove from circulation any works whose purpose is not to provide the reader with a precise and coherent idea of the world according to the National Socialist point of view and to instruct him as to the historical destiny of his race!

He also laid out for me a theory as to what he calls *le savoir-lire.* Instead of trying to remember as many things as possible, as most readers do, the opposite should be done, i.e., "reading with the memory off," as he says, in order to put out of the mind anything which is not "of the essence." And what, for him, is of the essence? Nothing but the "verities" that have been formulated "by the recognized masters of national thought."

Gralt was present at this conversation—I should rather say "at this monologue"—and he seemed to me somewhat embarrassed . . . As for me, I scarcely uttered any objections: just what it took to keep the speechifier going.

I sometimes reproach myself as if it were a kind of minor cowardice in me to shy away from any argument with Dr. Weissmüller. Then again, it's the only reasonable attitude. The advantage of a brain like mine over a thick head like his is that I learn a lot by listening to him, while he would learn nothing from me.

No illusions as to what he thinks of me. His politeness does not fool me. Without any doubt, he takes me for an ordinary specimen of a bygone age, a fossil contemptible twice over, both for belonging to the bourgeoisie and for displaying the form of intelligence he despises most, the sort of roving and elusive intellectual curiosity which tackles everything and settles nowhere, which inevitably leads to indifference or skepticism and makes a man unfit for any strong conviction, for adherence to any doctrine. One day he said to me, of Goethe—and it would be hard to compress more false ideas into so few words: "Goethe, that *eclectic intellectual,* who has done so much harm . . ." I suppose he places me in the anonymous crowd of the infinitely small "eclectic intellectuals," at the very bottom of the ladder of which Goethe, according to him, occupies the highest rung in spite of all. I could not wish for more flattering company . . .

Weissmüller asked me if I had read *Mein Kampf.* Upon my affirmative and reserved response, he asked me what I thought of that book and whether I did not find in it a clear and logical answer to all present-day problems.

He listened to me attentively. But he started when I described *Mein Kampf* as an "aggressive book":

"Aggressive?"

"Yes, aggressive. And the proof is that the author has never authorized the complete translation of it into any language. Since every nation of Europe is threatened in it with aggression, a truncated version has had to be provided for each of them, in which the passages about each one, the publication of which would have aroused their suspicion of Hitlerian designs, have been suppressed."

I had the impression that this commonsensical objection was completely new to him, and that he was quite struck by it. He made no reply, and hastily changed the subject.

III. HATRED OF GERMANY. ATROCITIES IN THE NAZI CAMPS*

During the First World War, I said "the Germans," and very rarely "the Boches." I fought them as best I could, I strove with all my might for their defeat; but I regarded them as an adversary rather than an enemy. They killed my two sons, and yet I came home in '18 without having ever known hatred. I criticized Poincaré's intransigent attitude. I wished Briand's peacemaking policy well and supported it with my votes, and until the emergence of the Nazis, I persisted in hoping for a rapprochement between France and Germany. It was at the time of Munich that I felt hatred seeping into me; it was in June of '40 that the acrid poison entered every fiber of my body; since the occupation I have suffered its incurable virulence like a damned soul, and every day worse. Romain Rolland seems to have gone through the same stages. That man in love with justice and harmony, but still more with liberty, was the warmest supporter of the Second World War, the fiercest opponent of Hitler's Germany. He remained in France during the occupation. I can imagine better than anyone what he must have suffered during the final years of his life. Throughout four years, forced into that humiliating proximity with the enemy, we could observe what the official supporters of Nazism were up to. Before our eyes, innocent people were arrested without explanation, were brutalized, imprisoned for months without being the object of any investigation and without being accorded the least opportunity to clear themselves. Free men, women, children, whose only sin was to belong to the Jewish race or to the Communist party, or to have been victims of a false denunciation, were, to our certain knowledge, hunted down like game, torn from their families, thrown into sealed railway cars, treated as forced laborers. We learned that whole populations had been driven out of

*In this section, Maumort is writing towards the end of the war.

their homelands, plundered of all their goods, and deported en masse, in defiance of all national or international law. In all our occupied towns we could see bands of bought policemen—impeccable in their uniforms, covered with military decorations, and proud of being the most active defenders of Great Germany and the new order—torturing patriots, executing hostages by the hundreds, killing prisoners without trials, burning peasants alive in their barns, separating mothers from three-year-old toddlers.

In this intermingling of the two nations, Germany's principles, goals, methods, and innermost character came to light. Through his presence on our soil, through the brazen show he made there of his true nature, the German revealed himself as forever deserving to be loathed. I cannot help it. I now hate him.

All the same, as far as possible I try to struggle against this spell that blinds, I keep my critical mind alert, in order to stay lucid and fair. Thus, until recently, despite everything we know the Germans to be capable of in their madness of racial hegemony, despite the crimes that their Gestapo has committed in our country, I persisted in doubting the appalling news that our Resistance press was spreading about the Nazi camps. I wanted at all costs to convince myself that it was exaggerated, biased.

This time, doubt is no longer possible. The advance of the Allies into Germany, and of our troops into Alsace, suddenly allows us to assemble a whole body of proof, of damning, indisputable testimony. The newspapers these days are full of astounding details. Not only do the horrors that had been decried turn out to be perfectly true, but their atrociousness surpasses in refinement anything that the morbid imagination of a bloodthirsty persecutor could delight in inventing. Our war correspondents have been able to take stock of several of those gruesome camps. The executioners acknowledged the facts with an alarming cynicism. They claim to have carried out orders, to have followed meticulously planned rules of extermination. No remorse: in putting to death, by the thousands, the enemies of the regime, as coldly as one crushes bedbugs, they flatter themselves that they did their duty as soldiers! They admit to having suffocated infants, pushed herds of women into the gas chambers, thrown the old and the sick, all the "useless mouths," into the crematorium, hung Jews and Communists by the jaw from butcher's hooks to torture them to death. Photos have been taken and reproduced. In them can be seen the gaping doors of the ovens, the rows of hooks, the instruments of torture, the huge rooms for mass asphyxiation, with the transom windows over which bent the medical commissions assigned to scientifically observe the form of the victims' death throes.

Faced with such an outbreak of systematic, organized cruelty, indignation is ludicrous, and hate becomes unjust. One does not hate an insane criminal:

society disarms him and locks him up. The civilized world must render Germany harmless until it has given unquestionable proofs of having been cured. A nation where it was possible to recruit such fanatical torturers and honor them as loyal soldiers must not be left at large for a long time to come.

AN ENDLESS DEBATE will take place about the responsibility of the German people for the heinous deeds of the Nazi leaders. The day is coming when the survivors of the disaster will swear to God that they were forced to submit to the regime and did not approve of it. Let us not be duped. It is not true. All of Germany, with rare exceptions, was Nazi. No government has been more often or more legally elected by an overwhelming majority of its people. Hitler was a god to nine Germans out of ten. And if he had continued to be victorious, he would be a god for the unanimous whole of the German people.

From 1935 on, the clamor coming from the other side of the Rhine warned us that no German could rest as long as France was not annihilated, enslaved, reduced to the role of a serf tilling the land for the benefit of the race of lords.

This time, any feeling of generosity, of pardon, is extinguished in French hearts. We soon forgot '70; we soon—perhaps too soon—forgot, in 1920, the violation and harsh occupation of Belgium, the gas attacks of 1915. This time, no. This was the last straw. We cannot forget the camps.

They will say, once again: "We didn't want that," and probably, for many, it will be true. They did not want it, perhaps; but, en masse, they allowed a handful of lunatics to want it for them, and they cheered them, idolized them, and blindly followed them to the end of their bloodthirsty insanity, until the final collapse. And if the monster had succeeded in enslaving Europe, they would all have joyously come along in its wake and trampled the vanquished nations underfoot.

A dangerous nation, as one says "a vicious dog," "a dangerous madman." To be rendered harmless.

PEOPLE SPEAK OF "two Germanies," the good one and the other. This was undeniable, *in the past.* The fundamental *domestic* feat of Hitlerism was its having tracked down and deported or *eliminated* all the combative elements of the "good Germany" that resisted Nazi doctrines, and its having *converted* all the halfhearted supporters of the "good Germany," who in turn heartily elected the regime because they preferred to surrender their democratic principles, etc., and promote the material growth, the conquest, the violence from which they profited and which flattered their national pride, their taste for hegemony, the German mystical belief in the superiority of the Teuton, the heady lure of *Deutschland über alles.*

God knows I am not in the least *racist.* I have always opposed those who wished to exterminate the Germans as an accursed race. After '18, with Weimar, I believed in the possibility of a democratic spirit in Germany. Some Germans did lean in that direction. Hitlerism drove them out or murdered them. It managed to remove them almost entirely from the Germany that survives. Hitlerism is a monstrous and collective phenomenon which was possible only because the Germans found their secret ideal in it. There was a unanimous urge to shout *Heil Hitler.* Those who did this solely out of cowardice are extremely rare.

I no longer have any faith in the German of today, poisoned by the reign of Hitler. It is impossible to change, to educate, a whole nation.

Men of my age, who knew the end of the nineteenth century, the European civilization of that time when reason, human rights, and the human being were sacred values, feel that the raging hordes came to sack a *holy patrimony*—or at least one that was more precious to us than anything in the world.

The mortal duel that was waged in the trenches of World War I seems to us almost as gentlemanly as the battle of Fontenoy compared to what the Wehrmacht together with the Gestapo have turned war into, a barbarous slaughter with the extermination of whole populations of women and children as its goal, and with old people led off into slavery, like cattle.

For a long time I refused to believe that the Germans were so different from the French. I found Maurras, Barrès, blinded by patriotic hate. *Is it my turn to be blind?*

No, the French would not have been capable of such widespread acquiescence to Hitlerian doctrine, whose cynicism and lack of scruples was obvious, whose savage methods were a debasement of civilized man. The French hold on to their critical sense, their taste for thinking for themselves. Would they have been able to accept that fanatical, *religious* side, that worship of Hitler? Would they not have been revolted by the promises Hitler did not keep, those speeches in which he coolly contradicted what he had said the day before? Without flinching, the Germans watched Hitler ally himself with Russia after his anti-Bolshevik campaigns, then resume anti-Soviet campaigns when he launched his attack on Russia. They slavishly went along with all his flagrant denials. They cheerfully agreed to become morons. They accepted the *Gestapo.*

I don't know if I will ever be able to overcome my aversion and have any dealings with a German, no matter who he may be.

Gévresin, one of whose nieces had married the owner of a big hotel in

Cahors that the Gestapo emptied out to make room for its "services," was able to obtain the names and civilian status of some of the good bureaucrats who worked there. We destroyed those notes at the time of the searches in Piérac. But I recall a few precise details that struck me. One of the chief torturers, particularly inventive, a man of thirty-five, was, in civilian life, a young professor of Romance philology in a German university. Another, who, during the interrogations, to hasten the moment of confession, forced his victims to walk by turns on a floor covered with ground glass and in a tub filled with heavily ammoniated water, was, in civilian life, attached to the manuscript department in a big library, and was an expert on medieval miniatures.

My father fought in '70. He retained a certain resentment against the Pruscots,* but he spoke of the Germans without hatred, and received German scientific journals.

I believe that from now on it would be impossible for me to enter into a conversation with a German, even if he were cultivated or learned, without wondering if, during the occupation, this fine fellow with glasses had not fulfilled his patriotic duty by conducting some "interrogation" of that sort . . .

IV. Conventional Doctrines of the General Staff†

Fortunately I published a few articles between 1925 and 1935 to protest the conventional doctrines of the École de Guerre and the general staff, to demand that our enormous defense budget be largely employed in the creation of a sizable air force and the formation of motorized units capable of transforming our shock troops into a true offensive army with armored vehicles. Without these articles no trace would be left of my predictions. Among the papers I have destroyed, what I regret the most is the huge gray file in which I kept my notes and many articles, all ready for the press, which no one wanted to publish in the technical journals. It is no consolation to be able to say, "I told you so . . ." But there is something unjust and aggravating to me in this thought that I was one of the very few military writers who understood the errors of the official doctrines, who clearly imagined what war would be like in the future, and that except for a few published articles (which were neither the most detailed nor the boldest), no evidence remains of my clairvoyance.

I am specifically thinking of the paper which I wrote just after the reoccupation of the Rhineland by German troops and which neither the *Revue*

*I.e., the Prussians.
†Here Maumort appears to be writing sometimes in 1942 or 1943, sometimes in 1940.

des questions militaires nor the *Bulletin technique de l'armée* was willing to print. In it I argued, in a way I believe convincing and which events have borne out, that if, at that moment, we had taken advantage of our lead in aviation, and if we had secured an air force with an overwhelming numerical and qualitative superiority, we stood a good chance of avoiding war. I believe it still. I do not say that this would have prevented the rearmament of Germany, but the Germans would have had a much harder time catching up to our lead, and they would probably not have succeeded if we had refused to let ourselves be caught. In any case, faced with a very powerful French air force, Germany would have hesitated a long time before risking a conflict. And I remember that, in this paper, I tried to assert that time won in these matters was a factor in our favor, for we might have seen Germany's and Italy's domestic problems shake their totalitarian regimes, as this had nearly happened several times; and by preventing those regimes from relying on a military superiority, we would have stripped them of their principal strong point. Among the works that I am sorry to have lost, there are also my two essays on pacifism, that of 1924 and that of 1933 or 1934; I think they complemented each other nicely. One of these days I ought to take the time to write a précis of those articles, according to my memory. The question of pacifism was one of the least clear of the period after World I. The activity of the true and reasonable pacifists, which might have been decisive, which might perhaps have brought about a great advance in civilization, was completely impeded and compromised by the cumbersome and showy pacifism of those naïfs who were the majority, and whose principal error was to imagine that the Europe created by the treaty of Versailles was already a world in which justice alone would be enough to keep the peace; in which it was not necessary to arm justice to have it respected; and in which one could dispense with force to protect human rights.

I think I was more sincerely pacifistic than anyone. I was harshly enough criticized for it. But I always fought against the harmful aberrations of the blind pacifists. In that essay of '34, I stated once again that in certain given circumstances—and the threat of a Hitlerian hegemony and the beginning, at that time, of German rearmament, placed us in just such a circumstance— it was necessary to have at one's disposal a strong military force, and to be able to use it, and to want to use it, if one wished to hold the hostile powers in check and to keep them from destroying us and our pacifism the moment they were let loose on us. The risk of war, which so many pacifists refused to consider, believing that they were already betraying peace as soon as they imagined the possibility of a war, this risk is inevitable in the political state of the present Europe. To want to rule out this risk, to deny it, is automatically to make war certain and assure defeat. In a world where gangsters still exist, if one wants to live in peace, or if one wants only to be able to live, one needs to be armed, and, furthermore, to be ready to use one's weapon. It is not a matter of setting up an absolute principle: it is a matter of looking an established fact in the face, against which nothing can be done, and which it is insane to tackle through trust. "Show strength so you don't have to use it," Lyautey used to say.

PEOPLE ARE BEING SENT to prison . . . Daladier, Gamelin, Reynaud, Blum . . .* There is a lot of talk about responsibility. The press, the radio, portray the French as thirsting for justice, demanding the conviction of all the abettors of the defeat for having "failed to fulfill their duties." I am not in a position to judge if the concern for justice is really so widespread, so active. It seems to me that, for the politicians who stayed in or have returned to power, the desire for revenge against their former bosses or opponents is much more pressing!

I am surprised that, in this commendable search for the responsible parties, nothing is ever said of those who by dint of their titles and their past were the important technical advisers to the Minister of National Defense, all those old respected leaders who, twenty years after the First World War, were deaf to all warnings, never wanted to let go of the theory of the defensive, refused to believe that a modern war would be a lightning offensive of tanks and airplanes, did nothing to allocate to the creation of a modern army that tremendous defense budget which was available to them and which no government, not even the most leftist, refused them. Who are they? It is impossible that Pétain, that Weygand, have completely forgotten which authorities, from 1919 to 1931, presided over the deliberations of the Conseil Supérieur de la Défense and of our Conseil Supérieur de la Guerre!

ANNOYED AT READING yet again in the press the unjust nonsense that the Vichy propaganda periodically spreads about the question of "those responsible for the defeat," I have just taken down from my bookcase that book by General Chauvineau (professor at the École de Guerre), published by Berger-Levrault in 1938, about which I wrote a long report which was my final work of that kind and which no military journal saw fit to publish. At the time I felt rather bitter about it. I think that if I could read my paper again today, I would, alas, feel quite vindicated. . . . But it was destroyed, along with the rest of my archives.

*Three high-level politicians (Édouard Daladier [1884–1970], Paul Reynaud [1878–1966], Léon Blum [1872–1950]) and a general (Maurice Gustave Gamelin [1872–1958]) whom the Vichy regime, seeking to pin the blame for the defeat on its predecessors, tried at Riom in 1942 and deported to German prison camps.

In any case, I still have this book by Chauvineau, and if it were not so sad to go back over that blindness of our great military leaders now that we are assessing just how fatal it was for us, I would savor my vindication at leisure . . .

But why attach any importance to Chauvineau's book?

Because it is introduced by an important preface, more than twenty pages long, signed by a name that compels attention: MARSHAL PÉTAIN; and this preface is dated *1938*.

This preface not only imparts to Chauvineau's nonsense the authority of one of the most undisputed military experts, but it brings to that nonsense the support of the great leader who today mercilessly condemns the "errors" of others. In it can be seen, once again, what ideas about the future war were held by the former victor of Verdun, the man who had for years sat at the head of our Conseil Suprême de Défense Nationale, as he shrugged off the warnings of those who, being better prognosticators of the future, kept on campaigning for an invincible air force and a formidable host of armored vehicles. The man who, today, carried to the top by the defeat that he let come about and was not able to foresee, thinks he has the right to look elsewhere for people on whom to blame our tragedy.

The title alone, in this month of August, 1940, is suggestive enough: *Is an Invasion Still Possible?* I'm opening the book at random. The margins are full of my indignant pencil slashes.

P. 28: "In France, a war involving a swift invasion, which is still called a war of movement, has had its day! And it is because Schieffen, faithful to bad military habits, wanted to wage that sort of war with us, that, even faced with an adversary as uninformed as he as to the dangers of the operation, he failed. All the more likely that he would fail now, faced with a country which has just learned its lesson from that grandiose experience, and with an army that has profited from the lesson to organize itself in accordance with the new and compelling demands of modern technique."

Poor Chauvineau! Where is he at this moment? Where is he hiding? What can he feel about himself and the damage that he and those like him have done to France?

What to think of a general-staff theoretician, backed by Pétain's high authority, who coolly declares, one year before the invasion of Poland, eighteen months before the invasion of France, p. 51: "The force of words brings about singular errors: popular imagination lends a magic power to *Motorization*. Taking its cue from a few military men, it sees in a motorized division a hard-hitting tool capable of freeing the offensive from the obstacles of a continuous front, and of allowing a return to Napoleonic exploits. Now, since speed and strength are, all things being equal, mutually exclusive, the more mobile a division is, the weaker it is as a striking force." He concludes with this general-staff axiom: "A motorized unit is a defensive tool."

P. 65: "Many military men after the war, taking their wishes for realities, think that, thanks to the rapidity of the preparation of future attacks, which seems to them a necessary outcome of the perfecting of offensive weapons and the use of assault tanks, they can prevent the creation of fortifications . . . A bigger mistake cannot be made."

Chauvineau informs us that no more than ten days is needed to create a fortified position able to protect its defenders against tanks. And, reassured, he concludes, p. 70: "In ten or so days [*sic*] we would outfit our frontier with a continuous barrier of active shelters, impregnable to cannons by virtue of their camouflage and to tanks by virtue of their resistance and impermeability to shells . . . Result: the machine gun, principal means of ground defense, will no longer be neutralized by the tank, and *this obliterates all the hopes founded on the action of the armored vehicle.* Confronted with a nation which has blocked its border in this way, *the offensive tank is worthless.*"

But one of the most appalling passages to read, one of the most egregious "prophecies-in-reverse," is the whole part that deals with large mechanized units: you think you are dreaming when you read "superior" assertions like these: "There exists in the use of tanks another tendency which cannot be passed over in silence: this aims at the formation of large, tank-based, mechanized units, capable of breaking through fronts and penetrating rapidly and deeply into the interior of the enemy country, to wreak havoc, destroy its communications and nerve centers, etc. One even hears it said that these tank raids could lead to a swift conclusion of the war." "Let us ask ourselves what tanks, *arriving in the region of Paris,* could actually do there . . ."

And everything that our High Command was capable of doing to imagine, anticipate, and prepare for the future war, is condensed in these masterly lines, p. 119: "The military ideal will thus gradually see its pretensions lowered until it is content with a defensive organization well-enough conceived to discourage any aggression. The great modern armed forces, whether on land, air, or sea, will then be like those earthenware animals that stare fiercely at one another at the entrances of certain homes."

When it comes to airplanes, the same inability to anticipate the future, the same submission to secondary or outdated objections, and the same positive self-confidence: "A Franco-Germanic air duel would generally be to the advantage of the French . . ." We've seen that, all right!

In his preface, Pétain completely endorses General Chauvineau on the matter of the offensive war. He denies that offensive warfare is at all effective. Even more, he claims that it has become impossible. This is the famous doctrine of the continuous front, born of the experience in the trenches in World War I, and which for twenty years has been the fixed and central idea of the whole French High Command.

P. xviii: "The continuous front is a consequence of increased manpower, supplied by the armed nation, and of technical properties of weapons capable of erecting barriers that cannot be breached by men or tanks.

"One detects certain tendencies to go back to the doctrine of the war of movement right from the start of operations, in pursuance of the ideas in favor before 1914. The experience of the war cost us too dear to return with impunity to the errors of the past. It will be the rare distinction of General Chauvineau to have shown that the continuous front is both based on the lessons of history and on the technical properties of our weapons and fortifications."

To the question which Chauvineau made the title of his book—"Is an invasion still possible?"—Pétain responded in the negative, with the same assurance as the author.

v. The True Nature of the Resistance: Indignation*

Very quickly, once the first weeks of upheaval which followed the exodus and capitulation were over, a majority of the French, although still very respectful of the Marshal's stature, felt that this government of defeat, kept in exile in Vichy, had arisen from an irreparable political error; that it ruled under the barely veiled supervision of the enemy; and that it would not be able to last without colluding more and more closely with the Germans. Discontent grew when people saw this government usurping the titles "revolutionary" and "national"—as if the revolutionary spirit was compatible with acceptance of the yoke; as if the national spirit could blossom with the backing of a foreign occupation; as if the cardinal requirement for a government to meet in order to claim to be "revolutionary" and "national" was not, first, that it be free. And, starting at the end of the summer of 1940, it became obvious that the country as a whole was grudging its trust in its compromised leaders, and was withdrawing it from them as the evidence mounted of their willing subjection to the conqueror.

In spite of all, the ideas of reconciliation, of "collaboration" might have been favorably received by French minds more eager for concord than revenge, if Germany had been prudent enough to hide its secrets better. But with such an onslaught of deliberate, organized, legalized cruelty, how would the French conscience, how would any human conscience, not have rebelled? How could the witnesses of such gratuitous iniquities, the powerless spectators of such unforgivable crimes, have been willing to extend a brotherly hand to a nation in which it was possible to recruit and to honor as loyal servants of the state those legions of torturers?

*Here Maumort is writing after the Liberation.

Make no mistake about it: even more than patriotism or the call of liberty, it is *indignation* that aroused the whole of France against Nazi barbarity!

The Resistance really was the kernel of France, the enduring heart of the motherland. And this heart had a unity, beat in unison. The error was to think that, in the normal course of events, the Resistance, by dint of its acquired strength and its right to the nation's gratitude, was also to become the rallying point of that whole multitude—the majority of Frenchmen— who resisted in their hearts, passively, without being militant, but who were often the timid, older, or pusillanimous brothers of the Resistance fighters.

Actually, reality proves that the role of the Resistance fighter must limit itself to resisting in time of oppression, but that his virtues, his beautiful courage, do not necessarily make him suited for everything. Particularly not for rebuilding France. This elite in a time of heroism may not be a nursery for the elites we need. [. . .]

As soon as the work of the Resistance was completed, the old ideological clashes reappeared, the old parties, the old set positions. Distrust, animosity, and dissension are rooted at the deepest level of the nation. [. . .]

Among the hopes of the Liberation was the hope that politics in France would never again be like what it had been in '38 and '39. That was the general wish. That wish has been betrayed.

The expected Revolution which was to be made by the entire nation has once again become the revolution of one class, of a single workers' party. Each party, instead of working for the nation, tries to enlist its supporters in order to prevail over the others. France is torn apart by one long election campaign, a bidding contest of demagogy, patriotism, revolutionary spirit, entitlement to run France. The Revolution was to take place in an atmosphere of victory and national reconciliation. At that moment, everything was possible. The Communists, it must be said, set a fine example with their ' concept of the general interest to which everything is subjected and for which they are ready—and prove themselves so—to make any sacrifice.

A revolution which has let its hour pass, a revolution deferred, is an aborted revolution.

Epilogue*

CHAPTER XXIII

What the Diary Was:
A Diary of a Happy Man

NONE OF THIS really belongs among my "reading notes". . . but why should I forbid myself these digressions, if I take pleasure in them? What does it matter if this notebook betrays its original purpose?

Now that it is open on my table, I have less taste for reading; this is a fact. Or rather, the temptation of writing beckons to me so strongly that I do not surrender so completely, so freely, as before to the interest of what I am reading: I am unconsciously looking for an observation to record, a passage to quote, an excuse, actually, to get out of my armchair and sit down in front of this notebook—I was going to write, this diary. And indeed, that is pretty much the form that, in spite of me, these "notes" are taking. So what? What is so surprising about that, anyway? In doing this, I am only returning to an old habit: a habit to which I have been faithful for fifty years, an *ingrained* habit if ever there was one, and one I would have retained, without any doubt, if circumstances had not forced me to give it up four years ago.

I have often missed it. Over the last months, I have even thought of

---

*André Daspre: Under this title, very different texts are assembled in two chapters: the notes on the end of Maumort, in Chapter XXIV, are preceded by a fragment in which the narrator explains the origin and function of the diary he has lost, and at the same time draws up a sort of balance sheet of his life. Without any doubt, the novelist conceived this fragment, which here forms Chapter XXIII, as an introductory text, the opening of the novel. But we know that he later modified his plan several times, particularly the composition of the first chapters. I have thus considered it preferable to place these pages here, where they appear as a conclusion, the last judgment of the narrator on himself and the world.

taking it up again. And I would have quite naturally decided to do so, I think, if I had not been deprived of my diary by that absurd theft of my tin trunk, if I had only had to pick up the thread again, to resume the daily task begun in my youth, to continue the notebook interrupted, in June '40, by the presence of the Germans. But, at seventy-five, to begin a diary! At the moment when nothing more is happening in my life! The diary of an idle, crippled, retired man. A journey around my room? No urge for that.

*

I so enjoy conversing with myself since I have had this notebook open on my table that, if I am not careful, the "reading notes" could become much less important than the digressions and the chatter . . . And why not? Chamfort* is right: one needs to yield to oneself and give in to one's propensities!

For how many hours, for how many hours like this one, on evenings like this evening, have I thus let my pen run over a notebook like the one before me? For as long as I can remember, or almost!

Since the beginning of my conscious life, in any case, since it was around my thirteenth year, after the death of my cousin Guy, that, for the first time, my instinct prompted me to confide to paper the feelings I had inside me. I freed myself of my sadness by making up romantic sentences about it. I can still see the black-bordered pages that I used to swipe from my sister Henriette for that purpose, and used to read over with emotion.

The first notebook dates from a little later. But this was not yet a diary. During my last year at the lycée, I had been seized by the urge to copy out, in my composition book, the ideas, the striking expressions, that I caught in my teachers' lectures or gleaned from my collection of selected passages. A kind of anthology, or "breviary," which I planned to expand throughout my life. I had not yet ventured to insert personal reflections in it. It only became a diary after my arrival in Paris, during my first year of university. So many things filled me with wonder in that new existence! The only way not to lose anything was to put down my impressions as they came to me. My notebooks were born, in short, of the fear I had of not being able to hold on to all the excitement that the present was offering me. I wrote it all down helter-skelter: quotations from my reading as well as remarks on literature or moral reflections, the things I admired at the time as well as those I loathed and rejected; I recorded my observations of the people around me, my schoolmates, my professors; I related my schedule, my outings in the capital, what I had seen and heard in the street, in the Latin Quarter, at the Sorbonne, at the theater, in Uncle Éric's salon; with no other aim than to give a

*Nicolas de Chamfort (1741–1794), French moralist famous for his epigrams and maxims.

form, a consistency, to the ephemeral, to fix through writing all that fluid wealth of daily life that I greeted with so much enthusiasm, and whose transitoriness I sensed. Already as a child, I was painfully aware of the passage of time; I wept in my bed, on the evenings after certain parties, at the memory of the joys that the day had brought me, and despaired over how little of them remained to me. I have always had that instinct of the ant who gathers in, that horror of waste and destruction, that tendency to hoard. Qualities increased, perhaps, by my nomadic existence as an officer, so little suited to accumulation. I have spent my life wanting to conserve: I collected documents, souvenirs, letters, notes, photographs, newspaper clippings, simply to prevent something that had been from disappearing, swallowed up by the past, by oblivion.

The hours I stole from my studies to fill the pages of my notebook were the best of all my days. (I loved to write, to catch a nuance, to find the right expression.) The best and probably the most productive for my development. Gradually, I gave in more to the temptation of focusing a large portion of my reflections on myself. I registered my plans, my resolutions, my hopes; I made judgments about my character; I strove to be honest, to analyze the real motives behind certain spontaneous acts, certain reactions. I did not spare myself criticisms. On one of the first notebooks I wrote, as an epigraph: *Pro remedio animae meae.** Which meant not only that the diary answered a need to pour out feelings, a natural taste for introspection, but also that it was for me a means to self-improvement, to intellectual and moral progress. There is nothing like that daily exercise for taking stock of one's possibilities and becoming aware of one's limits. Granted, in trying to define my character precisely, I did distort some of its outlines, but the problem was not serious, and was only temporary; the errors that I made about myself soon corrected themselves. The benefit, at any rate, was unquestionable. Through the complexities and contradictions of my nature, I ended up understanding what made it a whole: that by dint of which I was myself, and not someone else. "This fits me," I would say to myself, "and that doesn't." I was not often mistaken, and never for long. A sincere diary is an incomparable way of getting firmly set on your foundations, of staying authentically what you are.

It is also a hygienic habit, a healthy exercise. My inner life was like an account kept current. I felt constantly in order with myself. By giving a written form to the thoughts, the memories, that were weighing on my mind, I took a step back which allowed me to assess their worth and accord them their correct place. And, by the same token, I was liberating myself. Every night when I closed my notebook to go to bed, I had the feeling of having

*For the cure of my soul.

cleaned my own house, and of being perfectly available to welcome joyously what the next day would bring.

Joyously . . . Unlike most *private diaries,* which usually reflect more sadness than joy—because it is at times of crises, of moral dilemmas, of secret dramas that the author feels the need to open his heart—the tone of my notebooks, on the whole, was rather cheerful. Especially in those years of my youth, when I was discovering the world and tackling it with high spirits and the insatiable curiosity of a rubbernecker. (The tone darkened later, with age and adversity. But until around fifty, until the First World War and the death of my elder son, life was usually a matter of amusement for me. They were quite wrong who blamed me for seeing the black side of things. I did my best simply to see things as they are . . . Clear-sighted people are always taken for pessimists.)

At that age when one is pleased as Punch finally to have emerged from childhood, and when most young folk are inclined to consider themselves destined for greatness, the company of men who were intelligent in such various ways, and on whom fame conferred an additional prestige, taught me to keep my own counsel, to listen, and to evaluate myself without complacency. This marked me and made me modest for life. I have never liked to stick out. (Particularly as I soon noticed that a self-effacing attitude is one of the surest ways of maintaining the integrity and independence of one's inner life, which I cared for more than anything.) I chose the career of arms out of family tradition. And yet this was after some hesitation, and even a few detours (since, to be admitted to Saint-Cyr, the shortest route was not after all through the Sorbonne and a *licence ès lettres* . . .). I never dreamed of military glory, or of special honors. I knew there was no marshal's baton in my future. If I chose the colonial army, it was mainly to escape the dullness of the garrisons at home; and if, later on, I heartily participated in the conquest of Morocco, it was not to gather laurels on the battlefields and still less to hasten my advancement; it was only because I liked being on Lyautey's staff, in close contact with a great leader whom I'd had as colonel at Alençon and to whom I had become enthusiastically attached. No ambition, in a word, except that of doing well what I had to do, without drawing attention to myself. But this does not mean that I was like everybody else and totally lacked personality. Instead of ambition, I needed to satisfy several definite inclinations—among which, primarily, an always aroused curiosity and an innate tendency to meditation.

It would be too much to call my natural aspirations spiritual. Inner, perhaps . . . My friend Gévresin took a picture of me at Piérac on the bridge over the Célé, leaning on the rail, watching the water flow by. Of all the snapshots of me, this is one of those I like best, because it seems to me emblematic.

Since my adolescence, that has in fact been my constant position: leaning firmly on the rail, I dream away, watching life flow by; my own, my neighbor's, the world's. With no other concern than to stay as lucid as I can. With no other goal than to feed all my reveries, continually renewing their object; and to quench that curiosity about myself, about other people, and about things, which at first was a game, which became an obsession and very quickly a need. Along with a (not very conscious) hope of attaining a greater knowledge of mankind and, through that, a sort of wisdom. Strange confessions for an old soldier!

In fact, I have always lived on two levels: that of the man of action, that of the spectator. The man of action counted, certainly! I think I've proved it, and my service record makes it clear. As for the spectator, the gawker . . . Ah, how I prefer him to the other, and always have! To tell the truth, he is the only one of my two characters that I have thoroughly inhabited. I owe to him the pleasure that I have had in living. I owe to him the perpetual amusement that has given savor to my life. It is thanks to him that I have reached my age without being weary of anything, or almost . . . As curious as in the good old days. Neither embittered nor outraged. Worried about the immediate future, but who wouldn't be? Criticizing the world as it goes, but, at bottom, resigned to the ways things are because they serve as my entertainment. An old habitué of the bridge rail who knows that the water is sometimes clear and sometimes silty but that it flows on without ever stopping . . . Our lot is that of pieces of driftwood swept along by the current, bobbing in the eddies—and which perhaps, like me, find their zigzags entertaining. There is joy in moving, in being moved . . .

And I think I have figured out the secret of my equilibrium: my brain is built in such a way that I *have no need for certainty.* The bad fairy did not toss that curse into my cradle. It is quite an exceptional stroke of luck. I have the privilege—which in my generation was less unusual than today—of breathing easily amongst conjectures, contradictions, inconsistencies. Problems interest me without my having to solve them at all costs. Doubt is my climate. Nothing is simple or clear. One can never be sure of anything. This is something one has to get used to. I have devoted much time to thinking, to observing myself and observing others, to questioning myself and questioning others, to examining events, books—without, for all that, drawing any conclusions. I repeat: no need for certainty.

Obviously, this open-mindedness, this perpetual expectancy, would seem absurd—not to say criminal, because ineffective—to the realists of our time. Today's young people, who are by nature believers even when they are cynical, are madly searching for affirmation, and feel reassured only with collective affirmations; this ability I have of keeping my balance while suspending my judgment they would take for a dangerous symptom of mental illness.

That's how I am. And I want to add, *Thank God!** "God made me so, praise be to Him!" The experimental observation that everything that exists is in a state of constant transformation satisfies my philosophical cravings. Too easily, perhaps? So much the better for me. I don't know if one has to believe in *progress,* but it is impossible to deny *movement.* The whole universe is astir. I don't need to know where it is going, or even if it is going anywhere. It is enough for me that it goes! Its momentum, even if aimless, is, in my eyes, a justification, and I don't ask for more. What is life? To be quite honest, this is a question that I don't often ask myself. But when I ask it, my reason, which has never burdened itself with metaphysical concerns, readily accepts this hypothesis: life is in motion. Why look farther? Life may be nothing else than this universal soar without beginning or end.

*

A glimpse of what my life as a happy man has been like.

I have been a happy man. Through growing old and assessing lives other than my own, I have become aware that I was born under a lucky star. I have known painful griefs, hard ordeals, disappointments; for twenty-five years, since my retirement, I have lived in great solitude; nevertheless, if I look back I have no complaints about how fate has treated me; I even feel that I have everything I could have wished for. Probably that would surprise a lot of people! It is rare for a septuagenarian to announce in all sincerity: "I've had the life of a happy man."

Maybe someone else, weighing up the little I have accomplished in the course of my long life, would summarily decide that it is the life of a washout. For my part, I don't see it that way. And this is not self-delusion: the bitter taste of truth is sufficiently genuine and compelling in me that I would not hesitate to acknowledge my failure, if I considered my life to be one. (Why should we be ashamed of our defeats? Nothing is more foolish, unless it is to glory in our successes. Apart from very rare exceptions, failures and successes are equally the result of givens and of circumstances which do not depend on us. I am thinking of precise examples. I have encountered very few cases in which a man is unquestionably responsible for what he is.)

Is it that I did not have enough ambition to start with? Which would explain my not regretting that I missed my goals? Certainly I nursed no illusions, not even at the age of mad hopes. I never imagined that my destiny was to accomplish great things . . . To what is this due? Partly, no doubt, to this: that I was fortunate enough, starting at seventeen, to go live with my

*English in the original.

uncle Éric in Paris and to rub shoulders with what the world of letters, of the University, and of the academies then considered to be renowned intellectuals. Which encouraged modesty in a young man from the provinces who was thoughtful, rather shy, and not presumptuous.

The fact remains that at the time of which I am speaking I enjoyed life enormously. This showed between the lines of my diary. It did not contain only serious reflections. It was stuffed with witty remarks, observations taken from life, anecdotes. At night, after a page which seemed felicitous to me, I would sometimes seek out Aunt Ma in her little blue drawing room and read her a few passages. The freedom of my opinions did not shock her. She did not make fun of my flights of enthusiasm, or of my of bursts of indignation, or even of the occasional awkwardness in my style. She entered into the game with good grace, sometimes giving me advice. (By a tacit agreement, neither my aunt nor I ever ventured a reference to these readings in the presence of Uncle Éric. He never suspected the existence of my diary.)

I kept hardly anything secret from my sister. I remember, after that first year of Parisian life, spending the summer holidays here at le Saillant and giving Henriette a reading *in extenso* from my notebooks. My father, who always got up early, would retire right after supper. For as long as I can remember, the evenings were a time dedicated to endless talks and confidences between my sister and myself. We usually began by taking a long stroll in the park; then, when night had fallen, we would go up to Henriette's room. I would take my notebook out of my pocket and start to read. Dear Henriette! I can still see her in her low chair; the pink light of the lamp brightened the glow of her complexion and wreathed her beautiful Florentine adolescent's face with a halo. Motionless, her eyes lowered on her sewing, she listened without interrupting me, without asking a question. I sensed that she was moved and aquiver. A veil was lifted for her, and she was able to see what my life in Paris, during that long year of separation, had been like; my letters, though frequent, had only given her sketchy and misleading glimpses. But it was mainly to me that those evenings were a revelation! I had never had the leisure or the curiosity to reread those pages scribbled day after day. Their juxtaposition threw a completely new light on them. By reliving my student days one after another, I got an unexpected bird's-eye view of my inner life, I discovered its mysterious course, like those wadis that meander half buried through the sands, whose winding and unbroken track only an aerial photograph suddenly reveals and renders perceptible. How many forgotten details, how many meaningful incidents of which my memory had retained no trace, appeared to me once again, resurrected in all their freshness! (This is where I ought to put everything I wrote above about the usefulness of keeping a diary, for it was only after this rereading of the whole that I understood its incomparable effectiveness. There is no more accurate mirror for one who seeks to know his true face. And no other way of protecting the most precious part of one's life from daily destruction.) The experiment was conclusive.

I vowed that I would never give up this habit, and, despite all obstacles, in the bled, in the trenches, it is a resolution that I kept with perseverance for more than half a century. I held on to all those notebooks. I had more than a hundred of them . . . They were my reason for being, the proof that I had existed; they were the very substance and work of my life. How can I console myself, today, for having been forever deprived of them?*

CHAPTER XXIV

His End

[*According to André Daspre, Martin du Gard envisioned a quick, painless death for Maumort, either by suicide or by a fatal stroke. Of the first eventuality, he left the following sketch:*]

Following a first stroke, which leaves him paralyzed in one arm for a few days and subjects him for a week to the excruciating torture of aphasia, he gets better and gradually resumes a more or less normal life. But the specific threat is there, haunting, implacable. The sturdy old man is mortally wounded . . .

Methodically, he prepares his suicide by gas.

The note he leaves on his table, near the envelope containing his will: "Why extend the reprieve? Tomorrow can only be worse. I am cutting short the wait. Farewell to all."

Maumort.

[*The novelist had also foreseen the possibility that he himself might disappear before having finished his narrative. In his diary, on 15 May 1942, Martin du Gard wrote of his novel: "It is a work that can grow and be perfected indefinitely: a work that will never be finished for me, and that, however, may at any moment be interrupted by my death. An ellipsis and an editor's note will suffice: 'Here ends the manuscript of Colonel de Maumort, felled by a stroke on the night of . . .' "*]

*The story of the loss of Maumort's diaries is given in the first letter to his friend Gévresin— see pp. 611ff.

II

Letters of Lieutenant-Colonel de Maumort

(31 December 1944–January 1945)

LETTERS TO GÉVRESIN

[Translators' Note: Well into the writing of Lieutenant-Colonel de Maumort, *Martin du Gard had the idea of recasting the novel in epistolary
form. Setting aside certain chapters, like "The Drowning," which would
have remained unaltered, he would have attempted to rearrange most of the
sustained fictional memoir he had fashioned (that is, the bulk of the material printed so far in this volume), using its elements to produce a fragmentary and deliberately disjointed narrative in which the evocation of
memories would have occupied a progressively larger place. He would also
have added certain episodes, such as Maumort's return to le Saillant at the
end of the war. He hoped to attain a greater freedom, as the letter form
might allow him more easily to break into the narrative with digressions,
counterpoint disparate components, etc. It is impossible to know whether
this method would ultimately have satisfied him more than the one he originally chose. The nine letters he finished before his death give an excellent
sense of the effect he wished to create, and provide additional insights into
Maumort's life.]*

Letter I

Le Saillant par Menneville, Orne
Sunday, 31 December 44.

Your card, just received, has shaken me right out of my torpor! Very
touched by your good wishes, old pal! "Unforgivable," yes, you're right: it's
unforgivable of me not to have written you since I got back home, and several times, and at length, as was promised. But I may be a little less at fault
than it would seem: for, distrusting the postal service and the slowness of its
reorganization (and rightly so, since your card, postmarked the 24th, arrived
this morning, which means it took seven days to cross the eight hundred
kilometers that now separate us!) I had, on the sixteenth, the day after my
return here, entrusted to the driver of my ambulance—who assured me that
he would go right back to Cahors—a letter in which I brought you up to

609

date on my trip. He should have had it delivered to you the following Saturday, via the truck driver who does the weekly mail run from Cahors to Piérac. Did he forget? Did he lose my envelope? I'd thought I could count on him. He treated me with great solicitude during the five days of the trip. Five days and four nights, since, from the first evening on, the difficulty of getting me a bed—a bed that would be accessible to me—seemed so great that, having vainly awoken the porters of three different hotels in hopes of being given a room that wasn't on the third floor, I threw one of those fits that you can imagine and refused to go on looking; I spent the night in the ambulance, alone, at the back of a garage, on my cot. This was well before Limoges, in a deserted and barely lit town where the black ice stopped us around midnight, Uzerche if I'm not mistaken. And the truth is I found that this so simplified the search for a place to stay that for the next four nights I insisted on camping in the same way. I landed here on the fifth day, early in the afternoon, with a tramp's beard and without having slept in a bed since leaving Piérac!

What a homecoming, old friend! This return to le Saillant was a trial from which I still have not recovered. A hundred times worse than anything we might have expected . . . Let's not regret that lost letter: better that you didn't read it, it would just have upset you to no purpose: it was nothing but a cry of distress . . . I scribbled it the very night of my return, on the Boccas' kitchen table, by the light of a candle-end (our electricity was turned back on only last week, for Christmas, and Bocca hadn't found so much as a liter of kerosene for sale around here). You can imagine me, with my hip, perched awry on this wooden stool, exhausted, discouraged beyond all telling of it . . . I had just spent those first hours wandering around like a sleepwalker in the indescribable chaos of my old house, my dear old house, where nothing is where it used to be, in its accustomed place, where everything is soiled, broken, unrecognizable. You would need to know le Saillant for me to be able to describe to you, give you a sense of, the devastation! I was in a state of prostration that I scarcely dare admit to you and from which I still haven't really emerged after two weeks of trying to overcome this unprecedented depression. That doesn't sound like me, does it? But it is so. Ah, how stupidly I overestimated my strength in August, after the last German wave came through, when I wrote Bocca not to begin any ordering, any cleaning up, until my arrival!

Two weeks when I've hardly stopped thinking of you, sharing my torment with you, but having neither the wish nor the time to explain my silence to you, not even having the heart to confide my despondency, of which I am terribly ashamed, which I kept hoping I would master the next day . . . And then I needed not only to somehow make myself a little space that was more or less habitable in this shambles, but, on the moral plane, to struggle tirelessly with myself to live in this chaos, to resist the temptation to walk away from it all, to have myself taken someplace else, anywhere.

Nevertheless, the very touching welcome I was given by Bocca and his wife, their emotion at seeing me again, should have helped me get over that inexcusable attack of weakness more quickly. Only now am I beginning to feel the comfort I receive from the presence of those two souls who are so humbly, totally devoted, so attentive in showing me constant proofs of their almost animal attachment.

I firmly promised myself, when I began to write you, not to let myself start whining or go on too long about these material troubles, mostly curable when all is said and done. They would seem laughably insignificant to so many families without shelter, to so many disaster victims like those two old people I ran into the other day while going through Poitiers who were holding a bunch of big keys in their hands and who stopped us, wild-eyed, to tell us that they hadn't even been able to locate, among the ruins of their neighborhood, the site of what had been their house . . . But you see, dear friend, I haven't kept my promise. And I'm not done: I cannot bring myself to close this first letter without broaching this very night, regardless, the subject that causes me the most pain. Because if I bemoan finding everything upside down and destroyed in my house, it is not the only reason, or even the true reason, for my dejection: the real wound is elsewhere. I have suffered a loss (an absolutely irreparable one) whose haunting regret will probably never go away . . .

You remember my fury, in Piérac, the day the Germans came to search your house, when those two imbecile policemen, despite my protests, loaded into their van that big tin trunk I had been stupid enough to bring from le Saillant, full of letters, note cards, articles, eyewitness accounts, files of every variety, collected by me over half a century and to which I attached an inestimable documentary worth.* I have bitterly reproached myself for not having hidden it here, as I did the fifty or sixty diaries in which, since my youth, I had written down my daily thoughts and all the salient facts of my existence. And, rightly, the only thing that consoled me a little for that absurd burglary was—I'm sure I told you this at the time—the certainty that at least, after the war, I would find at le Saillant that irreplaceable collection of notebooks which constituted the private diary of my life, and of which the records stolen by the Gestapo were really only the supplementary notes, the supporting material.

I was all the more sure that I would recover that treasure since I myself

---

*Roger Martin du Gard: This trunk will be discovered in Germany and returned to the Colonel, who will find in it various precious and pertinent documents. (For example Xavier's diary, the history of the drowning . . .)

had stashed it safely away before leaving in August '40. It was I who had chosen the hiding place, I who got Bocca to dig that hole in the wall of our wine cellar—the driest, the soundest of any—I who wrapped each diary in tarlined paper that I thought was waterproof. And, on one of the nights that preceded my departure, it was I who buried the packages in the niche; who got Bocca to wall it up while I watched; who had him embed in the reconstructed wall a big iron wine rack that we stocked with empty bottles. We were proud of our work: no one could suspect a thing.

Alas! All it took was a drainpipe, on the outside, cracked by a freeze; a slow invisible seepage along the foundation wall: the watertight niche filled up like a cistern! When, the other day, we wanted to retrieve my dear papers, Bocca needed to fish them out of the mud with a rake! They had been reduced to a mucky mass, a shapeless and stinking amalgam. Four winters of rains, four years of fermentation in a closed space, had not only rotted and peeled off the wrappings but had also soaked each notebook through and through! Even as I write you, I still seem to smell that swamp odor, and my despair again grips my throat . . . You have no idea what can become of papers that steep for four years in stagnant water! It was all just a glob of blackish shreds which stuck to one's hands like pitch and which we put in a vat full of water. The next day, I was able to remove from it, with the help of a skimmer, a certain number of shapeless little lumps: notebooks slightly less liquified than the others, and which seemed to be eaten into only at the edges. Rose patiently dried them in the oven. I hoped to be able to open them. But the pages were so thoroughly stuck together that up to now I have found it practically impossible to separate them; especially as they fall apart at the merest touch. What good will it ever do me to have saved these scraps? The faded vestiges of writing that can be made out in places are barely decipherable. All the same, I thought I recognized the remains of a notebook in which I had collected information and memories for the book of which I spoke to you that I had long ago planned to write about Lyautey.

I need say no more about it. You know me, you know what this diary was for me. I would have been much better able to withstand learning all of a sudden that I was totally ruined. When I saw that hopeless putrefaction at the bottom of the niche, I was left stunned. If my fate was to die of a stroke, I would certainly no longer be of this world! Without the help of Bocca and Rose, I would never have been able to climb the stairs out of the cellar!

That was twelve days ago; twelve days during which I have tried to reason with myself, to accept the irreversible. I have yet to succeed. The moment I think about it, and I think about it constantly, my temples pound, I lose interest in everything. I did not know how much I cared about that diary. With it I seem to have lost whatever still connected me to life. You will tell me that my recollections still remain to me, that luckily my memory is still very precise, very accurate. Of course I repeat that to myself twenty times a day. But that is to talk a lot of hot air. Memories are nothing; drawings in the sand, compared to what that diary was, that monument which time had built and which had an existence of its own, independent of mine. Deprived of those notebooks, I feel dispossessed of myself, as if my personality had liquified along with them and as if I were now no more than an empty shell.

Tomorrow, a holiday. I realize that there will be no mail. I am dispatching Bocca to Menneville on the double, to send off these pages today. It has done me good to write you! You cannot imagine how much. I'll do it again tomorrow.

Tonight, faithful thoughts, apologies, and good wishes, dear old friend, and the hug for special occasions.

M.

P.S. Well played, we must admit, that offensive of von Rundstedt's! A brutal chomp out of our front between Aix-la-Chapelle and Trèves! Even though we have reason to hope since yesterday that their thrust is cut off, the stakes for them are such that they will surely make immense sacrifices to stay on the Meuse and stop our advance no matter what.

Letter II

1 January 45.

I did well, yesterday, to tell you my troubles at great length. I feel better this morning. And yet I hardly slept last night.

New Year's Eve! For as long as I can remember this night of December thirty-first has meant a lot to me. Even in the bled, I don't believe I ever saw the year change without meditating awhile, by myself, at some fireside, on the year that had passed. More than any of them, the one that just ended calls for a bit of contemplation. 1944! A date for the textbooks of future schoolboys: "the year of liberation," "the year of the Normandy landings," "the year of the campaign for France." (And, for me, the last year of that long brotherly stay with you.)

I celebrated the memory of a lot of those New Year's Eves last night, lying in the dark on a makeshift bed. Rose improvised it for me in a corner of the library by piling up the three least-soiled mattresses in the house on the wooden floor; by way of blankets, two greenish rep curtains that, throughout my childhood, I saw hanging in my father's study; and covering all, the remains of an incredible crimson plush portiere, trimmed with gold braid, brought by the Germans from I don't know where, a processional banner perhaps, which lends to my catafalque the ridiculous splendor of a royal bed . . . Outside, snow, a storm. Around me, the great empty house, echoing and quivering in the wind. Impossible to sleep a wink. Seventy-five in a few months. Quite old, quite lonesome . . . Yes, completely lonesome, since I left you! And even more so since all my papers are lost. The thing I cared for most—as much as for myself. And wasn't it myself, the best part of me, that diary where a half-century of my existence was written down in its smallest details, with its joys, its illusions, its enthusiasms, its disappointments, its sadnesses? As soon as I opened one of those notebooks, it was my very life I was reliving, day by day . . . But enough complaining!

Before going to bed last night, I had luckily taken the precaution of cramming logs into my big white tile stove (which you know very well, without your suspecting it, since it looks like a brother to the one in your dining room, the one by which we so cozily chatted away, on certain winter evenings, when you managed to persuade the gendarme's children to bring us back a few barrowfuls of dead wood from la Châtaigneraie; the one by which, in September—do you recall?—during that endless night that followed the last of our "war councils," we kept the punch warm till dawn, without any light, without daring to stir, hearts beating, ears pricked, waiting for Antonin and his brothers to come back, all four of whom we knew had gone off for the strike on the Bouessac bridge.)

I would be wrong to regret last night's insomnia. The fact is that it brought me less melancholy than serenity and courage; and I got up this morning in quite good spirits, actually, with an inexplicable sense of self-confidence and all sorts of plans in mind. At bottom, my return to solitude doesn't really scare me; as overwhelming as it has sometimes been these last few days, I tell myself that I am very used to it and that it has never hamstrung me—quite the contrary. A source of vigor, rather. We often agreed about that. You remember the Mogul:

Solitude où je trouve une douceur secrète . . .*

It's going on eight o'clock, I'm stopping to catch the broadcast. (How I missed the radio, those first days, until they turned the power back on!)

Rundstedt definitely does not seem to have succeeded in hanging on to the Meuse. If this morning's bulletin is to be believed, he could be forced

---

*"Solitude in which I find a secret sweetness . . ." From *Le Songe d'un habitant du Mogol* by La Fontaine (*Fables, Book XI, Number IV*).

to fall back for lack of support. Maybe even all the way to the Siegfried Line? . . . But I'll spare you my tactical insights. These mess-hall prognostications that we armchair strategists are so full of would really be ridiculous in this correspondence—completely. Don't worry, I'll take care to restrain myself.

What brings me much closer to you is the death of Romain Rolland. Tonight's broadcast will, I hope, give us a few details. You are certainly as saddened by it as I am. He was born in 1866, scarcely four years our elder. Yet another contemporary who passes away; and a great one. It was young Darcieux who got me to read *Above the Battle*. You were not yet at Headquarters with us. December, 1915, I think. We were billeting at Béthune. Darcieux had dug the book up somewhere, and he brought it to the mess.

What vituperation! They were all outraged, astounded. Far more removed, for certain, from a Rolland and his state of mind than from Neanderthal man.

If the author of *Above the Battle* had been shot, they would all have enthusiastically requested the honor of commanding the firing squad . . . As for me, I remember so well the first time I read it! I can even see the spot: a demolished evacuated village, whose name I have forgotten, between La Bassée and Lille. Headquarters had assigned me to supervise the relief troops. The trenches began right where the last houses stopped. My driver and I had to wait in a cellar near the first-aid post for night to fall. A very cold winter's day, calm, with no wind. Occasional explosions at the edge of the woods. From time to time, ambulance men, hugging the ruins of a sort of barn, guided some lightly wounded men, whom I heard moaning, towards the station, where they would get hastily patched up. (Mysterious caprices of memory! Not once in thirty years have I thought back to that gray late afternoon, to that dusty cellar, to that little one-street village with its roadway of big northern cobblestones, with a frozen cattle pond off to the right, in the middle of a little town square strewn with rubbish. And I can still see all that this morning, down to the slightest detail.) We had a bite to eat, then my driver lay down and I, standing, with my back against the wall, beneath the only basement window that let light into the nook, while waiting for night, the arrival of the troops, and the changing of the guard, took the book out of my map case and devoured about fifty pages of it. After those first four months of war, Rolland's call seemed to me like a personal message. A *revelation!* The word is not too strong.

1 January, evening.

I'm writing you by candlelight. A power failure; we have at least one or two every day. This one made me miss tonight's broadcast. I won't go to sleep, though, without chatting another moment with you.

Today was definitely better. The burden seemed lighter to me, my obsession less persistent; and having this half-written letter on my table, I felt much less alone. In the end, I shall have to accept the irreparable. Time will do its work, as your neighbor Lebel used to say. Only today do I foresee the possibility—the dawning, dare I write?—of resignation.

I spent this first day of the new year very quietly reading, shut up in my bedroom/dining room/study/library. I didn't want to disturb Bocca and his wife on a New Year's Day, and, given the state the house is in, I cannot dream of starting to tidy up all alone.

I have gone for years without opening Chateaubriand again. Why not today? It was really chance that placed in my hands this last volume of the *Memoirs,* the sixth in the Biré edition; bound in morocco, no less. Can you imagine that I picked it up the other day in the laundry room, where it was serving as a shim for a wobbly trestle! (No matter how insufferable that popinjay may be, such treatment was excessively disrespectful . . .) I was curious to open it. I want to reread it. A test of patience. Everything he says—commentary, judgment—is exasperatingly tendentious. Even so, I admit that the perfect ring of certain passages was not lost on me, and I was especially keen to revisit the political and social upheavals of that astonishing era, which I had somewhat forgotten. An era hardly less tormented, and, if less chaotic, scarcely less tragic than our own. Moving, I assure you, to observe those convulsions in the light of our recent experiences! And then how many penetrating remarks, once the author brings himself to break away, for a moment, from his overpowering person!

I wanted to copy out a few of these remarks for you, and had inserted bookmarks, but I realize that while having dinner I let most of these fall out. You'll have to make do with this one, on the "democratic leanings" of our fellow citizens:

"We obey a power that we think we have the right of insulting; that is all we need of liberty."

He also notes, rather amusingly, concerning Louis-Philippe—I quote from memory—that his tongue was "set in motion by a torrent of clichés." This reminded me of those redundant speeches which that ex-schoolteacher, whose name I forget, used to inflict on us—you know, that fat Sancho Panza who organized the maquis at les Roches and who got shot at the railroad crossing in Coursat?

I was going to wish you good night, but the return of the electricity has put me back in the saddle, so to speak. We won't have so many opportunities, now, to start a new year!

And you, how did you begin it, this year 1945? Here, I'll reconstruct what you did today in the greatest detail, like a psychic. You'll tell me if I'm clairvoyant. First, this morning, after the ceremony of the New Year's presents, you gave Prospérine the day off so that she could go be with her family at her niece's. At noon, you warmed up some leftover soup yourself on the stove in your study—I can very clearly see the white tureen with blue flowers on it— and, at the corner of your desk, made your lunch of some goat cheese, an apple, and a book propped up against the carafe. You woke from your nap just in time to receive a few visits. For sure, one from young Crétoy, to whom you lent your medical journals for December; one from M. Carnavert with his chronic loss of voice (an excellent exercise in attention for an old man's sluggish hearing); maybe also one from Dr. Jacquemin's children, come from Cahors for the holidays, with a supply of gossip about the little intrigues around the new prefect. Finally, if your godson is home on leave, between six and seven o'clock you put on a starched collar; then you gave some milk to the cat, locked the door to the garden, closed the shutters, and, hobbling along, your pocket swollen with a bottle of plum brandy, you set off in the snow, by the steep Clos-Vert path, to go dine at the Comtesse's; and I can see you, happy man, at that precise moment, doing justice to the vol-au-vent from Pouilloux's, with the traditional goose confit still to come!

Well, without pretending to compete with that citified social life, I too, in my bled, had the surprise, just imagine, of seeing my door open wide and having Bocca bring in visitors. Guess who . . .

My four farmers. That's what it is to have become the lord of the manor again! A touching visit: they came, together, to wish me *"la bonne ânée,"** as their fathers (and even, for two of them, their grandfathers) used to come to greet my father on the first of January. A ritual going back more than a hundred years, no doubt . . . I hadn't seen them for five years. How changed they seemed! Aged, like me; but not only aged, transformed. It is true that, even before I left le Saillant, since, after falling off a horse, I was forced to give up managing the land, and, as you know, to turn their smallholdings into farms, I had pretty much lost sight of them. All the same, those fat years of the occupation, that clandestine trafficking, that sudden wealth, seem to have changed them quite fast, and maybe not to their advantage . . . They appear even more self-satisfied, more narrow-minded and set in their opinions, more distrustful, if possible, of each other; wanting both to display their new affluence and yet to conceal their assets and cover up their material well- being, eager to denounce the scandal of the black market so as to prevent any hint of illicit gains; in short, more entrenched than ever in their stupidity, their cunning, their vanity. I was amused to see them come in, as in the past, one behind the other, according to age, looking cocky, both offhand and ill

*"Happy New Year," with a country accent.

at ease, in white shirts and Sunday jackets, keeping their round, snow-powdered hats screwed on their skulls, and no longer knowing how to address me because they had never got used to saying *"mon colonel"* and they don't want to say *"nout' maît',"** as they did at the time when I lived part of my day with them on the smallholdings. In the absence of any "hard stuff," since the occupiers had naturally cleaned out the cellar, Bocca went to draw two jugs of his cider; and, for want of glasses, he brought us a tray with a silver cup that had escaped the looting, a cracked teacup, and three iron mugs forgotten by the German orderlies. This did not stop us from drinking a very cordial toast. They naturally spoke to me about the "Fritzes," quite proud of the little tricks—cautious ones—they had played on them; on that score every one of them had a personal little story to tell, already ossified, with well-rehearsed winks and laughs in the right spot. You can well imagine that in order not to be outdone, I regaled them with a few select and only slightly embroidered memories of our maquis in the Lot. (Notably the story of the search of Dufay's house and the two bicycles.)

Here I desert you for Vicomte d'Outre-Tombe,[†] who, at this late hour, will be much better and more rapidly able than you to induce me to fall asleep.

Tibi,

M.

Letter III

Tuesday, 2 January.

I am sitting down this morning at my table to pass on my bad mood to you.

Bocca has just returned from Menneville with the bread and three local newspapers, the only ones to be found here for the time being. Yesterday's papers: typical first-of-January editions. I was hoping that the reduced format, the single sheet of cheap paper, would cut down the usual set pieces about the "new year," and the sunny forecasts. No such luck. Tomorrow, victory and peace! Tomorrow, the spectacular annihilation of the Axis! Tomor-

---

*"Our master," in country dialect.
[†]I.e., Chateaubriand.

row, the triumphant apotheosis of the democracies into a world standing fraternally together, under the liberal protection of the *United Nations*! And above all, tomorrow, prosperity! On this point, a touching unanimity! Prosperity! Our little prophets are not yet weary of having announced for six months that America in its generosity is tomorrow preparing to pour into our starving continent the fabulous stocks of wheat, meat, fat, coffee, and coal that its far-sighted philanthropy has, it seems, been hoarding on our behalf. In the meantime, the distribution of foodstuffs becomes more parsimonious every day: the bread ration is pathetic, and that of fat has even been reduced this month.

When it comes to "wishes," not one of these provincial editorialists dares wish that our country had a more coherent policy, a less inexperienced government than the youthful gang of ministers that we got this summer from Algeria . . . I'm furious! The attachment that the *général-président** has developed for his *Free France* companions is perfectly legitimate; but I am amazed by the blind trust that he seems to grant them in the political domain. Is it naïveté on his part? Soldierly indifference? The indifference of a great leader who has his war to conduct? That is no reason, because in the end what is at stake with this foolhardiness? Neither more nor less than the reorganization of France; which is to say, the future of the country. Don't spitefully remind me of the gladness with which I, unlike you, greeted the installation of this de Gaulle government. I still think that it is composed mainly of honest men, sincerely animated by the desire to do something new and to do it well. Their loyalty, their loyalism, their patriotic fervor, their courage, even their youth— so many guarantees that justified my hopes at the time. But, godammit! since I have seen them grappling with the problems of the moment, everything about their behavior exasperates me: their clumsiness, their inconsistencies, their sudden and absurd initiatives, at other times their incomprehensible inertia. We seem to be sailing through a storm with a crew of Boy Scouts who are prompted by the best of intentions but whose goodwill does not suffice to make up for their total lack of experience and political savvy.

In the general confusion that events have plunged us into, the management of domestic affairs (to mention only those) and the swift recovery of our country are jobs too delicate and urgent to serve without unfortunate consequences as an exercise, an apprenticeship, for that nursery of neophytes! I am almost at the point of missing our old leaders from before the war . . . And yet you know how little respect I have for our former parliamentary and governmental outfit. (It's not for nothing that I lived for more than ten years in close company with Lyautey.)

*Charles de Gaulle (1890–1970).

But I have better things to do than inveigh against our statesmen. Know that today, January 2, the first working day of the year, I got up all bushy-tailed and with my head full of wise and cheerful resolutions. No doubt the effect of my long letter to you, which Bocca just mailed in Menneville and which has freed me, it seems, from the most noxious part of the evil spell I have been under since my return.

You have often told me—and it is true—that my infirmities are not of the kind that affect the health. Mine, after all, remains solid. Though I may be lame in the hip, and I limp, I still feel enough enthusiasm to begin and enough strength to persevere. If I have a few years yet to live, I must make the best possible use of them. Last night I thought again about the creation here of that university foundation that we talked so much about together, these last months. The project must be examined closely. But first, put things back in order here; restore as much as I can this big house, devastated by four years of occupation but still sturdy and fit to render service to whoever knows how to use it. I feel I have duties towards this old family abode, which saw me come into the world and which—in the course of my nomadic life, and for twenty years in succession between the wars—has offered me its refuge and its peace. I have decided to start this very day. Hercules in the Augean stables! In a few weeks, with a little persistence and the Boccas' indefatigable zeal . . .

Letter IV

Thursday, 4 January, before dinner.

These pages have remained on my table since the day before yesterday. I wanted to do too much in these first days and I have exhausted myself. I have blessed you for having forced me to take those phials with me. My hip hurt so much that Rose had to give me a shot and help me get into bed. Today I have better conserved my strength. My fatigue is bearable, I have time to finish my letter before dinner.

The wind has shifted since noon. It's still snowing, but the storm has quieted down. My stove is drawing well. I feel that I'm getting back a taste for myself . . . However, I need to be better organized and especially to put my study back in order. The last German staff that stayed here removed all the furniture to turn it into a telephone exchange or something of the sort. They drilled holes in the partitions for their wires, which hang dismally along the walls. I avoid going in there. Besides, lacking coal to keep the furnace going,

I will have the least trouble withstanding the winter by taking refuge here in the library, thanks to this old white tile stove (which must date from my great-great-grandfather's time, which I never saw lit, and which Bocca got working again for my return). My library? Imagine a big gypsy caravan; I have my bed here, my armchair, the table where I eat, the table where I write, the table where I wash up, my tin trunks, my clothes piled on chairs. And all the walls covered with books, my books all around me. Because—did I tell you?—I found my shelves more or less full. A real miracle.

It's the only thing that escaped pillage. Out of respect or out of indifference? Doesn't matter. The huge joy I feel because of it deprives me of the right to complain about the rest. (I write this, but, ah! how far I still am from resignation.)

They emptied the clothes wardrobes and the linen wardrobes, stole all the blankets, almost all the bedding, most of the kitchenware. But let's try to be fair. Fortunately they left the furniture. But they wore out, dirtied, damaged what they didn't carry off.

The Boccas, relegated to their cottage, forbidden to enter the château, were helpless witnesses to this plunder. Each new wave of occupiers made the havoc worse by changing the allocation of the rooms as if on a whim. The entrance hall served by turns as the NCOs' canteen, as the secretaries' office, as the orderlies' dormitory; the dining room as the guardroom, as a smoking room for the officers, as a bedroom, as the game room; the drawing room as a refectory, the library as a mess, my bathroom as a kitchen, the ground floor rooms as garages for the motorcyclists. The doors, with numbers painted on them, are covered with cabalistic inscriptions. The entire house looks like an abandoned billet. I scarcely recognize it.

Helped by Rose, Bocca, and an old refugee woman from up north whom they took in, I am trying to conduct a preliminary straightening up. The old furniture of the Maumorts, devoutly maintained by so many careful generations, has not stood up to the numerous movings-about at the hands of soldiers: most of the tables and chairs are missing a leg, the marble tops of the dressers are chipped or cracked; big pieces of the marquetry have come unglued; all the armchairs are more or less burst, the drapes torn; my old white paneling is studded with nails and scarred by long blackish streaks whose origin I do not know; all the beautiful rugs that I brought back from Africa are threadbare down to the weft. And what a mess! Things are all over the place. Every drawer, every sideboard, every closet I open is full of disparate objects and junk, in which family souvenirs, photographs, chipped curios are mixed up with flotsam left by the invasion: tools, rags, record books, maps, mysterious diagrams, old cans, any number of tattered uniforms, even musical instruments, even this old gramophone and these broken records that I found today—along with a little pink satin shoe!—behind the chimney grate in a room upstairs. I am not exaggerating a thing. Bocca makes piles of all this stuff in the middle of the rooms, and, like rag-dealers, Rose and I spend hours shuffling through this jumble, picking it over, until the cold stiffens our joints and swells up our fingers like sausages. At certain moments, the strangeness of the situation and the unexpectedness of some discovery makes us laugh in spite of ourselves; but most often, our fatigue and disgust are such that we perform this grim task in silence, in a sort of stupor . . .

Interrupted by the arrival of Rose and her tray, then by the evening broadcast. (I could see you, simultaneously, at your own radio, wrapped in your old shepherd's cloak . . .)

Rundstedt, this time, seems out for the count. We don't know what our losses are, but at least they will serve some purpose. That fierce counterattack of the beast at bay, when the Allies already thought they could sound the mort, reminds them in time that the game is not yet over, that unity remains the first condition of success, and that it would be wise for them to wait at least until the moment of the quarry to show each other their teeth, as they already were starting to do before this alert . . . On the other hand, among the Fritzes the failure of this spectacular offensive, on which the army and the German people were obviously pinning enormous hopes, is going to further weaken the Wehrmacht's prestige, and this disappointment may very well help to hasten the collapse at home.

Speaking of the radio, did you listen carefully to Hitler's New Year's message the other day? Did you notice the insistence with which he again proclaimed that *Germany would never surrender*? And what do you say to his tirade about the "corruption" of the bourgeois regimes of the West? All the more painful to hear, when one thinks of the edifying spectacle that we are presenting at the moment to the enemy . . . "United" nations, "allied" armies—and dissension everywhere! In France, hardly four months after the "liberation," the internecine struggles are covertly resuming their virulence, and everywhere this truce among the parties to which we owe the effectiveness of the "resistance" is coming to an end . . . In Italy, in Greece, the Anglo-Saxons are shamelessly pursuing their own political ends . . . In Poland and the Balkans, Russia is pursuing its own, without even trying to hide it . . . In invaded Germany, even before victory is assured, a dash to conquer the "zones of influence" . . . We know what this means: these are the absurd and disastrous mistakes committed in 1919 and 1920 starting up again. Yet the Atlantic Charter, you recall, adamantly opposed every possibility of annexation; it solemnly affirmed the right of all nations to freely choose their form of government, to have a say in the outline of their future borders, etc. Who seems to remember it now?

Enough palaver for tonight. I'm going to bed. Good night, old pal.

Chateaubriand awaits me. I've got about fifty more pages to go. It won't be easy to make it to the end. Even when I admire him, he gets on my nerves . . . He really could use a bit more sense of the ridiculous. Judge for yourself:

"Whoever has read these Memoirs has seen what my fate has been. I had not swum a stroke from my mother's breast when torments already besieged me. I wandered from shipwreck to shipwreck," etc.

To be that obsessed with the desire to get sympathy or to show off! His whole life long he was the prey of deference to public opinion! He never made a move without wondering what people would think of it, without acting in such a way that his prestige would be increased by it. A preoccupation which reveals, in the end, a certain mediocrity of soul; but which sometimes may have allowed him to accomplish feats . . . A fine case of "Bovarysm"! I don't remember if your dear Jules de Gaultier* made use of it. And this leads me to a little examination of conscience. (Strongly recommended, at the moment of going to sleep.) I too, I too . . . The beam and the mote . . . (The beam is for him, the mote for me.) I have been only an apprentice "Bovaryst," next to him! I try to judge myself without indulgence, and do not seek to appear better—or simply other—than I am. But I cannot deny that I too have always been very sensitive to "what-people-will-say." Keen not to disappoint, even more than eager to give a good impression of myself. Which has often forced me, besides, to curb certain questionable instincts, and to act, if not by concealing my character (this has happened to me, of course, but very rarely; on this point I have the right to be fair to myself!), then at least by conforming to what was most estimable in myself; by staying, as much as possible, at my peak. "Moral" usefulness of Bovarysm.

Grant me that this concern with "what-people-will-say" is not exactly deference to public opinion: only the first stage of it. I see that, in me, this concern probably produced, indirectly, my deep love of solitude. That's right. Follow my reasoning: for the person who constantly worries about not disappointing his neighbor (provided, however, that he is also exempt from a need to shine, from any need to please; since, of necessity, the desire to show off supposes the presence of a potential spectator)—for this person, the elimination of others is inevitably a relief. Now, this is my case. Thus solitude brings to me more than to most other people an intoxicating sense of freedom. An indirect consequence of Bovarysm, and one that I don't think Gaultier saw.

Good night!

Quarter to one. Impossible to sleep. I've turned the light back on. I will

*Jules de Gaultier (1858–1942). Author of "Bovarysm: An Essay on the Power of Imagining" (1902). Gaultier finds this phenomenon present in almost all the characters of *Madame Bovary:* "The same ignorance, the same inconsistency, the same absence of individual reaction seem to make them fated to obey the suggestion of an external milieu, for lack of an autosuggestion from within."

finish my letter in pencil, in my bed. Strange how these blank pages attract me. I had forgotten how heady this pleasure of writing is—what Chateaubriand flatly calls "the nasty habit of paper and ink" (on an otherwise not stupid page on which, to excuse the length of a description, he explains that he didn't have *the time to make it short*).

It was Romain Rolland who kept me up. The devil if I know why I wrote you on January first that his book *Above the Battle* was a revelation for me. Odd how quickly one gives in to ready-made expressions . . . That word could not be less exact! The deep intellectual and moral renewal which has made me what I am and thanks to which we were so quickly able to become friends when we met in the 1st Cavalry Corps, does not date from 1914 at all, or from my reading of Rolland's book! It dates from seventeen years earlier! Very precisely: from the summer of 1897, from the time when my young officer's conscience balked at the scandals of the Dreyfus Affair. Yes, that was when I had the sense of a *revelation*. You never had to pull yourself up in that sudden way; the leftist circle into which you were born, your training among medical students with rather socialistic leanings, quite naturally prepared you to become a Dreyfusard right from the start. But I! Think for a moment about what my position was like at the time, in my squadron of spahis! Everywhere I looked, in the whole of the Constantine garrison, as well as in France among my friends and in-laws, I could find nothing but fanatics whose point of view I could not approve. Everyone around me was up in arms against the disgraceful Frenchmen who dared to call the word of our generals into doubt. They could not bear the idea that the government some-day might, "under pressure from the Jews," permit the reopening of the trial of a "traitor" duly convicted by a court-martial of French officers! I had to proceed alone, after much groping and anxious hesitation, to an impartial examination of the problem which lay before me and which I could no longer evade. I had to do my turnabout alone. I gradually discovered caste blindness and the irrational hatred of the racists, as well as nationalism and its narrow outlook, reasons of state, the patriotic lie, the conventional heroism valued in the army, the hypocrisy and cynicism of governments, the credulity of the masses, the actual indifference of most of my comrades to truth and jus-tice. Do you understand what that might have been like? Fortunately, I had always held independence of judgment to be sacred; and then, I was approach-ing thirty, I was at the age when the character is formed, when one's thinking, after the perplexities and swervings of youth, seeks a personal and stable ori-entation. In the space of a few months, I had to revise all my traditional ideas about institutions, the established order, the rights of man, the nobility of the military profession, the homeland—what else?—about everything!

The shock was such that I did not hesitate, after the trial at Rennes—whose proceedings, published in full by certain evening papers, I followed

daily—to request a two-year leave, to look for another occupation and dissociate myself as quickly as possible from that compromised officers' corps with
which I no longer wanted to have anything in common; and I would certainly have made my resignation final if, during my leave, the party of justice,
as we said at the time, had not triumphed and completely reorganized the
high command. I thus agreed to resume my place in the army because it
seemed to me purged, rejuvenated. (You and I have since learned to our cost
that "purges" only purge for a moment, and only on the surface; and that the
changed air very soon becomes polluted again, without one's being able to do
anything about it.) It was then that luck smiled on me: I got Lyautey for my
colonel, in Alençon. You know how fond I became, right away, of that
extraordinary man, the *Constable,** as it amuses you to call him. But in my
heart of hearts, I was not the same; I was no longer the neophyte, the impassioned, determined officer I had been before the Affair. In spite of the
ardor—the elation, sometimes—that I put into serving Lyautey in his campaigns of conquest, it was the chief, the great civilizer, that I loved to serve
more than the conqueror. At Rabat, at Casa, beneath my victor's dolman I
harbored—I would have qualms about writing: the heart of a *pacifist*;
that would be paradoxical, in spite of all, and would demand too many
qualifications and commentaries; but let's say: that of a pacifier, of a soldier-
colonizer, of a messenger of civilization, who was reluctant to admit the
supremacy of force, of a patriot who was not blinded by nationalistic idolatry. I add—and I would be curious to know if your own experience corrobo-
rates mine—that, between 1900 and 1914, this type of officer was not
exceptional, or even unusual, and that, during the final years of the war, in
1917, 1918, it was even much less so. (And does this perhaps explain 1940? . . .)

All this to underline that, at the end of 1914, when *Above the Battle* fell
into my hands, Rolland's book did not *reveal* anything at all to me; it simply
found in me a reader particularly predisposed to receive it. And if it meant so
much to me, it was not because it opened up new horizons to me but only
because it confirmed, buttressed, gave order to my latent convictions. How to
describe it? You did not know me at the very beginning of the war. I found
myself in quite an uncomfortable position. The colonial major that I was had
in no way been prepared by his African campaigns for that European war;
neither technically nor, what is more important, morally: he felt painfully disoriented in the atmosphere of a general staff of home officers, particularly in
a general staff of cavalry officers. Granted, I was pleased to be there; it was I
and I alone who had wanted to come fight in France; I had even had to battle for five days with the chief, to endure Homeric rages, in order to get

*The principal officer of the household of the early French kings, who evolved into the com-
mander in chief of the country's armies in the absence of the monarch. (*O.E.D.*)

Lyautey to post me to the first contingent sent from Morocco . . . (You know that he himself had decided to remain in Casa, to defend his conquest, whatever the cost; he knew that this was too recent, too fragile still, for him to accept being deprived of his troops, and had got it into his head not to let any members of his staff go. Moreover, he never forgave me for my stubbornness, which he practically considered a betrayal of him personally, indeed a sort of desertion . . .) Yes, it was I who wanted to be part of the fighting army, and I carried out my duty as best I could, but mechanically. My fervor subsided with the first skirmishes, at the Belgian border. I have never forgotten my first German. I was coming back from a mission one morning at dawn. Suddenly, a hundred meters off, I saw five or six Uhlans on patrol who were riding towards us on the deserted road, singing. To avoid an encounter and keep them at a distance for a moment, I jumped out of the car and, while my driver quickly made a U-turn, grabbed my carbine and, taking cover behind one of the trees at the side of the road, fired. I saw one of the riders bend over in his saddle and fall from his horse in a slump, while the others scattered over the plain at a gallop. Two hours later we were back at headquarters. I did not tell anyone about the incident, but for several days in a row, I kept thinking about that young man whom I had shot like a game bird. No, I could not bring myself to regard that war between whites, between brothers, as being really justified, really necessary; I fought it without believing in it, without liking it. You can guess the echoes that the voice of Romain Rolland awoke in me!

But enough of that. This time, I'm sleepy. Pardon this nocturnal improvisation . . . It was that inaccurate word *revelation* that kept me from falling asleep.

I will send this packet in three ordinary envelopes. I'll need big ones if I go on writing you with this logorrhea. Unfortunately, the "Journaux-Tabac," Menneville's only stationer, is completely sold out! You ought to send me some from Piérac.

Good night!

M.

Letter V

Tuesday, 9 January.

I just have the energy to wish you good night before snuggling down in bed. I haven't written you for five days, in spite of my eagerness to thank you for your card and your press clippings. I thought to do it on Sunday; but I was so tired that I stayed in bed in a half-somnolent state that I couldn't rid myself of the whole day. I tried to read that packet of articles which you were kind enough to clip for me, but I had such a hard time concentrating that I put off perusing them until later.

My excuse is that I'm dead beat, old pal; worn-out, crippled, bent double like an old woodcutter . . . These last few days I've pushed myself to my limits. I do much more than I should . . . But the work is advancing steadily! Since Thursday, in fact, I have assumed command of a veritable squad of movers. On his own initiative, Bocca went and chased down three workers that he knew in Menneville, three farmhands whom the winter months have left temporarily unemployed and who didn't mind coming to "the château" to do a few days' work out of the weather. One of them even brought along his wife and his sister to help. With seven, you can imagine that the clearing is making good headway!

Last night, all the rooms on the second floor were more or less put back in order, refurnished, with their tile floors mopped. Tonight a good third of the downstairs is already scrubbed, emptied of its garbage, and swept. The good old smell of bleach is wafting all the way into my library, mixed, alas, with insidious whiffs of stench from the courtyard where, for three days, a pyre worthy of the Ganges has been burning from morning to night, in which refuse of every kind smolders beneath the snow in an acrid, crawling smoke: rotten mattresses, greasy rags, old slippers, bits and pieces of worm-eaten furniture—a pile of horrors . . .

All these extra biceps ought to lighten my personal contribution: but not at all. I am forced to put in my eight hours, just like the laborers. I have to be on the spot to make decisions, control the operation, point out what I want to keep and what should be set aside for future repairs, show where the various pieces of furniture go, etc. I confess that, a while ago, I saw nightfall coming like a deliverance!

"M'sieu looks a fright," Rose told me when she brought the lunch pail. And do you know how she manifests her pity? In the most unexpected, touching, clever way: just now I saw her appear armed with an antiquated contraption, a big copper warming pan, rescued who knows how from the pillage, which she found the time to polish and has filled with embers. As I write this, she is running that dazzling, heat-giving star up and down between my icy sheets.

Good night. I yield to the irresistible call of that piping hot bed. May it cure my aches and pains!

Letter VI

Thursday, 11 January.

Dearest Friend,

The scrubbing has kept me busy since my letter to you of the day before yesterday, but I'll spare you the details. It makes me feel so good to see my Saillant arising from chaos day by day that my fatigue hardly matters. You should know I'm keeping my team until the end of the week and that on Sunday I hope I'll finally be able to return to a less abnormal life, in a house that will have been cleaned through and through. Hallelujah!

These last few nights I've finished reading your clippings. Not a one, of course, that didn't keenly interest me, and that didn't make me melancholically long for the nights full of unforeseen digressions that we would have had reading those articles together if I were still with you in your study, stretched out on the chaise longue with Diogène on my lap.

I'm sure you took a sly pleasure in cutting out for me the scathing sermon which that old ham Henri Tarens delivered on January first for the edification of his readers—I was going to write, his flock. What else is new! It's no great thing to tirelessly proclaim that a national recovery cannot happen without a total rectification of morals, and that any progress of a political order first depends on progress of a moral order. Who would dare contradict these truisms? In principle there's no choice but to agree. It would obviously be the ideal solution. And it's not a new song: from the beginning of time, moralists have sung us the same refrain: *Quid leges sine moribus?**

But you know my position, and Tarens isn't the one to dislodge me from it. If the *social* system was in fact only perfectible to the extent that human nature—that constant—can be altered at its core, cleaned of its flaws, and made exemplary, one would quite simply have to give up hope for the future. No, my friend; there is a problem with man as there is a problem with institutions, and luckily these two questions are not indissolubly linked, or even so dependent on one another as people like to think—or to say, so as to excuse themselves for not doing anything.

The wise lawmaker is the one who, for lack of anything better, begins by

---

* *Quid leges sine moribus vanae proficiunt?* (Horace, *Carmina*, III, xxiv, 35.) "What profit laws, which without morals are empty?"

accepting man as he is. Let's take the example that we have before us; the civilized world in its present situation. If those who have arrogated to themselves the power to guide our destinies merely ensured the majority of men an easier material existence by means of a few essential, well-known reforms which have been proposed and postponed a thousand times, and if they did not pretend to find a definitive solution to the complexities stemming from the war (a solution which, moreover, can never be attained, given the relativity of all things), it is likely that, by the same token, the moral values of individuals—which so preoccupy M. Tarens—would be improved. And if the effective contribution of our twentieth century was limited to that, admit with me that it would have done more than enough, that it would have well served the generations to come.

Back to Romain Rolland . . .

I had been shocked by how little importance our local press attached to his death: two or three news items and a few mentions the next day in an editorial: it wasn't much! I see with relief that this silence wasn't general and that the big Parisian papers did better. (Although I do sense certain reservations in the excerpts you sent me . . .)

Poor Rolland! I wanted to reread, at random, a few passages from *Above the Battle.* (The volume was misplaced; I thought for a moment that it had been stolen. Finally I spotted it. I'd know it anywhere! It's all dirty and falling apart. It did not leave my tin trunk for the first months of the war. An old relic! I hold it dear.) I can well guess—and can even understand—what the young folk (your friend Crétoy, for instance, or the Jovin brothers, or the more intelligent of our NCOs in the maquis) would think of this book if they should ever take it into their heads to open it. First of all, they would surely hasten to condemn what they have the least tolerance for today: an instinctive refusal to "get involved." Already in 1915 the superpatriots were accusing Rolland of refusing to take a position in the quarrel between the French and the Germans; some even blamed him for daring to publish, in the middle of the war, an apologia for the enemy. Nothing could be less true, however, or more unjust. If Rolland goes out of his way to distinguish each side's responsibilities fairly in what seemed to him a fratricidal conflict, his book nonetheless remains a painful but very clear indictment of the megalomania of Pan-Germanism and the damaging misdeeds of Prussian militarism. In the first weeks of the war, in August, on the day after the devastating fire started by the Germans in Louvain, he wrote to the playwright Gerhart Hauptmann: "This crime against honor, which arouses the contempt of every honest conscience, is too much in the political tradition of your kings of Prussia; it did not surprise me." Yes, I can imagine the reactions of young Crétoy and of his friends in the Cercle de la Jeunesse . . .

Everything—the cast of mind, the style, the sorrowful tone, the vocabulary reminiscent of 1848—everything would put them off this work of despair but also of moderation and justice . . . Even me, I confess, when I come to certain pages . . . Events have gone so very fast since 1915! Never has the breach between the immediate past and the present been so sudden, so general, so marked. Nevertheless, language like the following—which lends such dignity to the opening of the *Introduction*—affects me the same way it did long ago: "A great nation beset by war has not only its frontiers to defend, but also its reason. It must be saved from the hallucinations, the injustices, the stupidities unleashed by the scourge. To each his duty: to the armies that of guarding the soil of the homeland; to the intellectuals, that of defending thought . . . Someday, history will make a reckoning of each of the countries at war; it will weigh up the sum of their errors, lies, and hate-filled madness. Let us strive to make sure that in its eyes, ours will be slight." What do you think of that, my friend?

The generation that a Romain Rolland will help represent in the history of ideas is our own. Think of that. I grant you that we have no reason to be proud of the political legacy that our generation is leaving; but I am far from ashamed of its moral and intellectual legacy! "A generation of humanists," the young people say . . . "A generation of individualists," they will also say, with the same derogatory smile. Individualists is what we are—dyed in the wool.

In that era—our own—collectivism and technology had not yet combined to essentially transform the life of society, the relation of individuals to the community, the relations of people among themselves, and to alter the very concept of man. The individual, his thought, his free will, his tastes still mattered to everyone. Everyone, including the governments. Remember. When we said "European civilization," we were speaking of something factual, definite, perceptible to all, and of which there was only one possible interpretation. And, in that "civilized" Europe, one single notion of human rights was, except for certain nuances, universally accepted. In that era, an independent-minded man who, alone against the world, rose up somewhere against an injustice, might very well be ridiculed, even momentarily reduced to silence: he almost always ended up getting a hearing, commanding respect, winning over a large part of public opinion to his protest. Well, my friend, I wish I could be sure that that era is not gone for good . . .

An old man's talk, perhaps. (It's in *Choses vues,* I think, that Hugo notes that an old man who moans about his times is really only complaining about his age.) This is often true. I don't think it's true of us. Old man or not, is it possible today to accept without protest the world that these last ten years have made for us? The general disarray, the disorder of minds are blatant; all judgments are skewed: those of men in the street and men of state alike.

Mediocrity, even a certain baseness, has spread like an oil stain, laxly tolerated in the widespread lassitude. In every domain, spiritual virtues are in decline, weakened, unappreciated: and yet never have they been more indispensable for holding in check those evil forces—violence, money—which triumph openly and divert mankind not only from a considered effort to recover its balance, but also from a valid concept of the future.

Just look at what is happening here. In our France, still smarting from its wounds, impoverished to the point of destitution, starving, looted, reeling with humiliations that are not washed away in a day, do you make out, anywhere, signs of that moral greatness, that strength of soul, that patient and courageous wish for salvation which we must have if we want to rise out of our present chaos? And how many countries in the world, how many ruined, terrorized, enslaved populations lie even lower than us? To emerge from this general stagnation, we would need guides, "prophets"; the calls of those my old uncle Éric called "the great mediators," the Emersons, the Erasmuses, etc., would have to be heard in the land.

Romain Rolland might have been one such. Too late: he is no longer here to restore yet again, to those who have lost it, their faith in man. Who will arise in his place to defend and save the fundamental—and seriously endangered—values of that spiritual civilization for which, during half a century, he so steadfastly fought?

In your letter, to soothe our regrets, you seem to say that we could not have counted on him any longer, that he no longer had a part to play. It's possible.

Would he nevertheless have tried to make his voice heard once again in the midst of our uproar? Would he have had the courage to oppose this consent to violence and hatred that the sufferings we have endured has wrung from all of us, even the best? To rise once again "above the battle," above the fanaticisms that everywhere fight for possession of the masses and especially the younger generations? To preach, one more time, a true order, a just order, an order of tolerance and concord, to our partisan youth, too often uneducated, too exclusively drawn to infighting, but still generous, perhaps, and less corrupted, I hope, than misled? Would he even have had the physical strength? That demanding conscience which, for such a long time, through so many books, had lit the way for men of goodwill but which age seemed somewhat to have dimmed: would it have flared up again to utter one last cry of alarm in this universe gone mad? And had he, in the waning days of his life, kept enough freedom of spirit and of action to want to take on that role and defend those precious and fragile values which, in his heart, he had never stopped espousing? I cannot be absolutely certain of this. Those values, in many parts of the globe, are now considered outdated and harmful by important masses of believers, moved by a generous messianism; and we are not unaware that Rolland felt an anxious and sometimes trusting sympathy for these new crusaders . . .

But can it be asserted that this unrepentant, selfless idealist was incapable of one last stand, out of faithfulness to his secret self? However that may be, with him gone, I don't see anyone to succeed him in that role of scout. No matter how hard I look, I don't see anyone who could lay claim to the rights of independent thought with the same nobility and authority, with the same prestige of a life devoted to pure causes. Until yesterday, simply by his presence among us, Romain Rolland bore testimony that the human conscience, as it had been shaped by centuries of moral culture, had not foundered in our disasters. And that, more than anything, grieves me about his death.

Forgive me . . . I just reread, in a low voice, this effusive improvisation with that little chuckle of satisfaction which I know all too well, with that cheap vanity which belatedly warns me and calls me to order . . . Take your eloquence, Maumort, and wring its neck! . . . Alas, I must be incurable . . . To choose the words, chisel the sentences, round off the periods, polish the endings, this will always and in spite of everything be my propensity, my vice . . . The style of a valedictorian! If I had any sense of shame with you, I'd start my letter over again.

Yet my pain over the disappearance of Rolland is genuine, as you well know. The more one is sincere and convinced of what one is writing, the more sober one's language ought to be. Stendhal . . . Avoid pathos . . . Instead of that—badaboom, badaboom—I charge blindly ahead into "the rights of independent thought," "the human conscience," and other flashy clichés . . . Ah, that word *conscience,* Gévresin! There's nothing like it for ennobling a text! . . . How I've used it, misused it, abused it during my life! When it comes to abusing conscience, I'm a recidivist!

This reminds me of a quip by some Englishman (Bernard Shaw, maybe? unless it's D. H. Lawrence?) who claimed that conscience is usually only a reflex of fear—fear of laws, fear of opinion, fear of oneself . . .

Which is like what Montaigne suggests: that one need not proudly look to man's superior nature for the origin of the precepts that dictate his conscience to him but simply to social customs: when you come right down to it, a survival of the first police regulations! That's setting things straight!

I'll wind up my evening chat with that. Note, by the way, the quality of my new paper! And don't deny me mitigating circumstances.

If my unctuous grandiloquence needs excuses, I assign most of the responsibility to these beautiful, smooth sheets. Yes, indeed! This paper is so white, so glossy, that the pen glides over it effortlessly: it's as exhilarating as a skating rink: and you're immediately tempted to do endless "figure eights" on it!

A surprise from Rose, this vellum! The topographical bureau of the American division that was assigned to "clean up" the area this summer after the German retreat came to billet at le Saillant. But seeing the state it was in, they decamped within twenty-four hours. After they left, Rose found several reams of this luxurious paper, which she put aside for me and triumphantly brought out for my New Year's present on the first of January: "Monsieur can maybe use this *for his writings*." And how! We are nowhere near to producing anything similar in France. Graph paper, but so what? Long live the *American Army*!*

Good night, old friend. Much love.

M.

Letter VII

Sunday, 14 January.

Everything came off well, as expected, and your advice about sparing myself, dear doctor, arrives too late: I dismissed my slaves last night, with a bonus! The house is finally clean. Rose and I will finish putting things away without them; we have all winter for that. So this morning I treated myself to a long Sunday lie-in: eleven hours of well-earned rest beneath my purple-and-gold catafalque. (One of these nights I'm sure I'll dream that I'm the Blessed Sacrament, and wake up singing *Venite adoremus . . .*)

I'm feeling so sprightly today that after my lunch I gave in to the desire to go hobble around a bit in the park.

I have to tell you that the weather has completely changed since Thursday. No more snowy gusts, no more wind. It still freezes at night; but this afternoon the temperature was almost warm, in the sun. The statue of Diana, so light-colored in summer in its circle of greenery, seemed made of charred stone, under its half-melted cope of snow. In the alleys, the crunching under my feet of the dead leaves shriveled by the frost reminded me of the winters of my childhood. (It is often said that smells have a magic power to bring the oldest memories back to life; but what about sounds!) I went as far as the spot we call the *saut-de-loup,* where the surrounding wall, interrupted for ten or so meters to afford a view, is replaced, as in the old days, by a stonework

---

*English in the original.

ditch, deep enough so as to be almost impassable—by the cattle at any rate. From there you see Menneville in the distance, on its hillside. It might have been a landscape sketched in charcoal: the countryside, still white, criss-crossed with soot-colored hedges, climbs in a steady slope towards the town, whose roofs, overlapping one another, form a mass of a thick and velvety black which is outlined against the golden whiteness of the sky. (I'm doing my best here . . . It's to help you envision this clearly. I am saddened by the idea that you don't know this country where I was born, where I have lived so long, where I have now returned, to die! Let yourself take in my indulgent descriptions, while waiting for me to be able to send you photos.)

I came back through the terrace area. The big pool, still frozen, shone "matte" like a sheet of new aluminum. In that light, in that muffled silence, my Saillant had the radiance, the enchanted freshness of a fairy-tale palace. A fairy's wand seemed have conjured it out of the ground just at that instant. Some remaining snow, along the gutters, further darkened my big roof, whose stormy slate-blue and steely glints always remind me of the backs of certain fish; and in their stone frames, the bricks, enlivened by that pale sun, gleamed flower-pink. Let me tell you that the bricks of le Saillant are noth-ing like modern bricks; since the brickyards replaced wood fires with coal furnaces, the baking gives the clay a dull look, a rough surface, and a dark, purplish coloring like that of clotted blood. These seventeenth-century bricks, half as thick as ours, are made from a material as fine and as smooth as that of roof tiles; and they have a soft vermilion hue that turns the color of glowing embers at the end of the day when the sun sets the façade ablaze.

How attached I feel to this dear old building, to these tall trees, to these well-known surroundings! What a privilege to be from one special place on earth! To have a spot on the planet where nothing is unfamiliar to you, a blessed spot, full of family history, always unchanged, always ready to wel-come you. During my leaves in my colonial days, the moment I had set foot again on French soil a nostalgic impulse used to carry me to this living heart of my homeland: it was to le Saillant that I flew as fast as I could, like a hom-ing pigeon whose infallible instinct takes him straight back to his nest. Don't laugh at this easy lyricism. For the first time since my return, it seemed to me today, as I slowly made my way back to my house, that I was reliving one of those moments of the past, one of those exalted moments when the urgent call of le Saillant resounded in me. As soon as, from the road, leaning out the door of the car, I would glimpse, above the treetops of the park, the big bluish roof flanked by its two tall brick chimneys, I ceased to be an exile, a nomad. I recovered my place in the universe. Present and past came together and fused into one. I sank my roots back into my soil. I became like these trees, each of which I had known forever, and which were waiting for me here, embedded in this earth where their seed had sprouted . . .

I remember those homecomings! My sister would appear on the front steps and run to meet the car. Then I would enter my home, my own house. In silence, followed by Henriette, faithful guardian of our estate, who was as moved as I, I would walk through all the rooms at a leisurely pace, delightedly giving myself over to the magic of recollection, to that subtle memory of the senses, which are suddenly awakened by the creaking of a stair, the mustiness of cretonne in a room long closed off, the spicy smell of a pantry cupboard, the feel of a doorknob, of a banister, of the arm of an armchair, the shape of a lamp, the forgotten timbre of a clock. Nowhere else did I ever feel so fully myself, so refreshed, so ready to develop all the possibilities of my nature! You'll smile: I remember my emotion on the day when, reading the second part of *Faust*, I heard this fraternal echo: *Hier bin ich Mensch, hier kann ich es sein!*—which I translated thus: "Here I am a man, here alone can I fully be one!" Only a vestige of respect for the style of our residence—and also, I must confess, Henriette's adamant opposition—got me to give up the wild urge that I had for one whole summer (the first year that my sister and I were the owners of le Saillant) to have those words carved—in Gothic letters!—on the Louis XIII arch of the front door! My excuse is that at the time I was twenty-six . . .

Can you understand me, you old vagabond? You are just the opposite of me: rootless by nature, by habit, by taste, indifferent to the past, essentially detached from everything. Don't tell me otherwise. If you went back to live in your hometown, it was purely by chance—admit it. When you left the army and had to choose some place to settle, it seemed convenient to you to retire to that honest house in the Lot that your father had left you all furnished (which I don't believe you had set foot in since his death, what's more) and for which your agent had long been seeking a satisfactory tenant. But nothing sentimental drew you to Piérac. Except for your books (and maybe not even them, since you're down to a hundred and fifty or two hundred specialized volumes useful for your scientific curiosity), what matters to you in that house of your childhood? Would you even be able to inventory, from memory, that impersonal set of family furniture that you happened to ensconce yourself in twenty-five years ago? I don't blame you at all for being the way you are. I simply observe, from having shared your life in Piérac, that that paternal house is nothing more for you than a temporary domicile, a final camping ground, the last of your garrisons. And, this being the case, I strongly doubt that you can grasp the concrete—I will even say passionate—character of the bonds that tie me to this region, to this estate, to my trees, to my old pile, to everything that has accumulated in it over generations, to all the pieces of furniture, all the familiar objects, each of which, as far as I know, has always occupied a ritual place within these old walls and also a place in me, in my memories. How can I explain it to you? Think of certain times in history—and in our lives as officers—when we were uplifted, carried away by patriotic fervor. Well, my affection for le Saillant is a feeling of the same kind. I love le Saillant as we both love France. And what I feel when I come back here also resembles that emotion one feels at certain sacred spots, certain sanctuaries. Nor is it dissimilar to ancestor worship in Asia . . . Don't smile. There is a little of all that in my faithful old heart. But what I feel is much simpler, less religious, more tender. Yes, at the bottom of it there is a great depth of tenderness, do you see? A sort of filial tenderness. In comparison to which, I assure you, the pleasure of ownership, which you sometimes make fun of and which I don't deny, really plays only a minimal . . .

Something strange just happened to me, my friend. I put down my pen without even finishing my sentence, suddenly overwhelmed by an immense distress, and I remained motionless for a solid hour, my elbows set on the arms of my armchair, my nape heavy, my gaze fixed, my forehead bent low. The obviousness of my approaching end had abruptly weighed down on me. A horrible sensation of vertigo, the vertigo of a complete indifference. It is not true that I am still attached to anything at all. My life is over with, emptied of all content, devoid of all curiosity, of any possibility of illusion or hope: forever empty, sterile . . . My life drags along in the *gloom,* an unavoidable, definitive gloom, the gloom of an absolute loss of appetite. What do the coming days matter to me? Tomorrow no longer has any appeal for me. No use striving in vain: it's too late; nothing interests me anymore and nothing can ever interest me again, because age is putting me hopelessly out of the game, out of all games; because nothing *concerns me* anymore . . . The future of man, of society? I have too little faith in their perfectibility for the fate of humankind to make me forget my own. He who gets off at the next station has no reason to care about the journey that the travelers on board his train will have to make, after him . . . Powerless, deaf to every call, incapable of wanting anything. I do not even wish to be released from this gloom. I no longer have any desires, not even to die soon. I await my death in a barely conscious passivity, in a brutish stupor.

Rose brought me my tray. I chatted a moment with her, and I dined with good appetite. Nothing is changed, the mechanism hasn't broken down, I go on making the movements of a living person.

And I take up my letter where I left off, as if after an intermission; but with the inner—and indisputable—certainty of having had, during that intermission, the revelation of a blinding truth, compared to which everything else is only automatism and pretense. What was I telling you? My fidelity to things of the past, the devotion I have to this estate. They are sincere, they are real; but I do feel they belong to those obsolete sentiments that outlive the time when they were accepted and widespread. Vestiges of a bygone era, outdated mawkishness, sentiments that have become anachronistic! The moment is near when no one will feel them anymore, when they will be scarcely conceivable, when historians will study them scientifically, as they do today to describe the feudal state of mind or the customs of the Ancien Régime. Already many of those old estates, those châteaux, those manor houses which in my youth still studded the French provinces, are beginning to disappear or undergo radical alterations, either because the buildings have gone to ruin out of neglect or because those estates have been subdivided, sold off by plots, and the new use of those old houses by the State or one of its big agencies requires remodeling, the construction of additions or extra floors. Converted into sanatoriums, retirement homes, or reformatories, they are already unrecognizable.

That the château of yesterday is no longer on the scale of the individual of today is an obvious fact that I had not realized before the last war but that I've felt very deeply since my return to le Saillant. As dear as my shell is to me, and as happy as I am to find myself back in it, I no longer feel completely comfortable here. And in saying this I am referring to something entirely different than the material conditions of my moving in again, the damaged furniture, the torn curtains and rugs, the insulting discoveries I make each day, the German inscriptions that cover the doors. The discomfort I'm talking about is of a different order, a moral order, I almost wrote "social" . . .

Both moral and social, if you wish. Having come back home, as is my right, it's strange that I should have a "guilty conscience" about it. As if I were usurping a place which I am no longer altogether right in calling my own. A "guilty conscience" because I feel at odds with, opposed to, my times.

We cannot escape our times. Like it or not, our path is the one that history lays out for us. Well, for a quite a while now, and especially for the last quarter of a century, the path has taken a turn; and I haven't wanted to see it, I haven't been willing to follow the turn. In this sense I am an anachronism . . . The situation of a wealthy old man who lives alone with his servants in a château where he uses a few rooms at most and where half a dozen families with children could easily live in his stead; who has reserved for himself alone the enjoyment of a beautiful park, enclosed by walls, where no one can enter except by breaking in, where no mother from the neighborhood can come take her children for a walk without being liable to expulsion and a fine; who, to ensure his own well-being, has a hundred and sixty hectares of meadows, land, and woods being tended by farmers who owe him a part of their profits—such a situation, although it in no way transgresses against our institutions, presents a sight that may seem outrageous in the eyes of this new and less unjust society which is already emerging on the horizon and which will undoubtedly impose itself before long on the civilized world. I am painfully wrestling with this stifling contradiction.

This life of a gentleman farmer that my father and grandfather led, and that, before this war, seemed to me not just legitimate and honorable but excellently suited to the free man that I was and meant to remain, I see today as something blameworthy; it sanctions a scarcely acceptable opposition between the miserable condition of the masses and the advantages that a few fortunate people owe to a stroke of luck. It is clearly the shocking survival of an obsolete way of life which may still be allowed by the civil codes and protected by the law but which is already condemned by public opinion and will soon be forbidden; one of those privileges that is impossible to justify, and from which a well-born man cannot draw profit and satisfaction without suffering.

What I'm writing you here is sincere, although the words are carrying me, as always, beyond what I'm exactly thinking. At the same time that I'm building this case against profiteering capitalism, a voice in me protests against the severity of the indictment; I both accuse and defend myself, condemn and absolve myself. Tonight, privileges weigh on me, and I have the soul of a Tolstoyan hero who is ready to distribute his land to the serfs. Tomorrow morning, once again a landowner and glad of it, I won't rest until Bocca has fixed the breach that the frosts have made, these last few days, in the wall surrounding the park; or else I'll dream up some superfluous embellishment . . . For example, this afternoon, during my walk, I spent a long time thinking over a plan I was already entertaining before the war: to put a new allée, a rectilinear gap, right through the forest, in the direction of the pond, that would open in front of a certain bench where I like to go sit—I can picture it so clearly in advance, a long tunnel of greenery—and would allow the shimmering of the water to be seen in the distance . . . And I'm also sincere, I swear, when at certain times I denounce this social inequality of which it pains me to be the beneficiary and when, at other moments, I am pleased to feel that I am a landowner and to take on the maintenance of my property. It seems to me that I am thus obeying a sort of imperative; I have a debt to pay, I enjoyed this estate, which was created, planted, built by those who came before me at le Saillant; I do not have the right to lose interest in it, to get rid of it; I owe it to myself to be as vigilant as my ancestors were; I have inescapable duties towards these old trees, these old buildings . . . What name to give this moral obligation? The *sense of continuity*?

I know very well what would reconcile these inner contradictions. More than ever I am absorbed by this project for a posthumous "Foundation" which we have so often talked about and for which, you remember, we even went together to consult your *notaire* in Piérac. I would obviously have less of a "guilty conscience" if I were sure that, after my death, le Saillant would become the property of the University of Paris and would serve as a place of rest, retreat, and work for tired or convalescent students. I need to look more closely into the legal conditions for a bequest of this kind. For this I am sorry not to have your friend, Maître Fromelines, the attorney, whose goodwill and advice would be invaluable to me. The *notaire* in Menneville is a newcomer whom I don't know and who doesn't have a great press in the area. This is no reason, all the same, to delay working on my plan. If the good weather lasts a few days, I'll ask him to come see me.

Opened a book at random, while waiting for Rose and her tray: Chamfort. I happen on this: "We need to know how to do the stupid things our character demands of us." Amusing . . . On this score, dear friend, we have nothing to cede to Chamfort, wouldn't you say? I'm thinking of your hike through Scotland. Of the adventure of the princess . . . Of your idiotic duel with the Dutchman over the Zuider Zee . . . And as for me, how many stupidities of that kind could I fish up from my memory, if I tried a little? . . .

I read a fair amount of Chamfort in my youth. And you? Out of curiosity, I might add, more than any great enthusiasm. My uncle Éric (and all his colleagues at the University as well) set great store by him. And by Rivarol* (whom I myself would be tempted to prefer to the other—is this a heresy?).

Dined on porridge with milk, like a child. Don't complain, you can still find food without too much trouble, in Piérac! Here, let me tell you, feeding oneself is a real problem. Though I still occasionally get a bit of milk or butter, thanks to the farms. Not everyone can say as much. I also have some beans: the Boccas' harvest. But the supply is quickly running out. No meat. The bread is bitter, indigestible, and we barely touch our rations. Nothing reaches Menneville. The shops are empty and aren't getting restocked. And the shortage is all the more keenly felt since the population has increased by a third with those families of refugees, of war victims, that have settled in everywhere. People look at one another askance, being undernourished, poorly dressed, quarrelsome, and tired. All work is interrupted. I've had to give up on making the slightest repairs. The workmen don't even bother to come anymore. The locksmith has no more iron, the carpenter no more seasoned timber, the plumber no more lead, the painter no more paint or putty or windowpanes. It rains into all the houses for lack of roof tiles, slates, and laths. You can't get anything, not even a nail, not even a ball of string. Who would ever have thought such scarcity possible in France, and in this western region, one of the country's most prosperous? How long will this time of penance last? One sees no reason why it should stop . . . Are there any signs

*Antoine de Rivarol (1753–1801), French writer, wit, and conversationalist.

of improvement in the towns? Here everything seems forever blocked, at a standstill.

While lapping up my milk, a memory concerning Chamfort and my uncle Chambost-Lévadé, the terrible and endearing "Uncle Éric," came back to me. I've already spoken to you about this character, but the subject is inexhaustible . . . Have I told you that he had a genius for mortifying remarks? A professor's vice: his position allows him to indulge it, in a cowardly way, with total impunity . . . The scene took place at my uncle and aunt's, in their townhouse in the rue de Fleurus. I was about eighteen; I was living with them. It was on a Sunday, during one of their weekly at-homes. I don't remember how the subject of Chamfort came up. Marcellin Berthelot was there. My uncle Éric, although, as you know, he had been, with Leroy-Beaulieu, one of the founders of the École des Sciences Politiques, whenever possible expressed a haughty disdain for politics and politicians; so much so that he had been deeply shocked when his friend Berthelot had accepted a portfolio in the new government, the portfolio for Public Education, I think. He made a point of calling him *"Monsieur le ministre"* or *"Son Excellence,"* while continuing to address him by the informal "tu," and he riddled him with epigrams. That day, out of sheer spite, he had thought it witty to quote to his famous friend a quip of Chamfort's, and quite a silly one into the bargain: "Combine the talent of a monkey with that of a parrot, and you come up with a good minister." "A perfect professor, too," growled a throaty voice. It was old Renan, who, from the other end of the room, got in this quiet dig to defend his friend Marcellin. "Monsieur Renan," as people said back then . . . I see him so clearly, in that big wing chair to the right of the fireplace, where my aunt used to deposit him the moment he arrived; he seemed as much a part of the furniture as the clock and the solid bronze candelabra. He hardly ever missed a Sunday. He spoke little, heard everything without seeming to have listened, and from time to time raised a sleepy eyelid and in a courteous tone tossed off a little sentence that found its mark. I can see his broad face, soft and fleshy; a good-natured visage cast in gelatin . . . I remember his little wrinkled elephant's eyes and the sly smile that sometimes stretched his thick, sensuous lips. You can well imagine that I don't attach much importance to the impressions of the young provincial that I then was, stunned to find himself each week in the midst of one of the most intellectual and refined circles in the capital. That said, I have fewer qualms about giving you the main impression I have kept of M. Renan: the unaccountable juxtaposition of an extreme modesty and an incredible self-confidence . . . Let me be more specific: the unbelievable mixture of an obvious and almost childlike shyness in manners, with an immovable inner assurance. I will go further: with the almost monstrous serenity of a kind of patriarch, aware of his superiority and absolutely sure of himself. This roly-poly even seemed incapable of imagining that his knowledge, his perspicacity, the validity of his conclusions and certainties could ever be doubted! And this without any appearance of smugness.

I hand this testimony over to you for what it's worth; but isn't it puzzling that this living image of papal infallibility should have been left me precisely by this man whose name, like that of Montaigne, has become synonymous in people's minds with smiling skepticism and universal doubt?

It's been a long time since I thought about all that!

I'm grateful to Chamfort for having awakened these memories.

My father had sent me to Paris to continue my studies, and the Chambosts had offered to take me in at the rue de Fleurus. The townhouse no longer exists—it was torn down to open up the Boulevard Raspail. Happy times! I was living in the Latin Quarter. I was studying for both my entrance exam to Saint-Cyr and my *license ès lettres*. Every Sunday afternoon, in the huge room on the second floor, fitted out as a library, I saw *le Tout Paris* of the University and the Academies. (I was far from suspecting then that those thousands of volumes that covered the walls and that I gazed upon with the veneration of a student enthralled with reading would someday be left to me, and that I would reverently move them to le Saillant! . . .) Wicked tongues called the Chambosts' salon "the anteroom of the Institut"; and that reputation tickled my aunt's social pride so agreeably that she devoted a part of her life to trying to justify it. Not without success. The effectiveness of her sway was evident, and I saw the fruition of more than one appointment that had been discreetly prepared and cunningly ripened in the private conversations that she reserved for herself with the most influential of the Sunday regulars.

Letter VIII

Tuesday, 16 January.

My letter of Sunday kept on obsessing me. I wanted to write you again yesterday, but I had so much to do in the house with Rose.

What have I been, my whole life, when you come right down to it? A sort of outcast. Without essential affinities, without ties, without respect for the caste into which I was born, in which I have lived; but with no possible connections, alas, to the people of the working class, to whom my reticent sympathy is quite rightly suspect; to whom my habitual ways of thinking and living have never allowed me to get close. Midway between the aggressive have-nots, intoxicated with abstractions, who imagine they can get everything through a radical leveling, through the unlimited sacrifice of the individual to the collectivity, and who don't see that they are likely to destroy the whole human heritage before they satisfy their just demands; and the privileged by birth, obsessed with their own interests, blinded by their traditional rights to the point of having lost any notion of their responsibilities, their social duties, and who cling desperately to all of their advantages, unable as they are to perceive what it is unfair to want to defend, and what, for the general good itself, it would be legitimate to want to preserve.

I have been equally rejected by both sides: by the "society people," who considered me virtually a traitor because of my thirst for social equity, my severity with their narrow selfishness, my refusal to ratify the validity of their traditions; and by "the masses," who were annoyed by my manners and offended by my mistrust of superstitions and abstract doctrines, my independence towards parties, my taste for order, my insurmountable loathing of political improvisation and of overly hasty changes. God protect us from the biologist-theoretician of genius who would claim to teach us how to make a baby in nine days.

Yes, an outcast . . . And I have instinctively chosen most of my friends from among "outcasts" like me: born, usually, into the well-to-do class but having rejected its prejudices and its faults, and kept nothing but certain rules of courtesy, a certain way of behaving in one's relations with oneself and others, a certain knack for humor, a certain notion of moral elegance and of honor, an aesthetic rather than an ethic . . . Cultivated humanists, ready to engage in reasoned argument, careful to temper their most changeless convictions with a dash of skepticism; enterprising in thought, thoughtful in their actions; neither lukewarm moderates nor fanatical revolutionaries, but people in love with progress and fearlessly drawn to that persistent and continuous reform of judgments, of institutions, of laws, of social behavior, which is the very history of civilization.

It's too late. I am and will doubtless remain an idle old man, a superfluous man, a spectator. A prisoner of the class I was born into. Worried, contrite, but unable to free myself through a painful sacrifice. Too skeptical, as well, and for a long time now, to be better than a fence-sitter. Exactly: an old snail.

My only excuse is my age . . .

Letter IX

I am impatient to let you know. The Foundation project has just taken a big step forward in my mind.

It occurred to me that there is no reason—actually, a lot of reasons, but they are all suspect and bad—to postpone the carrying out of the plan until *after my death.*

The trick would be to manage to combine this carrying out with my presence at le Saillant. For I don't have the courage to give the place up, to go off into self-imposed exile yet again, to leave my shell and go end my days somewhere else. Even near you, I would miss le Saillant.

The plan would be: an agreement with the University to create here a house of retreat, convalescence, and work for the academics and students of Paris. I would leave the University the whole of the estate, buildings, land, meadows, and woods. But would the revenue from the farming be sufficient for the maintenance of the boarders?

This hypothesis strongly appeals to me. I would like for my books not to be dispersed. Studious young people would find the basis of a fairly complete general library here, around fifteen thousand volumes, which could be of great value to them. And it pleases me to think of all those happy young men, at the age of enthusiasms, scattered over the property in the spring and summer months, conversing in groups under my lindens, and enjoying the charm of this old park.

If I brought off this plan while still alive, I would need to keep only a few rooms for myself . . . Obviously, this would be a very different life for me; I would sacrifice my tranquillity, my dear solitude. But the feeling of no longer being a social parasite would be a significant compensation. And—who knows—the proximity of those young people would perhaps create around me an atmosphere which, on certain days, I might find quite pleasant.

What helps give validity to this plan is the thought that neither my sister Henriette nor especially my father would have been against it. I am inwardly convinced of this, although it might surprise those who knew them, who saw them leading their lives here as lord and lady of the manor. Don't forget that in 1865 it was my father who, breaking with all the local traditions and customs, canceled his tenant-farming leases one after the other to transform our four farms into smallholdings and that, to get this bold innovation accepted and have it carried out, he had to fight for years against everyone's conventions, mistrust, and disapproval. I do know that for him it was a way of satisfying his rural tastes, which were keen: he didn't like abandoning his estate to his farmers' initiatives or being unable to take part in the agricultural life of le Saillant in a personal, active, daily way.

But he was also following other motives of a general order. I understand him very well. It was a step taken towards a bit more social justice. (Will I have the courage to take one more step in that same direction?) Without any doubt he was loath to live off his rents as an idle gentleman and profiteer, like all the Maumorts before him, who were content to fill their money boxes with the crowns that the farmers came and lined up twice a year on the table in the entrance hall. I am sure that my father would be opposed to certain principles which would today be called democratic and which he never put into abstract or dogmatic terms but whose demands clearly influenced the way he conducted business on various occasions. By giving up the tenant-farming leases and replacing them with smallholding contracts, he too was securing "a better conscience" for himself.

The farmer always remains a stranger, almost an adversary. He is a man to whom you say: "I am the landlord. You are the farmer. You assume all the worries, all the responsibility; you lay out the capital and take all the risks. I merely lend you a piece of land that I hold by right of ownership. Work it with your own resources. Water it with your sweat so you can pay me a yearly cash fee that I set in advance and that you commit to give me no matter what. If the cow dies, if hail destroys your fields, if there are no apples this year, if drought or lack of rain threaten the harvest, too bad for you. I need to get paid."

The smallholder, on the other hand, is a collaborator. To each of his smallholders my father said: "Fifty-fifty. I'm *including* you in the farming of my lands. You'll work my soil, but at my expense: I'll provide you with the animals, the fertilizer, the machines. I'll help you with my presence and my advice. We'll run the business jointly. We'll share good and bad luck fairly: the risks, costs, and losses as well as the profits. I won't demand any rent from you, any set fees in cash. We'll simply go halves on what we harvest together."

I heard my father advocate that institution of smallholding a hundred times; he never got over the fact that none of his landowner neighbors followed his lead. He was not willing to separate the profit from the labor and the responsibility. He intended to pull his share of the weight. He needed to feel that the income he received from the sale of the cattle and the crop was earned through some participation on his part, and did not regard it solely as a right of ownership.

And in fact I always saw him rise at dawn and go off on horseback to oversee the field work on the spot. He liked only the company of his smallholders. He kept an eye on everything. He was demanding but fair. I think he was loved by them for his experience, his attachment to the earth, his reserve that was never haughty: "Our master isn't proud," they used to say. He always consulted them but did not ask any initiative on their part: he calculated and thought ahead on their behalf; and they accepted his instructions without argument, knowing full well that at the end of the year they would benefit from them.

This happened around 1860. My father moved into le Saillant right after his marriage, and the next year he drew up his first two smallholding contracts.

How different they were from what they later became, the relations between the "squire" and the local peasantry. Nearer, indeed, to feudal customs than to ours! In those days, the squire, rooted in his estate from generation to generation, traveling little, always present, dependent as any plowman upon the soil and the whims of the seasons, closely shared the life of the peasants. And, like them, he loved his own province, his own village, exclusively: an actual solidarity, a—how to say it . . . racial kinship?—truly tied him to those fellow denizens of his native soil. People did not burden themselves with many "social questions" at the time; but through instinct and education, the propertied class cared about the interests of the region, its prosperity, the needs of the country folk. My forebears at le Saillant protected the ordinary people thereabouts, helping them materially and morally in every kind of crisis.

"How times have changed . . ." By gaining their freedom—quite rightly, I admit—from all tutelage, the sovereign people have, by the same token, released from their traditional duties the descendants of those squires for whom altruism was often the case and who nearly all knew how to fulfill, without boastfulness or negligence, the social obligations they deemed incumbent upon them.

I don't want to paint too rosy a picture. If I compare the time of 1860, for instance, with 1900, 1910, or, even more, with 1930, there was, heaven knows, a greater gap between the rich and poor during the Second Empire than today: a distance and a formal respect, demanded by the former and accorded by the latter, which shocks our modern egalitarianism. But by living alongside the rich, the poor used to obtain constant advantages they are now denied. All in all, the daily aid given to the rural population by the landowners, real and effective at the time, has gradually disappeared.

We need to be fair to the past. I am not trying to defend at all costs the life and attitude of the bygone squires. Or to justify the unpleasant sense of "superiority" that the privileged few quite naturally inherited back then; but whatever may have been said about it, that sense was usually innocuous and contained no arrogance, because that superiority seemed to them in the order of things, it was an ancestral habit rather than an effect or a proof of their vanity—a superiority that it did not even occur to them to question and that seemed to them all the less debatable since it was recognized by everyone.

This is curious: in our part of the country, people at that time, with very rare exceptions, had no preconceived animosity against the "châteaux." They made a major distinction between the unostentatious affluence of those old families that had lived among them on the same land for generations and the showy luxury of the nouveaux riches whose origins they did not know and whose overnight wealth stirred up both distrust and envy. But the old village squire was part of the local heritage; they had known his father and his grandfather; they had long addressed him, with a respectful familiarity, by his first name, and were grateful to him for being there, for symbolizing the past, for representing the continuity of their region. When he had good qualities, they were proud of him. They appreciated his simplicity, his benevolence, his advice, his services: he often enjoyed a kind of attachment, or at least a fondness, a trust, that was not servile and that went hand in hand with esteem. These cordial tendencies were repaid in kind. Noblesse oblige: one behaves better knowing one is in the public eye and respected. If his situation, his education, his manners conferred authority upon him, the notable usually felt bound to justify it with his behavior, his affability, his devotion to the commonweal. The result of all this, it seems to me, was fairly good relations between the classes. No automatic denigration, on the part of the lower classes; little jealousy, by and large, since there was no real poverty around the château: the work somehow fed a man, and the hired hand in our provinces did not ask much more; he had not yet crossed the threshold of unrest to enter the stage of wage demands or revolt; he did not consider himself underprivileged or a victim of exploitation; his life was hard, frugal, but secure and tranquil; he did not feel persecuted; he thought himself happy enough not to want anything more.

Am I perhaps blinded by complacent illusions, which find in me a ground prepared by atavism and by age? *Laudator temporis acti . . .* It's possible. All was not idyllic in the country of "our master." The war shaped new generations of peasants, awakened, argumentative, rebellious, and demanding, but whose animal roughness has lost its edge, and who are no longer the "feral brothers" that Jules Renard portrayed.[†] I can feel that I am overdoing my picture a bit. It's probably not worth regretting what was. My grandfather's farmers, my father's smallholders were tough, vindictive, sometimes ferocious. Many of those calm thatched cottages, whose chimney smoke I used to watch peacefully rising in the twilight in my Lamartinian youth, harbored behind their bolted doors the fearsome secret of some

---

*"A praiser of past times." (Horace.)

† *"Frères farouches"*—a phrase borrowed by Renard from La Bruyère to describe the peasants.

family tragedy, an illegal confinement, a case of incest, or some long, unwitnessed agony . . . Yes, to keep myself from going on with this indulgent evocation of the past, I only need to recall the Perche of old, those barely suspected scandals, those questionable deaths, so many cruel mysteries that were never cleared up . . .

It doesn't matter. A certain social equilibrium, which may have borne the barbarous marks of the Middle Ages, existed at that time. It has been upset, that is a fact; and—this is another—it has yet to be replaced.

*

. . . I am stopping here, for tonight.* I have been suffering since this morning from a relentless headache, which at moments causes me a strange sensation of heaviness in my limbs, dizzy spells, blurred visions . . . At our age, dear old friend, any unusual and persistent indisposition makes the ears prick up, you know . . . I do not wish for death, but this world has nothing more to keep me, and truly, if I was sure of going "on the sly," of avoiding the ordeal of a painful death agony, ah, how I would let myself peacefully slip into the eternal nonbeing!

Editor's note: This unfinished letter is the last that Colonel de Maumort wrote. The old man seems to have had a premonition of his end. The day after he wrote these lines, his servant, entering his bedroom, found him dead in his bed. He had succumbed to a stroke while asleep. Around him all was in order. He does not seem to have struggled.

*What follows is a tentative ending for the epistolary version of the novel, left by Martin du Gard among his papers.

III

The Files from the Black Box

[*André Daspre: Literally, a black box (found among Martin du Gard's possessions at the time of his death), 15.7" x 19.7" x 15.7" in size, bearing the following inscription in white letters: "B[ibliothèque]. N[ationale]. R. M. DU GARD. Maumort. Notes. Quotations. At least three years." (This last remark meant that he wished for a delay of at least three years before access to the contents was granted to the public.) The black box holds seventy numbered folders, along with their table of contents, but only fifty-one of them have a title and contain a file. (For this reason, the reader will sometimes find gaps between the numbers of the folders—number 11, for instance, being followed by number 21.) The box held no novelistic material per se but rather a collection of very diverse documents which Martin du Gard needed in order to write his book and which he built up by going back to notes from old files, as well as by assembling a new set of materials intended especially for this novel. But it must be added that for the writer these files had a very general value and significance: on many essential points, it is certain that the notes of the black box express the heart of his thought. This is why Martin du Gard wished that these files be entrusted to his grandson, Daniel de Coppet, in the hope that he would benefit from this collection of reflections compiled over the course of an entire life. (Daniel de Coppet later gave the black box to the Bibliothèque Nationale so that the documents would be available to scholars.) Thus the publication of these files, as a postscript to the text of the novel, ought to permit not just a better understanding of the novelist's working methods but also a more precise knowledge of his ideas and his opinions on topics that particularly concerned him.]*

1. General Politics

1.1 *Politics. The statesman's complex.* The statesman. His supporters see in him only the apologist for an ideology, the defender of a noble cause, the servant of the public good. And his adversaries see in him only a cunning opportunist who uses a fictive ideology to satisfy base instincts, ambition, financial needs, an appetite for power and honors. And both sides are more or less right. But each considers only one aspect of the statesman, in whom there nearly always coexist an ambitious man who wants to satisfy his passions, his taste for domination, his desire to get rich *and also, almost always,* an idealist, a believer, capable of suffering martyrdom to defend his faith, what he thinks is the good of mankind.

It must be accepted as a fact that a coin has two sides; that a statesman, by definition, by nature, is both an unscrupulous social climber and a believer who has dedicated himself to the collective good.

1.2 *Politics.* For Maumort, all of politics turns on a single problem that must be solved: reconciling the needs of *individual freedom,* which are natural, legitimate, inviolable, and of the maintenance of *order,* which is indispensable to social equilibrium.

1.3 *Political life.* As soon as a good man—by this I mean an upright character, a soul that is noble and sensitive to lofty things, a steady mind, a just man—enters political life, the good men can count noses: there is one less of them . . .

When Lyautey entered politics, it was a false step, and he quickly got out.

1.4 *Maumort will say (universal suffrage):* The critical, disastrous illusion of our fellow citizens has been to fail to take their role as voters seriously enough. The same people who are the most careful when it comes to choosing a doctor or a lawyer for themselves vote without any attempt to discriminate, without any notion of the gravity of the consequences, electing braggarts, climbers, schemers, whom they know to be such, without attaching any great importance to it, without realizing that the Chamber is not a single entity but rather the gang they've elected, probably imagining that with men who, individually, are fairly mediocre figures, it is possible to form a political body capable of seeing far and bringing great things to pass. Will this illusion prove fatal to French democracy?

1.5 *Maumort (press):* People too often say that our contemptible press is the effect, the reflection of the "mentality" of the average man. They don't say often enough how much it is rather *the cause* of it.

1.6 *Politics. Advantages and dangers of democratic control of power.* Maumort, a born aristocrat, seesaws between his instinct, confirmed by experience, which tends to make him trust only in leaders who are responsible but not controlled by Caliban;* and his rational principles, which make him both fear absolute power and demand for the governed a right of control over those who govern them.

1.7 *The tyrants of democracy. Maumort thinks:* I am terribly wary of dictatorships—and scarcely less so of democracies. They are filled with dangerous men who have figured out that to win the naïve votes of decent folk it is first necessary to speak their language and borrow their colors. What do the "democratic" statements of a Clemenceau, a Roosevelt, a Churchill, a de Gaulle mean, when we know their lives, their acts? No, the instinctive tyrants do not require out-and-out dictatorships. Where there are power and honors, camouflaged tyrants can be found.

We saw this clearly in France when all the "republican" leaders, as soon as they rose to the top, demanded that the Chambers grant them "full powers."

1.8 I have never had a taste for adventure, although for many years I enjoyed leading the rather adventurous life of a colonial officer. But adventure was never for me anything but a fleeting distraction. In my heart of hearts, I love stability.

I love my freedom, and cannot picture it amidst either disorder or insecurity.

1.9 *Politics. Maumort: man of the left.* Maumort will say: My republican loyalty (unlike Lyautey, for example), my democratic convictions, correspond to something strong in me: the rejection of injustice and, even more, of institutionalized injustice.

But I must add that by defending these advanced political ideas, whose practical implementation would entail the abolition of all the advantages I owe to my birth, to my wealth, to my social situation as a well-to-do bourgeois, I am displaying an abnegation from which I inwardly derive a certain pride. It pleases me to think that I am working against my personal interest in the name of *moral* principles.

---

*In Ernest Renan's play *Caliban* (1877), the title character represents democracy.

When I think politics, it is of the others, the majority, the wronged, that I am thinking; and not of myself.

I.10   *Maumort the republican:* The republic, in the words of Suarès, was (for Péguy*) *the ideal city of free men* [see R. Sécrétain: *Péguy, soldat de la vérité,* Émile Paul, 1946].

To be a republican is to have put the love of freedom ahead of everything.

I.11   *Maumort and patriotism.* Maumort: At bottom, examined closely, patriotism—if you strip away its concrete reality, which amounts to very little—is an abstract idea.

A patriot who loves his country is like a lover who loves *love* and not this or that woman.

The concrete reality of patriotism is the natural, human attachment that we have for a piece of land, a neighborhood, our family, our social set, our language, our friends, certain habits, and, for some, an art, a particular culture, an intellectual and moral heritage.

If patriotism were only that, it would be a dupery for a citizen, a drafted soldier, a taxpayer, etc., to make so many sacrifices in its behalf. A discrepancy between that attachment and what is demanded in the name of that attachment (which is considered not as a personal fact but as a duty).

But the homeland is also a moral and social concept, justified by being presented as necessary for practical reasons (like taxes and military service). Yet this concept, if it did not contain a kernel of emotional, concrete reality, would be questionable. As one questions the validity of a government, of institutions, of laws. How was an anti-Nazi patriotic under Hitler? How, in the name of that patriotism, did he let himself be killed for a state he detested?

I.12   *Simplistic profession of faith:* "A Republican" as people used to say when I was fifteen, and "a Dreyfusard," that is, deeply enamored of freedom and hostile to all "reasons of state." Thus I have stood up against totalitarianism, whether it be called "Fascism," as it was yesterday, "Stalinist Communism," as it is today, or "American Bureaucratic Democracy," as it may be tomorrow.

I.13   *Maumort:* Until 1930, '32, '34, maybe, I was still able to get passionately involved, to become indignant. But this attitude melted away, day by day. Until I sank into a kind of misanthropic distress and hostile discouragement about everything. I knew what I had lost: *my faith in man . . .* And for

*Charles Péguy (1873–1914), French poet and philosopher.

good reason. For years I had been witnessing a sort of general deterioration of the world. The U.S.S.R., in which I had placed ingenuous hopes; Italy, which I had always adored; Germany, which, even after the First World War, I had not been able to hate or stop trusting, had been engulfed by a fanatical and totalitarian state control that dispelled my illusions. I saw Europe, poisoned, slowly rot. I saw the rebirth and infliction of everything that I had eradicated from myself, from my aristocratic origins—no, from my bourgeois origins, from what was bourgeois in my aristocratic origins. (The rest I kept, and I had no intention of getting rid of it.) Then, as I grew older, I was flooded with contempt for that whole dreadful world that I saw arise and prosper around me. No wish to fight back. What for? I was not on either side of the barricade anymore. Those whom I would formerly have wanted to defend were no better than those who had conquered them. Everything seemed to me ugly and wretched, deserving only a disgusted shrug. I turned away in order not to see, to forget. My Saillant, my library. I stopped replying to many old friends because in their letters they spoke to me only about politics. I preferred my solitude to those disappointing contacts. My old unbridled individualism filled me with sullen but intoxicating satisfactions. There can be a haughty grandeur, at the end of a life, in drinking deep of the failure of everything, losing interest in the world, thinking harshly, with despair: "After me, the deluge, since they wanted it, since they were stupid enough to want it, returning to dogmatic idolatries that we thought had been extirpated for centuries." This fanatical world that had taken over everything was no longer mine. I was outside the world of the "believers."

I.14 *The peasant and the defeat.* The peasant—that horrible caricature of a man (but, as they say, the "infrastructure" of the country)—has scarcely recovered, thanks to the armistice, from the cold sweats of the invasion.

I.15 *Maumort. The insomnia of the world.* It was Victor Hugo, I think, who said: "War is the insomnia of the world."

Never has the world suffered from insomnia as much as in the middle of the twentieth century. Never has the term seemed more exact to describe the anguish that hovers over adults and the elderly, and the anxious uncertainty that paralyzes the energies of the young, bars their future, and turns so many of them into impatient madcaps, pleasure-seekers, most of them unconsciously convinced that it is absurd to take anything seriously because they will not have time to bring anything to completion or to suffer the consequences of their acts and of the responsibilities they take so lightly, according to the opportunity, the temptation, or the mood of the day.

1.16 *Maumort:* In one sense, I can say that my happy life has been a cruel trial. My time—the era in which I have lived, the events to which I have been an involved witness, from the Dreyfus Affair down to the failure of the Liberation, with the First World War, the Russian Revolution, the fascistic regimes of Italy and Germany, etc. along the way—has constantly offended my idea of life, of the world, and of man. All the facts have proven me wrong. Everything I have been attached to has gone bust. My way of thinking has been incompatible with my times. The modern world was the opposite of that in which I could have lived harmoniously.

I don't have a "philosophy." I have never belonged to any system. All you can say of me is that I have had a few strong intuitions, predilections, a few deep-rooted ideas which have all been at odds with the prevailing climate.

2. INDIVIDUAL AND COLLECTIVITY

2.1 *Individualism and community. Maumort. The young man* will say:* What matters to me is not *to become* but *to do.* I don't care if I am somebody, if I have a personal existence. What I value most is feeling that I am contributing to a great collective enterprise. My private life is what it is, I deal with it as little as possible, my dream would be to have none at all, to be totally integrated, dissolved, depersonalized in the job to be accomplished. Your generation's personal ambitions seem childish to me. There is nothing comparable in me, I don't even understand the place it held in your life, this need to *realize yourself.* I like nothing better than this anonymity in which I live, in which I plan to die, provided that I have taken part in the great communal work of the nation, of Europe, of the new civilization, of mankind.

I have no desire to be myself, no particular wish I want to fulfill. I have no concern aside from the world I live in and the fate of the world after me. I don't count for anything. I have no individualistic inclinations. To me that even seems absurd, narrow-minded, petty, monstrous. I am only a fragment of a whole, a fragment that hasn't anything autonomous about it and doesn't want to have. It is the whole, the future of the whole, that alone interests and excites me.

To have been used, with every bit of my strength, to move the machine along a little—that is all I ask of life, and it requires the total gift of myself.

---

*André Daspre: Who is this young man? In all likelihood, these statements would have been put in the mouth of a young man to whom Maumort would have been opposed. . . . The novelist was deeply annoyed by certain young people after the Second World War who seemed to him to dismiss the values he respected most.

2.2   *Maumort. Good and evil:* There are two kinds of morality: ordinary morality, which is *social* morality, which is based on the human need to live in a united society, and which implies rules accepted by everyone, those rules themselves being based on whatever benefits or harms the community; in this domain, the immoral act is that which, if done by everyone, would go against the interests of all. And there is another, *individual* morality, more difficult to define, which has a connection to aesthetics. It is not enough for me to determine my actions according to the collective interest. Among the acts that do not damage society and that, in the eyes of social morality, are legitimate, there are a number that I forbid myself to perform in the name of this individual morality which I have within me. What is this morality based on? On a certain conception of my dignity, my private honor. In the same way, I may permit myself acts which, done by everyone, would be harmful to society, if I do not see anything reprehensible in those acts as concerns my personal conscience, and if, by performing them in certain circumstances where only I am involved, I can be certain of doing no harm to society: "It doesn't hurt anybody" is a sufficient justification.

2.3   *Maumort. Individualist:* There are words that have always made me shudder: the word "party"; the word "prison."

2.4   *Maumort's individualism:* Maumort always rebels against the common association of individualism with disorder, license, rejection of responsibility.

   He does not separate *freedom,* which he demands, from the *responsibility* that has always been its brake and its regulator against the abuses and excesses of moral liberation.

2.5   *Maumort. An individualist, beginning in boarding school (Prometheus):* An individualist! I remember with what touching exaltation I wrote, in my *rhétorique* class, a lyrical French composition about Prometheus, the great loner, the born enemy of all constraints, the adversary of all dogmas, the revolutionary nonconformist who wanted to be accountable for his thoughts and acts to no one but himself. I expected to cause a scandal. I had not counted on the Jesuitical diplomacy of my teacher, who merely read in class, in a tone of bombastic grandiloquence, the most turgid passages of my essay and set off the most humiliating hilarity against me . . .

2.6   *Maumort. Individualism:* There is an anarchic and blameworthy individualism but there is another that is legitimate and fosters progress.

· · ·

2.7   *Selfishness. Maumort, on himself:* So deeply individualistic that I have lived as a selfish man, making only a minimum of sacrifices for others.

2.8   *Maumort. Freedom of mind:* I am now almost certain of achieving the greatest hope of my entire life: I will die alone, more and more withdrawn into myself, but with complete *independence of mind.*

2.9   *"Mass man" and "the anarchic individual."* The people/mass as opposed to the collection of individuals. Individualism. Maumort:* Truly, by my nature and my tastes, as much as by reflection and experience, I am totally against this new ideal of a human being that the totalitarian ideologies have developed and that the theoreticians of planned economies advocate: what the Americans have dubbed *mass man,* as opposed to the man they call the *anarchic individual,* a throwback, in their eyes, to the era of liberalism. It seems to me obvious, and fortunate, that a civilized people tends to be no longer a herd, a human agglomerate, but a collection of distinct individuals.

Parable of the rice: I remember that, as a young lieutenant at Versailles who was sometimes assigned to supervise the kitchen, I initiated a minor revolution. I had noticed that on rice days, the pots came back half full of a whitish mush which the soldiers spurned and which was thrown in the garbage. I taught the cooks how to prepare the rice Asian-style, in such a way that instead of the sticky magma the soldiers had a moist, fluffy rice, the grains of which remained separate: firm, well cooked, and well drained. The success was immediate: the pots came back empty. I am reminded of this experience when I think of the human magma, the *mass man* of the totalitarian states. Instead of *mass-rice, individual-rice . . .*

2.10   *Duhamel in his* Souvenirs. *Individualism.* "(Philosophical) individualism: insofar as it teaches that the great human virtues—those that are the opposite of the animal and herd virtues—are essentially the virtues of the solitary man, individualism is a fruitful doctrine, a doctrine of wisdom, in a world racked by power plays. I have remained, and intend to remain, a very fervent individualist, and this fervor is not afraid to be evangelical. Yet I have never forgotten the commandments of social life. And if I remain unshakably individualistic through love of human destinies, I declare myself a disciplined individualist."

(Individualism, and not rebellious anarchy.)

---

*English in the original.

2.11   A genuine *individualist* eventually realizes that his principal, constant effort aims at reconciling in himself his violent need for independence and the exacting sense he has of his responsibilities.

2.12   Man is an individual being. Though he may live in society, he always remains an individual, and his strongest instincts are those that have to do with his individual life. As a social animal, man is incomplete, temporary, conventional: it is a varnish he has applied to himself and that does not take.

2.13   *Individualism. The revolution by the individualists:* A revolutionary alteration of the economic and social world is unarguably necessary—but it is by making partial revolutions in various domains that the total revolution, the revolution as a whole, will be accomplished or started on its way. Every human group has a collective mentality which is composed of the mentalities of its members. If we want to organize a new (or altered) world, with more freedom and happiness, it is man first of all, the initial unit, who must be changed into a free and morally happy individual.

   By fighting for the freedom of the individual against the collectivistic revolutionaries who deny it, we thereby work, *more than they do,* for the advent of a better world, in which the individual will be respected. If the future revolution is made by individualists enamored of freedom, the world that will be organized by them will reflect their way of thinking.

2.14   *Nietzsche:* "Become what you are."

2.15   *"On Pindar"* (Pontigny,* 1926): "Become what you are, once you have learned it."

2.16   Not *selfish* but *self-centered. Maumort:* I have always been firmly *self-centered.* Which, fortunately, does not at all mean that I am *selfish.*
   I am well aware that we do not readily admit our selfishness. I am well aware that I am selfish, as much as any man. I will thus say, more precisely: "I am not more selfish than the average, while being much more *self-centered* than most; while being as *self-centered* as it is possible to be."
   This calls for explanation, and some examination of conscience.
   I am not liable to excessive indulgence when it comes to myself. I have even always taken a certain satisfaction in knowing my faults: my taste for truth goes that far. I am all the more prepared to look into my vices of character and to pinpoint them since I do not much believe in the possibility that

---

*The abbey of Pontigny, where members of the intelligentsia of Europe met yearly for seminars on varied topics. Martin du Gard heard the saying of Pindar's quoted at one such gathering.

man can improve himself and since I am inclined to believe that man is not responsible for that set of good and bad traits which make up his nature and which result from a lot of factors that are more or less independent of his will: his heredity, his education, his circumstances. Therefore it would not do me much credit to accuse myself of selfishness, if I thought this corresponded to reality. No: when I examine myself, when I review my behavior at this or that moment of my past, I observe that I have only rarely displayed selfishness. I have always been sociable, obliging; I have known how to dedicate myself to certain people, certain tasks, to impose on myself certain sacrifices, often painful, out of natural altruism.

On the other hand, I am and have always been deeply self-centered. I mean by this a fundamental tendency to withdraw into myself, to be concerned with my development; to question myself and to observe myself living; to be sufficient unto myself; to be more interested in myself than in anything else. A fundamental tendency to be my own support, to do without the approbation of others, to pursue my own evolution very consciously and doggedly. Hence my natural taste for solitude, for communing with myself. Hence this need I have always had to keep my diary, this record of my thoughts and acts. When I am displeased with myself, a friend's forgiving appreciation does nothing to lighten the severity of my judgment of myself. And, by the same token, no matter what I have done, if, in the depths of my conscience, I find, in all clear-sightedness, an approval, then the condemnation of others, even if it be the condemnation of the whole world, though it may not leave me altogether indifferent, does not change my point of view one iota. If I approve of myself, the opinion of those I respect most will not change a thing.

During my entire life, I find examples of this inner balance, which depends only on myself. This is what I mean when I say that I am *self-centered*.

It is because I am deeply *self-centered* that I was able, as I turned twenty, to put my life on two different and simultaneous tracks: a practical life, a life of action, an officer's life, which was only a concession to external necessities and social conventions; and a private life, this one *self-centered*, unknown to anyone, led in isolation, a life of inner thought and intellectual and moral development. If I had not been so *self-centered*, I would have determined my future differently: either I would have devoted my intellectual abilities to attaining a place in society and would have tried to be a writer or a teacher, someone who makes a profession of thinking and expressing himself; or I would have put my whole intelligence at the service of my military career, and my ambition would have been to be a great military leader or an undisputed expert on military questions. No: I was *self-centered* enough to want to keep what was best in me for myself alone; I eschewed mentioning it or even letting it be seen; I accepted being, in the eyes of the world, merely a conscientious officer without professional ambition; and I saved for my own strictly private use a certain mental acuity, a certain intellectual merit, like a miser who will not let himself spend a cent so as to be able to enjoy the little treasures of his money box in secret.

It is also because I am deeply *self-centered* that I could, without suffering much as a result, allow a woman, even though I sincerely loved her, to distance herself from me, and, later on, could refrain from fighting my in-laws to regain possession of my sons. Here the distinction is very clear, and not specious. It was not at all out of *selfishness* that I acted in that way: it was because I was *self-centered.* It was not to recover my freedom that I accepted the slackening of my marital ties; on the contrary, the gradual estrangement of my wife caused me great emotional suffering. Nor was it out of *selfishness* that I left the task of raising my children to my mother-in-law; not at all to get rid of a delicate and demanding duty; I wanted nothing so much as to perform my role as a father. In those two cases, I yielded to circumstances; I was not willing to undertake a battle to win back my wife and force her to live with me, I was not willing to tear my sons away from a home where they were happy, because I preferred to sacrifice myself, to sacrifice my preferences, to those of my wife and my children; which is exactly the opposite of a selfish attitude. But if I was able to make those sacrifices with a minimum of inner torment and despair, it was because I was deeply *self-centered;* it was because, losing everything, I still was left with myself. It was because the solitude to which I was condemned by the near-desertion of my wife, then of my children, was inhabited by my own presence. It was because I had, in the force of my personal feeling, a higher interest, which, in those cruel times, furnished me with a supreme compensation.

It is because I was *self-centered* that I hardly suffered from a long career in the army without reward, without high rank, without honors. If the thought that I had failed in my life because after so many years of service I retired with the rank of colonel while all my peers were major generals or lieutenant generals, had fine commands, etc.—if this regret never crossed my mind, it was because I was *self-centered* enough not to attach any value to honors; it was because my basic interest was elsewhere: in myself, in my *self-centered* development.

And if today, at seventy, I feel that I have fully satisfied my ambitions and made a perfect success of this life that everyone deems a failure, it is because I was *self-centered* enough to think that a life in which I kept my mind free, in which my brain never stopped working and evolving, in which I always found in my inner reflection a constant activity, in which I continue to conduct my little cogitations as I please, is a life that is exceptionally full and satisfying.

Self-centered? I simply mean by this that the only great adventure of my life has been the *dialogue* that I carried on with myself; a dialogue that began with the awakening of my intelligence, that has never stopped, that still goes on; it was to preserve it that I entered the army, that I made no sacrifices to career ambitions, that I accepted the destruction of my home life. *Solitude* and *inner dialogue,* that is my whole life . . . And what I sought to attain through myself was *Man.*

3 and 4.* Freedom. Refusal to Become Affiliated. Dissociating Oneself

3.1   *1933.* I am loath to make *commitments.* Perhaps because I know that I am loyal? Because I believe in keeping my promises?

3.2   *To Jouhandeau†, March '34 (politics):* It is lucky that I am far away at this moment. I am not forced to take sides. I allow myself, *in petto,* to dismiss the supporters of all parties. There is such a gulf between myself and all politicians of whatever stripe that matters which divide them and set them against each other are for me niceties devoid of interest.

I too feel fiercely individualistic. Every Westerner is. But to know one's instincts and their strength is not necessarily to approve of them. I am ready for great personal sacrifices on the day when people who inspire trust in me put forward a clear, workable doctrine that I can believe effective. For the moment, alas, I am only "anti": anticapitalistic, antimilitaristic, antidemagogic, antistatist. And it is quite uncomfortable to have only negative positions, to know only what one no longer wants.

3.3   *November 1934.* I've never liked being a soldier. Today, I'm too old for it. I won't enlist.

3.4   *"Commune," November 1935, p. 337.* Marx, asked in a questionnaire, "Your favorite motto?," replied: "*De omnibus dubitandum.* Everything must be doubted."

3.5   *Refusal to join in:* I do not want to take an unqualified position regarding problems that my training has not prepared me to solve and the study of which has only, up to now, led me to recognize their discouraging complexity.

---

*André Daspre has combined the contents of these two folders into one, subsuming all of the entries as decimals of the number 3.

†Marcel Jouhandeau (1888–1979), French writer.

3.6   *Nice, Nov. '35:* I am beginning to think that the importance of economic well-being has been overestimated. It is not everything for man. People will soon realize that the socialistic totalitarian state leads to a gilded barracks, but a barracks nevertheless. That man, as much as he needs bread and butter, needs his *individual sovereignty* to be respected. That you maim him by interfering in his private life, his habits, his leisure activities; by making collective work a sacred duty, when it is nothing but forced labor; by imprisoning him within the borders of a country; by hiding the world from him; by forbidding him to protest, to compare, to think freely, to rebel, to be a nonconformist; by submitting him to brainwashing; by condemning him to a life of siege and dictatorship.

3.7   *Agree with Sartiaux* in thinking:* Isn't a spectator's life the best? At any rate, it is our lot. Why regret beliefs, passionate convictions, since we have spent thirty or more years of our life getting rid of them?

To take sides is a necessity of *action,* not of *thought* or of *art.* We can admire men of action, builders. But we are not of their "style." We cannot be everything at once. We have to know our limits and not mix types.

3.8   *Tocqueville, quoted by Marcel Arland† in "Le Promeneur," p. 233 [1944]. Tocqueville's liberalism.* "The dominant passion of Tocqueville," says Arland, "and perhaps his only real passion, is that of freedom. But he considers that freedom does not have less to fear from democracy than from royal absolutism. He not only dreads the brutal violence of the masses, but also and above all the *progressive leveling, the lowering and stifling of man* by the natural play of democracy. In defending freedom, it is human dignity he means to defend."

3.9   *Tocqueville (in* Democracy in America*):* "I appeal beyond the sovereignty of the people to the sovereignty of the human race."

"I believe freedom to be in danger as long as power finds no obstacle in its way that might check its advance and give it time to moderate itself. Omnipotence seems to me in itself something evil and dangerous."

"He accepts democracy," says Arland, "as an unavoidable development . . . Those who make a monster of democracy, he reassures and shows that it is not synonymous with despoilment and slaughter; those who throw themselves into it with their eyes closed, he warns of errors and possible dangers."

"Do you wish," adds Arland, "for an even more direct profession of faith?

---

*Félix Sartiaux, friend of Martin du Gard's.
†Marcel Arland (1899–1986), French writer and editor.

It will be found on this page, which Tocqueville probably wrote only for himself: 'My instinct, my opinions:

" 'I have an intellectual sympathy for democratic institutions, but I am *an aristocrat by instinct;* that is, *I despise and fear the mob. I passionately love freedom, respect for rights, but not democracy.* This comes from the bottom of my soul.

" '*I hate demagogy, the disorderly acts of the masses,* their violent and unenlightened intervention in affairs, *the envious passions of the lower classes,* the irreligious tendencies. This comes from the bottom of my soul.

" 'I am neither of the revolutionary nor of the conservative party. And yet, when all is said and done, *I belong more to the latter than the former.* For I differ from the latter as to the means rather than the end; whereas I differ from the former as to both the means and the end. Freedom is the first among my passions. This I hold true.' "

3.10   *Maumort:* If I want to be free, it is in order to have the freedom not to choose.

3.11   Ours will be the century of no *unity.* The fanatical beliefs, the ideologies clash in a chaotic free-for-all. I console myself for this by thinking that it is easier, in an atmosphere of heated contradictions, to remain open to all the intellectual possibilities and not to yield to the restrictive, impoverishing temptation of a certainty imposed by one's time.

I am almost inclined to go farther and to write that every ideological certainty is a lie—or, at least, a mistake by its very definition—to the extent that it limits us and closes off options. Once and for all let us get this idea out of our heads which the sectarians sow there for their own ends: that there is cowardice in not coming to a conclusion, in not deciding, in not making a choice. The truth is that it requires much more firmness of soul and moral courage to live with contradiction and doubt than to surrender oneself to the well-marked paths of a conviction.

3.12   *Maumort. To be above contradictions.* Instinctively, I have always been extremely reluctant to *choose.* Hesitation is an atmosphere familiar to me, and I have always considered absolute certitude to be an intolerable impoverishment. In so saying, I am exaggerating a bit. To maintain the contradictions of my thought and my nature is not an easy and comfortable position, but it has enormous compensations in the sense of inner nobility that it brings me. To unite the extremes in oneself, to be the living proof that the extremes are not irreconcilable, kindles an indescribable feeling of power and greatness. It is a summit from which one overlooks both slopes; and on it one breathes the air of mountaintops.

3.13 *Maumort will say (freedom):* I have passionately cherished and defended freedom. Out of reason, but also because of my nature. If I have always wanted freedom for everyone, it is also to some extent because I have always had an instinct to evade overly narrow rules and to consider this exemption a special right, with a very strong sense that my quality as a human being allowed me to live outside commonly accepted rules.

3.14 *Maumort. Freedom:* Everyone carries within himself his own definition of freedom. For Maumort, to be free is above all to defend his personality against society, to protect the integrity of his nature from social forces that tend to subjugate it, alter it, or paralyze it by intruding into the domains of private life. To be free is to have the right to be oneself while submitting to the laws of one's country.

3.15 *Colonel Maumort:* It took me a long time to understand that I deluded myself when I considered human society through the microcosm of an army regiment, and concluded that man likes to be commanded by a leader whom he respects and whose orders relieve him of all initiative. This is an error, which has the appearance of truth only in the temporary setting of a barracks. Outside, once past the gate, man likes to feel free, and he wishes for order to reign and ensure his safety but for this order to impose a minimum of constraints on him and to require of him only a slight and willing submission. It is in a regiment, or at school, that the adolescent, knowing that he is dragooned with no possibility of escape, assumes the appearance of a good obedient student in order to avoid trouble. As soon as he can do otherwise, he rises up and demands his freedom.

3.16 *Liberalism. Maumort's political credo:* Even in his own era, he basically thinks more or less what Tocqueville thought [see 3.9]: "I *am an aristocrat* by instinct. I have an 'intellectual sympathy' for socialism. *Freedom is the first among my passions.*"

3.17 *Maumort. Liberté, égalité, fraternité:* I demand, for the spiritual domain, a maximum of *liberty;* for the economic and the social domains, a maximum of *equality* and *fraternity.*

I am willing to see the triad restored to honor: *homeland, family, work*;* but that does not make me renounce the motto of the great republics: *liberté, égalité, fraternité.*

*Motto of Pétain and Vichy.

3.18   *Maumort:* To tell the truth, in the course of a long, varied and vagabond life, I have never encountered *fraternity* anywhere. Not even in the religious orders . . . A single exception: in war. I mean: in the trenches. Or more precisely: under fire. And that never lasted very long: the length of a "bad spell." But it was really fraternity that united the men, exposed to the same dangers, the same panic, the same agonies, and removed for a time from the world of the living . . . *morituri* . . . And back behind the lines, seeing how quickly and brutally the bickering started up again, I was very often surprised that after having tasted the deep delights of feeling they were brothers, the wolf-men could so easily, and without falling into despair over it, see the fraternity of the front line vanish . . .

3.19   *Antoine,* after the war, or Maumort?* [Below, this extract from an article by Abel Bonnard *(Journal des débats)* titled "Don't Adapt."]

"Don't adapt—this, I believe, is the true watchword of strong souls; or rather, adapt as little as possible, for we all accept our own time to some extent, since we live in it. But, given this, we must not renounce what we are on the pretext that most of our contemporaries are going off in a direction different from our own. The true proof of our vigor is to establish ourselves in our era, along with our ideas, our tastes, and our preferences. For then we too become one of the facts of the present. By keeping up certain ways of thinking, of feeling, of living, we carry them into the future and perhaps help to bring about their return. To regret is not always useless: our regrets for the past are seeds we toss into the future."

3.20   *The depersonalization of the individual in the mass.* The moment men are gathered and united by a common faith, everything that constitutes a person's individual worth, his greatest virtues, is paralyzed by the unavoidable phenomenon of collective hysteria. Each individual *is drained of his own personality* and yields to the laziness of no longer determining his own path or conduct. He loses that sense of responsibility that was his highest virtue, the principal element of his moral elevation. He no longer has to make the effort to think, to judge. He becomes part of an anonymous society. In the nameless group, he blithely, cravenly escapes from everything that makes human life and thought so difficult and so noble. Of course, in order to pay for that self-desertion, he accepts hard collective duties. But as hard as these may sometimes be, they are less of an effort—they are, despite all, less arduous, requiring less courage, than solitary duty (and the fact of being responsible to oneself alone). He has fled his essential task, *his true destiny as a*

---

*André Daspre: Probably Antoine in *The Thibaults.*

reasoning animal; he has delegated the sacred powers that he had over himself in order to become an anonymous fragment of a herd, guided only by his basic and hysterical instincts.

3.21   *The gaggle of geese:* Observe the stupidest animal in the farmyard: the goose. A goose goes out in the road by itself. Watch how it finds its way about in spite of everything, avoids the stone heap, discerningly searches for its food, locates the best spot in the pasture by itself. Observe this gaggle of geese together: they all seem to have lost their heads at once, they panic, rush this way and that, beating their wings, get bogged down in a mud puddle, bump into a stone heap, foolishly assault an impenetrable hedge, fall back into the ditch and splash about clucking with fear and anger, graze at random here and there, go right past the best spot without even noticing it. *The moment they form a flock, their stupidity alone seems to guide them,* they make only absurd, useless movements, *imitating each other.* The one in front walks aimlessly and all the rest follow, going where it has gone.

3.22   *Maumort: E. Mounier, "Esprit," March '47, p. 476. Against noncommitment.* "Certainly nothing is more tempting than to look down on things while congratulating oneself for not being tied to any convention, for fighting on two fronts, for receiving blows from the right and the left. An illusory ivory tower which takes itself for a command post! Freedom of mind has no need of a visible sign of separation, which imparts an overly enticing tranquillity. Freedom of mind has to be won in open combat, by struggling against doubt and protest."

5. JUSTICE

5.1   *The freedom to err!* What remains of freedom if the freedom to err is suppressed? It was precisely according to this principle that error cannot be free that the *Syllabus** was written against us!

5.2   *Maumort. Need for justice:* My constant effort to see clearly, to understand, is another form of the need for justice. To think straight is to honor justice.

5.3   *Justice: "Audiatur et altera pars."*† Let the other side also be heard.

---

*The *Syllabus,* issued by Pius IX in 1864, stigmatized as an error the view that "the Roman Pontiff can and should reconcile himself to and agree with progress, liberalism and modern civilization."

†St. Augustine of Hippo, in *De Duabus Animabus contra Manicheos.*

6. REVOLUTIONARIES

6.1   *Maumort. Revolutionaries do not work for evolution.* It is commonly thought that they do, and this is a deplorable error. I am more and more convinced that the march of the world and that uninterrupted movement over centuries which constantly presents the double phenomenon of an order of things that is coming undone and an order of things that is dawning, asserting itself, blossoming (and which is, strictly speaking, the evolution of civilization) happens according to a plan that has little relation to those cataclysmic accidents that are revolutions.

I am even inclined to think that those incoherent convulsions—to whatever degree, real or false, they may be connected to the appearance and development of new ideologies (and whatever they might have to contribute in the domain of social institutions)—mainly result in irreparable disasters, in wasted time, in a useless mess; and that, on balance, those periodic catastrophes have ended up delaying rather than accelerating mankind's evolution towards new thoughts and towards a better organization of the world.

6.2   *Revolutionaries.* Men of action are not always obtuse; but they are often very limited.

Revolutionaries, whether they are pompous and inane, or cynical and vain about their lack of scruples, or bloodthirsty and vindictive, or all these things at once, are always a demonic breed, in which all the superstitions and all the animal instincts of primitive man survive.

They are savages, bent on destruction, presumptuous, drunk with childish hopes, all the more fearsome in that they imagine they can wield ideas and claim to justify their inconsistencies, their brutalities, with short-sighted "principles," accepted without examination and applied with a fanatical frenzy.

Is an improvement of the human condition possible? This is not clear. If it were to happen, it would be through a slow and natural moral evolution, which would gradually create in man the wish, the power, the wisdom to master his instincts. One thing, at any rate, seems certain: that this moral progress would not come about through any sudden change, through disorder and revolt by the average man.

(This progress, which is simply the *evolution of civilization*—let us put aside the term "progress," which contains the idea of a steady improvement, since it is not certain that the future will be superior to the past—is produced by the *perpetual movement* of things that wear out and disappear and of things that arise and cohere. Just as walking is a fall constantly interrupted by the next fall.)

6.3   *The young (revolutionaries).* They are all conceited enough to think that the day of creation was the day they opened their eyes on the world.

6.4   *The revolutionaries' grudge.* At the heart of most revolutionaries, even the greatest, there is a secret grudge over having been crossed by society when they were young.

"The end result of physical nature and of the human masses left to their own appetites is this blind destruction of everything that the mind has created." (Boutroux.*)

6.5   *Revolution: violent disruption.* Which, at first, can only bring added misery to people.

6.6   *Louis Ménard.† Prologue d'une révolution (1849).* [Taken from an article titled "From 16 April 1848 to the Elections," published in Numbers 9–10 of 1948 of the magazine *Maintenant.*]

"A revolution that does not set out to *profoundly improve the lot of the people* is only a *crime* replacing another crime."

(In reality, every revolution is nothing but a takeover by people who want to replace the country's rulers and have their turn at exploiting the masses, but to arrive at that point and secure the help of those masses, they always promise them well-being, justice, freedom, and happiness . . .)

6.7   *Against revolutionaries.* In the face of all good sense and with no regard for the natural order, they hope for an improvement of their social condition by inducing *catastrophic events,* which can only produce fresh disasters and an economic disorder of which they will be the first victims. But it is the slowness of social evolution, held back by the propertied classes, that has pushed them to the limit and distorted their vision of things. Whose fault is it if they have lost all trust in a rational progress of institutions and mores?

6.8   *Revolutionaries.* The young don't mistrust "altruistic ideas" enough: they do not yet know that the nature of man is an insurmountable obstacle to their practical realization and that, by setting up these ideas as noble doctrines and trying to apply them, they will only manage to cause frightful carnage a thousand times worse than that of the most violent natural cataclysms or the most devastating epidemics. A thousand times worse for mankind

---

*Émile Boutroux (1845–1921), French philosopher.

†Louis Ménard (1822–1901), French writer and scientist. The publication of his *Prologue to a Revolution* caused him to be forced into exile for several years.

than are the evils or injustices that they think they are "altruistically" combating and that they hope in vain to cure!

R.M.G., 1793–1917!*

6.9　*Ernst Jünger,[†] "Clandestine Document During the War" (quoted by "La Tour de feu," p. 47)*. Lie of the totalitarians who want to create men's happiness through violence.

"The hand that wants to help man and free him from blindness must be unstained by crimes and violent acts."

The good that results from violence is in fact an evil, because it is a good poisoned by the virulent germs of its origin and will very soon degenerate.

6.10　*Revolutions and social disorder*. Do not be under any illusions as to the possibilities of a social equilibrium. As long as men are what they are, any organization of society implies an inevitable portion of disorder.

And, until now, history shows that revolutions have succeeded only at displacing, for a longer or shorter time, that *portion of disorder* inherent in every society.

7. COMMUNISM

7.1　*Communist tactics*. For a bourgeois, to lie, to pull the wool over someone's eyes in order to swindle him, to set traps for him, to cheat him every which way, to live and act behind a mask the better to attain one's ends, is called hypocrisy, duplicity, deceit, baseness, villainy. For a Communist, this is called "tactical skill" and is a source of pride.

March '36.

7.2　*The Communist faith*. They are prey to a sort of collective madness that reason is powerless to control.

7.3　Lenin used to say of capitalists and their position that they are "tangled." One sometimes wants to say that the Communists' position vis-à-vis the world is far too "simplified."

7.4　*Communism. European tragicomedy*. It is ridiculous to think that in our relatively democratic countries, where work is, all in all, elective and the

---

*Martin du Gard initialed many of these note cards "R.M.G."; in this case, he added the dates of the French Terror and the Russian Revolution, presumably as a wry comment.

†Ernst Jünger (1895–1998), German novelist and essayist, a formerly ardent militarist and nihilist whose outlook in midcareer changed to an equally ardent belief in peace, European federation, and individual dignity. *(Encyclopaedia Britannica)*

workers' standard of living is fairly high, there are Communists, admirers and promoters of the Stalinist regime (that is, of a fanatical military in the service of an imperialistic dictatorship that rules inexorably over a muzzled people condemned to forced labor and deprived of the most elementary well-being) who have made any serious contribution towards spreading an ideal of freedom, leisure, prosperity, etc. among the masses.

7.5 *Maumort. Communism.* To what extent must we reject the good feeling that Communists can, on the whole, inspire? Is it because those who disseminate the Soviet doctrine have fine qualities of character, of earnestness, the spirit of sacrifice, a sense of human brotherhood, that we are not supposed to dismiss the ideology they preach and the government they would like to set up?

Maumort has lived with Communists during the Résistance.

7.6 *Malraux and Communism.* For Malraux, Communism is simply a *religion,* born of the need to justify, for a humanity condemned to factory life by the economic development of society, the existence of the proletarian, which is "no joke," he says.

In Russia, two million bourgeois and one hundred forty-eight million proletarians, actual or potential. The establishment of Communism there has been easy.

In France, twenty-three million bourgeois and seventeen million proletarians, actual or potential. The situation is different. Revolution is impossible—except after a war, if Communism then appeared to be the only party capable of wanting peace and making it, which would win it twenty out of the twenty-three million bourgeois.

But when Communism, put in with the help of a war, had to start governing in the West, it would be forced, in its dealings with Westerners, to compromise itself in doctrine and in fact.

For Malraux, at the present moment, since he is French and an intellectual, to be a French Communist would be unthinkable, absurd. He is not a proletarian. This is a fact. His intellectual role is to understand everything human; with all of his intelligence, he leans towards Russian Communism, that experiment of one hundred forty-eight million men trying to bring dignity to their lives as forced laborers. But for him, the question of human dignity presents itself differently, since he is a French intellectual. And when he is told: "All intellectuals to the cotton front!"* he refuses and feels that he has to defend something else which is essential.

---

*I.e., in the sense that the Soviets were dispatching writers to the fields or factories to improve their perspective through direct contact with the labor force.

7.7 *Against Communism.* Mauriac says it very well (*Figaro,* 21 February '46): ". . . our essential disagreement with Communism is *not about the structure of society* but about the idea *that we have of the human being.*

"Our justice is not their justice. It is the defense of man that is at issue."

7.8 *Regarding Communism.* Like it or not, as Malraux has said, the great event of the First World War was the Russian Revolution. Communism is linked to contemporary social problems, and one can only adhere to one's concept of a social justice based on new foundations. In principle it has made itself the mouthpiece and enforcer of the world proletariat's just demands.

As opposed as one may be to the *methods* of Communism, one cannot, in good faith, confine oneself to a purely negative position towards it.

See the whole issue of *Esprit,* beginning of '46.

7.9 *"Renaissance," article against the Communist peril.* That mendacious ideology, which promises happiness and tyrannizes the individual down to the innermost recesses of his private life, which cripples a nation by stifling one after another of the values that permitted it to live and gave it a dignity, a moral personality, and a spiritual influence.

7.10 Lenin and Plekhanov. The mistake—which led to Stalinism—was to want Russia to pass without any transition from the autocratic regime to a socialistic one.

From an article in *La Nef* (February '50), signed by G. Alexinsky, a deputy of the Duma in 1905 and a collaborator with Lenin, I learn that the first Bolsheviks did not think they could bring off their social revolution in Russia and maintained that in Russia it was not necessary to go too far too fast or attempt anything but the installation of bourgeois democracy to start with.

Lenin shared this idea until 1914. It was only in 1917 that he thought it possible to make a purely socialistic revolution in Russia without passing through the stage of bourgeois democracy.

He was wrong. He would regret it today if he could see Stalin's Russia! Which confirms all too well the warning by old Plekhanov, the father of Russian Marxism, the founder of Russian social democracy, who had prophetically declared that if an attempt were made to create a socialist regime in Russia, for which Russia still lacked an economic and social foundation, the outcome would be a new Inca empire in which a socialist caste would oversee national production through bureaucratic and terroristic means.

7.11 *Maumort and Capitalism:* I was a socialist, especially after 1918. I thought that profound social reforms were essential, that the war had been the work of capitalism, the result of the capitalist system, and that capitalism was indefensible.

This lasted for ten years, during which I watched the Russian experiment with a cautious sympathy and a great curiosity.

It was around 1930 that I suddenly understood that the coming to power of the proletariat and the abolition of capitalism was producing social results worse than those of capitalism, since the individual continues to be fiercely exploited by the proletarian collectivity: an exploitation that leaves no hope, since the exploited one can no longer aspire to prevail over his boss because there are no more bosses and he is exploited by the working class itself.

8. HUMANISM. RATIONALISM

8.1   *For Maumort?*
    Gorky, *Europe,* June 1925: "Truth? It is a judgment suffused with a feeling of faith."
    (Which explains the skepticism of those who have no inclination to "believe." They are not even able to find truth in anything.)

8.2   *Racine:* "Do you think you can be holy and just with impunity?"
    "Do you think you can be *frank* and just with impunity?" Maumort will say to Gévresin, concerning the latter's problems with the town council of Piérac.

8.3   *Billy,** *Propos* (*Figaro,* 29 May 1939) quotes this passage from Suarès' *Vues sur l'Europe* (1939): "No generation† for a hundred years has been more open to all forms of foreign life and thought, to all works of art, all doctrines, every category of science and beauty, in Europe and Asia, in the present, in the past, everywhere."
    Billy adds: "It is true that the generation of 1890–1900, in France and elsewhere, achieved a kind of cosmopolitan culture unknown before it and which we shall not see again for a long time if indeed ever. That period was marked by a splendid blossoming of the aesthetic sensibility in the intellectual elite."

8.4   *Vauvenargues:* "Clarity is the good faith of philosophers."

8.5   *Joubert:*‡ "Clear ideas are useful in speaking, but we almost always act on some murky idea; they are the ones that run our lives . . ."

---

*André Billy (1882–1971), French novelist and literary critic.
†Here, as in the next paragraph, it is the generation of 1890–1900 that is in question.
‡Joseph Joubert (1754–1824), French moralist.

[Martin du Gard adds in pencil:] A clear idea is always a false idea. Thus errors easily win out; they have clarity on their side.

9. LIMITS OF THE KNOWABLE. AGNOSTICISM

9.1 *Maumort and reason.* I yield effortlessly to the guidance of my reason. I have scarcely any preconceived ideas. When I meditate on a subject, I do not believe I yield to the temptation of bending my reason to justify my propensities, I let my reason work freely and I surrender willingly to its arguments, to the reasoning of my reason.

Thus, in the course of my life, I have allowed to form in myself, through reflection, a certain notion of the universe which is constantly being changed, augmented, and completed. With enough distance to be the observer of this evolution, and enough passivity to foster the progressive stages of this work of thinking, this ongoing development.

9.2 *Maumort and the "why."* I have put much stock in science . . . It was not without consequences that at eighteen I heard M. Renan chatting with M. Berthelot . . . All my life, it has brought me precise observations, like a spyglass trained on phenomena which has allowed me to see a thousand things that I would not have noticed in the whole panorama. But as soon as scientists want to explain, they make suppositions . . . And the sense of life— the why of my presence in this world and the goal of my mission—still escapes me. My reason comes up against the incomprehensible at every turn. The more reasonable, and reasoning, I am, the more the incomprehensible manifests itself to me and envelopes me in its darkness. Why this thirst to understand, if my brain is condemned not to slake it?

Yes, but let's not make a drama out of it . . . This incomprehension has not really tortured me, because I am made in such a way that I still get more pleasure from looking than from understanding, and, in order to look, I have found the scientists' spyglass very satisfactory . . .

9.3 *Agnostic. Friendship of Vayron.* Maumort the philosopher.* I had by nature, I think, little inclination to take up this or that philosophical system, and Vayron's successive infatuations with Kant and then Spinoza had hardly any effect on me. It seemed to me, vaguely, that the adoption of a doctrine, however attractive it might be, would immediately deprive me of the easy freedom of nonpartisanship, of not holding any opinion, which I needed in order to follow my favorite instinct, which was to let my mind ramble with curiosity from one extreme to the other, as a spectator.

*Gustave Vayron, friend of Martin du Gard's.

There was also this. Unlike Vayron (and most young people), I had no hankering for certainty and in no way wished to find a truth which would satisfy me and to which I could dedicate myself. On the contrary. That hypothesis scared me. The only thing that really mattered to me was to be able to go on ruminating to my heart's content while sauntering in every direction, without constraint or restriction, and to avoid the trap of any certainty, which would forever have closed to me the pleasant path of conjectures.

9.4   *Agnostic. Maumort:* I am still surprised today, when I look at young people, to observe how rare, in the final analysis, are those who do not need to lean on a faith in order to live.

For me, it is a miracle how well I have always got along without it. In my time, I have known what it is to be concerned with metaphysical problems; like everyone, I have asked myself insoluble questions about our origin and our purpose, but with me this has never taken the form of an inner torment, an angst. And I have never aspired to a faith that would have freed me from these question marks by bringing me a solution to these enigmas.

Agnostic without pain: I do not know, I know that I do not know, and that is all. I accept my ignorance, I put up with it as with all the other imperfections inherent in the human condition. We come up against our limits at every turn: the limits of knowledge have never seemed to me particularly unbearable.

9.5   *Maumort. Tolerance. "Countertruths" and not "errors."* Since adolescence, I have made it a rule to call the opinions of those who do not think as I do "countertruths" rather than "errors"; and I have always done my best to make this essential distinction more than a matter of words, more than a healthy habit of thought, but instead a rigorous method, an unbreakable precept.

9.6   *Maumort's philosophy. To accept the limits of the knowable.* Due to a natural tendency that I find fortunate—since it spares me sterile spiritual torments—whenever my thinking comes up against the insoluble, the unknowable, I examine it with curiosity; then, as soon as I have clearly recognized it as such, I stop thinking about it, and refuse to bloody my nails in vain against that impassable wall.

This is not a piece of advice that can be given to those who lack this attitude. Many, on the contrary, hammer away at the insoluble and are fond of the state of mystical anguish into which this futile quest puts them.

·   ·   ·

9.7 *Maumort's philosophy. Metaphysical pangs. The* whys *and the* hows. I have had the luck to be naturally indifferent to the *whys* and interested only in the *hows*. I have never been tortured by metaphysical doubts, and I get along quite nicely without answers to the questions that obsessed Pascal. In other words, I have the good fortune to accept the limits of the knowable, without rebellion or despair. I take the universal enigma as a fact in the moral as well as in the physical domain. I have a good enough time observing man, beginning with myself, not to worry uselessly about his origins and his purpose, which will always elude us.

9.8 *Maumort (1887):* At that time, I naïvely thought that, given the pace of the discoveries of science and the investment of thinkers in a Europe that was stable and permanently safe from wars, I would not reach the end of my life without having solid answers as to most of the "great problems."

But I am still asking myself these questions . . . Is death the end of being, or only an unknown transformation?

Does mind depend on matter, or matter on mind? What is their exact relationship?

Does the world obey a law, or is it only a chaos in which forces clash at random?

Is man merely an accident in the cosmic immensity? Etc., etc.

So many insoluble enigmas.

11. The Jewish Problem

11.1 *Maumort. Status of the Jews. The Affair and the Jewish question.* (See Sécrétain, *Péguy,* p. 77 ff.) Maumort has always had a liking for the Jewish *leaven.* As a student, he already had many Jewish friends. He had noticed what the power of a Jew brings to a gathering of young people—and to society: the temperature immediately rises; any tendency to passivity, to bourgeois tranquillity, to frivolousness disappears. The Jew supplies the spark. He throws people's minds into confusion and makes the discussion more complicated, but he also feeds it, invigorates it with his contradictions and with his caustic, critical intellect. He causes the lifeless dough to rise. He exudes around him an intensity of life, triggers an acceleration of thought. Destructive, but always dynamic. He has a dramatic sense of things which comes to him from the astounding and terrible destiny of his race and which radiates warmth. He is a precious leaven of immoderation. He goes at once to extremes. Thanks to him, problems become complex, brains work; he is curious about everything, explores ideas through and through, with courage, abnegation, a personal disinterestedness that commands respect. He is dangerous like an explosive but useful like a force of nature. His mental quickness jostles everything, puts everything back in the crucible. He respects nothing, no tradition, no convention. He is an agent of propulsion in human civilization. Everything is a problem for him. He prevents us from falling asleep in immobility and indifference. He stimulates intelligences with his dynamic touch. Beside which his foibles are insignificant. Maumort admits to a certain practical anti-Semitism, he accepts that the state should try to rein in the Jews' worldly appetites, which are insatiable. It is the flip side of the coin. They can be annoying in business. But indispensable in the intellectual life of mankind.

It is a leaven of restlessness, which is necessary. They have suffered so much over the centuries that their energy as resisters and their vital need for protest and reparations need to be understood. They have a right to live, and the vitality of this fierce and combative people against the incredible fate that stalks them is full of grandeur and compels admiration. The eternal failure of this great people.

Maumort recalls having wanted to destroy an anthill, having fought for days against that tenacious will to survive that each night mended the damage he had inflicted during the day. He ended up giving in, ashamed to destroy that force, compelled to admiration before the mystery—which is that of *life.*

The nobility of the Jewish soul. Their kindness, their true Christian charity.

11.2   *Maumort. "Petit Niçois," 13 July '40. Concerning the Jews. The Jews' terror.* Use the following news item: A nephew of the physicist Einstein (Karl), a Jew, who had taken refuge in France, was interned in a camp near Bordeaux. Liberated after the Armistice but terrified at the idea of falling into the hands of the Germans, he slashes his wrists. Found in time and saved by French soldiers, in the Béarn. But while convalescing eludes the surveillance of the male nurses, flees, and throws himself into a torrent in the Pyrenees.

11.3   *Jewish question.* Maumort, at the time of the Dreyfus Affair, will have known an extraordinary Jew (maybe an officer like Mayer, a graduate of the Polytechnique), very intelligent, original, in a class of his own, having a *doctrine of salvation for the Jews* (the doctrine of G. Blumberg, founder of the magazine *Shem*).

To fight anti-Semitism by affirming the necessity for the Jews to recover their dignity by taking back the name of their race and by reconquering the land of the Hebrews.

Maumort will present a long summary of this strange doctrine and will contrast it with what Renan said: that the Jew is not an Oriental racial type; he is not descended from the Hebrews, but from *Europeans* converted to Judaism between 200 B.C. and the fifth and sixth centuries A.D.

11.4 *Maumort. Dreyfus Affair.* Without going so far as to say, as was done in Europe, that the French had a warlike temperament, I find there is something true in this. The French are *combative* by nature.

In the Dreyfus Affair, antimilitarism had a certain "military" character (likewise French anticlericalism, etc.). Let us suppose that the Affair had broken out in England. The advocates of a retrial and the opponents of the General Staff would have had a very different character, would not have worked up that very military passion against the army (embodied, for example, in a Péguy—one is hard put to imagine an English Péguy). I mean that, compared to the English, for instance, the French nation may seem to be a majority composed of military temperaments, the English nation being, if you like, a conglomeration of "civilians," minds that always prefer order and calm to a brawl, minds that do not ignite at every opportunity.

My newspapers are beginning to repeat daily that the fundamental cause of France's degeneration—and thus of our disaster—is the intrusion of the Jews into the nerve centers of the nation and their monopolization of the levers of command. This is obviously at the instigation of the Nazis, impatient to see the vague anti-Semitic movement, which had begun in France immediately after the Popular Front, spread and become more virulent. But as pressing as the German influence is, I do not think it suffices to explain this unanimity and insistence in the papers. The time is right. In the anguish and the ordeals that follow his defeat, the vanquished needs to throw the responsibility for his misfortune onto someone else. The Jew is there, the eternal scapegoat . . .

Anti-Semitism . . . I am very surprised to see the old adversary reappear. (I am wrong to be surprised. It is always the same adversaries that we see reappear. The clique gathered around Pétain in Vichy is just the same as what we used to call, in 1897 and 1898, the "General Staff." Same ambitions, same vanities, same amorality. And the same methods. And the same pretexts: reasons of state, the salvation of France. At bottom, it is always the Dreyfus Affair, which is only waiting for a chance to come back to life . . .)

In reality, French anti-Semitism is rather superficial in its form and content. Essentially contrary to the temperament and traditions of the country. In France, the true anti-Semites will always be few. People are anti-Semitic here for personal reasons, under the influence of false information and through self-interest; rarely out of principle. The best thing for the Jews would be for the attack that is emerging against them to be led by the Germans and driven by their propaganda, with their arguments and slogans. For to want to create a racial, Nazi-style anti-Semitism in France is an undertaking with small chance of success. The graft will not take. It is to hit French common sense on too sensitive a spot. A widespread popular movement inspired by racism is scarcely conceivable here.

I do not mean that a crusade against the Jews is practically doomed to failure. In the professions where they abound and where they excel—such as finance, commerce, the bar, medicine, the movie industry—mobs of colleagues and non-Jewish rivals, keenly interested in seeing the Jews stripped of their positions and having their access to these professions limited or forbidden, can easily be stirred up against them. This would end up producing many opportunistic crusaders and could make life very difficult for the Jews of France. But that is not really anti-Semitism. If it were decreed tomorrow that any man weighing two hundred and twenty pounds had to surrender his rations to the others and starve, it would be surprising to see how few thin people would stand up for the obese.

21. MAUMORT'S PHILOSOPHICAL DEVELOPMENT

21.1 *After Guy's death.* With Guy and Xavier I had an initial and vague revelation of *evil.* At Saint-Léonard, I had discovered and practiced it myself. Guy's sad end put me abruptly in brutal contact with *death.*

Evil, illness, death . . . It was the other side of life. That was the end of the world of my childhood, of the world, bathed in pure, harmonious, perfect light, in which my sister had reigned. The time of naïve illusions was irreparably gone, and I was driven out of paradise for good.

I had understood what the true, fearsome laws of life are.

21.2 *Maumort at boarding school.* To be blunt, until my arrival in Paris I had only mediocre, conformist, routine-minded teachers* who were limited by narrow conventions and had no opinions of their own. The best deserve no better epithet than that they were conscientious in their job. Lacking imagination, and mental freedom too. Not rising above any of the ready-made ideas they had to teach, or the subjects of their curriculum. Living off word lists and clichés.

I judged them only later. But at the time, as a student, I somehow sensed their deficiencies; enough, anyway, not to worship them, or blindly believe them. I was frustrated and hostile. Very inclined to contradict them and

---

*Presumably Maumort is referring to his teachers at Saint-Léonard, not his series of outstanding private tutors.

doubt their teaching. Impervious, and wanting to find something else, without knowing how or what. Thus, very much disposed to think for myself, as soon as I would be mature enough to do so, and well enough informed. This was what happened once I arrived in Paris. The discovery of contemporary thought, at the Sorbonne and in the gatherings at the rue de Fleurus, immediately triggered in me the need to go searching with these new guides, to orient myself in the universe, to seek my truth beyond the officially recognized truths.

It was in Paris that I encountered doubt—doubt, as a basis and a tool of knowledge—by listening to the discussions of my uncle, Renan, Berthelot, Taine, etc. Happy, suddenly released, to discover through these great models that it was permissible and even encouraged to question everything.

Thus my natural and still poorly justified unbelief derived excellent support from seeing Renan consider and reject dogmas.

That was when I began to admit to myself that metaphysics had never seemed to me anything but meager fare, and I dared to think that the ready-made ideas of my provincial teachers rested on a collection of absurdities.

21.3 *Maumort as an adolescent:* I got used to the unmistakable fact that there is really nothing good to expect from a life where evil rules and which is doomed to end in sickness and death. I became aware of the imperfection of everything, and that the happiness we dream of does not exist, for anyone.

Already at that time, my faith was so weak that I really did not believe in eternal life, in salvation. An unsatisfying existence, unachievable ambitions, a series of failures, and nothingness at the end of the final tumble: so did the human condition appear to me. Perhaps not with this clarity, but with the implacable force of the obvious.

Life is to tack between misfortunes and finally to fall into a black hole.

My schoolmates' carefree attitude seemed foolish to me.

That every life is destined to adversity and death seemed to me the supreme law, to which it was necessary to resign oneself. Nothing was more appealing to me than to find, in the Greek tragedies and the French classics, this recognition of that unavoidable fate that bends Oedipus, Philoctète, Prometheus, Phèdre and Hermione, Andromaque and Bérénice under its incomprehensible yoke. There lay the truth. Next to which, Bossuet and his *Universal History,* Pauline and Polyeucte struck me as *silly.*

I would have had to believe in eternal life to find any compensation in the poignant injustice of earthly life. And, when I discovered Vigny* and his haughty pessimism, I felt a sort of relief. Only there was an attitude worthy

*Alfred, Comte de Vigny (1797–1863), French soldier, writer, poet.

of a man, crushed by fate, facing it without hope, without bending, proud, irritated, disdainful, a victim of injustice, the only universal law; the nobility of hopeless rebellion. Defiance, the only answer to the silence of the deity. In Paris, in '87, this gloomy notion of things brightened considerably. I discovered that besides universal hardship, life also contained its beauty and its joys. I fell under its spell but without losing sight of the daily drama. Nearing the end of a life that has been happy, I am still at this same point.

21.4 *Maumort as an adolescent:* At seventeen, as a result of that bottomless nihilism into which I felt myself sinking, all the warmth that there was in my heart went out to mankind. I truly lived the *misereor super turbam.** I wept for human beings, all human beings.

And from that crisis of infinite pity something has always remained to me: this both passionate and indulgent interest I have had, starting at that time and lasting all my life, in human beings. A warm feeling, an emotional need to understand in order to excuse; a feeling that so cold an expression as *curiosity about others* would fall far short of describing. *Communion* would be less inaccurate; a compassionate communion, even when it was ironic. If I had been a novelist I would have truly loved all my characters, especially the most mediocre, and perhaps the most despicable.

21.5 *Maumort at the end of his adolescence, at the beginning of his active life. A certain nihilism. A certain nihilistic humanism.* I do not pretend that at twenty I had explored all of human knowledge, but the result was about the same. A thorough exploration of human knowledge would not have led me to a more absolute conviction that life had no meaning, or, at least, that our human condition condemned us to be forever unaware of such a meaning and to go without that explanation of the universe which would give man his reason to live.

I came to the obvious conclusion that life was not worth living; which was the final outcome of turn-of-the-century "scientism." And I took refuge in a transcendental attitude like Vigny's: I looked nothingness in the face, having no other compensation for this oppressive tête-à-tête than the sense of being clearheaded, the pride of preferring a discouraging truth to metaphysical illusions. If man has no destiny in the universe, better to know it than to delude oneself with vain hopes. These truths are bitter but salubrious.

Nothing was less tempting for me than the attitude of a Pascal, who, after having reached that level of development where one finds oneself confronting nothingness, and unable to tolerate the freezing glare of that obvi-

*To feel pity for the mob.

ous fact, capitulates, renounces logic, and consciously, deliberately, stoops to adopting a mindless faith in God.

Life has no sense, the life of mankind leads nowhere. God does not exist. The soul is not immortal. The individual personality is itself but an illusion. The very regret we have, despite ourselves, in finding only nothingness at the end of our quest, is a survival in us of the consoling errors of religions, which assured us of a destiny, showed us a path to follow and a goal at the end of the path.

I explored consoling religions and reassuring philosophical systems. I rejected those cures for the angst of nothingness. I preferred to suffer from the inevitable. I did not suppose that I could ever take refuge in metaphysical clouds. I was too repelled by obscurity and too much in need of clarity. How did it come to pass that I did not suffer so greatly from my nihilism? It was because I enjoyed the *game* of life. Refusing to deceive myself, I accepted the human condition within its narrow limits, and precisely in it I found a large enough variety of "diversions" to protect myself from all despair. Like an inmate condemned without appeal to life imprisonment, who would accept his incarceration with good grace because he would find in his prison a thousand distractions with which to while away the time, I submitted to the inevitable.

Thus did I come to terms with my destiny and find a *modus vivendi,* a practical and acceptable compromise, for my sojourn among men, not only in my material activity, my day-to-day occupations, my contact with the world, but above all in my spiritual activity, in the inexhaustible dialogue with myself, of which I never wearied.

21.6 *Maumort's philosophy as an adult: acceptance of social conventions.* I did not understand until much later why the nihilism I had come to at the end of my studies, when I entered the army, did not have tragic consequences in me and did not end up creating a profound despair in facing life.

There was, first of all, as a palliative, an antidote, my *youth* itself and my physical health. They saved me from a suicide like Werther's. The calm acuteness of my judgment led me to a complete negation; but practically, in reality, something solid remained to me: my taste for life and for its spectacle, my fellow feeling for people, my friendships, my hopes for a love life, the natural balance of my robust body—all sorts of benefits which were relative but positive and which I cheerfully put to daily use. I entered adult life stripped of all philosophical illusions, believing in nothing, not even believing that it was possible to believe; but, deprived as I was of the usual moral supports, I was nonetheless a strapping fellow of twenty-four starting off in life, and that start itself was a sufficient reason for living and a source of small joys. What I had before me was full of appeal: a new experience, regulated by precise duties, by many activities, by the responsibilities of a young leader, a career to follow, with no end of considerable amusements; to get to know a new milieu, to assume a certain social importance, to discover unknown countries, to campaign in the colonies, to plunge into exoticism, to taste heroism, to devote myself to a noble and useful task, *to live*!

This was already something, it was even a lot. But there was something else besides, something deeper that I did not understand until much later, that I did not even formulate until very late in the day, but that I sensed in myself, and from which I undoubtedly benefited at the time. What to call it? A "philosophy"? . . . No, but something that could be used to shore up my moral equilibrium: acceptance of social conventions; the ability (for lack of the universal order that my studies had led me to consider unobtainable, if not nonexistent) to make do with that *fictive order* that the centuries of civilization have ended up creating. The life of mankind was probably only a gratuitous game; but there were rules to this game. And by accepting the rules, it became possible, without believing in anything, to play the game of life courageously and cheerfully: the main thing was not to be deluded, not to take the conventionally established rule for the truth but only for a convention. Yet to go along with it willingly, to be able to act out one's part and play the game. Civilization rested on a fabrication with no basis whatsoever; but it was enough to accept the contemporary myths without illusion to be perfectly at ease in the world. I knew, for example, that common morality—and let's simply say "morality"—rests on nothing, that the distinction between good and evil is arbitrary; that it rules over society like the survival of the necessity for police and for organization. But morality rules, and it needs to rule so that things work and the complicated gears of the human community run smoothly. Thus there was no choice but to accept it, as something relatively valid.

The serious blunder would be to reject morality in the name of a transcendent spiritual attitude and so to find oneself sidelined. Everything is based solely on "con games." But everything has to be based on something. Therefore let us accept, with a smile, what is after all the very mild tyranny of the con games. Let us no longer try to scrutinize the illusory values whose universal acceptance makes for the cohesion of human societies. We know, once and for all, that they are illusory. Let us take them for what they are, in the privacy of our thoughts, but let us, like the common run of humanity, accept them with good grace, and we will enjoy, as those people do, the benefits of an accepted order. We will be in immediate agreement with the world of our time.

(I would now almost go so far as to say: it does not much matter if a law is just, so long as there is a law and a consensus among people as to the supremacy of that law.)

In reality, without formulating my practical philosophy in this way, without clearly perceiving it, I was already applying its principles. I constantly said to myself, when faced with social demands: an absurd convention in itself, or, at the very least, arbitrary; but a convention accepted by the majority. Thus, let us submit, without playing the wiseacre. For it is the only way to be able to live. And the absurd thing would be to have come into the world and not have found a way to live in it.

In fact, I had the smiling attitude of a minor Montaigne. I played the game nicely with everyone and without needless hostility.

A smiling philosophy, which made me happy; which made me even-tempered and easy to live with, I think, for those around me.

21.7 *Maumort as an adolescent:* Upon my arrival in Paris, my discovery—the first gleam at the end of that tunnel in which I felt myself lost—was that to think for oneself, to seek the truth, and to seek it through one's own means, off the beaten track and beyond the mental habits of the majority, was not only a right but a duty of conscience.

The right and the duty to reject what the official teachers taught, if I did not agree with what they taught. The right to judge the teachers. The right to prefer myself to them. I had a sudden revelation of the nobility there is in wanting to be oneself, and wanting to be only oneself.

And I immediately set out to question myself in all things in order to be as conscious as possible of who I was.

On certain days, at the beginning of that period, I felt a kind of iconoclast's intoxication in rejecting as nonsense certain things I had been taught to revere. I immediately stopped considering as respectable—and above all as necessarily true or correct—things that respectable people were teaching me or that I had been taught to respect. To separate a teacher's authority from the value of his teaching.

Not to believe what the preacher says for the sole reason that he has the reputation of an educated man with a superior intelligence. The right of *unlimited reappraisal.* I remember opening, in my mind, a huge category that I called "con games" into which, bit by bit, I disdainfully tossed nearly everything I had been taught to respect: the Catholic religion, popular morality, conventional distinctions between good and evil, official history, etc.

Which soon amounted to wiping the slate clean and starting all over again, in my compelling need for truth and the Absolute.

A violent, fervent, intoxicated iconoclast, and one who stopped at nothing. But I was not replacing my teachers with others. From the day when I dared to say to myself, "The Abbé X, professor of philosophy, is of no account, has no credibility, is a false and useless mind, a well-trained parrot, and everything he says has to be reexamined," I likewise said to myself while listening to Renan and Taine hold forth, "It is not because M. Renan believes this that it is good to believe it. He may be talking through his hat. Let's examine his assertions and convictions closely, without bias in his favor, to see what they're worth in themselves and what they're worth *for me.*"

This was monstrously impudent and prideful. But quite healthy. *I was forever cured of worshipping.* I have never again let anyone lord it over me. I have always examined an idea independently of the person who put it forward.

21.8   *Maumort. Brainwashing. Reaction of the critical mind.* It was starting from his experience of the Dreyfus Affair that Maumort really became resistant to all brainwashing. He understood that nearly everything one reads to keep informed about modern life is written by people of more or less dubious sincerity whose sole aim is to influence by appealing to the passions rather than to reason. Precisely the opposite of the scientific method, which sets outs the facts in order to come closer to the truth.

The aim is to make people take sides.

Systematic denigration of the opponent, by pasting a defamatory label on him: "Demagogue! Utopian! Foreigner! Gravedigger of the Republic! Antipatriot! Anarchist!" etc. Nowadays: "Fascist! Capitalist stooge! Arms dealer!"

Shameless use of noble sentiments: altruism, generosity, fraternity. In the name of truth, justice, progress (nowadays: democracy, liberty, right to work). Use of symbols: the flag, the cross, etc.

Use of catch phrases, presented out of context, often deformed, borrowed from great thinkers—Emerson, Goethe, Nietzsche, Jesus Christ, Confucius, Plato.

They appear to defend the "interests of the working class" or "the farmers," even though moved by the spirit of partisanship, domination, personal ambition. They invoke the family, the home.

The use of unverifiable or doctored statistics leads opinion astray; for example, to discredit an idea, a doctrine, to slander the private life of those who support that idea, smear their reputation, render them suspect.

Piling up of specious arguments to evade a precise, factual question.

Use of formulas that sway the public, such as: "You need to be really vile to . . . You need to be totally ignorant of the issue to . . ."

Appeal to a community spirit: "We patriots . . . We Catholics . . ."

Solution. Only one: at school, train the child's critical mind. Make him distrustful of all credulousness.

21.9   *Maumort is not a thinker. Maumort:* More than anything I admire *rigor* in thought.

But it is in vain that I have always tried to bring rigor to my mind. I remain deplorably superficial. Nothing of a *thinker*.

When it comes to life, I observe; when it comes to knowledge or books, I analyze, I understand. And this I do fairly well. I assimilate well what life brings me of experience and what books teach me. A good assimilator. And I am capable of "purring" without end over these acquisitions, of interminably chewing on my assimilations.

But to find the key to a problem with a well-conducted, in-depth meditation, no. I am not one of those people who rethink the world.

21.10   *Maumort as objective "thinker":* All my life I have made great efforts to be, above all else and in everything, objective. For a very long time I thought I was, and I awarded myself a badge for objectivity.

Today, when I think of those overviews, those "objective" meditations that filled the notebooks of my diary, I understand the extent to which I was deluding myself: it was pure subjectivity!

When I was "philosophizing" about general questions, I was actually interested in myself, in discovering and understanding myself.

And when I "philosophized" about others, it was more or less the same. I have always been infinitely more interested in men than in ideas.

21.11   *Maumort a "dilettante"? He will say:* I played the dilettante with my thought but not with life. I believed in the colonial cause, in the great role that France could play in Africa, in Morocco, and I devoted myself to it for years with all my might. At the time of the Affair, I risked permanently wrecking my career in order to take a stand. At the time of the Occupation, I did everything I could at my age on behalf of the Résistance. No, let's be fair: a dilettante perhaps, but I have taken my life seriously.

22. SKEPTICISM

22.1   *C. Bernard* wrote:* "In the sciences, faith is a mistake and skepticism progress." I add: "It is the same with everyday judgment and the way we lead our lives."

At twenty, our breviary was the *Introduction to the Study of Experimental Medicine.* The life and work of a Claude Bernard calmed our worries by giving proof that doubt is not the path of nihilism but—quite the opposite—that of discoveries, of intellectual progress, and of wisdom.

---

*Claude Bernard (1813–1878), French physiologist, author of *L'Introduction à l'étude de la médicine expérimentale* (1865).

22.2 *Nice, November '34.* I belong to an era when we had a need to understand and an inability to believe.

22.3 I have only *opinions* at a time when everyone has *convictions.*

A "traveler's" curiosity.

22.4 *Maumort:* On a great number of questions, the best arguments find me resistant: their main effect is to give me a better sense of the complexity of the problems they mean to solve: they make me more attentive, or even worried; but they do not persuade me. The fact that I can neither refute them nor accept them prompts me to think that the solution of these problems is something other than what I am being offered and what I have believed up until now.

To meet people who are better educated or cleverer dialecticians than I am is not enough to make me give up my intuitions. I suppose there is an answer; I regret not being able to arrive at it; but I hold to my positions, and I prefer the uncertainty of doubt to a conviction that everything in me rejects.

You can always counter a sophism with a sophism. You have only to find it.

22.5 *Fanaticism. Maumort and his guests:** I state yet again that if anything human remains alien to me, it is fanaticism.

I see it as Vice Number One, the great transgression against the mind. Different points of view are always reconcilable. The diversity of opinions would impart an intellectual richness to mankind if the intolerance of the sectarians did not turn that happy diversity into a poison fatal to the harmony of human societies.

22.6 *Maumort: The virtues of indifference.* It is a well-known phenomenon, and an unchanging one, that passion paralyzes reason. The climate of reason is relative indifference. We can only reason coldly. I have always observed that, during the time when a problem is at its most extreme, the solutions we think we will find to this problem are false and ineffective. It is only from the moment when a question has ceased to arouse a passionate interest that we have some chance of considering it in its entirety, analyzing its essence, seeing where the true difficulty lies, and discovering the real solution. In the heat of the moment, solutions are never anything but provisional, inadequate, unworkable. We understand clearly only what we have

---

*I.e., the German occupiers at le Saillant.

ceased to be interested in. This is true in arguments between individuals, in family and marital struggles, in misunderstandings of friendship and love. And it is true also in social clashes and conflicts between nations.

22.7 *Self-confident people. Maumort:* I have always felt an insurmountable distrust of those people who go along without ever seeming to let any inner hesitation slow or stop their momentum.

These people come fully prepared for any problem or question, all set with a precise and peremptory answer, just as if that question, that problem, had been the subject of a study to which they had devoted their entire life.

22.8 *Maumort:* Don't criticize me for being too skeptical! So few minds have skepticism within their grasp that it will never make up for the excessive credulity of the masses, and it will never dangerously tip the scale . . .

22.9 Fanaticism is so universal, so natural to man, that there is no point fearing that liberalism and tolerance will carry the day and make man incapable of action, decision, or initiative. These will never be anything but a weak and necessary antidote, a brake that slightly retards the blind thrust of the passions.

22.10 *Skepticism. Maumort:* Among minds that are inquisitive and naturally in search of truth, the greatest number unfortunately also have a compulsive need for certainty; without realizing that by running after the latter, they turn their back on the former.

The taste for certainty, so pressing in most people, seems to be a consequence of a noble appetite for truth. It is nothing of the sort. On the contrary, it is the search for truth that leads to a distrust of all certainty.

22.11 *Skepticism. Maumort:* Pascal—so engaging with his poignant anxiety—is hardly my man. I get along too well with Montaigne. Pascal would have called me a Pyrrhonist. And it is true. I think that supreme wisdom, though unimaginable, would coincide with the absence of all passion. And that, I was forgetting to say, wisdom seems to me the best form of human happiness. If I have not been able to—have not even tried to—rid myself of all passions, at least I have done my best to control them, if only by satisfying them in moderation. For I have always observed that any passion we satisfy usually has more of a tendency to wear itself out and lose its hold than to grow through practice, as the Church believes. But my true Pyrrhonism has been to avoid dogmatic statements all my life and to refrain from giving in to that common need for certainty, to that always disastrous need to believe which plagues most men, the weak and the mediocre even more than the great—although there are, to my knowledge, many Pascals in the intellectual world.

Nothing is entirely false. Our acts and our thoughts are the expression of our very diverse natures; of received influences; of the customs and the rules of the society in which we live.

22.12 *Maumort's philosophy. To accept man's inconsistency.* Used to considering myself with an indulgent curiosity as to the various tendencies and contradictions of my instincts and my feelings, I very early on acquired that essential notion of the diversity, the complexity, the *incoherence* of a human being, and I had no wish to fight that natural *inconsistency* of man; I immediately accepted it as a fact. This spared me those inner struggles that haunt the lives of so many adolescents. I did not go through "crises." I did not make a fetish of being logical with myself in every act of my life. What is more, I enjoyed that diversity, and I cheerfully assumed all the different and contradictory personalities I felt inhabiting me by turns. I was always sincere with myself, but successively. Thus I never insisted that one attitude in me was superior to another. I did not mutilate or harm myself by forcing myself to conform to this or that model.

I even quickly came to understand that by wanting to be rigorously consistent, we only succeed in limiting and impoverishing ourselves, becoming ossified. I downright relished surrendering myself to all my possibilities. In this I found the voluptuous satisfaction of freedom and inner richness.

22.13 *Maumort and experience:* As he grows older, Maumort learns to savor experience for itself. For a long time, as long as he still has some life ahead of him, what he likes in the experience he gains is what will help him in the future to live better, or more, or more usefully. When he has not much life left to him, the old man relishes the fruit of his experience for its own savor, which is much like the savor of wisdom. Knowledge will be of no further use to him. But he finds an immense satisfaction in it, all the greater since it is disinterested.

22.14 *Maumort. Liberalism like Rougier's.** I find in Rougier's book on *The Economic Mystiques* precisely the state of mind that suits Maumort, the doctrine that fits in perfectly with that old liberal bourgeois, born at the end of the Empire, opened to thinking through his contact with Renan, a man of

---

*Louis Rougier (1889–1982). His book *Les Mystiques Economiques* (1950) is subtitled "How One Goes from Liberal Democracies to Totalitarian States."

action and a soldier, a moralist, etc. An enlightened but not extreme socialist, loathing the stupidity of the masses and the illusions of universal suffrage; a proud spirit, a member of Lyautey's staff, with the temperament of a leader; unbelieving yet spiritual, fed on the principles of 1789, enamored of justice and clarity but contemptuous of demagogy, having a natural sense of grandeur; a true humanist, devoid of any humanitarian mawkishness, etc.

A major discovery. Maumort needed to be a great unrepentant liberal. Thanks to Rougier, he can be that in a superior way, without being thought of as a backward-looking reactionary, quite the opposite.

22.15   *Maumort. Duty of irony towards oneself.* Many people who are considered "modest" are simply "well-bred Frenchmen" who have been taught, quite young, that one of the their first duties was that of *irony towards oneself,* a rule of a specifically Franco-English code.

22.16   *Maumort.* Lyautey, who sometimes was annoyed by my skepticism, said to me one day: "There is in you a disconcerting contrast between the spirit of decision which you display in the slightest exercise of duty while on a campaign, and this indecisiveness which constantly appears in your conversation."

He wasn't stupid, Lyautey. I could have answered him that there were in me a will of decision and initiative on the plane of action and a wise will not to take sides, to remain independent, in the domain of the mind; and that this double and contradictory attitude was quite deliberate in me. In fact, this may have been what I did answer him.

23. MORALITY. GOOD AND EVIL

23.1   Resignation: virtue of the lazy.

I think that the people who pass for virtuous are the ones lacking the opportunity of temptation to do wrong.

23.2   *Maumort's morality.* In the attitude of uprightness and integrity that make this amoralist a man of principle, how to deny the role of conformity, the fear of consequences, the need for approval and social esteem, the desire to keep up his reputation, to stay on the right path, to avoid impairing a certain opinion (a "legend") that people whose respect he cares about have formed of him . . .

An *aesthetic* rather than an *ethic,* really.

.   .   .

A certain wisdom, too, which made him consider respectable society as a reality which must be taken into account, which there is no point in offending with behavior that is too free. A certain morality is as necessary, socially, as politeness.

23.3   *Maumort. Morality.* I have never had a sense of good and evil. At least I do not see morality in these terms. I would say rather that I have a certain feeling for values and for the hierarchy of values. Certain acts, commonly judged to be immoral, have never seemed so to me.

I judge actions not according to the scale of good and evil but according to a certain scale of values, which is to me a true scale. I strive towards everything that can develop in me the man that I am, that I am conscious of having the right to be. For me, this is the good. And I place in the category of evil certain constraints of common morality, because I have the feeling that they tend to diminish me.

23.4   *Maumort. Probity through lack of memory.* The man who has left me with the strongest impression of moral rectitude said to me one day:

"I've never had the slightest memory. I don't remember what I've done or said two hours afterwards. As a child, every time I wanted to lie, I contradicted myself, gave myself away, and got caught red-handed.

"Well, more than upbringing, this is basically what made an honest and trustworthy man of me. This total lack of memory gave me a life philosophy. I understood, very early on, that lies, shams, diplomatic scheming were not for me. I took on the habit of being frank, open, straightforward, and of always saying what is really on my mind.

"And this has worked extraordinarily well for me. It has given me, in everything I have undertaken, in all my contact with human beings, an absolutely exceptional strength. I am the one whose word is his bond and who is never doubted."

23.5   *Lying from an excess of imagination. Maumort:* There are many ways of lying. I have a friend who is particularly straight, honest, loyal, and even scrupulous. I quite surprised him the day I told him: "You're such a liar that no one can believe a word you say . . ." He became indignant; he is convinced that he is the frankest, most truthful person there is! And it is true that he has a horror of lying and that he never tries to conceal the truth. Yet all his life he has unconsciously bent the truth.

The explanation is simple: he has the mind of a romantic or a poet; *he thinks he is telling the truth, but he has far too much natural imagination to see and tell things as they are.*

23.6 *Inner reality.* I do not much like to moralize. Yet I am inclined to do so: it is my "Prudhomme" side. When I catch myself, I stop. Usually too late . . . "Why play the critic?" whispers an inner voice. "Haven't you always done what you wanted?"

Well, no. I may have appeared to be doing so, but it isn't true. My behavior has always been subject to a rule which was not, obviously, that of standard morality, which was . . . Here my pen is stayed. I cannot find words to express that general rule, that common denominator of my acts—of whose existence I am nevertheless so certain.

As I reflect upon this question of the common denominator, I think I can hazard this: I have always tried hard not to betray a certain "inner reality." Meaning what?

For someone with a certain level of intelligence, of character, of culture, his inner life, his emotional life, the particularity of his natural leanings, etc., constitute a whole, a structure, something which hangs together and whose elements are linked by connections that may be only partially visible but are undeniable and, for anyone who observes himself consistently, conscious and verifiable. This is what I call "inner reality."

I must proceed cautiously through this labyrinth into which I am venturing . . . Let us try to go further: this is not an abstract concept; for me, it is an indisputable reality. It is the core of my personality; my whole being is organized around it. And always has been: this is what forms an unbroken thread between the boy that I was and the old man that I am; it makes up my identity.

It is because this reality has an actual existence that, for me as I watch myself living, there is never any *contradiction* in myself; and not even any possibility of a contradiction. Although others, seeing me thinking and acting at various moments of my life can, from the outside, call this a "contradiction," I, who judge from the inside, feel that it only appears to be so. Others are wrong because they do not know everything. And when they think they pick up "seeming contradictions" of this kind, they commit the same blunder as if they were to say to the old man: "You will never convince me that you and that child who played with a hoop are the same person." Which surprises me as much as them but which still does not create any doubt in me. In fact, in each of us, everything is as closely connected as the links in a chain, everything is fundamentally and necessarily coherent; everything obeys an inner logic that is secret and sometimes subtle, but unfailing.

I have always been very attentive to this "inner reality." I have spent my life taking stock of it, jealously defining its boundaries. I was very careful to shield it from the influences that I sensed were opposed to it. To preserve the unity and integrity of our being is, to my way of thinking, the first of duties to ourselves. We need to carry our self-respect to that extreme. If I try to find what has usually determined my conduct, it is this self-respect, this need not to neglect or betray my inner reality. "Do what appeals to you, provided that you remain faithful to what is most authentic and most enduring in yourself."

I should now examine what relation exists between what I am saying here and the notion of conscience. But I have done enough introspection for tonight.

23.7   *Maumort.* The heart of human nature is intolerance and cruelty. This noted, there is no need to be surprised that most people have towards those who are different in their habits, their tastes, their ideas, their views, the instinct to consider them as adversaries and the desire to fight them by any means, to defeat and dominate them. Then, once they have triumphed, through force or cunning, the need to persecute them, with the hope of destroying them.

Intolerance and cruelty make the history of mankind a series of battles and persecutions.

A tiny minority, equally suspect to the bigots of all parties, escapes this law of nature. The free, liberal, tolerant, understanding, and skeptical man is bound to be isolated.

23.8   *Purity.* Let us pity the "pure." The etymology of "purity" is certainly *paupertas.**

24. RELIGION. THE PROTESTANTS

24.1   Aragon,[†] *Les Cloches de Bâle,* p. 420 [1934]. I rather like this statement by Aragon: "Churches did not impress him, they even always aroused a sort of disrespectful mirth in him, as if *in front of a clumsy magician whose tricks you see through.*"

24.2   Benda,[‡] "Sporades," *N.R.F.* October 35. "You have to understand that this woman is Catholic, and does not *want* to be happy."

24.3   1938. I am like Francis, the hero of a novel by Clarisse Francillon (*Le Plaisir de Dieu,* 1938, p. 32), whose Bible was always open to the chapter of

---

*Poverty. Martin du Gard is amusing himself with an imaginary etymology.
[†]Louis Aragon (1897–1982), French poet, novelist, essayist, spokesman for Communism.
[‡]Julien Benda (1857–1956), French writer.

Job at the verse: "It profiteth a man nothing that he should delight himself with God."

24.4   *God's common sense.* "Your God may have every perfection," he said to his old country priest, "but when we see how the world works, we have to suppose that the one who created it had no common sense at all."

24.5   *Maumort. As old Rosalie used to say:* It may have been the Good Lord who created the world, but surely it was the Devil who organized it.

24.6   *Maumort. Dr. Gévresin is wont to say:* Among the wonders of nature that should be used as proof of the existence of God, there is that miraculous invention of the sphincter.

We need only think of the mass of foul matter and putrid gases that each of us constantly walks about carrying in his bowels and to imagine what life in society and the charm of an elegant gathering would be like if Providence had not furnished all of us with the most sophisticated of hermetic seals.

24.7   *Maumort's religious life. No need of God.* To a friend from his youth, who has lost his faith and is suffering as a result, and who is surprised by Maumort's perfect poise in his lack of belief, Maumort answers: "It would not be right to call me a monster because my moral code manages without any religious belief or afterlife. I have no need of eternity.

"For thousands of years, hundreds of millions of civilized men, highly spiritual and moral, the Chinese, have lived without believing in another world, without God. But not without religiosity, without cultivating their religious feeling."

24.8   *Maumort and religion.* Maumort sometimes wondered how it came to pass that, being who he was, he was not harder on, or downright repelled by, the Catholic religion.

This probably results from the fact that his doctrine is rooted in a deeply pessimistic view of the world. Maumort and a Christian are in agreement, at the starting point, that man's life is a "vale of tears," in which injustices, undeserved suffering, and needless pain abound. This fundamental, reasonable pessimism is the basis of all the dogmas of Christianity: original sin and expiation, the difficulty of achieving salvation, the fear of death . . .

From that point on, the agreement ceases, of course. The unvarying responses of the Christian faith are absurd but touching. Maumort thinks it all right—for others . . . *So few men are equal to despair!*

So hard for them not to drown in it! Religion helps most of them see the world as it is—unjust and bad—and yet accept it thanks to a specious magic trick: God wanted it that way for your salvation.

"I am happy that, starting in my childhood and for my entire life, I have lived among believing souls. The great spiritual advantages that believers derive from their religion for their inner balance, the support it gives them in misfortune, are real assets whose value I have never underestimated.

"Happy, no doubt, those middling minds whom the absurdity of dogmas and all the irrationality of religion do not keep from believing. It is to my contact with them, although that contact has often made me suffer, that I owe my always having practiced tolerance. I do not know if I would have arrived at tolerance through reflection alone.

"Man's life is so miserable! More power to him if he manages to find solace by counting on the compensations of a future life. This is good social hygiene. Why forbid him these soothing illusions? To take away from a believer the support he finds in Providence, to open his eyes when he entrusts himself to divine kindness by pointing out all the evil, all the disorder that triumphs everywhere in the universe is to act like someone who reveals to a patient who is doomed and does not know it the mortal illness that is consuming him.

"The worship of truth does not justify pointless cruelties."

24.9   *Maumort. Protestant hypocrisy. How this constant hypocrisy is linked to the obsession with duty.*

A memory of an episode that happened with Coppet* in Figeac.

One evening, at dinner, a political conversation about the socialism of the S.F.I.O. Party,† the errors committed, the lack of a clear and easily absorbed doctrine, etc. I throw myself into a well-founded critique, and with all the more freedom since Coppet has always known of my sympathy for the Socialist Party, my friendship with Blum, my admiration for Jaurès, etc. Coppet defends socialism tersely and immediately turns the conversation in another direction.

The next day, finding me alone, he tells me:

"I want to go back to what you said yesterday, which I didn't at all like."

"But you yourself admit . . ."

"Yes, I agree almost entirely with what you think. But I don't say it. And that's the difference between us. Thanks to my upbringing, I have a sense of duty that has always been missing in you. Just because something is true is no reason to say it. Quite often it's even *a very good reason to keep your mouth*

---

*Marcel de Coppet, Martin du Gard's son-in-law.

†*Section Française de l'Internationale Ouvrière,* or French Section of the Workers' International, informally known as the Socialist Party.

shut. It is to do damage to a just cause, to betray a party that is our own and that we have to defend."

"Blindly? No matter what it does?"

"Blindly, in front of other people."

"But first off, we were among ourselves . . . And not at a public election rally . . ."

"It makes no difference. We were among family, and already there was too much of an audience. Neither your wife, nor mine, nor Daniel (he was eleven at that time) needs to know the weaknesses or the mistakes of the party. It's a question of *mental discipline* . . . You see, I have an absolute principle: never to open my mouth, no matter if it's one-to-one, without first thinking what influence my words will have on the person I'm talking to, and without choosing from among the ideas that I am about to express the ones that will steer him in the right direction, have a good effect on him. Never to speak casually."

"And sincerity?"

"There is a higher duty than being sincere. It is to serve, by every means, what you think is useful to progress, to the right social orientation, to the collective good. Always to think, before speaking, of the effect that our words will have, of the role that we want to play, of the ideas that we want to spread and see prevail."

24.10   *Protestantism.* The Protestant religion is less idiotic than the Catholic, but I think it corrupts man more.

Catholicism cannot be said to be a school for loyalty and frankness; but it cannot be said to be a school for deceitful behavior, either. I would say this about Protestantism.

To say that a Protestant is deceitful or hypocritical is a cliché. This is wrong, if one understands by it, as do those who repeat this cliché, that the Protestant dupes the people around him, that his virtuous words are knowingly uttered with the intent of misleading others. On that score, Catholicism produces as many duplicitous characters as Protestantism or as atheism.

When I think that the Protestant is a hypocrite, I very particularly mean that the Protestant has an extraordinary propensity for deluding himself.

The Protestant has a strong tendency not to see the selfish, calculating, petty reasons whereby he carries out this or that act and to persuade himself that his motives are austere and virtuous and that by behaving in the way he does he is obeying the moral duties that his religion has filled his head with. Example: a Protestant is someone who has the temerity to think and to say: "We don't eat well at home; but our cook is a poor creature we took in out of charity, to save her from poverty and prostitution, and we willingly sacrifice good food to perform this basic duty to our neighbor." And he believes it when he says it. He is truly oblivious to the fact that out of avarice he has leapt at the chance to hire an unmarried mother who is willing to accept a paltry wage in order to have a job and whose misfortune he exploits to treat her as a pariah, feeding her only scraps, making her sleep in a garret that no servant would want, and keeping her on duty for fifteen hours a day "to help her become rehabilitated through work."

A Catholic is perfectly capable of this miserliness and abuse. But he will not boast of it, because he is conscious of his bad instincts. He will not so easily fool himself. He will admit to it at confession, so aware is he of his low nature.

The Protestant angles for high office and is not afraid to say, in all good faith: " I consider it my duty to serve my country," etc.

24.11   *Maumort and atheism. He will say:* I have trained all my curiosity on the things of the human realm, on what concerns man, his individual and social behavior, his nature, his twists and turns. The cosmic mystery has always left me rather indifferent. I effortlessly accept it as unfathomable, unknowable. Whence my indifference to God. Faced with the mystery of the universe, I have always been repelled by religious explanations; I dismiss them rather than argue about them; they seem to me implausible and in fact of a very complex, imaginative naïveté and vaguely absurd. Even when I was a child, the priests' teaching had no real hold over my ability to believe. Something in me balked. God, the creation of the world and of man, the divinity of Christ and all that follows seemed to me like ingenious and unlikely fables. I somehow felt that "it wasn't serious."

I instinctively refused to let myself get bogged down in that religious hodgepodge, in which I saw nothing solid or probable. If not incoherent, at least coherent in a way that was very artificial and gratuitous and that did not satisfy my type of mind. Subtle and altogether inadequate explanations of a great surrounding mystery that I felt no urgent need to solve. I preferred that incomprehension to the poor hypotheses that were offered me by the Church.

24.12   *Maumort and Catholicism.* My religiousness—I will even say my belief (since I am reluctant to call by the name of "faith" that undivided hold that catechism lessons, my sister's fervor, and the example of everything around me at the time had on my simple child's mind)—was for me only one of the forms of my submission to the teaching and rules of my family. It gradually decreased along with that submission. The day when I felt independent enough to challenge orders and refuse to be blindly obedient, was, quite naturally, the day when I challenged dogmas and refused to practice religion.

24.13 *Maumort's antireligiosity.* It must be shown through what experiences Maumort came to hate all religious fanaticism.

1) In his childhood at le Saillant, he witnesses a first drama brought about by beliefs too confidently held.

2) Afterwards, he arrives in Paris, and, in the skeptical and Renanian society of Chambost, discovers the advantages of tolerance and lack of belief.

3) While stationed in Versailles (from 1888 to 1890) he is involved in a second drama caused by intolerant fanaticism. This time, with the perspective of his Parisian experience, he protests and fights in vain against the consequences of those fanatical attitudes.

4) Later (1897 and '98), the [Dreyfus] Affair offers him a new example of this clash of fanatical positions.

Thus the hatred for all partisan bigotry is implanted in him.

24.14 *Maumort's personal ideas on contemporary religious evolution.* Since World War I, and especially since 1940, the accumulation of suffering has caused an exacerbated revival of religiosity in the world that the Churches have taken advantage of as much as have the charlatans of occultism.

A regression of trust in scientific progress, a trust that, at the end of the nineteenth century, had drained the religious instincts.

All religiosity rests on the fact that it is primarily a practical means of relieving moral anguish or physical pain by means of formulas, rituals, which bring solace through hope.

In the great present upheaval of consciences, there is a general psychological disturbance; so many reasons for despair and uncertainty, so many families rent apart, ruined, so many fears for the future, so many bodies and souls enslaved that mental turmoil has thrown many of these unfortunates into the superstitiously receptive state of primitive man.

A resurgence of all the illusion-mongers.

One needs only to think of all the clairvoyants, astrologers, etc. whom the press never fails to publicize and who are secretly patronized by educated and cultivated people who would never have been seen going to fortune-tellers in the past. People's intelligence is no longer enough to protect them because they are depressed, dazed, anxious, disoriented, hungry for certainties that they can no longer find by themselves.

In this atmosphere so favorable to religiosity, the Catholic Church has found an opportunity for a comeback that seemed unimaginable in 1900.

Thanks to the separation of Church and State (1902), it has found both a means of propaganda (the Church as victim, martyr to anticlericalism, etc.) and a chance for inner purification. It has gained in spiritual power and worth what it lost in the temporal domain. More independent of the state authority. Fewer priests, but more faith.

Two phenomena to note:

1) Abundance of the faithful; return of the lukewarm and an increase in new converts.

2) Inner evolution of the Church, return to evangelical purity; a real revolution, begun by a young, fanatically Christian clergy scorning material goods, imbued with a revival of evangelical socialism, returning to the people, taking up the defense of the destitute. A horror of the clericalism of the great prelates. And, as the generation of the old 1900-style "prelates" disappeared, these new ideas penetrated the higher realms of the Church.

The Church of Rome frees itself from the *lower forms of piety* (Mauriac,* *La Pierre d'achoppement*) and recruits the faithful from among the intellectuals, the scientists (Lecomte du Noüy, etc.).

25. COSMOS AND NOTHINGNESS

25.1   *Adapting to nothingness. Maumort's nihilism:* Each of the paths of thought, each of the distant perspectives that it runs out into, always leads to nothingness.

But I am fortunate in being able to resign myself to nothingness. The despair that it arouses in me does not change a certain physical tendency—and a happy one—to want to live, to want to play the game of life, and even to like that game. To know that all is vanity, as in Ecclesiastes, does not prevent certain natures, like my own, from finding some sweetness in this vanity of earthly life, and from enjoying it. I manage to do without hope, to accept the limits of the unknowable, to resign myself to the inevitable, and to continue the course of my life with a disillusioned attitude but without losing my balance.

25.2   *The plan of the Creator.* The universe? An immense chaos of forces that intertwine and clash at random, giving birth to every possible phenomenon. No *plan*. If there were a plan, evil and pain would be unknown. It is *Homo sapiens* who wants to impose order at all costs and who fights against evil, injustice, suffering, and death.

Vigny is right: if there were a creative and responsible god, he would have to appear before man and justify himself.

---

*François Mauriac (1885–1970), French novelist, essayist, playwright; the book cited is *The Stumbling Block.*

25.3 *Life?* A series of possibilities, that is how it presents itself to man. If there is an order behind all these chance events, he knows nothing of it, can know nothing of it . . . And each of us throws himself into the game, and, from among the possibilities that offer themselves, chooses the makings of a personal destiny that is not too incoherent.

26. DEATH AND OLD AGE

26.1 *Death in Russia (February '31). Regarding Russia's materialism.* A fascinating investigation would be to find out how people die in Moscow. A survey of their last moments. What death is like without religion, among people who have truly been sterilized of the germs of religiosity through an entirely materialistic upbringing.

26.2 *Maumort.* I have long said, complacently, that I was "between two ages." I no longer am, alas. I am at the end of my time; and as I no longer count on the hereafter, I have no other "age" to reach except death.

26.3 *Maumort and nothingness.* I have arrived at an age when one lives daily in the solemn proximity of death. One is then aware of the emptiness of human ambitions, the emptiness of any success, the emptiness of moral values, the emptiness of life, the emptiness of death, the primal and total emptiness.

26.4 *Maumort facing death.* The anguish of nothingness, or the religious hope in an afterlife? I choose the anguish, and "choose" is quite an inadequate word . . .

Besides, although I have known the anguish of the void at that time when a man, around the age of forty, suddenly realizes that he is at the end of the ascending phase, spies the other, downhill slope, and goes through a period of vertigo and despair in the face of the brevity of a life, I left that stage behind a long time ago.

I do not know what terrors the hour of death has in store for me, but I know that it is no longer nothingness that causes me anguish—only the fear of the final physical and mental sufferings.

I maintain that if I were certain that my heart would stop beating some night in my sleep, I would have no more fear of death.

26.5 *Maumort.* I am like Chénier's* "young captive":

*André de Chénier (1762–1794), French poet and political journalist.

"Quoi que l'heure présente ait de trouble et d'ennui,
*Je ne veux point mourir encore."**

26.6. *The fear of death (June '48). Maumort:* In the business of the day, we almost manage to forget her, the gloomy bitch . . . Despite my lame leg and my little physical upsets I am sound enough in body and mind, spry enough, to enjoy living and all sorts of activities. But at dawn, or on sleepless nights (at that moment of intense inner lucidity that precedes complete bodily awakening), it is her time, and she never fails to appear! Her first care is to remind me of my age, and I am seized with dread: I always forget how old I am, and that the coming day is only a "probable" reprieve . . . I tell myself that tomorrow I will no longer be here; and the anxiety that takes hold of me, always the same, is intolerable. It has a double cause: what terrifies me is, on the one hand, the fact that I will soon not exist; and, on the other, that I do not know what my end will be like, what final suffering I will have to undergo before ceasing to be. Now, if there is nothing absurd about fearing the throes of death, what is absurd, and what reason should be able to protect us from, is feeling a bitter despair for the moment when we shall have ceased to be here. I weep, not only for my dying self, but for my dead self: nothing is more senseless, since this supposes that I imagine myself being dead, and aware of being so: which is the height of idiocy. On the contrary, I ought to find a supreme consolation in the certainty that the one thing, par excellence, from which I will never suffer, is precisely being no more. But these are the logical arguments of a man awake, when the soothing light of day and the exercise of my vitality stand between me and the specter of death. In the dark hours of the nightly rendezvous, I cannot defend myself from this *double* terror: the one, very legitimate, of mortal illness, of the death agony; and the other, really absurd and pointless, of the moment when I will have ceased to live, of precisely the moment when I am certain that I have escaped all possibility of pain for good.

26.7 *Maumort. Age.* Throughout these memories, he comes up against "nevermores."

Nevermore this feeling, this impulse, this desire, this hope, this bracing illusion . . .

Nevermore . . . This includes everything from the bicycle to love . . .

26.8 *Old age. Maumort.* I do not dislike the man I have become with age; I accept myself. I sometimes even want to say, like Goethe in his seventies: "I

*"No matter what trouble and woe the present hour holds,
   I do not want to die yet."

am different, but I do not feel inferior to the man I was." This thought, if I needed it, would help me bear the weight of the years. To tell the truth, I bear my old age easily. I even feel a certain pleasure in growing old. Yes, unquestionably, there is a great sweetness in living on, as I do, in the shadow of death.

26.9   *The "physical" warning upon waking up.* The true explanation for that special lucidity at the moment of waking up, which reveals to us some painful little spot in some part or other of the body that is not perceptible during the day, is, I think, that in the fully awakened state the multiplicity of the reactions of our consciousness to external perceptions prevents us from hearing that secret confidential communication of the body. In reality, that painful spot never stops "expressing itself," complaining, sending out its SOS. But we do not hear it. In that moment between sleeping and awakening, the hum of the world does not hinder us from hearing. In that external silence, in that absence of ordinary reactions, our sensitivity is naturally attuned to listening.

26.10   *Maumort:* I often think of what the priest in Menneville said to me one day, a man of experience, a confidant of family secrets: "You need to see things as the Good Lord made them. Death is a deliverance. It releases us from our loved ones. And it releases them from us . . ."

And he repeated, without making a point of it, in an undertone, his eyelids lowered: "It releases us from our . . ." etc.

26.11   *Before death.* At that unprecedented moment when, between the living person and the one who is going to die, no other dialogue is possible than that of looks, no other exchange than that of a silence full of thoughts and love.

27. FAITH IN MAN. STUPIDITY

27.1   *Maumort. Human stupidity.* It has excuses. Its principal cause is *ignorance,* according to the generally held views, and in this is found a very compelling cause for hope: the development of education, without perhaps ever completely eliminating stupidity, ought gradually to reduce it. This confidence was widespread in the last half of the nineteenth century and is still prevalent, despite the very poor results achieved by compulsory schooling. It is true that the education given in public elementary school to the vast majority of children is still quite rudimentary, quite uneven, and could be greatly improved; the results could unquestionably be much better.

But my experience as an army officer has made me skeptical. There were still a lot of illiterates among the recruits at the start of my career. That number has been falling. (To an incredibly inadequate degree, however! But let's go on.) What struck me is that this decrease in illiterates seemed to make little if any difference in the level of general stupidity. An unsurprising observation when the countless number of idiots that one meets among educated people and university graduates is taken into consideration.

It would be fairer to admit that human stupidity has two causes that may well be insurmountable. The first is the hellish complexity of reality; the second is the extreme difficulty that most people have in properly interpreting that reality, since a clear vision of it is always impossible to man, who, with his faulty senses, can never glimpse more than a partial view; and we all have an individual, incomplete idea of reality (and incomplete in different ways, according to one's particular nature, one's peculiar inability to grasp reality). This makes the general stupidity more excusable, certainly, but it also indicates that human stupidity is virtually irremediable.

To achieve a result, given that it seems scientifically proven that the acquisitions of individuals are not passed on hereditarily (but only through oral and written tradition), we would have to consider the question from the angle of selection. Imagine a humanity which, through processes of selection, favors only the reproduction of individuals whose ability to interpret reality is, through a freak of nature, appreciably better developed and richer than the average. There is no other way to keep stupid people from being born and to raise the level of human intelligence.

Time and again, I have observed that it was by no means among the illiterate that the stupidest people were to be found, and I strongly doubt that the total elimination of illiterates would have a conclusive effect on human stupidity.

27.2 *Human stupidity. The stupidity of clever people.* Stupid people do not have a monopoly on stupidity. We have all known lofty intellects, minds of great learning, who, in some domain, displayed an abysmal ignorance and looked manifestly idiotic.

I even seem to have noticed that the idiocy of an intelligent man could reach an unparalleled opacity, since it is generally exacerbated by a naïve arrogance, which comes precisely from the fact that a clever man usually finds it very hard to imagine that he may also be a fool.

27.3 *Maumort. Natural credulity:* I have always been astounded by the ease with which men believe things they have never seriously investigated and about which they do not have even the beginning of a proof. Note that many of them know they have been mistaken a hundred times over and are sincere enough to admit it, yet this thought doesn't at all make them doubt their impulsive beliefs of today.

Here again, at bottom: human stupidity.

What is the use of fighting prejudices? It seems that man cannot do without them and that any exploded prejudice is immediately replaced by another. Is even the one who attacks them exempt from them? He conceals his own. I still prefer the confession of that intelligent friend who always used to say: "I have hardly any prejudices, but I do have this one . . ."

27.4   *Maumort. Stupid generations.* It may not be true that in every age the same percentage of intelligence, taste, etc. exists in the world. There are generations that have less perceptivity, less taste, than others. There are ages in which common opinions are less stupid than in others; and ages in which people think little and badly.

27.5   *Maumort. Flawed logic.* Right after the "fanatics," the people you have to watch out for most are the ones with flawed logic.

Difficult to spot, because difficult to define. There is a tendency to place among the unsound thinkers all those that do not think as we do. What especially indicates unsound thinking, is that faculty, all too widespread, of extracting completely erroneous conclusions from a truth. This is the giveaway. To get trapped in an error by relying on an obvious truth is the certain mark of flawed logic.

Flawed logic can be joined to a very keen intelligence. In such a case it can be compared to a very sensitive barometer that would always be in movement but would never predict the weather correctly because it had not been properly adjusted.

27.6   *Maumort. Compulsory education.* I thought a lot about it while talking to my men when I was a young officer. Especially the reservists in the war.

I sometimes wonder if human stupidity is not on the upswing. An ignorant peasant from the time of La Fontaine who could neither read nor write may not have been markedly less stupid than such-and-such a farmer that I know, who has his *brevet élémentaire,** reads his newspaper every day and talks about it at the café, listens to the radio, goes to the movies several times a year, never misses one of his party's political rallies, has amorphous notions

---

*Diploma a student receives around the age of fourteen or fifteen.

about everything, and permits himself to lay down arguments with all the narrow-minded assurance of an imbecile.

The ignorant man of earlier times, who did not allow himself to reflect on much of anything, who followed his natural intuition, the advice of his elders, his local tradition, and who abided by customs, attained from the outset a certain sterling common sense which preserved him from the pretentious stupidity of today's average man, who receives everything and does not pull a single idea out of his own head.

In the past, he knew he was ignorant; now he thinks he is smart.

27.7 *Maumort:* I have often been sorry that I did not live in those days when humility was common and natural, and when most men, most women, and nearly all adolescents knew that they were not qualified to reason, or only about very few matters, and accepted not having opinions about everything and left it up to a few elite minds, who had given proof of wisdom, to supply, for the great problems that face mankind, the provisional solutions that great intelligences of every generation put forward.

27.8 *December '40. Human stupidity.* Every life that departs from the average is always, in the final analysis, dedicated to a struggle, eternally the same: the struggle against human stupidity. Stupidity, which begets baseness and malice. A struggle that begins very near yourself, in the home, in the family, and which expands, in widening circles, to your acquaintances, to strangers, to the public, to nations. And when you have thirty or forty years of futile struggle behind you, and you come to realize there is nothing to be done, that people's stupidity is a fundamental fact of life in society on this planet, as enduring, and as subject to influence, as the elements, as the sea or the rock, as the wind or the rain, you withdraw; and you finally discover that no one is a better example of this universal stupidity, against which you have quixotically fought, than yourself! The moment has then come for a smile and resignation: there is nothing for it but to curl up into a ball, smoke opium, and prepare for an easeful disappearance.

27.9 *Maumort. Faith in man.* It is true that man is an ugly monkey, and that you can go on forever describing his low instincts, all his mean, cruel, and despicable acts. But that there are men enamored of justice, devoted to the point of sacrifice, capable of reason, faithful in friendship, full of pity for suffering is enough to deny us the right to speak ill of man.

All the evil he does comes, upon close inspection, from stupidity. If we decided to fight stupidity as we have fought the plague, leprosy, alcoholism, and syphilis, who knows whether we might not succeed in improving the race?

27.10 *Faith in man. Maumort as an adolescent.* What I kept longest, before arriving at a general negation, was my trust in man, a naïve faith in human progress, in the unlimited perfectibility of humanity.

On this point I profited from the example of my uncle Chambost and his famous Sunday confederates. All those agnostic humanists and scientists were imbued with that faith.

I lost it quite fast. It seems to me that this happened at Saint-Cyr, in that daily contact with my fellow students, with man. And my whole life experience has done nothing to bring that supreme hope back to me.

27.11 *Maumort. Faith in man.* The sense I have of human stupidity and villainy is very close to despair and despondency. I try hard to hang on to the little faith that remains to me and is precious to me. I try hard to convince myself that the situation is not irreversible, that the perfectibility of the human animal remains true in itself, but that he is still only at the beginning of the beginning of the ascent, and that he will need thousands of years and thousands of steps backward in order to advance a single centimeter.

27.12 *Faith in man.* In the end, the hopelessness of man's perfectibility rests scientifically on the principle of the intransmissibility of acquired characteristics. Every child who is born is a specimen of the primitive human species. If the present adult differs from the cave-dwelling adult, it is not because he is essentially different but because he has benefited, after his birth, from the educational treasure amassed experimentally by successive generations over thousands of years: education allows him, in a few years, to pass through the stages of an age-old civilization whose acquisitions human society has securely and progressively transmitted. Which amounts to saying that every man of today is a primitive wild animal dressed up in the cast-offs of a line of collectors and improvers: it is not at all surprising that these fine outfits sometimes fall off, according to the circumstances, and leave the primitive man standing naked, prey to his basic instincts.

27.13 *One of the aspects of Maumort:* "I have seen everything dwindle and perish. My time is past, yet I do not despair of the world." (Around 1942.)

27.14 *October '44. Faith in man. To the young people of '44:* The underground "Éditions de Minuit" have published a certain number of Péguy's texts. Between 1900 and 1914, Péguy had already denounced everything that horrifies the "liberated" youth of 1944 . . .

The people of my generation have believed in a miraculous recovery several times already:

after the Affair,
after the publication of Wilson's Fourteen Points,
after February '34 and the advent of the Popular Front;
each time we were let down.

I am wholeheartedly with you. Your refusals and your wishes are mine. But don't ask me for enthusiasm anymore . . . I am skeptical as to the perfectibility of man and his institutions.

27.15   *August '48. Trust in life. Maumort:* I admire the younger generation when I see it full of vitality and hope. I know that it is pushed in that direction by the dynamism of youth. All the same, it deserves more credit than we do for trusting in life, since we old people know how beautiful and rich and exquisite life can be when the world has reached the balance and stability of a relative peace. We have known that; and our illusion was to take for a result achieved by progress what was only a fleeting moment of equilibrium and grace. We believed that this was civilization and that men who had attained that degree of development would not allow themselves to be thrown back into barbarism. How would the young know that? What we tell them of it appears to them the drivel of old men weeping over their own youth. They live in an atrocious world, which seems normal to them. Yes, those who are happy to live, those who hope, are praiseworthy, and we need to have patience with those who are not discouraged by the contemplation of the absurd. We have the advantage over them of knowing by experience that life can be beautiful, that progress is possible, that civilization is not completely a pipe dream, and that there are moments when the life of mankind is not assailed by every misfortune.

28. PROGRESS

28.1   *Is the evolution of humanity towards wisdom inconceivable?* In a community of reasonable human beings, the exercise of reason could assume the role that the religious or national mystique holds in modern societies. But a majority of reasonable human beings would be required* . . . (Why not suppose that the human species is heading towards this goal, and that the very slow progress that mankind is making over thousands of years is pointing towards *wisdom?*)

---

*Roger Martin du Gard: A majority with the will to pool what each person can attain of moderation, sound judgment, understanding, and wisdom to create an atmosphere of spiritual equilibrium and brotherhood in the community.

28.2 *Scientific progress.* The progress of science is denied. By whom? By the bulk of the people who think and write. But it is all too often forgotten that almost no one has the right to speak about science.

Who was Brunetière to declare the failure of science? What qualifications as a *scientist* did he have that would have allowed him to judge the work of scientists and not only to judge the work but also to rise above it, extract the laws of the whole, etc.?

Then what is happening? The ignorant (and I am speaking of Brunetière: I except Gourmont, Bergson, le Dantec, perhaps Maeterlinck) deny the progress of science because they see it roughly, from the outside, and only put their attention on the daily back-and-forth, the fluctuation of the scientific life, which advances today and tomorrow retreats, and seems to waver in place. Only scientists believe in science, and they are the only ones who can have an opinion.

28.3 *Science advances all the same, with detours. Maumort will say (example of detours):* In 1890, when I was twenty, we were still arguing passionately about Evolution. But Darwinism was in a bad way. Lamarck had been rediscovered and was being set against Darwin. The theories of the latter looked like ingenious but simplistic daydreams, whereas the transformism of Lamarck was a serious doctrine that satisfied the mind.

But then, in the last fifteen years or so, the wheel of science took another turn, and Lamarck fell back into obscurity, without any defenders. Since the progress of cellular physico-chemistry permitted the discovery, in the nucleus of the living cell, of *chromosomes;* and since it could be proven that these chromosomes held, within their *genes,* the entire genotype, there was no longer anything in transformism that could explain the evolution of the species: we now know that none of the transformations caused by either the environment or by organic activity is transmissible by heredity. We continue to accept the great law of evolution as valid; but, for lack of anything better, in order to explain it we resort to those mysterious and rare chemical accidents that are constantly happening in the genes of the chromosomes through an obscure but unquestionably observed phenomenon, accidents called mutations. And it so happens that this theory of mutations brings many of Darwin's hypotheses back into favor. Darwin gets the upper hand over Lamarck. This is how science works. None of its advances is ever definitive, but each of its steps forward contains a grain of truth.

I also witnessed the glorious rise of Freud's discoveries, then saw his theories about the role of the unconscious fall into disfavor. I do not doubt that the psychological science of the future will, in the brilliant and uneven contribution of Freud, sift out what must be kept and what must be rejected of his overly bold hypotheses.

28.4 *The miracle of civilization:* When we look back on the life of mankind, we see only a series of monstrous enslavements: slavery, serfdom, colonialism, racism. By what miracle has human *civilization* been able to make any progress through so many absurdities?

28.5 A. Maurois,* *Études littéraires* (Bergson). Against the finalistic doctrines: "The world of the living is not like a plan that is carried out but rather like a creation that goes on endlessly, following an initial movement."

29. Happiness

29.1 *January '33. Unhappiness exists. Happiness does not.* But there is *distraction,* and sometimes *pleasure.*

29.2 *An old man's past:* a long series of unrecognized or wasted moments of happiness . . .

29.3 *Schopenhauer; Maumort, Claire's death.* "Life is but a series of misunderstandings and lost moments of happiness."

30. Women. Love

30.1 *Le Tertre,† 1921.* The best of marriages is a purgatory. Definition of a purgatory: a hell that is not eternal.

30.2 *November 1929. Feminism.* Woman is an unfortunate and incomplete animal that can only live under supervision. Women's real misfortune began with their emancipation. All the emancipated women I have known were dying of it. The canary also clamors to be set free, but if you open his cage, he is doomed.

30.3 *Feminism.* The ideal type that today's "emancipated" woman is aiming at used to have a name which had an outright pejorative sense: *virago.* The society of tomorrow will no longer be made up of men and women but of men and *viragos.*

.   .   .

*André Maurois (1885–1967), French biographer and novelist.
†Martin du Gard's country house in Bellême, Normandy.

THE WOMAN and the cat are the only animals able to domesticate man. The woman often succeeds at it. The cat always.

30.4   *Antifeminism. Paradoxes of the misogynist.* The absurd dogma of equality between men and women. A five-year-old boy, if he has a sister or a girl cousin, already knows that between the two sexes there is an insurmountable lack of understanding. Man does not understand woman. He can use her for a thousand purposes in the same way he uses electricity, without ever understanding what he is using. We can even give this using of her the flattering name of collaboration, out of politeness. But let's not talk about equality. This is an incorrect and very dangerous notion for the peace between the sexes: since, for the woman, this notion of equality is only an incitement to resist, to rebel, to subjugate.

30.5   *Maumort. Superiority of the male. Regarding Bocca and Rose.* I am always struck by the stupidly domestic way in which the good Rose, the perfect servant, goes about her daily chores, without any concern for perfecting her technique (or of making her effort more efficient, either), working, it seems, almost without thinking, the way an ox ploughs or a horse trots along in its shafts. To watch Bocca working, or any laborer hereabouts, is always a keen pleasure for me; his movement is traditional yet at the same time ingenious, inventive, well thought-out with a view to improving his methods; both to do it better and to do it as easily as possible.

All in all, the woman is, due to her unchangeable nature, a domestic animal. She may acquire all the virtues of such a role; she will always lack some indefinable ingredient that spells superiority.

To the male, the spirit of enterprise and of invention, genius. To the male, that agent of all progress: the incessant need of something better, the quest for something else, something more. The woman accepts what is; the man goes forward.

And this is genetically written: towards the female ovum, motionless and receptive, the male launches his millions of adventurous, throbbing, vibrating, exploring spermatozoa.

30.6   *A misogynist. (Xavier?).* When I announced my marriage to him, he favored me with a card bearing these simple words: "Arise, ye wretched of the earth!"

30.7   *Maumort. Love and friendship:* The best thing about love is that feeling of *respect* and of *tender trust* that is the very essence of friendship.

.   .   .

30.8 *February '47. The liberated woman.* Reading the curious book by Marguerite Grépon, *Introduction à une histoire de l'amour* (J. Vigneau, 1946), written confusedly and in an awkwardly terse style that means to be simple and direct, and is obscure and convoluted, but is packed with ideas and suggestive insights.

On the evolution of women, their emancipation from the control of men, from the marriage laws, etc. A book that tends to reinforce my objections and only partially convinces me.

I think by "protesting," by wanting to emancipate themselves and have their "slavery" abolished, women have thought to gain something, when, in reality, they have mainly lost. By pretending to face men on equal terms (diplomas and sexual freedom) they have forfeited the game in advance. Neither physically nor intellectually did they have the means to win it. In the process, they deprived themselves of the relative happiness that a somewhat passive and quiet existence provided them.

Our grandmothers were, for the most part, docile, unassuming wives, who accepted their domestic and dependent lot, and derived many daily benefits from it; they were to some extent maidservant-mistresses, not without influence over men, and their role was not servile. They did not pass themselves off, as they do today, as equals and also as adversaries. They did not say: "All right, let's see who will end up the winner now!" like contemporary young brides. They found, in the modest acceptance of their fate, a daily chance to please and be loved.

We have known, in those earlier generations (before 1914), many decent women who enjoyed performing their duties as wife and mother, who played the part of collaborator and adviser at the side of their husband (who was not kept constantly on the defensive since the wife's attitude, in principle, was one of submission). They were satisfied with their life in second place, in the shadow of the man; and, all in all, most were happy.

The woman of today, who is filled with a brooding rebellion, a prideful fear of returning to subjection, has altered the peaceful atmosphere of the couple. There is no more trust and security. A tight game is being played. She wants to be independent and considers herself equal to the man, having the same rights as he to make decisions, express opinions, know what needs to be done. She has won freedom, she has lost her inner peace. Between equals, there is a secret state of war. This freedom, which the liberated woman feels to be precarious, threatened (because of her physical weakness, her need for affection from a man for whom love is only a fringe benefit) makes her *skittish*. A skittish person no longer knows happiness. The satisfactions of pride that freedom brings her are but a poor compensation for the pleasures of the shared life that she has compromised by refusing to be dependent.

Among these "liberated" women, I see only frustrated individuals tormented by demands they cannot truly satisfy, envious of the male's organic and intellectual superiority, and often devoured by an anarchic nihilism that goes nowhere. There is a core of despair in them that may be an unconscious regret for a lost paradise, an irremediable imbalance.

More "intelligent," granted, and more "cultivated" than their mothers were. And so what? This is not what gives them a good conscience and happiness; quite the contrary. Especially as this "intelligence," this "culture" is only a reflection of the male intelligence and culture. They are very ambitious and easily pass their exams, because they are receptive and hardworking. But this learned intelligence, of which they are so proud, is not worth much, and they feel this keenly when they come into contact with men's intelligence. Most of them struggle in vain and wear themselves out wanting to appear intelligent—without fooling anyone, not even themselves.

And it is not clear that this false intelligence is any further from stupidity than was the illiterate common sense of women in the past.

They strive to seem more than they are, more than their nature as women allows them to be; they make themselves insufferable with their excessive and ill-justified pretensions, they blame men, society, and life for that latent dissatisfaction which comes from their repudiation of true feminine qualities in order to sport the masculine qualities they will never really acquire, of which they are doomed by nature to acquire only the appearance. It seems to me that misogyny is making great inroads among men, especially among men of forty (when sexual passion cools and is less blinding), fed up with the dealings they have had with women. The man of forty has recovered from his illusions about women. (If he runs a business, he has observed that a woman is inferior to a man when she replaces him in certain positions: perfect, often, as long as she is second in command; mediocre if she is in charge of a division.)

There is no way out of this deplorable situation. Women will never again consent to being passive and trusting partners. They will not give up the prerogatives they have won. We will have to keep a very close eye on how things go in Russia, for example, to get an idea of what relations between men and women will become in the future, and to know what kind of society will be possible with "liberated" women . . .

30.9 *November 1951. Love, love . . .* (After a rereading of *Letters of a Portuguese Nun.* *) Love has always seemed to me something of a shameful sickness which it is impossible to talk about, embarrassing to hear about, and blatantly ridiculous to let people see. I have always restrained myself from

*By Mariana Alcoforado, 1699.

showing this sort of feeling to anyone, even to my private diary (even sometimes to the person in question . . .)

The confidences of people in love have always made me much more uncomfortable than any obscene exhibition. I am unable to take an interest in other people's love affairs: and the most famous novels of love bore me as much as children's books. Only one attitude to take, when you have "caught" love: hide! (As if you had eczema on your face.)

30.10   *Gévresin as misogynist.* Maumort relates an example of female stupidity and treachery, and adds:

"If Gévresin were here, he would not miss a chance to repeat how beautiful life on earth would be on the day when biologists learn how to produce children in their laboratories, when only males are created, when the female species disappears from the globe, and when liberated men organize an exclusively male world. On days when he is inclined to leniency, he is willing to concede that, for the sake of scientific curiosity, a few specimens of the female sex might be kept in zoos . . ."

31. PACIFISM. AGAINST VIOLENCE

31.1   *Peace.* Everything people are doing or propose to do on behalf of peace has my firm support. But I confess: it always seems to me I am watching doctors prescribe care for an incurably ill patient—or, with the best intentions in the world, administer haphazard treatments to one whose sickness has not yet been thoroughly diagnosed . . .

The peace that they are "consolidating" is not peace. Peace does not yet exist and never has existed on earth. What has been called peace up until now I call *truce;* better truce than war, admittedly.

But it is peace that matters to mankind, and peace is an entirely new and unknown relationship that involves creating a state of law between nations, condemning as a crime against humanity any recourse to violence and coercion; a relationship based on the absolute refusal of one nation to make war with another for any reason at all and backed up by an international court where every dispute between nations could from now on be resolved through negotiation and arbitration alone.

31.2   *The ideal peace.* Until now, the statesmen who have made peace have always done it as if they accepted *in petto* that wars are inevitable, that a peace is never more than a truce, that the cannons must not be destroyed but carefully put away. I dream of a peace that would be devised by people who, in their heart of hearts, are finally looking to do more than just "play for time."

31.3   *The pacifists. Maumort thinks:* In the ranks of the pacifists have enlisted first, by instinct, all the *cowards* (those who feel themselves to be such and those who do not believe themselves to be but in fact are, through and through). Altogether they form a sizable body, one that is convinced, and fervent, and persistent, and good at speechifying. But nothing more. Pacifism will begin to matter when it becomes the special province of the courageous or even the daredevils, those who cannot be stopped when they want to oppose something. As long as pacifism is the ideological refuge of the fearful, war, and the parties to war, among whom the courageous and the daredevils are not scarce, will not be met with any obstacle other than fine phrases.

31.4   *Maumort. Against stupid nonresistance.* The principle of nonresistance is dangerously utopian. It is to be hoped that this war will have made even the most obtuse pacifists understand that. The obstinate adherence to passivity, by ensuring the strong impunity and easy success, can only encourage them to violate justice. The lamb will never thwart the wolf's cruelty with his gentleness.

To resort to violence whenever no other means exist for opposing violence. A sensible pacifism can go no farther than that.

Cruelty dwells at the heart of human nature. This is a fact that must never be forgotten. Against cruelty, there is only one effective weapon: *law.* A law armed with power.

Nonresistance serves only to foster violence and hatred everywhere, by making it easy for force and oppression to carry the day. As if it were enough to repeat, "Death to war!" to establish peace . . . As if rational arguments, protests, appeals to conscience, even examples could protect us from unbridled force, and prevent oppression!

31.5   *Pacifism. Summer '47.* Notes for tackling the "pacifism" question.

How the pacifist ideal of 1875–1935, which was routinely accepted by everyone, fell out of public favor.

How the spread of conflicting ideologies has, in the last fifteen years, transformed people's mentality by bringing back *the spirit of the religious wars* that precludes any attempt at conciliation and any peaceable ideal.

How the frantic desire to see a cause triumph and to stamp out the enemy has supplanted the desire for peace in the younger generation.

It is the idea of happiness that has changed: people no longer imagine their happiness in the form of a lasting peace but rather in the form of a victory.

Pacifism has ceased to have meaning except for the survivors of a bygone era.

The "pacifist" position, which was that of the best European minds of my generation, the fruit of the idealistic humanism of the nineteenth century, the pacifism that we knew in France from 1875 until 1914 and from 1920 until 1935, and that was almost universal among intellectual circles is no longer possible, has lost all credibility with the younger generations. Why? It is a fact. But the cause?

Because the spirit of Europe, between 1930 and 1940, following the development of Soviet Russia and of the fascist regimes in Italy and Germany, became the spirit of the religious wars (the Spanish Civil War in '36 marks the moment when this spirit assumed its full growth, imposed itself on European minds).

Before that era, even at the time of the Balkan wars or the First World War, the majority of Europeans conceded that the human ideal was to live in peace and that wars which were unleashed by economic factors and the needs of territorial expansion and which threw nations into bloody and ruinous conflicts ran counter to the true wish of mankind: to work in peace. Peoples fought without hatred, dragged into wars by ambitions that had nothing to do with them; enemies or allies in spite of themselves, because of political games, they all considered themselves equally the victims, unconsulted, of baneful forces that compelled them to sacrifice their lives, their individual happiness, and their prosperity for illusory benefits which did not concern them.

THERE WAS UNANIMITY in recognizing, as an obvious fact, that war was a crime against humanity and an indefensible absurdity. Even those whose profession it was to make war, the military leaders, thought so. No one in the world wanted war. A few skeptics considered it a periodic and lamentable scourge that could never be completely eradicated. There were differing opinions as to the means that should be used to make wars impossible. But everyone agreed on one point: that war was an evil, and the worst of all those that our human condition inflicts on us.

Everything changed around 1935; and everything is radically changed today.

Today, for most adults between twenty and forty, if war is still an evil, it is not the worst. What they consider the worst of misfortunes is witnessing the political idea, the government and institutions they have embraced, fail. They will stop at nothing, including, of course, war, to ensure the triumph of the ideology to which they have devoted their partisan energies, their fervent belief, their religious fanaticism. What matters to them is not, first and foremost, avoiding an unprecedented global catastrophe; it is making sure that the Marxist system or the American capitalist system, the dictatorship of the proletariat or the economy of the Anglo-Saxon democracies, comes out on top.

This is what I call the spirit of the religious wars. The spirit that for two centuries put Europe to fire and sword: the Papists and the Huguenots mercilessly slaughtered each other and preferred the triumph of their cause to an existence of tolerance and concord. At that time, there was no more room for pacifism than there is today. No one wished for "peace above all," because, above all, each one wanted to win and to impose his version of the truth.

Just like us, Erasmus found himself at the end of a time when people had bet on reason and worked for peace and, like us, he saw arising and spreading an era of fanaticism in which his voice had become suspect and his attitude of conciliation and tolerance was considered cowardice. We too find ourselves straddling these two antithetical periods; we have known an age when pacifism was not considered absurd and was held as a noble ideal, endorsed in principle by everyone and almost attainable: the League of Nations was a first step, and we were already dreaming of something better— a World Federation with one law, one economy, one army, all of them international. But suddenly the spirit of the wars of religion again swept the world; and all our desires for peace, our attempts to achieve peace, the tremendous wish of a whole generation of civilized men became pathetic pipe dreams in the eyes of the rising generations, who had turned fanatical, resolving to fight mercilessly because they were determined to win, and who no longer spoke the same language as we do. No point trying for peace among men in a world where the only thing that matters to most is the triumph of one side and where, no doubt regretfully, but without backing down, the majority accepts the necessity of a war to crush the heretics, which is their fundamental goal.

31.6   *Peace. Maumort:* Clemenceau said that war is too important a matter to be entrusted solely to the military men.

This is true. But even more so for peace. And yet, would the civilian powers be equal to this task and understand their responsibility?

31.7   *Modern warfare.* War changed in character after the French Revolution. It was from the idea—perhaps monstrous—of the "armed nation" that the mystique of modern warfare was born, turning every war into a civil war, a total war, a holy war.

No comparison with the armed militias of the sixteenth to the eighteenth centuries. A victory strengthened the power of the government, but a defeat did not bring it down. Power was not *dependent on the outcome,* as it is today. Louis XIV could have lost Waterloo without losing the throne.

31.8   *Maumort and war.* Maumort is the opposite of a pacifist of the *Summer 1914* type.* An old soldier who believes in the law of universal warfare. Too intelligent not to want the world to achieve peace. But maybe in a thousand years. And not believing it.

   Sees all the horrors of war clearly. Does not defend it, and glorifies it even less. But thinks it natural to man (biological concept of the universe). And eternal. See Quinton (Alain), *Échec à la force,* pp. 63, 67, 68.

32. A Look at the World of the Past

32.1   *Vain recriminations against the past. Easy consolation.* There is nothing more childish or stupider than this sense of shame and scorn for our past that they† want to inculcate in us through propaganda. The sepulchral and quavering voice of the great marshal‡ lends itself, alas, better than any other to this type of confession and penitence. The regime that governed us until the day of the defeat had its defects, its mistakes, its abuses. Let's admit that it was worn out, let's admit that it needed changing. It had its drawbacks; it also had its virtues. Its major fault was its inability to reform its abuses. This is the only lesson to draw from recent French history. But let's not come down too hard on its abuses. Today's severity is too much like vengeance, like the need to make someone or certain persons responsible for our present misfortune. All governments have had abuses. But some have known how to fix them in time.

   It is a childish temptation to make facts prove too much. The savage who sees lightning strike his village supposes right away that his tribe has misbehaved and offended the gods.

   I do not want France to experiment with an entirely new system of government. It is a kind of experiment for which people generally pay with long periods of suffering. I want France to go back soon to the body of institutions that it built up in a century of successive tribulations and that represent precious acquisitions made with the help of time. In politics, improvise as little as possible. Don't look for innovations among your neighbors, even if those innovations have facilitated their victory. What we know of the neighboring regimes has nothing to tempt us. If we admit that the Third Republic had let its institutions slide over time, let's go back to work, I agree. Let's

---

*Martin du Gard is referring to his novel *Summer 1914.*
†I.e., the proponents of the Vichy regime.
‡Pétain.

try to rebuild the republic of Gambetta.* There was some good in it. It produced results. It lasted sixty years. It fit the French temperament well and was the natural expression of it.

32.2 *The cheerful France of 1900. A sensible mediocrity. Maumort:* When I recall how cheerful France was in 1900, with its lax but solid institutions, with its discipline that was loose but sufficient for maintaining order; with the elasticity that the instability of the regimes imparted to the government; with its essential loyalty to the republican system whose disappearance no one, not even the opposition parties, sincerely contemplated; with its familiar rapport, free from fear, between the citizens and the administration; with its patriotism that was steadfast but broadened and ventilated by internationalism; with its not too tempestuous social conflicts—then I say to myself that, in this almost nonperfectible world, the France of 1900 offered a relatively tolerable, relatively lasting solution to life in society. But the rest of Europe would have had to arrive at the same sensible mediocrity.

33. UPHEAVAL OF THE PRESENT WORLD

33.1 *Torturers. Maumort:* Man is fundamentally cruel. In Africa I saw incredible refinements in the ferocity of the *strong* against the *weak* that came from an instinctive drive the satisfaction of which gave the strong an intense sensual pleasure comparable to the satisfaction of the sexual instinct. And I am not speaking of the ferocity of the Arab, or even of the white NCO. I saw ferocity flash in the eyes of our best fellow *officers.*

Cruelty is a natural instinct.

"Yes," I will be told, "in Africa, in the army, with men who inevitably worship power."

No, everywhere. In our French schools, the child who persecutes the youngest boy or the class cripple, and pulls the legs off grasshoppers and the wings off cockchafers, and brings little live birds to the cat. And in our towns, the cook who scalds the rock lobster, puts snails on a fast for three weeks, slowly smothers the duck while folding its neck under its wing so that the flesh will be better, and gouges out the rabbit's eye with a knife point so that it will bleed before its throat is slit. And the carter who keeps kicking the horse that is falling under too heavy a load. And the muleteer who twists the mule's tail to make it go faster. And the concierge who beats her dog.

All torturers in the making.

---

*Léon Michel Gambetta, (1838–1882), French political leader; one of the chief creators of the Third Republic after the defeat of Napoleon III in 1870.

33.2 *Contemporary barbarism.* The men of the generation that was born with the century and who, fifteen years old during World War I, thought that the trenches and Verdun were the ultimate in horror, found themselves plunged (what with Hitler, the camps, the ovens, the dreadful Soviet regime, etc.) into an almost universal barbarism that, twenty years earlier, in 1919, no European could have believed possible. A return to the worst periods of history, to the horrors of the Inquisition, etc.

How to be surprised by the derangement of the civilized world, the confusion of minds, the cynicism of people and governments, etc.?

33.3 *Maumort and current events. The new warfare.* War, the great destroyer of morals . . . but what to say, then, about this *guerrilla warfare,* free, unpunished, and almost always without risks, which is waged in ambush, where you are invisible, elusive, fleeing at the least hint of danger, where you play like children, and where you can live outside the law with impunity, kill, attack from the rear, loot shops, rob travelers, while still being looked on as heroes?

How can this produce anything but a generation of unscrupulous adventurers and apprentice gangsters?

33.4 *Maumort in 1944.* Certain politicians of this time seem to me to accept the Communist program with the ulterior motive of rendering the Communist party powerless while appropriating and sanctioning the reforms that Communism would have inspired.

33.5 *Forecasts of war. October '46.* Am I as worried about the fate of Europe as ten years ago? I despair of the U.N. just as, ten years ago, I despaired of the League of Nations. I fear Stalin as much today as I feared Hitler in 1936, and I cannot help thinking that, just as we could have stopped Hitler in 1936, so we might also be able to stop Stalin with a preventive show of belligerence. Stalin is not only a Russian imperialist, as were Ivan the Terrible and Peter the Great; he is a Bolshevik who is not giving up the plan of establishing his absolutist regime throughout the entire world, starting with Europe. This is why he wanted the war in '39, and why he did not hesitate, in order to finally set it off, to sign his pact with Hitler, guaranteeing him half of Poland. And he will repeat his maneuver whenever he wants to, through the intermediary of a Yugoslavian, Bulgarian, or Polish stooge, or maybe a Chinese one. And on the day and at the hour of his choosing, he will force England and the United States into a war. Maybe not for four or five years, if his plans are allowed to ripen; but not much later. Already he has set up

Communism in Yugoslavia, Poland, and Bulgaria, and has completely over-run the Baltic states. Germany seems, if the recent elections are any indication, to be resisting the Russian influence a bit more than might have been expected. But we cannot be at all sure that this resistance will not be overcome within six months.

33.6   *Maumort. Indiscernible truth. Winter '47.* Until 1940, the man of my generation, the man who had lived for sixty years, had a very clearly defined sense of direction. As for me, the author of *Barois* and *Summer 1914* was quite the same man who had been drawn to Tolstoy and Romain Rolland (and not Barrès) around 1900, and the same who gave a pacifistic speech in Stockholm in 1937. Coherence, continuity in evolution. The writer of the left, a socialist sympathizer, and a pacifist.

In '40, a staggering blow to the skull, and all ideas hopelessly scrambled. Impossible to get back on your feet. Impossible to know what to think. This "truth" which had been leading the way for forty years, which was sometimes clearly visible and sometimes hidden for an instant by the bends in the road, but which always reappeared, and which we could follow simply by continuing to advance, vanished like a mirage. Sometimes we seem to glimpse it in the arid landscapes, strewn with pitfalls, where the Marxists inhumanly hold sway; and sometimes it appears, abandoned behind us, in that familiar and bourgeois landscape that has the charm of the homeland, where everything is steady, reassuring, on a human scale.

Between the disturbing world of violence and fanaticism, and the out-moded world of prudence, of liberalism, we wander among the gaping crevasses in an uninhabitable no-man's-land where there is no possible rest or balance. Where, in which direction, lies decadence, error? In which direction, future balance and nascent innovation? Are those who herald it in the East lying to us? We too would like to see it there, but we cannot manage it. And do those who in the West defend a past still full of appeal but smelling so strongly of the rottenness of things coming to an end have the right answer? That answer coincides so unreassuringly with our selfish motives . . . Which are the true prophets, which the gravediggers?

33.7   *The decomposition of the world. Maumort:* When I observe the current decomposition of the world, I remember a very curious conversation that I heard in my youth at one of my uncle Éric's Sunday at-homes, during which one of the guests—I think it was Renan—gave a witty talk on the Chaldean myth according to which the sun god of the Babylonians, Marduk, after having vanquished the monsters of chaos, fashioned the world with the putrefied remains of an enemy goddess whose name I have forgotten.

33.8 *Maumort. An epoch of "transition"?* How many times already in the history of civilizations has a hopeless disorder in institutions and mores been explained, if not justified, by the *new order* that was laboriously being brought into the world—a new order whose early signs eluded the investigations of the sharpest minds of those accursed periods?

Who knows what is germinating in the depths of this chaos?

33.9 *The birth of a new world.* It would be enough to have clearly understood that every life is a chaos in the process of organizing itself for one to contemplate the convulsions of the world at present with a less troubled eye.

I want to convince myself that these shocks, which are splitting the world open like a chestnut in the embers, have a meaning: the search for a new equilibrium, the laborious birth of a new "provisional" order.

(For a *different* equilibrium, rather than a new one—of a *different* provisional order.)

33.10 *Present-day problems.* The only thing that matters is to grasp in the present what is dying and what is demanding to be born. But who can claim to have an ear fine enough to discern, among all the cries that are ringing out in the seething course of events, which is the swan song and which the cock's crow?

34. THREATS FOR THE FUTURE. STATE CONTROL

34.1 *Maumort. The eclipse of intelligence.* We have all known those practical minds that, on the pretext of not being taken in by a lot of hot air, mistrust all ideas. These people feel their hour has come: a rare chance to blame the disaster on ideas and idealists and to plan a world where they would no longer be in an inferior position because intellectual activity would be suspect and kept hidden.

We may be heading towards a more or less lasting eclipse of intelligence—as is the case with countries under totalitarian regimes. It is so tempting for man's inherent stupidity and laziness to accept a few ready-made precepts, to make taboos of them and block the path of all those arduous intellectual investigations that might always shake the comfortable foundations of the existing order!

34.2 *Maumort. Against the state,* which increasingly tends to intrude in private affairs where society has no business as long as these affairs involve nothing harmful to the community.

But everything rests on this "harmful," and it should be clearly defined.

Because the state always makes these interventions in the name of defending the majority.

For the state, a minority cannot have the right to act and exist freely. In fact, for the state, any minority is, by definition, as a foregone conclusion, considered an active threat to the majority. The state does not treat minorities as fractions of the society that have a right to existence but rather as the enemy is treated in time of war—as an aggressive, dangerous, dissident group that must be exterminated.

34.3   *Maumort. State control.* The state is at the service of the individual. Individuals, gathered into a society, establish the state to regulate the relations among them, protect them, help them, ensure them greater happiness. The present idea of the Minotaur state, the state tyrannizing the individual in the name of an abstract idea of community, is ridiculous.

Something as absurd as my barrack-room sergeant who forced us to polish the soles of our dress shoes black and make them shine, as if the sole was not specifically designed to be in contact with the dust of the ground. Just as blatantly ridiculous.

34.4   *Maumort thinks:* The coming world will be a restricted, organized world from which any spirit of initiative, any exceptional personality will be excluded. The ideal of unflagging mediocrity.

Western humanity, since the Renaissance, has set itself problems and has sought solutions by propounding more and more hypotheses and asking questions. The spirit of invention has taken an incredible leap forward: in the last hundred and fifty years, it has had a field day. Civilization has demonstrated boldness in every domain. This was a time of investigation, of discoveries, of unfettered imagination, the era of personal initiatives.

It seems that this stage is drawing to a close; that everything is conspiring to impede the continuation of that "free play" . . . Discipline first! The coming times will see the man of imagination and initiative muzzled. Along with freedom, our successors will lose the right to give themselves up to inventive madness. Rules will be laid down, and in every arena man will be limited by barbwire certainties that he will no longer have the right, and will not be given the time, to overstep. Play will be stopped. Laws, constraints, *verbotens* will be imposed in the name of the collective good by social dictatorships. The watchword will no longer be *search,* or *invent,* but *organize.* Personality, eccentric genius, the right to think anything, to say anything, solitary research, originality, and diversity in minds will no longer be respected. A fixed pattern, a social type, from which no one will be allowed to deviate, on pain of being ostracized and left to die, will be imposed through education. It will be impossible to outdistance one's neighbor, to be adventuresome, to explore thought and the universe. Mankind will live a concentration camp or monastery existence in which everything is planned for the best, controlled, in which no law may be broken. The virtues prescribed and taught will be submission, conscientiousness, and energy in communal work, acceptance of the rules. Independence of mind and initiative in action will be crimes against the majority, against the state, against society. (The level of material well-being will be raised; but what produced the strength, the *drive* of civilization will be broken, or shackled for a long time. The ideal will be to achieve "a good average.")

After a few centuries in this utilitarian servitude, will the human species perhaps move towards an ideal of a complicated termitarium, a superior termitarium, where everyone will have his place, his role, his limited mission, his activity prescribed in advance, progressing through his life like a train on its rails? If there still arises a free and original spirit which education does not succeed in regimenting, it will be expelled by the community, done away with, or committed to an asylum.

34.5   *Much will be lost by suppressing anarchy.* The coming civilization will set up a stable world for us. Above all else, stable. (And stability is incontestably an element of well-being, of happiness.) Stability and security.

But at what cost! The price is terrible! Art only develops in social instability, in freedom. Art is a form of anarchy. An atmosphere of discipline paralyzes it, kills it. In a passionless civilization, where the reasons for rebellion are suppressed, art will quickly wither. A state of contented platitude. The tragic will be erased from the world. The man of tomorrow may never again feel a need for poetry, art, innovation. He will be satisfied but not curious. There will be no more yeast in a human dough that contains no freedom.

Unless such a strict discipline provokes violent individual reactions?

34.6   *Maumort. Could it be that history is always right? Forecasts.* Our children seem doomed to live in a hard world, where order will be imposed on everyone by a *prison discipline,* protected by a sort of *perpetual martial law.* It will not be enough to be obedient and work like a galley slave: a person will even have to *love this servitude fanatically,* and let it be known, and prove it through all his words and deeds. It is possible that people will adapt and that a contagious collective intoxication—which may not be without greatness, the greatness of any fervent abnegation—will make them consider that accepted slavery as the supreme nobility and the supreme happiness of the human condition and lead them to regard the relative freedom of earlier eras as a state of uncomfortable anarchy (very difficult to evaluate equitably what mankind will have lost or won in that transformation of social existence).

34.7 *Maumort. Is the predilection for peace universal?* It is surprising today to hear so many "average Frenchmen" of the so-called ruling or intellectual classes speaking as if, by and large, they preferred Bolshevism and its vast upheavals to the moderate and peaceful socialism of democracy. "It would be pointless to have lived through these heroic years," one hears it said, "in order to lapse back into the same dull and dreary turn-of-the-century republicanism!"

The mistake of people my age, Maumort will say, is perhaps to have believed that the great majority of men ask only to be able to work in peace, under a relatively free regime. The majority may have a taste for danger, adventure, risky innovations; and isn't it possible that they see only the boredom of regularity and security in the happiness that we want to provide them? Is there perhaps now in Europe a majority of young people who, having tasted violence, have found in it the satisfaction of their primitive instincts and aspire only to go on living a daredevil existence? Violent natures love violence; and there are many of them. And weak natures—of whom there are a still greater number—cannot keep from secretly feeling ashamed of their weakness, and they compensate for their nature by giving themselves the luxury, if not of extolling violence, at least of not grudging the violent a certain respect, and of getting fired up by incendiary speeches. A nation is composed of this dual element at times of revolution. People get intoxicated on the strength of others to make up for the strength they don't have themselves.

34.8 *Return to the war of religion (1947).* Our era can be compared to the one when Luther's Germany took on European Christendom and when Europe was split into two ideologies, fiercely determined, both of them, to triumph and subject the world to their law. Papists and Lutherans fought for several centuries and the wars of religion spread ruin, misery, terror, and perpetrated the worst iniquities, the cruelest massacres.

Between the Communism of Moscow and American democratic capitalism, what is beginning is a similar ruthless struggle, an outburst of hatred and violence, an appetite for exclusive victory, for total extermination of the enemy. The world is going to be plunged into horror and bloodshed for a long time to come.

34.9 *Maumort: I have chosen freedom.* As hard as one can be on the injustices and abuses that characterize the regimes of bourgeois democracy, the partial freedom that these regimes guarantee the individual is preferable to the pitiless disciplines and servitude that state Socialism imposes.

35. THE FUTURE OF FRANCE

35.3   *Maumort:* I see no reason why a man of high caliber should not find defeat to be at least as much a source of energy and moral elevation as victory.

35.4   *Maumort to the leaders:* May those who tomorrow will have the responsibility for public order and civil peace soothe hatreds and spare us the added useless misfortune that bloody reprisals would bring. There will be better things to do at the hour of recovery than to imitate our enemies by taking up their barbaric cry of: "We want heads!" Enough blood has been spilled over Europe. Let us tend to our wounds.

35.5   *The Third Republic. Maumort writes:* I read almost everywhere that the France of tomorrow, like all the countries of the civilized world, is bound to have a very authoritarian form of government, a planned economy, a pseudo-dictatorship more or less disguised as democracy.

I still don't believe a bit of it. The taste for freedom is deeply ingrained in Western man and firmly rooted in the French soul. But, if such a regime were to take over, we would soon realize to our cost the advantage of decades of republican politics and of our much-disparaged Third Republic. It is comfortable to live under institutions that are somewhat lax but respected all the same, in a country where the harmless quarrel of the government and the opposition serves as an outlet for the passions, keeps them from fermenting in the closed vessel from which all revolutions spring—and where the mediocrity of the parliamentary politics, the instability of the administrations, if they made it difficult to carry out great programs, turned the government into some big elastic entity, with blunted corners, which unruly revolutionaries found hardly any supporters to attack.

What nineteenth-century liberalism was, symbolized by the City of London, is not worth regretting. We owe to it the unjust exploitation of the working masses.

But state capitalism, or Stalinism, or the capitalism of Hitler's Germany, also leads to injustices, or even tyranny.

We will probably return, through revolution, to a government of freedom, which will be very different from the former liberalism because it will take account of social necessities and demands and will distribute incomes more fairly.

35.6 *The future of capitalism.* Are we finally going to witness the fall of capitalism?

I already thought so at the end of the other war, and indeed capitalism was reeling. But it quickly recovered; it came back to life everywhere—even in Russia, in a different guise—with a relentless vigor, more insatiable than ever for profits, more grounded than ever in social injustice. This time it seems mortally hit . . . but the monster dies hard! It has already digested many a revolution. Its tactics are subtle. It knows how to accept the inevitable and not go head-on against the institutions that condemn it and seem able to bring it down. It has digested universal suffrage. It has appropriated proclamations of social justice and inscribed "liberty, equality, fraternity" on its banks. It has no petty compunctions. It knows how to patiently survive and return to life, and to assume the colors of the times. It is not hampered by principles, it joins in the most hostile popular demands and finds a way to avoid having what is in fact its tyranny hobbled by ideological contradictions.

Is this the final phase? Will the interwar period, from 1920 to 1940, turn out to have been its swan song? The legal government, the state, relinquished real power to capitalism. It actually became the servant and the tool of capitalism's most brazen schemes, let itself be overrun and tamed by capitalism's corporations and gave up, in order to leave capitalism's hands free, the social reforms most obviously necessary and urgent if catastrophes were to be averted. With the total state control that the World War will produce everywhere, will this government, tomorrow, be able to escape the sordid dictatorship of money?

Perhaps.

But the state may also prove powerless to bring down capitalism, or may dread, in the wake of such a widespread cataclysm, that it will be weakened further by revolutionary explosions. (The enemy will not let itself be disarmed without a struggle, and will know how to foment unrest that can shake the stability of the state which attacks it directly.) Thus the state may try to find compromises and collude with capitalism—just as was done by the totalitarian states which had the will to destroy the capitalist system but could not in reality do without it even though they attempted to limit its power, and which finally had to cut a deal with it. (Neither Mussolini nor Hitler could get along without its support, and that support was not without compensations, skillfully concealed from the eyes of the masses.)

The most likely hypothesis is that the sovereign states of the future order, even if they ever achieve anything against the capitalists, will not be able to destroy capitalism and will use it as their principal strength. As we have seen in Russia, where the capitalism of the banks and corporations, spectacularly annihilated, became a state capitalism, while for the proletariat no great change occurred . . . (which should be looked into closely).

35.7 *Maumort. Birthrate.* A friend of Maumort's (Dr. Gévresin?) used to reply to birth announcements:

"If it's an accident, accept my condolences. If it's on purpose, you deserve to be disemboweled (if not worse . . .).

"I am against the increase in the birthrate, the present cause of the world's poverty and of wars. Better for France to perish, if its salvation depends on a surplus population for which it cannot ensure a comfortable standard of living, which perpetuates pauperism and unemployment, and which inevitably brings about those economic imbalances that produce bloody conflicts."

(See Bouthoul's book, *Millions de morts.*)

36. THE FUTURE OF EUROPE

36.1 *Maumort.* When all is said and done, the only valid watchword would be this: let this wretched humanity be as little *unhappy* as possible.

A big step would be taken if we could make man better. No effort by moralists and legislators in this direction should be discouraged. But if we doubt that man is perfectible—or, what comes to the same thing, if we think that the improving of human nature is an evolution so slow that it will take thousands of years—we can at least try to control society in such a way that the beastliness of the human animal is held in check. Against the ferociousness of the animal, we can always advocate the muzzle.

36.2 *May '41.* It seems to me that not enough thought has been given to the consequences that will result, whatever the outcome of the war may be, from the intermingling of the European populations and the profound changes that are taking place in Europe, among the victors and the vanquished alike, under the system of German servitude. And along with this convulsed Europe, which will rise again gasping for breath and essentially transformed, the rest of the world is evolving very quickly, the balance of power is changing month by month. The United States will probably be the great beneficiary of the upheaval. Its power is growing at a dizzying rate. It is likely that, in the future, it will form, along with England and all the dominions that have become independent, a huge Anglo-Saxon federation, which will have to deal with other forces, grouped perhaps around Russia, if Russia manages to pull into its orbit what remains of the totalitarian nations of Europe, readier to adopt Communism than the Anglo-Saxon democratic ideal. And what will Asia be, under the Japanese hegemony? An independent continent, or allied to Russia?

36.3   *Maumort. 27 July '41. The United States and Japan. Indochina.* The blaze is spreading, it will go round the world, and I will certainly not see the end of it. I think that America will finally have the last word and will be the "profiteer," more or less bled dry . . . but that will not be all: it will be necessary to pick up the pieces, sew things back up: a quarter-century of economic convulsions on the horizon, once the time of the bloody convulsions is over. A fine mess . . . As hard as one might be on this world that is collapsing, that of liberal economies and of money, its fall will be dearly paid for by mankind, and there is no guarantee that the shaky future which rises on so many ruins will be any better. Those who have a faith are lucky: I wish I could *hope*—for anything!

I am withdrawing into myself. Sieyès* answered, not without legitimate pride: "Well, I have lived" (if he had been able to say, "I have lived and worked well," he would have been a great example). The wise attitude, in this universal disaster that goes beyond any individual destiny, is not to lose interest in oneself: *it is to maintain oneself at a certain level.*

I do not expect that what my life has become today will change before my death. I am trying to come to terms with it in the least undesirable way possible in order to reach the end without idleness or despair. This diary saves me from both. No matter what happens, I hang on to it. It is my refuge. It will allow me to say, in my turn, on the day I have to pack up and go: "I have lived. I have left all the windows wide open to hear and see what was going on outside. But I have carried on with my own little existence, quietly, with dignity, and I have kept my balance in this earthquake . . . I have pretty much, as best I could, *maintained myself at a certain level.*"

36.4   *Maumort. Certain secrets about the war. About Germany.* From R. Cartier, *The Secrets of the War, Revealed by Nuremberg* (1947). Important revelations: there are various points on which our judgments need to be reappraised, notably:

1. *Hitler's strategic abilities.* Maumort could admire certain bold strokes demonstrating military genius: the invasion of Holland and the sudden thrust into Sedan and the Ardennes, supposedly impassable, that decided the

*Joseph Emmanuel Sieyès (1748–1836), French statesman.

fate of France. The masterly, unexpected, manifold way in which the invasion of Poland was conducted. And even the Russian campaign, which might have destroyed the Russian forces before allowing them to fall back (a plan that failed by chance: the early arrival and severity of the winter of '41–'42).

2. The threat of the invasion of England: a simple feint to hoodwink Russia and allay its mistrust. In fact, no landing had been contemplated. A show.

3. Hitler's intention in '40–'41 to attack Gibraltar and storm the Mediterranean. A plan that failed because Franco refused to let the German army come through.

Maumort has guessed this from the Allies' conciliatory attitude towards Spain, which indicated a major service rendered, etc.

36.5   *Maumort. Views on the military organization of Europe after '45.* See the booklet *Fédération 57* (October '49), a long, intelligent, and "military" article by General Montrelay.

36.6   *Europe. Maumort:* Europe does exist. It existed in the Middle Ages, in the eighteenth century. It is not an artificial, chance assemblage. Its intellectual cultures have family ties. Its languages as well. The languages of Western Europe have inherited a certain number of words coming from Greek and Latin, which gives them a family resemblance. And not only words, but common ideas, springing from a common culture, which also comes from Greece and Rome. The "Latin world" of former times.

36.7   *Maumort. European Federation.* The first time Maumort encountered this idea, it was in the mouth of Renan. He liked to speak about the ideas of "nation" and "race," which he differentiated with excellent and precise arguments. He said: "Nations are not eternal. They began, they will end. The European Confederation will probably replace them. But at the present time, the existence of nations is good, even necessary. *Their existence is the guarantee of freedom; which would be lost if the world had only one law and one master.*" (Renan, "What Is a Nation?" p. 309, *Speeches and Lectures,* 1887, pp. 277–310.)

36.8   *European asphyxiation.* Europe, deprived of the thousands of relative freedoms that give ease and play to the life of the individual, presents us with an unbreathable atmosphere where all functions wither. All of a sudden, the air has no more oxygen. Maybe the lungs of future generations will change and adapt. But for people of my age and for all those who have lived before the war in a free country where the idea of freedom held a place of honor and was more or less put into practice, it is the torture of asphyxiation.

.   .   .

36.9 *Maumort.* A great figure of a man "without a country"? No, a great figure of a *European.* But one who has no place in Europe yet.

36.10 *July '44.* Europe, as this war will leave it, will be like a vipers' nest. And plans for peace are being made . . .

36.11 We are also willing to accept force . . . but provided that it be deeply allied with justice, dignity, wisdom.

36.12 Equality of rights between nations is of major importance, since justice is possible only between equals. As soon as there is inequality, the strongest cannot resist abusing its power, and so much for justice.

38. Maumort's Conservative Tendencies

38.1 *Inequality.* Every organization of society comes up against the problem of *inequality* among men. Inequality in health, in strength, in intelligence. A law of nature.

It may have been a mistake to try to offset natural inequality through equality of rights. Men of unequal intelligences may not have anything to gain from equality of rights.

38.2 *Maumort. Conservative tendencies.* H. Guillemin, in his preface to Joseph de Maistre's* *Considérations sur la France* (1943): "Even as he spurs himself on to disparage the Republic, to prove it absurd, deceptive, inhuman, even as he tries to convince himself that the Revolution in itself is bad, completely bad, there remains deep within him an uneasiness, a qualm, a doubt, something like a premonition, like a voice that makes him ashamed of his short-sightedness, like a very hushed reproach of his conscience: *how do you know that what you take for wisdom is not just your prejudice?*"

38.3 *Maumort. Conservative tendencies. Maumort:* By nature, I rebel against any *destructive act.* It is as a *destructive act* that a revolutionary act incurs my distrust, my censure.

But once this instinctive shudder has passed, my reason intervenes with that often unsettling question: after all, was what has been destroyed so good that it was worth preserving?

Ah, how gladly I would accept a *constructive revolution!* . . . but those two words clash when placed side by side. Revolutions never do anything but destroy. It is always the counterrevolutions that construct. It remains to be

*Joseph de Maistre (1753–1821), French moralist and polemicist.

seen if these constructions, these new institutions—supposing that they are an improvement—could not have been set up through wise reforms, and without revolution . . . Look at Sweden . . .

Joseph de Maistre's epigram doubting the validity of his own arguments against the Revolution: "If Providence erases, probably it is in order to *write . . .*" (Chapter II, *Considérations sur la France.*)

38.4   *Maumort's conservative tendencies. The ideal republic. Maumort:* I think that if the majority of Europeans had to agree on a way to express the essence of their political opinions in one line, most of their votes would go to this negative formula: *down with all forms of tyranny.*

Yes, despite present appearances, the majority feels only mistrust for that "better" envisioned by the revolutionary Utopians—which is, particularly in this case, the "enemy of the good."

And what is the *good* in politics? A government of competent and moderate men, liberal institutions, just laws to which reason subjects itself without disapproval, social security, a polite struggle between parties, a sound currency—in short, a regime where the citizens' business proceeds in fairly good order, as human affairs go. Naïveté? I'm not so sure! . . .

I have known a time when political life in the nations of the West came close enough to fitting this description that it was possible to believe it could someday come true.

38.5   *Conservative tendencies.* I hold happiness to be the only thing that counts, and by "happiness," of course, I mean the feeling one has of it: he is happy who thinks he is and does not want to change.

When I remember how happy the villagers of my area looked (relaxed, well-balanced, satisfied, and jolly) when I was young, and when I now encounter people from the country and from my little town, when I see their worried faces, when I hear their demands, when I perceive the thoughts of hatred and revolt they harbor in their disgruntled heads, I am not sure whether to believe that the social institutions of our times have improved the condition of individuals and that the lower classes are happier since becoming emancipated and conscious proletarians . . .

38.6   *Maumort's conservative tendencies. Sovereignty of the people?* If we someday discovered that we were totally wrong about the question of the sovereignty of the people and that the mass of citizens will always be incapable of governing itself, the two last centuries of Western civilization would seem an eclipse of common sense, a tragic hiatus in the evolution of human society; two centuries squandered on the most chimerical experiments.

38.7   *Conservative tendencies. Against the revolutionary process. The aging Maumort:* Each day I feel the disharmony between my times and myself growing worse. There is only talk of revolution, of a new and better regime. The general ferment does not affect me. I am vaccinated against this revolutionary fever, contagious though it may be for a man like me who knows that all is not right in this world and who wants more order and justice.

Am I the one who lags behind? Or am I ahead of my contemporaries? Am I a backward old man, a fossil attached to outmoded values? Or rather am I a premature example of a coming reaction that will restore in people's minds a taste for order, security, sound judgment, balance, a happy medium?

Whichever it may be, this disharmony exists. The divorce between myself and this turbulent stage of social evolution that we are witnessing is complete. Whatever happens, I know for sure that a certain political romanticism will never again have a hold over me. I hate with a reasoned hatred the incoherence and barbarism of these revolutionary periods. I remain convinced that, by abandoning the way of slow and circumspect reforms in order to adopt that of violent and radical upheavals, those who want to lead the world towards a higher degree of civilization are moving in the wrong direction. They are jeopardizing the natural evolution of the civilized world by thinking it useful to take shortcuts.

By refusing to admire this brutal technique, by bestowing my approval on wise minds, on careful reformers, by dreading the triumph of extremists on every side as the worst danger, by preferring graduated changes to tumultuous upsets, I feel that I am in the tradition of true human civilization and that I am abiding by the laws of the species, whose defensive reactions are to eliminate the agents of disorder and disintegration who abuse, jeopardize, and finally block its natural development.

(1944)

38.8   *Maumort. Politics. Aristo-republican.* Maumort is of the *aristocratic republican* type.

He has (especially after the Affair) the ideas of a man of the left and the *sensibility* of a conservative. The Molé* type?

All his life he has been torn between these two contradictory tendencies.

*Louis-Mathieu, Comte Molé (1781–1855), French monarchist statesman who held office under Napoleon I, Louis XVIII, and Louis-Philippe.

Ready for the boldest social reforms. Very interested in the Russian Revolution and its beginnings.

But a great repugnance for the demagogic politics of the parliamentarians, a liking for order, for *the leader,* and, deep down inside, hard on "the masses"—what his grandfather called "the rabble" and his father "the Communards."

38.9 *Against doctrinaire improvisers. Maumort:* I have made no bones about criticizing the institutions and political practices of the Republic, and time and again I have had occasion to denounce the weaknesses and dangers of democratic regimes, but, all in all, I remain loyal to a social order whose value I have experienced and whose faults, which might be corrected, do not keep it from being the nearest thing to the ideal that I hold of present civilization.

What certain people have tried to replace it with is proving even less satisfactory, and the conditions of existence that these attempts of the new regime imposed on man seem worse to me than those imposed by the old system.

Besides, I mistrust those who think that, out of the blue, we can turn what exists upside down and found a new order from scratch. This is an idea of quixotic doctrinaires. May heaven preserve us in these matters from rash improvisers!

Maumort: In Paris, opinions change with the seasons, and it takes a certain courage, a certain firmness of judgment, to swim against the current and keep believing in an idea that has grown old, that has become commonplace and gone out of fashion, simply because one thinks that it continues to be true.

38.10 *In everything, be wary of improvisation. Maumort:* I am always wary, in every domain, but particularly in politics, of everything that is a rational, logical, global system and that follows an outline, satisfying to the mind, which is the result of human thought and of the will of many elite heads. Particularly in the domain of institutions, or in pedagogy. These brilliant innovations are always fragile because without roots.

At bottom, I am inclined to be a traditionalist. Which is not to defend the past or the status quo. I have faith in what evolves, what lives and changes and develops. But this needs to be the fruition of something that has existed for a long time and that is trying to develop by itself, obeying its own drive, without too many external, foreign additions.

The rest is merely a temporary success, usually shaky, born of the artificial impulse of a momentary need or a fashionable ideology. The rest is merely improvisation.

38.11 *Conservative tendencies. Against democracy.* It is disturbing to realize that, until now, an assembly of parliamentarians is scarcely more than a gathering of long-winded, bawling demagogues, whose brains have not been able to assimilate the abstract principles with which they are intoxicated and who will never derive from them reasonable institutions, a solid and viable regime, or measured rules for leading the nation. They make laws any which way, looking only at the immediate and incidental good that they think it urgent to bring about, and their blinders keep them from seeing the evil they do, the wrongs they commit, in the name of a specious social progress and a narrow concept of justice.

39. MISCELLANEOUS REFLECTIONS

39.1 *Knowledge of oneself and others.*

39.1.1 R. Martin Guelliot, *Le Spectateur,* April 1911, p. 176: "The illusion of constancy." "The prejudice of believing that man always remains true to form, that a sustained attention can be demanded of a healthy and intelligent man and that it be the same every day . . . This prejudice is very common; it could be called *the illusion of constancy . . .*"

39.1.2 *Maumort's thoughts, March '49. Instinctive camouflage in the presence of the person one is speaking to. Mimicry.*

How is it that I always have the impression that my friends have nothing to gain from my putting them in contact with one another?

I always hesitate to hold gatherings at which people are thrown together (although I am probably exaggerating the heterogeneous character of those occasions).

Isn't it mainly that I offer to each, in private conversation, a certain image of myself, rather different according to whom I am with, and that I find myself torn between these different aspects of myself when I am in the presence of several friends at once?

And it is also that I make a special effort to adapt to each of them. When my friends get together, the efforts I would have to make in order not to disappoint any of them are many and contradictory—in other words, impossible.

In this connection, I note a very pronounced phenomenon, similar to what I believe is called mimicry in zoology: an extraordinary and disturbing faculty for shaping myself within a few instants to the milieu I am occupying, to the people who are speaking to me. I am virtually unable to offer others a firm, well-defined personality as long as I perceive, through an instantaneous intuition, that this personality, though it happens to be my own, would put them off, offend them, annoy them. I think if I'd had to sleep on the ocean sands, like a sole, I would immediately have acquired brown spots. Renan confesses, I no longer remember where, to this inability to displease. His amiability must have been just as phony as mine.

39.1.3   False importance of the *face. Maumort:* It is the wearing of clothes that has given so much importance to *faces* (and to hands)—the only "authentic" parts offered to the evaluation of others. Hence, to judge a person's degree of beauty, we devote our attention almost exclusively to the face, as long as the body, under the material, is of satisfactory size and proportions. The habit is ingrained. We do not judge in other ways. He is beautiful, he is ugly, means: he has a pleasing face or his features are not appealing.

But each time I have had an opportunity to see a gathering of naked men (draft board, showers in the barracks, swimming on maneuvers), I have noticed that the point of view was totally changed. We then spontaneously judge the person according to the strength, the grace, the harmony of his body. For example, I was surprised, with one or another of my men whom I was used to regarding as particularly ugly, to find a handsome muscular fellow, with broad shoulders, well-defined pectorals, narrow hips, long slender legs. In that harmonious whole, his unattractive face hardly counted any more. And as soon as he was dressed again, I was surprised that, a moment before, I could ever have found him handsome.

39.1.4   It is in the tone of voice that the soul quite often reveals itself. I always wait to hear people speak before judging them.

39.1.5   *Maumort. Knowing others.* How could we know one another? We never show ourselves as we are, we hide our true faces even from ourselves. I have always vividly remembered that page of Vauvenargues in which he compares the world to a costume ball where the masks dance a quadrille together and part without having revealed who they are.

And so, in my relations with others I have always been at pains to remove my mask. It is often an initiative that induces others to do the same. And it is to my frankness, I believe, that I owe having received so many confidences. I did not hesitate to be the first one to reveal myself. And I have often seen mistrust melt away as a result.

39.1.6   *Maumort: Incommunicability.* It is only at the end of his life, after an appalling number of experiences, after a huge waste of illusions, that a man (even the most sociable, the most surrounded with affection, the best provided with friends) reaches this strange discovery: that all agreement between two people is, to a greater or lesser degree, but always, always, *the result of a misunderstanding*.

One of the bitterest, most indigestible, most difficult truths to accept . . .

39.1.7 *Maumort:* I have never committed great, lasting follies. Reason is for me what automatic brakes are on certain machines: it stops me on the slope of disorder, even when I no longer have a very good grip on the lever of reasoning.

39.1.8 *A friend of Maumort's. Pretending.*
The fellow who is only a "make-believe fellow," who pretends all his life. Pretends to be educated, pretends to be energetic, etc.

Has no children. Even when he makes love he only pretends to be reproducing.

39.1.9 *Vauvenargues. Letter to Mirabeau, 1740.* "But the hard and rigid man, blunt, full of stern maxims, intoxicated with virtue, a slave of old ideas that he has never examined deeply, an enemy of freedom—this man I shun and detest; to my mind this is the vainest, most unjust, most unsociable, most ridiculous type, the one most likely to let himself be hoodwinked by low and deceitful souls, in short the blindest, most biased, and most odious type to be found under the sun.

"A noble and ardent man, unbending in adversity, extreme in his passions, above all things human, with a boundless freedom in his mind and heart, pleases me most; upon reflection, I add to these attributes a supple and flexible mind and the strength to control himself when necessary."

39.1.10 *Maumort. Important people.* People are worthy of respect only insofar as they take life seriously, and their own in particular. But their company is bearable only if they have the good taste never to seem to do so.

(1952)

39.1.11 *Life in society.* Life would be more acceptable if it were not full of so many idle, talkative, indiscreet, and desperately "gregarious" "friends" . . .

39.1.12 *Maumort. Understanding the erring ways of humankind.* The most balanced man, as long as he has some imagination and some natural vigor, has had in his life—if only for thirty seconds—the taste for blood, a wish for murder or for emptiness, and the most perverse, sadistic sexual desires; and this makes it possible to understand how, without necessarily being a monster, a vigorous, violent man, whose moral brakes don't work well, can end up in court.

39.1.13 Simone Weil* writes in her notes to R. P. Perrin: "The crimes horrified me but did not surprise me; I felt myself capable of committing them; it was just because I felt this possibility in myself that they horrified me."

39.2 *Psychoanalysis. Sexuality.*

39.2.1 *An old homosexual.* Mme. Sokolnicka has treated an old man suffering from neurotic problems. He was a homosexual without knowing it who, for sixty whole years, had repressed his instincts, lived a normal life.

39.2.2 *Lie. (Xavier?)* A young woman with a very strong propensity to lie; great gifts for poetry, for literature. Liked to tell tales. Convinced a man that she loved him. Convinced the head of a theater that she had capital for renting and subsidizing that theater, etc.

She lied in particular after a strong emotion. Example: very moved to have suddenly found herself in the presence of the sea, the infinite horizon; once home from her voyage, she is asked if she saw the sea; *she claims she didn't get to see it.* She adamantly maintains that she saw nothing, that she does not remember. Out of a need for discretion, for hiding a deep emotion.

39.2.3 *Lying and onanism.* Rank† has observed that liars are generally onanists, onanists who are not suffering from any neurosis.

Psychoanalysts believe they have also noticed that among the great devotees of truth, most are onanists who have succeeded in overcoming their passion.

39.2.4 *A case of counter-lying.* A young man, whose female cousin committed suicide by throwing herself under a train and whose brother was killed in the war.

Haunted by the idea of guilt, responsibility. Insomnia. Refusing to speak for several days in a row. Tried to pick a fight with peasants he met on the road, in the hope of killing them and having remorse afterwards.

Thought himself responsible for his cousin's suicide. Had, since childhood, wished for his brother's death. All his dreams show the wish for his brother's death.

---

*Simone Weil (1909–1943), French writer and philosopher.
†Otto Rank (1884–1939), Austrian psychologist.

Constant lies. But, while the habitual liar tries to make a false thing real, this man was trying to make what had actually happened unreal through lying. (He spun yarns about the death of his cousin and his brother.) The ordinary liar tries to be believed. This young man, on the contrary, tried not be believed, to make the reality of the past implausible.

39.2.5 *A case of adaptation:* an impotent husband becomes a potent industrialist.
   [*R.M.G. note in pencil:*] A remark by Antoine.*

39.2.6 *The case of a child.* A boy of fifteen. At boarding school. Became a dunce, then fell ill: loss of memory, inability to work, in spite of his ambition to learn. He became extremely hypocritical, pretending to be very devout, very modest, mystical. Said he wanted to be a priest, out of a love of purity.

In reality, an intense, repressed sensuality. And unconscious homosexual instincts.

(In a dream he sees his mother so sick that he wishes for her death as a release, in order not to see her suffer. In fact, *he wished for his mother to be dead,* did not admit it to himself, and derived satisfaction from dreaming of her death as a release for her. A compromise between his wish for this death and the filial love he had acquired the habit of showing her.)

(As a child, lying next to his sister, he had been aroused. What he called "the blackest hour of his life." He dismissed this memory with horror. At each confession, he would return to this very old transgression and ask for penance.)

(At five, he had literally been sick.)

39.2.7 *Dream.* Those who say that they *do not dream* simply mean that *they do not remember* their dreams. Which is the sign of a very great resistance by the unconscious. The more serious a patient's case is, the more trouble he has remembering his dreams.

39.2.8 *Maumort. Inner demons.* I can still recall the dreamy gravity of her gaze and voice when that philosophical old madam, enriched by every possible experience, calmly stated to us:

"One has to have seen all that I have seen from close up, in France and elsewhere, to know this: that vices, surrender to every sexual instinct, debauchery reveal that underside of life of which most people know only the

---

*André Daspre: Which means that this remark might have been placed in the mouth of Antoine Thibault [from Martin du Gard's novel *The Thibaults*].

external aspect. And without that discovery, one cannot understand anything of the true nature of human beings.

"I now associate with men and women of the best social circles, free from all vices; I watch them live. Well, I, who know, perceive in their demeanor, in certain ways they have of thinking, in their judgments, in their behavior, in certain of their actions that are unexpected and as surprising to those who do not know as an undecipherable mystery—I clearly perceive the underside, of which I have experience. I read them like an open book. No one around them—usually beginning with themselves—suspects what they are, deep down in the secret authenticity of their being.

"Then too, some of the more reflective, observant, insightful ones seem at times to have a dim inkling of the vague ferments that are at work in them. For the whole of their normal, conventional, but obscurely unsatisfactory lives, they struggle, in their inner silence, against those murky instincts they sense in themselves.

"Most of you esteemed and respectable people harbor, beneath appearances of integrity and moral 'health,' hidden and unfulfilled vices. And these appearances, which you zealously cultivate, are only an invisible protective cocoon that you unconsciously spin to smother your demons.

"But I, who have lived trafficking with those demons, am not deceived by these appearances."

39.3 *Maumort's personality.*

39.3.1 *Maumort. Accepting oneself.* The secret of my inner peace (which seventy years—let's say half a century—of human life and reflections have never changed) rests on a *"loyal" and natural acceptance of myself.* "Loyal" comes from Montaigne: *To loyally enjoy one's being,* he writes. I did not take this secret from Montaigne, even though he possessed it before I did and it was one of the reasons that made him a chosen master of mine. I did not take it because I already possessed it, even as a child (despite a Catholic upbringing, despite examination of conscience and confession), long before having picked up Montaigne; I do not think it can be acquired. It is a gift of nature. It can be lost, it can be developed: but it can hardly be acquired.

And let it not be said that self-loyalty is an impediment to moral and intellectual improvement. Montaigne, who demonstrates the opposite in many places, can be consulted. For it is not a question of smugness, but of going along with propensities, with (perfectible) tendencies that one discovers in oneself; and this does not imply passivity.

The opposite is Pascal, the very model of the sincere man tortured and dissatisfied with himself.

39.3.2 *Maumort lives on good terms with himself.* A friend of Maumort's, a great traveler (for example an explorer met in Africa) to whom Maumort asks the reasons for his uninterrupted peregrinations, admits:

"It is because I hate myself and am trying to leave myself behind." And Maumort is surprised. Here is a feeling that, even at his worst moments, he has never had. He has always lived on good terms with himself. He is the only person with whom he has always and without exception got along.

39.3.3 *The taste for balance and peace. Maumort writes:* I have never had trouble living in peace with myself and have always done my best to live in peace with others. Peace is my climate. I am tempted to believe it is almost everyone's natural climate: all the people I have known who liked disorder and fighting were also, in some way, unbalanced individuals who had strayed from the norm.

39.3.4 *Maumort: The man "who has arrived" no longer learns anything.* There may be some vanity, some conceit, in thinking this, but I do think it: if I have reached my seventies with the mind of a schoolboy, with the receptivity, the true humility of one who is aware of his ignorance and always tries, on every occasion, to learn something, to reappraise his judgments, to constantly question the little he thinks he knows—I owe this, I believe, to the lack of ambition that has made me a failure in my century, a man without place, power, honors. All those I have met occupying high office, wielding some power, having to command, to hang on to prestige, had stopped learning, even if they had not finished reflecting. They had reached that level where one no longer has the time to go to school; they had to appear to know and not to doubt anything; and they had gradually come to convince themselves that they did know and to be satisfied with their certainties.

39.3.6 I was only at ease when withdrawn and alone in my shell, like a snail.

39.3.7 *Maumort. The lower man and the upper man.* The harmless and amusing breed of people who claim to read palms are accustomed to making a major distinction between the left hand and the right. The lines of the former reveal the *natural* destiny, the hereditary traits, the virtues and defects given at birth; the lines of the latter are more or less different; and these differences mark the *acquisitions,* the modifications in the original person, as a result of training, upbringing, life in society, individual will, fortuitous events.

This distinction corresponds to something real. "Two souls throb in my breast," says Faust. I sense two beings in myself. The first I, the natural I, primitive, the prey of its passions, its terrors, its instincts. And then a second I, which family upbringing, education, life in society, professional life, meditation, culture, and the will have gradually brought out. I feel that my personality is formed by the union of these two I's. And in my daily existence I am quite able to tell their reactions apart. I can say: "The one who just did this, felt that, gave in to anger, to sensuality, to laziness, to fear, is the lower man, the man of the natural depths." And I can say: "The one who resolved to do such-and-such and keeps at it, the one who performed a well-considered action, who exerted a certain influence, who achieved a certain aim is someone else, the upper man, the one I have created to the best of my ability." And throughout all of my "purring" life, I have never stopped developing the higher man at the expense of the primitive man. Or, more precisely, I have done my utmost to guide the instincts, the impulses of the lower man—in whom resides the vital, primal force—towards ends, results, and outcomes that will benefit the upper man.

It is generally the case that the upper man satisfies me more than the other and that I take some pride in my creation. But I sometimes also realize that the lower man was right to refuse, to balk, and he obeyed legitimate instincts; that I was mistaken to force him, to repress him, and to make him perform acts of which the upper man was wrong to be proud.

It is the same as in riding. The good horseman is obviously not the one who indiscriminately lets himself be led by his mount; but no more is the one who is constantly holding his horse back and leaves it no free initiative. The good rider is the one who accepts collaboration, who takes account of his animal's reactions, of the deep wisdom of certain instincts, but who does not surrender unreservedly to those instincts but instead analyzes them, judges them, guides them, steers them towards goals that he has in mind and that his mount is incapable of choosing.

39.3.8 Maumort repeats Stendhal's mot: "To be *true,* simply *true;* that is the only thing that matters."

39.3.9 My epitaph: "He lived in the sadness of a happy life."

39.3.10 *Maumort and ambition.* It has generally been said of me that I was not ambitious. Some have blamed me for this, as if it were a failing.

I have nothing against ambition or against the ambitious. I would rank it among a man's virtues rather than among his faults. But there is ambition and ambition. I think that the quality, the legitimacy, of an ambition can be measured quite accurately by the *means* it uses to satisfy itself. An ambition that does not hesitate to use mediocre means, or even despicable ones, thus reveals the measure of its worth. This criterion has never failed me, and I have always judged the ambitious not by their goals or by their motives but rather by what they were willing or refused to do to achieve their ends: their means, their methods, the relative uprightness of their ways.

40. Determinism and Free Will

40.1   *Chance.* Do not forget that nine times out of ten in life there is a total disproportion between cause and effects.

The most crucial events leading to irrevocable decisions almost always arise from some insignificant chance circumstance, from a fortuitous encounter.

Go back to this often, since it is an "oddity" in the eyes of an old man who is reviewing his life.

Take up Maumort's life again and show, at each decisive stage, that it was some little fact that suddenly changed its course, introduced new elements that totally altered it.

The most cautious, the most deliberate life is still a blind walk. Life is like a road that other roads are constantly cutting across slantwise; we grope our way forward, without seeing those many crossroads, those centers of communication, without being aware of the *choice* that is constantly presented to us. And without realizing it we start down roads whose direction is unknown to us, from which we can never return, towards destinations where chance has led us.

Another comparison: life is like that inextricable tangle of rails that we see as we ride the train out of a large station; rushing along those tracks at a speed that does not allow us to know where they are leading or to choose, we depend on unforeseeable shuntings, etc.

40.2   R. de Gourmont,* *Mercure de France* (1 August 1910), p. 416: "Everything that tends to dull this notion of the absolute dependence of man, an atom swept along in the whirlwinds of causes and effects, is only the childish protest of feeble brains."

40.3   L. Bourdeau,† "The Problem of Death," [op. cit.] p. 121: Individual freedom "is but a metaphysical illusion."

---

*Remy de Gourmont (1858–1915), French writer.
†Louis Bourdeau (1824–1920), French philosopher.

41. TODAY'S YOUTH

41.1 *Maumort and the young.* They appear to think that between the preceding generation and themselves, who went through June 1940, there can no longer be shared ideas or common ground in any area, either in politics or economics, of course, and not even in philosophy or literature. Are they right? As the young Christians who summarily swept away the whole tradition of the Roman Empire might have been right? Or are they too, like so many other generations of young people, victims of that illusion that persuades twenty-year-olds that they are seeing the world with new eyes, that it is obsolete and rotten, and that they will turn it upside down?

41.2 *Maumort. Youth. The prestige of continuity. Maumort will say to the young:* Of course, we judged our elders with a severity full of self-importance, and we too thought that our generation was exceptionally gifted and that it was arriving just in time to mend our fathers' mistakes and finally point the world in the direction of decisive progress . . .

But despite that cheeky criticism, we felt a natural deference towards those who had accomplished something before us. We had a deep sense that every achievement is deserving of respect, because every achievement is difficult and the least result is already a success in itself. And above all, the antiquity, the continuity, the lastingness of a tradition retained, even for the most iconoclastic of us, a mysterious prestige, an unquestionable worth, a secret and powerful authority.

Nothing is more natural, Maumort will say to the young, in this outburst of evil forces that is shaking the planet, than your need to cling to some life buoys, to some floating certainties. That is what castaways do. But if you yield to the temptation, you are lost.

41.3 *Maumort apologizes for being of his time.* What I just wrote would probably shock many young minds. I am aware of it, so much so that I am sometimes tempted to stifle certain thoughts that spontaneously come to me so that I won't think like a fossil. But what for? It's no use wanting to be up to date . . . I would only succeed in seeming to be so—and probably not very convincingly. I have always accepted myself as I was. I must accept myself today as age makes me. And I cannot reject the legacy of my times without running the risk of finding myself stripped of any heritage, of being nothing more than an empty old husk . . .

42. THE BOURGEOISIE

42.1 *Winter and spring '34.* What is really tearing me apart is that at this moment the voices of *reason* and *cowardice* are merged in me.

What *reason* counsels me, in the name of the oldest, the dearest, the most legitimate of my values (that is: not to take sides, to keep a cool head, to remain an arbiter, a scholar) is also what my liking for security, my age, my habits of comfort, and, to be honest, my pusillanimity prompt me to do.

My case must not be unique. Many among us—there are still some scrupulous ones—are on the brink of leaping at extremes that do not really attract them, in order at least to be certain that they are not surrendering to the insidious instinct for tranquillity.

42.2 *Maumort. The bourgeois.* My lineage continues, through me, in a single irresistible and unbroken stream. However much I want to be myself first and foremost, it is neither true nor possible: I am first and foremost my father's son and my grandfather's grandson. My own kicking and thrashing will not change that at all, or very little. I am an outcome, sometimes willing and sometimes reluctant; but however much we want to be of our times, we do not free ourselves from the breed of which we are born. However much we want to be like this or that person we admire, it is our brothers and not our peers that we will take after.

42.3 *On the bourgeoisie.* I have always refrained, says Maumort, from defending the bourgeoisie. As well as from blaming it. I know, from *birth,* what is mediocre about it; but I also know what is healthy about it. And if I had to plead its cause, I would insist on that faithfulness it brings to the principles of order, without which no society can remain balanced and avoid chaos.

I would compare the virtues of the bourgeoisie with those of classicism. It is a necessary dike against political romanticism and the social disintegration that is its consequence. Its existence seems to me like a proof of the instinct of self-preservation that ensures the salvation of the social animal. Its existence has been linked to the order of society, all through these last centuries. It has provided a counterweight to the destructive forces of the rabble's unruly appetites, to the apocalyptic frenzies of revolutionary ideologues of every stripe. It has perhaps saved culture for a while and permitted a high degree of civilization in the West. But its role may be over.

42.4 *Bourgeoisie.* The bourgeoisie of the nineteenth century, as it has survived into the twentieth, will probably disappear before the twenty-first, and because of the same defects that led to the demise of the nobility in the eighteenth: presumptuousness and a lack of will. But let us be fair to it: certain qualities that it had, at the time of its power, assure it an equitable judgment from history.

43. CONCERNING GERMANY

43.1 Tragic destiny of this nation, always hated because of a few obnoxious shortcomings that keep it from being liked for its high virtues. The Germans console themselves by thinking that others envy them their superiority, and for eighty years they have defied the world and tried to terrify it by parading their strength, by glorifying the monarchy, the army, and the fleet.

43.2 For the German people to feel the world's hatred is nothing new. From the beginning of time, the Pan-Germanists have been aware that their wish for power would call down on the Reich universal reprobation and hostility. And we know that the famous "nightmare of coalitions" already hovered over the old Bismarck's insomnia.

43.3 I liked Germany, and I liked the Germans. What sudden Circe changed that people into a horde of loathsome monsters?

43.4 *Ferocity.* La Bruyère: "It is something always novel to me to contemplate how ferociously men treat other men."

43.5 Rivarol: "The most civilized peoples are as close to barbarity as the most burnished steel is to rust."

51. INCLINATION TO MEDITATION. PURRING

51.1 *Maumort's purring.* He speaks much more than he writes and he certainly writes much less than he thinks. Thus it is when alone that he feels he is giving his full measure and is at his best. Which would suffice to explain the place that "purring" has occupied in his life.

51.2 *Purring.* The only moments of complete authenticity. At those times, Maumort is even more than a contemplative monk who surrenders himself, displaying himself openly to the eyes of his Creator, since he experiences the same surrender but is free of any fear of displeasing or saddening God: the surrender of a monk who, far from beating his chest, would accept himself as he is, without regret or pride. This is when Maumort feels a well-being that has its source in a perfect naturalness; he lets his mind roll unconstrained down the slopes of his nature.

51.3 *Maumort and his "purring."* The deep-rooted habit that he has of continually conversing with himself means that, unlike most men, even the most thoughtful, who live turned towards the outside, he has usually remained in a "conscious state." For most men, it is the unconscious state that is habitual.

51.4 *Maumort. "Purring."* To Saint-Gall, who asked me one day what I did with my evenings, I replied, laughing, *"I purr."*

He gave no importance to this retort. It was as if I had told him, "I do nothing," but, spontaneously and by chance, I had enriched my vocabulary with a term that delighted me—and which, half a century later, I still use to describe this exercise of mine, this gentle meditation, which has been the principal and most voluptuous occupation of my entire life. Half-rational, half-emotional. I would never have dared say to myself as I left the barracks or a meeting with friends, and as I hurried home to give myself up to my vice: "Now, let's think" or "Let's meditate." I would not even have dared say to myself: "Let's reflect." That would have seemed an insanely pretentious way to describe the kind of vague daydreaming that I was going to do, with a book on my knees. But I said to myself: "Let's *purr.*"

And during those solitary hours I spent curled up with myself, letting my mind voluptuously roam free, I really was like a satisfied cat that purrs.

Vauvenargues says somewhere: "to leaf through" one's thoughts . . .

51.5 *Maumort. Inclination to meditation. Ecstasy.* I do not know how to characterize this tendency towards withdrawal, towards solitary meditation. All the words seem to me pretentious and inaccurate: reflect, meditate, think, philosophize, etc. There was something of all that in the pleasure I took in *ruminating* by myself. But it looks too much as if I'm describing the meditative youth of a thinker, the childhood of a Leonardo da Vinci, a Descartes, a Pascal, a Vauvenargues. That would be ridiculous and false. I did not have the brain of a thinker, but I enjoyed playing interminably with this inner purring, which, if I had been more gifted, might have turned me into a philosopher. There was ecstasy in that pleasure. I could, without tiring, linger in that vagueness of mind that turns endlessly around itself.

51.6 *Maumort. Purring.* At that time of my youth, Maumort will say, there was so much confusion in people's minds, so many new prospects—it seemed—and, at the same time, so much uncertainty as to the direction in which our elders pointed us, that I saw nothing better to do than explore those vacant tracts and devote as much time as I could to that fascinating (and sterile) exercise which consisted of following every path that presented itself, one after the other, and of wandering according to my fancy among all the ideas of the time, without any hope, any desire, of finding a stable point in that shimmering diversity, without feeling any wish to settle in one spot. I did not think that one could do anything but rove, and the best thing was to do it without anxiety and enjoy it.

51.7   *Maumort as an adolescent.* I had no ambition to write, to express myself literarily, for an audience. First, I did not believe I had the necessary gifts; but even if I'd had them, or had been presumptuous enough to think myself capable of acquiring them, I don't think that it would have changed my plans. I was too self-centered to wish for the approbation of an audience. It was for myself alone that I wanted to learn, meditate, understand. Without entertaining any illusions as to the superiority of my intelligence. I never took myself for an original or deep "thinker." What I wished for, but passionately and tirelessly, was to clarify things for myself: only to become a man with just and clear ideas; to remove forever from my mind all that was vague and obscure; to understand myself perfectly and to grasp as many things as possible.

For me, to "understand" was to have the feeling that I had dispelled from a complex question everything that was conventional and imprecise and had arrived at the heart of the matter, at the essence, at the core of the problem, which I had thus rendered clear and orderly.

In my refusal to become a writer there was perhaps unconsciously a secret warning that someone who always likes to remain neutral, to see things from high up without taking sides, without passion, has nothing in him of what it takes to be an artist and a creator.

51.8   *Maumort and his daydreaming.* For this state of dreamy gawking before the running stream of a thought that flows and saunters along random associations—which was characteristic of me at an early age, which is still the main occupation and distraction of my old age—I have recently found an excellent definition in the *Cahier rouge* of Claude Bernard, who writes this: "Ideas develop spontaneously in the mind, and when you let yourself go with your ideas, you are like a man at his window who watches passersby. You watch your ideas pass by. This demands no effort, it even has a great charm."

That is exactly what I have experienced all my life. Claude Bernard adds severely: "What takes work and causes fatigue is to grab the idea by the neck as one would grab a passerby despite his desire to flee, to keep the idea in place, to fix it, to give it form."

Well yes, I knew that. That is why I never took myself for a thinker but rather for a sort of harmless crank: a waking dreamer.

Leibnitz: "Reflection is nothing but paying attention to what is in ourselves."

51.9   *Purring.* In purring, says Maumort, all that I have really done is to learn to know myself well, which is still the best way of learning about others.

51.10   *The question of the diary. Maumort.* Goethe says somewhere that there comes an age "when one can no longer talk to anyone but God." I feel, like him, that at my age, I no longer much enjoy talking to men. But I still enjoy talking to myself as much as ever. And it even seems to me that this pleasure has only increased with the years.

51.11   *Inner purring. Indulgence towards oneself leading to a sterile life. Maumort confesses:* My attitude, at the moment of our marital falling out, at the time of and after my widowerhood, no matter what the reasons I gave and am still giving myself—is mostly explained by my natural selfishness. This selfishness has fostered in me a prodigious instinct for avoiding suffering, an almost monstrous ability to become detached, a deep-rooted indifference. From adolescence on, I trained myself to be self-sufficient. It was in solitude, in a taste for withdrawal, for living inside myself, that, from the age of fifteen, I looked for and found the source of my happiness. Never happier than when nothing disturbed my inner purring.

Except during my engagement and the first years of marriage, I have never been very good at inconveniencing myself, at putting myself out for others. I asked little of others, and I meant to be treated in kind. Resistant to any emotional slavery, to any commitment which could upset or even disturb my purring. Under an appearance of gentleness, even friendliness, a deep-seated attitude of natural indifference to anything that did not concern my little inner life. My pleasure, to which I sacrificed everything, was to live withdrawn, playing in my corner with my thoughts and my daydreams, like those old maids who cloister themselves voluntarily in their little apartments and spend days doing nothing except handling, arranging, and caring for the objects, the thousands of useless knickknacks with which they have fashioned their narrow universe.

When I look back on my past, I am flabbergasted at having actually dedicated nine-tenths of my time to that perpetual inner retreat. I have sacrificed everything to it, absolutely everything, my affections, my family, my friendships, my career, my vague ambitions for the future. The active periods of my life—in Morocco, during World War I—are a minor part of my existence. All the rest has been swallowed up by the monomania for isolation and inner purring. Like those neutered cats who can and like to doze twenty hours out of twenty-four, rolled up in a ball and purring tirelessly from pleasure. I have led the life of a thinker, of a Benedictine, without doing anything with that mental concentration. A life that would be admirable if it had resulted in something. A selfishness and a withdrawal that would be justified if they had been the raison d'être and the source of a great work. But this monstrous withdrawal was sufficient to itself, and it was totally unproductive, for I am not pretentious enough to believe that my notes, my diary, had the slightest worth and could justify this intellectual onanism.

I have not known how to use the merit I might have had. I am like someone who is an active man, made for enterprise, initiatives, organization, and whose activity is spent in random sauntering.

51.12 *Maumort:* I am aware, as I sketch what is still a very accurate portrait of myself, that I would not use any other words or colors if I had to paint a "great thinker," a Montaigne or a Descartes . . .

I am risking ridicule, in order to be truthful.

All these descriptions are accurate. It is strictly true that only one thing has counted in my life: to think, to understand, to be curious about as many things as possible, to set in motion for my unique and tireless pleasure my thinking machine, in the same way as a Montaigne or a Descartes.

If this constant toil of my brain has only shed a weak light on the problems that arise for men, it is for lack of genius and I can do nothing about it. Nevertheless the truth of the matter is that I have only liked inner meditation; it is not my fault if my intelligence was not endowed with more power and penetration. The very meager result of my research in no way alters the fact that my only interest in this world was to try to understand. The flame has not stopped burning in the heart of the lantern; this is all I can claim. But it was a dark lantern that scarcely shone, I admit. This tiny gleam nevertheless has lit my entire life.

51.13 *Journal. Maumort. Shell.* I just remembered a moment ago the big flesh-colored shell, streaked with brown, that my grandmother brought back from some trip and which for so many years sat, as a curio, on the console table in my bedroom. Sometimes she would put its surface, cold and smooth as porcelain, to my ear, and tell me: "Listen . . . Do you hear the sound of the sea?" I had never heard the sea; but I made out a steady murmur in the depths of the shell, which brought to mind the wind of November under the doors, the rhythmic breathing of a sleeper.

Enclosed in my library, with this fat notebook of white paper, my dreams, and my memories, I am like the child of long ago who used to lean over the shell: I listen, tirelessly, to that long whisper which slowly rises from the depths of my past.

51.14 *Purring. Passive daydreaming.* This curious phenomenon of progressive development, sometimes continuous, sometimes intermittent, capricious, jerky; of the solitary mind inexhaustibly fertilizing itself.

Another image: those moments when I drew from myself an uninterrupted string of thoughts, as a spider endlessly spins his web.

51.15 *Maumort. Fishing.* Fishing for memories, a ledger line. Old fisher of memories. He should call his memoirs: *Memories of an Old Fisherman.*

I feel like an old railway carriage on a siding.

51.16 *Maumort.* I feel like an old well at the bottom of which life has left a bit of truth.

52. BENT FOR PSYCHOLOGY. CURIOSITY ABOUT HUMAN BEINGS

52.1 *Maumort. He can say:* I have always been passionately interested in what it is to be human, since *without any intent* (that is, with no other intent than to satisfy this curiosity) I noted everything that was happening in the present, in no particular order.

How strange it is that, after having burned all that, after having let go of, got rid of, freed myself from that past (to which I had given a form, an imprint, through writing) I cannot bring myself to accept this disappearance, this deprivation. This need to fish up the past and to make a new imprint of it does not let me rest. No matter how genuinely modest I am as to what I write, I cannot get the idea out of my mind that what I am recounting is fascinating in itself. And it is absolutely true that this is the only thing which now, when nothing but the present should interest me, fascinates me, to the detriment of everything else.

52.2 *For Maumort. About having memories distorted by the point of view of the present.* As he grows old, he doesn't tire of the surprise he feels observing the parallel development of all things—of people, families, ideas, institutions.

The evolution of people our age, like ourselves, whom we have known in their youth, in an earlier phase, and whose progress we have followed step by step, is a subject of endless meditation and interest. Usually, everything is unpredictable and yet at the same time—though we were not able to foresee it—appears to us, when we notice it, as necessary and such that we could and should have foreseen it if we had been able to distinguish the essential elements, the real causes, the true secret forces, the laws of nature.

Maumort: It is even more striking for me as I fish up my memories. For I discover with hindsight that it is only now that I begin to see clearly into the chaos of the past. Memories, as I write them down today, in the light of the present, with the clear awareness of what was and of what has come to pass, are different and infinitely better observed, truer, than what I noted then, at the actual moment. I see the origins of past events, their points of departure, their true directions, their secret and profound motives, which often escaped me at the time. I see their complete outlines, I untangle their real meaning; and this total understanding, which was hidden from me by the perspective of the present, was impossible for me at the time when I was both living and noting these occurrences. I remember my notes back then well enough to feel how rudimentary and incomplete they were, and distorted by too close a viewpoint. It is now, with the light of today and the knowledge of what followed, that I finally am approaching the confused truth of that time. I reconstruct reality, as it was and as I did not then perceive it.

52.3   *Maumort. About the diary. The keyhole. Maumort: I have spent a lot of time at the keyhole . . .* in order to observe myself zealously and others no less zealously.

52.4   *Object of Maumort's meditations: man.* If Maumort were to summarize in three lines the subjects which have occupied a whole life of solitary and insatiable reflection, he would say: *the entire effort of my mind has been confined to dismissing appearances in order to deepen the knowledge of myself and the knowledge of others.* Not a metaphysician in the slightest—no angst about the infinite—but rather a psychologist, a moralist: a boundless curiosity about all human types, beginning with the closest: myself.

52.5   *Maumort. Knowledge of man.* To know something of the depths of man, it is indispensable to undertake a lucid exploration of one's own depths, and I have long thought that this prerequisite was enough. I no longer think so. The contact with others, the display of their behavior in difficult and various circumstances, their confidences, opened many avenues to me that I would never have discovered in myself alone. But to understand others, we need to be used to analyzing ourselves and to have gone very far in that direction: what we discover in others also helps us very much to know ourselves. These two kinds of study are linked and those who do not pursue them simultaneously do not go far.

· · ·

52.6 *Experience. Maumort values what he calls his "experience."* Claude Bernard wrote: "Experience is always the conclusion of a process of reasoning whose starting point is observation." (Quoted by Fernandez, *N.R.F.*, May '43, p. 485.)

(He was obviously thinking about scientific experiments, about the laboratory, but this also goes for experience, i.e., the acquisition of wisdom in the course of one's life.)

52.7 *Maumort's philosophy. The inefficiency of intelligence, of knowledge.* *Maumort:* In observing myself without illusion, without pretension, I noticed early on that—in me at least—in spite of appearances, will and action never obeyed reasoning or intelligence but, on the contrary, were set in motion by my instinctual nature, and it was after the fact that I used my intelligence and my reason to give a flattering meaning to my feelings and impulses and to justify my actions. This observation has had no small part in leading me to become very skeptical regarding the value and the prestige of theories and of intelligence in general.

Intelligence only provides pretexts after the fact, justifications which satisfy our pride as reasoning beings. When by chance I obeyed my reason, it was because it simply happened through a felicitous and pleasing coincidence that I was spontaneously disposed by my instincts to act in that way. The powerlessness of intelligence is particularly blatant when it is a matter of good and evil. It is as impossible to be good because you have an understanding of what virtue is about as to become a creative artist the moment you understand, with your intelligence, what art is. To understand and to do, to know and to be, have nothing in common.

52.8 *A rough and difficult character (important).* Maumort is rough. An old soldier, intelligent and philosophical, with a very free mind, full of personal views, he retains a tough side, inflexible, slightly aggressive: *a difficult character.*

All his setbacks are explained in part by this *ornery attitude,* and also his isolation, his having few friends. He always frightened the circles in which he lived with his violent judgments, his blunt frankness, his natural, somewhat contemptuous severity, his haughtiness. *A quarrelsome wisdom.* Has always fallen out with everyone. Upright, rigid, understanding, and tolerant through effort and reflection, but abrupt in his relations, intransigent, surly, difficult to handle.

He has never been loved except by very rare friends. His peers, as a whole, hated him. They felt judged. The respect he inspired was usually not accompanied by affection. *The opposite of easygoingness.* Establish Maumort's difficult character right away.

"The docile, obedient, orderly, hardworking, unmischievous child that I was did not presage the ornery individual, with a difficult character, irascible, intransigent, not much loved by his peers, that I was to become at the age of puberty."

52.9   *Maumort. Virtue: the prolongation of a fault.* Goethe, in *Poetry and Truth,* remarks that our faults and our virtues are of the same essence, that our virtues are the blossoming prolongation of our faults, as the stem and the bloom of a plant are the prolongation, the blossoming in the light, of the roots that spread in the secrecy of the earth.

He adds that this is why we are usually aware of our virtues and why it is harder for us to notice our faults, since they dwell in the secrecy of our nature. He denied quite often that we can understand ourselves and stated repeatedly that others knew him better than he knew himself.

This is questionable, and I prefer what he used to say to Lavater: that man, in observing himself, notices more readily what he lacks than what he possesses, his shortcomings rather than his virtues; that he is more tormented by his imperfections than delighted by his qualities.

Elsewhere, in *Iphigenia,* Goethe says the following: "Man rarely thinks highly of what he does, and what he does, he hardly ever knows how to value."

Still elsewhere, he says *(Aphorisms):* "How to learn to know oneself? Never through meditation but through action. Try to do your duty, and you will immediately know who you are."

52.10   *To be curious is the opposite of being stupid.* "*À qui peu bée, peu vient.*" It is to old Ernestine that I owe my knowledge of this delightful proverb. Henriette often told me that, as a child, I wore out everyone in the house, including herself, with my constant and unexpected questions. Only Ernestine always answered. And when she heard my sister making fun of my "How?"s and "Why?"s Ernestine corrected her: "Let him do it, dear. The one who's the most curious is never the stupidest. *À qui peu bée, peu vient.*" Henriette and my father amused themselves by repeating this proverb, which they had never seen written out, and which, phonetically, I am almost sure they did not understand any more than I did. "*À qui bébé, peu vient,*" we would stupidly go on repeating.

It was Xavier de Balcourt, one day when Ernestine's proverb had come up in the conversation, who got us to repeat it, looked into how to write it, sought out its meaning, and finally enlightened all of us. Certain things make a lasting impression, one doesn't know why. I remember that evening when Xavier, after having questioned Ernestine and having got her to repeat the sentence ten times, put on the right track by the very exact intonation that the old woman gave it, had an inspiration: "I've got it! *À qui peu bée*, whoever fails to investigate, who has no curiosity, desire, appetite, *peu vient*, obtains little, remains poor . . ." He got great enjoyment from his discovery, and so did we.

I have never forgotten this proverb of Ernestine's. It is very wise. Indifferent people don't get anywhere. You must yearn deeply to receive; desire deeply to obtain; put a lot of passion into your quest, if you want it to be fruitful.

This proverb has stayed with me all my life. I have applied it to myself many times. I have never wanted to be modest in my ambitions. When it seemed to me I desired the impossible, I thought: *À qui peu bée, peu vient!* and I went forward despite everything. This gave me good results, almost always.

52.11   *On the lookout. Maumort confesses:* I am able to remain a whole hour behind a shutter, watching someone live who is not doing anything interesting but who thinks he is alone, who does not know he is being watched. Such a spectacle delights me, thrills me, fascinates me. I am like people of the yellow race: I like to spy—on anybody, for no reason, for fun.

52.12   There is a book by Barbusse*, the hero of which condemns himself to live as a prisoner in a hotel room because he has discovered a crack in the wall which allows him to see and hear everything that is going on in the next room. From the first pages on, as soon as I understood the subject, I felt myself blushing, as if I had been caught doing something wrong.

52.13   *Maumort. 1883.* In his youth, not much taste for novelty. More curious about people than about things. Little desire for travel and change of scenery. And in his curiosity about people, more inclined to observe those he already knew well than to be on an endless quest for new relationships.

52.14   *Maumort:* I don't know how much sincere love there is in me for my fellow man. But isn't this need to make myself loved by him already a proof of my feeling for him?

52.15   *Maumort's memory.* A surprising memory, precise, evocative, providing a thousand unexpected details (which explains the exactitude of the recollections, the descriptions).

---

*L'Enfer (The Inferno), by Henri Barbusse (1873–1935).

Maumort: Goethe maintains that at sixty a man has already drunk from the waters of Lethe. This does not apply to me. I would almost say: quite the opposite! The older I get, the less I have of certain of my faculties (imagination, reasoning, stamina in work—especially imagination) and the more it seems my memory remains keen, standing on ruins, never tired of projecting its movies. And this is probably due to the fact that as I get older I exercise it even more, since I take even more interest—the only interest left to me—*in remembering.*

52.16 *Maumort, on the subject of the memory. Different memories. He could say:* I have it from a Jewish friend that the Talmud distinguishes four kinds of *memory:*

—That which retains only the latest impressions, what is recent, and forgets the rest.

—That which, on the contrary, seems already full, does not record the present in a lasting way, and contains only old memories.

—That which retains everything equally and is an inexhaustible receptacle, cluttered with memories.

—That which chooses with discrimination, like a demanding collector, and keeps only the quality pieces.

The first is like a blackboard erased with a sponge. The second is like a notebook with no more blank pages. The third is like a general store, like a load of household garbage. The fourth is like a filter.

52a. READING

52a.1 *Maumort's reading. Quotations from reading.* One of Maumort's characteristics is to have owned a huge library and to have read enormously.

Insist strongly at the beginning on the joy that he has in finding his books intact, in reordering them, in having those he bought in the Lot sent to him, in starting to read again. And then, he constantly writes down quotations from his reading. We must feel that he spends the greatest part of his days reading. And he quotes excerpts: "I picked up the second volume of the *Letters* of Seneca again. I find this in it: (quotation) which relates to what I was thinking the other day . . ." I only need to draw copiously from my vast collection of "quotations." An excellent way to use them. And, by means of the selection of these texts, I will draw a much more thorough and subtle portrait of the mind, the taste, the inclinations of Maumort while giving the readers the pleasure of finding there a ready-made anthology.

He buys books. He will say: "I have sent off to replace such-and-such a book that I can no longer find." And later on, he will draw quotes from it.

52a.2   *Pontigny, 1923: education of Paul Desjardins (Uncle Éric).** His encounters with foreign authors:

—At twenty, Emerson; quest for oneself.
—At twenty-six, Tolstoy: *War and Peace, Anna Karenina;* G. Eliot, *Middlemarch.*
—At thirty, Dostoyevsky.
—At thirty-five, Ibsen.
—At forty, Nietzsche: *Beyond Good and Evil.* Forbidden fruit.

52a.3   *Memory of childhood reading. Maumort:* A curious thing for me, who was to become such a great reader, that I only began to read, to like to read, very late. I was never one of those children who, as soon as they can read well enough to do it effortlessly, dive madly into any printed matter they can lay their hands on. On the contrary. Most of the books I was given I began and didn't finish. I found them totally uninteresting. The Bibliothèque Rose† bored me stiff. And I did not acquire a taste for reading until I was fourteen or fifteen, when I could read adult books.

I preferred life to books, the spectacle of the world to the best-told fiction. I especially remember the extreme interest I took, as a child, in the activity of workers. I could sit for half a day, attentive and silent, in front of the workbench of a carpenter who came to do some repairs at le Saillant, or watch a farmer's wife as she baked bread. One summer, we had the furniture in most of the bedrooms reupholstered, and an upholsterer came to live in one of the outbuildings for two weeks. I did not leave his side. I was ten. Soon he entrusted me with small tasks, showing me the tricks of the trade. Those two weeks count among the best memories of my holidays.

Since that time, the only thing I have preferred to reading is my *purring.* These two pleasures, besides, were often fused. I picked up a book, read twenty pages, then kept it open in front of me; but, with my head between my palms, twisting a lock of hair on my right temple, I went off into an interminable reverie.

52a.4   *Maumort. Reading.* The arrival of the Chambosts' library at le Saillant brought about a profound evolution in my intellectual life. I lived in the midst of books. Apart from my sustained reading, I fell into the habit of taking a book off the shelf at random, on the spur of the moment, for half an hour of leisure and reading, of entering into contact with a mind of the past,

---

*Paul Desjardins (1859–1940), teacher, principal model for Éric Chambost-Lévadé.
†A collection of books for children.

even if only for an instant. I lived in the daily company of an elite of thinkers who had a life different than mine, other educations, other tastes, other tendencies, other orientations, other truths.

The multiplicity of those different readings made my mind supple, and precisely at the age when it usually becomes ossified. By agreeing with them one after another, because I understood their points of view, I achieved an extraordinary tolerance, I lost a certain ignorant smugness, I understood much, and I judged everything more impartially.

Not only did my library educate me, at an age when the mind has a tendency to withdraw into itself, but it made me better.

Cite titles: Emerson, Montaigne, Goethe, Rousseau, Voltaire, Diderot, Vauvenargues, Saint-Évremond, Bossuet, Tolstoy, Dante, Chesterton, Shakespeare, Gibbon, La Bruyère, Ibsen, Plato, Kierkegaard, Descartes.

52a.5   *Maumort as reader:* I have strolled about in this library for twenty years like a customer in a clothes store; I try on this and that, until I have found something that fits me: my mood, my size that day. The miracle is that my size (mood) is sufficiently changeable so that, over time, I have read and reread all my books, or just about.

53. Taste for Solitude

53.1   *Maumort. Solitary old age.* Each human being is alone. I already understood this at fifteen. But there are degrees in this human isolation. The most impermeable of all isolation is that of the people who, throughout their evolution, never cease to strive to be as lucid as possible. It is also the most dignified, the proudest, and the one that permits the achievement of a sort of serenity.

Wisdom, that late fruit which ripens so slowly and can only be picked at the very end of the harvest, in *solitude.*

53.2   *Maumort. Solitude.* I don't know how to express this sensation of joyous intensity, of vitality, that solitude and "purring" always bring me. It is only at those moments that I feel that *each minute has its full share of life.*

53.3   *Maumort's total solitude. Maumort:* There is something monstrously abnormal in my solitude. Without a wife, children, nephews, relatives, almost without friends. Alone in the world, to an extent that may be unique. Alone in the middle of a universe that is highly populated, but only by memories. Alone in the world, in a world gone by.

That's how it is. Up to me to make the most of this fact.

53.4   *Maumort. "Use the terrain." (Paul Maunoury).* A military expression, very often employed by Maumort, which contains the whole philosophy of a skeptical and level-headed man who is always trying to adapt himself to what is happening, to draw some advantage out of what is inevitable.

53.5   *Maumort. "My" silence.* I don't like southerners. I enjoy *my* silence too much. In order to think, they always need the *agora* or the *forum.* No other type of human being so lacks—I won't say just a need or a taste for solitude, but even a sense of what it is.

53.6   *Solitude. The beyond.* I believe—if we admit the hypothesis of a beyond—that after death the reward of the just will be to be able to live eternally alone, free to be with themselves and in silence. This supreme luxury, is, I think, the paradise reserved for the best. The punishment of the wicked will be lack of privacy, impossibility of escaping the group, perpetual merging with the crowd. Hell is the constant contact with others, with their rules and their "infernal" din; one of the tortures of hell will be the uninterrupted cacophony of the radio, invention of Satan.

(1949)

53.7   *Musician:* "Do you like music?" "To tell the truth, I generally prefer silence . . ."

53.8   Fabre-Luce,* *Fils du ciel,* pp. 160–161 (Gallimard, 1941): "How, after having freed ourselves from traditional moral rules, can we keep our purity? Is it through solitude? Is it through action?

"It is after having cut the mooring ropes that we begin to make discoveries in ourselves.

"Solitude is never anything but a point of balance, soon left behind, between a world of living beings and a world of specters . . ."

53.9   *Maumort:* My life as an old man, my life as a recluse, has been so quiet these last years, in this solitude, that I've sometimes felt myself slipping into a forgetfulness of all the things of the world as one sinks into quicksand. Sometimes I've reached the point where I got so used to this solitary and desireless life that I no longer thought about the passions, the forces of instinct which rule the hectic existence of men; a little more and I would have doubted their existence, a little more and I would have wondered if they

*Alfred Fabre-Luce (1899–1983), French writer.

were not fictions, inventions of a mind that deforms, exaggerates, conjures up ghosts.

And now, with this diary which throws me back into the past and makes me relive the emotions, the jolts, the whole fire of my youth, it is as if all the demons suddenly filled my solitude and my confinement, and I ask myself through what blindness I had come to forget or to doubt their sovereign powers. "Evil is the active force created by instinct," says William Blake.*

53.10   *Maumort. The Appian Way.* A septuagenarian who looks back over his past life is like a stroller whose path is strewn with graves. I daren't compare my trivial existence to the majestic Appian Way . . . : in any case, a path in a cemetery.

53.11   *Gravity.* Maumort likes this sentence from Vigny's *Journal intime:* "Once you are alone, descend to the bottom of your soul, and you will find, sitting on the last step, *gravity* awaiting you."

53.12   *Islam and silence. Maumort:* Islam has revealed to men this *wisdom of silence,* of which the European has no knowledge.

The Arab knows that silence is a force, and makes it a point of pride to keep quiet.

53.13   *Maumort.* Chadourne tells me that what is impossible for cured tuberculosis patients who have spent five years in a sanatorium is not so much to go back to active life as to resume an interest in life outside. They are always a little like foreigners in transit among their families and compatriots, less sensitive to events and bereavements.

This is exactly Maumort's state of mind. Because of his age and his long years of withdrawal from the life of others.

54. MAUMORT. FONDNESS FOR WITHDRAWAL. ATTITUDE OF A SILENT SPECTATOR

54.1   *Maumort could say to the occupiers:* In gagged France, very few intellectuals (and especially few among those who count) have bowed fawningly and paid court to the masters of the hour. Like those prisoners behind bars who have no other means of protest but the hunger strike, many French intellectuals mounted a silence strike and nobody mistook the meaning of those abstentions, neither their usual readers, nor public opinion, nor the

---

*This is a literal translation from the French. Blake's actual line goes: "Evil is the active springing from Energy." (*The Marriage of Heaven and Hell,* Plate 3.)

people in power: one only needs to see how the official press has slung mud at them—to the extent of trying to make them the persons most to blame for this military defeat.

For several years we have lived in exile in our own country, like animals that feel the earth shake: motionless, cooped up, waiting. But there is a ripening in this wait: and a real virility as well, in this temporary and silent acceptance.

Gagged, powerless, we have seen an accumulation of mistakes, which were not all inevitable consequences of the defeat, and we are impatient to be able to participate in a collective effort which would have our complete support.

Fabre-Luce, *Journal de la France*, I, 90 [events of March 1939 to July 1940]: "The free spirits are no longer of any use; they dedicate themselves to silence."

Like so many others, I dreamt of the brotherhood of man and believed that this generous impulse, which has existed from time immemorial, was finally going to steer towards stable relations a humankind that I wanted to believe had quieted down. Alas! *Homo homini* more of a *lupus* than ever!* The discouraging spectacle that the world has presented to my mature years is that of constantly more violent demands, and of merciless battles ruled by force and never by reason; of an unleashing of sectarian hatreds that throw individuals, social classes, parties, peoples, races, and continents into conflict one against another. The emergence of that brotherly, hardworking, and peaceful world, to which the destiny of thinking man is leading us, has been postponed until future millennia. The reign of Confucian morality is still not in sight. How to reject the hard lesson of the facts?

I have nothing to say. I am made in such a way that even in this period when passions are in control and when none but fanatical ideologies confront each other, I can only come out with moderate words. It would probably take more than the calamities and the disasters of this time to get me to give up this ideal of moderation and tolerance in which I think I see the best prefiguration of justice.

54.2 *The attitude of the spectator in times of revolution. Tocqueville "memories" (of 1848).* "I felt that we were all in the midst of one of those great (democratic) floods, where the dikes that individuals and even parties want to set up only serve to drown those who build them and where nothing is left to do for a while but to study the general characteristics of the phenomenon."

---

*The Latin saying *Homo homini lupus* means "man is a wolf to man."

54.3 *Maumort and recent events:* While the bloody insanity continues to spread, while partisan fury, useless cruelty, ideological confusion reign, how to keep one's serenity, how to avoid the pain of a sterile pity, how to resist despair? One would need to have enough strength to apply the saying of Dante: *Guarda e passa,* "observe and move on . . ."

54.4 *Nothing good to expect from chatterboxes. Silence.* When the storm blows, the mind has no other refuge than silence. Ecclesiastes: "A time to keep silence and a time to speak." Pascal: "One must keep silent as much as one can."

Silence is not synonymous with submission. There are people who are not made for getting into fights. Descartes says that he would rather "be a spectator than an actor in all the comedies playing in the world."

Montherlant wrote to Faure-Biguet* in 1919: "And I so keenly feel the intellectual poverty of those who demand that we take sides!"

54.5 *Silence.* We are in one of those chaotic times in history when certain independent minds, those who have a taste for order as well as a reverence for freedom, are condemned to an attitude of silent spectators, caught up as they are in preserving the integrity of their inner life from those upheavals.

54.6 *As a man of his times, Maumort will say:* The defeat, the armistice, and the shapeless chaos that followed have definitely put me on the sidelines. In May '40, if I opened a newspaper or a magazine, I would get annoyed but would want to argue all the same—I still felt somewhat a part of my time.

Today, no—it's over. I am irrevocably out of it. *I no longer feel contemporary.*

54.7 *Maumort. A disconcerting period:* A strange time . . . Its events have an extravagant, unexpected, disconcerting character. Such a remark in the mouth of a young man might provoke the response that such has always been the case, and that man, incapable of prescience, has always been surprised by what happens. But I have lived long enough to maintain that this has not always been so. The extraordinary made its debut in the current world in 1914. Before that date, things that occurred had often not been foreseen in detail, but they were among the expected things, the various hypotheses that could have been formulated, without one knowing which would come to pass. Today events defy any hypothesis. This must have been the case at certain times of violent crisis in the history of mankind. People alive

*Henry de Montherlant (1896–1972), French novelist and playwright; Jacques-Napoléon Faure-Biguet (1893–1954), French literary critic.

in 1789 and 1793, witnessing the history of their times, must have experienced the same disorientation.

54.8 *Maumort's retirement. Maumort on his retirement and his old age at le Saillant:* If there is idleness in my selfish existence, it is an idleness which remains substantial and which has the merit, at least, of being quite pleasant.

54.9 *Maumort. Resignation. Don't complain. "A well-bred man eats anything"* (Max Jacob, *Conseils à un jeune poète*, 1945, p. 107). M. Jacob, p. 78: "Courteline said to Jules Renard: 'Don't get embittered!' "

54.10 *Maumort:* I have this double disposition of being able to be sometimes a man of action and sometimes an attentive, impassioned, but passive spectator. And on occasion I move very quickly from one state to the other. I have been this way since my adolescence. With a secret preference, it seems to me, for the attitude of an observer. A preference, in any case, which has increased with age and which is such that now I truly do not wish for anything but to watch current events carefully and understand them well.

54.11 *Maumort.* Not very talkative. A gaze both intense and serene, a penetrating gaze that inspires trust, a *silent gaze.*
     Gives the impression of a beautiful building, of a beautiful inner architecture. That impression of balance which is given by a beautiful monument, a Greek temple, a Renaissance façade.
     In him, the balance of the world.
     And also, in this balance, there is the exact opposite of the (slightly hysterical) dynamism of the party-joiners, the fighters, those who are possessed and set in motion and propelled forward by a single fixed, dominating, proliferating idea. The fighter is in a state of imbalance, like a man walking. Maumort is a man at rest, the motionless guardian of a flame sheltered from disorderly winds.
     Our era has lost its balance.

54.12 *Maumort. Contemplative order.* "A man of action, that is what I have been during most of my life. For thirty years or so, speculation was for me only a luxury that I pursued outside a terribly active life. But for the last twenty years, it has been the opposite. I have dedicated the best of my time to thinking. And since my accident two years ago I have completely entered the *contemplative order.*"
     No. He has always "purred."

55. TENDENCIES TO ARISTOCRATISM (ESOTERICISM)

55.1   *Maumort. Aristocratism. Pascal:* "Nobility is a grand thing: it is twenty years won at a stroke." (He meant that a man of simple birth, in order to make his merits known, to receive an important office, had to expend twenty years' worth of efforts from which the noble is exempted thanks to his power, his connections, his position in society, his money.)

552.   *Maumort. Aristocracy.* There is something *uncultured,* in spite of everything, in a man of common birth, Maumort will think, no matter what his level of education, culture, refinement, and worth. True culture agrees best with the inheritance of an ancient tradition, the innate habit of certain material advantages, certain privileges. I even wonder if this absurd, groundless, and indefensible feeling of social superiority has not furthered in me this interest I take in myself, which might have turned into the basest selfishness but which in me has mainly led to reflection, to study, to cultivation, *to the cultivation of myself,* to introspection.

55.3   *Maumort. Aristocracy.* Maumort does not believe in the virtues of aristocracy by birth. For him, the aristocracy can only be the elite of the nation, those who have risen to the first rank thanks to their merits, their intelligence, their work. But, all the same, he has, on account of his birth, an unconscious satisfaction, an involuntary pride. Though he knows that it is nothing to his credit to have been born a Maumort, he likes it. He is happy to have had *that good fortune.* It seems to have conferred on him a certain set of character traits that he holds in particularly high regard. He well knows that his worth, to the extent that he has any, is based on something else: his education, his studies, the cultivation of his mind, his intellectual life. Of course, but he almost thinks that his birth has predisposed him to acquiring those values, and he is grateful to it for that. He cannot consider it an unimportant asset. It is something very close to *heredity.* An *inborn* predisposition.

55.4   *Aristocratism.* The basic thing is to accept yourself, in your own nature. Not as you are, but as you are by nature. If you're a plum tree, don't try to produce apples but rather get from your sap the best sort of greengage . . . *"Begin by having self-esteem,"* says Nietzsche, *"everything else flows from that." The Will to Power,* II, aph. 440.

To remain like oneself, in one's own truth, one's own nature, and seek to improve oneself. Convinced of my right to exist, without mutilation or fakery. Having sensed very early on that common conventions and rules were detrimental to the integrity of my personal consciousness; and that the moral dogmas of society threatened to stifle my vital forces to no purpose.

55.5 *Maumort on morality.* One has to accept oneself, explore oneself, make the most of oneself. This has been the rule of my life. Everything is allowed, on condition that one can, in everything that one allows oneself, keep one's self-esteem and feel that, in doing so, one remains true to oneself and to one's real nature.

What do the rules dictated by standard morality matter? We well know that they are *relative,* that they vary according to times and places, and that any rule can be countered by another, just as valid. We only owe them a minimum of submission, what we grant, out of politeness and sociability, to the conventions accepted by the majority. We have to remove our hat upon entering a church and our shoes upon entering a mosque. All our obedience to morality is of the same order: to avoid needlessly scandalizing our neighbor, out of the duty to be sociable.

55.6 *Aristocratism. Maumort:* At bottom, I have always obeyed *my* law, defended *my* truth, followed *my* morality, without, however, openly infringing *the* accepted law, truth, morality—out of politeness, out of concession to social norms, and with no missionary zeal, without trying either to adapt my law, my truth, my morality to the law, the truth, the morality of the masses, or to have my law, truth, morality prevail over theirs.

55.7 *Maumort. Aristocratism.* To have a firm grip on myself, to watch myself and see myself clearly, without cheating, to avoid assigning false reasons to the acts I am about to perform, and then . . .

Then, I don't say "complete freedom," but "great, very great freedom." I don't say, "everything is allowed," but: "Almost everything is allowed if I act consciously." To know myself for what I really am. And this brings to mind something that Degas said to one of his students. He leans over the sketch: "But, my boy, your left arm is much too long." The student hesitates and stammers: "Maître, I wanted that . . . It's on purpose . . ." "Ah," replies Degas, "if it's on purpose, that's another thing entirely. I haven't said a word. Go on, go on . . ."

55.8 *Maumort. Individualism. Aristocratism. Good and evil.* This anarchic tendency, this anarchic aristocratism, goes far back. In our year of *philosophie* at school, five of us formed a secret *Pentabolic* society, which we placed under the protection of the ancient philosopher Archeleus, of whom it had been said to us, by an imprudent teacher, that he was the founder of a philosophical doctrine according to which good and evil did not exist in themselves, in a natural way, but only in a conventional way. For Archeleus, moral laws were nothing more than arbitrary rules imposed by the chief, the tyrant, the one with the power, the one who was strongest, or by the majority (which amounts to the same thing). The distinction between the just and the unjust already seemed to us an entirely personal opinion, the prerogative of the individual, a right of the free mind. To each his own morality. Not as suits his wishes, but as suits his conscience. For our *"pentabolic"* doctrine prided itself on being lofty, and we debated endlessly and with laudable punctiliousness in order to determine what were, by our lights, the limits of good and evil. In short, if my memories do not delude me, we did not categorically object to any sort of behavior as long as our action did not injure anyone. And we forbade whatever caused others to suffer. Hence we came to the conclusion that a certain amount of hypocrisy was permissible and even advisable, since if we forced the spectacle of a scandal upon others it would harm them by going against their conformist idea of good and evil. Everything was allowed to the superior man who we judged ourselves to be, on the condition: 1) that he be aware of his action, and in harmony with his personal conscience, 2) that this action make no one suffer, 3) that this action be kept secret so as not to shock the *pecus*.*

55.9 *Thoughts of Maumort. In praise of hypocrisy.* Politeness is a *social* necessity, the most important of all. And there is no politeness without hypocrisy. Which amounts to saying that hypocrisy is of vital importance in human relations.

One needs to be brutally frank with oneself and amiably hypocritical with everyone else. The only thing that matters is that this hypocrisy be *conscious* and within bounds. It is less a matter of deceiving others than of not needlessly wounding them.

55.10 *Maumort.* Quite impervious to what-people-will-say-of-him, and indifferent to the disapproval of the Saint-Gall circle.

He had early acquired the habit of relying on his reason, on his conscience, and of spurning commonly accepted rules.

This without ostentation, still less defiance. On the contrary, a certain diligence, not just in playing something of the hypocrite, but in hiding, or at least keeping to himself, what did not need to be said. The avoidance of scandal was for him an elementary form of politeness.

*The herd.

55.11 *Maumort. Aristocratism. "Social politeness."* To reconcile a legitimate moral freedom with the rules honored by the society in which one lives.

At a certain level of intelligence and culture, the individual is perfectly justified, in the conduct of his private life, in taking into account only the dictates of his own conscience; on the condition, however, that he exercises with discretion the freedoms that his conscience grants him and that he is careful, out of concern for social solidarity, not to upset consciences less evolved than his own.

A certain degree of civilization corresponds naturally to a certain degree of *civility.*

55.12 *Barrès.** Cahiers, Volume XIII (Unpublished; "Table ronde," Jan. '50) (apropos the ring of Gyges,† which renders its wearer invisible):* "We should not reveal ourselves to those who would not understand." The entire text of the paragraph is: "Beautiful image of the ring of Gyges. If he turned it, he was invisible. I have taken advantage of this possibility again and again. We should not reveal ourselves to those who would not understand."

To use this quotation without it appearing to come from me, Maumort will say: At Lyautey's, in the rue Bonaparte, I met some friend of Barrès's, who told us this. (I have forgotten the name of the teller, but I have not forgotten Barrès's comment.)

Barrès would have said, more or less, to someone who quietly reproached him for concealing something: "The ring of Gyges. What a beautiful image! You had only to turn it to become invisible! Well, I admit it, I have taken advantage of this possibility again and again . . ." and, after a time, thoughtful: "We shouldn't reveal ourselves to those who wouldn't understand."

55.13 *Maumort. Aristocratism.* Every epoch has its own ideal of man, whether it be *the knight, the monk, the corteggiano, the gentleman,* the *honnête homme,* or today, *the specialist, the technician!* When it's not the shrewd operator, the self-made man! There is no longer any ideal of man.

55.14 *Maumort. Concerning le Saillant. Or maybe aristocratism?* I spent the first twelve or thirteen years of my existence confined to le Saillant. For more than ten years, when I was at the age when impressions are indelible,

---

*Maurice Barrès (1862–1923), French writer and politician.

†King of Lydia in ancient times. In Plato's *Republic,* Gyges was a shepherd who found a ring that made him invisible and used it to seduce the queen and murder the king.

le Saillant was my only window on the world. Those impressions were constantly rekindled by constant returns to le Saillant during the years of my active life. At the age of retirement, I have come home to walk in my former footsteps, and once again le Saillant has enclosed me in its universe.

Well, one doesn't live with impunity in such intimate, avid (amorous, I might say) contact with such a special universe, where the harmonious proportions of the building, the beautiful symmetry of the façade, the pure style of the interior decoration, of the antique paneling, the volume of the rooms provide a continual satisfaction to one's reason, logic, and taste and make such a fine match with the noble disposition of the two terraces, with the ordered grace of the allées in the park, where the alignment of the tall trees and the pale statues at the intersections confer a simple, stately dignity upon the allées without being solemn, and where silence reigns, away from all the rumblings of the world—an exceptional silence undisturbed even by the barking of a dog, the lowing of cattle, the banging of a barn door, the distant call of a human voice, etc.

55.15   Aristocratism. A term to use in this context: *a style of life*. For Maumort, this aristocratism is definitely a *style of life*.

55.16   *Stendhal and the lower classes ("Brulard," p. 150):* "I abhor the rabble (when it comes to communicating with them) at the same time that, under the name of the *people*, I passionately desire their happiness. My friends, or rather my so-called friends, start with that when they cast doubt on my sincere liberalism. I loathe whatever is dirty; but as far as I can see the people are always dirty."

P. 156: "I love the people, I detest the oppressors, but it would be a torture for me to live with the people. My skin is much too delicate. A boundless horror for anything that looks *dirty,* or *dank,* or *blackish.*"

55.17   *Maumort and the "people."* In this, we are true Maumorts, my sister and I.

Stendhal confesses somewhere that he passionately wishes for the happiness of the people and for a stop to be put to their unjust oppression but that he abhors the rabble and that contact with the lower classes is a torture to him.

I admit to being exactly like him.

Unlike so many of my class and upbringing, I sincerely approve of all the egalitarian social laws and am personally ready to make any sacrifice so that the condition of mankind can finally and truly be on an equal footing, so the intolerable social injustice can cease and the workers' lot can be as good as that of the bosses.

But to live with the people, to find myself mixed in with them, at close quarters, is very unpleasant to me. I am much too refined in my habits and my tastes not to feel unbearably ill at ease in working-class circles. One can love the people and not be able to stand their ongoing company. One can love the populace and not like to live with the individuals who compose it. Their ways of being and of thinking, their ways of being happy or unhappy, their desires, their welfare, their joys, their emotions, their sensitivity, their reactions are not my own, and I am a foreigner among them. My climate is not theirs. Whenever circumstances have forced me into contact with them, I have suffered from it. I have always felt diminished, lowered, by it. I am capable of camaraderie, of warmth, there is no haughtiness in my attitude, no stupidly aristocratic disdain. I concede that many common folk are worth much more, morally, than "society" people. I give them their full due, and my respect is sincere. But we are not of the same kind, there's nothing to do about it, and I can no more live with them than with Africans. Everything about them shocks me one way or another.

And I detest the peasant, because I know him well. He may be the salt of the earth and the strength of a nation. But his vices are beyond redemption. His virtue, peasant virtue, those wholesome virtues that literature exalts because it invents them, I have hardly ever encountered. In no other class is the individual so *crude,* so selfish, so meanly self-interested, so crafty, secretive, underhanded, and squalidly vile; so basely vulgar, incapable of generosity and high-mindedness, so devoid of natural nobility, so cruel to his fellow man.

55.18 *Maumort.* Have another look at the chapter on aristocratism after having reread Fabricius Dupont, *Manifeste des inégaux,* Ed. des Gazettes, Paris, '49.

56. PESSIMISM

56.1 *Maumort. Pessimism.* "The truth about life is despair," says Vigny. (Secrétain, *Péguy,* p. 247.)

56.2 *Maumort's pessimism.* Deep down, I have never been a pessimist, although it could justifiably be said of me that I was the opposite of an optimist. I have had the luck, which is perhaps only an effect of a good physical harmony, the benefit of a robust nature, to be able to turn a hard and lucid eye on life and the human condition *without ever going so far as to disparage one or the other.*

56.3   *Pessimism.* Maumort: too fundamentally *realistic* not to be pessimistic, but also too realistic not to make the best of his pessimism and accept life, man, the world as they are and take pleasure in them.

56.4   *Maumort. Pessimism.* A level-headed pessimism. He does not unrestrainedly blacken mankind. But he only gives humanity, taken as a whole, a grade of seven or eight out of twenty.

    The honorable mediocrity of man. Even in many distinguished individuals who have played a role, wielded some influence, enjoyed some fame, there is, when you look closely, only a *noble mediocrity.*

56.5   *Maumort's pessimism.* I know from experience that it is wise to *distrust pleasant thoughts* and that the most clear-sighted, most disillusioned of men always remains foolishly ready to mistake his hopes for reality. If that gives proof of a "pessimistic" nature, then I am a "pessimist." And I even try to be one, since I am always quick to doubt my judgment whenever I see that its first impulse has been to offer me conclusions I would be pleased to take as valid.

56.6   *Love of life and pessimism.* The contradiction is to love life, instinctively to judge it precious, and yet be forced, by one's reason, to deem it bad, incoherent, absurd.

It may be in this contradiction that the whole force of life resides, and life itself. Antinomy, alternation, contradiction, conflict between polar opposites—this is the very law of life, its *condition.* Instinct versus reason: essential condition of life for man. Life would essentially be this *balance* (temporary, and constantly modified) between opposing forces.

    He who loves life must logically love contradiction, constraint, this tug of war between two opposites.

To obtain this unstable and perpetual balance of the *happy medium.* That, in the end, is the philosophy of *compromise.* Truth resides in this compromise, in the middle course, in this oscillation, in this rejection of the *extreme,* the *excessive.*

    But let us acknowledge that everything that has been done in the world has been done by the extremists, the fanatics . . . that a perpetual balance would amount to a stagnation of mankind, and perhaps a mortal paralysis. Yes, but let's quickly add that if the extremists had not always been curbed, both by opposing extremists and by people with level heads, mankind would have run to ruin.

To progress through life like a tightrope walker—supple, and equipped with a good balancing pole.

56.7   *Maumort. Lyautey.* With no illusions as to men, he had the transcendent pessimism of great men of action, which, far from discouraging them in their undertakings, is for them one more reason to set about and work relentlessly at their tasks.

56.8   *Pontigny, 1926. Pessimism and optimism.* There is in every complete man a reasoned pessimism that is in fact counterbalanced by a vital optimism (e.g., Montaigne).

Luce* is a fine example of an intellectual, since he possesses to the highest degree that vital optimism which permits one to live and which, in complete human beings, fortunately acts as a counterweight to the reasoned pessimism that their intelligence imposes on them.

56.9   Valéry,† *Regards sur le monde actuel* [1931], p. 102: "The most *pessimistic* judgment about man and the world, and life and its worth, accords wonderfully with the *action* and the *optimism* that life demands." ("My 'pessimism.' ")

70. The Art of the Novel

70.1   *1910. Man: a succession of men.* Base all psychology on the biological law that a living being is a succession of movements, that there is no absolute unity among all the acts of a life (see Le Dantec, *Influences ancestrales,* p. 217). That the same name disguises different and successive men. Instead of making men all of a piece, study lives, *the series of men in a single man,* and show the diversity that the same personality can assume according to its age and the prevailing circumstances.

Study biographies rather than moments of the life of a fairly steady individual. In this way, come closer to reality.

And don't be afraid to show that a man of fifty can be very different from what he was at twenty, can have a whole other idea of good and evil, etc. Indeed this is the modern trend. But we are still far from applying it in literature with the complexity that it has in reality.

---

*Marc-Elie Luce, character in Martin du Gard's *Jean Barois,* a respected humanist and free-thinker.

†Paul Valéry (1871–1945), French poet and critic.

70.2   *May 1914. On board the* Équateur *(returning from Naples).* It is on a boat that we really understand what a novel is, its goal, its limits, its true social role. The point is *to tell a story* (to entertain, almost), to take a normal person, whose private life is hard and usually dull, out of his humdrum existence. This is the origin of the novel and what the fundamental definition of a novel must encompass. I am too used to considering the novel only as a work of art, having its raison d'être in pure art. That is not what it is. Bloch* is right. The novel has its place among the needs of man, like [illegible word] or play. If the gentleman reading a stupid novel in the bow could get the same enjoyment out of reading another novel whose subject would touch him as deeply, would captivate him as thoroughly (main objective: to escape from the humdrum), and which, in addition, would bring him moral or intellectual benefit, that would be even better. But above all, tell a story— captivate. The novel is a social need, less dangerous than aspirin and more active than the chaise longue—don't forget it. In the same way that a play *must* absolutely be dramatic, *theatrical,* so the new novel *must* open up the possibility of taking flight out of your private life, must seize you and carry you away, almost gaily. And if it is not first and foremost captivating, it is nothing: for this interest that it must have is the basis, the vehicle, and the only vehicle for everything that you want to put into it later.

70.3   *July 1920. Panorama (πᾶν δρῶ, I see all). Panoramic art.* A novel which would be to current novels what a panorama is to a painting.

August 1920. Monologues. Rereading Stendhal, I think that what brings out J. Sorel[†] with such extraordinary vividness is in part his continual *monologues.* He is constantly discovering his inner thought, and that is the only way to show a person naked to his very depths. The art would be to assign just the proper depth to each of the characters by assigning just the proper amount of monologues to each. Antoine[‡] will have to soliloquize much more than all the others; and this alone will put him by himself in the foreground of the book.

70.4   *September 1920. Great subjects seen over time.* What is fascinating about the mystery of things and people is the *transformations* in their situations. To have a keen enough imagination and a sharp enough observation to know and conjure up the situation of a family at a given moment and to place this vision side by side with a new image that this family presents ten, twenty years later. There you have the tragedy, the mystery, of life. To picture

---

*Jean-Richard Bloch (1884–1947), French writer.
†Julien Sorel, protagonist of Stendhal's *The Red and the Black.*
‡Antoine Thibault, one of the main characters in Martin du Gard's *The Thibaults.*

young parents, children, a given state of affairs, and twenty years after, these same people, the ones who are still there, what they have become, the new structure that the eternal kaleidoscope, as it implacably turns, has composed with these little oddments . . .

That is what gives interest to a novel, the story of a short, detached episode.

70.5 *Innovative writers, and writers who implement.* Sainte-Beuve distinguishes between the *primitive, ground-breaking, original* writers and the *studious, smooth, docile* geniuses. (On the one hand Homer, Aeschylus, Dante, Shakespeare, even Molière. On the other, Horace, Virgil, Racine.)

It is a similar distinction that I make when I always distinguish between those who are *innovators,* who bring forth the new and open up possibilities, and those who are *end results,* who perfectly implement what has been innovated (often imperfectly) by others.

Gide, Claudel, Péguy, Proust are pioneers. The other great contemporaries carry things out and originate nothing. Posterity retains only the former.

70.6 *Literature.* The mark of a great work: *to create a myth* (the Cid, René, Rastignac, J. Sorel). What novelist will create for the generations to come the myth of the man of tomorrow?

70.7 *June 1925. The parts of* The Thibaults. I would like for people to be able to say of *The Thibaults,* of its *different parts,* what Rilke said (*Rev. Genève,* May 1925, p. 535) of Rodin's works: that most of the time, in front of a work by Rodin, *we don't dare give it a name* (limit it, circumscribe it).

70.8 *October 1928.* From a conversation with Jean Prévost about the writing of a book—its momentum, the appeal there is for the reader in rediscovering the very movement of the creator's ideas—I draw some personal reflections.

When I write a carefully wrought letter, to Coppet for example, I am in a state of inner pressure; I am controlling both the sequence of the ideas and the choice of the vocabulary; I often make happy finds; the obligation to leave nothing to chance, to express my whole idea as I go, makes me work in a way that is not at all like the state of mind I am in, even during intense visions and trances, when I scribble a rough draft, in which I only put down the ideas, any way they come, in profusion, the good and the bad, retaining the right to later sort through this jumble.

And afterwards, when I return to this jumble and pick from it whatever I need for the finished bouquet, I don't even bother to remember that inner movement that drove me at the time. That movement is thus always lost, with my present method. This may be rather serious. I manage to produce a fairly good dish with the leftovers. But what would the piece be like if it stayed whole?

This remains to be seen.

I might avoid that very slow and painful toil which I force myself to do. I would work with more fire. And I might give my books the benefit of that natural verve which, I am told, often runs through my letters.

In practical terms, facing a chapter to do:

1. Put down briefly, without sentences, at the moment of the first vision, the whole scene (as I was doing, but more schematically).

2. Don't let the notes stagnate or go cold. Immediately get down to composing the *final version* (which I will correct and recorrect, of course). But avoid writing, as I do, a draft *A,* that I know will be formless, that I leave formless, then a *B,* a *C,* etc. *Don't accept formlessness. Try to give a form immediately.*

But this is to lose the incomparable, secret, irreplaceable *collaboration of time.* Is good wine made with this year's vintage?

70.9   *August 1928. The young.* Yes, they all have a great talent: but it's the same.

70.10   From *International Literature,* organ of the International Union of Revolutionary Writers:

Moscow, 31 December 1933.

Monsieur R. Martin du Gard,

The congress of Soviet writers will take place in the month of May 1934. This congress will be an event of the highest importance, not only in the life of Soviet writers but in the entire U.S.S.R.

At a time when Soviet writers examine their work, experience the effectiveness of their principles and their method, confront their ideas in anticipation of future work, deepen their means of close participation in the socialist structure by toppling the final obstacles; at a time when Soviet writers are particularly attentive to the perspective of writers from the capitalist countries, we would be happy to hear your voice.

It would be necessary for Soviet writers and our public opinion to become acquainted with your opinion as to the present situation abroad and the situation of the U.S.S.R. and its literature.

This is why we are asking all those who sympathize with our writers, our artists, our scientists, to kindly answer the following questions:

1. Have the existence and the successes of the Soviet Union played a part in your outlook? Have the October Revolution and the Soviet structure prompted changes in your outlook? In what way and how much have they influenced your ideas and your writings?

2. What is your opinion of Soviet literature?

3. What are the moments and developments of capitalist culture that have most held and influenced your mind?

The International Union of Revolutionary Writers will put out a special issue of its magazine *International Literature* devoted to the Congress of Soviet Writers, in which the answers will be published.

We would be grateful if you would answer before 15 April 34.

The secretariat of the I.U.R.W.,

S. DINAMOV, S. LUDKIEWICZ, BELA ILLES, M. MOUSSINAC.

Unsent response to a survey on the Russian novel (1934):

Although I never respond to surveys, I did not want my abstention in this case to give the impression that I am not one of those to whom you address your appeal, one of those who "sympathize with the writers, artists, and scientists of the U.S.S.R.," since I very warmly count myself among them.

My opinion on young Russian literature is limited to a few works translated these last few years into French.

I have been struck by the sense that they are a potentially undeniable literary force. An overdisciplined force—and poorly disciplined, perhaps. The political faith that sustains your young people also paralyzes them. And that spirit of protest, of generous propaganda, that animates them, often threatens to blind them. A writer must be able to express himself with independence, without surrendering, without giving way to collective suggestions. The great ones are almost always loners.

Your young writers all have great talent; what worries me slightly is that they all have the same one: a partisan talent. Each of them seems to proclaim: "I write to convince!" Pardon me, but I am one of those who persists in thinking that your great Chekhov, that colossus, was right when he said: "When I describe horse thieves, I don't need to add: it's bad to steal horses." And I also think Montaigne was wise when he informed us: "I don't teach, I tell stories. And besides, it may be that by telling stories, without wanting to teach, we teach best."

The assurance of someone who thinks he has the truth in his pocket is rarely persuasive. We distrust the reasoning of someone who is convinced. Thinking is the opposite of believing; to reflect is first of all to reject what we would immediately be tempted to take as indisputable; to reflect is first of all to deny. The first rule, says Alain, the rule of rules, is the art of challenging what is appealing. What your young writers lack, it seems to me, in order to be considered thinkers and direct the thought of others, is *the spirit of doubt.*

In all their books, the characters appear mainly as mouthpieces. Mouthpieces not only of an author, which already would be serious, but of a regime. (Do I need to add that the merit of that regime is not for a moment in dispute here?) In those novels by young Russians, the ideas do not issue naturally from the characters who express them, are not born of them, supported by them; they are characters who seem to be ghosts upheld by abstractions. And, in the same way, when these characters act, their actions contribute more or less arbitrarily to a doctrinaire demonstration by example.

I believe that it is neither by its dialectical force nor by the soundness of the convictions expressed by the author that a novel lives and touches hearts; it is the quantity and the quality of profound life that it has been able to capture and render unforgettable to the reader. What counts—have you forgotten, children of Tolstoy, of Chekhov, of Gorky?—is the *sense of life,* that human, general je-ne-sais-quoi which is and will remain meaningful for everyone, in all times and places.

One can understand, besides, the temptation which your young authors are yielding to. A brain is always driven to fill its work with the issues of the day that obsess it, with everything that people are talking about at the time it is writing.

Yet the past ought to teach us that there is no material more perishable than current events: it is always that element which often fascinated contemporaries and attained a fragile renown that, in a work made to last, decomposes soonest and often brings about the disintegration of the whole. A fish rots starting with the head, goes a Chinese proverb. A novel dies starting with the thesis. Even the best of the best provide fearsome examples of this: Tolstoy, Balzac, George Eliot.

It goes without saying that any great work forces us to think. But in an indirect, suggestive, almost involuntary way, and for that reason all the more effective. If we admit that it can pose problems, at least I think that it does not have to resolve them. The supreme difficulty for the artist is precisely to separate what is time-bound from what is permanent, what is the current, short-lived debate of contemporary humanity from what is the anguishing enigma of eternal humanity.

It is in fact with this human anxiety that every truly great work has quivered since the Greek tragedians. An impassioned questioning; but with no answer. The answer is always a topical improvisation.

70.10a   *Questions of topicality in the novel.* It is tempting to shape one's oeuvre out of the serious problems being debated in one's time. It seems legitimate to enrich one's work with the contribution of contemporary thought and experience. This is a stupidity which is always fatal . . . The social question clutters the work of Balzac. Historical questions, that of Tolstoy. In *Middlemarch,* everything that is a general idea about medicine, political life, even the dissidence of religious sects, is so much dead weight. The whole difficulty consists in distinguishing between what belongs to eternal man and what to contemporary man.

Therefore, beware of the war and everything that is a contemporary problem or event.

70.10b   Stendhal, *Le Rouge et le Noir,* p. 373, chap. LII: "Politics is a stone tied to the neck of literature . . . It is a pistol shot in the middle of a concert."
   J.-R. Bloch.*

70.11   *1935. Ripeness of subjects:* How many modern books leave me unsatisfied, as if I am confronted with something imperfect, unfinished, in which the elements have not attained the harmony of their development.

A subject is like a fruit. As good as it may be to start with, it only becomes flavorsome when it has ripened well.

70.12   *Realism. Aragon, October '37:* "Many people, and particularly writers, confuse realism with painting from nature . . . They do not think, as I do, that *realism is above all an attitude of mind in the novelist, which is the result of his concept of the world.*"

70.13   *1947. Separation of substance and form:* Valéry said somewhere: *Thought, by its very nature, lacks style.*

He was reflecting, obviously, on the thought of the "thinkers," philosophical thought.

I would tend to say that any *idea,* by nature, lacks style; that every idea exists *independent of form,* or, more exactly, independent of a precise, unique form; *that an idea is born formless* and can be dressed in a number of different forms.

This is what happens for me. The idea is born in me formless, naked; in order to *capture* it, to *hold* it, I at first use any form at all, whatever words

---

*André Daspre: Martin du Gard was afraid that the political involvement of his friend Jean-Richard Bloch would have unfortunate consequences for Bloch's literary work.

come to mind. And it is *later,* by means of a second effort, assiduous and of an aesthetic order, that I seek out a form for it that suits it well, that fits it closely, that brings out its particular shape.

70.14   *Substance and form:* The example of *translation* helps nicely to clarify my point of view on the separation of substance and form.

I have already noted somewhere the role that must have been played, in my natural tendency to separate substance from form, by the fact that at the time of my apprenticeship I was reading mainly *Tolstoy* (and also Eliot, Hardy, Dickens, Ibsen, D'Annunzio—foreigners whose ideas and intentions I received devoid of any formal adornment).

I note this as well. I am convinced that when the great believers in the indissolubility of substance and form (Gide, for example) read their own writing in a translation, they suffer, they no longer recognize themselves . . .

As for me, I reread *The Thibaults* in German (trans. Eva Mertens) with *almost more pleasure* than in my French version. I found my ideas, my objectives, intact, stripped of the screen of *my style,* and as if seen through a transparent pane which brought out their intellectual and psychological content.

70.15   *Novel.* A process which would be copied from reality—in life we at first form an extreme and simplistic idea of a person, then we gradually correct it—would consist of presenting characters in full color, then shading them off to their true tone. Or, conversely, colorless, and color them in bit by bit.

Such and such a criminal would at first be a man who has excuses, then a wretch whom life has betrayed yet who has remained decent. And such and such an honest fellow, seen more and more closely, would become practically a scoundrel.

70.16   See Aragon's *Le Libertinage,* notably *La Femme française.* I notice how much it adds to the interest of the reading not to have all the keys, to be faced with the characters and their actions not as we usually are with the characters of a novel, but as we are with real people and their difficult-to-interpret actions, about whom we have only scraps of information, and often contradictory ones. Yet, in the spectacle of life, even when we don't understand everything, there is a logic, a secret connection, something that does not seem gratuitous.

To convey this, I don't think it is at all a matter of inventing in an incoherent way. On the contrary, one should establish the reality very solidly, create profoundly true individuals, assemble their actions with the greatest possible attention to reality.

And, afterwards, remove big pieces, break up the weft with big gaps, drop explanations of transitional acts, and this somewhat randomly, by sometimes taking out even essential things.

We would then have the impression that we get when we discover characters, or an adventure, in real life. The impression of grasping bits and pieces, one, two, or three aspects of the matter; but never the impression of clearly possessing the whole of the solution.

It is this impression of wholeness that now must be fought. Before very long, those books in which everything is exposed, analyzed, laid out will no longer seem readable.

70.19   *Vigny:* "Art is *selected* truth."

70.20   *Montesquieu, quoted by Gide:* "To write well, you have to leave out the intermediary ideas."

70.21   *Psychology of a novelist:* The typical, significant expressions are not those that we hear and jot down but rather those that we *invent.*

70.22   Broaden the life of characters by presenting many tangential thoughts and secondary concerns beyond and sometimes in complete opposition to the central issue.

70.23   *May 1920. Verger [d'Augy].** At bottom, what makes a character in a novel interesting is not so much the particularities of his personality as the *insistence* with which the author displays the character in all his aspects. Insist, don't pass over anything.
[*In pencil:*] Proust.

70.24   That we might say of a book, as of a beautiful river: *it has a current.*

70.25   Jean Prévost, *La Création chez Stendhal* (1942); *Stendhal's technique.*
P. 236. Stendhal takes pains to give to the *narrative* "the very rhythm of the thought and the action" which he is describing. Hence the "extreme speed of the sentence" and the "concise choice of details." Law: *"For each moment, one detail and only one."*

---

*Estate owned by Martin du Gard's parents in Sancergues, in the Cher *département,* south of Paris.

P. 237. He quotes the descriptions. "He avoids in descriptions anything opaque or static" that interrupts or slows things down.

Pp. 237–238. "French clarity comes easily to someone who hasn't much to say. Freedom with sentences can be obtained by working as a copy editor . . . The difficulty begins when you need to blend diverse or opposing elements into a short text."

P. 239. *Adjectives.* "He prefers to put the words *grace, beauty* [nouns] into a sentence rather than the adjectives *graceful, beautiful, charming.*"

Hostility towards adjectives. "He allows himself the most completely trite adjectives" that only give "background color" to the scene, to the emotional state.

P. 240. "Any studied epithet would have stopped the reader, diverted his attention from the action, would have made him think of the author. The sentence would have felt altered, touched up. Stendhal hates *sentences that the reader looks at* rather than having them simply *become a part of him . . .* From the moment he admires an epithet, the reader is no longer *in* the book: he is outside of it."

P. 241. "Stendhal guesses correctly, and he thinks everyone else guesses too, that a sentence of Balzac's is never written in one go. 'I suppose,' he says of Balzac, 'that he writes his novels in two stages: first sensibly,* then he dresses them up in fine style.' "

---

*Roger Martin du Gard: Badly put. "Spontaneously" is what he ought to have said, "in a natural, cursory style; and the entire mind absorbed in the logic of the action." (I'm not sure that this is so true for Balzac. But how obvious in so many others, Chateaubriand, Flaubert, A. France, etc.). The important thing is not that a page be written in one go, but that the work of retouching be sufficiently thorough that the retouches erase all sign of the retouching, and so that, by dint of work, the style has the ease, the quick flow of spontaneity.

ROGER MARTIN DU GARD was born on March 23, 1881, in
Neuilly-sur-Seine, France. Trained as a paleographer, he turned
to fiction in his early twenties, and in 1913 produced his first
major work, *Jean Barois*. In 1920 he embarked on an eight-part
family saga, *The Thibaults,* receiving the Nobel Prize in 1937 for
its seventh volume, *Summer 1914,* a narrative of the tribulations
of the Thibault brothers as they face the approach of the First
World War. A prolific author who lived in the country and
devoted himself almost solely to his vocation, he also wrote several plays; a brilliant novella about incest, *Confidence Africaine;*
a book memorializing his long friendship with André Gide;
and one of the century's great diaries. It was during the years
between the German occupation of France in 1940 and his
death in 1958 that Martin du Gard composed *Lieutenant-
Colonel de Maumort.* The book's inclusion in the prestigious
Pléiade series when it first appeared in 1983 confirmed its status
as a classic.

LUC BRÉBION, Ph.D., is a writer, translator, and lecturer on
aesthetics who divides his time between the United States and
France.

TIMOTHY CROUSE, author of *The Boys on the Bus* and
numerous articles in *Rolling Stone, Esquire,* the *Village Voice,
The New Yorker,* and other publications, is currently working
on a book of stories and a novel.

A NOTE ON THE TYPE

THIS BOOK was set in Adobe Garamond. Designed for the
Adobe Corporation by Robert Slimbach, the fonts are based on
types first cut by Claude Garamond (c. 1480–1561). Garamond
was a pupil of Geoffroy Tory and is believed to have followed
the Venetian models, although he introduced a number of
important differences, and it is to him that we owe the letter we
now know as "old style." He gave to his letters a certain elegance and feeling of movement that won their creator an
immediate reputation and the patronage of Francis I of France.

Composed by Creative Graphics,
Allentown, Pennsylvania
Printed and bound by Quebecor Fairfield,
Fairfield, Pennsylvania
Designed by Virginia Tan